THE RISE OF NAGASH

Other Great Stories from The Old World

• THE WAR OF VENGEANCE •
Nick Kyme, Chris Wraight & C L Werner
Book One: *The Great Betrayal*
Book Two: *Master Of Dragons*
Book Three: *The Curse Of The Phoenix Crown*

• THE TYRION & TECLIS OMNIBUS •
William King
Book One: *Blood Of Aenarion*
Book Two: *Sword Of Caldor*
Book Three: *Bane Of Malekith*

• ELVES: THE OMNIBUS •
Graham McNeill
Book One: *Defenders Of Ulthuan*
Book Two: *Sons Of Ellyrion*
Book Three: *Guardians Of The Forest*

• GOTREK & FELIX: THE FIRST OMNIBUS •
William King
Book One: *Trollslayer*
Book Two: *Skavenslayer*
Book Three: *Daemonslayer*

• KNIGHTS OF BRETONNIA •
Anthony Reynolds
Book One: *Knight Errant*
Book Two: *Knight Of The Realm*

• EMPIRE AT WAR •
Dan Abnett, Nick Kyme & Darius Hinks
Book One: *Riders Of The Dead*
Book Two: *Grimblades*
Book Three: *Warrior Priest*

THE LEGEND OF SIGMAR
Graham McNeill

Other Great Stories from Warhammer Age Of Sigmar

• GOTREK GURNISSON •
GHOULSLAYER
GITSLAYER
SOULSLAYER
Darius Hinks

BLIGHTSLAYER
Richard Strachan

VERMINSLAYER
David Guymer

REALMSLAYER
David Guymer

SKAVENTIDE
A Novel By Gary Kloster

THE LAST VOLARI
A Novel By Gary Kloster

THE HOLLOW KING
A Cado Ezechiar Novel By John French

THE ARKANAUT'S OATH
A Drekki Flynt Novel By Guy Haley

HAMMERS OF SIGMAR: FIRST FORGED
A Novel By Richard Strachan

GODEATER'S SON
A Novel By Noah Van Nguyen

THE RISE OF NAGASH

Mike Lee

A BLACK LIBRARY PUBLICATION

The Rise of Nagash first published in 2012.
'Picking the Bones' first published digitally in 2012.
This edition published in Great Britain in 2025 by
Black Library, Games Workshop Ltd., Willow Road,
Nottingham, NG7 2WS, UK.

Represented by: Games Workshop Limited – Irish branch,
Unit 3, Lower Liffey Street, Dublin 1,
D01 K199, Ireland.

10 9 8 7 6 5 4 3 2 1

Produced by Games Workshop in Nottingham.
Cover illustration by Jaime Martinez.
Map by Nuala Kinrade.

A CIP record for this book is available from the British Library.

ISBN 13: 978-1-83609-200-1

See Black Library on the internet at

blacklibrary.com

Find out more about Games Workshop
and the worlds of Warhammer at

warhammer.com

Printed and bound in the UK.

THE WORLD OF LEGEND

Across the Old World mighty nations flourish. Beneath the soaring peaks of the Worlds Edge Mountains, industrious Dwarfs work their mines to fuel their forges. From gleaming white-stone harbours and bustling ports, sleek Elven ships ply the azure waters of the world's oceans. In the fair lands of Bretonnia, chivalrous knights pursue noble quests and launch bold crusades into distant lands and, at the heart of the Old World, in the lands of the Empire, the teeming masses of humanity bustle in the wide avenues of their great cities.

Yet not all is well amongst the civilised races of the world. Mighty princes and powerful warlords raise glorious hosts without number, marching to war against those that should be their closest allies in the name of conquest and power. Whilst Elven warships battle the charnel fleets that sail from the accursed Land of the Dead, the humble peasants of Bretonnia cower within their meagre hovels, hiding from the bestial horrors of the Brayherds that stalk the lands. Amongst the mountain peaks, throngs of stalwart Dwarf warriors muster in valiant defence of their ancestral homes against the relentless advances of brutal and warlike Orcs and Goblins. And in the frozen north, where the Winds of Magic blow strong and the whispers of the Chaos gods haunt the dreams of mortals, the lost and the damned grow in number with each passing season and the Champions of Chaos grow hungry for the time when they will lead their armies south, bringing ruination to the civilised lands of Men, Dwarfs and Elves.

This is a dark age, a bloody age, and from this age heroes of legend will rise to challenge the gathering forces of chaos and destruction.

CONTENTS

Nagash the Sorcerer 11

Nagash the Unbroken 343

Nagash Immortal 547

Picking the Bones 915

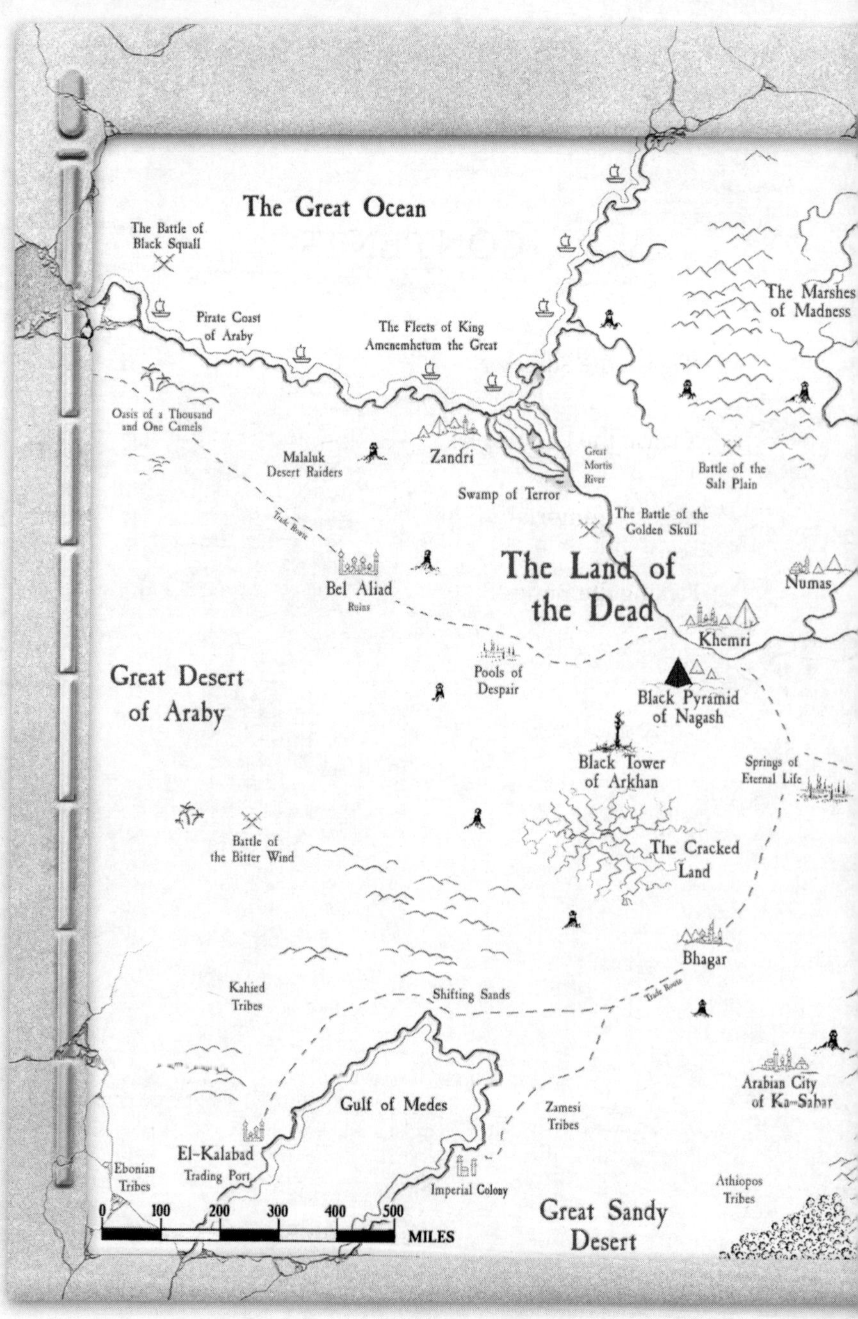

The Great Ocean
The Battle of Black Squall
Pirate Coast of Araby
The Fleets of King Amenemhetum the Great
The Marshes of Madness
Oasis of a Thousand and One Camels
Malaluk Desert Raiders
Zandri
Great Mortis River
Swamp of Terror
Battle of the Salt Plain
The Battle of the Golden Skull
Trade Route
The Land of the Dead
Bel Aliad
Ruins
Numas
Khemri
Great Desert of Araby
Pools of Despair
Black Pyramid of Nagash
Black Tower of Arkhan
Springs of Eternal Life
Battle of the Bitter Wind
The Cracked Land
Bhagar
Kahied Tribes
Shifting Sands
Trade Route
Arabian City of Ka-Sabar
Gulf of Medes
Zamesi Tribes
El-Kalabad
Trading Port
Ebonian Tribes
Imperial Colony
Athiopos Tribes
Great Sandy Desert
0
100
200
300
400
500
MILES

The Plain of Bones
Desolation of Nagash
The Sour Sea
Nagashizzar
Below which lies the Cursed Pit
Misty Mountain
Blight River
The Broken Teeth
The Fortress of Vorag
Ruins
Battle of the Grey Hag
The Straits of Nagash
Red Cloud Mountain
Mortis Tarn
Cursed Lahmia
The Bitter Sea
Doom Mountain
The Battle of Phar's Legion
Ash River
Battle of the Mighty Flame
Devil's Backbone
Gulf of Fear
Lybaras
Resting Place of Queen Khalida
Mahrak
City of Decay
Quatar
Palace of Corpses
Charnal Valley
Doom Glade Swamp
The Cursed Jungle
Battle of the Old Gods
Mount Arachnos
Crater of the Walking Dead
Temple of Skulls
Lost Plateau
Rasetra
KEY TO MAP OF THE LAND OF THE DEAD
Settlement
Battle
Necropolis
Oasis
Fleet
Jungle
Trade Route
Volcano
Tower Delineating Borders of Nehekhara

NAGASH
THE SORCERER

DRAMATIS PERSONAE

KHEMRI, The Living City
Thutep, priest king
Neferem, queen
Sukhet, Thutep's son
Nagash, grand hierophant
Amamurti, heirophant of Ptra
Ghazid, grand vizier
Arkhan, **Raamket** and **Shepsu-hur**, dissolute minor nobles
Khefru, servant to Nagash
Malchior, **Drutheira** and **Ashniel**: druchii wizards

ZANDRI, City of the Waves
Nekumet, priest king
Amn-nasir, Nekumet's son
Shep-khet, hierophant of Qu'aph

LAHMIA, City of the Dawn
Lamasheptra, priest king
Lamashizzar, Lamasheptra's son

KA-SABAR, City of Bronze
Akhmen-hotep, priest king
Suseb the Lion, the king's champion
Pakh-amn, master of horse
Memnet, grand hierophant of Ptra
Hashepra, high priest of Geheb
Sukhet, high priest of Phakth
Khalifra, high priestess of Neru

RASETRA, former colony of Khemri
Rakh-amn-hotep, priest king
Guseb, grand hierophant of Ptra
Ekhreb, champion of Rasetra

LYBARAS, City of Scholars
Hekhmenukep, priest king of Lybaras
Shesh-amun, champion of Lybaras

MAHRAK, City of Hope
Nekh-amn-aten, hierophant of Ptra
Atep-neru, hierophant of Djaf
Khansu, hierophant of Khsar
Nebunefer, priest of Ptra

QUATAR, The White Palace
Nemuhareb, priest king, Lord of the Tombs

NUMAS, Breadbasket of the Kingdom
Seheb and **Nuneb**, twin priest kings
Ankh-memnet, hierophant of Ptra

BHAGAR, A trading town
Shahid ben Alcazzar, prince

BEL ALIAD, A trading town
Suhedir al-Khazem, prince, Keeper of the Hidden Paths

BOOK ONE

ONE

A PRAYER BEFORE BATTLE

The Oasis of Zedri,
in the 62nd year of Qu'aph the Cunning
(-1750 Imperial Reckoning)

Akhmen-hotep, Beloved of the Gods, Priest King of Ka-Sabar and Lord of the Brittle Peaks, woke among his concubines in the hours before dawn and listened to the faint sounds of the great army that surrounded him. Sounds carried far in the desert stillness; he could hear the distant lowing of the oxen as the priests moved among the herds, and the whickering of the horses in their corral at the far side of the oasis. From the north came the reassuring tinkle of silver bells and the ringing of brass cymbals as the young acolytes of Neru walked the perimeter of the camp and kept the hungry spirits of the desert at bay.

The priest king breathed deeply of the perfumed air, filling his lungs with the sacred incense smouldering in the tent's three small braziers. His mind was clear and his spirit untroubled, which he took to be a good omen on the verge of such a momentous battle. The chill of the desert night felt good against his skin.

Moving carefully, Akhmen-hotep disentangled himself from the arms of his women and slid from beneath the weight of the sleeping furs. He sank to his knees before the polished brass idol at the head of the bed and bowed before it, thanking the shedu for guarding his soul while he slept. The priest king dipped a fingertip in the small bowl of frankincense at the foot of the idol and anointed the brow of the stern, winged bull. The idol seemed to shimmer in the faint light as the spirit within accepted the offering, and the cycle of obligation came full circle.

There was a scratching at the heavy linen covering the entrance to the chamber. Menukhet, favoured servant to the priest king, crawled inside and pressed his forehead to the sandy floor. The old man wore a white linen kilt and fine leather sandals whose wrappings rose almost to his knees. A broad leather belt circled his waist, and a leather headband set with semiprecious stones sat upon his wrinkled brow. He'd wrapped a short woollen cape around his narrow shoulders to keep the cold from his bones.

'The blessings of the gods be upon you, great one,' the servant whispered. 'Your generals, Suseb and Pakh-amn, await you without. What is your wish?'

Akhmen-hotep raised his muscular arms over his head and stretched until his hands brushed the tent's ceiling. Like all the people of Ka-Sabar, he was a giant, standing almost seven feet tall. At eighty-four he was in the prime of his life, still lean and strong despite the luxuries of the royal palace. His broad shoulders and the flat planes of his face bore the scars of many battles, each one an offering to Geheb, God of the Earth and Giver of Strength. The Priest Kings of Ka-Sabar had long been accounted as fearsome warriors and leaders of men, and Akhmen-hotep was a true son of the city's patron deity.

'Bring me my raiment of war,' he commanded, 'and let my generals attend upon me.'

The favoured slave bowed his shaved head once more and withdrew. Within moments, half a dozen body slaves entered the chamber, bearing wooden chests and a cedar stool for the king to sit upon. Like Menukhet, the slaves were clad in linen kilts and sandals, but their heads were covered by hekh'em, the fine ceremonial veils that kept the unworthy from viewing the priest king in all his glory.

The slaves worked swiftly and silently, preparing their master for war. More incense was cast upon the coals, and wine was offered to Akhmen-hotep in a golden cup. As he drank, nimble hands cleaned and oiled his skin, and bound his short beard into a queue with braided strips of glossy leather. They dressed him in a pleated kilt of the finest white linen, placed red leather sandals upon his feet, and set around his waist a belt formed of plates of hammered gold, inlaid with lapis lazuli. Wide gold bracelets, inscribed with the blessings of Geheb, were pressed around his wrists, and a bronze helmet crowned with a snarling lion was set upon his shaven head. Then a pair of older slaves placed his armour of woven leather bands around his powerful torso, and a broad necklace of gold, inlaid with glyphs of protection against arrow and sword, around his neck.

As the armourers finished their tasks a pair of veiled slaves entered the sleeping chamber with trays of dates, cheese and honeyed bread for their master to break his fast. They were followed by a pair of armoured Nehekharan nobles, who fell to their knees before the priest king and touched their foreheads to the floor.

'Rise,' Akhmen-hotep commanded. As the generals straightened, sitting back on their haunches, the priest king settled onto his cedar chair. 'What are the tidings of the foe?'

'The army of the usurper has encamped along the ridge north of the oasis, as we expected,' answered Suseb. Akhmen-hotep's champion was called the Lion of Ka-Sabar, and was tall even among his own people; at a crouch, his head was nearly level with the seated priest king, forcing him to bend his neck ever so slightly to show proper deference. The champion carried his helmet tucked beneath one powerful arm. His handsome, square-jawed face was clean-shaven, as was his dark-skinned head. 'The last of their warriors arrived only a few hours ago, and they appear to have suffered greatly on their long march.'

Akhmen-hotep frowned, and asked, 'How do you know this?'

'Our sentries along the northern perimeter can hear groans and fearful murmurs rising from the enemy camp,' Suseb explained, 'and there are no signs of tents or campfires being lit.' The priest king nodded.

'What do our scouts report?'

Suseb turned to his companion. Pakh-amn, the army's Master of Horse, was one of the wealthiest men of Ka-Sabar. His black hair was curled into ringlets and oiled, falling over his sloping shoulders, and his armour was ornamented with lozenges of gold. The general cleared his throat. 'None of our scouts have returned as yet,' he reported, bowing his head. 'No doubt they will arrive at any time.'

Akhmen-hotep waved the news away with a sweep of his hand.

'What of the omens?' he asked.

'The Green Witch has hidden her face,' Pakh-amn declared, referring to Sakhmet, the baleful green moon, 'and a priest of Geheb claimed that he saw a desert lion hunting alone among the dunes to the west. The priest said that the lion's jaws were dark with blood.' The priest king scowled at the two generals.

'These are fine portents, but what of the oracles? What do they say?' he asked. It was Suseb's turn to bow his head regretfully.

'The Grand Hierophant assures me that he will perform a divination, after the morning's sacrifices,' the champion said. 'There has been little opportunity up to this point. Even the senior priests are occupied with menial tasks–'

'Of course,' Akhmen-hotep interjected, grimacing slightly at the memory of the shadow that had fallen over Ka-Sabar and the other cities across Nehekhara barely a month past. Every priest and acolyte touched by that tide of darkness had died within moments, leaving the great temples decimated.

Akhmen-hotep was in no doubt that the foul shadow had been spawned in blighted Khemri. All of the evils plaguing the Blessed Land for the last two hundred years could be laid at the feet of the tyrant that ruled there, and the priest king had vowed that Nagash would at long last answer to the gods for his crimes.

The priests of Ptra greeted the dawn with the blare of trumpets. On the plain to the north of the great oasis, the assembled warriors of Ka-Sabar's Bronze Host shone like a sea of golden flames. To the east, the weathered line of the Brittle Peaks was etched in harsh, yellow light, while the endless, rolling dunes of the Great Desert off to the west was still cloaked in shadow.

Akhmen-hotep and the nobles of the great army gathered by the waters of the oasis, glittering in their martial finery, and offered up sacrifices to the gods. Rare incense was burned to win the favour of Phakth, the god of the sky and bringer of swift justice. Nobles cut their arms and bled upon the sands to placate great Khsar, god of the desert, and beg him to scourge the army of Khemri with his merciless touch. Young bullocks were brought stumbling up to Geheb's stone altar, and their lifeblood was poured out into shining bronze bowls that were then passed among the assembled lords. The nobles drank deep, beseeching the god to lend them his strength.

The last and greatest sacrifice was saved for Ptra, mightiest of the gods. Akhmen-hotep came forward, surrounded by his towering Ushabti. The priest king's devoted bodyguards bore the marks of Geheb's favour; their skin was golden and their bodies moved with the fluid power of the desert lion. They stalked around the priest king with massive, two-handed blades gleaming in their taloned hands.

A great pit had been dug at the edge of the oasis, in full view of the gathered army, and seasoned wood brought all the way from Ka-Sabar had been piled in it and set alight. The priests of the sun god surrounded the blaze, chanting the Invocation of Going Forth to Victory. Akhmen-hotep stood before the hungry flames and spread his powerful arms. At his signal, shouts and screams shook the air as the Ushabti dragged a score of young slaves forward and cast them into the flames.

Akhmen-hotep joined the chanting of the priests, calling upon Ptra to unleash his wrath upon Nagash the Usurper. As the smoke darkened above the fire and the air grew sweet with the smell of roasted flesh, the priest king turned to Memnet, the Grand Hierophant. 'What are the portents, holy one?' he asked respectfully.

The high priest of Ptra shone with the Sun God's reflected glory. His short, round frame was clothed in a robe woven with threads of gold, and golden bracelets pinched the soft flesh of his brown arms. Upon his chest lay the polished golden sun-disk of the temple, inscribed with sacred glyphs and showing the likeness of Ptra and his fiery chariot. His fleshy face was covered in a sheen of sweat, even at this early hour.

Memnet licked his lips nervously and turned his face to the flames. His deep-set eyes, shadowed by a thick band of black kohl, betrayed none of the priest's inner thoughts. He studied the shapes in the smoke for a long time, his mouth set in a grim line.

Silence fell upon the scattered nobles, broken only by the hungry crackle of the flames. Akhmen-hotep frowned at the Grand Hierophant.

'The warriors of Ka-Sabar await your word, holy one,' he prompted. 'The foe awaits.'

Memnet squinted at the curling ribbons of smoke.

'I...' he began, and then fell silent. He wrung his podgy hands.

The priest king stepped close to the smaller man.

'What do you see, brother?' he asked, feeling the expectant stares of a thousand nobles weighing upon his shoulders. Cold fingers of dread tickled at his spine.

'It... it is not clear,' Memnet said hollowly. He glanced up at the king, and there was a glint of fear in his dark-rimmed eyes. The Grand Hierophant glanced back at the sacrificial fire. He took a deep breath. 'Ptra, Father of All, has spoken,' he said, his voice gathering strength as he fell into the ceremonial cadences. 'So long as the sun shines on the warriors of the faithful, victory is certain.'

A great sigh passed through the assemblage, like a breath of desert wind. Akhmen-hotep turned to his noblemen and raised his great bronze khopesh up to the sky. The light of the sun god blazed from its keen, curved edge.

'The gods are with us!' he cried, his powerful voice carrying over the murmurs of the throng. 'The time has come to cleanse the stain of wickedness from the Blessed Land! Today, the reign of Nagash the Usurper will come to an end!'

The assembled nobles answered with a great cheer, raising their scimitars and crying out the names of Ptra and Geheb. Trumpets sounded, and the Ushabti threw back their golden heads and roared, baring their leonine fangs at the cloudless sky. North of the oasis, the serried ranks of the great army took up the cry, clashing their weapons against the faces of their bronze-rimmed shields and shouting a challenge in the direction of the enemy camp, more than a mile away.

Akhmen-hotep strode back in the direction of his tents, calling for his chariot. The assembled noblemen followed suit, eager to join their warriors and reap the glory that awaited them. No one paid any more heed to Memnet, except his fearful and exhausted priests. The Grand Hierophant continued to stare into the flames, his lips working soundlessly as he tried to puzzle out the portents contained within.

A mile distant, along the rocky ridge that sat astride the ancient trade road leading to far-off Ka-Sabar, the warriors of Khemri lay like an army of corpses upon the dusty ground.

They had marched night and day, burnt by sun and frozen by darkness, driven by the lash of their generals and the implacable will of their king. League after league passed beneath their sandalled feet, with scant pause for rest or food. Years of famine and privation had rendered their bodies down to little more than sinew and bone. The army moved swiftly, winding down the road like a desert adder as it bore down on its foe. They travelled light, unburdened by the weight of a baggage train or extravagant retinues of priests. When the army stopped, the warriors sank to the earth and slept. When it was time to move again, they rose silently to their feet and shuffled onwards. They ate and drank on the move, eating small handfuls of raw grain and washing it down with sips of water from the leather flasks at their hips.

Those that died on the march were left by the side of the road. No rites were spoken for them, nor were any gifts offered to propitiate Djaf, the god of death. Such things had long been forbidden to the citizens of the Living City.

The corpses withered under the merciless heat of the sun. Not even the vultures would touch them.

As the light of dawn stole across the stony earth and the warriors of the Bronze Host shouted the names of their gods to the sky, the warriors of Khemri stirred from their exhausted slumber. They raised their heads and blinked dully at the sound, turning their dust-streaked faces to the oasis and the shining army that awaited them.

A dry, rustling sound, like a chorus of swarming locusts, rose from the shadows of the dark pavilions erected behind the army's silent ranks. Moving slowly, as though in a dream, the army of Nagash rose once more to its feet.

'It's as if they're marching to their deaths,' Suseb the Lion declared, watching the shambling ranks of the enemy army descend from the ridge and form up at the edge of the shimmering plain.

The tall champion stood beside his king in the bed of Akhmen-hotep's armoured chariot, taking advantage of the slight elevation to look over the heads of their assembled troops. Double lines of archers formed the front ranks of the army, their tall bows of wood and horn held ready as the enemy slowly drew within range. The companies of spearmen, nearly twenty thousand in all, waited behind them, stretching like a wall of flesh and bronze nearly two miles long. Gaps between the companies created lanes for the bands of light horsemen and charioteers that the priest king chose to hold in reserve at the rear of the waiting host. Once the Khemri army broke, he intended to unleash his cavalry upon the fleeing warriors and slaughter them to a man.

No quarter would be asked, and none given. Such was not the usual way of war in the Blessed Land, but Nagash was no true king. His nightmarish reign in the Living City was an abomination, and Akhmen-hotep intended to erase its taint for all time.

The priest king and his bodyguard were drawn up at the centre of the battle-line, athwart the old trade road. The priests and their retinues were still streaming out of the oasis and making their way to the rear of the army, wreathed in clouds of incense and bearing the icons of their gods before them. Hashepra, bronze-skinned Hierophant of Geheb, had arrived first, and was already deep in prayer. His bare chest was striped with sacrificial blood, and his deep voice was intoning the Invocation of Unconquerable Flesh.

Akhmen-hotep studied the mass of dark figures that was flowing sluggishly onto the plain before his army. Spearmen and axe-men gathered together in ragged companies, intermingled with small bands of dusty archers. Their shambling march kicked up a haze of dust that masked the movements of other units still on the ridge. The priest king thought he saw small units of cavalry moving slowly along the ridge line, but it was difficult to tell for certain.

There was some kind of activity behind the centre of the enemy host. It looked like a mass of slaves, carrying a number of dark shapes, palanquins, perhaps, and arranging them in groups at the crest of the ridge. The sight of them sent an unaccountable chill down the priest king's spine.

Suseb sensed the king's disquiet.

'Your strategy has worked to perfection, great one,' he said. 'The enemy is exhausted, and their ranks have been thinned by their headlong march. See how far the people of the Living City have fallen! We have nearly twice as many companies at our command.' The champion pointed to the army's flanks. 'Let us order our left and right wings forward. When the battle is joined we can encircle the Usurper's army and grind them to dust.'

Akhmen-hotep nodded thoughtfully. He had counted upon this when he'd raised the banner of war against distant Khemri and called upon the other priest kings to unite against the Usurper. Nagash would not tolerate defiance. He'd shown that at Zandri, more than two hundred years ago. So, Akhmen-hotep had made no secret of his advance on the Living City, knowing that Nagash would hasten to meet him before his spark of rebellion could ignite the rest of Nehekhara. Here, then, was the fiend, hundreds of leagues from home, having pushed his army past all human endurance in a fit of tyrannical fury.

Nagash had played directly into his hands. It was like a gift from the gods, and yet, Akhmen-hotep could not shake a powerful sense of foreboding as he watched his foes array for battle.

'Have there been any reports from our scouts?' the king asked.

Suseb paused.

'None, great one,' he admitted, and then shrugged. 'Likely, the Usurper's patrols chased them into the desert during the night, and they are still making their way back to us. No doubt we will hear from them soon.' The priest king's lips drew into a grim line.

'And no news of Bhagar, yet?' he asked.

Suseb shook his head. Bhagar was the closest Nehekharan city, still little more than a merchant town, perched at the edge of the Great Desert. Its princes had pledged their small army to Akhmen-hotep's cause, but there had been no sign of their forces since the Bronze Host had begun its slow march. The champion shrugged.

'Who can say?' he said. 'They might have been delayed by sandstorms, or perhaps Nagash sent a punitive expedition against them as well. It matters little. We don't need their help against a rabble such as this.' Suseb folded his powerful arms and glared disdainfully at the Usurper's approaching warriors. 'This won't be a battle, great one. We will slaughter them like lambs.'

'Perhaps,' the priest king said. 'But you have heard the stories from Khemri as well as I. If half of what the traders say is true, the Living City has become a dark and terrible place, indeed. Who knows what awful powers the Usurper is consorting with?' Suseb chuckled.

'Look around, great one,' he said, indicating the growing assembly of priests with a sweep of his hand. 'The gods are with us! Let Nagash consort with his daemons; the power of the Blessed Land burns in our veins!'

Akhmen-hotep listened and took heart from Suseb's words. He could feel the power of Geheb burning in his limbs, waiting to be unleashed upon the foe. With such blessings at their command, who could stand against them?

'Wise words, my friend,' he said, gripping Suseb's arm. 'The gods have delivered the foe into our hands. It is time for us to strike the killing blow. Go, and take command of the chariots. When I give the signal, grind the enemy beneath your wheels.'

Suseb bowed his head respectfully, but his handsome face was lit with a joyful grin at the prospect of battle. The Lion leapt gracefully from the chariot, and immediately one of the Ushabti and a tall, keen-eyed archer took his place in the king's chariot.

Alone with his thoughts, Akhmen-hotep resumed his study of the approaching enemy force. He was a skilled and experienced general; the sight of the enemy's silent, shambling ranks should have filled him with eager joy. Once again, he tried to shake a creeping sense of dread.

The priest king beckoned to one of his runners, and said, 'Inform the Master of the Bow to begin firing as soon as the enemy comes into range.'

The boy nodded, repeating the order word-for-word, and ran off towards the battle-line.

Akhmen-hotep turned his face to the fierce light of the sun and waited for the battle to be joined.

The warriors of Khemri poured down off the ridge like water spilling from a cup, spreading in a dark arc across the white plain and flowing inexorably towards the Bronze Host. Hollow-eyed nobles paced along behind their ragged companies, cymbals clashing and drums pounding, setting a funereal pace. Squadrons of bedraggled horsemen followed behind the footmen, slipping like ghostly shadows in and out of the dusty haze kicked up by the infantry's marching feet.

Horns wailed along the length of the opposing battle-line, barely a hundred and fifty yards distant. The archers of Ka-Sabar stood twenty yards ahead of the regular infantry: three thousand men, arrayed in three companies, with a dozen arrows per man driven into the sand by their feet. At the signal, the archers plucked the first of their arrows from the sand and fitted it to their powerful composite bows. Bronze arrowheads glinted angrily as they were aimed into the cloudless sky. The archers paused for a single heartbeat, muscles bunched along their arms and shoulders, and then a single, piercing note from the signal-horn rang out and the bowmen loosed as one.

Bowstrings hummed, and three thousand reed arrows, sped by prayers to Phakth, god of the sky, fell hissing among the enemy ranks.

The warriors of Khemri crouched low and raised their rectangular shields. Arrowheads punched through laminated wood with an angry rattle. Men screamed and fell, shot through the arm or leg, or collapsed lifeless to the broken ground. The infantry slowed momentarily beneath the awful rain, but continued to press grimly forwards. Within moments of the first volley, a second was arcing skyward, and then a third. Still the enemy pressed forwards, their companies withering slowly under the steady rain of fire.

Then came the thunder of hooves, and several squadrons of light horsemen charged out of the haze towards the line of archers. The cavalrymen wielded compact horn-bows of their own, and the Khemri warriors unleashed a ragged volley as they bore down on the bowmen. Arrows sped back and forth across the killing ground. Horses and men went down in a spray of dirt and rock, but the bowmen of the Bronze Host shrugged off the enemy fire. Protected by the invocations of their holy priests, most of the Khemri arrows broke or glanced harmlessly from their bare skin.

Still the horsemen bore down on the thin line of archers, heedless of the appalling losses inflicted by the bowmen. Bronze scimitars flashed in the riders' hands as they closed in. At thirty yards the archers fired a last volley into the front ranks of the horsemen, and then turned and raced for the safety of their battle-line.

An eager cheer went up from the front ranks of the Bronze Host as they made ready for the enemy charge. The Khemri horsemen lashed at the flanks of their mounts, but the weary horses could not catch up to the fleeing bowmen. Frustrated, they reined in less than a dozen yards from the shouting infantry, and then wheeled about and withdrew, leaving several hundred of their fallen brethren littering the battlefield.

The sacrifices of the cavalry, however, bought time and distance for the Usurper's infantry, who were almost upon their foes. With a final clash of cymbals and a rattle of hide drums the silent companies surged forwards, brandishing stone axes and short-handled maces above their arrow-studded shields. The two armies came together with a hollow crash of flesh, wood and metal, punctuated by fierce shouts and the screams of the dying.

The warriors of the Bronze Host moved back not a single step from the force of the enemy's charge. Filled with the vigour of Geheb, their patron god, they splintered shields and shattered bones, dashing their foes to the ground. Decades of pent up anger against the tyrant of Khemri found its voice in a hungry, wordless roar that reverberated from the warriors of Ka-Sabar. Akhmen-hotep and the chanting priests felt the echoes reverberate across their skin and were awed by the sound.

Dust was thickening around the churning mass of warriors, making it difficult to see. Akhmen-hotep scowled, studying the rearmost ranks of his footmen. They were pressing forwards, eager to join in the killing, which he took to be a good sign. The priest king sought out the priests of Phakth. He saw them a short distance away, shrouded in plumes of fragrant incense.

'Glory to the god of the sky, who sped our arrows in flight!' he shouted. 'Will great Phakth stretch forth his hand and wipe the dust from our eyes?'

Suhket, High Priest of Phakth, stood in the centre of the chanting priests, his shaven head bowed in prayer. He opened one eye and arched a thin eyebrow at the priest king.

'The dust belongs to Geheb. If you would have it lie still, importune him instead of the Hawk of the Air,' the priest said in his nasal voice. The priest king scowled at Sukhet, but did not press further. Instead, he turned to his trumpeter.

'Sound the general advance,' he commanded.

Horns wailed, echoing up and down the line. The champions of the infantry companies raised their blood-streaked swords and shouted orders to their men. Shouting, the warriors took one step forward, and then another. Bronze-tipped spears jabbed and thrust, streaming blood, and the exhausted warriors of the Living City gave ground.

Step by step, the warriors of Ka-Sabar drove the enemy back the way they had come. They climbed over the bloodied corpses of the fallen until blood stained the wrappings of their sandals up to their ankles. Meanwhile, the companies at the far ends of the battle-line began to curve inwards, trying to surround the retreating enemy. The Khemri light cavalry harassed the flanks of the spearmen with arrow fire, but did little to slow the inexorable advance.

Akhmen-hotep gestured to his charioteer, who took up the double reins and lashed the team of horses into motion. The chariot rolled forward with a clatter of bronze-rimmed wheels, keeping pace with the advancing army.

A runner appeared from the right flank, his face flushed with excitement. 'Suseb asks permission to attack!' he cried in a piping voice. The priest king considered this for a moment, cursing the dusty haze. Finally he shook his head.

'Not yet,' he answered. 'Tell the Lion to bide his time a little longer.'

So, the advance continued. The Bronze Host moved inexorably across the plain, drawing slowly but steadily closer to the ridge line. Akhmen-hotep's chariot bounced and lurched over the corpses left behind by the fighting. The priests of the city were far behind him, hidden by the dust of the advance, while the churning haze continued to mask the fighting to the fore. He could hear the rattling of chariot wheels off to his left and right, and the nervous whicker of horses as the cavalry kept pace with the footmen. The priest king listened intently to the timbre of battle, waiting for the first signs that the enemy companies were broken and in full retreat.

Despite the steady, remorseless slaughter, the warriors of the Living City refused to break. The closer they drew to the silent, black pavilions lining the ridge, the harder they fought. They pressed against the shields of the enemy spearmen, as though the death looming before them was preferable to what waited at their backs.

Within an hour, the fighting was nearly at the foot of the low ridge line. From the rocky summit, the battle resembled nothing so much as the swirling edge of a sandstorm, lit from within by hard glints of flashing bronze.

Figures waited silently on the slope, watching the approaching storm. Companies of heavy horsemen waited among the dark linen tents, their banners hanging listlessly in the hot, still air. Smaller bands of heavy infantry, clad in leather armour and bearing bronze-rimmed shields, knelt stoically before the great pavilions, awaiting the call to battle.

A group of priests stood together at the centre of the line, outside the largest of the tents. Tall and regal, they wore the black robes of Khemri's mortuary cult, circlets set with sapphires and rubies adorning their shaved heads, and their narrow beards bound with strips of hammered gold. Their dusky skin was pale, and their hawk-like faces were gaunt, but dark power hung over them like an invisible shroud, causing the morning air to shimmer around them like a mirage.

These terrible men waited upon a stooped, elderly slave that crouched at their feet and watched the progress of the battle on the plain below. Blind and nearly toothless, the slave's blue eyes were clouded with milky cataracts, and his brown skin was dried and wrinkled like aged parchment. His bald head was cocked to one side, balanced precariously on his scrawny neck. A thin line of drool hung from his trembling lips.

Slowly, the wrinkled head straightened. A ripple went through the assembled priests, and they shuffled forward, their faces expectant. The slave's mouth worked.

'It is time. Open the jars,' he said, in a voice ravaged with pain and the weight of too many years.

Silently, the priests bowed to the blind slave and went inside the tent. A pair of sarcophagi stood within, carved from glossy black and green marble, fit for the bodies of a mighty king and his queen. Baleful glyphs of power were etched upon their surfaces, and the air surrounding the coffins was as cold and dank as a tomb. The priests averted their eyes from the dreadful figure carved upon the king's sarcophagus, kneeling instead before eight heavy jars nestled at its feet.

The priests picked up the dusty jars in their hands and carried them out into the open air. Each of the clay vessels vibrated invisibly in their grasp, sending a deep, unsettling hum reverberating through their bones.

Slowly, fearfully, the priests set the jars down on the uneven ground. Each vessel was sealed shut with a thick band of dark wax, engraved with rows of intricate glyphs. When all of the jars were in place, the men drew their irheps, the curved ceremonial daggers used to remove the organs of the dead for interment. Steeling their nerves, the priests cut away the wax seals. At once, the buzzing grew louder and more insistent, like the drone of countless angry wasps. The heavy clay lids rattled violently atop the jars.

Nearby, horses shied violently away from the unsealed vessels. With trembling hands, the priests reached forwards and pulled the lids away.

Akhmen-hotep raised his hand to signal his trumpeter. Now was the time to send the chariots and horsemen forwards to break the enemy line once and for all.

All at once, the swirling haze of dust was swept away. The priest king felt a cold wind rushing over the skin of his upraised arm, goose bumps prickling his bare flesh.

The pall of dust flowed up the rocky slope of the ridge in a single, indrawn rush. For a dizzying instant, Akhmen-hotep could see the battlefield in every detail. He saw the struggling companies of enemy foot-sloggers, reduced to ragged bands of tormented warriors forced back almost to the very foot of the ridge line. Beyond them, the priest king saw the rocky slope, leading upwards to a long line of black linen tents, and squadrons of rearing, plunging horsemen.

Then he saw the priests and their tall, heavy jars. The dust formed whirling cyclones over the open vessels, and then Akhmen-hotep watched them darken, turning from a pale tan to deep brown, and then to a slick, glossy black.

A seething, whirring drone radiated down the rocky slope and washed over the combatants, sinking through armour and flesh, and vibrating along their bones. Horses bucked and screamed, their eyes white with terror. Men dropped their spears and clapped their hands over their ears to try to shut out the awful noise.

The priest king watched in growing terror as the ebon pillars stretched upwards and poured out a pall of roiling darkness that spread like ink across the sky.

TWO

SECOND SONS

Khemri, the Living City,
in the 44th year of Khsar the Faceless
(-1968 Imperial Reckoning)

On the seventh day after his death, the body of the Priest King Khetep was taken from the temple of Djaf, in the southern quarter of the Living City, and borne within an ebon palanquin to the House of Everlasting Life. The palanquin was carried not by slaves, but upon the shoulders of Khetep's great Ushabti, and the king's mighty champions marched with their heads hung low and their once-radiant skin stained with ash and dust.

Throngs of mourners crowded the streets of the Living City to pay homage to Khetep as the palanquin passed by. Men and children fell to their knees and pressed their faces to the dust, and mothers wept and tore at their hair, calling to Djaf, god of the dead, to return their monarch to the land of the living. Water drawn from the River Vitae, the great Giver of Life, was cast upon the sides of the palanquin amid tearful prayers. Potters brought out the cups and bowls that had been fired on the day of Khetep's death and dashed them to pieces on the street in the wake of the priest king's passage. In the merchant's quarter, wealthy traders tossed gold coins into the dust before the cortege, where the polished metal caught the light of Ptra's holy fire and blazed beneath the Ushabti's marching feet.

By comparison, the streets of the noble districts surrounding the palace to the north were silent and still. Many of the households were in mourning, or preparing the exorbitant ransoms expected to redeem their lost kin after the disastrous defeat outside Zandri a week before. The atmosphere of sadness and dread settled over the procession like a shroud, weighing heavily on the shoulders of the devoted. Khetep had ruled over Khemri for more than twenty-five years, and through a mix of diplomacy and military prowess he'd forced the cities of Nehekhara to put aside their feuds and live together in peace. Nehekhara had enjoyed an age of prosperity not seen since the great Settra, five hundred years before.

All that had been swept away in the space of a single afternoon on the banks of the Vitae. Khetep's great army had been broken by the warriors of Zandri, and the Ushabti had failed in their sacred duty to protect the king. The news had spread across the Blessed Land like a dust storm, sweeping all before it, and the future was uncertain.

The silent procession made its way into the palace grounds, where the king's household lined the great avenue leading to Settra's mortuary temple. Noblemen and slaves alike prostrated themselves in the dust as the palanquin approached. Many wept openly, knowing that they would soon be joining their great king on his journey into the afterlife.

Settra had built his temple to the east of the palace, facing downriver where the Vitae led to the foot of the Mountains of the Dawn, and symbolic of the journey of the soul after death. The avenue led to a massive, roofed plaza, supported by ranks of huge sandstone columns that led all the way to the temple's grand entrance. The shadows beneath the broad cedar roof were cool and fragrant after the fierce, dry heat of the day. Their footsteps echoed strangely among the columns, transforming their heavy, measured tread into mournful drum beats.

A thirty foot high doorway stood open at the far end of the plaza, densely carved with sacred glyphs and flanked by towering basalt statues of fearsome warriors with the heads of owls, the horex, servants of Usirian, the god of the underworld.

A procession of solemn figures strode from the shadows beyond the great doorway as the Ushabti approached. The priests were clad in ceremonial robes of purest white, and their dusky skins were marked with hundreds of painted henna glyphs, sacred to the cult. Each priest wore a mask of beaten gold, identical to the burial masks of the great kings who lay in their tombs in the sands to the east, and wide belts of gold adorned with topaz and lapis lazuli encircled their waists.

The priests waited in silence as the Ushabti laid the palanquin down at last and drew open the heavy curtains that concealed the priest king's body from view. Khetep had been tightly wrapped in a white burial shroud, his hands folded across his narrow chest. The great king's shrouded face was covered in an ornate burial mask.

For the only time in their lives, the great Ushabti sank to their knees and prostrated themselves before someone other than their king and master. The mortuary priests ignored the mighty champions. They drew near the palanquin and carefully removed the body of their exalted charge. Two by two they bore the shrouded corpse upon their shoulders, and took it into Settra's temple, where only the dead and their eternal servants were allowed.

Once upon a time, the services of the mortuary cult were reserved for the Priest Kings of Khemri alone. Over time, their practices had spread across all Nehekhara, and grew to encompass noble families who enjoyed the priest kings' favour. Now, even the lowliest families could purchase the services of a priest to attend upon their loved ones, though the price was steep. No one begrudged the cost, even though a man might scrimp and save for a lifetime for the privilege. The promise of immortality was a gift beyond price.

The priests carried the body of the king into the depths of the great temple, through vast, sandstone chambers whose walls were covered with intricate mosaics depicting the great Pilgrimage from the East and the Covenant of the Gods, wrought more than seven centuries before. On those walls, great Ptra led the people to the great, life-giving River Vitae, and Geheb sowed the dark earth with rich crops to make them healthy and strong. Tahoth the Wise showed the people the secrets of shaping stone and raising temples, and when the first cities had been built, glorious Asaph rose from the reeds beside the river and beguiled the people with the wonders of civilisation.

Another chamber lay beyond these wondrous halls, low-ceilinged and dark. Smooth red sandstone gave way to glossy blocks of polished basalt, joined together so cunningly that no seams between the stones were visible. The carvings were highlighted here and there with faint touches of silver dust or precious crushed pearl: landscapes of fertile plains and a wide river, presided over by a mighty range of mountains that dominated the distant horizon. The details were vague, made all the more ephemeral by the shifting light of the oil lamps that flickered around the marble bier at the centre of the room. The Land of the Dead was a beguiling image, like a mirage of the deep desert, beckoning seductively to the viewer only to fade once he drew near.

The priests laid the body of the king upon the bier, and reverently pulled away the linen shroud. Khetep's body had been cleaned by his attendants at the battlefield, and the priests of Djaf had further washed it in a solution of ancient herbs and earth salts. The great king's angular face appeared serene, though the cheeks and eyes were already sunken and there was a strange, bluish-black tint to his thin lips.

A silent procession of acolytes filed in and out of the room as the priests worked. They bore clay pots of expensive ink and fine brushes of camel hair to paint Khetep's skin with glyphs of preservation and sanctity, as well as jars of raw herbs, perfumed water and still more earth salts. Finally came a procession of four young priests carrying intricately carved alabaster jars that would store Khetep's vital organs until his eventual resurrection.

The senior priests worked swiftly, preparing the body for preservation. The priests of the city temples had declared that the coronation of Khetep's heir and his sacred marriage must proceed at sunset, only seven hours away, so there was little time before the dead king's interment. Once the burial shroud was removed, they gathered in a circle around the bier and faced the statues of Djaf and Usirian, which flanked a ceremonial doorway on the eastern wall of the chamber. The senior priest, Shepsu-het, raised his stained hands and prepared to utter the Invocation of the Open Door, the first step in securing Usirian's permission to one day return Khetep's spirit to the Blessed Land.

Just as the priest began to speak he felt a chill race down his spine. The back of his neck prickled beneath the weight of a cold, inimical stare, much as a mouse might suffer under the unblinking gaze of a cobra.

Shepsu-het turned to face the shadowy figure standing in the chamber's entrance. The other priests followed suit, and sank quickly to their knees as they recognised the figure.

Nagash, son of Khetep, Grand Hierophant of the Living City's mortuary cult, favoured the kneeling priests with a disdainful glare.

'What is the meaning of this?' he demanded in a clear, resonant voice.

The senior priests looked to one another apprehensively, their disquiet evident in the set of their hunched shoulders and furtive movements. Finally, they turned to Shepsu-het, who gathered his courage and spoke.

'Time is of the essence, holy one,' he said, his old voice muffled by the mask he wore. 'I thought you would wish us to begin the rites at once.'

Nagash considered the priest for a long moment, and then favoured Shepsu-het with a mirthless smile. At only thirty-two, Nagash was the youngest Grand Hierophant of any city in Nehekharan history, and his physical presence filled the funeral chamber. He was tall for the people of Khemri, and preferred the attire of a warrior prince to the staid robes of a priest. His white linen kilt was bound with a broad belt of fine leather, studded with rubies and gold ornaments in the shape of scarabs. Fine sandals of red leather covered his feet, and a wide-sleeved open robe covered his broad shoulders and the upper part of his muscular arms. His broad, tanned chest bore the scars of battle, earned in the wild years of early adulthood and still stark against his nut-brown skin.

He had his father's handsome features but none of Khetep's warmth, with a square chin and an aquiline nose, but a pair of eyes the colour of polished onyx. His narrow beard was bound in a queue with strips of hammered gold, in the manner of the royal household, and his scalp was shaven and oiled to a lustrous sheen.

'Once again, you demonstrate why *I* am Grand Hierophant instead of you,' Nagash said, stepping deeper into the room. He moved with a jungle cat's grace, gliding almost soundlessly across the stone floor. 'You are an old fool, Shepsu-het. I choose to attend upon my father alone.' He waved his arm at the doorway behind him. 'Begone. If I need the assistance of a pack of prattling monkeys, I shall send for you.'

The senior priests quailed before Nagash's forbidding stare. They rose quickly, as one, and shuffled out of the room. Shepsu-het went last, his expression unreadable beneath the smooth, golden features of his mask. As he departed, the figure of a young priest slipped quietly through the doorway into the chamber. Unlike Nagash, the young man was conservatively attired in a white robe and simple gold belt, but his scarred face was lit with an impudent grin, and his brown eyes were sharp and calculating.

'That one means you trouble, master,' he murmured, watching Shepsu-het disappear from sight.

Nagash stepped around the foot of the bier and folded his arms, studying the body of his dead father in detail.

'I suppose you think I should kill him,' he said absently.

The young priest shrugged, and said, 'He must be a hundred and fifty years old. There are herbs that could find their way into his wine: simple things you could find in the temple kitchens, but deadly when combined in the right way. Or an asp could wind up underfoot in the priests' baths. It's been known to happen.'

Nagash shrugged slightly, listening with only half an ear. His attention was focused on the body before him, looking for clues that would reveal how the priest king had died. Khetep's skin had a yellow tinge from the natron wash the priests had given the corpse, but it could not fully disguise the body's grey pallor. Though well advanced in years, at the age of one hundred, Khetep still possessed a measure of the fighting strength he'd enjoyed in his prime. Nagash studied the formation of the king's muscles, noting with a frown the dark lines of the corpse's veins and the body's distended belly.

'Too much wine and luxury,' he muttered. 'Your defeat was written in the sagging lines of your body, father. Your glories made you weak.'

The young priest chuckled, and said, 'I thought that was the point of glories, master.'

Khefru was the first son of a wealthy merchant family, who had enjoyed spending his father's coin on wine and games of dice. He'd got the scar that disfigured the left side of his face in a drunken knife fight outside a gaming-house. His opponent, the son of a powerful noble in Khetep's court, died a few days later. Rather than face execution, Khefru had begun a new life in the mortuary cult. He was a terrible scholar and an indifferent priest, but possessed a sharp wit and a singular bloody-mindedness that Nagash found useful. He'd chosen Khefru as his personal servant on the same day he'd become Khemri's Grand Hierophant.

'Glory is for fools,' Nagash declared. 'It's a poison that saps the will and diminishes one's resolve. Khetep learned that to his cost.'

Khefru arched an eyebrow at his master, and said, 'No doubt you would have ruled differently.'

Nagash glared balefully at the young priest. At sixteen he'd followed his father's army east through the ancient Valley of Kings, and then south towards the steaming jungles that, according to legend, had been the birthplace of their people. For three years Khetep had fought against the hordes of lizardmen that lurked there, beginning construction of the great fortress of Rasetra as a bastion against their constant raids against the allied city of Lybaras. When Khetep was stricken down with the fever, Nagash assumed command of the expedition. For almost six months he'd led his father's warriors in a merciless campaign against their enemies, finally culminating in the brutal battle that had broken the backs of the local lizard chieftains and pacified the region.

For those six months, he'd ruled like a king, and held the land in an iron grip, but when Khetep had recovered enough to begin the long trek home, he'd given Rasetra to one of his generals, and brought Nagash back to the Living City with him. The surviving members of the expedition had been forbidden to speak of Nagash's brief rule. He had been praised as a mighty warrior, but no more, and upon their arrival in Khemri the king sent Nagash to Settra's temple to begin his studies. Now, thirteen years later, Rasetra was a small but thriving city with a priest king of its own.

The Grand Hierophant rested his palm on the hilt of the jewelled irheps at his belt.

'If noble families passed their inheritance to their first-born, as they do in the barbarian tribes to the far north, things would be very different indeed,' Nagash said. 'Instead, fortunes are passed to second sons, and we are shut up in temples.'

'The firstborn are given to the gods, in return for the Blessed Land they have given us,' Khefru said, reciting the old saying with no small amount of bitterness. 'It could be worse. At least they don't sacrifice us, like they did in the old days.'

'The gods should take goats, and be content,' Nagash snapped. 'They need us far more than we need them.'

Khefru shifted from one foot to the other, suddenly uncomfortable. He glanced worriedly at the grim-looking statues on the other side of the room.

'Surely you don't mean such a thing,' he said quickly. 'Without them, the land would wither. The ancient compact–'

'The ancient compact sold us a bowl of sand in exchange for eternal servitude,' Nagash declared. 'The gods offered to make our fields bloom and hold the desert at bay in exchange for worship and devotion. Think on that, Khefru. They were willing to give us paradise in exchange for prayers and the gifts of our firstborn. The gods were *desperate*. Without us, they were weak. We could have enslaved them, bent them to our will. Instead, we are in bondage, giving them strength that we could better use ourselves. Real power lies here, in *this* world,' Nagash said, tapping the marble bier for emphasis, 'not in the next. Settra understood this, I think. That was why he sought the secret to eternal life. Without the fear of death, the gods would have no hold over us at all.'

'A secret that has eluded the mortuary cult for more than five hundred years,' Khefru pointed out.

'That is because our sorcery depends upon the beneficence of the gods,' Nagash said. 'All our rites and invocations are fuelled by their energies. Do you imagine they will help us escape their clutches?' The Grand Hierophant clenched his fists. 'Do not think I flatter myself when I say I possess the greatest mind in all Nehekhara. In thirteen years I have learned everything the cult knows about the process of life and death. I have the knowledge, Khefru. What I lack is *power*.'

As he spoke, Nagash's eyes grew fever-bright, and his voice rose until it was almost a shout. The intensity of the Grand Hierophant's emotions stunned Khefru.

'One day you will find it, master,' the young priest stammered, suddenly afraid. 'No doubt it's only a matter of time.'

Nagash paused. He blinked, and seemed to collect himself, and said, 'Yes. Of course. Merely time.' The Grand Hierophant glanced down at his father's body. He drew the curved bronze knife at his belt.

'Bring the first jar,' he commanded. 'I won't have Shepsu-het accuse me of failing in my duties.'

Khefru went quickly to the waiting alabaster jars and picked one carved with the likeness of a hippo. The canopic jars were made to hold the dead king's four vital organs, the liver, lungs, stomach and intestines, and were carved with glyphs that would preserve them until such time as they were needed once more.

The young priest set the heavy jar beside Nagash, and murmured a prayer to Djaf, god of the dead, before pulling off the lid. Nagash held the bronze blade over his father's belly. He paused briefly, savouring the moment.

'No sign of a wound at all,' he observed. 'Perhaps his heart gave out in the heat of battle.' Khefru shook his head.

'It was sorcery, master,' he said. 'I heard that the army of Zandri called down a spell that smote the priest king and his generals, far behind the battle-line. None of the wards laid by our priests could stop it. When Khetep fell, our army lost its heart, and the Zandri warriors hurled our men back in disarray.'

Nagash considered this, and said, 'But Zandri's patron is Qu'aph. That does not sound like the subtlety of the Serpent God.'

'Even so, master, this is what I was told,' Khefru said, shrugging.

Scowling, Nagash reached down and made the first cut, slitting the abdomen from navel to sternum. At once, the king's belly deflated, spilling a foul, bubbling flood of tarry fluid over the edge of the bier and onto the floor.

Khefru reeled back from the stinking liquid with a muttered curse. Nagash stepped back as well, frowning in surprise. After a moment, the viscous flood subsided, and the Grand Hierophant stepped carefully through the sticky pool back to Khetep's body.

Using the tip of his knife, he added four perpendicular cuts to widen the incision, and pulled one of the flaps of skin aside. The sight of what lay within caused Nagash to hiss in surprise.

The priest king's organs had been fused together by some magical force.

His intestines and stomach were shrivelled into a knotted ball, until there was no way to tell where one ended and the other began. Likewise, the diaphragm and lungs had been warped into bulbous masses of diseased flesh. It was as though a great cancer had eaten Khetep from within.

The Grand Hierophant knew of no god who could do such a thing.

Gingerly, Khefru eased up to the table. When he saw what had become of Khetep, his face twisted in disgust.

'What foul sorcery could do such a thing?' he gasped.

Nagash was no longer listening. The Grand Hierophant was bending low over his father's corpse, studying the great king's twisted remains with rapt fascination. A strange, hungry gleam shone from the depths of his dark eyes.

By noonday, the great plaza outside the palace was full of noblemen and their retinues, waiting to offer gifts for Khetep's interment and to pledge their fealty to his heir. Small tents of brightly coloured linen had been erected by the royal household to shield the nobles from the worst of the sun's heat, and slaves bustled to and fro with jugs of watered wine cooled by the cisterns deep beneath the palace. The stink of sacrificial animals hung heavy in the still air, as each of the noble families sought to outdo their rivals with lavish gifts of lambs, oxen and even a few precious horses. Nagash scowled forbiddingly at the noxious spectacle as he and Khefru made their way to Settra's Court. He knew that by the end of the ceremonies the grand plaza would resemble a stockyard on market day. The stench would linger for weeks.

The crowd grew thicker the closer they came to the king's audience chamber. A dozen of Thutep's Ushabti bodyguards lined the broad steps leading into the echoing hall, resplendent in their polished gold breastplates and gleaming swords. The faces of the devoted were young and fierce. Still little more than acolytes, their skin shone with Ptra's holy blessing, but their bodies had yet to develop the perfectly muscled physiques of the Great Father's chosen warriors. A hectic knot of palace slaves stood behind the rank of bodyguards, bearing wax tablets and rolls of fine parchment. They circled around a tall, dignified figure of middle years, wearing the gold circlet of Khetep's grand vizier.

Nagash moved effortlessly through the multitude, like a crocodile knifing through the dark waters of the Vitae. Slaves scattered from the Grand Hierophant's path and prostrated themselves on the hot, filthy ground, while their masters fell silent and bent their heads in respect. Khetep's eldest son ignored them, one and all.

The Ushabti bowed their heads in turn as Nagash glided smoothly up the sandstone steps, and the palace servants withdrew swiftly into the shadows of the court. That left only the grand vizier, who folded his hands calmly and awaited Nagash's approach.

'The blessings of the gods be upon you, holy one,' Ghazid said, bowing his head respectfully to the Grand Hierophant. Though at least a hundred and ten, the grand vizier was still lean and fit, with the quick, hawk-like energy of the desert tribes from which he was born. Legend said he'd been a bandit in his early years, but had allied himself with Khetep when the young priest king had tried to bring the desert tribes to heel. Khetep quickly found himself confiding in the bold, clever tribesman, and when the army returned to Khemri, Ghazid went with them. In short order Ghazid was named grand vizier, and he had served the royal household ever since. He proved to be an able advisor and stalwart friend to the king, and many believed that much of the city's resurgent glory could be rightly attributed to him. His keen blue eyes missed nothing, and he feared neither man nor beast. Nagash had hated him since childhood.

'Pray, reserve those well wishes for yourself, grand vizier,' Nagash said with a cold smile. 'I come to tell my brother that the rites for our great father are complete. He will be laid to rest in the Great Pyramid in just a few hours, in accordance with the wishes of the priests.' The Grand Hierophant bent his head in a semblance of respect. 'It will be yet another loss to Khemri when you go into the darkness alongside him.'

'Alas, holy one, you are misinformed,' Ghazid replied smoothly, 'no doubt due to your grief and the duties of your station. Alas, Khetep has forbidden me from accompanying him into the underworld. As he lay dying on the battlefield, he commanded that I remain to guide his son through the early days of his reign.'

'I... see,' Nagash replied. 'Such a thing is unprecedented. It is a great honour, of course.'

'And a great responsibility,' Ghazid added. His blue eyes regarded Nagash steadily. 'Times of peace and prosperity tempt otherwise reasonable people to make rash decisions.'

The Grand Hierophant nodded gravely, and said, 'Wise words as ever, Ghazid. I can see why my father valued your counsel so much.'

Ghazid waved his hand dismissively. 'Your father never truly needed my counsel,' he replied. 'If anything, he often brooded too much over his decisions. If I did anything for him, it was to prompt him to take action when the situation warranted it. Better a swift blow to kill a viper before it can rear up and threaten to strike.' Nagash's eyes narrowed thoughtfully.

'Well said, Ghazid. Well said.'

The vizier smiled, saying, 'I am pleased to be of service, as always,' he replied, bowing his head once more. He stepped aside, gesturing to the court's open doorway. 'Your brother is receiving offerings from the city's embassies as we speak. He will be pleased to hear your news.'

Nagash nodded brusquely and resumed his swift pace, passing between the massive sandstone columns supporting the roof of Settra's Court and into the presence of the towering basalt statues of Asaph and Geheb, who stood to either side of the towering doorway. Geheb stood to the doorway's right, his left hand clutching the sickle of the harvest and his right hand held up in a gesture of warding, keeping out spirits of misfortune or malevolence. Asaph held her hands crossed over her breast in greeting, her glorious face serene and inviting. Gold leaf decorated the goddess's headdress and the bracelets upon her wrist, and shone from the curved blade in Geheb's hand. The idols were a display of enormous wealth and power. The rough basalt alone had taken ten years and cost the lives of more than four thousand slaves to bring it from the Brittle Peaks to the east, but they paled in comparison to the great hall that lay beyond.

Settra's Court was a rectangular chamber more than two hundred paces long and forty paces wide, bordered by great columns of polished marble that supported a ceiling forty-eight feet above the gleaming stone floor. The sandstone walls and floor had been faced with square sections of rich, purple marble, shot through with veins of onyx and gleaming gold that glowed in the light of scores of polished bronze oil lamps situated along the length of the chamber. The air inside the grand, echoing space was cool and fragrant, perfumed with costly incense burnt in braziers near the grand dais at the far end of the hall.

In ages past, Settra's Court had been the grandest audience chamber in all Nehekhara, surpassed only by the extravagance of the White Palace at Quatar some centuries after Settra's death. In these times, the entire nobility of Khemri could fit inside the lofty space, with room to spare for their families and slaves. Today, however, the audience chamber was crowded nearly to bursting, the murmur of voices mingling together in a steady, surf-like roar that echoed in the space between the huge pillars. Even Nagash was, for a moment, taken aback by the sheer spectacle that lay before him.

During Khetep's reign his tireless efforts to unite all of Nehekhara, if not as an empire then as a confederation of allied city-states, had involved so much negotiation and statecraft that the other Nehekharan cities had been obliged to create permanent embassies within the Living City. Delegates from each of these embassies filled the hall, each of them bearing lavish gifts to accompany Khetep into the afterlife and cement their relationship with his successor. From where he stood, Nagash could see a delegation from Bhagar in their black desert robes and head wrappings, whispering to one another in the company of a dozen slaves bearing urns of rich spices brought by caravan from the south. Nearby, the golden-skinned giants of Ka-Sabar folded their massive arms and watched the proceedings intently, beside them open chests containing ingots of polished bronze. Farther down the hall on the right, the Grand Hierophant spied a crowd of courtiers and noblemen clad in the silk robes and long kilts of distant Lahmia. Their expressions were guarded as ever, but Nagash noted the weariness that hooded their eyes and dulled their expressions. No doubt many of the Lahmians had escorted Thutep's young bride up the great river to Khemri, a difficult journey in the best of times, but all the more gruelling when it had to be done in haste. Idly, he wondered what other gifts the rich and decadent Lahmians had brought to honour his dead father.

At the moment, the attention of the Lahmians, and indeed that of nearly everyone else in the chamber, was focused on the great procession currently making its way towards the grand dais. Ranks of noblemen clad in plain, white kilts and shoulder capes were being led forward, escorted by tall Ushabti with gleaming green skin and long, fine black hair. Nagash recognised the devoted with a start. They were the chosen warriors of Zandri, the architect of Khemri's defeat.

Khefru had noticed the procession as well, and whispered, 'What can this mean, master?'

Nagash gestured to his servant for silence. Frowning, he slipped quickly to the right and began working his way through the deep shadows behind the pillars along the great wall. Dozens of royal slaves bustled past them in the darkness, each intent on his own business and unaware of the personage who moved in their midst.

'Nekumet, the Priest King of Zandri, is a thoughtful and devious man,' Nagash hissed. 'He invited the war with Khemri over those absurd trade disputes last year, and now he seeks to supplant us as the pre-eminent power in Nehekhara. This is but the next step in his grand strategy.'

The Grand Hierophant moved as swiftly as his station allowed, reaching the far end of the audience chamber in a few minutes, where the shadows were watched over by alert, keen-eyed Ushabti. The young bodyguards bowed their heads at Nagash's approach and let him slip quietly into the crowd of viziers and courtiers in attendance at the foot of the dais.

Nagash noted at once that the viziers were troubled men. They whispered quietly to one another, their hands moving in urgent, impassioned gestures as they discussed the events unfolding before them. Impatient, the Grand Hierophant pushed his way through the crowd of grey-bearded officials until he was nearly standing before the king's throne.

The throne of the Living City was ancient, carved from an elegant, fine-grained dark wood not found anywhere in Nehekhara. Legend said it had been brought from the jungles south and east of the Blessed Land, during the mythical Great Migration, while some claimed it had been built from wood taken from the south in the early years of Settra's reign. It rested at the top of the grand dais, beneath a massive statue of Ptra, the Great Father. Reaching nearly to the ceiling, the idol was made of sandstone plated in sheets of hammered gold. The sun god's right hand was clasped against his chest in welcome, while the left hand was held out in a gesture of warding, protecting the Priest King of Khemri from the evils of the world.

There was also a lesser throne upon the dais, set off to the right and two steps lower, closer to the floor where Khemri's citizens attended upon their king. In the early days of the Living City, Khemri's patron god was Ptra, and under the auspices of the Sun God, Settra the Great was able to forge Nehekhara into a mighty empire. This was not enough for the mighty king, however, and in time, his power and his pride grew so great that he believed that he could find a way to defy death, and reign over the Blessed Land until the end of time. That was when the city's mortuary cult was born, more than seven hundred years ago, and in Settra's lifetime its high priest supplanted Ptra's, becoming Khemri's Grand Hierophant.

The ruling house of Khemri still owed a tremendous obligation, not just to Ptra, but to all the gods of the Blessed Land. Though the people of Nehekhara first encountered the gods near where the city of Mahrak now stood, many hundreds of leagues to the east, it was at Khemri, upon the banks of the River Vitae, that they entered into the great covenant that gave birth to the Blessed Land. Ptra and the gods swore to provide a paradise for the Nehekharans to live in, so long as the Nehekharans worshipped them and raised temples in their name. In addition every noble house would provide their firstborn as a gift to the gods, to serve as their priests and priestesses. In Khemri, the firstborn child was given to Ptra as the living embodiment of the great promise sworn between men and gods.

When Settra founded the mortuary cult he risked breaking the sacred covenant that made his glorious empire possible. Since he could not give his firstborn child to the gods, he chose to honour his promise in another way, by taking a priestess of Ptra as his wife. Settra's queen, the great Hatsushepra, was a daughter of the royal court of Lahmia. Ever since, a daughter of Lahmia was wed to the Priest King of Khemri to ensure the prosperity of the Blessed Land.

The queen's throne sat empty. Khetep's wife, Sofer, was praying at the temple of Djaf in preparation for joining her husband that afternoon, but there was someone standing *beside* the lesser throne, her hand resting almost possessively on its ornately carved arm. The strange breach of decorum caught the Grand Hierophant's eye, and he glanced up at the figure on the steps, less than a dozen feet away. Nagash's breath caught in his throat.

She was very young, Nagash noted at once, still a long way off the full flowering of her beauty. Her lithe body was clad in glorious yellow silk, brought all the way from the strange land that lay across the seas east of Lahmia. Bracelets of delicate, honey-coloured amber decorated her brown wrists, and a necklace of gold and fiery rubies encircled her slender neck. She had a small mouth and a pointed nose that accentuated her high, fine cheekbones and large, almond-shaped eyes that were the colour of polished emeralds. Despite her youth, she stood beside the empty throne with great poise and dignity. She was serene and utterly radiant. In time, Thutep's betrothed might become the greatest queen Nehekhara had ever known.

Nagash had never felt beguiled by a woman at any point in his life. The thought of emotional attachment or dependency was repellent to him, and could only be a hindrance to his ambitions, and yet, the moment he saw the queen, Nagash found himself gripped with a terrible, burning desire. His hands, hidden within the depths of his voluminous sleeves, clenched into grasping claws. The thought of the horrors he could inflict on such sanctified flesh nearly swept every other ambition out of the Grand Hierophant's mind. Only the thunderous cheer of the assembled throng brought Nagash out of his cruel reverie and focused him once more on the matter at hand.

The priest king's throne also stood empty. Thutep, the heir apparent, stood at the foot of the dais before a richly dressed dignitary from Zandri. Nagash's brother still wore the ceremonial finery of a royal prince, clad in a kilt and shoulder cape of white linen worked with gold thread. Gold bracelets were clasped around his brown arms, and a circlet set with a single ruby rested upon his brow. Though he did not possess the refined features of his father and older brother, Thutep's face was expressive and his eyes twinkled with easy charm. The ambassador from Zandri, whose sea-green robes were decorated with fine pearls and smooth, teardrop-shaped emeralds, bowed deeply to the king. The ambassador's dark hair and beard were tightly curled and glistened with fragrant oil, and his face was lit with a happy smile.

Nagash scowled as he recognised many of the faces of the young men who stood in serried ranks behind the ambassador. Many of the men bore livid bruises on their limbs or chests, and several sported fresh bandages spotted with blood. To a man, their faces were downcast, their chins hanging low in shame. They were the noblemen taken prisoner in the disastrous defeat just a short month ago. Nagash grasped the nature of Zandri's plan at once, and eyed his brother speculatively.

'The people of the Living City thank Nekumet, your great king, for this expression of charity and mercy,' Thutep declared, his hands clasped across his chest as he bowed, deeply. 'Let their return signal a new era of peace and prosperity for the people of the Blessed Land!'

Cheers rang out, once more. Khefru leaned close to his master, saying, 'Zandri is giving back all their prisoners without asking even a token ransom? It's madness!'

Nagash was careful to keep his bitter dismay secret.

'Not at all,' the Grand Hierophant said. 'The gesture wasn't made for Thutep's benefit, but for the other ambassadors.' When Khefru gave his master a blank stare, Nagash shot him an irritated look. 'Can't you see? It's a carefully calculated insult, and Nekumet's opening diplomatic gambit. By making a great show of handing back our noblemen without demanding a punishing ransom, he's telling the rest of Nehekhara that we're no threat to him.' He took in the entire chamber in a sharp sweep of his hand. 'Khetep is dead, and the jackals are circling, looking to grab whatever influence they can. Zandri just leapt to the front of the pack, and Thutep is too naïve to see it.'

Suddenly, Thutep turned, as though he'd caught the sound of his name. His gaze alighted on Nagash, and after a moment, his smile widened.

'Welcome, brother,' he said, beckoning to the Grand Hierophant. 'I'm glad you were here to witness the end of our feud with Zandri. Now the past can be put aside and forgotten.' Nagash favoured the ambassador from Zandri with a cold, implacable stare.

'I have come to tell you that our father's body has been prepared for its journey,' he said to his brother. 'We will bear him to the Great Pyramid an hour before sunset, in accordance with the wishes of the priests.'

The ambassador heard the news and his expression grew sombre. He bowed his head to Thutep, and said, 'Although we marched to war against your father, he was a bold warrior and a great king, and we mourn his death along with the rest of Nehekhara. We would therefore humbly offer a gift on behalf of the people of Zandri, to accompany Khetep on his journey into the afterlife.'

Thutep received the news with a grave nod. 'Very well,' he said. 'Let us see this gift.'

The ambassador beckoned, and a stir went up at the far end of the procession. The former prisoners, who were awaiting Thutep's leave to return to their families, were brushed to either side by a knot of burly, bare-chested slaves, dragging a trio of black-garbed figures, whom they deposited quickly at the ambassador's feet before hurriedly withdrawing.

Nagash studied the three figures carefully. They were tall and slender, clad in a strange combination of tattered woollen robes and some kind of dark leather armour that covered their torsos and abdomens. Two of them were female, with long, white hair that hung in unkempt tangles down to their waists. The male's hair was black as jet, almost as long and equally tangled. Their skin, what little Nagash could see of it, was whiter than alabaster. Their features were fine-boned and delicate, with pointed chins, sharp noses and angular cheekbones. They were beautiful, in a strange, almost dreadful way, and for all that they appeared fragile compared to the Nehekharans around them, they carried an aura of menace that somehow unsettled him. The male glanced up at Nagash. His expression was slack, and his black eyes were vacant. All three of them had been heavily drugged.

Curious whispers spread through the court. Thutep stared at the strange creatures with a mix of fascination and revulsion, as though he had come upon a clutch of cobras.

'What are they?' he asked.

'They call themselves druchii, great one,' the ambassador said quickly. 'Their ship grounded off our coast during a terrible storm only a few months ago, and they have served as slaves in the royal household ever since.'

At the sound of the word 'slave,' the male druchii turned his head to the ambassador and hissed something in a sibilant, snakelike tongue. The man from Zandri blanched at the sound, but quickly recovered.

'They are a wonder, are they not?' he said. 'It is our king's wish that they attend upon Khetep's spirit in the afterlife.' Thutep was taken aback by the offer. Material goods were one thing, an outsider offering slaves for the service of a dead king was something else.

'Well, it's certainly a generous gift,' he said slowly, unwilling to give offence.

Nagash watched the entire exchange with increasing interest. What was the Zandri delegation playing at? Obviously there was much more to this than met the eye. Then he noticed one of the females steady herself and bend her head in concentration. She tried to speak, slurring the words of her chilling language, but nevertheless Nagash sensed a faint wave of power emanate from her like an icy desert wind.

He stiffened, suddenly alert. Could it be?

The Grand Hierophant turned to Thutep.

'Zandri's offer is unprecedented,' he said, struggling to keep his voice even, 'but that does not make it unwelcome. I say we should accept their gift in the spirit it was given, great one.' Thutep beamed.

'So be it,' he declared. 'The slaves should be conducted to the temple,' he said to Nagash. 'Will you see to it?' Nagash smiled.

'I should like nothing more,' he replied.

THREE

THE BLACK VIZIER

The Oasis of Zedri,
in the 62nd year of Qu'aph the Cunning
(-1750 Imperial Reckoning)

Shouts of anguish and fear rent the air above the battlefield as unearthly darkness rolled like a swift tide down the rocky slope and across the bloodstained sands. Akhmen-hotep, Priest King of Ka-Sabar, watched the companies of enemy infantry find new strength as the terrible shadow swept over their heads. They surged forwards against the front ranks of the Bronze Host, chopping and stabbing fiercely at the giant warriors before them. Whether their new-found ferocity was born of courage, or terror, the king could not say.

The chariot beneath Akhmen-hotep lurched backwards as the driver cursed and wrestled with his frenzied horses. The terrible, droning sound pulsed and sawed rhythmically around the struggling warriors, making it difficult to think. The priest king saw warriors in twos and threes racing past his chariot, running away from the fighting, back towards the sunlit oasis. His companies were wavering, their courage pressed to the limit by the sudden change of circumstance.

Darkness engulfed the ranks of the enemy warriors and swept over the battle line. Men cried out in terror. More and more warriors in the rear ranks of Akhmen-hotep's companies turned and fled rather than face the sorcerous shadow.

The priest king cursed and looked around in growing desperation. The tide of blackness would sweep over him in seconds. He had to act quickly and regain control of his troops before their resolve collapsed entirely.

His Ushabti bodyguards were already reacting, drawing their chariots around the priest king in a tighter defensive formation. Akhmen-hotep caught sight of his remaining messengers, standing just a few yards behind his chariot and eyeing the coming darkness with palpable dread.

'Runners!' he called out, beckoning to them. 'Here! Quickly!'

The four boys gladly raced for the safety of the chariot. Akhmen-hotep held out his hand. 'Up here! Grab hold,' he shouted above the din. As they climbed aboard, he stole a quick glance to the east, searching for Suseb's company of chariots. If the front lines broke, the Lion and his men would have to countercharge Nagash's warriors to give the infantry time to retreat and re-form their units. The chariots, however, were nowhere to be seen. The dust was rising once again, and all the priest king could see were vague shapes dashing back and forth through the haze.

There was no time to waste. He had to issue orders to his men at once, or they would take matters into their own hands. The priest king tasted bile in the back of his throat as he searched for his trumpeter's chariot. Thankfully, the man had kept his head and ordered his driver to remain close to Akhmen-hotep's left.

'Sound the call to withdraw!' the priest king shouted. Five yards away, the trumpeter nodded and put his bronze horn to his lips.

The long, wailing note rang out across the battlefield, and then the tide of unearthly shadow swept over them.

Akhmen-hotep felt a chill wind brush across his bare neck, and the air above him rustled and clattered with the whir of insectile wings. For a few moments, the priest king was blind as the spreading cloud blotted out the blazing sun, and a wave of childlike terror closed like a vice around his throat. Sounds became strangely magnified in the darkness. He heard the savage curses of his driver and the terrified panting of the horses over the clash of arms, and the shouting of warriors from the battle-line dozens of yards distant. If anything, it sounded as though the fighting had redoubled its intensity, coming from every direction at once.

The priest king's eyes gradually adjusted to the change, and details of the battlefield took shape around him. The shroud of darkness above the warriors was in constant, seething motion, which allowed just enough light to seep through so that the plain was plunged into a sort of perpetual twilight. He could see the faint gleam of the spears and helmets of the Bronze Host, still struggling with the warriors of the Usurper. His companies were giving ground, slowly but surely, but the command to withdraw had restored some of their former spirit and discipline. Still, from what the priest king could see, there were scores upon scores of stragglers staggering across the battlefield. Akhmen-hotep took heart from the fact that many of them seemed to be heading back to their companies along the line, but others were milling about in apparent shock or confusion.

All was not lost, the priest king reckoned. Off to the south, he could still see the oasis, bathed in Ptra's light. If the host could fall back to the sunlight in good order, they could stand their ground and repel the Usurper's sudden assault, but Akhmen-hotep knew they could not do it without help.

The priest king glanced down at his messengers, and asked, 'Which of you is the swiftest runner?' All four boys looked to one another. Finally, the smallest of them raised his hand.

'They call me Dhekeru, great one,' he said, with a small amount of pride, 'because I am as fleet as a mountain deer.' Akhmen-hotep smiled.

'Dhekeru. That's good.' He laid a broad hand on the boy's shoulder. 'Go and tell the priests to hurry north and join us. The gods must be with us if we are to prevail.'

Dhekeru nodded. The young boy's face was set in a determined scowl, but the priest king could feel the runner's little body trembling in his grip. Akhmen-hotep gave the boy's shoulder a reassuring squeeze, and then Dhekeru was gone, leaping from the back of the chariot and dashing off into the gloom.

The priest king straightened and tried to take stock of the battle. The battle-line was a swirling mob of silhouettes just to the north. Experience told him that they had fallen back perhaps fifty yards so far, and were giving ground quickly. More screams of terror rang through the air, and confused shouts echoed up and down the line.

Akhmen-hotep frowned. There were still more stragglers stumbling across the plain behind the retreating army. Where were they all coming from?

Then, something heavy crashed against the side of the chariot to the priest king's right, next to his bowman. The archer let out a startled shout and stumbled backwards as a figure tried to climb over the bronze-armoured side. Akhmen-hotep saw a bloody hand reach for the bowman and grab hold of his leather armour, and then, to the priest king's horror, the figure hauled back with surprising strength and pulled the archer over the side.

Horses screamed in terror. Akhmen-hotep heard the driver curse fearfully and crack his whip, jolting the chariot forwards. The priest king staggered, groping for the khopesh by his side as the silhouetted figure dragged itself further over the rim of the chariot and reached out to him. A terrible stink emanated from the attacker, and Akhmen-hotep smelled bitter blood and ruptured bowels, like a freshly killed corpse.

Then the figure drew nearer with a gurgling hiss, and the priest king peered through the gloom and realised that was exactly what it was.

It was one of the Usurper's tormented soldiers, clad only in a ragged, bloodstained kilt. Its chest was misshapen, having been crushed by the bronze-shod wheel of a chariot, and a spear point had torn open the warrior's cheek before deflecting downward into the base of its neck, leaving a gaping, bloody hole. A flap of bloody skin dangled from the side of the creature's pallid face, and the priest king could glimpse pale bone as its jaw gaped in another reptilian hiss.

Before the creature could reach him, Akhmen-hotep's Ushabti stepped between them with a liquid growl and a blur of his ritual blade. Bronze rang against bone and the undead monster fell back over the side of the chariot. Its severed head bounced once off the vehicle's wooden bed and disappeared into the darkness.

The sounds of battle raged all around them as the rest of Akhmen-hotep's retinue found itself under attack. A chariot raced past, heading south, with a trio of clawing fiends hanging from its sides. The priest king realised that one of the creatures was wearing the leather and bronze harness of his own army.

Akhmen-hotep choked back a cry of horror. Nagash's unholy powers were far greater than he imagined. The dead rose from the bloodied earth to do his foul bidding!

One of the messengers let out a terrified scream. The priest king whirled, but the boy was gone, snatched into the darkness. The other children wailed in terror, crowding towards the front of the chariot. At the priest king's side, his devoted bodyguard stood with his feet wide apart and his ritual sword raised, ready to protect his master against any foe, living or otherwise.

They heard the sound of splintering wood and the frenzied cries of maddened horses off to their left. Akhmen-hotep saw that one of the chariot drivers had lost control of his animals and the panicked beasts had turned too tightly, flipping the chariot onto its side. His stomach fell as he saw a flash of bronze cartwheel across the sand. It was the trumpeter's signal-horn. More than a dozen walking corpses were converging on the broken chariot and its stunned occupants. They reached the chariot's archer first, chopping his unconscious form to pieces with their stone axes.

Akhmen-hotep heard the chariot's driver shriek in terror, but then the Ushabti assigned to protect the trumpeter reared up among the undead warriors with a leonine roar and laid about them with his ritual sword. The giant warrior sent broken bodies spinning through the air with each sword-stroke, reaping a terrible harvest among the blasphemous throng, but more and more of the fallen warriors were closing in from all sides, brandishing bloodied weapons or reaching for the devoted bodyguard with grasping, claw-like hands.

Akhmen-hotep fought to keep his balance as his chariot turned sharply about and began to head back in the direction of the oasis. He craned his neck, trying to see what was happening along the battle-line. From what he could see, the withdrawal had ground to a halt, and his companies were being attacked from in front and behind, sowing deadly confusion through the ranks. The priest king clenched his fists in frustration; with his trumpeter gone, he had no way of communicating with his men. He thought of poor, brave Dhekeru, racing unarmed across a plain swarming with the walking dead, and his expression turned bleak.

There was nothing more he could do. Their survival rested in the hands of the gods.

Back along the shadowed ridge, the air trembled with another seething, locust-like drone. Each of the silent tents surrounding the army's central pavilion contained an upright sarcophagus of polished basalt, attended upon by a cowering knot of dull-eyed slaves. The rising drone spurred these wretched figures to fearful action, clawing at the heavy stone lids and pulling them aside.

Serpentine hisses and cruel, hungry laughter welled up from the depths of the stone coffins, causing the slaves to fall upon their knees and press their faces to the rocky ground. Pale, black-veined hands grasped the rims of the sarcophagi, and one by one, a score of monsters who wore the shapes of men climbed from their cold beds and stepped out into the welcoming darkness.

They moved with the arrogance of princes, who knew no law but their own. Their skin was white as chalk, and their lips and fingertips were bluish-black with the stain of old, dead blood. Rings of gold and silver glittered on their clawed fingers, and jewelled circlets rested upon their alabaster brows. All of them were garbed for war, with studded leather bindings covering their torsos and skullcaps of hammered bronze.

One among them was taller than the rest, gaunt and vulture-like even in his fine armour and heavy, black cape. His tent stood at the right hand of the great pavilion, and he wore the ornate circlet of a vizier upon his bald head. The noble's cheeks were sunken, emphasising his sharply angled cheekbones and pointed chin.

Arkhan the Black looked out upon the battlefield and was pleased with what he saw. His lips drew back in a malevolent grin, revealing a mouthful of stained, pointed teeth. The Vizier of Khemri ran a blue-black tongue over those jagged points as he felt the unspoken commands of his master.

'It shall be done,' he whispered in a thin, croaking voice. Then he beckoned to a messenger waiting in the shadow of the master's pavilion. 'Go to the Master of Skulls and tell him to begin,' he told the frightened boy. Then he turned and strode swiftly to a waiting squadron of heavy horsemen formed up on the slope before his tent.

Horses and riders alike hung their heads and trembled at the undead lord's approach. Arkhan's mount was a half-mad black mare, branded with sorcerous glyphs that bound it to his will. It rolled its eyes fearfully at its master's approach, tossing its head and clashing its chisel-like teeth as the warrior climbed gracefully into the saddle. The vizier turned to his men, smiling cruelly at the way they flinched beneath his stare.

'The Bronze Host has been laid against the anvil,' he growled. 'Now comes the hammer.'

Arkhan pointed a clawed finger at his trumpeter, and said, 'Signal the cavalry to wheel right. We will charge their left flank and put them to flight.'

The Usurper's vizier drew a wicked-looking bronze scimitar from its scabbard and put his heels to his horse's flanks. It lurched forwards with a tormented squeal, and the ranks of heavy horsemen followed suit. All along the ridge-line, Nagash's immortal champions took charge of their warriors and heeded the wailing call of the trumpet.

* * *

Arkhan's messenger raced between the funereal tents and picked his way across the rocky summit until he disappeared behind the ridge's northern face, out of sight of the battling armies. There, along the opposite slope, waited a dozen wheeled war machines built of heavy cedar logs and ensorcelled bronze nails.

A single, dust-covered tent waited beside the ancient trade road, which ran squarely between the line of war machines and their silent crews. A short, broad-shouldered man with small, dark eyes set in a round, jowly face emerged from the tent at the boy's approach, and replied to the vizier's message with a single grunt. He was a master engineer, chosen by Nagash to master the secrets of the fearsome machines as depicted in ancient manuscripts looted from a necropolis in far-off Zandri. For his success, Nagash tore out the man's tongue so that he could not share what he had learned with anyone else.

The Master of Skulls dismissed the messenger and walked up the road. The crews of the war machines went to work at once. Some bent to the task of cranking back the throwing arm of each catapult, while others turned to the dozen large wicker baskets and pulled away their lids, revealing heaped piles of leering skulls marked with clusters of arcane glyphs.

Within minutes, the catapult arms had been locked back, and their leather baskets filled with their grisly ammunition. When all was ready, the engineer raised his hand and let out a wordless, ululating cry.

Flickering green fire burst from each of the catapult baskets, and the chief of each crew hurriedly pulled back on the lanyards. The catapult arms banged against their braces, and hundreds of fiery, shrieking skulls streaked through the darkness over the ridge.

Akhmen-hotep brought his khopesh down upon the skull of one of his fallen soldiers as the corpse-thing tried to claw its way onto his chariot. The enchanted bronze sword sheared away the top of the warrior's head, splattering brain matter onto the king's bare shins. The thing collapsed, sliding from the back of the chariot, while the king's bodyguard hacked apart two more that were trying to climb aboard from the other side.

The king and his retinue had been retreating steadily across the plain, hoping to find the city priests making their way north from the edge of the oasis. Corpses assailed them from all sides. Many were crushed beneath the chariot's wheels, but others tried to leap upon the backs of the horses or get inside the chariot. The last two messenger boys had been dragged away by the undead creatures, and the horses were staggering from exhaustion and scores of minor wounds. Most of his Ushabti were still with him, as far as he could see, but they were almost half a mile away from the struggling army, and still there was no sign of Ka-Sabar's holy men.

Suddenly, the priest king heard a strange, piping chorus of unearthly cries coming from the direction of the ridge. Akhmen-hotep looked back the way they'd come, and saw a flickering rain of fiery green orbs arcing down onto the struggling companies.

The hail of screaming skulls scattered widely over the clashing armies, falling among friend and foe alike, but where the warriors of Khemri were inured to their horror, the Bronze Host was not. The grisly missiles exploded among their ranks, showering them with blazing fragments and filling their ears with shrieks of agony and despair. Beset on all sides by warriors living and dead, including the bloodied corpses of their kinsmen, the Bronze Host had been pushed far beyond the limits of its courage. Cries of horror went up from the men, and the embattled companies began to disintegrate as the warriors turned their backs upon the foe and ran for their lives.

Too late, Akhmen-hotep saw the trap that the Usurper had laid for him. Nagash had drawn his forces across the plain, through a field littered with Khemri dead, and the panicked warriors of the Bronze Host would retreat into the murderous arms of those they had already slain. The priest king's mind reeled at the disaster unfolding before him.

Just as all hope was lost, the piercing note of a trumpet sounded on the right flank, and the rumble of chariot wheels shook the ground behind the retreating army. Suseb the Lion had seen the peril as well, and he led his warriors in a sweeping charge across the battlefield. Akhmen-hotep watched as the champion and his two hundred chariots rumbled out of the haze, their scythed wheels tearing through the undead warriors caught in their path. Archers fired from the backs of the chariots, sending bronze-tipped arrows through the skulls of the slow-moving monsters as they rode past.

The chariots thundered off to the left flank, leaving a swathe of mangled bodies in their wake. Many of the army's companies were in full flight, but at least Akhmen-hotep had a chance to rally the survivors and perhaps turn the tide of battle once more, if only he could find the damned priests!

'Keep going!' the priest king called to his driver. The charioteer lashed his whip and drove his staggering horses into a trot, heading further south towards the oasis.

Arkhan the Black watched a second wave of shrieking skulls streak through the air overhead and fall upon the enemy's fleeing ranks. The centre had broken, but the flanks were still holding out against the onslaught. Somewhere behind the enemy lines he heard the wail of trumpets, and the muted thunder of chariot wheels. Was Ka-Sabar's heavy cavalry making a hasty retreat, or a desperate countercharge? At this distance, there was no way to tell.

Gripping the reins, the vizier surveyed the twenty squadrons of heavy horse massed along the western end of the ridge. Five hundred yards to the south, the left flank of the enemy army was locked in a relentless struggle with the Khemri infantry. They were heedless of the danger gathering like a cobra on the slope before them.

They would sweep down in an unstoppable wave, riding through their troops and crashing against the weakened ranks of the enemy like a thunderbolt. The infantry would break, and the slaughter would begin. Arkhan imagined the spray of hot blood against his skin, and shivered with anticipation.

Arkhan raised his curved sword and bared his blackened teeth. 'Charge!' he cried, and brazen trumpets wailed. Slowly at first, and then gathering speed in an avalanche of flesh and bronze, five thousand horsemen bore down on the unsuspecting warriors of Ka-Sabar.

Trumpets howling like the souls of the damned, the horsemen of Khemri thundered down the rocky slope towards the beleaguered companies of the Bronze Host. Arkhan the Black lashed at his enchanted mount, drawing ahead of his charging warriors in his hunger to bathe in human blood. The air rang with frenzied shouts as the heavy horsemen gave vent to their anger and fear and hurled themselves into the storm of battle.

The wings of the Bronze Host had curled inwards during the course of the battle as the warriors sought to encircle the smaller Khemri army; its battle-line curved into a long, glinting crescent, with the ends still struggling to force their opponents in towards the army's centre. This presented the charging horsemen with an opportunity to turn the tables on the spearmen of the enemy's left flank, striking the companies both from the front and the side.

The warriors of Ka-Sabar were tough and resolute fighters, however, skilled in the arts of war. Even as Arkhan's cavalry reached the base of the ridge, the enemy companies sensed the danger bearing down on them and tried to shift their lines to face the new threat. With his one good eye, Arkhan saw the ranks of spearmen waver and fragment as they tried to disengage from the relentless attacks of the Khemri infantry and prepare for the shock of the cavalry attack, but Nagash's footmen, both living and dead, drove inexorably against the struggling enemy formations. They dragged down shields and impaled themselves on spears, forcing their way among the giant warriors and breaking their cohesion still further. Seconds before impact, Arkhan saw the looks of despair on his enemies' faces as they realised that their frantic manoeuvres had been for nought.

Laughing cruelly, Arkhan led his horsemen through the thin ranks of his infantry and into the midst of the warriors of Ka-Sabar. Khemri footmen, too exhausted or too preoccupied to avoid the charge, were smashed aside by the weight of the horses or trampled beneath their hooves. Their deaths were meaningless to him, for within moments their corpses would rise and begin the assault anew.

The vizier's first blow was struck against one of his own men, his scimitar flashing down and smiting a staggering axe-man who stood between him and his chosen foe. The blade bit deep at the juncture of the man's neck and shoulder, spinning him off his feet with a scream and a welter of blood.

The smell of it maddened Arkhan. Roaring hungrily he spurred his horse forward into the thicket of spears before him, his blade sweeping left and right in devastating strokes. All around him, the charge of the Khemri horsemen crashed home, fracturing the companies into knots of desperately struggling men. Swords and axes flashed, hacking down at spear hafts and crashing against the edges of bronze-rimmed shields. Spearmen fell with shattered skulls or torn throats, or clutching the stumps of severed arms. Horses thrashed and screamed, impaled on bronze spearheads or pulled to the ground by the fearsome strength of the giant warriors. To Arkhan's right, a veteran spearman grabbed the reins of a rearing warhorse and jerked its head with such power that its neck broke with a brittle crunch of bones, and then stabbed his spear through the rider's chest as the dead mount collapsed to the ground.

Even astride his powerful horse, Arkhan found himself looking his towering opponents nearly eye-to-eye. Even as they reeled from the force of the cavalry charge, they struck at the vizier from every side. A flashing spear point drove into his left side, just beneath the ribs, and another punched through his right thigh and dug into his horse's ribs. Hissing like a viper, Arkhan decapitated a man to his right and took a hand off a spearman to his left. His sword flashed and spun, scattering ribbons of steaming blood in a wide arc as he toppled one foe after another. The necromantic power burning in his veins lent him equal strength and greater speed than his enemies, and his foes toppled like wheat before the vizier's bloodstained blade.

The enemy recoiled from Arkhan's terrible might, shouting the names of their gods or crying out in dismay. A flung spear struck the vizier full in the chest, piercing his lung. He tore it free with his left hand and hurled it back with a bloody sneer, and then stood high in the saddle and began to chant in a harsh, sibilant hiss. The air around Arkhan crackled with invisible power as he spoke the necromantic spell, and the men he'd slain began to stir. Streaming blood from their terrible wounds, the dead warriors climbed numbly to their feet amid the horrified cries of their kinsmen.

The shock of the terrible charge and the fate of their fallen brothers were too much for the enemy to endure. The spearmen broke, piling back upon the company next to them and disrupting the formation in their haste to escape. Arkhan's horsemen rode the spearmen down as they tried to flee, spurring their horses forward into the press and hacking away with their bloodstained swords. The panic of the fleeing men was contagious, affecting every warrior they came into contact with. The advancing cavalry had barely reached the second enemy company when it, too, wavered and broke in the face of the onslaught. They, in turn, fell back against the third company in line, their numbers so great that even stalwart warriors were swept away in the press.

Exultant, the horsemen continued their advance, sowing terror and panic among their foes. Several squadrons had already worked their way around the growing mob of fleeing troops and had encountered a screen of light cavalry. The enemy riders fired a volley of arrows point-blank into the flanks of the Khemri horsemen, toppling more than a score of men from their saddles or sending their mounts thrashing to the ground. One of Arkhan's squadrons wheeled to face the light cavalry and made to charge them, but the horsemen of Ka-Sabar broke off at once, galloping south for the safety of the oasis.

The third company was struggling to hold together against the tide of their retreating comrades. The formation had already fragmented into large bands of isolated warriors, but these men were made of sterner stuff than their fellows, and struggled to stand their ground against all odds. Horsemen circled them like wolves, darting in and striking a few swift blows before dashing away again, but the longer reach of the spear and the strength of the men of Ka-Sabar worked to their advantage. Dead men and horses were piling up around the grim spearmen, slowing down the weight of Arkhan's charge and allowing the retreating warriors the opportunity to escape. Cursing hatefully, the vizier weighed his options. The cavalry's charge had all but spent its strength. Should he withdraw, regroup, and charge again, or summon his fellow immortals and grind these stubborn holdouts into the dust?

Arkhan hesitated, and in those few moments his opportunity was lost. With the thunder of bronze-rimmed wheels and the deadly hum of bowstrings, a dark mass of armoured chariots charged out of the haze from behind the centre of the retreating enemy army, rushing to the rescue of the wavering left flank.

Arrows buzzed through the milling crowd of horsemen, wreaking deadly havoc among their ranks, and then the scythe-armed chariots plunged into their midst. The whirling blades mounted on the chariot axles, each as long as the blade of a sword, tore through the legs of the Khemri horses, mortally wounding dozens and filling the air with their chilling screams. Great bronze scimitars flashed in the hands of the warriors riding in the backs of these heavy war machines, cutting down horsemen and walking corpses alike.

The force of the enemy charge shocked Arkhan's horsemen. The bronze-sheathed chariots of Ka-Sabar were unlike the lighter, swifter machines found in the armies of other Nehekharan cities, and in the hands of a competent commander their impact was devastating. A cheer went up from the Bronze Host at their sudden appearance, and the wavering spear companies appeared to regain a measure of their lost courage. Arkhan knew that he had to act quickly before the chariots caused so much damage that he would have to withdraw back to the ridge. The thought of facing his master and admitting his defeat was too terrible to contemplate.

Arkhan uttered a savage curse and spurred his wounded horse forward, galloping headlong into the midst of the enemy chariots. Arrows buzzed angrily around him. One buried itself in his shoulder, but he scarcely felt the blow. He was searching among the thundering war machines, seeking the champion who led them. If he could find that man and slay him it would surely dismay the rest.

He saw the man almost at once: a lean, dark-skinned giant at the forefront of the enemy attack, wielding a two-handed khopesh as though it were no more than a hollow reed. The champion was already splashed with gore, and a dozen horses and their riders lay smashed and bloodied in his wake.

Arkhan knew that this was Suseb the Lion. It could be no other. Ka-Sabar's Master of Horse was accounted as one of the greatest living warriors in all Nehekhara.

The vizier smiled coldly. He had been murdering men like Suseb for a hundred years before the Lion was even born.

Across the battlefield, the mighty champion caught sight of the vizier's dark form. The Lion's eyes widened at the sight of the pale immortal.

Arkhan raised his bloody scimitar in challenge and put his spurs to his horse's flanks.

FOUR

THE FICKLE TIDE

The Oasis of Zedri,
in the 62nd year of Qu'aph the Cunning
(-1750 Imperial Reckoning)

Akhmen-hotep heard the thunder of hooves to the west and gritted his teeth in helpless rage. Pakh-amn's light cavalry was retreating from the Usurper's sudden attack. The shouts and screams from the far end of the battle-line had merged into a formless, toneless roar of pure noise. It was not the dull metal clatter of battle, but the sound of pure butchery. If the left flank had not already collapsed, it was teetering on the brink.

Men were pouring past the priest king's chariot in an apparently endless flood, their faces slack with terror and exhaustion. Behind them came an inexorable tide of walking death, a new army of undead flesh, animated by a soulless, evil will.

He had shouted himself hoarse, trying to rally his men and return them to the fight. At first, he enjoyed some success, collecting stragglers here and there and ordering them back into threadbare companies, but as soon as the shambling corpses appeared, they lost their nerve once more.

Unless something could be done to hold the undead creatures at bay, the Bronze Host would be utterly destroyed, and if the fearsome warriors of Ka-Sabar were no match for Nagash the Usurper, Nehekhara was surely doomed.

There had been no sign of the priests in the long retreat across the plain. Akhmen-hotep resigned himself to the fact that young Dhekeru had stood no chance against the horrors lurking in the darkness. All that remained was to reach the oasis and make his stand, hoping that the foul stain of darkness would not spread further.

Then, a pearlescent glow flared to life, just a few yards ahead of the retreating chariot. The driver called out in alarm, but the priest king laid a reassuring hand on the frightened man's shoulder. He could hear the sound of voices mingled in a steady, determined chant.

'The priests!' he cried, his heart lifting. His message had won through after all!

Within moments, Akhmen-hotep and his Ushabti led their chariots past a line of Neru's white-robed priests, all standing fearlessly in the path of the oncoming creatures and chanting the Invocation of the Vigilant Sentinel. The pearly light of the moon goddess radiated from their skin, pushing back the darkness and giving the frightened warriors a place of refuge. Beyond the line of stalwart priests, Akhmen-hotep spied their High Priestess, Khalifra, offering prayers and sacrifice to her goddess. Farther off, he saw Memnet and the priests of Ptra, gathered in grim debate with Sukhet and the priests of Phakth.

A booming, bull-like voice rose above the distant roar of battle and the confused shouts of the retreating warriors. Hashepra, the iron-thewed high priest of Geheb, was bellowing to the soldiers of the Bronze Host.

'Darkness comes and darkness goes, but the great earth is not moved,' he called. 'Stand fast, like the mountains, and Geheb will bless you with the strength to defeat your enemies!' The power of Hashepra's voice and his stern, intimidating presence had the desired effect on the men, restoring their courage and stopping their headlong flight. Slowly, but surely, discipline was being restored, but would it be in time?

Strange, unearthly moans rose from the gloom as the first of the undead reached the barrier of moonlight cast by the priests of Neru. The creatures hesitated, raising their bloody limbs to shield their faces from the glow. They hissed and cried, but for the moment they could advance no further. Akhmen-hotep offered a prayer of thanks to the Heavenly Consort, and then directed his driver to take him to Memnet.

The priests of sun and sky put aside their heated words at the priest king's approach, but Akhmen-hotep could see the strain etched deeply on their faces. He dismounted from his chariot before it had fully stopped and rushed up to the grim-faced men.

'Thank all the gods that you got my message,' he began. Memnet frowned. 'Message? There was no message.'

'When we saw the darkness unleashed, we knew that we would be called upon,' Sukhet interjected, 'though none of us could have expected the blasphemous sorceries the Usurper now possesses.'

'I see,' Akhmen-hotep said quietly. 'What about this foul darkness? Can you not disperse it?'

'It is all we can do to keep it from spreading further,' Sukhet snapped, giving the king a sour look. 'It is no mere cloud of dust or ash, but a living thing, perhaps a swarm of beetles or locusts, marshalled by diabolical intent. It rides upon the wind, and cannot be easily swept aside.'

'Then what of the Great Father's light?' Akhmen-hotep asked the Grand Hierophant. 'Can you not invoke Ptra to burn this devilry from the sky?'

'Do you not think I have tried, brother?' Memnet said bleakly. The Grand

Hierophant's face was pale, and his eyes were wide with fear. 'I have made entreaties. I have made sacrifices. I fed my body servants to the flames, but Ptra does not heed me!'

Akhmen-hotep shook his head, and said, 'You're not making sense. The covenant–'

'What the Grand Hierophant means is that we are being interfered with,' Sukhet said darkly. 'I do not know how.' He cast a worried look in the direction of the distant ridge. 'There is sorcery at work unlike anything I have ever known. It is the foulest sort of magic, the work of the devils!'

'Then you must strike at it with all the power you have available!' Akhmen-hotep said. 'Call upon the lightning! Sear the sky with Ptra's fire! Strike at the Usurper with all the wrath of the gods!'

'You don't know what you are asking,' Sukhet answered, genuinely shaken by the priest king's demand. 'The price of such power–'

'Pay it!' the king commanded. 'No cost is too great to rid the Blessed Land of such a monster! He has bled our cities white, terrorised our people and emptied our treasuries, and if we are defeated here, do you imagine that Nagash will be content with a ransom of gold, or ingots of bronze? Have you forgotten what he did to Zandri, back in the days of our fathers? That will pale in comparison to the vengeance he will wreak upon us for our defiance.'

'But the omens,' Memnet moaned. 'I tried to warn you. While the sunlight shone, we had our way, but now–'

Akhmen-hotep took a menacing step towards his older brother.

'Then make it shine again,' he snarled.

The Grand Hierophant started to protest, but suddenly a faint, skirling sound rose wild and clear above the tumult, echoing from the dunes to the west. Heads turned, searching for the source of the sound. Sukhet, whose ears were keener by the grace of his god, cocked his head attentively.

'Horns,' he said, 'but made of bone, not bronze.'

'Another trick of the Usurper?' Memnet asked.

'No, not this time,' Akhmen-hotep said. His face creased in a triumphant smile. 'The princes of Bhagar have arrived at last!'

Three-quarters of a mile distant, hidden from sight by the Usurper's unnatural shadow, four thousand robed horsemen rode out of the blinding desert sands, hastening to the fight. The merchant princes of Bhagar had sent every fighting man they could spare to aid their allies in the struggle against Nagash, and there were no better horsemen in all the Blessed Land. In ancient times, they had been bandits, preying upon Nehekharan caravans and slipping like ghosts back into the dunes, but in the time of Settra they had been tamed and welcomed into the Empire. Since then, they had prospered as traders, but they had never forgotten their warlike ways.

The horsemen of Bhagar knew the Great Desert as a man knows his first wife. They were privy to its changing ways and its fierce temper, its hidden gifts and shadowy secrets, and yet, as they rode to the aid of Ka-Sabar, they were bedevilled again and again by fierce sandstorms and false trails that cost them precious days amid the burning sands. When their outriders caught sight of the spreading darkness staining the horizon, they had feared the worst, and pushed their fiery desert steeds to the utmost.

Led by the bold Shahid ben Alcazzar, first among equals in Bhagar and called the Red Fox by his kin, the desert horsemen plunged fearlessly into the unnatural darkness hanging over the great plain, and found themselves behind a swirling mass of cavalrymen threatening the Bronze Host's left flank. Calling upon the spirits of their ancestors, they winded their bone war horns and raced into battle. The lead riders drew short, barbed javelins from quivers hanging by their knees and let fly into the packed mass of heavy horsemen, while those further behind unlimbered powerful composite horse bows and thick, red-fletched arrows. The powerful missiles could punch through a wooden shield at forty paces, and the riders knew how to use them to deadly effect.

The sudden attack sowed death and confusion among the enemy ranks, and the squadrons of heavy horsemen scattered before the onslaught. Swift as a pack of wolves, the desert raiders wheeled about and dashed back the way they'd come, leaving a hundred dead cavalrymen littering the bloody ground. Then, after a hundred yards they stopped, turned about, and came at the enemy once more, weaving effortlessly among the heavier warhorses and toppling men from their saddles. Furious, the Khemri horsemen tried to give chase, and the desert raiders began, slowly but surely, to draw them off to the west, away from the embattled spear companies.

Arkhan heard the wailing horns of the desert riders just as he began his charge, and realised the peril his warriors were in. They were caught between two enemy forces, and if the chariots could regroup and charge his men once more, they could very well break under the pressure. Without warning, the tide of battle threatened to turn against them.

Hissing like an adder, the vizier bore down on Suseb the Lion. The champion of the Bronze Host likewise ordered his chariot forward, raising his mighty khopesh. The archer beside him raised his bow, but Suseb stopped him with a forbidding glare. This would be a battle between heroes, or so the Lion thought.

As the distance between them dwindled, Arkhan began to chant. He felt the dark power bubbling in his veins, and at the last moment he stretched out his left hand and unleashed a storm of crackling ebon bolts at the occupants of the chariot. Screams and shouts of fury answered the vizier as he veered away from the onrushing chariot and its scything blades.

After a dozen yards, he swung about and saw that the champion's armoured chariot had come to a halt. Its driver lay at Suseb's feet, his body a smoking husk, and the Lion was struggling to untangle the chariot's reins from the corpse's shrivelled hands. The champion's archer, meanwhile, leapt from the back of the chariot and stood between Arkhan and his foe. The vizier laughed at the sight and spurred his mount forward.

The bowman was a man of courage. His face was a mask of rage, but he moved with calm efficiency, drawing a long reed arrow to his cheek and letting fly at the onrushing immortal. Arkhan jerked the reins at the last minute, trying to dodge aside, and the arrow struck him in the left arm instead of burying itself in his heart.

Before the archer could draw another arrow, Arkhan was upon him. His scimitar hissed through the air, and the bowman's headless body fell forward into the dust.

The archer's death had given the Lion the time he needed, however, and with an angry cry he lashed the reins and the chariot lurched into motion once more. Suseb handled the huge machine masterfully, turning it in a tight circle, but not before Arkhan dashed past. Once again, his scimitar whirred in a decapitating arc, but the blade shivered in his hand as though he'd struck solid teak. The Lion, it appeared, ranked high in the earth god's favour.

Despite the speed of Arkhan's charge he still felt the wind of Suseb's blade slicing through the air a fraction of an inch behind him. He continued on past the champion for less than ten feet before hauling furiously on the reins. His steed tossed its head angrily and pawed at the earth as the vizier hauled it back around for another pass.

Suseb was still struggling to control the chariot with one hand while looking over his shoulder at Arkhan. He was bringing the war machine about, but too slowly. Grinning like a devil, Arkhan bore down on the Lion's back, sword poised above his head. Once again he began to chant. Wisps of foul, black vapour began to curl from the edge of his blade.

The Lion watched the vizier approach with an expression of stoic resolve. At the last moment, Arkhan's sense of triumph turned to trepidation. When Suseb let go of the chariot's reins he knew that he'd been tricked. The champion became a blur of motion, spinning on his heel and bringing his massive sword around in a whirling, backhanded blow.

It was only the immortal's unnatural reflexes that saved him. He tore at the reins, once more, and the warhorse's charge was halted for the space of a single moment. Suseb's blade fell in a glittering arc, passing before Arkhan instead of through him, and sliced through the animal's thick neck instead. The horse's headless body lurched drunkenly to the right, sending mount and rider crashing full-force into the Lion's chariot. There was the sound of splintering wood and tearing metal. Arkhan struck the side of the war machine in a bone-crushing impact and knew no more.

A cheer went up from the beleaguered ranks of the Bronze Host at the sound of Bhagar's war horns. Their allies had arrived in the nick of time, just where they were needed. Akhmen-hotep felt a wild surge of hope. Could they snatch victory from the jaws of defeat?

The priest king regarded Memnet and Sukhet once more.

'You see? The gods have not abandoned us!' he said. 'Now it is up to us to show that we are worthy of their aid. Call upon their power, and let us destroy the Usurper once and for all!'

A terrible look came over Sukhet's face as he heard Akhmen-hotep's plea, but he nodded nevertheless.

'So be it,' he said in a leaden voice, and led his priests some distance away to begin the invocations.

The priest king turned to Memnet, and asked, 'And what of you, Grand Hierophant? Will the Great Father Ptra aid us in our time of need?'

Memnet stepped close to the king.

'Don't take that tone with me, little brother,' he said in a low voice. 'Did you not hear Sukhet? The gods are not soldiers to be commanded, like your warriors. They will exact a heavy price for such power, and *we* will be the ones to pay it, not you!'

The king was unmoved.

'If you fear to call upon your god, Memnet, then go and bend your knee to Nagash. Those are the only choices any of us have left.'

Memnet's face twisted into a mask of rage, so sudden and so intense that the Ushabti took a protective step towards the king, his fleshy hands clenching into trembling fists. The Grand Hierophant's jaw bunched angrily, but when he spoke, it wasn't to utter imprecations against the priest king. Instead, he began to chant in a heated voice.

Akhmen-hotep saw beads of sweat gather on Memnet's round face, and then felt a puff of hot air brush against his skin that quickly became a whirling, restless wind. The clacking, chattering cloud of darkness overhead roiled like a stormy sea. Narrow spears of fierce sunlight stabbed through the churning mass, touching the ground for an instant before the shadow swallowed them. Black, smouldering shapes fell to the earth around Akhmen-hotep and his warriors in a steadily building rain. The king realised that they were the husks of tomb scarabs, each as large as a grown man's fist.

Memnet's voice grew louder, rising over the howling wind in counterpoint to Sukhet's piercing, nasal voice. The priest of Phakth, the sky god, sounded as though he were in terrible pain.

Akhmen-hotep started as he felt his ears pop, and then he heard his soldiers cry out in fear and awe as a forked bolt of lightning crashed down on the distant ridge.

The crash of thunder that followed sounded like the end of the world.

Arkhan's eyes snapped open at the crescendo of noise, the thunder's concussion so great that for a moment the vizier thought someone had struck him.

He was lying on his back a few yards from the twisted wreckage of his enemy's chariot. The impact of his dead horse had splintered the war machine's left wheel and flipped the heavy vehicle onto its side, and the four horses that had drawn it were galloping away in terror, dragging the broken yoke behind them. Horses and men were screaming all around him in the gloom, and his cavalry, beset from two sides, were struggling to survive.

Cursing, Arkhan struggled to regain his feet. His right leg was weak and stiff. Belatedly, he realised that a dagger-sized shard of bronze was jutting from his right thigh. He tore it free with his left hand and forced himself upright. A shudder passed through the immortal, and he felt the familiar, dreadful ache begin in his guts. The exertions and the wounds he'd received had consumed much of his master's vital elixir, and a deadly lassitude began to steal along his limbs.

Feeling a tremor of fear, Arkhan surveyed the wreckage of Suseb's chariot. Had the champion survived?

He saw the mass of wood and metal shift. Twisted bronze plates groaned and popped, and Arkhan felt a surge of dread as the Lion's head and shoulders struggled into view.

Desperate, the vizier raised his sword and chanted the Incantation of Summoning. The dark magic was fickle, resisting his control due to his weakened state, but three of Arkhan's dead cavalrymen stirred and struggled to their feet.

'Kill him!' the vizier commanded, pointing to Suseb.

The undead warriors lurched forwards. One cavalryman pulled a javelin from his chest and hurled it at the pinned champion. It struck Suseb in the left shoulder, piercing his armour but not the blessed flesh beneath. The Lion roared in anger and redoubled his efforts, pushing himself onto his knees. With his right hand, he tore a jagged piece of bronze plate from the wreckage and hurled it end-over-end at the nearest walking corpse. The impact crushed the revenant's skull, dashing it to the ground.

Cursing, Arkhan charged in alongside his remaining warriors, hoping to slay the champion before he could free himself.

One of the dead cavalrymen lunged at Suseb, chopping down at him with an axe. The stone blade glanced from the Lion's skull, leaving a shallow gash along the side of his head. The other reached for the champion's throat with bloodied hands. Suseb grabbed the empty-handed creature by the arm and hurled it into the axe-wielding warrior's path. The clumsy revenants tangled together and fell in a squirming heap, and before they could rise again the Lion snatched up his massive khopesh and cut through both bodies in a single, ringing stroke.

Sensing an opening, Arkhan leapt forwards and slashed at Suseb's face. The champion saw the blow coming and tried to twist away, but the scimitar left a deep slash across the warrior's brown cheek. The vizier laughed at the sight of the wound, but his triumph was short-lived. The Lion's khopesh flickered through the air, and the immortal darted backwards barely in time to avoid having both legs cut from under him.

With a lusty roar, Suseb flexed his powerful legs and burst free from the wreckage. His huge sword wove a deadly pattern through the air as he advanced fearlessly upon the vizier.

'Vile, godless coward,' he growled. 'It's a disgrace to stain my blade with such an unworthy foe, but I'll do it gladly if it will rid the world of you and your ilk.'

Arkhan spat a swift incantation and hurled a bolt of necromantic power at the Lion. It struck Suseb full in the chest. The champion bellowed in pain, but continued his implacable advance.

Another bolt of lightning smote the earth, this time striking in the midst of a company of Khemri warriors near the centre of the battle-line. Shouts of wonder and dismay were drowned in the peal of thunder that followed.

Then, to Arkhan's horror, a shaft of sunlight pierced his master's shroud of darkness and glinted from the Lion's blade. His cold flesh trembled at the sight, and for the first time he feared the possibility of defeat.

An angry wind rushed northward across the battlefield, howling with the fury of a god. Lightning scourged the earth like a taskmaster's lash, clawing along the ridge line amid a growing hail of burning scarab husks. More and more sunlight made its way through the writhing cloud, striking down the walking dead wherever it touched.

Within the black pavilion, a crowd of slaves grovelled in the dust before the king's grim sarcophagus and begged for their deliverance. In the shadows at the back of the chamber, the Usurper's ancient slave turned his blind face skywards and uttered a terrible, croaking laugh.

There was a hiss of air and the grating of stone, and the lid of the king's sarcophagus slid open. A shrieking chorus of tormented spirits and a gust of freezing air washed over the terrified slaves, who raised their hands in supplication to their lord and master.

Nagash the Immortal, Priest King of Khemri, stepped from his ensorcelled coffin amid a whirling nimbus of shrieking souls. Wreathed in roiling, ethereal vapour, the master of the Living City paid no heed to the worshipful entreaties of his slaves. Green bale-fire blazed from his sunken eyes and crackled along the staff of dark metal clutched in his left hand. The faces of the four skulls that topped the fearsome stave glimmered with unearthly power, blurring the air around it.

The king's handsome, lined face and strong hands were the colour of alabaster, gleaming like polished bone from the folds of his dark, crimson robes. His bald head was covered by a skullcap of hammered gold, inscribed with strange glyphs in a tongue unknown to civilised men.

Cowering slaves scattered from the immortal king's path as Nagash turned to the smaller sarcophagus that waited beside his own. The figure carved upon its surface was serene and beautiful: a goddess of the Blessed Land in the bloom of her youth.

A cold smile bent the necromancer's thin lips. He stretched forth his right hand, and the spirits surrounding him flowed down his arm and played across the coffin's surface. The marble lid shivered, and then slowly drew aside.

A faint, tortured moan rose up from the depths of the sarcophagus. Nagash listened, savouring the sound. His smile turned cruel.

'Come forth,' he commanded. The king's voice was bubbling and raspy, wheezing up from a pair of ruined lungs.

Slowly, painfully, the figure emerged. She was clad in priceless samite, with a queen's golden headdress set upon her brow. Bracelets set with brilliant sapphires hung from her fragile wrists, wrinkling the dry, parchment-like skin beneath. She clutched her claw-like hands painfully to her withered chest, and her head was bowed beneath the weight of her royal finery. Wisps of faded, brittle hair had escaped from the folds of her headdress and curled against her sunken, yellowed cheeks. Time had eaten away the gentle curves of her face, leaving only sharp edges and a thin, almost lipless mouth. Her joints creaked like dried leather as she moved, drawn to the necromancer as though by an invisible cord.

Bright, beautiful green eyes shone like emeralds from the queen's mummified face, etched with suffering so deep that it defied human comprehension.

The slaves grew silent as their queen walked among them. They buried their faces in the dust and pressed their hands to their ears to shut out her pitiful cries.

Nagash waved his hand once more, and the tent's heavy flap was pushed aside. He led his queen into the raging tumult, heedless of the wrath of gods or men. The necromancer looked out across the battlefield, and his smile twisted into a hateful sneer.

'Show them,' he commanded his queen, and she raised her withered arms to the sky and let out a long, heart-rending wail.

Akhmen-hotep felt the change, more than a mile away. The wind and the lightning stopped in a single instant, so suddenly that the king found himself questioning his senses. Then the rustling darkness overhead seemed to swell, filling his ears with its buzzing drone, and the priests began to scream.

He had turned his back on Sukhet and Memnet when the fire and lightning had begun, leaving them to their incantations while he tried to gauge their effect upon the battle. Now he whirled at their agonised cries, and saw that both men had fallen to their knees. A shiver went down the king's spine at the look of absolute horror writ upon their faces.

'What is it?' he asked. 'In the name of all the gods, what's happened?'

For a moment, it seemed that neither man heard him. Then Memnet whispered, 'We are undone.'

'Undone?' the priest king echoed. Mounting fear tightened like a fist around his heart. 'What does that mean? Tell me!'

'The Daughter of the Sun,' Memnet groaned. The Grand Hierophant's skin was flushed, and his eyes bright with fever. Akhmen-hotep could feel heat radiating from him in palpable waves.

'Neferem?' the priest king asked, surprised. 'What of her? Does she still live?'

'He has enslaved her!' hissed the Grand Hierophant. 'Nagash has bound her, body and soul!'

The news stunned Akhmen-hotep.

'That's not possible. She's the covenant made flesh. Her spirit binds the *gods.*'

'Do not ask me how,' the Grand Hierophant said. He sounded like a frightened child rather than a living embodiment of Ptra. He stretched a trembling hand to the north. 'I can feel her, brother! You cannot imagine her pain. The things he has done to her... I cannot bear it!'

'Then we must do something!' the king declared.

'Our power cannot touch her,' Memnet cried, 'nor can the blessings of the gods be arrayed against her. Look! Even the light of Neru fails in her presence!'

Horrified, Akhmen-hotep turned his gaze to the north. Memnet was right, the Consort's potent ward had failed, and the undead were closing in once more. The acolytes of the goddess had retreated to their high priestess, their faces pale with shock. Khalifra was weeping openly, her hands clenched to her belly as though stabbed.

The king's body felt cold and leaden. With a shock, he realised that even Geheb's gift of strength had failed him.

The gods had abandoned the men of Ka-Sabar.

Suseb's massive sword crashed against Arkhan's guard, hard enough to drive the vizier to his knees. The immortal struck the ground hard and rolled aside barely in time to avoid another blurring stroke aimed at his head. In desperation, Arkhan threw a backhanded slash at the champion's ankle, but the scimitar turned awkwardly in his hand and glanced off Suseb's calf. Arkhan realised, with a shock, that the champion's blow had bent his prized blade.

Arkhan kept rolling, narrowly avoiding another cut that struck a glancing blow against his shoulder. The Lion was as swift and as strong as his namesake, his god-given gifts rivalling even those of the Ushabti. Thinking quickly, he flipped onto his back and threw out his left hand, spitting words of power. A single bolt of energy leapt from his fingers and struck the champion in the chest. Suseb let out a pained grunt, but his stride never wavered. The vizier's power was almost spent.

'You cannot escape judgement so easily,' the Lion roared. 'The time of your reckoning is at hand!'

Suseb reached the vizier in a single, swift step and brought down his terrible blade. Once again, Arkhan tried to parry the blow, but this time his weakened scimitar snapped with a discordant clang.

The immortal threw the broken blade aside and threw up his empty hand.

'I yield!' he cried, sliding his left hand behind his back to the dagger concealed in his belt. 'Have mercy, Lion of Ka-Sabar! Nagash will pay any ransom you choose!'

Suseb's face lit with righteous anger as he spoke. 'You dare to plead for mercy, servant of the Usurper? If the gods see fit to spare you, let them stay my hand!'

The Lion drew back his blade. For the briefest instant, he seemed to stagger, as though the sword was suddenly heavier than before, and Arkhan saw his opportunity. His left hand snapped up in an underhand throw, and there was a heavy *thunk*, like a knife sinking deep into wood.

Suseb paused, his mouth hanging open. Slowly, his gaze fell to the hilt of the dagger jutting from his chest. Hurled with superhuman strength, the needle-sharp blade had driven deep into his body.

The champion took a half-step forwards, his face etched with strain as he tried to draw one more breath, but the dagger had pierced the Lion's heart. Suseb's great sword tumbled from his grasp, and the champion sank slowly to his knees.

Arkhan bared his jagged teeth in a slow, wicked grin. Slowly and deliberately, he rose to his feet and picked up Suseb's blade. Then he bent down and whispered softly in the Lion's ear.

'It seems the gods have spoken,' he said.

Cries of dismay went up from Suseb's men as the vizier brought the heavy blade down on the Lion's neck. Weak as Arkhan was, it took two clumsy blows to hack the champion's head from his shoulders.

Akhmen-hotep heard the shouts of despair from the army's left flank and knew that the battle was lost. The acolytes of Neru had fled, bearing away their high priestess as the marauding undead closed in. The king's Ushabti had dismounted and encircled him with bared swords, awaiting his command.

Hashepra, high priest of Geheb, approached the king. The burly priest's face was stricken, his tanned cheeks wet with tears, but his voice was as strong as ever.

'I have four companies of spearmen formed up and waiting for your orders, great one,' he declared. 'What would you have us do?'

The priest king felt cast adrift in the unnatural darkness. The foundations of his world had been torn away in a single morning, leaving him bereft.

'Save yourselves,' he said numbly. 'Order the trumpets to sound the retreat. Nagash has won the day.'

Hashepra recoiled in surprise, as though Akhmen-hotep had struck him. The priest started to protest, but there was no denying the disaster unfolding around them. Finally he nodded and went to pass the word to the trumpeter.

The Ushabti led the priest king back to his chariot and sped him away, in the direction of the oasis. Memnet had disappeared, evidently carried away by his own priests.

Akhmen-hotep caught sight of Sukhet's corpse as the chariot passed by. The priest of Phakth lay upon his back, his face a mask of despair. The living embodiment of the god of justice had slit his own throat.

An hour later, Arkhan limped up the rocky slope in the direction of his master's pavilion. The last surviving companies of the Bronze Host had fought their way out of the darkness and fallen to their knees in the bright sunlight of the oasis. Nagash's undead minions halted at the shadow's edge, unable to pursue any further. The vizier doubted there were more than a hundred living Khemri warriors scattered across the entire plain.

Nearly a dozen alabaster-skinned figures waited hungrily outside their master's tent. They glared at Arkhan with barely concealed hatred as he brushed past his brethren and entered the master's tent unannounced.

Nagash waited within, surrounded by his retinue of ghosts and attended upon by his queen and his slaves. Three immortals knelt at their master's feet, gulping noisily from golden goblets held in their trembling hands.

Arkhan smelled the heady perfume of the life-giving elixir and fell to his knees. He crawled through the dust to Nagash's feet, the ghosts circling him, touching his skin with fingers of ice and keening in his ears.

'I bring news of your victory, master,' he said hoarsely.

'Speak, then,' Nagash said coldly.

Arkhan ran his tongue over his cold lips. The thirst was terrible. Every vein in his body was shrivelled and aching. With an effort, he continued, 'The Bronze Host is in flight, and Bhagar's horsemen have been forced to quit the field.'

'Your cavalry pursues them even now,' Nagash said.

'Even so, master, even so,' the vizier replied, raising his eyes to the king. The queen stood to Nagash's right and a little behind the necromancer. Arkhan avoided her unblinking, agonised stare. 'We should recall our horsemen at once, before they become too spent,' he said. 'The Bronze Host is in disarray, fleeing for their lives down the trade road to Ka-Sabar. At least half their number lies dead on the plain below. If we pursue them, we might destroy them utterly–'

The king shook his head.

'There will be no pursuit,' Nagash declared. 'The army must return to Khemri at once. The Kings of Rasetra and Lybaras have risen against us as well, and even now their armies are marching through the Valley of Kings.'

Arkhan was taken aback by the news. For a moment, even his dreadful thirst was forgotten.

'What of our allies at Quatar?' he asked

'I have sent a message to Priest King Nemuhareb,' Nagash replied. 'He is marching to block the western end of the valley, and is certain that he can turn back the rebels.'

The vizier studied his master's face.

'You are not convinced,' he said.

'We must confront this rebellion from a position of strength,' the necromancer replied. 'This battle today was but the first of many. I foresee a long, bitter war to come. We must gather our allies and prepare for the storm.' A hungry glint shone in Nagash's dark eyes. 'We will deal with Ka-Sabar later. Before we are done, all Nehekhara will lie beneath our heel, and Settra's great empire will be restored!'

'From your lips to the gods' ears,' Arkhan might once have said. Now, the vizier only smiled, and asked, 'What would you have me do, master?'

'For now, drink. Then go and summon your errant horsemen. We depart for Khemri at dusk,' Nagash said, stretching forth his hand.

Ghazid, the king's blue-eyed slave, shuffled from the darkness at the far side of the tent with a golden goblet in his wrinkled hands. The vessel brimmed with a thick, crimson liquid. Arkhan's hands clenched as it drew near.

The vizier tore the goblet from the mad slave's hands and gulped greedily at its contents, all thoughts of war and conquest forgotten.

FIVE

A STORM OUT OF THE EAST

The Valley of Kings,
in the 62nd year of Qu'aph the Cunning
(-1750 Imperial Reckoning)

Something was moving beyond the Gates of the Dawn.

It was almost noon. Rakh-amn-hotep, the first of his name, Priest King of Rasetra, rubbed a calloused hand over his shaven scalp and squinted in the fierce sunlight. The air shimmered in the confines of the Valley of Kings, flashing brightly against the drifting clouds of chalky dust stirred up by the movement of the allied army. The fine, glittering dust had become their worst enemy during the long, punishing march down the winding valley. It clung to the skin, clogged throats and eyes, and sawed at the axles of the chariots. From where the king stood, surrounded by his Ushabti atop a low hill just off the wide temple road, he could see great clouds of dust shrouding the narrow pass at the western end of the valley, concealing whatever dangers might be arrayed against them.

Something was out there. That much was certain. But what?

Rakh-amn-hotep hooked his blunt thumbs into the arm holes of his heavy scale shirt and tried to shift it into a more comfortable position. It had been a long time since he'd marched through the sands of central Nehekhara, and he could stand the heat, but his skin was afire from the thick layer of dust chafing beneath the weight of his armour. The priest king was a short, very stout man, with a wide barrel chest and a blunt, pugnacious face. The point of a lizardman's spear had left a permanent dimple in his left cheek, creating the illusion of a smile. He was a savage, cunning man, cruel to his enemies and relentless when his anger was aroused, and the Priest King of Rasetra was frequently angry about something. His small city, situated near the edge of the steaming southern jungles, was constantly under threat from tribes of savage lizardmen. Not a year went by when the Rasetrans weren't fending off raiding parties, or leading punitive expeditions into the wilds to burn villages and take hostages from the larger tribes.

Years of fighting against the tribesmen had left their mark on the priest king and his warriors. They wore longer, heavier kilts of thick cotton that stretched below their knees, overlaid with cured leather taken from the massive thunder lizards that crashed their way through the thick jungle growth. Their torsos were covered in thick shirts of scaly lizard hide, with overlapping, bony plates to turn aside tooth or claw. The strange armour lent Rasetrans a savage, exotic appearance, which contrasted dramatically with the simple, conventional attire of their allies.

The city of Lybaras, on the other hand, was not known for its prowess in war. Their patron was Tahoth, the god of knowledge and learning, and their wealth, such as it was, stemmed from their great academies and craftsmen rather than from fierce raids or conquest. Their nobles had little use for jewels or fine clothes, but rather, invested their fortunes in scrolls and strange tools, vessels of rare glass and arcane devices of bronze and wood.

From where the King of Rasetra stood, it was difficult to tell a Lybaran noble from a slave. Both favoured a simple, dun-coloured kilt and functional leather sandals, with a dark brown cape that hung below the waist. The only difference, Rakh-amn-hotep noted with a scowl, was the amount of glass baubles and metal trinkets the nobles carried wherever they went. Even their Ushabti were strange, their bodies bearing none of the physical blessings of the other gods, and their weapons a motley assortment of sticks, knives and coils of tightly braided rope. Only their eyes betrayed their divine nature. They were a piercing, almost luminous grey, as hard and incisive as sharpened stone. Nothing seemed to escape their notice, much less catch them unprepared.

Hekhmenukep, Priest King of Lybaras, stood amid a bustling throng of chattering viziers and nervous scribes just a few yards to Rakh-amn-hotep's right. The king was peering intently through a long, wooden tube rimmed with polished brass, balanced on the bare shoulder of a waiting slave. Hekhmenukep was tall and lean to the point of being skeletal. His kilt hung listlessly down to the top of his bony knees, and the fall of his cape only accentuated the slope of his narrow shoulders. A fine gold chain lay around the king's long neck, from which hung a strange assortment of glass discs edged in copper, silver and brass wire. He looked more like a mason than the ruler of a mighty city, Rakh-amn-hotep mused.

'Well?' the King of Rasetra demanded. 'Do you see anything or not?'

The viziers surrounding Hekhmenukep shifted uneasily at Rakh-amn-hotep's peremptory tone, but the king himself appeared unfazed.

'The sunlight turns the dust into a swirling curtain,' he said, squinting into his strange contraption. 'There are flashes of light and the occasional shadow, but it's difficult to discern what any of it means.' The priest king straightened. 'Perhaps you would care to try?' he offered, gesturing at the tube.

Rakh-amn-hotep scowled at the strange object.

'I know little about Tahoth and his ways,' he grunted. 'I doubt he would bless me with any special sight.' The comment drew a laugh from Hekhmenukep.

'There is no need for special prayers in this case,' he said. 'Merely look into the tube. The glass will aid the working of your eye.'

Rakh-amn-hotep was dubious, but the need for information spurred him to try. On the level ground west of the hill, the armies of Rasetra and Lybaras were hastily turning off the road and forming their battle-line to the shrill wailing of trumpets. Somewhere up ahead, in that swirling mass of dust at the end of the valley, was the army's advance guard of light horsemen. Half an hour ago, a rider from the advance guard had come galloping down the road with a message from his commander: enemy troops had been sighted at the Gates of the Dawn. There had been no word since. Had the light horsemen encountered a small detachment of troops and driven them off, or were they fighting for their lives against the entire army of Quatar?

He'd known from the beginning that the march down the valley would be a race against time. The Valley of Kings was an ominous place, fraught with old magics and restless spirits that haunted the tombs of the ancient Nehekharans. Nothing grew there, and the nearest water was almost a hundred leagues away. The high, sheer walls of the valley forced travellers to traverse it from one end to the other. The eastern end, known as the Gates of the Dusk, was guarded by the city of Mahrak and its army of warrior priests. The western end, known as the Gates of the Dawn, was guarded by the Tomb Guard of Quatar. Rakh-amn-hotep knew that if their campaign were to have any chance of success, they would have to reach the Gates of the Dawn before Quatar got word of their approach and moved to block the mouth of the valley. If the Tomb Guard controlled the Gates of the Dawn, the allied army would either have to risk a brutal, bloody assault or else turn around and retreat back the way they'd come. Since leaving Mahrak, the allied army had moved with surprising speed down the winding valley, thanks largely to the Lybarans' strange, floating wagons. Suspended high above the valley floor by the hot desert wind, the wagons were able to carry the army's supplies and keep pace with the troops instead of being slowed to a crawl by unruly teams of camels or oxen. The army had covered almost a hundred leagues in just the first five days, and Rakh-amn-hotep had dared to believe that his gamble would succeed.

How the gods laughed when men dared to hope, the priest king mused sourly. He strode over to Hekhmenukep's odd invention and reluctantly peered into the end of the wooden tube.

At first, all he could see was a blurry circle of white. Frowning, he started to pull away from the tube, and suddenly the image cleared somewhat. Rakh-amn-hotep grew still, and noticed that he was seeing the swirling clouds across the valley almost as clearly as if they were just a few yards away. The priest king glanced back at Hekhmenukep.

'How is it that the gods share such power without requiring something in return?' he asked.

The King of Lybaras folded his thin arms and smiled. Like a tutor addressing a young student, he said, 'Tahoth teaches us that the gifts of creation are hidden in the world around us,' he said. 'If we are clever, we can uncover their mysteries and claim them for our own. In this way, we honour the gods.'

Rakh-amn-hotep tried to make sense of this, but gave up with a shrug. When they made camp that night he would make a sacrifice to Tahoth and consider the debt settled.

When he turned back, the King of Rasetra found that he'd lost the image once more. Frowning, he carefully drew back from the tube until once again the far end of the valley came into view.

Dust and more dust, the king observed irritably. Then he saw a glint of bronze wink from the murk, a reflection from a helmet, perhaps, or the tip of a blade. Then a vague shadow darkened the haze for a fleeting instant. Large and swift-moving, it was undoubtedly a man on horseback.

'The advance guard is engaged,' he muttered darkly, 'and they're fighting on our side of the valley mouth.' Rakh-amn-hotep rubbed his scarred chin thoughtfully. Years of battlefield experience suggested what was happening behind the curtain of dust. The advance guard numbered five thousand light horsemen, more than enough to overwhelm a small garrison of unprepared infantry within the space of half an hour. Instead, they were still fighting, riding madly back and forth through the thick haze rather than pushing their way through the mouth of the valley as they'd been ordered.

'Khsar flay their hides,' Rakh-amn-hotep cursed. 'The Tomb Guard has beaten us to the Gates of the Dawn.' Hekhmenukep's eyes widened in surprise.

'How is this possible?' he exclaimed. 'We moved faster than any army has ever marched, and our scouts encountered no sentries along the way.'

'Who can say what powers the foul Usurper possesses?' said a sharp voice behind the two kings. 'He has ruled unjustly in Khemri for more than two hundred years. It would not surprise me if every evil thing in Nehekhara is his to command.'

The kings turned as Nebunefer the Just struggled the last few yards up to the summit of the hill and limped painfully into their midst. The elderly priest was covered in a fine dusting of grit, coating his seamed face and dulling his bronze skullcap. He was attended by half a dozen senior priests and priestesses, each one raised in the great temples of Mahrak, the City of the Gods. Each of the hierophants wore fine linen robes in a variety of rich colours, from the Sun God's gleaming yellow to Geheb's mix of dark brown and vivid green. Rakh-amn-hotep noted their fierce expressions with secret amusement. How long had the Hieratic Council at Mahrak urged restraint in the face of Nagash's mounting crimes, saying that the gods would see justice done? That was before the shadow spread from Khemri, felling thousands of priest and acolytes all across Nehekhara. Within days of that terrible event, the council was beating the drum of war. Using the Hierophants of

Rasetra and Lybaras as go-betweens, they had hammered out a hasty alliance between the three cities and opened their immense coffers to finance a campaign to liberate Khemri once and for all.

Unfortunately, gold was all that the Hieratic Council seemed willing to provide. Rakh-amn-hotep had requested a contingent of Mahrak's fabled warrior-priests to accompany the allied army, but Nebunefer and his small retinue were all that the city could spare.

'If Nagash knows we're coming we could be facing the combined armies of Khemri and Quatar,' Rakh-amn-hotep growled. 'We can't possibly defeat them both.'

Nebunefer shook his head decisively, saying, 'Our spies in Khemri report that the Usurper has taken his army south to fight the Bronze Host of Ka-Sabar. The massacre of holy men across Nehekhara has spurred Akhmenhotep to declare war against the Living City.'

Hekhmenukep nodded thoughtfully.

'That's welcome news,' he said, 'but what of the remaining cities?'

'Numas and Zandri side with Nagash, along with Quatar,' Nebunefer replied. 'Of the minor cities, Bhagar will probably follow Ka-Sabar, while Bel Aliad remains loyal to Khemri.'

'And what of Lahmia?' the King of Rasetra asked. 'Their army is as large as mine and Hekhmenukep's combined.'

'We have sent an embassy to Lahmia to urge them to action,' Nebunefer said, shrugging, 'but so far they remain neutral.'

'Waiting to see which side gains the upper hand,' Rakh-amn-hotep grumbled.

'Perhaps,' Nebunefer said. 'Lahmia has ancient ties to the Living City. It is possible they are reluctant to take up arms against Neferem.' Hekhmenukep frowned.

'No one's seen Neferem for more than a century. Surely she's free of Nagash by now,' he said.

'No,' Nebunefer said uneasily. 'The Queen of the Dawn is not dead. We would know it if she were.'

Suddenly, a chorus of wailing trumpets echoed up and down the allied battle-line. Rakh-amn-hotep turned back to the swirling chaos at the western end of the valley. He could see the black specks of figures dancing at the ragged edges of the cloud. Scowling, he put his eye to Hekhmenukep's device to try to see who they were. For a few moments, all he could see was a panorama of boiling dust, but then he caught sight of a horseman of the advance guard. The warrior's horse was lathered and the rider was covered in dust. As the king watched, the warrior fitted an arrow to his bow and fired into the swirling dust, before retreating a dozen yards from the edge of the cloud. The same thing was happening all along the length of the dust cloud as the battered squadrons of light horsemen withdrew in the direction of their army.

Within moments, Rakh-amn-hotep saw why. A wall of white shields took shape out of the haze, growing larger and more distinct from one moment to the next. Slowly, inexorably, the first companies of the Tomb Guard advanced into the valley to meet their waiting foes.

'What is it?' Hekhmenukep asked. 'What do you see?'

For a moment, Rakh-amn-hotep could not believe his eyes.

'The King of Quatar is impatient,' he said. 'Instead of waiting for an assault, he's chosen to come and fight us here.' He shook his head in wonder. 'Nemuhareb has made a reckless mistake. With luck, we can make him pay for it.'

'How?' the King of Lybaras asked.

Rakh-amn-hotep glanced through the viewing-tube again. Strange as it was, he had to admit it was a damned useful tool. He gauged the speed of the enemy's march and reckoned they had another half an hour before the Tomb Guard was in range. The king turned back to Hekhmenukep, and asked, 'How quickly can your war machines be made ready?' The King of Lybaras looked to his viziers.

'Thirty minutes,' he said. 'Perhaps a little less. They should only be half a mile behind us at this point.' Rakh-amn-hotep smiled.

'Then we're going to get to see if they're half as clever as you claim they are,' he replied, and then called out to the messengers waiting at the bottom of the hill.

The next thirty minutes passed in a flurry of movement as the allied army prepared for the coming battle. Companies of archers advanced twenty paces in front of the infantry and made ready to fire. Behind them the battle-line stretched for a mile and a half across the valley, with the Temple Road running roughly down its centre. The infantry companies of Rasetra took up the army's centre and left flank, while the warriors of Lybaras took up the right. The beleaguered light horsemen of the advance guard withdrew off to the north, further reinforcing the right flank. The army's heavy cavalry waited a hundred yards behind the left flank: some two hundred Rasetran chariots, drawn by vicious, two-legged jungle lizards instead of horses. The warriors of Rasetra had been using the lizards in battle for more than a hundred years, but this was the first time they would be employed against another Nehekharan army. Rakh-amn-hotep kept them well back, hidden behind a low ridge just out of sight. His champion, Ekhreb, would lead them into battle.

Behind the left flank, the Lybarans were still wrestling their catapults into position. They had brought eight of the massive war machines with the army, and their crews were hastily readying piles of stone to load into their broad wicker baskets.

The full weight of Quatar's Tomb Guard marched against the allied force. Quatar's patron was Djaf, the god of death, and the city's warriors were justly feared for their prowess on the field of battle. Their infantry wore white-painted leather armour and carried heavy wooden shields, and their massive swords were capable of splitting a man in two with a single blow. It was said that their Ushabti bore the faces of jackals, and could kill with the lightest touch of their blades.

The Tomb Guard advanced on a wide front, with companies of archers interspersed among the heavy infantry. A large force of light horsemen and two great companies of chariots rode behind them. The light cavalry and one company of chariots swung to the north, threatening the allied right flank, while the remaining chariot company was held back in reserve, close to the Priest King Nemuhareb and his retinue.

Rakh-amn-hotep studied the enemy army carefully. The Tomb Guard was easily the size of his combined force, and had more heavy cavalry. He turned to his trumpeter.

'Signal the archers to fire when ready,' he said, and then turned to Nebunefer. 'Do you imagine the King of Quatar will follow the old customs, or will he fight us to the death?'

'It would depend on whether he has any of Nagash's lieutenants among his retinue,' the old priest said, shrugging. 'We should know soon enough once you spring your trap.'

The King of Rasetra grunted to himself.

'Assuming it works,' he muttered.

Down on the field, the archers drew back their bows and began to fire. Showers of arrows darkened the sky and fell among the warriors of Quatar, who raised their shields to protect them from the deadly rain. Here and there a warrior fell with an arrow lodged in his chest or his neck, but the rest continued to press forward. The enemy archers returned fire while still on the move, and Rakh-amn-hotep was impressed at the steadiness and accuracy of their volleys. Bowmen from both sides fell as the archery duel began in earnest.

To the right, the first of the catapults lofted its load of stones high into the air with a muffled bang. The projectiles spread out in flight, each as large as a man's head, and fell among the advancing infantry. Shields splintered and men were dashed to the ground, but the advance continued. Rakh-amn-hotep turned to Hekhmenukep.

'What of the other war machines?' he asked.

The King of Lybaras responded with an enigmatic smile. 'They will make their appearance known when they are ready.'

Rakh-amn-hotep frowned. When they were ready? What kind of an answer was that? Concealing a flash of irritation, he gestured once more to his trumpeter.

'Signal the left flank to advance,' he ordered.

The horn rang out at once. On the left flank, the warriors of Rasetra marched forward, raising their shields and readying heavy, stone-headed maces. The archers in their path fired off one last volley before gathering their unspent arrows and retreating down the narrow lanes between the infantry companies. When the last bowmen had passed, the companies closed ranks and presented a solid front to the enemy. Within minutes their shields were studded with arrow shafts as the Quatari bowmen continued their fire.

Moments later, the two forces on the left came together in a grinding crash of flesh, metal and stone. The echoing roar of battle resounded across the open ground, in counterpoint to the steady banging of the catapults off to the right. On that flank, the enemy light horsemen were trying to push around the edge of the allied lines, but so far the cavalry of the advance guard was keeping them at bay. The enemy infantry was staggering under the hail of heavy stones, but with great determination they continued to press forward. Behind them, the chariots made ready to add their power to the inevitable charge.

Rakh-amn-hotep studied the course of the battle so far and was satisfied. The troops on the left were struggling against the Tomb Guard, and the Rasetran companies were already shrinking as a steady stream of wounded men staggered away from the fight and sought safety behind their battle-line. The king looked for the Quatari reserves. The chariots were still in the rear, close to the enemy king.

Long minutes passed. The companies in the centre met with a grinding roar, while the enemy advance on the right foundered under the ceaseless bombardment. On the left, the Rasetran companies were starting to waver. Still there was no sign of the remaining war machines. Rakh-amn-hotep shot a worried glance at Hekhmenukep, but held his tongue.

Another minute passed, and the first companies on the left flank began to fall back. The Tomb Guard pushed forward, hacking relentlessly with their heavy blades. The carnage was terrible. Men fell with their skulls split or their arms hacked away, and rivers of blood stilled the clouds of dust around the struggling warriors.

The retreat on the left began to gather speed. As one company fell back, the ones on either side hurriedly withdrew as well. Within moments, the whole flank was falling swiftly to the rear.

Rakh-amn-hotep heard the faint wail of trumpets in the direction of the enemy centre. The reserve chariots were moving, bouncing quickly across the rocky ground towards the left flank. The enemy king sensed victory.

'Order the left flank to begin a general withdrawal,' he ordered.

Events on the ground, however, were moving with a speed of their own. The retreating companies were picking up speed, stumbling over themselves in their haste to escape the blades of the Tomb Guard. The enemy pressed forward hungrily, and more horns wailed as the Quatari chariots raced to join the impending slaughter.

Rakh-amn-hotep turned to the trumpeter.

'Send the signal!' he shouted.

The complex notes rang out across the battlefield. At once, the retreating companies picked up the pace and curved backwards, like a gate swinging on a hinge, to clear the path for the Rasetran chariots. Rakh-amn-hotep heard a wild, moaning cry of jungle horns as his heavy cavalry swept over the ridge and bore down on the unsuspecting Tomb Guard.

Then, a great commotion went up on the right flank. The King of Rasetra turned to see a pair of towering dust plumes rising up behind the enemy battle-line, nearly in the midst of the advancing Quatari chariots. A faint, thready hiss carried over the tumult of battle, and huge shadows moved within the cloaking dust. Then there was a rending crash, and the king watched with amazement as a chariot and its horses were hurled like toys into the air.

The Lybaran war machines had made their appearance at last.

They crawled from huge pits in the soft earth on clanking legs of wood and bronze. Steam, heated by the blessings of Ptra, hissed in bronze pipes and drove segmented legs and huge, sweeping pincers. A tail the size of a battering ram curled over each machine, lashing out and smashing chariots to flinders with each blow. Fashioned in the shape of enormous tomb scorpions, the constructs fell upon the rear of the enemy companies with disconcerting speed and power. Within moments, chariots and infantry alike were in full retreat.

On the left, the charge of the Rasetran chariots had inflicted a similar shock. The Quatari infantry staggered under the sudden counterattack, and the chariots had broken through their lines. The Quatari chariots, meanwhile had fallen into disarray, their horses terrified by the huge, fanged lizards drawing the enemy cavalry. A wild melee was in progress, but the Quatari forces were caught between the Rasetran chariots and their infantry, which had begun to advance once more.

The final blow came on the right flank. The enemy light horsemen panicked at the sight of the huge Lybaran war machines and quit the field. Seeing their opportunity, the horsemen of the advance guard swept around the Quatari flank and bore down on the enemy king and his retinue. Surrounded, cut off from retreat, Nemuhareb, Priest King of Quatar, offered his surrender.

The way to Khemri had been opened.

SIX

DEATH AND LIFE

Khemri, the Living City,
in the 44th year of Khsar the Faceless
(-1968 Imperial Reckoning)

In the waning hours of the day, Khetep, Priest King of Khemri, was brought forth from the House of Everlasting Life to begin his journey into the afterlife. The body of the king was wrapped in strips of the finest white linen, each one marked with the Glyphs of the River and the Earth in careful, precise script to sustain Khetep's flesh against the passage of ages. The hands of the king were folded across his chest, and a long, golden chain called the ankh'ram was twined about his wrists. The chain would anchor Khetep's spirit to his body so that he could find it again after centuries in the afterlife. His gold burial mask, shaped with care during the king's life by the finest craftsmen in the Living City, shone warmly in the late afternoon light. Garlands of fragrant blossoms surrounded the king's body, filling the air with their vibrant perfume.

The palanquin was borne by eight priests clad in white robes and a cape made of fluttering linen strips that symbolised the resurrection of the flesh. Their faces were hidden behind serene golden masks, and their movements were slow and ritually precise. Thirteen white-robed acolytes followed the palanquin, their heads covered in white ash and their eyes painted black with kohl, chanting the Invocation of Going Forth Into the Dusk to the beat of hide-wrapped drums. Last of all strode the Grand Hierophant in all his funereal splendour, bearing in his left hand the great Staff of the Ages. Nagash wore the ritual white robe and cape, its fabric strips embroidered with sacred glyphs in golden thread, and a golden pectoral inscribed with the sun, the jackal and the owl. White ash covered the Grand Hierophant's face, lending an otherworldly cast to his coldly handsome features.

A silent multitude awaited the slow-moving cortege in the great plaza outside the temple. Thutep and the royal household waited upon the right side of the procession, their regal finery clashing with the rough smudges of ash that blackened their cheeks and forehead. A hundred servants waited behind the household, bearing the grave goods that would accompany Khetep into the afterlife.

All those who had served the king in life stood to the left of the procession, and would continue to provide for him in death. Two score elderly servants and scribes, all of them bearing the respective tools of their trade in neat, cloth-wrapped bundles; more than a hundred slaves, their eyes hollow and their expressions bleak; and last of all, the stoic figures of the two dozen Ushabti that had survived their king's last battle on the banks of the River Vitae. The Ushabti stood in a hollow square formation, clad in all their battle finery, their gleaming ritual swords held ready. Within the square stood the trio of barbarians that the Priest King of Zandri had given to honour the death of Khetep. The druchii were still bound in chains, their expressions dulled by the effects of drugged wine. The barbarians stood apart from one another, their heads unbowed and their dark eyes smouldering with hate.

Moving to the measured beat of the drums, the cortege made its way across the plaza and into the city proper, followed by the mournful throng. They walked in echoing silence. The shops were all shuttered and the great bazaar had been emptied; even the distant docks, normally bustling with life, were empty. The people of the Living City had paid their respects to their king in the morning, as, by ancient law, they were forbidden to witness the final journey to his crypt. The gold coins scattered by the merchants earlier in the day still lay in the dusty street, untouched by beggar or thief.

At the centre of the city the cortege turned east, making their way beyond the city walls through the Gate of Usirian into the fertile fields beyond. To the north, a flock of herons took wing from the reeds along the banks of the Vitae, paralleling the cortege for a short way and then sinking back out of sight. To the east, the land sloped gently upwards. In the distance, the largest of the tombs were already visible, crowding the horizon like the rooftops of a sprawling city. Above them all loomed the Great Pyramid, its sloping sides painted crimson by the light of the setting sun.

The road was well-kept, formed of packed sand and stone, and tended to yearly by citizens as part of their compulsory service to the king. Within half an hour they came upon the first of the shrines: a tall, basalt statue of Usiris, just a few paces off the side of the road. Offerings of food and wine had been left at the statue's feet by travellers on their way to or from the great necropolis. Further on, the procession passed shrines to Neru and Djaf, Ualatp the Carrion God and even the dreadful Sokth, God of Poisoners. Everyone had a reason to fear one god or another as they made their way into the great city of tombs.

After an hour on the road, the cortege reached the rough edge of the necropolis. The procession crested a low hill, and the plain before them was crowded with small, square tombs, built of sandstone and crudely ornamented with sacred scripts or religious imagery. These were the vaults of the poor, those who spent their entire lives saving enough coin to purchase the ministrations of a mortuary priest. One tomb might hold thirty or forty bodies: an entire extended family, stacked one atop the other like mud bricks. The vaults grew in a chaotic sprawl across the uneven ground, often built by the families themselves, on whatever plot of clear, mostly level ground they could find. Some of the crude tombs had broken open over the years, allowing vermin and scavengers to eat away at the bodies inside. Huge, black vultures glided low across the tops of the tombs, or perched on the weathered roofs and eyed the procession with frank interest as the sarcophagus went by.

The road ended, for all intents and purposes, and the cortege was forced to wind its way carefully through the maze of narrow lanes and blind alleys between the shabby crypts. It was not unheard of for citizens to become lost if they wandered too deeply into the necropolis, and those that could not find their way out by nightfall were sometimes never seen again. However, the priests knew every twist and turn of the great city, for, in many ways, the necropolis was as much their home as the House of Everlasting Life.

The further in they went, the larger and finer the tombs became. They came upon grand structures of basalt or sandstone, inscribed with glyphs of protection and engravings of the gods in all their forms. Here were entombed the families of prosperous merchants or tradesmen, surrounded by shrines and statuary that both proclaimed their piety and forced their neighbours to keep a respectful distance. Even then, the crypts were crowded as closely together as possible, filling every square foot of available space.

Finally, as the sun was casting long shadows among the jumbled stone crypts, the procession reached a great plain at the centre of the necropolis, where the great kings of old built their tombs. The black tomb of Settra rose at the centre of the plain: a massive, square structure of black marble as large as the palace in Khemri. The great king and his household were contained within, as well as slaves, soldiers, bodyguards, chariots and horses, all in readiness for the day when they would be called to walk upon the earth once more. The doors to the great tomb were made of stone plated in raw gold, and the massive walls were carved with thousands of potent glyphs and invocations against harm.

Settra's Tomb took twenty years to build, and more than two thousand slaves perished before the labour was done. Every king that followed sought to outdo him, spending vast sums to create ever larger and more lavish crypts to proclaim their greatness to future generations. Thus it was that Khetep began building his tomb from the first day he became Priest King of Khemri. The Great Pyramid took twenty-five years to complete and cost the lives of close to a million slaves. No one but the king knew how much treasure had gone to build it. On the very day of its completion Khetep had ordered its chief architect strangled and entombed in a special chamber within.

The structure dominated the western edge of the plain, rising more than four hundred feet into the air and dwarfing every tomb around it. There were eight separate levels within the pyramid and two more tunnelled into the earth below it: room enough for an entire dynasty and their households.

A broad path of white stone led to the Great Pyramid's entrance, which had been built to resemble the façade of Settra's Court. At the top of the steps waited a score of mortuary priests, like silent ghosts lingering in the shadows of the great statues of Neru and Geheb, a dozen tall urns of wine resting on the stones before them.

A dozen armed priests from the temple of Usirian stood vigil outside the tomb, their faces hidden behind gold owl-masks. As the procession came to a stop at the foot of the steps, the leader of the horex stepped forwards and called out in a loud voice, 'Who comes here?'

Nagash raised the Staff of Ages and answered, 'The king has come. His time on earth has passed, and his spirit goes forth into the dusk. This is the house where he will take his rest.'

The horex bowed deeply and stepped aside.

'Let the king come in,' their leader intoned. 'A place has been made for him.'

Silently, the palanquin bearers made their way past the guardians and up the steps into the tomb, accompanied by the acolytes who would assist the priests in completing the interment.

Nagash climbed the steps to the tomb and took his place beside the wine-bearers. The Grand Hierophant turned to the waiting throng and spread his arms.

'The king has gone into his house,' he intoned. 'Where are the faithful, who will honour and serve him for all the ages to come?'

At once, a tall, dignified figure stepped forwards from the throng and ascended the wide steps. Khetep's wife, Sofer, wore a gown of samite bound by a belt of gold set with sapphires and emeralds. Her long, black hair was bound up in tight curls and oiled, and the circlet of a queen sat upon her brow. She was no more than a hundred and twenty years old, and her face was still unlined and beautiful. The queen stood before Nagash and said, 'I am Khetep's wife. My place is by his side. Let me go in and lie with him.'

Nagash bowed his head respectfully and stretched out his hand. Khefru emerged from the crowd of waiting priests, bearing a golden goblet. He filled the cup with poisoned wine and passed it to his master. The Grand Hierophant held out the wine to his mother.

'Drink, faithful wife,' he said with a smile, 'and enter your husband's house.'

Sofer looked at the goblet and hesitated for just a moment. Then she drew a deep breath and took the poison from her son. The queen closed her eyes, drained the goblet dry, and handed it back to Nagash. Immediately, another priest came forwards and took her by the hand. He led her into the crypt, where linen wrappings and a sarcophagus awaited her.

Next came the Ushabti. Each one took the poisoned cup almost gratefully, glad to escape the accusing eyes of the living and resume their watch upon the king. Even before the last of the devoted was gone, a stir went up among the slaves as they sensed that their time was drawing near. More than one had to be dragged up the stone steps and forced to drink the sacred wine, much to the consternation of the royal household.

When the last of the slaves had been taken into the crypt it was time for the sacrifices. Once more, Nagash spread his arms before the diminished crowd, and proclaimed, 'Let us make offerings to Usirian, he who leads the souls through the darkness, so that Khetep may enjoy a peaceful journey into the afterlife.'

Nagash turned to Khefru.

'Bring forth the barbarians,' he commanded. Khefru nodded and gestured to three of the waiting priests. They quickly descended the steps and took hold of the insensate druchii. The barbarians hissed and spat like angry cats as they were dragged before the Grand Hierophant.

Khefru stepped forwards with the cup. At once, the two females began to curse at Nagash in their cruel, sibilant tongue. The male bared his teeth in a silent snarl.

'Kill us and be done with it,' he said, 'but know this: he who slays us will be cursed, now and forever more. His lands will turn to ash, and his flesh will shrivel from his bones.'

At this, Khefru hesitated, until Nagash spurred him to motion with a heated glare. The druchii made no move to resist, and when the cup was placed to their lips they drank their measure, staring Nagash in the eye all the while. One by one, they sank to the stones and grew still.

By the time the last sacrifice had been made it was nearly twilight. Thutep and the royal household were left to race north though the necropolis, guided by fleet-footed acolytes until they made their way to the river's edge. There, his bride awaited.

While the cortege bore Khetep to his tomb, a different kind of procession left Khemri in a fleet of richly appointed barges, working their way downstream to prepare for the wedding. All of the Nehekharan ambassadors were present to bear witness, as well as all the noble families of the Living City.

Thutep reached the reed-choked banks of the Vitae just as the last rays of sunlight touched the water with flashes of mellow gold. Neferem stood in the shallows, her hands crossed over her breast in greeting, a smile upon her radiant face. She was the gift of the Sun and the River, the daughter of the Earth and the bearer of beauty and wisdom. Thutep waded ponderously through the water to take her hand and lead her to shore, where Amamurti, Hierophant of Ptra, waited.

When the marriage was sealed and the covenant between the Nehekharans and the gods had been renewed, a great cheer went up from the assembled nobles, and the new king took his queen aboard the royal barge and bore her back to the celebrations that awaited them in Khemri.

No one noticed that Nagash was not among the well-wishers accompanying his brother back home. He stood in the shadows by the river bank, watching the barges pole away upriver. The white moon had risen, and bats swooped low over the shore, hunting insects. Further downstream a crocodile slid into the water with a faint splash.

The Grand Hierophant smiled faintly and made his way back to the necropolis.

Reed torches dipped in pitch hissed and spat from the sconces along the walls of the stone chamber. It was a large room, forty paces to a side, but unfinished, the walls still undressed sandstone, and the chamber completely bare except for the three bodies stretched out on the floor.

The stone door to the chamber grated open. Khefru stepped inside, holding his torch high. Nagash followed swiftly behind him.

The Grand Hierophant walked quickly to the three lifeless druchii and studied them for a long moment.

'There were no problems?' he asked Khefru.

'None, master,' the priest replied with a smirk. 'I just waited until everyone had left for the city, and then dragged them inside.'

Nagash nodded thoughtfully. He knelt first beside the druchii male and pulled a tiny vial from his belt. He pulled open the barbarian's mouth, carefully, and poured two drops of greenish liquid on his tongue. Then he moved on to the first of the females. He had just finished with the second when the male drew in a great, whooping breath and sat bolt upright. The barbarian spat a stream of curses in his native tongue, and his eyes were wild as he looked around the room.

'Where am I?' the barbarian asked. He spoke passable Nehekharan, though his accent made him sound like the hissing of a cobra.

'Deep beneath the earth,' Nagash replied. 'You are in a vault in the lowest recesses of the Great Pyramid.' The barbarian frowned.

'The wine...' he began.

'You drank from a different urn than all the rest. Khefru made sure you drank a potion that created the illusion of death, rather than inflict it outright.'

'For what purpose?' the druchii asked warily.

Nagash smiled, and said, 'For what other purpose? You have something I want. I'm prepared to make a trade in order to get it.'

'What is it that we could possibly offer you?'

'The Priest King of Zandri slew my father with sorcery: dark, fearsome magic that our priests had no means to prevent.' He glanced knowingly at the barbarian. 'You performed that spell for him, did you not?'

'Perhaps,' the druchii said, smiling coldly.

Nagash glared at the barbarian, and said, 'Don't dissemble. The facts are obvious. Nekumet doesn't possess the skill to master such magic, and the effects of the spell were unlike anything I've ever seen. He persuaded you to use your sorcery to aid him in battle, and then, when he realised the true extent of your power, he betrayed you.'

'Go on,' said the druchii, his smile fading.

'Nekumet didn't want your blood on his hands. I expect you threatened to curse him, too, at some point in your captivity, so he sent you to Khemri instead. That way, we would kill you and suffer the consequences instead.'

'Clever, clever little human,' the druchii hissed, 'and all of this theatre was simply to satisfy your curiosity?'

'Of course not,' Nagash snapped. 'I want the secrets of your sorcery. Show me how to wield the power you command, and in return I will set you free.'

The druchii laughed.

'How delightful,' he said with a sneer. 'Nekumet said almost exactly the same thing. Why should I trust you?'

'Why, isn't that obvious?' Nagash asked, his smile widening. 'Because you're forty feet below the earth, in a tomb designed to kill those who wander its halls.' The Grand Hierophant folded his arms. 'I've already buried you alive, druchii. The only choice you've got left is to give me what I want.'

SEVEN

THE WRATH OF NAGASH

The Khemri trade road,
in the 62nd year of Qu'aph the Cunning
(-1750 Imperial Reckoning)

The Usurper's army was more dead than alive after the bloody battle at Zedri. The bodies of the dead, animated by Nagash's sorcery, could move only in darkness, and so the host rose at sunset and marched until just before dawn, when they would pitch the tents in the centre of the army for their master and his champions. When the sunlight broke over the Brittle Peaks to the east, the rotting corpses sank slowly to the earth, until the trade road resembled nothing so much as a corpse-strewn battlefield. Meanwhile, the dwindling ranks of living horsemen and warriors ate what they could and slept in shifts, waiting for the next attack.

Although they had arrived too late to turn the tide of battle at Zedri, the horsemen of Bhagar were determined to make Nagash's army pay dearly for its victory. Moving invisibly among the dunes, the desert raiders shadowed the slow-moving host and bit at its flanks in an endless series of hit-and-run raids. They would ride out of the desert in a sudden rush, flinging javelins and firing arrows into the enemy ranks, and then turn and flee back into the desert west of the trade road before an effective defence could be organised. When Arkhan's horsemen tried to pursue, they more often than not rode into a carefully laid ambush. Losses mounted, but to the desert raiders' chagrin the dead would simply rise up and march back to the Usurper's encampment.

As the days wore on, the raiders' tactics evolved. Scouts would follow the progress of the army at night, and report back to Shahid ben Alcazzar just after dawn. The desert wolves would then strike the camp at around noontime, knowing that they would be facing less than a third of the Usurper's warriors. Sometimes they ambushed Arkhan's mounted patrols. At other times they would seize a few score of Nagash's lifeless warriors and drag them off into the sands, where they would be dismembered and set ablaze.

At still other times they would strike for the heart of the encampment, attempting to reach the tents and the monstrosities slumbering within. Each time, the raiders managed to penetrate a little further into the camp.

Nearly a week after the great battle at the oasis, the Red Fox judged that it was time to strike in earnest. Five days of constant skirmishing had left Nagash's living warriors exhausted, and their numbers were only slightly larger than the numbers of ben Alcazzar's remaining horsemen. The Prince of Bhagar summoned his chieftains and laid out his plan.

Dawn on the sixth day found the army of the Usurper encamped across a rocky plain where the road passed close to the foothills of the Brittle Peaks. The desert to the west receded at this point, until the edge of the sands lay several miles distant. For the first time, the living remnant of Khemri's army was able to relax somewhat, believing that their camp was far more secure.

Behind the line of distant dunes, ben Alcazzar and two-thirds of his chieftains gathered before Ahmet ben Izzedein, Bhagar's Hierophant of Khsar. The desert prince and his chosen men bared their arms and made long cuts with their bronze daggers, letting the blood flow into a golden bowl at ben Izzedein's feet. The god of the desert was a hungry one, and his gifts were given only to those who were willing to make personal sacrifices on his behalf.

Ahmet ben Izzedein knelt before the bowl and began to chant the Invocation of the Raging Wind. Drawing his knife, he added his own blood to the bowl, and then drew up a fistful of sand and blew it in a hissing spray across the surface of the crimson pool.

At once, the desert wind stirred around the assembled warriors, raising a pall of stinging sand into the air. By the time they had leapt into the saddles of their graceful steeds the whirlwind was raging around them. Their war shouts were lost amid Khsar's hungry roar, but their bone horns cut like blades through the noise and sent the raiders sweeping over the dunes and racing across the rocky plain towards the enemy army.

The living warriors of Nagash's host saw the hissing cloud sweeping down upon them and knew what it portended. They leapt, fearfully, to their feet, reaching for their weapons or the reins of frightened horses. Trumpets blared in alarm, and the warriors of the Living City responded as swiftly as their exhausted bodies would allow. Within minutes, ragged bands of heavy cavalry were racing headlong into the storm, while spear companies formed up amid the decaying bodies of their kinsmen and prepared to receive the enemy charge.

Of all the gods, Khsar the Faceless was the least inclined towards humankind, and honoured the great covenant grudgingly at best. His gifts were often two-edged, and his worshippers called upon him only when they must. The raging storm called up by the Hierophant ben Izzedein lashed at both friend and foe, concealing the battle between the raiders and the cavalry in a hissing, knife-edged maelstrom. Riders literally crashed together out of the murk, striking at one another with a handful of frenzied blows, before pulling apart and disappearing once again. The screams of the dying were torn apart by the hungry wind, and the bodies of the dead were reduced to scoured bones within moments.

The desert raiders of Bhagar were in their element, however. With their faces hidden by their head scarves in a sign of devotion to their god, they read the shifting pattern of the winds and knew how to peer through the haze to find their foes. They rode with supernatural skill, as though their steeds could read their very thoughts. The desert horses were a breed apart, thought to be the only gift Khsar ever truly gave to his people, and they were prized above rubies by their masters. Time and again the raiders clashed with their foes, and more often than not they left a horseman of Khemri reeling in the saddle or bleeding out his life upon the ground.

Riderless horses stumbled out of the storm, galloping for the relative safety of the Usurper's camp. The spear companies watched the storm draw steadily closer and clenched their weapons fearfully. Their champions snarled orders to tighten the ranks, forming a solid wall of shields and spears in the face of the raging wind.

The sandstorm swept over the warriors in a hissing, blinding wave, stabbing at their eyes and clawing at every inch of exposed skin. The front ranks recoiled, as though from the impact of an enemy charge, but the rear ranks ducked their heads behind their shields and pushed back, keeping the line intact. Javelins flew out of the murk and fell among the ranks, sticking in shields or sinking through leather and into the flesh beneath. Men screamed and fell, their cries both painful and joyous, as though death was not so much an end as a release from the horrors they had endured.

Riders appeared like ghosts out of the storm, rearing their mounts before the shield wall and slashing down with scimitar and axe. They hacked off spearheads and dented helms, and, here and there, they bit into unprotected arms or necks. More men fell, but before their fellows could react, the riders had turned about and disappeared once more into the whirlwind.

Still, the line held, forming an arc of bronze between the storm and the silent pavilions along the road behind them. Warriors shouted encouragement to the men in front of them and leapt forward to fill the gaps left by their dead comrades. Their courage was desperate and unrelenting, each man knowing what would happen to their families at home if they failed to keep the raiders at bay.

They were so determined to stand in the face of the whirlwind that they failed to notice the silent band of raiders sweeping over the foothills to the east and charging into the opposite side of the camp. Only a handful of heavy horsemen stood in their path, and they quickly fell, riddled by arrows from the raiders' powerful horse bows. The raiders swept over the corpse-strewn ground and raced for the undefended tents just a few hundred yards away.

Shouts of alarm and strident trumpet calls rose from the centre of the camp. Slaves staggered from the tents into the bright sunlight, brandishing knives and wooden clubs in defence of their masters. The men of Bhagar cut them down like reeds, or pinned them to the earth with their barbed javelins, but the slaves' sacrifice delayed the attackers for a few, precious seconds. As the last of them fell, the air seethed with the hissing of countless wings, and the raiders cried out in dismay as a swirling pillar of scarabs spread above the cluster of tents and blocked the noonday sun.

Arkhan hurled the heavy lid of the sarcophagus aside and leapt to his feet, his brain aching from his master's blistering command. The sounds of battle were very close, and the vizier understood at once what had happened. Snatching Suseb's blade from the hands of a kneeling servant, the immortal dashed out into the unnatural darkness.

Two javelins struck him at once, punching into his chest from both the left and the right. The vizier staggered under the twin blows, but stretched out his left hand and hissed a dreadful incantation. A storm of magical bolts sped from his fingertips and slashed through the mass of horsemen before him, pitching men and horses shrieking to the ground.

A desert raider swept in from the right, slashing at Arkhan with his scimitar. The vizier spun on his heel, swinging his massive bronze khopesh and cutting off the horse's forelegs. The screaming, thrashing animal crashed to the ground and pitched the rider from the saddle. The raider landed nimbly and whirled to face Arkhan, but the last thing he saw was the immortal's flashing blade as it crashed into his skull.

Javelins and arrows buzzed through the air, and the shouts of horsemen filled the air. The raiders were among the tents, striking at anyone they could find, and the screams of men and horses echoed through the darkness as the immortals rose from their sleep and joined the swirling battle. Snarling a savage curse, the vizier leapt at the enemy. Fuelled by the fire of Nagash's unholy elixir, Arkhan plunged into the reeling crowd of desert raiders before him. Men fell dead from their saddles or found themselves pinned beneath the thrashing bodies of their mounts as the vizier cut a bloody path through their midst.

Then came a rising chorus of wailing, angry cries, and an eerie green glow suffused the darkness to Arkhan's left. The ghostly chorus swelled to a maddening crescendo, quickly joined by the frenzied screams of living men. A shock went through the crowd of raiders surrounding the vizier, and then suddenly they were gone, galloping madly in the direction of the desert. Arkhan whirled, searching for the cause of their sudden retreat, and saw Nagash, surrounded by almost a score of writhing, screaming men. The necromancer's hands were raised to the sky, and his eyes blazed with baleful light as he unleashed his retinue of ghosts upon his foes. As the vizier watched, the spirits wound around the shrieking men like snakes, pouring through their open mouths and into the corners of their eyes in search of their living souls. They left behind shrivelled, smoking husks, contorted in poses of agonising death.

The sudden, unnatural darkness and the wrath of the awakened necromancer set the desert raiders to flight. The sandstorm was already receding as the worshippers of Khsar fled back to the safety of the dunes. Arkhan raised his stolen sword and jeered at the fleeing raiders. Then he nearly staggered beneath his master's wordless, furious summons.

The vizier made his way swiftly across the battlefield and fell to his knees before the king. His mind raced, trying to puzzle out Nagash's sudden fury.

'What is your bidding, master?' he asked, pressing his forehead to the ground.

'Quatar has fallen,' Nagash declared. 'Nemuhareb and his entire army have been overthrown.' The ghosts surrounding the necromancer echoed his rage, hissing like a clutch of angry vipers. 'The rebel kings have placed him under arrest and seized control of the city.'

The vizier was stunned by the news. Seizing the city? Such a thing was unheard of. Battles between kings were settled on the field of battle, and the loser paid a ransom or other reparations to the victor. Sometimes territory or other rights were forfeited, but unseating a king and taking his city was unprecedented.

'These rebels have no respect for the law,' Arkhan replied carefully, running his tongue over his jagged teeth. It also went without saying that the enemy was within a few weeks' marching distance of Khemri, far closer than Nagash's own battered army.

'They think to weaken me by depriving me of Quatar,' Nagash said, 'but instead they have delivered themselves into my hands. The Kings of Numas and Zandri will not stand for the seizure of the White Palace, and will gladly join their armies with mine to drive the rebels back across the Valley of Kings.' The necromancer clenched his fist and smiled hungrily. 'Then we will march on Lybaras and Rasetra in turn and bring them to heel. This will be the first step in building a new Nehekharan empire.'

Arkhan gazed across the battlefield at the remnants of Khemri's conscript army. Nearly all of the Living City's resources had gone into Nagash's grand design for the last hundred years. This pitiful force of infantry and cavalrymen was the most that could be mustered to challenge Ka-Sabar, and that army was a horror-stricken remnant of what it had been. The vizier knew all too well how heavily Numas and Zandri had been called upon to provide tribute to fund construction of the living god's mighty pyramid. Their armies would be in little better condition than Khemri's, and while Nagash's terrible power could bestir the bodies of fallen warriors, Arkhan could see that the exertions of the campaign had drained even the king's prodigious reserves of strength. With Rasetra and Lybaras in control of the White Palace, they were in a precarious position indeed.

'Numas and Zandri will need time to raise their armies,' Arkhan said, 'and time is something we do not have in abundance. Our foes are in position to reach Khemri even now, while these desert wolves dog our every step–'

The priest king cut him off with a cruel chuckle.

'Do you doubt me, vizier?' he asked.

'No, great one!' Arkhan replied quickly. 'Never! You are the living god, master of life and death!'

'Indeed,' Nagash replied. 'I have defied death and laid the gods low. I am the master of this land, and all that it contains.' The necromancer stretched out his hand, pointing a pale finger at Arkhan's head. 'You look about you and see calamity, our small army in tatters, surrounded by our foes, but that is because your mind is weak, Arkhan the Black. You let the world bend you to its whims. That is the thinking of a mere mortal,' he spat. 'I do not heed the voice of this world, Arkhan. Instead, I command it. I shape it to my will.'

Nagash's cold, handsome face was alight with passion. The cloak of spirits surrounding him writhed and wailed in despair, and Arkhan could feel the power of the grave radiating from the king like a cold desert wind.

The vizier pressed his face to the dust once more.

'I hear you, master,' he said fearfully. 'Victory will be yours, if you will it.'

'Yes,' Nagash hissed. 'So it will. Now rise, vizier,' he said, abruptly turning away and striding in the direction of his pavilion. 'Our foes have made their move. Now we shall counter it.'

Arkhan fell into step behind the king. Every now and then his boot would fall upon one of the desert raiders that Nagash had slain, their bodies crunching like burnt wood beneath his feet.

'Summon your horsemen,' the king said. 'You will ride at once to Bhagar and visit my wrath upon the home of the desert princes.'

The vizier nodded, fighting to keep his face from betraying his trepidation. After the bloody battle at Zedri and the constant skirmishes since, he was left with just under three thousand cavalrymen, living and dead.

'It will be a long ride through enemy territory,' he replied, dreading the idea of crossing harsh desert terrain that his foes knew all too well. He and the other immortals would have to bury themselves deep in the sand to escape the sun's merciless glare.

'You will conquer Bhagar in five days' time,' Nagash declared. Arkhan's good eye widened.

'But we would have to ride day and night,' he said, before he could catch himself.

The necromancer paid no heed to the vizier's impertinence, saying, 'You will take two of the Sheku'met along with you. Use only one at a time, to preserve their strength.'

Arkhan looked up at the swirling, chittering shadow overhead. The Jars of Night were a potent tool, but the great scarabs had to be fed a steady diet of flesh to maintain their sorcerous bond. There had been no lack of food on the battlefield of Zedri, and since then Nagash had set the scarabs to feast upon the bodies of his undead warriors. Arkhan had watched soldiers covered in a writhing carpet of beetles, still marching stolidly down the trade road as the scarabs burrowed deep into their putrefying organs and flensed the skin from their skulls.

'It will be done, master,' the vizier replied. There was nothing else to say. 'What of you and the rest of the army?'

'The Master of Skulls will take charge of the living warriors and return the army to Khemri,' Nagash said as they reached the great pavilion. Slaves prostrated themselves at the king's approach, and a pair of moaning spirits flew from the king's side to peel back the tent's heavy linen entry flap. The tortured figure of Neferem stood just inside, and when the king beckoned, the queen shuffled painfully to his side.

'I shall return to Khemri at once,' Nagash said, 'and summon the Kings of Numas and Zandri to a council of war.' The king turned to Arkhan. 'Remember, you must seize Bhagar in five days' time: no more, no less. When the moon rises on the fifth day, this is what you must do.'

The vizier listened to the king's instructions without expression. He fixed his gaze on the necromancer's glowing eyes and tried to push the image of Neferem from his mind.

'As you wish,' he said, when Nagash was finished. 'Bhagar's fate is sealed.'

The king fixed his vizier with a soul-searching stare, and seemed content to find none. 'Remember, Arkhan the Black, go and bend the world to my liking, and you will continue to enjoy my favour.'

Then the living god raised his hand to the sky and shouted a string of rasping syllables with his ruined voice. At once, the swarm above him thrummed and spun like a gyre balanced on the necromancer's palm. The leading edges of the great shadow shrank inwards as a torrent of flashing, buzzing scarabs descended in a swirling column around Nagash and his queen. The two figures grew indistinct, and then disappeared altogether.

Arkhan felt the desert air rush past his shoulders, drawn from all directions towards the seething funnel before him. Then, in an instant, the pillar of glittering chitin leapt skywards like the cracking lash of a taskmaster's whip, drawing a column of roiling dust in its wake.

Nagash and the Daughter of the Sun were gone.

The vizier studied the empty space where the king had been, and a bleak look passed across his scarred face. Around him, slaves rose quickly to their feet and went to work striking the tents they had raised only a few hours before. Overhead, the living shadow began to constrict further as the insects, freed from Nagash's will, began to settle to the earth in search of food. The steady approach of sunlight shook Arkhan from his reverie. Slowly at first, and then with growing speed, he began issuing orders.

Within two hours the vizier and his horsemen were heading west, into the unforgiving desert. A restless cloud of hungry scarabs swirled over the centre of the column, shielding Arkhan and his immortal lieutenants from Ptra's searing light.

By mid afternoon, the army was on the march again, shuffling wearily north along the old trade road.

The companies of the dead, no longer animated by the will of their master, were left to fester in the hot desert sun. More than one weary soul looked back at the still figures and envied their fate.

A ribbon of seething, chittering shadow passed low over the Living City shortly after dusk. It raced over the top of the southern wall, past the huddled sentries crouching atop the battlements, and down the neglected streets of the Potter's Quarter. The rooftops of the crumbling, mud-brick homes were deserted, despite the heat of the long day, and not even dogs prowled among the piles of refuse strewn down the narrow lanes. The Merchant Quarter was likewise silent and shuttered tight. The squares of the Grand Bazaar were empty, its stalls dilapidated and its flagstones covered with sand. Only the noble districts further north showed any signs of life, where the city watch patrolled the streets in large, well-armed groups past barricaded courtyards and high walls topped with shards of broken pottery and glass. Even the sprawling complex of Settra's Palace was dark and empty of life. The only light to be seen anywhere on the horizon was off to the east, beyond the city walls, where serpentine flickers of indigo-coloured lightning crawled along the sides of a massive, black pyramid that rose from the centre of Khemri's great necropolis.

The hissing swarm of scarabs wound like a serpent towards the great palace, shedding streamers of smoking insect husks as it went. Finally, it plunged like an arrow into the great plaza outside Settra's Court and poured a flood of wriggling, dying beetles onto the silent square. Their life energies spent on the gruelling northward flight, the last of the scarabs clattered lifelessly to the ground around Nagash and his queen.

Even as the king came to earth, hundreds of slaves were hurrying down the steps from the court and abasing themselves before their master. In their wake came a pallid immortal clad in a crimson-dyed kilt and red leather sandals. The warrior's torso was wrapped in strips of banded leather armour, and wide leather bracers covered his forearms. A cape of flayed human skin fluttered in his wake as he strode swiftly up to Nagash and sank to his knees in supplication.

The priest king acknowledged the immortal with a nod.

'Rise, Raamket,' he commanded. 'How has the city fared in my absence?'

'Order has been restored, great one,' the immortal said at once. Raamket had broad, blunt features, like a rough-hewn statue, with heavy brows and a bulbous, oft-broken nose. His dark eyes held little imagination or wit, but were cold and steady as stone. 'There have been no further riots since the army went south.'

'And the ringleaders?'

'Some have been captured,' Raamket said. 'Others took their lives before we could seize them. The rest have fled the city.'

'How can you be so certain?' Nagash asked, his eyes narrowing in suspicion.

Raamket shrugged, and said, 'Because we have not found them, master. The city has been searched thoroughly, from one end to the other.' A faint smile crossed the immortal's stolid face. 'I personally questioned many of the city's merchants. They swore that many of the priests fled east, towards Quatar.'

Nagash considered the news. 'Relax our patrols,' he ordered, 'and then offer a double ration of grain for anyone that offers information on dissenters still hidden in the city. If there are any rebels left they will grow bold once they learn that the White Palace has fallen.'

Raamket's dark eyes glittered at the sudden news.

'The east has risen against us?' he asked. The savage immortal sounded pleased at the prospect.

'Lybaras and Rasetra have chosen to defy me,' the king answered darkly, 'and I suspect they are not alone.'

Nagash set off quickly towards the steps to Settra's Court, leaving the servants to surround the queen and escort her into the palace. Raamket fell into step behind his master. 'How shall we deal with these traitors?' the warrior asked.

'Send messengers to Numas and Zandri,' Nagash commanded. 'Summon the kings to attend upon me at Settra's Court in four days' time to attend a council of war. Quatar will be retaken, and then the east will drown in a sea of blood.'

Raamket smiled, revealing white teeth filed to needle-sharp points, and said, 'It will be done, master.'

EIGHT

RED RAIN

The desert city of Bhagar,
in the 62nd year of Qu'aph the Cunning
(-1750 Imperial Reckoning)

On the morning of the fifth day, Arkhan's horsemen crested the dunes east of Bhagar and found Shahid ben Alcazzar and his horsemen awaiting them just beyond the green expanse of the city's caravanserai.

The vizier reined in his rune-marked warhorse at the top of the furthest dune and spat a stream of incredulous curses into the shadow-bound sky. He had pushed his warriors relentlessly, pausing only at dawn and dusk to open the Jars of Night and then seal them up again. He killed horses and men by the score along the way, returning their corpses to the ranks when their exhausted bodies could withstand no more. Still others were sacrificed to the ravening scarabs. Their bones now gleamed white in the preternatural gloom, knit together by black sorcery alone. All so that he could outpace ben Alcazzar's horsemen and strike at their home before they could mount a proper defence, and yet they had still managed to outpace him!

When he'd run out of curses to hurl at the uncaring heavens, Arkhan sat back in his saddle and took quick stock of his situation. His horsemen, almost two thousand in all, were spread in a rough arc along the line of dunes to his left and right. Five hundred yards distant, the desert raiders waited in a ragged line, grouped around the fluttering banners of their chieftains. Arkhan's advance guard, consisting of little more than two hundred horsemen, formed a thin screen in the middle ground between the two forces.

'Signal Shepsu-hur to fall back,' the vizier ordered, gesturing angrily to his trumpeter. Nodding wearily, the musician brought the horn to his lips and blew a complex series of notes. Within moments, the advance guard was withdrawing across the rolling terrain. Arkhan noted that the desert raiders made no attempt to pursue.

Shepsu-hur left his horsemen at the bottom of the dune and spurred his struggling mount up the sandy slope to make his report. The immortal was wrapped in bindings of linen and leather from neck to toe, covering nearly every inch of his exposed skin. Only his ruined face was left uncovered, revealing the terrible injuries he'd received in the battle at the palace only a few weeks before. No amount of Nagash's sorcerous elixir had been enough to seal up the gaping wounds in the nobleman's cheeks and forehead, or restore his shrivelled lips and the ragged stub of his nose. Charred bone showed through the tear in the immortal's square chin as he spoke.

'The horsemen arrived less than an hour ahead of us,' the maimed immortal rasped. 'Some of them withdrew into the city when we arrived.'

'No doubt telling their kin to flee into the desert,' Arkhan said. He knew that some of the citizens would escape; it could not be avoided. The people of Bhagar were devout followers of Khsar, and they knew the ways of the desert well. Most, however, were trapped. If they tried to run, his men would ride them down. 'How many riders?' he asked.

Leather wrappings creaked as the immortal shrugged.

'Perhaps three thousand,' he said, 'but their horses are blown. They pushed themselves past the point of exhaustion getting here ahead of us.'

'Then this won't last long,' the vizier said, nodding grimly.

Drawing his huge khopesh, Arkhan called to his trumpeter. 'Sound the charge!' he commanded. 'We will press on to the city, regardless of the cost!'

Trumpet notes sang their clarion call along the dunes, and the mass of horsemen started to move down the sandy slope. Shepsu-hur wheeled his mount and raced ahead to catch up with his squadron. Arkhan kneed his warhorse forwards at a trot, his attendants closing ranks around him.

Bhagar was a prosperous city, but a small one. Its princes had nothing to fear from bandits, and it had never been so wealthy as to attract the attention of the larger cities to the north and the east. As a result, its leaders had never seen the need to spend vast sums building a wall around the city. Now, its horsemen tried to form a living barrier against the vizier's warriors, but Arkhan could see how the proud raiders slumped in their saddles, and the heads of their magnificent horses hung low to the ground. Better for Shahid ben Alcazzar to have preserved his men, Arkhan thought. He might not have saved his city, but at least he might have lived to avenge it another day. Now the proud desert prince would die along with them.

The Khemri horsemen spread out across the rolling, sandy terrain as they reached the bottom of the dunes, the immortals leading the way, followed by the grim, silent corpses of men that had belonged to their squadrons. The living cavalrymen fell behind, unnerved by the dead comrades riding in their midst. Far ahead, the proud desert horses of their enemies tossed their heads and pawed at the sand as the scent of rotting flesh reached them.

Still, the desert raiders waited, taking no action as their foes drew nearer. Arkhan peered through the gloom with his one eye, trying to locate ben Alcazzar and his retinue. What was the prince's standard? The vizier couldn't recall.

Three hundred yards... two hundred and fifty. Maddened shouts and wailing cries went up from the immortals, and the horses quickened their pace to a canter. A shadow passed over the desert raiders as the leading edge of the scarab cloud swept over them. Arkhan watched them become forbidding silhouettes, standing starkly against the lush greenery of the caravan oasis at their back.

Then, a figure at the rear of the desert horsemen raised a shining scimitar to the heavens. It caught the last of the sunlight, flashing with Ptra's angry fire, and then Arkhan heard a faint shout that cut through the mounting thunder of hoof beats.

A hot wind hissed through the oncoming cavalry. Arkhan felt its rasping touch slide across his cheeks. Then the hissing rose to a full-throated roar, and the world disappeared in a raging maelstrom of sand.

Arkhan raised a hand to his face with a bitter curse. Horses and men screamed in surprise and fright. The sandstorm lashed at exposed skin with a million invisible knives, clothing and even leather fraying beneath its unrelenting touch. The vizier's ensorcelled mount reared and tossed its head in pain. Arkhan pulled savagely at the reins and fought to keep his seat.

The onslaught lasted only a few seconds. It crashed through the Khemri force with all the power of a cavalry charge, and when the wall of sand had swept past, the heavy cavalry was scattered and disoriented, their forward momentum lost. The next sound they heard was the deadly hum of arrows and the spine-chilling wail of the desert raiders as they charged in behind Khsar's savage wind.

Shahid ben Alcazzar was called the Red Fox for a reason. Though nearly spent, the horsemen of Bhagar were far from helpless.

A hail of arrows and throwing javelins raked the stunned Khemri force. Men and animals fell to the ground, dead or thrashing in their death throes. Then the charge of the desert raiders struck home, and bronze clashed against bronze in a swirling, furious melee.

The ferocity of the Bhagar attack might have broken the Khemri force at the outset, had the riders all been living flesh and blood, but the immortals and their dead warriors were impervious to fear and contemptuous of javelins and arrows. The living cavalrymen reeled from the attack, but the dead raised their weapons and fought on.

A trio of panicked cavalrymen raced past Arkhan's plunging mount. With a snarl, the vizier cut them down with a volley of sorcerous bolts, and then spat Nagash's dread incantation and returned their corpses to the battle. The horses' smoking bodies clambered awkwardly upright, and the blackened husks of their riders climbed back into their saddles. The cavalrymen turned their melted faces to the vizier for a moment, and then, as one, they wheeled about and charged into the fray.

With a shout, a desert raider broke free from a pair of Khemri horsemen and bore down on Arkhan, his dark eyes blazing with hate. The vizier brought his horse around and called upon the power of Nagash's elixir. His blood burned, and the attacking rider seemed to move in slow, languid motion. Arkhan swatted aside the rider's blade and then slashed open his chest as the warrior lumbered past, once more uttering the arcane incantation that would bind the dead to his bidding. The raider's blood-soaked corpse had barely struck the ground before it was moving once more, rising clumsily onto its feet and staggering off in search of its former kinsmen.

Across the battlefield, the dead rose from the ground and threw themselves at the living. The men of Bhagar cried out in terror as the bloody corpses clung to their legs, snatched at reins or struck at them with knife and fist. The raiders slashed at the undead with swords and axes, severing arms and caving in skulls, but for every corpse that fell, another waited to take its place, and the men of Bhagar had precious little strength left after their long, wild ride across the desert.

Still the battle raged, with neither side willing to give ground. The forces were intermingled, and there was no telling who had the upper hand. Arkhan looked around for his trumpeter, and found the boy on the ground a short distance away with an arrow through his eye. With a snarl, the vizier realised that he scarcely needed the horn any more. The dead would do his bidding according to his will, and there were more of them joining his side with every passing minute.

Suddenly, Arkhan heard a whistling roar off to his right, and a plume of dust and sand rose like a fist into the sky. Men and horses were caught up in it and flung through the air like toys. The vizier bared his jagged teeth. That had to be the city's Hierophant of Khsar, and ben Alcazzar would no doubt be somewhere close by. Spurring his horse with a shout, Arkhan headed towards the slowly collapsing pillar of earth with the surviving members of his retinue in close pursuit.

Once again, he called upon the power of the elixir in his blood, and Arkhan waded through a sea of turgid bodies and drifting blades. He cut down everything in his path, be it enemy or friend. Every man he slew rose in his wake and rejoined the battle, their expressions still fixed in the agonising moment of death.

After what seemed like an eternity of slaughter, Arkhan came upon a knot of desert horsemen surrounded by a rising tide of slashing, snapping corpses. The vizier recognised ben Alcazzar at once, with his black leather armour and flowing head scarf. The prince rode a fiery white warhorse whose flanks were near pink with gore, and his scimitar was red and notched nearly to the hilt. He was surrounded by a dozen of his kinsmen, who slashed and stabbed at the encircling horde with grim, silent determination. The warriors had learned that a corpse without a head would not rise again, and they plied their blades like executioners, striking down one slow-moving undead warrior after another. The mindless corpses were already being forced to climb over the mounded heaps of their fellows in order to reach their prey. Arkhan noted with surprise that two of the headless bodies near the prince had the alabaster skin of immortals.

Next to ben Alcazzar sat a brown-robed man on a dusty steed, wielding a curled wooden staff instead of a blade. As the vizier watched, the man pointed his staff at a cluster of nearby riders and bellowed an entreaty to Khsar. At once, the sand beneath the riders exploded upwards with a roar like a storm wind, hurling their broken bodies more than thirty feet into the air.

Cursing, Arkhan cast around for something he could throw. He caught sight of the body of a warhorse nearby with a javelin jutting from its side, and rode over to grab it. The barbed shaft did not come free easily, even with the vizier's more-than-human strength, but finally he held the blood-stained weapon in his hands.

There was another blast of air just a few dozen paces to Arkhan's right, sweeping up half of the vizier's retinue and crushing the life out of them. With a savage shout, Arkhan turned in the saddle and hurled the javelin at the hierophant with all of his might.

The priest saw the weapon streak towards him at nearly the last moment and raised his staff in a desperate attempt to block Arkhan's throw. Had the javelin been cast by a mortal hand, the priest might have succeeded; as it was, the hierophant simply wasn't fast enough to keep the weapon's bronze head from punching into his chest and hurling him from his saddle.

Shahid ben Alcazzar saw the priest fall, and followed the path of the javelin back to Arkhan, some ten yards away. The vizier met the prince's dark eyes, smiled, and then spoke the Incantation of Summoning.

A moment later the prince's horse reared in fright, and ben Alcazzar staggered as the corpse of the priest tried to pull him from the saddle. The two figures struggled for a moment. Then, with a savage cry, ben Alcazzar drew back his sword and buried it in his older brother's skull.

As the priest's body fell limply to the ground, the prince glanced wildly around, and saw only a sea of grasping, bloody hands and slack, lifeless faces. Some of those who reached hungrily for him were once his friends or his cousins. Finally, ben Alcazzar turned back to Arkhan and shouted, 'Enough! Stop this tide of horrors, and I will yield!' The prince reached up and tore away his head scarf, revealing the anguish etched deep into his handsome face.

Arkhan raised his hand, and with a single thought his undead warriors retreated a step and grew still. Across the battlefield, the clamour of battle abruptly tapered off. The vizier edged his horse forwards until he was just a few yards from the prince. He smiled.

'What will you give so that your people may survive?' he asked.

'Take whatever you want,' ben Alcazzar said thickly. Tears stained his tanned cheeks. 'There is gold enough in Bhagar to make you a king, Arkhan the Black. I'll pay any price you name.'

Arkhan's dark eyes glittered.

'Done,' he said, and the fate of Bhagar was sealed.

The kings arrived in Khemri at roughly the same time, early on the evening of the fifth day after Nagash's return. The twin Priest Kings of Numas, Seheb and Nuneb, travelled south through the fertile river lands north of the Vitae with a mounted retinue of Ushabti, viziers, scribes and slaves. They crossed the great river by ferry, arriving at the empty city docks just as the royal barges of Zandri were poling their way to shore. The viziers of the two royal parties eyed one another with diplomatic reserve, and then hissed sharp orders to their slaves to begin disembarking as quickly as possible.

Within minutes, the square began filling with horses, chariots, palanquins and scores of frantic slaves as each procession sought to gain the advantage of precedence over the other. Zandri's chief vizier took the tactical step of ordering the king's wardrobe to be left aboard his barge, saving nearly half an hour of unloading. Not to be outdone, the chief vizier for the horse lords noted the surreptitious manoeuvre and sent a message across the river that only the chariots of the twin kings should be brought across, consigning the rest of the retinue to walk the rest of the way to the palace. Gold was pressed into the palms of the ferrymen to redouble their efforts, and bargemen were pulled from their duties and pressed into service unloading the royal household. Slaves lost their footing and fell into the river, and no one could spare a moment to aid them.

In the end, despite heroic efforts and great sacrifice on both sides, the kings reached the docks at very nearly the same time. The viziers had fought to a draw, bowing curtly to one another across the open square.

It was only then that the functionaries noticed the unease of the royal bodyguards, and realised how silent and dark the Living City had become. They looked around the deserted wharves, lit only by Neru's silver glow, and wondered at all the rumours they had heard about Khemri's ageless king.

No sooner had the royal personages set foot on the docks than a single, pale figure appeared at the southern edge of the square. Raamket, approached the three kings, his cloak of flayed skin spreading like ghastly wings around his shoulders.

'Nagash the Living God welcomes you,' he said, bowing deeply. 'It is my honour to escort you into his presence.'

Before the shocked kings could offer a reply, the vizier beckoned to the twin Kings of Numas, and then turned and set off at a brisk stride towards the palace. The order of precedence had been set, and a hissed command from the vizier set the royal chariots rattling forwards across the paving stones, leaving Amn-nasir and his scowling retainers to follow as best they could.

The procession made its way down the empty streets of the noble district, wondering at the walled compounds and bronze-studded gates. At the palace, the great gates stood open, but no guards stood watch at the entrance. Likewise, the great plaza outside Settra's Court was deserted, save for swooping bats and scuttling lizards hunting among the drifts of sand. There were no trumpets to announce their arrival, nor white-robed acolytes to bless them with salt and the joyous clash of cymbals. Unnerved, the twin Kings of Numas stepped from their chariots and joined Raamket at the steps to Settra's Court to await Amn-nasir's arrival, leaving their viziers to mutter fearfully and oversee the unpacking of gifts to present to Khemri's king. The twin kings' keen-eyed Ushabti, clad in white kilts and leather armour ornamented with medallions of turquoise and gold, surrounded their royal charges and glared forbiddingly into the deep shadows surrounding the square.

Fifteen minutes later, the Zandri delegation wound its way into the plaza, and Amn-nasir joined his royal peers with as much affronted dignity as he could manage. The Priest King of Zandri was stocky and walked with the rolling gait of a lifelong sailor. At the venerable age of a hundred and twenty, his years at sea were long behind him, but his frame was still lean and strong. By contrast, the twin horse lords were tall and fey, with darting eyes and sharp, angular features. Bands of hammered gold decorated their slim arms, and their black hair was bound in identical horsetail queues. The rulers of both cities owed their wealth to trade: slaves from the wild north in the case of Zandri, and herds of fine horses raised on the plains around Numas. Together, they represented the richest cities in all of Nehekhara, and they remained so because they allied themselves with the Priest King of Khemri.

Raamket wasted no time on ceremony. As soon as Amn-nasir joined them, the vizier bowed silently and led the way past the tall pillars and into Settra's Court. The statues of Asaph and Geheb were lost in shadow, their feet covered by piles of charred and broken stone.

Beyond, the great hall was as dark as a tomb. The only light came from the Priest King of Khemri, sitting upon the ancient wooden throne and surrounded by the restless glimmer of his ghostly retinue.

Raamket stepped swiftly into the hall, his sandals whispering softly across the marble floor. The three kings stared at one another uncertainly, all thought of precedence forgotten, until by silent agreement they entered the court together with their bodyguards close behind. Their footsteps echoed in the vast space, and the Ushabti nervously fingered their weapons as they felt unseen eyes watching them from the darkness along the length of the hall.

At the foot of the dais, Raamket fell to his knees before his master. The swirling nimbus of glowing spirits regarded the three kings with empty eyes and faint, fearful moans. Their funereal glow silhouetted the lower legs of the great statue of Ptra behind the wooden throne, revealing jagged scars and pockmarks blasted into the gold-plated sandstone. To Nagash's right, the ghostly luminescence outlined the edge of the queen's lesser throne. From time to time, the ebb and flow of the unearthly light would play across the bony tip of a shoulder clad in spotless samite, or the edge of a resplendent golden headdress.

Nagash slouched upon Settra's ornate throne, resting his head on the palm of his hand in contemplation. He studied the three kings coldly, his eyes like flecks of polished obsidian. 'Greetings, kings of the north and west,' the necromancer rasped. 'The Living City welcomes you.'

The regal twins of Numas paled at the sound of Nagash's ruined voice, and could not manage a reply. Amn-nasir, older and made of sterner stuff, mastered his deep unease and said, 'Your summons came as a great surprise. We thought you were far to the south, answering the challenge of Ka-Sabar.'

'Circumstances to the east compelled my return,' Nagash replied. 'No doubt you have learned of the battle at the Gates of the Dawn.' Amn-nasir shot a sidelong glance at the twin Kings of Numas.

'There are rumours,' he admitted. 'It is said that the Tomb Guard has been overthrown, and the Priest Kings of Rasetra and Lybaras have seized the White Palace.'

'It is no rumour,' Nagash declared. 'Hekhmenukep and Rakh-amn-hotep, that treacherous son of Khemri, have broken the ancient code of warfare laid down by Settra and deposed Quatar's rightful ruler. Now they are poised to march upon the Living City.' The Priest King of Khemri straightened slowly upon the ancient throne and stared intently at his guests. 'This is no mere feud between kings. These reckless men have invited chaos upon all of Nehekhara, and we must give answer to them!'

'But... what would you have us say?' Nuneb stammered. 'Your warriors are many days away, are they not?'

'And we have neither the gold nor the time to raise an army,' Seheb added.

'It is the same with Zandri,' Amn-nasir said. 'As you know very well, great one.'

'Once a crocodile tastes human flesh, it wants nothing else,' Nagash growled. 'These outlaw kings have taken Quatar, and intend to seize Khemri next. Do you imagine they will stop there? If we do not stand together against them they will surely conquer us one by one.'

'What of Lahmia?' Seheb asked. The young king's gaze flicked nervously to the hunched silhouette upon Neferem's throne. 'Where does Lamashizzar stand?'

'Or Mahrak?' Nuneb said. 'Surely the Hieratic Council will repudiate what Rasetra and Lybaras have done.'

'The Hieratic Council,' Nagash said with a bubbling sneer. 'Hekhmenukep and Rakh-amn-hotep are their pawns. They intend to destroy me, and because you are my allies, they will supplant you as well!'

'Is this because of what you did to Khemri's temples?' Amn-nasir asked. 'Or does it have to do with the darkness that fell across Nehekhara several weeks past? The one that slew so many young priests and acolytes?'

'It is because the Hierophants of Mahrak see me as a threat to their corrupt rule,' Nagash said, his eyes narrowed angrily at the Priest King of Zandri.

'Because you are a living god?' Amn-nasir asked archly.

A flicker of triumph shone in the necromancer's dark eyes, and he replied, 'Because I have conquered death itself.'

'Be that as it may, it does not change the fact that the armies of Rasetra and Lybaras are within a few weeks' march of Khemri,' the Priest King of Zandri said, unmoved. 'The warriors of Zandri have not fought a battle in centuries. Our weapons are dulled and our armour lies in tatters.'

'Numas is little better,' Seheb said. 'Our nobles are poor, and our treasury all but exhausted.' He spread his hands helplessly. 'We would need years to rebuild our neglected army.'

The Priest King of Khemri listened to the kings, and nodded.

'Then you shall have it,' he said. 'I shall keep our foes at bay while you prepare your cities for war.'

Seheb and Nuneb glanced nervously at one another, and then looked to Amn-nasir. The Priest King of Zandri eyed Nagash warily.

'How is such a thing possible?' Amn-nasir asked.

Nagash rose to his feet and smiled mirthlessly down at the three kings. 'Go home and ask your priests, Amn-nasir. Ask how their gods used to punish those who defied them. Then consider how fortunate you are to be an ally of Khemri.'

Within hours the three kings were gone, heading back to their homes with their gifts still in hand and their minds troubled with thoughts of war. Darkness fell heavy upon the Living City as midnight drew near, and an ebon palanquin borne by a dozen pallid and shuffling slaves made its way from Settra's Palace through the empty streets, heading in the direction of the Gate of Usirian. To the east, the night sky was lit with strange, shifting lights and crackling lashes of indigo-coloured lightning.

Inside the swaying conveyance, Nagash sat cross-legged upon the cushions with the Staff of the Ages by his side and a great book lying open before him. Dark glyphs and arcane diagrams stood out starkly from the brittle pages of yellow papyrus, lit by the swirling aura of spirits that surrounded the King of the Living City. The necromancer traced their curving lines with a meditative fingertip, preparing for the ritual to come.

The slaves carried their master down the long road towards the necropolis, their feet slapping rhythmically on the clean-swept stones. The broad fields to the south of the road, once vibrant with grain, now lay mostly fallow. To the north, along the banks of the river, the reeds grew unchecked. The ancient shrines were abandoned and showed signs of neglect, and the slaves gazed fearfully into the darkness, wondering what evil spirits might be watching them from the shadows.

At length, they drew near to the vast city of the dead. The crowded tombs shone beneath the shifting veils of light that hung above the centre of the necropolis: strange, ominous curtains of green and purple that seemed to coalesce out of the air and twist in strange patterns above the enormous pyramid at the city's heart. Greater than Settra's Tomb, greater even than the Great Pyramid of Khemri, the sloped sides of Nagash's Black Pyramid towered above them all. Wrought from black marble quarried in the Mountains of the Dawn, the pyramid was darker than the night; indeed, the eerie storm of lights swirling above it made no reflection in its matte black surface. Ribbons of indigo lightning curled and crackled up the pyramid's four sides, coming together at its needle-pointed peak and coruscating through the sheets of colour swirling high above. Power radiated from the monument in palpable waves, washing over the surrounding tombs and down the twisting lanes of the necropolis.

The slaves bore the palanquin to the base of the ebon pyramid and sank silently to their knees, their limbs trembling not from inertia, but from pure, atavistic fear. Nagash emerged from the palanquin at once, the great book hanging in the air by his side, and strode swiftly through the monument's shadow-haunted archway.

Beyond lay a narrow corridor of close-fitting black stones, carved with row upon row of carefully ordered glyphs. No golden statues or colourful mosaics adorned the walls of the crypt, and no torch sconces broke the seamless procession of arcane symbols. The Black Pyramid was no palace to house the body of a dead king; it was built to tap the energies of the otherworld.

The vast structure held more than a hundred rooms, both within the pyramid and dug deep into the earth beneath. Terrible spells of misdirection and death had been laid upon its corridors and intersections, and all the devious arts of Khemri's tomb builders had been brought to bear to kill unwanted intruders with subtle, deadly traps. Only Nagash knew them all, and he made his way swiftly down the dark hallways and through huge, echoing chambers crowded with occult tomes and centuries of arcane experiments. He made his way towards the very centre of the pyramid, to a small room of stone that lay precisely beneath the peak of the towering structure more than four hundred feet above. The chamber was pyramidal in shape, the floor and walls each constructed of a single slab of black marble, carved with hundreds of sigils and glyphs. A vast, complex sign had been incised into the stone floor and inlaid with gold by the priest king. He had spent twenty years learning the art of its construction before hazarding the attempt. No one else could be trusted with such a delicate, precise task.

Nagash stepped carefully across the lines of the great symbol and stood in its centre. Midnight was almost at hand. At the heart of the pyramid he could sense the movement of the moons and stars overhead, moving in their careful, measured paths. Currents of dark magic, drawn through the air from the very crown of the world, swirled and seethed against the tomb's black flanks.

Raising his hands to the sky, Nagash spoke the first words of the great ritual in his broken, rasping voice.

Far to the south, the sky was clear, with a vault of glittering stars high overhead. Neru, the bright moon, was sinking low to the west, and baleful Sakhmet, the Green Witch, shone cruelly overhead as Arkhan and his warriors led the people of Bhagar out onto the plain between the city and the caravanserai.

Shahid ben Alcazzar and his desert princes had been bound with ropes, along with their families and slaves, and surrounded by a cordon of undead riders. Behind them came the traders, the craftsmen, the farmers, beggars and thieves: all the people of the city, in a shuffling, heartbroken mass. They were bound in huge slave coffles that stretched for more than a mile, leading back along the trade road into the heart of the city.

The remnants of Arkhan's mounted force waited upon the plain with the city's wealth gathered in their midst: a stamping, wide-eyed herd of magnificent desert horses, the wondrous gifts of Khsar. In Nehekhara, where a noble's status was measured in part by the number of horses in his stable, the herd was practically worth its weight in gold. The princes and their sons wept openly at the sight of their beloved companions in the hands of their foes.

Ben Alcazzar walked at the head of the vast procession, surrounded by his wives and children. His face was like stone, but his dark eyes were full of pain. Any price, he had said to Arkhan upon the battlefield, with the blood of his own brother staining his hands: anything, so that his people might survive. Terrible as his fears had been, he'd never dreamt it would come to this.

Arkhan waited with his horsemen upon the plain. Less than two thousand remained, and nearly all of those were bloodied and dead. The desert raiders had fought like daemons to defend their home, plunging knives into their foes even as they died. More than a quarter of the immortals accompanying the force had been slain, their decapitated bodies buried under piles of the enemy dead. The vizier's force had been wiped out twice over, he estimated, and only dark sorcery and pure, black will had saved the day.

The desert princes were led out into the centre of the plain by the undead horsemen. The slave coffles were herded to the left and right some fifty yards distant, forming long processions of weeping, distraught figures. Arkhan nudged his horse forwards, followed by Shepsu-hur and a score of grim-faced immortals bearing naked blades in their hands. The vizier could feel the blood start to pound in his veins, a slow, relentless rhythm, pulsing like a dark tide through his brain. Words, too faint to understand, whispered dreadfully in his ears.

Arkhan reined in before Shahid ben Alcazzar. The desert prince watched him approach, and for a moment the fire of defiance lit his dark eyes.

'May all the gods curse you, Arkhan the Black,' he said in a voice grown hoarse with sadness. 'What mercy is this, turning my people into slaves?'

'At least they will survive,' the vizier said coldly, 'for a time, at least. Such is the mercy of Nagash.'

The pulse was growing stronger, rippling through his body in waves. The other immortals felt it, too, their bodies swaying in their saddles, caught in the grip of its power. Arkhan's hand tightened on the hilt of his blade.

'I have kept my promise,' he said, baring his jagged teeth. 'Now you must pay the price.'

Shahid's defiant expression faltered. He glanced down at his chained hands.

'You have taken my freedom,' he cried. 'What more must I pay?'

The words were ringing in Arkhan's ears, rasping and insistent. His vision reddened under the pounding of blood in his temples, and his reply came out as a wordless growl as he raised his sword to the sky.

Behind the vizier, bronze flashed in the green moonlight as the horsemen drew their curved daggers and plunged them into the necks of the desert herd. Horses screamed and tossed their heads, scattering ribbons of steaming blood across the sands, and still the knives flashed and fell, slaughtering Bhagar's priceless steeds.

Howls of shock and despair went up from the people of the city as they saw their horses slain. Shahid ben Alcazzar's face turned ashen at the sight. The shock of the slaughter pierced his heart deeper than any blade. Arkhan saw the light go out of the desert prince's eyes long before his sword plunged into ben Alcazzar's neck.

Screams and wailing pleas went up from the chieftains and their households as the immortals waded in among them, their swords hacking down left and right in brutal, bloody strokes. Men threw themselves in front of the falling blades, protecting their wives with their last breaths, and mothers tried to cover the bodies of their stunned and silent children. The fetlocks of the immortals' horses turned red with steaming gore.

The people of Bhagar rent their clothes and tore at their hair in misery as they were forced to witness the massacre. As terrible as the blood-letting was, worse still were the spectral figures that rose in torment from the mutilated bodies and were drawn into a swirling pillar of shrieking souls that rose into the starlit sky and sped in a twisting ribbon off to the distant north.

A howling wind stirred the space within the Black Pyramid, stirring Nagash's robes as the necromancer's ritual neared its peak. Dark magic flowed down the sides of the great crypt, drawn by the arcane symbols carved into its vast flanks, and were channelled through conduits worked cunningly into the stone. The power flowed into Nagash, and with it he reached out with his will across hundreds of leagues and seized upon the death energies of Bhagar's noble houses and their enchanted steeds. He drew their tormented spirits to him, down into the black stone of the pyramid, and fed them to the ritual he had painstakingly built.

Above the massive pyramid, the night sky grew heavy with dark, swirling clouds. Indigo lightning leapt from the black stone into the sky, kindling unholy fires deep within the boiling mist. Pain, agony and death, distilled from a thousand tormented spirits, was poured into the growing storm.

Deep in the pyramid, Nagash raised the Staff of the Ages to the stone peak above him and shouted a single, arcane syllable. There was a flash of light, and a rushing chorus of wailing souls, and then, in an instant, the roiling storm overhead vanished, leaving the world stunned and silent in its wake.

Hundreds of leagues distant, sentries pacing the walls of Quatar noticed the dark clouds gathering over the city from the west. Many of them were from Rasetra, and were used to the sudden storms of the southern jungle, so they paid little heed to the building storm.

Slowly and steadily, the clouds piled up over the city, blotting out the stars above. Hours later, the first, heavy drops began to fall. They pattered thickly against the stones and splashed on the helmets of the soldiers. Some turned their faces towards the sky and tasted the rain on their lips. It was warm and bitter, tasting of copper and ash. They wiped their chins and, holding up their hands to the guttering torches, they saw that their palms were slick with blood.

Red rain fell across Quatar, staining the White Palace crimson and filling the streets with puddles of gore. It fell upon the citizens sleeping on their roofs and spattered the faces of the priests who hurried from their temples and stared wide-eyed at the heavens.

The ghastly downpour lasted until a minute before dawn. When it was done, the entire city was steaming like a sacrificial altar.

By nightfall the first people began to sicken and die.

NINE

SECRETS WITHIN THE BLOOD

Khemri, the Living City,
in the 44th year of Qu'aph the Cunning
(-1966 Imperial Reckoning)

The emissary of Quatar approached the king's throne to the beat of hide drums and the tolling of a deep, bronze bell, leading a procession of courtiers garbed in bone-coloured linen and fine, golden masks. Behind them came a score of pale-skinned barbarian slaves, naked but for colourful strips of cotton tied to their throats and arms like the feathers of singing birds. They carried open chests of sandalwood and polished bronze in their calloused hands, filled with gold coins, precious spices and other exotic treasures. It was mid-afternoon, and the air inside Settra's Court was hazy with swirling clouds of incense. The grand assembly had been in progress for more than four hours, and the city's nobles were casting impatient glances towards the dais and shifting uncomfortably from one foot to the other. Outside, a new acolyte had taken up the role of the Ptra'khaf, summoning the wealthy and powerful to attend upon their king in a sweet, singsong voice. Nagash fancied he heard a note of desperation in the young boy's call.

The Grand Hierophant moved amid the deep shadows behind the court's towering marble columns, watching the games of state play out on the grand processional before the dais. In Khetep's time, the court would have been easily three-quarters full during the monthly grand assembly, with the second sons of every noble family and emissaries from all of Nehekhara's cities in attendance. The last time the chamber had known such a throng had been on the day of the old king's interment, but, two years later, the great hall was little more than a third full. Ghazid and the king's servants had spread out the attendants from the dais to nearly the middle of the room to make the assembly seem larger than it truly was.

'Beware of nobles bearing gifts,' Khefru murmured over Nagash's shoulder. 'It looks as though old Amamurti has decided he's had enough. I wonder if he'll head back to the White Palace, or decamp to Zandri's court next?'

Near-invisible in the deep shadows, Nagash sneered in the direction of the emissary and his entourage, and said, 'Judging by the richness of his gifts, Amamurti will be boarding a barge for Zandri by sunset. He'll regret his lavishness once he reaches the coast. The old goat will have to pay dearly to gain Nekumet's favour over the embassies already camped there.'

From the moment of Khetep's death by the banks of the Vitae, Khemri's power and influence had slipped like grains of sand from the weak hands of his successor. Rasetra's envoy had been the first to take his leave of Thutep's court, amid promises of eternal goodwill and support for Khemri's policies. Then the desert princes of Bhagar had departed, followed by the envoys of Bel Aliad and Lybaras. Within months, word reached Khemri that the dignitaries had taken up residence in Zandri instead, paying homage to Nekumet's court. Slowly but surely, the locus of power was shifting away from the Living City for the first time in history, and for all his impassioned speeches and lofty ideals, Thutep seemed powerless to stop it.

Even Khemri's noble houses had begun to lose their respect for the king's authority. None of the most powerful families chose to attend the royal summons to the grand assembly. At first there had been elaborate excuses and sincere regrets, but now they simply ignored the call of the Ptra'khaf in favour of other pursuits. Many of the lesser houses had followed suit, and as the Grand Hierophant surveyed the bored-looking nobles gathered in the hall he found that he recognised less than half of them.

Not that Nagash had been a fixture in Thutep's court since his brother's ascension. For the last two years he had spent nearly every night in the secret chambers within the Great Pyramid, seeking to master the sorcerous arts of the druchii. He'd spent months learning their degenerate tongue, and hours listening to their hissing discourses on the nature of magic. Everything they told him confirmed his beliefs: the gods were not the wellsprings of the world's power. Magic permeated the land, invisible and omnipresent as the desert wind. Those that were sensitive to its touch could direct its flow, providing they had a keen mind and a potent will. So the druchii said, and yet, despite his every effort, Nagash felt nothing.

The Grand Hierophant paused beside the rounded bulk of a marble column, his handsome face hidden in shadow.

'A court full of jackals and mangy dogs,' he observed, studying the crowd with a sour expression. 'Who are these fools?'

Khefru stepped up to his master's side, and said, 'Third and fourth sons, mostly, with no prospects or inheritance. Most of them are here because of public debts or other minor crimes. Your brother requires them to attend the grand assembly to help atone for their misdeeds.' The young priest smirked. 'I know many of them quite well.'

'Such as?' the Grand Hierophant asked, his eyes narrowing thoughtfully.

'Well,' Khefru murmured. He nodded his head at a group of noblemen standing on the opposite side of the hall. 'Take that pack of rats over there,' he said. 'You won't find a worse lot of drunkards and gamblers in all of Khemri. The tall one in the middle is named Arkhan the Black. He'd cut his own mother's throat for a bag of coin.'

Nagash arched a narrow eyebrow, and said, 'Arkhan the Black?'

'If we were close enough to see his teeth, you wouldn't have to ask,' Khefru said, chuckling softly. 'He chews jusesh root like a common fisherman, and he's got a smile like a smashed wine cup. Spends most of his ill-gotten coin on favours at Asaph's Temple, and word is that he has to pay double before any of the priestesses will go near him.'

'My brother makes a mockery out of all of us,' Nagash hissed, shaking his head in disgust. His hands clenched angrily at the thought of his father's blasted corpse and the terrible power that had destroyed him: power that remained stubbornly out of his reach! Bile burned at the back of his throat at the thought of all he could do with but a *sliver* of that awful strength. He turned to Khefru. 'Any one of these will do,' he said with a disdainful sweep of his hand. 'Promise whatever you must, but be discreet.'

'I know just the person, master,' Khefru said, nodding quickly. 'You may rely upon me.' The expression on his face told Nagash that the young priest knew very well what would happen in the event that he failed.

Nagash dismissed Khefru with a curt nod of his head and the two parted ways, the young priest slipping silently into the rear of the crowd while the Grand Hierophant continued his journey through the shadows towards the great dais. The envoy of Quatar had reached the far end of the hall, and his deep, practised voice was echoing from the columns and the high, dark ceiling.

'Great King of the Living City, on behalf of Quatar I offer up these treasures and a coffle of fine northern slaves to you as a measure of our esteem. It is with great regret that we must take our leave of you, and we hope that these gifts will recommend us fondly to you in our absence.'

It was nearly mid-afternoon, and once the emissary had been given leave to depart, the grand assembly would conclude. Then, Thutep's queen would be brought forth to offer blessings upon any children born since the last new moon. Nagash planned to settle in the shadows and watch the Daughter of the Sun for a time. He had not seen her since Khetep's interment, but he thought of her often. She was exquisite, a perfect blossom tended in the temples of Lahmia since her youth, and unlike any woman he had ever known. The Grand Hierophant wondered what it would be like to possess one such as her.

Lost in his covetous reverie, Nagash failed to notice the white-robed figure waiting in his path until he was nearly on top of her. She wore the ceremonial vestments of a matron of Ptra, her stout figure entirely concealed except for her strong, wrinkled hands, which were clasped tightly at her waist. Her face was concealed behind a gold mask that glimmered faintly in the reflected light of the court's oil lamps. The matron bowed deeply at Nagash's approach.

'The blessings of the Great Father be upon you, holy one,' she said in a deep voice. The matron spoke with a Lahmian's singsong accent. Nagash scowled at the woman.

'I require no blessing from you, matron,' he replied curtly. The answer seemed to amuse the matron.

'Be that as it may,' she said. 'I stand before you on behalf of the queen. Neferem wishes to speak with you.'

'Indeed?' Nagash murmured, his handsome face betraying a hint of surprise. 'This is an unexpected honour. When am I to meet with her?'

'Now, if it please you,' the matron answered, gesturing into the darkness beyond the dais. 'She waits in the antechamber beyond the great hall. Shall I escort you there?' Nagash let out a snort.

'I was born in these halls, woman. I can find my own way,' he said, and left the matron bowing awkwardly in his wake as he strode swiftly off into the gloom. His dark eyes were pensive as he contemplated the reasons for this surprise summons. The Daughter of the Sun did not, as a rule, hold private audiences with anyone save the king.

The shadows grew deeper as Nagash passed by the great dais. Thutep was perched at the edge of Settra's throne, smiling politely at the Quatari emissary as the man continued his lengthy farewell speech. A small crowd of bodyguards and functionaries waited upon the king's pleasure in the darkness just past the dais. Nagash moved swiftly past them and approached a trio of wide-spaced stone doors set into the chamber's far wall. Statues of the gods stood watch beside each of the doorways: Neru at the door to the far left, Ptra in the centre, and Geheb to the right. A pair of Ushabti stood guard at the centre door with their huge ritual swords in their hands, their skin glowing softly with the sun god's blessing. A matron waited with them, poised and patient. She bowed gracefully as Nagash came forwards, and she spoke quietly to the devoted, who nodded solemnly and stepped aside. The Grand Hierophant acknowledged the matron with a passing glance and pushed the stone door open.

The antechamber was small and brightly lit, with more than a dozen oil lamps guttering in niches from the sandstone walls. Fine Lahmian rugs, imported from the Silk Lands to the east, covered the floor, and the air was thick with a haze of pungent incense. Low divans had been arranged in a loose circle in the centre of the room, all facing towards a cushioned chair ornamented in gold leaf. Neferem, Daughter of the Sun, sat facing the door, her back straight and her arms resting lightly on the arms of her chair. She wore the dazzling golden headdress of Khemri's queen, and a broad pectoral of gold studded with gemstones and lapis lazuli lay upon her breast. Her eyes were shadowed with dusky kohl, and her skin shone like bronze in the firelight. She smiled slightly as Nagash approached, and the Grand Hierophant was surprised to feel his pulse quicken in response. A fool like Thutep did not deserve such a wife!

Nagash approached the queen, taking note of the half a dozen matrons resting upon their knees at a discreet distance on the far side of the room. He bowed smoothly before the Daughter of the Sun.

'You summoned me, holy one?' he said.

'The blessings of the Great Father be upon you, Grand Hierophant,' Neferem replied, in a voice as dark and rich as honey. She spoke with the musical accent of the Lahmians, and her every movement was graceful and poised. The queen indicated a divan to her right. 'Please, sit. Would you care for wine, or perhaps some food?'

'I do not partake of wine,' Nagash said. 'It clouds the senses and corrupts the mind, and I can abide neither.' The Grand Hierophant settled on the edge of the divan. 'But I thank you, nonetheless.'

Across the room, the matrons shifted uncomfortably, but the queen was unruffled.

'My husband was speaking of you the other day,' she began. 'He has seen very little of you since your great father's death.'

Nagash shrugged. 'My brother and I have never been close,' he said, 'and my duties with the cult demand much of my time.' His eyes narrowed thoughtfully. He had been careful to conceal his trips to the Great Pyramid these last couple of years. Was it possible Thutep was spying on him?

'I certainly understand the demands that gods and men place upon the priesthood,' the queen said with a knowing look, 'and as the Grand Hierophant of Khemri's Mortuary Cult your influence extends beyond the Living City, to liche priests all across Nehekhara. Some might even say your power rivals that of the Hieratic Council in Mahrak.' Nagash smiled faintly.

'All men die, holy one,' he said. 'That alone is the source of our influence.' He waved his hand dismissively. 'The great mysteries of life and death occupy my interest. I have no time for the petty politics of the priesthood.'

Once more a stir went through the silent matrons. Neferem studied the Grand Hierophant for a moment, resting her chin on the tips of her fingers, and said, 'But the kings of Nehekhara rely upon priests for their insight and wisdom, do they not?'

'Some more than others,' Nagash observed. 'The Priest Kings of Lahmia are notably indifferent to the demands of their holy men, for example.'

'That depends upon the advice, I think,' the queen countered, 'and its source.' Nagash folded his arms across his chest and regarded Neferem coolly.

'And what advice would you have me give, holy one?' The Daughter of the Sun smiled at him.

'Your brother has a bold vision for the Blessed Land,' she said. 'Your father brought an era of peace and prosperity to Nehekhara. Thutep wants to build upon that and unify the land once more.' Nagash arched an eyebrow at the queen.

'He would restore Settra's empire?'

'Not an empire,' Neferem said, 'a confederation of equals, bound by ties of trade and mutual self-interest.' Her eyes glittered with passion. 'We are all one people, Grand Hierophant, bound to the gods in a covenant of faith. The Blessed Land belongs to all of us. Settra's empire only hinted at the glories we could achieve once our rivalries were put aside.' The Grand Hierophant let out a derisive snort.

'You would have the people of Khemri believe that they are the equal of those flea-bitten horse thieves in Bhagar? It's outrageous!' Neferem straightened in her seat, and her beautiful face took on a haughty cast.

'They *are* equal,' she said, 'and both cities could profit from such an understanding. What has Nehekhara gained from centuries of warfare except stagnation and death?'

'Death is the way of the world,' Nagash said. 'Why should a man trade for something when he can seize it instead?' The Grand Hierophant rose to his feet. 'Khetep understood this. The Priest Kings of Nehekhara yielded to his authority because he was a great general, and they feared the might of his army.'

'And look at how long his achievements lasted after his death,' Neferem answered. 'Khemri's court is all but emptied. Fear can compel men, but it cannot bind them together for long.'

'Not without constant reinforcement,' Nagash hissed. 'Thutep surrendered what authority Khemri possessed when he chose not to seek revenge against Zandri for the death of our father.' He gestured sharply in the direction of the court. 'The great houses disdain him, and he does nothing. At this point, I would not be surprised if more than one of them was plotting against him. How does he expect to forge a grand confederation of kings when he cannot manage his own court?' The queen stiffened.

'And what would you have him do?'

'What I wish is not relevant,' Nagash snapped. 'If Thutep hopes to rule over Khemri, he must spill his share of blood. Heads must roll, both here and abroad. That is how cities grow wealthy and powerful, not because they went to their neighbours and begged for aid.'

Neferem's jaw tightened fractionally at Nagash's contemptuous tone, but her voice was steady as she spoke. 'I can't deny that my husband's vision grows harder to achieve with each passing day,' she said. 'We are not blind to Zandri's ambitions, Grand Hierophant. I hoped that you could be persuaded to intervene on your brother's behalf. If the other cities would agree to help form a united front against Nekumet–'

'To what end? So they could throw away their swords and become a nation of merchants?' Nagash's lip curled in distaste. 'And you thought I would lend my voice to such foolishness? You insult me, holy one.'

Neferem's face grew still.

'Then I regret having given offence,' she said neutrally. 'I shall take up no more of your time, Grand Hierophant. My husband had spoken to me at length of your brilliance, and I know what it is like to put aside ambition and serve the needs of a temple. I had hoped to give you a role in shaping the future of Khemri.' The Grand Hierophant bowed deeply to the queen.

'For me to shape the future of Khemri I would require a crown,' he said coldly. 'For now, that privilege belongs to the Priest King of Zandri.'

Nagash turned on his heel and took his leave of the queen. The startled whispers of the matrons followed after him as he returned to the shadows of Settra's Court. While he had been with Neferem the grand assembly had concluded, and the hall buzzed with the murmur of voices as the young nobles of the city hurried out into the sunlit afternoon in search of better entertainment. A handful of nervous young mothers clutched their babes at the foot of the great dais, awaiting the blessing of the Daughter of the Sun. Thutep was already gone, having exited the court through Neru's door at the rear of the chamber.

The great dais was deserted. Nagash paused nearby.

'A crown,' he murmured thoughtfully, looking up at Settra's throne.

Unnoticed by the dwindling crowd, Nagash climbed the stone steps and stood beside the ancient chair. He rested his hand on the arm of the throne and contemplated the backs of the milling nobles, his eyes full of dark and terrible thoughts.

The druchii warlock frowned at the centre of the chamber's stone.

'You're certain this faces directly north?' Malchior said in his sibilant tongue. Nagash glanced up from the pages of the book.

'Of course,' he said. 'The pyramid is precisely aligned with the four corners of the earth. It's vital to maintaining the aura of preservation within the tomb. Have you no understanding of geomancy in your homeland?'

'Geomancy,' the warlock sneered, 'how quaint.' He stepped forwards and laid a black-gloved fingertip against the sandstone. 'Never mind the fact that this material is a poor conductor of magic. Marble works far better.'

Nagash scowled at the pale-skinned figure. Two years of imprisonment had done little to blunt the arrogance of the three druchii. Once they had accepted the terms of Nagash's agreement they had quickly demanded everything from fine foods to books and other entertainments, which they seemed to regard as nothing more than their due. The Grand Hierophant had humoured them, within reason. Over time, their prison had expanded to include more than a dozen adjoining chambers, and he had taken pains to furnish them so that they would enjoy some measure of comfort.

The great chamber where he had first revived the druchii had become their work room, and the margins were crowded with bookshelves, tables and chairs. Nagash crouched in the centre of the space, with a large, leather-bound book open before him. The thick pages were covered in copious notes dictated by the druchii and copied down in Nagash's hand. Since he had begun his training, Nagash had committed everything he'd been taught to paper, both for his own reference and to ensure that his tutors remained honest. A horsetail brush and a small pot of ink sat on the floor beside his knee.

'Marble, and gold,' Drutheira hissed. The lithe, white-haired witch was lounging like a sunning cobra on a low divan across the chamber, tracing a set of Nehekharan glyphs with an elegantly pointed fingernail. 'This cursed land is too far from the north. I can barely sense a glimmer of power here.'

'Perhaps it is this pyramid,' Ashniel said, raising her dark eyes from the book she was reading and regarding Nagash hatefully. The druchii straightened, extending her slim white arms over the reading table in a catlike stretch. 'We should be teaching you out in the open air, not shut up in this awful barrow.' Nagash grunted in amusement as he reached for the brush and ink.

'So the lion said from the hunter's pit,' he replied. 'Perhaps the fault lies in your perceptions, druchii; the pyramid is a potent focus for mystical energies. The mortuary cult has interred our kings in such crypts for centuries to maintain the invocations of restoration.'

Within the first few days of their imprisonment, the barbarians seemed to have appointed roles for themselves. Malchior took on the lion's share of Nagash's tutelage, setting a difficult and demanding pace of lectures and exercises. Drutheira assisted Malchior during the more complicated lessons, but preferred to focus her energies on more physical pursuits, and despite repeated failures, her attempts at seduction continued unabated. Meanwhile, Ashniel treated the Grand Hierophant with nothing but contempt, keeping to her books and reading voraciously about Nehekharan culture, religion and, most importantly, the construction of their crypts.

It was clear to Nagash from the beginning that Malchior and Drutheira were meant to distract him, each in their own ways, while Ashniel kept to herself and looked for a way to free them from Khetep's tomb. The hateful witch had been careful to cover her tracks, but not quite careful enough, and Nagash and Khefru had found evidence that Ashniel had managed to breach the first layer of traps surrounding their apartments and was making slow but steady progress exploring the lower level of the crypt. The battle of wits, keeping one step ahead of the witch by changing the location and nature of the traps, had become a diverting pastime for Nagash and his favoured servant.

The Grand Hierophant dipped the brush in the black ink, consulted the tome open before him, and began to paint the sigil on the floor.

'You are certain this will work?' he asked, tracing the complicated lines with care.

'I am certain of nothing in this place,' Malchior growled. The warlock folded his arms and watched the sigil take shape on the stone floor. 'Drutheira is right, this land is a desert in more ways than one. The winds of magic are very weak, scarcely stirring the aether, and, as I've said often enough, your kind has a feeble grasp of magic at the best of times.'

The warlock let the implication of his statement hang in the air between them: you may not be capable of this. Nagash clenched the brush tightly in his hand and focused on crafting the sigil.

'If this does not work, what then?' he asked curtly. Malchior shrugged.

'There is nothing else,' he said. 'This ritual isn't even an accepted part of our magical lore. It's the sort of thing practised by shade-casters and gutter witches, who lack the will to harness the winds of magic.' He spread his hands. 'If this attempt fails, the fault lies with you, human. I've tried everything I can think of.'

Then, a murmur of voices echoed from the passageway beyond the work room. Nagash glanced up from his work as Khefru entered the room with a hooded figure in tow.

'Here he is, master,' Khefru said with a bow. 'Allow me to present Imhep, of the House of Hapt-amn-kesh. He should serve your purposes in every particular.'

The hooded figure swayed slightly on his feet. Imhep reached up and bared his head with shaking hands. He was young, only sixty or so, with large, watery eyes and a receding chin. A short, black wig sat askew on his shaven head.

'It is an honour, Grand Hierophant,' he said in a slightly slurred voice. 'Your servant said you requested me personally?'

'Did you drug him?' Nagash asked, frowning at Khefru.

'Well... yes,' the young priest replied. 'I thought it prudent, all things considered.' The Grand Hierophant glanced worriedly at Malchior.

'Will that cause problems?'

The notion seemed to amuse the druchii, who said, 'That depends on how much effort you intend to put into your lesson.' He pointed to the flowing black lines. 'Just be careful that the fool doesn't scuff your hard work with his plodding feet.' Imhep was glancing around the dimly lit chamber with befuddled interest, taking special note of the two witches.

'What... That is... How may I be of service to you, holy one?' he asked. 'My friend Khefru mentioned a reward of some kind.'

'He has debts,' Khefru interjected. 'Imhep is something of a gambler, you see.'

Nagash eyed the young noble closely, noting the lack of rings or other jewellery, and the man's worn kilt and sandals.

'I take it he's the sort that loses a great deal. Won't his debtors inquire after him?' Khefru shrugged.

'Perhaps, but what will they learn? No one saw me with him, master. I was most careful.'

'We had some very fine wine,' Imhep said, his slack face quirking into a grin. 'Where was that again, friend Khefru?'

Nagash bent and finished the sigil with a few deft strokes of his brush, and then beckoned impatiently to his servant.

'Bring him here,' he said, 'but be careful of the glyphs.' Khefru took Imhep's arm and led the drugged man across the room as though he were a child.

'Mind your step,' he told the noble as they approached the edge of the sigil. 'That's it. Right into the centre.'

Imhep swayed drunkenly in the middle of the circle, forcing Nagash to grip his arms and hold him steady.

'Forgive me, holy one,' the young man said with a chuckle. 'I'm not certain how much help I am going to be at the moment. As I said, it was very fine wine.'

'Get that cape off him,' Malchior commanded. At a nod from Nagash, Khefru darted forwards and jerked the cape from Imhep's shoulders, revealing the noble's narrow, bony chest.

'Careful!' Imhep barked. 'That's my good cape! I'll be needing that back.' The warlock paced slowly around the edge of the sigil.

'Where are the implements?' he asked. Imhep turned his head at the sound of Malchior's voice.

'What's the barbarian saying?' he asked.

Khefru reached into his belt and drew out a pair of long bronze needles. The young noble's eyes widened.

'Merciful Ptra! What are those for?'

Malchior glided like a snake towards Khefru, his eyes glinting. He reached out and delicately pulled them from the priest's grip.

'Yes,' he murmured. 'These will do.' He turned to Nagash. 'Hold him.'

Nagash seized Imhep's lower jaw and wrenched his head around, until they were looking eye to eye. The noble let out a startled cry, which turned to a scream of agony as the druchii stepped inside the sigil and drove the first needle into Imhep's lower back.

The young noble collapsed to his knees, shrieking in agony. Nagash watched as Malchior put his free hand against the side of Imhep's head and bent it to the side, exposing the tendons of the noble's thin neck. With a hungry smile, the warlock plunged the second needle into the juncture of shoulder and throat, and Imhep's entire upper body went rigid. Malchior worked the needle deeper into Imhep's chest.

'Remember our discussions on nerve clusters and their uses,' he said dispassionately. 'This will keep your subject alert and suffering, but unable to interfere.' Nagash looked into Imhep's eyes, drawn by the gleam of pain radiating from their depths.

'And the suffering is important?' he asked.

Drutheira chuckled.

'It is not *vital*,' she admitted, 'but it is certainly entertaining.' The warlock frowned at the interruption.

'We were speaking of sandstone earlier,' he said. 'Some physical objects channel and store magic better than others, but none work so well as flesh and bone. Humans, as I said, have a poor grasp of magic, but like all living things, their bodies accumulate power over time.' Malchior traced a fingernail across Imhep's cheek. 'Can you feel it?' he asked.

Fascinated, Nagash reached out and laid a hand on the noble's forehead. He cleared his mind and tried to employ the techniques the warlock had taught him. After a moment, he shook his head, and said, 'I feel nothing.'

Malchior smiled.

'Touch your fingers to the needle, then,' he said.

The Grand Hierophant's gaze fell to the needle jutting from Imhep's torso. Tentatively, he reached out and laid a finger on its round end. The noble stiffened, his eyes widening in pain.

The metal trembled against Nagash's fingertip. It was cold to the touch... and then he felt it, like a faint thread of fire pulsing against his skin.

'Yes,' Nagash whispered. 'Yes...' A terrible, hungry light grew in his eyes. 'At last.'

The warlock loomed over Imhep's shoulder, his face lit with ghastly joy.

'Give me your knife,' he said.

Nagash's hand fumbled at his belt. The pulse of power sent a tremor through his frame, quickening along with Imhep's pulse. He handed over his curved knife without hesitation, ignoring Khefru's quiet protest. Malchior pulled away the noble's wig and cast it aside.

'Now we shall draw that power to the surface,' he said, laying the point of the knife against Imhep's scalp. 'Hours of agony will shape it, and strengthen it as your victim struggles to survive. When the time is ripe, we will cut his throat and his life force will pour over your hands. Then your education will begin in earnest.'

Slowly, carefully, the druchii began to cut into Imhep's skin. Nagash watched the warlock work. After a moment, he turned a page in his book and began to make careful notes.

TEN

TIDINGS OF WAR

**Ka-Sabar, the City of Bronze,
in the 63rd year of Ptra the Glorious
(-1744 Imperial Reckoning)**

The wind from the east in the City of Bronze was called Enmesh-na Geheb, for it was the eastern quarter of the city that contained the majority of Ka-Sabar's complex of foundries. The Breath of Geheb reeked of cinders and the smell of scorched copper, as ingots of ore carved from the Brittle Peaks were melted in great crucibles and combined with bars of nickel to produce high-quality bronze. For centuries Ka-Sabar had been known as a city of industry, and had made its wealth by trading everything from belt buckles and wheel rims to fine swords and scale armour. In these dark days the demand for her goods was greater than ever. The city's furnaces lit the eastern skies by night, and her smithies were shrouded in a perpetual mantle of acrid smoke. Heavily armed caravans made their way down the trade road from Quatar bearing chests of gold and silver, and returned laden with swords and axes, scale shirts and shields, bronze-tipped spears and baskets of arrowheads. Rasetra and Lybaras were spending enormous sums, much of it borrowed from the Hieratic Council in Mahrak, to equip their growing armies. Akhmen-hotep's viziers were stunned at the huge influx of wealth, but the king understood the desperation that drove such furious spending. He, too, had been feverishly rebuilding his shattered forces after the devastating defeat at Zedri, six years earlier. So long as that unholy monster Nagash ruled over the Living City, not a single soul in Nehekhara was safe.

News of the slaughter at Bhagar had arrived with the first of the desert city's hollow-eyed refugees, less than three weeks after Akhmen-hotep had returned to Ka-Sabar. For weeks the city was paralysed with terror and grief, and its citizens looked to the north with mounting dread as they awaited the arrival of the Usurper's nightmarish horde. Then a messenger travelled the trade road bearing letters from the Kings of Rasetra and Lybaras. They had risen up against the Usurper and taken Quatar by storm, and were poised to liberate Khemri! Akhmen-hotep swiftly drafted a letter declaring his support for the western kings and then spent the rest of the day in the Temple of Geheb, thanking the gods for his people's deliverance.

A month passed with no news as Ka-Sabar mourned its dead sons and contemplated the future. Akhmen-hotep sent one messenger after another to the White Palace, seeking word from his new-found allies. None returned. Finally, after six long months, the king despatched a small force of his Ushabti and a squadron of horsemen to Quatar to learn what they could.

Two months later, the Ushabti returned, on foot, bearing a tale of horror and despair. On the very night of the slaughter at Bhagar, the skies above Quatar had wept blood, and within days the entire city was consumed by a plague the likes of which the Blessed Land had never known before. The sickness struck man and animal with equal ferocity, maddening them with a violent, savage fever. Within a week the city was consumed in an orgy of murder and destruction. The allied armies were decimated, torn apart from within as entire companies succumbed to the fever and turned upon their fellow warriors. The Kings of Rasetra and Lybaras had been forced to flee the city, abandoning their armies for the safety of Mahrak at the other end of the Valley of Kings. According to rumour, they intended to raise more warriors and return with a contingent of warrior priests from the Hieratic Council to cleanse the city and resume the advance upon Khemri, but as the months turned to years, it became clear that the priests at Mahrak could not find a way to counter the curse that had befallen the city.

Akhmen-hotep had no doubt that Nagash was the source of the terrible plague. The thought chilled him to the depths of his soul. Grimly, the king began to rebuild his shattered army and prepare for the worst.

Nagash did not stir from Khemri in the wake of the terrible plague. Although the armies of his enemies had been devastated, it appeared that the Usurper's army had fared little better. To make matters worse, a season of terrible sandstorms had risen from the Great Desert and swept across central Nehekhara, making travel all but impossible for weeks on end. The result was a stalemate of sorts. A tattered remnant of the western armies still held the White Palace at Quatar, while Nagash was free to work his evils in the Living City. The fate of the Blessed Land hung in the balance as both sides raced to rebuild their devastated forces and start the war anew.

The vizier rose slowly into view as he ascended the sandstone steps leading to the council hall, his robes fluttering in the hot wind blowing across the city from the east. Slanting beams of sunlight shone on the functionary's bronze skullcap and glittered from the gold rings adorning the man's wide, scarred hands. He bowed low to the king and the small group of nobles who sat or paced around the windswept chamber.

'The emissary from Mahrak has arrived, great one,' he said.

Akhmen-hotep turned at the sound of the vizier's rough voice. He was pacing, as was his wont, striding along the wide flagstones beside the short, squat columns that supported the eastern edge of the council hall's roof. The chamber had no walls, resting as it did atop the royal palace in the centre of the city, which was itself at the summit of one of the Brittle Peaks' many foothills. The King of Ka-Sabar could look out across the width and breadth of his domain, from the forges spread in a smoking crescent to the east to the brooding stone temples of the gods that filled the Priests' Quarter to the west. A fine layer of soot coated the round sides of the eastern columns, and swirling drifts of sand and grit blew across the small chamber's stone floor, reminding the king and his nobles of the earth god whom they worshipped.

The king's chair, a massive thing made from pieces of petrified wood and heavy bronze fittings, faced the stair from the far end of the room. A score of smaller chairs were arrayed in a rough circle before it, reserved for the city's major nobles and the king's closest allies. Less than half were occupied.

On the left hand of the king's chair sat Memnet, the Grand Hierophant of Ptra. On the right slouched Pakh-amn, the king's Master of Horse, along with half a dozen young sons of the city's noble families. A great many of Ka-Sabar's great lords had not returned from the debacle at Zandri, and the mantle of leadership had fallen on largely inexperienced shoulders. Neither Khalifra, the Priestess of Neru, nor Hashepra, the Hierophant of Geheb, were in attendance, and the king felt their absence keenly. The emissary's sudden arrival had left Akhmen-hotep with little time to gather his advisors, and the religious leaders were rarely seen outside their temples these days. The new Hierophant of Phakth, a priest named Tethuhep, had not been seen in public at all. His spokesman claimed that Tethuhep was occupied with prayers for the defence of the city, but Akhmen-hotep suspected that Sukhet's successor was not yet ready to assume his official duties.

Truth be told, Pakh-amn and Memnet were in little better shape. It was plain to Akhmen-hotep that both men had been deeply scarred by the horrors they had witnessed six months before. The Grand Hierophant was a gaunt, hollow-eyed figure, his face aged beyond his years since the fateful battle. Though still a powerful and influential figure in the city, Memnet had grown increasingly distant and withdrawn with each passing year. Pakh-amn had suffered even worse since his return to the city. Akhmen-hotep had made no secret of the young noble's precipitous withdrawal from the battlefield, and his early return to Ka-Sabar, more than three days ahead of the king, caused many in the city to question Pakh-amn's courage. For more than a year after the battle he was absent from the king's court, and rumours circulated that he had turned to the milk of the black lotus to escape the pain of his disgrace. He, too, was sunken-eyed and brooding, his fingers trembling as he held a cup of wine with both hands.

Akhmen-hotep studied the council for a moment, and then nodded gravely to his vizier.

'Bring him forth,' the king commanded. The vizier bowed once more and withdrew down the stairs. Less than a minute later they heard the measured tread of the king's Ushabti, and four of the devoted rose into view, escorting a very old priest, who wore the vibrant yellow robes of a servant of Ptra. Despite his advanced years, the emissary moved with surprising confidence and strength, and his dark eyes were keen and bright. His gaze fell upon Memnet, and the Grand Hierophant leapt from his chair as though stung.

'Nebunefer! The blessings of Ptra be upon you, holy one,' Memnet stammered. The Grand Hierophant clutched at his hands and bowed deeply. 'This is an unexpected honour–'

Mahrak's emissary forestalled Memnet with an upraised hand.

'Be still,' he commanded roughly. 'I haven't come to inspect your coffers, Grand Hierophant. I bring tidings to your brother the king.' Nebunefer inclined his head respectfully to Akhmen-hotep. 'Blessings of the Great Father be upon you, King of the Bronze City.'

'And to you,' Akhmen-hotep replied neutrally. 'It has been some time since an emissary arrived from the City of Hope. Do the desert storms scourge Mahrak as well?' Nebunefer arched a thin eyebrow at the king.

'The storms are our creation, great one. The Hieratic Council has gone to great lengths to keep the blasphemer in Khemri at bay so that you and your allies can recover from your terrible losses.' The king considered Nebunefer for a moment.

'We thank the council for its aid,' he said carefully. 'Does this mean that Mahrak is ready to send its warrior-priests into battle against the Usurper?' Nebunefer gave the king a terse shake of the head.

'The time is not yet right,' he replied. 'The Kings of Rasetra and Lybaras have raised new armies and are ready to resume the crusade against the blasphemer.'

'Ah. I see,' Akhmen-hotep said. 'So the Hieratic Council has at last cleansed Quatar of its terrible curse?' The emissary paused.

'The plague has been allowed to run its course,' he replied. 'Many of the city's noble families survived, including Nemuhareb and the royal family, as well as a few hundred soldiers that had been quartered inside the White Palace, but the rest suffered terribly.' Akhmen-hotep nodded gravely.

'The caravans from the north brought terrible stories: streets covered in ash and human bones, houses barricaded from within and filled with mutilated bodies, and Charnel pits filled with burned skulls. In truth, Quatar is a city of the dead.'

'And so the monster's army grows,' Pakh-amn said, raising his red-rimmed eyes to stare at the emissary. His voice was little more than a croak, and his teeth were stained a dark blue from years of drinking the milk of the lotus. 'The dead in their tens of thousands are his to command, priest. Quatar is under siege even as we speak!' For a brief moment Nebunefer was taken aback by the vehemence in Pakh-amn's voice.

'The Hieratic Council has heard the stories of the battle at Zandri,' he said, 'and steps have been taken to put the citizens of Quatar beyond Nagash's reach. The surviving members of the city's mortuary cult worked day and night to seal the dead into carefully warded tombs in the city necropolis.' The emissary turned his attention back to the king. 'What is more, the accounts of fighting at Zandri and Bhagar tell us that either Nagash or one of his so-called immortals must be present to raise the bodies of the dead, and he will not have that opportunity at Quatar.' The king clasped his broad hands behind his back and looked out across the eastern quarter of the city, feeling the breath of Geheb against his skin.

'You said that Rasetra and Lybaras have raised new armies.'

'Rasetra marches for the Valley of Kings even as we speak. Rakh-amn-hotep has mustered every warrior his city possesses, and even includes companies of savage jungle beasts in his army. Hekhmenukep and the warrior-engineers of Lybaras have emptied their fabled arsenals and are hastening to Quatar with a legion of dreadful war machines to counter the blasphemer's undead horde. Within the month they will be encamped outside Quatar, and will march upon the Living City as soon as the signs are propitious.'

Pakh-amn muttered darkly into his wine cup and took a long swallow. Akhmen-hotep shot the nobleman a hard look, but said nothing. Instead, he drew a deep breath and turned to Nebunefer.

'What does the Hieratic Council want from Ka-Sabar?' he asked. The emissary smiled faintly at the king's frank manner.

'Our spies in Khemri have reported that Nagash has not been idle since he laid his curse upon Quatar. He has bent the Kings of Numas and Zandri to his will and emptied his coffers to raise a mighty army. They are marshalling on the plains outside the Living City, though the constant storms have slowed their movements considerably.' Nebunefer paused. 'It is possible that the army is intended for Ka-Sabar, great king, but the council thinks it more likely that they will head for Quatar first and seal off the Valley of the Kings.' Akhmen-hotep nodded.

'Nagash is no fool,' he said. 'If he can hold Rasetra and Lybaras at bay by seizing the Gates of the Dawn, then he can deal with us at his leisure.' The king considered the situation. The size of the eastern armies would work against them on the march, slowing their progress almost to a crawl. The armies of the Usurper, on the other hand, were closer to Quatar, and could move with much greater speed. Nagash did not have to burden himself with food and water for his troops, after all. The thought sent a shudder down the king's spine.

'The next few weeks will be crucial,' Nebunefer continued. 'Rasetra and Lybaras must safely cross the Valley of Kings. Once they have reached the plains beyond, the advantage in battle will be theirs. Thus, we must take steps to draw Nagash's attention away from Quatar for a time.' A heavy silence descended upon the council chamber, broken only by the hissing breath of the god. Memnet glanced fearfully from his brother to Nebunefer.

'What would you have us do, holy one?' he asked in a wavering voice.

'We propose attacking Nagash from an unexpected quarter,' the emissary replied, his dark eyes glinting. 'For all his supposed genius, the blasphemer is also a petty and arrogant king. Any defeat, no matter how small, is an insult to his overweening pride, and he will be compelled to respond.' Nebunefer spread his hands. 'The Bronze Host is in an ideal position to launch such a blow.' Akhmen-hotep frowned at the man.

'And where would you have us strike?' he asked.

'At Bel Aliad, on the other side of the Great Desert.'

Pakh-amn let out a choking sound, spraying wine over the rim of his tilted cup. The haggard nobleman's gasping coughs quickly dissolved into mirthless laughter as he lurched drunkenly from his chair. Many of the council's young noblemen looked to one another in embarrassment and dismay, but some few joined Pakh-amn in laughter, believing they understood the point of the joke.

'A daring plan from a bunch of cowering priests,' Pakh-amn spat, fixing Nebunefer with a hateful glare. 'Your precious council sits on perfumed cushions and leaves us to do battle with the armies of the damned! You've heard stories of what happened at Zandri, but you weren't there! The sky didn't boil with darkness over your head! Your friends weren't turned into hissing, clawing corpses!'

Akhmen-hotep took two long strides across the council chamber and smote the Master of Horse on the side of the head. The nobleman was knocked from his feet, his empty goblet clattering musically across the stones. Swords flashed as the king's Ushabti stepped forwards, ready to act upon Akhmen-hotep's command.

'Shame me once more, Pakh-amn, and I will kill you,' the king said coldly. 'Now begone. The council has no further need for you.'

At a nod from the king, the four Ushabti stepped forwards and surrounded the nobleman. Pakh-amn climbed unsteadily to his feet, rubbing his hand over the red welt left by the king's open hand. With a last, hateful look at Nebunefer, the Master of Horse was escorted swiftly from the hall.

The king waited until Pakh-amn had disappeared from sight before bowing his head to the emissary.

'My apologies,' he said. 'Ka-Sabar means no insult to our honoured allies. That said, surely you must appreciate the... challenges... of such an undertaking. As you said, Bel Aliad lies on the other side of the Great Desert. Travelling around it would take months, and would bring us dangerously close to Khemri along the way.'

'We do not propose travelling around the desert, but through it,' Nebunefer replied. 'There are ancient routes across the sands that caravans used to travel in centuries past.'

'Many of the oases along those routes have long since dried up,' the king said, 'and they would not have been enough to support an army in any case.' The emissary smiled.

'The desert holds more secrets than you know, Akhmen-hotep. The bandit princes of Bhagar could and did move large bands of horsemen across the desert virtually at will, and we know that there are almost a hundred Bhagarite refugees here in the city. Put the question to them, great one. They can lead you across the desert.'

'Why should they?' the king asked. The question took the priest aback.

'Why? For revenge, of course,' he said. 'Nagash must pay for what he did to Bhagar. Do you not agree?' Akhmen-hotep ignored the emissary's question.

'And if we attack Bel Aliad, what then?' he asked.

'You occupy the city for a time,' the emissary said. 'Loot the homes of the noblemen and the spice markets. Slay those who support the blasphemer in Khemri. When word reaches the Living City that you have conquered the city, Nagash will be forced to order his army to move against you. From Bel Aliad you could threaten the city of Zandri, and that is something that he cannot allow. By the time his warriors arrive, you will have already disappeared back into the desert, and the blasphemer's army will have been drawn hundreds of leagues in the opposite direction from Quatar.'

Nebunefer's proposition deeply unsettled the king. Occupy the city? Loot its riches and slay its leaders out of hand? That was the way of barbarians, not civilised Nehekharans, but the Usurper had done far worse at Bhagar, and would not stop there. As king, he had a duty to defend his people, regardless of the cost. He could only hope that the gods would forgive him when it came time for his soul to be judged. Akhmen-hotep turned to his brother. 'What say you, Grand Hierophant?' he asked.

Memnet blanched under the king's searching gaze. The Grand Hierophant was but a shadow of his former self. Gone was the proud, confident religious leader that six years ago had demanded vengeance for the deaths of his fellow priests. He had come away from the battlefield at Zandri a changed man, wounded to his very soul by what he had seen and done. He had grown distant from the king since then, and had never spoken of the price he'd paid for calling down the fires of his god against the Usurper.

The Grand Hierophant tucked his hands into his sleeves and once more glanced fearfully from the king to Nebunefer. With an effort of will, he gathered his courage and said, 'Lead us, oh king, and we will follow.'

Akhmen-hotep drew a deep breath and nodded gravely. Outside, the breath of the god fell still.

'Then it is decided,' the priest king said. 'Sound the trumpets and call forth our warriors. The Bronze Host marches once again to war.'

ELEVEN

THE GAME OF KINGS

Quatar, the White Palace,
in the 63rd year of Ptra the Glorious
(-1744 Imperial Reckoning)

Rakh-amn-hotep, Priest King of Rasetra, clenched the railing of the sky-boat with his scarred, stubby fingers the moment he heard the warning grumble of the wind spirits overhead. Sure enough, there was a crackle of canvas and the huge air bladder contracted along its thirty-yard length, pitching the wooden hull of the sky-boat downwards like a ship cresting the peak of a towering wave. The king bit back a startled shout as the craft descended in a swift, graceful arc out of the Valley of Kings and over the crescent-shaped wall of the Gates of the Dawn.

Standing at the prow of the sky-boat, Rakh-amn-hotep felt hot, chalky wind buffet his face and watched the dusty ground race past with terrifying speed. They were past the fortifications sealing the western end of the valley in less than a minute, and through teary eyes he could see the gleaming stones of the Temple Road winding down the gentle slope towards the city of Quatar. The walls of the city and the central palace were a faint cream colour, Ptra's blessed sun having bleached away much of the ghastly red stains left by Nagash's cursed rain. If the god was kind, within another ten years there would be no sign of the nightmare that the Usurper had inflicted upon the city.

The great plains of central Nehekhara stretched beyond the city, a vast, rolling vista of sandy soil marked with trade roads in lines of white stone. To the king's relief, the air bladder overhead swelled once more in answer to the chorus of chanting priests at the craft's notional stern, and the sky-boat levelled out several hundred feet above the ground. Fighting to control his lurching stomach, the king could see the sharp-edged flanks of the Brittle Peaks stretching in a vast line to the north and south, and the broad ribbon of the life-giving River Vitae winding off to the west, towards the distant sea. The southern flank of the river was bordered with a thick band of vibrant green, while to the north stretched the rich fields of the Plains of Plenty, where the horse lords of Numas tended their herds and harvested the grain that fed much of Nehekhara.

To the king's relief, he saw no columns of dust or swarms of metal-clad figures making their way across the plains towards Quatar. The rolling plains were empty, all the way to the glinting, mist-wrapped Fountains of Eternal Life, many leagues to the north-west. Nagash's armies still had not stirred from the fields outside Khemri, which lay hidden behind a smudge of ominous purple clouds just at the edge of the north-west horizon. For the moment at least, Quatar and the forces encamped outside it were safe.

A vast, orderly camp had sprung up in the wide fields west of the city. Lines of dun-coloured tents were laid in neat rows, organised by company and arrayed around a central square containing parade grounds, supply tents and portable smithies. Neat columns of unhitched chariots filled an open square near a makeshift horse corral, and three adjoining fields were filled with huge, hulking shapes wreathed in tendrils of steam and thin wisps of darker sacrificial smoke. Rakh-amn-hotep saw huge catapults, war scorpions and towering giants made of carved wood and bronze plates. The army of Lybaras had arrived with all its strength, and it was a fearsome sight to the battle-hardened king.

The air spirits hissed and grumbled overhead, and with a creak of timbers and a groan of cables the great sky-boat swung around and began to descend. Rakh-amn-hotep saw that they were making for a large plain to the south of the Temple Road, less than a mile from the perimeter of the Lybaran camp. Three other sky-boats were already grounded on the sandy plain, unloading jars of supplies to long lines of waiting slaves. The sky-boats were hidden beneath the vast bladders of canvas, which contained the air spirits that kept the craft aloft. Built from modified river boat hulls, they hung beneath the bladders from a web of stout cables thicker than a man's arm. Each hull could carry a huge amount of cargo in its holds, including an entire company of soldiers, if their stomachs were up to the trip.

When the Lybaran sky-boat had found the Rasetran army a week ago and offered to carry Rakh-amn-hotep ahead to Quatar, the king had left much of his baggage behind and loaded the boat with a mixed company of Ushabti and heavy infantry. Their frightened cries and queasy groans had been a never-ending source of amusement to the sky-boat's small crew. The king didn't envy the slaves who would be given the task of washing out the cargo holds.

The craft sank in a slow, graceful arc towards the field, drifting slightly south and gliding to a stop with a crunch of sand and gravel, just like a river boat sliding up to the shore. By the time that one of the boat's acolytes had thrown a rope ladder over the side, the first of the king's Ushabti were staggering up onto the deck and turning their faces gratefully to the sun. Smothering a wry grin at their discomfort, the king ordered his troops to disembark first. He did not have long to wait.

During the disembarkation, a trio of chariots arrived from the city, driven by members of Hekhmenukep's royal household. One of the king's viziers climbed carefully down from the lead chariot and waited patiently for Rakh-amn-hotep to descend from the sky-boat. He bowed low as the King of Rasetra stepped clear of the ladder.

'My master the Priest King of Lybaras sends you greetings, great one,' the vizier said. 'He asks you meet with him in the White Palace, where he would offer you some refreshment after your journey.'

The stout king planted his feet on the sand and swayed drunkenly. His body felt like it was still falling through the air, and his knees were as weak as a newborn's.

'Lead on,' he said with a distracted wave, and tried to concentrate on walking the ten yards to the waiting chariots without pitching forwards onto his face.

Once the king and his Ushabti were aboard, the chariots wheeled around in a tight circle and clattered across the landing field towards the Temple Road. The ride smoothed out considerably once they reached the road's stone surface, and soon the drivers had their horses dashing down the road at a ground-eating canter. After the heady rush of air travel the pace seemed sluggish to the men of Rasetra.

Within half an hour the stained walls of Quatar loomed before the chariots, and Rakh-amn-hotep saw that the city gates were open and empty of traffic, even though it was early afternoon. Only a handful of warriors stood guard upon the walls, and the king noted that they wore the dun kilts of Lybaran soldiers rather than the bleached white of Quatar's tomb guard.

He had heard that the city had suffered greatly in the grip of Nagash's foul curse, but Rakh-amn-hotep had no idea what that truly meant until the chariots passed through the open gate and onto an empty street that had once led to the city's bustling marketplace. The houses and shops lining the road were covered in a fine layer of white ash, and many doorways were streaked with soot from fires set during the plague. Piles of desiccated refuse lay heaped in the narrow alleys or along the sides of the street, but there were no animals rooting through the mess in search of a meal. A heavy pall of silence hung over the scene, muffling even the rattle and squeak of the chariot wheels. The acrid reek of burnt wood and charred flesh permeated the still air. Far off to the north-east, pillars of grey smoke rose languidly into the sky as the priests of the mortuary cult committed still more corpses to Ptra's cleansing flames.

The plague had been over for more than a year, and the survivors were still dealing with the bodies that had been left behind.

They rode on through the empty bazaar, stirring up clouds of ash and dust, and then through the Merchants' Quarter. Here the king's experienced eye saw the telltale signs of past violence. Many of the homes had been looted by bands of maddened plague victims, and piles of broken furniture and shattered pottery lay in drifts outside the smoke-stained doorways. Ominous stains against the walls of some homes hinted at the dire fates of their owners.

As bad as the destruction was in the Merchants' Quarter, the noble districts beyond had suffered even worse, as though the citizens pinned the blame for their misery squarely on their king and his supporters. All of the homes had been broken into and burned, and even the walls of some estates had been torn open by frenzied work with picks and spades. Walls had been toppled and roofs had fallen in when their wooden supports had finally burned through. Some time in the past, workers had cleared a path through the debris in the centre of the street, and the chariots were forced to ride single file past mounds of broken bricks and charred, splintered wood.

It was only when they were nearly upon the stained walls of the White Palace that they came upon the first signs of life. The grand structure, built to rival then ultimately surpass the glories of Settra's palace in Khemri, was surrounded by small ornamental parks and wide squares set with fountains that were fed by springs running beneath the city. The parks were filled with weathered, ash-covered tents and ramshackle huts made from crumbling mud bricks, and gaunt, hollow-eyed figures in tattered robes clustered wearily around the dust-covered fountains, washing clothes or filling jugs with water. The few survivors of the plague years watched the chariots roll past with expressions of misery and dread.

The White Palace rose like an island of stability amidst the squalor and despair of Quatar. Though its walls still bore the stains of Nagash's vile curse, the palace had been completely untouched by the chaos and savagery that had gripped the rest of the city. Warriors of Quatar's royal household stood guard at the palace gates, garbed in white leather armour and bearing their huge, curved swords. They bowed their heads gravely as the chariots rolled past, and the procession continued on down a wide avenue lined with towering statues of Djaf's jackal-headed servants. To the west, Rakh-amn-hotep could see the white bulk of the mortuary temple, while to the east rose the forbidding Palace of the Dusk, the temple to the God of Death. The palace lay ahead, a sprawling structure faced with white marble that towered like a sphinx above every other building in the city.

Rakh-amn-hotep's escort carried him down the wide avenue and into a small square that opened before the palace's wide steps. There, arrayed in serried ranks ten men deep, waited a company of warriors clad in the heavy scale armour of Rasetran infantry. A tall, broad-shouldered warrior whose skin glowed with the might of the sun god stood at their head. The champion raised his sword in salute as the chariots approached, and as one, the warriors let out an exultant cheer at the sight of their king.

The chariots reined in before the assembled troops, and Rakh-amn-hotep ordered his driver to turn around so that he could better see and be seen by the Rasetran warriors. Smiling fiercely, the king raised his arms in greeting.

'Stalwart souls!' he cried. 'It has been too long since I have seen your faces, and I rejoice to see you in such fine spirits. For six long years you few have held this city in the face of calamity. For six long years you alone stood between the monster at Khemri and the kingdoms of the east. All of Rasetra knows of your brave deeds! Your names have been spoken with honour in the temples, and your families have been richly rewarded by my hand in gratitude for your service. Our brothers and cousins are on the march, shaking the earth with their fury. Soon they will stand among you, and we will march east to finish the work we started so long ago!'

Once more, the warriors let out a great cheer and clashed their maces against their shields in salute. Their faces split in proud smiles to hear of the king's esteem, and only the hard look in their dark eyes hinted at the ordeal they had been forced to endure. Ekhreb, the king's champion and commander of the detachment, sank to one knee as the king descended from the chariot.

'None of that, by the gods!' Rakh-amn-hotep declared, waving his hand impatiently at his champion. 'For all that you and your men have faced, you should never be asked to bow to another man again.' The king strode forwards and gripped the champion's arms, nearly dragging the taller man onto his feet.

'Welcome back, great one,' Ekhreb replied in a deep voice. The champion was powerfully built, blessed with the strength and vitality of one of Ptra's favoured sons. His face was wide and his jaw square, and his dark eyes glinted beneath a heavy, jutting brow. Sunlight shone on his shaven head, and gleamed from the gold rings in his ears. His wide mouth quirked in a wry grin. 'Six years is too long to be without your presence.'

'You are too kind, my friend,' Rakh-amn-hotep replied.

'Not at all. We thought you'd be back within the year. In fact, you said something along those lines just before you left.'

'It's possible that I might have been a bit optimistic in my estimate.'

'We came to that same conclusion after the fourth year or so.' The two men chuckled, and then the king's expression turned serious once more.

'How bad was it?' he asked quietly. The grin left Ekhreb's face, and his expression turned bleak as he struggled for the right words. Finally he sighed.

'It was terrible,' he said. 'None of us will lead virtuous lives after this. There is no hell that the gods can make that could equal what we faced here in Quatar.' Rakh-amn-hotep grimaced at the look in his champion's face. He looked over the ranks of jubilant men at Ekhreb's back.

'Is this all that remains? Barely a company of men out of forty thousand souls?' The champion nodded.

'Only the gods know how many deserted and headed for home during the early months. We tried to stop them, but once the fever took hold of the populace it was all we could do just to stay alive. The Lybaran army was all but destroyed within the first six months. We survived only because we fell back and shut the palace gates against the mob.' Ekhreb shrugged. 'Would that I could regale you with tales of courage, but the truth is that we hid behind these walls and prayed for our survival. Eventually we realised that the plague couldn't find its way into the palace.' Rakh-amn-hotep frowned.

'Why was that?' he asked. Ekhreb's expression darkened.

'We wondered about that as well,' he said. 'In the end, the only explanation that made any sense was that Nagash didn't want it to. Nemuhareb fears that the Usurper has a special fate in mind for him and his family.' The king's frown deepened.

'Has Nemuhareb caused any trouble?' Ekhreb shook his head.

'None,' he said. 'He is a broken man, drowning his nightmares in wine and the milk of the black lotus. We're the only reason he hasn't been deposed.'

'I'm surprised there is anyone willing to take his place,' Rakh-amn-hotep muttered darkly. 'How many citizens are left?'

'The gods alone know,' Ekhreb replied. 'Less than a thousand, for certain. We have search parties combing each district of the city, and we're still finding bodies. The city is one vast tomb. It will take generations for the city to recover, if at all.' The king nodded.

'I can see why the Lybarans chose to camp outside the walls,' he said.

'What of our own army?' the champion inquired. 'When will they arrive?'

'It will be some weeks yet,' the king said with a sigh. 'We were still several days from the Valley of Kings when the Lybaran sky-boat found us. It's been slow going, all the way from Rasetra. We've got sixty thousand infantry and horsemen, plus another twelve thousand barbarian troops and their thunder lizards.' Rakh-amn-hotep shook his head. 'I never should have let Guseb talk me into bringing the lizards along. So far, they've been more trouble than they're worth. Fortunately, it appears that Nagash is in no hurry to march on the city, which had been my greatest cause for concern.'

'You can thank Hekhmenukep and Nebunefer for that,' Ekhreb said.

'Nebunefer?' the king asked, his eyebrows rising in surprise. 'What's that old schemer doing back here?'

'He arrived with the Lybarans,' the champion replied, 'and then left almost at once for Ka-Sabar. Rumour has it, they've hatched a plan to keep Nagash distracted while we marshal our forces.'

'I'm not sure I like the sound of that,' the king said, scowling up at the palace. 'Come on, old friend,' he growled, beckoning to Ekhreb. 'Time to find out what our allies have been up to while I've been away.'

The black tower rose like a blade of stone in a swirling sea of sand. Just on the edge of the Great Desert, it was constantly assailed by the storms that howled across the hot dunes. The great blocks of basalt that comprised the tower's outer surface had been smoothed to a mirror finish by the scouring sand. The sound it made against the stone was like the hissing of a hundred thousand hungry snakes, seeking the slightest crack or flaw to work their way inside.

Yet, work on the tower continued, even in the teeth of the raging wind. Day and night it went on. An army of slaves shaped stones and carried them to the base of the tower, where still more labourers dragged them up a vast, spiral ramp that wound sinuously around the tall spire to a height of more than two hundred feet. The ramp was made of wood and hides, and lashed together with thick coils of rope, and it wavered and trembled appallingly in the storm. It had collapsed many times, toppled by raging gales of wind or sawn through by the abrasive sand, and each time, scores of labourers were crushed beneath the weight of fallen timbers and splintered stone.

The lucky ones did not rise again. Most, however, pushed aside the fallen beams or clawed their way out through the sand, digging with ragged hands or the pointed tips of finger bones. Some squirmed right out of the ragged scraps of flesh and muscle that had once clothed their gleaming bones. Their strength was born of pure, relentless will, lashing at their trapped souls like a scourge.

The people of Bhagar did not know hunger, or pain, or fatigue. The last of them had died more than three years before at the feet of Arkhan's black tower, fitting the foundation stones into place. The breath of their god raged impotently around them, scourging their bodies and hollowing out their eyes, and yet the tower continued to grow.

Constructing the tower had been an idea of Arkhan's for some time, dating back to the early construction of his master's mighty pyramid. When he found himself in possession of several thousand slaves after the conquest of Bhagar, the vizier saw his opportunity. While his master focused on raising his armies at Khemri, Arkhan proposed building the citadel to guard the city's southern approaches against another attack from distant Ka-Sabar, or perhaps even a revolt in the Spice City of Bel Aliad. The Undying King considered this, and agreed.

In truth, Arkhan wished to distance himself from Nagash for an entirely different reason: namely, the king's life-giving elixir. He chafed at the power that Nagash had over him by virtue of that terrible draught, but still its sorcerous formula eluded him. If he were to continue to serve the king from his seat at the black tower then Nagash would have no choice but to show the vizier how to craft the elixir for himself, or so he had thought.

Every six months a courier arrived from Khemri bearing a sealed chest that contained six vials of the elixir, just enough for one drink per month. The privation left him weak and thirsty all the time, and despite his best efforts he could never save enough of the liquid to study its properties for any length of time.

For the first two years after the slaughter at Bhagar the slaves had dug deep into the rocky soil with crude picks and shovels, creating the first of the tower's many floors more than fifty feet underground. Arkhan summoned stonemasons from Khemri to guide the slaves in their work, while his undead horsemen stood watch from the surrounding dunes. Later, the slaves were sent back to their home city and set to work demolishing their homes for the stone needed to shape the tower's foundation.

The deepest of the underground vaults was set aside for Arkhan. Although nothing like the grand eminence of his master's marble crypt, the chambers served the immortal's immediate needs. It had taken most of a year to move his household from the Living City to the distant tower due to the raging storms, and many loyal servants perished along the way. The rest he killed with poison as soon as they arrived. They waited upon him in the gloom of his sanctum, their shrivelled bodies wrapped in robes of blackest linen and wrought with arcane sigils of preservation.

Arkhan was within his inner sanctum, poring over scrolls of arcane lore and studying the ruby depths of one of his precious vials of elixir when he heard a faint, hissing rustle in the dark corners of the room. For the briefest instant he thought that the questing sand had finally found its way inside the black tower, driven by the implacable hate of Khsar the Faceless, whose people Arkhan had murdered. Pure terror coursed through the immortal's veins. Then, in a flash he snatched up a guttering lamp and advanced across the room, banishing the deep shadows before him.

Lamplight glittered on shining black carapaces. Scarabs were pouring from cracks in the stonework and flowing in a seething carpet across the sanctum's floor.

Arkhan took a step back, clenching the vial of elixir tightly in his hand as he prepared to cast a fiery incantation. The scarabs came together in the centre of the chamber, leaping into the air with a dry clatter of wings and swirling into a seething, glittering cloud.

The words of the incantation died upon Arkhan's lips as the cloud took on a familiar shape.

'Loyal servant,' said a voice from the depths of the rustling cloud. It was born of scraping mandibles and buzzing wings, scrabbling legs and dusty carapaces, but its identity was unmistakeable. Stunned, Arkhan bowed before the visage of Nagash.

'I am here, master,' the vizier said, tucking the vial into his sleeve. 'What is your command?'

'Our enemies march against us once more,' the necromancer said. The vague outline of Nagash's face turned towards the vizier. 'New armies are gathering at Quatar, and the Bronze Host crosses the Great Desert to strike at Bel Aliad.'

'Crossing the desert? Impossible!' Arkhan exclaimed. 'The storms–'

'The storms are the work of the craven priests of Mahrak,' Nagash hissed. 'They hope to hinder our efforts and conceal the movements of their troops. Even now, refugees from Bhagar are leading the warriors of Ka-Sabar along the secret pathways of the desert tribes. They will reach Bel Aliad within a fortnight. They do not know, however, that there is a traitor in their midst, one who has worshipped me for many years, since the defeat at Zedri. He will deliver the Bronze Host into our hands, and then the City of Bronze itself!'

Arkhan's mind raced as he considered the sudden turn of events.

'My warriors stand ready, master,' he said. 'What would you have us do?'

'Take your undead horseman and ride for Bel Aliad,' the necromancer said. 'Once you arrive, this is what you must do.'

The necromancer told Arkhan of his plan in hissing, crackling tones. The vizier listened with his head bowed low, contemplating the downfall of Akhmen-hotep and the people of Ka-Sabar.

TWELVE

DESIGNS UPON A CROWN

Khemri, the Living City,
in the 44th year of Geheb the Mighty
(-1962 Imperial Reckoning)

The slave girl knelt on the stone floor in the centre of the magical circle, her body rigid with agony as Nagash intoned the Incantation of Reaping. Only two days before, she had arrived in the Living City on a slave ship from Zandri, taken in a raid on the barbarian lands to the far north. Bright blue eyes stared up at Nagash in mindless terror. Her mouth gaped wide in a frozen shriek of pain, revealing fine, white teeth and a squirming tongue. Her shoulders trembled as she struggled for breath. The Grand Hierophant had been careful to allow her muscles just enough flexibility for her to breathe enough air so that she could remain conscious and alert. It had taken many months and countless experiments before he was capable of such precise control.

Nagash's powerful voice echoed from the stone walls of his sanctum beneath the Great Pyramid as he continued the remorseless, savage chant. He spoke in Nehekhem, not in the debased, snake-like tongue of his prisoners. His knowledge of their barbaric magic had grown in leaps and bounds in the three years since he'd slain that hapless fool Imhep. The spilling of blood, the unwinding of a living spirit from its bindings of flesh and bone, these things were second nature to him now.

The words of the ritual rang like the tolling of a bell, rising in tempo as Nagash focused his will upon the slave girl's labouring heart. Her heartbeat began to hammer in time with his chanting voice, and the air between them crackled with invisible power. The Grand Hierophant clenched his fists and felt the warmth of the girl's life force against his skin. His voice rose to an exultant shriek as the chant rose in tempo, and wisps of smoke began to curl from the slave's pale skin. Her trembling ceased. Veins stood out starkly at her temples and along the sides of her throat. Nagash felt the beat of her heart rise to a glorious crescendo. Then her body gave a single, violent spasm and exploded into a column of hissing green flame.

Nagash plunged his hands into the seething inferno, feeling the power race along his skin as he seized the slave girl's throat. With an inhaled breath and an exertion of will, he drew her life force into him. His veins burned, and her final cries rang soundlessly along his bones. It was over in a moment, and her body, drained of every dreg of power, collapsed in a heap of steaming bones at Nagash's feet.

This was but a prelude, a gathering of strength for the real work that was about to begin. Wrapped in ethereal mist and glowing with unholy energy, the Grand Hierophant stretched out his arms once more and turned his attention to the wooden cage just a few feet beyond the edge of the magic circle. Dusky figures stirred inside, half-hidden by the shifting shadows cast by the room's guttering oil lamps. They were siblings, a young man and a woman in the full bloom of youth and of noble birth, whom Khefru had found in the wine houses near the docks. The discovery had been a stroke of luck. Nagash's requirements for his next experiment had been very specific, and he had been forced to wait months for the pair to fall into the young priest's clutches.

With the last syllables of the Incantation of Reaping still echoing in the chamber, Nagash began his next ritual. The first phrases were simple enough, serving to focus the Grand Hierophant's concentration, but grew swiftly in cadence and complexity as the first stages of the transformation began.

He had learned very quickly that there were limits to the power of a human soul. When Imhep breathed his last and poured out his lifeblood onto Nagash's hands, the Grand Hierophant felt his veins turn to fire and believed himself a god, but that wondrous energy faded all too quickly. A single human life could fuel a minor druchii spell, but no more. Malchior had responded to his frustrations with a shrug. A soul was but a puff of breath compared to the wild winds of magic that fuelled the druchii's greater rituals.

The warlock had known this all along. It was yet another of the barbarians' devious traps. Malchior could fulfil the letter of their agreement by teaching Nagash the incantations and rituals of druchii magic lore in the full knowledge that the Grand Hierophant would never amass enough power to attempt the more potent spells. Such an effort would require scores, if not hundreds of souls, a process that was far too unwieldy to perform in a single rite, and on too large a scale to avoid notice by Thutep and the city nobles. No doubt Malchior hoped that Nagash's lust for power would tempt him to recklessness and self-destruction. Instead, the Grand Hierophant began to apply his new-found powers in another direction, namely the accumulated arcane lore of Settra's mortuary cult.

For more than two thousand years, the cult of eternal life had plumbed the dark mysteries of life and death. Their ancient tomes were filled with theoretical rituals to harness the soul and manipulate the invisible workings of flesh and bone. Until now, however, their practical rites were minor in comparison to those of the druchii, because the liche priests depended on the gifts of the gods to fuel their incantations. All that had changed when Imhep had poured out his lifeblood over Nagash's hands.

This new incantation was based upon an older rite found in the cult's body of arcane lore. Nagash had spent the better part of a year altering and refining the ritual to suit his plans. Now he would put it to the test.

The arcane chant rolled like thunder from Nagash's tongue, driven by the energies stolen from the slave girl. He focused on the two shadowy forms crouching at the far end of their cage and extended his hands towards them. At once, the young siblings collapsed to the floor, moaning in fear and pain. Power flowed from his fingertips and played across their naked forms.

Nagash performed the incantation for nearly an hour, until the last vestiges of stolen energy sped from his fingertips. As the rite concluded, he spoke a single name.

'Shepresh,' he said, and lowered his arms. Silence fell, punctuated by soft, choking sounds from inside the cage and the swish of an ink brush from the corner of the sanctum to Nagash's left.

Khefru continued to note his observations in a huge, leather-bound book for several long minutes after the rite was completed. Nagash's erstwhile tutors were absent. Since he had begun to apply his new-found abilities to the lore of the mortuary cult, the Grand Hierophant found that he required the presence of the druchii less and less. Soon, Nagash suspected that their long-term arrangement would finally come to an end.

The young priest made a final note with his brush and glanced up at his master.

'Was the rite successful?' he asked. Nagash spared a final glance towards the mewling figures at the bottom of the cage and waved dismissively.

'It is too early to tell,' he said, striding carefully from the circle. 'The transformation has only begun to take root. I shall know more when I return later tonight.' The Grand Hierophant folded his arms across his chest. 'Have you seen to the preparations inside the city?'

Khefru nodded gravely as he capped the ink-pot and set his brush aside. The past six years had taken a toll upon the former noble. Though still very young by Nehekharan standards, the priest had grown haggard and sunken-eyed in service to his master's increasingly dangerous pursuits. His face was sallow and puffy from too many nights spent in wine houses searching for his master's victims, and he'd taken to shaving his head to conceal the streaks of grey that had begun to sprout at his temples. The long scar on the left side of his face cut a jagged white furrow across his fleshy cheek.

'All is in readiness, master,' he replied. 'The house has been made ready, and the slaves know their tasks.' Nagash studied Khefru warily.

'You sound reluctant,' he said. Khefru closed the tome carefully and lifted it from the writing table.

'It is not for me to say, master,' he answered, returning it to a shelf laden with similar volumes.

'True enough,' the Grand Hierophant replied. 'Tell me, nonetheless.' The young priest considered his words carefully.

'What you are contemplating is reckless,' he began. 'These men are cowards and fools. They will betray you in an instant–'

'They will have far more to gain from me than from my brother,' Nagash cut in. 'Just as you did, if you recall.'

'That's not how they will see it,' Khefru persisted. 'They have no power, no wealth or influence. Thutep and the great houses would crush them, and they know it. No amount of persuasion will convince them otherwise.' Nagash smiled coldly.

'Persuade them? Hardly. When the time comes, they will have persuaded themselves.'

Khefru's gaze drifted to the cage at the far side of the room. His expression grew strained.

'Haven't we tempted fate enough?' he asked. 'I've lost count of all the people we've killed. Rumours are starting to spread through the river districts.'

'Fate?' Nagash spat. 'Fate is a notion that weak minds use to excuse their failures.' The Grand Hierophant stepped close to the young priest. 'Have you grown weak, Khefru? Our work has only just begun.' The young priest met Nagash's eyes, and his face went pale.

'No, master,' he said quickly. 'I'm not weak. Command me, and I will serve.' Nagash studied Khefru's face for a long moment.

'Let us go, then,' he said, and turned away.

Khefru watched the Grand Hierophant leave the dimly lit chamber and begin the long, winding trek to the surface. A wet, gurgling cough came from the deep shadows within the cage. With a last, dreadful look at the squirming forms inside, the priest hurried quickly after his master.

It was approaching midnight in the world beyond the crypt. Neru hung, bright and full, above the vast necropolis, limning the stone structures in ghostly silver light and creating pools of inky blackness in the narrow lanes between, while Sakhmet, the Green Witch, shone baleful and red just above the eastern horizon. Nagash and Khefru made their way alone among the houses of the dead, listening to the chatter of jackals among the poorer crypts to the south-west. They encountered no dangers on their trek to the distant road. In times past it was not unknown for gangs of thieves and grave robbers to prowl among the vast city of tombs, but that had come to an end within the last few years. Rumours abounded in the city that something dark and terrible had taken root in Khemri's necropolis, and those who braved its streets after dark were never seen again.

The Grand Hierophant had certainly not lacked for subjects in the early days of his studies, nor had his tutors lacked for entertainment.

They walked in silence along the mortuary road, past neglected shrines half-covered in sand and marked with bird droppings. Bright moonlight painted the slopes of the distant dunes and silhouetted the broad sweep of a heron's wings as it took flight from the river bank to the north. A pack of jackals followed the pair a short way from the necropolis, their low-slung forms loping along the crests of the dunes and their eyes shining like polished coins as they studied the two men. With every mile, the scavengers edged closer and closer to the pair, until finally Nagash turned and fixed the largest of the pack with a challenging glare. The pack leader held the necromancer's stare for a few moments, and then let out a ghoulish, yapping cry and disappeared over the crest of a sand dune with the rest of the pack close behind.

The gates to the Living City were shut for the night, but the Grand Hierophant was allowed in without so much as a challenge. By ancient tradition, the priests of Settra's cult were allowed to come and go through the Gates of Usirian at any time of the day or night, owing to their duties among the crypts outside the city. Beyond the gate, the streets of the Temple district were quiet. Distantly, the two men could hear the faint chants of the priestesses of Neru rising from their temple compound as they went about their nightly vigil, warding Khemri from the spirits of the wastes.

Just beyond the temple district, Khefru led his master to a pre-determined alley, where a palanquin and eight nervous-looking bearers waited. Nagash was ushered quickly inside and the bearers set off at once, making their way into the Merchant's District and turning north, where wine houses and dens of vice lined the side streets just south of the city's wealthy neighbourhoods.

Here the streets were still well-travelled, even at such a late hour. Groups of drunken men staggered to and from the taverns and gambling houses, or crouched outside the shops and passed jars of beer or played games of dice. Young, grubby-faced children ran along the lanes, offering to help the drunkest souls find their destinations, and relieving them of their coin along the way. Fights broke out as dice games grew heated or drunken arguments got out of hand. Small bands of dour city watchmen prowled the area armed with lanterns and stout, bronze-capped staves, scattering the worst troublemakers with angry shouts and sharp blows to the offenders' shoulders and legs.

The palanquin made its way unnoticed among the late-night revellers and scowling watchmen, finally turning right down a narrow alley close to Coppersmith Street. Khefru jogged ahead of the palanquin to a recessed door lit by a small, hanging oil lamp. The priest rapped softly as the bearers lowered the palanquin to the ground. With a rattle of bolts, the door swung open just as Nagash emerged into the night air. Glancing warily up and down the dark alley, the Grand Hierophant stepped quickly through the doorway into a small, rubbish-strewn courtyard. Two of Nagash's household slaves bowed low to their master and quickly secured the door behind him.

The Grand Hierophant took in the courtyard with a single, disdainful glance. Sand covered the cracked flagstones, and weeds grew in the stagnant water of a long-dead fountain. Rats scuttled through the shadows along the foot of the pockmarked walls.

'This hovel was the best you could find?' he asked Khefru.

'You wanted anonymity, did you not?' Khefru said archly. 'Would you have preferred a manor in the noble districts, in full view of every gossiping slave and meddlesome widow?' He surveyed the decaying home with a satisfied nod. 'Places like this are common near the seedier quarters. Nobles or traders buy them up and use them for trysts, and then sell them off again when the mood suits them. The locals see people come and go from them at all hours and don't think twice, and it's just down the street from some of your guests' favourite haunts.'

'Fine, fine,' Nagash snapped. He turned to the two slaves. 'Are all in attendance?' he asked.

'The last arrived an hour ago, master,' one slave said as he shot the last bolt home.

'No doubt they've drunk most of the wine by now,' Khefru said darkly. 'Not a good way to begin a conspiracy, master.' The Grand Hierophant ignored the priest's impertinence.

'Take me to them,' he commanded the slaves.

Nagash followed the two men across the courtyard and through an open doorway, into a narrow, unfurnished corridor lit by a pair of guttering oil lamps. More slaves were bustling up and down the passageway, bearing empty jars of wine or platters of half-eaten food. The sound of a muffled voice emerged from the far end of the corridor, followed by raucous laughter.

The slaves led the Grand Hierophant down the passageway and through a series of small, empty rooms cluttered with bits of broken furniture. Each room was more brightly lit than the last, until Nagash found himself in a well-lit antechamber adjoining the house's large common room. The buzz of voices and the clink of metal cups sounded from the other side of a pair of curtained doorways on the opposite side of the antechamber.

Nagash waved the slaves aside and, with a brief glance back at Khefru, he straightened his robes and stepped quietly through the nearest doorway.

Unlike the rest of the house, the common room had been richly appointed with furnishings from the Grand Hierophant's apartments at the royal palace. The floor was covered in fine rugs made in distant Lahmia, and fine divans set with silk cushions had been arranged in a rough circle around an imposing chair made of dark, polished wood. A dozen young noblemen lounged on the divans or sprawled on the rugs, drinking wine and picking at scraps of fish or fowl from copper plates laid out among the revellers. The aromatic smoke from expensive incense curled from braziers in the corners of the room.

Heads turned as the Grand Hierophant entered the room. Faces flush with wine and ribaldry wore expressions of bemusement, and then surprise, as the guests recognised the man who had come late to the feast.

Nagash stepped forwards, pausing beside the chair of dark wood reserved for the dinner's host. As the drunken voices fell silent, the man reclining in the chair straightened with a chuckle.

'What now? Will we have dancing girls?' he asked, glancing over his shoulder. 'With skin as pale as moonlight and hair as black as–' His lecherous smirk turned to wide-eyed shock as he saw who stood beside him.

Nobleman and priest stared at one another for a long moment. Then Arkhan the Black began to laugh. The Grand Hierophant's expression turned grim.

'Do I amuse you?' he asked in a quiet voice. Arkhan smiled, revealing his ruined teeth.

'We were speculating who our mysterious host might be,' he said, lapsing once again into laughter. 'Raamket thought it might be another attempt by the king to keep us out of the wine houses.' He raised his glass to Nagash. 'And here you are.'

Raamket, a dark-eyed brute of a man with the face of a dockside brawler, glared daggers at Arkhan. The other nobles burst into drunken laughter at their friend's discomfort. Another noble, a man named Meruhep, fished a baby eel from a bowl in his lap and studied it in the lamp light.

'Our friend Raamket seems to know a bit too much. Perhaps we have a spy in our midst!' he said, tilting his head back and noisily slurped the eel down.

More laughter filled the room. Nagash waited in silence until the merriment died away. He eyed Arkhan coldly. After a moment, the nobleman's smirk faded and he rose sullenly from the chair. Nagash settled gracefully into the seat.

'A crude attempt at humour, but the sentiment is accurate,' the Grand Hierophant said. 'In fact, the reason you are here is because you know first-hand how misguided and dangerous my brother's rule has become.' Arkhan snorted into his wine cup.

'The only danger I can see is death by boredom,' he said. 'Those Grand Assemblies get more excruciating by the month.'

'My brother treats you all like children,' Nagash said. 'It's humiliating, not just for you, but for Khemri as well, because it reveals to the world that our king is a weak man.'

'What would you do in his place?' Meruhep asked with a smirk. 'Drag us all into the bazaar and cut off our hands?' The Grand Hierophant ignored the question.

'Thutep has convinced himself that humans are innately compassionate and charitable,' he said. 'He thinks that if you sit through enough royal courts the virtues of civic responsibility will seep into your heads like drops of cool water. He fancies that he can persuade the kings of Nehekhara to put aside centuries of warfare out of enlightened self-interest and the temptations of trade.' The words dripped like venom from Nagash's tongue. 'And how has our city profited in the last six years? The great houses of Khemri ignore his royal summons whenever they see fit and act according to their own interests. Entire neighbourhoods in the noble districts lie empty because the embassies of our brother cities have been seduced away by Zandri. The City of the Waves has usurped Khemri as the greatest city in Nehekhara for the first time in centuries. And for what? So that Thutep can negotiate lower grain prices with Numas and import rugs tax-free from Lahmia. That is what we have traded our pre-eminence for, beads on an abacus.'

Several of the nobles shifted uneasily at the vehemence in Nagash's speech. One of the men, a handsome, easygoing rake named Shepsu-hur, leaned back on his divan and eyed the Grand Hierophant warily.

'If things are as dire as you paint them, holy one, why haven't the great houses moved against Thutep?' he asked. 'Wasn't that how your dynasty came to exist in the first place?'

Nagash gave Shepsu-hur a sharp glance, but then a reluctant nod. Khetep had been of royal blood, but he was not the son of Rakaph, the previous king. When Rakaph had finally died his wife, Queen Rasut, had defied ancient law and claimed the throne for a short time, fearing that the kings of Numas or Zandri would try to supplant her infant son and claim the city for their own. Ultimately, the Hieratic Council of Mahrak managed to persuade Rasut to yield the throne and return to Lahmia, where she died a short time later. Khetep, Rakaph's trusted vizier, was appointed to rule the city as its regent until Rasut's son reached adulthood.

Within a month of Rasut's death, her young son died of a sudden fever, and Khetep became Priest King of Khemri.

'For the moment, the current situation favours the great houses,' Nagash continued. 'Under my father's rule, their power and influence were kept in check, but now they can flout the king's law and build their fortunes however they choose.' He shrugged. 'No doubt in time one of the houses would believe itself strong enough to seize the throne, but they will never get the opportunity. Zandri means to become the pre-eminent power in Nehekhara, but for that to be possible, Khemri must be forever broken. King Nekumet is gathering his strength even now. In a short time, perhaps a few years, he will grow bold enough to march against us. When that happens, the Living City will bow its knee to Zandri and forever become its vassal.'

The assembled noblemen did not know how to respond to Nagash's bald declaration. Many looked to their wine cups or glanced surreptitiously at their fellows. Only Arkhan ventured a reply.

'These are grim tidings indeed, holy one, but what do you expect us to do about it?' he asked. 'We have no power, wealth or influence.' The nobleman gave the Grand Hierophant a ruined grin. 'I suppose we could challenge Nekumet to a drinking contest, or a game of dice. How would that be?'

Raamket glowered at Arkhan.

'I wouldn't try,' he muttered. 'I've seen the way you throw dice.'

The room erupted in gales of laughter at Arkhan's expense. The nobleman bared his blackened teeth and snarled drunken oaths at his friends, and for a few moments all the talk of kings and conquests was forgotten. Nagash simply sat, patient and unblinking as a snake, until finally the laughter died and the faces of his guests were solemn once more.

'Power is a fluid thing,' he continued, as though the interruption hadn't occurred. 'It changes hands more easily than one might think. Surely my brother is a prime example of that.' Nagash studied each of the assembled nobles in turn. 'You are powerless now, that is true, but that could change.' Arkhan leaned forwards, setting his cup on the floor.

'You could arrange such a thing?' he asked.

The Grand Hierophant smiled coldly. 'Of course,' he replied. 'The old ways are coming to an end. Khemri will have a new king, and he must be served by cruel and ruthless men, men who are not afraid to bloody their hands and make people fear the Living City once more.' Nagash studied his assembled guests in turn. 'You can be wealthy and powerful beyond your wildest dreams, if you are the ruthless men I seek.' Meruhep noisily slurped down another eel.

'You're a fool if you think you can become king,' he sneered. 'You're a priest. The Council at Mahrak would never allow it.'

'Those frauds have no power over me!' Nagash snarled, his hands clenching the grips of his chair. 'Their authority is a lie, and one day I will cast them into the dust. They have bound us to the will of the false gods for long enough!'

The young noblemen stared wide-eyed at the Grand Hierophant, too shocked to speak. Meruhep shook his head disdainfully, fishing about in the bowl at his lap. After a long moment, Arkhan broke the silence.

'I am a ruthless man, holy one,' he said quietly, 'but you knew that already, or else I would not be here.'

'I am as well,' Raamket said heatedly. 'See if I am not.' Shepsu-hur chuckled softly.

'I can be ruthless when the mood takes me, holy one,' he said.

One by one, the other nobles added their voices to the chorus. Arkhan had been correct, Nagash had chosen each man carefully, based on recommendations from Khefru. For all their youthful bravado, they were desperate and wretched men, deep in debt and lost in their vices. The promise of wealth and power tempted them beyond reason, and none of them had much to lose beyond their wasted lives.

Only one man held his tongue. Meruhep's expression turned more and more scornful as the cacophony around him grew. He set his bowl aside, sloshing wine and limp eels onto the floor.

'You are all fools!' he snapped, glaring angrily at his fellows. The young noble pointed angrily at Nagash. 'He has no power! His cult is a sham, made to satisfy the vanity of a king. Do you think the great houses will sit idly by and let him depose his brother? Do you imagine even Thutep will be merciful when he learns of this? No. Your heads will sit atop spikes outside the palace.' Meruhep turned back to Nagash. 'And believe me, the king will find out, one way or the other. These things never remain secret for long...'

The young noble stopped in mid-sentence, his brow furrowing. For a moment, it looked as though he'd lost his train of thought, and then his eyes widened and he doubled over with a gasp of pain that quickly gave way to agonised screams.

Men scrambled to their feet with surprised shouts. Some threw their wine cups to the floor, fearing some kind of poison. One man, a distant cousin of Meruhep, tentatively approached the stricken noble's side, but stopped dead when he caught the look on Nagash's face. The Grand Hierophant was staring intently at the writhing nobleman, his lips moving in a silent recitation.

Shepsu-hur caught the look on Nagash's face as well. His gaze fell on Meruhep, and his eyes widened in horror.

'Blessed Neru,' he said, pointing to the floor. 'The eels!'

The assembled nobles followed Shepsu-hur's gesture. Meruhep's overturned bowl lay in the centre of the floor, and a knot of boiled eels writhed and snapped like a clutch of snakes in the spreading pool of wine.

Cries of horror and dismay filled the common room, and the young men recoiled in terror from Meruhep's thrashing body. Within seconds, his screams turned to gurgling, gasping cries, and blood began to soak through his linen robes. His movements became uncontrolled, turning into death spasms as the eels chewed through his abdomen.

Within a few minutes, Meruhep was dead, lying in a pool of his bodily fluids. Long, pale shapes squirmed through the blood and bile, falling still one by one. When the last of the creatures had returned to lifelessness, Nagash raised his eyes to the shaken crowd.

'No doubt you all understand the need for secrecy in this endeavour,' he said calmly. He beckoned to the shadows at the corners of the room, and slaves rushed forwards to drag Meruhep's body away. 'For the moment, you need do nothing but wait.'

Nagash raised his hand again, and Khefru appeared from the antechamber. The young priest carried a roll of papyrus in his hands.

'At present, all I need from you are your names,' said Khefru. 'Write them down on this scroll, along with the names of any other noblemen whom you believe can be persuaded to our cause.'

Khefru went to Arkhan first, handing over the papyrus and reaching for an ink brush tucked into his sleeve. The nobleman was staring at the trail of blood left behind by Meruhep's corpse with a mixture of avid interest and revulsion. With an effort, he tore his gaze away from the nightmarish scene and glanced at the blank papyrus.

'Do we… do we sign this in blood?' Arkhan asked hesitantly. The question surprised Nagash.

'Blood?' he said archly. 'Certainly not. What do you take me for, some kind of barbarian?'

Hours later, Nagash emerged from the decrepit house and directed the palanquin bearers to return to the necropolis. They did so fearfully, their footfalls echoing down the city's deserted streets. It was nearing the hour of the dead, when Neru's light was nearly gone and the spirits of the wastes could roam the land in search of prey. Sakhmet burned brightly, just above the western horizon, and the bearers kept throwing frightened glances over their shoulders, as though the Green Witch was dogging their heels. When they finally returned to the Great Pyramid, Khefru had to promise to double the men's wages to keep them waiting among the jackal-haunted tombs.

Nagash noticed none of this. He rose from the palanquin without a word and dashed swiftly inside the huge tomb. The oil lamps were still burning inside his sanctum. He snatched one up and rushed forwards, holding it high above his head and banishing the shadows that concealed the contents of the wooden cage on the opposite side of the room.

Mewling cries of terror greeted Nagash as he reached the enclosure. Yellow light gleamed from the wide, maddened eyes of a young man, who had pressed his trembling body into the furthest corner of the cage to try to escape the fate that had befallen his sister. Her body lay almost at the Grand Hierophant's feet, surrounded by a pool of congealing blood and bodily fluids. Her skin had swollen like a sausage and then burst, spilling a foul slurry of cancerous flesh and reeking blood onto the stone floor. The stained bones amid the gore were the only indication that the corpse was even human.

Nagash fumbled quickly at the lock securing the cage door. Then he reached in and seized the young man by the hair. He dragged the screaming figure out of the cage like a butcher selecting a kid for the slaughter, and examined every inch of his naked body.

The Grand Hierophant smiled. The young man, Shepresh by name, was completely unharmed. The curse that had slain his sister had not touched him, despite the noble blood they shared.

Still smiling, Nagash dragged the mewling figure into the ritual circle to begin the Incantation of Reaping once more. Then, Khefru entered the room, carrying the rolled-up papyrus they'd brought from the meeting.

'The names!' Nagash said, stretching out his hand. 'The names! Bring them here!'

The hour of the dead was at hand, and there was terrible work to be done.

THIRTEEN

THE TWO-EDGED BLADE

Bel Aliad, the City of Spices,
in the 63rd year of Ptra the Glorious
(-1744 Imperial Reckoning)

The Bhagarite horseman raced effortlessly down the narrow lanes of the army camp, glimmering like a ghost in the predawn gloom. Silver bells attached to the leather tack of the desert horse made a strange, unearthly counterpoint to the animal's drumming hoofbeats, sending a shiver of dread through the warriors of the Bronze Host as he raced towards the centre of the camp. New recruits rose from their bedrolls and stumbled out into the horseman's wake, wondering what all the urgency was about, while the veterans shared grim looks and reached for their whetstones, or began making last-minute repairs to their armour.

The Bronze Host of Ka-Sabar was encamped at the western edge of the Great Desert, their tents spilling in a great crescent from the mouth of a narrow wadi that had sheltered them for the last ten miles of their trek. The journey across the dunes had taken many weeks, even with the unerring guidance of nearly a hundred Bhagarite riders. They marched by night and took shelter during the searing heat of the day, and within the first week even the strongest warriors looked out across the endless expanse of sand and feared that they would never find their way out again. Their guides were as good as their word, however, and the Bronze Host was never more than three days from a desert oasis or a hidden cache of sealed water jars, preserved food and even feed for their horses. The guides entered each oasis and opened each cache with an eerie, keening wail, drawing their knives and slicing their cheeks in an offering to their faceless, hungry god. By the time the army reached the far edge of the desert their guides were pale and wide-eyed, shivering as though with fever and muttering prayers to Khsar under their breath.

The Bhagarites had guided the army to a rocky plain just a mile from the Spice Road that ran along the western edge of the desert, little more than five miles from Bel Aliad. As the warriors of the Bronze Host stumbled onto the plain like men woken rudely from sleep, the Bhagarites wrapped themselves in funereal robes of the purest white and wound their headscarves round their heads in the complicated arrangement called the Eshabir el-Hekhet, the Merciless Mask. They prepared to avenge their slaughtered kin in an orgy of righteous bloodshed.

The order to attack had not come. Instead, Akhmen-hotep ordered the army to make camp and offer prayers to the gods. They had just completed a gruelling trek across the merciless sands of the Great Desert, and even the Bhagarites reluctantly admitted that the army could stand to wait a day and regain some of its strength.

One day passed and then two. A third day came and went, and still the army did not stir. The Bhagarites grew restless. Did the priest king not realise that sooner or later a caravan or a shepherd could stumble across the camp and send a warning to their foes? They tried to make their case to the king, but Akhmen-hotep was unmoved. He sent the riders from the camp, ordering them northwards to scout the terrain and bring back news of the city and its people.

Five days after the army's emergence from the desert, a Bhagarite horseman was riding for the king's tent as though the howling spirits of the waste were hot upon his heels.

The rider came upon Akhmen-hotep and his generals as they were beginning their morning prayers. A young bull, one of five precious animals brought with them across the desert, had been sacrificed to Geheb. Hashepra, the Hierophant of the Earth God, was standing before the kneeling noblemen, his muscular arms outspread and the bloody sacrificial knife held high. Two young acolytes, neither one more than twelve years old, held the great bronze bowl with trembling hands to catch the dying animal's blood.

Heads rose curiously at the sound of the hoofbeats, and the king's Ushabti rose to their feet and formed a forbidding line in the rider's path. The Bhagarite reined in a discreet distance from the bodyguards and leapt gracefully from the saddle.

'Great king!' the horseman cried. 'Your camp has been discovered! The warriors of Bel Aliad are assembling on the plains south of the city and making ready to attack!'

Startled shouts and calls to battle rang out from the assembled nobles, some even going so far as to dash off across the camp to ready their warriors for the coming battle. Among their number, only Akhmen-hotep remained on his knees, his hands held out in supplication and his head bent in prayer. Those noblemen nearest the king eyed Akhmen-hotep, worried, uncertain what they should do.

Among them was Pakh-amn. The Master of Horse was still out of favour with the king, but Akhmen-hotep insisted that he be brought along when the army marched on Bel Aliad. By ancient custom, the Master of Horse was one of the king's chief generals in times of war, and Akhmen-hotep had commanded that all the old traditions be upheld. For his part, Pakh-amn had performed his duties with cold-hearted diligence and devotion.

The Master of Horse took in the unfolding scene and drew a deep breath. 'What is your command, great one?' he asked stiffly. His cheeks were still hollow and his eyes sunken from the touch of the lotus, but his voice was sober and strong.

Akhmen-hotep did not answer at first, his lips moving in a silent prayer. He passed his hands over his face and across his shaven scalp, as though washing himself clean of fear and doubt.

'We shall finish making our obeisance to Geheb,' he said quietly, 'and then we shall summon the Grand Hierophant and offer sacrifices to Ptra so that he will guide us to victory.' As he spoke, the king bent his head to Hashepra. The hierophant nodded and beckoned to his acolytes, who brought forward the wide, brimming bowl. Pakh-amn's stained lips pressed into a thin, angry line.

'Time is of the essence,' he said. 'The enemy could be upon us within the hour. Since they willingly serve the Usurper, I doubt they will trouble themselves with lengthy prayers to the gods.'

'All the more reason for us to demonstrate our devotion,' the king replied calmly. 'We are not fighting for glory, or for gold. We are fighting to defend the Blessed Land, and to honour the covenant between gods and men.'

'The warriors of Bel Aliad will not appreciate the distinction,' Pakh-amn said sourly, 'when they are scattering our disorganised companies and setting fire to our tents.' Unperturbed, Akhmen-hotep accepted the sacrificial bowl and raised it to his lips. When he passed it back to the acolytes his chin was wet with blood.

'What happens today is the will of the gods,' the king said. He looked pointedly at the waiting acolytes. 'Will you show your devotion to the Earth God, Pakh-amn, or do you intend to continue the debate and delay the army further?'

Pakh-amn glared hotly at the king. He started to reply, but caught himself at the last moment, and instead reached impatiently for the red-rimmed bowl. Casting apprehensive glances to the north, the rest of the assembled nobles followed suit.

The early morning sunlight rested like a red-hot iron across Akhmen-hotep's face and neck. Around him, the Bronze Host surged forwards to the tramp of thousands of feet and the heavy beat of drums. The air above the army was thick with swirling dust that coated a man's throat and gummed up his eyes. They were three miles north of camp, advancing in a steady, if ragged line towards the City of Spices and its waiting army. As it happened, Pakh-amn's fears had been for naught. Although the warriors of Ka-Sabar had taken more than two hours to form up and make ready to depart, the army of Bel Aliad was no faster. By the time the two armies came within sight of one another the defending army had managed to travel just a single mile.

They came together on a rocky plain bordered by the Spice Road to the west and the desert fringe to the east. Akhmen-hotep could just see the walls of Bel Aliad rising along the horizon to the north. The fighting men of the City of Spices were advancing in rough order, slowly but surely driving back the hundred Bhagarite horsemen who were trying to screen the Bronze Host's approach. Bel Aliad boasted its own light horsemen. The city had been originally founded by exiles from Bhagar, after all, more than four hundred years past, but their mounts were ordinary animals bought from Numas, rather than gifts from the desert god. Their squadrons advanced in fits and starts, wheeling across the plain like flights of angry birds before racing back to the safety of their advancing army. The desert horsemen retreated slowly but steadily, greeting the enemy movements with derisive jeers and the occasional bowshot.

The main body of the enemy army numbered eight thousand strong, or so the Bhagarite scouts claimed: a large force, but like their light cavalry, it lacked quality. Bel Aliad was the smallest city worthy of the name in all of Nehekhara. To defend itself from desert raiders and to protect its numerous merchant caravans, the city's princes spent a fortune maintaining a standing army of sell-swords and hired thugs. Their bowmen were drawn from the fearsome sea archers of Zandri, and their two large City Companies were bolstered by four thousand northern mercenaries, hired from the barbarian tribes and brought south aboard chartered merchant ships to take up arms under Bel Aliad's banner.

The barbarians were huge, stinking, hairy brutes, clad in matted furs and long, oily tunics cinched with wide leather belts around their waists. Though primitive and ignorant of the proper arts of war, these mercenaries were fearsome fighters with shield and spear, or wielding deadly, leaf-shaped bronze swords brought from their rugged homeland. Leading the army were the merchant princes and their retainers, who disdained the cavalry tactics of their ancestors and instead fought from the back of light, swift chariots like other civilised armies.

Against this army the Bronze Host could muster only four thousand men, plus the hundred Bhagarite horsemen who had served as their guides. Six years had not been enough time for Ka-Sabar to restore its shattered forces, for the heavy infantry companies of the City of Bronze demanded lengthy training and conditioning to fight with spear, shield and scale armour. Akhmen-hotep had managed to field only two full infantry companies, plus a large force of five hundred chariots and a thousand trained bowmen. The rest of his army was comprised of loose companies of warrior-aspirants who had been pressed into service as improvised light infantry. Each aspirant carried only a small, round shield, a short sword and a quiver of light, barbed javelins, identical to the hunting weapons that many of them had used as children. They had been drilled relentlessly on the training fields outside the city, but no one knew for certain how effective they would be on the field of battle.

When the Bronze Host had left Ka-Sabar, it had been generally hoped that they would not see action at all. Now the companies were ranged just ahead and to the sides of the slow-moving heavy infantry, each man holding a javelin loosely in his hand. The army's bowmen formed a long line behind the heavy companies, their bows strung and ready, while behind them came the army's chariots.

The army of Bel Aliad had come to an unsteady halt across the plain, and was re-forming its companies. Two lines of mercenary archers were far out in front, their arrows placed and ready to fire. Behind them crowded noisy mobs of barbarian warriors, their faces painted with blue and red dyes and their shaggy faces alight with the prospect of bloodshed.

At the sight of the Bronze Host, the mercenaries began to clash their weapons against the rims of their shields and howl like a pack of hyenas, filling the air with strange war cries spoken in their guttural tongue. Akhmen-hotep thought he could see the standards of the City Companies, beyond the milling barbarians, and a roiling plume of dust that had to come from the army's chariots. Bel Aliad's light horsemen crowded around the army's flanks, threatening to charge once again at the thin line of Bhagarite cavalry occupying the middle ground between the two armies.

Raising his hand, Akhmen-hotep ordered the army to halt. Trumpets sounded, and the king turned and leapt from the back of his armoured chariot. His Ushabti joined him at once, ringing the priest king in gleaming bronze. Pakh-amn dismounted his chariot nearby and hastened to the king's side, along with his other generals, members of his retinue and Ka-Sabar's religious leaders. Hashepra was garbed for war, clad in bronze scale armour and bearing his customary hammer, and Khalifra, high priestess of Neru, carried a blessed spear in her slender hand. Only Memnet was unarmed, his face pale and waxy in the fierce light of day.

The king waited until the assembly had gathered and nodded gravely.

'The blessings of the gods be upon you,' he said to them. 'The day of battle is upon us, and so far, all is proceeding as expected.' Pakh-amn folded his arms.

'You mean to say you planned this?' he asked. 'Instead of sweeping down on Bel Aliad and taking it by storm, you wanted to fight their army in the open field, where their greater numbers would tell against us?' Akhmen-hotep eyed the Master of Horse coldly.

'You expected us to steal upon Bel Aliad like thieves in the night and slaughter its citizens while they slept? That is the way of the Usurper, Pakh-amn. We will fight the men of Bel Aliad according to the proper rules of war, as the priest kings have done since the time of Settra. Quarter will be given if asked, and ransoms will be claimed.' A stunned expression crossed Pakh-amn's face, followed by one of dawning comprehension.

'That's why you tarried in camp for so long,' he said scornfully. 'You wanted them to discover us. Why didn't you just send a messenger inviting them to battle? Wouldn't that have been the civilised thing to do?' Hashepra took a step towards Pakh-amn, glowering forbiddingly at the young nobleman.

'You forget yourself once again,' he warned. 'Here, on the field of battle, you can be slain outright for such talk.'

'No doubt that would suit the king well,' Pakh-amn snapped, 'but it won't change the truth of what's before us. Have you all forgotten what happened at Zedri? The old ways are gone! If we don't accept that, Nagash will destroy us!'

'The old ways are all that separate us from that monster!' the king cried. 'If we abandon our beliefs and fight like the Blasphemer, how are we any better than him?' He raised his fist to the sky. 'So long as we live, the old ways survive! So long as I draw breath, the Blessed Land lives within me.' Pakh-amn's dark eyes glittered with contempt, but he bowed to the king.

'Lead on, then,' he said, 'for so long as you live.'

Hashepra growled angrily and began to raise his hammer, but the king stopped him with a raised hand.

'Return to your chariots!' he commanded his warriors, and then turned to the assembled hierophants. 'Remain here and summon the powers of the gods to aid us,' he said. 'If Bel Aliad has truly turned to Nagash, there will be no priests among them. Your blessings may well turn the tide in our favour.' Khalifra folded her arms regally, but her face was lined with strain. The beautiful priestess seemed to have aged decades since the terrible battle at the oasis.

'We will give what we can,' she said gravely. Hashepra folded his powerful arms and nodded as well.

'If Bel Aliad has turned to Nagash, they won't need priests,' Memnet said in a leaden voice. 'They will have the Usurper's power to call upon.' The king looked his older brother in the eye, and a bleak look came over his face.

'Then we will have to trust in courage and god-given bronze,' he said. 'That is all any man can do.'

Akhmen-hotep considered his gathered generals, particularly his belligerent Master of Horse. The defeat at Zedri had left wounds that ran deeper than flesh. He knew that the confidence of the army was shaken, nearly to the point of rebellion. Pakh-amn in particular had been badly scarred by what he had seen. Could he be trusted? For a fleeting moment, Akhmen-hotep was tempted to remove the Master of Horse from his position and send him back to camp, but immediately he realised that doing so would send the wrong signal to the rest of the army. If they saw that the king's faith in them was so shaken that he would arrest one of his generals, their resolve might vanish like wax under the midday sun. He had to believe that there was still strength in the old ties of duty and piety, that the covenant between men and gods was still strong, and that there were some things in the world that not even Nagash the Usurper could sweep aside.

Drawing a deep breath, the king made his decision. He beckoned to his trumpeter. 'Order the Bhagarites to probe the enemy horsemen to the right,' he said, 'and then withdraw to the rear by way of the desert.' Hashepra frowned as he listened to the king's order.

'You would deprive us of our light cavalry at the start of battle?'

'Our guides have clad themselves in white once more, and wear the Merciless Mask,' Akhmen-hotep said. 'They hunger for vengeance, but I will not allow our cause to be tainted by a massacre of innocents. The Bhagarites will have to bide their time until Nagash and his immortals are made to account for their crimes.'

The trumpeters raised their curved, bronze horns and blew an intricate series of notes. As the sounds faded, the king turned to Pakh-amn.

'I will lead half the chariots forward, comprising the centre of the army,' the king said. 'When we start to move, and the dust fills the air, take the remaining half and head for the left flank. Take care to conceal your movements behind the aspirant companies, so that the enemy does not suspect you are there. I'll draw the attention of the prince and his chariots. Wait and watch for the opportune moment to strike.'

Pakh-amn stared into the king's eyes, and seemed to understand what Akhmen-hotep was giving him. He nodded slowly.

'I will not fail you, great one,' he said.

'Then return to your chariots,' the king ordered, 'and may the gods grant us victory.' As the generals and the king's retinue raced to their posts, Akhmen-hotep turned to the hierophants. 'Will the gods lend their favour today, holy ones?' he asked quietly. 'I drank deep of the bull's blood this morning, and yet I felt nothing. Geheb's strength does not burn in my veins.'

Memnet refused to meet his brother's eyes.

'I warned you,' he said softly. 'I told you at the oasis that there would be consequences for presuming upon the power of the gods.' Hashepra gave the Grand Hierophant a sour look, and then bowed his head to the king.

'Fear not, great one,' he said. 'Geheb has not forgotten his favoured sons. You will feel his presence among you as you race forth to battle.'

Khalifra touched the king's muscular arm and smiled warmly.

'Neru is always with us, great one,' she said. 'Her light ever burns in the darkness. Do not fear.'

The Priest King of Ka-Sabar bowed to the holy ones, and his heart felt light. Smiling, he turned and strode quickly for his chariot, trailed by his leonine Ushabti. With every step, his doubts and fears were swept away by the measured tramp of feet and the clatter of arms and armour. The clamour of the battlefield beat against his bones like a drum. For a moment, he was able to forget the horrors he had witnessed, and the great suffering that the Blessed Land had witnessed in the course of his life. For a moment, he was back in the times of his father, and his father's father, waging war for wealth and power, and the glory of his gods.

Akhmen-hotep climbed aboard his heavy chariot and grasped the hilt of his gleaming sword. He signalled his trumpeter with a flourish.

'Order the army to advance!' he called.

Trumpets called across the battlefield, and as one the companies of the Bronze Host began to move. As the king's chariot lurched forwards with a rumble of bronze-rimmed wheels, Akhmen-hotep stood tall and surveyed the disposition of his and the enemy's forces. The City Companies of Bel Aliad were mustered behind a rough line of four large mercenary bands. Between the two large infantry units Akhmen-hotep could see a profusion of banners, no doubt adorning the chariots of the merchant princes and their leader: Suhedir al-Khazem, the Keeper of the Hidden Paths.

To the far right of the enemy line, Akhmen-hotep could see a swirling smudge of dust. The Bhagarites were withdrawing towards the desert, hopefully drawing the enemy light horsemen on that flank along with them. Mirroring the Bel Aliad formations on the other side of the plain, the two heavy companies of the Bronze Host marched at the centre of the battle-line, and in between them advanced half of Ka-Sabar's feared chariots. Pakh-amn and the other half of the chariot force were already on the move, shifting off to the left behind two marching companies of aspirants. Still further back came the host's company of archers, still hidden from the enemy's view.

The warriors of the Bronze Host continued forwards, advancing slowly but steadily. The king peered off to the left, trying to catch a glimpse of the enemy light cavalry on that side, but he couldn't see them. Shouted warnings from the ranks of the infantry companies brought the king's attention back to the front, and he saw a cloud of dark, flickering reeds arcing high into the sunlit sky ahead of them. Men cursed and raised their round-topped wooden shields, and the warriors in the chariots crouched low behind the bronze-clad walls of their machines. The arrows fell, whirring malevolently through the air, and Akhmen-hotep felt his skin prickle with heat as the blessings of Geheb came upon him.

Bronze arrowheads cracked against shield faces or smacked into scale and leather armour. Men grunted and stumbled beneath the fearsome rain, but the warriors plucked the arrows from their vests and tossed them contemptuously aside. Shafts struck their tanned skin and glanced aside, turned by the power of the God of the Earth. Cheers went up from the Bronze Host as they discovered that Geheb was with them. Akhmen-hotep bared his teeth and signalled to his trumpeters again.

'Order the aspirants forward!' he cried. 'Archers, make ready!'

Two signals rang out along the length of the host, and were answered by lusty shouts from the young men of the aspirant companies. Javelins ready, the lightly armoured warriors quickened their pace, jogging swiftly across the plain towards the mercenary archers and footmen. The Zandri bowmen, shaken by the failure of their first volley, made ready to fire again, while the barbarian troops howled like beasts and shook their weapons eagerly as they watched the light infantry approach.

The enemy bowmen fired off one more volley, and then swiftly retreated down prepared lanes between the barbarian mobs as the aspirants drew near. At sixty paces, the javelin throwers quickened their pace. At fifty, they drew back their arms and hurled a shower of barbed weapons at the waiting barbarians. The javelins fell among the mercenaries, sticking into shields or punching through furs and thick tunics. Men roared and fell to the ground, clutching at the wooden shafts.

At forty paces, the aspirants drew more javelins from their quivers and let fly, and then again at thirty. At twenty paces they cast again. Then, they turned tail and ran back in the direction of their lines. Jeers and obscenities followed, until, seventy paces away, the aspirants turned, drew more javelins, and advanced once more. Flights of javelins fouled the mercenaries' shields, inflicted terrible wounds and killed a few score men, and again, just as the aspirants were nearly within reach of the barbarians' weapons, they turned and ran.

On the fourth such attack Akhmen-hotep heard trumpets and the sounds of battle off to his left. The enemy light horsemen had intervened on that flank, attempting to run down the light infantry companies. In the centre and on the right, however, the barbarians had taken all they could stand. Prodded to the point of distraction, the mercenaries abandoned all sense of discipline and charged forwards, eager to strike back at the javelin throwers.

Their job done, the aspirants turned tail and kept on running, drawing the barbarians across the plain towards the heavy infantry of the Bronze Host and the bowmen behind them.

Akhmen-hotep raised his sword.

'Archers, make ready!' he ordered. The king watched as the line of mercenaries rushed towards his companies in a seething wave of flesh and bronze. At fifty yards he brought down his blade. 'Fire!'

A rain of deadly arrows leapt from the rear of the Bronze Host and fell among the charging mercenaries, sowing death through the swarming mobs. Men fell by the hundreds, and for a moment the pursuit faltered in the face of mounting casualties. The mercenaries were more than two hundred yards away from the rest of their army, however, beyond the reach of their bowmen and the support of the City Companies. Trumpets blew urgently from the midst of the enemy chariots, vainly trying to call the warriors back and re-form their disorganised companies, but Akhmen-hotep was not about to give them the chance.

The Priest King of Ka-Sabar threw back his head and gave a fierce shout. 'Warriors of the Bronze Host! Strike now, and redeem your honour! For the glory of the Earth God, charge!'

The earth shook with the roar of two thousand voices and the thunder of hooves as the army of Ka-Sabar sprung its trap.

FOURTEEN

THE BLOODSTAINED SANDS

The Western Trade Road,
near the Fountains of Eternal Life,
in the 63rd year of Ptra the Glorious
(-1744 Imperial Reckoning)

'Someone is signalling,' Ekhreb said, straightening gracefully from the low, leather-covered divan and gesturing with his wine cup at the sky.

Rakh-amn-hotep glanced up from his maps with a weary grunt, squinting into the dust-stained air. The Kings of Rasetra and Lybaras had made their midday camp in the shelter of a pair of dunes just off the side of the western trade road, drawing the huge, creaking wagons of the Lybaran court into a defensible circle beneath the shade of a small grove of palm trees. Within the circled wagons the Lybaran servants had spread thick rugs over the sandy ground and set out tables and divans for the comfort of the kings and their generals. When the King of Rasetra had first laid eyes on the massive wagons he'd sneered quietly to Ekhreb about the soft ways of Hekhmenukep and the Lybaran nobles, but after more than a week on the march to Khemri, the bellicose Rasetran had to admit that there were far worse ways to conduct a campaign.

For all their zeal to reach the Living City and cleanse the Blessed Land of Nagash and his minions, the movement of the allied armies had been dreadfully slow. It had taken almost two weeks for the Rasetran army to make its way along the Valley of Kings, even with the help of the Lybaran sky-boats, and once the two armies were united at Quatar, the march slowed nearly to a crawl. The heavy catapults and other war machines crafted by the Lybarans frequently broke down, requiring hours to replace warped axles or broken wheels, and the jungle auxiliaries of the Rasetran army could only face the searing heat of the desert for short periods of time before they had to rest and take on more water.

The allied armies stretched back along the trade road for many miles. Like an inchworm, the tail end of the host would leave its camp in the morning, and by evening it would be settling into the camp of the army's lead elements from the night before.

At such a slow pace, the kings and their retinues rose from their furs at dawn, lingered over their morning meals and devotions and got a start on the business of the day while the troops marched slowly past. When the last elements of the army came into view by late afternoon, the court would spend an hour or two consulting with the commanders of the rear-guard and baggage train. Then, as the sun set behind the veil of dust to the west, the camp would travel for a few hours and catch up with the army's lead companies.

According to Rakh-amn-hotep's original estimations, the allied armies should have been on the outskirts of Khemri by now. As it was, they were still roughly two days' march from the Fountains of Eternal Life, little more than halfway to their goal. The two forces, and the Rasetran auxiliaries in particular, were consuming supplies at a staggering rate, especially fresh water. The huge thunder lizards had to be literally doused with it at regular intervals to keep their thick skins from drying out, to the point that their handlers had been on half-rations for days so that they could keep their charges alive.

'What now, by all the gods?' Rakh-amn-hotep grumbled, peering up at the silhouetted bulk of the Lybaran skybox. The contraption was very small by comparison to the great sky-boats: a box, slightly smaller than a chariot, suspended by cables from a spherical bladder filled with air spirits. The whole thing could be loaded into the back of one of the huge Lybaran wagons, and was drawn out each time the kings made camp. The box was kept tethered to a pair of wagons by a length of stout rope, and raised to a height of more than a hundred feet.

The Lybarans kept a trio of boys up in the box at all times, scanning the countryside for miles with their clever seeing-tubes and watching for messages from the army's vanguard. As Rakh-amn-hotep watched, one of the boys raised a platter-sized dish of polished bronze and caught the rays of Ptra's glorious light, aiming a series of brilliant flashes off to the west. After a moment, the boy lowered the signalling device and the lookouts watched intently for an answer. Ekhreb took a sip of wine and wiped the sweat from his eyes.

'Perhaps it's just the cavalry reporting that they've reached the springs,' he said. The king snorted in bitter amusement.

'Your optimism never ceases to amaze me,' he said. Ekhreb shrugged philosophically.

'I survived six years at Quatar. Nothing much worries me any more.'

'That's right. Rub some more salt in the wound,' the king growled. He levered himself to his feet and shrugged his heavy scale coat back into place. 'You keep going on like that, and I'll petition the Grand Hierophant to make you priest king instead of me. Then I could go live the carefree life of a king's champion.'

'Gods forfend!' Ekhreb said in mock horror. 'You're far too ugly to be a proper champion.'

'Don't I know it,' the king said with a chuckle. His grin faded as one of the boys climbed fearlessly over the edge of the skybox and slid nimbly down one of its long ropes. The young messenger disappeared from sight behind one of the hulking wagons, and Rakh-amn-hotep made his way across the expanse of rugs to await the boy's arrival next to the Lybaran king.

As he did nearly every day of the march, Hekhmenukep sat before a low, broad table covered in sheets of papyrus inscribed with all manner of arcane diagrams and invocations. Half a dozen of his retainers crowded around the edges of the table, deep in discussions about strange subjects of engineering or alchemy, while the king studied the diagrams through one of his bronze-rimmed disks and made annotations with a fine-haired ink brush. A slave knelt at Hekhmenukep's left, holding a wine goblet for the king's refreshment, while another stirred the air above the royal scholar's head with a fan made of peacock feathers. He seemed entirely at ease, immersed in a world of ratios and calculations. Rakh-amn-hotep felt a bitter surge of envy at the Lybaran's detachment.

Hekhmenukep glanced up from his work just as the messenger wound his way nimbly past the parked wagons and raced past the watchful Ushabti into the king's court. The Lybaran king glanced bemusedly from Rakh-amn-hotep to the wide-eyed boy.

'Yes? What is it?' he asked.

'There is a sun-sign from Shesh-amun,' the boy said, referring to the Lybaran champion in charge of the allied vanguard. 'He says: enemy horsemen east of the sacred springs.'

'Damnation,' Rakh-amn-hotep growled, his scarred hands clenching into fists. 'Is the enemy present in strength?' The messenger took a step back at the king's fierce tone.

'A thousand pardons, great one. He did not say.'

'Shesh-amun wouldn't have reported otherwise,' Hekhmenukep said calmly. The news did not please the Rasetran king. He turned to Hekhmenukep.

'I thought you said that the Bronze Host was drawing Nagash's army to Bel Aliad,' he said

'Indeed,' the Lybaran king replied, and then gave a thoughtful shrug. 'Perhaps Nagash chose to split his forces instead. If so, that could still work in our favour.'

'If we were in possession of the sacred springs, I would agree with you,' Rakh-amn-hotep growled. 'As it is, our stocks of water are very low. If we don't get to the springs very soon, the heat will kill our troops quicker than Nagash could.'

Hekhmenukep frowned. 'How long?' he asked.

The Rasetran king bit back a surge of irritation. How could he not know the needs of his own army?

'A day or two. Certainly no more,' Rakh-amn-hotep declared, 'and it's nearly mid-afternoon now.' The king began to pace across the rugs, considering his options. If they were very, very lucky, the enemy cavalry was nothing more than a scouting force, or the vanguard of the Khemri army. Reaching a decision, he glanced back at the Lybaran king. 'I'm going forward to take command of the vanguard and see what we're facing,' he declared, and then turned to Ekhreb. 'Gather up a mixed force of light infantry and bowmen, plus all the horsemen you can lay your hands on, and join me as quickly as you are able,' he ordered. Ekhreb nodded, rising swiftly to his feet.

'What is your plan?' the champion asked.

The question seemed to amuse the Rasetran king. 'My plan?' he said. 'I'm going to head down the road with all the warriors I can muster and kill every living thing between me and the springs.' He slapped Ekhreb on the shoulder. 'Don't tarry, old friend,' he said, and hurried from the camp, shouting for his charioteers in a gruff voice.

Warning shouts rose above the clamour as trumpets wailed across the battlefield and Bel Aliad's barbarian troops let out a ragged, hungry shout. Akhmen-hotep hefted his notched and bloodstained khopesh and bellowed hoarsely, 'Here they come again! Make ready!'

Horns blared, signalling the Bronze Host and the distant priests, and with a clatter of metal and wood the infantry companies made ready once more. The battle had raged for hours, ebbing and flowing across the corpse-strewn plain. Akhmen-hotep's plan to put the barbarian mercenaries to flight with a single, swift charge had failed, and despite heavy losses the barbarians had refused to break. They fought with a reckless courage that bordered upon desperation.

More than once over the course of the bloody battle, the king wondered what fearful things the merchant princes had told them about their overlord in Khemri. Had it not been for a timely charge by Pakh-amn's chariots on the left flank, the army would have been surrounded during the first attack. The Master of Horse had proven his worth time and again over the course of the day, driving off cavalry attacks and saving the light infantry on his flank from utter destruction.

Except for the discipline and skill of the veteran companies of the Bronze Host, the battle would have already been lost. Time and again they withstood showers of deadly arrows and the crushing weight of the barbarian infantry attacks. The enemy mercenaries had been reduced to four ragged companies, and the fire from the Zandri archers had dwindled, suggesting that they were running low on arrows.

A unit of light horsemen still lurked at the edge of the enemy's right flank. They had already caught Akhmen-hotep's light infantry in two surprise charges and mauled them severely, and were watching for another chance to strike. The king regretted having sent the Bhagarite horsemen to the rear and had despatched a messenger to recall them, but that had been nearly two hours ago, and they had yet to reappear.

As the weary veterans closed ranks and readied their spears, Akhmen-hotep caught sight of a ripple of movement across the battlefield. Bel Aliad's chariots and its two City Companies, which had been held in reserve since the battle began, were marching forward in the centre of the enemy battle-line. It was late in the afternoon, and his troops were exhausted, as were the enemy mercenaries. The merchant princes had come to the conclusion that the next attack would decide the battle. Looking over his battered troops, the king thought that they were probably right.

'Messenger!' Akhmen-hotep cried, and a boy dashed up to the side of the king's chariot. 'Tell the archers to concentrate their fire on the City Companies,' he ordered. The runner repeated the order word-for-word and dashed off to the waiting bowmen. For a moment, the king debated on sending another messenger back to the priests, to beg for one more appeal to the gods, but he changed his mind with a shrug. The gods were not blind. They could see how desperate the situation was. If they withheld their power the war was already lost. The king swept his blade down in a wide arc.

'Forward!' he called to his men, and the formation of chariots began to move. They were a few dozen yards behind the main battle-line, positioned between the two veteran companies. The gap was currently being covered by a small company of light infantry the king had shifted over from the left flank. The weary aspirants felt the chariots approaching and gratefully withdrew. Their capes were torn and bloodstained, and many of them carried bent or splintered javelins recovered from the bodies of the slain. A few raised their weapons in salute to the king as they filed past the advancing chariots and went into reserve.

The clamour of the enemy troops grew louder as the barbarians picked up the pace. Their savage nature drew them to battle like moths to a flame, and they began to outstrip the measured pace of the City Companies. Then the first volley of arrows from the Ka-Sabar archers hissed overhead, plunging in a deadly rain among the enemy infantry. Men staggered, pierced through their thin leather vests or bronze skullcaps. The screams of the wounded galvanised the mercenaries, who had suffered one terrible volley after another for most of the day. Their hoarse war cries turned to frenzied screams as they broke into a wild charge, hoping to come to grips with their enemies before the archers could fire again.

Men shouted orders among the veteran companies, and the Bronze Host steeled itself to receive the charge. Akhmen-hotep felt a glimmer of hope as the mercenaries broke ranks with the city troops. He watched the advancing chariots carefully, waiting to see how the merchant princes would react. The line of war machines hesitated for a moment, and then a ragged chorus of war-horns sounded and the chariots surged forwards, trying to lend their weight to the mercenaries' attack.

Akhmen-hotep smiled fiercely. It appeared that the gods were smiling on them after all. The king studied the pace of the charging enemy troops, waiting for the moment when the mercenaries had committed to their attacks.

The enemy infantry swept in from left and right, converging on the solid ranks of bronze-armoured spearmen. They ignored the aspirants, having learned from bitter experience that the javelin men would only fall back in the face of their charge and leave them exposed to further arrow fire. For their part, the aspirants waited patiently, hefting their barbed weapons. Once the melee began, they would rush in and hurl their shafts point-blank into the mercenaries' flanks.

The two forces came together in a thunderous crash of wood and metal. Both veteran companies staggered under the impact, but the strength of Geheb filled them, and they bore up beneath the assault. Barbarians fell beneath the Host's stabbing spears or were dashed to the ground by bronze-rimmed shields, but they pressed forwards in a bestial frenzy, hacking with notched axes and blunted blades. Though their limbs were hard as teak and their bodies clad in fine bronze scales, here and there a foeman's weapon would find its mark, and a warrior of Ka-Sabar would topple to the ground.

In that moment of contact, while the barbarians were focused on the enemies before them and the City Companies were struggling beneath a hail of arrows, the chariots of the merchant princes were in the middle ground between the two forces, alone and unsupported. Akhmen-hotep grinned fiercely and raised his sword.

'Charge!' he ordered.

Trumpets wailed, and with a fierce shout the heavy chariots of the Bronze Host thundered forwards, passing between the struggling infantry companies and crashing into the mingled flanks of two barbarian companies. Heavy, bronze-rimmed wheels and scythe-like blades tore through the milling troops, crushing limbs and splitting torsos. Bowstrings hummed as archers fired into the howling mass of warriors. At such close range the powerful arrows punched clean through their targets and often struck the man next in line. Noblemen and Ushabti lashed out at the mercenaries with their curved swords, striking down at their exposed heads and shoulders and inflicting terrible wounds.

The barbarians gave way before the fearsome charge within moments, retreating away to either flank of the terrible chariots, and Akhmen-hotep drove them onwards, through the enemy battle-line and directly at the advancing merchant princes. The nobles of Bel Aliad saw the huge bronze war machines bearing down on them and their formation came to a panicked halt, like a caravan in the face of a sudden, vicious sandstorm. Though greater in number than the chariots of Ka-Sabar, they were far lighter and no real match for the veteran warriors of the Bronze Host. Several noblemen around the edges of the formation tried to turn their machines around and scurry out of the way of the oncoming wall of flesh and metal, while others surged forwards in a bold display of resolve. The result was disorder and chaos, robbing the formation of much of its strength at a critical moment.

Arrows snapped back and forth through the air as bowmen of both formations traded shots. One arrow struck the lip of Akhmen-hotep's chariot and ricocheted, striking him in the hip. The king swatted the arrow away as though it were a stinging fly. Horses and men screamed as other arrows found their marks, but the sounds were lost in a swirling, crashing roar as the formations came together.

Akhmen-hotep heard his charioteer let out a warning yell, and the chariot swerved to the right. An enemy chariot swept past, almost too fast to follow. The scythe-like blade fixed to the hub of the heavier Ka-Sabar chariot struck the enemy machine in the flank and ripped the wicker hull apart in a shower of splintered reeds. The bowman in the chariot let fly a wild shot that snapped past the king's head, and then they were lost in the dust of the swirling melee.

The battlefield shook with the clash of arms and the screams of the dying. To Akhmen-hotep's left, the Ushabti in his chariot lashed out with his ritual sword at a passing enemy machine, his fearsome strength slashing open the enemy chariot's hull and chopping apart its driver. Off to the right, lost in the haze, there was a splintering of wood and a broken chariot wheel soared through the air behind the king's speeding chariot.

Akhmen-hotep leaned against the front of his chariot and tried to make sense of the confusion around him. He searched for the blurry shapes of banners, trying to find Bel Aliad's leader. One quick challenge could end the battle, if the merchant princes still possessed a shred of honour.

A rumble of wheels thundered in from the right, and a Bel-Aliad chariot charged out of the dust. The charioteer angled his machine expertly, passing the king's vehicle on the right quarter. The archer in the back of the chariot drew his bow and fired, just as Akhmen-hotep lashed out with his sword. The arrow struck the king at the rounded part of his shoulder, punching through the bronze scales and sinking deep into the flesh beneath, but not before the king's sword had sliced through the charioteer's right arm. The man let out an anguished scream and fell onto his side, causing the horses to veer suddenly to the left and flip the chariot over.

The king pulled the arrow free with a snarl and cast it aside, feeling hot blood spread across the inside of his armour. As near as he could reckon, they had penetrated nearly all the way through the enemy formation. He heard a distant, surf-like surge of noise, to his left, but it was too far away to matter to the king at that moment. He glanced wildly in every direction, looking for a sign of the enemy leader.

There! Off to the right and a few dozen yards ahead, he spied a knot of stationary chariots flying a profusion of brightly coloured banners. It had to be the enemy prince and his bodyguards. Akhmen-hotep brought them to the attention of his charioteer by gesturing with his sword, and the man swung the war machine around. They bore down on the enemy like a hurled spear, aimed directly for the chariot in the centre of the group.

The prince and his retinue saw the danger at once, but there was little time to get their horses moving. Two of the bodyguards tried to push forwards and bar Akhmen-hotep's path, but their horses could not get moving quickly enough. Instead, the king's chariot struck the prince's machine like a thunderbolt, smashing the wicker hull to pieces and flipping it onto its side.

Akhmen-hotep leapt from the still-moving chariot and rushed towards a tall, lean warrior clad in burnished bronze armour and desert robes of brilliant yellow and blue. His men, an archer whose arm had been clearly broken in the crash and his unarmed charioteer, both threw their bodies into the king's path, but Akhmen-hotep hurled them aside like children. Still, it bought the prince enough time to draw his blade and prepare for the king's attack.

The prince of Bel Aliad was a brave man, but no warrior. His scimitar slashed at Akhmen-hotep's face in a clumsy, backhand blow that the king smashed contemptuously aside. His return stroke blurred through the air and came to rest against the prince's throat.

'Yield to me, Suhedir al-Khazem,' Akhmen-hotep growled, 'or prepare to greet your ancestors in the afterlife.'

The prince swayed on his feet. His sword fell from his trembling hand.

'I yield. By all the gods, I yield!' he said, sagging to his knees, as though overcome by a terrible burden, and reaching up to pull away his yellow head scarf. The prince's face was youthful but haggard, gaunt and pinched with strain. 'Spare my people, great one, and all the riches of Bel Aliad will be yours!' Relief washed over the King of Ka-Sabar, but he kept his expression stern and inscrutable.

'We are not monsters,' he said to the prince. 'You have dealt with us honourably, and we will treat you in kind. Signal your men to cease fighting, and we will discuss terms of ransom.'

The prince called to his trumpeter, and gladly gave the order. From the look on the man's face, Akhmen-hotep thought that he was happy to have lost the battle. He no longer had to heed the orders of the monster that crouched on the throne at Khemri.

Horns sounded again and again, cutting through the din of battle. It was several long minutes before the clamour subsided and the dust began to settle. A cheer went up from the Bronze Host, and then was suddenly cut short by confused shouts and angry cries. Bemused, Akhmen-hotep looked to the prince, but Suhedir al-Khazem looked mystified as well.

The rumble of a chariot approached hurriedly from the north-west. Within moments Akhmen-hotep spied Pakh-amn's battered chariot racing towards them across the battlefield. As he drew nearer, the king could see the stricken expression on the young noble's face.

'What is it?' Akhmen-hotep cried as the chariot rumbled to a halt. 'What has happened?' Pakh-amn looked in dread at Suhedir-al-Khazem, and then addressed his king.

'The messenger has returned from camp,' the nobleman replied. Akhmen-hotep frowned.

'Well? What of it?' he asked.

'He could not find the Bhagarite horsemen,' Pakh-amn said in a grim voice. 'The camp guards said they never arrived.'

The king was confused for a moment.

'But where else would they go?' he began, and then his blood ran cold. Slowly, he turned, casting his eyes to the north, in the direction of Bel Aliad. Suhedir al-Khazem, listening to the exchange, let out a despairing cry.

The first tendrils of smoke were rising above the distant City of Spices.

FIFTEEN

LESSONS IN DEATH

**Khemri, the Living City,
in the 45th year of Ptra the Glorious
(-1959 Imperial Reckoning)**

The great architects of Khemri had spared no expense to provide for the late King Khetep's every spiritual need in the afterlife. They built vaults within the Great Pyramid to hold tall jars of grain and dried fish, candied dates, wine and honey. There were rooms filled with luxurious furnishings, and chests of cedar wood packed with rich garments for the king to wear. Another chamber held a brace of mummified falcons and the king's favourite bow, in case he wished to go hunting in the fields of paradise. Still other chambers contained the king's mummified horses, and a great chariot made of bronze and gilded wood.

There was even a long, low chamber containing a fine river boat, complete with mummified oarsmen, in the event that the mighty king desired to ply the great River of Death.

The finest chamber of all was built far above the king's burial vaults, set in the very heart of the Great Pyramid. There, the architects had built a glorious throne room, complete with soaring columns and flagstones of polished marble. A noble dais stood at the far end of the throne room, and upon it stood a single throne, wrought not of wood but of darkest, polished obsidian. Flanking the throne stood towering statues of Ptra and Djaf, their faces stern, but their hands raised in welcome.

More statues were interspersed among the columns that ran to either side of the chamber: Neru and Asaph, Geheb and Tahoth, all of the gods of Nehekhara, each one awaiting the arrival of the dead king's spirit. For the throne at the far end of the room was not meant for Khetep, but for Usirian, the baleful god of the Underworld.

It was in this great hall that Khetep would come to be judged by the gods. If he had lived a virtuous life, he would be allowed into the golden fields of paradise. Otherwise, Usirian would drive the king's spirit into the howling wastes of the Underworld, there to suffer for all time, or at least until such time as the mortuary priests could summon back his soul and return him to the land of the living.

It was here that Nagash would summon his noble allies, more than forty in number, and, presiding from Usirian's black throne, he would work to undermine his brother's tenuous rule. If Arkhan, Raamket or the other young nobles were discomfited by the necromancer's profound display of sacrilege, none of them were foolish enough to share it. There was also the fact that he had kept his word and made them all very rich, very powerful men.

It had been three years since they had signed their names in that run-down house off Coppersmith Street, and in that time a terrible plague had swept through the great houses of Khemri. The sickness literally dissolved its victims from the inside out over a period of days or sometimes weeks. Vast fortunes were paid to the temples of Asaph and Tahoth to cure the sick, but the best that the priests could manage was to prolong the agony of the afflicted. No one survived the plague's touch, and the healers could not fathom how the sickness spread. Slaves, guards and functionaries were untouched, and only those born of noble blood seemed to be at risk. All, that is, except for those whose names were written on Nagash's list.

As the death toll mounted and the great houses became decimated, many vital positions in Thutep's court, some of which had been kept in the same family for centuries, were left vacant. Finally, the desperate king had little choice but to hand these titles to the only noblemen who still answered the call to the Grand Assembly. Khemri's fortunes were fading all too quickly. Other than a brief show of esteem from the other great cities upon the birth of his young son Sukhet five years before, the Living City had been all but forgotten by its peers.

'How fares the caravan trade?' Nagash asked, studying the assembled nobles over steepled fingers. The braziers in the great throne room had been lit, casting long fingers of light past the towering columns and throwing the ominous shadows of the stone gods across the marble flagstones. Khefru moved silently among the necromancer's allies, providing refreshment to those who wished it.

Shepsu-hur plucked a goblet of wine from the priest's wooden tray as he went past. Thutep had named him master of the gates, which gave him responsibility over levying taxes on the merchant caravans that came and went from Khemri. This included the river traffic from Zandri and the grain shipments that came south from Numas.

'Prices have nearly doubled in the bazaar,' he said, sampling the wine. 'Grain, spices, bronze: traders from every city are making life hard in the marketplace.'

The necromancer nodded.

'Zandri's work,' he declared. 'King Nekumet is tightening his fist around us. He's convinced the other kings to raise tariffs on exports to Khemri in order to choke off our trade.' Nagash turned his gaze to Raamket. 'No doubt it has increased smuggling tenfold.'

Raamket folded his thick arms. The burly nobleman had been appointed master of rods, making him responsible for the City Watch. With Nagash's help, Raamket had quickly used his authority to establish control of Khemri's criminal gangs as well.

'The gangs on the docks and the south gate district are doing a brisk trade,' he said with a chuckle. 'They plan on passing the goods on to the traders in the marketplace at half again the normal rate, a bargain these days, but the gangs will grow rich off it.' Nagash shook his head.

'No,' he said. 'Inform the gangs to sell their goods at the same price as the foreign traders. It serves our purpose for the city to suffer for a while.' Raamket frowned at the news.

'They won't want to hear that,' he said.

'If they won't listen, then relieve them of their ears,' the necromancer said. 'When the time comes for Thutep to yield his crown, it would be... preferable... if the populace supported his removal.' He turned to Arkhan. 'What is the mood of the people at present?'

Arkhan waited until Khefru approached, and then took a goblet. He drained half of the wine in a single draught and glowered at the rest. As master of the levy, it was his responsibility to maintain the yearly census and ensure that every adult citizen fulfilled his annual civil service. In times of war, he would also be required to marshal the spear levies that would form the bulk of Khemri's army.

'The rumours are circulating, as you requested,' he said. 'The great houses are being punished by the gods for permitting Thutep to bargain away Khemri's pre-eminence. It didn't take much effort to get people to start repeating it.'

Shepsu-hur sipped his wine thoughtfully. 'If we make the people think that the plague is the work of the gods,' he said, 'won't that drive them into the arms of the priesthood? I thought that was something we didn't want.' Nagash smiled coldly.

'They can give the priests all the coin and devotion they wish,' he said, 'so long as the holy men are helpless to stop the plague.' The necromancer leaned forwards upon the ebon throne.

'Thutep's time on Settra's throne has nearly run its course. The people are restive. A few more weeks of hunger and destitution and they will be ready for my brother to fall. For now, we must recoup our strength and prepare for one last outbreak of the so-called plague. This time, the sickness will spread beyond the great houses and afflict the city merchants. That should be sufficient to ignite the fires of unrest.' Nagash waved a dismissive hand. 'Tomorrow is the new moon. Return here at midnight with your offerings and we will perform the Incantation of Reaping.'

With that, the audience was at an end. The noblemen drained their goblets and set them on the marble floor. Then, they retired from the echoing chamber without a word. Moments later, only Khefru remained, dutifully picking up goblets and setting them on a wooden tray balanced upon his hip. Nagash studied his servant thoughtfully.

'There is something you are not telling me,' he said. Khefru shook his head.

'I don't know what you mean, master.'

'I can see it in the stiffness of your posture and the way you carefully avoid my gaze,' the necromancer said coldly. 'Don't insult me with your pitiful attempts at subterfuge, Khefru. It would not be wise.'

A faint shudder caused the young priest's shoulders to tremble. He paused for a moment, collecting himself, and then set down the wooden tray and straightened. 'I fear you are growing too bold, master,' he said. 'Thutep isn't as blind or as foolish as you think. The disappearances are gaining more and more attention. Your supposed allies are dragging dozens of victims off the streets each month for your rituals–'

'Arkhan and the rest must learn the rudiments of the necromantic arts if they are to be useful to me,' Nagash growled, cutting him off, 'and the curse requires a great deal of power to maintain it through the turning of the moon.' The necromancer shifted irritably upon the throne. 'The energy dissipates too quickly. It's like filling a wine jar using one's bare hands.'

'But the risk...' Khefru began, spreading his hands helplessly. 'Your allies are growing too bold. They're seizing the first victims they come upon, and many of them have families who take note of their disappearance. I know for a fact that people have gone to the temples begging for a formal inquiry. It's only a matter of time before a wealthy merchant or a neighbourhood full of grieving families pays the priesthood enough to start a serious investigation. After that it's only a matter of time before the king becomes involved.'

'And what of it?' Nagash snarled. 'We've spent the last three years stripping away the king's power. The great houses are all but extinct, and my men control all the vital functions of the city. If anything, I expect we could find a way to turn the inquiry to our own ends, embarrassing the priesthood as a pack of corrupt, meddling fools.' As he said this, Nagash saw Khefru blanch. The necromancer leaned forward intently. 'Ah. Now I see the heart of it. After everything we have learned, everything we've done... you're still afraid of the priesthood.'

'No... no, it's not them,' Khefru stammered. His sallow face grew pinched with fear. 'I fear no man in this world save you, master, but what of the gods? We've cheated Djaf and Usirian of dozens of human souls. By now, their wrath must be very great.'

'And yet they have done nothing,' Nagash said scornfully. 'Do you know why? Because we stand to usurp them of their power. We are plumbing the secrets of life and death, Khefru. Without the fear of dying, and the threat of judgement, the gods will lose their hold over mankind.'

'Yes. Yes, I see all that,' the young priest said, his knife-scar accentuating the pained look on his face, 'but we're not immortal yet. Death still waits for us, and beyond that, divine judgement. We… we've done awful things, master. There is no hell in Usirian's teachings terrible enough to suit our crimes.'

'Leave such things to me, Khefru,' Nagash said coldly. 'All things in due time. For now, we must focus on taking Thutep's crown. Do you understand?'

Khefru nodded reluctantly. 'I understand, master.' He bowed quickly, and returned to his work. The young priest gathered up the wine cups and made for the side passage that led down to the lower levels, where Khetep's crypt and Nagash's study were located. Just as he reached the columns along the north side of the room, he paused.

'One more thing, master,' he said. 'Your guests have made a great deal of progress exploring the crypt over the last few days. I believe Ashniel has almost found the way out. Should I introduce the next set of traps?' Nagash leaned back upon the throne, his face lost in thought.

'Leave that to me as well,' he said.

The braziers had been left to burn out in the Great Pyramid's grand throne room. Nearly four hours past midnight they gave off a sullen red glow that lent the huge chamber an ominous blood-hued cast. The ruddy light scarcely reached above head-height along the towering stone columns, and pooled on the broad steps of the great dais.

Silence stretched through the chamber's chill air, broken only by the furtive sounds of burrowing tomb beetles. Then there was a faint sound, like the whisper of skin across stone, and a thin hissing that nearly resolved into words.

Dark forms moved in the shadows beyond the columns on the north side of the room. The sibilant whispers rose again, like a conversation between a trio of vipers. Then a lithe shape glided from the darkness and stepped into the centre of the throne room. Pale hands reached up and pulled back a black cotton hood, revealing the sharp-edged features of Ashniel, the druchii witch. She turned slowly in place, as though trying to deduce where the chamber was in relation to the rest of the huge pyramid, and how close she might be to freedom.

Within moments, Ashniel was joined by her companions. Drutheira had her hood back, letting her white hair tumble across her narrow shoulders. Her ethereal beauty had been transformed into a tight mask of strain, and she clutched an improvised dagger chipped from a broken shard of obsidian. Malchior limped along in her wake, cursing softly under his breath. The shaft of a barbed dart jutted from the druchii's left thigh, and every step left a small pool of blood gleaming upon the marble. Clearly, Ashniel's mastery of the crypt's many traps still left something to be desired.

The three druchii came together and whispered once more, clearly arguing about which way they should go. Then a cold voice echoed from the darkness, transfixing them with its predatory intensity.

'You're very close,' Nagash said from the darkness surrounding the ebon throne.

Cloth whispered against stone as the necromancer rose to his feet and slowly descended the steps into the ruddy light. In his left hand he held the Staff of the Ages, and his dark eyes were intent upon the barbarians. Nagash smiled, a gesture devoid of warmth or humour.

'Shall I tell you which direction to go?' he asked, pointing to the doorway at the far end of the hall. 'When the spirit of the dead king was judged and accepted into paradise, he could leave the Great Pyramid and travel to the afterlife. So the architects built a long, sloping corridor there, to facilitate his passage.' Ashniel gave Nagash a look of purest hate.

'A pity that a spirit has no need for an actual door,' she hissed. 'The passageway is purely symbolic, and ends at a stone wall.' She drew herself to her full height and sneered at the necromancer. 'I've spent a great deal of time reading about your people's bizarre burial rites.' The witch turned and pointed into the shadows along the chamber's southern wall. 'There will be another doorway there, leading into the upper vaults. Beyond that will be the corridor to the outside.'

Nagash inclined his head mockingly. 'The passage awaits, witch. All that stands between you and your freedom... is me.' He spread his arms expansively. 'Defeat me with your sorceries, and you may go free.'

Malchior took a limping step towards the dais. 'What kind of trick is this?' he spat, but the movement was nothing more than a feint. Quicker than the eye could follow, the warlock threw up his hand and hissed a stream of liquid syllables that caused the air to crackle with magical power.

Nagash reacted without hesitation, bringing around the Staff of Ages and chanting an abjuration just as a bolt of blue-white light shot from Malchior's hand. The destructive spell leapt at Nagash. Then it seemed to unravel midway to its target as it encountered the necromancer's counter-spell and dissipated with a thunderous *crack*!

As the ragged tendrils of sorcerous energy washed over him, Nagash switched tactics, thrusting his open hand forwards and barking out a spell. There was a flash of heat, and darts of glimmering fire stitched the air between the necromancer and the druchii. The barbarians scattered, deflecting the magical bolts with counter-spells. The darts etched molten craters in the marble flagstones and blew fragments from the towering stone columns that flanked the throne room.

Ashniel circled to Nagash's left, spitting out a blasphemous incantation and hurling a bolt of hissing blackness from her open hands. Nagash turned it aside with another quick counter-spell. It struck the Staff of the Ages and deflected past the necromancer with a thunderous roar, striking the ebon throne of Usirian and melting it into a steaming puddle of liquid rock.

Malchior struck Nagash a moment later, hitting the necromancer in the side with a spear of crackling energy. Nagash, still focusing on his counter-spell, was able to dissipate most of its power, but the rest of the spell's energy raked across his ribs like a lion's claws, and set his robes ablaze.

The necromancer staggered. With a roar, he barked a stream of syllables. The fire licking at his robes guttered and went out, channelled into a whipcord of flames that he unleashed upon Ashniel. The witch severed the stream of energy with contemptuous ease.

Suddenly, a storm of whirling shadows surrounded Nagash. A pale figure emerged from the darkness, appearing to dance past the necromancer, and fiery pain tore through the necromancer's arm. Nagash whirled, but Drutheira was already out of reach, vanishing into the magical darkness with a hateful laugh. Blood poured down his arm from a gash left by the witch's dagger.

The air in the chamber quivered with the crash and roar of sorcerous power. Another bolt of power tore through Drutheira's cloak of shadow, and Nagash felt his entire left side explode in pain as the spell grazed his hip. It spun him around like a child's toy, nearly pitching him from the dais. He landed hard on his right side, sparing him from a stream of crackling darts flung by Ashniel.

Nagash bit back the pain that clawed at his nerves and tried to collect his wits. The druchii were far more experienced with sorcery than he was, but he'd thought that without raw magic – the winds of magic, as they called it – to draw on, he would be able to counter their spells with ease. Clearly, the barbarians hadn't shared everything they knew. Nagash, however, possessed secrets of his own.

Once more, the inky shadows closed in around him. The necromancer abandoned his counter-spells and clutched the staff with both hands, watching for a telltale flicker of pale skin.

Drutheira seemed to dance through the darkness towards him, approaching Nagash from the side. He let her draw close, and then lashed out at her with his staff. The witch saw the blow coming and tried to leap aside, but the necromancer caught her right ankle and caused her to stumble. She fell with a screech, rolling painfully down the stone steps of the dais.

As she fell, Nagash rose to one knee and barked out a counter-spell that scattered the shadows like smoke. His throat was tight and painful and his body was starting to tremble from strain. Immediately, he felt a sense of pressure against his skin and he brandished the Staff of the Ages in front of him as bolts of power struck him from the front and the side. Claws of fire tore at the side of Nagash's face, and he was deafened by twin concussions that hammered at his body. Agonising pain lanced into his chest, as though iron fingers tore deep into the flesh and muscle beneath his skin.

For a dizzying instant Nagash wavered on the edge of unconsciousness.

He clawed his way back by sheer force of will and sought out the wounded figure of Malchior, still standing at the centre of the throne room. Clenching his right fist, the necromancer began to chant.

Nagash knew that the barbed spike in the warlock's leg was tainted with poison, a painful, debilitating venom that was even now coursing through the druchii's veins. Somehow the warlock was able to continue fighting despite the agony of the poison, but now the necromancer enhanced its virulence tenfold. The druchii stiffened in mid-chant, his muscles tightening like cables beneath his skin. Foam burst from the warlock's mouth, and he toppled over and began to writhe across the cratered stone, until a flurry of searing bolts from the necromancer's fingers tore the druchii's body open like knives. Boiling blood spattered across the floor, and the warlock's flayed body stilled.

Nagash wasn't finished with Malchior yet. He tasted blood as he spat the Incantation of Reaping and consumed the warlock's soul. Malchior's life essence flowed into him like a river of ice, banishing the pain of his wounds and filling his veins with power.

Drutheira lay at the foot of the dais, doubled over in pain. She had landed on her right arm, which was bent at an awkward angle. With a snarl, Nagash jabbed a finger at her and spat a vicious spell. The witch threw up her good arm and screamed a counter-spell, but the force of the necromancer's attack struck her like a desert storm. Drops of blood appeared on the witch's pale skin, spreading rapidly as her flesh was stripped away in twisting ribbons by a furious magical wind. In the blink of an eye the witch was shredded, her entrails spread in a gory fan behind her steaming bones. Once again, Nagash chanted the Incantation of Reaping and ate the barbarian's life essence.

A bolt of searing power smashed into the necromancer, but Nagash scarcely felt it. The energy dissipated like smoke, cancelled by the inrush of power from Drutheira's soul. He turned to Ashniel, who still stood near the chamber's southern wall, and unleashed a rippling string of magical bolts. The witch countered his attacks with fearsome speed, deflecting many of the bolts and dissipating the rest. Crackling detonations split the stones and sent puffs of dust into the air around the druchii, but Ashniel was unharmed.

With a screech, the witch struck back. Nagash felt the dais beneath him start to shift and give way. He focused his will on the stones, which were turning black and melding together like the maw of a gaping pit. The necromancer barked a counter-spell and poured his newly gathered energies into the incantation, fixing the stones once more into solidity.

Before Ashniel could launch another attack, Nagash unleashed another torrent of bolts at the witch. Once again, she deflected them with almost casual skill. More concussions reverberated across the chamber, sending razor-sharp flecks of stone whickering through the air.

Ashniel staggered beneath the onslaught, but she gave the necromancer a malicious smile.

'A clever trick, human,' she shouted, 'but those two were amateurs compared to me. Your attacks are potent but clumsy, and your energies are finite. I can counter your spells indefinitely, and when you have exhausted yourself, I will make a new pair of gloves from your hide.'

Nagash's face twisted in rage and he began to chant again. A wild, howling wind rushed from the necromancer, roaring down the dais towards the witch. Ashniel threw up her hands and the wind curled around her. The flagstones beneath her feet erupted in fragments, and the sharp echoes of splintering stone filled the air.

'You see?' she said with a laugh. 'Your spells can't touch me.'

Nagash drew a deep breath. The power of the druchii souls was fading, leaving his throat feeling raw and torn.

'What makes you think that spell was meant for you?' he croaked.

Ashniel's smile faltered. Her eyes narrowed warily, and with a hiss like an angry cat she whirled to see the cracked and splintered feet of Asaph, goddess of love.

Baffled, she spun back to Nagash, just as the head of the goddess landed on her. The stone head, the size of a chariot, smashed to pieces, crushing the druchii to a pulp.

Nagash uttered the Incantation of Reaping one last time, and drank deep of Ashniel's life essence. Pain faded, replaced by the cold bliss of triumph.

The necromancer surveyed the scene of carnage. Veils of dust hung in the air, tinged red by the banked light of the braziers.

'My thanks for the lesson,' Nagash said with a smile.

SIXTEEN

THE CREEPING DARKNESS

**Bel Aliad, the City of Spices,
in the 63rd year of Ptra the Glorious
(-1744 Imperial Reckoning)**

By the time Akhmen-hotep and his warriors reached Bel Aliad, the Bhagarite horsemen had killed every living thing they could. Bodies lay in heaps along the narrow streets, cut down as they tried to flee the swift-riding desert raiders. When the panicked citizens fled into their homes the merciless Bhagarites flung torches and looted oil lamps through the windows and waited with their bows at the ready. Old men, women and children lay huddled by the doors of their homes, pierced by arrows and spears. The Bhagarites had waded into the slaughter until their white robes and the withers of their horses were drenched in innocent blood.

The stench of spilled blood hung heavy in the air, even in the famous Spice Bazaar. The brightly coloured awnings of the spice market had been slashed apart, and a king's ransom worth of exotic herbs had spilled from broken urns and been trampled into the dirt. Bel Aliad had been cast to ruin in the space of a single afternoon. The desert raiders had cut out its heart to answer for all that they had lost, and now, the horsemen sat their mounts and stared dumbly at the horror they had wrought, their sword-arms hanging limp and their dark eyes empty of thought or feeling.

Akhmen-hotep strode heavily into the Spice Bazaar, surrounded by his Ushabti and Pakh-amn's light horsemen. They'd left their chariots at the edge of the town, for there had been no way to guide the heavy war machines down the streets without riding over Bel Aliad's massacred people.

The king's bloodstained sword quivered in his hand as he saw the milling figures of the horsemen. Rage and despair flooded through Akhmen-hotep, and when he tried to speak all he could manage was a wordless roar of anguish that echoed in the corpse-strewn square. The desert horses shied at the terrible sound, tossing their heads and backing away from the advancing king, but the Bhagarites stilled the animals with leaden voices and slid from the saddles with funereal grace. They walked a few steps towards the king and carefully laid their swords on the ground beside their feet.

Some of the men reached up and tugged their headscarves loose, baring their necks, while others pulled open their gore-spattered robes and revealed their heaving chests. They had avenged their murdered kin, and now prepared to join them in the afterlife.

At that moment, Akhmen-hotep would have gladly obliged them. He stared into their dead eyes and felt sick with fury.

'What infamy is this?' he cried. 'These people did nothing to you! Do you imagine your loved ones are pleased with what you've done? You've murdered mothers and their babes! This is not the work of warriors, but of monsters. You're no better than the Usurper!'

The imprecation struck the Bhagarites like the lash of a whip. One of the horsemen screeched like a desert cat and snatched up his blade, but he took no more than two steps towards the king before one of Akhmen-hotep's Ushabti stepped forwards and cut him down. The king's bodyguards swept forwards in a single mass, their ritual swords flickering, but they were halted by a commanding shout, not from Akhmen-hotep, but from Pakh-amn, the Master of Horse.

'Stay your hands!' the young nobleman shouted. 'The lives of the horsemen are for the king to take, not your own!'

True to their oaths, the devoted paused, awaiting their master's order. Akhmen-hotep turned at the sound of Pakh-amn's approach, glaring up at the nobleman as he reined in his horse beside the king.

'Do you mean to plead for their lives, Pakh-amn?' he snapped. 'Their lives are forfeit for what they have done!'

'Do you think me blind, great one?' the nobleman shot back. 'I have seen the slaughter just the same as you, but their executions must wait if you and I hope to see Ka-Sabar once more.'

Akhmen-hotep bit back a savage reply. As terrible as it was to hear, Pakh-amn was right. Without the Bhagarites they would never find their way back across the trackless sands of the Great Desert, and the king's duty to his people came before all other considerations. Justice for the people of Bel Aliad would have to wait.

'Seize them,' he told the Ushabti in a hollow voice. 'Take away their horses and their swords, and return them to camp.'

The Ushabti lowered their blades reluctantly, but did as the king commanded. The desert horsemen offered no resistance as their hands were bound behind their backs with rope taken from their saddles, and strange hands took hold of the bridles of their sacred horses. As far as they were concerned, their lives were at an end.

'We should take them back by a circuitous route,' Pakh-amn suggested. 'Lest the city nobles catch sight of them. I'll round up some troops and see about putting out the fires.' Akhmen-hotep nodded heavily.

'What will I tell Suhedir al-Khazem?' he asked, unable to take his eyes from the torn and twisted bodies filling the square.

The Master of Horse drew a deep breath. 'We will say that some of our horsemen got carried away during the battle and that there was some looting. Nothing more. If we tell them the truth there will be a riot.' Even battered and disarmed, the city nobles and the surviving members of the City Companies made for a large body of men, and the terms of ransom that the king offered meant that they would be held in camp under minimal guard. The barbarian mercenaries would be chained into slave coffles and marched back with the army: such were the wages of war in the Blessed Land.

Akhmen-hotep considered this, and nodded. The prince and his men would have to be told the truth eventually, but not today. He did not have the heart for it.

'See to it,' he said wearily, and waved Pakh-amn away.

The king stood alone in the blood-soaked square as the Bhagarite horsemen were led away and Pakh-amn snapped orders to his horsemen. His broad shoulders sagged, and Akhmen-hotep sank to his knees among the bodies of the innocent.

'Forgive me,' he said, bending down to press his forehead to the hot stones. 'Forgive me.'

The setting sun was red as fresh blood as it sank behind the mists above the Springs of Eternal Life. The hazy white clouds roiled slowly in the hot air, winding in thick tendrils around the tops of the high dunes just a few miles distant from where Rakh-amn-hotep stood. He was coated in a paste of sweat, dust and grit from the swirling cavalry skirmishes of the late afternoon, and his left shoulder ached from the sting of a horseman's arrow that had penetrated a few inches past the heavy scales of his armoured vest. His throat and nostrils were caked with mud, and it felt as though his eyes would stick shut if he closed them for more than a few moments. To his tired mind the mists seemed to curl and stretch towards him like the welcoming arms of a lover. He longed to feel that cool, clean touch, but it remained just out of his reach, guarded by a long, thin line of Numasi horsemen and Khemri spears.

The enemy force stretched along the base of a line of low dunes running roughly southwards, with their left flank standing astride the Western Trade Road that led to the Living City. The bulk of the enemy cavalry had withdrawn to the north side of the road, no doubt to discourage flanking efforts in that direction. The Numasi cavalrymen were devils on horseback, almost the equal of the desert princes of Bhagar, and despite being significantly outnumbered they'd got the better of the Lybarans in most of the day's skirmishes.

Rakh-amn-hotep had pressed them hard, believing at first that the Numasi cavalry was no more than a large scouting party sent to gather intelligence on the situation at Quatar. The enemy had retreated slowly but steadily in the face of his advance, sometimes wheeling and dashing forwards to unleash a volley of arrows or clash swords with a squadron of Lybarans who pressed too close. He had been certain that they would eventually break off and retreat north and west once the day was nearly over, but now he realised bitterly that the horsemen were merely a vanguard like his own, and they'd held him up just long enough for the rest of their force to form up for battle.

The majority of the Lybaran cavalry was arrayed in a broad crescent to either side of the Rasetran king: close to three thousand light cavalry and a striking force of fifteen hundred heavy cavalry. The heavy horse was situated to the king's left, still relatively fresh at the end of the day. Rakh-amn-hotep had kept them and his Ushabti in reserve, unwilling to wear them out on constant pursuits when he might have need of them later. To the king's right, the horses of the light cavalry squadrons waited with their heads drooping and their flanks dappled with foam. Their riders poured precious water from the leather flasks at their hips onto thick cotton rags and held them up for their weary mounts to lick.

Rakh-amn-hotep scowled up at the lowering sun. There were perhaps two hours left before sunset. If they could not find a way to break through the enemy line it would mean another day out in the sands, consuming the last of the army's water. The Usurper's troops appeared to number at least fifteen thousand men, including the two thousand Numasi cavalry they'd skirmished with earlier, mostly light infantry and a few companies of archers. The Rasetran king would generally be tempted to put his faith in Ptra and try a massed charge, but the majority of his force was all but exhausted. Did they have enough strength left to break the enemy line?

The king turned and beckoned to the commander of the Lybaran contingent, who stood with his retinue only a few paces away. Shesh-amun was one of Hekhmenukep's staunchest allies, and despite his advanced years he carried himself with a young man's strength and vigour. He was lean and rangy like old leather, his skin burned almost black by long decades labouring under the desert sun. The champion was a bluff, forthright man who did not suffer fools gladly, and didn't think so much of himself that he couldn't be persuaded to listen to reason. The Rasetran had warmed to him at once. Rakh-amn-hotep leaned over the side of his chariot as Shesh-amun approached.

'We need to get past these jackals,' the king said quietly. 'Are your men up to one more fight?'

'Oh, they'd welcome the chance to fight someone that doesn't wheel away and run at the first sign of trouble,' Shesh-amun growled. 'Those Numasi horse thieves have got their blood up, but I suspect that was the whole point.' The champion turned his head and spat into the dust. 'They're willing, and the horses, too, but don't be surprised if they start dropping dead if the fight goes on too long.' The Rasetran king nodded grimly.

'Well, promise them all the water they can drink, if only we can break through and reach the springs. Maybe that will keep them alive a few moments more.'

'I'll pass the word,' Shesh-amun said. Just as he began to turn away, a horn sounded beyond the dunes to the east of the weary horsemen. The champion peered off into the distance. 'Are you expecting someone?' he asked. Rakh-amn-hotep straightened and looked eastward. Sure enough, a winding ribbon of dust was rising from the direction of the trade road.

'Indeed I am, but I'd nearly given up on him,' he said. 'Reinforcements are coming,' the king told Shesh-amun. 'Ready your men for action.'

The champion bowed quickly and hastened off to spread the word. Minutes later Rakh-amn-hotep heard the rumble of hooves, and a squadron of light cavalry raced over the dunes to join the line of weary horsemen. Tired cheers went up from the vanguard as the reinforcements began to arrive, and the king waited for the sight of Ekhreb's chariot among the column of troops. He saw it at once, bouncing along in the light cavalry's wake. Rakh-amn-hotep raised his sword in greeting, and the light chariot angled off the line of march and reined in beside the king.

'I left you back at camp three hours ago!' Rakh-amn-hotep shouted to the champion. 'Did you get lost? All you had to do was follow the damned road!' Ekhreb leapt from the back of the chariot and reached the king in two quick strides.

'That's rich,' the champion replied mildly. 'You, lecturing me about arriving late. I marshalled six thousand men for you on two hours' notice. Shall I send them back to camp?'

'Don't be churlish,' the king replied. 'I can have you beheaded for that, you know.'

'So you've said,' Ekhreb replied. 'Many, many times.' Rakh-amn-hotep caught sight of a company of Rasetran light infantry jogging over the dunes to the east.

'What have you brought me, exactly?' he asked.

'A thousand light horsemen, four thousand light infantry, and a thousand of our jungle auxiliaries,' Ekhreb said. 'I thought the scaly-skins might strike some fear into the enemy's hearts.'

'No archers?' the king asked sharply. The champion made a visible effort not to roll his eyes.

'You said nothing about bowmen, great one.'

The king bit back a sarcastic reply. Ekhreb was right, after all.

'We'll have to rely on the bows of the light cavalry then,' he muttered. Ekhreb folded his arms and stared at the distant enemy line.

'Not much of a force,' he said. 'It seems that Akhmen-hotep's diversion was successful.'

'Perhaps,' the king replied, 'but it doesn't need to be very large, so long as they keep us from the springs.' Rakh-amn-hotep studied the enemy dispositions and made his plans. 'Form the infantry into line right here,' he told his champion, 'and put the auxiliaries on the right.' Then he beckoned to Shesh-amun. When the Lybaran arrived, he told him, 'Pull your light horsemen back over the dunes behind us, and start circling around to our right, towards the road.' Shesh-amun frowned.

'But they'll be expecting that,' he said. The king waved his concerns away.

'Sometimes we must give the enemy what he's looking for,' he told the champion. 'Don't commit your men to pitched battle unless you must. Just push as far as you can around the edge of their line. I'll give you ten minutes to get your riders moving before we advance.'

Though clearly still doubtful, Shesh-amun bowed to the king and began shouting orders to his troops. Ekhreb had already passed the king's commands to the allied reinforcements. The light infantry companies were already forming a rough line before the allied cavalry, and the dark green shapes of the jungle auxiliaries were moving between the king's chariots and the Lybaran light cavalry. The lizardmen were huge, hulking creatures, their scaly skins tattooed in strange spiral patterns that stretched across their rolling muscles. They carried massive clubs in their taloned hands, made of heavy pieces of wood studded with jagged chips of glossy black stone. Human skulls hung from rawhide cords around their naked waists, and their powerful, wedge-shaped heads bore a fearsome resemblance to the great crocodiles of Nehekharan legend. The trained warhorses rolled their eyes and shifted nervously at the creatures' acrid stink, but the lizardmen paid them little heed.

As the infantry were forming up for battle the light horsemen on the right flank began to slowly withdraw over the dunes to the east. Rakh-amn-hotep expected some kind of reaction from the enemy line, but the Usurper's troops made not a sound.

Ekhreb folded his muscular arms and surveyed the troops' movements with a practised eye.

'Where do you want me?' he asked the king.

'You?' Rakh-amn-hotep grunted. 'I want you right beside me, of course. That way you can't claim you got lost heading to the battle.' Ekhreb gave the king an arch expression.

'I live to serve, great one,' he said wryly. 'What now?' Rakh-amn-hotep counted off the minutes in his head.

'Order the centre and the left flank forwards,' he commanded. 'The heavy cavalry will charge along with the infantry.'

The champion nodded and passed the orders at once. Trumpets sounded, and the ragged line of warriors raised their shields and marched towards the foe, followed by the light horsemen a dozen yards behind. Across the broken ground between the two armies, the enemy bowmen waited in two long skirmish lines before the infantry companies. As the king watched the distance between the two forces shrink he found himself wishing for a few Lybaran sky-priests to spoil the enemy's aim. The thought stirred a faint twinge of suspicion in the king's mind: where were the enemy sorcerers? He'd heard the stories of what had happened at Zedri, years before. Now that his forces had been committed, he found himself wondering what terrible surprises the Usurper's army had in store.

The air darkened above the closing armies as the enemy bowmen loosed their first volley. The Rasetran infantry quickened their pace at once, throwing up their wooden shields against the deadly rain. The shower of arrows struck their targets with a dreadful rattle of bronze against wood. Men screamed, and gaps showed in the advancing companies, but the rest pressed on. More arrows flickered through the air as the light horsemen returned the enemy fire, shooting high over the heads of the advancing infantry. Far to the left, a low rumble began as the heavy cavalry spurred their mounts into a ground-eating canter, and the enemy companies on that flank lowered their glinting spears to receive the inevitable charge.

The enemy bowmen fired a second volley and then withdrew to safety as the Rasetran warriors bore down upon them. Rakh-amn-hotep nodded thoughtfully.

'All right,' he said to Ekhreb. 'Order the auxiliaries to attack.'

Ekhreb called out, and a heavy drum answered, beating out a low, dreadful cadence. With a hiss like a desert wind, the company of lizardmen rose from their haunches and loped towards the enemy battle-line, covering the ground swiftly with their long strides. The air filled with screeches and dreadful, warbling cries as the jungle warriors advanced, and Rakh-amn-hotep was pleased to see the troops on the left waver at the sound.

All along the battle-line the warriors of the opposing armies crashed together in a resounding clatter of wood and bronze. The screams of the dead and dying carried clearly above the din, and badly wounded men began to break away from the struggling companies and stagger back the way they'd come. On the left, the heavy cavalry thundered home against the enemy shield wall, flinging broken bodies back onto their fellows as they drove a wedge into two of the enemy companies. Swords flashed down in brilliant arcs, splitting skulls and cleaving torsos, and frenzied horses reared and lashed at the screaming throng with their terrible hooves.

On the right, the lizardmen leapt at their foes with a bloodcurdling chorus of hissing screeches and inhuman wails. Their scaly skin turned aside all but the strongest spear-thrust, and their war clubs smashed wooden shields and bones alike into ragged splinters. The king watched the enemy infantry reel in terror from the onslaught, but the majority of his attention was focused on the light horsemen still further down the right flank. Their horses were rearing and screaming at the scent of the strange lizardmen, but as yet they held their position at the opposite end of the road. A few of the cavalrymen loosed wild shots into the frenzied creatures, to no discernible effect.

Minutes passed, and the fighting continued. The enemy forces had wavered under the initial ferocity of the allied attack, but they had regained their resolve and their greater numbers were beginning to tell against the Rasetran infantry. The heavy cavalry on the left were being slowly surrounded by a sea of roaring, stabbing warriors and were trying to extricate themselves from the mob. The infantry companies on the left and in the centre were being driven back by the sheer weight of their foes. Only on the right were there still signs of success, as the lizardmen took a terrible toll of the lightly armoured humans. Rakh-amn-hotep, however, knew from experience that the lizardmen could not sustain such efforts for long, especially in this searing heat. Before too much longer they would start to falter, and he would have to pull them back or risk seeing them overwhelmed.

Then the king caught a glimpse of movement further to the right. A squadron of the enemy cavalry was wheeling away, heading further off to the north. A minute later another squadron followed, and then another. They had spotted the flanking movement by the Lybaran horsemen and were moving to counter the attempt, leaving the battered infantry on the right without any support.

Rakh-amn-hotep smiled and drew his sword.

'Time to end this,' he growled. To Ekhreb he said, 'The Ushabti will advance upon the right,' pointing his sword at the junction where the enemy right met the centre. 'Push through and drive for the springs!'

As one, the Ushabti shouted the name of Ptra the Glorious and raised their gleaming blades to the sky. With a peal of trumpets the company started forwards, gathering speed as the charioteers lashed the flanks of their horses. As they rumbled forwards the chariots altered their formation, stretching into a wedge aimed like a spear at the vulnerable point of the enemy line.

The earth shook beneath the thundering wheels of the war machines. Rasetrans in the rear ranks of their struggling companies saw their king approach and raised their voices in a lusty cheer that spurred the efforts of their fellows. For a brief moment the allied line surged forwards a single step, and then the chariots smashed into the battle-line. Light infantrymen were smashed aside by teams of charging horses, or trampled beneath hooves and bronze-rimmed wheels. Bowstrings snapped as archers in the chariots fired point-blank into the massed enemy troops, and the armoured figures of the Ushabti reaped a terrible harvest with their huge, sickle-shaped swords. Rakh-amn-hotep chopped down with his sword and smashed a screaming warrior's skull. Then he swept aside the jabbing point of a spear.

'Keep going!' he roared to his charioteer, and the man cracked his whip with a will, shouting to Ptra to strengthen his arm.

The infantrymen reeled from the impact, and the battle-hardened Rasetrans pressed the advantage, driving the wedge still deeper into the line. The enemy troops on the right flank were cut off from their neighbouring companies and left to the mercy of the ravening lizardmen, who tore heads from the dead and dying and crushed them in their terrible jaws. Without the support of the light cavalry, the spearmen began to waver, and a moment later their resolve failed them and they began to run, stumbling and clawing up the slope behind them. The jungle warriors gave chase, hissing and screeching their savage war cries.

Rakh-amn-hotep roared in triumph.

'Wheel right!' he ordered, and slowly the chariots began to press upon the unprotected flank of the companies in the enemy centre. Arrows scythed into the sides and rear of the enemy formations, and panic took hold. When the enemy warriors saw that their left flank had crumbled they turned and ran, and within minutes the slopes were swarming with fleeing troops. The Rasetrans snapped at their heels like wolves, slaying every man they could reach. Exhaustion alone held back the struggling allied troops, and was all that kept the retreat from becoming a blood-soaked rout.

Relief and a sense of triumph flooded the king's tired body. The battle had lasted less than half an hour, judging by the height of the sun. Ptra's burning orb had vanished into a pool of crimson light along the western horizon. With luck, the king thought, the vanguard would reach the life-giving pools by nightfall.

The Rasetran infantry clambered up the slope after their foes and disappeared over the summit of the dunes. For the cavalry and the chariots it was harder going, as the sands gave way beneath the plunging hooves of the horses. Rakh-amn-hotep was busy contemplating how he would press the pursuit with fresh elements of the army's light cavalry when his chariot finally crested the rise, and slid to an awkward halt.

Rakh-amn-hotep threw out a hand to steady himself at the sudden stop, a curse halfway to his lips, when he realised that the entire allied pursuit had pulled up short. The survivors of the enemy army were running pell-mell across a wide, rocky plain, in the direction of the springs, And, with a cold sense of realisation, the king saw why.

Across the broad plain, arrayed at the very edge of the mist-wrapped springs, stretched a line of infantry and bowmen that ran from one end of the horizon to the other. The bloody sunlight shone on thickets of spears and round, polished helms, tens of thousands strong. Huge blocks of heavy cavalry waited beyond the line of spears, and smaller squadrons of light horsemen prowled along the front of the battle-line like packs of hungry jackals.

'In the name of all the gods,' Rakh-amn-hotep whispered in awe. Now he understood. The enemy force he'd just defeated was just the vanguard for the Usurper's main host.

Ekhreb reined in his chariot alongside the king. 'What do we do now?' he called.

Rakh-amn-hotep shook his head at the legions of silent warriors waiting across the plain.

'What can we do?' he said bitterly. 'We must retreat and carry news back to the rest of the army. Tomorrow we must summon all our strength and fight for our very lives.'

BOOK TWO

SEVENTEEN

ATTACK AND RETREAT

Bel Aliad, the City of Spices,
in the 63rd year of Ptra the Glorious
(-1744 Imperial Reckoning)

The date wine was thick and cloyingly sweet. Akhmen-hotep grimaced as he raised the cup to his lips and took another draught. Inside the king's tent, the air was cold and still. No oil lamps had been lit, nor were there any coals banked against the night's chill. Only a pair of wide-eyed slaves attended upon the king, kneeling fearfully at either side of the tent's entrance.

Akhmen-hotep's tent faced west, letting in long, slanting beams of moonlight as the linen entry flap was pulled aside. Outside, the camp was quiet save for the distant music of Neru's acolytes as they performed their midnight vigil. The king raised his eyes to the round figure silhouetted in the moon's cold radiance.

'What do you want, brother?' he asked, in a voice roughened by many cups of wine.

Memnet did not reply at first. The Grand Hierophant stood in the entryway for a few moments, letting his eyes adjust to the gloom, and then shuffled wearily inside and settled in a chair close to the king. He gestured, and a slave crawled swiftly across the sandy floor to press a cup into the high priest's hand.

'I thought you and I could share a drink,' Memnet said thoughtfully, sniffing at the strong smell of the dates. He made a face. 'No water for the wine?' Akhmen-hotep took another sip.

'I do not drink it for the taste,' he said quietly.

The Grand Hierophant nodded, but said nothing. He took a tentative sip of the wine, before saying, 'You cannot blame yourself for what happened. It's the nature of war.'

'War,' Akhmen-hotep growled into his cup. 'This is not war as our fathers knew it. This... this is grotesque!' He drained the dregs and glared at one of the slaves, who crawled forwards with a fresh jug of wine. 'And the harder we fight, the worse it becomes.' He turned abruptly, causing the slave to slosh the syrupy wine over the king's hand.

'What is happening to us, brother?' Akhmen-hotep asked. His handsome features were etched with despair. 'Have the gods forsaken us? Everywhere I turn, all I see is death and ruin.' He held the brimming cup before him, his dark eyes bleak. 'Sometimes I fear that even if we do defeat the Usurper, we'll never be free of his taint.' Memnet stared into his cup for some time. He took another sip.

'Perhaps we are not meant to be,' he said quietly. The king grew very still.

'What do you mean?' he asked.

Memnet did not answer at first. His expression grew haunted, and Akhmen-hotep saw how ravaged his features had become since that fateful day at Zedri. The priest's face was like an ill-fitting mask, resting uneasily upon his skull. He took a deeper draught of the wine and sighed heavily.

'Nothing is eternal,' he said at last. 'No matter what we believe.' The high priest sat back in his chair, turning the polished cup in his hands. 'Who remembers the names of the gods we worshipped in the jungles, before we came to the Blessed Land? No one. Not even the oldest scrolls in Mahrak speak of them.' He glanced up at the king. 'Did they abandon us, or did we abandon them?' Akhmen-hotep scowled at his brother.

'Who knows?' he said. 'That was a different age. We are not the people we once were.'

'That is my point,' the high priest said. 'You ask if the gods have forsaken us. Perhaps it would be better to ask if we have grown estranged from them. Nagash may be the herald of a new age for our people.'

'How can you say that?' Akhmen-hotep snarled. 'You, of all people!' Memnet was unfazed by the king's accusatory tone.

'The role of a priest is about more than making sacrifices and collecting tithes,' he said. 'We are also the bearers of deeper truths. That is the charge that the gods lay upon us.' His gaze fell to the shadows upon the ground. 'Those truths are not always pleasant to hear.'

Akhmen-hotep considered this as he peered into the depths of his cup. Despair ate at him, draining the colour from his face. Then, slowly but surely, his expression hardened. His brows drew together and his lips pressed into a thin, determined line.

'I will tell you what I think,' he said slowly. 'I think that the truth is what we make of it. Else, why would we have need for kings at all?' He raised the cup to his lips and emptied it in one long swallow, and then held the empty vessel up to his eyes. His fist tightened, the tendons on the back of his scarred hand growing as taut as cords as he slowly crushed the metal cup. 'Nothing is preordained, so long as we have the courage to fight for what we believe.' He tossed the lump of metal onto the ground. 'We will cast down the Usurper and drive his spirit into the wastes where he belongs. We will make this land right again, because I am the king and I command that it be so!'

Memnet raised his eyes to the king and studied him for a long moment. His eyes were like dark pools, depthless and inscrutable. A ghost of a smile flitted across his face.

'I expected no less from you, brother,' he said.

The king made to reply, but faint sounds beyond the confines of the tent made him pause. He scowled, listening intently. Memnet cocked his head to one side and listened as well.

'Someone is shouting,' he said.

'Not just one,' the king answered thoughtfully. 'Perhaps it is Pakh-amn, leading his soldiers back into camp. They've been putting out fires in the city all evening.' The Grand Hierophant stared at the dregs in his cup.

'Keep a close eye on that one, brother,' he warned. 'He grows more dangerous every day.'

Akhmen-hotep shook his head dismissively, saying, 'Pakh-amn is young and proud, to be sure, but dangerous?' Yet even as he said it, he recalled the tense confrontation just before the battle today. *Lead on then. For so long as you live.*

'He has regained some of the respect he lost at Zedri,' the high priest said. 'His cavalrymen cheered his name when the battle was done.'

'And what is wrong with that?' the king asked, though he could not help but feel a twinge of apprehension.

'The Master of Horse has made it plain that he opposes the war against the Usurper,' the Grand Hierophant said. 'Who can say what he might do if he found himself in a position of influence over much of the army?'

The shouts were still distant, but growing more intense by the moment. Finally the king could stand it no longer.

'What would you have me do, brother?' he asked, reaching for his sword. 'Pakh-amn served me well on the battlefield today. I have no reason to suspect him.'

'Nor will you, if he is clever,' Memnet pointed out. 'Watch him closely. That is all I ask.'

Akhmen-hotep glowered at the priest. 'Bad enough that we must guard against the schemes of the Blasphemer,' he growled. 'Now you would have me question the honour of my noblemen.'

Before Memnet could reply, the king snatched up his sword from a nearby table and strode swiftly out into the cold night air. With an effort of will he tried to banish his brother's dire observations from his mind as he hurried in the direction of the voices, flanked by four Ushabti who had been standing guard outside the king's tent.

The shouts carried easily in the chill air, coming from the western edge of the camp. Akhmen-hotep quickened his pace at the sounds of alarm that were spreading among the tents of the Bronze Host. Men were stumbling out into the darkness, their armour half-on and their weapons in their hands. A flash of movement to the king's right drew his eye. He saw a pair of

Neru's acolytes stumbling down an adjoining lane, half-carrying a third acolyte between them. Their ceremonial garments were speckled with blood. Muttering a curse, the king broke into a run.

As he drew near the edge of the camp, Akhmen-hotep began to encounter groups of panicked men running the other way. Their kilts were stained with dust and soot, and their faces were pale with fright. The men were blind to the presence of the king in their midst, rushing past him like a flock of startled birds, intent on nothing more than running east as quickly as they could.

Five minutes later the king found himself at the edge of the sprawling camp. He came upon a scene of chaos and confusion. A nobleman on horseback was shouting orders and trying to control his plunging mount at the same time, while a small group of warriors was pulling open the crude enclosure holding the barbarian prisoners they'd taken in battle. A second enclosure, built to contain the imprisoned members of Bel Aliad's City Companies, had already been opened, and the prisoners were milling around the moonlit plain in confusion.

Akhmen-hotep ran up to the shouting horseman, realising at the last moment that it was Pakh-amn.

'What is going on?' he shouted up at the Master of Horse.

Pakh-amn twisted in the saddle and stared wide-eyed at the sudden appearance of the king. 'They're coming!' he said hoarsely.

'What?' the king asked. He looked around, trying to make sense of the scene. 'Who is coming?' The young nobleman eyed the throng of milling prisoners and cursed under his breath. He leaned down until his face was just inches from the king's.

'Who do you think?' he hissed. 'The people of Bel Aliad have risen in their multitudes, great one. They set upon us as we were leaving the city and killed a third of my men. The rest of us ran the entire way back to camp, but even so, we haven't much time. The dead are rising from the battlefield, too, and are heading this way even as we speak.'

Akhmen-hotep felt his blood turn to ice as he heard the news. 'But there were no sorcerers in the city,' he protested numbly. 'Suhedir al-Khazem swore an oath on it.'

'Go and see the carnage at the city gates if you don't believe me,' Pakh-amn snarled. 'Old men with their stomachs torn open, mothers with slit throats and trampled children. They came at us out of the side streets and alleys and tore my men apart with their bare hands!'

The king's shock melted beneath the young noble's acid tone. He glowered up at the Master of Horse, and replied, 'Even so, we have the wards. The priests of Neru–'

'Are dead or dying,' Pakh-amn shot back. 'They were ambushed a short while ago as they walked their circuit. We heard hoof beats off to the north, probably light horsemen armed with bows. Neru's holy wards have no power over a flight of arrows.'

The king gritted his teeth at the news, remembering the trio of wounded acolytes he'd seen earlier. He considered the unfolding situation quickly, and his heart sank at the realisation that he'd been caught in the jaws of a trap. The battle they'd fought earlier in the day had only been a prelude, meant to wear his men out and swell the numbers of the enemy's forces even further. The king drew a deep breath.

'It's good that you thought to free the prisoners,' he said heavily.

Pakh-amn bared his teeth. 'If the gods are good, the fiends will go for them first and give us time to get out of here,' he hissed. The nobleman's cold-blooded tactic took the king aback.

'We'll form up the host here,' he said, 'between Bel Aliad and the camp. Perhaps we can find some spare weapons and arm the City Companies–'

Forgetting himself completely, Pakh-amn glowered at the king.

'Are you mad?' he snapped. 'Even had we the time to form up the army, the men are exhausted and the horses are blown, and the dead won't bother forming into companies and marching to battle. They'll lap around our flanks and swarm like ants over the camp.'

'Then what would you have me do, Master of Horse?' Akhmen-hotep growled threateningly.

Pakh-amn blinked at the king's tone, perhaps realising how far he'd overstepped his bounds.

'We must flee,' he answered, his voice more subdued, 'right now, while there's still time. Gather the Bhagarites and see if they can lose us among the sands.'

The king's lip curled in distaste, but there was some sense in the young noble's words. If he offered battle he risked playing further into his enemy's hands. The thought of such an ignominious flight went ill with the king, but they'd done what they'd come to do. They'd fulfilled their obligation to their allies. Now, their only obligation was to themselves and their city.

To the king's left, a group of barbarians began to shout, pointing off to the west and babbling in their guttural tongue. Akhmen-hotep stepped away from Pakh-amn's horse and peered westward.

At first, it seemed as if the broken plain was slowly undulating, like sluggish waves along the surface of a river, but as the king's eyes adjusted to the shadows he could make out round, drooping heads and slumped shoulders, dark and tattered beneath Neru's silver light. A shambling mob of figures limped and lurched its way silently towards the camp. Some brandished axes or spears, while others reached for their distant prey with bare and bloodied hands. The leading edge of the horde was less than a mile away, advancing at a slow, relentless pace. Akhmen-hotep felt their mindless hunger like a cold blade pressed against his skin.

The men of the City Companies saw the undead creatures too. Some of the men called out tentatively to the approaching figures, thinking that their kin had come to pay the ransom for their release.

In a few more minutes the slaughter would begin, and panic would spread like a desert wind through the camp. If they were to have any chance to escape at all, the king knew that they would have to act quickly. Sick at heart, the king turned back to Pakh-amn.

'Go and rouse your horsemen,' he told the young nobleman. 'You'll have to be our rearguard as we try to withdraw.'

Pakh-amn stared at the king for a long moment, his dark eyes hidden by shadow. Finally he gave a curt nod and kicked his horse into a gallop. The king watched the Master of Horse disappear deeper into the camp, and then began issuing orders to his bodyguards.

'Rouse the company commanders at once,' he told them. 'Tell them to muster their troops and gather everything they can carry. We move out in fifteen minutes.'

The Ushabti bowed quickly and raced off into the darkness. Akhmen-hotep looked around and saw that the mercenaries were already gone, fleeing pell-mell off to the south. The warriors of Bel Aliad were heading westwards in a ragged mob, calling out to figures that they vaguely recognised among the approaching horde.

Burning with shame, Akhmen-hotep said a short prayer to Usirian, that their souls might find their way safely into the afterlife. Then he turned and raced for the centre of the camp.

The walking dead of Bel Aliad were methodical in their work. They stumbled after their screaming kinsmen, dragging them to the ground and stabbing them with spears or tearing them open with tooth and claw. The warriors of the City Companies fled in every direction, but they were weary from a long day of battle and terrified beyond reason at the sight of the bloodstained monsters that had once been their wives and children. Some tried to fight, taking up rocks or pieces of wood and striking in vain at the tide of relentless corpses. Others tried to hide amid the broken ground, cowering behind boulders or burying themselves in drifts of sand, until clumsy, grasping fingers closed around their throats. Still others begged for mercy, appealing to those among the horde whom they knew by name. In every case, the result was the same. The men died, slowly and terribly, and then, within minutes, they rose anew and joined in the hunt.

When the men of the City Companies were no more, the undead army combed the darkness for the pale-skinned northmen. The hulking barbarians swore wild oaths and called upon their rough-hewn gods as they fought, smashing skulls and breaking bones even as cold, dry teeth closed upon their throats. For all their struggles, the horde claimed them as well.

The last to die were the city's proud rulers. They stumbled from the empty camp of the Bronze Host and found their people waiting for them on the broken plain. Silently, reverently, the dead of Bel Aliad surrounded the princes and tore them limb from limb. Suhedir al-Khazem was eaten alive by his three daughters, watching in mute, insensate horror as they dug their fingers into his abdomen and tore his entrails free.

All the while the Bronze Host of Ka-Sabar was fleeing further and further into the desert, carrying only what the weary soldiers could sling upon their backs. They moved in silence, casting fearful glances back at their abandoned tents and wondering when the first packs of shambling corpses would find their trail, and the long hunt would begin.

Sitting atop his rotting horse on a sand dune to the north, Arkhan the Black watched the army retreat into the merciless desert, and smiled. For a moment, just before the city's dead reached the enemy camp, he'd feared that Akhmen-hotep would offer battle instead of retreating. That would have complicated his master's plans. Fortunately, the doomed king had chosen to enter the trap instead.

The immortal waited with deathless patience until the last of the enemy warriors had vanished across the rolling hills of sand. Then he nudged his dead mount forwards with a creak of old leather and a rattle of bones. At once, his squadron of skeletal horsemen followed, their harnesses rattling hollowly in the waning moonlight.

EIGHTEEN

SEALED IN STONE

Khemri, the Living City,
in the 45th year of Ptra the Glorious
(-1959 Imperial Reckoning)

The wails of drugged and terrified victims created a shrill counterpoint to the furious chants echoing in the great throne room deep within the Great Pyramid. Nagash stood within a carefully marked ritual circle, not far from where the barbarian witch Drutheira had met a gruesome end not twenty-four hours before. Khefru had worked frantically to clear away the bodies, and then find an unmarked part of the floor where he could inscribe the ritual circle. Only the remnants of Asaph's shattered head, and the grisly remains beneath, still remained as proof of the magical duel waged on the previous night.

The braziers were burning brightly, and clouds of incense hung above the gathered nobles. All forty of Nagash's allies were in attendance, in two groups of twenty. While a score of the noblemen stood around the perimeter of the circle and joined in the invocations, the rest kept a close watch on the waiting sacrifices. Many of the victims were slaves, bought in the market near the docks that very day. Others were drunkards or gamblers, who had the misfortune of being in the wrong place at the wrong time when one of Nagash's men passed by. Their senses were dulled by wine or black lotus root, or numbed by the mild narcotic mixed with the burning incense, but even so they could not help but be aware of the terrible fate that awaited them.

Nagash led each ritual, his powerful voice rising to a crescendo as the victim caught within his grip began to burn. He drank deeply of their souls and wove the energy into the greater incantation that he'd begun hours earlier, feeding the curse that continued to plague the noble-born of Khemri. Beneath his ritual robes his torso was bandaged from his shoulders to his waist, and his cheeks were burned from the touch of the druchii's sorcery. His arms, particularly the one that Drutheira had cut, ached down to the very bone. It was all he could do to move them, much less grip each squirming slave and tear free his soul. What sustained him was the memory of his victory over his erstwhile tutors, and the knowledge that the throne he'd coveted for so long was nearly within his grasp. Another week, perhaps two, enough time for the plague to claim the last of the city's high nobility and provoke the angry citizens to riot, and he would be ready to make his move.

The victim within his hands went limp, his screams dwindling to a breathless whimper as his body burst into a hissing plume of green flame. Nagash felt the sorcerous fire lick up his arms and threw back his head in exultation as the young man's lifeforce passed through him. Not for the first time, he felt the heady, fleeting rush of youth and wondered if there might be some way to make that vigour his own.

Nagash scarcely felt the slave's body crumble to ash in his hands. He added the stolen life-force to the fabric of the curse and brought the Incantation of Reaping to a conclusion. The necromancer swayed slightly, drunk from the taste of so much power. By his count they had sacrificed half of the night's bounty so far.

'You are dismissed,' he told the men standing around the circle. 'Go and send the others to me.' Then he beckoned to Khefru, who waited in the shadows near the dais. 'Wine,' he commanded.

The servant approached with a small jug and a goblet made of beaten gold. Nagash snatched the jug from Khefru's hand and raised it to his lips. He drank deep, slaking his burning thirst.

'Better,' he said huskily, handing the jug back to his servant. The vessel fell through Khefru's slack fingers and smashed upon the stones, mingling wine with the piled ash of the sacrifices.

'Clumsy fool!' Nagash snarled. 'Sop it up at once. Drink it down if you have to! If your act of carelessness breaches the ritual inscriptions...' The necromancer paused, suddenly noticing the look of dumb horror on the young priest's face. Nagash cuffed his servant on the ear. 'Have you not heard a single thing I've said to you?' Khefru's sallow face had turned pale. He pointed a trembling finger at the knot of wailing victims.

'That girl there,' he said. 'The young one, with the gold circlet around her arm.'

Nagash scowled irritably at the huddled mass of wretches. After a moment, he caught sight of the one to whom the priest referred. She was very young, supple and strong, with a slightly exotic cast to her eyes. He reckoned a girl like her must have been worth her weight in silver on the block.

'What of her, damn you?' he asked.

'She's no slave,' Khefru said, his voice thick with dread. 'Can't you see? She's Lahmian. I've seen her before. She's one of the queen's personal servants!' The news gave Nagash pause.

'Surely not,' he said, studying the girl more closely. 'Perhaps she was taken in a raid, part of some caravan bound for Lybaras, or possibly even Mahrak.'

'No!' Khefru moaned. 'I've seen her at the palace! What slave would be put on the block with a gold circlet still around her arm?' Forgetting himself, the priest gripped Nagash's left arm. 'I warned you about this, time and again! Someone, perhaps Shepsu-hur, perhaps Arkhan, got lazy and careless, and took the first person that caught his fancy, and now we're undone! The queen won't rest until she's learned who took her maid!'

Nagash shook off Khefru's panicked grip. He beckoned impatiently to the second group of nobles, which, interestingly, contained both Shepsu-hur and Arkhan.

'Quickly!' he snapped. 'Bring her first, the young one, with the gold circlet on her arm. Now!' Khefru's eyes widened in horror.

'You can't mean to kill her?' he asked. The necromancer's hands clenched into fists.

'Do you imagine we can send her back to the palace, after all she's seen?' he hissed. 'Gather what's left of your courage, you simpleton. We've almost reached the end. In another week, two at most, none of this will matter any more.'

To Nagash's surprise, Khefru refused to yield. 'You can't do this!' he said. 'I won't–'

Before he could say any more, a fierce shout rang across the throne room from the south side of the chamber, followed by cries of surprise and fear from among Nagash's minions.

The crowd along the south side of the chamber seemed to recoil from a fierce, golden radiance that shone between a pair of columns at the midpoint of the room. Nagash saw Arkhan, who was leading the second group of noblemen and dragging the young maid by the arm, glance to his right and turn pale with shock. Weeping in relief, the maid tore loose from Arkhan's grip and ran towards the light.

Nagash turned on his heel and dashed up to the dais, climbing the cracked stone steps until he could see over the panicked, milling mob. At once, he found himself staring into the angry eyes of his brother, Thutep.

The young king was dressed as though for war, armoured in a bronze breastplate and woven leather bands that covered his arms and legs. He carried a gleaming khopesh in his right hand, and the golden headdress of Settra rested upon his brow. Thutep was surrounded by a dozen of his Ushabti, and it was from them that the golden light of Ptra shone like a lamp, chasing back the room's dreadful shadows. The devoted were armed and armoured, too, and their handsome faces were set into masks of righteous rage. Within the protective circle of the bodyguards, a few paces behind the king, stood the regal figure of Hapshur, the High Priestess of Neru. The priestess clutched her slender staff of office and gazed angrily at the tumult that surrounded her. On Thutep's left side, the queen's young maid knelt at the king's feet, her forehead pressed to the flagstones.

When Thutep saw his brother, his handsome face twisted into a mask of grief-stricken rage.

'Ghazid tried to warn me about you,' he said to Nagash, his powerful voice cutting through the clamour like a knife. 'He said you were a threat, not just to me, but to Khemri. And gods, now I see that he was right all along!'

Nagash smiled coldly at the king. 'That was your trouble all along, brother. You were always too sentimental, too afraid to hurt those around you. You wanted to be loved,' he sneered, 'but for a king to rule, he must be feared.'

The necromancer spread his arms wide, encompassing the entire chamber. 'No one in all of Nehekhara fears you, brother. Least of all me.'

'Heretic!' Hapshur cried, brandishing her staff at Nagash. 'You are an abomination before the gods, and a traitor to your priesthood! The hour of your reckoning is at hand!'

Thutep pointed his curved sword at Nagash, and said, 'There is no escape, brother. Companies of the City Watch surround the pyramid, and we know where all the exits lie. In the name of Ptra, the Great Father, you and your followers are under arrest. When the sun rises tomorrow you will be put on trial for your crimes in the temple square at Khemri, and the servants of the gods will pass judgement upon you.'

Moans of despair rose from Nagash's minions, but the necromancer felt only a rising tide of icy rage.

'You would have a reckoning then, brother?' he said. 'So be it.'

The necromancer flung out his hand and spat a string of arcane syllables, unleashing a torrent of sizzling, glowing darts that streaked over the heads of his men and chewed Hapshur apart. The high priestess let out a single, lingering shriek as her body was shredded by sorcerous teeth. Thutep and his bodyguards were all caught in the fine spray of blood and minced flesh.

'Destroy them!' Nagash commanded.

Faced with such a display of power, his men did not hesitate to obey. The noblemen drew knives and swords and rushed at the king's bodyguards from all sides, but despite heavily outnumbering the dozen glowing bodyguards, Nagash's men were completely outmatched. Blessed by Ptra with superhuman speed and strength, not to mention a lifetime devoted to mastering the arts of combat, the young devoted met the noblemen with a fierce shout of joy and began a terrible slaughter.

As young and relatively inexperienced as the Ushabti were, their skill and ferocity were appalling. Noblemen fell like ripe wheat, most cut down before they could even lay a single blow. Unless something was done, the battle would be over in moments.

Nagash hissed the Incantation of Reaping and drank in the life energy of the slain noblemen. With their raw souls bubbling in his veins, he threw out his hands once more and unleashed spell after spell, hurling bolts of pure darkness into the tight circle of bodyguards. Each bolt found a mark, sinking effortlessly through the armour of the devoted and rending flesh and muscle beneath. The Ushabti staggered beneath the blows, but fought on, sustained by their vows to Ptra.

The necromancer's minions grew more cautious, focusing their efforts on the most wounded bodyguards. An Ushabti reeled as one of Nagash's bolts peeled back the right side of his face. Sensing an opportunity, one of the noblemen lunged forwards, hacking his blade into the bodyguard's throat. Even as the devoted fell, his sword licked out in a backhanded swipe that cut his attacker in half, and the two men died at nearly the same moment.

Nagash reaped the dying nobleman's soul and continued to punish the devoted with a barrage of lethal magic. When the Ushabti surged forwards, trying to use Nagash's men to shield them from his spells, he opened pits of shadow at their feet. When the survivors reeled back to safer ground, he speared them with bolts of sizzling black flame. It wasn't just Nagash that the Ushabti had to worry about, for Arkhan and a few of the more magically adept nobles joined in too. They flung darts point-blank into the beleaguered Ushabti, striking them from unexpected directions and creating more opportunities for their fellow nobles.

Thutep stood his ground through it all, shouting encouragement to his men. More than once he tried to join the fight, only to be pushed back by his men. Their courage and devotion were a wonder to behold, but one by one the devoted were overwhelmed. Within minutes after the fight began, the last Ushabti succumbed, his sword buried in the chest of another of Nagash's men.

The surviving noblemen clambered over the bodies of their dead compatriots and closed like jackals around the king. Thutep glared defiantly at the necromancer's henchmen, his sword held ready. On impulse, he glanced down at the girl, still cowering at his feet, and murmured a quick command. Fleet as a deer, she leapt thankfully to her feet and raced into the shadows behind Thutep, fleeing to the surface and safety.

It was the last free act that Thutep ever made. At that moment, Nagash cast a powerful spell that gripped his brother's mind in a vice. He stiffened, his face growing slack with horror as Nagash exerted his will over the king.

The necromancer's henchmen saw the king's transformation and stayed their hands. Most reeled back in exhaustion, grateful beyond words that the battle was done. A circle of torn and bleeding corpses surrounded the king and his fallen bodyguards. Slightly more than half of Nagash's men were dead, and the rest counted themselves lucky not to be among them.

Nagash descended from the dais, still pinning his brother in place by sorcery and the weight of his prodigious will. He approached his brother, his cold features lit with triumph. The necromancer stood before Thutep, his eyes blazing. Slowly, deliberately, he reached up and lifted away the king's royal headdress.

Thutep's body trembled with outrage, but he could not make his muscles obey. The necromancer smiled.

'Go on,' he said. 'Strike me down. You still hold your sword. All you need is the will to use it.' Nagash took his time arranging Settra's headdress upon his brow, and then reached down and took Thutep's sword hand by the wrist. 'Here. Let me help you.'

He raised Thutep's sword arm and placed the curved edge of the khopesh against his throat. 'There. All you need is a simple flick of the wrist and you'll slice open the artery. What could be simpler than that? Go on. I won't stop you.'

Thutep's entire body trembled. His eyes were wide and unblinking, his face flushed with effort. A single tear coursed down his cheek. The khopesh did not move.

Nagash sneered in disdain.

'How pathetic,' he said, and turned away. 'Seize him, and follow me.'

All at once, the force gripping the king vanished. Thutep, still straining at his bonds, all but fell into the arms of Nagash's minions. His sword was plucked from his hands and his arms twisted behind his back. The king hung limply in their grip as the noblemen followed Nagash from the hall.

They took the king through the north passage, down into the depths of the pyramid where their father Khetep was laid to rest. The dead king's crypt was one among many, set aside for not only his wife, his bodyguards and his servants, but for his children as well. The Great Pyramid was meant to house not just one king, but an entire dynasty.

Nagash led the way into the crypts, lighting the path with a pale grave-light that seemed to emanate from his skin. Thutep quickly realised what was happening, and began to struggle with his captors.

'You can't do this, brother,' he said. 'The people won't permit it! You're a priest, consecrated to the gods. You can't sit upon the throne!'

'I am consecrated to no god, brother,' Nagash spat. 'I served the will of Settra, king of kings, but that time is past. Tonight, a new era has been born. It's a pity you won't see its glories unfold.'

Thutep only struggled harder, until two men had to take hold of each of his arms and drag him along the dank stones.

'You're mad!' he cried. 'The other kings will rise against you! Can't you see that?'

'I understand the political realities far better than you, little brother,' Nagash snapped. 'Let them come. I will be ready for them.'

Nagash paused. They had come to the end of a long passageway, lined with smooth, blank walls. The architects had left them unadorned on purpose, so that after Thutep died a host of artisans could come and create elaborate mosaics that would depict the glories of his reign. At the end of the passageway stood a narrow doorway, flanked by two stone horex. A huge slab of stone rested against the wall to the right of the opening.

The necromancer's light penetrated some way into the burial chamber, revealing a small room with more bare walls and a pedestal intended to hold the king's sarcophagus. Nagash gestured, and his men shoved Thutep inside. He landed hard against the stone pedestal and whirled, his expression still defiant.

'Do you have the nerve to kill me with your own hand, brother?' he snarled. 'Or will you stand there in the corridor and send in your jackals to finish the job? The gods do not countenance the murder of a king. It has been that way since the dawn of civilisation. By striking me down, you will damn yourself.'

Nagash only laughed while his men went to work around him.

'I have no intention of killing you, brother,' he said. 'Nor will any of my men raise a hand against you. I wouldn't dare, but not for the reason you might think. You see, there's another law I have to be wary of, even older than the one you described: the one that says that a man's murderer is forbidden to marry his widow.'

The look of shock and anguish on Thutep's face was priceless. Nagash savoured every moment of it, right up to the point that Arkhan and his men pushed the stone slab into the doorway and buried the king alive.

NINETEEN

BLOOD AND WATER

The Fountains of Eternal Life,
in the 63rd year of Ptra the Glorious
(-1744 Imperial Reckoning)

The priests were kept busy throughout the night as the army prepared for battle. Neru's acolytes paced the sprawling perimeter of the allied camp, raising their eyes to the face of the goddess and filling the cold air with song to keep the spirits of the wastes at bay. Around the campfires, hammers clattered against bronze as warriors made last-minute repairs to chariots or mended their battle-harnesses. Men prayed as they worked. Some called upon Ptra to drive their enemies before them, while others beseeched mighty Geheb to lend them the strength to overcome their foes. Still others made worship to ashen-faced Djaf, God of Death, praying that their blows struck clean and true. The rattle and murmur of the enormous host mingled with the cries of oxen, goats and lambs as the priests led their charges from the sacrificial pens and dragged them before red-stained altars in the centre of the camp. The clamour of the army ebbed and flowed across the sands like the restless breath of a vast, elemental beast.

The army of the Usurper waited little more than three miles away, across rolling dunes and a broad, rocky plain. Small campfires flickered among the hundreds of dark tents, and from time to time the nervous whicker of a horse would reach the ears of the allied sentries, but otherwise the enemy camp was eerily still.

At the centre of the vast encampment, ringed by scores of watchful Ushabti, Rakh-amn-hotep listened to his scouts' reports and contemplated the field of battle for the coming day. Long after he'd dismissed his captains to their tents, the king perched on a camp stool and brooded over the large map arrayed before him, studying the positions of his and his enemy's troops. From time to time his champion, Ekhreb, would rise from his chair near the entrance to the large tent and fill the king's empty cup with a mix of herbs and watered wine. At the far side of the tent's central chamber the King of

Lybaras reclined upon a dust-stained divan. The papyrus sheets resting in his lap fluttered slightly as Hekhmenukep snored, his chin resting upon his narrow chest.

Two hours before dawn the army's slaves rose from the cold ground and began preparing the morning meal. Bowls of grain porridge were passed out to the thousands of grim-faced warriors, along with a palm-sized piece of unleavened bread and a single cup of water. Among the tents of the noblemen, those who could bring themselves to eat breakfasted on bread and olives, goat's cheese and river fowl. Their wine was thick and resinous, for no water could be spared to thin it.

Half an hour before sunrise, as the sky was paling to the east, the army began to muster. Horses thundered down the camp's narrow lanes as the kings despatched the first orders of the day to their companies. File leaders bellowed orders to their troops, drawing them from their tents and forming them into lines. The rumble of man-made thunder and a furious shriek of steam sounded in the north-eastern quarter of the camp, setting the Rasetran cavalry rearing and stamping in fright as the Lybaran war machines stirred to life. Six huge figures reared slowly into the brightening sky, their heavy armour plates grating and groaning as they shifted against one another.

The earth shook as the giants climbed ponderously to their feet. Their faces, carved from wood and sheathed in burnished copper, bore visages meant to win the favour of the gods: a snarling hound's face, in honour of Geheb; the cunning, enigmatic jackal favoured by Djaf; or Phakth's haughty, cruel falcon. The warriors of Rasetra and Lybaras stared in awe as the great engines hefted massive stone maces and took their first steps towards the battlefield. Few noticed that the army's war scorpions were nowhere to be seen. Like their patron, Sokth, the stealthy machines had slipped away in the night, leaving only piles of churned sand to show where they had been.

The stirring of the war machines brought answering bellows from the south-eastern quarter of the camp, as the living war machines of the Rasetran army raised their armoured snouts and challenged the distant giants. The thunder-lizards were massive, humpbacked creatures, with squat legs the size of tree trunks and powerful, lashing tails that were knobbed at the end like maces. The beasts were sluggish in the early morning chill, despite sleeping on sands heated by the warmth of a score of blazing fires. Their handlers, lean, agile lizardmen from the southern jungles, prodded the creatures to their feet with long, spearlike sticks and clambered up their sides into howdahs of wood and canvas fitted to their armoured backs. Packs of lizardman auxiliaries crowded the field around their massive cousins, whispering to one another in their hissing, clacking tongue. Some showed off the bloodstained skulls they had taken in battle the day before, inviting their fellows to taste the trophies with flicks of their dark, forked tongues.

Just as the first rays of sunlight broke over the far horizon, a chorus of trumpets pealed from the centre of the camp and the infantry began to move. The forward edge of the battle-line, twenty thousand men, formed into ten companies stretching nearly five miles from north to south, advanced under the watchful stares of their noble commanders and the leathery curses of their file leaders. The cavalry rode in their wake: eight thousand light horsemen, five thousand heavy horse and two thousand chariots, plus another twenty thousand reserves and auxiliaries. Behind them, striding through swirling clouds of dust, came the titanic war machines of Lybaras and the bellowing thunder lizards of Rasetra. Last of all came the multicoloured processions of the army's priests: servants of Ptra and Geheb, Phakth and Neru, and even priests of Tahoth the Scholar in their gleaming vestments of copper and glass.

The armies of the East marched to battle with the rising sun at their backs and the shadows of night retreating before them.

The bow of the sky-boat pitched and rolled as the sun churned the air above the rolling dunes, making Rakh-amn-hotep glad that he had resisted the urge to eat a hearty breakfast before heading for the battle-line. Beside him, Hekhmenukep swayed like a palm tree in a storm, relaying instructions to his signallers as easily as if he were reclining in his tent back at camp. The King of Rasetra gripped the bow rail in one white-knuckled hand and resolved not to embarrass himself in front of the scholar-king.

Scores of Lybarans crowded the decks of the sky-ship as it floated along behind the advancing army. Four teams of signallers lined the ship's rails, clutching their dish-shaped bronze reflectors and periodically gauging the angle of the blazing sun. Behind them, a company of archers sat crosslegged down the centre of the deck, their long bows resting within easy reach as they chatted or played at games of dice. At the stern, surrounding the sky-boat's complicated set of rudders, two dozen young priests chanted invocations to the air spirits that kept the vessel aloft. Farther off to the east, trailing well behind the advancing army, came the remainder of the Lybaran sky-boats, the seven stately craft casting long shadows across the rolling terrain beneath their keels.

Two hundred feet below, the allied army advanced steadily across the broken plain towards their waiting foe. At such a distance, none of the rumble and clatter of an army on the march reached Rakh-amn-hotep's ears, which only served to deepen his unease.

'I feel like a spectator up here,' he said, half to himself. He glanced at Hekhmenukep. 'Are you certain this will work? What if the army can't read our signals?' The King of Lybaras gave Rakh-amn-hotep a condescending smile.

'There are Lybaran signallers with every company,' he said, as though reassuring an anxious child. 'We have spent centuries refining this system in elaborate games of war. It cannot fail.' Rakh-amn-hotep stared thoughtfully at the Lybraran king.

'How many times have you used it in a real battle?' he asked. Hekhmenukep's confident smile faltered a bit.

'Well...' he began.

'That's what I was afraid of,' the Rasetran king growled. For a fleeting moment he considered asking Hekhmenukep to be set down with the rest of the army, but having orders issued from the ground *and* the air would only increase the risk of confusion. Scowling, he turned his attention to the battlefield below and tried to work out the enemy's dispositions.

From Rakh-amn-hotep's vantage point, the army of the Usurper was laid out before him like tokens on a battle-map. Companies of blue-clad Zandri archers formed a skirmish line some fifty yards in front of a veritable wall of enemy spearmen, anchored on the trade road to the north and stretching for more than four miles in a shallow crescent to the south. The enemy companies were less numerous, but individually larger than the allied formations, five ranks to the allies' three. The king spied still more companies held in reserve behind the front rank, reinforcing the enemy centre and right. As near as he could reckon, the combined forces of the Usurper outnumbered the allied infantry by more than twenty thousand men. Large squadrons of Numasi light horsemen prowled along the flanks of the enemy army, alert for any attempts to sweep around the battle-line, and a large block of heavy horsemen waited behind a set of dunes along the enemy's left flank. Two more formations waited at the rear of the Usurper's force, but they were cloaked in the mists rising from the Fountains: chariots, or perhaps even catapults, the king surmised.

'Seventy, perhaps eighty thousand troops,' Rakh-amn-hotep mused. 'It appears that Ka-Sabar's diversion to the south wasn't as successful as we hoped. That must be all the fighting men of Khemri, Numas and Zandri combined.' He leaned against the rail, studying the formations more carefully. 'Still no tents, as reported at Zedri. Where are the Usurper and his pale-skinned monsters?' Hekhmenukep considered this.

'Perhaps they are hidden in the mists surrounding the fountains,' he suggested.

'Perhaps,' Rakh-amn-hotep agreed. 'At Zedri, he revealed himself only when his army was on the verge of defeat. It's possible that he thinks he can carry this battle on the strength of his army alone.' The king folded his arms and scowled at the enemy troops.

'No. There's more to it than that. Something is wrong here, but I can't put my finger on it.'

Hekhmenukep joined the Rasetran king at the rail and spent several long moments surveying the broken plain. Finally he said, 'Where are the bodies?'

'Bodies?'

The Lybaran king indicated the plain with a sweep of his hand, and said, 'This is where you fought the enemy vanguard yesterday, correct? You told me that there were hundreds of dead from both sides.'

'More on their side than ours,' Rakh-amn-hotep interjected.

'But what happened to the bodies?' the Lybaran asked. 'The plain should be covered in bloating corpses and flocks of vultures, but there's nothing there.' Rakh-amn-hotep considered this.

'That's it,' he said at last. 'Yes, it must be! Nagash used his damnable sorcery to animate the dead and...' He swept his gaze across the battlefield, looking for clues. 'He could have marched them into the mists to conceal them as a reserve force.'

'Why not simply bury them in the ground where they fell?' Hekhmenukep suggested. 'Then they could spring up behind us as our companies advanced.'

The Rasetran king shook his head, and said, 'The ground is too rocky to allow it, and we'd see the churned ground from here besides.' Once again, he studied the enemy's dispositions. 'The enemy has reinforced its lines in the centre and on their right, leaving the left flank relatively weak. They want us to throw our weight against the left, drawing us forwards as their companies retreat, and then counter-charge with their heavy cavalry to stop us in our tracks. That leaves us overextended and weak on their right flank, ripe for a counter-attack from the south.' Rakh-amn-hotep pointed off into the dunes beyond the enemy's right flank. 'The dead are waiting out there in the sands,' he declared. 'That's what Nagash is planning. I'd wager my life on it.'

Hekhmenukep considered this, before saying, 'I can't fault your reasoning, but how do we counter it?'

'We shift the bulk of our reserves to the south,' the Rasetran king ordered. 'Alert the commanders to watch for counter-attacks. Then we see about turning the tables on the Usurper's forces to the north.'

Rakh-amn-hotep began to issue instructions to the waiting Lybaran signallers, his commands growing swifter and more assured as the pieces of his battle-plan fell neatly into place. Within minutes the signal-men were at work, flashing messages to the troops on the ground, and the Rasetran king grinned fiercely as the allied army went into action.

Even with the wonders of the Lybaran sun-signals, rearranging the dispositions of the allied army took up much of the morning. Huge clouds of dust churned above the plain, masking the movements of the allied companies as they headed to their new positions. Other than a few desultory probes from enemy light horsemen to the south, the Usurper's army made no move to interfere with the allies' manoeuvres.

Rakh-amn-hotep sipped watered wine from a golden goblet as the army completed its final adjustments along the great plain. Hekhmenukep waited alongside the Rasetran, contemplating the waiting enemy forces.

'Four hours, and they've barely moved,' he said. 'It's as though we don't matter to them at all.'

'Oh, we matter,' Rakh-amn-hotep said, 'but it doesn't profit them to come out and challenge us. Remember Nemuhareb's mistake at the Gates of the Dawn? He could have sat and defended the fortifications at the gates and probably driven us back, but his pride got the better of him. Nagash knows that time is on his side. He's got the fountains at his back. All he has to do is hold us at bay, and the heat will do his work for him.' The Rasetran took another sip of wine. 'That's why we have to risk everything on one, fierce assault,' he said. 'We break through his lines with our first attempt, or probably not at all. Each successive attack will be weaker than the one before.'

A signaller on the starboard rail flashed an acknowledgement to the forces on the ground. The nobleman in charge of the team strode quickly to the waiting kings and bowed deeply, before saying, 'All is in readiness, great ones.'

Rakh-amn-hotep nodded.

'Very well,' he said, and smiled at Hekhmenukep. 'Time to roll the dice,' he said, turning to the signaller. 'Send the order to begin the advance.'

The command was passed among the men, and within moments all of the bronze discs were flashing the signal in hot bursts of light. The kings heard the wail of war-horns on the plain below, and with a muted roar the vast battleline of the eastern armies began their attack.

Rakh-amn-hotep had shifted the entire weight of the allied infantry southwards, arraying them against the centre and right flank of the Usurper's host. Ten thousand Rasetran warriors marched in the front ranks, striding shoulder-to-shoulder with their broad wooden shields raised before them. Their dark faces were painted in vivid streaks of yellow, red and white, in the manner of the barbaric lizardmen, and fetishes of feathers and bone joints were bound to the heads of their stone maces. At the rear of each company marched groups of Rasetran archers, clad in heavy, ankle-length coats of lizard hide. Each archer had a slave who paced alongside him, carrying bundles of bronze-tipped arrows so that the bowmen could draw and fire on the move.

Smaller companies of Lybaran light infantry marched behind the Rasetrans, armed with heavy swords and hatchets. They advanced close behind the heavy infantry, like jackals pacing behind a pride of desert lions. Their task was not to confront living foes, but to wield their blades against the bodies of fallen warriors, both allied and friendly, who were left in the wake of the army's advance. Still farther east, the infantry reserves of the army were arrayed in a crescent covering the advancing army's southern flank, watching for signs of a surprise attack from the dunes.

As the battle-lines advanced, the Lybaran catapults went into action, sending rounded stones the size of wagon wheels arcing over the heads of the allied troops. The projectiles ploughed into the packed ranks of the enemy infantry, crushing everything in their path amid sprays of splintered wood, flesh and bone. The screams of wounded and dying men rose above the muted tramp of marching feet.

When the allied companies were two hundred yards from their foes, the feared Zandri archers drew back their bows and darkened the skies with volley after volley of arrows. Bronze arrowheads crackled against the shields of the Rasetran infantry, or buried deep into their thick, scaly coats. Here and there a warrior fell as a reed shaft found its way through a chink in their heavy armour, but soon the Rasetran archers were returning fire against the Zandri bowmen, and the intensity of the enemy fire began to subside.

The enemy archers gave ground before the advancing allied host, continuing to fire until they had exhausted their small store of arrows. Then they retreated behind the safety of their battered infantry companies. The Rasetrans continued their slow, steady advance, conserving their strength in the blistering heat, until the two armies came together in a slow, grinding crash of arms and armour. The enemy infantry met the allied warriors shield-to-shield, jabbing at their foes with long, darting spears, while the Rasetrans hammered away at the lightly armoured troops with their brutal stone-headed weapons.

The hard-bitten jungle warriors sowed terrible carnage among their less-skilled foes, their armour shrugging off all but the strongest blows. The enemy line bowed beneath the onslaught, but before long the heavy infantry began to tire beneath the weight of their gear and the heat of the sun, and the advance began to falter. Enemy reserves streamed to the centre and right, shoring up the Usurper's battleline.

'The advance is faltering,' Hekhmenukep said. 'Your men can't keep this up for much longer.'

Rakh-amn-hotep rested his hands against the rail of the sky-ship and nodded. He could clearly see that the push on the centre and the enemy right could not succeed, for the heavy infantry was trying to force its way into a veritable sea of enemy troops. The attack had done its job, however, drawing off much of the Usurper's reserve troops, leaving the enemy left flank even more vulnerable than before. The enemy commanders on the ground could not see the concentrations of the opposing armies as he could, and, with the advantage of his god-like vantage point, he knew exactly where and when to strike. Had his foe been anyone else, the Rasetran king might have pitied him.

'Any sign of attack from the south?' he asked.

Hekhmenukep shook his head, saying, 'Nothing yet.'

'Then they've waited too long,' Rakh-amn-hotep said. Satisfied, he turned to the signallers. 'Signal for the attack on the enemy left to commence.'

Down on the battlefield, the Lybaran scholar-priests read the winking signals and raised their hands to the towering figures before them. Singing incantations and carefully worded commands, they unleashed their charges upon the enemy line.

Timbers creaked and giant mechanisms rattled and groaned as the six giant war machines lumbered forwards against the enemy's left flank. Packs of huge lizardmen and their lumbering war beasts loped in their wake, filling the air with furious shouts and ululating war cries.

The skirmish line of enemy archers faltered at the sight of the advancing war machines, and when the first volley of arrows clattered harmlessly against their wood and bronze frames, the bowmen beat a hasty retreat behind the dubious safety of their spearmen. The Khemri infantry held its ground as the giant engines approached, perhaps trusting in their Eternal King to deliver them.

The giants covered the intervening distance in a few dozen strides and waded into the packed warriors, hurling broken, screaming bodies skywards with every sweep of their legs. Their huge maces swept down like pendulums, carving bloody swathes through the press. Frantic, screaming warriors hurled themselves at the giants, stabbing their spears into the joints between the engines' heavy plates, but their weapons could not penetrate deep enough to hit their vulnerable joints. The war machines never slowed, driving steadily deeper through the shattered enemy companies, and into the deep, bloody furrows ploughed by their feet came the wild lizardmen, who fell upon the stunned warriors with their savage, stone-tipped mauls.

Panic raced like a sandstorm through the enemy's left flank, and the Usurper's broken line reeled backwards in the face of the overwhelming assault. As the Khemri champions tried to re-form their retreating companies the ground beneath them exploded in a shower of rock and churned sand as the Lybaran war scorpions sprang their ambush. Terrified warriors were chopped to pieces by bronze-edged pincers or crushed to pulp by the scorpions' lashing stingers. Within the space of a few minutes, organised resistance collapsed as the Khemri spearmen lost their courage and fled westwards.

As the enemy's left flank collapsed, receding from the giants in a swift-flowing tide, the air overhead was rent with unearthly shrieks and arcs of flickering green flame that rose from catapults concealed in the mist to the rear of the enemy host. Clusters of enchanted, screaming skulls rained down upon the striding giants, shattering against their wood and bronze plates in bursts of sorcerous fire. Within moments, two of the huge machines were wreathed in flames as burning fragments found their way through gaps in their armoured plates and ignited their vulnerable skeletons. Their advance slowed as the building heat softened their bronze gear wheels and ate at their bones. Thick copper cables snapped under the building stress, lashing like giant whips and bursting the engines apart from within. A giant with the jackal-headed visage of Djaf died first, blowing apart in a shower of jagged metal and splintered wood as its steam vessel burst in a thunderous explosion. A falcon-headed giant fell next as its bronze knee joints broke apart, toppling the machine forwards onto a dozen retreating Khemri spearmen.

Horrified, the Lybaran priests chanted frantically to their war machines, commanding them to withdraw, but not before two more of the giants were struck multiple times and set on fire.

Devastating though the barrage was, it was not enough. As the last two surviving giants withdrew, the lizardman auxiliaries pressed their attack amid the lashing war scorpions, and the enemy's left flank continued to disintegrate. Farther west, trumpets sounded as the Numasi heavy horse were ordered into action to try to save the day.

Hekhmenukep uttered a stream of vicious curses as the fourth giant shuddered to a stop and blew apart, showering the battlefield with fragments of molten metal.

'I told you they weren't suited for this kind of battle!' he said in dismay. 'The giants were meant as siege weapons, to break down the city walls once we reached Khemri!'

'If we break the Usurper's army here, a siege will be unnecessary,' Rakhamn-hotep snapped. 'Your machines served us well. The enemy flank is shattered, and victory is within our grasp.' The Rasetran king pointed westward. 'Unleash your sky-boats on the enemy's catapults and take your revenge, Hekhmenukep. It's time to strike the killing blow.' With that, he turned to the signallers and began issuing a third string of orders to the troops on the ground.

The King of Lybaras shook his head sadly at the burning wreckage littering the battlefield to the north-west.

'Such a terrible waste,' he said, watching decades of labour turn to ash before his eyes.

The Numasi horsemen knew that something had gone terribly wrong by the frantic sound of the trumpets calling them to battle. Spurring their horses, they crested the ridge to the east and saw devastation and disaster unfolding before them. Undaunted, they closed ranks and charged into the teeth of the enemy advance.

Eight thousand of the finest heavy cavalry in Nehekhara swept down upon the marauding lizardmen, their spear points glittering balefully in the noonday sun. Like an avalanche of flesh and bronze they bore down on the howling barbarians, until the last moment, when the galloping horses caught the acrid stink of the lizardmen and recoiled in confusion and fright. Horsemen cursed and fought their suddenly panicked mounts, and chaos spread through the cavalry's ordered ranks just as the charge crashed home.

Huge lizardmen were dashed to the ground, impaled on spear points or trampled by frenzied horses. Some of the barbarians pulled the screaming animals down with them, their reptilian jaws clamped around the horses' necks. Men were smashed from their saddles by stone mauls or dragged to the ground by powerful, clawed hands. The huge thunder lizards bellowed and lashed at the cavalrymen with their massive tails, crushing man and horse alike.

Like two maddened beasts, the formations tore at one another in a wild, swirling melee. The lizardmen and their war beasts were individually more powerful and resilient, but they were also vastly outnumbered. The master horsemen of Numas quickly regained control of their mounts and pressed their advantage against the barbarians, using the speed of their horses to launch coordinated attacks against their slower foes. One after another, the barbarians sank to the ground, their thick hide pierced by dozens of spears.

Tormented past endurance by the spears of the horsemen, one of the thunder lizards let out a panicked roar and turned tail, thundering back the way it had come. Herd beasts at heart, the rest of the massive creatures followed suit, chasing after their retreating cousin. The Numasi cavalry, severely mauled by the fight, staggered to a halt and tried to re-order their scattered formation, until an ominous rumble to the east warned them of impending doom.

The Rasetran chariots, two thousand strong, rumbled across the plain at the spent Numasi horsemen. Arrows fell among the exhausted heavy cavalrymen, pitching warriors from their saddles and killing horses. Filled with dread, their commanders ordered the cavalry to withdraw in the face of the onrushing chariots in the hope of buying time to organise a countercharge, but in short order the withdrawal turned into a full retreat as the decimated warriors lost their courage in the face of the enemy's relentless advance.

Behind the charging Rasetran chariots, five thousand Lybaran and Rasetran heavy cavalry raced across the plain and turned southwards, driving into the enemy's centre. Struck in the flank by the massed cavalry charge, the enemy companies wavered, and then broke. Trumpets signalled frantically from the rear of the Usurper's army, and the remaining reserves rushed forwards to form a rearguard and cover the army's retreat. Overhead, the sky-boats of Lybaras glided past the fleeing enemy troops, heading for the Usurper's catapults. As they passed above the siege engines, warriors hurled baskets full of stones and sharp pieces of metal over the side, raining destruction down upon the war machines. Panicked by the sudden, deadly rain, the catapult crews broke and ran, fleeing into the concealing mists of the fountains.

Across the plain, the armies of the east raised their bloodied weapons and cheered, shouting the names of their gods into the pale blue sky. Behind the exhausted heavy infantry, the warriors of Lybaras continued their grim work, plying their heavy blades across a vast field littered with the bodies of the dead.

Cheers resounded from the decks of the sky-boat as the enemy's beleaguered rearguard withdrew under a steady hail of arrow fire into the fountains' concealing mists. Hekhmenukep turned to his ally and bowed in admiration.

'The victory is ours, Rakh-amn-hotep,' he said. 'Your strategy was without flaw.'

The Rasetran king shrugged. 'Who couldn't triumph with machines such as this at their command?' he said, rapping a knuckle against the rail of the floating vessel. 'I could see the enemy's every move laid out before me, as if I was playing a game of Princes and Kings. Perhaps we've found the answer to Nagash's vile sorcery at long last.'

On the plain below, the allied cavalry was pacing after the retreating enemy like a pack of wolves, edging closer and closer to the swirling clouds and their promise of sweet, life-giving moisture. Hekhmenukep gestured towards the horsemen with a wave of his hand. 'Will you order a general pursuit?' he asked.

Rakh-amn-hotep shook his head. 'Much as I would like to ride the enemy into the ground, our troops are tired and half-dead of thirst,' he said, 'and we must see to the bodies of the dead before we press on.' He nodded towards the swirling mists. 'We'll press forwards with the cavalry, seize the fountains, and tend to our wounded by the sacred springs.' The Fountains of Eternal Life, an ancient gift from the Goddess Asaph, were legendary for their healing properties, and only the great River Vitae was more revered in Nehekharan lore. Hekhmenukep nodded in agreement.

'Now that the sky-boats have emptied their holds we could press ahead with the horsemen and take on water while the rest of the army deals with the dead and wounded,' he said. The Rasetran king considered this.

'A reasonable plan,' he said. He waved to the nearest signaller. 'Send word to the cavalry and the chariots to continue the advance.'

Orders were relayed to the horsemen and the seven sky-boats drifting at the edges of the mists. As the kings' vessel pulled alongside, the entire armada began a graceful descent into the pearly white clouds. Men crowded around the rails of each ship, eager for the first, blessed caress of cool, damp air.

Rakh-amn-hotep watched the mist rise past the keel of the sky-boat and sweep silently over the rails. It wound around his outstretched arms and passed like a veil across his face, but instead of feeling life-giving moisture against his parched skin, he felt only dry, dead air and the smell of dusty smoke against the back of his throat. Hekhmenukep coughed, and other members of the crew cried out in bewilderment.

Moments later, the sky-boat sank through the layers of mist and broke into open air, less than a hundred feet above the ground. Rakh-amn-hotep blinked his dry, stinging eyes and looked out across the great, hilly basin and its silvery pools of sacred water. What he saw filled him with horror.

The great basin, wrought by a holy union between Asaph and mighty Geheb, contained dozens of irregular pools, lined by winding paths covered in rich, green moss. The sacred, silver waters had been defiled, however. Each pool had been filled with the rotting corpses of the men slain in battle the previous day. Billowing stains of blood and bile desecrated Asaph's life-giving pools, covering their surface in a scum of foulness and corruption. The retreating warriors of the Usurper's host were filing back across the basin. Their former panic had subsided, and their companies were slowly re-forming as they withdrew down the once-sacred paths.

Men fell to their knees aboard the sky-boat, stricken dumb by the enormity of Nagash's crime. Hekhmenukep's hands trembled upon the rail.

'How?' he stammered, unable to tear his gaze away from the desecration. 'How could he do this?'

Rakh-amn-hotep could not answer. No words could suffice.

A vast sea of tents lay across the great basin, surrounded by companies of heavily armoured swordsmen. Concealed from the sun by the fountains' tainted vapours, Nagash's pale-skinned immortals stood in plain view, surrounding a great black tent that crouched like a spider at the centre of the camp.

The Rasetran king stared down at the distant gathering of monsters, and in that instant he felt the weight of a vast and soulless regard, like a cold knife pressed against his skin. For the first time in his life, the warrior-king felt truly afraid.

Then, from the midst of the pale immortals, a whirling column of darkness soared high into the air. It struck the swirling clouds and spread outwards, like a pool of boiling ink. As the leading edge of the wave sped towards the drifting sky-boats, Rakh-amn-hotep heard the rising buzz of locusts.

'Turn us around,' he said breathlessly. 'Do you hear? Turn us around! Hurry!'

Men began shouting all around the king as the swarm of ravening insects swept over the sky-boat. Rakh-amn-hotep staggered, feeling thousands of tiny legs scrabbling at his skin as the wave washed over him. They battered his face, clawing at his eyes and biting at his face. He roared in anger and revulsion, sweeping futilely at the swarm with his arms. Stinging pain lanced across his bare hands and wrists. He staggered backwards and fell to the deck, crunching hundreds of hungry insects beneath him.

Above the raging drone of the swarm and the scream of terrified men, the Rasetran king heard a crackling, tearing noise overhead. Blood streaming down his face, Rakh-amn-hotep clawed the insects from his eyes long enough to glimpse a roiling carpet of locusts ravaging the great bladder that kept the sky-boat aloft. As he watched, the canvas split and unravelled like a rotting carpet, releasing the air spirits trapped within.

There was an ominous creaking of timbers, and then Rakh-amn-hotep felt his stomach lurch as the sky-boat plunged to the ground.

TWENTY

THE LONG, BITTER ROAD

The Great Desert,
in the 63rd year of Ptra the Glorious
(-1744 Imperial Reckoning)

The skeletal horsemen attacked again just before dusk, riding down upon the retreating army with the blood-red sun at their backs. The desiccated horses and their riders seemed to glide across the sands. Their bodies, baked by the desert heat, were nothing but tattered leather, bone and cured sinew, and together they weighed not much more than a living man. Warriors at the head of the column barely had time to shout a warning before the first arrows struck home.

Screams and hoarse cries from the head of the army stirred Akhmen-hotep from his stupor. He and the survivors of the army had been on the march since midnight, fleeing ever deeper into the desert after the nightmarish attack outside Bel Aliad. The enemy cavalry had harried them every step of the way, sweeping through the disordered column at will and leaving a trail of dead and wounded men in their wake. Barely thirty in number, the undead horsemen weren't numerous enough to cause widespread destruction, but what they lacked in numbers they made up for in tireless, hateful determination. Fearful of being overtaken by the vengeful dead of Bel Aliad, Akhmen-hotep had kept the army on the march, all through the night and into the searing heat of the day. Now they staggered drunkenly across the sands, delirious from exhaustion and the merciless lash of the sun.

The king raised his head at the clamour from the front of the host.

'Shields!' he yelled hoarsely as the first of the enemy riders came into view. The skeleton's mount was in full gallop, and Akhmen-hotep could see its shoulders working through ragged holes in its hide and hear the faint slap of its cracked hooves against the soft ground. Ribbons of parchment-like skin flapped like gory pennons from the rider's bleached skull as it raced along the length of the column. Its recurved horn bow was held at the ready. As the king watched, the horseman drew back the string in one smooth motion and loosed an arrow as it shot past one of the army's remaining chariots. There was a bloodcurdling scream and one of the chariot's horses collapsed to the ground.

Cursing through parched lips, Akhmen-hotep staggered towards the galloping rider. Shouts filled the air around him, but the king paid them no heed. All that mattered to him at that moment was stopping the damned monster before it killed another of their horses. Roaring in frustration and anger he raised his heavy khopesh and swung at the skeletal rider, but the horseman was still out of reach. His blow went wide and the raider swept past, readying another arrow for a victim further down the line.

'Here I am!' Akhmen-hotep cried as the rider galloped away. 'Turn about and face me, abomination! Slay the King of Ka-Sabar, if you dare–'

Suddenly the king felt a powerful hand clamp around the back of his neck, and he was hauled backwards off his feet as though he were nothing more than a child. A weapon hissed through the air. Akhmen-hotep smelled musty leather and bone dust, and then he heard a terrible *crunch!* Something sharp struck his cheek and glanced away, and then he saw the smashed pieces of a skeletal horse and its rider tumble across the sand in front of him.

'Have a care, great one,' the deep voice of Hashepra, Hierophant of Geheb, rumbled in the king's ear. The huge priest sidled backwards, his hammer at the ready, drawing Akhmen-hotep along with him. 'Master yourself, lest you shake the confidence of your men. We're in a tough enough position as it is.'

Akhmen-hotep struggled against the roar of impotent rage building in his throat. Another enemy horseman rode past, his body pierced by arrows. As the king watched, the creature drew one of the long shafts from its chest, fitted it to its bow and fired it at a living horse. The strange, almost absurd image filled the king with frustration and despair.

'By all the gods, how are we to fight these things?' he whispered hoarsely. 'Every man we kill rises again. Every kinsman we lose turns his dead hands against us.' With an effort, he planted his feet and twisted out of Hashepra's grip. 'And for every one of these monstrosities we slay, ten more spring up in its place.' He turned to the hierophant. 'Tell me, priest, how does a man defeat a foe as numberless as the sands?'

The Hierophant of Geheb stared into the king's eyes for a long moment, and Akhmen-hotep saw a reflection of his own despair in the priest's face.

'The gods alone know,' he said at last, and then he turned away. 'Come back to the chariots, great one. The enemy has passed us by for the moment. It will be dark soon, and there is much for us to discuss.'

Akhmen-hotep watched the priest trudge wearily back to the line of battered chariots less than a dozen yards away. The bleak look in Hashepra's eyes had chilled him to the bone. 'The gods know,' he said, and tried to draw some strength from the words. 'The gods know.'

Dazedly, the king joined Hashepra back at his chariot. During the chaos of the retreat, the war machines had been pressed into service as makeshift wagons to carry whatever supplies they could salvage from the camp, as well as providing transport for wounded priests and nobles. Two figures rested uneasily among sacks of grain and jars of water in the back of the king's chariot. Khalifra, High Priestess of Neru, had been made as comfortable as possible among the cargo. The stub of an arrow jutted from her left shoulder, and her face was drawn and feverish as she slept. Memnet sat beside her, his sallow features bathed in sweat. The fat priest had a damp cloth pressed against Khalifra's brow.

'We must make camp soon,' Memnet was saying as Akhmen-hotep approached. 'The men and animals are past exhaustion. If we continue any further we will kill more men than the enemy will.'

'If we stop, the enemy will attack us in strength,' the king said wearily. 'They will overwhelm us.'

'We don't know if there are any more of them out there besides the damned horsemen,' Hashepra said. 'Great one, we have to stop sooner or later. Better now while we've still got the strength to defend the camp.'

'Also, we must take stock and see how many men we have left,' Memnet pointed out. 'Not to mention our supplies.'

'And we must talk to the Bhagarites,' Hashepra continued. 'We will need to find a supply cache or an oasis soon.'

'All right, all right,' Akhmen-hotep said, raising his hands in surrender. 'We'll camp here, and move on before first light tomorrow. Pass the word to the men.'

With the decision made, the king's strength seemed to leave him. His limbs felt as heavy as lead, and at that moment he wanted nothing more than to crawl into the dubious shade beneath the chariot and sleep. Hashepra began issuing orders to a group of messengers waiting nearby when the sound of hoofbeats approached them from the rear of the column.

Akhmen-hotep whirled, thinking Nagash's horsemen had decided to turn around and strike them again, but even as he raised his blade the king saw that both horse and rider were figures of flesh and blood rather than leather and bone. As the horseman drew near, Akhmen-hotep saw that it was none other than Pakh-amn, and it occurred to the king that he hadn't seen the Master of Horse since the attack the night before.

'Where have you been?' he asked without preamble as the young nobleman reined in his exhausted mount beside the chariot. Pakh-amn's face betrayed a flash of irritation at the king's tone.

'I've been organising a rearguard and taking stock of our situation,' he replied curtly. 'I thought you might like to know the state of our army, great one.' Hashepra bridled at the young noble's peremptory tone, but Akhmen-hotep forestalled him with a wave of his hand.

'Well. Let's have it then,' he said to the Master of Horse.

'We've got two thousand five hundred men left, more or less,' the young noble said, 'though close to a third of them are wounded to one degree or another. No one has any camp gear to speak of, though perhaps a quarter of the men managed to escape camp with a couple of days' worth of food stuffed into their belt-pouches.' Pakh-amn nodded in the direction of the chariots. 'Hopefully you enjoyed better luck with the baggage train before we fled.'

'That remains to be seen,' Akhmen-hotep replied. 'What about the Bhagarites?' Pakh-amn's expression turned grim.

'Whether it was the will of the gods or Nagash's own design, the Bhagarites suffered dearly during the night,' he answered. 'Some of the men swear that the skeletal raiders went out of their way to kill the desert bandits. Out of the hundred that accompanied us from Ka-Sabar, less than twenty remain.' He shrugged. 'Perhaps if they'd still had their swords when the attack began, they could have better defended themselves.' Hashepra's face darkened with rage.

'It's time someone knocked some manners into you, boy,' he said quietly.

'Enough, holy one,' Akhmen-hotep declared. 'Remember what you said about setting an example for the men. The Master of Horse offends no one but his ancestors with such petty behaviour.' Pakh-amn let out a derisive snort.

'Petty?' he said. 'I merely speak the truth. If the king is not strong enough to face it, then he's no true king at all.'

'There is truth, and then there is sedition,' Memnet said. 'The king could have you executed for such talk, Pakh-amn.'

The Master of Horse glared at the Grand Hierophant, and said, 'I can think of perhaps a thousand men who would disagree with your opinion, priest.'

Akhmen-hotep stiffened. Suddenly, Memnet's warning from the night before echoed in his mind. *Who can say what he might do if he found himself in a position of influence over much of the army?*

If he gave the word, Hashepra would strike the young nobleman down with a single blow from his hammer. Just as the command rose to his lips, Pakh-amn turned to him and said, 'Forgive me, great one. Like you, I'm very tired, and my nerves are on edge. But I am happy to say that all is not yet lost.'

'And how is that?' the king asked.

'I have been speaking to the Bhagarite survivors,' the nobleman said. 'They know of a supply cache a day's ride from here.'

'A day's ride is two or more days on foot,' Hashepra countered. 'Half the army will be dead before we get there.' Pakh-amn nodded.

'Unless we empty the chariots and send them ahead to gather supplies,' he said. 'I could take the remaining Bhagarites as guides and outriders, plus a few hundred picked men. Then in a day's time you march with the rest of the army and meet us halfway back on the return leg. It would be difficult, but not impossible.'

Akhmen-hotep paused, rubbing at the grit surrounding his eyes as he tried to think through the nobleman's plan. It seemed sound... if he could trust the Master of Horse. Could he risk sending off all his chariots and most of his guides under Pakh-amn's command? Even if he chose someone else to lead the expedition, how could he know for certain if the man wasn't one of Pakh-amn's sympathisers? The Master of Horse could then slip away in the night and join his compatriots, leaving the army to its fate and returning safely to Ka-Sabar.

The king looked to his brother for advice. Memnet said nothing, but the look in his dark eyes spoke volumes. Akhmen-hotep sighed and shook his head.

'We can't risk the chariots, or the guides,' he said. 'We'll ration our supplies and head for the oasis as best we can.'

Pakh-amn's eyes widened at the king's decision, but then his jaw clenched in anger.

'So be it,' he said tightly, 'but men will die needlessly as a result. You will regret this decision, Akhmen-hotep. Mark my words.'

The nobleman spun on his heel and strode swiftly to his horse. Akhmen-hotep watched him go, debating the idea of ordering Pakh-amn's arrest. Would arresting him prevent a mutiny, or provoke one?

The next thing he knew, Hashepra was gently shaking his shoulder.

'What shall we do, great one?' the hierophant asked.

Akhmen-hotep shook himself, as though waking from a dream. Pakh-amn's galloping horse was already a long distance away, heading back to the rear of the host.

'Make camp,' the king said dully. 'Then pick some men you trust and have them go over the supplies. We'll start rationing right away. Send runners looking for any servants of Neru that might have survived. We could use a ward to protect the camp once it gets dark.' Hashepra nodded.

'And then?' he asked. The king shrugged.

'Then we try to survive the night,' he said in a hollow voice.

Sensations slowly penetrated the darkness: throbbing pain in his chest, shoulders and back, and then the swelling roar of thousands of shouting voices. Cool, slightly oily water lapped against his lower legs, caressing his parched skin. For an instant, his brain was seized with competing sensations of pure terror and giddy relief.

After a moment, the cacophony of noise surrounding Rakh-amn-hotep resolved into the familiar noise of the battlefield. Wounded men screamed all around him, begging for help, while off in the distance hundreds of men shouted lustily for the blood of their foes. The Rasetran king realised in a daze that they were probably referring to him.

Blinking slowly, the king found himself lying on his stomach at the edge of one of the great sacred pools. He couldn't remember how he'd got there. The last thing he knew, he'd watched the sky-ship's air bladder come apart, and felt the deck drop away beneath him as the great craft plunged earthwards.

Wincing, Rakh-amn-hotep got his hands underneath him and tried to push himself upright. A stabbing pain lanced through the right side of his chest. More than likely, he'd cracked a rib at some point during the crash. No doubt he'd been thrown clear when the wooden hull crashed to the ground. By the gods' own grace he'd just managed to clear the deep pool at his feet. Had he landed three feet shorter he would have surely drowned in Asaph's sacred water.

No, not sacred any more, the king corrected himself. With a hiss of revulsion he jerked his feet from the corpse-choked water and wiped at the oily residue of human rot clinging to his skin. This close to the water the stench of corruption was tangible, coating the back of Rakh-amn-hotep's dry throat.

Coughing raggedly, the king rolled over and tried to take stock of his surroundings. The wreckage of the sky-boat lay just ten yards or so away, its shattered timbers partially covered by a tattered shroud of canvas and a carpet of seething, chewing insects. To his horror the king saw struggling figures buried beneath the mass of locusts. One lifted a hand skywards, as though beseeching the gods for help. Three of the man's fingers had been gnawed down to the bone.

Few of the other Lybaran sky-boats had fared any better. Rakh-amn-hotep could see broken hulls scattered across the eastern curve of the great basin, and dozens of dazed and injured men were trying to escape the wreckage.

To the west, waves of sound reverberated across the basin from the massed warriors of the Usurper's host. From what the Rasetran king could tell, the retreating companies had fetched up against Nagash's hidden reserves, and the Usurper's immortal champions were angrily re-forming their ranks. The great mass of disordered troops was the only thing standing between the allied survivors and Nagash's eager companies. That would change in a matter of minutes.

Rakh-amn-hotep staggered over to a group of Lybarans crawling away from the ruins of his sky-boat.

'Where is your king?' he asked hoarsely. 'Where is Hekhmenukep?' When the stunned crewmen stared wordlessly at him, the Rasetran applied his sandal to their backsides. 'On your damned feet!' he ordered. 'We have to get out of here, but no one leaves until Hekhmenukep is found!'

The king's commanding voice sent the crewmen scrambling back the way they'd come, hurriedly searching around the wreckage of the sky-boat.

'Get the wounded moving!' Rakh-amn-hotep called after them. 'Any men who can't move must be carried!'

As the crewmen searched, the king turned his attention to the survivors of the other sky-boats. Many flocked to the sound of his voice, and he put them to work as well. Large swathes of torn canvas were gathered off the ground to provide crude litters for the most seriously wounded, and the king began sending small groups eastwards as soon as they were organised.

'Over here!' one of the Lybarans called, waving frantically. 'He's here! The king is here!'

Hekhmenukep was lying only a few yards from the smashed prow of the sky-boat. Miraculously, he had escaped the ravages of the locust swarm, while two men who had come to earth a few feet closer to the crash had been reduced to glistening skeletons. When Rakh-amn-hotep reached the king, two of Hekhmenukep's subjects were trying to help him to his feet. The Lybaran ruler was pale and hunched with pain, and flecks of bright red foam tinged the corners of his mouth. Rakh-amn-hotep muttered a curse.

'A rib has pierced one of his lungs,' the veteran warrior said. 'Set him on a piece of canvas and get him back to the army as quickly as you can. Don't worry too much about his comfort. Right now, speed is what matters.'

As the crewmen hastened to obey, the air shook with the bellow of war-horns and the mingled voices of thousands of eager warriors. Across the basin, the Usurper's army was on the move once more.

The Rasetran king growled like an old, scarred hound. They had run out of time.

'Get moving,' he said to the remaining men. 'Help the wounded as much as you're able. Now, go!'

The Lybarans needed no further urging, fleeing for their lives in the face of the advancing army. In moments, the king stood alone, in the face of the Usurper's distant horde. Beaten but unbowed, he turned his back on his foes and headed off after his men.

Behind him, the Usurper's warriors let out a wordless roar of bloodlust and surged forwards, breaking ranks in their eagerness to catch up to the Lybarans. The enemy warriors were more than half a mile away, and were forced to follow the twisting trails that surrounded the poisoned fountains, but the same could be said for Rakh-amn-hotep and his men, many of whom could barely move. With every passing moment, the bestial sounds of pursuit grew louder in the king's ears.

Then, up ahead, Rakh-amn-hotep spotted horsemen wending their way carefully among the pools. They were Lybaran light horsemen, the leading edge of the pursuit force that had followed the retreating enemy companies into the basin. As he watched, the horsemen helped their fellows onto the backs of their horses and began to head back the way they'd come. The litter bearers had no choice but to struggle onwards with their burdens, but now they marched under the protective gaze of the light horsemen.

One of the cavalrymen spotted Rakh-amn-hotep and spurred his horse forwards with a shout. He reined in alongside the king and slid from the saddle without hesitation.

'Your champion waits with the Rasetran chariots yonder,' he said breathlessly, nodding his head in the direction of the mists to the east. 'Take my horse, great one. The enemy is nearly upon us.'

Rakh-amn-hotep glanced back the way he'd come and was shocked to see enemy spearmen less than a hundred yards away. 'Get back in the saddle,' he ordered. 'Two can ride as well as one. Besides, I'm like to fall off if I try to ride this beast by myself.'

The cavalryman leapt gratefully back onto his horse's back and with an effort helped the king up behind him. An arrow hissed through the air off to their right, and then another. The horseman hauled on the reins and spurred his mount away from the advancing host. He wove his mount through the press of retreating figures with great skill, occasionally splashing through shallow pools to circumvent larger knots of men.

Many minutes later they reached the far end of the basin and its tendrils of swirling mist. A hundred Rasetran chariots waited there in a kind of rear-guard, their narrow wheels and considerable weight preventing them from penetrating further into the basin's rough terrain. Ekhreb waited nearby, ordering litter bearers to load their charges aboard the chariots as they arrived. The champion's expression relaxed considerably when he saw his king approaching.

Rakh-amn-hotep dropped gracelessly from the saddle and clasped the cavalryman's wrist in thanks before walking over to Ekhreb.

'The damned Usurper was a few steps ahead of us all along,' he snarled. 'The battle on the plain was just meant to exhaust us and use up the last of our water. Now he's poisoned the only water source for fifty miles. If we stay here his reserves will break us by nightfall, and then there will be a slaughter.' Ekhreb listened to the dire assessment calmly.

'What would you have us do?' he asked. Rakh-amn-hotep gritted his teeth.

'We retreat again, damn it. Back to Quatar, though the gods alone know how we're going to make it. Nagash will pursue us. He'd be a fool not to. We'll draw him against the walls of the city and try to break him there.'

'What if the Usurper is still thinking a few steps ahead of us?' the champion asked. Rakh-amn-hotep scowled at the champion.

'Well, if it makes you feel any better, we'll all probably be dead of thirst long before that becomes a problem.' he said. Ekhreb chuckled in spite of himself.

'Now look who's the optimist,' he said, and lead the king to his waiting chariot.

The tent flaps of heavy canvas swept aside, allowing only the weak grey light of the misty basin into the gloom of Nagash's tent. Raamket hurried inside, grateful to escape even the faint glimmer of Ptra's searing rays. Most of his body was shielded by leather wrappings and armour, leaving only his head and hands exposed. His cloak of human skin fluttered like vulture's wings in his wake as he approached the Undying King and sank to one knee.

'The enemy host is withdrawing, master,' the immortal said. 'What is your command?'

Nagash sat upon the ancient throne of Khemri, displaced from Settra's palace for the first time in centuries. The king's brooding figure was wreathed in the sepulchral tendrils of his ghostly retinue, their faint cries weaving a fearful threnody in the oppressive shadows. The necromancer's vassal kings waited upon Nagash's pleasure: Amn-nasir, the once-proud King of Zandri, sat in a low-backed chair at Nagash's left and drank wine laced with the black lotus, his expression haunted. The twin Kings of Numas sat next to one another on the necromancer's right, whispering apprehensively to one another. At the rear of the tent the Undying King's marble sarcophagus sat beside his queen's. Neferem's sarcophagus was shut. Ghazid, the necromancer's servant, knelt beside the stone coffin and stroked its polished surface with a trembling, wrinkled hand, whispering in a thin, reedy voice.

The Undying King rose to his feet amid a swirl of tormented spirits and strode to the opening of the tent. With a gesture, the mantle of spirits glided forwards and pulled the tent flap aside.

Nagash stared from the shadows into the failing light of day and smiled.

'We march to Quatar,' he declared, 'where we will grind these rebel kings beneath our heel.'

TWENTY-ONE

THE ELIXIR OF LIFE

Khemri, the Living City,
in the 46th year of Ualatp the Patient
(-1950 Imperial Reckoning)

The Priest King of Khemri folded his arms and scowled at the large parchment map spread before him.

'Where are they now?' Nagash asked of his vizier.

Arkhan the Black moved quickly around the corner of the long table and stood beside the king. The nobleman referred quickly to a note scrawled on ragged parchment, and then traced his finger along the length of the Great Trade Road, west of Khemri.

'According to the latest reports from our scouts, the Zandri army is here,' he said, pointing to a spot approximately a week's march from the Living City.

The other half a dozen noblemen attending upon the king, including the thuggish Raamket and a weary-looking Shepsu-hur, leaned over the table to better hear Arkhan over the sound of voices and the shuffling of pages in the King's Library. Traditionally a silent, solitary haunt for the king and the royal family, the library occupied almost an entire wing of the palace. In his youth, Nagash spent many years poring over ancient tomes in the library and prowling through the dim, dusty archives in the wing's sub-levels. Now that he was king, the large sandstone chamber had become his chamber of office, where he conducted much of the business of the kingdom.

Though it was already well into the evening, the room was crowded with scribes, messengers and harried-looking slaves, all going about their business under the disapproving glare of the library's senior clerk. It had been much the same for days, ever since the Bhagarite trader had arrived at the palace with valuable news to sell: King Nekumet of Zandri had mustered his warriors and was preparing to liberate the Living City from the clutches of Nagash the Usurper. For the first time in eighteen years, Khemri was at war.

News of the impending attack had not come as a great surprise. Indeed,

Nagash had been expecting such a move for quite some time and had been making the necessary preparations. The news of Thutep's fall had spread across Nehekhara like a storm wind, prompting cries of outrage and dismay in the palaces of the other great cities.

It was not so much the act of removing Thutep that was so abhorrent, for the young king had been widely viewed as foolish and naïve, but the fact that Nagash had violated the covenant of the gods by claiming the crown. As firstborn, his life belonged to the gods, and thus he had set a dangerous precedent that the other kings could not abide. To make matters even worse, he had forbidden Thutep's wife, Neferem, to join her husband in the afterlife, as custom demanded, jeopardising the covenant and offering a grave offence to the gods.

Nagash had lost count of the number of angry delegations sent from the holy city of Mahrak to demand his immediate abdication in favour of Thutep's son. Meanwhile, he suspected, the Hieratic Council had been sending envoys to the other cities in the hope of raising an army to remove him from the throne by force. Until now, however, the Kings of Nehekhara had preferred to bide their time and hope that the gods, or more likely, Khemri's angry populace, would step in and save them the expense of a costly military campaign.

For nine years, the gods had been strangely silent, and the people of Khemri had accepted Nagash's rule with a kind of stunned passivity. His rise to power marked the end of years of plague, and had ushered in an era of calm and stability. The king replenished the ranks of the nobility by elevating prominent members of the merchant class, and suppressed crime through quiet arrangements with the city's criminal elements. Dissenters were quickly identified and dealt with quietly by Raamket's agents, allowing the king free rein to pursue his immediate goals.

Nagash had known from the first that it would only be a matter of time before King Nekumet felt strong enough to march on Khemri. Now the labour of the past few years would be put to the test.

'What have we learned about the composition of the army?' the king inquired. Arkhan consulted his notes again.

'Our scouts report eight thousand foot soldiers, a mix of regular spear companies and barbarian auxiliaries, as well as two thousand archers and fifteen hundred chariots.'

Sidelong stares and uneasy murmurs passed among the noblemen. The Zandri army was nearly twice as large as Khemri's. Nagash nodded thoughtfully.

'King Nekumet has assembled an ideal force to combat ours' he said. 'Clearly his spies have kept him well-informed.' He glanced up at Raamket. 'What of our own troops?'

'The last of our spear companies and archers left the city by mid-afternoon, as you commanded,' the nobleman said. 'The light horsemen and chariots are finishing their final preparations even as we speak.' Nagash acknowledged the report with a curt nod, and then turned to Shepsu-hur.

'And what of your forces?' he asked. The handsome nobleman gave the king a rakish smile.

'All stands in readiness,' he said easily. 'We can leave at any time, great one.'

Nagash studied the map for a few moments more, and then nodded in satisfaction.

'There is nothing more to discuss, then,' he said. 'The cavalry will depart in two hours, as planned. Shepsu-hur, you will leave Khemri an hour after midnight. Be at the rendezvous here,' the king continued, indicating a point along the banks of the River Vitae, 'by dawn.'

Shepsu-hur bowed to the king, and the rest of the noblemen took this as their cue to depart. Arkhan quickly rolled up the map of Nehekhara and departed with a hasty bow. Two hours left precious little time to make ready, and there was still much to be done. Nagash dismissed them from his mind at once, returning his attention to the books and parchments that had been covered by the vizier's map.

Books and scrolls on architecture lay atop a broad sheet depicting a monumental pyramid, larger by far than even the Great Pyramid. The pyramid contained more than a dozen levels of carefully arranged chambers, more than half of which penetrated well below ground level, and the margins of the architectural plan were filled with precise measurements and lists of materials that would go into the pyramid's construction. Tonne upon tonne of black marble, plus hundreds of pounds of silver and jars of crushed gemstone.

The cost of the building materials alone would beggar the great cities of Nehekhara twice over. Yet every bit was absolutely vital, in Nagash's estimation. Based on everything he had learned from the druchii, plus the observations of his experiments over the last decade and a half, it would take nothing less to draw the winds of dark magic to Nehekhara and store their power for his use.

The cost of such an undertaking did not concern him, but was a relatively trivial problem, as far as Nagash was concerned. What confounded him, time and again, were the calculations of labour that would be required to build such a massive edifice. The king traced a fingertip along a series of figures in the lower margin of the plan, arriving once again at the inevitable conclusion: *two hundred to two hundred and fifty years.*

Nagash placed his palms on the tabletop and revisited his calculations once again, trying to find a way to complete his grand design in less than a single lifetime. So keen was his concentration that it was several long minutes before the king realised that the library chamber was completely silent.

Frowning, the king glanced up from his work to find Neferem and her retinue of maidens standing in the centre of the room. The Daughter of the

Sun was dressed in her royal finery, complete with the ceremonial headdress and heavy golden sunburst worn by Khemri's queen. Her green eyes were limned with kohl, and her lips had been dusted lightly with crushed pearl, but such adornments seemed cheap compared to Neferem's natural beauty. Not even the cold glare of contempt she focused on the king detracted from her tremendous presence.

Everyone in the chamber: slaves, scholars, even the querulous senior librarians, had fallen to their knees and bent their heads to the floor in her presence.

'Leave us,' Nagash commanded, and the attendants hastened from the room.

The king studied Neferem appraisingly. After almost twenty years she had fully blossomed into the legendary beauty the gods had meant for her to be, and despite himself Nagash felt the hunger of desire all the more keenly.

'I see you've finally put off those damned mourning robes,' he observed. 'You look like a queen once more. Does this mean you've changed your mind?'

Neferem ignored the king's question.

'I want to see my son,' she said. Her voice had deepened over the years, roughened by an ocean of bitter tears.

'That's out of the question,' Nagash said coldly.

'You're taking Sukhet to war with you,' the queen replied, her voice quavering with barely repressed anger. 'He's still just a child, you soulless monster.'

'I'm well aware of Sukhet's age,' the king replied. 'Believe me, I would just as soon leave him here, for he will no doubt be a burden on my retinue during a very difficult campaign, but you give me little choice. How else can I guarantee you won't do something stupid while I'm gone?'

Neferem's eyes shone with tears. Defiantly, she held them back, and spoke with as much dignity as she could muster.

'My place is with my husband,' she said. 'You of all people should know that.'

'You will join him in time, never fear,' Nagash replied. 'How quickly that happens depends entirely on you.'

'I will never marry you!' Neferem cried. The tears came. Hot with rage, they traced streaks of black down her perfect cheeks. 'Your pathetic obsession sickens me. Hold me prisoner in this palace for another hundred years and it will only deepen my hatred of you.'

Nagash was around the table and halfway to the queen before he knew what was happening. His hand was raised, ready to strike. Neferem's maids wailed in terror and despair, lunging forwards to put their bodies between Nagash and their beloved queen. The Daughter of the Sun never flinched, but simply glared at the king as though daring him to strike her.

The king went completely still, legs frozen in mid-stride. He breathed deeply, and forced his fist to unclench.

'Shut up, you braying cows!' Nagash snarled at the whimpering maidens, and then stared hard at the queen. 'Your feelings for me do not matter in the least,' the king said through clenched teeth. 'And we shall see how stubborn you are after fifty years have passed, and your son has forgotten everything about you.' He inched closer. 'The choice is yours, Neferem. Submit to me, now or later.'

A shudder, born of anger and sorrow combined, wracked the queen's body. Black tears fell from her cheeks and spattered on the stone floor, but Neferem did not yield.

'Let me see my son,' she said again. 'Please. Let him have his mother's blessings before he leaves for war.'

Nagash regarded her for a moment, considering her request. He took another step closer, his face mere inches from Neferem's. He looked into the queen's eyes and smiled.

'Sukhet has no need of your blessings,' he said softly. 'He will be at my side the entire time. Think on that while we are away, Neferem, and be content.'

Two hours later, the last elements of Khemri's small army departed from the Living City in a fanfare of trumpets and the thunder of hooves. Arkhan the Black was given command of the squadrons of light horsemen, while Nagash rode at the head of the chariots, manned by the recently elevated noble sons of the new great houses. By the king's side stood Sukhet, a solemn-looking child of fifteen years who wore his father's ill-fitting armour as he rode into battle. Out through the city's western gate they went, down the Great Trade Road, in full view of however many spies King Nekumet had inside the city. Delegations from the city's temples watched the king depart, their blessings unspoken. Nagash had made no offerings to the gods before leaving for war, nor had he requested the company of the priesthood to support the army. Such a thing, as far as they knew, was unprecedented.

On into the deep desert night they rode, making good time down the broad, paved roadway. It wasn't long before the swift-moving horses caught up with the tail end of the army's infantry. Nagash called a brief halt to impress upon the company commanders the need to make the upcoming rendezvous on time, and then the cavalry pressed on.

An hour after midnight, the horsemen reached the main camp of the Khemri army, close by the banks of the River Vitae. There the king conferred one last time with Arkhan, who would assume command of the entire cavalry force, and then there was nothing to do but wait for the coming dawn.

Shepsu-hur arrived exactly on time, just as the first rays of light were breaking across the Brittle Peaks to the east. The huge, broad-bellied cargo haulers wallowed like hippos on the wide river, their hulls and long, spider-like oars backlit by the rising sun. No sooner had the first of the cargo ships pulled up to shore than the king gave the order to embark.

Over the course of the day, four and a half thousand men struggled through the shallow waters along the riverbank and climbed aboard Shepsuhur's fleet. By late afternoon all fifteen ships were loaded, leaving just the light horsemen and chariots behind. Arkhan and the cavalry would continue west along the road to harass King Nekumet's forces and hold the attention of his army.

Four nights later, the fleet of cargo haulers slipped unseen past the watchfires of the Zandri army and continued on to the sea.

The ships from Khemri reached the mouth of the River Vitae at just past dawn of the sixth day and nosed out into the heaving, blue swells of the Great Ocean. From there, it was only a few miles to the harbour of Zandri. The cargo haulers worked their way past the breakwater in a disorderly mob and made for the first empty piers they could find. The bleary-eyed harbour master and his apprentices didn't know what to make of the sudden arrivals at first. Were they part of a slaving expedition or a trading fleet that had arrived ahead of schedule? The ships flew no flags, and were no different in design from the coastal trading ships that Zandri used. So the harbourmaster scratched his head and checked his records, and the first ships had already tied up and were disembarking troops before he realised what was happening and sounded the alarm.

The Khemri army took the city by storm. With its entire army far off to the east, Zandri was virtually defenceless in the face of Nagash's attack. The few companies of the city watch that attempted to contest the landings were broken within an hour, and then Nagash's troops descended upon the helpless inhabitants of the city.

The sack of Zandri lasted for three horrifying days. Nagash's forces systematically looted and burned their way from one end of the city to the other. The great slave markets were emptied and their human chattel loaded onto the Khemri ships. The city's noble houses were pillaged and the families enslaved. Warehouses were emptied of valuable goods until the army's ships could hold no more. The rest were put to the torch, along with two-thirds of the ships tied up in the harbour. Through it all, the embassies of the other great cities took refuge in the city temples and looked on with abject terror as Nagash took his revenge for all the humiliations that King Nekumet had heaped upon Khemri.

On the morning of the fourth day, the traumatised survivors of the city crept furtively out into the streets to find their tormentors gone. The cargo haulers, packed with loot and thousands of slaves, had slipped their moorings and departed during the night. Nagash's army, meanwhile, had passed through Zandri's eastern gate and set out upon the Great Trade Road after King Nekumet and his warriors.

Nagash set a brutal pace for his army, marching them all day and halfway through the night in an effort to catch up with the Zandri forces. They camped by the side of the road and ate whatever they had to hand before catching a few hours' rest. Then, they rose at dawn and started the process again. Along the way they overtook a number of merchant caravans heading east with supplies for the Zandrians and relieved them of their burdens.

Two gruelling weeks passed before the Khemri army's scouts located the fires of the Zandri camp. The enemy's march had been slowed nearly to a crawl by relentless attacks from Arkhan's cavalry troops, and there were signs that their supplies were running low. With all of the Zandri scouts drawn eastwards, searching in the wrong direction for Nagash's army, King Nekumet had no inkling that the bulk of Khemri's forces were camped just a few miles along the road behind his troops.

As the Khemri army settled wearily onto the sands to either side of the road, Nagash ordered his men to erect a tent for him a few hundred yards further west, away from the bulk of the army. Sukhet, the young prince, was left in the care of Raamket, and the king sent Khefru to go and fetch one of the scores of slaves that the army had brought with them from Zandri. The battle would begin in earnest after first light, but Nagash intended for the opening moves to take place in the cold hours of darkness.

Creating the ritual circle was difficult on the uneven ground in the centre of the tent, and reminded Nagash of the near-insurmountable problem he would face on the morrow. His army was still outnumbered two to one, and his men were nearly exhausted by the long march. The use of sorcery would be vital in the coming battle, but how could he draw upon the necessary life force to cast his spells? He would be too far from the battle-line to make use of the deaths of his and Nekumet's men, and an elaborate ritual circle would be difficult to create and maintain on the open ground. It was a problem he had yet to find a solution for.

Nagash had just completed the circle when Khefru returned, dragging a young slave along with him. The young man, a long-limbed northern barbarian, was near catatonic with exhaustion, hunger and fear. He stumbled into the tent like a sacrificial bull, dull-witted and uncomprehending of his fate. The king pictured Khefru slitting the barbarian's throat and emptying his blood into a copper bowl, just like those simpering fools in the Zandri camp.

The king paused, suddenly frowning in thought. Khefru caught the change in his master's demeanour and gave the barbarian a worried glance.

'Is he not suitable?' the priest asked. 'He's strong and healthy, I assure you.'

Nagash waved Khefru to silence. His mind raced, considering the possibilities. The king nodded to himself and dragged his foot through the ritual circle, obliterating its carefully formed lines.

'What are you doing?' Khefru asked, his brow furrowing in confusion.

'Get that tunic off of him,' Nagash ordered. He went to a cedar chest by the tent flap and drew out a brush and a bottle of ink. 'Then go find me a copper bowl. I want to try an experiment.'

The priest shook his head in bemusement, but did as he was commanded. Nagash used a pair of copper needles to freeze the slave in place, and then began to paint the ritual symbols of the Incantation of Reaping directly onto the barbarian's pale skin. By the time Khefru returned with a suitable bowl, the slave's body was covered in hieroglyphic patterns.

'What in the name of all the gods?' Khefru asked, staring at the slave's body.

'The name of the gods, indeed,' Nagash said. During the process he'd made refinements to the ritual markings, tailoring the incantation to the new process he'd envisioned. 'The answer was right in front of me all along, Khefru. The priests drain the blood of the sacrificial bull and share it with the king and his men before battle. Why?' Khefru frowned thoughtfully.

'So that they can receive the benefits of the ritual,' he said.

'Exactly,' Nagash said. 'And why the blood? Because it contains the animal's life essence. Do you see? The power lies in the blood!' The necromancer straightened and drew his curved dagger. 'Come here and ready the bowl.'

The king reached up and grabbed a handful of the slave's hair, bending the head forwards and placing the blade of the knife under his chin. Khefru had just enough time to get the bowl in position before Nagash slit the barbarian's throat from ear to ear. As the steaming blood poured into the bowl he began to chant the Incantation of Reaping.

Moments later the slave's lifeless body toppled onto the ground. Nagash wiped the dagger clean using the slave's hair, and then held a trembling hand over the bowl. His eyes lit with avarice.

'I can feel it,' he whispered. 'The power is there, in the blood!' He held out his hands. 'Give it to me! Quickly!'

Khefru offered up the bowl, and without hesitation Nagash brought it to his lips. It was hot and bitter, dribbling over his chin and staining his robes, but the taste set his nerves on fire. The slave's vigour flooded into him, filling the king with strength unlike any he'd known before. Greedily, he took deeper and deeper draughts, until the blood ran in thick streams down his chest.

Nagash let the empty bowl tumble from his fingers. Power radiated from his skin like heat from a forge.

'More,' he hissed. 'More!' The look he turned upon Khefru sent the young priest stumbling from the tent in terror.

Burning with stolen vitality, Nagash threw back his head and uttered a terrible, triumphant laugh. Then he began to weave the incantations that would seal Zandri's doom.

TWENTY-TWO

SPIRITS OF THE HOWLING WASTES

The Great Desert,
in the 63rd year of Ptra the Glorious
(-1744 Imperial Reckoning)

The skeletal horsemen attacked the army's makeshift camp many times over the course of their first night in the desert, and did so every night thereafter.

They would ride out of the darkness, dry hoofbeats near-silent on the shifting sands, and fire a volley or two of arrows into the press of men before whirling around and vanishing back into the night. Warriors would jerk awake at the screams of wounded men and scramble to their feet, believing that the undead hordes of Bel Aliad had caught up with them at last. Reeling with exhaustion, shivering with fear, they would clutch their weapons in white-knuckled hands and search frantically for the source of the attack, but by then the enemy was long gone. Cold and frustrated, the men of the Bronze Host eventually wrapped themselves back in their short cloaks and tried to calm down enough to sleep once more. Then, an hour or two later, the horsemen would attack once again.

Sometimes the riders fired at random into the camp. Other times they sought out specific targets. They shot at any priest they could see, especially the handful of Neru's acolytes who had survived the attack outside Bel Aliad. The ward they laid around the camp kept the undead riders at a distance, but the magical invocation had to be maintained in a constant, nightly vigil. Akhmen-hotep was forced to send a heavily armoured escort with the acolytes to shield them from enemy arrows as they walked the perimeter beneath the gleaming moon.

It was a hazardous duty, and one or more of the acolytes' bodyguards were wounded each night, but without the protective ward the army was vulnerable to more than just Nagash's horsemen. The Great Desert was home to a multitude of hungry and malevolent spirits that preyed upon the living, and their howls could be heard among the dunes when the moon's light was dim.

Each dawn, the army would find itself a little diminished from the day before. Wounded men died in the night, overcome by their wounds or sickened by the chill air. Khalifra's fever worsened as an infection set in around the barbed arrow in her shoulder. She lingered, raving, for four more days, but despite Memnet's constant ministrations the high priestess finally succumbed. Her body was prepared as best as her acolytes could manage and wrapped in scavenged linen for the long journey home.

The bodies of the common warriors were removed from the camp by a special detail overseen by Hashepra, the Hierophant of Geheb. Out of sight of their comrades, the men methodically dismembered the corpses and removed their organs, so that Nagash could not add them to his blasphemous ranks. Hashepra commended their spirits to Djaf and Usirian, and their mutilated bodies were buried beneath the sands.

There was little water and even less food to keep the army going. Within three days they had to begin butchering the wounded horses and ration the meat carefully so that every warrior had at least something to eat. Nothing was wasted. Even the blood was collected carefully in Geheb's great sacrificial bowls and given to the men a swallow at a time. The constant night attacks nevertheless took their toll, sapping the men's strength and slowing their pace.

It was eight days before the Bronze Host reached the first of the Bhagarite supply caches. The surviving desert raiders had turned sullen and belligerent since the retreat from Bel Aliad. They were furious with the king for taking their swords and leaving them to the mercy of the city's undead citizens, and yet paradoxically resentful that they had not yet been allowed to die and join their kin, as they'd expected. The warriors of the host regarded them with naked hostility, blaming the Bhagarites more than Nagash for their present misery. After one of the guides was set upon by a gang of warrior-aspirants and nearly beaten to death, the king was forced to use his Ushabti to guard the Bhagarites from his warriors.

After more than a week in the desert, hungry and fleeing from an implacable army of the dead, Akhmen-hotep's men were becoming their own worst enemies.

'How much?' the king asked, sitting in the cool shade cast by the gully wall. His voice was a dry, rasping croak, and his lips were cracked by thirst. Like the rest of the army, he drank only three cups of water per day, and the last drink had been more than four hours ago.

The army had reached the third of the Bhagarite supply caches: a series of hidden caves among the narrow defiles of a range of sheer sandstone cliffs that rose like weathered monuments from the desert sands. When they'd arrived the warriors had scrambled like lizards into the shade of the twisting gullies, heedless of the serpents and scorpions that no doubt sheltered beneath the rubble at the base of the cliffs. Many of the warriors had cast aside their heavy bronze armour days ago, next went the shields, and even their polished helmets. Some didn't even carry weapons any longer, having divested themselves of every bit of unnecessary weight that they could manage. They were ragged, filthy and dull-eyed, little more than animals preoccupied with survival in a hostile land. Only the king's Ushabti maintained their weapons and harness, still true to their sacred oaths of service to their god and their king. The leonine devoted seemed untouched by the privations of the brutal retreat, sustained in body if not in spirit by the gifts of mighty Geheb. They were the king's strong right hand, and perhaps the only thing that held the army together after all that it had suffered.

Hashepra sighed, wiping dirt from his hands, and glanced over his shoulder at the low cave gaping on the far side of the gully wall.

'There's a spring inside, thank the gods, but only eight jars of grain,' he said.

Akhmen-hotep fought to hide his disappointment. Beside him, Memnet shifted silently on his haunches. The Grand Hierophant had lost a great deal of weight over the course of the campaign. His once-round face was sunken-cheeked, and his wide girth had shrunk so quickly that the skin hung from his waist like a half-empty sack. Though he could have claimed a greater share of the food as his proper due, the high priest had taken even less than the king. If anything, the nightmarish journey across the sands seemed to have made the Grand Hierophant stronger and more assured than ever before, and Akhmen-hotep had found himself depending heavily on his brother as the situation worsened.

'The caches are getting smaller,' the king said wearily. Hashepra nodded.

'Honestly, I don't think the Bhagarites expected to live long enough to worry about a return trip,' he said. 'I expect we exhausted the major caches on the way to Bel Aliad. All that's left are bandit hideouts like this one.'

Akhmen-hotep ran a wrinkled hand over his face, wincing as he brushed the sores on his forehead and cheeks.

'Eight jars won't last us more than a couple of days. How far to the next cache?'

The Hierophant of Geheb grimaced, and said, 'Three days, more or less, but the Bhagarites say it lies north of here, not east.'

'And the closest one further eastward?'

'A week at least, they said.'

The king shook his head.

'We'll have to kill more of the horses. How many are left?' he asked. Hashepra paused, trying to think. Memnet raised his head and cleared his throat with a hoarse cough.

'Twelve,' he said.

'Twelve horses, out of a thousand,' Akhmen-hotep murmured, musing bitterly on so much lost wealth. The retreat had been more ruinous than any battlefield defeat. The king couldn't imagine how his city would recover.

'The Bhagarites still have twenty,' Memnet replied. 'We could start with them instead.'

'The horsemen would sooner give up their right arms,' the king said, 'and the horses are the only thing we have that ensures their cooperation.'

Hashepra sank down onto his haunches beside the king.

'The men won't see it that way,' he said quietly. 'They already grumble that the Bhagarite horses are being fed while the army goes hungry. Soon you might be forced to put a guard upon them as well.'

Akhmen-hotep glanced worriedly at the priest, and asked, 'Have things got as bad as that?' Hashepra shrugged his powerful shoulders.

'It's hard to tell,' he said. 'My acolytes have heard some talk here and there. The men are hungry and afraid. They don't trust the Bhagarites, and they resent your protection of them.'

'But that's madness,' the king hissed. 'I don't like it any better than anyone else, but without the Bhagarites we won't make it out of the desert alive.'

'This doesn't have anything to do with logic, great one,' Hashepra said, shaking his head. 'The men are barely rational at this point.'

'No.' Memnet interjected. 'It's not the men who are the problem. It's Pakh-amn. He's turning them against you, brother, and you're letting him do it.'

Akhmen-hotep scowled at the ground between his feet. He hadn't seen very much of the Master of Horse since their first night in the desert. The young nobleman kept to the back of the army, claiming that he maintained a rearguard in case Nagash attacked the column in force, but it had been weeks, and such a threat had yet to materialise.

Hashepra eyed Memnet dubiously, and said, 'Pakh-amn is an arrogant rogue, perhaps, but no traitor. He's served the king ably since we left Ka-Sabar.'

'Has he? I wonder,' the Grand Hierophant said. 'He enjoys the admiration of the warriors, without being forced to make the difficult decisions to keep the army alive. Has he made any effort at all to curtail the men's resentments?'

Hashepra had no answer to the priest's question. Akhmen-hotep set his jaw stubbornly. 'A mutiny wouldn't improve our odds of survival,' he protested.

'Pakh-amn doesn't want an army; he wants a throne,' Memnet said. 'He wouldn't care if he walked out of the desert alone, so long as Ka-Sabar was his.'

'Enough!' the king snapped, cutting off his brother with a curt wave of his hand. 'I've heard this all before. If Pakh-amn means to move against me, let him come. In the meantime, let's clean out this cache and move on. We're wasting precious time.'

The king climbed unsteadily to his feet. As one, his Ushabti rose gracefully from the shadows and followed along in Akhmen-hotep's wake as he made his way back to the army's remaining chariots. Hashepra watched the king go, his expression thoughtful.

'There is something sinister at work here,' he mused. 'The acolytes of Neru have found places where their nightly wards have been tampered with. Someone is stealing out of the camp late at night, but so far the sentries have been unable to catch who it is.'

Memnet glanced up at Hashepra, his expression intent.

'Have you told the king?' he asked.

'Not yet,' the hierophant said. 'I have no interest in starting a witch hunt. The army's morale is fragile enough as it is. My acolytes and I are investigating the matter quietly. Tell me, do you have any evidence of Pakh-amn's intentions?'

'No,' Memnet said, shaking his head. 'The Master of Horse is too clever for that. All we can do is watch for signs that he is about to make his move. I fear that we will have little warning, which is why I have begged my brother to take action before it is too late.'

Hashepra nodded.

'Well, now at least I have a direction to look in,' he said, rising to his feet. 'I'll keep a close eye on Pakh-amn and see what the man is up to. Perhaps I can uncover enough evidence to expose him.'

'I will pray to the gods for your success, holy one,' Memnet said, nodding, but the Grand Hierophant did not sound too hopeful.

Three days later, Hashepra was dead. His acolytes found him in the early hours of the morning, wrapped tightly in his cloak. When they unwound the tattered fabric they discovered a giant black scorpion nestled in the hollow between the hierophant's shoulder and neck. He had not been the first man to perish in such a way since the retreat began, for Sokth's children were fond of taking refuge among the living and tormenting them with their terrible stings. The venom of the black scorpion turned the body as rigid as stone, and Hashepra had died in agonising silence, unable to make a single sound as the poison worked its way to his heart.

The news of Hashepra's death filled the rest of the army with super-stitious dread, and men took to giving offerings to Sokth from their already meagre rations, in the hope that the God of Poisoners would spare them. Akhmenhotep tried to prevent the practice, arguing that fear was a poison all its own, but the men would not listen, and thus grew weaker still.

In the end, the king was forced to slaughter four more of the precious horses and ration the meat and blood carefully to get the army to the next bandit cache, only to find that the caves had been emptied a long time before. The anger and despair among the men had been palpable, and resentment against the Bhagarites nearly led to a riot. Only the king's Ushabti managed to keep the desert guides alive. That night, however, two of their horses were killed and butchered, evincing wails of horror and bitter curses from the desert horsemen when the bones were discovered the following morning. The perpetrators of the deed remained a mystery.

On the night of their fifteenth day in the desert, the acolytes of Neru and their exhausted bodyguards were slain in a brutal ambush just before dawn. The men, well-practised in watching for signs of mounted attackers, were caught unawares when a dozen skeletal archers rose from the sands on the other side of the camp's protective ward and fired into their midst. The heavy infantry were the first to die, shot through the throat or pierced in the back at nearly point-blank range. Then the ambushers turned their bows on the fleeing acolytes. By the time reinforcements arrived the skeletons had disappeared, and the army had lost what little protection it had against the hungry night.

From that point forward, Akhmen-hotep was forced to keep half the army awake while the other half snatched a few hours' sleep, rotating the groups every four hours. Attacks from the skeletal horsemen continued, and casualties mounted. Warriors who were caught sleeping on watch forfeited their food ration for the next day, which was tantamount to a death sentence. With so few chariots remaining, men who could no longer march had to be left behind.

Slowly but surely, the spirits of the desert closed in. Nightmares plagued the sleeping men, and strange figures stalked the edges of the camp beneath the moonlight. Men sometimes rose from sleep and tried to walk off into the sands, swearing they heard the voices of their wives or children. Those who succeeded were never seen again.

The Bhagarites led the army to one empty cache after another, and bore the king's recriminations with looks of sullen contempt. The number of horses dwindled, until by the twenty-fourth day the last of the chariot pullers was dead. According to the guides, the next cache was more than five days away. The Bhagarites would no longer say for certain how many more days it would take for them to reach the far side of the desert.

Days passed, and the rations dwindled. Groups of men began lurking around the picket line where the last Bhagarite horses were kept, despite the warning glares of the Ushabti who had been set to guard them. Desperate as they were, none of the warriors dared to try their luck against the devoted, but the same could not be said of the Bhagarites.

On the thirtieth night of the retreat, while strange, savage creatures paced and howled in the darkness beyond the edge of the camp, the desert raiders commended themselves to Khsar and slipped away from the handful of Ushabti that still guarded them. Though the devoted were more than capable of fending off the advances of their starving kinsmen, their powers were not equal to the guile and stealth of the Bhagarites, who were horse thieves of nearly supernatural skill. The raiders had reached the pickets and climbed bareback onto their mounts before the devoted knew what was happening.

Shouts of alarm rang out across the camp as the desert riders spurred their beloved horses past the surprised bodyguards out into the sands. A few of the men tried to chase after the riders, but none got very far. Khsar's divine animals were still as swift as the desert wind, and fled like smoke from the warriors' outstretched hands. Their riders, free at last, threw back their heads and stretched their arms up to the sky, feeling the pounding of the hooves and the whisper of the wind against their skin one last time.

Without food or water, the last men of Bhagar and their beloved horses rode into the trackless desert, commending themselves into the embrace of their faceless god.

After the men of Bhagar were gone, there was nothing left but to march eastwards and pray to the gods for deliverance.

The army dwindled swiftly, like grains of sand spilling from a broken glass. Men died in the night, taken by madness or hunger, or simply fell to the ground during the march and refused to get up again. The hostility of the warriors subsided, along with all other emotions. They had been emptied of thought and feeling by the desert, and now waited only to die.

Then, when the Bronze Host was at its weakest, Nagash's horsemen struck the deadliest blow of all. On the night of the thirty-second day they slipped easily past the unseeing sentries and left their handiwork to be discovered by the stunned warriors at the first light of dawn.

Ten jars of grain and fifteen jars of water were left in plain sight, distributed evenly around the ragged camp. The men fell upon them in a frenzy. When the jars were empty, they broke apart the thick vessels and licked the insides clean.

Then, with a little food in their bellies, the warriors of the Bronze Host sat down and thought about what the strange gift meant.

Akhmen-hotep awoke with a start. Overhead, the night sky was bright and clear, scattered with a sweep of glittering stars.

He hadn't meant to sleep. The king sat up, blinking owlishly into the darkness. A handful of his Ushabti surrounded him, staring watchfully around the camp. The rest were walking the perimeter, alert for the enemy's next move. If the skeletons meant to repeat the tactic of the night before, the king meant to stop it.

His bodyguards were under strict orders to drive off the skeletons and destroy any food or water they left behind. Akhmen-hotep knew that it was the only way to deal with the danger. The rations were deadlier than any spear or knife. With them, Nagash could tear the Bronze Host asunder.

Suddenly, three of the Ushabti rose to their feet, blades at the ready. A figure was approaching, picking his way carefully past knots of sleeping men. As he drew near, the king saw that it was Memnet. Waving for the devoted to relax, the king rose to meet his brother.

Akhmen-hotep saw that the Grand Hierophant was upset. His haggard face was pale, and his eyes were wide with fear.

'The time has come,' he whispered. 'They are making their move even now!'

Fear, and worse, a terrible despair, swept through the king.

'Who?' he asked.

Memnet wrung his shaking hands, saying, 'A score of lesser nobles and their men, a hundred warriors, perhaps more. The water and food were the last straw. They believe that if they treat with Nagash they will be allowed to return to Ka-Sabar in peace.'

Akhmen-hotep nodded grimly. If he summoned all of his bodyguards, he could cut the heart out of the conspiracy. A dozen Ushabti had little to fear from a hundred starving warriors.

'Where is Pakh-amn?' he asked.

'Here I am,' the Master of Horse answered.

Pakh-amn and a dozen noblemen were approaching the king and his guards with weapons in their hands. The young nobleman's face was taut with anger.

'Your men have turned against you, great one,' he declared. 'The consequences of your folly have caught up with you at last.'

Akhmen-hotep heard the sounds of fighting and the screams of dying warriors echo from across the camp. His bodyguards were under attack by the men they had been trying to protect.

'Did you think to cut my throat while I slept?' he snarled at Pakh-amn. 'Or did you plan to give me as a gift to your new master in Khemri?' The accusation struck the young nobleman like a blow. He paused, his expression stricken. Seizing the opportunity, the king reached for his sword. 'Kill them!' he commanded his Ushabti, and the five bodyguards charged forwards without hesitation, their ritual blades flashing.

Shouts of alarm and the clash of blades filled the air as Pakh-amn and the noblemen recoiled from the Ushabti's fierce assault. Men fell like wheat before the blades of the devoted, cut down by blurring strokes that sliced effortlessly through their armour. Pakh-amn fought furiously, shouting curses as he turned aside one attack after another. A ritual blade landed a glancing blow against his sword-arm, and then another bit deep into his thigh. The nobleman staggered, but fought on, parrying furiously as blood poured over his knee and spattered onto the sands.

Within moments Pakh-amn's warriors had been cut down. The Master of Horse lasted a few seconds more, but it was clear that the wound in his leg had cut the artery and his life was draining away. He stumbled, and an Ushabti's sword cut deep into his chest. With a groan, Pakh-amn sank slowly to the ground.

Akhmen-hotep walked over to the fallen nobleman. His heart was heavy, but his face was a mask of rage.

'Go and aid your brothers,' he told the devoted. 'Return to me as swiftly as you can.' With a snarl he kicked the sword from Pakh-amn's hand. 'I'll deal with this one.'

The Ushabti raced silently into the darkness. Akhmen-hotep watched the pulse of blood streaming from Pakh-amn's leg steadily weaken. The Master of Horse stood on the threshold between this world and the next.

'You damned fool,' Akhmen-hotep said. 'I would have honoured you when we returned to Ka-Sabar. Why couldn't you have settled for that? Why did you have to try to claim my throne as well?' A strange expression came over Pakh-amn's bloodless face.

'You've gone...' the young nobleman whispered, blood leaking from the corner of his mouth, 'You've gone mad... great one. The gods have... abandoned you... at last. I came... to save you.'

The king's angry expression faltered.

'You're lying,' he said. 'I know what you've planned. Memnet warned me.' He turned to his brother. 'Tell him–'

The knife felt cold as it slid into his chest. The pain was breathtaking. Akhmen-hotep's mouth opened in shock as he stared into his brother's eyes.

Memnet, once the Grand Hierophant of Ptra, glared angrily at his brother.

'I tried to tell you,' he said. 'I tried. Back at Bel Aliad, do you remember? The old ways are gone, brother. Nagash has become the master of death. He has overthrown the gods! If we are to prosper, we must worship him. Why couldn't you see that?'

The king's knees buckled. He fell, dragging Memnet's knife from his trembling hands. Akhmen-hotep landed on his back, next to Pakh-amn's body. The Master of Horse was staring skyward, the tracks of his tears drying at the corners of his dead eyes.

The Priest-King of Ka-Sabar turned his eyes to the stars, seeking the faces of his gods.

Arkhan the Black rode out of the desert with a hundred of his horsemen at his back. The fighting in the camp had ended. The Ushabti had wrought a fearsome vengeance for the death of their king before they too had succumbed. Bodies lay everywhere, providing bloody testament to the Bronze Host's last battle. The vizier bared his black teeth in a gruesome smile.

Men prostrated themselves as the immortal and his retinue approached, cowering and trembling with terror. Some clawed at their faces and moaned like children, their sanity having fled at last. Of the four thousand warriors that had followed Akhmen-hotep on his ill-fated expedition, less than five hundred still survived.

The immortal guided his undead mount down a long, corpse-choked lane that ran all the way to the centre of the camp. Memnet the traitor awaited him there, standing over the body of his brother. Blood still stained the fallen priest's hands.

Arkhan reined in his decaying horse before Memnet and gave the wretch a haughty stare.

'Kneel before the Undying King of Khemri,' he commanded.

Memnet flinched at Arkhan's voice, but he raised his head in a gesture of defiance.

'I kneel only before my master,' the traitor said, 'and you are not him, Arkhan the Black.'

The immortal chuckled. Suddenly, a harsh, rasping wind rose among the company of skeletons at his back. Memnet first took the sound to be a kind of laughter, and perhaps it was, but the sound came not from desiccated throats, but from the stirring of insects that poured from empty eye sockets and gaping mouths, or crawled from the depths of ragged wounds. The swarm took flight, swirling into a column of seething life that descended before Memnet and assumed the image of Nagash.

'Bow before your master,' rasped the voice of the necromancer.

Memnet fell to his knees with a cry of fear, saying, 'I hear you, mighty one! I hear and obey! All has been done as you commanded,' he said, gesturing to the body of the king. 'See? Akhmen-hotep, your hated foe, is no more!' The head of the construct seemed to regard the dead king, and then turned to face Memnet once more.

'You have done well. Now rise, and claim your reward,' he said. Wringing his hands, Memnet struggled to his feet. Arkhan dismounted and stepped forwards with a sneer of contempt. Reluctantly he held out a vial of red liquid.

'Immortality is yours,' the king said. 'Take it, and go forth to rule Ka-Sabar in my name.'

Memnet took the vial and gazed at its contents with a mixture of awe and revulsion. 'As you command, Undying One,' he replied. 'My men will require food and water to complete our march.' Arkhan threw back his head and laughed. Memnet cringed at the awful sound.

'We have given you all the food we had,' he said coldly. 'Fear not. Your warriors will soon have no need for it.'

'Do you remember all I taught you?' the necromancer asked.

'I remember,' Memnet replied. 'All the dreams... they are still locked in my head. I know the incantations, master, every line, every syllable.'

'Then drink the elixir, and power over the dead will be yours,' Nagash declared. 'Drink. Your army awaits.'

Memnet stared at the vial for a moment longer, and then pulled off the stopper and drank the elixir in one swallow. A shudder wracked his wasted frame, and with a cry he fell to the ground, writhing and convulsing as the elixir burned through his veins.

Arkhan turned away from the spectacle with an expression of disgust. He looked westwards, where the rest of Memnet's army was slowly approaching over the dunes. All the corpses of Bel Aliad, men, women and children, plus the city's slaughtered mercenaries and the Bronze Host's battlefield dead, shuffled silently across the sands. The desert sun had rendered them down to nothing more than scraps of leathery flesh and bleached bone, and they numbered in the thousands.

The image of Nagash wavered and broke apart, transforming once again into a column of rasping, whirling insect life. It sped across the sands, engulfing Arkhan's form, and then like a desert cyclone it recoiled into the night sky, taking the immortal with it.

When Memnet's senses finally returned he was alone except for the broken souls of his brother's army and the raw, grinning faces of his own.

TWENTY-THREE

THE WHITE GATES

The Western Trade Road,
near Quatar, the City of the Dead,
in the 63rd year of Ptra the Glorious
(-1744 Imperial Reckoning)

Like a wounded giant, the allied army stumbled and lurched its way along the winding road back to Quatar, leaving a trail of flesh and blood with each ponderous step.

Rakh-amn-hotep kept the army in camp during the worst heat of the day and on the march at night, believing that the Usurper's pursuing army couldn't manage a major attack beneath Ptra's blazing sun. There had been probing attacks by Numasi cavalry at dawn and dusk, but each time they were rebuffed with little loss. Nagash's main force, as far as the Rasetran king could gather, was at least half a day's march to their west, following them doggedly along the trade road.

Rakh-amn-hotep believed that Nagash was biding his time, like a jackal waits for its prey to weaken in the desert heat before closing in for the kill.

The defeat at the Fountains of Eternal Life haunted the Rasetran king, a man who had spent his entire adult life on the battlefield. He had plotted and planned the western march for more than two years, and in the end Rakh-amn-hotep had discovered that he wasn't even fighting the same sort of battle that his enemy was. He had read all the accounts of the battle at Zedri and believed himself a better general than either Nagash or Akhmen-hotep, but he had still made the fatal error of fighting the Usurper as though he were a mortal king in command of a civilised army.

Nagash, however, was not swayed by furious assaults or swift cavalry movements. The thought of seeing thousands of his citizens, the lifeblood of his city, cut down on the battlefield was little more than an irritation to him. He could suffer blows that would have crushed a mortal king, only to rise once more.

Rakh-amn-hotep had begun to despair that they would ever be rid of Nagash.

More than three weeks after the battle outside the Fountains, the king could only think of keeping the army alive for one more day. The retreat had been a bitter, gruelling ordeal, without a doubt the hardest march of Rakh-amn-hotep's long life. Surviving those first days after the battle had been the hardest. With the water casks empty, the king had ordered his Ushabti to comb the army for every drop of liquid they could find. They confiscated all the remaining wine carried by the army's noblemen, and all the sacrificial libations brought by their multitude of priests.

The cavalrymen kept themselves alive by turning to the old bandit trick of drinking a cupful of their horses' blood each day. Even so, the warriors and animals of the host weakened quickly, and many of the wounded succumbed within days. It was only by the constant efforts of the Lybaran priests that their king, Hekhmenukep, still clung to life.

With the Lybaran sky-boats destroyed by Nagash's sorcery, the allied army paid the price of travelling without a proper baggage train. There were few wagons to draw upon, forcing Rakh-amn-hotep to send detachments of light cavalry on a long, dangerous march off to the north to try to draw water from the River Vitae, many leagues away. The cavalrymen were harassed by Numasi horsemen the entire way, but their courage and determination kept the army going long past the point of collapse.

Still, both armies had suffered greatly in men, animals and materiel. The Lybarans had seen every one of their war machines destroyed, for those that had survived the battle had exhausted their energies and couldn't keep pace with the army's swift retreat. Rather than allow the constructs to fall into the Usurper's hands, the army's engineers had breached the binding wards that kept the machines' fire-spirits in place. The resulting eruptions blew the engines apart in thunderous blasts of wood, metal and steam. Some of the senior Lybaran engineers, men who had devoted much of their lives to creating these wondrous machines, gave themselves up to the fires.

The Rasetrans suffered as well, particularly their jungle auxiliaries. The rationing of water amounted to a virtual death sentence for the giant thunder lizards, whose bodies were already taxed near to breaking point by the dry climate. The last of the great beasts died within a week after the battle, and the numbers of lizardmen dwindled swiftly thereafter. During the long night marches the chill desert air carried the eerie, keening sounds of the barbarians' death songs as they mourned the loss of their kin. The song died away a bit at a time, each and every night, until finally it was heard no more.

All that remained of the once-proud allied army was a bedraggled horde of wasted men and horses, and Rakh-amn-hotep had to concern himself with keeping his warriors from casting away their heavy weapons and armour to lighten their load on the march. He had already instituted severe punishments for warriors who were found to have abandoned their wargear, and still, each night the rearguard came upon bundles of leather armour and helmets, bronze swords and spears. The king would have begun ordering the offenders impaled if he'd had any wood to spare. He would be damned if he got the army back to Quatar only to find that they'd thrown away all the tools they would need to keep the city out of Nagash's hands.

The army was close to the White City, thank the gods, and the Brittle Peaks dominated the eastern horizon, their jagged flanks a dull black against the deep blue vault of the heavens.

Rakh-amn-hotep's chariot was heading westwards, back along the army's long, sinuous line of march. The king spent most every night ranging back and forth along the length of the allied host, checking the state of the companies and reminding the nobles of their responsibilities. It was a routine born of long habit, forged in the jungle campaigns south of Rasetra, and it had served the king well in the past.

They were nearly at the centre of the slowly marching column, passing alongside what was left of the baggage train and the huge wagons of the Lybaran court. Priests paced alongside the creaking wagon that held Hekhmenukep, their heads bowed as they prayed for the king's survival. As Rakh-amn-hotep's chariot rumbled past, one of the holy men straightened and beckoned to the king, nearly stepping out into the chariot's path.

Rakh-amn-hotep stifled a disapproving frown and touched the chariot driver on the shoulder, signalling him to stop. The weary horses needed little encouragement, their heads drooping as they snuffled about in the dust in search of something that might contain a few drops of moisture.

The Rasetran king squinted in the darkness at the approaching priest.

'Nebunefer?' he said, recognising the envoy from Mahrak. 'Since when did you become a healer?'

'One doesn't need the gift of healing to pray for the health of a great king,' the old priest said stiffly. His voice was rough and leathery, and his haggard face seemed even more careworn and stern after the privations of the long retreat, but the gleam in his dark eyes was as indomitable as ever.

The Rasetran king nodded grudgingly and kept his doubts to himself. Nebunefer had kept to the army's contingent of priests since their departure from Quatar, but Rakh-amn-hotep had little doubt that the old schemer was still somehow in close contact with the members of the Hieratic Council back in Mahrak and his spies scattered across Nehekhara.

'How is Hekhmenukep doing?' he asked.

'His condition is grave,' the old priest replied. 'His servants fear that an infection has settled into his lungs.' Nebunefer folded his arms and stared up at the king. 'The king needs the services of a temple, and very soon, or I fear he will not survive.' Rakh-amn-hotep gestured to the east.

'Quatar is almost in sight,' he replied. 'We should reach its gates early tomorrow night.' Nebunefer was unmoved.

'Tomorrow night may well be too late, great one. If the city is so close, we should press on. We could be in Quatar before noon.' The Rasetran king bristled at the note of command in the priest's voice.

'The men are exhausted,' he growled. 'If we keep them going past dawn, into the full heat of the day, we could lose many of them. Are the lives of a few hundred warriors worth the life of a king?' Nebunefer raised a thin eyebrow.

'I'm surprised you would ask such a question, great one.' Rakh-amn-hotep let out a snort.

'Right now I need spearmen and cavalrymen, not kings,' he said.

'But the king isn't just one man, as you well know,' Nebunefer countered. 'He represents his fighting men as well. If Hekhmenukep dies, there is no guarantee that the Lybaran host won't take his body home and leave you to fight Nagash alone.'

The old schemer had a point, Rakh-amn-hotep admitted sourly. He turned and stared off to the east for a moment, trying to gauge the remaining distance to Quatar. He knew that another contingent of horsemen was due back from the river sometime near dawn. It might be enough.

'We'll see how things stand as we get closer to dawn,' the king said at last. 'If the men are able, we'll move on. Otherwise, you may have another day of praying to do.'

For a moment it seemed that Nebunefer would continue the argument, but after catching the hard look in the Rasetran's eye, he merely bowed to the king and went off to catch up with Hekhmenukep's wagon.

Rakh-amn-hotep watched him go, and then tapped his driver's shoulder.

'Turn us around,' he growled. 'Let's get back to the head of the column.'

The driver nodded and popped the reins, chiding the horses back into motion. They turned in a bouncing arc eastwards and rejoined the trade road once more. Rakh-amn-hotep paid little attention to the trudging men as the chariot rumbled down the column, his mind preoccupied with weighing the risk of a forced march against the very real possibility of losing Hekhmenukep and the Lybarans in the process.

He hoped the night didn't have any other surprises in store.

When Arkhan received the summons he was more than three miles to the east, prowling along the trade road with a squadron of Numasi horsemen and nipping at the heels of the retreating enemy army. The cloud of locusts that swept down upon the immortal out of the darkness had spooked the still-living Numasi and their horses. Arkhan glared contemptuously at his erstwhile allies as the insects hissed and spun round his head.

'Return to my tent, favoured servant,' Arkhan heard in the rustle of chitin and the buzz of papery wings. 'The time of retribution is nigh.'

Arkhan turned command of the squadron over to its Numasi captain, ordering them to close and engage the enemy rearguard throughout the night. Then he turned, wheeled his undead horse around and raced off into the darkness.

The army of the Undying King was arrayed in a crescent formation that stretched for more than three miles from tip to tip, its outstretched arms reaching hungrily for the fleeing enemy host. Most of the warriors in the front lines were long dead, their flesh turned leathery by the desert air and their corpses home to burrowing scarabs and black desert scorpions. They advanced slowly and stolidly after their foes. When the king and his immortals halted the army at dawn they stood in ordered ranks, baking in the heat, until the time to march came once again.

By contrast, the remainder of the host, less than a third of Khemri's city levies and what was left of the allied armies of Numas and Zandri, followed a few miles behind the vanguard along the trade road, their heads bowed with hunger and fear. The living trembled at the sight of the walking dead, furtively making signs to ward off evil when they believed none of Nagash's immortals were looking. The Undying King drove them without mercy. Wounds were not tended, nor were they fed more than a meagre ration of water and grain each day. Nagash cared little about the condition of their flesh, for when the time came his warriors would fight, one way or the other.

The companies of living warriors averted their eyes and clutched their spears with trembling hands as Arkhan raced past. He came upon his master's pavilion near the rear of the column, arrayed on a level patch of sand a few hundred yards from the road. Other tents had been pitched nearby, and Arkhan saw many of the army's engineers labouring at a frantic pace under the stern gaze of several of the king's immortals. He had heard rumours of Nagash's new battlefield innovations, and presumed that they were being made in anticipation of the coming fight at Quatar.

More than a score of undead mounts waited outside the master's tent as Arkhan approached, and he carefully concealed a frown of disapproval. Since rejoining the army a few weeks past, he'd taken pains to avoid his fellow immortals. The years of solitude in his black tower had left him impatient and mistrustful of the company of others, particularly of his own kind. Steeling himself, he slid from the saddle and entered his master's tent without a passing glance at the slaves cowering outside.

The tent's main chamber was crowded with kneeling figures, all waiting upon the king. Arkhan spied Raamket, garbed in a fresh cloak of flayed human hide, and the bandaged figure of Shepsu-hur. The immortals studied Arkhan with the flat, hungry stare of a pack of jackals, and he bared his broken teeth in return.

Nagash, the Undying King, sat upon Khemri's ancient throne at the rear of the chamber, flanked by his uneasy allies. Arkhan could see at once that the campaign had left its mark on the three kings. Amn-nasir, the Priest King of Zandri, was nearly catatonic, his eyes glazed and his expression slack under the effects of the black lotus. Seheb and Nuneb, the twin Kings of Numas, had kept their wits so far, but both of the young men were anxious and uncharacteristically withdrawn. One of them, Arkhan couldn't tell which, kept biting at his nails when he thought no one was looking. The immortal could smell the blood on the king's fingertips from across the chamber.

The vizier marched past the kneeling immortals and sank to his knees directly at Nagash's feet. He could hear the faint moans of the necromancer's ghostly retinue swirling above his head.

'What is your command, master?' he asked.

Nagash straightened upon the throne.

'We draw close to Quatar,' the Undying King declared, 'and the time has come for the craven King of the White City to pay for his surrender at the Gates of the Dawn.' The necromancer stretched out his hand. 'I shall send you forth with these immortals to Quatar's great necropolis, and there you will raise up an army of vengeance to take the city from our foes. When the rebel kings of the east reach Quatar's walls, you will be there to bar their path and seal their doom.'

Now, Arkhan understood the strategy behind the necromancer's slow pursuit of the enemy army. He had been herding them onwards to Quatar, where he planned to trap them against the walls of the city and crush them without mercy. The vizier glanced back at the kneeling immortals. With so many together, they could raise a considerable army among the houses of the dead, easily enough to overwhelm Quatar's meagre garrison, and afterwards, who knew? The White City would be in need of a new king.

The vizier smiled and bowed his head to Nagash. 'It shall be as you command, master,' he said. 'We are your arrow of vengeance. Release us, and we will fly straight to your enemy's heart.'

The Undying King gave the vizier a grim smile.

'I count upon it, loyal servant,' he said. Then he beckoned, and slaves appeared from the shadows bearing goblets brimming with crimson liquid. 'Drink,' Nagash commanded. 'Fill your limbs with vigour for the battle to come.'

Arkhan was on his feet in an instant, feeling the sudden tension in the air as the immortals reacted to the presence of the elixir. A slave stepped before the vizier and offered him the first taste. Arkhan found himself staring into Ghazid's blue eyes as he took the vessel in both hands and drank deeply, his body shuddering with the taste of power.

The rest of the immortals surged forwards like jackals around a corpse. Ghazid watched them drink and cackled with glee, his eyes glittering with madness.

The howling swarm sped across the face of the moon in the early hours of the morning, passing undetected over the heads of the enemy army retreating to the east. Faster than the flight of a night hawk, they sped to the great plain at the foot of the Brittle Peaks, where the towers of Quatar rose like white sepulchres beneath the stars. Ribbons of smoke curled into the night sky from the poorer districts of the city, where victims of the plague were still being found and given to the flames.

The swirling, seething swarm passed over the near-deserted city and its furtive sentries, seeking the vast complex of tombs that spread along the foot of the mountains east of Quatar. The huge swarm seemed to hover over the necropolis for a moment, billowing this way and that as though searching among the maze of crypts. Then the living cloud gathered itself and hurtled southwards, crossing the road leading from Quatar to the Gates of the Dawn and settling among the shabby, crumbling tombs of the city's poorer citizens.

Smoking husks of dead insects showered down among the tombs as the immortals came to rest after their long flight from Nagash's pavilion. Arkhan paused for a moment to check his bearings and gauge the height of the moon. It was less than three hours until dawn, he reckoned. There was little time to lose.

Hissed commands passed among the immortals. They fanned out quickly among the tombs, spacing out in an arcane pattern that they had been taught centuries past. Arkhan stood in the centre of this sorcerous web, his veins brimming with inhuman power. He reached out with his senses and felt the currents of magic rippling through the air. Even hundreds of leagues distant he could feel the pulse of the Black Pyramid like the thundering heart of a god.

Arkhan raised his hands to the black sky and began the great invocation, and one by one his fellow immortals joined in, until the air shook with their dreadful voices. Dark magic spread like a stain among the tombs, seeping irresistibly past the cracked facades and flowing over the shrouded bodies within. The vizier knew that the poor could not afford the elaborate protective wards that were typically worked into the tombs of the nobility, making his task that much easier.

The ritual continued for more than an hour, growing in complexity and power until Arkhan thought that he could feel the energy humming along his skin. Faint curtains of dust rose above the countless tombs as their contents began to shift and press at the thin stone walls. Portals cracked apart and collapsed in a shower of rubble as the first warriors of Arkhan's new army shambled out into the darkness.

Hundreds upon hundreds of skeletal figures clawed their way from their tombs, their eye sockets lit with tiny sparks of grave-light. Tattered, filthy wrappings fluttered from their limbs as they shuffled silently westwards in response to Arkhan's will. In the broken ground outside the necropolis they formed into rough companies, directed by the subordinate efforts of the remaining immortals. Within two hours the army of the dead numbered thirty thousand strong, testing Arkhan's necromantic powers to the very limit.

The sky was paling to the east. Arkhan knew that at dawn his control would weaken, as he was forced to take shelter from the sun's rays. Soon the people of Quatar would look pleadingly to the east, begging for deliverance from the ghastly horde that swept over their walls.

Not one would live to see the dawn.

TWENTY-FOUR

THE BLOOD OF PRINCES

Khemri, the Living City,
in the 46th year of Ualatp the Patient
(-1950 Imperial Reckoning)

The Priest King of Khemri stood beneath the blazing noonday sun and tried not to think of blood.

He stood upon an overseer's platform at the edge of the Plain of Kings, watching the labourers at work on the foundations of the Black Pyramid. At Nagash's command, the great plain at the heart of Khemri's necropolis had been transformed. His plan for the pyramid made use of every last hectare of available space set aside for future kings, and demanded still more besides. Scores of smaller crypts had been disassembled and relocated to other parts of the necropolis in order to make room for stone-carving yards, staging areas and rubbish piles. A wide avenue had been built running north from the great plain, requiring the demolition of still more crypts so that huge blocks of marble could be brought from the barges tied up along the river. At the moment it was being used to remove hundreds of cart-loads of sandy soil as Nagash's army of slaves excavated the pyramid's subterranean chambers. When it was complete, the Black Pyramid would dwarf every other structure in the necropolis. Indeed, it would be the largest single structure anywhere in Nehekhara. The king's ambitions required nothing less.

Nagash folded his arms tightly around his chest. Despite the heat of the day, his bones felt brittle and cold, and an aching weariness began to sap the strength from his limbs. He would need to feed again soon. Months of experimentation had allowed Nagash to refine the process of leeching vitality from living blood, but its effects were all too fleeting. Depending on the quality of the source, the king could enjoy a few days of youthful vigour, or a week at most.

The benefits were astonishing. Nagash could not remember possessing such strength or clarity of thought in his entire life, but each time the tide of blood receded he was left feeling weaker and more wretched than ever before. No amount of food or rest could take away the awful chill that settled into his bones, or the alarming weakness that left him as helpless as a child. The only answer was to find another source of blood.

Fortunately, the king had those in plentiful supply.

There were half a dozen slave camps situated around the edges of the city's necropolis, enclosed by perimeters of trenches and spiked wooden barricades and patrolled by horsemen from the king's army. Since the sack of Zandri, more than thirty thousand labourers had been assembled for Nagash's grand scheme, including the bulk of King Nekumet's army and two-thirds of his citizens. Still more were arriving each day, as Nehekhara's other great cities sent tribute to ensure that they didn't suffer the same fate as Nekumet and his people.

The battle on the road to Khemri had been swift and decisive, thanks in no small part to Zandri's large force of mercenary troops. The superstitious northern barbarians had no faith in the gods of the Blessed Land, and as such they enjoyed no protection from the incantations of Neru's priestesses. That left them vulnerable to Nagash's sorceries, and over the course of the night he had tormented the warriors with all manner of ghostly visions and portents of doom. By midnight the barbarians were panicked and on the verge of riot, and when Nekumet and his noblemen attempted to restore order, the mercenaries rose up in revolt.

Chaos tore through the enemy camp as the Zandri army turned upon itself in hours of confused, brutal fighting. By dawn, the surviving mercenaries had managed to escape the Zandri camp and blundered southwards, deeper into the desert. Nekumet's remaining troops were exhausted, hungry and dispirited, and their camp all but destroyed. At dawn, the dazed survivors began to salvage what they could from the wreckage, and then Nagash's army appeared in full battle order on the road behind them.

Despite everything they had endured the night before, Nekumet's troops still managed to form up and offer battle, but before long they found themselves under attack from Arkhan's cavalry as well, and the Zandrian battleline quickly disintegrated under the pressure. By mid-morning King Nekumet offered his terms of surrender to Nagash, but the King of Khemri refused. There would be no terms. Zandri would surrender unconditionally, or they would be slaughtered to a man. Dismayed, Nekumet had no choice but to comply.

By the end of the day, the survivors of Zandri's army had been disarmed and bound into slave coffles for the long march to Khemri. Nekumet, stripped of his crown and royal robes, was dressed in sackcloth and sent home on the back of a flea-bitten mule. It was only when he'd arrived at Zandri's broken gate that he learned what Nagash had done to his city.

News of the battle raced across Nehekhara like a storm wind, borne by the shocked ambassadors fleeing the ruin of Zandri. In Khemri, crowds of citizens turned out along the great avenues to cheer the return of their conquering king. The Living City's pre-eminence had been restored in a single, brutal stroke, and Nagash's great work could begin in earnest.

The king surveyed the scope of the excavations once more and nodded thoughtfully. A small retinue of scholars and slaves stood next to him, bearing copies of the pyramid's plans for Nagash's reference. To the king's right stood Arkhan the Black, clad in fine robes and wearing gold rings stolen from the defeated Zandrian nobles. He had been rewarded well for his efforts against Nekumet's army, and was the king's chief vizier, charged with overseeing the construction of the Black Pyramid. Also, he had been the first of Nagash's vassals to taste the king's life-giving elixir and enjoy the vigour of youth once more.

Nagash gauged the progress of the excavations and judged that they were proceeding well.

'Continue as planned,' he told his vizier. 'The excavation will proceed night and day until completed.'

'Does that include our citizens, or just the slaves?' the vizier inquired carefully. To speed construction further, Nagash had ordered the city's criminals put in the slave camps, and every citizen due to perform his annual civil service was sent to the construction site. Until the massive structure was finished, Khemri's roads and infrastructure would go untended.

Nagash considered the question and waved his hand expansively.

'Save the most difficult and dangerous tasks for the slaves,' he said, 'but everyone must still do their part.' Arkhan bowed.

'It shall be as you say,' he replied, 'but deaths among the slaves will increase. We have lost a sizeable number already due to hunger and disease.'

'Disease?' the king frowned. 'How is that possible?' The vizier shifted uncomfortably on his feet. He, too, was showing the first pangs of hunger; his eyes were sunken and his hands trembled slightly with cold.

'The priests of Asaph and Geheb have not been especially diligent in cleansing the camps of sickness,' he said. 'I have complained to the hierophants, but they claim that their priests are occupied with other matters.'

'Such as trying to undermine my rule,' Nagash growled. The temples of the city had been a constant nuisance since his ascension. They sent elders to the Grand Assemblies, calling on him to relinquish Neferem and agree to step aside as soon as Sukhet reached adulthood. Their acolytes spread rumours among the populace that the gods were displeased with his rule, and would punish Khemri unless he was forced out. No doubt they were taking their orders from the Hieratic Council at Mahrak, which had a vested interest in maintaining its authority over Nehekharan affairs. If he thought he could get away with it, Nagash would have gladly sent his warriors to clean out the temples and put the damned priests to work in the slave camp, but unfortunately the council still held too much power and influence over the other great cities, and so for the moment he had to endure their interference.

A chill wracked the king's powerful frame. He folded his arms tighter and scowled down at the pyramid's foundations.

'Any workers who perish, especially those who die at the excavation site, are to be added to the pyramid's inner structure. Bury them in the substrate. Mortar the walls with their blood and bones. Exactly how you do it isn't important, so long as their deaths are part of the pyramid's construction. Do you understand?'

The vizier nodded. Of all the king's vassals, Arkhan had the strongest grasp of the principles of necromancy. The death energies contained within the pyramid would help attune the structure to Nagash's invocations, and make it more receptive to the faint winds of dark magic.

'It will be done,' he said, bowing once more.

Satisfied, Nagash was about to take his leave and return to his studies at the palace when he caught sight of Khefru hurrying up the steps to the overseer's platform. Like Arkhan, the young priest had also been the recipient of the king's sorcerous elixir, though in Khefru's case he participated only at the king's express command. The servant's reluctance baffled Nagash, but it was clear that Khefru's ravaged health had benefited as much as the rest from the infusion of sorcerous vigour.

The young priest approached the king and bowed. Nagash studied the man intently.

'Why aren't you at the palace?' he asked. Among other things, Khefru was responsible for keeping watch over Neferem and her son, who were isolated from one another in different parts of the palace. Khefru paused for a moment to catch his breath. Under the harsh light of the sun, his skin was a pale, unhealthy yellow.

'An advance party arrived in the city an hour ago, with word that a royal delegation from Lahmia was on the way. King Lamasheptra is expected to arrive by late afternoon, and will request an audience at this evening's Grand Assembly,' he said.

The king's expression darkened.

'Where, no doubt, Lamasheptra will insist upon seeing his sister Neferem, and her son.'

'The advance party didn't specifically mention such a request,' the young priest said carefully. Nagash glared at the man.

'Don't be an idiot,' he snarled. 'Why else would the Lahmian king leave his flesh-pots and travel halfway across the country?' A faint shiver gripped Nagash's frame, which he quelled with gritted teeth. For a moment he wondered if perhaps there was time to feed before meeting with Lamasheptra, but the notion smacked too much of weakness, and he forced it aside. 'Frankly, this comes as no surprise,' he continued. 'It was only a matter of time before Lamasheptra managed to gather his courage and come here to test the strength of the old alliances.' He glowered at Khefru. 'How many warriors has he brought?'

'A handful of Ushabti and a squadron of horsemen. No more,' the priest said with a shrug.

Nagash nodded. 'Then he won't be planning on doing anything reckless. Very well,' he said, waving impatiently at Khefru. 'Inform Neferem and Sukhet that they will be attending the Grand Assembly this evening. Who knows, perhaps the sight of her son after so many years will break Neferem's resolve at long last. That would almost make the evening's farce worthwhile.'

The Lahmian delegation arrived at Settra's Court with a fanfare of trumpets and the rhythmic tinkle of ankle bells, accompanied by the whisper of silk and the patter of soft flesh on polished marble. Conversations stopped and heads turned as half a dozen dancing girls wove their way down the gleaming aisle, swirling through twisting ribbons of orange, yellow and red like beguiling sun-spirits. Jaded noblemen from all over Nehekhara forgot what they'd been saying a moment before as they caught tantalising glimpses of bared shoulders, rounded hips and dark, flashing eyes.

Behind the dancers came the Lahmian king, striding along the aisle in a blissful cloud of narcotic incense. Lamasheptra was lean and graceful, his steps as light and swift as the dancers that preceded him. He was a young, handsome man, little more than a child. The Kings of Lahmia married very late in life, claiming that they served their goddess best by drinking deep of all the decadence their city had to offer. Lamasheptra still had many decades of worship left in him, with a smooth, unlined face the colour of dark honey and limpid brown eyes. He had a sharp nose and a full, sensuous mouth framed by a close-cropped beard, and tightly curled black hair that hung well past his shoulders. Unlike the custom of most young nobles, Lamasheptra wore soft, flowing yellow silk robes that hung open at the chest, and patterned silk trousers. Gold rings glittered on his soft fingers, and an earring set with a gleaming ruby hung from his left earlobe. The assembled nobility stared at the Lahmian king as though he were some kind of exotic animal, and Lamasheptra revelled in the attention.

Not too long ago the king's court was an echoing, empty space, even during King Thutep's Grand Assemblies. Now, the space was as full as it had ever been. Throngs of newly raised nobility, bedecked in gaudy kilts and half-capes, stood and gaped at the Lahmian procession, while the ambassadors of Numas, Rasetra, Lybaras and Ka-Sabar stood in tight, apprehensive groups and whispered amongst themselves. The first emissaries had begun arriving within a month after the king's victory over Zandri, and they had listened fearfully as Nagash instructed them on the new state of affairs in Nehekhara. After what had happened to Zandri, none dared gainsay the man some called the Usurper.

At the far end of the great hall, gathered like a pack of baleful jackals, stood the king's chosen, his viziers and captains, those who served him first and best. They watched Lamasheptra and his retinue approach with the sharp stares of predators. In their midst, perched upon the dark throne of Settra the Great, sat Nagash the king. His eyes were intent upon the approaching Lahmians, but his face was coldly neutral.

A dozen steps from the dais the swirling dancers stopped and bowed, their silken ribbons rippling sinuously around them like tongues of flame. Lamasheptra passed among them and approached to the foot of the stone steps, so close that Arkhan and Shepsu-hur had to bow and give way for the king to pass.

Lamasheptra spread his hands in greeting and gave Nagash a dazzling, practiced smile.

'Greetings, cousin,' he said to the Usurper. 'I am Lamasheptra, fourth of the name, son of the great Lamasharazz. It is an honour to meet you at long last.'

'Then I am pleased for you,' Nagash said coolly. His smile did not reach the depths of his dark eyes. 'It has been some time since the sons of Lahmia attended upon the King of the Living City. I had begun to believe that you and your father meant to offer me insult.' Looks of shock flitted across the faces of the dancers, but Lamasheptra would not be baited.

'It is a long journey to the Living City, cousin,' the Lahmian king said smoothly. 'You may as well say the slow-moving river or the sandy road means to mock you.' Nervous laughter rose from the crowd, earning warning stares from the king's chosen. Lamasheptra pretended not to notice. 'I would not dream of offending a cousin of mine, especially one who has earned for himself such a fearsome throne.'

'Well said,' Nagash replied, his voice full of soft menace. 'What, then, is the reason for this timely visit?'

'What else, cousin? Duty and loyalty,' Lamasheptra said, 'and love of family. Before my blessed father died, he made me swear before the goddess to offer his blessings to his nephew Sukhet, whom he never knew. He also bade me give his farewells to his sister, Neferem. And so, to honour my father, I have made this long journey.'

'For Neferem, and for Sukhet, but not for me, your cousin?' Nagash asked.

Lamasheptra laughed, as though Nagash were the soul of wit. 'As though I could ignore the great Priest King of Khemri! Naturally, I have come to honour you, and assure you of Lahmia's continued esteem.'

'Nothing would please me more,' Nagash replied. 'For centuries, Khemri has treasured Lahmia's esteem greater than any other city's. I assume, then, that Lahmia will join the other cities of Nehekhara in providing a small token of this esteem.' The Lahmian's smile did not waver.

'One cannot put a price on esteem, cousin,' he said. 'What sort of token would satisfy you?'

'A thousand slaves,' Nagash said with a shrug. 'Surely a modest gift for such a wealthy city.'

'A thousand slaves a year?' Lamasheptra asked with a frown.

'Certainly not,' Nagash replied with a chuckle. 'A thousand slaves a month, to help with the great work I am building in Khemri's necropolis, and in the interests of peace, of course.'

'Peace. Of course,' the Lahmian replied, 'and a smaller price than Zandri was required to pay, I'm sure.'

'Indeed so,' Nagash said. 'I'm pleased to see you understand.' The Lahmian nodded.

'Never fear, cousin. I understand a great many things,' he said. Then he nodded to the lesser throne at Nagash's right. 'What I do not see is my noble aunt and her son. I have heard so many stories of Neferem's legendary beauty, and I have longed to witness it for myself.' He bowed slightly in the direction of the throne. 'I have a gift for her from the people of Lahmia, to show their continued love and devotion for the Daughter of the Sun. I trust you will permit me to present it to her?'

'We are always pleased to receive gifts from the great cities,' Nagash said dismissively. 'Bring it forth, and let us see it.'

Lamasheptra smiled broadly and beckoned to his retinue. A small figure slipped from the midst of the bodyguards, courtiers and slaves and hurried to the base of the dais. Nagash saw that it was a young boy, scarcely more than fifteen years of age, but he wore the bright yellow robes of a priest of Ptra. The boy stood at Lamasheptra's side and bowed deeply to Nagash.

The King of Khemri glowered at the boy. 'Is this some kind of jest?' he asked.

'An understandable reaction, cousin,' Lamasheptra said with a chuckle, 'but I assure you, Nebunefer here is a fully sanctified priest. The priests at Mahrak proclaim him to be the most gifted young man of his generation, and that the Great Father has a special destiny in mind for him. For now, though, he will wait upon the queen and see to her spiritual needs, since she is unable to attend the rites at the city temple.'

Nagash fought to conceal his irritation. The Lahmian fop was a clever one, he had to admit, but what were his motives? Had the Hieratic Council bribed him to send their little spy into the palace, or was Lamasheptra a willing ally of the damned priests?

He could refuse the gift, of course, but doing so would suggest weakness, and Mahrak would simply send one after another until they forced his hand. Nagash eyed the boy suspiciously. Nebunefer's face was open and confident, full of the self-assurance of youth. The king wondered what the boy's blood would taste like, and smiled.

'Welcome, boy,' Nagash said to Nebunefer. 'Serve the queen well, and in time, you will be rewarded.'

Nebunefer bowed once more. Lamasheptra's eyes glittered with triumph.

'Where is my beloved sister and her son?' he asked. 'I had thought to find her here, presiding over her guests and loyal subjects, as good rulers ought.'

Nagash considered Lamasheptra for a long, silent moment. Then he raised his right hand and beckoned to the shadows behind the throne.

Whispers rose from the darkness, followed by the sound of shuffling feet. The first person to appear was not Neferem, nor even Sukhet, but an old man, limping and broken, as though his bones filled his skin like shards of clay. His head was bald and scarred, his lips slack and twitching, but his blue eyes were sharp and fever-bright. Ghazid, the last Grand Vizier of Khemri, turned and beckoned to the shadows like a child calling for his playmates. He was ignorant of the staring faces in the crowd. The looks of horror and pity had no meaning for him any more. Nagash had spared his life on the night that he had buried his brother alive, but not out of mercy. He had given the old man into the hands of his vassals, who had tortured him inventively for many years. Age and great pain had worn away his once-sharp mind, until he was little more than a child in an old man's body. Then Nagash had returned him to Neferem and Sukhet as a gift.

Ghazid beckoned a tall, noble-looking young man out into the light. He was clad in noble finery, with a kilt and cape of purest samite and a prince's golden headdress on his brow. Sukhet had the handsome features of his father and the fierce demeanour of his illustrious grandfather, with piercing eyes and a strong, square chin. Gasps rose from the assembled crowd at the sight of him. Even Lamasheptra seemed struck by the young man's regal bearing.

Sukhet, son of Thutep, carried himself with great dignity and poise. He stepped past the great throne as though it were empty and descended the stone steps until he stood before the Lahmian king. A ripple of unease passed through the king's chosen at the sight of the young prince. Arkhan in particular eyed Sukhet as though he were a form of especially venomous snake.

Lamasheptra smiled warmly at Sukhet, apparently ignorant of the apprehensive stares of the noblemen around him. He started to speak, but the words dried up in his throat as he saw the Daughter of the Sun emerge from the darkness behind Nagash's throne.

She wore a simple gown of purest white, cinched by a girdle of leather and burnished copper that hung lightly upon her hips. Her long, black hair had been washed with scented oils and pulled back in a thick braid that hung nearly to her waist. The queen's green eyes were vivid in their kohl-darkened orbits, but no other balms or tinctures had been added to her face. Her feet were bare, as was her brow: the heavy golden cape and wondrous headdress of the queen had been left behind, along with the gold bracelets and rings that she had brought with her from far-off Lahmia. Neferem, Queen of the Living City and Daughter of the Sun, cloaked herself in anguish and loss. Her face was a pale mask, beautiful but still, like the image carved upon a sarcophagus.

The queen was not the young maiden she once had been. Life and loss had left their mark upon her features, ageing her well beyond her years. Gasps filled the echoing court at the sight of her, and even Lamasheptra was taken aback. The king staggered a half-step back, as though the sight of her were a physical blow. For the briefest instant, his brown eyes glanced at the man upon Khemri's throne, and then slowly, reverently, the King of Lahmia sank to his knees before Neferem.

In a rippling whisper of cloth, the rest of the court followed suit. Some knelt gracefully, while others simply fell to their knees in wonder. Within moments the only men standing were the king's chosen, who looked to one another with shifting, apprehensive stares, and the queen's son, Sukhet.

The prince turned, and saw his mother for the first time in nearly a decade.

Nagash studied the pair over steepled fingers and fought to stifle his anger. This had been a mistake. He should have arranged a private meeting between Lamasheptra and Sukhet instead of permitting this spectacle. He'd thought to demonstrate his control over Thutep's wife and heir by allowing them a brief moment at court, but he hadn't counted on the enduring superstition and sentimentality of the populace.

Sukhet stared into his mother's eyes, and in that moment he forgot himself. All dignity fled as he rushed to his mother and reached for her hands. Neferem reached for him as though in a dream, a slight frown of bemusement penetrating her shock. The prince took her hands in his and touched his forehead to them in a sign of reverence.

The King of Khemri paid no mind to the maudlin scene. His eyes were on Lamasheptra alone. The Lahmian was watching mother and son with an awestruck expression that could not quite hide the calculating look in his dark eyes.

At that moment Nagash realised that Sukhet had to die.

They came for him in the dead of night, when the rest of the palace was sleeping. Sukhet's cell was two levels beneath the sprawling palace, in a cramped chamber formerly reserved for storing expensive spices and wines. The entire section had been abandoned decades ago, back in Khetep's time. Only Khefru and Ghazid came and went through its darkened corridors these days, and Nagash's servant alone had the key to Sukhet's chamber.

Khefru led the way, holding an oil lamp in one trembling hand. The priest moved unerringly through the labyrinthine hallways, until he finally came upon an unmarked door of heavy, scarred teak. Khefru fumbled in his robes for several long moments before producing a long rod of tarnished bronze that he fit into the door's massive wood and bronze lock.

The mechanism turned with a loud clatter. As Khefru started to pull the door open, Arkhan the Black stepped forward and shoved the servant roughly aside, sending the oil lamp crashing to the floor. Behind the vizier, Raamket and Shepsu-hur rushed silently into the cell.

The chamber was small, barely twelve paces by six. A narrow bed was set against one long wall, with a cedar chest at the end for the prince's clothes. Opposite the bed stood a narrow table with a single chair and a small oil lamp, where the prince would take his meals or read books brought to him from the library. Though he was allowed to walk the grounds of the palace within carefully proscribed limits, the small room had been Sukhet's home for nearly ten years.

Ghazid rose from his pallet just inside the door, his battered face gaping in terror. He let out a wordless, childlike cry of fear as Raamket seized his arms and hurled him out of the way. The servant hit the stone wall beside the table and crumpled into a senseless heap.

Sukhet bolted from the narrow bed as the two noblemen closed in on him. Raamket reached him first, closing a powerful hand around the prince's left arm. Sukhet's right arm flashed downwards in a blurring arc, and Raamket let out a roar of pain. The handle of a small eating knife jutted from the man's collarbone, just a few inches to the right of his neck.

Shepsu-hur stepped forwards and smashed his fist into the prince's face, breaking his aquiline nose and splitting his lip. Sukhet's head jerked back and hit the wall over the bed, and the young man collapsed.

Raamket and Shepsu-hur grabbed the prince's legs and dragged him roughly onto the floor. Ghazid, regaining his senses, cowered against the wall and began to wail in terror. Sukhet spat blood and tried to tear himself free from the grip of his assailants, but then a shadow fell over him from the doorway of the cell.

Nagash loomed over the young prince with a pair of long, copper needles clutched in his hands.

'Hold him still!' he snapped. The coppery smell of spilled blood hung in the close air of the chamber, making the king almost dizzy with hunger.

Shepsu-hur and Raamket tightened their grip on the prince's arms, their faces contorted with effort. Nagash lunged forwards like a striking snake and drove the needles home. Sukhet's body went rigid with agony, the sight of which made Ghazid wail all the louder.

'Shut him up!' Nagash snarled, and Raamket began to beat the old man. At a nod from the king, Shepsu-hur stripped away the prince's tunic and threw it aside.

'The ink!' Nagash commanded, turning and stretching his hand to Khefru, who still stood in the corridor beyond.

The young priest hesitated, clutching the brush and ink pot in his hands. A look of dread marked his sallow, puffy features, but he had been given a taste of the king's elixir more than once, and a faint gleam of hunger shone in his eyes.

'Surely there is another way,' Khefru stammered. 'We can't do this, master. Not to him.'

'You dare to question me?' the king hissed. 'You, of all people? He is flesh and blood, just like all the others you stole off the city streets. He is no different from the slaves whose blood you drained, and then sipped from a golden cup!'

'He is a prince!' Khefru cried. 'The son of Thutep and the Daughter of the Sun. The gods will not forgive us!'

'The gods?' Nagash said incredulously. 'You little fool. We are gods now. The secret of immortality is ours.' He gestured to the stricken prince. 'His body is charged with divine power. Imagine how much sweeter, how much more potent it will be. We might not need another taste for a hundred years!'

Anguish wracked Khefru's face. 'If it's divine blood you want, then kill a priest!' he cried. 'If he dies, you lose your hold on Neferem, and Lahmia may well declare war against us. Is that what you want?'

'Neferem will not hear of this,' Nagash said coldly, 'until such time as I choose to tell her. Neither will Lahmia be told.' He took a threatening step towards Khefru. 'Sukhet has to die. He is too dangerous to be allowed to live. Did you not see how the people reacted to him at court?'

'But the queen–' Khefru stammered.

'The queen does not rule here!' Nagash roared. 'Don't tell me you have fallen under that witch's spell, have you? Have you? Because if you would rather I took the blood of a priest, I will open your veins here and now.'

Khefru recoiled from the king's malevolent voice, straight into the arms of Arkhan, who held him in an iron grip. The priest glanced up into the vizier's ghoulish face, and the courage went out of him. With trembling hands, he held out the ink and brush to the king.

Nagash took the instruments and turned back to the prince's rigid body. His eyes shone with avarice.

'Have a bowl ready once I've finished with the glyphs,' he said as he knelt beside Sukhet. 'I don't want to waste a single drop.'

Hours later, Nagash swept down the darkened corridor outside the queen's chambers, his robes billowing behind him like the wings of a desert eagle. Blood roared in his temples and burned along his veins: stolen blood, hot with the vitality of youth and the divinity of royal birth.

The guards standing outside the queen's door were hard-bitten men, cruel and incorruptible. As the queen's jailers they were prepared to die at a moment's notice to keep the queen's chambers sacrosanct, but they all quailed like frightened children at the sudden appearance of the king. They looked into Nagash's eyes and glimpsed the terrible power burning in their depths, like the fiery gaze of Usirian. As one, the guards sank to their knees and pressed their foreheads to the stone, their bodies trembling in fear. The king paid them no mind, sweeping past them like a storm wind and knocking the heavy door open with a brush of his left hand.

At once, a chorus of frightened shouts arose from the maids sleeping in the great antechamber beyond. They rose from their couches in terror, crying out the name of their mistress and begging the gods for aid.

'Silence!' Nagash cried, clenching his left hand into a fist and reciting an incantation in his mind. At once, the shadows of the great room thickened like ink and swallowed the women up in an icy embrace. He glided across the piled rugs, past their silent and quaking bodies, and burst into Neferem's bedroom.

The chamber was luxuriously appointed, with a gleaming marble floor and a high terrace that looked northwards towards the great river. Neferem had risen swiftly from her bed and covered her naked body with a silk sheet. Her black hair was unbound and spilled across her bare shoulders, and her eyes gleamed like a cat's in the moonlight. For the first time, a look of real fear shone upon Neferem's face.

Once more, Nagash looked upon her and was gripped with desire. With the power seething in his body, power drained from her son's veins he knew that he could take whatever he wished from her. He smiled a jackal's smile.

'I've been thinking,' he said slowly.

Neferem said nothing. Her body was taut with tension. All at once, Nagash realised that she had positioned herself with her back almost to the terrace across the room. If he took one step closer, he was certain she would throw herself from the balcony. The thought only made him want her even more.

'When I saw you at the assembly today, alongside your son, I realised that what I had done to you was wrong,' Nagash said. He indicated the bedroom with a wave of his arm. 'It isn't right to keep you locked up here, like a caged bird. I cannot possess you in such a way. Your will is strong, nearly as strong as mine, and you have already said that you would sooner die than submit to me. Every year that passes only draws you further from my grasp, until one day you will shed your mortal flesh and join your husband in the afterlife.'

A wary look came over Neferem's face. Her body relaxed very slightly.

'What you say is true,' she replied. 'If you thought to break my will by reuniting me with Sukhet this afternoon, it did just the opposite.'

'Oh, I know,' the king said. 'Your will is very strong, nearly as strong as mine. I see that now. And so, I'm here to set you free.'

The Daughter of the Sun gave Nagash a bewildered look.

'What do you mean?' she asked.

'I mean you have a choice,' the king said with a smile. 'Here and now, I swear an oath before the gods not to harm Sukhet from this moment forward. I will not use him to compel you ever again.' He took a slow step forwards. 'You are free to choose your own fate. Either remain here as you are and rule alongside me, or drink this, and life as you know it will end.'

Nagash raised his right hand. In it he held a small golden cup, half-full with dark liquid. The elixir was still warm, fresh from Sukhet's young heart. The queen considered the cup. Her face became very still and calm.

'You swear that Sukhet will be safe?'

'From this moment forward he may do as he wishes,' Nagash said. 'I swear it, by all the gods.'

The Daughter of the Sun nodded, and came to a swift decision. 'Give me the cup, then,' she said.

'Are you certain?' Nagash asked. 'Once you have drunk from the cup, there will be no turning back.' Neferem raised her chin and gave Nagash a haughty look.

'I have never been more certain of anything in my life,' she replied. 'Let the darkness come. I weary of this sad and terrible life.' The necromancer smiled.

'As you wish, o queen,' he said, and handed the cup to her. 'Drink deep, loyal wife. The effect will be swift and painless.'

TWENTY-FIVE

THE ROAD OF BONES

Quatar, the City of the Dead,
in the 63rd year of Ptra the Glorious
(-1744 Imperial Reckoning)

The army of the east had marched through the night and on into the sunrise, hastening their steps towards the City of the Dead.

The first companies crested the high dunes at the western edge of the Plain of Usirian just before midday, and when they saw the white city shimmering in the searing light they raised their hands to the sky and thanked the Great Father for their deliverance. They lurched and stumbled down the sandy slope, breaking ranks as they succumbed to the promise of cool water, fresh food and a pallet in the shade where they could sleep without fear. The noblemen in command of the companies made a half-hearted effort to restore discipline, but their throats were caked in dust and after weeks of strict rations they were hungrier than they had ever been in their lives. When the subsequent formations reached the edge of the plain and saw the headlong rush for the city they joined in, until by the time Rakh-amn-hotep reached the dunes with the army's centre he saw a veritable flood of tanned bodies pouring across the rocky ground towards Quatar's stained walls.

The king reined in his chariot with a stream of bitter curses. The leading edge of the mob was more than a mile away. There was no stopping them, but Rakh-amn-hotep vowed that he would have their commanders whipped before the day was out. His presence at the dune crest kept the rest of the army in line. He could see temptation in the eyes of the men, but one look at the king's furious expression was enough to remind them of their training, and their discipline held as they continued on to Quatar.

Rakh-amn-hotep waited there as the rest of the host filed past, baking in the still, dusty air as he watched for the leading elements of the army's rearguard. The long, terrible retreat would not be done until the last man of the last company passed through the city gates.

The king's chariot driver wiped his gleaming brow and pulled a thin leather flask from his belt. He offered it first to the king, but Rakh-amn-hotep stoically declined.

'Drink your fill,' he told the man. 'I can wait.'

When the creak and rumble of chariot wheels reached the king's ears several minutes later it took Rakh-amn-hotep by surprise. He found himself blinking dazedly to the west.

'So soon?' he murmured. 'By the gods, is this all we have left?'

The army's remaining chariots and its squadrons of heavy horsemen rode past the king in good order, tired but proud of their hard duty covering the army's retreat. The Rasetran chariots were pulled by horses, taken from the supply train when their swift jungle lizards had perished in the heat. The charioteers raised their weapons in weary salute to the king.

Ekhreb, the king's champion, appeared with the last of the rearguard squadrons, riding in the saddle of a dust-stained mare.

'What did you do with your chariot, you damned fool?' the king asked.

'Traded it to a bandit princess for a cup of cool water,' the champion replied in a deadpan voice.

'She didn't try to entice you with her other charms?'

'She may have tried. I was too busy drinking.'

The king managed a weary chuckle, and asked, 'What did happen to your chariot?' Ekhreb sighed.

'We hit one too many rocks cutting back and forth across the road. The left wheel was cracked through. Fortunately, the cavalry has plenty of spare horses.'

'Any signs of pursuit?' the king asked, but the champion shook his head.

'Not since dawn,' he said. 'We were probed by some Numasi horsemen just before the moons set, but they withdrew off to the west just before daybreak.' Rakh-amn-hotep nodded thoughtfully.

'They assumed we'd make camp at daybreak, like normal,' he said. 'Now they're more than half a day's march behind us. That's the first good news we've had in weeks.'

'And not a moment too soon,' Ekhreb agreed. He gestured at the distant mob streaming across the plain. 'The men are at their breaking point.'

'Only half of them,' the king replied testily. 'It's a disgrace, but the officers are to blame. After we've had a day's rest I intend to sort things out, believe me.'

'And there will be much wailing and gnashing of teeth in the city of Quatar,' the champion said with a rueful grin. He watched the running figures for a moment, and then his brow furrowed in bemusement.

Rakh-amn-hotep was just about to order his chariot forwards again when he caught the look on his champion's face.

'What is it?' he asked.

'I'm not sure,' Ekhreb said. 'Does the city look strange to you?'

* * *

At the far end of the Plain of Usirian the city of Quatar shimmered like a desert mirage. Its white walls, once stained with the red rain of Nagash's terrible plague, had been bleached by years of relentless sunlight, and they shimmered with heat like clay fresh from the kiln. The City of the Dead gleamed like a new sepulchre, and the men of the allied army rushed towards it with open arms and hoarse shouts of joy.

None of the exhausted warriors noticed that Quatar's gates were still shut, at a time when there ought to have been a meagre but steady flow of traffic into and out of the city. Nor did they wonder at the lack of smoke hanging over the rooftops. The hearths and clay ovens had all gone cold during the night.

The warriors made it to the cool shadow of the city walls and fell to their knees, gasping, and in some cases weeping in relief. Red-faced noblemen shouted up at the battlements, calling for a guard to throw open the gates. After a moment, the rest of the men took up the shout, calling loudly enough to wake the dead.

In the darkness of the city's eastern gatehouse half a dozen pallid figures were startled awake by the clamour. They cursed in surprise at the sound of hundreds of shouting voices, and in their fear and confusion they commanded their warriors to awaken.

All along the broad walkway running atop the western wall, thousands of skeletal warriors began to stir. Bleached skulls rose from the stone walkway, turning this way and that in search of their foes. Bones clattered and scraped as they reached for bows and arrows or bundles of bronze-headed javelins. There were no shouted commands, nor the strident call of war-horns. Silent and purposeful, the undead warriors climbed to their feet and took aim at the helpless men below.

The first hissing flight of arrows went almost unnoticed by the warriors on the plain. Men toppled over dead with scarcely a sound, or collapsed in shock as the pain of their wounds took hold. The groans of the dying were drowned by the cheers and desperate pleas of their comrades for several seconds more, until a ragged volley of javelins darkened the sky overhead and fell in a deadly rain among the reeling mob. Shouts of relief turned to frightened screams as scores of men were wounded or slain. Warriors shouted in panic and confusion. Some waved their arms wildly at the gaunt silhouettes atop the wall, believing that the city's defenders were firing on them by mistake. Officers shouted conflicting orders, some acting on instinct and trying to form the men into companies, while others screamed for a full retreat and fled back towards the rest of the army. The men caught in between, dazed with exhaustion and hunger, were cut down where they stood.

When the first arrows started to fly, Rakh-amn-hotep could not believe his eyes. He rubbed his hand across his face and squinted into the harsh light, convinced that he'd been mistaken. Then he heard the faint sound of screams and the strident call of horns from the centre of the army and the awful truth struck home.

'Gods above,' the king said softly, his voice numb with despair. 'Nagash has taken Quatar. How in the name of all that is holy...'

Ekhreb cursed, reaching for his sword.

'What do we do, great one?' he asked.

The world seemed to spin around the king. He swayed on his feet, clutching the side of the chariot to steady himself.

'Do?' he echoed, his voice filled with dismay. 'What can we do? That monster is always one step ahead of us! It's as though he knows our every thought–'

'If that were true his men would be right on our heels, herding us to slaughter,' the champion snapped, his tone so sharp that it struck the king like a blow. 'Get a hold of yourself. Nagash is no all-seeing god. He's taken Quatar, but we're not encircled yet. We still have room to manoeuvre, but the men need direction. What are your orders?'

Rakh-amn-hotep recoiled from the champion's stern tone, but Ekhreb's words had their desired effect. Anger replaced shock and despair, and the king began to think.

'All right,' the king growled. 'Let's get ourselves out of this mess.' He stared at the distant city and shook his head bitterly. 'We can't retake the city, not in the shape we're in.' Once more, despair threatened to overwhelm him, but the Rakh-amn-hotep pushed the feelings aside. 'We'll have to continue the retreat.'

The champion nodded. 'South, down the trade road to Ka-Sabar, or north, towards the River Vitae?' he asked.

'Neither,' Rakh-amn-hotep growled. 'If we go north, Nagash can trap us against the river and destroy us. And Ka-Sabar lies too far to the south. Without supplies we'd lose more than half the army on the march.' With a bleak look on his face, he pointed further eastwards, beyond the City of the Dead. 'No, we'll have to circle around Quatar and risk the Valley of Kings. It's more defensible, and Mahrak lies at the far end. We know we can find safe haven there.'

The king did not point out that such a retreat would spell the doom of the great crusade against the Usurper. Nagash would pursue them eastwards, and from this day forward the armies of the east would be fighting, not for the sake of Nehekhara, but for the survival of their people. The alliance would very likely end, as each king sought to make his own peace with Khemri.

Rakh-amn-hotep looked out across the Plain of Usirian and felt the tides of the war turning, flowing inexorably from his grasp.

'Form up your horsemen and chariots,' he told Ekhreb, and pointed off to the south-east. 'You'll lead the advance around the southern edge of the city in case the enemy tries to block our path to the valley. If no one challenges you, ride on to the Gates of the Dawn and seize the fortifications. There are cisterns and storehouses within the walls. We'll take all we can carry and see if the Lybarans can find a way to collapse the gates behind us. That might buy us another day or two.'

Ekhreb accepted Rakh-amn-hotep's orders with a curt nod. After all he had seen during the battle at the fountains and the grim retreat afterwards, the thought of destroying the ancient Gates made no impression on him at all.

'What about you?' he asked the king. The Rasetran nodded at the chaos spreading across the plain.

'I'm going down there to rally those damned fools and get them moving,' he said. He held out his hand. 'Get going, old friend,' he told his champion. 'I'll see you in the valley beyond the Gates of the Dawn. By then I'll have figured out a proper punishment for giving me the sharp side of your tongue.' Ekhreb gathered up his reins.

'You could relieve me of command and send me home,' he offered. 'It would be a terrible disappointment, but I imagine I could live with it.'

'Couldn't we all,' the king retorted, and the two warriors parted ways, racing to pull their army back from the brink of destruction once again.

Arkhan awoke in darkness, feeling the stirring of his skeletal warriors like the buzzing of wasps within his brain.

He was sitting upon the Ivory Throne of Quatar, his pale face and hands stained black with drying blood from the entertainments of the night before. A handful of immortals slept upon the blood-spattered floor around the throne, surrounded by the detritus of their revels. Most of the vizier's undead brethren had scattered across the city with the coming of the dawn, seeking their own solitary havens to wait out the light of day. It appeared that he was not the only immortal growing ever more solitary and mistrustful as the years went by.

The vizier experienced a moment of disorientation, like a man wakened suddenly from a dream. He could sense a portion of his makeshift army in action off to the west, probably the bowmen he'd situated along the city wall. Though the undead were extensions of his will, his ability to sense their activities was vague at best despite his growing skill. At the moment the connection was more tenuous still, and with a start he realised that it was midday, and the hateful sun was almost directly overhead.

The other immortals were beginning to stir, peering warily into the darkness of the throne room. Raamket rose swiftly to his feet, swathed in a fresh kilt and a knee-length coat of soft flesh. Nagash had been very specific as to the fate of Nemuhareb, the Priest King of Quatar, but less so with the rest of the king's family. The immortal had stripped away the skin of Nemuhareb's children with care.

'What is happening?' Raamket hissed. Clothed in human skin and dappled with dried gore, the noble's voice was thin and fearful as a child's.

'The enemy is here,' Arkhan snarled, leaping from the throne. Behind him came a rustle of flesh and the faint drip of blood as the wind of his passing stirred what was left of the Lord of Tombs. At the command of the Undying King, Nemuhareb had been skinned alive, and his hide, with its nerves carefully and magically preserved, had been stretched across a standard pole and painted with necromantic runes using the king's heart blood. When Nagash's army eventually marched from Quatar they would carry the flayed skin and tormented soul of Nemuhareb before them as a warning to those who would defy the will of Khemri.

'The damned eastern kings force-marched their armies the rest of the way to Quatar instead of waiting one more day as Nagash expected,' Arkhan continued, his anger growing by the moment. He cursed himself for a fool. After weeks of hounding Akhmen-hotep and the Bronze Host across the Great Desert he'd allowed himself to indulge in too much celebration after his easy conquest of Quatar. Now, instead of Nagash's army pinning their foes against the city walls and slaughtering them, Arkhan was faced with stopping the eastern armies with the scrapings taken from the city necropolis. The archers and javelin throwers on the walls were the best-armed troops he had, and his immortals were imprisoned inside their own havens for as long as the sun burned overhead.

The vizier's blood-smeared hands clenched into impotent fists. Furious, he sent a single, burning command to his undead army.

At this point there was nothing left for Arkhan to do but kill as many of the easterners as he could.

The eastern end of the Plain of Usirian had been transformed into a killing ground. Hundreds of dead and dying men littered the rocky field beneath the walls of Quatar, and still the arrows arced through the blazing sky. The survivors of the allied armies' ill-fated lead companies were in full flight, trampling one another in their haste to escape the rain of death. As they ran, bony hands burst from the loose soil and clutched at their ankles. Men fell screaming as the earth heaved and countless skeletons burst from the ground among the panicked troops and set upon them with jagged teeth and claw-like fingers.

Those few that survived the jaws of Arkhan's fearsome trap retreated back to the main body of the eastern host and sent tremors of terror and despair through the ranks. Men wavered, already pushed to the limits of their resolve by the hardships of the long retreat. Officers shouted encouragement and uttered blistering oaths to try to keep their warriors in line, but for a few, desperate moments the allied army teetered on the brink of collapse.

Then, just as all seemed lost, the sound of war-horns carried through the din and the earth rumbled like a drum under the beat of thousands of hooves as the army's weary cavalry swept down the column's right flank and charged once more into the fray. They smashed through part of the shambling horde of skeletons, smashing their bodies to pieces and grinding them under their hooves before swinging to the south and circling around the enemy-held city.

Though the charge had only stopped part of the enemy attack, it restored some of the army's lost courage and halted the mindless spread of panic. Moments later Rakh-amn-hotep reached the centre of the army, riding past the frightened companies and galvanising them with his presence. He roared imprecations at the retreating warriors, halting them in their tracks through the sheer, indomitable force of his presence. Oblivious to the arrows hissing through the air around him, he sent the shattered companies marching to the rear of the column and formed a battleline to receive the advancing horde.

The skeletons attacked in waves, clawing mindlessly at the shields and helms of the exhausted spearmen, but with the king at their back the companies stood their ground and they hurled back one assault after the next. Men in the rear ranks picked up rocks and hurled them at the shambling skeletons, smashing skulls and splitting ribcages.

After weathering five separate attacks, Rakh-amn-hotep passed a command to his signallers, and the army began to advance. The companies pressed forwards, a step at a time, carving a path through the skeletal horrors and slowly working their way around the perimeter of the city towards the Gates of the Dawn.

Arrows continued to rain down on the warriors from the walls of Quatar, but the range was great, and few found their mark. Rakh-amn-hotep rolled up and down the length of the advancing army, encouraging them to keep pushing forwards against the tide of bones.

One hour passed, and then another. Weary beyond reason, the army fought on, passing south of Quatar and then forcing their way eastwards. The Rasetran king turned his attention to forming a rearguard from the mauled companies at the back of the column, standing with them and holding off what remained of the undead attackers while the rest of the host retreated safely beyond their reach.

The fire of the archers dwindled steadily as their supply of arrows ran low, and less than two hundred skeletons remained on the sun-baked plain to challenge the retreating host. The ghastly mob made one last attempt against the rearguard, and this time the eastern warriors responded with such fury that not one of the grisly warriors survived.

Alone and unchallenged upon the field, the rearguard raised their spears and offered praise to the gods and to Rakh-amn-hotep for their victory, but when the warriors turned to salute their king they found his chariot empty. Rakh-amn-hotep lay upon the ground just a few yards away, his chariot driver kneeling at his side. An arrow, one of the very last fired from the city walls, had taken the bold king in the throat.

TWENTY-SIX

THE CITY OF THE GODS

Quatar, the City of the Dead,
in the 63rd year of Ptra the Glorious
(-1744 Imperial Reckoning)

So long as he drank his master's elixir, Arkhan the Black was immortal. Thus, pain applied in just the right way could be made to last a very, very long time.

The vizier writhed and gurgled in a sticky pool of his own fluids, smothered by a wet, chitinous blanket of tomb beetles. His clothes and most of his skin had long since been eaten away, and the flesh beneath chewed to a pulp as the scarabs worked their way into the tender organs beneath. When he tried to keep screaming, the air whistled tunelessly through the gaping holes in his throat, and all that emerged from his gaping mouth was the rustling, tearing sound of hundreds of pairs of mandibles.

Nagash sat straight-backed upon the throne of Quatar with the hide of its former ruler stirring at his back. His immortals, as well as the vassal Kings of Numas and Zandri, all waited upon the king as he meted out his displeasure on the vizier. Nagash's undead champions watched Arkhan's suffering with wary, subdued expressions. Never before had they been shown the agonies that one of their own kind could be made to endure, and, to a man, they all feared that they could be next. For the kings, however, the horror was even worse. Seheb and Nuneb had collapsed early on, their eyes wide and feverish with shock. Their Ushabti had little choice but to take the twin kings by the arms and hold them bodily upright until Nagash declared the audience to be at an end. Amn-nasir drank and drank from the goblet clutched in his trembling hand, but no amount of wine and crushed lotus could banish the scene unfolding at his feet.

The beetles had been at work for more than an hour, and yellowed bones could be seen amid the tattered scraps of red meat still clinging to Arkhan's frame. With a rustle and a swirl of the necromancer's ghostly retinue, Nagash stretched forth his hand and the swarm of beetles fled the vizier's ruined body in a chittering tide, racing across the marble floor and over the sandalled feet of the immortals.

'You failed me,' the Undying King said. He rose to his feet and approached Arkhan's ravaged form. 'I delivered our enemies into your hands, and you let them slip away.'

Arkhan's body shivered and twitched. He turned his shredded face to his master. Blood and other fluids pooled in the empty eye sockets. His jaw worked clumsily, driven by just a few remaining shreds of muscle, but the only sound he could manage was a thin, tortured wheeze.

The Undying King held out his hand, and Ghazid, his servant, appeared from the shadows behind the throne. The blind wretch carried a wide copper bowl brimming with a thick, steaming crimson fluid, and he walked with exaggerated care, as though fearful of spilling a single drop. A shiver went through the immortals as they smelled the elixir. One or two even forgot themselves and took a step or two towards the bowl, their blue lips drawn back in a rictus of thirst. Nagash stilled them with a single look.

For several long minutes there was only the swish of the servant's feet upon the stones and Arkhan's jagged, whistling breaths.

It had been barely seven hours since the ambush outside the city walls. The main body of Nagash's host had arrived within two hours after sunset. As soon as the king realised he'd been deceived he'd driven his troops forwards with merciless zeal, but by then it was already too late. The armies of the east had withdrawn far up into the Valley of Kings, and the Lybarans had managed to collapse the Gates of the Dawn behind them. The king's skeletal horde was digging its way through the rubble with the untiring energy of the living dead, but it would be hours, perhaps days, before a path could be cleared to allow the army through.

The plain outside the City of the Dead was carpeted with the bodies of the fallen. Perhaps five thousand enemy troops had been killed in the battle, but many more had managed to escape. The Undying King had not been pleased by the news.

Ghazid came to a halt beside his master. Nagash glanced down into the bowl's depths, and placed his palm against the red, turgid surface.

The necromancer's gaze fell to the vizier's ruined body. His ghostly servants reached out to Arkhan, winding ethereal tendrils around his arms and legs, and then picking him up off the floor. He hung upright before his master, dangling awkwardly like a smashed puppet. Blood ran from the chewed flesh in long, ropy strands.

Nagash stepped forwards and pressed his bloody hand to Arkhan's raw face. The immortal stiffened, bones and cartilage crackling wetly as the sorcerous mixture went to work restoring the vizier's body. Limbs twisted and popped, pulled back into place by knitting muscle and tendons. Blood poured in a rush from split arteries and veins as Arkhan's heart gained strength, pouring onto the marble, and then slowing steadily as the vessels closed and were covered by a pale film of skin.

More cartilage popped in Arkhan's throat. The vizier's chest swelled with an agonised breath, and he let out a single, tortured scream.

The Undying King took his hand away from Arkhan's face. The red print of his palm and fingertips vanished in moments, like water soaked into parched earth. Arkhan shuddered convulsively, and then spoke. His words came haltingly as his lips grew back to cover his teeth.

'We... did... all,' he stammered. 'All that... could... be done.' Arkhan shuddered again. Newly formed eyes rolled in their sockets. 'They... came in daylight.'

'Better you had burned and done my bidding!' Nagash cried, and the braziers guttered as though caught in a desert wind.

'Slay me then!' Arkhan said. 'Cast me to the flames if it please you, master.'

Nagash gave his vizier a calculating stare.

'In time, perhaps,' he said. 'For now, you will continue to serve me. We march upon Mahrak as soon as a path to the valley has been cleared.'

A stir went through the assembly, and Amn-nasir's face rose from the depths of his goblet.

'Mahrak?' he asked hoarsely, as though the name made little sense to him. Seheb let out a groan. Nuneb stiffened.

'We cannot,' Seheb said, his lips trembling with fear. 'We dare not march upon the City of the Gods! You go too far–'

'No city in Nehekhara has need of two rulers,' Nagash said coldly, turning and fixing Seheb with a contemptuous stare. The necromancer pointed to Nuneb. 'Bring him here.'

At once, half a dozen immortals moved towards the twin kings. Their Ushabti moved to shield the kings, their hands darting to the swords slung across their backs.

'No!' Seheb cried. The young king fell to his knees. 'Forgive me, great one! I... I misspoke. I merely meant to say that we have thrown back the invaders. The west is secure, and our cities have been neglected for many years.' He cast about fearfully, looking to Amn-nasir for support and receiving only a hooded stare in return. 'If you would complete the destruction of Rasetra and Lybaras, so be it, but what purpose would it serve to attack Mahrak?'

'Who do you imagine we do battle with, you little fool?' Nagash snarled. 'Do you think these petty kings would dare defy Khemri alone? No, Mahrak is the heart of this rebellion. The Hieratic Council fears me, for I have learned the truth about them and their feckless gods.' The necromancer raised his bloodstained hand and clenched it into a fist. 'When Mahrak falls, the kings of the east will bow to me, and a new empire will be born.'

Seheb stared up at the Undying King, his eyes bright with fear. The immortals were only a few steps away, waiting on Nagash's command. Steeling himself, he pressed his forehead to the marble floor, as a slave would before his master.

'As you command, great one, so shall it be,' he said. 'Let Mahrak be brought to its knees before your might.'

Nagash considered the twin kings for a moment more, and then waved the immortals away.

'The last battle is almost at hand,' he said, as the pale figures returned to their places. 'Serve me well, and you will prosper. Immortality itself will be yours.'

Another wave of the necromancer's hand, and his spirits released Arkhan. The vizier landed in a heap, still too weak to stand, but his skin was whole once more. Nagash studied the fallen vizier and nodded thoughtfully.

'Great shall be the wonders of the coming age,' he said.

The gods alone saved the armies of the east, or so its warriors believed.

They had found the Gates of the Dawn abandoned, a thing unheard of since Settra's time, hundreds of years past. Ekhreb and his riders took the fortifications without incident, and found its storehouses well stocked with food, water and supplies, enough to sustain the army on the long march to Mahrak. The companies each drew their own stores as they passed through the gates into the Valley of Kings, and were even able to steal a few hours' rest while the Lybaran engineers searched for a way to bring the fortifications down.

While they waited, the rumour spread that Rakh-amn-hotep, the Rasetran king, had been killed by an arrow, fighting alongside the rearguard outside Quatar. Hekhmenukep, the Priest King of Lybaras, still clung to life, but none knew for how long. The host's surviving nobles began to talk of returning to their homes. For the space of a few hours that afternoon, the army once again teetered on the brink of destruction.

Then the news spread through the ranks: Rakh-amn-hotep still lived! The enemy's arrow had wounded him gravely, but by luck alone the shaft had missed the major arteries. The rearguard brought him into the fortifications, where the army's priests took him under their care.

Then, when the Lybaran engineers had done their work, trumpets blared from atop the fortifications, and the army was assembled in ranks on the western side of the wall. Amid a fanfare of horns, a column of chariots rode through the gates and passed slowly down the length of the column. Cheers went up from the weary Lybarans as they saw their king riding in the lead chariot. Hekhmenukep's fever had broken over the course of the afternoon, and he had ordered his Ushabti to prepare his chariot so that the men could see that he was well. He managed little more than to stay upright as he rode all the way to the front of the army, but the gesture had the desired effect. Their morale restored, the army resumed their long retreat eastwards, towards Mahrak. Behind them, the ancient fortifications built by the first king of Quatar collapsed in a rumble of grinding stone and a rising pall of chalk-white dust.

The destruction of the gates bought the army two full days. The allied host made good use of the time, racing all night and half the next day along the broad, dusty road that ran the length of the sacred valley. They camped in the shadows of the oldest tombs in Nehekhara, where the tribes laid their chiefs to rest before the creation of the great cities. There was great power invested in the ancient tombs, and the priests of the allied armies drew on that power with a willingness they'd never demonstrated in the march to the west. They summoned desert spirits and wove cunning illusions to trap and confound their pursuers, while mounted raiders laid bloody ambushes for any enemy horsemen that pressed too closely to the retreating column.

Two days after the battle at Quatar the sky to the west turned dark as pitch, like the heart of a raging sandstorm, and the allied army knew that Nagash and his forces had entered the Valley of Kings. Cloaked in howling blackness, the immortals and the companies of the dead pursued the allied armies without pause. As the undead horde stumbled onto the traps laid by the priests the valley shook with peals of thunder and strange, unearthly roars, and lurid flashes of lightning lit the edges of the dust clouds as the armies marched at night.

Slowly but surely, the gap between the two armies closed. The immortals learned to defeat the priests' illusions, and their necromantic powers allowed them to banish or destroy the spirits sent against them. They ransacked the ancient tombs to find more bodies to replenish their ranks, leaving nothing but rubble and ruin in their wake. With each passing night, they drew closer to their quarry, until the army's rearguard was locked in constant skirmishes with Numasi scouts and light infantry.

The terrain in the Valley of Kings was, however, favourable to defensive fighting. Clusters of stone crypts prevented massed cavalry charges and provided defensible positions for infantry and archers. There was no room to outflank the allied rearguard, and the defenders could fall back from one line of improvised fortifications to the next. The undead attackers pressed hard against the rearguard, and losses mounted, but the stubborn defenders succeeded in keeping Nagash's troops away from the main body of the retreating host.

Two weeks later, with roiling dust clouds looming at their backs, the vanguard of the eastern armies reached the Gates of the Dusk, and the warriors of the east fell to their knees and thanked the gods for their deliverance.

The Gates of the Dusk were older by far than their distant cousins to the west, some scholars even claiming that the great stone obelisks marking the entrance to the valley predated the Great Migration, though none would speculate on who could have raised such towering structures, or why. The massive stone pillars, eight in all, rose more than a hundred feet above the valley floor, and were arrayed side-by-side along the ancient road that wound along the base of the valley. During Settra's time, low walls had been built from the sides of the valley up to the base of the obelisks, but construction was halted shortly thereafter when a terrible plague swept through the work parties. The architects took this to be a sign of the gods' displeasure, and no further attempts were made to fortify the eastern end of the valley. A sprawling village of stone and mud-brick buildings that once supported the labourers still stood a quarter of a mile to the east of the great gates. Over time, it had been taken over by the temples of Djaf and Usirian as a stopping place for pilgrims who sought to visit the tombs of their ancestors within the valley. The village bustled with activity as the armies of the east filled the narrow streets and looked for places to make camp.

Rakh-amn-hotep had been carried into the centre of the village and placed in an abandoned manor that had once belonged to a Lybaran royal architect. He was brought aboard an improvised palanquin layered with cloaks and cushions, and his Ushabti carried him with the utmost care. Ekhreb and a squadron of horsemen kept onlookers and well-wishers at a distance as the king was brought into the manor.

While his miraculous survival was well known among the rank and file of the army, and, indeed, served to inspire the warriors many times during the hard march down the valley, what was not commonly known was that the bronze arrowhead had lodged deep in the king's spine. Rakh-amn-hotep could move his eyes and manage a weak grunt if asked a simple question, but that was all. For all intents and purposes he was a living man trapped in a lifeless body.

The king's servants made Rakh-amn-hotep as comfortable as they could in a secluded part of the house, while Ekhreb and the army's captains gathered and began making plans to defend the Gates of the Dusk from Nagash's horde. Rakh-amn-hotep lay in the dim light of half a dozen oil lamps and listened to the murmuring voices in the manor's common room, while a dozen priests dressed his wound and washed his body in warm water and scented oils.

It was almost dawn. The army was almost fully encamped at the gates, with only the last squadrons of the rearguard still arriving from the night's skirmishes. Suddenly, the king heard a commotion in the street outside the manor, and surprised shouts at the manor door. Conversation in the common room abruptly ceased, and the priests attending the king shared worried glances as the commotion near the front of the old house increased.

Rakh-amn-hotep's hearing had grown as sharp as a bat's since his injury. He could tell that the voices were moving, heading deeper into the house. After a few moments it became clear that they were, in fact, coming his way. His gaze fell upon the room's single wooden door.

The assembled priests climbed nervously to their feet as footfalls sounded in the corridor beyond. The door latch rattled, and Ekhreb stepped swiftly inside. The champion was still covered in white dust from the road, and there was an agitated expression on his handsome face. Ignoring the startled looks from the priests, he approached the king and bowed.

'Nebunefer is here, with a delegation from the Hieratic Council at Mahrak,' he said gravely. 'They wish to see you.'

The two men locked eyes. It was a shameful thing for a man to be seen in such a crippled state, much less a king. Ekhreb looked willing and ready to send the delegates back to Mahrak if the king so wished.

After a moment, Rakh-amn-hotep drew a deep breath, and let out a single grunt: *Yes.*

Ekhreb bowed his head once more, and returned to the doorway.

'The Priest King of Rasetra welcomes you,' he said into the darkness.

The priests in the room bowed their heads and withdrew quickly to the edges of the room, and then sank to their knees as Nebunefer strode through the doorway. The aged priest had dispensed with his dust-stained robes, and wore the golden vestments of a high priest of Ptra. Behind him came four cloaked and hooded figures, their features completely hidden in layers of gauzy cotton.

The delegation approached the king's side and bowed deeply. Nebunefer raised his hands.

'The blessings of Ptra the Glorious be upon you, great one,' the priest intoned. 'Your name is spoken with reverence in the temples of the great city, where it rises like pleasing music to fill the ears of the gods.' Nebunefer turned and indicated the hooded figures with a sweep of his hand. 'The Hieratic Council has been informed of your heroic deeds, great king,' the priest said gravely, 'and they wish to give you this gift as a token of their gratitude.'

Nebunefer bowed once more and stepped aside. As one, the figures reached up and drew back their hoods. Several of the priests in the room gasped in surprise.

Rakh-amn-hotep found himself staring up at four identical golden masks, each one shaped by a master craftsman to capture the essence of a goddess. They were breathtaking in their perfection, from their almond-shaped eyes to the sleek curves of their cheeks and the promise of their full lips. The hammered gold glowed under the lamplight, and in the shifting shadows it seemed as though the masks smiled lovingly down upon the king. Black shadows pooled at the base of the priestesses' long, pale throats. Each young woman wore a necklace of black asps to guard her virtue and show her devotion to the goddess Asaph.

The priestesses gathered around the king's head and stretched forth pale hands decorated in sinuous henna tattoos. Rakh-amn-hotep felt their cool touch as they peeled away his bandages and brushed lightly at his face. Then they laid their hands upon his wound and in a single voice they began to chant.

The incantation was a long and arduous one, requiring a combination of timing, finesse and power. The priestesses' hands wove a delicate web around the king's wound, teasing the bronze arrowhead away from Rakh-amn-hotep's spine and knitting the flesh together in its wake. By the time they were done the oil lamps had burnt out and bright morning sunlight was slanting into the room from the corridor beyond.

Three of the priestesses drew up their hoods and withdrew to the doorway. The fourth studied the king in silence for a moment, and then bent towards him until her perfect golden mask was scant inches from his face. The flickering tongues of asps tickled the king's chin.

Large, dark eyes looked into the king's. The priestess exhaled, and Rakh-amn-hotep could somehow feel it through the mask, as though it had slipped past the goddess's rounded lips. Her breath was warm and soft, and smelled of vanilla.

'Rise,' the priestess whispered. 'Rise, and give glory to Asaph.'

With that, the priestess withdrew, drawing her hood up over her head and slipping silently from the room with her retinue at her back.

Rakh-amn-hotep watched them go. He breathed deeply. A faint tremor passed through his body. His fingers twitched. Then slowly, painfully, the king pushed himself upright. He swung his legs over the edge of the palanquin and took another deep, racking breath. Then he pressed his hands to his face.

'Glory be to Asaph,' he said in a ragged voice.

'Glory be to Asaph,' Ekhreb echoed solemnly. Nebunefer smiled.

'I am glad to see you well, great king. Given all you and your people have done in the long war against the Usurper, this was the least that we could do.'

The Rasetran king lowered his hands and gave the priest a forbidding stare.

'About damn time,' he growled. Nebunefer's smile faded.

'Excuse me?'

'There are perhaps a thousand men between here and the Fountains of Life whose bones are bleaching in the sun because our healers could not save them,' the king said. 'Where were the priestesses of Asaph then?' With a grunt, the king levered himself to his feet. 'Where were the priests of Mahrak when a plague of madness was raging through Quatar? We have marched and fought and bled for your sake, Nebunefer. Nagash is nearly upon your doorstep, and it's past time for you and your holy men to join the fight.'

The old priest bristled at the king's tone.

'We have opened our coffers to you and Hekhmenukep,' he snapped. 'We paid for your armies twice over!'

'You can keep your damned gold!' Rakh-amn-hotep shot back. 'We would have fought that monster even had it beggared us!' The king took a step towards the old man, his anger rising. Then he caught himself. With an effort, he took a deep breath and continued. 'You marched with us, Nebunefer. You were at Quatar. You've seen the bodies. Tens of thousands of dead men… Even if we win, our cities may never be the same again. If the Hieratic Council had been with us in the west–'

'It isn't as simple as that, great one,' Nebunefer said.

'I've heard the stories of the battle at Zedri,' Rakh-amn-hotep said. 'I know that Nagash's defilement of Neferem has given him the power to negate your invocations, but by the gods! The things that your priests might have done to sustain us, far from the battle line...'

'You know far less than you imagine,' Nebunefer hissed. He started to say more, and then paused. The old priest stared hard at the holy men ringing the room. 'Leave us,' he commanded.

When the priests were gone, Nebunefer glanced warily at Ekhreb, but Rakh-amn-hotep folded his arms stubbornly, and said, 'He deserves to hear this as much as I do, perhaps more so.' Nebunefer frowned, but finally he shrugged his bony shoulders.

'Very well,' he said with a sigh. 'Do you know why Neferem renders our invocations powerless?'

The Rasetran king considered the question, and then answered, 'Because she represents the covenant between the gods and men, which is why Settra coerced the Hieratic Council into allowing his marriage to the Daughter of the Sun, hundreds of years ago. He sought to bind the sacred covenant governing all of Nehekhara with his household, and to prevent the council at Mahrak from ever turning their powers against him.'

'But,' Nebunefer said with a raised finger, 'the great king didn't fully appreciate the significance of his marriage. The Daughter of the Sun does not represent the sacred covenant, she is the covenant made flesh.'

Rakh-amn-hotep scowled at the priest, and asked, 'Why would the gods do such a thing?' Nebunefer smiled faintly.

'As a sign of faith,' he replied. 'Faith that our ancestors would honour their promise to give offerings and worship to the gods.' The king nodded thoughtfully.

'And Nagash has claimed this covenant for his own. Gods above, he's a usurper in more ways than one.'

Nebunefer shook his head ruefully, and said, 'For all his vaunted intelligence, Nagash doesn't seem to fully appreciate what he's done. If he wished, he could command the powers of the gods, in exchange for sacrifice and worship. As terrible as things have been, but for the Usurper's arrogance it could have been far worse.'

'That remains to be seen,' Rakh-amn-hotep growled. 'Since Neferem represents the covenant, she is the conduit for the gods' power. But such things work both ways.'

The old priest nodded. 'Our offerings do not reach the gods, nor do their gifts bless us in return,' he said. 'Nagash has cut us off from our power, great one. We have not acted until now because we cannot.'

The king's hand strayed to his throat. 'But what the priestesses just did...' he began.

Nebunefer sighed. 'A lifetime's devotion to the gods transforms us. Our souls become charged with the power of the divine. Now, that is all we have left.' He nodded towards the door. 'Those four priestesses gave up part of their souls so that you could walk again.'

'Great gods,' Rakh-amn-hotep whispered. 'How are we to stop this monster? His army will be here an hour after sunset. We must hold him at the Gates of the Dusk.'

'We cannot hold Nagash here,' Nebunefer said. 'The gates are poorly fortified, and your armies have been badly mauled already.'

'My men don't lack for courage,' the Rasetran king growled, 'especially now that the beast is breathing at their door.'

Nebunefer chuckled.

'After all that your warriors have done, no one will ever question their courage,' he said, 'but if they remain here they will be overrun by dawn. Ask your man here if you don't believe me.'

The king looked to his champion. Ekhreb scowled, but nodded reluctantly.

'He's right, great one,' he said, 'Those walls weren't built high enough or broad enough to stop a determined army, and the men have nothing left to give. They will fight if you give the order, but they won't last for long.'

'What would you have us do, then?' Rakh-amn-hotep asked the priest with a sigh.

'Withdraw,' Nebunefer replied. 'Return to your cities and rebuild your armies.'

'And what about Nagash?'

'Nagash means to conquer Mahrak,' the old priest said. 'He has dreamt of humbling us for a very long time, and now he has the chance.' He faced the king. 'You are right, great one. The time has come for us to pay our tithe of blood. We will fight the Usurper at the City of Hope until you and Hekhmenukep can return and break the siege.'

'That could take years, Nebunefer,' the king replied. 'You just said yourself that the Hieratic Council is powerless.' Another faint smile crossed Nebunefer's face.

'I never said the word powerless, great one. We still have our Ushabti, and the city is protected by wards that even Nagash would be hard-pressed to break. Fear not. We will hold out for as long as we must.'

Rakh-amn-hotep began to pace around the dimly lit chamber. His knees felt weak, but after he'd learned what had been done to restore his limbs, he didn't think he'd ever sit down again.

'What of Lahmia?' he said. 'Those libertines have done nothing, even when Nagash took their royal daughter and slew her son. How long do they think they can sit by and watch Nehekhara burn?'

'We have sent emissaries to Lahmia many times,' Nebunefer said. 'So long as Neferem is tied to the Usurper, they refuse to act.' The king chuckled bitterly.

'For me, that would be more than enough reason to act.' He glanced at Ekhreb. 'What is the hour?'

'An hour before noon, great one.'

Rakh-amn-hotep sighed. There was much to do, and little time.

'I want our forces on the march by mid-afternoon,' he told his champion. Ekhreb managed a grin.

'Another long march,' he said. 'The men will start to regret all those prayers for your swift recovery.'

'No doubt,' the king said, 'but at least this time they'll be heading home.' Rakh-amn-hotep turned to Nebunefer. 'Any supplies you could give us–'

'They are on the way here even now,' the priest interrupted. 'You can take the wagons, as well. We'll expect you to return them in due time.'

The king nodded to Ekhreb, who bowed low and hastened from the room. Moments later he could be heard barking orders to the captains waiting in the common room.

Nebunefer bowed low to Rakh-amn-hotep.

'With your permission, great one, I must depart,' he said. 'There is much to be done in Mahrak before the Usurper's army arrives.' The king nodded, but his expression turned grave.

'I cannot speak for Lybaras, but I and my people will not abandon you. That said, I can't guarantee when we will return. You may have to endure for a very long time.'

Nebunefer smiled, and said, 'With the gods, all things are possible. Until we meet again, Rakh-amn-hotep. In this life, or the next.'

TWENTY-SEVEN

THE UNDYING KING

Khemri, the Living City,
in the 62nd year of Qu'aph the Cunning
(-1750 Imperial Reckoning)

The evening air blowing through the open entryway of Settra's Court was pungent with the reek of cinders and scorched flesh. Faint shouts and terrified screams sounded in the distance. Khemri, the Living City, was on fire.

'Explain this,' Nagash said to his immortals. His cold voice echoed faintly in the cavernous space. 'This is the third night in a row that there have been riots in the Merchant Quarter.'

The black-robed noblemen, a hundred in all, shifted uneasily around the darkened court and stole wary glances at one another. Finally, Raamket stepped forwards and ventured a reply.

'It's the same as always,' he grunted. 'The harvest was poor. Trade has suffered. They crowd together in the marketplace like sheep and bleat the same things, over and over again. When darkness falls, they grow bold enough to cause trouble.' The nobleman shrugged. 'We kill the rabble-rousers when we catch them, but the rest of the herd never seems to get the message.'

'Then perhaps you're being too selective,' the king snapped. He leaned forwards on his throne and glared down at Raamket. 'Send your men through the quarter and kill every man, woman and child you find. Better yet, impale them on spikes around the city wells, so that every matron who has to come to draw water can listen to their cries of agony. Order must be restored. Do you understand? Kill however many you must to put an end to this disgraceful unrest.'

Arkhan the Black stood at Nagash's right hand, close by the dais. He took a long drink from the goblet in his hand and stared into its depths.

'Killing that many people will be counterproductive,' he said grimly. 'Our labour pool is small enough as it is, to say nothing of the city watch or the army. Every citizen we put to death only places more strain on those who survive.'

The emptiness of Settra's Court attested to the vizier's observation. Where the hall was once packed with obsequious nobles and scheming ambassadors, now only the king and his immortals remained, along with a handful of slaves and Nagash's silent queen. One way or another, the Black Pyramid had consumed everyone else.

It had been an epic labour, far in excess of the king's worst predictions. Quarrying the marble and transporting it alone had occupied tens of thousands of workers and required expert stonesmiths to properly select and shape the massive ebon blocks. Accidents and misfortune took their toll, both at the quarry and at the construction site: a cable snapped, or tired labourers grew inattentive, and men died in shrieking agony beneath tons of black marble. In the first ten years, Nagash had used up half the slaves he'd taken from Zandri, and more continued to die every day.

Nevertheless, the work went on. When setbacks occurred, Nagash ordered his taskmasters to work deep into the night. The city watch sent a steady stream of gamblers, drunkards and thieves to the slave camps outside the necropolis to try to stem the growing tide of casualties. When the criminals ran out, they sent anyone they caught on the streets after dark. The great cities also continued to send their monthly tithes to Khemri, buying peace with the Usurper with a steady flow of blood and coin.

Still, it wasn't enough. Construction fell behind schedule, year upon year. No one in Khemri believed that the structure would be completed in Nagash's lifetime. Years passed, but the King of the Living City did not seem to feel the passage of time, and neither did the king's chosen vassals, whose power and wealth in the city increased with each succeeding decade. Rumours were whispered among the lesser nobles of the court: had Nagash unravelled the deepest mysteries of the Mortuary Cult? Had he been blessed by the gods to lead Nehekhara to a new golden age?

Then Neferem began appearing at the king's side during his Grand Assemblies, seated upon the lesser throne and assuming the duties of a queen, and the rumours took a much darker turn.

As the years passed and the number of deaths continued to mount, the annual civil service for Khemri's citizens was extended from a month to six months, and then up to eight. Fields outside the city grew fallow for want of farmers, and Khemri began to spend a great deal of gold importing more grain from the north. Trade suffered for want of craftsmen and artisans, and prices increased. Khemri's new golden age lost its lustre quickly.

Lahmia was the first of the great cities to withdraw its ambassadors and renege on its monthly tithe. Others followed quickly: Lybaras, then Rasetra, Quatar and Ka-Sabar. They had calculated that Khemri didn't have enough population left to raise a proper army to enforce their claims, and they were right. The king vowed that work on the pyramid would continue, regardless of the cost. Nagash modified the civil service decree once more, so that every father and eldest son in every household in the city, common or noble, would serve continuously until the massive edifice was complete.

The court emptied quickly. A few noble families tried to flee the city entirely, making for the dubious safety of the east. Nagash ordered a squadron of light horsemen sent after them, offering a hundred gold coins for the head of every man, woman and child they caught. It was a gamble, of sorts, for there was no way to be certain that the horsemen would follow orders once they had left Khemri behind, and Nagash could not send an immortal to command them. For as much as the king and his chosen vassals had become ageless and powerful beyond mortal ken, they nevertheless paid a steep price for their gifts. The light of Nehekhara's sun burned their skin like a firebrand and sapped their terrible strength, forcing them to seek refuge in the deepest cellars or crypts during the day. The problem had confounded the king for decades, and the answer continued to elude him. It was as though Ptra himself opposed Nagash's will, scourging him and his immortals with fire.

'The priests,' Nagash muttered darkly. 'They are the ones to blame for this.'

He knew it to be true. The priests were immune from conscription or civil service, and they spent their days skulking in their temples and looking for ways to undermine him. They asked after Sukhet continually, and Nagash suspected that they had spies in the palace searching for where he was kept.

Arkhan shifted uncomfortably.

'No doubt you are right, master, but what can we do? Attacking them is tantamount to attacking Mahrak, and if we did that, then the whole country would rise up against us.'

Nagash nodded absently, but his gaze drifted to Neferem. The queen sat straight-backed in her chair, showing no reaction to what was being said. He wondered if perhaps she was in league with the priests as well.

The gift of the elixir to Neferem had been a necessary one. He was determined to possess her beauty, if he had to take a thousand years to wear her down. Nagash had seen how the elixir had affected the will of his vassals, who were helpless to resist its seductive pull, and he hoped that she would succumb as well. Though it made her more agreeable in general, the queen's will was entirely unaffected.

She had, however, stopped pestering him with questions about her son. That at least was a blessing.

The problem, the king suspected, was that duplicitous priest Nebunefer. Nagash was certain that he was a spy sent by Mahrak, and he could come and go freely from the palace now that the king and his immortals had to sleep through the day. Something was going to have to be done about that man, the king decided, something quick and fatal, and it was going to have to happen soon. Mahrak could protest all it liked.

Then, shadows passed across the open entryway to the court. The immortals were immediately on their guard, their hands straying to the swords at their belts. Nagash frowned curiously. When was the last time a citizen had appeared at one of the Grand Assemblies? Twenty years? More?

'Come forward,' the king called out. His voice rang sharply through the stillness. 'What do you have to say?'

There was a few moments' hesitation, before a solitary figure appeared in the entryway. He approached the dais with slow, faltering steps, silhouetted by the moonlit entryway behind him. Nagash could tell at once that it was an old man, bent and nearly broken by the weight of years. When he was three-quarters of the way down the long, echoing aisle, the king recognised who it was, and felt a surge of anger.

'Sumesh? Why aren't you at the pyramid? What's happened?'

A stir went through the immortals as the pyramid's last surviving architect shuffled painfully into the king's presence. Sumesh was more than two hundred and thirty years old, positively ancient by Nehekharan standards. Though Nagash had ensured that he was a very wealthy man, Sumesh was haggard and his body twisted with age. His gnarled hands trembled and his shoulders were bent.

Sumesh did not answer at first. The architect strode up to the foot of the dais and carefully knelt upon the stone before turning his face up to the king.

'Great one,' he said in a quavering voice, 'I have the honour to inform you that the last stone was fitted into place an hour past. The Black Pyramid is complete.'

For a moment, Nagash could not believe his ears. A glimmer of triumph shone in his dark eyes.

'You have done very well, master architect,' he said. 'I am indebted to you, and will ensure that you are well rewarded.'

No sooner had the words escaped his lips than Arkhan stepped behind Sumesh and cut his throat from ear to ear. The immortals growled hungrily as the old man's blood poured out onto the marble steps, and his corpse collapsed face-first onto the stones. Nagash studied the spreading pool of crimson at his feet and smiled.

'It appears that a solution has presented itself,' he said.

The king dispatched his orders at once. The slaves were ordered back to their camps and given an extra ration of food and wine. Arkhan, Raamket and the rest of the immortals were sent out into the city streets to put an end to the rioting by any means necessary. Then Nagash left the queen in the care of Ghazid, and had Khefru lead him through the fire-lit streets to the necropolis, where the new pyramid waited.

It could be seen for miles along the road to the necropolis, towering high above the petty crypts and seeming to swallow the light of the moon. The Black Pyramid was darker than the night, its edges knife-sharp against the indigo sky. Arcs of pale lightning would occasionally crawl across its polished surface, sending pulses of invisible power washing over Nagash's skin.

The pyramid was a collector and an attractor of dark magic, and for two hundred years it had glutted itself on the spirits of tens of thousands of slaves. That energy coursed through its glossy stones, stored for a single purpose: a ritual unlike anything Nagash had ever performed.

The palanquin crossed a vast plaza made of close-set marble flagstones and stopped before a featureless, unadorned opening at the base of the pyramid. It was no more than a square opening in the side of the great structure, just wide enough for two people to enter side-by-side. Nagash and Khefru passed through the opening and were swallowed by the darkness beyond.

At a gesture from the king, the corridor beyond was suffused with a pale green grave-light that seeped from the very stones. The floor, walls and ceiling of the passageway were intricately carved with thousands of hieroglyphics, placed with exacting care by expert stonemasons. Nagash ran his fingers along the carvings as he climbed the sloping corridor, tasting the enormous power roiling within the structure.

'Yes,' he whispered. 'The alignment is complete. I can feel the energies building.'

Khefru strode along six paces behind the king. His face was a mask of dread.

'Sumesh outdid himself,' he said quietly. 'He finished months ahead of schedule.'

'So he did,' Nagash said, and chuckled at the realisation. The power coursing through him was far sweeter and more potent than any wine, and he drank deeply of it.

He led Khefru upwards through the nacreous light, through a twisting maze of corridors and stark, empty chambers that pulsed with necromantic energies. Both master and servant navigated the labyrinth with the ease born of familiarity. Nagash had moved his arcane researches, and later, his abode, into the pyramid five years before, as the work parties laboured to complete the upper quarter of the structure. The labourers knew full well the extent of the deadly traps sown throughout the pyramid, and knew better than to trespass beyond the unfinished areas of the construction site.

Finally, the king reached the heart of the vast pyramid: the ritual chamber. It was a large, octagonal room whose walls curved upwards to form a faceted dome above a complex ritual circle some fifteen paces across, carved directly into the marble floor and inlaid with crushed onyx and silver. Thousands of complex hieroglyphs had been carved into the gleaming walls, each one painstakingly designed to focus the death energies stored within the pyramid and channel them into the ritual circle. Nagash stood in the doorway for a moment, studying the interplay of energies that flowed across the graven walls and the circle-inscribed floor. Finally, he nodded in grim satisfaction.

'It is perfect,' he said with a jackal's smile. Nagash walked reverently across the room and took his place in the centre of the ritual circle. 'Go to the sanctum and gather my books,' he ordered his servant. 'There is much work to be done, and not much time before the dawn.'

Khefru still lingered at the chamber's entryway, his expression troubled.

'What ritual, master?' he asked in a dull voice.

'The one that will usher in a new age,' the king said, fully intoxicated by the power at his command. 'The false gods must perish to make way for mankind's true master.'

With his back to Khefru, Nagash could not see the look of horror etched into the servant's ravaged features.

'You... you cannot think to slay the gods, master. It's not possible.'

Even as he said it, Khefru cringed, expecting a furious tirade from his master, but it appeared that Nagash was in a magnanimous mood.

'Kill them? No. At least, not at first,' he said calmly. 'First we must starve them of the power they have stolen from our people. When the priests of Nehekhara are dead, the temples will empty and the gods will no longer receive the worship that sustains them.'

Khefru said, aghast, 'That would break the covenant! Without that, the land will die!'

Nagash turned to his servant.

'After all this time, you still don't understand, do you?' he said, as though speaking to a child. 'Life and death will have no meaning once I am master of Nehekhara. There will be no fear of hunger or disease. Think of that! My empire will be eternal, and one day it will spread across the entire world!'

Khefru could only stare in shock at the king's pronouncement. After a moment, the triumphant glow waned from Nagash's face.

'Now go,' he said coldly. 'It is well past the hour of the dead, and there are many preparations to be made.'

The king laboured for several hours in the ritual chamber, laying the groundwork for his incantation. Khefru stood at the margins, taking precise notes as ordered and fetching arcane powders and paints from the sanctum many levels below. His face, backlit by the flickering energies that surrounded his master, was thoughtful and deeply troubled.

Finally, when dawn broke above the distant mountains, Nagash called a halt.

'It is almost complete,' he said. 'By tomorrow at midnight, the incantation will be ready.'

As the sun rose into the sky overhead, Nagash left the ritual chamber and followed a twisting passageway down one level to his crypt. Many of his immortals had taken up residence in the lower levels of the pyramid, at the king's command, and were probably already secured in their stone sarcophagi.

The crypt was a pyramid in miniature, with four slanting walls that came to a point over the king's resting place. Powerful incantations were carved into each of the walls and the symbols filled with powdered gemstone to enhance their longevity and potency. They glowed with an inner light as Nagash entered the chamber.

At the centre of the room stood a low stone dais, and upon it rested a marble sarcophagus fit for a king.

Khefru rushed forwards as Nagash strode to the dais, stepping up to the sarcophagus and gripping the stone lid. With supernatural strength he lifted the covering clear with a smooth, practiced motion and set it aside.

Inside the stone coffin were perfumed cushions and sprigs of aromatic herbs, laid aside for the comfort of the king. Nagash climbed inside without hesitation and lay down. The marble enclosure channelled the energies of the pyramid and helped restore his mind and body while he drifted in a kind of cataleptic trance.

As soon as he was settled, Khefru lifted the lid once more and prepared to set it into place. At the last moment, he hesitated. Nagash glanced impatiently at his servant.

'What is it?' he snapped. 'I can see the questioning look in your eyes. Out with it.'

'I...' he began. 'I beg you to reconsider this, master. Your pyramid is finished, but Khemri as a whole is weak. If you strike out at the priests, there will be no turning back.' The king's face hardened into a mask of rage.

'With the power at my command, I can take a thousand men and defeat every city in Nehekhara. They would not tire, would not fear, would not falter, for they would not die. You're a fool, Khefru. Once I thought you an ambitious man, but the truth is that you have always been a coward. You don't have the strength to stand up to the fates and choose your own destiny.'

Khefru stared down at the king for a moment longer, and his expression fell.

'Perhaps you're right, master,' he said, as he slid the stone lid back into place. 'Sleep well.'

Nagash awoke to a strange, scratching sound above him. For a moment, he did not understand what he was hearing. His mind was still immersed in heady dreams of vengeance and conquest. Had he imagined the sound? Was it borne from dreamlike vistas of burning cities and plains of bleached bone?

Then a thin trickle of stone landed upon his chest and he knew that this was no dream, but something altogether worse. Someone was drilling a hole in his sarcophagus.

There was a scrape of metal as a tool was removed from the breach. His mind raced as he tried to understand what was happening, and then something thick and cool fell in a steady trickle onto his chest.

Lamp oil, he realised with a growing sense of horror. Someone meant to burn him alive inside his coffin.

With a wordless snarl, he shoved hard against the stone lid, but the covering was held fast. More heated shouts occurred above him, and the pouring oil abruptly ceased. The next thing to come through the bore-hole would be a red-hot coal.

Seething with anger, Nagash put his hands against the lid of the sarcophagus and roared a furious incantation. The power of the pyramid flowed into him like a torrent and the stone lid exploded with a flash of heat and a thunderous detonation.

The blast, in such a confined space, stunned and blinded the king. For a fleeting instant there was a flare of searing agony, and then a rush of air and the hissing of flames. The blast had ignited the oil soaking into his robes! Nagash screamed in anger and pain, breathing in a gust of flame that raked red-hot talons down his throat and into his lungs.

Deaf and blind, Nagash could do nothing but call upon the pyramid's power once more. A cold gust of wind erupted from the sarcophagus, snuffing the flames and tearing the oil-soaked robes from his torso. The king croaked another incantation and he burst from the smoking coffin like a bat, his arms spread wide as he leapt straight up into the air.

Men were screaming in the small chamber, a confusing babble of orders, sacred oaths and bitter curses. Nagash fetched up hard against the ceiling and tried to force his eyes to function. Power boiled into his eye sockets, causing still more pain but clearing the spots of colour from his vision.

The smouldering corpses of young men lay scattered around the king's chamber, their bodies torn by shrapnel from the exploding stone lid. Four men, who had been standing close to the entrance and had escaped the worst of the blast, were fanning out into the room and raising their hands as though to abjure the king. Nagash felt their power at once, and then recognised the robes they wore. Priests!

One of the men, a young priest of Ptra, raised his hands and uttered a sharp invocation. There was a flare of golden light, and a spear of flame jetted from the man's open hands.

With a curse, Nagash dodged to the right, croaking out a banishment spell even as he tumbled through the air. The holy flame struck the ceiling and seared his face and hands before it collapsed under the weight of his counter-spell. Without hesitation, Nagash flung out his hand and sent a flurry of ebon darts from his fingertips. They pierced the young priest like arrows, catching him in the right arm, chest and neck. He collapsed, writhing and choking on his own blood.

A booming voice roared out words of power, and Nagash felt the air tremble around him. Stone shards on the floor quivered, and then streaked through the air towards him. Once again, the king used his power of flight to dive across the room and escape the lethal hail. Pellets dug painfully into his legs, but the worst of the blast passed him by.

The surviving priests were all focusing on him. Abruptly, the wind supporting him rebelled, as though gripped by another man's will. Nagash was caught unawares and sent plunging to the ground, just as another bolt of flame tore through the spot where he had been, He landed painfully on his side, listening to the angry shouts of the priests as they tried to coordinate their attacks.

Lying on the stone floor, Nagash was partially hidden behind his smouldering sarcophagus. He glimpsed the legs of one of his attackers and snapped out a fierce incantation. At once, the floor beneath the attacker turned into a pit of darkness, and the priest had time for one terrified scream before he disappeared from sight.

The king heard the startled shouts of the two surviving attackers on the opposite side of the sarcophagus. Their voices dropped to a whisper as they discussed what to do next. Nagash cast around quickly, looking for some means to turn the tables on the two priests. His gaze fell upon a trio of bodies to his left, and he was suddenly reminded of his last conversation with Khefru, only a few hours before. On impulse, he stretched out his hand towards the bodies and began to improvise.

The power of the pyramid flowed through his fingertips towards the corpses. For a moment, nothing happened. Then, one of the dead men stirred. Slowly, clumsily, the corpse rolled onto its stomach and tried to clamber to its feet.

There were more nervous whispers on the other side of the coffin, and then silence. Nagash gathered himself, watching the shambling corpse intently. As it swayed unsteadily to its feet, the priests saw it and attacked. A gust of wind seized the corpse and pulled it up into the air above the sarcophagus, where a spear of flame pierced its chest and set it alight.

The two priests cried out in triumph just as Nagash rose quietly on the right side of the coffin and raked the attackers with a storm of necromantic bolts.

As the dead men collapsed to the ground, Nagash lurched towards the entryway. With the rush of battle fading, a flood of agony threatened to overwhelm him. Cursing, he drew upon the pyramid still more, silencing the pain and trying to heal his wounds.

A figure stood just outside the entrance. Nagash came up short, his right hand rising with a hiss.

'It's me, master,' Khefru said. The servant stepped into the room, a look of shock and surprise on his face. 'I... I tried to get to you in time,' he stammered. 'They got here just ahead of me.'

'Indeed,' the king growled. His voice, issuing from a flame-scarred throat, sounded almost bestial.

Khefru stared at the king's burned body, momentarily transfixed by the enormity of what had happened.

'You're hurt,' he said shakily. 'Please. Let me tend to your throat.'

He stepped closer, tentatively touching the king's burned neck with his fingertips. The gesture covered the movement of his right hand, which thrust a needle-pointed dagger straight into the king's heart.

The two men froze, locked in a grim tableau. Khefru grunted, trying to force the knife deeper, but Nagash had seized his wrist. The point of the knife had penetrated little more than an inch into the king's chest.

'Did you think I would not guess?' Nagash said to him, the growl in his voice nothing to do with his injuries. 'How else could the priests have reached my chambers?'

A flicker of fear played across Khefru's face, and then his expression hardened as he surrendered to the inevitable.

'You went too far,' he snarled. 'You were the most powerful priest in Khemri! You could have lived a rich, indolent life. Instead you threw it all away for this... this nightmare! It's obscene!' he cried. 'Can't you see what you've become? You're a monster!'

Khefru heaved on the dagger with the last reserves of his strength, trying to finish what he'd begun, but the weapon did not budge an inch.

Nagash reached up with his left hand and placed it on Khefru's chest.

'Not a monster,' he said. 'A god, a living god. I am the master of life and death, Khefru. Alas, you were too faithless to believe me. So now I must show you.'

The king clenched his left hand and drew upon the power of the pyramid. Khefru stiffened, his eyes widening and his mouth gaping in a silent scream. Nagash began an incantation, shaping the words as he went along and focusing his will with singular intent. The servant's body began to convulse.

Nagash drew his left hand away from Khefru's chest, and as he did so, he drew a glowing filament of energy along with it. The king's eyes never left Khefru's as he slowly and remorselessly drew his servant's soul from his body. As he did so, Khefru's stolen youth fled with it, causing his body to shrivel and decay before Nagash's eyes. When he was done, nothing but a stream of dust trickled from his clenched right hand.

Khefru's ghost floated before the king, moaning softly in terror and pain.

'Now you will serve me forever more,' Nagash said to the spirit. 'You are bound to me. My fate is now yours.'

The king turned and found Arkhan and the other immortals standing outside the doorway to the chamber. They were weak and disoriented, having been roused rudely from their slumber.

'What has happened?' Arkhan gasped. Nagash eyed his men coldly.

'We have been betrayed,' he said.

Filled with icy rage, Nagash climbed the twisting ramps to the pyramid's ritual chamber. His mind worked swiftly, creating a picture of what his enemies intended. Khefru's betrayal was no isolated thing. He had approached the priesthood and offered to lead them to the crypt chamber, but Nagash had no doubt that the priests had bigger plans of their own. Even now they would be in the palace, searching for Neferem and persuading her to take control of the city. It was not an assassination, but a coup.

His enemies had acted prematurely, no doubt surprised by the early completion of the pyramid. With more time to plan and gather their resources, the priests might have succeeded. Instead, they had failed, and their doom was sealed.

The king hastened into the ritual chamber and gathered his concentration. All the elements were in place. He had but to utter the incantation, and the age of gods and priests would come to a terrible end.

Power built within the Black Pyramid as Nagash's incantation began. Every slave who died during its construction, more than sixty thousand souls, was focused by the king's fury into a single, terrible spell.

Above the pyramid, the sky began to warp, and then darken. Black clouds boiled into existence where none had been before, lit from within by savage bursts of lightning. The density and power of the unnatural storm grew more and more intense, casting its shadow in a spreading pool across Khemri's necropolis. Where it fell, the dead trembled uneasily in their graves.

For more than half an hour the energy grew in power, until it seemed that the sky would split beneath its awful weight. Then, with a hideous, piercing scream the storm burst in an irresistible wave, racing in a series of ebon ripples across the sky.

The shadow of Nagash's fury spread to every corner of Nehekhara in the space of just a few minutes. Darkness fell across the great cities, and every priest or acolyte touched by the shadow died in a single, agonising instant. Only those who by sheer fortune were shielded by stone survived the lash of the necromancer's power.

Nagash knew at once that his ritual had only partially succeeded. He'd moved too quickly, and his focus had been tainted by his anger and his lust for revenge. Thousands had died, to be sure, but it was not yet enough.

The reserves of necromantic power inside the temple were weakened, but enough remained for a single invocation. Nagash uttered the words of power, and a pall of dust and shadow spread from the necropolis and fell upon Khemri, cloaking the Living City in artificial night.

The king turned to his immortals. To Raamket he said, 'Take two-thirds of the chosen and drown the temples in blood! Slay every holy man or woman you find!'

To Arkhan, Shepsu-hur and the rest, Nagash simply said, 'Follow me.'

Dozens of robed bodies littered the plaza outside the royal palace. Nagash led his twenty-five men straight to Settra's Court, where he found the queen and the high priests of the city. They were bickering like children, each one with a differing idea of what to do next. Most were ashen-faced, on the verge of panic after the king's shadow had fallen across the city.

Nagash and Neferem's eyes met across the length of the vast, shadowy court. The queen's face lit with an expression of pure hatred, and the priests turned to face the king with mingled expressions of anger and dread.

'Kill them,' Nagash commanded his men, 'all but Neferem. She belongs to me.'

The immortals did not hesitate. Swords and knives leapt from their scabbards as they raced down the length of the court. The high priests all began to talk at once, throwing up their hands and uttering a bewildering array of invocations, but Nagash was prepared for them. Shadows raced across the marble tiles, and sped from the darkness beyond the tall pillars flanking the centre aisle. They swept down on the priests like vultures, freezing their hearts just as they had stolen the will of Thutep, the former king.

The high priests of the living city were made of sterner stuff than Nagash's late brother. Amamurti, the aged high priest of Ptra, threw off the king's fist of shadow and hurled a spear of flame the length of the hall. It struck Shepsu-hur full in the chest, setting him ablaze in an instant. The immortal screamed in terror and pain, his skin melting like tallow in the heat. He staggered, pawing desperately at his chest and face, and then with an effort of will he collected himself and continued to run, closing the distance with the man who had wounded him.

Another immortal toppled to the floor with his legs nearly cut out from under him by a handful of stone projectiles. Wind buffeted the warriors, threatening to pull them off their feet. Arkhan caught sight of the Hierophant of Phakth and stopped his invocation with a hurled dagger. The high priest fell to his knees, clutching at the knife that had sprouted from his throat.

Before the hierophants could ready another wave of spells the immortals were upon them. Swords flashed, and men were torn asunder. The Hierophant of Djaf met the charge head-on, cutting one immortal down with a single stroke of his sword before another buried his knife in the high priest's eye. Arkhan reached the fallen Hierophant of Phakth and despatched him with a swift stroke of his blade.

Nagash paced along the aisle in the wake of his warriors, already casting a new incantation. As the priests fell he tore their life essences from their bodies and bound them as he had done to Khefru. One by one their moaning forms were drawn through the air towards the king and formed an unnatural retinue around his body.

The High Priestesses of Asaph and Basth fell next, their heads severed as they tried to fight back-to-back against the immortals. The Hierophant of Tahoth fell next, pleading for mercy as Arkhan slit his throat. The rest fell back, climbing the dais and forming a barrier between the queen and Nagash's men. As they did, the High Priest of Sokth took a dagger in his leg and fell onto the steps. An immortal leapt on him like a desert lion and sank his teeth into the man's face.

That left only Amamurti and the Hierophant of Geheb. The high priest of the earth god was already bleeding from half a dozen wounds, but he continued to fend off his attackers with brutal sweeps of his bloodstained hammer. One immortal grew too bold and tried to cut at the hierophant's knees. The high priest smashed the warrior aside with a blow from his hammer, but that created the opening Arkhan was looking for. Swift as a viper, he leapt forwards and brought down his gleaming khopesh, and the hierophant's hammer, along with his arm, bounced wetly across the stone steps.

The Hierophant of Ptra called out the name of his god and hurled a gout of hissing flame down the steps at the advancing immortals. Three of them were struck full-force and collapsed in heaps of blackened bones and bubbling flesh. Before Amamurti could cast another invocation he was struck by three flung daggers, one of which pierced his heart. The high priest sank slowly to the dais beside Neferem's paralysed form, his life essence bleeding from his eyes and gaping mouth.

Nagash stepped slowly through the carnage. With a wave of his hand he snuffed the flames that were scourging Shepsu-hur's body, and then climbed the steps until he stood eye-to-eye with the queen. For the first time Nagash noticed the terrified form of Ghazid, crouched fearfully in the shadow of Settra's throne.

The king's gaze returned to Neferem. The Daughter of the Sun was quivering with rage, struggling to break the hold that Nagash had over her. Once upon a time she might have succeeded, but decades of drinking Nagash's elixir had taken its toll on her will.

'Where is that snake, Nebunefer?' the king growled. 'I know he had a hand in this treachery.'

'He is not here,' the queen answered defiantly. 'I sent him away, in case the priests failed to kill you.' She tried to move, to advance upon him with clenched fists, but Nagash's will held her fast. 'Whatever happens here, at least he will survive to raise the other great cities against you!'

'You dare defy me, your rightful king?' Nagash roared.

'You killed my son!' Neferem said through clenched teeth. Her voice seethed with hatred. 'Khefru told me everything.'

'Did he tell you that you drank Sukhet's blood an hour later?' Nagash replied. 'Yes. You owe your continued youth to his murder.'

Tears leaked from the corners of Neferem's eyes, but the hatred on her face remained.

'Kill me and be done with it,' she hissed. 'It doesn't matter now. You've spilled the blood of holy men, Nagash. The gods will engineer your ruin far better than I.'

'You think this is terrible?' Nagash said, indicating the pile of torn and bleeding bodies. The ghosts shifted around him, wailing piteously. 'This is but the prologue, my foolish little queen. I have not yet begun to sow the seeds of slaughter across Nehekhara. When I am done, Mahrak will lie in ruins, and the old gods will be cast down forever. And you will stand by my side and watch me do it.'

Nagash's left hand shot forwards and closed around Neferem's throat.

'From the moment I saw you, I knew that I had to possess you,' he said. 'That time has now come.'

Neferem started to speak, but suddenly her body stiffened as Nagash began to chant. Power coursed through the queen's body, bursting from her eyes and mouth in a torrent of glowing green light. Her lifeforce was torn from her, flowing to Nagash in a slow, inexorable stream. A faint, tortured scream rose from the queen's throat: a sound of terrible anguish and pain that seemed to go on and on.

Tendrils of smoke rose from Neferem's skin. Her flesh shrank and her skin wrinkled like dried leather. The flow of energy from her body began to dwindle. Her shoulders drooped and her head bobbed on her almost-skeletal neck, but somehow the queen continued to survive.

Nagash drew the life from her until he could take no more. In the space of a minute, the Daughter of the Sun had been transformed into a living horror, her body somehow sustained by the bindings of the sacred covenant. Her withered legs gave out beneath her, and Neferem sank painfully to the dais, right beside Settra's throne.

The king studied Neferem in silence. His immortals stared at the king and his queen with horror and awe. Behind the king's throne, concealed in darkness, Ghazid held his head in his hands and wept.

TWENTY-EIGHT

THE CITY OF THE GODS

Mahrak, the City of Hope,
in the 63rd year of Ptra the Glorious
(-1744 Imperial Reckoning)

Blue-grey smoke wreathed the thousand temples of the city of Mahrak, filling the air with the fragrances of sandalwood, frankincense and myrrh. A riot of horns, cymbals and silver bells echoed and re-echoed down the narrow streets and across the great plazas where the faithful gathered for prayer and sacrifice. Priests slaughtered herds of oxen, goats and lambs, casting their flesh and blood into the flames. In some households, young slaves were fed cups of wine laced with the black lotus, and then were led to the sacrificial bonfires that burned before the great Palace of the Gods. Across the City of Hope, beseeching hands were cast skywards, imploring the heavens for deliverance from the terrible darkness approaching from the west.

The people of the city had good reason to believe that the gods would intervene. At the centre of the city, surrounded by a walled plaza in the heart of the Palace of the Gods, lay the Khept-am-shepret, the miraculous Sundered Stone that saved the seven tribes from extinction during the darkest days of the Great Migration.

Bereft of their ancient homes, bereft of their gods, weakened unto death by the sun and the endless, scorching sands, the tribes had come to this great plain and found that they could walk no more. In ages past their gods had been the spirits of the trees and the jungle springs, of the panther, the monkey and the python.

Here, in this great, empty wasteland, the tribes in their desperation prayed to the sun and the blue sky for salvation, and Ptra, the Great Father, was moved by their pleas. He stretched forth his hand, and a great boulder in the tribes' midst split apart with a sound like a thunderbolt.

Stunned, the tribes gathered around the sundered stone, and saw fresh, sweet water come welling up through the sharp-edged cracks. The tribes drank, cutting their hands on the knife-edged stones and thus offering their first sacrifices to the gods of the desert. In the days that followed the great covenant was pledged and the Blessed Land was born.

Mahrak began as a collection of temples, one for each of the twelve great gods, and a glorious palace where the tribes could come together and offer worship on the high holy days of the year. Slowly but surely, the city grew up around these great structures, as cities are wont to do, first with districts of modest dwellings to house the workers building the temples, and then with marketplaces and bazaars where traders could come and ply their wares. Then, as centuries passed and the tribes spread across Nehekhara to found other great cities, Mahrak increased in wealth and influence as distant rulers sought the wise counsel and prayers of the temples.

The temples were gargantuan affairs, having grown along with their burgeoning fortunes: Geheb's temple was a mighty ziggurat that dominated the horizon to the east, lit at its summit by a roaring flame that had not been extinguished in four hundred years. Nearby, Djaf's temple was a sprawling complex of low, massive buildings built from slabs of black marble, while to the west, beyond the perfumed gardens of Asaph, the ivory tower of Usirian rose from the midst of a sprawling, intricate labyrinth formed by walls of polished sandstone.

The Palace of the Gods, the seat of power of Nehekhara's Hieratic Council, sat at the feet of a massive pyramid that rose more than two hundred feet into the sky. At its summit sat an enormous disk of polished gold that caught the sun's rays and reflected Ptra's glory in a shimmering beacon that could be seen for leagues across the eastern plains. All of the temples, even the broad field of black obelisks erected in obeisance to dreadful Khsar, the Howling One, glittered with ornaments of gold, silver and polished bronze, surrounded by crowded neighbourhoods of mud-brick buildings whose narrow streets only saw sunlight when Ptra's light hung directly overhead.

Mahrak was the oldest, largest and most splendid of Nehekhara's great cities, home to thousands of priests, priestesses and scholars and the tens of thousands of traders, craftsmen, labourers and pilgrims who served them. Many of Nehekhara's wealthiest families maintained residences in the city, and in centuries past a constant stream of noble visitors made their way to the city in search of blessings or advice. That had been before the rise of the Usurper in Khemri.

To the west, the swirling, blue-black clouds were already past the Gates of the Dusk and bearing swiftly down upon the City of the Gods. Standing upon the battlements near Mahrak's western gate, Nebunefer tucked his thin arms into the folds of his robes and nodded in grim satisfaction. The armies of Rasetra and Lybaras were withdrawing to the south-east, the dust of their passing still hanging in the late afternoon air along the southern horizon, but the Usurper's army showed no signs of pursuing them. Nagash wanted a final reckoning with the council and he would have it, regardless of the cost. Nebunefer hoped the price would be more than the Usurper could afford to pay, not that such a thing would stop him.

A hot wind gusted over the battlements, full of grit and the musty smell of the grave. A thin line of warriors stood along the walls, awaiting the arrival of the foe. Mahrak had never needed an army before, and even as the Usurper grew in power at Khemri, the Hieratic Council refused to consider raising one. That would have been tantamount to admitting that Nagash's power exceeded that of the gods. Each temple did have its own corps of Ushabti, however, and there were no finer warriors in all of the Blessed Land.

The devoted were the paladins of the gods, men who dedicated their lives to serving their deity and protecting the faithful from harm. In return for their devotion the gods gave them wondrous and terrible gifts, in proportion to the strength of each Ushabti's faith and the worthiness of his deeds. In other Nehekharan cities the Ushabti guarded the priest king, who was a living embodiment of their god's will, but in Mahrak the devoted guarded the temples and the persons of the Hieratic Council, who by virtue of their station were second only to the gods.

In distant Ka-Sabar the Ushabti of Geheb were tawny-skinned giants with leonine fangs and lambent eyes; in Mahrak, however, Geheb's devoted were transformed into towering, manlike lions, with a desert cat's fearsome strength and speed and hands tipped in deadly claws. The devoted of Djaf had the heads of ebon jackals and the cold touch of death in their fingertips. Ptra's Ushabti were golden-skinned titans too beautiful and terrible to look upon. Their voices had the pure tone of trumpets, and their hands could shatter swords.

By ancient tradition each temple mustered no more than two score and ten of these holy warriors, and they gathered along the wall in all their glory: six hundred holy warriors against Nagash's thousands.

As mighty as Mahrak's Ushabti were, they were not the city's only defences. Vast and ageless powers had been woven into the city's walls and foundations: spirits of the desert and divine servants of the gods, who stirred awake at the approach of Nagash's horde. These guardians were not bound by the covenant, at least not in any direct sense, and thus they could not be turned aside by the will of the Daughter of the Sun. The Usurper was about to learn that the gods, though bound, were still far from helpless.

A stir went through the ranks of the devoted along the battlements to Nebunefer's right. The old priest turned and caught sight of three imperious figures clothed in vestments of yellow, brown and black advancing down the length of the wall towards him. Nebunefer bowed deeply at the approach of his master, Nekh-amn-aten, Hierophant of the great Ptra. Flanking the high priest were Atep-neru, the inscrutable Hierophant of Djaf, and the scowling, belligerent Khansu, Hierophant of Khsar the Faceless.

'This is an unexpected honour, holy ones,' Nebunefer said. 'No doubt the devoted will draw inspiration and courage from your presence.'

Nekh-amn-aten waved the priest to silence with an irritable hand gesture. 'Spare us the platitudes,' the hierophant growled. 'All that time spent among kings has thoroughly corrupted you, Nebunefer. I've never heard such simpering drivel in my life.'

Nebunefer spread his wrinkled hands and smiled ruefully. The hierophant had been born in Mahrak, and had never once gone abroad. As far as the old priest knew, this was the first time Nekh-amn-aten had set foot on the city wall.

'No doubt you are right, holy one,' he said diplomatically. 'The courts of our allies are rife with all manner of ease and comfort, certainly nothing like the stern life we enjoy here.'

Khansu glowered at Nebunefer's impertinent tone, but Nekh-amn-aten seemed not to hear. Tucking his hands in the sleeves of his heavy cotton vestments, the hierophant stepped to the edge of the battlements and stared out at the roiling clouds that bruised the western horizon.

'I never should have let you talk me into this,' he said sourly. 'We ought to have kept our allies close by and let Nagash focus his attentions on them.'

'To what end, holy one?' the old priest asked with a sigh. 'The armies of Rasetra and Lybaras have fought like lions, but their strength is spent. If they had remained, as Rakh-amn-hotep was determined to do, we would be standing here witnessing their slaughter.'

Nekh-amn-aten grunted irritably, and said, 'And Nagash would have spent much of his army's strength destroying them, perhaps leaving him too weak to challenge us.'

The anger Nebunefer felt at the hierophant's callousness, surprised him. Perhaps he had spent too much time among the priest kings after all.

'The advantage is ours, holy one,' he said forcefully. 'We will let the Usurper break his teeth against our walls, while our allies rebuild their armies and return to finish what they have begun.' Atep-neru turned to Nebunefer.

'How long will that be, priest?' he asked in a sepulchral voice. 'Two months? Ten? A year, perhaps?'

Khansu growled irritably, and said, 'A year? What foolishness. The campaigning season is nearly done. Once Nagash sees he cannot breach our defences he will make for Lybaras, or perhaps withdraw to Quatar.'

Nebunefer took a deep breath and fought to conceal his irritation. How many times must he repeat himself?

'What does Nagash care for seasons of war?' he asked. 'His warriors are not needed back in Khemri to gather in the harvest.' The old priest shrugged. 'His miserable subjects can all starve to death for all he cares. Indeed, in death they would become more useful to him still. No, he will remain here, on this side of the Valley of Kings, until all the eastern cities have burnt or bowed before him. And make no mistake, he will start his campaign here. He knows we have sent Rasetra and Lybaras against him, and may even suspect that we were behind the attack on Bel Aliad. If he conquers Mahrak, the war could end in a single stroke. Mark my words, he will attack us with everything he possesses, and if he cannot overcome our defences we could be facing a long and protracted siege.'

Nekh-amn-aten clasped his hands behind his back, still staring out at the spreading clouds.

'How long can the city withstand such a siege?' he asked. Atep-neru tapped a long finger against his chin.

'We will not lack for water,' he said. 'Our cisterns are full, and the Sundered Stone remains a wellspring for the faithful. If we ration the supplies in the storehouses, we could last for three years if we had to.'

Nekh-amn-aten turned to Nebunefer. 'Three years,' he echoed, his expression darkening. 'Do you think it will come to that?' The old priest thought back to the last time he spoke to the Rasetran king. *You may have to endure a very long time.* Nebunefer met his master's worried gaze.

'Only the gods can say,' he replied.

The armies of the Undying King reached the holy city just a few hours past nightfall, pouring over the dunes in a hissing tide of dry leather and dusty bones. The ranks of the undead had swelled dramatically over the course of the relentless march through the valley. Skeletal archers from Zandri formed skirmish lines ahead of the clattering spearmen, and bony Numasi horsemen paced silently behind the tireless battleline, escorting Nagash's immortal captains. Further back, towards the rear of the silent, rattling horde, other, more terrible creations lumbered across the sands, driven by the will of their implacable masters.

When Nagash's vast host had left Khemri for the Fountains of Eternal Life it had been comprised entirely of living, breathing men. Now, less than a quarter of that number remained. Packs of jackals loped in the army's wake by night, and great flocks of carrion birds wheeled silently above them by day. The pickings for the scavengers were scarce, but the presence of so much death and decay nevertheless proved too great for them to ignore.

A terrible, keening wind whistled through the undead ranks, plucking at frayed tatters of clothing and torn pieces of leather or parchment-like human skin. Its breath sucked veils of sand and dust into whirling patterns that rose above the bleached skulls of the warriors and fed the roiling mantle of darkness that shrouded the host from the burning touch of the sun.

The constant, howling dust storm forced the immortals and the living warriors of the army to march with their shoulders wrapped in capes with desert cowls drawn tightly around their faces. The men of Zandri and Numas were numbed and half-deafened by the constant roaring of the storm, and more than one horse had to be put down after the fine, swirling grit had put out their eyes. It had been the same for weeks on end as Nagash drove them along the dreadful valley in pursuit of the armies of the east.

They had expected to find their foes holding onto the Gates of the Dusk in a last, desperate attempt to keep the Undying King at bay. For the last few days the army had been at a forced march, hoping to reach the end of the valley and catch their enemies unawares, but when the vanguard of skeletal horsemen reached the gates they'd found the low walls abandoned and the village beyond eerily silent. The immortal commanding the vanguard had angrily sent a messenger in search of a living Numasi horseman with enough of a brain to make sense of the tracks they'd found on the other side of the town. From what the exhausted cavalryman could tell, they had missed their foes by only a few hours. When Nagash received the news he ordered the army forwards in full battle array, expecting to catch the allied armies at the gates of Mahrak.

At a silent command, the vast western host clattered to a halt just over a mile from the walls of the holy city. Nagash's immortal captains reined in their mouldering horses and raised their heads, sensing the currents of power coiling restlessly through the sands ahead. Halfway between Mahrak and the invading army ran a shifting, tenebrous line of demarcation where Nagash's veil of shadow pressed against the city's ancient wards. Beyond that restless line of darkness the plains before the city were pale and gleaming beneath Neru's silver light.

The sky above Mahrak was a cobalt tapestry, woven with threads of glittering diamond. Watch-fires burned from great braziers atop the city walls, bathing sections of the battlements in pools of molten orange light. There was no mob of panicked soldiers struggling to pass through Mahrak's western gate, which puzzled the immortals. But for the potent energies encircling the city, Mahrak seemed surprisingly quiet.

Hours passed while the rest of the army moved into position and messengers were sent from the vanguard to make their report to the Undying King. Once again, the weary Numasi riders were brought forwards, and still more hours passed before the riders established that the allied armies had circled around the city to the south and were withdrawing in the direction of their homes. As the news filtered down to the king's immortals, many assumed that they would continue the pursuit, and shifted their tireless horsemen further down the battle-åline to the south.

Nagash's orders, when they were issued at around midnight, caught many of his captains by surprise. The Numasi horsemen were ordered to secure the army's flank to the south-east and keep a watch on the allied armies' retreat, and the reserve companies were brought forwards and arrayed behind the main battle-line. Quartermasters and their slaves went to work pitching tents and creating corrals for their wagon horses a quarter of a mile behind the army, while armourers unpacked their portable forges and siege engineers went to work hauling their ponderous engines in the direction of the waiting city. Groaning wagons rolled along in their wake, laden with baskets of grinning skulls and casks of reeking pitch.

The attack on the City of the Gods would begin in the hours just before dawn.

Arkhan the Black paced through the predawn darkness, wishing for a horse.

The hungry wind had eased considerably over the last half an hour, leaving his ears ringing and his nerves unsettled by the lack of sound and pressure. Much of the swirling dust had settled, and had he a mount he could have observed the army from one end of the battle-line to the other, which was entirely the point. The captains would need the visibility to command their companies, and the siege engineers would need to observe the fall of their artillery during the march to the walls.

More than eighty thousand corpses stood in tight ranks twenty deep, arrayed in a rough crescent formation that stretched for nearly three miles north to south. Another forty thousand spearmen waited in reserve, surrounding the firing positions of fifty heavy catapults. In between the main battleline and the reserves were squadrons of undead horsemen and their immortal captains, plus five thousand skeletal archers. The bowmen would march close behind the spear companies, raking the enemy battlements with a steady rain of arrows while the assault troops attacked the main gate. Only when the gate had fallen would the cavalry spring into action, charging through the gap to sow chaos and death across the City of Hope.

Arkhan noted that none of the Undying King's living allies would take part in the attack. The Numasi remained off to the south-east, ostensibly guarding the army's flank from the withdrawing eastern forces. Zandri's troops had been placed upon the northern flank and allowed to remain in camp until further orders.

It was clear that Nagash did not trust his vassals, particularly where Mahrak was concerned. The vizier understood his master's growing paranoia all too well.

Since the debacle at Quatar, Arkhan hadn't commanded so much as a scouting party. Indeed, the king had forbidden him to so much as wear his sword and armour during the long march. He was not even allowed to ride a horse. Short of ordering him to march naked behind the army's baggage train, Nagash had subjected Arkhan to every possible humiliation. The vizier had come to suspect that the only reason he hadn't been destroyed outright was so that he could serve as a constant reminder to the rest of Nagash's captains.

For a while, Arkhan had believed that the punishment would cease, eventually, and he would return to favour once again. Now, he wasn't so sure, and he wondered what, if anything, he was going to do about it.

The vizier strode down the length of the battle-line behind the waiting horsemen, seeking one immortal in particular. Most of the pale figures he spotted threw a mocking salute or sneered in contempt. Arkhan kept his face neutral, but made a note of each and every slight. If I can fall, so can you, he thought, and when that happens, I'll be waiting.

Finally, near the centre of the line, he caught sight of the one he was seeking. Shepsu-hur was sitting in the saddle of his skeletal warhorse, his bronze helmet resting on the saddle between his thighs and his hands busy running a whetstone along the edge of a sharply pointed knife. He stiffened slightly and turned in the saddle, as though sensing the weight of Arkhan's stare. Bits of dry linen flaked away from his burned limbs as he moved, and his ruined face cocked curiously to one side as he saw his former master. After a moment's consideration the maimed champion sheathed his knife, brought his horse about and approached the vizier. Like most of Nagash's immortals, Shepsu-hur no longer bothered using reins: a dead horse cared nothing for a bridle, being directed solely by the rider's will.

'Not long now,' Arkhan said by way of greeting as the immortal approached. Shepsu-hur nodded, his dry leather wrappings crackling and creaking as he moved.

'I'm surprised you won't be joining us,' he said in his ravaged voice. 'I expected Nagash to return you to command in time for the assault. It's foolish not to make use of your talents when so much is at stake.'

The words of rough praise would have heartened a mortal, but Arkhan felt only resentment at his master for the obvious slight.

'It's been weeks,' he growled. 'Nagash has forgotten me, I expect. I'm sure that Raamket or someone else began scheming to take my place the moment I fell out of favour.' Shepsu-hur nodded gravely.

'Raamket's the one, which I'm sure comes as no surprise. You did yourself no favours by keeping to that tower of yours for so many years.' The vizier nodded.

'True enough,' he said. He eyed Shepsu-hur and wondered if the immortal had ever chafed under Nagash's bond as he had. Was he the only one who had sought to free himself from the master's chains? Surely not.

'How many allies do you think Raamket has among the court?' he asked. The champion shrugged, sending another shower of brittle cloth tumbling to the ground.

'Not many, I expect. He was never that popular, especially in the beginning, but now that he has the master's ear that will no doubt change.' Shepsu-hur studied Arkhan thoughtfully. 'Why do you ask?'

'Just considering my options,' Arkhan said carefully.

Shepsu-hur nodded. As the immortal started to reply there was a shout from the rear of the army and a series of heavy *thuds* rumbled along the length of the battle-line as the catapults went into action. Streaks of livid green light arced over the waiting spearmen as bundles of enchanted skulls plunged towards Mahrak's walls.

Horns boomed hollowly nearby, and Arkhan saw a flare of sorcerous fire a few score yards to his right. A phalanx of withered corpses bearing white-faced shields and great swords had appeared along the slope of a high dune at the rear of the waiting horsemen: the corpses of Quatar's royal bodyguard, bound into Nagash's service and bearing the flayed standard of their former king. The Undying King stood behind the ranks of the Tomb Guard, surrounded by his spectral retinue and attended closely by Raamket and a handful of slaves. Beside Nagash walked the broken figure of Neferem, her withered face twisted into a mask of silent grief.

Arkhan felt the necromancer's unspoken command buzzing in his brain like a swarm of ravening locusts. A stir went through the waiting horsemen. Shepsu-hur straightened in his saddle.

'It begins,' he rasped, reaching for his helm. The immortal nodded to Arkhan before slipping the helmet onto his head.

'We'll speak of Raamket and his allies again once the battle is done,' he said.

The catapults fired again, hurling their screaming projectiles at the city. With a clatter of bone, wood and metal the first spear companies began to move, rolling in a silent, inexorable tide towards the city walls. Arkhan felt the earth tremble at the tread of eighty thousand pairs of feet.

'How long, do you reckon?' he asked the champion. Shepsu-hur looked towards the City of Hope.

'An hour. Perhaps less. Once the gate is breached, the city is doomed.' He shrugged. 'Perhaps they will surrender before it comes to that.'

'Is Nagash interested in surrender?'

The immortal looked down at Arkhan and gave him a fanged smile.

'The Undying King has said that every man who brings him a living priest will be paid his weight in gold. The rest are to be slain out of hand.' The vizier was surprised at the news.

'Slain? Not enslaved?' he asked. Shepsu-hur shook his head in reply.

'Today, the age of the old gods comes to an end,' he said. 'The temples will burn and the faithful will be put to the sword.'

'The men of Numas and Zandri will be outraged,' Arkhan declared, thinking back to the reaction of the kings in the palace at Quatar. 'They may well revolt.'

Shepsu-hur wheeled his horse around. The immortal glanced back over his shoulder.

'The men of Numas and Zandri may well be next,' he said, and went to rejoin his troops.

Arkhan watched the cavalry set off behind the implacable spearmen and looked beyond, to the silent walls of the City of the Gods. Invisible energies crackled through the air, swirling above the marching army like a building storm. A breeze plucked at the vizier's robes, kicking up tendrils of dust and grit. Arkhan couldn't say if it was Nagash's doing, or whether some other force was stirring as the army began to march.

* * *

Atop the nearby dune, Nagash the Undying King watched his army press forwards and contemplated Mahrak's doom.

Bale-fires were burning across the plain where bundles of screaming skulls had fallen short of the city walls. As the necromancer watched, the catapults launched another salvo, and this time many of the projectiles found the range. They burst against the walls in sickly green showers of bone and broken sandstone, or struck the battlements in blazing sprays of fire.

The spear companies were moving at a slow, measured pace, advancing in a broad line towards Mahrak's western wall. They had nearly reached the demarcation line where the necromancer's shroud met the city's defensive wards.

Nagash turned to his queen.

'Cast them down,' he told Neferem, pointing towards the starlit field. The Undying King was already gathering his power, drawing upon the energies of the Black Pyramid, hundreds of leagues distant. When the wards fell, his sorcerous shroud would rush in, and darkness would fall upon the City of Hope.

The first ranks of spearmen reached the city's wards. Neferem raised her withered arms and let out a long, despairing cry.

Down on the plain below, the breeze began to strengthen, pulling ribbons of sand into the air towards the waiting city. The spear companies continued forwards under the fire of the catapults, followed by thirty squadrons of light cavalry led by a third of his immortals. In their wake came thousands of skeletal archers, their tall bows held at the ready. They would do the majority of the fighting once the companies reached the walls, shooting at the city defenders as they fired down at the milling spearmen.

The march of the spearmen had sent a steady, rolling drumbeat across the sandy ground, but that tempo was punctuated by slow, heavy footfalls. *Thump... thump... thump...*

They crested the line of dunes just as the catapults fired another salvo at the city. Eight towering figures, each sixteen feet tall and crafted of fused bones and cable-like sinews, the bone giants wielded enormous clubs, fashioned from ships' masts cut down and banded together with thick strips of bronze. Fashioned after the complicated metal giants of Lybaras, they would assault the city's gate and hammer it down, paving the way for the cavalry to begin the slaughter.

The wind was continuing to strengthen, drawing more and more dust into the air above the plain. The necromancer's mantle of shadow was starting to unravel, drawn inexorably into the building vortex.

Thousands of skeletons marched forwards, their battered helmets and spear tips gleaming dully under the fading starlight. The city's wards had not fallen.

For a fleeting instant, the Undying King was stunned. He sharpened the force of his command, quickening the pace of his troops. The bone giants increased their stride, gaining swiftly on the advancing companies.

Overhead, the clouds of dust were boiling, their insides lit from within by a furnace-like glow. The wind had risen in power to an angry, lion-like roar. Then came a deafening *crack*, like a boulder splitting in the sun, and fire began to rain down upon the living dead.

Tumbling pieces of rock the size of wagon wheels arced from the clouds on trails of blazing crimson, landing among the tightly ranked spearmen and hurling their pieces skywards in plumes of dirt and flame. Each impact reverberated across the plain like a hammer blow, one falling atop another so quickly that they merged into a titanic, thunderous roar.

Huge holes were gouged in the spear companies, but the skeletal warriors did not feel hesitation or fear. Driven by the invisible lash of their king's will, the spearmen closed ranks and continued to press forwards. Bodies struggled onwards, their wrappings burning away as they walked. The catapults continued to fire, but as the skulls streaked through the clouds the bundles were burst apart and hurled earthwards, landing upon the skeletons below.

Furious, Nagash whirled upon his queen. He seized Neferem by her hair and wrenched her head around, cracking the desiccated skin of her neck.

'Break their power!' he commanded. 'Break it!'

Neferem raised her arms feebly, her face warped by pain and terror. She wailed like a lost soul, crying her torment to the heavens, but to no avail.

The immortals had penetrated into the wards, and as the fiery stones fell around them they quickened their pace, weaving their way past the struggling spearmen and racing for the gate. The giants followed suit, in some cases ploughing ruthlessly through any spearmen caught in their path. One giant was struck squarely in the forehead by a plunging stone, shattering its misshapen skull. The headless construct staggered for a moment, and then righted itself and continued on.

When the charging horsemen were less than a hundred yards from the city walls the sandy ground before them heaved and burst, throwing a curtain of dust high into the sky. The cavalry, going too fast to stop, plunged into the billowing wall and disappeared from view.

For a moment, Nagash could see nothing, and then a small shape came spinning out of the cloud like a flung potshard. By luck, it hit a bone giant in the chest and shattered in a spray of fragments. Belatedly, the necromancer realised that the shape had been one half of an undead horse.

The dust was starting to thin out, and large, dark shapes could be seen stirring within its depths. More bits and pieces were flung from the cloud, like fragments scattered by the sweep of heavy blows.

The giants had nearly reached the curtain of dust. They raised their clubs and swung them in broad, ponderous sweeps, cutting roiling wakes through the shroud and revealing massive, leonine shapes whose flanks were the colour of the desert sands. One of them rounded on the giants and leapt forwards, paws outstretched.

It struck the giant in the chest, talons shattering the fused ribcage and digging furrows in the construct's pelvis. The monster was easily as large as the giant, with a lion-like body and a powerful, lashing tail, but the head of the beast was not a lion. It had a russet mane and slitted yellow eyes, but the face was that of a man.

The sphinx bared massive fangs and lunged at the giant's neck, snapping the knobbly vertebrae in a single, powerful bite. The construct toppled beneath the monster's weight and the sphinx tore it apart with sweeps of its sabre-like claws.

More sphinxes leapt from the settling dust cloud, their pelts covered in crushed pieces of bone and pale shreds of tissue. They dashed among the remaining giants, too fast for their clumsy weapons to touch, and tore at their legs with tooth and claw. One by one, the constructs crashed to the ground and were ripped to pieces.

Clouds of arrows arced across the plain and landed among the sphinxes as the surviving archers drew into range. The monsters raised their heads and snapped at the arrows as though they were no more than stinging flies, and then returned to their grisly work.

The spearmen were still pushing forwards under the hail of fire, but now they advanced singly, or in scattered knots of five or ten warriors. Their companies had been shattered, and the archers were suffering beneath the heavenly assault. The plain was carpeted in smouldering bones and broken bits of weapons and armour.

Baring his teeth in a silent snarl, Nagash raised his face to the heavens and roared in anger. Down on the field the surviving skeletons staggered at the sound, turned about and began to withdraw.

The sphinxes paced the broken ground at the foot of Mahrak's walls like hungry cats, staring balefully at the rest of the necromancer's forces. The remains of the cavalrymen and their immortal captains crunched beneath their paws. Not one of the riders had survived.

The huge beasts tossed their heads and roared defiantly at the retreating skeletons, their human-like faces both wrathful and triumphant as they stood among the broken bones of the horde.

Beyond the City of Hope, the first rays of dawn were breaking.

TWENTY-NINE

THE LORD OF THE DEAD LANDS

Mahrak, the City of Hope,
in the 63rd year of Djaf the Terrible
(-1740 Imperial reckoning)

The slaves began their work at dusk, edging warily across the shadow line as soon as the sun disappeared behind the sorcerous clouds to the west. They worked in groups of fifty or sixty, with a third of their number dragging hand carts while the rest scooped up armfuls of broken bones or torn leather harness and loaded up the conveyances as quickly as they could. Companies of skeletal archers watched over the bone gatherers from just behind the demarcation line, ready to shoot any slave who lost his nerve and tried to return before their cart had been filled. The closer the scavengers got to Mahrak's walls the more fearful they became.

Arkhan the Black stood atop the same low dune where Nagash had unleashed his first attack on the city of priests, and watched the progress of one particular band of bone gatherers who were a few hundred yards farther ahead than the rest. A scribe sat on the sands nearby with a portable writing desk balanced on his knees, ready to record the vizier's observations. Behind them the vast tent city of the besiegers was stirring, rising from the long day's slumber and making ready for another tedious night watching the shadow line and waiting for the city to fall.

Four years after the catastrophic opening of the siege, the western plain of Mahrak was carpeted in splintered bone, torn armour and broken weapons. Uncounted thousands of warriors had been hurled at the city, only to be smashed by fiery stones or shattered beneath the paws of the city's elemental guardians.

Company after company had been fed into the waiting maw of the city defences, using every conceivable tactic that Nagash and his captains could devise. They launched elaborate feints and flanking moves, hoping to overwhelm the defending wards. They supported the assaults with fierce bombardments and scores of lumbering bone giants. They even crafted burrowing constructs to try to tunnel across the killing field, all to no avail. The defences of Mahrak were as tireless and fierce as Nagash's undead attackers, and as the months turned into years the plain outside the city became a vast field of bones.

The carnage had grown so severe that the besiegers had to start using slaves to clear lanes through the debris to permit the movement of troops. Cart-loads of bones were dumped in huge liche-fields to the rear of the army, where the king's acolytes would pore through the wreckage for suitable parts to reassemble useful warriors or larger siege constructs. Further west, scavenging parties combed the necropoli of Khemri, Numas and Zandri, breaking into peasant crypts and raising new conscripts to restore Nagash's battered army.

The cost of maintaining the siege had grown so severe that the stored energies of the Black Pyramid had been dangerously depleted. Raamket had been sent back to Khemri after the first year of the siege to gather fresh souls for sacrifice. Rumour had it that barges of northern slaves were shipped downriver from Zandri every month to die in the depths of the pyramid.

The Undying King had made it clear to his vassals: if it took ten years, or ten thousand years, the siege of Mahrak would continue until the City of the Gods was no more.

Arkhan peered into the deepening gloom beyond the shadow line and gauged the progress of the scavenging party.

'Two hundred yards,' he said, and the scribe's brush whispered across the papyrus. 'Nothing yet.'

The party was well ahead of the other scavengers, wading through drifts of splintered bone that rose almost to their knees. The sky above the slaves remained clear, as expected. For the last year the besiegers had begun probing the city's wards in various ways, gathering information on how they operated in the hope of finding a way to unravel them. They had learned that groups of a hundred men or less could cross the shadow line without triggering the rain of fire and could move safely up to a quarter of a mile from the city. Once past that, however, they fell prey to the sphinxes.

There was some debate as to how many of those desert spirits protected Mahrak. Various observers claimed no more than half a dozen, while others insisted there was at least a score. The trouble was that the spirits came and went at will within the quarter-mile zone just outside the city walls. They could disappear into the sandy soil and emerge from a dust cloud hundreds of yards away, striking with terrible speed, before vanishing once again. Despite their best efforts, Nagash's troops had yet to injure a single sphinx, much less slay one.

The siege wasn't entirely one-sided, however. If Nagash's warriors couldn't enter Mahrak, they could at least make certain that nothing got out. Numasi patrols had intercepted numerous foraging parties over the last two years, and after sufficient torture, the prisoners had confessed to the desperate conditions inside the city. Mahrak's food stores had been exhausted long ago. The horses were gone, as were all the rats. Fighting had broken out around the temple of Basth when mobs of starving citizens went after the temple's sacred cats. Mahrak's fearsome Ushabti, the most terrible holy warriors in all of Nehekhara, found themselves turning their powers upon the city's faithful in a desperate effort to maintain order.

Initially, Nagash had been pleased by the news. It seemed as though the city might fall at any time, but the king's anticipation soon turned sour. Mahrak continued to endure, night after awful night, while to the south the Kings of Rasetra and Lybaras were no doubt rebuilding their broken armies to offer battle once more.

The sound of hooves on the far side of the dune caught Arkhan's attention. He stole a glance over his shoulder and saw a messenger wearing a hooded desert cape slide clumsily from the saddle of a sickly looking mare. Frowning, Arkhan turned his attention back to the slaves creeping towards the distant city. Whatever the rider had to say, he'd hear it soon enough. It was unlikely to be of much significance.

The messenger took his time climbing the rounded dune, his breath rattling noisily in his throat. Arkhan heard the man's laboured footfalls draw near, until he could smell the oily stink of sickness seeping from the wretch's pores. The vizier's pale lips curled in distaste. When the man spoke, his voice was a wheezing rattle.

'First we offer bones. Now we sacrifice flesh and blood to the lions of the desert,' he said. Arkhan felt a cold flash of irritation. Once upon a time he would have made the man suffer dearly for such impertinence.

'Have you a message for me?' he growled. 'Or have you chosen to risk your life by wasting my valuable time?' The messenger surprised him with a phlegmatic chuckle.

'The sands of time are running swiftly through our fingers, Arkhan the Black,' he said quietly. Irritation gave way to outrage. Arkhan rounded upon the messenger, his pale hands clenching into fists, and found himself staring into the sallow, haunted face of Amn-nasir, the Priest King of Zandri.

The immortal fought to keep the shock from his face. He stole a wary look at the nearby scribe, who was watching the exchange with dreadful fascination.

'Leave us,' Arkhan told the man. 'I'll relay my observations personally to the king.'

The scribe started to object, but thought better of it when he saw the look of menace in Arkhan's eyes. Without a word, he snatched up his materials and hastily withdrew down the far side of the dune. When the scribe was out of earshot, Arkhan turned back to the king.

'What is the meaning of this?' he hissed.

Amn-nasir's sunken eyes widened fractionally at the vizier's tone, although perhaps it was simply Arkhan's words making their way through the fog of wine and lotus root gripping the king's mind. Amn-nasir managed a fleeting smile, revealing a mouth full of stained, rotting teeth.

'I wished to see for myself how far the king's proud vizier has fallen,' he said softly. Some of Arkhan's former anger returned. He spread his arms wide.

'Then look,' he sneered. 'Drink deep, great one.'

The priest king's smile returned. A bright thread of drool slipped from the corner of his mouth, and he wiped at it absently with a trembling hand.

'Not even the mightiest among us are safe from Nagash's wrath,' he observed.

Arkhan bit back a sharp reply. What point was there in denying it? Amn-nasir had watched him writhe like a worm in the palace at Quatar. He thought back to Shepsu-hur's last words, before he'd ridden to his doom beneath the walls of Mahrak.

The men of Numas and Zandri may well be next.

A distant rumble sounded from the direction of Mahrak, followed by the faint sound of screams. With a curse, Arkhan turned back to the plain and saw that the carnage had already begun.

Three sphinxes reared above the panicked slaves, lashing out at the screaming men with huge, blood-slicked paws. Bodies spun through the air like straw dolls, split wide by the monsters' talons. It looked as though half the slaves were already dead, and the rest were fleeing in panic back towards the shadow line.

'Come on,' Arkhan murmured angrily. He studied the plain of bones around the fleeing slaves carefully. 'Rise up, damn you!'

One of the sphinxes seemed to leap lazily forwards among a knot of terrified slaves, crushing several beneath the weight of its paws and catching another in its fangs. The monster bit the slave in two, spat out the pieces, and then started to lunge for another victim, when suddenly the ground heaved around the struggling slaves and the sphinx jumped skywards like a startled cat.

Massive, low-slung figures erupted from the earth on either side of the sphinx. Jagged pincers the size of a grown man snapped at the monster's legs, and segmented tails made of gleaming bone stabbed at the creature's flanks with stingers as long as swords. Three bone constructs, wrought in the shape of huge tomb scorpions, surrounded the desert spirit and stabbed its flanks again and again, eliciting terrible, human-like roars of rage and pain.

The wounded sphinx retreated, dragging a paralysed hind leg and snapping defiantly at the scuttling constructs. The scorpions pressed forwards relentlessly, spreading out to attack the creature from three different directions at once. A sudden gust of wind across the plain kicked up a cloud of sand around the struggling figures and the sphinx's pack mates attacked. The leonine monsters coalesced out of the swirling sands and leapt onto the scorpions, snapping at the constructs' tails with their powerful jaws. Bone splintered and fragments were hurled into the air as the spirits savaged the constructs.

Within seconds, the ill-fated ambush was over. The six monsters paced around the shattered constructs for a few moments more, and then they turned their backs on the fleeing slaves and withdrew into the churning clouds of sand. Their dusky hides merged with the swirling dust, and then disappeared from view.

Arkhan studied the broken bodies of the scorpions and shook his head irritably. Six months of incantations and labour, all gone in moments. The vizier grimaced.

'Well, we managed to hurt one of the beasts this time,' he muttered bitterly. 'That's progress, I suppose.' Amn-nasir grunted scornfully, which in turn triggered a fit of painful coughing.

'Nagash has made a grave miscalculation,' the king finally said. 'He has kept us here for years, while our cities slide into ruin and our enemies grow in strength. If we had marched on Rasetra and Lybaras at once, we would have ended this war in a month. But now–'

'What?' Arkhan interrupted, his eyes narrowing suspiciously. The king hesitated.

'Every man has a limit to what he can endure,' he said, his voice almost too faint for the immortal to hear. The vizier studied the king's tormented face.

'We either endure, or we perish,' he replied.

'All men perish,' Amn-nasir said. 'Sometimes a good death is preferable to a wretched life.'

Arkhan shook his head.

'You had your chance to rise up against Nagash many years ago, but you bowed your knee to him instead. Now it's too late,' he said.

'Perhaps,' the king said enigmatically, 'and perhaps not.'

'Stop playing children's games,' Arkhan snapped. 'Speak plainly, or not at all.'

'As you wish,' Amn-nasir said. 'The Priest King of Lahmia is on his way here, with an army at his back.' The vizier's eyes widened.

'Are you certain?' he asked, knowing how foolish he sounded even as the question passed his lips. Amn-nasir grinned again, enjoying Arkhan's surprise.

'My scouts spotted them yesterday. They will be here on the morrow,' he replied.

The failed ambush was forgotten. Arkhan's mind raced as he tried to grasp the implications of the Lahmians' impending arrival.

'An army,' he murmured. 'Why? Is Lamashizzar coming to side with Nagash, or with the people of Mahrak?' Amn-nasir shrugged.

'The Lahmians are famous opportunists. No doubt Lamashizzar senses that the balance of power is shifting, and seeks to exploit it for his own ends.'

Arkhan considered this, before asking, 'How large is the Lahmian army?'

'Perhaps fifty or sixty thousand troops,' the king replied, 'a mix of infantry and heavy cavalry, all clad in strange, outlandish armour.'

The vizier shook his head. Nagash had more than twice that number camped outside Mahrak.

'If Lamashizzar pits himself against the Undying King he will be destroyed,' he said.

'If he fights alone, yes,' Amn-nasir said, nodding slowly.

The immortal and the king stared at one another for a long, fraught moment.

'Are the men of Numas contemplating revolt as well?' Arkhan asked quietly.

'I do not speak for Numas,' Amn-nasir replied, his expression inscrutable. Arkhan stepped close to the king.

'You're a fool to tell me this,' he hissed. 'Nagash would reward me well for such information.' Amn-nasir was unmoved by the threat.

'Now who is playing children's games?' he said. 'Do you imagine that your master is capable of gratitude after all this time? Even if you whispered all I've said into Nagash's ear and he somehow trusted you enough to act upon it, do you truly think it would change anything?'

'Why talk to me at all?' the vizier snarled. 'You're right. I have no influence or power any more. The king sets me to menial tasks when it pleases him, and provides me only enough sustenance to eke out a weak, miserable existence.' He thought to say more, but shame held his tongue. For years he had been given little more than drops of the master's precious elixir, leaving him in constant torment. In desperation, he had taken to supplementing his meagre sustenance with the blood of animals. The bitter blood of horses, jackals, even vultures, partially lessened his terrible thirst, but did nothing to restore his vitality.

More than once over the last few years, Arkhan had contemplated disappearing into the desert and making his way back to Khemri. He knew where Nagash's arcane tomes were hidden, deep within the Black Pyramid, and somewhere in their pages were the formulas for creating the dreadful elixir. Those formulas would free him from Nagash's clutches forever, but the long, burning leagues between Mahrak and the Living City daunted him in his weakened state.

'You know more about Nagash and his powers than anyone,' Amn-nasir said, 'and you have every reason to desire his downfall. This is your chance, possibly your only chance, to be free of him. If you went to Lamashizzar and offered to share Nagash's secrets, it might be enough to sway him.' Arkhan frowned.

'Sway him?' The vizier felt his anger returning. 'All this bold talk of revolt is a fantasy, isn't it? You haven't spoken to Lamashizzar at all. For all you know, the Lahmians think Mahrak is on the verge of collapse and they're coming here to curry Nagash's favour. You want to use me as your stalking horse, stirring up the notion of rebellion and gauging Lamashizzar's reaction before you risk your own skin.'

For the first time, Amn-nasir's bleary eyes widened in anger.

'Think what you like, vizier,' he said coldly. 'I never claimed to know Lamashizzar's mind. But that doesn't change any part of what I've said to you.' The king reached up with his palsied hands and pulled up his desert hood.

'You and I know better than anyone what Nehekhara will become if Nagash triumphs,' Amn-nasir said. 'Mahrak cannot endure much longer, and no doubt Lamashizzar senses this. When that happens, darkness will spread across the east, and the Undying King will become the lord of a dead land. We stand upon the brink, Arkhan. This is our last chance to draw back from the brink of ruin.'

Arkhan did not reply at first. He stared out onto the bone-covered plain, and thought of Bel Aliad, and Bhagar, and even of Khemri.

'Lord of a dead land,' he murmured. He took a deep breath. 'I must think on this, great one. You say that Lamashizzar will arrive tomorrow?' The vizier glanced back at the king, but Amn-nasir was gone, already climbing back onto the saddle of his sickly mare. Arkhan watched the king go, and contemplated the future.

A dozen leagues south-east of Mahrak ran a broken range of flat-topped hills, separated by narrow, steep-walled canyons and treacherous gullies. For centuries the terrain had been a haven for eastern bandits, until Nagash's father Khetep had ruthlessly cleansed it on his southern campaigns, more than two hundred years ago. Many of the steep hills were honeycombed with caves, some containing hidden wells and supply caches built by bandit gangs. A clever general could hide an army in that rugged landscape, which is exactly what Rakh-amn-hotep had done.

It had taken more than three months to move the companies of warriors into position. They moved by night to conceal the dust of their march and burned no fires save for a handful of meagre ovens set deep in the back of the hill caves. First the cavalry arrived, establishing a picket to keep Numasi scouts at bay and standing guard over the caches of supplies transferred by swift-moving wagon teams sent ahead of the infantry companies. By the time the Rasetran king arrived at the sprawling encampment, more than forty thousand warriors had been assembled, awaiting the call to battle. In the weeks that followed, another twenty thousand troops had arrived, bringing the army to nearly its full size.

The host was but a pale shadow of the proud force that had marched upon Khemri four and a half years ago. There were no lizardmen from the deep jungle and their massive beasts of war, nor were there squadrons of swift chariots drawn by hissing, saw-toothed reptiles. Every horse in Rasetra had been pressed into service, and every old veteran and callow youth had been armed and cased in heavy scales and fed into the crucible of war. This was the seed corn of his people. If this last campaign failed it would mean the end of his city. No one would be left to work the mills, or the smithies, or keep the market square going. Within a generation the jungle would claim Rasetra once more.

Rakh-amn-hotep reckoned that the same could be said of Lybaras. The warriors of the scholar-city had been arriving for the last month, and there was no mistaking the old men and clumsy young scribes filling the ranks of their spear companies. He imagined the huge libraries and schools of engineering and philosophy echoing and empty. The great war machines and wondrous sky-boats of Lybaras were no more, and would perhaps never be seen again.

A gentle wind was blowing off the mountains to the west and Neru was high and bright in the sky as the Rasetran king stood atop a low ridge and watched for the army's last expected arrivals. His Ushabti stood close by, wrapped in desert robes and hoods to conceal their divine gifts. A pair of scribes crouched at the base of a large boulder, comparing supply lists and making notations on wax tablets with dull copper styluses. Ekhreb stood to one side of the scribes, studying their notations carefully, and then went to the king's side. He nodded his head to Rakh-amn-hotep and the tall, slender figure standing at the king's right.

'All is in readiness,' the champion said quietly. 'The companies have drawn their supplies for the march, and will be ready to move at first light.' Rakh-amn-hotep nodded gravely.

'The picket is secure?' he asked. Ekhreb nodded.

'The Numasi haven't been patrolling as aggressively for the last few months. When they send out patrols at all, they rarely stray more than a few leagues from camp.' He sighed. 'Hopefully that doesn't mean that Mahrak has finally capitulated.'

There had been no word from the City of Hope for a very long time. Small scouting patrols had managed to steal close to Mahrak over the years and bring back news of the siege, but Rakh-amn-hotep had called off the missions just before he began sending his troops northwards. He didn't want to risk having one of his scouts taken prisoner and revealing the army's position.

After a moment the stout king shook his head.

'If Mahrak had fallen, Nagash's host would be bearing down on Lybaras right now,' he said. Secretly however, the king's instincts told him that the city was close to collapse. That they had endured as long as they had was a grim sort of miracle. He thought of Nebunefer, and wondered if the old priest still lived.

A stir went through the Ushabti. One of them pointed southwards, and the king peered into the gloom.

'Here they come,' Rakh-amn-hotep said portentously.

The plume of dust raised by the column was a faint smudge in the moonlit sky. Rakh-amn-hotep first spied a small squadron of chariots, no doubt the king's Ushabti, and then came a single, darkly painted wagon, drawn by a team of six horses. A final company of spearmen marched doggedly across the rough terrain behind the Lybaran court wagon.

As the king watched, a pair of Rasetran scouts broke cover from a shadowy defile further south and rode out to meet the column. There was a brief exchange, and one scout led the wagon and its bodyguards towards the ridge where Rakh-amn-hotep waited. The remaining scout wheeled his horse around and guided the spear company towards a nearby gully, where the troops could eat a decent meal and catch a few hours of sleep before the march began the next day.

Rakh-amn-hotep gestured to his companions and began walking down the ridge towards the oncoming wagon. The Lybaran Ushabti arrived first, dismounting from their chariots and bowing their heads respectfully to the Rasetran king as he approached.

The wagon, the last, battered remnant of Hekhmenukep's splendid mobile court, rattled to a halt a few moments later. Slaves raced around to the back of the conveyance, pulling its wooden doors open and placing a set of steps on the ground just as the Lybaran king emerged.

Hekhmenukep had healed well since the battle at the fountains. Deep wrinkles crowded the corners of the priest king's eyes, and he moved with greater care than he might have done years before, but otherwise he seemed in good health. He climbed down onto solid ground and approached Rakh-amn-hotep, trailed by an earnest-looking young man in royal robes.

'Well met, old friend,' Hekhmenukep said sombrely. He turned and gestured towards his companion. 'Allow me to present my son and heir, Prince Khepra.' Khepra stepped forwards and bowed to the Rasetran king.

'It is a great honour,' he said, his voice grave and his expression full of youthful seriousness. Rakh-amn-hotep nodded courteously to the young man.

'In return, let me introduce my own son,' he said, indicating the slender, robed young man standing nearby. 'This is Prince Shepret.'

At the sound of his name the robed figure stepped forwards and bowed. He drew back his desert facecloth, revealing sharp, aquiline features and startling green eyes.

'The honour is ours,' Shepret said. Though physically almost exactly the opposite of the stout, craggy-featured Rasetran king, Shepret's steely tone and brusque manner was just like his father's. Hekhmenukep smiled at Rakh-amn-hotep.

'It appears we think alike, you and I,' he said

'Indeed,' the Rasetran king replied. 'About time for the younger generation to make their mark in the world.' But Hekhmenukep could not mistake the look that went with Rakh-amn-hotep's words.

Both men understood that this was the last chance to save their homes. If they failed to break Nagash at Mahrak, the cities of the east were doomed.

Better that their sons fight and die on the battlefield than bend their knees to the Usurper.

'I trust you've taken good care of my troops these last few months,' Hekhmenukep said, changing the subject.

The Rasetran king nodded. 'All is in readiness,' he said. 'Now that you've arrived we will march at first light tomorrow. There's no sense waiting any more than we must and risk a chance discovery by Nagash's scouts.'

Hekhmenukep nodded. 'And the Usurper suspects nothing?' he asked.

'As far as we can tell, he has no idea we're here,' Rakh-amn-hotep replied. 'His attention is focused entirely on Mahrak, and his Numasi allies are doing a poor job of securing his flank. We'll hit the Numasi encampment tomorrow like a thunderbolt, and drive through and into Nagash's positions before they know what is happening.'

'What of Zandri's army?' Hekhmenukep asked. 'Is there any sign of them?' Rakh-amn-hotep shook his head.

'We assume they are further north, guarding the Usurper's northern flank, too far away to make much difference once the attack begins. By the time they are able to join the battle the outcome will have already been decided.'

Hekhmenukep considered the plan and nodded. Both kings knew that their forces were badly outnumbered. Surprise was essential if they were to have a hope of defeating Nagash's horde.

'Let us pray that we can avoid notice for just a few hours more,' he said. 'The future of all Nehekhara depends upon it.'

Thirty yards away, two men lay behind another rocky ridge line, listening intently. The voices of the two kings carried easily through the cold night air. Eventually, the party climbed aboard the Lybaran court wagon and the procession made its way up into a hidden valley, where the bulk of the allied army waited.

The two Numasi scouts waited for more than half an hour, long after the last echoes of the wagon's passage had faded away. Slowly and carefully, they eased from their camouflaged holes and slipped like shadows down to the base of the ridge, where their horses waited. Without a word, the two men climbed into their saddles and parted ways, racing across the desert to carry the news to their master.

THIRTY

THE END OF ALL THINGS

Mahrak, the City of Hope,
in the 63rd year of Djaf the Terrible
(-1740 Imperial reckoning)

The Lahmian army reached Mahrak by mid-morning of the next day, arriving with a fanfare of trumpets and the liquid flutter of hundreds of yellow silk banners. Squadrons of heavy cavalry came first, riding around the northern perimeter of the besieged city in a sinuous column of brightly coloured pennons. Silver pendants worked into the horses' harnesses glittered icily in the bright sunlight, contrasting with the strange, coal-black scale shirts and greaves that the cavalrymen wore. Behind the heavy horsemen rode smaller squadrons of horse archers riding sleek, lean-limbed mounts. Short, powerful horse bows rested across their wooden saddles, similar to the fearsome weapons of the vanquished Bhagarites.

Behind the horse archers, long columns of spearmen marched under various silk banners that announced the identities of their noble patrons. The footmen wore dark metal armour similar to the cavalry, and their swords and spear-tips were fashioned from the same ore.

At first glance, the final Lahmian infantry companies appeared to be spearmen as well, except that they bore no shields and were smaller in number than the standard foot companies. Each warrior marched with a long pole held against his shoulder, but upon closer observation it became apparent that these weapons were not spears. In fact, they hardly looked like weapons at all. One-third of the object was indeed a pole of hard wood, nearly as thick as a man's forearm and capped at the end by a bulb of dark metal. The rest of the object's length was made of unpolished bronze and held in place with more dark metal bands. Artisans had carved the bronze to resemble the scaly hide of a fearsome lizard, and the object's bronze tip resembled the leering, fanged mouth of a crocodile. The carved jaws were parted, opening to reveal dark hollows within.

The Zandrian outriders who met the Lahmians studied the strange warriors with a mixture of curiosity and dread. It was well-known that Lahmia was a distant and exotic place, and its people traded with mysterious barbarians in the Silk Lands in the far east. What they saw only confirmed their expectations.

The army came to a halt within only a few hundred yards of the Zandri positions and quickly began to stake out a perimeter as though preparing to make camp. Into their midst came a procession of brightly coloured wagons that no doubt contained the Lahmian king and his retainers. The newcomers appeared to take little notice of the gaunt, staring Zandrians, or the bone-covered plain stretching westwards from Mahrak's walls and the roiling clouds of darkness hanging in the sky beyond.

The same could not be said of the people inside the besieged city. When the first yellow banners were seen to the north, word spread like a desert storm through Mahrak's filthy, corpse-choked streets. By the time the Lahmian army had drawn up before the Zandri encampment half a dozen tall Ushabti had climbed atop the city's northern wall, bearing a frail, robed figure who weighed little more than a child. Slowly and carefully, they set Nebunefer onto his feet and helped him lay his wrinkled hands upon the battlements for support. Then the withdrew to a respectful distance.

Nebunefer watched the wagons of the Lahmian king roll into view, followed by a long line of heavily laden supply wagons. The old priest's mind was still sharp, almost preternaturally so, these days. Starvation had a tendency to focus one's thoughts, he had come to learn, at least for a short time.

From the evidence, it was clear that Lamashizzar had no intention of lifting the siege. For ten long years the Lahmians had watched the war against Nagash unfold, refusing to commit to one side or the other. Nebunefer believed that they were waiting to see which side gained the upper hand before committing themselves. Now, apparently, they had made their decision.

An Ushabti approached and bowed to the priest, offering a small clay cup brimming with steaming liquid. Nebunefer took the cup in both hands, grateful for its warmth despite the bright, mid-morning sun. He took a small sip of the tea, Lahmian tea, he noted sadly, imported at great cost from the Silk Lands and purchased for the temple storehouses years before. The tea had a delicate, floral taste when combined with water from the Sundered Stone. It was all that the priesthood had left. They steeped the tiny leaves until nothing was left, and then ate those as well.

No one knew how many of Mahrak's citizens were left. Hundreds had died in riots as the food supplies dwindled, and many hundreds more succumbed after everyone became too weak to fight. Entire families had retreated into their homes, sending out the youngest and strongest in search of food, or when hope ran out, to loot an apothecary's shop for a fast-acting poison. There wasn't a single apothecary shop left intact anywhere in the city. It was only by the selfless efforts of the priests of Geheb and Asaph that a plague had not broken out years before.

Rumours were rife of cannibalism in the poorer districts of the city, as desperate, starving families fell upon the wasted corpses piled in the streets. The Hieratic Council declared such an offence punishable by death, but little effort was made to hunt for the perpetrators. No one really wanted to know if there was any truth to the tales.

Nebunefer sipped his tea slowly, wincing at the cramps that gripped his belly from time to time as he watched the Lahmians organising a royal procession to greet the Usurper. As he watched, his mind drifted back to the last time he'd spoken with the Rasetran king. He wondered what had become of Rakh-amn-hotep, and where he was now. Much could happen to a man in four years. Perhaps the king still intended to keep his old promise. If so, Nebunefer feared that the Rasetrans would not arrive in time.

'I thought that I might find you here,' said a sepulchral voice close to Nebunefer's ear.

The old priest blinked for a few long moments, unable to puzzle out where the sound had come from. He turned his head in a daze and saw the pale, hollowed-out face of Atep-neru, the Hierophant of Djaf. The long siege had turned the priest even more cadaverous than he had been to start with, but the privations of hunger didn't seem to plague him as much as Nebunefer or the other priests.

'Atep-neru, it's good to see you,' Nebunefer said. His voice was a thready whisper, despite the Lahmian tea. 'It's been some time since you left the precincts of your temple. I had begun to fear the worst.' He gestured towards the north. 'You've come to see the arrival of the Lahmians, I expect.' The Hierophant of Djaf frowned worriedly at the old priest.

'Nothing of the kind,' he said. 'I've come to summon you to the Palace of the Gods. There are important decisions to be made.' Nebunefer sipped his tea and winced as another cramp seized his guts.

'I have nothing useful to add,' he said, shaking his head wearily. 'Nekh-amn-aten speaks for our temple, as always. He can decide for himself.'

'Nekh-amn-aten is dead,' Atep-neru said flatly. 'He took poison sometime during the night. By right of seniority, you are now the Hierophant of Ptra.'

Nebunefer could not bring himself to reply at first. He looked down at the cup in his hands and waited until the terrible pain in his heart subsided.

'I pray that Usirian will judge him kindly,' he said at last. Then the old priest took a deep breath and straightened. 'What decisions must be made?' Atep-neru folded his thin arms.

'Nekh-amn-aten insisted upon defiance against Nagash,' he said. 'Now that he is gone, Khansu is advocating a rash and destructive response.'

The old priest nodded in understanding. The Hierophant of Khsar had grown increasingly intemperate and erratic as the siege wore on.

'What does he suggest?' he asked.

'An attack, of course,' Atep-neru said. 'With not just the Ushabti, but every person left in the city. A last gesture of defiance, while we still have the strength to fight.'

Nebunefer shook his head, and said, 'That would be no fight. Just glorified mass suicide.'

'My thoughts exactly,' Atep-neru said. 'Khansu is a fool, but he's won a number of council members over to his side. I need your support to suggest a more rational course of action.'

'Such as?' the old priest asked.

'Why, surrender of course,' Atep-neru replied. 'Something we should have done long ago and spared our people much suffering.' The hierophant spread his hands. 'Nagash must see that we are at an impasse. Every day the Usurper lingers here, he and his allies see the fortunes of their home cities dwindle. I'm certain he would be willing to negotiate an end to the siege.'

'Assuming that were true, what of our allies? We would be betraying them.' Nebunefer replied with a sigh. Atep-neru's frown deepened.

'Our allies have abandoned us,' he snapped. 'It's been four years, Nebunefer. They are not coming. No one is going to save us but ourselves.'

Nebunefer stared up at Atep-neru and saw the absolute conviction in the hierophant's eyes. The old priest sighed, feeling more weary than he'd ever felt in his long life. He turned, looking out at the Lahmian camp once more, and shook his head sadly.

'Go on,' Nebunefer said. 'Convene the council at the Palace of the Gods. I...' He stared down at the depths of his cup. 'I'll just finish my tea.' The hierophant nodded curtly.

'I'll see you at the palace, then,' he said. 'Don't keep us waiting long. With Lamashizzar here, our position becomes more perilous by the moment.' Atep-neru turned on his heel and hastened towards the battlement stair.

Nebunefer watched the hierophant go, and then turned back to the Lahmian army. He watched their silk banners ripple in the desert wind, and sipped the last of his tea. The sense of loss he felt cut clean through him, like a flashing blade in the heat of battle.

This would be Mahrak's last day. The city's brave resistance was at an end, whether it be thrown away in a single, doomed charge or traded like cheap cloth in the marketplace. Those were the only options that remained.

The old priest drank the last, bitter dregs and studied the empty cup for a long moment. Then he stretched forth his hand and let it fly, casting it in a plunging arc over the city wall.

There was, Nebunefer realised, a third option.

The Lahmians did not bother sending a messenger to the tent of the Undying King and waiting to be invited to an audience. Within an hour of their arrival a procession was organised and set off towards the centre of Nagash's camp. They announced their coming with the blare of trumpets and the clash of cymbal and bell, filling the air with a riot of celebratory noise. The warriors of Zandri stood aside as the procession marched through their encampment, marvelling at the dark-armoured horsemen and the black lacquered palanquin, leading a procession of brightly clad retainers carrying dozens of bundles and wooden chests.

News of the army's arrival raced through the camp, drawing Nagash's remaining immortals from their posts to attend upon their master. The king's Tomb Guard, hastily mustered to full strength as the procession approached, stepped aside and allowed the pale-skinned nobles to file hurriedly into their master's cavernous tent.

Arkhan the Black slipped in among them and sidled towards the shadows in the far corner of the dimly lit chamber. He searched the growing crowd for any sign of Amn-nasir or the twin Kings of Numas, but Nagash's mortal vassals were nowhere to be seen.

The Undying King was already present, sitting upon Khemri's throne at the far end of the chamber and attended by his blind servant Ghazid. Neferem was absent. Even her small throne had been hastily removed.

Speculation was rampant. Arkhan listened to the sibilant whispers of his fellow immortals. Many reasoned that Lamashizzar had reached his majority and come to swear his allegiance to Nagash. Others speculated that the young king would challenge their master for the return of Neferem. Still others believed that Lamashizzar hoped to intercede on behalf of the priests of Mahrak. Arkhan folded his arms and settled down to watch the audience unfold.

The blaring horns and ringing cymbals drew near. A hush fell over Nagash's court. At a quiet order from the Undying King, Ghazid limped down the aisle between the waiting immortals and made his way outside the tent.

The music outside stopped. Then, after a few moments, it began again, softer and more melodious. The tent flaps were drawn aside, and a score of colourful musicians entered, filling the dark chamber with the crystal notes of silver flutes, cymbals and bells. The Lahmians took no notice of the ghastly assemblage filling the shadowy expanse of the chamber. They spread quickly to either side of the opening and continued to play as the first courtiers began the long procession towards Nagash's throne.

Each silk-clad noble approached the Undying King with a handsome gift: bolts of the finest silk, chests of delicate jade or gilt necklaces decorated with gleaming gems. The courtiers bowed before the throne and stepped alternately left or right, forming ranks that ran the length of the aisle all the way back to the tent's entrance.

After several long minutes, when the last courtier had bowed and strode smoothly to his appointed place, there was another bright flare of trumpets and a rising crescendo from the musicians at the entrance. Then, in the silence that followed, Lamashizzar, the young Priest King of Lahmia, entered the crowded tent.

Word had reached the besieging army just last year that Lamasheptra, former King of the City of the Dawn, had finally succumbed to the strain of a long life of indolence and excess. Very late in life he had sired a son and daughter by one of his wives, and his heir, Lamashizzar, had only just reached adulthood. The young king walked straight-backed and proud towards Nagash's throne, clad in an ornate version of the dark scales worn by the rest of his army. The Lahmian king wore no helm, allowing his long, curly black hair to spill across his squared shoulders and frame his lean, handsome face. His large, brown eyes were sharp and bright, like a hawk's, and the young king favoured Nagash's court with a warm, dazzling smile. A curious wood and metal club was cradled in his left arm, like a sceptre. Like the objects carried by his men, the king's club was worked in the shape of a grinning crocodile with a gaping, polished maw.

The Lahmian king approached Nagash without the slightest sign of fear, and bowed respectfully at the foot of the throne. The Undying King regarded Lamashizzar with a cold, baleful stare.

Nagash's lip curled into a sneer. His ghostly retinue keened fearfully.

'You forget your place, boy,' Nagash said. 'Kneel in the presence of your betters.'

The hateful tone of the necromancer's voice cut through the air like a knife. Then a stir went through the immortals as the Lahmian king threw back his head and laughed.

'The years have treated you unkindly, cousin,' Lamashizzar said. 'Do your eyes fail you after so many centuries? I am no boy, but the king of a great city, the same as you, and so I greet you warmly, and offer these gifts to show you my esteem.'

Shocked hisses rose from the court. Many looked at Lamashizzar with frank astonishment, thinking the young man deranged. Arkhan sidled closer, now even more interested in the exchange. Nagash straightened. His hands closed on the arms of his throne.

'What is the meaning of this?' he asked coldly.

Lamashizzar looked surprised, and said, 'Meaning? Why, merely to reaffirm the close ties between our two cities. I have watched your campaigns with great interest, cousin. It shamed me to see you stymied so long here at Mahrak, so my first act as Lahmia's king was to raise an army and march to your aid.'

Arkhan saw Nagash's face drain of colour. The necromancer leaned forwards slightly.

'You are here to aid me?' he asked.

'Oh, yes,' Lamashizzar said. As he spoke, his demeanour changed slightly. The mirth drained from his features, and his voice took on a hard edge. 'For the love we have for Khemri, and for my aunt, your queen, the warriors of Lahmia are prepared to deliver Mahrak into your hands. What the gods have denied you for four long years we will give you in the space of an afternoon.'

A shocked silence fell upon the court. Arkhan watched Nagash intently, expecting violence. Instead, the ghost of a smile touched the necromancer's lips.

'What is your price?' the Undying King asked.

Lamashizzar bowed once more.

'I wouldn't dream of taking advantage of you in such a dire circumstance,' the young king said. 'I merely want Khemri and Lahmia to enjoy the close relationship our cities have had since the time of mighty Settra.'

Nagash's expression hardened once more. 'Enough dissembling,' he growled. 'What is it you want?'

The young king spread his hands.

'What else is there worth sharing?' he asked, turning to survey the gathered immortals with a smile, but Arkhan saw the cold, calculating gleam in Lamashizzar's eye.

'We want power,' the Lahmian said, turning back to Nagash. 'Share with us the secret of eternal life, and Mahrak is yours.' The baldness of the demand shocked even Nagash.

'You forget yourself,' declared the Undying King.

Lamashizzar slowly shook his head.

'Oh, no,' he countered. 'I assure you, cousin. I have forgotten nothing. It is you who have lost your way and brought your kingdom to the brink of destruction.'

The young king pointed eastwards, towards Mahrak, before continuing, 'You have defeated one army after another, but this city of priests continues to defy you,' he said. 'The plain of bones outside testifies to their power. Eventually they will all starve, perhaps in another six months, perhaps in another two years, but even then the city will not fall. You won't be able to cast down its gates and loot its great temples, and your enemies will take heart from this and continue to resist you while your own cities fall to dust.'

'And you imagine that you can triumph where I cannot? You are a fool!' Nagash spat.

Lamashizzar smiled once more, but his eyes were intent.

'Then our bones will litter the field outside Mahrak, and you will have lost nothing,' he said.

The assembled immortals watched, rapt, as the two kings vied with one another. The Undying King was furious, but Lamashizzar was undaunted. The young king had considered his position carefully, and was confident he held the upper hand. Arkhan studied Nagash's expression closely, and was surprised to find a hint of tension that he'd never seen before. It was possible that Lamashizzar was right.

As Nagash considered the young king's offer, the tent flap was pulled aside and an immortal rushed into the chamber. Heedless of the tension in the room, the captain bowed to the king and said loudly, 'The Hieratic Council has sent a representative to treat with you under a flag of truce!'

Lamashizzar listened to the news and his eyes widened with surprise. His triumphant smile faltered. Behind him, Nagash's grip on the throne relaxed. His eyes glittered like a viper's.

'Your offer of assistance is noted,' the Undying King said to Lamashizzar, 'but will not be required.'

The Lahmian king turned back to Nagash and bowed.

'Then I shall take my leave of you,' Lamashizzar answered smoothly. 'Perhaps later we may speak again.'

Nagash smiled. The spirits surrounding him whirled about in fear.

'Oh, most assuredly,' he said. 'We shall speak again very soon.'

Lamashizzar spun on his heel and beat a dignified retreat with his retainers close behind him. Their rich gifts lay where they left them, forming crooked lines all the way back to the tent's entrance. Nagash watched the Lahmians go, savouring their dismay.

When the last courtier had fled, the necromancer beckoned with a clawed hand.

'Bring me this emissary,' he commanded.

Minutes later, the tent flap swept aside again, and a pair of immortals escorted a wrinkled old man into the chamber. They held the emissary by his arms as they led him down the aisle towards the throne so that his sandalled feet scarcely touched the ground. To Arkhan, the frail, withered mortal looked like nothing more than a dust-covered beggar, but Nagash took one look at the emissary and rose swiftly to his feet.

The immortals reached the throne and forced the emissary to his knees before the Undying King. Nagash looked down on the old man, his face lit with triumph.

'This is an unexpected gift,' he said. 'I thought to find you cowering in some temple deep within the city, or hiding behind those fools who make up your so-called council. Did they send you to me as some kind of peace offering, Nebunefer? A gift to persuade me to stay my wrath?'

Nebunefer put a hand on his bent knee and slowly, painfully, levered himself to his feet. Once more, the immortals reached for him, but this time the old priest met them with a stern glare. Waves of heat radiated from his skin, which glowed like metal drawn from the forge. The two undead champions recoiled, hissing warily.

The old priest turned his attention back to Nagash.

'I have come to negotiate on behalf of the people of Mahrak,' he said in a voice that was little more than a whisper.

Nagash's eyes narrowed thoughtfully. 'The citizens have defied the council and wish to surrender?' he asked.

Nebunefer sneered at the Undying King.

'You pompous ass,' he rasped. 'I'm here to negotiate the terms of your surrender.'

Heads turned. The immortals gaped at the old priest's bravado. Then, one by one, they began to laugh, until the darkened chamber shook with the racket. Nagash silenced them with an unspoken command.

'Your precious city teeters on the brink of destruction, and you come here to mock me?' the necromancer hissed.

'You think this is a jest?' the old priest snapped. 'Think again. Your siege has been an utter failure. In four years you haven't got within ten yards of the city walls. There are hundreds of thousands of bones strewn between here and Mahrak's gates. Truth be told, we've lost count of the number of assaults we've defeated.' Nebunefer folded his arms. 'The city will not fall to the likes of you, Nagash. The gods will not allow it.'

'The gods,' Nagash sneered. 'Those disembodied charlatans. Their time is done. The empire to come, my empire, will be eternal.'

Nebunefer let out a wheezing laugh, and said, 'Settra thought the same thing, and now the beetles are burrowing into his guts. You won't be any different, Nagash. You're just another petty tyrant who will rise and fall like all the rest, and when you die the gods will await you in the place of judgement. No doubt they're looking forward to seeing you.'

'No god may stand in judgement over me!' Nagash roared. 'I have burned their temples and slain their priests! Soon their precious city will be mine, and then their names will be forgotten for all time!'

Nebunefer shook his head.

'You are a fool,' he said, 'an arrogant, deluded fool who thinks himself the equal of the gods. Yet you aren't clever enough to understand one simple fact: so long as the covenant exists, the gods cannot be overthrown. They are bound to us, just as we are bound to them, and nothing you can do will ever change that. Can't you see? Your pathetic crusade against the gods was doomed from the beginning!'

The old priest was goading the necromancer. Arkhan saw that at once, but could not understand the point to it. Nagash, however, was blind to this. How often had he dreamt of getting his hands on Nebunefer after the treachery that night in the royal palace? Now he had the old priest in his clutches, and Nebunefer had stoked the king's hatred to the boiling point.

Nagash's hands clenched. He took a step towards the priest, and then froze. His eyes widened, and his expression turned to one of dawning triumph.

'Of course,' he whispered. 'The answer was right in front of me all along.'

The Undying King let out a savage cry of joy and lunged forwards, seizing the old priest by the throat.

Nebunefer's eyes widened. He grabbed Nagash's wrists, trying to pry himself from the necromancer's grip, but he was no match for the king's unnatural strength. Nagash lifted the priest off the ground and shook him like a rag doll.

'I could not see it!' Nagash said, laughing like a devil. 'I had the power of the gods in my clutches and never realised it! Mahrak is doomed, Nebunefer, and you will die knowing that you made its destruction possible!'

Nebunefer continued to struggle, tearing at Nagash's wrists with his failing strength. Pure hatred glittered in the old priest's eyes. Then, there was a brittle *crack*, like the snapping of a rotted branch, and Nebunefer's head rolled back at an unnatural angle.

Nagash tossed the dead priest's body aside.

'Bring me the queen!' he roared. 'The fall of the old gods is at hand!'

At that moment the tent flap was pulled aside once again. A messenger staggered inside, stained with dust and half-dead with fatigue.

'The armies of Rasetra and Lybaras are coming!' he gasped. 'They will be here within the hour!'

Surprised hisses rose from the immortals. Nagash, the Undying King, merely smiled.

'They will be too late,' he said.

Little more than a league to the south-east, the allied armies swept across the rolling plains like a storm wind, bearing down on the Numasi encampment. Eight thousand cavalrymen made up the host's vanguard, led by Ekhreb, with the rest of the army advancing close behind. Huge plumes of dust were kicked skywards by their advance, but stealth had been cast aside in favour of pure speed. If the gods were with them, the Numasi would not have time to form a proper defence.

Ekhreb felt the wind upon his face as the horses raced across the plain, and felt a surge of savage joy. The weight of all the bitter defeats seemed to fall from his shoulders at long last as they closed for one final battle with the enemy. Here, at last, the advantage was theirs. The battle would belong to them.

Riding in the midst of the allied horsemen, Ekhreb guided his powerful horse up a high, sandy dune and plunged down the other side. Beyond sat another broad plain, perhaps half a mile across, ending in another tall set of dunes. Dark clouds swirled past the distant slopes, and the tops of Mahrak's temples dotted the northern horizon.

In between, arrayed across the plain, were squadrons of Numasi horsemen: twelve thousand cavalry, drawn up and arrayed for battle around the standards of their twin kings.

At the sight of the allied vanguard the Numasi drew their swords. Sunlight glinted on a thicket of polished bronze. In an instant, Ekhreb's joy turned to ash. Somehow they had been discovered. Rakh-amn-hotep's gamble had failed.

In the centre of the enemy battle-line, the twin kings raised their hands. War-horns bellowed out a single note, and the Numasi began their advance.

Horns wailed across the vast camp of the besiegers, calling the undead host to war. Immortals scattered from the tent of the Undying King, almost too fast for the eye to follow. They leapt onto their skeletal horses and sped off in a dozen directions, already composing the intricate series of orders that would reposition tens of thousands of troops to deal with the sudden arrival of the enemy.

There had been no word from the Numasi kings to the south, but fragmentary reports indicated that the cavalry had already assembled and advanced to meet the foe. Nagash's captains chose a line of low ridges a few hundred yards behind the Numasi encampment to place their initial battle-line; companies of spearmen were hastily shifted south-east and formed up along the forward slope of the ridge line, while messengers were sent racing northwards to summon Zandri's archers for immediate action. Within minutes, the bulk of Nagash's army, fully a hundred thousand undead infantry and horsemen, was on the move, angling south-east to present a wall of bone and metal before the advancing eastern forces. Farther behind the battleline, siege engineers plied the lash against the backs of their slaves as they struggled to orient their massive catapults towards the attacking enemy.

Amid the chaos, eight huge companies of skeletal warriors, the army's entire reserve force of forty thousand troops, stirred beneath Nagash's furious will and began to march towards the shadow line. The Undying King stalked behind them, surrounded by his Tomb Guard and a large retinue of slaves. A score of the terrified servants carried the stone sarcophagus of Nagash's queen upon their bare shoulders.

Arkhan the Black trailed behind the grim procession, fiercely wishing for his armour and sword. He was tempted to race back to his threadbare tent and garb himself for battle despite Nagash's spiteful orders; better to be tortured again than to have his head cut off by a chance encounter with an enemy horseman.

Not that he had any idea what he might do if he were armed and armoured. Who would he fight? Part of him entertained the thought that he could still win back the Undying King's favour if he acquitted himself well in battle, but to what end? A return to slavery, begging at his master's hem for droplets of his terrible elixir?

Power crackled invisibly through the air. Horns wailed, and the earth shook beneath the tread of tens of thousands of marching feet. To Arkhan, it felt as though the world's foundations were shifting beneath him. Moving as though in a dream, the vizier was pulled along in his master's wake.

The army's reserve companies clattered to a halt mere inches from the shadow line, the warriors' rotting faces lit in shifting tides of light and darkness wrought by the warring sorceries. To the west, distant but growing ever nearer, came the heavy tread of giants.

Nagash appeared in the midst of the skeletal companies, his robes flapping in the charnel wind rising behind the undead army. In his left hand he held the mighty Staff of the Ages, wreathed with the tormented spirits of the king's ghostly retinue.

The necromancer stepped to the edge of the shadow line and felt the power of the city's wards seething across his skin. As the queen's sarcophagus was set upon the ground behind him, he turned and stretched forth his right hand. The spirits surrounding the staff flowed across the stone coffin and pulled aside the lid, and then drew out Neferem's withered body. She hung in their grasp like a broken doll, trailing scraps of filthy linen and tattered skin. Ghazid, standing close by the coffin, turned his blind face to the queen's drifting form and wailed in misery.

Nagash drew his queen to him. The shadow line roiled in response to Neferem's presence.

'You are the key,' he said, looking down upon the queen's tormented face. 'You are the covenant made flesh. Go, and open the gates of the city.'

The necromancer set Neferem on her feet. She swayed unsteadily, her shrivelled face turning this way and that, like a lost child. A tortured moan escaped her lips. Then, with a rough shove, Nagash drove her across the shadow line.

At once, a fierce wind sprang up around the queen, and the air crackled loudly with building tension. His face set in a hateful mask, Nagash followed a few steps behind Neferem. Moments later, his warriors followed suit, penetrating the wards in their thousands.

Arkhan bared his ruined teeth at the sudden surge of energies that rose from the sands around Nagash and his warriors. Even the slaves felt it, and they cried out and covered their faces, expecting to feel the merciless wrath of the gods at any moment. Ghazid let out another despairing wail and lurched forwards, his hands raised to the heavens.

The wind's fury rose with each step that Neferem took, scattering drifts of bleached bones and drawing plumes of sand and dirt into the air. Waves of heat began to rise from the ground, even as the building clouds covered the face of the sun.

Undaunted, Nagash drove Neferem and his troops forwards. He could sense the strain building on the city's wards as their carefully worded incantations were forced to deal with a paradox. The wards were made to protect the faithful from those who threatened the City of the Gods. By virtue of Nagash's bond, the undead queen was both.

Dark clouds seethed angrily overhead, and the stink of brimstone permeated the air. Flashes of orange light blazed within the clouds, and the first streaks of fire began to fall on the advancing companies. Fierce thunderclaps smote the sky with each falling stone, as though the wards were starting to crack beneath the strain.

Blazing stones carved fiery paths through the advancing companies. One burning projectile fell like an arrow directly at Neferem and Nagash, but even as it plummeted earthwards the rock began to break apart, until it exploded harmlessly a dozen yards from its intended target. A wave of fierce heat washed over the queen, curling her dried robes and parchment-like skin. Nagash raised his staff skywards and roared in triumph.

With every step, the roaring wind and blazing heat grew stronger. The churning motion of the clouds increased, and the hail of fire dwindled. The insides of the clouds were rent by successive concussions that shook the air over the advancing troops. Arcs of violet lightning lashed at the plain like a taskmaster's scourge.

They were nearly halfway to the city walls when the sphinxes appeared. They emerged like wraiths from the whirling dust, roaring and snapping their jaws fearfully at the terrible image of the queen. The scouring dust had shredded her priceless robes and torn away the queen's golden head-dress, and her skin began to unravel like rotting thread. Still she pressed on, lashed by the storm and by Nagash's furious will. Her cries were lost in the roaring of the desert spirits and the fury of the wind. Tossing their fear-some heads, the sphinxes withdrew before her like whipped dogs.

The heat had grown intense, like standing at the very mouth of a great furnace. Nagash saw his robes begin to smoulder, and staggered to a halt. His troops came to a stop behind him, but Neferem he drove ever forwards, pressing relentlessly against the ancient wards. Behind the necromancer, the shadow line was contracting, its border fraying beneath the onslaught. Unholy darkness flowed like ink in its wake.

There was a peal of thunder, and for an instant Neferem was wreathed in a halo of savage lightning. Her body burst into flames, but Nagash's will drove her still onwards. Her arms drooped as fire ate through the tendons and leathery muscle, and her lustrous hair burned away in a sudden shower of sparks.

A figure lurched past the Undying King and staggered into the searing heat. Ghazid, faithful to the last, followed in his queen's wake. His skin blackened in moments and his robes caught fire, but the former vizier did not falter.

The sphinxes howled and writhed in torment as the magical wards began to shatter under the strain. The building heat grew so intense that the air itself seemed to glow. Neferem was visible only as a skeletal silhouette, wreathed in orange and violet fire.

From more than half a mile away, Arkhan felt the tension in the air like dull knives raking at his skin. The slaves around him fell dead, blood streaming from their ears and eyes.

Then, without warning, the pressure vanished, bursting like a bubble, and a deafening silence fell across the field of bones. Neferem was gone, her body turned to ash. Ghazid's blackened corpse lay just a few yards away, one outstretched hand still reaching for his beloved queen.

Drifts of dirt and sand fell in rattling curtains across the plain. With a last, dwindling roar, the sphinxes turned to ribbons of smoke and were scattered by the ebbing wind, and darkness fell upon Mahrak, the City of the Gods.

Out on the plain of bones, Nagash raised his hands to the sky and roared in triumph.

'The age of the gods is at an end!' he cried. 'From this day forwards, the people of Nehekhara will worship their Undying King!'

Nagash swept down his ancient staff and his skeletal warriors swept forwards. Among them marched three towering giants, who raised their massive clubs and advanced upon the city gate. Within minutes, the slaughter of Mahrak's citizens would begin.

A blare of trumpets sounded to the south-east, and Arkhan realised that the armies of the east had arrived, just in time to watch Mahrak's fall.

Suddenly the vizier staggered beneath the savage lash of his master's will. From across the charnel plain, Nagash commanded the immortal, *Seek out Amn-nasir and command him to attack the Lahmians at once.*

The vizier struggled to reply, but the necromancer had already turned his thoughts elsewhere. Arkhan found himself on his knees, surrounded by the bodies of dead slaves. Their tormented faces stared up at him, their expressions of fear and pain no doubt mirroring his own.

Arkhan the Black staggered to his feet and set off in search of the King of Zandri.

The final destruction of the Daughter of the Sun reverberated across the City of the Gods and then spread outwards, across the warring armies and on to the far corners of Nehekhara. Every priest and acolyte, every bold Ushabti, felt it like a blade of ice, sinking without warning deep into his heart. When it withdrew they felt the power of the gods flow out of them like their life's blood, a wound that no healing hand could stanch. Helpless, horrified, they knew that the covenant had been broken, and they felt the gods receding from them forever.

It was the beginning of the end. Nehekhara was blessed no more.

Rakh-amn-hotep and Hekhmenukep also felt the breaking of the covenant, and knew what it portended. Their Ushabti cried out in horror, tearing at their beards and beating their breasts in vain as their god-given powers began to fade.

The kings guessed what the terrible change portended, but neither man said a word. Their warriors were still advancing, mere minutes away from clashing with the Usurper's undead horde.

It was the end of all things. All that remained was to fight until the darkness overwhelmed them.

A cheer went up from Nagash's immortals as the bone giants reached the gates of the city to the north-east. The siege was over, and the final victory was at hand.

Across the killing ground in front of the undead battleline, squadrons of swift Numasi horsemen were falling back before the advance of the eastern armies. A solid wall of Lybaran and Rasetran spearmen more than two miles long drove the enemy cavalry back through their own encampment and towards their own lines. When the advancing spearmen were fifty yards from the waiting skeletons, the twin kings signalled their men and the Numasi broke into a full retreat, falling swiftly back through narrow lanes between the undead infantry, and forming up to the army's rear.

As soon as the Numasi were out of the way, companies of undead archers stepped forwards and raised their black bows. Clouds of reed shafts darkened the skies over the killing ground, and the final battle was joined.

To the north, the Zandri encampment was a scene of pandemonium. Men fell to their knees and begged the gods for forgiveness, or shook their fists and shouted curses at the bone giants and skeletons assaulting Mahrak's walls. The ponderous blows of the giants echoed across the plain as they battered down the city gates.

Consumed with grief and rage, many of the Zandri fighting men turned on Arkhan with fists and knives as he tried to fight his way to the king's tent. Snarling with rage, he ignored their feeble blows and hurled the fools out of his path. Once or twice an arrow hissed past, but the vizier paid them no mind.

Another fight seemed to be brewing outside Amn-nasir's tent. Messengers from Nagash's captains were arguing furiously with the Zandri king's attendants and bodyguards, who were half-mad with anger. The vizier noticed a dozen silk-clad Lahmian retainers standing apart from the raging dispute. They eyed Arkhan warily as he shoved through the press and plunged through the tent entrance.

Amn-nasir and Lamashizzar stood in the main chamber, surrounded by a dozen stricken-looking Ushabti. The bodyguards turned on Arkhan at once, drawing their terrible blades, but both kings swiftly intervened.

As the Ushabti withdrew, Amn-nasir bowed his head gratefully to Arkhan. Lamashizzar regarded the immortal inscrutably. Arkhan sensed that he had interrupted another heated debate.

'Have you made your decision?' Amn-nasir asked. Arkhan turned to the King of Lahmia.

'You offered the might of your army in return for the gift of eternal life,' the immortal said. 'The Undying King will never reveal the secrets of his elixir to you, but I can.'

With a splintering crash, the gates of the city crashed inwards. As one, the surviving skeletons outside Mahrak's walls surged forwards, spilling clumsily through the opening as the giants turned their attention to climbing over the sandstone battlements.

Beyond the broken gates lay an open square, where the resolute figures of six hundred holy warriors stood. Mahrak's Ushabti commended their souls to gods that no longer heard their prayers, and rushed forwards to fight and die according to their vows. They struck the skeletal horde like a ravening wind, shattering the undead attackers by the hundreds. When the bone giants swung over the city walls the Ushabti hacked at their massive legs until one by one they collapsed to the ground.

The defenders of the city fought like heroes of legend, but their strength ebbed with every blow and more and more of the enemy spears found their marks. One by one, the great Ushabti fell, crushed by giant hands or bled dry by scores of terrible wounds. Slowly but surely the survivors were driven back from the gates by the relentless press of skeletal bodies. Nagash guided his warriors expertly, using alleys and side streets to isolate and surround the defenders, before burying them beneath a tide of metal and bone.

By the time the last Ushabti fell, all three giants and nearly fifteen thousand skeletons had fallen before their flashing blades, a last, doomed gesture of faith and honour in the face of all-consuming night.

Heedless of fallen heroes or forsaken gods, the thousands of remaining skeletons marched on the city temples. Nagash, surrounded by his Tomb Guard, made his way towards the Palace of the Gods.

Screaming skulls traced glowing arcs of sorcerous fire over the battlefield as the armies of east and west tore at one another with spear, axe and sword. The warriors of Rasetra and Lybaras fought like devils, carving deep into the ranks of the undead, but their companies were sorely outnumbered. The allied kings had committed every company available into the battle-line, and still the enemy troops were lapping inexorably around the companies fighting along the flanks. Slowly but surely, the undead army pressed forwards, closing around the allied troops like the jaws of a crocodile.

Sensing that they had the upper hand, the immortals sent half their number and their cavalry escorts galloping off to the right flank. The Numasi kings watched them go, and realised that the pivotal moment was at hand. Once the cavalry swept around the allied flank, the fate of the army was sealed.

Seheb and Nuneb took up their reins and waved to their captains. Without any fanfare the cavalry squadrons began to move, edging towards the army's right flank. As the immortals and their light horsemen crossed in front of the advancing Numasi cavalry, the twins sent another signal. Blades flashed from their scabbards, and the squadrons increased their speed to a canter.

Pale heads turned at the approach of the Numasi horsemen. The immortals grinned like jackals, raising their weapons in salute.

Seheb and Nuneb grinned back, returning the salute. Then their swords swept down in a vicious arc.

'Charge!' the twins cried, and their kinsmen replied with a blood-curdling roar and the flare of trumpets.

The Numasi cavalry took the immortals and their horsemen in the flank, isolating the undead squadrons and smashing the warriors to the ground. For a few, crucial moments the immortals were caught off-guard by the sudden reversal, and their surprise was reflected by the lack of resistance by their warriors. The skeletons were reaped like wheat by the veteran horsemen, and the pale-skinned captains soon found themselves beset by dozens of flickering blades.

Snarling in fear and rage, the thirty immortals tried to hack their way free of the press and rejoin their comrades, who watched the battle helplessly more than a mile away. Little more than a handful succeeded.

On the opposite side of the battlefield, Ekhreb and the waiting allied cavalry stirred at the sound of the Numasi trumpets.

'That's the signal,' the champion told his lieutenants. 'Let's go.'

Ekhreb was still somewhat in shock over the Numasi kings' surprising offer of parley. He had been on the verge of ordering the allied vanguard to charge the enemy horsemen when the twin rulers suddenly lowered their weapons and rode forwards under a sign of truce. They told the Rasetran champion that they had seen enough horrors in service to Nagash, and had repudiated their oaths to serve him. The whole army was ready to switch sides, if the eastern kings would have them.

The trouble was that there was no time for discussions. The armies were on the move, and even with the support of the Numasi horsemen, the advantage of surprise was fast slipping away. Ekhreb had to decide whether the twin kings could be trusted. One look into their haunted eyes was enough to convince the scarred champion. He knew what they were feeling all too well.

The allied cavalry rode westwards along a shallow gully pointed out to them by the Numasi horsemen. It concealed their movement for more than a mile, emptying the squadrons out on the enemy army's far right flank. The skeletons had already advanced well forwards, sweeping inexorably around the flank of the smaller eastern army. That left their rear ranks exposed to the sudden appearance of the allied cavalry.

The Numasi were moving further east, sowing confusion along the rear of the enemy battleline. Seheb and Nuneb had been as good as their word. With a fierce grin, Ekhreb raised his heavy sword.

'For Rasetra! For Lybaras! For the glory of the gods! Charge!' he commanded.

With a wild roar the allied cavalry thundered forwards, their swords glimmering balefully in the gloom. The undead spearmen, focused on the enemy infantry in front of them with mindless zeal, did not realise their peril until it was far too late.

Nagash found himself at the edge of the great plaza that stretched before the Palace of the Gods when he heard the faint clamour of trumpets to the south-west and the exultant roar of thousands of living men. He paused, just as he was about to give the order for his Tomb Guard to storm the palace of the decadent priests, and focused his attention through the eyes of various undead champions in his host. What he saw brought a stream of blasphemous curses to his lips.

The Numasi had betrayed him! Already they had killed half of his immortals or put them to flight, and were bearing down hard upon the rest. The right flank of his vast army had been hit by a surprise charge of enemy cavalry and wavered on the brink of collapse. So far, his army's centre and left flanks were holding, but with his captains under direct attack they could not guide his mindless companies effectively.

Pure, venomous fury welled up within the necromancer. How he had longed to burst open the doors of the Palace of the Gods and watch those fools on the Hieratic Council come crawling on their bellies, pleading with him to spare their worthless lives. Now he was to be cheated of his rightful reward, a mere hundred yards from his goal!

There were, however, more pressing matters at hand than simple entertainment. His reserves were out of position, rampaging through Mahrak's streets and wrecking the city's temples. He would have to assume command of the companies on the battleline and then extricate his warriors from the city immediately. With their added numbers he would have more than enough troops to stop the attack on the right flank and regain the initiative against the enemy. First, however, he needed to restore his battered forces to full strength.

Drawing upon the power of the Black Pyramid, Nagash began the Incantation of Summoning. Across the city, Mahrak's dead citizens began to stir.

Out on the charnel plain, the right flank of Nagash's army rallied briefly under the lash of the necromancer's will, but pressure from Ekhreb's cavalry and the Rasetran spearmen drove the skeletal companies back. The surviving immortals, freed from the strain of fighting and simultaneously directing the huge host, drove the Numasi horsemen off to the west and kept the allied troops from completely turning the right flank. Nagash's troops were effectively cut off from their camp, and slowly but surely they were being driven back against Mahrak's implacable walls.

The immortals stared furiously off to the north, wondering where the Zandri army was. Nearly a dozen messengers had been sent demanding their support, but none of the riders had returned.

In the swirling chaos of battle, the immortals failed to notice that the army's catapults had fallen silent, nor could they see the smoke rising from their tents in the sorcerous gloom.

While the warriors of Zandri were overrunning Nagash's encampment, Lamashizzar's troops formed up and advanced southwards, closing in on the necromancer's forces from the north. The warriors had furled their brilliant yellow banners and smudged their faces with ash, concealing them somewhat under the pall of shadow covering the city. They had reached to within a hundred yards of the enemy's struggling right flank just as Nagash's first mob of reinforcements came stumbling through Mahrak's shattered gate.

Observing his army's progress from the back of a coal-black mare, Lamashizzar ordered his companies of dragon-men forwards.

* * *

Nagash hurled Mahrak's dead headlong at the advancing enemy troops, seeking to bog down their advance under the weight of thousands of shambling bodies. The wasted corpses of men, women and children stumbled through the gate and threw themselves upon the eastern spears, while the Undying King marshalled his skeletal companies inside the city and sent them back out through the gate in good order.

The king came last, leading his Tomb Guard. His immortals took heart at the sight of the Undying King, and redoubled the efforts of the companies on the centre and left. The battle had been raging for more than two hours, and the eastern troops were weakening steadily. Nagash gathered his reserves on the right and prepared for a counter-assault. Controlling such a huge force and maintaining the mantle of shadows overhead was fast draining his magical reserves, leaving him little in the way of power to devote to destructive spells. That would come later, once he'd hurled back the enemy assault and regained the offensive.

Then the king noticed the black-armoured troops advancing slowly from the north, nearly perpendicular to Mahrak's western wall.

The damned Lahmians! Either they had put the men of Zandri to flight, or else Amn-nasir's men had turned traitor like the cowardly Numasi. Regardless, the necromancer knew that they had to be dealt with immediately, or else they would leave his army with no room left to manoeuvre. They would be trapped against the walls of the city and ground to pieces by forces advancing on three sides.

Nagash shifted the army's reserve companies to the north, anchored in the centre by his elite Tomb Guard. With another set of unspoken commands he returned control of the main army to his immortals, and then headed north in the wake of his bodyguards. The Undying King drew on the last of his dwindling reserves and began to chant a fearsome incantation.

At Lamashizzar's command, four companies of dragon-men rushed out in front of the set ranks of the spear companies and formed into tightly packed blocks, four ranks deep. The front rank of each company dropped to one knee, allowing the rank behind to rest their dragon-staves on the shoulders of the men in front.

Five companies of skeletal warriors advanced upon the dragon-men in a thunderous rattle of wood, metal and bone. It was a fearsome sight to behold, but the dragon-men were the elite of the Lahmian army, handpicked for their intelligence and strength of will. Few people had the nerve to handle the deadly and unpredictable dragon powder made by the alchemists of the far east.

The skeletons approached in tight formation, advancing implacably upon the Lahmian lines. As they approached, the dragon-men drew lengths of smouldering cotton rope from bottles at their waists. They blew steadily upon the wicks to keep the burning ends lit as the distance to the enemy dwindled.

Two of the four companies aimed the mouths of their dragon-staves at the centre of the enemy line. The white shields of the troops in the middle made for excellent targets in the faint light.

At fifty yards, Lamashizzar ordered the dragon-men into action. Each warrior touched his burning wick to a tiny hole drilled in the side of his stave. Two thousand dragons spat tongues of fire, and sent balls of lead the size of sling stones crashing through the enemy ranks in a wash of brimstone and an ear-splitting crescendo of man-made thunder.

The sound was appalling. Nagash had never heard the like. It was followed by a terrible, rending clatter as a hail of invisible projectiles tore through the dense formations of his troops. Shields splintered, and limbs and torsos exploded in a shower of fragments. The terrible hail ripped through the companies from front to back, buzzing malevolently through the air like river hornets. A fearsome impact struck the king in the left shoulder, punching like a fist through cloth, muscle and bone. The words of his incantation were swept away in a furious tide of searing pain. Nagash staggered, his right hand rising to his shoulder and coming away slick with viscous blood. A hole the size of his thumb had been punched through his robe and vestments, and the cloth surrounding it was soaking with gore.

For a moment the necromancer's view was obscured by a pall of stinking black smoke. When it cleared, he was stunned to see the extent of the damage wrought by the Lahmian attack. His Tomb Guard had suffered the worst, nearly three-quarters of the heavy company having been blown apart. Nearly a third of his remaining companies had also been destroyed. The survivors were still moving doggedly forwards, but the enemy companies were moving, shifting so that their front two ranks traded places with those behind them, and more of the terrible staves were being brought to bear on his warriors.

Trumpets sounded in the north-east. Nagash could hear a rumble of hooves, and knew that the Lahmians had committed their cavalry. The black-armoured horsemen charged past their spear companies on the Lahmian right flank and slashed through the risen corpses of Mahrak, scattering the last of Nagash's reinforcements and sealing his army's doom.

Ahead of the king his skeletons had almost reached the front ranks of the Lahmian fire-throwers, but the enemy had readied their second volley. Furious, Nagash struggled to force the pain aside and summon forth his power, but even as he did so, he knew that he would be too late.

Overhead, the mantle of shadow was weakening, admitting thin shafts of bright, golden sunlight. Shouts of terror and dismay went up from the king's immortals. Nagash, the Undying King of Khemri, roared out a bitter curse as the world before him erupted in blooms of hungry flame.

EPILOGUE

THE CASKET OF SOULS

Khemri, the Living City,
in the 63rd year of Djaf the Terrible
(-1740 Imperial reckoning)

Two months after the Battle of Mahrak, the Army of Seven Kings arrived at the outskirts of Khemri. There were no armies to contest their approach, nor cheering throngs with vessels of sacred water to welcome their liberators. The fields outside the great city were barren, and its gates open and untended. Vultures perched on the battlements, and jackals stole furtively down the sand-choked streets. It was a desolate, haunted place, marked by centuries of terror and steeped in innocent blood. The army's scouts, hardened veterans one and all, refused to enter the city at all except when the sun was high and bright overhead.

It had been a long and arduous pursuit from the charnel fields outside the City of the Gods. At Mahrak, the dragon-men of the Lahmian army had shattered Nagash's reserves and sent a terrible shock through the rest of the Usurper's host. As the allied armies began to tighten their grip around the undead horde, the pall of shadow hanging over the city began to unravel. Shafts of lambent sunlight pierced the gloom, heartening the allied warriors and filling their enemies with dread. The rumour spread among the eastern armies that Nagash had been slain, and a great shout of triumph went up from their ranks as they forced the Usurper's skeletal horrors back against the walls of the ravaged city.

When the sun burst through the failing shadows the surviving immortals in the Usurper's army knew that all was lost. Their only hope of survival was to break through the ever-tightening encirclement and try to get away. The immortals gathered their remaining cavalry, and with a wail of war-horns they threw themselves at the allied warriors stretched across the western edge of the plain. These were the spearmen and cavalry of the allied armies' right flank, who had seen the hardest fighting of the day and were on the verge of exhaustion.

The sudden enemy charge caught the warriors by surprise, and despite a bitter fight the immortals managed to punch through their lines and break out to the west. They fled through the chaos and flames of their encampment and raced for the Gates of the Dusk, hoping to lose themselves in the Valley of Kings before the mantle of darkness came completely apart.

The immortals sacrificed entire companies of infantry to hold their pursuers at bay. Fewer than ten thousand undead infantry and horsemen reached the Valley of Kings, leaving the bones of more than a hundred thousand warriors littering the fields to the east. By the end of the day the terrible army of the Usurper had been all but completely destroyed.

There were no thoughts of giving chase at first, for merely lifting the siege of Mahrak had been daunting enough. Their victory had been greater and more total than they had believed possible. Men were sent south to gather supplies for the long trek eastwards, and in the meantime, the kings turned their attention to the devastated city and its citizens.

They soon discovered that Mahrak was a city only in name. Its homes and marketplaces were empty, and fires burned out of control in many of its temples. Late in the evening after the battle had ended, the city's few survivors emerged from the Palace of the Gods and wept for their salvation. Half of the once-mighty Hieratic Council, plus a few hundred distraught priests and starving citizens were all that remained. A great many of the priests died on that first night, unable to bear the knowledge that their gods were lost to them forever.

Out on the charnel plain, companies of soldiers combed the battlefield in search of survivors. The bodies of the dead immortals were taken into the city and hurled into a roaring bonfire lit in the plaza outside the Palace of the Gods. The body of the Usurper could not be found, nor that of his vizier, Arkhan the Black.

So, the allied armies set off in pursuit of the last remnant of the Usurper's host. They chased the fleeing army down the Valley of Kings, encountering stubborn resistance from enemy rearguard troops and suffering constant ambushes from parties of skeletal horsemen. The bulk of the Usurper's surviving companies fought a bitter holding action at the Gates of the Dawn, but the allied troops forced their way through the ruins after three days of hard fighting. Outside the gates of Quatar the pursuers came upon the Usurper's terrible battle standard, woven from the living skin of King Nemuhareb. Someone had planted it so that it faced towards the city's deserted streets. Why it had been abandoned like that, none could say.

Some prisoners were taken on the trade roads west of Quatar, mostly terrified merchants carrying ingots of bronze from Ka-Sabar to Khemri. From them, the allied kings learned of the treachery of Memnet, the former Hierophant of Ka-Sabar, and of his nightmarish rule over the City of Bronze. They also learned that Raamket, one of the Usurper's chief lieutenants, still held the Living City with a small garrison of immortals and undead warriors. The host continued on, preparing for one final battle outside the walls of Khemri, only to discover a city of ghosts and silent, echoing streets.

Raamket and his garrison were nowhere to be found. The great palace of Settra was empty. There were signs that it had been looted more than once, and after the last attempt someone had tried to set it on fire. The allied scouts suspected that Raamket and his warriors had fled more than a week before, perhaps to Zandri, or to Numas, or even down the Spice Road towards Bel Aliad. None could say for certain. When the garrison left, the city's few remaining inhabitants had fled also, leaving the city to the scavengers.

On the second day after reaching Khemri, allied patrols were ambushed by skeletal warriors inside the city's necropolis. For the rest of the day, allied infantry forced their way into the city of the dead, fighting a bloody cat-and-mouse game with undead horrors lurking among the crypts.

Soon it became apparent that the Usurper's last remaining troops had established a ring of defences around the Black Pyramid. It took two more days of difficult fighting before the last of the undead warriors were destroyed, and the kings turned their attention to the pyramid and the secrets it contained.

Shouts and bestial snarls echoed up from the darkness. A warrior, his face gleaming with sweat beneath his conical helmet, turned away from the featureless entrance of the pyramid and shouted, 'They're bringing out another one!'

The seven kings rose from their chairs beneath the shade of a great pavilion tent erected a dozen yards from the entrance to the pyramid and stepped once more into the blazing sunlight. A thousand warriors filled the great marble-flagged plaza outside Nagash's pyramid. They had been standing watch outside the entrance since dawn, observing the heavily armed hunting parties and teams of engineers that had come and gone from the crypt over the course of the day. They straightened their tired shoulders and readied their weapons once more as the pyramid surrendered another of its monsters.

The immortal shrieked in pain as he was driven out into the sunlight. He was tall and powerfully built, with a bare chest and gaping jaws dripping ribbons of dark blood. The hunting party had bound the undead noble's arms behind his back with loops of heavy rope, and then driven the points of two stout spears into his back, just beneath the shoulder blades. With two men on each spear they drove the monster into the plaza, towards a blood-stained patch of paving stones near the centre. The decapitated bodies of twelve other immortals were laid out side-by-side nearby, their pale skin blackening in the heat of the day.

At the place of execution, the hunters bore down on their spears and forced the howling immortal to his knees. The kings approached, trailed by their bodyguards and champions. Hekhmenukep and Rakh-amn-hotep walked side-by-side, accompanied by Khansu, the Hierophant of Mahrak and de facto master of the ravaged city. The kings of the west, Seheb and Nuneb of Numas and Amn-nasir of Zandri, walked some distance apart from the eastern kings, each man lost in his thoughts. Lamashizzar, Priest King of Lahmia, kept entirely to himself, sipping wine from a golden cup and speaking softly to a number of veiled attendants. When they were close enough to clearly see the immortal's face, they came to a stop.

Rakh-amn-hotep studied the monster's features for several moments, and then shook his head.

'I don't know him,' he said. He turned to Amn-nasir. 'Who is he?'

The King of Zandri frowned. His body was more gaunt and wasted than ever, and his left eye twitched feebly. Rumour had it that he was trying to wean himself off the black lotus, but the struggle was taking a fearful toll.

'Tekhmet, I think,' Amn-nasir croaked. 'He was one of the captains at Mahrak. A minor lord and an ally of Raamket. No one of importance.'

'Traitor!' the immortal hissed, spitting gobbets of blood onto the stones. 'The master will have his revenge upon you! You and the cowards of Numas! All of you will suffer an eternity of pain!'

Rakh-amn-hotep nodded curtly to Ekhreb. The champion stepped forwards, a huge, bloodstained khopesh resting against his shoulder. At the sight of the blade the immortal began to writhe and howl in fear, pushing back against the spears until the points burst through his chest. Ekhreb reached the immortal in four measured strides, and without ceremony he swung his heavy sword in a flashing arc. Tekhmet's head bounced twice along the stones, and came to rest near Amn-nasir's feet.

The men of the hunting party pulled their weapons from Tekhmet's body and bowed to the rulers, their chests heaving with strain.

'That is the last of them, great ones,' their leader said. 'We've emptied all the crypts at the base of the pyramid. Many looked like they had been abandoned some time ago.'

Rakh-amn-hotep nodded, and said, 'This was boldly done. Rest assured, you and your men will be well-rewarded for what you've done today.' The men of the hunting parties had all been volunteers, willing to brave the depths of Nagash's pyramid in search of the king and his servants. Over the course of the day more than half of them had met grisly ends in the confines of the brooding crypt.

Khansu studied the bodies stretched out on the paving stones.

'Thirteen,' the hierophant said. 'That still leaves more than a dozen of the fiends unaccounted for, including Raamket and that devil Arkhan, to say nothing of Nagash.'

Rakh-amn-hotep saw Amn-nasir stir uncomfortably, and realised that the King of Zandri was staring at Lamashizzar. The Rasetran king scowled at the Lahmian.

'Were you going to say something?' he asked.

Lamashizzar shrugged. 'The rest of the immortals have no doubt gone into hiding elsewhere. Perhaps to Ka-Sabar, or even to Zandri or Numas. Didn't those merchants we caught on the trade road mention that Arkhan had a citadel somewhere north of Bel Aliad?' The young king shook his head. 'This war is far from over, my friends. Mark my words: we'll be hunting the last of Nagash's immortals for many decades to come.'

Hekhmenukep folded his arms thoughtfully, and said, 'But if that's true, then it's clear that Nagash is no longer in control. He must be dead, or at least gravely injured.'

'He was with the Tomb Guard outside Mahrak's gates,' Lamashizzar said. 'I would swear to it. The Usurper was struck down by my dragon-men, along with his bodyguards. Either his immortals recovered his body and brought it back with them, or it's buried beneath heaps of bones outside the City of the Gods.'

'Nagash wasn't left behind at Mahrak,' Rakh-amn-hotep said doggedly. 'I had a thousand men searching at the foot of the walls. No. He's here somewhere. Tekhmet and the other immortals returned here for a reason.'

One of Hekhmenukep's engineers emerged from the depths of the pyramid and approached the assembled kings. The Lybaran bowed to Hekhmenukep and said nervously, 'We believe we've found the king's chamber, great one. It's in the upper levels, just beneath the ritual chamber at the centre of the pyramid.' The scholar pulled a cloth from his belt and wiped the sweat from his face. 'The approach to the chamber is guarded by a number of deadly traps. For your own safety, I beg you to reconsider entering the room. Surely a cadre of champions could accomplish the task just as well.' Hekhmenukep shook his head, but it was Rakh-amn-hotep who answered the engineer.

'Enough of our men have died inside that damned crypt today,' the Rasetran said. 'This one thing we must do ourselves.'

The engineer bowed again and backed away, returning to wait by the entrance to the pyramid.

Rakh-amn-hotep surveyed his fellow kings. 'Gather your swords,' he said gravely. 'It's time Nagash paid for his crimes.'

A servant stepped up to the Rasetran king and handed him his sword. Rakh-amn-hotep took it without a word and headed off to the pyramid's entrance with Ekhreb following a pace behind. When he was halfway there he felt a tug on his sleeve.

The king turned and saw Amn-nasir. The King of Zandri was unarmed, and his expression was grave. Amn-nasir cast a worried glance back at the other kings, still some distance away, and then said, 'There is something we must speak about, Rakh-amn-hotep.'

The Rasetran bit back a surge of anger, and said, 'I understand your reluctance, Amn-nasir, but it's important that we face Nagash together.'

'No!' the King of Zandri replied. 'It's not that! There is something you must know about Lamashizzar, and what happened during the battle at Mahrak. The Lahmian is not to be trusted!'

Rakh-amn-hotep scowled at Amn-nasir. 'What in the name of the gods are you talking about?' he asked.

Amn-nasir started to speak, but Ekhreb made a faint warning gesture. 'Lamashizzar is coming,' he said quietly.

The Zandrian nodded. 'We'll speak more tonight,' he told Rakh-amn-hotep, and then stepped aside as they were joined by the remaining kings.

For a moment, the Rasetran was tempted to press Amn-nasir further, but he noted that the sun was sinking towards the horizon and he had no desire to be caught in the pyramid after nightfall. Whatever the king wanted to tell him, it paled next to what waited for them in Nagash's sanctum.

'All right,' he said, gesturing to the engineer. 'Take us to the chamber.'

The nervous engineer led the seven kings into the depths of the great crypt, navigating by virtue of an oil lamp and a complex map scrawled on a large piece of parchment. Rakh-amn-hotep was conscious of few details as they worked their way through the maze of corridors, dimly lit chambers and winding ramps. The darkness of the place had a weight to it, pushing back against the feeble light of the lamps and hanging like a shroud over the king. From the hunched shoulders and apprehensive expressions of the other rulers, the Rasetran could tell that they felt it, too.

After what seemed like an eternity, the engineer stopped at the foot of a long, sloping passage that angled upwards for almost sixty feet before ending at a pair of towering double doors. Lamps had been laid at ten-foot intervals along the passageway, illuminating dozens of chalk marks on the intricately carved walls and along the floor. A group of equally nervous Lybarans waited at the foot of the passageway, staring apprehensively up at the doors.

'The corridor is lined with many different kinds of traps,' the lead engineer said. 'We've marked all the triggers we can find with chalk, but...' He shrugged helplessly.

The Rasetran nodded, asking, 'And no one has been in the king's chamber?'

'Blessed Tahoth! Of course not!'

'Good,' Rakh-amn-hotep said. He drew his sword and began to carefully make his way up to the doors.

It was no small feat to avoid the telltale chalk marks inscribed on the floor, requiring a slow and careful dance along the passageway. The doors at the end of the corridor were made of basalt. Their surfaces had been carved in a bas-relief of Nagash, holding the Staff of the Ages and looming over a multitude of kneeling kings and priests. Scowling, Rakh-amn-hotep put a hand against the door on the left and pushed the heavy portal open.

Beyond was a four-sided chamber whose basalt walls angled inwards to form a second pyramid. Walls, floor and ceiling were inscribed with thousands of intricate hieroglyphs, inlaid with crushed gemstones that glittered balefully in the lamplight. An intricately carved marble sarcophagus rested upon a stone dais at the centre of the chamber.

Waves of magical energy pulsed inside the chamber, setting Rakh-amn-hotep's nerves on fire. Faint echoes, cries of terror and misery, rose and fell in his ears. Each step across the chamber sent waves of despair coursing up the king's spine.

Gripping his sword tightly, Rakh-amn-hotep approached the dark sarcophagus. Some instinct told him that the casket was not empty. The final reckoning with the Usurper had come at last.

The Rasetran king waited by the side of the sarcophagus until all seven kings stood by his side. All but Amn-nasir were armed, and they held their weapons ready.

Rakh-amn-hotep laid his hand on the edge of the casket's lid. Each of the other men did the same.

'For Ka-Sabar and Bhagar,' the Rasetran said. 'For Quatar, and Bel Aliad, and Mahrak.'

'For Akhmen-hotep and Nemuhareb,' Hekhmenukep added. 'For Thutep and Shahid ben Alcazzar.'

'For Nebunefer, loyal servant of Ptra,' Khansu said. 'And for Neferem, the Daughter of the Sun.'

Rakh-amn-hotep raised his sword.

'Let justice be done!' he cried, and heaved upon the casket's lid. The top of the sarcophagus slid aside, and a torrent of locusts and glittering beetles poured from the darkness, filling the air with the dry rustle of wings.

The kings staggered away from the casket, batting furiously at the rushing wall of insects. The sound of the swarm in the confined space was nearly deafening, Then, just as suddenly as it appeared, the cloud of insects was gone, racing down the passageway behind them.

Stunned, Rakh-amn-hotep ran a trembling hand across his face. For a moment he'd been transported back in time, when another swarm had swept over his sky-boat above the Fountains of Eternal Life. He shook away the awful memory and stepped back to the casket once more. This time he threw his full weight against the stone lid and sent it crashing to the floor. Sword ready, the Rasetran peered inside.

The sarcophagus of the Undying King was empty.

An entire company of swordsmen was left to guard the pyramid once night had fallen. A bonfire had been built in the centre of the great plaza, and the bodies of the immortals had been consigned to the flames. Later, after the seven kings had given up and returned to their encampment outside haunted Khemri, a team of workmen barred the pyramid entrance with a massive block of granite that had been found elsewhere in the necropolis. It was merely a temporary measure, for on the morrow the Lybaran engineers would set to work sealing up the pyramid in earnest, ensuring that its evil powers could never be used again.

That mattered little to the small group of men who crept up to the far side of the pyramid shortly after midnight. There was more than one entrance into the great crypt, if one knew where to find them. The leader of the group touched a series of faint indentations on the pyramid's smooth surface and a narrow portal slid open with only the faintest grating of stone.

Once inside, the group lit small oil lamps and followed their guide through a maze of narrow passageways and vast, echoing chambers that led them inexorably towards the centre of the pyramid. Finally, their path ended when they came to a blank wall at the far end of a long, sloping corridor. The guide ran his fingers over the stone until he found a tiny indentation. There was a faint click, and a section of the wall swung inwards.

The cloaked figures slipped silently through the doorway. Their guide was already moving around the large chamber beyond, lighting a series of larger oil lamps with a practised ease born of long familiarity. The expanding glow revealed shelves heaped with scrolls and thick, leather-bound books, as well as broad tables cluttered with a plethora of arcane objects made from glass, metal and bone. Elaborate skeletons, some human, others bestial, were fixed together with wire and stood on display in various corners of the room. The men looked around the chamber in awe, amazed at the sheer wealth of knowledge contained within.

One man in the middle of the group reached up and pulled back his hood. Lamashizzar raised his oil lamp high above his head and stared covetously at the many bookshelves.

'You never said there would be so much,' he whispered. 'We'll never get them all out.'

'We don't need all of them,' Arkhan said. The immortal worked his way across Nagash's library until he stood before an apparently bare stretch of wall. He felt the stone carefully for the hidden lever, wary of the booby traps set in the wall around it. Finally he found what he was looking for, and with a gentle tug a part of the wall swung open, revealing a niche that contained four leather-bound tomes. The immortal's lips pulled back in a ghastly smile. 'The other books are just records of Nagash's experiments. These are the ones that contain all the things that he learned, including the secret of his elixir.'

Arkhan felt his pulse race as he closed his hands around the books. Here at last was the knowledge he craved. He would return to his tower with the books and unravel their secrets, starting with the formula for Nagash's life-giving elixir. Already the hunger was so great that it cut into his guts like a knife. Soon he would regain his full strength, and then he would plumb his master's more esoteric spells. Who could say what might happen after that? The power of the old gods was broken, and the land devastated by war. The people of Nehekhara would need a new leader for the dark times to come.

'You said that the pyramid was to be sealed,' Arkhan said to the Lahmian king as he placed the books in a leather bag that hung from his shoulders. 'What will the kings do then?'

'The hunt will continue,' Lamashizzar replied. 'Rakh-amn-hotep intends to march on Ka-Sabar next. Seheb and Nuneb have said they intend to return to Numas and scour the city for signs of your fellow immortals, while Khansu and Hekhmenukep plan to return to Quatar. There is talk that one of the Lybaran king's sons may become king of the city.'

Arkhan nodded absently, still with his back to Lamashizzar and his men. There were only five of them, and with his preternatural senses he could place each and every one of them around the large room. His hand reached down and drew a narrow dagger that he'd concealed in his sleeve. Weak as he was, he was still a match for five normal men.

'What of Amn-nasir? Aren't you afraid he might tell someone about our little arrangement?' he asked.

Lamashizzar affected a sigh, and said, 'Unfortunately, the King of Zandri suffered a terrible accident as we were leaving the pyramid earlier today. I'm afraid I accidentally triggered one of Nagash's many traps, despite the chalk marks left by the Lybaran engineers. Tragically, Amn-nasir was right behind me. The poisoned darts missed me, but one of them struck him in the arm. He died before we could get him back to the surface.'

The vizier's smile widened. That was one loose end he had no need to worry about. Once Lamashizzar and his men were dead, he would take Nagash's tomes and disappear into the desert.

'Such exceptional treachery,' the vizier said approvingly. 'I suppose I shouldn't be surprised.'

Quick as a snake, the immortal spun and leapt for the first Lahmian. The man barely had time to shout before Arkhan seized him by the shoulder and spun him around. He slit the man's throat with a swipe of his dagger and started towards Lamashizzar.

Suddenly there was a flash of orange light and a clap of thunder. A heavy impact smashed into Arkhan's chest, just above his heart.

The immortal staggered. He looked to the Lahmian king, who was holding a miniature version of a dragon-stave in one outstretched hand. Smoke curled from the dragon's bronze jaws.

Arkhan's gaze fell to the blackened hole in his chest. Darkness pressed in at the corners of his vision. He tried to speak, but his lungs refused to draw breath. Slowly, the immortal sank to the floor.

The Lahmian king walked over to Arkhan's prone body and carefully studied his face. 'Take the monster and as many books as you can carry,' he said to his servants in a steely voice. 'I want to be on the way back to Lahmia by mid-morning.'

Lamashizzar reached down and pulled the books from Arkhan's bag. While his servants looted the necromancer's library he opened the first of Nagash's arcane tomes and began to read.

Hundreds of leagues to the north-east, where the Plains of Plenty gave way to the broken foothills of the Brittle Peaks, the boiling cloud of locusts used up the last of its strength and plunged earthwards on a trail of smoking insect husks. With a harsh, chittering buzz the last of the insects struck the wasted ground and burst apart in a hideous clatter of chitin and boiling fluids. Wreathed in the vapour of thousands of shattered locusts, a human figure staggered from the centre of the dying mass and stumbled forwards for a few, painful steps before collapsing to his knees.

He could not say for certain how he'd come to this wasteland. Memories flitted at the edge of his awareness like ghosts, haunting him with meaning and then vanishing when he tried to seize them.

Agony stabbed through him like a hot knife. His left arm was curled tightly against his chest, like a rope that had been wound too tight. A ragged hole had been blown through his upper arm, shattering the bone and causing the muscles to constrict. Two more holes had been driven into his chest, one to the right of his breastbone, just below the lung, and the other a hand's span above his navel. Bile and other fluids leaked from the wounds, reeking of corruption.

His face was burning with fever. He reached up with his good hand and pressed it to his forehead, where he found another awful wound. A ragged hole had been punched into his skull, close to the temple. The edges of the bone were splintered, sinking like needles into his fingertips. The touch set his head to pounding and sent more waves of hot agony pulsing through his brain.

There had been a battle. He could hear the sounds of it in his head: the clatter of bronze and the dry rattle of bones as dead men advanced towards the enemy; an army, his army, marching into a wall of orange flame and bursting into fragments, and then a series of invisible blows striking him one after another, plunging him into darkness.

He remembered hands pulling at him, dragging him through the blackness, and an eternity of shouting voices and the tumult of battle. When light finally returned, it was grey and unfocused. Dark figures flitted above him, and he could hear harsh whispers that once or twice rose into vicious shouts.

Look at him! His flesh doesn't heal, no matter how much blood we give him! What kind of sorcery is this?

We'll take him to the pyramid. There is power enough there to make him whole.

Slay him! Take his blood for our own! If we don't scatter, the eastern kings will kill us all!

Coward! Go, then, and be damned! When the master is whole again, how you will suffer!

The arguments continued until he could take no more, and he cursed at the voices with words of power until they fled like startled birds.

Later, much later, he was carried into cool, throbbing darkness. Power, soft and sensual, caressed his skin and sank into his wounds. The voices came back, whispering entreaties: *call upon the pyramid, master. Heal yourself. Please! The enemy draws near!*

He called, and the power flowed into him, but it lapped uselessly over his wounds. He tried to force it to heal him, but it would not obey no matter what he tried. It was as though the secrets to wielding the power had been taken from him somehow, leaving him bereft.

Much had been taken from him, of that he was certain.

Some time later there had been cries of fear, and the sounds of battle once more. A voice called out to him to flee, and then fell silent. For a long time afterwards, there was only darkness.

Then he heard strange voices, full of anger and the promise of destruction. His enemies had found him at last. Anger and terror consumed him, until the power building beneath his skin threatened to tear him apart. Stone grated on stone, letting in a blade of burning light, and then came the rising sound of wings.

Nagash turned his head this way and that, taking in the panoramic sweep of the wasteland. Nothing moved among the broken stones and lifeless sand. With a sound that was half-groan, half-growl, he forced himself painfully to his feet and turned around, looking back at the trail of broken husks that stretched towards the green horizon to the south-west.

His bones were cold and his muscles weak. Only the pain kept him going, denying him any chance of peace. Nagash sought the power that he'd felt in the cool darkness of the pyramid, but there was nothing there. He was as broken and empty as the smoking carapaces at his feet.

Clenching his one good hand, Nagash the sorcerer threw back his head and howled his rage at the heavens. He cursed the green land at the edge of the world that had once been his.

Reeling, exhausted, he spun around and glanced northwards, into the wastes. His foes had consigned him to this place somehow. No doubt they expected him to die, and his spirit to be lost forever in this empty land.

That was when he glimpsed it: a whisper of power, far off among the broken peaks to the north-east. It was faint and ephemeral, twisting effortlessly away from his mind as he tried to focus on it. Not that it mattered. The power was there, beckoning to him in the midst of the wasteland.

His face set in a grim mask, Nagash took one halting step forwards, and then another. Pain lanced through his frame, but he drew strength from it, driving his legs forwards with bitter strength. A cold wind wracked his body and sent fingers of ice into his wounds, but he embraced the pain gladly.

The wasteland would sustain him, and one day, he would revisit it upon his foes until all the world was nothing but howling spirits and dry, bleached bones.

NAGASH
THE UNBROKEN

DRAMATIS PERSONAE

LAHMIA

Lamashizzar, priest king
Neferata, queen
Khalida, ward of the royal household
Ubaid, Lamashizzar's grand vizier
Tephret and **Aaliyah**, handmaidens of the queen
Abhorash, the king's champion
Ankhat and **Ushoran**, wealthy and powerful nobles
Zurhas, Adio and **Khenti**, dissolute minor nobles
W'soran, a scholar, formerly of Mahrak
Prince Xian Ha Feng, emissary of the Eastern Empire

THE OTHER CITIES

Shepret, king of Rasetra
Khepra, priest king of Lybaras
Anhur, prince of Lybaras
Naeem, priest king of Quatar
Amunet, queen of Numas
Teremun, priest king of Zandri

PROLOGUE

NEW BEGINNINGS

Lahmia, the City of the Dawn,
in the 63rd year of Khsar the Faceless
(-1739 Imperial Reckoning)

Small, soft hands gripped her and gently shook her. Voices whispered urgently in her ears, calling her back across the gulf of dreams, until the Daughter of the Moon stirred at last from her slumber and opened her heavy-lidded eyes. It was very late. Neru hung low on the horizon, sending shafts of lambent moonlight through the tall windows of the bedchamber. The golden lamps had been turned down, and only the faintest hint of incense still lingered near the room's tiled ceiling.

The sea breeze stirred the gauzy curtains surrounding her bed, carrying ghostly sounds of revelry from the Red Silk Quarter, down by the city docks.

Neferata, Daughter of the Moon and the Queen of Lahmia, rolled onto her back and blinked slowly in the gloom. Tephret, her most favoured handmaiden, was crouched by the head of the queen's sumptuous bed, one slim hand still resting protectively on Neferata's naked shoulder. The queen irritably brushed the touch away, her own fingers slow and clumsy from the effects of too much black lotus and sweet, Eastern wine.

'What is it?' Neferata murmured, her voice thick with sleep.

'The king,' Tephret whispered. The handmaiden's face was hidden in shadow, but the outline of her slender body was tense. 'The king is here, great one.'

Neferata stared at Tephret for a moment, not quite able to make sense of what she'd heard. The queen sat up in bed, the silken sheets flowing over the curves of her body and pooling in her lap. She shook her head gently, struggling to think through the clinging fog of the lotus. 'What time is it?'

'The hour of the dead,' Tephret replied, her voice wavering slightly. Like all of the queen's handmaidens, she was also a priestess of Neru, and sensitive to the omens of the night. 'The grand vizier awaits you in the Hall of Reverent Contemplation.'

The mention of the grand vizier cut through the mists surrounding Neferata's brain at last. She swung her slender legs over the edge of the bed, next to Tephret, and let out a slow, thoughtful breath. 'Bring me the *hixa*,' she said, 'and my saffron robes.'

Tephret bowed, touching her forehead to the top of Neferata's feet, then rose and began hissing orders to the rest of the queen's handmaidens. Half a dozen young women stirred from their sleeping cushions at the far end of the room as Neferata rose carefully to her feet and walked to the open windows facing the sea. The surface of the water was calm as glass, and the great trading ships from the Silk Lands rode easy at their anchors in the crowded harbour. Specks of red and yellow lantern-light bobbed like fireflies down Lahmia's close-set streets as the palanquins of noblemen and wealthy traders made their way home from an evening of debauchery.

The lights of the Red Silk District, as well as the more upper-class District of the Golden Lotus, still burned brightly, while the rest of the great city had sunk reluctantly into slumber. From where Neferata stood, she could just see the sandstone expanse of Asaph's Quay, at the edge of the Temple District and just north of the city harbour. The ceremonial site was bare.

The queen frowned pensively, though she'd expected no less.

'There was no word from the army?' she asked. 'None at all?'

'None,' Tephret confirmed. The handmaiden glided swiftly across the room and knelt beside the queen, offering up a small box made from fine golden filigree. 'The king's servants are in an uproar.'

Neferata nodded absently and plucked the box from Tephret's hands. She carefully opened the lid. Inside, the *hixa* stirred torpidly. Neferata gripped the large, wingless wasp between thumb and forefinger and pressed its abdomen against the hollow beneath her left ear. It took a few moments of agitation before she felt the *hixa's* sting and the prickling tide of pain that washed across her face and scalp. Blood pounded in a rising crescendo at her temples and behind her eyes, finally receding several seconds later into a dull, throbbing ache that set her teeth on edge but left her alert and clear-headed at last. There was no better cure for the lingering effects of lotus and wine, as the nobles of the city knew all too well.

She placed the *hixa* back in the box with a sigh and handed it back to Tephret, then raised her arms so that her maids could wrap her body in ceremonial robes of welcome. Tephret set the golden box aside and hurried to a cabinet of gilded ebony that contained the queen's royal mask. Made of beaten gold and inlaid with rubies, polished onyx and mother-of-pearl, it had been crafted by the artisan-priests of Asaph as a perfect likeness of the queen's regal face. It was the face she was required to show to the rest of the world. In time, it would serve as her death mask as well.

It would have taken hours for Neferata to fully prepare herself for her husband's return; she impatiently waved aside the proffered golden bracelets and necklaces, and glared at the maids who tried to paint her eyes with crushed beetle shell and kohl. The instant her girdle was pulled tight and the royal mask set carefully upon her face, she snatched up Asaph's snake-headed sceptre from Tephret's hands and hurried from the bedchamber. A servant dashed ahead of Neferata, her bare feet slapping on the polished marble tiles as she held up a bobbing lantern to light their way.

Neferata moved as swiftly as her confining robes would allow, but it still took ten long minutes to traverse the labyrinth of shadowy corridors, luxurious rooms and ornamental gardens that separated her apartments from the rest of the palace. It was a world apart, a palace within a palace that served as both sanctuary and prison for the women of the Lahmian royal bloodline. Not even the king himself could enter, save on certain holy days dedicated to the goddess Asaph and her divine revels.

There were only three small audience chambers where the queen and her daughters were allowed to interact with the outside world. The largest and grandest, the Hall of the Sun in its Divine Glory, was set aside to celebrate weddings and childbirths, and was open at various times to both the royal household and the common folk of the city. The smallest, a dark vault of green marble known as the Hall of Regretful Sorrows, was where long, solemn processions of Lahmian citizens would come to pay their last respects to a dead queen before her journey to the House of Everlasting Life.

In between was the Hall of Reverent Contemplation, a medium-sized chamber built from warm, golden sandstone and inlaid with screens of lustrous, polished wood. More temple than audience chamber, it was here that the king and the noble families of the city – as well as a handful of common folk, chosen by lot – would gather to pay homage to the queen and receive her blessings for the coming year.

By the time Neferata arrived at the hall the great golden lamps had been lit, and incense was curling in dark, blue-grey ribbons from the braziers that flanked the royal dais. A red-faced servant, glistening with sweat, was single-handedly trying to unfold the delicate wooden screen that was meant to shield the royal presence from unworthy eyes. The queen stopped the servant in her tracks with a curt wave of her hand as she stepped from behind the elegantly carved wooden throne and approached the robed figure resting upon his knees at the foot of the dais.

Like the queen, Grand Vizier Ubaid had taken the time to don his ceremonial saffron robes to welcome the king's return. His shaven pate had been freshly oiled and matched the mellow tone of the room's polished wood. Neferata could barely make out the coiling tattoos of Asaph's sacred serpents that wound sinuously about the sides of Ubaid's head and neck. She couldn't help but note that the thin coating of fragrant oil effectively concealed any signs of nervous sweat on Ubaid's high forehead.

The grand vizier bowed low the stone floor as Neferata descended the broad steps of the royal dais. 'A thousand, thousand pardons, great one–' he began.

'What is the meaning of this, Ubaid?' Neferata hissed. Her husky voice sounded harsh and menacing within the golden confines of her mask. 'What is he doing here?'

Ubaid straightened, spreading his hands in a gesture of supplication. 'I swear, I do not know,' he replied. 'He arrived little more than an hour ago with a small retinue and a handful of slaves.'

Like most Lahmian nobles, the grand vizier had a slender neck, high cheekbones and a prominent jaw-line. Years of rich living hadn't softened him, like many of his peers, and despite being of middle age his body was still slender and strong. Many at court suspected him of being a sorcerer, but Neferata knew that he was simply very good at keeping up appearances. He had even taken to wearing golden caps on the ends of his little fingers, each one ending in a long, artificial nail in the fashion of bureaucrats from the Silk Lands across the sea. The affectation did nothing to improve the queen's mood.

'Where is the army?' she demanded. 'The last report said they were still three days' march away.'

Ubaid shrugged helplessly. 'There is no way of knowing, great one. Likely they are still somewhere on the trade road, west of the Golden Plain. Certainly they are nowhere near the city itself. The king appears to have hurried on ahead of the host.'

As well as the majority of his noble allies, Neferata observed, growing more irritated by the moment. Absolutely nothing about Lamashizzar's expedition to Mahrak had gone according to plan, and now he was risking the ire of people whose goodwill he would desperately need in the years to come. 'And where is the king now?' she asked coldly.

The vizier's carefully composed expression cracked somewhat around the edges. 'He's... in the cellars,' he answered in a subdued voice. 'He went there straightaway with his men–'

'The *cellars*?' Neferata snapped. 'Why? To inventory the jars of grain and honey?'

'I...' Ubaid stammered. 'I'm sure I can't say–'

'Asaph's teeth!' the queen swore. 'I was being sarcastic, Ubaid. I know perfectly well what he's doing down there,' she said. 'Take me to him.'

Ubaid's eyes widened. 'I'm not certain that would be proper, great one–'

Neferata straightened her shoulders and glared down at the grand vizier, her golden face implacable and cold. 'Grand vizier, the king has flouted ancient tradition by returning to the city in this... unorthodox... fashion. By custom and by law, he hasn't *officially* returned, which means that I continue to rule this city in Lamashizzar's name. Do you understand?'

The grand vizier bowed his head at once. Over the last year and a half he'd been exceedingly careful to conceal his true feelings about the king's secret dispensation of power. By rights, Ubaid should have been the one to rule Lahmia in Lamashizzar's absence; the queens of Lahmia were not meant to sully themselves with mundane affairs of state. Now, eighteen months later, Ubaid understood what had persuaded the king to make such a scandalous choice.

'Please follow me, great one,' he replied smoothly, and rose to his feet.

The great palace was honeycombed with a network of hidden passageways, built for the use of the household's many servants, and Ubaid led the queen through a veritable labyrinth of narrow, dimly-lit corridors and dusty storage rooms as they made their way to the cellars. Neferata could barely see where she was going within the confines of her mask. The servant's lantern bobbed in the darkness ahead of her like some teasing river spirit, luring her onward to her doom.

Finally she found herself descending a series of long, narrow ramps, and the air turned cold and damp. Gooseflesh raced along the skin of her neck and arms, but she suppressed the urge to shiver. Then a few minutes later she felt the weight of the narrow passageways fall away to her left and right, and she realised that they'd entered a large, low-ceilinged space. Neferata glimpsed stacks of rounded, clay jars sealed with wax, and heard the distant sound of voices somewhere up ahead.

Ubaid led her through one interconnected cellar after another, past jars of spices, salt and honey, bolts of cloth and bricks of beeswax. The sense of space began to shrink again, and the queen reckoned that they were heading into a much older part of the cellars. The voices grew more distinct, until she could clearly make out her husband's hushed, urgent voice.

Suddenly, the grand vizier halted and stepped aside. Neferata rushed ahead and emerged into a small, dripping chamber stacked with wide-bellied wine jars bearing the royal seal. A handful of torches guttered from the walls, casting strange, leaping shadows across the floor.

Lamashizzar, Priest King of Lahmia, City of the Dawn, stood over an opened wine jar and gulped greedily from a golden drinking bowl. His rich, silken robes were grimed with the dust of the road, and his tightly curled black hair was matted and limp with sweat. Half a dozen noblemen stood around the king, all of them travel-stained and reeling from fatigue. Several drank along with the king, while the rest stole apprehensive glances at the slaves working feverishly at the far side of the room. None of them noticed the sudden appearance of the queen.

Neferata studied the men for a long moment and felt her irritation sharpen into icy rage. She took another step into the room and drew a deep breath. 'This is an ill-omened thing,' she declared in a cold, clear voice.

Startled cries rang off the stone walls as the noblemen whirled, their dark faces pale and eyes wide with shock. To Neferata's profound surprise, many of them reached for their swords; they caught themselves at the last possible moment, hands hovering over the hilts of their blades. Yet they did not relax. None of them did. Instead, their eyes darted between Neferata and the king, as though uncertain how to proceed.

Now it was the queen's turn to stare in amazement. Some of the men she knew to be Lamashizzar's closest supporters, while others, though Lahmian, were strangers to her. All of them shared the same tense, hard-edged expression, the same fevered glint in their eyes.

They look like cornered animals, Neferata thought, thankful that the all-enclosing mask hid her startled reaction. Is this what war does to civilised men?

The king himself was no less stunned to see his queen. His handsome face was sallow and drawn; his eyes were sunken and his cheeks hollowed out from poor eating and little sleep, but his gaze was sharper and more penetrating than ever. Lamashizzar lowered the drinking bowl. Red wine trickled thickly down the sides of his sharp chin.

'What in the name of the dawn are you doing here, sister?' he rasped.

'I?' Neferata snapped, her anger managing to overcome her growing unease. 'More to the point, what are *you* doing here?' She advanced on Lamashizzar, her hands clenched into fists. 'There are sacred rites to be observed. The king may not return to the city without first performing the Propitiations of the East. You must thank Asaph for the blessing she gave when you first set out to war!' Neferata's voice grew in volume along with her ire, until her voice rang like a bell within the confines of the mask. 'But the army isn't expected for days yet. Asaph's Quay is bare of offerings from the citizenry. The proper sacrifices have not been made.'

Without warning, the queen lashed out, striking the drinking bowl from the king's hand. 'What happened?' she hissed. 'Did you drink all the wine you plundered from here to Khemri? Couldn't you have waited two more days to slake your thirst? *This is an offence against the gods, brother.*'

For a moment, no one moved. Neferata could feel the tension crackling like caged lightning in the air. The king glanced past Neferata. 'That will be all, Ubaid,' he said to the grand vizier.

Ubaid bowed and hastily withdrew, his robes rustling as he fled from the cellar as quickly as his dignity would allow.

Lamashizzar stared at the queen, his eyes depthless and strange. He raised his hand and laid the tips of his fingers against the mask's curved, golden cheek.

'The gods do not care, sister,' he said softly. 'They no longer hear our prayers. Nagash the Usurper saw to that on the plain outside Mahrak. Did you not read any of my letters?'

'Of course I did,' Neferata replied, suppressing a chill at the mention of Nagash's name. She and Lamashizzar had been born during the height of the Usurper's reign, when the former Grand Hierophant of Khemri's mortuary cult had held all of Nehekhara in his iron grip. It was only when the kings of the east had risen in revolt against Khemri that they had learned true horror of the Usurper's power, and though they eventually triumphed, the cost of victory was almost too terrible to contemplate.

Angrily, she pushed aside the king's hand and stalked past him. At the far end of the chamber, the slaves stopped what they were doing and abased themselves at her approach.

'It doesn't matter if the covenant has been broken or not,' Neferata continued. 'In matters of state – and religion – perception is every bit as important as reality. Lahmia was spared from the worst excesses of Nagash's rule, but the war has disrupted trade with the west for more than ten years now. Fortunes have been lost – to say nothing of the enormous debt we now owe the Emperor of the Silk Lands. If the people had *any* inkling of the deal we struck to obtain their dragon-powder there would be rioting in the streets.'

'That was Lamasheptra's doing, not mine,' Lamashizzar pointed out, bending to retrieve his drinking bowl.

'It doesn't *matter*,' Neferata insisted. 'Father is dead. *You* are the one on the throne, now. The people look to *you* for reassurance. They need to believe that the Usurper's reign of terror is over and that a new era has begun. They need to know that Lahmia will prosper once more.'

The queen's tirade had carried her nearly all the way across the chamber. The slaves were still as statues, their previous labours forgotten as they pressed their foreheads to the earthen floor. They had been in the process of shifting scores of dusty wine jars and dismantling wooden shelves to create a cleared space for–

Neferata came to a sudden halt. Her eyes widened behind the golden mask as she saw the linen-wrapped bundles resting on the earthen floor. 'What–' she stammered, suddenly at a loss for words. 'Brother, what is all this?'

Behind her, Lamashizzar dipped his bowl in the open jar. He stared into its ruby depths, and an ironic smile tugged at the corners of his mouth.

'The dawn of a new era,' he said, raising the bowl to his lips.

They were not jugs of plundered wine or wrapped brinks of lotus leaf. Neferata saw that at once. Each bundle had roughly square sides, some reaching as high as her knees. The linen wrappings were stained brown by countless leagues of travel, and were bound with braided twine. She went to the closest one. Slaves scattered from her path like frightened birds as she knelt beside the parcel and tugged at its bindings with long-nailed fingers. As she did, a stir went through the assembled nobles. Neferata heard angry growls and choked protests, until finally one of the men could contain himself no longer.

'Stop her!' the nobleman snapped. Neferata didn't recognise the voice. 'What is she even doing outside the Women's Palace? She should be in her proper place, not–'

'She is the *queen*,' Lamashizzar said, in a voice as cold and hard as Eastern iron. 'She goes where she wills.'

Neferata listened to the tense exchange with only half an ear. Her dark fingers teased the twine knot apart, and a corner of the linen wrapping fell away to reveal–

'Books?' the queen said. Her eyebrows knitted together in a frown. They were thick tomes of expensive Lybaran paper, bound in a strange kind of pale leather that sent prickles of unease racing down her spine.

'The books of Nagash,' Lamashizzar explained. 'Smuggled from his pyramid outside Khemri. All his secrets: his plans, his studies, his... his experiments. It's all there.'

Neferata felt her heart grow cold. She rose and turned to face the king. 'I don't understand, brother,' she hissed. 'You were supposed to forge an alliance with the Usurper. With the power under your command you could have broken the siege at Mahrak and handed the east to Nagash! He would have agreed to any terms–'

'No,' Lamashizzar said flatly. He took another long draught from the bowl, his face haunted with memory. 'You weren't there, sister. You didn't see the... the *creature* that Nagash had become.'

'We knew he was a sorcerer–' Neferata began.

'He was a *monster*,' Lamashizzar said darkly. 'None of the rumours we'd heard came anywhere close to the truth. Nagash was no longer human, and what he'd done to Neferem–' The king's words dried up in his throat. Finally, he shook his head. 'Believe me, Nagash would have never honoured the terms of an alliance, much less shared the secrets of eternal life.' He gestured at the stacks of linen-wrapped volumes with his drinking bowl, sloshing thick wine onto the floor. 'So. Better this than nothing at all.'

Neferata spread her hands. 'Indeed? Are you a sorcerer now?' she shot back. 'I'm certainly not.'

'You were trained by the priestesses of Neru,' Lamashizzar said. 'You know how to perform incantations, how to create elixirs–'

The queen shook her head. 'That's not the same thing,' she protested.

'It's enough,' Lamashizzar said. He lurched forward, seizing Neferata by the wrist, and pulled her after him as he wound his way drunkenly through the collection of plundered tomes. Beyond the linen-wrapped books lay another shape, stretched out against the dank stone wall. 'We also have *this*,' the king said proudly.

It was a corpse. It had been inexpertly wrapped, and the linen bindings were devoid of the ritual symbols of the mortuary cult, but the shape of the body was unmistakeable.

The king gave his sister a conspiratorial smile. 'Go on,' he said, squeezing her wrist with surprising strength. 'Take a look.' His eyes glittered like glass, sharp and fever-bright.

Lamashizzar's hand squeezed harder. Neferata clenched her jaw and sank slowly to her knees. She heard the slaves shift nervously behind her as she stretched out her free hand and began to gingerly pull away the wrappings that covered the corpse's head.

The face took shape by degrees: first a man's beak-like nose, then a prominent brow and deeply sunken eyes. Next came sharp-edged cheekbones and a long, square jaw that gaped in a grimace of agony, revealing a mouthful of jagged, blackened teeth.

The corpse's skin was pale as a fish's belly and covered in a patchwork of fine scars. The veins at his temples and along his neck were black with old, clotted blood. The very sight of it filled the queen with revulsion. Neferata recoiled from the ghastly visage. 'What in the name of all the gods–'

Lamashizzar pulled her close. 'He is the key,' the king hissed, filling her nostrils with the sour reek of wine. 'This is Arkhan the Black. Do you know the name?'

'Of course,' the queen said with a grimace. 'He was the Usurper's grand vizier.'

'And one of the first immortals,' the king added. 'But he fell from favour during the war and betrayed Nagash on the eve of the great battle at Mahrak. He offered me the power over life and death if I would side with the rebel kings against his former master.' Lamashizzar gave the queen an almost boyish wink. 'After the battle, I hid him in my baggage train during the long march to Khemri. No one suspected a thing. The others thought he'd fled westward with the rest of the Usurper's immortals, so once we'd reached the Living City and the Usurper's troops made their last stand in the city's necropolis, I paid some soldiers to spread the rumour that Arkhan had been seen fighting to the bitter end at the foot of his master's pyramid. No doubt the story's taken on epic proportions since then.'

'And Arkhan actually held to his bargain?' she asked.

The king smiled. 'As much as I expected he would. He led me to the books, deep in the heart of the Black Pyramid.'

'Then you killed him.'

Lamashizzar's smile never faltered. 'Is that what you think?'

Neferata's expression hardened beneath the mask. With a savage jerk, she tore her wrist from the king's grasp. 'You're drunk,' she hissed. 'And I am not in the mood for games, brother.'

That was when the smile faded from the king's face. Slowly, deliberately, he lowered his hand and set the bowl of wine upon the floor. His eyes bored into hers. 'Then perhaps I should make it plain for you,' he said quietly. He spoke again, in that voice as hard and cold as iron. '*Bring them.*'

There was a commotion behind Neferata, and the slaves began to wail in terror. She froze at the sound, and watched as Lamashizzar leaned forward and tore away the linen bindings wrapping Arkhan's torso. The immortal's chest was even more scarred than his face, but what was worse was the blackened, thumb-sized hole in Arkhan's breast, just above his heart.

'He was swift, but the bullet in my dragon stave was swifter still,' Lamashizzar said. His nobles crowded around him, dragging the terrified slaves over to Arkhan's body. 'It's still there, buried in his heart. Here. Let me show you.'

The king crouched over the body and pressed his fingers deep into the wound. There was a thick, liquid sound, and Lamashizzar grunted in satisfaction. When he drew his hand away his fingers were covered in a black fluid as thick as tar. A fat, round metal ball was gripped between his fingertips. He held up the bullet and studied it for a moment.

'You see?' he said. 'Such a wound would have killed one of father's mighty Ushabti, much less a mere mortal like you or I. But to Arkhan it was nothing more than an *interruption*.'

The king bent close to the immortal's face. His voice dropped to a whisper. 'He's still in there,' Lamashizzar said, but whether he said it to Neferata or to the immortal himself, the queen could not be certain. 'Locked in a cell of flesh and bone. So long as his heart cannot beat, Nagash's elixir cannot circulate through his limbs, nor fan the flame of his cursed soul.'

The look on the king's face sent a shudder through Neferata. This was not the libertine who had led his father's army to Mahrak. The things he had seen on the field of battle – and possibly within the pages of the books he'd stolen from the Usurper's crypt – had left an impression in the young king's mind. Blessed Neru, she thought. What if he's gone mad?

Lamashizzar chuckled to himself, entirely oblivious to his sister's mounting unease. 'I have had many discussions with the former vizier on the journey home, and I believe we have reached an understanding. He will serve us, unlocking his former master's secrets and teaching us how to create the elixir for ourselves. If he serves well, then we will share the draught of life with him. If not...' he paused, and his expression grew hard. 'Then we will send him back into his cell, and we shall see how long it takes for an immortal's body to collapse into dust.'

The king tossed the bullet aside, then nodded curtly to his noblemen. Without a word they drew knives from their belts and began slitting the slaves' throats.

Hot blood sprayed through the air. The slaves thrashed and choked, pouring out their lives onto Arkhan's still form. As they died, Lamashizzar picked up the pale leather tome and began turning its pages.

'The world has changed, sister,' Lamashizzar said. 'The old gods have left us, and a new power has risen to take its place – a power that now we alone possess. We shall usher in a new age for Lahmia and the rest of Nehekhara. One that we shall preside over until the end of time.'

At their feet, the blood-soaked body of Arkhan the Black drew in a terrible, shuddering breath. His bruised eyelids fluttered, and Neferata found herself staring into a pair of dark, soulless eyes.

The Wasteland, in the 63rd year of Khsar the Faceless
(-1739 Imperial Reckoning)

Night came swiftly to the wasteland.

As the last rays of Ptra's hateful, searing light disappeared behind the jagged fangs of the Brittle Peaks, stealing away the heat of the day and filling the narrow gullies with inky shadow, the hunters of the dead spaces began to stir from their lairs. Deadly vipers slithered from beneath rocky overhangs, tasting the air with their darting tongues. Scorpions and huge, hairy spiders crawled from their daytime burrows and began their hunt, seeking sources of heat against the contrasting coolness of the rocky ground.

In one shadow-haunted gully, half a dozen lean, spotted shapes came nosing along the broken ground, tracking the scent of death. The jackals had been following the trail for many nights; it had rambled and looped back upon itself many times, like the path of a beast lost in madness and on the verge of collapse. Now the hunters sensed that the prey had been run to ground at last. Sniffing at the chill air, they edged towards a low overhang carved deep into the gully wall.

Within the darkness of the overhang, a bundle of rags stirred fitfully at the jackals' approach. The scavengers paused, ears forward, watching as a single, bony hand groped its way painfully from beneath the overhang. The skin was blackened and leathery, the nails yellowed and splintered by months of scrabbling over rocks and burrowing in the dry earth. The skin of the knuckles was split, peeled back like shreds of dry parchment to reveal grey flesh inlaid with grit.

The jackals watched as the long fingers arched, digging into the earth for purchase. There was a rustle of fabric and loose dirt. A trio of sleek, black lizards bolted from beneath the overhang, startled as their refuge began to shift beneath them.

Slowly, shakily, the figure dragged itself out into the night air. First an emaciated arm, then a bony shoulder, then a thin torso clad in grimy robes that had once been the colour of blood.

A bald head, blackened and blistered by the sun god's merciless touch, emerged from the shadows: a man's face, once handsome, now ravaged by the elements and the horrors of war. Dark eyes, set deep in bony sockets, regarded the jackals with feverish intensity. The man's face was gaunt to the point of being skeletal, his cheeks and nose frayed by brushes with rock and the mandibles of burrowing insects. A ragged hole, wide as a man's thumb, had been punched into his forehead, close to the left temple. At one time the ghastly wound had grown infected, causing the flesh to swell around the rim of splintered bone and the veins to distend with corruption.

The jackals lowered their heads and began to whine softly as the figure continued to drag itself from its refuge. This was not what they expected. Indeed, their would-be prey exuded a sense of *wrongness* that their animal brains couldn't quite comprehend.

Death hung over the man like a shroud. In addition to the awful wound in his head, his left arm was coiled uselessly against his chest. Another hole had been blown through the upper limb, shattering the bone and constricting the muscles into immobile knots. The scent of old bile rose from a puncture in the man's belly, and another wound in his chest carried the reek of old infection.

Dead, the jackals' minds said. The man ought to be dead long since. And yet still the leathery muscles worked, creaking like old ropes. The eyes still burned with an almost feral rage. Thin, cracked lips drew back from blackened teeth in a snarl of challenge.

Nagash the Usurper, Undying King of fallen Khemri and for a time the master of Nehekhara, pressed his palm against the stones and grit of the gully floor and with a bubbling growl pushed himself to his feet. Once upright, he swayed slightly as he turned his head to the gleaming face of the moon and let out a long, ululating howl of hate.

The jackals flinched at the awful sound. It proved too much for the leader of the pack, who let out a nervous bark and sped from the gully with the pack hard on its heels.

Nagash continued to howl long after they were gone, emptying the last dregs of air from his lungs in a long, wordless curse against the living world. The exertion left him shivering and weak, his skin burning with a fever that had no basis in the sicknesses of living flesh.

Like the jackals, he turned his face skyward, casting about for spoor. The scent of power hung above the emptiness of the wasteland, emanating from the slopes of a dark, brooding mountain that always seemed to lie just beyond the far horizon. It had a flavour unlike anything he'd ever tasted before; not dark magic, which he knew well, nor the fitful heat of a human soul. It was something furious and unfettered, primal and alien at the same time. It shone like a beacon in the emptiness, promising him vengeance against those who had betrayed him and cast him out into the wastes. He thirsted for it, and yet, like a mirage, it seemed to recede into the distance with every step he took. Lately, even the scent of it had grown vague. It was getting harder and harder to sense it past the pain of his ravaged body and the fever buzzing in his skull.

You're growing weaker, a voice said. *Your power is almost spent. Darkness waits, Usurper. Darkness eternal, and the cold winds of the Abyss.*

Nagash whirled, hissing with rage. She stood just a few feet away, her translucent body silhouetted by moonlight. Neferem, last Queen of Khemri, looked much as she did the day she died: a withered, ravaged husk of a woman, transformed into a living mummy by Nagash's sorceries. Only her eyes, large and brilliant as cut emeralds, hinted at the beauty that had been taken from her. Her ghostly figure was clad in ragged samite, and the golden headdress of a queen rested precariously upon her brow.

The Usurper reached out with his hand and clenched it at her like a claw – but his febrile mind failed him. The words of power that once bound the ghosts of Nehekhara to his will had been somehow stolen from him. Rage and frustration boiled inside his brain.

'*Witch!*' he hissed. His voice sounded somewhere between a growl and a groan. '*I am Nagash the Immortal! Death cannot claim me! I have passed beyond its grasp!*'

So have we all, Neferem replied soundlessly. Her eyes glittered with hate. *You saw to that at Mahrak. The paths to the Lands of the Dead are no more, swept away when you used me to undo the sacred covenant with the gods. Now none of us shall ever know peace.* Her shrivelled face contorted into the ghastly semblance of a smile.

Especially you.

Snarling with fury, Nagash whirled about, tasting the air for traces of the otherworldly power. It seemed to lie just beyond the line of peaks to the east. He lurched forward, scrabbling one-handed at the loose scree lining the gully slope. The Usurper scaled the steep incline with an awkward, spider-like gait. When he was almost to the top, he turned back to Neferem's vengeful spirit.

'*You haunt me at your peril, witch!*' he croaked. '*When I find the dark mountain I will have the power to consume souls and command the spirits of the dead as I once did! I'll feast upon you, then, and silence your moaning forever!*'

But the queen did not hear him. She was gone, as though she'd never been there.

Nagash searched for Neferem amid the shadows of the gully for a long time, muttering bitterly to himself. Once, he called her name, but her spirit would not be summoned so easily. Finally he turned and scrabbled the rest of the way up the slope.

At the summit, Nagash saw only a broken sea of foothills, stretching off to the horizon. The dark mountain had receded from him once again. He turned his face skyward, casting about for the trail once more, and then continued his limping course eastward.

Hours later, when the pale moon was close to its zenith, another pack of scavengers came sniffing into the gully where the Usurper had been. They circled about the rocky overhang, hissing and chittering to each other in their own strange tongue. As with any pack, it was the largest of the creatures that decided their course, cuffing and threatening the rest into submission. They too continued eastward, moist noses bent low over the rocks as they followed Nagash's strange, unliving scent. They loped and lurched and scrabbled along, sometimes on four legs, sometimes on two.

Nagash had so far passed beyond the grasp of death, but not beyond the jaws of constant, grinding agony. Every step, every movement of arm or head, sent waves of vivid, aching pain reverberating through his wasted body. The awful wounds he'd suffered hardly troubled him at all – or at least, no more so than the agony that gripped the rest of his frame. It was a consequence of the elixir, he knew. The magical potion – wrought from blood and life energy stolen from innocent, anguished victims – allowed him to retain the vigour of youth for hundreds of years, and was the key to creating an empire unheard of since the age of Settra the Magnificent.

Normally, it would also heal nearly any injury, no matter how severe, but not since that fateful day at Mahrak, when the army of Lahmia had thrown in its lot with the rebel kings of the east and unleashed their strange weapons on him and his unliving host. He remembered the wall of fire and a crescendo of thunder from the ranks of Lahmia's black-armoured warriors, and then watching the massed ranks of his corpse-soldiers disintegrating before him. The traitors had turned on him just as he'd won his greatest triumph. Mahrak had been cast down and the sacred covenant with it. The power of the priesthood and their parasite deities had been swept aside, so that only he, Nagash the Undying, remained.

As he made his way slowly down the rubble-strewn slope of another dark ridgeline, Nagash heard a wheezing breath in his ear. It had a rasping, ragged tone, like wind blowing across the end of a broken branch.

You are no god, a man's voice sneered. *Do you remember what I said to you in your tent at Mahrak? You are a fool, Nagash. An arrogant, deluded fool who thinks himself the equal of the gods. And look at you now: a madman, clad in rags, stumbling blindly through a dead and pitiless land.*

Shouting in rage, Nagash whirled at the voice, but his footing slipped and he tumbled head over heels to the bottom of the treacherous slope. He fetched up painfully against a small boulder. His limbs were twisted awkwardly beneath him, and at first they refused to obey his will.

As he struggled to force his body into action, Nagash became aware of a ghostly figure glaring down at him from a little further upslope. Nebunefer was a frail, ancient little man, clad in the same threadbare robes he'd worn on the day he'd died. His wrinkled head lay at an unnatural angle, the stub of broken vertebrae jutting painfully against the taut skin of his bent neck. Like Neferem, the old priest's eyes glittered with pure hate.

How the mighty have fallen, Nebunefer said. *You dare to call the mighty Ptra a parasite? He created the earth, and everything that lives upon it. What little power you possess was stolen, ripped from the souls of the innocent. It's finite, and the last sands of the hourglass have almost run out.*

'Not yet, you old fool,' Nagash snarled back. *'If you were still flesh, I would wring your neck a second time! Watch.'*

His limbs felt leaden, his joints frozen like corroded bronze, but Nagash would not be denied. Slowly, clumsily, he forced his good arm to work, and then his legs. Minutes later, he stood shakily on his feet again, but Nebunefer was gone.

'Jackals,' he spat into the darkness. *'We'll see who laughs last.'*

It took more than an hour for Nagash to climb the opposite slope, snarling curses and burning with fever all the while. His limbs were growing stiffer by the moment. He drove himself onward with nothing more than the belief that the dark mountain was just ahead, right over the top of the next ridge.

It had to be.

He would not succumb. He would not fail. He was the rightful King of Khemri, heir to Settra's throne, and by extension the master of all Nehekhara.

A faint wind hissed along the ridgeline, just a few yards out of reach. A voice drifted down to him, riding on the sandy breeze.

Usurpation is not a right, brother.

Thutep stood at the crest of the ridge, his face turned towards the moon hanging low overhead. His older brother seemed damnably at peace, staring up at Neru's beaming face. Only his fingertips, worn down to stumps of splintered bone, hinted at his last, awful moments, buried alive inside his own tomb.

'*The strong have the right to rule,*' Nagash hissed. '*You were weak. You did not deserve the throne. Khemri's fortunes suffered under your reign.*'

Thutep shrugged, never taking his eyes from the moon and the open sky. *That was the will of the gods,* he said. *You were a priest, and a prince of the realm. You wanted for nothing–*

'*Nothing except an empire,*' the Usurper said bitterly. '*Had I been first-born, the people of Khemri would have served me gladly, and the city would have prospered. If you would blame anyone, blame those damned gods you so adore. It was they who made me no more than a second son. It was their will who ultimately sealed you inside that tomb.*'

His brother had no answer to that. By the time Nagash reached the summit, Thutep was gone.

Beyond the ridge was a broad, rocky plain. The dark mountain, and its promise of power, might have loomed among the company of a dozen other peaks along the horizon to the east. Beyond their jagged summits, the sky was already paling with the light of false dawn.

There was nowhere to hide. No caves, no overhangs, no brush-covered depressions to crawl into and escape the fire of the sun. Nagash knew it would sear his skin in minutes, but that was of little concern to him. Far worse was its effects on the elixir. The older he and his immortals had become, the more that sunlight sapped the strength of their stolen vigour. When he and his armies marched to war, they moved in a perpetual darkness wrought by fearsome sorcery. Even at the peak of his powers, Nagash doubted he would have survived a full day's exposure to the sun.

As things were now, he didn't think that he'd last more than a few minutes.

Gritting his teeth, Nagash began scraping at the baked ground. Ptra could not have him. He would sooner cover himself in dirt like an animal than concede defeat to god or man.

May I be of service, great one?

The voice was soft and too sincere, the kind of tone a servant would take to mock his master to his face. It sounded right by Nagash's ear. With a monumental effort, he turned his head and glanced up at the ghostly figure kneeling by his side.

Khefru was holding out his hand to Nagash, as though to help him stand. The former priest, who had helped Nagash learn the secrets of necromancy and later conspired with him to seize the throne, smiled down at his former master through a mask of flame. As the Usurper watched, the priest's body became wreathed in sorcerous fire, just as it had centuries past when Nagash had learned of Khefru and Nekerem's betrayal.

'*Traitor,*' Nagash hissed. '*Snivelling coward! Enslaving your spirit was too good for you! I should have consumed you utterly when I had the chance.*'

To Nagash's surprise, the ghost's burning face turned bitter. *More is the pity,* Khefru said. *Better oblivion than an eternity wandering in the cold places of the world. You'll understand soon enough.* The former servant turned, gauging the time until dawn. *Not long now.*

But the Usurper refused to be cowed by the spirit's ominous words. '*Let it come!*' he said. '*What do I care if I'm freed from this broken husk of a body? You were never a match for me in life, Khefru – not you, nor Thutep, nor even Nebunefer or Neferem. You shall be my slave again, you cur. Watch and see.*'

Khefru's smile broadened as the flames bit deep into the flesh of his face. *Do you imagine that it's just the four of us? Oh, no, great one. We're just the ones who could reach you the easiest. There are others out there in the shadows, waiting for your demise. All the people of Mahrak, slaughtered in their thousands and cast adrift, without Usirian to judge them or Djaf to conduct them to the afterlife. All the soldiers of both sides who fell in the final battle, and all the skirmishes who came after, and all the common folk who perished in the famines and plagues that wracked the land afterwards. You cannot imagine so many,* the former servant said. *But you will have all eternity to entertain them.*

This time, Nagash watched the spirit go. Khefru simply stood up and walked away, without so much as a backwards glance. He headed westwards, into the fleeing shadows, and dissipated like smoke.

The scavengers heard him raving long before they actually saw him. He was lying face down in the middle of a rocky plain, spitting curses in a tongue they didn't understand and directed at nothing they could see. The wasteland had obviously driven the hairless one mad, not that it made any difference to them. His meat would taste the same regardless.

The four of them were starving. There had been six of them once upon a time, when they'd been sent from the tunnels of the Great City to scour the World Above for the hidden gifts of the Great Horned One.

During the second year of their great hunt, they'd seen the claw of their god trace a green arc across the sky, and had followed its trail into the depths of the wasteland, where they'd found a scar gouged in the packed earth and a handful of treasures nestled together like a clutch of new-laid eggs.

Great was their fortune, or so they'd believed. Great would be their glory when they returned with their bounty to the clan master! But tracing their steps back out of the cursed waste had proved much more difficult than they'd bargained for. After the first few months the food had run out, and hunting in the rat-forsaken wasteland was slim. Mad with hunger, they'd turned on one another, and the two weakest had become food for the rest.

When the last of that meat ran out, more than a month ago, the four hunters had spent weeks waiting for one of their fellows to slip up and become the next meal, but none of them were so careless. Finally, growing more and more desperate, one of the band began gnawing at the Horned God's sky-gift, in hopes of gaining the upper paw over his companions. Out of self-preservation, the other hunters began to nibble their share of the god-stone as well. It tore like a knife through their guts and set their nerves on fire, but it lent them enough vigour to survive and keep the stalemate going.

The hunters ate of the god-stone sparingly, fearing the wrath of the clan-master when they finally did manage to return to the city. Their fur was falling out in patches, and awful, glowing lesions appeared on the raw skin beneath. Catching the scent of the hairless one was a gift from the Horned One himself, they reasoned. They hoped to find enough meat on the prey's bones to last them until they could escape the wasteland and make their way home.

When they caught sight of the prey's shrivelled, leathery body they began squabbling over the spoils at once. Knives were drawn. Threats were spat. Alliances were formed and broken in the space of minutes. Finally, the leader of the little band put an end to the bickering and declared that each hunter was entitled to one of the prey's limbs. Once those were cut off, the torso would be divided four ways, and then they'd all get turns sucking the sweetmeats out of the skull. With dawn looming close on the horizon, the band grudgingly reached an agreement. They shuffled about the hairless one, choosing which limb they wanted and scheming how to steal the rest when an opportune moment arose.

The leader of the pack hefted his knife and flipped the prey onto his back – the better to get at the entrails when the time came. To their surprise, the prey was still alive, its eyes widening at the sight of the knife in the pack leader's hand. The hunters chuckled. The meal would come with a little entertainment as well.

Hissing expectantly, the pack leader bent down and grabbed the bony wrist of the prey's one good arm. He started to stretch it out for a clean cut when the hairless one reared upward with a howl and sank its teeth into the hunter's throat!

Flesh tore. Hot blood sprayed across the rocky ground, and the pack leader let out a choking squeak. The hairless one was clumsy and slow, but the hunters were weak themselves and stunned by the sudden ferocity of the attack. They barely had time to react before their would-be prey grabbed the knife from the dying pack leader's hand and buried it in the chest of the hunter to his right. Then, with an exultant howl, the hairless one leapt upon the third hunter and the two fell to the ground, stabbing wildly at one another with their knives.

In the space of just a few seconds, the pack had been all but destroyed. The realisation proved too much for the fourth hunter's fragile courage to withstand. It abandoned its pack-mates and fled squeaking into the pre-dawn shadows.

Nagash pulled the crude knife from the monster's throat. Dark blood bubbled from the wound. He bent over it at once, gulping down the hot liquid as the creature shuddered in its death throes.

The power! He could taste it in the vile thing's blood. The Usurper drank deep, marvelling at the fire that raced through his withered limbs.

When the monster was dead he leaned back, chest heaving, face bathed in gore. His emaciated body shuddered as successive waves of agony wracked it, but he welcomed the sensation for what it was. A semblance of power was coursing through his form once more, restoring to him a small amount of vitality.

One day he would thank Khefru for the incentive to try his luck with the beasts. Had he not been so persuaded to survive, the battle might not have gone half so well as it did.

The Usurper glanced about the plain, looking for where the last of the monsters had gone, but the creature had vanished from sight.

What monsters were these? For the first time, Nagash could study his attackers in detail. They looked like nothing so much as diseased men with the heads and naked tails of *rats.* They were even dressed in filthy kilts made of some sort of woven plant matter, now frayed and begrimed with the dust of the wasteland. Silver earrings glittered from their rodent-like ears, and one wore a thin, gold bracelet around its right wrist. Each of them carried bronze knives of surprising quality, as well made as anything forged in distant Ka-Sabar.

The only other possessions they carried were rough, leather bags, tightly-knotted and secured to their leather belts. Nagash reached down and tugged at the one on his last victim's belt – and felt a shock of power like a live coal burning in the palm of his hand. He dropped the bag with a start. Then after a moment's thought he carefully sliced open the side with the point of his bloody knife.

At once, a sickly green glow emanated from the slit. Working carefully with the knife, Nagash opened it further and dumped the bag's contents onto the ground.

Two small lumps of glowing green stone, each about the size of his thumb, rolled onto the hard ground. The light they cast was intense. Where it touched his bare skin it set his nerves to tingling.

Nagash reached down and carefully picked one up. Heat suffused his fingertips, radiating from the stone in a steady, buzzing stream. He inspected the stone carefully, and was shocked to find what looked like teeth marks chiselled into its rough surface. The creatures were *eating* the rock? That explained the traces of power in their blood.

The Usurper's heart began to race. The creatures must have come from the dark mountain. How else could they have come by the same power he sought? No other explanation made sense.

Already, the pain was fading from his limbs, settling into a dull ache that pulsed like a hot ember in his chest. He considered the glowing rock for a moment more, and abruptly reached a decision. Setting the stone back on the ground, he took the hilt of his knife and broke it into three smaller pieces.

With only a moment's hesitation, Nagash picked up the smallest piece and swallowed it.

Fire burst along every nerve in the Usurper's body. His muscles swelled with power; his scalp tingled until it burned. Nagash's mind reeled under the onslaught. It was far wilder and harder to channel than any power he'd known before, but the intensity was still nothing like the enormous energies he'd wielded in the past. It raged through his body, wreaking havoc on flesh and bone. He seized it with his will and directed the raging torrent where he wished it to go.

There was a crackle of bone and a creak of decayed sinew. The Usurper threw back his head and howled his suffering to the sky as his ruined left arm knit back together. Next, foul smelling smoke poured from the holes in his torso and forehead. He doubled over, still shrieking in pain, as flesh and organs were shifted aside.

Thump. Thump. Thump. One after another, three small, dark metal balls thudded to the ground, wreathed in pale greenish steam.

Seconds later, Nagash the Usurper was whole again, in body if not in mind.

The first rays of dawn were breaking over the distant peaks. With a trembling hand, Nagash gathered up the rest of the stones and tucked them back into the slit pouch. As he quickly dragged the bodies of the creatures over to him, he could sense that more stones resided in the pouches of the other creatures he'd killed.

It wasn't much, but it would be enough, the Usurper vowed. The stones would sustain him and guide him to the great mountain, where he would learn to master its fearsome power.

As Ptra's light burned overhead, Nagash curled up on the rocky ground, shielded beneath the bodies of those he'd slain, and dreamed of the doom that would befall Nehekhara.

ONE

BALANCE OF POWER

Lahmia, the City of the Dawn,
in the 70th year of Basth the Graceful
(-1650 Imperial Reckoning)

The yellow silk roof of the Hall of Rebirth rippled like a great sail in the freshening wind blowing from the coast, and its polished cedar timbers groaned like a great ship at sea. The comparison seemed particularly apt, Neferata thought bitterly, given the legion of shipwrights that had been hastily drafted to build it.

Preparations for the great Council of Kings had gone on for three solid months, beginning on the very day that the fateful news had arrived from Ka-Sabar. Even as word raced through the winding city streets that the City of Bronze had fallen at last, and the long war against the Usurper had finally come to an end, King Lamashizzar was already digging into the city treasury in anticipation of his royal peers' arrival. Commissions by the hundred flowed from the palace and descended like flocks of sea birds on the astonished city merchants and trading factors: jars of fine wine by the hundreds; casks of beer by the *thousands;* cunning gifts of gold, silver and bronze; bales of silk by the ton and a queen's ransom in fine spices and rare incense.

And that was only the beginning. Swift trading ships plied the fickle seas between Lahmia and the Eastern Empire's trading cities to bring back the finest, most exotic delicacies that the Silk Lands could produce, while the dockyards were stripped of every able hand to build a vast tent city on the Golden Plain. As spring gave way to summer it seemed as though every able-bodied man, woman and child was working feverishly to complete the king's grand design.

When the rebel leaders finally arrived, in the last month of summer, they were met at the edge of the Golden Plain by Lamashizzar himself, at the head of a richly-dressed panoply of courtesans, artists, musicians and servants. After being showered with small gifts – from rings and bracelets to fine swords and splendid chariots – the rulers were conducted across the great, fertile plain to the sprawling city of silk tents set aside for their servants and retainers. The gentle breezes that caressed the plain turned the tent city into a rippling banner of festive colour: sea green for Zandri, gold for Numas, blue for Lybaras and brilliant red for Rasetra.

The royal processions descended upon their encampments with weary delight, and allowed a few hours to rest and refresh themselves before the celebrations began in earnest. Then, at sunset, Lamashizzar and his panoply summoned his royal guests with a blare of golden trumpets and led them in a triumphant procession through the streets of his city.

The people of Lahmia commemorated the end of the war for seven ecstatic days, and from the halls of the palace to the mean streets near the dockyards, the king's royal guests were treated like saviours. They wanted for nothing, except perhaps a few hours' rest here and there between revels and enough room in their baggage to carry all of Lamashizzar's rich gifts back home with them.

It was only at the end of the week, when the king's guests were thoroughly worn out and more than a little overwhelmed by the Lahmians' wealth and generosity, that Lamashizzar convened the Council of Kings to decide the future of Nehekhara.

The great Hall of Rebirth had been built by the city's carpenters and shipwrights in the space occupied by the palace's grand royal gardens. In fact, the wooden structure encompassed the gardens themselves, creating the illusion that the council chamber was surrounded by a tamed wilderness. Brilliantly coloured songbirds, many imported at great cost from the Silk Lands, filled the space with music, while fountains burbled serenely just out of sight. Servants came and went along hidden paths, bearing refreshments to the guests, who sat around a huge, circular mahogany table in a clearing at the far end of the garden. The effect of so much vibrant, harnessed life on the desert rulers was nothing short of stunning.

The entire spectacle, from start to finish, had been calculated as carefully as any military campaign, Neferata understood. It was couched to tempt, seduce and intimidate the rulers of east and west, and muddle whatever alliances they might have forged against Lahmia's interests. It was also stupendously, ruinously *expensive*. The city's treasury was virtually empty. All of the wealth that their father Lamasheptra had so carefully built during the dark years of Nagash's reign was gone. Their last reserves had been thrown away on a single, extravagant throw of the dice. There was not enough gold in the coffers to make even a quarter of the coming year's payment to the Eastern Empire; if Lamashizzar's negotiations did not bear fruit, the City of the Dawn faced certain disaster.

While the king gambled with his city's future, Neferata was left to watch the proceedings from a broad balcony that spanned the rear of the great hall and overlooked the great council table. Her handmaidens lounged on silk cushions and ate candied dates while they gossiped in hushed tones about the scandals from the previous week's celebrations. A delicate fog of incense curled just above their heads: myrrh spiced with black lotus, to relieve the boredom. Servants knelt at the fringes of the chamber alert to the queen's every need. A low table, with sheets of paper and an ink brush, had been hastily set beside her as she studied the visiting rulers from behind a polished wooden screen.

As precarious as Lahmia's future might be, judging by the appearance of their guests it was evident to Neferata that the other great cities were in a far worse state. During his unnatural reign, Nagash the Usurper had recreated the Nehekharan Empire in principle if not in name, subjugating the other great cities through the power he held over Khemri's hostage queen, Neferem.

For centuries, each city had been forced to pay tribute to the Usurper in the form of gold and slaves, driving them to the brink of ruin. When the priests of Khemri – at the urging of their superiors on the Hieratic Council in Mahrak – finally attempted to unseat Nagash and end his blasphemous reign, the Usurper retaliated with a terrible curse that struck down two-thirds of Nehekhara's priesthood in the space of a single day.

It was that one act of infamy that finally caused the priest kings to rise up in revolt, but the Usurper fought back with dark magics and terrible atrocities that devastated the Blessed Land and slaughtered thousands. Yet even when the Usurper's army was finally defeated, close to a dozen of his immortal lieutenants escaped destruction and continued to bedevil the land for decades.

Rather than celebrate their hard-won triumph at Mahrak, the Priest Kings were faced with a long, gruelling campaign of terror and attrition as they hunted down every last one of the Usurper's minions. Since Nagash's body had never been found, it was secretly feared that one of them still possessed the Usurper's corpse and, if given the opportunity, might be able to restore the dreaded necromancer to life. It had taken ninety years to finish the task, slaying the last of Nagash's immortals after a lengthy siege at Ka-Sabar, the City of Bronze.

The long years of war had left an indelible mark on each of Nehekhara's rulers. They were gaunt from strain and deprivation that no amount of easy living could ever erase. Few wore jewellery, or gilt adornments on their robes of state, and the fine fabrics of their ceremonial attire seemed shabby and worn. Even now, amid the verdant luxury of the great hall, their expressions were haunted and fretful, as though they expected fresh horrors hiding in every shadow.

Neferata was vividly reminded of that night in the cellars, now decades past, when Lamashizzar and his cabal had returned from the war. *And they'd scarcely fought more than a handful of battles, while these men and women have known nothing else their entire lives,* she thought.

Yet as beleaguered and broken as these rulers might be, they were not to be underestimated, the queen knew. When the doors to the great hall were opened, Lamashizzar's guests had filed through the gardens in solemn procession, led by the Priest Kings of Rasetra and Lybaras and the young Queen of Numas. Each of the three rulers bore a sandalwood box in their hands, and when they reached the great council table they set the boxes before the smiling Lahmian king and drew forth their contents.

The severed heads of Raamket, the Red Lord, and Atan-Heru, the Great Beast, had been treated with nitre and the sacred oils of the mortuary cult, and looked much as they had at the moment of their deaths. Their pale skin was mottled with burns from the touch of the sun, and their lips were drawn back in savage, almost bestial snarls, revealing teeth that had been filed to points and stained brown with human blood. The third head, by comparison, was round and fleshy as a suckling pig's, with small, beady eyes hidden by a thick band of kohl.

Memnet, the former Grand Hierophant of Ka-Sabar, who murdered his king and served Nagash in exchange for eternal life, had wailed like a babe as he was dragged before the headsman. An expression of craven terror was still etched on Memnet's jowly face.

The heads still sat in the centre of the table, their hideous expressions turned to face Lamashizzar. The message – to Neferata, at least – was clear. *We've done our part, while you sat in your city by the sea. Now you'll help us rebuild, or there might be one more head on this table by day's end.* At this point, it was difficult to say whether Lamashizzar's display of wealth had successfully undermined his guests, or simply strengthened their resolve.

The queen bit her lip in irritation. We should be deciding this on the battlefield, she thought. We can always make more soldiers. Gold is much harder to come by.

It was mid-afternoon. The council had been in session for almost five hours, during which time Lamashizzar enquired of the needs of each of his guests and made offers of assistance in the form of monetary loans and trade agreements. Dizzying sums of gold were haggled over, while scribes hurriedly drafted copies of proposals that would govern the flow of goods across Nehekhara for generations to come.

Trade with the Eastern Empire would rejuvenate the Blessed Land's economy, and open up a vast new realm of markets for Nehekharan goods – and all of it would pass through the City of the Dawn. Each of the rulers had been given the chance to speak, and a brief lull had settled over the table while each of the council members took stock of their current positions. Off to the east came a distant grumble of thunder as a late-summer rain shower made its way towards the coast.

Neferata heard a rustle of cushions behind her, followed by a familiar cat-like tread as her young cousin Khalida came to sit beside her.

'Great Gods, is it finally over?' the girl asked, slumping theatrically onto the queen's lap. 'We've been trapped in here *forever*. I wanted to go out riding before the rain came in.'

Neferata chuckled despite herself. Khalida hadn't the least interest in courtly gossip or affairs of state. At fifteen she was tall and coltish, full of so much restless energy that even the sprawling Women's Palace wasn't large enough to contain her. She was much like her father, Lord Wakhashem, a wealthy nobleman and close ally of King Lamasheptra, who had secured a strategic marriage to Neferata's aunt Semunet. Both had died when Khalida was very young, and according to tradition she had been returned to the keeping of the royal family until such time as a husband could be found for her. She was passionate about horses, archery – even swordplay – and had little interest in the finer aspects of courtly behaviour. Lamashizzar dismayed of ever finding a nobleman who would take Khalida, but Neferata was secretly proud of her.

The queen reached down and stroked the girl's dark hair. She kept it in dozens of tight, oiled braids, like the Numasi horse-maidens of legend. 'The real work has scarcely begun, little hawk,' Neferata said fondly. 'Up until now, the council has merely argued matters of taxes and trade. Trivial matters, in the grander scheme of things.'

Khalida looked up at the queen. The goddess Asaph hadn't blessed her with the radiant beauty that Neferata and most of the Lahmian royal bloodline possessed. She was striking, in a fierce, angular way, with a sharp nose, a small, square chin and dark, piercing eyes. She frowned. 'Trivial compared to what?'

The queen smiled. 'Compared to power, of course. The decisions made here will determine the balance of power in Nehekhara for centuries to come. Each of the rulers seated below us has their own idea of how that balance should be struck.'

Khalida took the end of one of her braids between her fingers and twirled it thoughtfully. 'Then who decides which idea is best?'

'We do, at the moment.' *And Lamashizzar had best exploit this opportunity to the fullest.* Neferata took Khalida by the shoulders and pulled her gently upright. 'Pay attention to something other than horses for a moment and I'll try to explain.'

Khalida sighed heavily. 'If it will make the time go faster.'

The queen nodded approvingly. 'It begins with Khemri,' she said. 'Since the time of Settra the Magnificent, the living city was the centre of power in Nehekhara. Even after Settra's empire fell, the Living City and its mortuary cult exerted tremendous political and economic influence from one end of the Blessed Land to the other. Their interests were guaranteed before all others, and that translated to power, comfort and security. Next in line came Mahrak, the City of the Gods, then Ka-Sabar, Numas, Lybaras, Zandri, Lahmia and Quatar.'

'Numas was more powerful than Lybaras?' Khalida exclaimed. 'They're farmers, mostly. Lybaras had airships!'

'The Numasi provided the grain for most of Nehekhara,' the queen said patiently. 'You can't eat an airship, little hawk.'

'I suppose,' the girl said. 'But what about us? Why were we so low on the list?'

Neferata sighed. 'Because we were so distant from Khemri, for starters. Zandri was closer, and was somewhat richer due to the slave trade. And unlike other cities, we preferred to keep to ourselves.'

'But Nagash changed all that.'

'That's right. Khemri is nothing but ruins now, as well as Mahrak, and most of the other cities suffered greatly thanks to the Usurper. Now that the war is over, everything lies in flux.'

It was then that King Lamashizzar's voice rose above the muted murmur of the hall. 'My honoured friend, Priest King Khepra; do you wish to address the council?'

A heavy wooden chair creaked as Khepra, Priest King of Lybaras, rose slowly to his feet. The son of the late King Hekhmenukep looked much like his illustrious father: he was tall and lean, with narrow shoulders and a square-jawed, hangdog face. Unlike his father, though, Khepra's arms and shoulders were thick with muscle, and his hands and face bore the scars of dozens of battlefields.

Like the kings of Lybaras before him, Khepra wore a fine gold chain about his neck, hung with a bewildering assortment of glass lenses bound in gold, silver or copper wire. It was a relic from a more prosperous, peaceful age, when the engineer-priests of Lybaras crafted wondrous inventions for the greater glory of Tahoth, patron god of scholars.

The king nodded to Lamashizzar. 'Great king, on behalf of your esteemed guests, I wish to thank you for this splendid display of generosity on our behalf. I'm also grateful to see that all of us have come together today to ensure the continued prosperity of our great cities, and the land of Nehekhara as a whole. It is a welcome beginning, but there are still very serious matters that require our attention.'

Neferata's eyes narrowed. 'Now it begins, little hawk. Watch the faces of the rulers around the table. How are they reacting to the Lybaran king?'

The young girl frowned, but did as she was told. 'Well... they're looking curious, I suppose. Politely interested.' She paused, her head tilting slightly to one side. 'Except for the King of Rasetra.'

'Oh?' the queen asked, smiling faintly.

'He's not even looking at Khepra. He's pretending to sip his wine, but really he's watching everyone else.'

Neferata nodded approvingly. 'Now you know who is truly asking the question. King Khepra is speaking on Rasetra's behest, while King Shepret can devote his full attention to gauging the reactions of his rivals.'

Rasetra and Lybaras had been close allies during the war, and had borne the brunt of the fighting from beginning to end. Whatever it was that Rasetra was now after, King Shepret could almost certainly count on Khepra's support in the council. She'd tried to warn Lamashizzar to find a way to drive a wedge between the two kings; if he didn't one of the other kings wouldn't hesitate to try.

Neferata turned to the table at her side and picked up the waiting ink brush. She wrote hurriedly in the sharp-edged pictographs of the Eastern Empire's trading cant: *Divide Rasetra and Lybaras, or they will outmanoeuvre you!*

She paused, tapping the end of the brush against her lower lip as a thought occurred to her. *King Khepra's son is in need of a wife. Perhaps Khalida?*

She plucked a pinch of fine-grained sand from a tiny box by the ink-pot and scattered it across the pictographs to help set the ink, then held out the page for a servant to carry downstairs to the king.

'While we now have plans in place to ensure the stability of our own homes, there are still three cities that are desolate and devoid of leadership,' the King of Lybaras said. 'We cannot sit idly by and watch them fall to ruin.'

'Generous words from a man who just spent the last four years desolating one of the very cities in question,' Lamashizzar replied good-naturedly. The other rulers laughed at the gentle jibe, but for a moment King Khepra was put on the back foot. He faltered for a moment, unable to come up with a proper response.

'The city of Ka-Sabar is the least of our concerns at the moment,' King Shepret said in a flat voice. He was lean and muscular, with his late father's broad shoulders, but where the legendary king Rakh-amn-hotep was stout and pugnacious, Shepret had the aquiline features of an up-country patrician. Though he was just over a hundred years old, well into middle age, his thick black hair only showed a few streaks of grey, and his green eyes were as vivid and sharp as cut emeralds. 'The Living City has lain in ruins for almost a century.' He set down his wine cup and turned his piercing gaze on Lamashizzar. 'Now that the war is over, we must reclaim the city and restore the rightful order of things.'

Agitated murmurs rose around the council table. Khalida grinned. 'Lamashizzar made Shepret state his own case,' she said proudly. She glanced sidelong at Neferata. 'That is what happened, right?'

Neferata sighed. 'With Lamashizzar it's difficult to tell, sometimes. But possibly, yes.'

'But why does King Shepret care about restoring the Living City? Doesn't he have enough worries with the lizard folk?'

The queen gave her young cousin an appraising stare. Apparently Khalida wasn't as oblivious to matters of state as she appeared to be. Rasetra was the smallest of the great cities, but because of its proximity to the deadly southern jungles and its tribes of Lizard Folk, their army was second to none. But the war had bled Rasetra white, and now the city was fighting for its survival against growing attacks by lizard war parties.

Neferata considered the question carefully. 'It's not entirely unexpected,' she said. 'Rasetra was originally settled by Khemri, just a few hundred years ago. When King Shepret talks of putting another king on Khemri's throne, he means one of his own sons. They're directly related to the old royal family, and have an unassailable claim. It would give Rasetra a powerful ally on the western side of the Bitter Peaks, and allow it to exert its influence across all of Nehekhara.'

At the council table, Lamashizzar cleared his throat, and the murmurs fell silent. 'That's a very noble goal, honoured friend,' the king said, 'but also a daunting one. Khemri lies empty now. Only jackals and restless ghosts prowl the city streets.'

King Shepret nodded. As a young man, he'd been with his father's army when they'd reached Khemri, just a few months after the battle at Mahrak. He'd seen the city's sand-choked streets firsthand. 'According to my sources, many of Khemri's citizens fled to Bel Aliad, hoping to begin a new life there.' He shrugged. 'They could be resettled again, with the proper incentive.'

Khalida let out a snort. 'At the end of a spear, he means.'

The girl was absolutely right, Neferata realised. She turned quickly and took up the ink brush again. *Give Shepret what he wants,* she wrote. *Give him Khemri.* A servant scurried forwards and plucked the message from the queen's outstretched hand.

Khalida watched the servant go. 'Does the king actually follow your advice?'

'It's been known to happen,' Neferata replied.

'Is it true you actually ruled the city when he was fighting against Nagash, all those years ago?'

The question took Neferata aback. 'Who told you that?'

'Oh,' Khalida said, suddenly uncomfortable. 'No one in particular. Everybody knows it - inside the Women's Palace, at least.'

'Well, it's nothing that needs to be repeated elsewhere,' the queen warned. 'Other cities may treat their queens differently, but here in Lahmia, such things are not done.' She paused, uncertain of how much she should reveal. 'Let's just say that it was a difficult time, and we were at a delicate stage of negotiations with the Eastern Empire. I... consulted with Grand Vizier Ubaid on a number of important matters while the king was away. Nothing more.'

Khalida nodded thoughtfully, and turned to regard the council once more. 'Shepret would have been right about my age back then,' she mused. 'He looks so *old* now. Yet you and Lamashizzar still look as young as thirty-year-olds.'

Neferata stiffened. You see much more than I give you credit for, little hawk.

For the last nine decades, Lamashizzar and his cabal had been hard at work deciphering Nagash's tomes and trying to replicate his elixir of immortality. For the first few years the king had consulted her regularly, and despite her misgivings, she'd helped explain the necromancer's basic methods in crafting potions and performing incantations. Relinquishing control of the city to Lamashizzar had been much harder to bear than she'd imagined; experimenting with Nagash's books had at least given her something to *do*. Returning to a quiet, cloistered life in the Women's Palace seemed like a fate worse than death.

It had taken them four years of trial and error before they managed to create a very weak version of the elixir. After that, Lamashizzar no longer summoned her from the Women's Palace. She received a small bottle of the potion every month, which managed to slow the process of ageing, but nothing more. As far as she knew, Lamashizzar and his noblemen still experimented with the process, in an unused wing of the palace. She had no idea what had eventually become of Arkhan, the king's immortal prisoner.

'My brother and I have been very fortunate,' Neferata replied, as casually as she could manage. 'The blessings of Asaph run strong in the royal bloodline. They always have.'

Khalida chuckled. 'I hope I'm half so lucky when I'm a hundred years old,' she said.

'Time will tell,' the queen replied, eager to change the subject. 'What's was King Teremun saying just now?'

The young girl blinked. 'Ah... I think he asked Shepret what he meant by restoring the rightful order. Something to that effect.'

As Neferata considered the question, Shepret turned to the King of Zandri and replied. 'The will of the people has been worn thin by a century of warfare. We need to send a clear sign that the age of Nagash is no more. There needs to be a new king on Settra's throne, and a Daughter of the Sun at his side.'

Neferata drew in a sharp breath. That was clever, Shepret, the queen thought. Very clever indeed.

It was a proposal almost guaranteed to win Lahmia's support. From the time of Settra the Magnificent, the Priest Kings of Khemri were married to the eldest daughter of the Lahmian royal line. The Lahmian king's first-born daughter was called the Daughter of the Sun, because she was the living embodiment of the covenant between the gods and the people of the Blessed Land. The marriage was meant to create a union between the spiritual and temporal power of Settra's throne, and it had been one of the cornerstones of Khemri's power ever since.

Clearly, the King of Rasetra was proposing an alliance with Lahmia, one that, in theory, would benefit both cities. It was also something that none of the other great cities would stand for.

As if on cue, Queen Amunet of Numas turned in her chair to face Shepret. She was the daughter of Seheb, one of the twin kings of the city, and the only survivor after the vicious cycle of fratricide that occurred in the wake of the twins' sudden deaths. She had eyes as black as onyx and a smile like a hungry jackal.

'You're putting the chariot before the horse, King Shepret,' the Queen of Numas said dryly. 'Lamashizzar and his queen have to actually produce children before your dream can become a reality.'

The rest of the council responded with nervous laughter – all except for the sickly King Naeem of Quatar, who planted trembling hands onto the tabletop and pushed himself to his feet. Naeem was of an age with his peers, but as a young acolyte he'd been among those trapped at Mahrak during Nagash's ten-year siege, and he'd never truly recovered from the suffering he'd endured there. His body was painfully gaunt, his head bald and his cheeks sunken. When he spoke, his voice was little more than a whisper, but his rheumy eyes burned with conviction.

'King Shepret speaks of restoring the proper order of things, but his priorities are misplaced,' Naeem declared. 'The greatest of the Usurper's crimes was that he broke the sacred covenant between the people and their gods. The blessings that have sustained us for millennia are slipping away. The sands press a little closer to our cities each year, and our harvests are dwindling. Our people suffer a little more each year from sickness, and do not live the same span of years as our ancestors. Unless we find a way to redeem ourselves in the eyes of the gods, within a few hundred years Nehekhara will be a kingdom of the dead.'

Khalida's eyes widened. 'Is this true?'

Neferata's lips pressed together in irritation. 'I haven't had the opportunity to measure the size of our fields lately,' she answered. 'It certainly sounds ominous enough, but remember that Naeem was a priest long before he became a king, so his convictions are more than a little suspect.'

The young girl frowned. 'What does that mean?'

'Wait and listen.'

Down at the council table, Lamashizzar spoke. 'What, then, would you have us do?' he said to Naeem.

From the look on Naeem's face, the answer seemed obvious to him. 'Why, the people must first be reminded of their duty to the gods!' he replied. 'We must spare no effort to rebuild Mahrak, and restore the Hieratic Council to its proper place in Nehekharan society.'

'Now we get to the heart of the matter,' the queen said to Khalida. 'Naeem has been listening to those bitter old buzzards that have roosted in his court.'

Throughout the history of Nehekhara, the Hieratic Council had presumed to speak on behalf of the gods themselves, issuing edicts and meddling in the affairs of kings from their seat of power at Mahrak. With temples in every one of the great cities and religious advisors in all of the royal courts, their wealth and influence had been tremendous. Their grip on Nehekharan society had finally been broken by the Usurper, and since the fall of Mahrak the remnants of the council had taken refuge at Quatar, where they continued to issue dire warnings about the passing of the old ways. As far as Nefereta was aware, none of Nehekhara's rulers seemed willing to listen to their harangues any more. Their divine powers had faded, and the glories of the Ushabti, their holy champions, were nothing more than a fading memory. Their day was done.

Lamashizzar raised a placating hand. 'Your piety does you great credit, King Naeem,' he said smoothly, 'and I'm sure that all of our friends here would agree that we would like to see the council restored to Mahrak one day. Of course, I don't need to tell you, of all people, how our cities have suffered during this long war–'

'If it wasn't for the Hieratic Council, none of us would be sitting here today!' Naeem shot back. His watery eyes widened in righteous indignation. 'It was they who forged the great alliance between Rasetra and Lybaras! They who financed the building of the armies and the engines of war! We owe them–'

'No one here has claimed otherwise,' Lamashizzar replied, his voice taking on a steely edge. 'Just as no one here has claimed to possess the resources to rebuild Khemri, either.'

Neferata straightened. Don't be a fool, brother, she thought. You have a golden opportunity here. Don't squander it!

'For a century, everyone here has given much in the service of the common good,' Lamashizzar continued, conveniently overlooking the fact that half of the cities represented at the table sided with Nagash up until the very last moment outside Mahrak. 'I think the gods would forgive us if we now focused on regaining our strength, if only for a short while. Vast restoration projects are, in my opinion, a bit premature at this point. Does anyone disagree?'

The King of Quatar glared archly at the assembled rulers, but even Shepret sat back in his chair and stared silently into his wine cup. Neferata clenched her fists in frustration.

'Then we are all in agreement,' Lamashizzar said. 'But I thank both King Naeem and King Shepret for making their concerns known to us. I'm confident that when the time is right, we will no doubt revisit these proposals and give them due consideration.' Smiling, the Lahmian king rose to his feet. 'For now, though, may I suggest we adjourn and refresh ourselves before the evening's feast?'

King Naeema looked as though he would protest Lamashizzar's suggestion, but he was pre-empted by Queen Amunet and Fadil, the young King of Zandri, who rose to their feet without a word and took their leave of the council. Servants and scribes rose to their feet, swarming around the table, and the King of Quatar had no choice but to gather up his retainers and leave with what little dignity remained to him.

'Thank Asaph,' Khalida said with a sigh. 'King Naeem looked like he was ready to argue all night long.' She turned to Neferata, her expression hopeful. 'Shall we return to the Women's Palace now?'

'Go on,' Neferata told her. 'Take the maids with you. I'll be along presently.'

Khalida's eyes widened. 'I– I mean, I don't think that's very wise–'

'I must speak to Lamashizzar,' the queen said, anger seeping into her voice. 'In private. Do as I say, little hawk.'

The young girl shot to her feet as though stung, and within moments she was herding the bemused handmaidens from the balcony. As soon as they were gone, Neferata snatched her mask from a nervous-looking servant and stormed down the stairs to the lower floor.

She found Lamashizzar along one of the twisting garden pathways that led from the council space. The king was surrounded by a number of senior scribes, who were presenting drafts of various trade agreements for his approval. He looked up as she approached, and the self-satisfied smile on his face vanished.

'I must speak to you,' Neferata said icily. 'Now.'

The king's eyes narrowed angrily, but Neferata met his stare without flinching. After a long moment he dismissed the scribes, who wasted no time withdrawing down the garden path.

'I'm starting to think W'soran was right, all those years ago,' he growled at her. 'You seem to have a problem with understanding your place, sister.'

Neferata stepped close to him, turning her masked face up to his. 'Did you read a single thing I wrote, brother? I made the words as simple as I could,' she hissed. The vehemence in her voice surprised even herself, but she was too frustrated to hold it back. 'Give. Khemri. To. Shepret. Is that too complex an idea for you to grasp?'

'Why in the name of all the gods would I do such a thing?' Lamashizzar snarled. 'Hand control of Khemri to Rasetra? It's ridiculous!'

'It was the perfect opportunity to cripple our most dangerous rival!' Neferata shot back, her voice echoing within the confines of the mask. It took all of her self-control not to tear the damned thing off and fling it into her brother's smug face. 'Don't you see? Rasetra hasn't the strength to rebuild Khemri *and* keep the lizard folk at bay simultaneously! Shepret's greed would have been his undoing. All we had to do was sit back and give him our blessing!'

'And deprive ourselves of a major trading partner? Are you insane?' the king snapped. 'Has the black lotus permanently dulled your senses? These trade agreements will pay our debt to the Eastern Empire and cement Lahmia as the centre of power in Nehekhara.'

'Are you really as naïve as all that?' the queen replied. 'Our *honoured friends* won't abide by those agreements one moment more than they have to. As soon as they've restored their cities and rebuilt their armies, they'll form a coalition and force us to negotiate terms that are more to their liking. Did you learn nothing from the war with Nagash?'

The king's hand shot out, seizing Neferata's jaw and gripping it with surprising strength. 'Don't speak of things you know nothing about,' he warned. 'I should never have let you advise Ubaid in my absence. It put too many dangerous ideas in your head.' He shoved her roughly backwards. 'If you know what's good for you, you'll concern yourself with more proper matters, like providing me with an heir. Or would you rather I stopped sending you bottles of elixir every month? I can always marry Khalida once you're dead and gone.'

Lamashizzar's words cut through Neferata like a knife. And it was no empty threat, she could see the truth of it in his eyes. She was trapped. He could withhold Nagash's elixir any time he liked and simply wait for her to die.

Rapid footfalls sounded down the garden path. Neferata turned to see a pair of royal guardsmen appear, obviously drawn by the heated exchange. Lamashizzar acknowledged them with a curt nod.

'The queen has grown overexcited from the events of the day,' he told them. 'Conduct her to the Women's Palace at once, and inform her maids that she's to be given a draught to help her rest.'

Lamashizzar took the queen by the arm and handed her to the guards as though she were a child. Neferata felt herself moving, as though in the grip of a dream, as the warriors took her back to her gilded prison.

TWO

THE BURNING STONE

The Bitter Sea,
in the 76th year of Asaph the Beautiful
(-1600 Imperial Reckoning)

As it happened, using the glowing stone never did lead Nagash to the slopes of the dark mountain. If anything, it confused his course further, leading him ever deeper into the heart of the wasteland. It was a mystery that took him more than a hundred years to solve, during which time he was forced to re-learn the sorcerous arts that had made him master of Nehekhara.

The properties of the glowing rock – over time Nagash simply called it *abn-i-khat*, or 'the burning stone' – were similar in principle to the winds of magic he'd learned from his druchii tutors centuries ago, but not as easily manipulated using the rituals he'd mastered in Khemri. As near as he could tell, it wasn't truly a stone at all, but a physical manifestation of pure magic. If he used a fragment of stone as the locus of a simple ritual, the mineral consumed itself, converting to a dry, ashy substance that flaked away from its outer surface. The conversion was proportional to the amount of energy used, so far as he could determine; more than once he bitterly regretted the lack of paper and ink to document his observations. He'd learned over time how to ration the stone perfectly: a single thumbnail-sized chip provided him with enough strength and mental acuity to fulfil his needs for as much as a month, provided he didn't need to draw unduly upon its power. The flecks sustained him far better than his elixir ever did, but its chaotic energies sometimes caused his thoughts to become unmoored, or his perceptions to shift in unexpected ways.

If not kept under careful control, the stone wrought physical changes as well. His skin had retained its leathery texture, but it had taken on a green-tinged alabaster tone. As soon as he'd understood the stone's transformative properties he focused his attention on channelling it to good use as much as possible; now he was stronger and swifter than ever before, and virtually tireless for days at a time. Lately his skin was growing mottled with faintly luminescent deposits around his shoulders and midsection, leading him to wonder how much of the stone he ate was accumulating in his bones and organs. Would there eventually come a point where its energies became too concentrated for him to control? He reluctantly conceded the possibility, even as he continued to consume the glowing stone.

Time had no meaning in the trackless expanse of the wasteland. Nagash no longer marked the passage of days, focusing all his attentions on unlocking the powers of the stone and shaping rituals to harness its power. The first rite he experimented on was creating a resonance between a fleck of stone and the source it had stemmed from.

The results were initially very disappointing. Over time, as he began to grasp the mineral's properties more closely, the experiments became merely baffling. It wasn't that the resonance failed to draw him in a distinct direction – it pointed him in a multitude of directions at the same time, including straight up and straight down. Following the many paths the ritual revealed to him caused Nagash to cross and re-cross the length and breadth of the wasteland. From time to time he would find pieces of stone, sometimes buried deep beneath the ground, but none led him towards the dark mountain. After a time, he began to think that the fickle energies of the stone were somehow *purposely* leading him astray.

Then one night, he saw a streak of green light arc across the starlit sky, and another piece of the puzzle fell into place.

Whatever the *abn-i-khat* was, it truly was not of this earth – or at least not part of the earth that Nagash knew and understood. He marked the plunging arc of green light as a soldier might trace the fall of an arrow shot, and then began a long and arduous trek to find where the stone had fallen. Eventually he came upon a shallow crater dug into the earth. Pieces of the green stone were nowhere to be found, but large, rat-like footprints were in abundance. The beasts had made it to the site mere hours before he did. Nagash tried to track them further, but soon lost their spoor across the hard, rocky terrain. After that, he resolved to kill the rat-beasts wherever he found them, for clearly they coveted the stone at least as much as he did.

Nagash mulled over everything he'd learned, and concluded firstly that if he'd been able to detect the power radiating from the mountain at such a distance, it must contain a much larger collection of *abn-i-khat* than he'd ever seen before, and its chaotic energies made magical divination difficult, if not impossible. So he abandoned his ritual and let his instincts guide him, heading ever eastward over the ridges and foothills and leaving his senses open for concentrations of magical power.

It was the hazy glow to the north-east that drew him first – a faint, greenish luminescence that limned the crooked lines of the mountain peaks, almost too faint to see against the paling of the early morning sky. He was well beyond the foothills now, crossing the first of the Brittle Peaks, and the sensations of power seemed to shift directions like the fey mountain wind.

Like everything else about the wasteland, the glow seemed just a few miles distant, but it took him nearly a fortnight to reach the last of the intervening peaks. From there, Nagash found himself staring down upon a broad, dark sea. The night was early, and the glow he'd seen on previous nights wasn't in evidence yet, allowing him to see a long way in the clear mountain air. Marshlands glittered frostily beneath the moonlight along the sea's south-eastern shore, while a broad crescent of watch fires flickered along the coastline to the north and north-west.

None of that mattered to Nagash. To the east, hard by the shores of the gloomy sea, rose the dark slopes of the mountain that had called to him for more than a hundred years. It was larger and far more imposing than the broken peaks that surrounded it; tendrils of steam leaked from fissures along its flanks, glowing faintly green in the darkness. It dominated the horizon for miles, crouching at the edge of the sea like a brooding dragon from some barbarian myth.

Looking upon the mountain, Nagash realised he had never actually seen it with his own eyes before that moment. The shadow of the power buried at its heart had somehow etched itself upon his mind's eye. Now he understood why it had always seemed to hide, just out of his grasp, no matter how hard he tried to reach it. All this time he'd been chasing a phantasm, a ghost of the true mountain. The notion both intrigued and troubled him.

Nagash reckoned that there could be dozens, perhaps even scores of stone deposits hidden within the mountain. How could they have been gathered all in one place? His gaze strayed to the constellation of watch fires lining the northern coast. Perhaps it was the rat-things. They were gathering up the stones faster than he. It all had to be going somewhere.

He would have to learn more before proceeding. The secrets of the mountain would be his, no matter what; he would need every bit of power he could muster to re-conquer Nehekhara and punish those who had defied him. If the rat-things stood in his way, then he would deal with them as well.

It took most of the night for Nagash to descend the far slope of the mountain and make his way to the outskirts of the marshland. In the early hours before dawn, when the night was coldest, a thick blanket of glowing mist rose from the marshlands and along the shores of the distant sea. The vapours curled and shifted across the surface of the water, though there was no wind to stir them; the unearthly light created the illusion of half-formed shapes capering and whirling madly within the mist.

The marsh terrain was more dense and treacherous than Nagash realised. He sloshed through foul-smelling, scummy water that rose up to mid-thigh in places. It was unnervingly warm, and where it touched his skin he felt the faintest brush of sorcerous energy. The necromancer considered the tendrils of steam writhing like serpents across the flank of the distant mountain.

If there were enough burning stone buried within the mountain to taint the neighbouring sea, his vengeance upon the living world would be great indeed.

He wound between hummocks of thick, yellow marsh grass and stunted trees, listening to slithering, splashing creatures hunting through the mist. Strange howls and high-pitched cries echoed from the moss-covered branches of the trees, and once he saw a pair of faintly glowing yellow eyes regarding him intently from the shadows to the left of his path. But the creatures of the marsh shunned him, as all living beasts did. More than once he heard something huge rise up in the mist ahead of him and go thrashing off into the water at his approach. When the sun finally broke over the horizon, hours later, he crawled into a muddy hollow formed by the thick roots of a half-dead tree and waited for nightfall.

Voices and the sounds of thrashing water roused him from his meditations, many hours later. Darkness had fallen, though the moon was still low in the sky, and as he crept to the edge of the tree's sheltering roots he could see a yellow haze of lantern light playing upon the surface of the water.

The voices sounded human, guttural and strained with effort. There were at least two speakers, perhaps three, calling out to one another in a barbarian tongue unlike anything Nagash had heard before. It was difficult to tell how far away the voices were, the sounds echoing flatly from the surface of the water and the surrounding trees.

Nagash eased carefully from his hiding place, head low, and searched for the source of the noise. The thrashing continued unabated, punctuated by grunts and muffled blows. It was coming from beyond a screen of moss-covered trees just a few dozen yards away. The glow of lanterns seeped between the gnarled trunks, flickering crazily as struggling figures moved past the source of the light.

The necromancer still carried two of the large bronze daggers he'd looted from the corpses of the rat-things so many years ago. He drew one of the blades from his leather belt and crept from tree to tree until finally he caught sight of the source of the noise.

Peering through a screen of hanging moss, Nagash saw a wider patch of water just past the hummock where he stood. Perhaps ten yards away a low, flat-bottomed boat had poled up close to another small, tree-covered hummock, and within the globe of light cast by the lantern set at its bow, four men were wrestling with the thrashing body of what appeared to be a huge, whiskered fish. Two of the men stood up to their waists in the murky water, their arms thrown around the fish's scaly flanks as they tried to heave it up into the boat. A third stood in the boat and tried to grip the creature's flat, toothy head, while the fourth tried to kill it with blows from a short, thick club. From where Nagash stood, it was difficult to tell which side was winning the fight.

The men were barbarians; that much he saw at once, but they had little in common with the tall, fair-haired northerners sold on the slave block at Zandri. Their bodies were short and squat, thick with muscle but deformed in different ways. He saw hunchbacks and misshapen skulls, long, ape-like arms and bulging, knobby spines. Their heads were hairless, and their skin was a sickly, pale green. The men in the boat wore simple, belted kilts of rough leather that hung below their knees, and their chests were decorated in swirling scar patterns similar to Nehekharan tattoos.

So it wasn't the rat-creatures who inhabited the north shore after all, Nagash realised. Clearly these barbarians had lived close to the tainted waters for much, if not all their short, squalid lives. The mutations wrought by the burning stone appeared pervasive. The necromancer's eyes narrowed thoughtfully. With a little patient study, these men could teach him a great deal.

Sticking to the deep shadows, Nagash crept around the edges of the wide pool while the barbarians struggled to finish off their prey. The noise of their struggles masked his movements, until finally he reached the far side of the hummock next to their boat.

The sounds of thrashing abruptly ceased. Nagash heard the barbarians whooping and laughing, and then the sounds of feet tramping through foliage just a few yards away. Carefully, he eased through the undergrowth towards the sounds.

Within moments, lantern light was seeping between the mossy trees. Nagash heard the scrape of wood on soil, and then a meaty *thud* on the ground nearby. Peering around the bole of a gnarled old tree, he saw that the barbarians had grounded their little boat and dragged their monster catch up onto dry land to clean it and cut away the meat. The fish was huge – easily six feet long – and almost as thick as a human torso. The scales along its back were a dark grey, grimed with muck from the bottom of the pool, and its wide mouth was full of small, black, triangular teeth.

The two men who had wrestled the thing from its hiding place beneath the water had pulled on heavy, oiled leather cloaks and stood tiredly over their catch, their mud-streaked chests heaving, filthy water streaming down their legs. One of their companions was digging a leather-wrapped bundle out of the bottom of the boat, while the fourth man was busy tying the craft to the branch of a nearby tree.

Sensing his opportunity, Nagash slipped silently from the shadows beneath the tree and crept across the small clearing where the men had set down their catch. Being careful not to startle the barbarians, he walked quietly up behind one of the cloaked men. At the last moment, just as Nagash came within arm's reach, the man must have sensed his presence. The barbarian whirled about, his powerful hands poised to seize whatever was creeping up behind him. The man must have been expecting an animal of some kind, because when he saw Nagash, his beady eyes widened with surprise.

Before the barbarian could recover, Nagash darted in quickly and slashed his throat with the rat-beast's dagger. Blood splashed across the clearing and the man collapsed with a choking scream.

Nagash turned on the second cloaked man just as the barbarian leapt at him with a guttural shout. He managed to get his left hand around the man's throat as they crashed together, nearly knocking him from his feet. A stubby-fingered hand seized Nagash's knife wrist and held it in a vice-like grip, while jagged fingernails clawed for his eyes. Nagash tightened his grip on the barbarian's throat and tried to pull his knife hand free, but the man refused to let go. A knobby fist smashed into the side of the necromancer's skull; he responded by driving his knee into the barbarian's groin. The man roared in pain, but doggedly hung on.

The barbarian who had been tying off the boat snatched up a fallen branch and charged across the open ground towards Nagash, and the fourth man wasn't far behind. The tide of the battle was rapidly turning against the necromancer, and the very idea infuriated him. With a snarl, he drew upon the power of the burning stone.

Fiery strength surged through him. His hand closed about the barbarian's neck, crushing the man's spine. Nagash hurled the body like a children's doll straight into the third man's path. Both man and corpse tumbled across the ground in a tangle of limbs.

Nagash pounced on the man before he could pull himself free and drove his dagger through the barbarian's eye.

The last man stopped dead in his tracks, mouth agape in shock. Without thinking, Nagash flung out his hand and hissed a stream of arcane words – and the power of the stone responded. The man's body went suddenly rigid, as though gripped in a giant's invisible fist. The necromancer hissed in satisfaction.

'*Good,*' Nagash murmured, feeling the power crackling through his outstretched hand. '*Yes. Very good.*'

He rose slowly, careful to maintain his focus on the impromptu spell. It was more difficult than it once was; the magic was more potent, but less controlled, and fought against his will every second.

Nagash approached the man carefully. The cloth bundle was still clutched in the barbarian's hands. The necromancer reached up and carefully prised it from the man's fingers. The objects wrapped up in the greasy cloth clinked metallically.

He smiled. Kneeling down, he set the bundle on the ground and unrolled it. The tools within gleamed in the lamplight. The necromancer nodded grudgingly. Crude implements, but suitable to the task. Satisfied, Nagash turned his attention back to his prisoner.

'*I have many questions,*' he told the terrified barbarian. '*This is a strange land, and there is much I do not know about you and your people.*'

He drew a long, curved flensing knife from the pouch and inspected the bronze blade in the lantern light.

'Fortunately, I expect you will be a font of useful information,' the necromancer said. He rose to his feet and studied his subject carefully. He raised his left hand, and with a slight gesture, the barbarian's arms rose from his sides.

Nagash's smile widened. It had been a very long time since his last vivisection.

'We shall begin with the muscle groups,' he said to the man, and went to work.

THREE

A SILKEN BETRAYAL

Lahmia,
the City of the Dawn,
in the 76th year of Asaph the Beautiful
(-1600 Imperial Reckoning)

The Eastern priests crouched before the queen like great, yellow bullfrogs, backs slightly arched and palms pressed to the marble floor as they filled the Hall of Reverent Contemplation with their buzzing, wordless song. Their eyes were squeezed shut in concentration, perspiration gleaming beneath the brim of their outlandish felt hats as the six elderly men emitted a basso drone that Neferata could feel against her skin. The delegation from the Silk Lands seemed to find it uplifting, judging by the beatific looks on their faces. She found the noise deeply unnerving – and it just seemed to go on and *on*. For the first time, Neferata was genuinely glad that she was required to wear a mask in public. The longer the Eastern *throat music* went, the more horrified she became.

The audience with the Imperial delegation had begun in a civilised enough fashion, with little of the outrageous fanfare that usually accompanied the arrival of a member of the Celestial Household. Normally, the first Imperial attendants would arrive well before dawn to decorate the Hall of Reverent Contemplation with silk hangings, lacquered screens and an unbroken line of royal carpet stretching all the way to the palace gate. Priests would walk from one end of the hall to the other, chanting prayers to chase away evil spirits and promote harmony, then give way to a procession of musicians and artists whose task was to tune the vibrations of the space in a manner that was pleasing to Celestial ears.

When the delegation itself finally arrived, many hours later, it would be accompanied by a small army of courtiers, bureaucrats and servants that would fill the cramped chamber to capacity. By the time that Neferata met the delegates face-to-face, it was only the relative placement of the throne-like chairs that made it clear who was actually giving an audience to whom.

By contrast, the current ambassador had arrived with very little fanfare, appearing at the palace gates promptly at midday and pausing only long enough to have a brilliant blue carpet unrolled at his feet before continuing onward to the hall. He was accompanied by a very modest retinue: five bureaucrats, a handful of courtiers, and a young woman clad in rich robes whose face was painted white as alabaster. The entire delegation could be seated in a comfortable half-circle before the royal dais, lending the proceedings an unusually intimate, almost conspiratorial air.

Of course, all the usual Imperial proprieties had to be observed. The audience had begun with a lengthy recitation of the queen's lineage, followed by an even longer recitation of the ambassador's ancestry. The ambassador, speaking through his senior bureaucrat, then offered a very appreciative and long-winded greeting, bestowing upon Neferata the acknowledgement of the Imperial Court and the hopes of continued harmony with the City of the Dawn.

Tea was served. The strange Eastern concoction, served in tiny ceramic cups, still tasted like little more than heated bathwater to Neferata, but she'd learned to nod politely and listen with feigned appreciation as the ambassador's courtiers spoke at length of the refinement of the leaves and the delicacy of its flavour.

Once the cups had been collected and a prayer offered to the Eastern gods in thanks for the tea's many blessings, it was time for the customary tokens of esteem. Neferata accepted a fine Eastern bow and a quiver of arrows on behalf of the king, as well as a half-dozen scrolls of poetry, three chests of fine silk robes and a prince's ransom in exotic spices from the far corners of the Empire. This time the ambassador even brought a gift for the queen's lovely cousin, whom the king had required to attend the audiences as part of her courtly education. A servant presented Khalida with a magnificent falcon, taken from the Emperor's personal stock. Evidently, the last ambassador had overheard Neferata's pet name for her cousin, confirming the queen's suspicion that the delegates from the Imperial court spoke perfectly good Nehekharan, and insisted on translators for their own inscrutable reasons.

After presenting the gifts, a light meal of Eastern delicacies was served, followed by more tea and polite conversation that lasted for two long hours. Then came a period of digestion and restful contemplation that normally would be accompanied by soft music or recitations of poetry. Neferata grimaced as the droning of the priests continued, and wondered if perhaps the Eastern Empire's culture was on the decline.

Meeting with the delegates from the Eastern Empire was the only official function left to Neferata. King Lamashizzar hadn't opened the palace to his citizens on the high holy days in many decades, and the temples no longer had the power to influence court affairs as they once did, so Neferata now spent the vast majority of her time locked inside the Women's Palace.

The only reason she was still allowed to receive the Easterners was because Lamashizzar had never had any patience for the Silk Lords' tedious social rituals, yet couldn't risk offending his erstwhile allies by fobbing them off on one of his viziers. It was the primary reason she'd been given so much authority when the king had taken the army to Mahrak. At the time, the risk of a royal scandal paled in comparison to a diplomatic incident with the Empire.

Since the war, official visits from the east generally only happened once a year, when an Imperial delegation arrived to collect Lahmia's annual payment for the shiploads of iron and dragon-powder that Lamasheptra had purchased more than a century before. The next scheduled payment wasn't due for another three months, so the unannounced arrival of an Imperial vessel had caused considerable curiosity among the members of the Lahmian court.

Something was definitely going on, the queen knew, studying the resplendent figure of the Eastern ambassador. The Empire didn't send a prince of the blood all the way across the Crystal Sea on a mere social call.

Xia Ha Feng, August Personage of the First Celestial House and Scion of Heaven, was young and very handsome, in the coldly detached manner that all the Silk Lords affected. He was clad in layered robes of blue and yellow silk. The outer robe was embroidered with sinuous, bearded serpents whose scales were picked out in tiny garnets, and whose belly plates were fashioned from lustrous mother-of-pearl. The prince's raven-black hair was oiled and pulled back in a severe topknot, and a circlet of gold rested upon his brow. Long, artificial fingernails, also crafted of fine gold, capped all ten of the prince's fingers. Though a mark of refinement and wealth in the Silk Lands, the affectation seemed sinister, even monstrous, to the queen. She wondered idly where the young prince fell in the line of succession to the Imperial throne. Despite hundreds of years of trade and diplomatic relations with the Silk Lands, the Eastern Empire was still largely a mystery to the Lahmians. It was reputed to be vast in size, but foreigners were forbidden to travel beyond a handful of sanctioned trade cities situated along their western coast.

The Silk Lords claimed that their civilization was far older and more advanced than that of the Nehekharans, but Neferata, like most Lahmians, doubted the truth of this. If the Eastern Empire was so old and powerful, why were they afraid to let foreigners see it?

All at once, the priests' disquieting song came to an end. Rather than build to a satisfactory conclusion, like proper music did, the droning simply *stopped.* The priests bowed low to the queen and swiftly withdrew. Neferata blinked dazedly in the sudden silence, uncertain how to respond. She stole a surreptitious glance at Khalida, who sat upon a lesser throne to Neferata's right. Over the last half-century, the little hawk had blossomed into a tall, elegant young woman, though somehow she'd never outgrown her love for horses, hunting and war. She remained one of Neferata's favourites, though once the queen had given birth to her own children they had grown inexorably apart. Soon she would be leaving the City of the Dawn altogether, for Lamashizzar had arranged her betrothal to Prince Anhur, the son of King Khepra of Lybaras, during the last round of trade negotiations.

The young princess was sitting very straight in her chair. Like Neferata, her face was hidden behind a serene golden mask, but the queen could see that her chin was bobbing ever so slightly as she fought to stay awake.

As one, the Imperial delegates nodded their heads and gave a contented sigh as the priests silently left the hall. The prince turned to the bureaucrat at his right and spoke softly in his native tongue. The functionary listened intently, then bowed his head to Neferata.

'The Scion of Heaven hopes that this gift of song is pleasing to your ears, great queen,' he said in flawless Nehekharan. 'The music of the mountain priests is reserved only for the gods themselves, and those whom Heaven deems worthy.'

'I can't imagine what I might have done to deserve such an honour,' Neferata replied smoothly. She thought she heard a tiny, muffled snort of amusement from her cousin. 'The Scion of Heaven is as discerning as he is generous.'

The Eastern prince listened to the translation and inclined his head to the queen. He spoke again, very softly, and the bureaucrat smiled. 'The Scion of Heaven would be honoured to share the gifts of the gods with you whenever you desire, great queen.'

The statement sent a prickle of alarm racing up Neferata's spine. 'The Scion of Heaven's generosity is truly boundless,' she answered calmly. 'The court is always honoured to receive a visit from the Celestial Household, and we hope he travels to Lahmia often in the coming years.'

As the functionary related the queen's words, the prince smiled for the first time. The look in his dark eyes as he spoke reminded Neferata very much of the cold, predatory stare of the falcon he'd given to Khalida.

'The Scion of Heaven has no plans to travel in the foreseeable future, great queen,' the bureaucrat replied. 'And he is looking forward to sharing the fruits of our civilisation with you in the coming months.'

Neferata straightened slightly on the throne. 'Do I misunderstand?' she asked. 'Are we to be graced with your august presence for a lengthy stay?'

This time the functionary didn't bother to translate. 'The Scion of Heaven will take residence in Lahmia,' he replied. 'His factors are seeking appropriate lodgings near the palace even as we speak.'

For a moment, the queen forgot all sense of Eastern decorum. 'Will he be staying long?' she asked.

The bureaucrat frowned ever so slightly at the forwardness of such a direct question, but he replied smoothly, 'The Scion of Heaven wishes to broaden his education of foreign cultures, and hopes to gain a deep understanding of your ancient and noble traditions.'

He means years, Neferata thought with alarm. She hesitated, composing herself and considered her reply. 'This is unprecedented,' she said carefully. 'And a momentous event in the history of our two peoples.'

The prince's smile widened as the bureaucrat translated. His reply was delivered with carefully modulated deprecation. 'The Celestial Household merely wishes to become closer to our Western neighbours, and hopes to offer what meagre aid we can in this time of transformation and rebirth.'

Neferata's unease deepened. 'We are naturally deeply grateful to the Emperor, and appreciate his interest in our people's wellbeing,' she replied.

The bureaucrat bowed deeply. 'The Emperor of Heaven and Earth is a dutiful son, and is responsible with the gifts that the gods bestow upon him,' he replied. 'A momentous event in Guanjian province has enriched the Empire, and he has taken it as a sign from Heaven that he must turn his attentions to our neighbours who are in need.'

'That is very comforting to know,' the queen replied, though she felt anything but. 'Might one inquire as to the nature of this blessed occurrence?'

The functionary beamed proudly. 'Imperial surveyors have discovered gold in the mountains of the province! Even the most pessimistic reports suggest that the vein is larger than any found in the Empire's history. Within two years, three at most, the Imperial treasury expects to benefit from the gods' great bounty.'

Neferata felt her blood run cold. Now she understood the reason behind the prince's sudden arrival. 'Truly, the fortunes of the Celestial Household are a wonder to the rest of the world,' she replied, as calmly as she could manage.

Prince Xian rose gracefully from his chair and clapped his hands together. His translator bowed once again. 'The Scion of Heaven thanks you for the graciousness of your welcome, and hopes that this audience is but the first of many to come.'

Neferata rose to her feet. 'The august personage of Prince Xian is always welcome,' she said, 'and we hope that he will grace us again with his presence soon.'

The queen remained standing as the prince and his entourage departed. When they were gone, Khalida leaned back in her chair and sighed. 'What an insufferable bunch of fops,' she growled. 'I think I fell asleep at some point during the meal. Did I miss anything?'

Neferata drew in a deep, silent breath. 'No, little hawk. You didn't miss anything at all.'

The prince's message had been for her and the king alone. Among the Silk Lords, even betrayal was delivered by polite implication.

Rain hissed against the thick glass windows, obscuring the view of the predawn city and the sea beyond. Within the bedchamber, Neferata's handmaidens lay sleeping. Every now and then, one of them would whisper or sigh, deep in the grips of a lotus-fuelled dream. The queen had pushed the bottle of dream-wine on her maids, insisting that they should all drink a cup before she partook herself. It was a rare luxury for the maids, who were expected to be ready to serve the needs of the queen on a moment's notice. Neferata appeared to sip from her own cup, but scarcely let the bitter liquid touch her lips.

Tephret was the last to succumb. The elderly handmaiden had held on until well past midnight, until finally Neferata had been forced to feign sleep herself before Tephret would finally give in herself. The queen had lain in her bed for several hours afterwards, grim thoughts whirling through her head as she listened to the rain steal over the slumbering city. Finally, not long past the hour of the dead, she rose and slipped on a robe, then lit a small oil lamp and sat down at her writing desk.

The words had not come easily. *The Eastern devils have laid a trap for us,* she'd written in deft brush-strokes. *Within two to three years, the value of gold in the Empire will plummet.*

On the surface, the statement seemed innocent enough. She chewed the end of the ink brush. Did she need to spell it out for Lamashizzar? She sighed. *As a result, our annual payment to the Empire is certain to increase well beyond our capability to pay.*

What had possessed their late father Lamasheptra into entering such a potentially disastrous deal with the Eastern Empire would remain a mystery for the ages. He had concocted the scheme not long after Nagash seized the throne at Khemri and made the queen – Lamasheptra's daughter Neferem – his hostage. After years of secret negotiations in the Imperial trade cities across the sea, the Imperials agreed to share with Lahmia the same arms and armour that equipped their own fearsome legions. This included enough of the Easterner's mysterious and explosive dragon-powder to equip an army of warriors, as well as weapons to employ them, which alone would be enough to make Lamasheptra's forces the dominant military power in all of Nehekhara.

In return, the Emperor demanded a staggering sum, equivalent at the time to ten tons of gold per year for the next *three hundred years,* and required nothing less than the sovereignty of the city itself as security for the trade. If Lahmia failed to make even *one* payment to the Empire, the city would become an Imperial possession from that day forward. Lamasheptra accepted the deal without qualm, despite the fact that the amount of money owed to the Empire each year was greater than the city's yearly tax revenue.

Perhaps the old king had planned to supplement his payments with plunder taken from Khemri; possibly he thought to exact tribute from the other great cities once the fearsome power of his army became known. As it turned out, the delivery of the promised arms and armour had taken more than a century. The final shipment, consisting of the dragon-powder itself, reached Lahmia some five months after Lamasheptra's death, and the young king Lamashizzar proved far too cautious with the powerful weapons he'd inherited. Meanwhile, the city treasury had dwindled steadily away. It was only through several shrewd trade deals with Lybaras, Rasetra and Mahrak during the war that Lahmia was able to survive at all.

Of course, the Empire had never intended to deal fairly with Lamasheptra. They'd done everything in their power to make it difficult for the city to fulfil its financial obligations, and now that there were only a few years left before the debt was fully paid, the Silk Lords had gone to extreme measures to ensure that Lahmia would be theirs.

Neferata was sure that the discovery of the gold mine was a lie. The Imperial household would flood the market with coin from their own treasury to convincingly drive down the value of their currency long enough to force Lahmia into default, after which point things would gradually return to normal again. It would cause a short period of suffering for the Empire's subjects, but it would be a small price to pay for a strategic foothold in Nehekhara.

The question, Neferata thought, is how do we get out of the trap before it snaps shut?

The complex web of trade deals that Lamashizzar had built after the war had produced dividends, and greatly increased Lahmia's influence across Nehekhara, but it wouldn't be enough if the Empire demanded more gold. The only way to save the city from the hands of the Easterners was to either seize more wealth from Lahmia's neighbours, or defy the Silk Lords, and Neferata was certain that Lamashizzar hadn't the nerve to do either.

To be honest, she wasn't even certain if her brother *cared* what happened to the city any more.

The confrontation in the council chamber, now a half-century past, had ended whatever feelings of affection Neferata had for her brother. There was a time once when she thought she might have loved him, when she thought he would stand up to centuries of hoary tradition and treat her as a co-ruler instead of a mere possession. Now she knew better. All he wanted from her were heirs to continue the dynasty, while he fumbled after the secrets of immortality. Nothing else mattered.

Well, Lahmia mattered to her. Neferata would be damned before she saw the City of the Dawn become a plaything for foreign lords. She could rule the city with a surer hand than her brother ever could.

The queen set aside the ink brush and listened for a while to the sound of the rain on the windowpanes as she turned the problem over in her mind. Always, she came back to the same conclusion.

Something had to be done. If Lamashizzar wouldn't take action, then she must.

Neferata took up the sheet of paper and considered it for a long moment. Her expression hardened. Slowly, carefully, she fed the paper to the flame guttering in the oil lamp on her desk.

It was no more than an hour before dawn when Neferata rose from her place by the window and dressed herself in a dark robe and slippers. She left her black hair bound up and pulled on a black wool cloak, then picked up a small gold box from her dressing table and tucked it into her girdle. Her golden mask was left on its wooden stand, its smooth curves masked in shadow.

Her maids were still sleeping soundly, though she knew that they would begin stirring as soon as it was light. There wasn't any time to waste. The queen slipped quietly from her bedchamber and hurried down the dark halls of the palace towards the Hall of Restful Contemplation.

She moved as quickly as she dared, keeping to little-used passageways as much as she could. Twice she saw the telltale glow of a lantern crossing down an adjoining corridor, but each time she found a pool of deep shadow to hide in before the sleepy servant girl passed by. Within minutes she was standing before the tall bronze doors of the audience chamber. The metal surface was cold to the touch as she pulled one of the doors open just wide enough to slip through.

Heart racing, she dashed down the length of the hall and pressed her ear to the outer doors. Would there be guards on the other side? She had no idea. After listening in vain for several long moments, she gave up and decided to take a chance. She grasped the door's heavy brass ring and opened it just a bit. The corridor beyond was dark and empty.

Neferata felt a faint thrill as she slipped across the threshold into the palace proper. Now she was officially an escapee, in violation of royal and theological law. *But only if they catch me*, she reminded herself, and grinned in spite of herself.

The going was slower once she emerged into the palace proper; she was far less familiar with its layout, and not accustomed to its routines. At least there were no guards about. Once upon a time the halls would have been patrolled by the king's Ushabti, who were as swift and deadly as Asaph's terrible serpents. She had only the vaguest memories of them now, from when she was a young girl. Neferata remembered their silent, graceful movements and their depthless, black eyes. All that remained of them now were the great statues that guarded the royal tombs outside the city.

Once again, she kept to deserted hallways and managed to avoid the few servants who were up and about at such an early hour. It took her nearly half an hour to make her way to the far side of the palace and the dusty, deserted wing where Lamashizzar hid his darkest secrets. The main doors to the wing were locked, but Neferata expected as much. Within a few minutes she located the entrance to the servants' passageways and felt her way into the oppressive darkness that lay beyond.

Cobwebs brushed ghostly fingers across the queen's face. The narrow corridor was windowless, and dark as a tomb. Neferata listened to rats scuttling across the floor up ahead and cursed herself for not thinking to bring a candle stub to light her way. Gritting her teeth, she reached out with her hand until she found the wall to her left and let that guide her onwards.

The air was cold and dank. Now and again her fingertips brushed across a slimy patch of mould. Once, something large and many-legged darted out from underneath her fingers, and it was all she could do not to let out a startled shout. For all she knew, the king or his companions could be nearby. If they caught her now, Neferata didn't care to speculate what they might decide to do with her.

After about twenty feet, her hand encountered a wooden doorframe. She continued on, counting each doorway as she went. It had been more than a century since she'd last stood inside Lamashizzar's improvised sanctum, but she knew it was in the centre of the wing, far from any windows that would reveal the telltale glow of oil lamps burning far into the night. When Neferata reached the tenth doorway she stopped and tried the latch. It moved with a faint screech of tarnished metal, the sound deafeningly loud in the oppressive darkness. She paused, hardly daring to breathe, but several seconds passed without any sounds of movement other than the scampering of rats.

The door opened with only the tiniest sound of wood scraping through the grit that had accumulated on the sandstone floor. Enough predawn light filtered through windows on the eastern face of the palace wing to provide some definition to the interior of the building. She saw that she was in a narrow corridor facing eastwards that connected to a wide central passageway that ran the entire length of the wing.

Moving as silently as she could, Neferata crept to the end of the servants' corridor. The walls of the central passageway had been stripped of their hangings, and every piece of art and furniture had been removed many years ago; they had all been surreptitiously sold in the city marketplace during lean years to help pay off the debt to the Silk Lords.

The thick dust that had settled in the central passageway had been churned by the regular passage of sandalled feet. Peering through the gloom, Neferata followed the muddled tracks down the wide hall until they stopped outside an otherwise unobtrusive door to her right.

Heart pounding, she laid her hand on the latch. This was the point of no return; once she crossed the threshold, there would be no turning back.

This is not for me, she reminded herself. This is for Lahmia.

The latch gave an oiled click as she pressed it. She pushed the door open with her fingertips, smelling the faint scent of incense and the tang of spilled blood.

There was still a faint red glow emanating from a banked brazier on the far side of the room. Neferata paused in the doorway, taking in everything she could see. There were more tables than she remembered, most of them covered in stacks of paper, collections of papyrus scrolls and jumbled piles of leather-bound books. Wooden chairs and tattered divans were scattered about the room, with wine goblets and trays of half-eaten food set nearby.

The queen's lips curled in distaste. It resembled nothing so much as the cluttered library of a wealthy young dilettante.

Convinced that Lamashizzar and his cronies were nowhere about, Neferata stepped inside and shut the door behind her. She navigated carefully around the room until she reached the brazier, and within a few minutes she'd stoked it carefully back to life.

The glow of the burning coals reached into the far corners of the large room, revealing still more shelves and wide, utilitarian tables set with dusty ceramic jars and glass bottles filled with exotic liquids and powders. They were set to either side of a cleared patch of floor that had been scrupulously swept clean of dust and grime and inlaid with a complicated magical symbol the likes of which she had never seen before.

It took a moment before Neferata spied the figure sprawled in one corner on the other side of the sorcerous circle. The queen searched the tables around her for an oil lamp. Finding one, she lit the wick using a coal from the brazier, and, summoning up her courage, she crept closer to the king's prisoner.

Arkhan the Black hadn't changed one bit in the last hundred and fifty years. He was clad in filthy rags, and his bluish skin was covered in grime, but his face looked exactly as it had when she'd first set eyes on him all those years ago. A thick, iron collar enclosed the immortal's neck, connected to a heavy chain that had been bolted deep into the wall. At his side, an upended wine goblet spilled a thick trickle of dark fluid onto the floor.

The immortal's lips were stained black by lotus root. Though his chest did not rise and fall as a living mortal's would, Neferata knew that Arkhan was deep in a drugged slumber. From the very beginning, Lamashizzar kept his prisoner under control by feeding him a mixture of his weak elixir and enough lotus root to kill a half-dozen men. When he wasn't needed to translate Nagash's esoteric writings, Arkhan was kept in a stupor so he couldn't escape.

Staring at the immortal's slack features, Neferata wondered how much of his sanity still remained. She consoled herself with the thought that if Arkhan was of no further use to Lamashizzar, he would have been disposed of without a moment's hesitation.

The queen took a deep breath and drew the gold box from her girdle. Opening the filigreed lid, she withdrew the *hixa* and pressed it to Arkhan's neck. It took several attempts before the insect's abdomen arched and drove its sting into the immortal's flesh.

For a moment, nothing happened. Neferata expected Arkhan to groan as the wasp's venom burned away the effects of the lotus, but the immortal didn't so much as tremble. His eyes simply opened, as though he'd only been lightly dozing, and he fixed her with a dull, listless stare.

Neferata expected Arkhan to wonder at her presence, but the immortal said nothing. The unnerving silence stretched for several long minutes, until finally the queen could take it no more. Without thinking, she reached out and gripped his arm, and to her surprise, Arkhan the Black flinched from her touch.

The Queen of Lahmia struggled to give the ghastly creature a friendly smile. 'Greetings, Arkhan of Khemri,' she said. 'Do you remember me? I am Neferata, Queen of Lahmia, and I have a proposition for you.'

FOUR

THE BARROW-LANDS

Cripple Peak,
in the 76th year of Asaph the Beautiful
(-1600 Imperial Reckoning)

Nagash understood now why the barbarians favoured their long, oiled cloaks. It was the rain: the steady, invasive, unrelenting rain.

North of the great sea, the coastline was a mix of flat, marshy plains and rolling hills girdled with stunted, grey-green thorn trees. The larger of the barbarian villages squatted atop these bald hills, their squalid mud and grass huts crouching like clusters of toadstools beneath the never-ending sheets of rain. Smaller villages or clan-like communities hunched amid the yellow weeds of the marsh plains, connected by winding, waterlogged foot paths worn by generations of hunters and raiding parties. The barbarians avoided travelling along those paths at night, Nagash found, for the humans were not the only hunters who favoured the paths when the moon was high in the sky. More than once, the necromancer heard the caterwauling of great cats out in the darkness, and the bellowing of a fierce creature that sounded bestial but had the timbre of a human voice. Sometimes he would hear stealthy footsteps creeping through the tall weeds as he walked the paths at night, but none came close enough to threaten him.

It had taken weeks to make his way up from the southern marshes to the sea's north coast. Since then, Nagash had moved more cautiously among the barbarian settlements, gathering information about them where he could and then moving on. They were a primitive, suspicious people, hostile to outsiders and capable of the kinds of treachery and cowardly viciousness common to the poor and the weak-willed.

The barbarians were little better than animals, subsisting on what little food they could scrape from the land or catch in the dark, bitter waters of the sea. They clad themselves in rough leather and worked with crude tools of wood and stone for the most part, although occasionally Nagash would peer from the shadows into the open doorway of a village hut and spy a tarnished bronze sword or spearhead hung from pegs close to the crude stone hearth. The style of the metal weapons was crude by Nehekharan standards but entirely functional, and obviously kept as treasures by the barbarians. He suspected they were battle-trophies, since the villagers had nothing of substance to trade with. That meant there was another, more prosperous and advanced barbarian culture somewhere nearby.

Virtually all of the barbarians he observed bore the mark of the burning stone in one fashion or another. The waters of the Sour Sea - or so Nagash called it, because it was dark and bitter with mineral salts from the *abn-i-khat* - permeated everything in the region and warped it in uncontrolled ways. Physical deformities were commonplace: most were minor, and a few even seemed beneficial. One night, as he'd crept up to peer into the doorway of a village hetman's dwelling, he was surprised to find himself staring at a young boy of eight whose eyes shone like a cat's in the reflected glow of the hearth-light. The child saw through the darkness with ease, raising such a hue and cry at Nagash's appearance that the entire village rose up in arms to try and capture him. The pursuit had lasted most of the night, and they'd come close to catching him a number of times.

At first, his interest in the barbarians had been more a matter of survival and a certain degree of scholarly curiosity, but the more Nagash learned, the more he saw the potential that lay before him. Here was a vast source of magical power, one that might even rival that of the Black Pyramid in Khemri, and a primitive people who could provide him with soldiers and slaves.

He would not necessarily have to return to Nehekhara to continue his quest for domination. His empire could begin again here, along the shores of the Sour Sea.

The barbarians were a fractious and tribal lot, not dissimilar to the desert tribes he had known in the past. They were led by whoever was strong enough and brutal enough to cow the rest into submission, supported by a strong cadre of kinsmen and allies who served as the hetman's warband. They posed little threat to Nagash; even the larger, hilltop tribes were still isolated from their neighbours, and could be brought down one at a time. No, what concerned him most were the totem-shrines of polished wood that every village boasted, and the treatment of the itinerant priests that tended them.

The totems were columns of carved wood more than fifteen feet high - no small feat in a land where the trees grew like gnarled fists and were no more than eight or nine feet tall - and were shaped to resemble tall, powerfully-built men and women. There were four to eight figures carved into each totem, always in pairs, facing outward from the trunk in poses that Nagash supposed were meant to convey strength, wisdom and prosperity.

The craftsmanship was crude by Nehekharan standards, and there was no common iconography from one totem to the next that might suggest anything like a pantheon. The only common factor he could discern was that none of the figures bore the deformities common to those who worshipped them. Villagers made offerings of food and simple, carved tokens to the shrines, and Nagash suspected that, given the location of the totems at the centre of each village, they were the focal point of the barbarians' important ceremonies.

The priests who tended the shrines travelled from village to village, never staying in one place for more than a few days at a time. Like the priests Nagash had known in Khemri, these holy men got the best of everything. Their leather kilts were well made and often decorated with pieces of metal or polished stones, and carried polished wooden staves that they wielded both as weapons and badges of office. They were uniformly tall, well-fed and physically fit, and not one of them bore the slightest trace of disfigurement. The holy men travelled in groups of six or eight, usually with an older priest attended by a pair of functionaries and two or three young acolytes. When they stayed at a village they slept in the hetman's hut, even if it meant the hetman and his family slept outside that night.

From what Nagash could tell, the priests' duties involved anointing the totem shrines with oils and performing prayers over them, collecting tribute in the form of food, beer, clothing and tools (which the acolytes carried on their backs when the priests left) and occasionally meddling in the affairs of the villagers themselves. They decided who could marry whom, settled certain disputes involving inheritance, and in one case ordered the death of a young man whose ravings suggested that exposure to the burning stone had rendered him mad.

The priesthood's influence and authority could be problematic, Nagash realised. More importantly, their lack of deformities hinted that they'd learned to control the worst effects of the *abn-i-khat*, just as he had done. Potentially that made them very dangerous indeed.

The barbarian villages grew larger and more elaborate as Nagash drew closer to the great mountain. The broad hillsides had been crudely terraced, and ranks of round-roofed huts sprawled down and across the sodden fields, where crops of rice and tubers were nurtured in paddies of bitter water. The tracks were wider and better travelled, and the woodland more sparse. Only the constant rain worked in his favour, giving him reason to conceal his face beneath the dripping hood of his cloak and discouraging conversation with the barbarians he encountered on the muddy tracks. There were times, on moonless nights, when he would attach himself to larger groups of travellers and follow along with them in silence for many miles, little more than another vague, cloaked shape in the darkness.

Now he stood beneath the dripping branches of a small copse of trees, close to the point where the northern coast began to curve south and east towards the mountain, and watched a strange procession make its way down the switchback trail of one of the largest barbarian villages Nagash had seen yet. Normally the crude customs of the barbarians were of no interest to him whatsoever; what caught his attention this time were the dozens of glowing green lights that accompanied the procession down the dark trail.

The necromancer clutched his sodden cloak tightly around his ever-thinning frame and edged back into the shadows of the wood as far as he could manage. As far as he could tell, the procession would make its way down the muddy trail directly past where he stood, which also meant that they were heading towards the mountain.

The procession was a long one. He reckoned that he was almost two miles from the village. The tail end of the line was still working its way down the hillside when he began to hear the low, mournful chanting of voices emanating from around a curve in the track to his left. Minutes later, a familiar glow began to seep around the muddy track, followed by a pair of young priests wearing fine robes and carrying gnarled wooden poles in their hands. The acolytes' heads were bared to the bitter rain as they led the procession down the track, their faces turned downward and their shoulders heaving as they led the rest in the funereal chant. The green light emanated from globular sacks of hide hung from the ends of the wooden poles. Each hide sack had been scraped until they were translucent and then filled with water. Glowing green shapes stirred within, occasionally darting and swimming from one end of their prison to the next.

Behind the priests and their heavy lamps came a large group of chanting, bare-headed holy men, all clad in rough vestments of cloth and hide that were decorated in glittering bits of metal and precious stones. Their faces had been painted with glowing oil that highlighted their handsome, unmarred features.

After the phalanx of chanting holy men came a column of groaning acolytes bearing a rough, wooden palanquin. Upon the palanquin rode an arrogant old man that Nagash knew had to be the barbarian high priest. He sat upon a straight-backed throne, wreathed in layers of heavy robes festooned with chains of actual gold and a kind of polished, ruddy copper. A circlet of gold rested upon his brow, inset with a glowing oval stone. The piece of *abn-i-khat* looked to be the size of a bird's egg; Nagash could feel its crackling power from a dozen yards away. His hands clenched hungrily at the sight of it. Had he more power at his command, he might have been tempted to lay waste to the holy men and take the stone for himself.

The high priest went by, heedless of the necromancer's feverish gaze. Behind him came another set of lantern-bearing priests, followed by a funereal procession uncomfortably similar to those Nagash had once presided over in Khemri.

There had been a battle, Nagash realised at once. The barbarians followed the priests in family groups, arranged by order of prominence within their village. Their fine clothes had been covered in grey ash, and many of the women had cut away their hair in a gesture of grief. They carried the dead upon their naked shoulders, resting in a woven litter made from swamp reeds. The corpses were naked, and Nagash was surprised to see that none of the litters contained trophies or grave gifts to aid their spirits in the afterlife. The tribe needed absolutely everything they could get just to survive. The dead, however honoured in life, clearly had to fend for themselves afterwards.

A pair of lantern-bearing priests marched at roughly even intervals along the length of the great procession, filling the air with their droning chant. Nagash watched the line snake its way south-eastward, apparently heading for the broken plain at the foot of the great mountain. Intrigued, Nagash waited for the end of the procession to go by, then fell into step behind him. The darkness and the steady, drizzling rain hid him effectively from view.

They passed through rocky, flat terrain, devoid of any signs of life. To Nagash's surprise, the path widened after a time and became paved with irregular, flat stones. Totem shrines appeared at intervals along the crudely-built road. Their faces had been painted some time earlier with the same glowing oil that adorned the priests, lending the carved faces an eerie semblance of life.

Hours passed. The barbarians walked for miles in the dark and the rain, growing steadily closer to the mountain. Eventually, Nagash saw a glowing, greenish nimbus in the air some distance ahead. After about half a mile he could see a line of tall, formidable-looking structures that stretched across the path ahead. More glowing orbs hung at intervals along their length, or shone from the slits of windows set into their flanks. Before long Nagash realised that he was looking at a strange kind of fort. From what he could tell, it was a series of long, high-walled buildings made of mud, brick and wood, connected end to end and stretching from a rocky spur to the north-east all the way to the shore of the Sour Sea, perhaps two miles to the south-west. A single, wide gateway provided the only access between the barbarian villages and the sea's western coast. It was also the first real attempt at fortification Nagash had seen in the entire region.

The procession led through the wide gate and into the lands beyond. There were acolytes waiting to shut the gates as the last of the mourners passed by; they had just begun to push the heavy, wooden portals closed when Nagash appeared out of the darkness and rain. They stared at the cloaked and hooded figure uneasily, but made no move to challenge him.

Nagash strode down the long, torchlit tunnel between the first and second gates as though he had every reason to be there. He studied the iconography carved into the support beams and the archways: more perfect faces, and occasionally something akin to a falling star, superimposed against a stylised mountain.

When he emerged from the second gate, Nagash strode a few more yards and then turned to stare back at the fort. There were more windows on this side, as well as long, roofed galleries that allowed the inhabitants to view the mountain and the wide plain. He could see more priests and acolytes up there, standing alone or in small groups, watching the procession continue towards the foot of the mountain. At once he realised that the huge structure was both temple and fortress combined. From here they could control the barbarians' access to the mountain and the evident power it represented.

Nagash looked up at the priests, smug and comfortable in their fortress of wood, and his lips drew back in a ghastly smile. One day he would show them the true meaning of power.

The procession continued across the plain for another ten miles before leaving the stone road and travelling across the rocky ground between rolling mounds of earth and stone that Nagash had come to realise weren't broken hills at all.

There were hundreds of them, crowding the plain before the mountain and spreading along the eastern coast as far as the eye could see. The barrow mounds varied in size: some were not much bigger than a rude barbarian hut, while others were the size of hillocks. He supposed the priests constructed them, for no one else had access to the plain. Their foundations were shaped from fitted stones, and then were roofed over with a cunning arrangement of rocks and packed earth. The older ones were hills in truth, covered over with yellow grass and even a few small trees.

It was a necropolis of sorts, similar in some ways to the great cities of the dead in far-off Nehekhara. As he worked his way among the great barrows his mind reeled with the possibilities. Here, sealed in earth and stone, was the beginnings of an army. All that he lacked was the power and the knowledge to bring them forth.

Upon leaving the road, the procession had spread out among the barrow mounds. Each family followed a pair of lantern-bearing priests to the mound that had been built for their kin. Nagash ignored them, making for a collection of glowing orbs farther across the plain that lay almost at the feet of the mountain itself. That was where the high priest and his retinue were to be found.

There were almost a dozen families gathered around the priests; no doubt they represented the kinfolk of the hetman and his warband. The bodies they'd carried for so long had been laid side-by-side before the dark entrance to the mound. Each corpse was naked. Their hair had been shorn close to the scalp, and their physical deformities had been covered in dark ash, so that they practically vanished in the gloom. All of the men bore ghastly wounds; Nagash had seen such things often enough to know the marks of spear and axe, expertly delivered. The hetman and his chosen warriors had gone to do battle with a far superior foe, and been dealt a bitter defeat.

Nagash kept his distance, sticking to the shadow of an older mound as he watched the high priest rise from his chair and spread his arms over the dead men. In a guttural yet powerful voice, the old man began to speak. Nagash didn't understand the words, but the cadences and the inflection were all too familiar. A rite of some sort was being performed. After a few moments, the senior priests joined in, and he could feel the currents of invisible power growing between them.

The chanting went on for many long minutes. The ritual was a simple one. It made no use of magical symbols or carefully-inscribed circles, just torrents of raw power drawn from the high priest's circlet and, cleverly, the deposits glowing from the skin of the fish held in the priests' lanterns. Slowly, steadily, the rite built to a crescendo – and then he saw one of the corpses start to twitch.

A wail went up from the crowd. As if in response, another corpse began to twitch. Then another. Soon, all of them were trembling with invisible energies.

There was a crackle of dead joints as, one by one, the dead men sat upright. They moved like statues, stiff and awkward, driven by unseen hands. A number of the mourners cried out again. Some tried to crawl across the wet ground, reaching for their kin, and had to be dragged back.

The corpses paid them no heed. First the hetman clambered slowly to his feet, followed by his retainers. Then, without a backwards glance, they walked slowly through the doorway of the waiting barrow.

To Nagash's surprise, the chanting of the priests continued – and then he realised that the wailing of the barbarians was being echoed from all across the plain. The high priest wasn't just animating the bodies of the hetman and his retainers – he was interring all the dead at once. Nagash's mind raced. How many bodies had there been? A hundred? More? Enough to constitute a small army, he was certain.

The high priest and his followers weren't holy men. They were necromancers as well, drawing upon the power of the burning stone to command the bodies of the dead. And for the moment, they were far more powerful than he.

FIVE

THE WORD OF KINGS

Lahmia,
the City of the Dawn,
in the 76th year of Djaf the Terrible
(-1599 Imperial Reckoning)

Arkhan the Black dreamt of riding beneath an endless desert sky, with nothing but the stars and the gleaming moon to watch over him. The Bhagarite stallion seemed to float across the rolling dunes, its hooves thudding softly like the beat of a living heart. Silver bells were woven into the stallion's mane, jangling a fine counterpoint to the horse's stride, and a dry wind caressed his skin, smelling of dust and faded spice.

There was no end to the sands, no end to the emptiness of the desert night. It was a benediction, a gift that he knew he did not deserve. And yet, when rough hands seized Arkhan and shook him awake, the pain of the longing he felt was worse than any wound he'd ever known.

He found himself lying on his side, cheek pressed against the grimy floor of the king's hidden sanctum. His eyelids felt stiff and brittle, like old paper. The immortal opened them with effort and peered up at the robed figure kneeling beside him.

W'soran's bald, bony head and long neck reminded Arkhan of nothing so much as a vulture. His wrinkled face, with its deep-set eyes, hooked nose and receding chin, would not have looked out of place on a statue of the Scavenger God himself. Once upon a time, he might have even been a priest of Ualatp. Arkhan knew that the man had come to Lahmia from the ruined city of Mahrak, more than a hundred years before, and had ultimately thrown himself on the generosity of Lamashizzar's court when none of the city temples would have anything to do with him. Without doubt he possessed a wealth of arcane knowledge and sorcerous ability that none of Lamashizzar's other allies could equal, which explained how he'd found his way so quickly into the king's secret cabal.

Cold, black eyes studied Arkhan with dispassionate interest. 'It's taking more effort to wake him with each passing night,' W'soran observed. He gripped Arkhan's shoulders and upper arms, testing the rigidity of the immortal's muscles and joints. 'No obvious signs of morbidity, but his vigour is clearly waning,' he said with a sour expression.

Arkhan heard sounds of movement at the far end of the room. An oil lamp flared, filling the space with orange light and the faint reek of melting tallow. 'Perhaps we're giving him too much lotus these days,' he heard Lamashizzar say.

W'soran grunted, bending closer and peering into Arkhan's eyes as though searching for signs of deception. 'He's being given the same amount as always,' he stated flatly. 'So, therefore, his ability to recover from its effects has diminished. He's weakening.' His small, dark eyes narrowed. 'Or...'

Arkhan heard footsteps draw nearer. A wine bowl clunked down onto a nearby table, followed by the dry rustle of papers. 'What?' the king said irritably.

W'soran stared into the immortal's eyes for several long moments, as though he could reach inside Arkhan's mind and read its contents like a dusty scroll. Arkhan gave the man a flat, predatory stare. His expression was unequivocal. *Given half a chance, I'd tear your head off your scrawny neck.*

It was nothing that W'soran hadn't seen every night for decades. What he didn't know was that, for the first time in a century and a half, Arkhan was strong enough to actually do it.

W'soran straightened, his knees popping noisily. He'd been well advanced in years when he'd first come to Lahmia, and Lamashizzar's elixir could not completely halt the implacable march of time. He shrugged his knobby shoulders.

'Perhaps the elixir is less effective as the physical body ages,' W'soran muttered, turning his back on the immortal. 'His flesh and organs are four hundred years old. It's possible that we are approaching the limits of your arcane prowess.'

There was no mistaking the accusatory tone in W'soran's voice. Lamashizzar did not reply at first, but Arkhan could feel the sudden tension in the air between the two men.

'Come here, Arkhan,' the king said coldly.

The immortal's eyes narrowed in concentration as he drew his legs up underneath him and pushed himself to his feet. His limbs were stiff and clumsy – not due to the effects of the lotus root, but rather the months of *hixa* stings he'd been receiving from Neferata. The wasp's venom collected in his muscles rather than passing away as it would in a living body, making even the simplest movements difficult. He tried to turn its debilitating effects to his advantage, letting it slow his movements to something approximating the lassitude that the king and his cohorts had come to expect. If Lamashizzar had even the slightest suspicion that he no longer had complete control over his prisoner, Neferata's scheme would come to naught, and he would never be free again.

The king was standing before a long, wooden table set just a few feet to one side of the room's ritual circle, his expression preoccupied as he tried to bring some kind of order to the pile of papers and scrolls spread before him. More figures moved about in the shadows at the far end of the room, murmuring in low voices and passing jars of wine between one another. Lamashizzar was accompanied by nearly his entire cabal: beside W'soran, the immortal recognised the tall, muscular outline of Abhorash, the king's champion, as well as the reclining forms of Ankhat and Ushoran, his oldest and most powerful allies at court. The king's grand vizier, Ubaid, stood apart from the other men, politely refusing offers of drink and waiting to do the king's bidding. Opposite the doorway, young Zuhras poked at the banked coals of a brazier with the point of his dagger, stirring them back to life. Grinning slyly, he speared one of the small coals on the point of his knife and used it to light the small, clay pipe dangling from his lips. The acrid scent of Eastern pipe smoke began to spread throughout the chamber.

That left only the two libertines, Adio and Khenti. Arkhan suspected they were chasing whores or losing their money in the gambling dens of the Red Silk District. Likely they would stumble in later, reeking of sour wine and cackling like hyenas to claim their share of Lamashizzar's elixir. Why the king hadn't lost patience with them and had their throats cut remained a mystery to Arkhan. He knew all too well that Lamashizzar would turn on anyone that he considered a threat.

Iron chain links rattled dully as Arkhan shuffled across the floor to stand before the king. Arkhan studied the man warily. Outwardly, Lamashizzar had aged somewhat, with grey hair streaking his temples and a fleshiness to his face that bespoke years of self-indulgence, but he still held himself with the easy assurance of a younger, fitter man. The effects of the elixir had left its mark on the king in more ways than one, Arkhan knew. He could see it in Lamashizzar's stiff shoulders and the swift, almost furtive movements of his eyes. The immortal had seen that look many times, in the court of the Undying King. The hunger for immortality turned the strongest men into beasts, making them savage, suspicious and unpredictable. If what the queen had told him was true, Lamashizzar cared little for the fortunes of his kingdom any more. Mastering Nagash's terrible incantations was his one and only obsession, which made him very dangerous indeed.

Arkhan clasped his hands together and bowed his head. The iron rim of the collar dug into his scarred neck. 'How may I serve, great one?' he asked his captor. The words burned like molten lead on his tongue.

'Is it true?' the king asked. He never took his eyes from the occult diagrams laid out on the table. 'Does the elixir no longer sustain you as it once did?'

The immortal considered his answer carefully. He knew that the moment he was no longer useful to Lamashizzar, the king would have him killed. 'I do not deny that it is harder to shake off the effects of the lotus,' Arkhan replied. 'It is possible that the learned W'soran is right. Certainly there is much more to be learned from Nagash's tomes. You have scarcely scratched the surface of the Undying King's power.'

From the moment that he had awakened in the cellars of the royal palace, Arkhan knew that his only hope of survival was to give up Nagash's secrets grudgingly, giving Lamashizzar just enough power to whet the king's appetite while he waited for an opportunity to escape. But Lamashizzar was no fool, he saw to it that Arkhan had no personal access to Nagash's books, and the only sustenance allowed to him was the same thin gruel that the king and his cohorts drank. It left him with barely enough strength to move, much less break free from the iron collar that the king had riveted about his neck. Even the black lotus had given him little relief; he was so weak that the potion brought no dreams, only cold oblivion.

W'soran seized on Arkhan's reply. 'Listen to him, great one,' he said. 'We must go back to the source and start again.' He stepped forward and laid a hand on one of Nagash's books. 'Follow the Usurper's instructions to the letter. We *know* that the rituals work – Arkhan here is proof of that!'

'And they also led to the Usurper's downfall!' Lamashizzar snapped. 'Everyone knows the horrors that took place in Khemri before the war. How long do you think we could prey upon palace servants and criminals before people began to take notice?'

'You can buy slaves from the East!' W'soran exclaimed. 'No one would care what you did with them! Or round up the hundreds of beggars clogging the streets in the lower districts! You're the *king*, or have you forgotten?'

The words had scarcely passed W'soran's lips when there was a rasp of metal and suddenly Abhorash was standing beside the king, his iron sword held loosely at his side. There was no expression on the champion's broad, heavy-boned face: he had the look of a man about to kill a snake that had slipped inside his house.

Lamashizzar said nothing to either of the two men. He simply met the older man's stare until W'soran finally looked away.

'I apologise, great one,' W'soran growled. 'My words were intemperate and ill-considered. I meant no disrespect.'

'Of course,' the king replied, but there was an edge to his smile that belied the graciousness of the answer. He gave a sidelong glance to Abhorash, and the warrior obediently – although not without some reluctance – slid his sword back into its scabbard. It was only then that Arkhan realised how tense he had become. His hands had curled into fists, and his jagged teeth were on edge. Just like Nagash's court, so long ago, he thought. How we circled each other then, like hungry jackals, ready to sink our teeth into the weak the minute their back was exposed.

Arkhan saw the champion relax slightly. Lamashizzar returned his attention to the papers on the table, and just when it seemed that he confrontation was over, Lord Ushoran took a sip from his wine bowl and said, somewhat offhandedly, 'Our guest from Mahrak does have a point, cousin.'

The king turned, as did Abhorash, both of them with almost the same look of irritation on their faces. W'soran's eyes narrowed as he tried to divine the real purpose behind Ushoran's words. Lord Ushoran was infamous for his intrigues, both in and out of court; mostly the king tolerated it because Ushoran came from one of the oldest families in Lahmia, and because the nobleman was smart enough not to involve any members of the royal family in his schemes.

Though distantly related to the king's household, Ushoran wasn't blessed with Asaph's gifts of beauty and charm; he had the sort of face that blended easily into a crowd, with close-cropped dark hair and unremarkable brown eyes. Arkhan gathered that Ushoran had gone to some effort over the decades to keep the cabal's activities out of the public eye. Lamashizzar believed him capable of anything.

'Do you now question my claim to the throne?' the king asked with a brittle smile.

Ushoran chuckled. 'Certainly not, cousin. I merely wish to point out that our progress has been almost nonexistent these past fifty years. We continue to age, albeit very, very slowly, and possess nothing like the power that his ilk–' the nobleman gestured to Arkhan with his wine bowl– 'displayed during the war.' He shifted slightly on the divan. 'It cannot be argued that you aren't following Nagash's incantations as they were intended.'

'Blood is blood!' Lamashizzar snapped, giving in to his anger at last. 'It carries life in it, whether it's from a goat or from a man! And no one will raise a hue and cry if we decide to sacrifice an animal once a month – if anything, they'll likely laud us for our piety! This way raises less suspicion. You all know that.'

Next to Ushoran, Lord Ankhat straightened and swung his legs over the edge of the divan. He was less the dilettante than Ushoran, though his family name was just as old and respected. Though small in stature, he was still trim and physically fit, with piercing eyes and a sharp mind that has hampered only by his notorious impatience. 'I know that power is meant to be *used*, or else it is worthless.' Ankhat said, fixing the king with a steady gaze. 'If we had the full power of the Usurper at our command, we wouldn't need to fear the other cities.'

'I'm certain Nagash thought the same thing,' Lamashizzar retorted, glancing back at Arkhan as if for confirmation. When the immortal gave no obvious sign of agreement, the king continued.

'It's different now,' Ankhat persisted. 'The other great cities are but a shadow of their former glory, and the power of the priesthood is broken forever. They wouldn't dare defy us.'

'Not separately, perhaps, but together?' Lamashizzar shook his head. 'An alliance of the great cities would destroy us as surely as it doomed Nagash.'

Ankhat snorted in disgust. 'Who would lead such an alliance? All the great kings are dead. All except you, that is.'

The king ignored Ankhat's clumsy praise. 'All we need is time,' he said. 'Every passing year, the cities of Nehekhara grow ever more dependant on our trade with the East. Our influence reaches all the way to distant Zandri, and as far south as Ka-Sabar. In another hundred years, perhaps two, no one will dare to move against us. There is no need for bloody gambles and ruinous wars. All we have to do is wait, and everything we want will fall into our hands.'

For a moment, no one spoke. Even the stolid Abhorash seemed uncomfortable with the king's vision. The very idea of restraint was alien to these men, who were accustomed to getting what they wanted with a snap of their fingers. Yet they could not bring themselves to gainsay the king. At least, not for now.

But for how much longer, Arkhan wondered. How long until they start to feel the creeping approach of time, and become obsessed with their fading vitality? How long until they realise that Lamashizzar's carefully reasoned caution is a mask for something far more simple and straightforward. The man is weak. He inherited his power from Lamasheptra, and the one time he tried to gamble with it, he lost his nerve. If I hadn't arrived at his tent outside Mahrak, he might never have committed his army to battle at all, and Nagash would very likely have won.

It still galled the immortal that he'd let Lamashizzar turn the tables on him inside the Black Pyramid. Even a weak man can be dangerous in the right circumstances, he reminded himself. Greed can sometimes be a courage all its own.

W'soran took a deep breath and folded his hands at his waist, not unlike a priest lecturing a group of acolytes. 'You mention animal sacrifice and piety, great one,' he said. 'Yet you fail to mention that the greatest of holy rites specify the spilling of *human* blood instead.' He spread his hands. 'If the lifeblood of a goat is no more potent than that of a man, then why do the gods make a distinction?'

The king turned and glared at W'soran, his brow furrowing as he searched for a proper rebuttal, but here the former libertine was out of his depth. Finally he turned to Arkhan.

'Is he right?' Lamashizzar asked.

The immortal affected a shrug. 'I'm no more a priest than you are, great one,' he answered carefully. He was treading in dangerous waters now. If Lamashizzar ever bothered to read Nagash's commentaries more attentively, he would see the truth of what W'soran was getting at right away. 'It's certainly possible that W'soran has the right of it, but that isn't really the point, is it? The question is whether creating the elixir from animal blood is potent enough to grant immortality or not. And that is something we have yet to prove one way or the other.' Arkhan gave the king a black-toothed smile. 'Certainly there is still room for improvement in your performance of the incantations.'

Lamashizzar gave Arkhan a hard, penetrating stare, and for a moment the immortal thought he'd overplayed his hand. Then, abruptly, the king grinned ruefully. 'There you have it,' he said, turning back to his cohorts. 'It's all my fault.'

Ushoran chuckled politely. 'Spoken like a true king,' he said, raising his wine bowl in salute. The others joined in, and Arkhan allowed himself to relax. He approached the table and pretended to study the ritual symbols. He could see places where he could suggest miniscule changes to the geometries that would suggest areas of improvement without providing any real benefit to the elixir.

The immortal bowed to the king, and smiled his ghoulish smile.

'Shall we begin, great one?' he said.

Raw, burning pain gnawed at Arkhan's nerves, banishing the thick fog of the lotus root. His muscles quivered like plucked bowstrings. Arkhan groaned, baring his ruined teeth against the pounding agony, and with an effort of will forced his stiff eyelids open.

She was standing over him, bathed in warm light from the oil lamp in her right hand. A tiny frown pulled at the corners of her perfect lips.

'Are you well?' Neferata asked. Her voice was dusky and sweet, like rich honey. Even in his wretched state, the sound of it was riveting. Large, almond-shaped eyes narrowed in concern. She raised a slender hand, and for a moment, the immortal thought she might actually reach out and lay her palm against his head, like a mother might to a sick child. The queen seemed to catch herself at the last moment, her hand pausing scant inches from his brow.

'It is nothing,' Arkhan grated. Even his jaw muscles were stiff now, despite the taste of the king's elixir he'd received little more than an hour ago.

The immortal tore his gaze away from the queen's face and used the end of the iron chain to pull himself to his feet. For a moment he leaned against the grimy wall and tried to orient himself. It felt as though he'd only just choked down the bitter bowl of wine and lotus root that W'soran had forced on him. He blinked in the dim light, still expecting to see the king and his cohorts moving about the chamber. 'What time is it?' he mumbled.

'Scarcely an hour before dawn,' the queen replied, a note of tension creeping into her voice. 'The king was here much longer than usual. I had to hide in an adjoining room until he and W'soran left. I think they were arguing.'

Arkhan managed a nod. 'W'soran is growing impatient,' he said. 'The old vulture covets not just Nagash's elixir, but the rest of his incantations as well. The others are starting to agree with him.'

Neferata's dark eyes narrowed thoughtfully. 'All of them?' she asked. She turned and walked back to the paper-strewn worktable where her husband had stood just a couple of hours before. Every movement was sensuous and fluid, almost hypnotic. Like one of Asaph's sacred serpents, Arkhan thought. The sight of her filled him with a bewildering mix of wonderment, hunger and terrible dread.

She was so like Neferem, he thought, and yet so unlike her at the same time. The women of Lahmia were famous for their seductive beauty, but the daughters of the king bore the likeness of the goddess herself. But where Neferem's staggering beauty had been tempered by her role as the Daughter of the Sun, Neferata's allure was darker and far wilder, like Asaph herself. A single look from her could topple kingdoms, the immortal thought. No wonder the kings of Lahmia keep their daughters locked away and their queens hidden behind golden masks.

'Well, Abhorash still seems loyal, but that's to be expected,' Arkhan said. 'Ushoran and Ankhat, on the other hand, are tired of Lamashizzar's half-measures. They were at Mahrak. They know how feeble the king's elixir truly is.'

Neferata stood beside the table and studied the arrangement of the papers carefully, noting their precise order carefully before picking through the pile. Lamashizzar would know if a single sheet was out of place when he returned the following night. 'What of Ubaid?'

The immortal shrugged. 'I confess I do not know. Lamashizzar only brought him into the cabal because he needed the grand vizier's help to maintain his secret. Since then he's been very circumspect with his opinions.'

'Typical,' the queen observed. 'But somewhat encouraging, nonetheless. And the others?'

Arkhan snorted. 'The young libertines? Irrelevant. Their loyalties belong to whoever supplies them with the elixir. Frankly, you would be better off without them.'

Neferata carefully peeled back several pages until she came to a yellowed sheet depicting a complex ritual circle. It was one of several versions of the Incantation of Immortality that Arkhan had tried to recreate from Nagash's books. To the immortal's unending irritation, the Undying King had not committed a definitive version of the ritual to paper, no doubt to keep its secrets firmly under his control. Lamashizzar could scarcely tell the difference between one page and the next without Arkhan's help, but Neferata's training with the priestesses of Neru gave her a degree of insight that her brother lacked.

Since she'd begun her secret tutelage under Arkhan, some eight months before, the queen's skill in the necromantic arts had grown by leaps and bounds. Sneaking into the cabal's sanctum each night, right on the heels of the king and his cohorts, she learned more in a few stolen hours than Lamashizzar had managed in more than a century.

Of course, it helped that Neferata was far less squeamish about the nature of the blood she used.

The queen studied the page intently. After a few moments, she took a piece of chalk from a clay bowl on a nearby shelf and began making precise adjustments to the circle laid out on the sanctum floor.

'Things are coming to a head quicker than I expected,' she said as she worked. 'We must be ready very soon now.'

Arkhan caught himself staring at the queen, watching the way her body moved in the lamplight. He took a deep breath and closed his eyes. 'If this ritual succeeds, then you will have all the power you need,' he told her. Together, they had already created versions of the elixir that were several times more potent than anything the king had made. The immortal licked his lips. 'Much depends on the quality of the base material, of course.'

Neferata gave Arkhan a sharp look. 'The blood of a royal handmaiden is sufficient, I should think.'

The immortal smiled. 'Younger is better than older,' he said. 'Of course, a live victim is better still.'

The queen made one last change to the circle and rose to her feet. 'And why is that?' she asked, as she inspected her work.

'The more youthful the blood, the more of life's vigour it contains, of course,' Arkhan replied.

'And using a live victim in the ritual grants even more vigour?'

Arkhan hesitated, uncertain how much he should reveal. Neferata had already gleaned far more secrets from him than he'd been willing to share. 'In a manner of speaking, yes.'

'Well, that will have to wait for another day,' the queen said. 'For now, we must be content with what we have.'

She moved past him, to a table at the far end of the room – one well out of reach of his iron chain, Arkhan could not help but note. Neferata picked up a small ceramic jar, not much larger than a nobleman's wine bowl, and carried it to the centre of the ritual circle. The immortal felt his turgid pulse quicken. Neferata never told him how she obtained the blood from her handmaidens, and, in truth, he didn't really care.

Neferata knelt beside the jar and placed a number of additional marks around its circumference, then retreated to the edge of the circle. 'The sun will rise soon,' she said, raising her arms towards the ceiling. 'Let us begin.'

Arkhan moved to the far side of the circle, taking care not to drag his iron chain across the sorcerous glyphs. He raised his own arms – stiff and yet trembling, all the same – to mirror Neferata's own. And then, together, they began to chant.

The words of power now rolled easily off Neferata's tongue, and the air began to crackle with invisible energies, harnessed to a force of will as great as any Arkhan had ever known save for Nagash himself. The immortal echoed every syllable, adding his will to her own, until the ritual circle seethed with power.

The incantation was long and complex, stretching for many long minutes, and Arkhan felt the energies of the ritual building to a furious crescendo. The jar began to tremble, its lid rattling maniacally as gusts of steam billowed from the contents within. His lips peeled back in a ghastly, feral snarl as he smelled the fragrant odour of the rapidly quickening elixir. Arkhan threw back his head and cried out the words of the incantation in an exultant voice. The centuries seemed to unwind within him, and for a single instant he was once more a mighty warrior, a master of magic and conqueror who once made all Nehekhara tremble with fear.

And then, immortal and queen cried out as one, and the ritual culminated in a shower of lambent sparks from the glyphs inscribed on the surface of the jar. Neferata staggered, momentarily stunned by the force of the power she'd commanded, but Arkhan's senses were razor-sharp. In an instant he was inside the circle, feeling the residual energies of the incantation burn across his skin as his hands closed about the curved surface of the jar.

He felt the queen's eyes upon him. They cut through his raging thirst like a knife. He clutched the jar tightly, imagining that he could feel the strength of the elixir through the glazed walls of clay. If he drank it dry, it might give him the strength enough to tear open the collar and finally escape.

Then again, it might not, and then where would he be? Neferata would not take such a betrayal lightly. And she already knew more than enough to continue studying Nagash's books without him, whether she realised it yet or not.

Arkhan sank slowly to his knees. With an effort of supreme will, he raised the jar to Neferata, as a servant might proffer wine to his master. 'Here, great one,' he said in a hollow voice. 'Drink of the fruits of your labour. Drink, and be restored.'

Neferata smiled at him, and Arkhan was secretly ashamed how it made his dead heart lurch in his chest. She came to him, graceful as a serpent, and took the jar from his unwilling hands.

The queen raised the steaming vessel to her lips and took a long draught. A delicious shudder went through her slender frame. 'Oh,' she whispered. '*Oh!*'

Arkhan watched in silence, gripped by a helpless despair. She would drink it all. He knew it. Months ago, she'd sworn to share every draught of elixir they made, just as Lamashizzar had promised him long ago. But promises meant nothing to kings and queens, except when it suited them. Nagash had taught him that lesson well.

He was surprised, therefore, when the queen lowered the jar to him once more. 'Here, favoured servant,' she said with a regal smile, her lips red with the sweet wine of stolen life. 'Take your due.'

It took all the remaining willpower he had not to snatch the jar from Neferata's hands. Still, they trembled as he brought the rim of the jar to his lips and drank.

The elixir flowed into his mouth like molten metal, setting every nerve alight. He stiffened, gulping greedily, as he felt a fraction of the old power return to his wasted limbs. It was a shadow of what he'd once felt as the Undying King's right hand, but it was still greater by far than anything Lamashizzar had wrought.

When he was done he sat back on his heels, gasping for breath. The queen was studying him, her dark eyes thoughtful. He met her gaze directly, too intoxicated for the moment to be cowed by her supernatural beauty.

'Why, great one?' he asked. 'What do you wish to gain from all this?'

Neferata's lips curved in a crooked smile. 'Besides eternal youth and power?' she asked.

'Yes.'

The queen's smile faded. 'Lahmia is in peril,' Neferata replied, 'and her king is too weak and too foolish to protect her. So I must instead.' She cocked her head and regarded him appraisingly. 'What of you? What do you wish, now that Nagash is dead and gone?'

Arkhan did not reply for a moment. He felt the power coursing through his veins and drew a heavy breath. 'What do I want? I want to ride a horse again, and cross the desert sands beneath the moonlight.'

Neferata quirked a delicate eyebrow. 'Is that all?'

The immortal gave her a tight-lipped smile and hefted a length of iron chain. 'Forty-seven links,' he said. 'That equates to exactly twenty-three and a half paces. For the past one hundred and forty years, that has been the length and breadth of my entire world. What I wish for, great one, is nothing less than paradise.'

Neferata considered this, and then, to Arkhan's utter surprise, she reached down and laid a hand upon his cheek. Her skin smelled of sandalwood, and was warm as a summer breeze.

She bent close to him, and her eyes seemed to swallow him whole. 'I know what it's like to live every day as a prisoner,' she said softly. 'Keep your oath to me, Arkhan the Black, and I swear you will see your wish fulfilled.'

Then she was gone, retreating from the circle and returning the ritual materials to the way they were as Lamashizzar had left them. Arkhan hadn't felt her pluck the jar from his hands. He hadn't even noticed it was gone until minutes after she'd departed.

It was a long time before Arkhan crawled from the circle and curled up like a dog at the base of the sanctum wall. When his mind finally quieted enough to let him sleep, he dreamt of endless, moonlit sands, and the music of silver bells. The warm desert air caressed his face, smelling of sandalwood.

SIX

THE BARROW-THIEF

Cripple Peak,
in the 76th year of Djaf the Terrible
(-1599 Imperial Reckoning)

Now that he had reached the mountain at long last, Nagash's great work began in earnest. His first months were spent combing its slopes, crawling into each fissure like a spider and searching for ways to reach deeper into its heart. He'd hoped that the deposits of *abn-i-khat* would lie close to the surface, and that the vents were signs of ancient impacts that would point the way to the burning stone, but within the first few days he realised that his theory was only half-right. The fissures were mostly shallow crevices that narrowed quickly as they plunged even deeper into the rock. They weren't the scars of multiple impacts, but the marks of a single, giant impact some incalculable time in the past. The burning stone had been driven deep into the mountain's guts, cracking its granite flanks like a dropped wine bowl.

He searched the mountain systematically, starting at its foot and working upward in a rough spiral. By day he took refuge in one of the deeper fissures, breathing in the glowing vapour in an attempt to replenish some of the power he'd expended. Already, his exposure to the burning stone was beginning to take its toll. He found that he needed to ingest more of the *abn-i-khat* to maintain his strength, which left his skin ravaged by terrible lesions and glowing traces of the mineral in his bones. The luminescence penetrated his flesh, revealing the workings of his muscles and the shrivelled knots of organs nestled in his chest, but so long as his mind remained sharp and his limbs obeyed his will, he paid the changes little mind.

Finally, many weeks later, he found a fissure almost two-thirds up the mountain that sank crookedly into the stone for more than twenty feet, then opened into a wide, low-ceilinged cave that glowed with residue from centuries of subterranean vapours. From that moment on, the mountain was Nagash's fortress, his sanctum from the burning sun and the meddling of feeble-minded men.

Nagash spent months searching the tunnels that branched from the great cave, discovering a vast, tangled network of passageways that honeycombed the fractured mountain. He marked the passageways with hieroglyphs using the point of his bronze daggers, slowly building a map of the labyrinth as he made his way ever deeper into its depths. He scraped residue from the rock walls and collected the dust in the hood of his cloak, and conceived of different ways to strain the mineral from the steam that billowed from the deepest parts of the mountain, but he could not find a way to reach the deposits themselves. The tunnels would have to be extended; exploratory shafts would have to be sunk deeper into the earth, and structures built to haul the stone to the surface. He would need an army of slaves to conquer the mountain and plunder its treasures, and so the necromancer turned his attention back to the surface once more.

It was very late, and though well past the rainy season the mountainside was wreathed in thick layers of mist. Luminous ribbons of steam caused the cooler layers of mist to writhe and dance, teasing the eye with ghostly images in the fog. Nagash paused at the lip of the fissure and listened. It was deathly silent along the slopes of the mountain and the barrow fields below. In the distance, he could hear the lapping of waves along the rocky shore of the Sour Sea.

The necromancer clutched his tattered cloak about his chest and made his way down the slope. Power crackled along his withered veins. He'd ingested the last bits of his scavenged stone and a healthy pinch of the cave-dust as well, to ensure that he would have ample strength to complete the ritual he'd planned.

At the foot of the mountain he paused again, his senses stretched to the utmost. For the last week he'd crept among the barrows, observing the activity of the priests while he searched for the likeliest spot to attempt his experiment. He'd learned that groups of acolytes, led by one or more senior priests, would patrol the northern edge of the wide plain for several hours each night. They rarely ventured further south, where the barrows were much older, and they hastened to return to the temple fort before the hour of the dead. He suspected that the patrols were more of a punishment for lazy acolytes than a genuine attempt to guard the barrow fields from intruders. He'd crossed paths with the patrols more than once during his explorations, and they'd never even suspected he was nearby. Nagash had listened to their nervous chatter often enough that he thought that he was beginning to understand parts of their bestial language.

He'd decided that it was best to attempt the ritual after the patrols had returned to the temple, to minimise the risk of discovery, but that served to limit how far he could travel from his mountain lair and still make it back before dawn. Satisfied that there was no one about, Nagash headed north and west, among the newer barrow mounds.

The barrow where the high priest had interred the hetman and his warriors was still relatively unspoiled. Streaks of mud had drained down over the stone foundations during the rainy months, and a layer of sallow, sharp-edged grass had grown atop the mound, but the wooden cover that had been placed over the entrance was still easily accessible. The cover, round as a wagon wheel and made from layers of planed wood, had been wedged into the stone frame and the cracks filled with packed earth.

Nagash stepped into the shadow of the barrow mound's entrance and stretched forth a gaunt, faintly glowing hand. The power flared along his limbs as he focused his will upon the wooden cover. Words of power fell like stones from his lips as he unleashed a short, concentrated spell.

Green light licked from the necromancer's fingertips and played across the surface of the wood. At once, the planks blanched, crackling from within as the energies ate through the living matter. The sound of decaying wood spread, growing in volume and intensity, until the entire cover collapsed with a hollow crash. Nagash hastened through the entrance, his bare feet kicking up dry clouds of dust with every step.

Beyond the opening was a short tunnel made of fitted stones that led into the centre of the mound. Nagash moved easily in the darkness, his eyes having long since adapted to the conditions of the deep tunnels beneath the mountain. After thirty feet or so, the tunnel gave way to the barrow proper: a dome-like chamber made of stone and packed earth that stank of mould and decay. There was nothing in the way of ornamentation on the walls, or the rotting platforms of wood and leather upon which the corpses were laid. It was a far cry from even the meanest of Nehekhara's crypts.

The hetman's body lay on a platform in the centre of the mound, surrounded by the bodies of his chosen men. The damp and the ravages of beetle and worm had worked their harm upon the corpse, causing flesh and muscle to liquefy and slough away from the bone. Much of the skin covering the hetman's skull had been chewed away, revealing part of a cheekbone and the warrior's gap-toothed jaw.

Nagash's lip curled in distaste. *Amateurs.* He'd hoped to find the corpses in better condition. It was easier to send power twitching through muscle than to animate bare bone. Looking about, he saw that none of the other bodies were in any better condition, so with an irritated grimace he drew his dagger and bent to work.

The damp earth made carving the ritual circle a simple task, though filling in the magical symbols was much harder to do with the necessary precision. He had to cut deeply into the dirt to chisel out the proper lines, taking far more time than he'd intended. By the time he was ready to begin, he reckoned that dawn wasn't more than an hour away. He hadn't even properly begun, and already the experiment had run into trouble.

Tucking away his dagger, Nagash stepped up to the edge of the circle and raised his arms. He began with a long litany of curses, focusing his anger and his desire by calling up the names of all those, living and dead, who had wronged him and cast him out into the wasteland. *Khefru. Neferem.*

Nebunefer. Hekhmenukep. Rakh-amn-hotep. Lamashizzar... The litany went on and on, until finally he was hissing with rage. At some point the names gave way to words of power, and the dank air crackled with the force of the necromancer's will.

He drew deeply of the power he'd absorbed, pouring it into the circle and the hetman's body. '*Rise,*' he commanded. '*Rise. Your master commands it!*'

Slowly the chamber became suffused with a greenish glow, emanating first from Nagash, and then from the hetman's body itself. Green light pooled within the corpse's eye sockets. A tremor went through the rotting flesh: muscles constricted, stirring colonies of beetles and wriggling worms.

Nagash watched in triumph as the corpse's spine arched. One arm lolled off the side of the platform, spilling rotting flesh onto the floor. Then, slowly, as though pulled by an invisible tether, the hetman sat upright. The skull oriented on the necromancer, its bare jaw working as though trying to speak.

'*Rise!*' Nagash ordered. '*Come forth!*'

The corpse paused for a moment, as though uncertain of its strength, and Nagash redoubled his focus. The hetman's body shuddered under the lash of the necromancer's will, and haltingly swung its legs over the edge of the frame. Wood snapped beneath the shifting weight, all but tumbling the corpse to the floor. It tottered unsteadily on bare, uneven feet for a moment, but then it seemed to find its balance. Slowly, steadily, its back straightened. The corpse turned carefully on its heel to face its summoner, bale-lights flickering where its eyes had once been.

Nagash's lips peeled back in a ghastly, triumphant grin. Cruel laughter bubbled up from his chest. And then the hetman's corpse raised its bony arms and lurched forward, reaching for his throat.

He was so certain of his control over the corpse that at first he didn't recognise his peril. It was only when the hetman's grasping fingers were scant inches from his throat that Nagash backpedalled in shock. '*Back!*' he commanded with a sweep of his hand, pouring still more energy into the spell.

But the corpse did not cease. It staggered forwards, fingers grasping, bony jaws clicking hungrily together. Snarling, Nagash tried to push the monster's arms aside. It tottered unsteadily for a moment, but recovered with disturbing speed. With every passing moment it seemed to grow in strength and intelligence. Cursing the chaotic energies of the *abn-i-khat*, Nagash angrily banished the energies of the ritual.

He expected the corpse to collapse at his feet. Instead it leapt forward, seizing Nagash by the throat. Bony digits dug deep into the necromancer's own unliving flesh, clawing into the waxy muscle beneath. Stunned, Nagash struggled in the hetman's grip. He stared into the bale-fires that still burned in the corpse's eye-sockets, and suddenly realised that it was being directed by a will other than his own.

The faint sound of chanting echoed down the dark tunnel from the barrow entrance. The priests! They hadn't been so careless or so blind as he'd thought.

As he struggled with the hetman, Nagash saw that the bodies of the retainers were starting to move as well. The energies of his ritual had dissipated, but he pressed his hand against the hetman's chest and lashed out with his will. The corpse staggered slightly, but resumed the attack almost at once.

Had he been a living man, Nagash would already have been dead. As it was, he would be surrounded within moments and torn to pieces by the rest of the hetman's retinue.

Rage consumed the necromancer. He, who had mastered the energies of the Black Pyramid, and once commanded armies of warriors both living and dead, laid low by a handful of corpses and a pack of bawling savages? It was unthinkable!

With a roar, Nagash drew upon his diminished reserves of power and felt his limbs burn with unnatural strength. He seized the hetman's right wrist with his left hand and squeezed, shattering the small bones and tearing its clenching hand free, then drew one of his bronze daggers and drove it through the corpse's forehead. The monster staggered, but did not fall. Snarling, Nagash wrenched the knife left and right until the vertebrae snapped, then tore the corpse's head from its shoulders. At once the body collapsed, falling apart as the sorcery that had animated it was suddenly dispelled.

Nagash had time to draw his second knife before the hetman's retainers closed in. There were five of the shambling creatures, their eyes burning with malice as they reached for him with claw-like hands. He slashed with his heavy blades, severing fingers and shearing through hands, but still the corpses closed in. They jabbed at him with splintered bones and snapped at him with their rotting jaws. He smashed the skull of one leering corpse, obliterating it like a rotting melon, and then shattered the knee of another. It fell at his feet, wrapping its mauled arms around his legs.

Another arm slipped around Nagash's throat and tightened with frightening strength, while a fourth creature fastened its jaws on his left arm. He felt himself being dragged off his feet. Snarling, he kicked at the creature holding his legs and succeeded in crushing its neck and shoulder with one savage blow. It fell back, one arm hanging uselessly at its side. Free of its grasp, Nagash twisted at the waist and drove his dagger into the throat of the creature whose teeth were savaging his side. Rotten flesh parted like damp cloth; he twisted his wrist and the monster's head came loose with a wet, popping sound.

The last of the corpses crashed into him, hands pressing on his chest. Nagash fell backwards, slashing wildly with his blade as he fell. He landed on his back, and the creatures fell atop him, pinning him down and tearing at him with their jaws. The necromancer writhed and kicked. Teeth sank into his cheek, tearing at the waxy flesh. Nagash brought up his left-hand blade, driving it so deeply into one corpse's ribcage that it became hopelessly entangled. Enraged, he let go of the dagger's hilt and drove his hand deeper, past the shrivelled organs and leathery muscles until his fingers closed around the creature's spine. He squeezed, crushing the vertebrae, and then shoved the crippled monster aside. Moments later, the last corpse collapsed with its skull crushed beneath the pommel of his dagger.

Growling like a beast, Nagash kicked himself free of the corpses and staggered back to his feet. Grisly wounds had been gnawed into his face, chest and arm, but he felt no pain. His flesh burned and his bones shook. Smoke curled from the ragged ends of skin hanging from his cheek.

He burst from the barrow mound with a Nehekharan war cry on his lips, his eyes blazing with wrath. Half a dozen priests were waiting outside, standing in a semi-circle and chanting, their arms raised to the sky. Perhaps a dozen acolytes attended upon them, holding aloft lantern-globes that were already half-dead from the strain of the priests' incantation.

Nagash flung out his hand and spat words of power. Arcs of green fire burst from his fingertips, spearing half of the priests. They fell screaming, their skin blackening as they burned from the inside out. Lantern poles toppled as the acolytes fled in panic, the globes bursting as they hit the ground.

The rest of the priests recoiled in shock and horror. He waited for them to strike back, unleashing searing blasts of their own, but no such counter-strike came. Nagash advanced on them, dagger poised. He slashed out with the blade, and one of the savages toppled with his throat slashed open. The last two turned to flee, wailing and babbling imprecations to the heavens. Nagash leapt upon them, hacking and stabbing until both lay silent and broken at his feet.

Nagash staggered, bloody and torn, chest heaving with exertion. His power was all but spent, his flesh savaged by combat and the fire of the *abn-i-khat*. He could still hear the screams of the acolytes, fading in the distance off to the north-west. Nagash threw back his head and howled after them. I'm coming, he thought savagely. There's nowhere you can run in this forsaken place that's safe from me!

Muscles quivering, he turned, heading back for the safety of the mountain – and saw that he was not alone. A single acolyte stood watching him, eyes wide and jaw agape with fear. He was young, scarcely old enough to be a man, and he clutched his lantern-pole with a white-knuckled grip.

When Nagash's merciless gaze fell upon him, the acolyte sank slowly to his knees and bowed low. The necromancer studied him for several moments, debating on what to do. Finally he simply nodded silently and walked away. Truth be told, he wasn't certain he had enough strength left to kill the young man and still make it back to the foot of the mountain.

Power. It all came down to power. He'd thought he'd had enough, and nearly paid for that mistake with his life. As he lurched across the lifeless plain towards the distant mountain, with dawn less than half an hour away, Nagash vowed that he would not make the same mistake again.

SEVEN

THE RIGHT OF QUEENS

Lahmia,
the City of the Dawn,
in the 76th year of Djaf the Terrible
(-1599 Imperial Reckoning)

'Please, great one. Try one of these.' Tephret reached for a golden bowl with one ancient, palsied hand and tried to fish out a few candied dates. 'You'll waste away if you don't eat something.'

A light supper had been laid out for the queen at the edge of the small pond that served as the centrepiece of the palace garden. Neferata leaned against the bole of a small ornamental tree, surrounded by a constellation of golden dishes laden with uneaten sweetmeats and Eastern delicacies. It was late spring, the rainy season, but the night was surprisingly clear. Neru shone high in the sky, and drops of rain from the evening's rainstorm glittered like diamonds on the blooming garden flowers. The night air was warm and heady with their perfume. Large fish swam in lazy circles just beneath the surface of the water, their opalescent scales glimmering ghostly white beneath the moonlight. If she listened very closely she could hear the whisper of the currents they stirred in their wake.

Neferata stilled Tephret's hand with a gentle touch and a warm smile. They were alone in the great garden, she'd sent her other handmaidens away as soon as the dinner had been laid out.

'These foreign foods have lost their savour, I'm afraid,' she said to Tephret. The woman's skin was soft and wrinkled beneath the queen's fingertips. At a hundred and sixty-five years of age, her most favoured handmaiden was nearing the end of a long and faithful life. The queen had watched her grow from a nervous slip of a girl into a grey-haired old woman, and in all that time, Tephret's devotion hadn't wavered.

Had she ever wondered why her mistress had never lost the bloom of youth? Had she ever resented Neferata's enduring beauty, even as her own faded with the passage of time? If she did, Tephret had never let it show.

Other handmaidens had come and gone over the decades, but she had remained, until now the queen could not imagine life without her.

Tephret returned the queen's smile, her rheumy eyes glittering. 'Shall I catch you a fish, then?' she said, and a sudden memory made her chuckle. 'Do you remember that time when you gave little Ismaila that bowl of Rasetran liquor, and she got so drunk she waded out into the pond and tried to catch the fish with her hands?'

'And she nearly drowned half of us trying to get her out,' Neferata added. 'I had weeds in my hair, and a frog went down the front of your robe.'

'That's right!' Tephret exclaimed, her face lighting up. 'I didn't realise it until we got back to your bedchamber, and then we spent half the night chasing the little thing around the room!' She threw back her head and laughed, transported by the memory, and Neferata joined in.

'Oh, she was such a silly one,' Tephret said, wiping tears from the corners of her eyes. 'But a good girl, bless her. What ever happened to her?'

Neferata sighed. 'Oh, her family had her married off to some petty lordling. Suheir, I think his name was. It was years and years ago, now.'

'Years and years,' Tephret echoed, shaking her head. 'It seems like that was just yesterday to me.'

'I know,' Neferata replied softly, feeling a sudden pang at the wistful look in Tephret's eyes. She gently gripped the handmaiden's arm. 'It must have been hard for you, watching all the other girls go on to raise their own families.'

'Oh, no,' Tephret replied, slowly shaking her head. 'I had no such illusions. I had no family after all, no one to search out a suitable husband.'

'I could have,' the queen said. 'I *should* have. It was my responsibility. I just couldn't bear to part with you.'

The handmaiden smiled, a little sadly. 'That's very kind of you to say, great one.'

'No,' the queen said. 'Call me Neferata. Nothing more. Tonight, let's talk as friends do. All right?'

At first, Tephret didn't quite know what to say. Finally, she nodded. 'You have been a friend to me,' she managed to say. 'Perhaps the only friend I've really known. Does that seem strange?'

'Not to me,' Neferata said, and felt tears prickle at the corners of her eyes. 'Here,' she said, picking up a wine bowl. 'Drink with me, and let's talk a little more about old times.'

The handmaiden hesitated for a moment. Tephret had never much enjoyed the taste of wine, and had always been the one to keep her head when Neferata and the rest of her handmaidens were deep in their cups. She started to speak, perhaps to voice a polite refusal, but then she met the queen's eyes and her resolve melted away. Without a word, she took the wine bowl in both hands and raised it carefully to her lips.

Neferata smiled to herself as she watched her handmaiden drink. Once upon a time, she could have ordered Tephret to partake of the wine, but now she could command others with nothing more than a gentle suggestion. Moreover, they *wanted* to obey, as though nothing might please them more. It was another gift of Nagash's elixir, she knew. It had manifested itself over time, growing in power as she and Arkhan continued to refine the necromancer's formula. Until now, the queen had been careful to use her newfound gift sparingly, but tonight, she would test it to its limits.

They sat and talked quietly for hours. Tephret drank wine while the two of them talked of times past, while Neferata kept a careful watch on the moon's stately progress overhead. As the hour drew close to midnight, she took a deep breath and said, 'How long has it been since you left the Women's Palace, Tephret?'

The handmaiden paused, her lips working silently as she tried to puzzle through the question. It was fairly late, by the queen's standards, and Tephret had consumed the better part of an entire jar of wine.

'Blessed Asaph, let me see...' the handmaiden muttered. 'It would have been the sixty-second year of Geheb, I believe. That was the year I was presented to the king, and he made me your handmaiden. I was just eight years old. That was...'

'More than a hundred and fifty years ago,' the queen observed. She considered Tephret for a moment, then reached over and plucked the empty bowl from the handmaiden's grasp. 'Walk with me,' Neferata said, taking Tephret's hand and gently pulling the old woman to her feet.

Tephret frowned in bemusement. 'Where? Is it time to return to the bedchamber, or do you wish to visit your cousin Khalida?'

The queen shook her head. 'Khalida is gone, remember?' she reminded Tephret. 'She was married to Prince Anhur, years ago. Now she rules as Queen of Lybaras.'

'Oh, of course,' Tephret said, chiding herself. 'Forgive me, great one. My memory plays tricks on me sometimes.'

The queen squeezed her hand. 'There's nothing to forgive, except that you forgot to call me by my name. Now come.'

'Where are we going, then?'

'Into the palace proper,' the queen replied. 'You've been shut up in here too long, Tephret. It's time to set you free.'

To the queen's surprise, Tephret stopped dead in her tracks, pulling against the queen's grip with surprising strength. 'We can't!' she said, her eyes widening. 'It's not allowed!'

Neferata turned, stepping close to the aged handmaiden and peering deep into her eyes.

'Do you trust me, sweet Tephret?' she asked.

The handmaiden fell silent, a reply half-formed on her trembling lips. She met the queen's eyes and relaxed at once.

'With my life,' she answered faintly. 'But... but what will the king's servants say? What about your mask?'

'They will say nothing,' Neferata said firmly. 'Tonight of all nights, we will go wherever we wish, and we will not hide who we are. Do you understand?'

'No,' Tephret said, shaking her head. 'But that's no matter. I go where you go.'

Neferata squeezed her hand and smiled. 'That's right, dear one. Just follow me.'

The queen led her most favoured handmaiden down the lamplit corridors, through rooms and galleries that they had both known all their lives. Servants made way for the pair, marvelling at how queen and handmaiden walked hand-in-hand, like close friends. They spoke to one another as they walked, sharing memories and laughing softly at one another's tales.

They passed through the Hall of Reverent Contemplation, still lost in times past. Tephret barely paused when the queen reached the end of the hall and pulled open one of the heavy outer doors. As luck would have it, a pair of palace servants were just passing the chamber as the queen emerged. One of the servants, a younger woman, took one look at the queen and fainted. The other was transfixed, his eyes wide and his jaw hanging open as Neferata approached.

'Tend to your companion,' she said, peering into the servant's eyes. 'And tell no one of what you saw.'

Trembling, speechless, the servant fell to his knees and pressed his forehead to the floor as the queen and her companion glided past.

Tephret followed the queen like an obedient child, clutching the queen's hand and staring openly at the unfamiliar surroundings. Neferata felt giddy, her pulse racing as she openly walked the halls that she'd been forced to skulk through for nearly a year. Other servants crossed her path, and each one she left prostrate on the marble tiles, stunned and quivering in shock. She relished their stunned, slack-jawed expressions, their instant subservience. This is how it shall be from this night forward, she swore to herself. I shall walk these halls whenever it pleases me. I shall see my children again. And no one will dare say otherwise.

Moving openly, Neferata covered the distance to the abandoned wing of the palace much faster than expected. For a moment, all she could do was stand at the servants' entrance. Her heart was in her throat.

Tephret was weaving on her feet. The late hour and the wine were weighing heavily on her. 'What are we doing here?' she said bemusedly.

The queen drew a deep breath. 'I have a gift for you,' she said. 'It's not much further now.'

The handmaiden peered through the doorway. 'It's so dark in there.'

'I know,' Neferata said. 'I know. Just hold my hand. Everything will be all right.'

And with that, her course was set. She could not turn back now. If nothing else, her pride wouldn't allow it.

Tephret followed her into the darkness without hesitation. She said not a word as they walked through the dust and debris, nor did she fret at the sounds of creatures scurrying just out of sight. All she did was tighten her grip on the queen's hand, and pressed on.

Neferata scarcely paused as she pushed open the door to the sanctum, as though she was entering nothing more than a room inside the Women's Palace. She took Tephret to the banked brazier, and then stirred the coals to sluggish life.

The handmaiden turned slowly in place as the orange light filled the room. Her gaze drifted past the laden bookshelves, the stained divans and the cluttered worktables. Neferata saw the look of innocent wonder on her face and realised that the old woman was looking for the gift she'd been promised. She watched as Tephret's eyes moved to the ritual circle at the far side of the room... and then she saw the huddled form of Arkhan, just at the edge of the light. Immediately, Tephret turned towards the immortal and then gripped the queen's arm.

'Someone's there!' she hissed, her voice quavering.

'I know,' the queen said. 'It's all right, Tephret. There's nothing to fear.'

Arkhan stirred, his head rising slowly at the sound of the handmaiden's voice. He leaned forward, into the firelight, and Tephret saw his face.

'Oh!' Tephret cried, her eyes widening in terror. She pressed a hand to her mouth, even as her voice built to a scream. 'Oh, merciful gods. Asaph protect us!'

Neferata batted Tephret's hand aside and seized her by the chin. 'Hush!' she commanded, turning the handmaiden's head so she could stare into her eyes. 'Do not be afraid. There is nothing to fear, do you understand?'

Tephret's voice fell to a whimper. Neferata heard a rattle of heavy, iron links, and then Arkhan spoke.

'What's going on?' he demanded. 'What's *she* doing here?'

'It's time,' the queen told him, never taking her eyes from Tephret. 'It's been a month. Lamashizzar will gather the cabal together to create his elixir. Correct?'

'Yes,' Arkhan replied. 'But what does that have to do with her?'

'Then this is the moment we've been waiting for,' Neferata replied. 'But before we confront the king, we'll need to be at the peak of our strength.'

The immortal let out an exasperated sigh. 'All right, but that doesn't explain–'

Neferata tore her gaze away from the handmaiden and fixed Arkhan with her stare. 'Months ago, you told me that the elixir can be made even more powerful using a living vessel.' A small part of her mind was surprised at how calm she sounded.

Arkhan was taken aback. 'No,' he stammered, shaking his head. 'You misunderstand. She... she's too old–'

'What's that got to do with anything?' Neferata snapped. 'She's alive, and she's here. If you are half as skilled as you claim to be, you should be able to make this work.'

A moan slipped past Tephret's trembling lips. She was weeping now, trembling from the strain of containing her fear. 'What's going on?' she asked in a fearful, almost childlike voice. 'What are you talking about? I don't understand...'

Neferata touched a finger to the handmaiden's lips. 'Hush, dear one,' she said, and forced a smile. 'You're about to receive your gift.'

She took Tephret's hand and led her across the room. She held the handmaiden's gaze the entire time.

'You've done so much for me,' Neferata said to her. 'For so many years you've served without hesitation or complaint. And now, dear one, I'm going to set you free.' The queen manoeuvred her into the centre of the circle and placed her hands on the woman's cheeks.

'Don't be afraid,' the queen said, drawing on the power of the elixir coursing in her veins. 'Everything is going to be all right. Stand here but a moment, and then no one in all Lahmia will ever command you again. Do you understand?'

Slowly, by degrees, Tephret relaxed. When she spoke again, her voice sounded small and frail. 'I understand, Neferata.'

The queen smiled, tasting tears on her lips. 'That's right, dear one.' She leaned forward, touching her forehead to Tephret's. 'You've done so very much for me, for so many years. You've earned your rest. Part of you will be with me always,' she said, and then stepped back until she stood outside the circle.

Arkhan was waiting for her. The immortal's expression was strange and troubled. 'You do not understand,' he said, so softly that only she could hear. 'If you truly love her, then you must not do this.'

The queen studied Tephret for a moment, then shook her head. 'No,' she said. 'It's too late for that. I need her, this one last time.' She turned to the immortal, and bore down on him with the full weight of her stare. 'Do what you must,' she told him. 'The king will be here in little more than an hour.'

Arkhan stiffened. 'Very well,' he said in a hollow voice. 'Prepare yourself, great one.'

Neferata nodded, wiping more tears from her eyes. 'I am ready,' she said.

The immortal bowed to her, then went to a nearby table. She watched, surprised, as he picked up a small knife and tested its edge against the ball of his thumb.

She was not prepared for what happened next. She was not prepared at all.

The sound of footfalls echoed through the darkness. Neferata focused on the sound. Her senses were sharp as a razor; she could hear nine distinct sets of footsteps. One moved with catlike grace, which she took to be Abhorash, the king's champion. Two more were loose-limbed and clumsy. The drunkards could be virtually anyone.

The steps drew closer, then suddenly there was a hiss of surprise, and everyone stopped, just outside the sanctum door. Neferata heard

Lamashizzar's voice, whispering urgently. Doubtless he'd seen the light of the brazier seeping beneath the sanctum door.

She heard a rasp of metal – it rang faintly, and she could tell it was sharp iron by the note, as distinct as a musical tone. Then came the catlike tread, and after a moment the door to the chamber swung slowly open. Abhorash entered, sword ready, with the king and the rest of the cabal close behind.

Neferata waited for them at the edge of the ritual circle, her head held high. Arkhan stood to one side, his hands clasped behind his back. Behind them, Tephret's bloody remains still lay sprawled in the centre of the circle. The queen's hands were spread at waist level, palms out, like a welcoming goddess. Her linen robe, from neck to sleeves, was stained crimson, and her chin was red with fresh blood.

Abhorash, the grim, implacable warrior, recoiled from the sight of Neferata with a cry of shock and wonder. Even Lamashizzar, who had known her all his life, was momentarily stunned by the sight of her naked, bloodstained face. The rest of the cabal looked upon her as though she was the vision of a vengeful goddess, come to wreak a terrible judgment upon them. Ubaid sank to his knees with a groan, his face filled with rapturous terror.

Given the scene spread before him, it was a wonder that the king could manage find his voice at all.

Lamashizzar took a halting step towards Neferata. 'How dare you!' he said. The words welled up from his throat in a choked whisper. 'This is an outrage. An offence against the crown!'

Neferata met his gaze without flinching, yet it was not her husband she saw. Her mind's eye could see little past the horrors of the hour before. She could still hear the echoes of Tephret's screams in her mind. She had lingered for a very long time, given the hideous things Arkhan had done to her. The queen had watched every agonising second of it. She had owed poor Tephret that much.

'This,' Neferata said in a leaden voice, 'is for the future of Lahmia. You have forgotten your duties to your people, brother, so I am taking matters into my own hands. Starting now.'

Lamashizzar's face went pale with rage. 'You stupid, arrogant bitch!' he growled. He rushed towards her, seizing both of her arms and shaking her roughly. 'When I get you back to the Women's Palace I'm going to flog you within an inch of your life! Do you hear–'

Neferata's small, slender hand moved too fast for mortal eyes to follow. She laid her palm against the king's chest and pushed, and Lamashizzar was hurled backwards as though he were nothing more substantial than a straw doll. Abhorash dodged nimbly aside, leaving the king to crash into the drunken forms of Lords Adio and Khenti. They fell to the ground in a tangle of thrashing limbs.

'I am the queen,' she said coldly. 'And from this night forward, there is no place in this palace that is barred to me. You shall remain king over Lahmia, brother, but know that I am Queen of Lahmia, and when I speak, you will take careful heed of what I say. Henceforth, we shall rule this city *together*. Do you understand me?'

Lamashizzar broke free of the paralysed libertines. His face was a mask of hatred, but Neferata could see a glimmer of fear in his eyes. Still, he managed a defiant snarl.

'Seize her!' he ordered Abhorash. 'She has gone mad! Strike her down!'

'He will do no such thing,' the queen replied calmly. She glanced at the king's champion and smiled. 'These men are mine now, brother – each and every one of them. They will serve me gladly, because I can give them something you cannot.'

That broke the spell. W'soran stirred, his eyes alight. 'The elixir!' he hissed.

Neferata nodded. 'I will offer you the power that you have so long craved,' she said. 'And in return, you will serve me as you would your king.'

Abhorash stirred. 'I want nothing of power,' he said in a deep voice.

The queen took a step towards him, well within reach of the champion's sword. 'No, you crave something far more elusive. You crave *perfection*,' she said. 'It's not enough to be the champion of the king; there are six others in Nehekhara who can rightfully claim such a title. No, you want to be the greatest of warriors, the epitome of fighting men. That's why you accepted the king's offer in the first place, didn't you? So that you could have all eternity to hone your skills beyond mortal ken.'

The mighty warrior blanched at the queen's unsparing assessment. The others looked at her as though she was an oracle, never pausing to think that, through Arkhan, she had more than a century's worth of knowledge about their every hope and desire.

She surveyed the assembled noblemen. 'Lamashizzar has failed you for the last time,' she said to them. 'Bow to me, and I will give you all that you desire. The choice is yours.'

W'soran did not hesitate. He sank to his knees and prostrated himself before the queen. Ankhat and Ushoran followed suit, and the three young libertines, Adio, Khenti and Zuhras followed suit. Ubaid, already kneeling, simply nodded deferentially to the queen, as he had done so many times before.

That left only Abhorash. The queen turned to regard him with a raised eyebrow. He held her stare for a long, silent moment, then slid his sword back into its scabbard.

Lamashizzar, who only moments before had been the undisputed ruler of the greatest city in Nehekhara, could only look on in helpless fury.

'What is it you want, sister?' he snarled.

Neferata smiled.

'For now, fetch a hammer and an iron chisel,' the Queen of Lahmia said, savouring her triumph. She pointed a bloodstained finger at Arkhan the Black. 'You're going to set him free.'

EIGHT

THE EYE OF THE BURNING GOD

Cripple Peak,
in the 76th year of Djaf the Terrible
(-1599 Imperial Reckoning)

After the ambush at the barrow, the priests organised large hunting parties to comb the plains and the mountain slopes to find Nagash's lair. For weeks they searched the mountain, sending acolytes down into the fissures as far as they could manage. Almost a score of them died in the attempt, overcome by the concentration of glowing vapours, and their bodies were never recovered. Despite their best attempts, the hunters never came close to him; he'd become far too adept at navigating the labyrinth of tunnels and caves beneath the deeper fissures. Whenever they drew too close he would simply retreat deeper into the maze until the hunters lost their nerve and withdrew.

Eventually, the barbarians' hunger for vengeance faded, and they abandoned their hunt. The stormy season was about to begin, and the older priests had no desire to spend day after day out on the mountain slopes in the rain. They retreated back to their temple fort and doubled the patrols out on the barrow fields, in case the terrible grave robber should return again.

Nagash spent weeks studying the movements of the patrols out on the plain, sometimes moving among them on nights when the rains were heavy and the brassy notes of thunder rumbled across the surface of the Sour Sea. He'd come to realise that the priests were not true necromancers; their skills were limited and extremely crude compared to his. What they lacked in sophistication they made up for in numbers and raw power, though, and the priests he encountered on the plain took their duties very seriously indeed. They were sharp-eyed and vigilant, even under the worst conditions, and they knew the plain far better than he.

If it came to battle, Nagash had no doubt that he would win, but the fight would cost him resources he could ill afford to spare. Though he spent nearly every day combing through the tunnels in search of more dust, there was now little left to scavenge. He'd filled his cloak hood to almost three-quarters full; perhaps two pounds, more or less, and mingled with all manner of impurities. It was his sole source of strength, unless he managed to find a way to reach the deposits buried deeper inside the mountain.

Thus, Nagash was forced to surrender much of the barrow fields to the priests, restricting his activities to the southern edge of the plain where they rarely patrolled. The barrow mounds there were very old, many having collapsed altogether under the weight of centuries and their contents long gone to dust. Any corpses left within the mounds would be nothing more than bones, and much harder for him to control, but for the moment they would have to serve.

Nagash searched the southern barrow fields for some time, examining the barrow mounds carefully before he found one that suited his purposes. Like the rest, its stone foundation had settled into the earth over the centuries, completely burying its entranceway, but the weeks of steady rain had softened its earthen roof enough that he could dig through it with his bare hands. Night after night, he clawed at the soft ground, tearing it away in chunks and casting it aside. Flashes of green lightning illuminated him as he worked, revealing his grotesque, almost skeletal figure. Sickly emerald light seeped from his bones, revealing the dark, rope-like muscles working beneath his tattered skin. More skin hung like torn parchment from his cheeks and forehead, revealing the leering skull beneath. The necromancer's eyes had long since rotted away, boiled from within by the heat of the burning stone. All that remained were twin, green flames, flickering coldly from the depth of sunken eye sockets. His limbs were held together not by sinew, but by sorcery and willpower alone.

Finally, late one night, Nagash's efforts bore fruit. His fingers tore through the last layers of root and soil covering the barrow, releasing a hissing cloud of noxious air that would have slain a breathing man within moments. Redoubling his efforts, Nagash widened the hole far enough to allow him to slither his way inside.

He had chosen this particular barrow because it was one of the largest ones still intact on the southern end of the plain. Nagash hoped it had belonged to a great warlord or hetman, and thus hold the remains of a large retinue that he could raise as well. What he found was far better than he'd hoped for.

Nagash slid through the muddy channel he'd carved in the barrow's roof and found himself in a moment of freefall as he plunged some twelve feet to the barrow floor. He landed hard, snapping his right collarbone like a dry twig; irritated, Nagash focused his will on the surrounding muscles to pull the broken ends of bone back into place, and then healed the break with a small measure of his power. Frowning, he bent down and laid a hand on the barrow floor. It had been laid with crude paving stones, now cracked and slimy with age.

Lightning flickered high overhead, casting a shaft of brilliant green light through the hole in the barrow's roof. It pierced the gloom, revealing a carved stone bier at the centre of the barrow. Laid upon the bier was the skeleton of a once-powerful man, clad in a mouldy shell of thick leather armour. A belt of heavy gold links hung loosely about the warrior's shrunken waist, and a circlet of gold, tinged black with corruption, lay against the corpse's bony brow. The warrior's hands were folded over the hilt of a long, black sword that had been laid atop his chest. It was straight and double-edged, and it seemed as though it had been shaped from a single piece of obsidian. Crude glyphs had been carved into the surface of the blade and then filled with a familiar green dust. The *abn-i-khat* still glowed faintly after so many years.

Nagash turned about slowly, his burning stare taking in the rest of the chamber. There were no less than a dozen other skeletons interred with the warlord, laid on stone biers and arrayed in a circle about their lord with their feet pointing towards the walls of the mound. Ten of the skeletons were clearly warriors, clad in rotting leather armour and carrying crude stone weapons of their own. The other two appeared to be female, judging by the tattered scraps of fabric and the tarnished golden jewellery that adorned their fingers and necks. Wives perhaps? There was no way to tell, and it mattered little to him at any rate. So long as they could dig, they would be of use to him.

Taking out his dagger, Nagash began to carve a ritual circle into the barrow's stone floor. It was different in design and intent than the one he'd used months before, and similar to the arcane circles he'd placed in the Black Pyramid at Khemri. This circle would not contain magical power; it would broadcast it in very specific ways.

When the circle was complete, Nagash took a moment to inspect it and make certain that every line, every symbol was correct and properly aligned. Then he retreated to the far side of the chamber and pulled a tightly closed bag from his frayed leather belt. Very carefully, Nagash opened his makeshift bag and studied the glowing dust contained within. It was slightly less than half-full at this point.

A growl rose from his ravaged throat. Power. In the end, it all came down to power – and the willingness to use it.

Nagash raised the bag, tilted back his head, and poured a stream of glowing dust down his throat.

A whirlwind of fire burst inside his chest and went howling up into his brain. The entire world seemed to shudder under his feet. When he finally lowered the bag, he could hear the thunder of rain on the earthen roof of the barrow and feel the slightest wrinkles in the leather of the bag clutched in his hands. His gaze pierced the gloom of the barrow, until every detail of the dank chamber was sharply etched in his brain.

That's when Nagash realised that the walls of the chamber were not raw earth, as he'd supposed. The builders instead had covered it with a kind of lime mixture, creating smooth, white surfaces that they had then decorated with paint. He saw crude representations of battles between human tribes, focusing on the triumphs of a tall, dark-haired man with piercing eyes: no doubt the very warrior whose bones now resided in the tomb. Of greater interest to Nagash was the woman depicted next to the warlord, whose eyes flashed with green fire and who flung bolts of burning energy to slay the warlord's foes. His gaze turned once again to the two female skeletons, whose corpses were arrayed by the warlord's head – and then he saw the mural that had been painted on the wall above them.

Fiery eyes blazing, Nagash approached the fading mural. At its feet he stared up at the curving wall and the image of a dark, broad-shouldered mountain, looming up over a bare, rocky plain. A long, burning line, like a spear, had been driven into the mountain's side, piercing it to its heart. At the centre of the wound there burned a green, lidless eye.

Nagash's burning heart raced. Quickly, he turned and stepped into the ritual circle. Raising his arms before the warlord's corpse, he focused his mind by hissing out the names of those he hated. Then, with visions of dark vengeance glimmering in his brain, he began the incantation of awakening.

The necromancer infused every arcane syllable with power until his shrivelled lips were ragged and the air clashed like a cymbal with every word he spoke. Nagash turned his implacable will upon the ancient corpses. *Rise,* he commanded. *Your master summons you. Rise!*

More power washed over the skeletons, stirring flakes of decaying leather from their armour and scattering scraps of moulding cloth – then the blackened bones began to emit a faint, green glow. There was a crackle of decaying hide and the creak of bending sinew, and Nagash saw the warlord's hands tighten on the hilt of his blade.

'*Rise!*' Nagash said aloud, his voice rising to a furious howl. '*The Undying King commands you!*'

There was a rasp of metal and bone. Slowly, the warlord rose at the waist, like a man sitting up from a long slumber. Tiny points of green fire glittered from bony eye sockets as the skeleton regarded Nagash.

Around the barrow chamber, the other skeletons were doing the same. They rose from their beds of stone and studied Nagash in cold, pitiless silence. The necromancer clenched his fists in triumph.

'*Come to me!*' he ordered.

Bones clattered as the warlord and his retinue slid from their biers and walked haltingly to stand before Nagash. With every passing moment they seemed to stand a little straighter, their movements a little stronger and more assured. Their bones radiated the chill of the grave, and ancient malice gleamed in their flickering eyes.

Nagash pointed a bony finger at the painting on the far wall. '*Now, show me,*' he told his ghastly retainers. '*Take me to the burning eye.*'

* * *

The undead took no notice of the rain, or the mud, or the sprawl of barrow mounds that had risen up across the plain since their death. They led Nagash across the barrow field to the east, and then skirted the southern slope of the mountain until they reached a path that only they could somehow perceive. Nagash wondered if the warlord and his retainers saw the mountain as it had been at the time of their deaths, or if they were simply following the course of ancient memories, heedless of the reality laid before them.

They climbed steadily up the slope through the darkness, and the more that Nagash studied the surrounding terrain, the more he began to see faint remnants of a roadway, and the outlines of foundations that might have once supported wooden structures. He'd paid them no mind during his initial searches, focusing on natural caves and fissures instead. Now he began to see telltale clues of a large complex - a palace perhaps, or a temple - that had once been built into the side of the mountain, many hundreds of years ago.

His servants led him to a wide depression in the mountain's flank, its edges rounded in places by the passage of years. He spied more outlines of foundation stones, now that he knew what he was looking for. Once upon a time, a huge, wooden structure had been built here - and perhaps there had been tunnels as well, burrowing into the mountainside. Clearly this was the place where the huge piece of burning stone had impacted, then was buried by hundreds of tons of shattered rock and smouldering earth. Apparently the barbarians' ancestors had witnessed the fall of the great stone and had decided to worship it, a tradition now aped by their debased descendants.

The warlord climbed the slope without hesitation, certain of his bearings even in the darkness and rain. At the base of the depression was a wide, rounded shelf of earth that Nagash now realised had been excavated in ages past to form yet more building foundations. The rain-slicked skull glanced left and right, as though expecting to see squat, wooden towers, or tall statues flanking the entrance to a hallowed place of worship. After a moment's hesitation, the warlord continued forward, marching stiffly for another thirty paces into the depression before coming to an abrupt halt by a steep slope of grassy earth.

Nagash smiled in satisfaction. '*Dig,*' he commanded. At once, the skeletal women stepped forward and began clawing at the slope. The warriors paused long enough to set aside their weapons before joining in as well.

By the time dawn broke through the scudding clouds overhead, the skeletons had carved a small cave out of the muddy earth. Nagash took refuge within and stood watch while his servants worked tirelessly through the day. By late afternoon, the skeletons were digging up squared-off pieces of stone that must have once belonged to a building's foundation. By late evening, they'd reached the broken pieces of a collapsed stone arch. Whatever passage the archway had once anchored had collapsed during the intervening centuries.

That night, Nagash went out into the barrow fields once more and returned with another dozen skeletons to add to his workforce. Less than a handful of dust remained in his bag. It was all or nothing now. They had to reach the burning stone. They *must.*

The skeletons worked through the night and into the following day. They shored up the walls with piles of broken stone and packed earth as the shaft descended at a steep angle into the side of the mountain. Then, during the third night, the skeletons clawed through a layer of earth and rock and broke into a narrow tunnel made of closely-fitted stones.

Nagash heard the hollow clatter of bony feet against flagstones and pushed his way to the front of the group. Sensing his thoughts, the skeletons paused and stood aside to let him pass.

The necromancer stood on a broad, stone staircase that sank still deeper into the side of the mountain. The walls of the staircase were carved with intricate reliefs, depicting men and women carrying offerings of food and grain down the stairs to set before the waiting god. Nagash descended the slimy steps as quickly as he dared, trying to gauge how much further the staircase went before they reached bottom.

After only a few minutes, the steps led to a small antechamber. Four thick stone columns supported the antechamber's low ceiling; they had been carved with reliefs depicting a pair of men and women, their hands held against their chests in a gesture of supplication. They reminded Nagash of the totem statues in the barbarian villages to the north-west, though these figures were not quite so idealised as the others. Wide, earthen bowls were scattered across the antechamber floor. The offerings that had once been heaped inside them were nothing more than dust now.

Nagash crossed the small chamber and came to a tall, rectangular doorway. The wooden doors that had once sealed the portal lay in heaps of dust across the wide threshold. He stepped through the drifts, scattering them with his bare feet, and entered a much larger rectangular chamber. This room's ceiling was supported by four pairs of squat stone columns, each one carved to represent a man or a woman kneeling in worship towards an undefined point at the far end of the chamber. There, in the darkness, Nagash sensed a steady buzz of magical power.

The necromancer walked carefully past the ancient pillars. Those on the left were male likenesses, he noticed, and the ones to the right were female, and each pillar represented the same person as the one before it, but with a critical difference. As Nagash progressed across the chamber, the carved figures grew stronger, more handsome – more perfect in shape. By the time he stood at the far end of the chamber, he was flanked by a pair of stone gods, still poised in supplication before an invisible god.

There was a pair of tall doors at the far end of the chamber, made of a grey metal that blended cunningly with the stone surrounding them. Nagash ran his hands across the surface of the doors, and was surprised to find them warm to the touch. There were four holes in each door at shoulder-height, arranged to accept a man's fingers. Without hesitation, the necromancer slid his bony fingers into the holes and pulled on the great doors.

At first, the metal panels refused to budge. Nagash let out an impatient hiss and called upon his ebbing power. His muscles burned, and he heaved upon the doors with all his might. There was a crack of corroded metal, then a squeal of hinges, and the doors began to move. They were immensely heavy, Nagash realised, far heavier than bronze, though not quite as heavy as gold. As they swung open, a fierce green glow poured out over Nagash and spilled into the ancient hall.

The necromancer felt his skin prickle at the touch of the sorcerous light. Beyond the heavy metal doors was an alcove of rough stone that had been chipped away to reveal a hemisphere of glowing, green stone as large as a wagon wheel. Aeons past, some foolhardy barbarian had braved the stone's searing touch to carve the semblance of a pupil and an iris into the surface of the stone, transforming it into an unblinking, blazing eye.

Nagash raised his hands covetously to the eye of the burning god and began to laugh. It was a sound of madness and murder, of devastation and despair. It was a ringing portent of ruin for the kingdoms of men.

Far up the tunnel, where the storm winds were rising, the warlord and his retainers heard the terrible sound and awaited their master's bidding.

NINE

AMONG THIEVES

Lahmia,
the City of the Dawn,
in the 76th year of Khsar the Faceless
(-1598 Imperial Reckoning)

It wasn't the tireless white horse of his dreams, but the chestnut-coloured Numasi warhorse was as fine as any animal Arkhan had ever ridden. Long of leg, with a broad chest and powerful hindquarters, the stallion had been bred for agility, strength and stamina – qualities meant to keep it and its rider alive on the battlefield. Presented as a gift from the Horse Lords to the King of Lahmia, the animal had been stuck in a stable, surrounded by sleek-limbed palfreys meant for nothing more demanding than an occasional hunt or ceremonial parade. The immortal had taken to the sullen, snappish creature at once; both of them had been locked away and largely ignored for far too long.

They passed through the palace gates at a trot, barely eliciting a response from the royal guard, and followed the broad processional that wound downhill amid the grand villas of the city's elite. It was just past nightfall, and the city's young lamp-lighters were still making their rounds down the narrow city streets. One boy with a long, reed taper had to leap nimbly to the side to avoid a bite from Arkhan's horse as he went by. Sounds of music and conversation flowed from the open windows of the walled villas as nobles gathered for an early evening meal before heading out into the city for a long night of debauchery. For the moment, the streets were relatively clear, and the immortal made good time. He was already impatient for the wide road and the rolling hills west of the city.

It had only been six months since Neferata had ordered the king to set him free – she'd forced him to wield the chisel personally, to Lamashizzar's utter humiliation – and already his memories of the last hundred and fifty years were fading away, like a long and tortured fever-dream. Neferata had chosen to maintain her quarters in the Women's Palace, far from her husband, and had been careful not to make too great a spectacle of her own newfound freedom. Where he'd once been confined to a single corner of a large, dingy room, Arkhan now had the run of the entire palace wing. Servants had been ordered to clean the corridors and begin refurnishing a suite of rooms, and he had been provided with a fine wardrobe of rich, dark silks and fine leather accoutrements.

Neferata had even gone so far as to provide him with a sword – not the curved, bronze khopesh that most Nehekharan warriors favoured, but a heavy, double-edged weapon made from dark Eastern iron. It was more than just a gesture of trust and esteem, Arkhan knew. The queen was also demonstrating her authority, both to him and to the rest of Lamashizzar's small cabal.

The queen gave him a weapon as a sign that she had nothing to fear from him. She opened the king's stables to him to show that she understood he had nowhere else to go.

After a short while the processional reached the bottom of the great hill and entered the city's eastern merchant quarter, where fine goods from all over Nehekhara were sold to the city's nobles and wealthier merchants. Business was still brisk, despite the hour. Trade with the west was finally on the rise again, with caravans arriving every few months from as far away as Numas and Zandri. Small crowds of citizens and servants browsed through the lamp-lit bazaars, buying bronze goods from Ka-Sabar, leather saddles from Numas or exotic spices from the jungles south of Rasetra. Merchants in the short capes and linen kilts of the desert cities haggled with silk-clad Lahmians and even a few haughty-looking Imperial traders, looking for luxury goods to carry back to their homeland. At one point, Arkhan heard a loud crash and a series of hoarse shouts across the wide square, and turned to see a pair of city guardsmen dragging a struggling, spitting young urchin away from a Rasetran spice trader's stall. If the young thief was very lucky, the city magistrates would only sentence him to a year's labour on a Lahmian merchant ship, otherwise, he'd be chained to the rocky shoreline north of the city and left for the crabs to eat.

Beyond the merchant district sprawled the cramped districts that were home to the city's many artisans and labourers. Here the streets were mostly quiet, as the tradesmen and their families retired to their rooftops or their small, walled courtyards after a long day's work. Children ran about or played games in the cool of the evening, enjoying a few precious hours of freedom. One group ran past Arkhan, led by a tall boy wearing a ghastly clay mask. They were pursued by another group of children brandishing sticks and wearing crude circlets or crowns woven from river reeds. They were intent on catching the masked boy, while his companions brandished sticks of their own whenever the pursuers drew too close.

'After them!' the young kings shouted gleefully. 'Death to the Usurper and his minions! Death to Nagash!'

The masked figure turned and made an obscene gesture at his pursuers, sparking more laughter and threats. Arkhan reined in his horse as they dashed across the street in front of him. The grotesque mask turned his way for a brief instant, and then the boy was gone, leading his young immortals into the shadows of a nearby alley.

Arkhan was still shaking his head in bemusement when the tightly packed mud-brick homes gave way to the cruder, sprawling mass of huts and wicker enclosures that crowded up against the range of rounded hills at the western edge of the city. The people here were mostly descendants of refugees from distant Mahrak, left to eke out a miserable existence among Lahmia's outcasts. Beggars, whores and would-be thieves skulked around the fringes of the trade road, eyeing the immortal's rich attire with predatory interest. Arkhan gave the boldest of them a black-toothed grin and they quickly looked away, seeking easier prey.

He spurred the warhorse to a canter, eager to be free from the stench and squalor of the dispossessed. Within minutes he was heading up into the wooded hills, leaving the noise and the lights of the city behind at last. Scraggly trees pressed close to the trade road, and the sky was just a narrow band of stars and moonlight overhead. Arkhan breathed in the cool air, fragrant with cedar and pine, and gave the horse its head. The stallion leapt eagerly into a gallop, and for a while he was able to put aside thoughts of formulae and incantations and simply feel the wind upon his face.

They had made great progress in the past few months, now that Neferata was in the position to obtain human subjects for their experiments. It was easy enough for Arkhan to snatch a beggar or a whore from the edge of the city, drug them with lotus root and slip back with them into the palace in the dead of night. Afterwards, the body could be dumped amid the condemned thieves north of the city and within a few days there would be nothing but bones, picked clean by the hungry sea. So long as they were suitably cautious, the city's refugee population would keep them safely supplied for hundreds of years. Their mastery of Nagash's complex ritual was still far from complete, but the elixir they created was more than potent enough to ensure the continued loyalty of Lamashizzar's cabal.

As usurpations went, the queen's move was as clever as it was subtle. Unbeknownst to the rest of the city, Lamashizzar had been transformed overnight from a king to a mere figurehead, issuing Neferata's edicts in his own name. He couldn't expose Neferata's scheme to the rest of the city without implicating himself in the practice of necromancy, and he couldn't move against her in secret without being opposed by the rest of the cabal.

Now that Ushoran, Abhorash and the rest had been given a taste of what the elixir could really do, they would have to be idiots to want a return to the thin gruel of goat's blood offered by the king. So far, Lamashizzar had accepted the new balance of power with what little grace he possessed, spending most of his time drinking and sulking in his quarters. It was possible that the coup had broken his nerve completely; Neferata seemed to think so, but Arkhan wasn't so sure. Losing a crown was one thing; losing control over Nagash's elixir was something else again.

He rode on, up into the hills and onto the edge of the great Golden Plain, where countless farmers reaped harvests of grain, corn and beans from the fertile soil. The vast fields now lay dormant and bare, awaiting the return of the spring. Arkhan reined in the warhorse and stared in silence, savouring the wide-open expanse. The crushed white stone of the trade road glimmered like a mirage beneath the moonlight, beckoning him ever westward, towards the Brittle Peaks and the lands beyond

The stallion slowed to a walk, its flanks heaving from the long ride, and Arkhan let the horse choose its own pace as they continued down the road. He was tempted, as he was every night, to simply keep going, past Lybaras and the desolate streets of Mahrak, through the Valley of Kings and the distant Gates of the Dawn. From there, he could slip past hated Quatar, and then to the citadel he'd built in the southern desert, or even to the deserted streets of Khemri itself.

The Black Pyramid remained at the centre of the city necropolis; the great crypt had been built to defy the ages, and would endure long after the sun had gone dark and cold. There were secret ways inside that no mortal knew of, and with the proper sacrifices, the dark winds of magic could be his to command once more.

And then... what? The memory of Nagash's terrible reign was still fresh in the mind of most Nehekharans. If the kings of the great cities knew he still survived, they would spare no effort to destroy him. He could either cower in the shadows like a rat and hope to escape their notice, or else try to raise an army and defy their combined might for as long as he could.

Lahmia, on the other hand, held out the promise of immortality and the comforts of a wealthy and powerful kingdom. He had little doubt that, under Neferata's capable leadership, the city would become the undisputed centre of power in all of Nehekhara. Within a few centuries it might even become the seat of a new empire, something that not even Nagash had been able to achieve.

When that day finally arrived, Neferata would need a strong right hand to lead her armies in the field and expand the borders of her domain; a faithful and ruthless lieutenant - perhaps, in time, even a consort.

Listen to you, he sneered. Arkhan the Black, bald-headed and broken-toothed, consort to the Queen of the Dawn. What a fool! The damned woman has you under her spell. Can't you see that? The farther away from her you can get, the better!

Except, of course, that he had nowhere to go.

Brooding on his fate, Arkhan continued down the road for more than an hour, passing farmers' houses and dark, fallow fields. Dogs barked in the distance; owls hooted, hunting prey, and bats flitted across the face of the moon. After a while, he came to a section of the plain that was still subdivided by stretches of dense woodland. Each time he came upon a stand of trees he paused and took a deep draught of night air.

Soon enough, his preternatural senses detected a faint hint of cooking fires and sizzling grease. He turned off the road and headed south, down a game trail that led deep into the shadows beneath the trees. The horse picked its way forwards carefully: even Arkhan had a hard time seeing much farther than the stallion's drooping head. Yet it wasn't long before the immortal could feel that he was being watched.

The camp was large and cunningly concealed within the thick trees. Undergrowth had been cleared away to create a series of linked clearings, then used to make a cluster of lean-tos and overhangs surrounding a small, banked cook fire. More than a dozen gaunt, filthy men – as well as a number of women and children – all clad in a motley collection of robes and desert kilts stood and stared warily as he emerged from the woods into the firelight. The women gathered the children and retreated swiftly into the next clearing down the line, while the men drew battered swords or hefted spears at his approach.

Arkhan reined in and gave them all a long, calculating look. Lips pulled back in a predatory grin. 'Well met, friends,' he said. 'I smelled wood smoke as I was passing along the road. Is there room for one more traveller around the fire?' He drew a fat wineskin from one of his saddle hooks and showed it to the men. 'I've two skins of Lybaran red I'll be happy to share in exchange for a hot meal, and then I'll be moving on.'

From where he sat, it was difficult to tell how many people occupied the camp: it could be anywhere from a few score to as much as a few hundred. Bands such as these moved like nomads up and down the plain, never staying in one place for too long lest they draw unwanted attention from the city. Mostly they stalked along the edges of the trade road, preying on merchant caravans for food, trade goods and horses. Arkhan had been seeking out their camps for several months. Many of the bandit gangs had grown adept at hiding in the woods and hollows scattered across the plain, but he'd learned his trade hunting Bhagarite desert raiders, and there were only so many places a large group could make camp without attracting attention.

The brigands cast questioning glances at a short, stocky man standing closest to the fire. He studied Arkhan for a moment, then nodded curtly. 'You can sit by me,' he said, and the rest of the men lowered their weapons. 'We've grain mash and a little rabbit we can share. Where are you headed?'

Arkhan slid easily from the saddle and tossed the wineskin to the brigand leader. He shrugged. 'Oh, here and there. You know how it is.'

He might not have any place he could truly go, but in this, Arkhan was far from alone.

* * *

The brigands drank every last drop of Arkhan's wine, and in return gave him a bowl of greasy stew and some news about the comings and goings of bandit gangs across the plain. The immortal chewed his gristle thoughtfully and listened to every word. Much of it was lies and exaggerations, he knew, coupled with a few honest facts about rival gangs, in the event he was a spy for the city guard. Later, when he'd returned to the palace, he would compare what he'd learned with the notes he'd taken from previous encounters, and look for common threads.

As the hour drew close to midnight, he took his leave of the brigands. Their leader and his lieutenants, who'd gotten the lion's share of the wine, made no protest, friendly or otherwise, as he said his farewells and led his horse back into the dark woods in the direction of the trade road. He could sense the movements of other bandits pacing him through the darkness, all the way to the edge of the wood line and beyond. They shadowed him across the bare fields, their brown capes blending with the dark earth. Most likely they were making sure he wasn't reporting back to a waiting troop of city guardsmen, but it was also possible that they meant to avail themselves of his fine horse and expensive iron sword. It had been tried a few times before.

They followed him all the way to the trade road, but pressed no closer than a few dozen yards. Once the horse was back on stable footing, the immortal swung into the saddle and waved farewell to his erstwhile shadows before setting off towards the city at a brisk trot.

He gauged that the camp contained a good hundred or so bandits, and a third as many women and children. It was one of the largest such gangs he'd encountered to date. There were enough armed men wandering the Golden Plain to amount to a small army; most were fairly organised and they were all heavily-armed. All they lacked was a strong leader to unite them under a single banner.

The more such gangs he encountered, the more Arkhan believed that his plan had merit. He could start with the largest gang, gain their loyalty through a mixture of charisma, fear and bribery, then begin forming ties with other, smaller groups. With the right mix of ruthlessness and reward, he could build an organisation fairly quickly, and having an armed force at his command occupying the Golden Plain would give him an outside source of power that he currently lacked. That was a lever that he could apply to any number of inconvenient obstacles.

Before he knew it, Arkhan was at the edge of the plain and heading downward through the wooded hills. The lights of the city glimmered on the horizon, unimpeded by the barrier of high city walls. Of all the great cities of Nehekhara, only Lahmia disdained such fortifications. Siege warfare had been unheard of before the war against the Usurper, and old King Lamasheptra trusted in his dragon men to keep the city safe. He wondered if the queen would take steps to correct her father's mistake.

Suddenly the stallion tossed its head, checking its stride and snorting in surprise. It was the only warning the immortal had before the arrows struck home.

Two powerful blows struck him on the left side, one just below his ribcage and the other in the side of his thigh. Searing pain stole the wind from his lungs. He pitched forward against the horse's neck, tasting blood in his mouth and fumbling at the reins. Gritting his teeth, he tried to spur the horse forward, only to find that his left leg wouldn't move. The arrow had passed completely through his thigh and buried itself in the thick leather of his saddle, pinning it in place.

A third arrow hissed out of the darkness, missing him by a hair's-breadth, then a fourth punched deep into his left shoulder. This time he cried out, cursing at the ambushers. He'd grown careless during his long confinement, letting himself walk into such an obvious trap. With the moonlight glowing on the white stone road he might as well have hung an oil lamp around his neck. The archers could see him clearly, while he was all but blind.

The warhorse sidestepped, tossing its head and snorting at his confused commands. Even if he managed to get the animal under control the archers would put an arrow in its neck before he'd gone half a yard. As near as he could reckon, he only had one option left. Gritting his teeth, the immortal grabbed the arrow jutting from his thigh and tore it free, then simply let himself fall from the saddle.

He landed on the right side of the horse, striking the road with a bone-jarring crunch that consumed him with another wave of blinding pain. Pure reflex forced his limbs to work, rolling him off the road and into the brush. He fetched up against a tangle of briars and lay still, pretending to be dead. Were it not for the elixir coursing through his veins, he likely would have been.

The stallion bolted as he fell, galloping down the road and out of sight. For a moment, nothing moved. Arkhan bit back waves of agony and listened for the slightest signs of movement.

Before long he heard quiet footsteps edging from the tree line on the opposite side of the road. It sounded like just two men. The bandits must have left camp long before he did in order to set up such an ambush. How had they known he would be heading back towards the city?

He heard the men make their way cautiously nearer. His right hand, shielded beneath his body, edged towards the hilt of his sword.

The ambushers paused in the middle of the road, just a few yards away. 'Not so tough as we thought,' one of them said. Arkhan thought he recognised the voice.

Arkhan heard the rasp of a sword being drawn. 'He'll want proof,' said another familiar voice. 'We'll take back his head. Roll his body out of the brush.'

The two men drew nearer. A hand gripped his right shoulder and pulled. Arkhan rolled onto his back, drawing his iron blade with a bestial snarl.

The two ambushers cursed, their faces exposed by the same lambent moonlight.

They weren't bandits at all. Arkhan found himself staring at Adio and Khenti, two of the king's young libertines.

Arkhan cursed. He'd been a fool. An utter and complete fool.

The two libertines stared back at the immortal with wide eyes. Khenti still clutched a powerful Numasi horse bow in his left hand, while Adio had left his on the white stone roadway so he could grip a curved, bronze khopesh in both hands. They were both clad head to foot in dark, cotton robes and short cloaks. Neither wore armour, as far as Arkhan could tell. No doubt they'd expected to kill or incapacitate him with a volley of arrows, then collect their trophy and ride back to the city. Had they been proper archers, they likely would have succeeded.

Careless, the immortal thought angrily. He'd all but planned the ambush for them. The cabal knew about his nightly rides out to the plain, and a few coins in the hand of the right stableboy would tell them exactly when he left. All they would have to do is ride the same route and pick out the best place to lie in wait.

The two fools hadn't killed him yet, but the powerful, broad-headed arrows had done their damage. His left leg felt leaden and unresponsive, and the arrow in his left shoulder made it difficult to move his arm. The third arrow had sunk deep into his vitals. It and the shaft in his shoulder had snapped when he'd rolled off his horse, leaving two bloodied and splintered stubs jutting from his robes. Agony washed over his body in cold waves, but he scarcely felt its bite. Pain held no power over him any more, not since the war. Not since Quatar.

He only had moments to act; if he was still on his back when Adio's shock wore off, even a pampered Lahmian libertine would have little trouble hacking him to pieces. Gritting his ruined teeth, he rolled onto his right side and then, using just his sword arm and his right leg, he pushed himself onto his feet. The moment he put any weight on his left leg it began to buckle. Desperate, he drew upon the power of the queen's elixir to lend him strength and speed.

For an instant, the immortal felt his veins catch fire, but the heat began to fade almost at once. Neferata's potion was powerful, but it still had its limits. Darkness crowded at the corners of his eyes, until for a moment he feared that he'd drawn too much and he was about to do Adio's work for him. The pain ebbed, held for a dizzying instant... and then swept back in again, pushing the threatening shadows aside. His leg remained weak, but at least the muscles responded to his will. It would have to be enough.

Adio was already lunging forward with a choked cry. He was a tall man, with long, lean arms, narrow shoulders and bony knees. His brown eyes were wide with fear, bulging above a long, hooked nose, and his narrow lips were stained by years of exposure to lotus root. His swing was swift enough, but lacked skill. Arkhan parried it easily with his iron blade and countered with a swipe to the nobleman's throat, but after more than a century his skill was little better than Adio's. The libertine clumsily blocked the strike and fell back towards the road, his sandals scuffing across its stone surface. The clash of bronze and iron galvanised Khenti as well. With a startled shout the paunchy nobleman turned and ran back the way he'd come.

Cursing, Arkhan charged after his would-be ambushers. He would have just as soon see Adio break and run as well, but the nobleman either didn't like his odds in a foot race, or was possessed of much more courage than the immortal had given him credit for. Adio threw another wild swing that missed the immortal by more than a foot, then abruptly shifted direction, swinging around to the immortal's left. Arkhan tried to match Adio's movements, but his wounded leg hindered him. The libertine slashed at him again, and Arkhan's sword was too far out of position to block it. The bronze blade gouged across the immortal's upper left arm, leaving a shallow cut through the muscle. Had the blade been sharper, it would have cut him to the bone.

Snarling, Arkhan planted his right foot and spun on its heel. The iron sword flickered in the moonlight, arcing around to catch Adio from an unexpected direction. The libertine reacted with surprising speed, just barely raising his curved sword in time to block the heavier blade. Still, the nobleman let out a high-pitched shriek as Arkhan's weapon sliced open Adio's sword arm just above the elbow.

Then a powerful blow hit the immortal in the back, punching into his torso just beneath his right shoulder. Arkhan staggered, shouting in surprise and anger. Khenti hadn't been running away at all; the pudgy little bastard had simply been getting enough room to start firing arrows again.

You've gotten soft in a century and a half, Arkhan thought, as Adio regained his balance and rushed at him, khopesh raised high for a skull-splitting blow. In a moment of cold clarity, Arkhan wondered if this was how he was going to finally die, struck down by a callow young gambler and left in a ditch for the vultures.

The khopesh swept down, its nicked edge whistling through the air. Arkhan's limbs moved without conscious volition, driven by instincts honed on countless battlefields. His iron sword swept up in a sweeping block, meeting the khopesh just past the height of its arc. There was a discordant clang, and the lighter bronze weapon snapped in two.

Adio reeled backwards, staring in shock at the ruined sword, and Arkhan was on him like a wolf. A backhanded blow from his heavier sword shattered the nobleman's right elbow, eliciting a scream of raw agony. The cry turned to a bubbling wail as the immortal's second stroke slashed Adio's throat all the way to the spine. The libertine fell backwards, his left hand trying to stanch the dark blood pouring from the gaping wound. He had no sooner hit the ground than the immortal was standing over him, sword raised. Arkhan ended the nobleman's thrashings with a single blow to the head.

Another arrow hissed out of the darkness, flying a handspan over Arkhan's bent back. The immortal pulled his blade free from Adio's shattered skull and turned, throwing back his head and howling like a fiend as he charged across the road.

His wounded leg hobbled him, turning his charge into a headlong stagger, but Arkhan pushed forward as quickly as he could. His bloodcurdling shout echoed from the dense trees. It was a calculated move, meant to rattle Khenti. Every second brought the immortal closer to his foe, and it took nerves of stone to calmly draw and nock an arrow in the face of a charging enemy swordsman.

Arkhan glimpsed movement across the road, then heard a muffled curse. Teeth bared, he oriented on the sound and tried to increase his pace. A moment later he could make out Khenti's head and shoulders, then the raised arm of his horse bow. The immortal was close enough to hear the *twang* of the bowstring, then Khenti's arrow smashed into his chest. It missed his heart but pierced his left lung; Arkhan staggered, but the sight of Khenti reaching for another arrow spurred him forward once more.

Crying out in fear, Khenti fumbled for another shaft from the hunting quiver at his hip. Arkhan reached him in eight long steps and smashed the bow from the nobleman's hand with a sweep of his sword. Forgetting the khopesh at his side, the libertine made to turn and run, but Arkhan's left hand seized him by the throat and held him fast. The point of his iron sword came to rest against Khenti's chest, just above his heart.

'I have some questions for you,' Arkhan grated. Flecks of dark ichor stained his pale lips. 'How long you live depends on how well you answer.' He drove the point of his sword a fraction of an inch into Khenti's chest for emphasis. The young nobleman moaned in terror.

'Who else is part of this?' the immortal demanded. He didn't know whether to be relieved or insulted that Lamashizzar had sent the two libertines to kill him. Had Abhorash been waiting for him instead, his headless body would already be cooling by the side of the road. Did that mean the king's champion might not be a part of the plot, or was he being reserved for a more important task?

Khenti squirmed in Arkhan's grasp. His puffy features were pale and mottled with fright. 'The king–'

Arkhan shook the nobleman like a dog. 'I *know* the king's involved, you idiot,' he snarled, revealing ichor-stained teeth. 'Who else?'

'I – I don't know,' Khenti stammered, his tiny eyes very wide. 'I swear! He claimed there were others, but he wouldn't name them!'

Which could mean anything, Arkhan mused angrily. It was entirely possible that Adio and Khenti were the only ones stupid enough to turn on Neferata, and the king lied to lend them some extra courage.

The immortal's grip tightened. 'Is the queen in danger?' he said. 'Was this just about killing me, or does the king have plans for Neferata as well?'

Khenti let out a groan. Tears of fright rolled down his round cheeks. 'It's too late,' he said pleadingly. 'She's already dead. You were – *ghurrrk*!'

The libertine's body spasmed. Arkhan hadn't realised he'd stabbed the man until the point of his blade burst from Khenti's back. The nobleman's body sagged in death, and the immortal let it sink to the ground. He left his blade sticking out of Khenti's chest, reached up with his right hand and grimly pulled the arrow shaft from his chest. The arrow in his back was more problematic. He groped at it for several moments, only succeeding in breaking off the shaft close to his torso. The exertion left him reeling. He turned his face to the night sky. How much stolen life did he have left, he wondered. More importantly, what should he do with it?

If Neferata was dead, there was nothing left for him in Lahmia. Lamashizzar would have him killed on sight. On the other hand, if Khenti was wrong, and the conspirators hadn't yet reached the queen...

For a long while he stood, staring up at the sky, feeling cold and weak. He tried to think about endless, rolling dunes, and the citadel he'd built in the middle of the empty desert, but Arkhan's mind kept coming back to the startling touch of a hand against his cheek, and the queen's depthless eyes staring into his own.

It was possible Khenti was wrong. In fact, it was more than possible. There could still be a chance to reach Neferata before Lamashizzar's trap could spring shut. Or so Arkhan cared to believe.

'Damn me,' he snarled up at the cold face of the moon. 'First Nagash, and now this.' He bent forward and pulled his sword from Khenti's chest. 'When will I ever learn?'

Gritting his teeth, Arkhan staggered down the trade road, towards Lahmia. With luck, his damned horse wouldn't have run too far.

TEN

THE HOUR OF THE DEAD

Cripple Peak,
in the 76th year of Khsar the Faceless
(-1598 Imperial Reckoning)

The storm was the worst of the season by far, and it broke upon the shores of the Sour Sea with little warning.

It had been a cloudy, windy day, with sudden gusts of rain interspersed with long periods of drizzle – nothing out of the ordinary for that time of the year. But shortly after sundown the wind picked up, howling like a chorus of hungry ghosts across the barrow fields, and flickers of lightning danced behind the roiling clouds out to sea. The barbarians along the north coast heard the ominous rumble of thunder, saw the height of the waves dashing against the shore, and rushed to their low, rounded huts. Lowland tribes flocked to the hills, begging the hetmen for shelter from the coming storm.

The reaction was altogether different among the Keepers of the Mountain, as the barbarian priests were known. Their lookouts reported the rising winds and the ominous clouds to the High Keeper, and after a moment's thought he ordered the patrols of the barrow fields doubled until the storm had run its course. The High Keeper was an old and cunning man, or he never would have risen to claim the God's Eye in the first place. The elder Keepers were certain that the grave-robbing monster who'd killed their brethren had been driven away by their hunting parties, but the High Keeper wasn't convinced. He was certain that the creature was still close by, perhaps hiding somewhere on the mountain in spite of his order's best efforts to find it. If so, the storm would draw it out of hiding. The wind and the rain would conceal its movements, providing the perfect opportunity to resume its grisly deeds. And when it did, the Keepers would be waiting.

A few hours later, well past nightfall, the storm broke upon the coast in all its fury. The wind raged, lashing at the men out on the barrow fields with blinding sheets of rain. Visibility dropped to twenty feet, then fifteen, then ten; had the Keepers not known the plain like the backs of their hands, they would have been utterly disorientated. Even still, the patrols could do little more than huddle together against the furious gale and creep from one mound to the next, trusting that the Burning God would lead them to the monster if it were about.

Then, around midnight, with the storm still scouring the plain, the patrols spied a pillar of green fire blazing fiercely to the south, towards the older barrow mounds. The sight lifted the Keepers' hearts. At first, they believed their prayers had been answered, and, in a bitterly ironic sense, they were right.

The four patrols made their way independently southward, converging on the source of the god's own flame. They had learned their lesson after the first disastrous encounter with the monster. The ostentatious lantern-globes had been left behind, and the acolytes had been armed with bronze swords and spears from the fortress's ancient armoury. The Keepers in each patrol had been entrusted with even more precious treasures: reliquaries of tarnished bronze, each more than a thousand years old, containing polished spheres of god-stone to fuel their invocations. It was more raw power than any of the Keepers had ever seen, much less controlled. Each patrol felt confident that they could deal with the monster on their own, and pressed forward as quickly as they could in hopes of securing the glory for themselves.

Nagash stood in the eye of the raging storm, shielded on all sides by a whirling column of power. Beyond the pillar of fire, the tempest roared, clawing at the shield like a frenzied beast, while within the air was still, and silent save for the scratching of his dagger through the damp earth. Where the bronze knifepoint passed, the earth was left blackened and smouldering by its touch.

The chunk of *abn-i-khat* burned like molten lead in his shrivelled stomach. He had carved a piece of stone the size of his fist from the centre of the Burning God's eye and had forced it down his throat, and the tempest raging within his flesh made the storm above seem as gentle as an evening breeze. He could feel every nerve, every muscle fibre, every inch of flesh and bone with sharp-edged detail. He felt every blade of grass beneath his feet, and every tiny mote of power within them – he could even feel the lingering vestiges of life force in the hide cloak that lay across his shoulders. A veritable sea of sensations raged within him from one moment to the next: it might have been pain, or pleasure, or a mingling of both. Nagash could not tell any longer. He was long past the point of making distinctions between the two.

Yet his mind was absolutely, utterly clear. His thoughts were gleaming and sharp-etched as obsidian, and beggared the lightning for speed. What mighty deeds could he have accomplished in Khemri with such clarity of thought? The power of the Black Pyramid paled in comparison.

The site he'd chosen for the great ritual was a flat region surrounded by four barrow mounds near the exact centre of the plain. He'd chosen the spot not only because it would allow him to cast his invocation over the entire area, but also because the pathways around the barrows would serve to channel the barbarian patrols in predictable ways. Nagash had no doubt that they would appear, once his work began in earnest.

There were more of them than he expected, and by either luck or design they struck at more or less the same time. Thin cries rose and fell amid the howling gale as sword- and spear-wielding acolytes charged blindly across the open ground towards the beacon of flame. Behind them, tiny pinpoints of green light glowed like sullen coals as a dozen priests brandished their bronze reliquaries and made ready for battle.

The necromancer straightened, gauging the acolytes' approach. To his mind, they seemed ponderous and slow, stumbling haltingly across the wet ground towards him. When they were halfway to him, he raised his dagger skyward and reached out with his will.

Slay them!

Blinded by eagerness and lashing curtains of rain, the acolytes did not register the figures rising up from the dark ground until they'd charged in among them. The skeletons reared up with disturbing speed, rain coursing from their age-darkened bones, and closed in on the barbarians from all sides. Obsidian blades flashed, severing limbs and spilling entrails. Bony hands grabbed at the acolytes, dragging them to the ground by their robes or by their hair. Leering skulls closed in, jaws snapping, their eye sockets alight with green flame. In moments, the acolytes' bloodthirsty shouts had turned to confused and agonised screams, punctuated by the clang and clatter of blades as the survivors rallied and fought for their lives.

It took several long seconds for the priests to grasp what was happening, and when they did their response was potent but poorly coordinated. Nagash felt a ragged volley of invocations from across the field as the priests tried to seize control of his warriors. Here and there one of the skeletons stumbled beneath the onslaught, and the acolytes lashed out at them, smashing several to pieces. The barbarians took heart, sensing that the tide of battle was about to turn - and then Nagash raised his left fist skyward and hissed a dreadful invocation of his own.

An ominous rumble echoed through the clouds overhead, followed by stuttering flashes of lightning. Moments later, the priests were stunned by a single arc of burning, green light that plunged to earth and struck the barrow mound between them with a sputtering hiss. Another glowing mote fell from the bruised clouds, then another, and then there was a clap of thunder and a shower of burning hail the size of sling stones plunged down upon priests and acolytes both.

Men fell dead with their skulls dashed in or their necks broken. Others shrieked in agony as their robes burst into greenish flames that the rain could not quench. The priests scattered under the onslaught, running in every direction to escape the attack, and the sight of their panic unnerved the beleaguered acolytes, who tried to break free from the clutches of the undead and escape into the darkness. Many were cut down as they tried to flee, or were dragged to the ground by claw-like hands and torn apart. The last thing the survivors heard as they fled for their lives was the sound of soulless, mocking laughter riding the howling wind.

The skeletons made no effort to pursue the fleeing barbarians. Heedless of the sizzling hail, those undead warriors with no weapons of their own began plucking weapons from the bodies of the dead, while the warlord and his skeletal retinue went about killing the wounded that had been left behind. Perhaps a third of their number had been destroyed in the fighting, their bones scattered across the smouldering ground.

The losses mattered little to Nagash. Close to forty-five dead barbarians littered the battleground, some still burning as the magical fire consumed their flesh. They would more than make up for the numbers he had lost.

Grinning cruelly, Nagash returned his attention to the ritual circle. His army had only just begun to grow.

The great circle took another hour to complete, while the wind and the rain raged unabated over the barrow fields. As the hour of the dead approached, Nagash cast aside his bronze dagger and drew the oilskin bag from his belt. He bent over the great circle and poured the last of the stone dust into the channels he'd burned into the earth. When he was done the ritual symbols glowed with latent power.

It was time. The necromancer tossed the bag aside and stepped into the centre of the circle. He felt each tiny tremor of energy in the web he'd created – a net of sorcerous power that he merely had to speak the proper phrases and draw tight over the plain.

Nagash looked out across the open ground. Skeletal figures waited in the darkness, silent and patient as death itself; the hetman stood among them, his rune-sword glinting balefully.

Clenching his fists, Nagash threw back his head and began to chant, spitting the arcane words into the sky. The arcane symbols within the ritual circle blazed with light, and the bruised clouds recoiled overhead, receding in every direction as the power of the necromancer's invocation spread in a great wave across the barrow plain.

Power flowed in a torrent from Nagash's body, racing across the fields and sinking like claws into the hundreds of barrow mounds. The energies sought out every corpse, burrowing into rotting flesh and yellowing bones and stirring up the ghosts of old memories buried within. The spell was attuned to the worst passions of the human soul: anger, violence, jealousy and hate, and it lent those memories a semblance of life.

Bodies trembled. Limbs twitched. Dead hands clenched, scattering dust from decayed joints. Pitiless flames burned in the depths of old, dead eyes.

Nagash felt them stir, hundreds of them, caught within the strands of his sorcerous web. Ragged lips pulled back in a triumphant snarl. '*Come forth!*' he shouted into the tumult. '*Your master commands it!*'

Sealed up in their earthen barrows, the dead heard Nagash's command, and they obeyed.

Hands clawed at muddy earth, or tore at wooden boards. The earthen surfaces of the barrow mounds rippled and heaved. Flashes of lightning silhouetted the stark outlines of skeletal figures dragging themselves free from their graves.

Silent figures shambled out of the stormy night, drawn by Nagash's command. When the southern barrows had been emptied, and a horde of more than a thousand skeletons stood at his back, the Undying King stepped from the glowing circle and ordered his army to advance.

The undead horde marched northwards, growing in size as it went. Keepers and acolytes who'd panicked and lost their bearings in the storm were the first to die, their terrified screams rising and then quickly vanishing amid the howling wind. The revenants let the bloodied corpses fall where they were slain and continued onwards, towards the temple fortress to the north. Within minutes the mutilated bodies began to twitch, preparing to join the implacable advance.

The lookouts had all retreated into the safety of the fortress the moment the storm had broken, so there was no one to witness the emptying of the sacred barrows. It was only when the survivors of the slaughtered patrols came stumbling out of the darkness that the rest of the order became aware of the doom that approached. Concealing his fear, the High Keeper ordered his brethren to the armoury, and them commanded that the ancient alarm-horns to be sounded, summoning aid from the villages to the north-east. The great horns had not been blown for hundreds of years, and only two out of the dozen instruments still worked. The urgent, wailing notes sounded for more than an hour, rising and falling with the wind. The hetmen nearest the fortress heard the call, but their warriors refused to leave their families and brave the fury of the storm. When dawn came, they would march, but until then the Keepers would have to fend for themselves.

Believing that reinforcements would soon arrive, the Keepers emptied the armoury and barricaded the southern gates. Lookouts were ordered out onto the walls, but there was little to see in the darkness and the rain until the walking dead were almost upon them.

The men guarding the gates heard the first shouts of terror from the acolytes atop the walls, and then, moments later came the eerie sound of fingers scratching against the wood. One of the Keepers, hoping to encourage the others, laughed at the pitiful noise.

At once, the scratching fell silent. The men held their breaths, hands tightening around the unfamiliar grips of their weapons. A young voice up on the wall was babbling in fright, begging for the Burning God to save them.

And then the Keepers felt an invisible wave of power wash over them, and the southern gates began to rot before their very eyes. Iron-hard planks cracked and splintered, filling the corridors with clouds of dust and snuffing out the torches. And then the scratching began again, louder and more insistent, followed by the sound of rending wood.

Within seconds, pairs of flickering, greenish fires shone out of the gloom. Claw-like fingers raked across the Keepers' wooden barricades. Men screamed and called out to their god for aid, while those in front who had no way to escape hefted their weapons and threw themselves at their foes. Bronze and stone blades hacked and stabbed. Ancient bones cracked and splintered, and blood spattered across the walls.

The Keepers of the Mountain were no cowards. Though unused to battle, they stood their ground and defended the fortress with strength and determination. The gateways limited the number of enemies that could be brought to bear against them at any one time, and for a while they managed to hold the invaders at bay. Some of the senior Keepers arrived with reliquaries of god-stone, and tried to hold back the undead by force of will. At some of the gates they were successful, holding the corpses fast so that their brethren could strike them down.

Yet the enemy was implacable. They knew no fear, nor pain, nor fatigue. When their legs were smashed, they dragged themselves across the floor and grabbed at the Keepers' legs. When their arms were torn off they snapped at the Keepers' flesh with their broken teeth.

Worst of all, every brother who fell rose up and joined their ranks. Before long, the Keepers found themselves fighting against the savaged corpses of men whom they'd known for years or even decades. It was too much for any sane mind to take.

At one gate after another, exhausted Keepers were overwhelmed, and resistance began to collapse. Acolytes fled, shrieking in terror, to the deepest parts of the fortress. They hid themselves in wooden chests, in dry cisterns and bins of dusty grain, trembling and weeping and whispering prayers for their deliverance right up to the moment that bony hands seized them and dragged them to their doom.

The main gate on the temple's south face was the last to fall. Most of the order's senior priests were marshalled there, aiding in its defence, and they had already thrown back three successive assaults. They had learned enough from the last few attacks to try a different strategy: instead of hurling their energies at the army en masse and trying to halt it in its tracks, the priests were focusing their will on isolated elements, attempting to seize control and turn them against the rest of the undead horde. Though Nagash's force of will far eclipsed any of the individual priests, he found it difficult to control his army and resist a score of individual attacks simultaneously, and the cursed priests were starting to inflict significant damage.

A cheer went up from the priests as the third assault foundered. Piles of shattered corpses clogged the gateway, and the stink of blood and spilled entrails hung heavy in the air. The defenders had paid dearly since the gate had fallen, but they'd learned hard lessons since the first assault began. More barricades had been erected to break up the undead advance, and the priests had organised themselves to operate in three groups. One group fought while the second performed the grim task of destroying the corpses of their brothers who fell in battle, so that they could not be turned against them. The third group rested and tended the wounded, or formed a new set of barricades for the defenders to withdraw behind. It was a potent and effective defence; so long as they kept their heads, they could hold the gate almost indefinitely.

Nagash struck them just as the defenders were rotating groups. All at once, the piles of old bones glowed a furious green and then exploded, filling the tunnel with jagged splinters. Men fell screaming, their bodies raked by the needle-like fragments, and the rest reeled back in shock. Before they could recover, Nagash himself burst through the gate, his hideous body wreathed in sorcerous flame. He spat words of terrible power, and darts of fire shot from his fingertips – where they struck, men collapsed in agony, their bodies consumed from within. Behind the necromancer came his retinue of ancient warriors. The undead warlord stepped past Nagash and began slaughtering the stunned priests with his rune-sword.

The surviving defenders recovered quickly, retreating back to another set of barricades and forming another, smaller defensive line. Nagash caught a glimpse of the High Priest and his senior servants clustered behind the barricade, along with perhaps a few score acolytes and holy men. They had been driven back almost the length of the tunnel; the north gate stood only ten yards behind them.

Nagash's hands clenched in anticipation. Teeth bared in a feral snarl, he advanced on the defenders.

The acolytes and the younger priests gaped in terror at his approach, their pale faces lit by the greenish flames wreathing the necromancer's body. Skeletons poured into the tunnel behind Nagash, filling it with the dry clatter of bones.

The High Priest saw his opportunity. Here was the chance to stop the attack in its tracks, if the glowing abomination could be destroyed! His old voice rang with authority as he shouted exhortations to the elders, and at once they linked their voices in a sacred chant. The rest of the defenders took heart from this, standing shoulder to shoulder and raising their weapons once more as the enemy approached.

Nagash flung out his hand and spat an angry invocation. A blast of green fire sped down the tunnel – and the priests responded, focusing their energies in a crude counter-spell. The bolt disintegrated a few feet from the terrified defenders, leaving them unharmed.

Smiling, Nagash hurled another bolt. Then another. Cold, mocking laughter echoed down the tunnel.

The priests deflected the second blow, and the third, but each one seemed to get a bit closer before breaking apart. A fourth bolt came close enough to singe the robes of the defenders. Lines of strain appeared on the faces of the holy men as they tried to withstand the onslaught.

A fifth blast was deflected. Then a sixth. Thunder reverberated in the confined space, deafening human ears. The seventh blast broke up with a blinding flash, close enough to cause the defenders' robes to smoulder. One of the senior priests slumped silently to the ground, blood streaming from his nose, eyes and ears.

The eighth blast slew five acolytes before the rest of its energy was dissipated. Another senior priest collapsed with a groan, clutching at his chest. The defenders' lines wavered, and then an acolyte, his mind overwhelmed by horror, hurled himself at the oncoming skeletons with a wordless shriek of terror and rage. Another acolyte succumbed, then another, and then the defenders' lines broke as they launched a last, desperate charge into the face of certain death.

Nagash blasted a charging acolyte point-blank, scattering burning body parts back down the tunnel towards the High Priest. The elders of the order began to waver, their minds strained to the breaking point by the contest of power. His laughter took on a harsher, wilder edge as he hurled a final bolt, straight at the High Priest's face.

The holy men summoned the last of their strength, and the bolt dissipated with a thunderous crash less than a foot from where they stood. The concussion hurled men's bodies against the tunnel walls, breaking old bones and crushing skulls. Others were slain instantly by the sudden flash of heat, their bodies charred beyond recognition.

Only the High Priest survived, his body largely shielded from the blast by the men in front of him. His robes smouldering, the old man tried to crawl backwards, away from the necromancer.

Nagash loomed over the barbarian, bending low and seizing him by his wrinkled neck. He pulled the old man up until their faces were scant inches apart. The High Priest stared into the necromancer's burning eyes and saw in them the death of all living things. Nagash's fist clenched; old bone snapped, and the High Priest's head lolled to one side. The barbarian's feet thrashed spasmodically for several seconds more, then went still.

Slowly, Nagash lowered the old man's body until his feet touched the stone floor. He released his grip, and the High Priest remained upright. Green flames flickered in the depths of his glazed eyes. Gripped by the necromancer's will, the old man sank to his knees, then reached up with wrinkled hands and gripped the golden circlet set upon his head. Haltingly, as though some part of the old priest's soul still struggled within the broken frame, the corpse removed the circlet and offered it to Nagash.

The necromancer took the symbol of the order in his bony hands, and, grinning cruelly, he twisted the soft gold until the setting holding the *abn-i-khat* burst apart. Nagash plucked the burning stone from the circlet, and tossed the mangled gold band aside.

The storm raged through the night and into the dawn of the next day, finally spending the last of its strength well past daybreak. As soon as the winds had dropped off, the hetmen of the nearby villages summoned their warriors and set off as quickly as they could down the muddy tracks towards the temple fortress.

When they arrived, the great fortress was silent and still. The gates along the north face were shut and locked, and no amount of shouting would bring one of the Keepers out onto the wall. Finally, one of the hetmen ordered runners to fetch a tall ladder from his village, and they sent a young lad scampering up to the top of the wall to see what he could find.

The warriors waited in silence as the boy disappeared from sight. The minutes stretched, one after another, and the hetmen exchanged nervous glances. After half an hour, they knew something had gone terribly wrong.

Finally, the main gate swung open. The boy appeared, trembling and pale. No amount of questions, cajoling or threats could make him relate what he'd seen inside, and nothing on earth could get him to go back in again.

Weapons ready, the hetmen led their troops into the fortress. At once, they saw that a terrible battle had raged inside the walls. Blood was splashed on the walls and the floors, and the stench of death hung heavy in the air. A mere ten yards from the north gate, one of the hetmen let out a cry of dismay and picked up a mangled band of gold. The other village leaders recognised it at once. If the God's Eye had been taken, it meant that the High Keeper and the order had been destroyed.

And yet, no matter how hard they looked, the villagers found no bodies inside the temple fortress. None at all.

ELEVEN

NECESSARY SACRIFICES

Lahmia,
the City of the Dawn,
in the 76th year of Khsar the Faceless
(-1598 Imperial Reckoning)

Ubaid bowed his tattooed head at the queen's approach. 'All is in readiness, great one,' he said, as though he were speaking of nothing more untoward than a palace feast.

Neferata acknowledged the vizier with a nod. It was fast approaching midnight; the audience with Xia Ha Feng had lasted much longer than she'd expected, but it had been important not to appear rude and hasten away too early. She needed the august personage to be receptive to her overtures, to believe that he could win her confidence and thus gain a lever to use against the king. So long as he believed that he had power over her, she was free to lay the trap that would ultimately ensnare him – and possibly the whole Eastern Empire as well.

A thin line of warm light shone beneath the door to the sanctum. Ubaid had been busy for hours, preparing for the ritual. The grand vizier was the only member of the cabal that she permitted into the chamber; the rest were now required to pay their respects and receive their draught of elixir in the funereal confines of the Hall of Regretful Sorrows. She'd chosen the location for the express reason that it was the least used of the queen's three audience chambers – and also because she wanted Lamashizzar and his former allies to never forget that she alone now stood between them and the realm of the dead.

Lamashizzar, of course, was furious at the thought. She knew that it was dangerous to provoke him in such petty ways; he lacked ambition, but he could be ruthless when his pride was offended. Perhaps, in time, she would release him from the obligation, but right now he needed to kneel before her and acknowledge her authority. He needed to be humbled. He needed to know what it was like to live at the whim of another. It was the one concession to her feelings that she allowed herself to make.

For the most part, she had been careful not to abuse her power. For all their reputation for decadence, in some ways the people of Lahmia were just as hidebound as other Nehekharans. None outside the palace knew that she no longer confined herself to the Women's Palace, and none other than the members of the cabal knew that the city was ruled by anyone other than its king.

Neferata intended it to remain that way. Nagash might have believed that he could rule as an Undying King in Khemri without tempting the wrath of the other great cities, but she knew better. Now that she had access to her children once more, she had plans to ensure that, to all outward purposes, the ruling dynasty would continue as before. When her son Lamasu reached marriageable age, she would find him a proper wife, and then it would be time for Lamashizzar to join his ancestors in the afterlife. Naturally she, as the dutiful wife, would appear to drink from the poisoned cup and join him in his journey to the underworld, and to all intents and purposes she would be dead and gone.

The trick would be to convince the other members of the cabal to engineer their own deaths as well. Already their long lives – and miraculous vitality – were giving rise to unwelcome rumours both at court and even as far away as neighbouring Lybaras. According to Lamashizzar's spies, Queen Khalida had hinted at suspicions of her own on more than one occasion, though she'd never come out and publicly accused her royal cousins of any unnatural dealings.

Neferata had tried to reach out to Khalida on more than one occasion, hoping to use their past friendship to build strong ties between the two cities, but so far the Lybaran queen had found compelling reasons not to accept any of her cousin's invitations to court.

At some point she would also have to decide what to do about Arkhan. For now, his knowledge of Nagash's sorcery still outweighed the risk of keeping him alive, but that balance was shifting fast. She was starting to grasp the finer nuances of the Usurper's incantations. Soon she would allow W'soran to begin studying the more esoteric aspects of Nagash's necromantic lore, using it to both control him and expand her own base of knowledge through his studies. Once that was underway, Arkhan would only be useful for his sword arm and his ability to procure victims for the cabal, two functions that she was certain Abhorash and Ushoran could perform just as well. It had been pathetically easy to win over the monster's loyalty, though it had required her to open herself to Arkhan far more than she would have liked. Neferata was already looking forward to the day that she could order Abhorash to put an end to the whole tiresome business.

The queen pushed open the sanctum door and hastened within, mindful of the sands hissing through the hourglass. Ubaid had laid out the ritual implements and lit the incense in preparation for the incantation. The sacrifice had likewise been prepared and awaited her in the centre of the circle.

His wounds had been cleaned and he'd been given a potion that would banish his fatigue and leave him awake and alert for the ceremony to come.

He was part of an experiment that Neferata was conducting in an attempt to better refine the outcome of Nagash's ritual. Arkhan had found him amid the squalid refugee districts west of the city: a young man, relatively fit and healthy enough to survive a full week of suffering. The subject was chained to an iron ring that had been set in the ceiling at the centre of the ritual circle, and the dark stone around his toes was layered with thick spatters of blood. The incisions that covered his body in precise, intricate patterns had been inflicted according to the diagrams provided in Nagash's tomes, and represented the culmination of the torturer's art. The wounds left every nerve in the victim's body throbbing and raw, but the injuries themselves were not serious enough to kill.

According to the necromancer's experiments, no victim had survived the nightmare of constant pain for more than eight days. By Neferata's estimation, at seven days the victim's energies would be at their peak; past that point they would start to ebb as the body began to fail.

Now would come the true test. Neferata crossed to the worktable at the edge of the circle. The razor-edged torture knives had been scrupulously cleaned and set aside on a clean linen cloth. In their place, Ubaid had set out the curved sacrificial blade, the golden bowl and the jewel-encrusted goblet that she used to drink the first draught of the elixir. The heavy tome containing the great ritual lay open to the proper page at the table's edge, but she hardly spared it a glance. She'd learned the necessary phrases and gestures by heart a long time ago.

Neferata breathed deeply, drinking in the delicate incense that permeated the room. She reached down and touched the blade of the sacrificial knife; the sharpened bronze was cold to the touch. The queen smiled, tracing a fingertip along the narrow, wooden hilt, then picked it up. It felt light and comfortable in her hand.

She entered the circle with care, and sought the young man's eyes. His gaze was fixed upon her, both terrified and hopeful all at once. A faint groan escaped his lacerated lips.

The queen held him with her gaze. Arkhan had taught her to draw upon the power inherent in the elixir. She used it now, and watched a spark of longing catch fire in his eyes. He drew in a deep, shuddering breath, and from the expression that crossed his tortured face, she knew that the agony wracking his body had been transformed into something far sharper, far sweeter and much more agonising than anything he'd felt before. How she had made him suffer in the last few days of his life. And yet he *loved* her, with all his heart and soul. He ached for her, through and through.

Smiling, Neferata placed the knife in her belt, and drew so close to him that she could feel his laboured breathing against her cheek. She stretched, almost languidly, reaching up to undo the chains that held his wrists. He staggered as the bonds were released, yet he did not fall. Her gaze held him upright.

Her smile broadened. 'You have pleased me,' she told him, and the words sent shudders through his frame. 'Now there is one last thing you must do, and then, my sweet, you will be with me forever.' She drew out the knife. 'Will you do this for me?

His mouth worked. Broken sounds issued forth, until tears of frustration gleamed at the corners of his eyes. Finally, he managed a shaky nod.

'I knew you wouldn't fail me,' she said softly. 'Take this,' she said, and held out the knife.

The young man reached out a trembling hand and grasped the gleaming blade. 'Good,' Neferata whispered. 'Wait here.'

She retreated to the edge of the circle. The hour had come. Ubaid appeared at her side, silent and ready.

Neferata raised her hands. Her eyes had never left her victim's. 'Now,' she told him. 'Repeat after me.'

And so she began to chant, slowly and purposefully, and the man in the centre of the circle joined in. She drew him into the ritual, weaving his pain and passion into the incantation, and he surrendered himself to it willingly, eagerly. At that moment, he wanted to give her everything her heart desired.

The incantation built slowly and steadily. Minutes passed into hours, until time lost all meaning. The climax, when it came, took both of them by surprise.

'Now!' she gasped. 'The knife!' Neferata raised a trembling finger to her throat, right over the pulsing artery. 'Give me your heart's blood!'

A beatific smile crossed the young man's scarred face. He brought the knife to his throat and sliced it open with a single, graceful motion. Ubaid was beside him at once, the golden bowl held in his upraised hands.

The man stood there, bleeding his life away, his face transported in ecstasy. She held him with her gaze until his heart ceased to beat, and his lifeless body collapsed to the stone floor.

Neferata let out a long, shuddering breath. Her nerves were afire. She reached for the golden goblet as Ubaid rose from the victim's corpse and brought her the brimming, steaming bowl.

Slowly, carefully, the grand vizier poured a measure of blood into the gleaming cup. Neferata inhaled the heady scent. It was sweeter than any fragrance she'd ever smelled before.

Suddenly, there came a sound in the corridor outside the sanctum. It sounded to Neferata like the scuff of sandal leather across stone. Ubaid frowned, and carefully set the sacrificial bowl upon the floor. The dagger he drew from his belt was anything but light and utilitarian. He circled around the bowl and moved quietly towards the closed door.

Neferata turned to watch him go. Something was wrong. She thought of Lamashizzar, and felt a sudden sense of foreboding.

The goblet was warm in her hands. She stared down at the still surface of the elixir, sensing the power seething in its depths. Neferata raised the cup to her lips and drank deep. The taste was painfully bitter, yet it filled her with a power the likes of which she had never known before.

Ubaid was struggling with someone at the door. Was it Lamashizzar? She could not tell, and at that moment, she did not care. Neferata let out a throaty chuckle. 'Stand aside,' she said to Ubaid. 'Let him pass.' Whoever it was, he would bow at her feet and beg her forgiveness for the unwelcome intrusion.

The grand vizier retreated from the doorway, and a lone figure staggered into the room. It took her a moment to recognise who it was.

'Arkhan?' she asked. She could smell the stink of blood on his robes. 'What is the meaning of this?'

The immortal lurched towards her. As he stepped further into the light, she could see the bloody stubs of arrow shafts jutting from his shoulder and side. His ghastly face was paler than usual, and the iron sword she'd given him was held in his hand. Its edge was dark with dried blood.

'The king is moving against you,' Arkhan croaked. He sounded as though he was at the very limits of his strength. 'Lamashizzar sent Adio and Khenti to murder me on the trade road. He means to kill you as well.'

Neferata shook her head. Arkhan wasn't making sense. She laughed softly, drunk with sudden power – and then a cold spike of pain lanced through her heart.

The queen had time for a single, startled gasp before the poison took hold and dragged her down into darkness.

Arkhan watched in horror as Neferata collapsed. The golden goblet tumbled from her hand, spilling the last, thick dregs of elixir at her feet. He lurched towards her, his body stiff and clumsy from his wounds. 'Help me!' he snarled at the grand vizier as he collapsed to his knees beside the queen.

'There is nothing to be done,' Ubaid replied in a dead voice.

Neferata lay upon her side, head resting on one out-flung arm. Her skin was cold to the touch. Arkhan rested his fingertips against her slender throat, but could not feel the pulse of her heart. He brought his cheek close to her lips. There was barely a whisper of breath.

The immortal's gaze went to the dented goblet. There were scarlet drops of elixir beading its rim. As he watched, they turned dull red, then black. Realisation sank into him like a knife. It was one thing to murder a man on the trade road and leave his body in the ditch; killing a queen was something altogether more risky. Her body would be handled by the priests of the mortuary cult, and viewed by thousands of grieving citizens. Her death would have to appear natural.

'This cannot be,' Arkhan snarled. 'No poison in all Nehekhara could overcome Nagash's elixir.'

'It is the venom of the sphinx, a poison both natural and super-natural,' Ubaid said. 'Even before the fall of Mahrak it was vanishingly rare. The gods alone know how Lamashizzar obtained it.' The grand vizier approached the queen. His expression was inscrutable as he studied Neferata's still form. 'According to the old texts, the venom attacks the blood, rendering it lifeless. Death is instantaneous.' He shook his head. 'It's a wonder that the queen is alive at all.'

Something in Ubaid's dispassionate voice kindled a black rage in Arkhan's heart. He surged to his feet, seizing the grand vizier by the throat. The immortal could feel the last vestiges of elixir boiling in his veins. Dimly, he was aware that Ubaid still held a knife in his hand, but the immortal scarcely cared. The point of his own sword was scant inches from Ubaid's belly.

'Why?' Arkhan growled.

The grand vizier glowered at the immortal, but his expression was bleak. 'Because, like Abhorash, I serve the throne,' he replied. 'Lamashizzar is weak and feckless, but Lahmia has survived such rulers before.' Ubaid squirmed a little in Arkhan's grasp. His voice rose in frustration. 'The queen did not keep her word. Instead of advising the king, she usurped his power entirely. It's not right–'

Arkhan's hand tightened around Ubaid's throat. 'She thinks only of this city! Lahmia will prosper under her rule! And for this, you *betray* her?'

Ubaid's eyes widened in anger. 'Who are you to judge me?' he hissed. 'Arkhan the Black, who betrayed his own king in favour of the Usurper, then even turned upon Nagash when it suited your purposes. What do you know of loyalty, or devotion?' He spread his arms. 'Kill me, if you wish, but you may not presume to pass judgement on me.'

Arkhan's grip tightened on the hilt of his sword. His mind whirled. Snarling in disgust, he turned and shoved the grand vizier towards the door. Ubaid staggered a dozen paces, an uncomprehending look on his face.

'I will leave it up to the queen to decide your fate,' Arkhan said coldly. 'Now go.'

Ubaid shook his head. The snake tattoo on his neck seemed to slither in the shifting light. 'Don't you understand? The queen will never wake. The elixir's power may slow the venom for a time, but it's just a matter of hours now. Days at the most.'

'*I said get out!*' Arkhan roared, and took a step towards Ubaid. The grand vizier saw the murderous look in the immortal's eyes, and his nerve finally deserted him. Tucking his knife back into his belt, he fled the room with as much dignity as he could muster.

Arkhan listened to the grand vizier's footsteps retreat down the corridor. He swayed on his feet. I must be out of my mind, he thought. How did I let Neferata do this to me?

He spun on his heel, surveying the chamber. Ubaid would go back to the king and report what had happened, and the king would swoop in like a hawk to seize the queen's body and reclaim Nagash's tomes. There was no time to waste.

With a trembling hand, Arkhan slid his iron blade back into its scabbard, and limped over to the golden bowl. The immortal knelt, placed his hands against the bowl's curved surface, and raised it to his lips. The liquid inside was still warm and fragrant.

He drank it all; it was far more than he needed, filling his innards to bursting, but he was careful not to waste a single drop. Stolen vigour seethed through his veins. The power of the elixir staggered him; it was nearly as powerful as Nagash's own, and far sweeter. Grinning mirthlessly, he plucked the remaining arrow stubs from his torso and cast them aside.

The immortal searched through the room until he found a large, linen sack, then filled it with a half-dozen carefully selected tomes. If the elixir was potent enough to resist the effects of the sphinx's poison, then perhaps there was a chance to defeat it entirely. First, however, he needed a place where he could work in relative safety. At the moment, only one option seemed open to him.

Arkhan knelt carefully and took the queen in his arms. Her body was already stiffening, as though in death, and felt as light and brittle as old paper. Once again, the immortal was struck by the sheer folly of what he was doing. He ought to be fleeing the city with as many of Nagash's books as he could carry. Once on the Golden Plain he could escape Lamashizzar's wrath with ease.

The immortal looked down at the queen's unconscious form and was reminded once again of Neferem, another daughter of Lahmia who was a pawn of kings and suffered for centuries while he stood by and watched.

Neferata didn't have to set you free, he reminded himself.

Cursing under his breath, Arkhan carried the queen from the room. With luck, he could make it to the Women's Palace before the king realised that she still lived.

It appeared that King Lamashizzar hadn't entertained the possibility that his wife might survive the poisoned cup. There were no palace guards roaming the corridors as Arkhan hastened to the southern edge of the palace. Just to be safe, he crossed into the Women's Palace via the rarely used Hall of Regretful Sorrows. The immortal fought down a sense of grim foreboding as he bore the queen's body past the great marble bier where the queens of Lahmia had been laid in state for millennia.

The Women's Palace was echoing and empty. For more than a century, the sprawling sanctuary housed only Neferata herself, along with the bare minimum of servants and handmaidens that protocol demanded the king provide. And yet his presence in the dusty halls was detected almost at once. Within minutes, the immortal found himself surrounded on all sides by pale, outraged women, some of whom were armed with small, wicked-looking knives. Had he been alone, he had no doubt that they would have set upon him like a pride of angry lionesses. Only the sight of the queen's motionless corpse held them at bay. They paced alongside him in mute shock for close to an hour while he wandered aimlessly through the sprawling palace.

Finally, his patience stretched to the breaking point, he turned to the women and asked where the queen's bedchamber lay. They stared at him as though he were mad – all but one young woman, dressed in fine robes, who stepped forward and silently beckoned for him to follow.

Her name was Aiyah. Much later, Arkhan learned she had served Princess Khalida as one of her handmaidens during the last year she'd lived at the palace. Despite her youth, she was calm and controlled in the face of catastrophe. She led Arkhan to the queen's chambers, then banished the crowd of servants to the outer corridor while the immortal laid out Neferata's body on the bed. The handmaiden returned as the immortal was unpacking Nagash's tomes, and waited quietly by the door. No protests, no tedious questions or hysterics. She simply waited, patient and composed, ready to serve the queen in whatever capacity she could. Arkhan's first instinct was to dismiss her, but the more he considered the difficulties of trying to work inside the confines of the sanctuary, the more he had to admit that he was going to need her help.

He knew that it wouldn't be very long before Lamashizzar learned where he'd taken the queen: hours, perhaps a day at most. So Arkhan told the handmaiden a partial truth – that the king had conspired to poison Neferata because he resented her claims to equality. Aiyah accepted the story without comment while the immortal took ink and brushes and began to inscribe out a ritual circle on the bedchamber floor. At some point during the process, the handmaiden slipped quietly from the room again, and he knew that his tale was winging its way through the Women's Palace. Arkhan reckoned that once the story was known, the palace servants would block any attempt by Lamashizzar to enter the sanctuary in search of the queen. As it was, the palace guard would baulk at any command to enter the forbidden halls of the palace; even though the palace was technically open now, hundreds of years of tradition carried a weight that was very difficult to overcome. That left only the king's fellow conspirators, and Arkhan was certain he could deal with any of them save for Abhorash – if the king's champion was even involved. He still had no idea how deep the conspiracy went.

The rest of that first night was spent sitting vigil at the queen's side and poring through the Usurper's tomes in search of an incantation or ritual that might banish the poison from the queen's blood. Hours passed, and Neferata began to turn pale. Her breath was still very faint, and only Arkhan's preternatural senses allowed him to hear a heartbeat. So far, the elixir was holding the poison at bay, but she was clearly weakening. As dawn began to break, far out to sea, Arkhan was no closer to finding a solution. He had Aiyah draw the curtains tight across the tall windows and continued his search. By the time night fell once more, he still had nothing to show for his efforts, and the queen's condition was becoming steadily worse.

Growing desperate, Arkhan set the books aside and placed the queen's body inside the ritual circle. Aiyah watched the immortal spread open three magical tomes on the floor by the circle, then gather up the inkpot and horsehair brush once more.

'Undress her,' he said to the handmaiden, and then began riffling through the pages of the three books.

The young woman hesitated. 'What do you intend to do?' she asked coolly.

Arkhan shot the handmaiden a hard stare. 'She will need help to overcome the poison in her veins,' he said. 'So far, her... blood is strong enough to at least slow the venom's progress.' He paused, studying a detailed drawing of a human figure on one yellowed page. After a moment he shook his head and continued his search. 'So I must find a way to increase her vigour enough to overcome it.'

The handmaiden took a step towards the circle and frowned. Her dark eyes lingered on the strange markings painted on the floor. 'I could send for an apothecary,' she offered. 'The priestesses of Neru have tended to the health of the royal line for centuries. They have experience with poisons–'

'If I thought there was an herb or potion that could save her, I would have carried her to the temple myself,' Arkhan snapped.

Aiyah took a deep breath. 'But this,' she began. 'What you're doing–'

'What I am doing is trying to save your queen,' the immortal said. He paused in his search, studied another image, and nodded to himself. Arkhan removed the inkpot's ceramic stopper. 'The longer we wait, the weaker she becomes,' he told her.

The handmaiden hesitated a moment more, brows knitted in consternation, before making her decision. She knelt carefully within the circle and began to deftly pull away Neferata's robes.

Arkhan laid out the runes with care. The work took hours, winding in intricate ribbons from Neferata's scalp to her toes. The immortal was conscious of each minute slipping away; it seemed to him that her skin was growing steadily cooler beneath his touch.

It was well past the hour of the dead by the time the preparations were complete. Arkhan stood and pressed the book into Aiyah's, hands. 'Go and stand at the edge of the circle, by her feet,' he said. 'When I begin, repeat the words as I say them. They are marked on the page there.'

Aiyah looked dubious, but accepted the tome nonetheless. 'Is that all?'

'Do you wish the queen to live?' he asked.

'Of course!'

'Then make that uppermost in your mind,' Arkhan told her. 'Think of nothing else. With luck, it will be enough.'

Arkhan took his place on the opposite side of the circle. Standing at the head of the queen, he spread his arms and began to chant.

The ritual was little different from the incantation of reaping that was used to create Nagash's elixir. He had made several modifications to the arrangement of the runes to account for the elixir already present in her body. He wasn't interested in transmutation so much as enhancing what was already there. In theory, the problem seemed simple enough.

Drawing on the surfeit of elixir filling his body, Arkhan poured a steady stream of power into the incantation. At once the air grew heavy above the circle, and he saw the queen's body begin to tremble. Tiny wisps of steam curled from the sigils painted on her skin.

The immortal felt the elixir boil inside him and directed the released energy into the arcane words rolling from his lips. And, within the circle, Neferata's body suddenly spasmed. Her back arched painfully, arms splayed and chest thrust skyward. Arkhan could see the tendons in her neck and along the backs of her hands grow taut as bowstrings; her mouth gaped, emitting a billowing gout of black vapour.

Arkhan watched as the queen's skin began to change. Her rich, brown skin, already pale, began to lose all trace of colour, taking on the cold tone of bleached linen or alabaster. He stopped the incantation abruptly, fearing that he might already be too late. The backlash of forces tore through him; he staggered, his hand going to his chest as invisible knives tore through his vitals. A thin trickle of ichor ran down his chin.

The immortal sank slowly to his knees. Neferata's body had gone limp again, shrouded in tendrils of steam. The runes painted on her skin had already begun to fade, running together in dark blue threads that formed pools on the stone floor. Aiyah sank to her knees, her eyes wide with shock. She crawled gingerly into the circle and laid a trembling hand against Neferata's flank. The handmaiden jerked her fingers away as though stung.

'She's cold,' Aiyah said. 'Colder than the desert night. What happened? What have you done?'

Arkhan stared at the queen's near-lifeless form. The runes had all but melted away in the heat that had radiated from her skin. Beneath the bluish tinge of the ink, he could see that her veins had turned black at her temples and throat.

The immortal rubbed the back of a hand across his lips. It came away slick with a film of ichor. Anger and revulsion roiled in his chest. What horror had Lamashizzar unleashed?

'I don't know,' Arkhan said in a hollow voice.

Five more days went by. Arkhan never relented, searching through Nagash's books again and again for something he could use to defeat the sphinx's venom. The queen scarcely breathed now; her flesh was cold and stiff as marble. Her heart still beat, stubbornly driving the elixir through her veins, but it had grown inexorably weaker with each passing night. Every ritual he attempted, no matter how great or small, only seemed to worsen her condition. It seemed that the sphinx's deadly venom had somehow bonded with Neferata's ensorcelled blood, transforming it from within. Any attempt to increase the elixir's vigour empowered the poison as well.

Now, as the seventh night fell upon the city, Arkhan believed he knew the answer. He sat at Neferata's writing desk and studied the words and symbols of the incantation one last time, checking carefully to ensure he'd made no errors. Satisfied, he took the large sheet of paper and set it on the floor at the edge of the circle. Next, he laid out the tools for the ritual with care, and then went to kneel at the queen's side. The immortal took her limp body in his arms and carried Neferata to her bed. He laid her body gently upon the silken sheets, and then returned to the freshly-drawn ritual he'd made. Arkhan took off his sword belt, and then let his robes fall to the floor. He turned to Aiyah and spread his arms.

'Follow the diagrams exactly,' he said to her. 'The symbols and their positions are crucial, or the energies will not conduct properly.'

The handmaiden nodded, but Arkhan could see the weariness and apprehension in her eyes. She had laboured every bit as hard as he had, yet without the benefits of the elixir to sustain her. When she wasn't participating in Arkhan's rituals she was trying to glean information about Lamashizzar and the other members of the cabal. Despite her best efforts, however, there was no way to find out who had chosen to side with the king in the wake of Neferata's disappearance. All that could be learned was that the king was incommunicado, conferring with his advisors. Arkhan knew he was simply waiting for news that the queen had succumbed at last. With luck, the king's strategy could be used against him. He had ceded the initiative to Neferata, if only she could make use of it.

This was their last chance. If this ritual failed, Arkhan was certain that the queen would not last until the dawn.

Aiyah stepped forward, brush and inkpot in hand. She studied the paper carefully for a moment, then dipped the brush in the inkpot and went to work. Her brushstrokes were tentative at first, but her confidence increased steadily as the hours went by and the ribbons of arcane symbols wove their way along Arkhan's skin. Still, it was close to dawn by the time the last symbols were inscribed upon the immortal's flesh.

'Well done,' Arkhan said, and hoped it was true. There was no way he could tell for certain. 'Now, quickly, take your place at the circle. There is very little time left.'

The immortal went and stood in the centre of the circle. 'No matter what happens to me, do not falter,' he told the handmaiden. 'Complete the incantation, no matter what. Do you understand?'

Aiyah nodded. Her eyes were now wide with fear.

'Then let us begin,' he said gravely. 'We are almost out of time.'

As before, they chanted the incantation together. At once, the immortal felt his veins begin to burn as the ritual tapped into his remaining reserves of elixir. But rather than draw out the stolen power, this ritual was meant to shape it instead, transforming it into a tool designed for a very specific purpose. Arkhan gritted his teeth as stabbing pains shot through his torso and limbs. His vision began to dissolve into a reddish fog, and a hollow roaring filled his ears. His skin drew painfully tight, until he thought it would split apart, but through it all, his chant never faltered. He'd suffered far worse in the past.

Time lost all meaning for the immortal. The incantation went on forever, and the agony only grew worse, until it was as boundless as the desert itself. Arkhan's voice was little more than a ragged howl of pain, but he still spat out the words that kept the incantation going. His entire body was afire; a small part of his mind was certain that his flesh and bones were melting in the heat.

An eternity passed. He did not feel the culmination of the ritual when it finally arrived; for him, there was only a shift in the roaring whirlwind that filled his ears, signifying that Aiyah had finished her chant. It took several long moments before she could make him understand anything else.

'Now?' her voice echoed in his skull. It sounded small and far away.

Arkhan tried to see beyond the red mist that filled his vision. He nodded, or at least he thought that he did. 'The... knife...' he gasped. The words sounded impossibly loud.

Aiyah let the page fall from her fingers. Her gaze fell to the small, curved knife at her feet. The edge, honed to a razor's sharpness, gleamed bright in the lamplight. When she tried to speak again, her voice caught in her throat. 'Are – are you certain?'

The immortal responded with a tortured groan that made the handmaiden flinch. 'Do it!' he moaned. His eyes were orbs of dark red, the pupils completely obscured, and yet she could feel the weight of his stare. 'This is... her only hope,' Arkhan continued. 'She is certain... to die... otherwise.'

Aiyah took a deep breath. Swiftly, she bent and took up the knife. It felt terribly heavy in her hand.

She crossed to the bed. But for her unnaturally white skin, the queen might have been sleeping, lost in a deep lotus-dream. Aiyah laid a trembling hand upon the queen's forehead, grimacing at how cold she felt.

'Asaph forgive me,' the handmaiden said faintly. Then she took the knife and sliced open the side of Neferata's throat.

Black liquid, hot and foul-smelling, poured from the wound and spread across the silken sheets. Neferata shuddered faintly, then went deathly still.

'It's done,' the handmaiden said, stepping back from the bed to avoid the rain of droplets pattering on the floor.

'Good,' the immortal replied. He climbed unsteadily to his feet. He beckoned to her. 'Help me. Quickly.'

Aiyah hurried to Arkhan and took his outstretched hand. She led him, stumbling, to the queen's side. The immortal knelt beside her, leaning in until his face was inches from hers. He nodded. 'Not long now,' he rasped. 'Hand me the blade.'

Aiyah handed over the knife and stepped back, wringing her hands. 'I never imagined there would be so much,' she said, staring in horror at the spreading pool of ichor. 'I've killed her. She's going to die!'

'It must be done,' Arkhan insisted. 'Her blood has been corrupted. Can't you see? We have to remove it, or she is doomed.'

The immortal watched in silence for another minute, watching the flood of ichor slowly ebb away. When it had become no more than a trickle, he took the knife in his left hand and pressed the point into the skin of his right forearm, just behind the wrist. He cut deep, slicing open one of the major veins. There was no pain. All he could feel now was fear.

The knife clanged to the floor. Left hand trembling, he cupped the back of Neferata's head and raised it from the sodden pillow. 'Live, oh queen,' he said, his voice shaking as he pressed the pulsing wound to her pale lips. 'Drink of me, and live.'

Arkhan felt her body tremble as the ichor touched her lips. His skin tingled as her lips brushed the inside of his forearm; they moved against his skin, almost like a kiss, and then she began to drink.

'Yes... yes!' Arkhan breathed. The red mist began to recede. '*Drink!*'

And she did. Hungrily, greedily, with gathering strength, she drew the liquid from the wound. Her mouth opened, teeth pressing into his flesh. Arkhan clenched his fist. As he watched, the cut in her neck closed up with startling speed.

'It's working!' he gasped. 'Aiyah, do you see? It's working!'

The roaring in his ears was receding. Within seconds he could see clearly again, and the pain had begun to fade. Arkhan's muscles felt loose and weak, and a chill settled into his bones. Neferata still drank from him, her eyes clamped tightly shut.

And then, without warning, her body began to convulse. Arkhan felt the muscles in her neck writhe like serpents. She tore herself from his grasp, her mouth agape and her chin stained dark with fluids. The queen thrashed upon the bed, arms and legs flailing. A cloud of steam boiled up from her throat, followed by a long, terrible howl.

Arkhan watched in horror as the queen's body began to change. Her flesh shrivelled, stretching the skin across her bones, and her lustrous, black hair grew faded and brittle. Neferata's eyes sank into their sockets, and her cheeks turned gaunt, transforming her face into a ghoulish, bestial mask.

Shrieking in agony, Neferata reached for him with one flailing hand. It clawed at the sheets, just inches away, but Arkhan could not bring himself to touch her.

Neferata's screams turned to a choking rattle. She collapsed back upon the bed. Her head turned towards Arkhan, and the immortal saw that her eyes were wide and staring. They were still vivid green, but the pupils were slitted, like those of a cat.

She stared at him for barely a moment, her expression filled with pain, and then all the air went out of her lungs and her body went limp. Arkhan heard Aiyah let out a long, heart-wrenching moan.

Neferata, Daughter of the Moon and Queen of Lahmia, was dead.

TWELVE

APOTHEOSIS

Cripple Peak,
in the 76th year of Khsar the Faceless
(-1598 Imperial Reckoning)

The slaughter of the barbarian priests had been more than just an act of vengeance on Nagash's part; it had served a pragmatic purpose as well. The mountain would become the seat of his power, just as the Black Pyramid had been in Khemri. From here he would raise the armies that would cast down the kings of Nehekhara. He envisioned sprawling mines, foundries, armouries and great laboratories from which he would continue to master the arts of necromancy. The construction alone would last centuries, and occupy his undead army both day and night. Eliminating the priests was necessary to keep them from interfering in his designs, and to swell the ranks of his workforce.

Construction began the night after the battle at the fortress temple. The undead rose from their beds across the barrow plain and converged on the south face of the mountain. Guided by Nagash's will, they began constructing the first stage of fortifications around what would be the first of many mine complexes. Within the first month the southern barrows had been dismantled, and the foundation stones hauled up to the mountain to help form the first buildings. Earth and stone excavated from the mountain were used as well, but Nagash knew he would need much more before he could say the great work was well and truly begun. The fortress would take many centuries before it was complete, and much of it would be underground, sheltered from the burning light of the sun.

At the same time, Nagash kept a close watch on the temple fortress. He knew that he hadn't managed to kill every member of the order. At any given time close to a hundred junior priests and acolytes were travelling between the barbarian villages, tending to each of the totem statues and performing the ceremonial duties of the order. Sure enough, almost two months later, a few score of the holy men returned to the fortress and began making it fit for habitation again. That night, he sent a large force to slay them and add their numbers to his own. Nagash especially savoured the irony of using the undead members of the order to slay their younger brethren and deliver them into his hands. After that, no one else attempted to take residence in the great fortress. Nagash suspected that the superstitious barbarians thought it to be haunted and, in a very real sense, they were right.

Surprisingly, the burials on the barrow plain continued. The families of the deceased would cross the Sour Sea in boats, making landfall just after sunset and bearing their dead kin to a spot on the northern end of the plain. They would bring tools with them, and under the moonlight they would dig a deep hole in the ground and lay the body inside. Then, to Nagash's amusement, they would turn their attention to the mountain and utter some kind of absurd prayer before filling up the hole again. Once the family had gone, Nagash would summon up the corpse and find a place for it on one of his work parties.

A year passed. Work on the mountain continued, and then the rainy season returned. Not long after, burials on the plain increased sharply. Scores of bodies were brought across the sea and laid to rest, usually in large groups. Nagash noted that the corpses were men of fighting age, and all of them had been slain by sword, spear or arrow. The barbarian tribes were at war again, though against whom Nagash did not know. One night, Nagash saw an orange glow on the horizon to the north-west, and realised that one of the larger hilltop villages was on fire.

Another wave of burials occurred, twice as large as the ones before. The war continued unabated, Nagash reckoned - and the barbarians were losing badly. Their loss was his gain, he reasoned. And then something unexpected happened.

One night, in the midst of another spate of burials, a small group of men made their way across the barrow plain in the direction of the mountain. They were dragging a large sledge behind them, bearing a large, cylindrical object wrapped in ragged sheets of muslin.

The men hauled the sledge over the muddy ground, until they reached the eastern edge of the plain. There, virtually in the shadow of the mountain, they took up tools from the sledge and went to work digging a deep hole. When one of the men judged the hole deep enough, he gestured for his companions to proceed, then he knelt before the hole and bowed his head, spreading his arms as though in supplication, or in prayer.

The rest of the men returned to the sledge and pulled away the muslin sheets. Then they took their places to either side of the cylinder and lifted it from its cradle. Struggling under the weight of the object, they inched towards the hole. Finally, after long minutes of effort, they let the end of the cylinder drop into the cavity and pushed the object upright. The kneeling man rose to his feet, his hands turning upwards in a gesture of triumph, as the men shovelled loose earth into the hole and stabilised the object. Once they were satisfied that the object was secure, the men gathered their tools and began the long trek back to the shore.

Nagash had observed this through the eyes of several of his servants, who stood watch over the plain to mark the arrivals of the burial parties. The object left at the foot of the mountain intrigued him. When the men had disappeared to the west, he sent one of the undead sentinels to inspect it.

What the sentinel found was a totem-statue, similar to those found in the barbarian villages. But where the other statues were four-sided and depicted two pairs of men and women, this statue was carved to represent one figure only.

The workmanship was crude. Nagash, looking through his servants' eyes, stared at the statue for some time, until he saw the suggestion of a cloak about the figure's shoulders and realised that the skeletal monster carved into the wood was meant to be him!

Nagash didn't know what to make of the statue. Was it some pathetic attempt at an abjuration, meant to forbid him from trespassing upon the plain, or was it simply a crude attempt at defiance on the part of the barbarians? At length, he decided to wait and see if the men visited the statue again.

And visit they did, just a few nights later, when the next wave of burials landed upon the shore. Nagash watched the men approach the statue, and this time he noted that the men were young and clad in robes – and, most importantly, bore none of the physical deformities that marked the rest of the villagers. They were members of the old order that Nagash had thought extinct!

To his amazement, the men surrounded the statue and laid plates heaped with offerings at its feet. They knelt in supplication and offered up prayers, then anointed the statue with oils. The whole ritual took almost an hour, and then the men hurriedly withdrew.

Nagash continued to study the statue throughout the night, trying to puzzle out the meaning of the ritual offerings and prayers. Were they actually offering up adulation and worship, or were the offerings more of a bribe to keep him from interfering in their business? The fact that the ritual coincided with another round of mass burials wasn't lost on him, but the timing didn't argue one way or the other.

He continued to watch and wait, though now he made sure that a small group of warriors were always kept close by the statue each night. The men returned each night that a burial took place, laying out more offerings and taking care of the great statue. On the fifth visitation, Nagash's patience was rewarded.

As the men gathered about the statue and laid out their offerings, another group of men and women approached from the north, where the latest round of burials were taking place. They accosted the supplicants, brandishing cudgels and shouting threats. The leader of the supplicants – a young man whose mannerisms seemed strangely familiar to Nagash – seemed to try reasoning with the second group, but his arguments fell on deaf ears. There were more shouted threats, and finally the supplicants chose to depart. The second group pursued them for a while, waving their clubs in the air, then, satisfied, they returned to the sombre ceremonies to the north.

The confrontation suggested a great many things to Nagash. The supplicants considered Nagash a god, and sought to worship him, but their newfound devotion wasn't popular with the rest of their kind. What was it they hoped to accomplish? Had the confrontation convinced them to abandon their heresy? The questions only served to pique his interest further.

Another week passed before the next spate of burials occurred. Again, the supplicants journeyed across the plain to kneel before the statue. This time, Nagash was ready for them.

The supplicants had no sooner begun their rite when a much larger group of villagers came charging out of the darkness, brandishing cudgels and knives and shouting threats at the kneeling men. The young leader of the supplicants rose to his feet and approached the villagers, but it was clear to Nagash that the mob wouldn't be interested in talking this time. They were out for blood.

Nagash issued a series of commands to the warriors that lay in wait just a short distance from the totem statue. They rose silently from their places of concealment and crept towards the unsuspecting barbarians.

The leader of the supplicants started to speak, but a burly villager stepped from the crowd and lashed out with his cudgel, striking the young man in the head and knocking him to the ground. The attack galvanised the rest of the mob; they rushed forward, shouting furiously, and fell upon the other worshippers. The holy men fell to the ground, covering their heads with their arms to ward off the avalanche of blows.

No one saw the undead warriors until it was too late. Half a dozen skeletons appeared out of the darkness, stabbing at the villagers with spears or slashing with tarnished bronze blades. Shouts of anger turned to screams of fear and pain as the mob was cut apart by the remorseless skeletons. The survivors reeled away from the attackers and fled into the darkness, abandoning their wounded compatriots to their fate.

The leader of the mob lingered a moment too long, pausing to deliver a final, vicious kick to the leader of the supplicants before trying to make good his escape. As he turned and prepared to run, he found himself face-to-face with a leering skeleton; the flat of the undead warrior's blade crashed into the side of his head, knocking him senseless.

The fight was over in seconds. Nagash's warriors surveyed the scene of carnage for a moment, and then a pair of the skeletons seized the leader of the mob by the shoulders and dragged him away. Two more of the warriors went to the leader of the supplicants, who was trying to force his battered body to stand upright. They seized him by the arms and dragged him away as well.

The remaining two skeletons hefted their weapons and slew the wounded villagers one by one. As the supplicants watched in horrified wonder, their oppressors died screaming – then, with the last of their lifeblood still flowing from their wounds, the corpses rose to their feet and followed their killers into the night.

A single tower reared up from the ugly sprawl of buildings, mine works and fortifications that now girdled the mountain's southern flank. Five storeys tall, square and built from stone, it would have been thought crude and artless in the civilized cities of Nehekhara, but it dominated the surrounding countryside and provided good fields of view over the southern barrow fields and the mountains to the south-east. It was no palace, but it allowed Nagash to oversee the labours on the mountainside and continue his necromantic studies in solitude until such time as a proper sanctum could be built.

The top storey of the tower was a single, windowless chamber, lit only by the pulsing green glow of a huge chunk of burning stone that rested on a crude metal tripod at the left of Nagash's new throne. The high-backed chair had been wrought of wood and bronze, shaped to resemble the Throne of Settra that had once rested in Khemri. The necromancer sat back in the tall chair, his hands steepled thoughtfully, as his warriors dragged the two barbarians into his presence.

The former leader of the village mob struggled in the skeletons' grip, spitting curses and roaring oaths in his bestial tongue. Blood flowed freely from a cut at his temple, but otherwise he appeared none the worse for his experience. The young supplicant, on the other hand, had been beaten within an inch of his life. He hung almost limply from the bony arms of the warriors. It took all of his strength to hold his head upright and look about in dull wonder at the shadowy interior of the tower.

With a mental command Nagash directed his warriors to drag the mob leader into the centre of a ritual circle he'd prepared some time before. They forced the man to his knees. When he tried to rise, one of the skeletons dashed him to the floor with another blow to the head.

The supplicant was deposited on the floor a short distance from the circle, at the very edge of the light shed by the chunk of burning stone. His wide-eyed stare fell upon Nagash, and immediately the young man bent forward, prostrating himself before the throne. The gesture triggered a memory: this was the young acolyte he'd seen outside the barrow during the ambush. Nagash smiled thinly. His instincts had been correct. This one could prove useful.

Nagash rose slowly from the throne. He was clad in robes that had been looted from the temple fortress, which concealed much of the changes that time and the *abn-i-khat* had wrought upon his body. It was only his hands and his face that hinted at the horrors concealed beneath the rough-spun cloth. His flesh, once paper-thin, had begun to liquefy under the heat emanating from his bones, giving it a sickly, gelid appearance. Muscles and tendons glistened in the open air where the flesh and skin had been worn away, and only the barest shreds of flesh remained at cheek and brow to lend the hint of life to Nagash's skeletal face.

He approached the leader of the villagers, whose eyes widened in pure terror. The barbarian screamed curses at the necromancer, his voice rising in pitch as his sanity neared breaking point. When Nagash entered the ritual circle, the barbarian surged to his feet, but before he could take a single step, the necromancer seized him by the throat.

Wide-eyed, gasping, the barbarian began to thrash and kick. Nagash spoke a single word, and the villager's muscles contracted savagely, putting so much stress on his limbs that the long bones of his arms and legs broke like dry twigs. His curses became shrieks of agony, growing ever more shrill and frenzied as the necromancer reached up with his left hand and began methodically pulling away handfuls of the barbarian's black hair. When the man's scalp was bald and bleeding, Nagash pulled a knife from his belt and began carving runes into the barbarian's skin.

The preparations took almost half an hour. When it was complete, Nagash dropped the villager in a heap at the centre of the circle and then withdrew. Once outside the circle, the necromancer raised his arms and began to chant. At once, the sigils etched into the circle flared into life, and the spell began to unravel the barbarian's mind and soul.

It was a variation on the ritual of reaping that he'd perfected in Khemri, and then reconstructed from memory in the years he'd spent wandering the wasteland. The difference between this version and the original was the way it separated the constituent elements of a victim's spirit. As he tore the villager's soul from his body, Nagash picked the elements he wished and discarded the rest, like a lord picking at a resplendent feast.

The barbarian's memories meant nothing to him; he cast those aside with a contemptuous flick of his wrist. Nagash learned that the man was an apprentice woodworker by tasting the flavour of his skill with chisel and saw. Those, too, he cast aside.

There! Nagash tasted the rough flavour of language in the stew of the man's thoughts. He drew that out and consumed it. Crude, guttural words came and went in his mind, etched one by one into his memory.

Finally, the necromancer consumed the barbarian's life essence. He tasted its potency and compared it to the power of the burning stone. Nagash's lip curled in distaste.

'*Disappointing,*' he sneered, as the shrivelled corpse collapsed onto the floor. With a wave of his hand, he sent a flow of power back into the sack of bones and sent it shambling off to the mines.

Nagash turned to the supplicant, who had watched the entire ritual in terrified silence. The necromancer searched his memory for the right words.

'*Who are you?*'

The supplicant pressed his forehead to the floor. 'Ha... Hathurk, mighty one,' he stammered.

'*Hathurk,*' Nagash echoed. '*Who are you to worship me? You served the temple once.*'

The necromancer expected the former acolyte to equivocate, but instead, Hathurk nodded matter-of-factly. 'I served the Keepers of the Mountain,' he admitted readily. 'In time, I would have become a Keeper myself. But their time is finished. The words of the Ancients have been fulfilled.'

'*How so?*'

Hathurk dared to glance up from the floor. 'The Ancients told us that one day the mountain would wake,' he explained. 'The god would come forth. And now you are here.'

Interesting, Nagash thought. '*Where are the words of the Ancients...*' he paused, realising that the barbarians had no words for the act of writing. '*How were the words of the Ancients preserved?*'

'They were passed down, generation to generation, from Keeper to acolyte.'

Nagash nodded thoughtfully. 'And do the village hetmen know these tales?'

Hathurk shook his head. 'They were not worthy, mighty one. They are ignorant, superstitious folk.'

'*Indeed,*' Nagash said.

Sarcasm was lost on the likes of Hathurk. The supplicant nodded quickly. 'They know of you, though,' he continued. 'We have travelled between the villages, spreading the word of your coming. We told the hetmen that it was you who came for the Keepers, because the High Keeper refused to accept that the words of the Ancients had been fulfilled.'

'*Do they believe?*' Nagash asked.

The supplicant shook his head. 'Not yet, mighty one. They are stubborn and set in their ways. But,' he added quickly, 'the war season has begun, and the tribes of the Forsaken have come down from the northlands with fire and sword. Without the Keepers to aid them, the village warbands have suffered many defeats. Already, two villages have been destroyed, their women and children slaughtered in their homes. The other hetmen are talking openly of an alliance against the Forsaken, but even that will not be enough. They will need the power of the mountain if they are to prevail.'

Nagash considered this. More vassals were needed to labour in the mines and seek out sources of stone and timber for constructing the fortress. Empires grew on a steady diet of conquest.

The Undying King crossed the sanctum and settled once more upon his throne. His eyes guttered thoughtfully.

'*Tell me more,*' he said.

THIRTEEN

BLOOD FOR BLOOD

Lahmia,
the City of the Dawn,
in the 76th year of Khsar the Faceless
(-1598 Imperial Reckoning)

'The queen! The *queen!*' Aiyah wailed in horror. 'Blessed gods, what have we done?'

Arkhan reeled backwards, away from the bed and Neferata's withered corpse. The sight of her left him speechless. He shook his head, stunned at the enormity of what had happened.

'I don't understand,' he finally managed to say. 'There were no mistakes. The ritual should have worked. *It should have worked!*'

The immortal rubbed his face with a bloodstained hand. Belatedly, he realised that his arm was still bleeding. With an effort, he focused his will and sealed the wound shut. He felt weak and stiff. His limbs were cold. He'd given her almost every ounce of vigour he possessed. *All for nothing,* he thought bitterly. *She looks no better than Neferem now.*

Arkhan forced himself to close his eyes. He took a deep breath and forced the image of the dead queen from his mind. Almost at once, his sense of regret dissipated, like the heat of the desert at sunset, leaving his mind sharper and clearer than it had been in years. Neferata was gone, and the glamour she'd cast on him had faded along with her. Arkhan was both surprised and ashamed at how keenly he felt the loss. Bitterness and hatred welled up to fill the void it had left behind.

He was himself again. And the way ahead was clear.

The immortal rose slowly to his feet and went to collect his robes. Aiyah was curled into a ball at the foot of the queen's bed, sobbing despondently.

'That's enough,' he said as he dressed. 'She's gone. All the wailing in the world won't bring her back.'

By the time he had tied on his sword belt, the handmaiden had mastered herself. She sat up, rubbing at the tracks of kohl that stained her damp cheeks. 'What would you have me do?' she asked.

Arkhan grabbed a carry-bag from the floor beside Neferata's writing desk and began stuffing Nagash's books inside. 'That's your concern now,' he said. 'If I were you, I'd gather up some changes of clothing and as many of the queen's trinkets as I could carry, and then steal a fast horse from the royal stable. Any number of merchant caravans would be happy to let you ride along with them, for the proper fee. I wouldn't advise riding the trade road alone.'

The handmaiden stared bemusedly at him. 'Leave the city?' she said dully. 'Where would I go?'

'Anywhere but here, you little fool,' he snarled, slinging the bulging bag over his shoulder. 'Unless you're keen to drink from a poisoned cup and follow your queen into darkness.'

Aiyah watched him as he headed for the chamber door, her expression full of dread. 'Where are you going?' she asked.

'To see the king,' Arkhan growled. 'There's something I've been wanting to give him for a very long time.'

The halls of the palace were quiet in the small hours before dawn. Arkhan slipped from one shadow to the next, his pale face hidden by a desert scarf and his hands concealed by dark leather gloves. He disliked the notion of creeping through the palace like a rat, but he suspected that if Lamashizzar knew he was coming, the feckless king would go into hiding, and the immortal did not have time to waste hunting for him across the sprawling royal compound. He meant to settle accounts with the king and be well away from the city before daybreak. There were secluded spots on the Golden Plain where he could lie up until nightfall and contemplate his next move.

Arkhan didn't plan on going far. He'd already come to that conclusion. With the queen dead and the king soon to follow, there would be chaos and confusion among the noble houses as the most prominent lords vied to rule the city as crown regent until Lamashizzar's young son reached adulthood. The process could last for weeks, even months – more than enough time for him to knit the plains outlaws together into something resembling an army. With a little luck, the city nobles would still be scheming against one another on the night his cutthroats came scrambling over the city walls.

The streets of Lahmia would run with rivers of blood. Her villas would go up in flame, as would the ships filling her harbour. The sack of the city would take days, and when he was done, not one stone would be left standing atop another. Then Arkhan would lead his howling mob eastward, and woe betide anyone or anything caught in their path. The petty cares of mortal men filled him with contempt; he wanted nothing more than to scourge mankind for its callowness and stupidity, to bury all of Nehekhara under a pall of suffering and despair. By the time he was done, the survivors would look back on the reign of Nagash with *envy*.

The immortal moved as swiftly as he dared, encountering few servants and even fewer palace guards as the crossed the royal compound towards the king's quarters. The royal apartments were a collection of luxurious chambers for the ruler, his children and his favoured concubines, connected by a sprawling network of common rooms, libraries, small shrines and meditative gardens. It occupied the entire north-west corner of the palace compound, with views looking out across the city proper and the wide, blue sea. What little he knew of it came from Neferata, and she'd only lived there during her early childhood. He had no idea where the king's bedchamber lay, but he'd spent enough time in the royal palace at Khemri to know how such places operated. *When in doubt, follow the servants,* he thought.

Once past the great central palace garden and the royal audience chamber, Arkhan passed through the palace's smaller privy chambers, where the king met with his councillors to conduct the day-to-day business of the city. From there he came upon a series of increasingly well-appointed passageways. He began to encounter more and more sleepy-eyed servants, hurrying about on one errand or another in anticipation of the coming day. Before long, Arkhan came to a tall, wide doorway, flanked by basalt statues of Asaph and Ptra. Hieroglyphs carved into the stone lintel proclaimed, *Here dwell the most favoured of the gods, the mortal seed of Asaph the Beautiful and great Ptra in His Glory.* With a wolfish smile, the immortal drew his iron sword and crept across the threshold.

Beyond the great doorway was a small, silent antechamber, with passageways leading off in three directions. Arkhan continued through the doorway on the opposite side of the room, and soon found himself in a small, shadow-filled garden. Narrow paths wound among the ornamental trees and clusters of ferns. Somewhere a fountain chuckled to itself, and captive songbirds chirped sleepily in the branches. Was this the central garden for the royal apartments, or just one of several? Arkhan's confidence began to ebb. He couldn't afford the time to search every path and passageway until he found the king. The first hints of false dawn were already paling the sky overhead.

Suddenly, he caught the sound of soft voices approaching him from behind. Arkhan slipped off the path as quietly as he could and hid behind the bole of a palm tree. Moments later, a pair of bare-chested slaves walked past, murmuring to each other in quiet tones. One carried a polished bronze bowl filled with steaming water, while another bore clean cotton cloths and a small, bronze shaving knife.

The immortal was surprised. He had no idea that Lamashizzar had become such an early riser. Arkhan waited until the men had disappeared from sight before easing himself back onto the path and following along in their wake.

It took several minutes to reach the far side of the garden. The paths wound a meandering course through the lush foliage, creating the illusion that the garden was much larger and more secluded than it actually was, and effectively concealed the routes into and out of the open-air space. It had been so cunningly designed that Arkhan hadn't realised he'd reached the opposite edge until he rounded another sharp turn in the path and came upon another tall, imposing doorway, flanked by a pair of royal guards.

Arkhan froze, his sword held low at his side. The two men were clad in lacquered iron armour and polished skullcaps, and were armed with heavy, straight swords like the one he carried. Neither man saw him at first; his dark clothing blended well with the shadows, and it was clear that their senses were dulled from a long, quiet watch.

They were less than fifteen paces away. Arkhan gauged the distance carefully, and drew upon what little remained of the queen's elixir. Strength swelled in his limbs, and he dashed forward, almost too quickly for the eye to follow. His blade whickered through the air. The first man barely had time to register the movement before his head toppled from his shoulders. Blood sprayed across the second man; Arkhan saw his eyes widen in shock, stunned by the speed and ferocity of the attack. The hesitation was fatal.

Arkhan paused just long enough to drag the two bodies beneath a nearby stand of drooping ferns, then crept carefully through the doorway into the king's personal apartments. Beyond was another dark antechamber, thick with a fog of cloying incense. He glimpsed low divans and wooden tables arranged together in tight clusters around the room. Empty wine jars and bronze trays littered with scraps of food covered most of the tables.

On the opposite side of the antechamber was another open doorway, filled with the shifting orange glow of lit braziers. Arkhan paused at the threshold and glimpsed what appeared to be another long rectangular chamber. There was a set of tall blue-painted doors on the far side of the room, and the doorway was carved with intricate hieroglyphs of protection, wealth and good fortune. The king's bedchamber had to lie on the other side of those doors, he reckoned. Arkhan steeled himself, acutely aware of how little vigour remained to him. He would have to make this quick. The thought galled him, but better swift vengeance than none at all. Tightening his grip on his bloodstained sword, he raced for the doors.

The guards rushed him the moment he stepped across the threshold.

There were six of them, waiting with swords drawn, three to either side of the doorway. Doubtless one of them had heard something as he'd despatched the guards at the edge of the garden, and they'd lain in wait for him. Now they leapt at him with triumphant shouts, moving quickly to cut him off from the king's bedchamber.

Arkhan had little time to curse his own carelessness, and no choice but to draw upon the elixir once more. The guardsmen were swift and skilled, but lacked experience; in their haste they got in one another's way, fouling the sweep of their own swords. The immortal gave them a bestial snarl and struck first, ducking low and spinning on his heel to strike at the man just behind and to his right. The heavy iron blade slashed across the guard's thigh, through the narrow gap between the edge of his armoured skirt and the top of his iron greaves. The sword sliced through flesh and muscle and left him thrashing on the floor in a spreading pool of blood.

The guardsman to Arkhan's immediate left chopped downwards with his sword. He parried the blow swiftly and drove the man back with a feint to his throat. The warriors shouted curses at him and at one another. A blade scored across his back, and another jabbed into his side, just above his hip. Arkhan scarcely felt the blows. He whirled left and slashed upwards, catching another guardsman's sword wrist and severing his hand. The man reeled backwards with a scream and slipped in the dark blood pouring from the other guard's leg.

Two down, but now the other guards had more room to manoeuvre. Arkhan sidestepped a fearsome downward slash, and then had to whirl out of the way of a thrust angling in from his far left. Then a powerful blow on his back cut deep into his shoulder blade and nearly sent him sprawling. This time he felt the sharp pain of broken bone, but he sealed the wound with a thought and kept fighting, lunging upwards and catching a guard in the throat with the point of his sword.

The remaining guards circled around him, harrying him with a flurry of strikes that were meant to test his defences and keep him off-balance. He kept moving, turning in place and batting the attacks aside, waiting for his moment. A warrior lunged at him from the right, thrusting at his sword arm. He turned on his heel, sweeping the point aside with his own blade and causing the man to stumble slightly forwards. The guard saw his peril and moved swiftly to regain his balance, but it was already too late. Arkhan's blade flashed, and the guard's head bounced across the floor.

The two surviving guards struck at once, hitting him from behind. One sword bit deeply into his right hip, its edge grating against bone, while the other stabbed into his back, just below his left shoulder blade. Arkhan staggered, tasting blood in his mouth. He turned, almost tearing the sword from the grip of the man who'd stabbed him, and slashed his blade across the man's face. The guard fell with a scream, clutching at his ruined eyes. His sword was still trapped in Arkhan's back, lodged between his ribs.

With a savage jerk, the last guard tore his blade free from Arkhan's hip. Seeing his foe gravely wounded, the guard rained a storm of ringing blows down upon the immortal's guard. Sparks flew as the iron blades clashed, and the immortal's counter-blows began to slacken. The guard cut him three times in swift succession, once above the right elbow, once in the left thigh, and once across the chest. Sensing triumph, the warrior redoubled his attacks, aiming a lightning-fast blow at Arkhan's neck that the immortal barely turned aside. The block left his torso unprotected, and the guard leapt forward with a shout, thrusting his sword straight at Arkhan's heart.

But the blow never struck home. Arkhan had given him the opening to draw him in, then spun on his heel and let the guard's sword go past him. His own blade smashed into the side of the man's head, shattering his iron skullcap and driving shards of bone into his brain. The warrior was dead before his body hit the floor.

Arkhan staggered, nearly toppling as well. The battle had lasted only a few seconds, but no doubt it had woken everyone in earshot. The alarm would be spreading through the palace even now. He groped at his back, fumbling for the sword that jutted from his ribs. It took several more agonising seconds to pull it free, and then a moment more to focus his will and use just enough power to seal the wound. He had very little remaining now. If he used much more he might not have enough strength left to escape.

It would be enough, he thought, gritting his ruined teeth. *It would have to be enough.*

Arkhan lurched forward, gathering speed, and shoved open the doors to the king's bedchamber.

The room was large, much more so than the queen's, and dominated by a wide bed piled with silken pillows. Two braziers along the walls to the left and right had been recently stoked to life, revealing rich, painted carvings etched into the sandstone that depicted the great journey of the Nehekharan people from the southern jungles millennia ago. Tall, basalt statues of Ptra and Asaph stood watch over the royal bed, their stone faces uncharacteristically smiling and beneficent. More padded divans and low tables were clustered around the edges of the room, along with a little-used writing table near the tall windows on the room's opposite side. Gauzy window hangings shifted lazily in the breeze blowing in from the sea.

The two body servants cowered at the foot of the bed, their eyes wide with terror. The upended bowl and the bronze knife gleamed at their feet. Arkhan ignored them, searching the room for the king. Just then, the wind shifted, drawing back the window hangings, and he caught sight of a silhouette between two of the windows. The figure moved suddenly, raising his right arm.

Arkhan was faster. His left hand shot up, fingers outstretched, and he spoke a single word. The last vestiges of his power flowed through his fingertips, and the silhouette stiffened.

A slow, cruel smile crossed the immortal's face. 'Did you imagine I'd forgotten?' he told the king. 'Oh, no. That little trick won't work a second time.'

He forced his stiff limbs to move, making his way haltingly across the chamber. When he passed the great bed, the two servants bolted from the room. He could hear their hysterical shouts receding in the direction of the garden. As he drew nearer to the windows he could see the king clearly now. Lamashizzar was clad in a silken sleeping robe, stained here and there with splashes of wine. The strain of the last week had taken a toll upon him: his face was gaunt and sallow, and his eyes were sunken deeply in their sockets. Arkhan saw that the king's lips were stained from the steady use of lotus root. How long had Lamashizzar kept himself here, surrounded by guards, waiting for word that Neferata had died?

The short dragon-stave was gripped in the king's outstretched hand. A faint wisp of smoke rose from the wick held in his left hand. The little red coal had burned very close to his fingers, but the king could not let it go. He stared at Arkhan, his expression transfixed, as a bird watches the dreadful approach of the cobra.

Arkhan stared deep into the king's eyes, savouring the terror he saw there. 'As you can see, I've learned a few tricks of my own,' he said. 'It took some time to perfect the technique, but I knew I'd need it when this day finally came. Thanks to you, I had plenty of time to practice.'

Never taking his eyes from the king, Arkhan set his sword carefully upon the floor. He straightened, his ghastly smile widening. 'There's something I've been wanting to share with you for a very long time,' he said. 'You know, it was very clever of you, shooting me in the heart with that damned stave of yours. When the bullet pierced, I honestly thought you'd killed me. Everything went black, but then I realised that I could still hear and feel everything around me. How I screamed then. How I raged. After a while, I even begged. I called upon gods I'd forsaken centuries ago, praying for the mercy of death. Naturally, it never came. It was the worst torture I'd ever felt, and if you knew anything about my past, you'd know just exactly how profound that statement is.'

Arkhan reached up and carefully took hold of the dragon-stave. One by one, he plucked the king's stiff fingers from the haft of the weapon. 'Do you know what sustained me in that darkness? The only thing that allowed me to keep what little sanity I had left was the slim hope that one day, I'd visit the same awful fate upon you.'

He took the weapon carefully from the king's hand. 'It was worth it, teaching you the secrets of the Undying King's elixir. Without it, my vengeance would not have been possible. Now, when the bullet strikes your heart, you'll know the same smothering darkness, the same helplessness. The same despair.'

The immortal pressed the gaping muzzle of the dragon to Lamashizzar's chest. A faint tremor shook the king's body. His eyes widened a tiny, terrified fraction. It would have taken a prodigious, desperate exertion of will to manage even so small a movement.

Arkhan plucked the wick from the king's left hand, and blew softly upon the end. The tiny coal blazed to life.

'When your servants find you, they'll think you've been slain, of course,' the immortal continued. 'Doubtless, they'll summon the mortuary priests, who will bear your body to the House of Everlasting Life and prepare you for the ages to come. If you're lucky, you'll die when they remove your heart and seal it in a canopic jar. If not... you'll have a very long time to regret you ever dreamt of crossing me.'

Arkhan touched the wick to the stave's touch-hole. 'The queen is dead,' he said to Lamashizzar, 'but at least she's free. I hope you rot in darkness until the end of time.'

The weapon discharged with a flash and a muffled *thump*. The impact knocked the king from his feet. He hit the wall and slid to the floor, his body going limp. Arkhan knelt, staring into the king's wide eyes, and then reached up with his fingertips to slowly push them shut.

Arkhan studied his handiwork a moment more, then rose and tossed the smoking weapon aside. The sky beyond the windows was paling. He was nearly out of time.

Snatching up his sword, he made his way across the bedchamber. His mind was already racing ahead, planning his route to the royal stables, when he heard a loud commotion in the chamber beyond.

Arkhan reached the doorway and saw a score of royal guardsmen dashing into the chamber from the direction of the garden, led by the king's champion. Abhorash's face was pale with fury. Two long iron swords gleamed in his scarred hands.

There would be no escape. Arkhan knew that at once. He was spent, and Abhorash was too skilled an opponent to be taken in by his tricks. For a moment, the immortal thought wistfully of the warhorse waiting in the stables, and the feel of the desert wind on his face.

He had his revenge upon the king. That would have to be enough.

Raising his sword, Arkhan went to meet his fate.

The scope of the tragedy was immense, the carnage terrible to behold. The royal apartments looked like a battlefield, heaped with the mangled remains of Lamashizzar's valiant guard. Though Abhorash, the king's champion, had slain the assassin in the end, it was a bitter victory for the people of Lahmia. Lamashizzar, the great king, was dead.

It was a crushing blow for the royal household to bear. Functionaries and servants alike were overwhelmed by the news, not realising that it was only a fraction of the greater catastrophe. Only Ubaid, the grand vizier, and the few remaining servants of the Women's Palace knew that Neferata was dead as well.

For a handful of hours, just after dawn, Ubaid held the fate of the city – and by extension, all of Nehekhara – in his hands. His first act was to order the king's champion to seal off the palace, allowing none to enter or leave upon pain of death. One of the queen's handmaidens was already missing, probably having fled in the small hours of the morning, but the rest of the household was kept from spreading the word to the city at large. Orders were given not to inform the king's children of his death, at least not yet. That bought the palace precious hours to organise a proper response.

After careful consideration, the king's privy council was summoned. Lords Ankhat and Ushoran answered the call at once, as well as the old scholar W'soran. Lord Zuhras, the king's young cousin, could not be found for hours, having gone drinking with his friends in the Red Silk District the night before. It was mid-morning by the time his servants brought him, pale and trembling, to the palace gates.

While the council met in secret to discuss the shocking turn of events, the priests of the mortuary cult were quietly summoned to begin their ministrations to the dead. Rituals began at once for the great king, preparing his body for transfer to the House of Everlasting Life. The protocols for the queen were different. By tradition, her body was to be washed and clothed by her handmaidens, and at dusk they would bear her upon their shoulders to the Hall of Regretful Sorrows. There she would be given into the keeping of the priests, who would tend her while her body lay in state for the proscribed three days and three nights. Only then, after the citizens had been given time to pay their last respects, would Neferata join her husband in the House of Everlasting Life.

Shortly before the appointed hour, just as the sun was setting far out to sea, Ubaid, the grand vizier, appeared at the door to the queen's bedchamber.

The last of the queen's handmaidens - half a dozen women ranging in age from youthful to elderly - were crouched on their knees around the perimeter of the queen's bed. The traditional preparation of the body had lasted for almost the entire day, and most of the handmaidens were slumped and silent with exhaustion. The rest rocked slowly on their heels, keening softly in mourning.

Ubaid stood in the doorway and carefully surveyed the room. He'd been told what the handmaidens had found when they'd entered the room that morning, but all traces of Arkhan's desperate rituals had been scrupulously removed. The ritual circle had been scrubbed away, along with the pools of dried blood that had stained the floor around the bed. The bedclothes themselves had been stripped away, and now lay in a tightly wrapped bundle in one corner of the room. The grand vizier made a mental note to have them burned before the night was out.

Neferata lay on a bare white mattress, her body wrapped in a fine cotton robe that had been marked with hieroglyphs of protection and anointed with sacred oils. Her arms were folded across her chest, and her golden mask had been laid across her face. Only the bare skin of her hands, marked with intricate bands of henna tattoos, showed how cruelly wasted her body had been at the time of her death. The sight of it sent a pang of guilt through the grand vizier, but he stifled it with an effort of will. What was done was done. His responsibility now was to look to the future, and ensure the continuation of the dynasty.

One of the older handmaidens caught sight of Ubaid and straightened. 'You shouldn't be here!' she said. 'It's not proper!'

'These are not proper times,' Ubaid replied. He approached the bed. As one, the handmaidens scrambled to their feet, forming an implacable barrier between him and their charge.

The grand vizier addressed the old handmaiden. 'Forgive the intrusion,' he said, inclining his head respectfully. 'I meant no disrespect. This has been a hard day for us all, and I wanted to make certain that the queen and her quarters had been seen to properly.'

'We know our duty,' the handmaiden said, folding her arms indignantly. 'Do you imagine we would allow any slight to her honour?'

'No, naturally not,' Ubaid replied. 'It must have been hard, preparing the queen and... restoring her chamber to its proper appearance. Did you manage all of it alone?'

'Just the six of us,' she replied grimly, though her head was held high. 'We couldn't trust such an important task to anyone else.'

'Yes, of course,' the grand vizier said, inwardly breathing a sigh of relief. He studied each of the handmaidens in turn, committing their faces to memory. All of them would have to die. Hopefully they would all choose to follow the queen into the afterlife, but if not, he would take matters into his own hands. Once they were gone, there would be no one left who knew the real circumstances of Neferata's death.

The cabal – what was left of it – could continue its work in secret. Ubaid had little doubt that W'soran would be able to take up where the queen left off. Lord Ankhat or Lord Ushoran would be named regent, and life in the city would go on much as before. In fact, the grand vizier thought, the opportunities for power and influence for the surviving cabal members would be even greater.

Ubaid took a step back and composed himself, then bowed solemnly to the handmaidens. 'It is time,' he said. 'The priests and the privy council await in the Hall of Regretful Sorrows. Let the people of Lahmia look upon Neferata one final time, and weep.'

The handmaidens grew subdued at the grand vizier's solemn words. The old one sighed and gestured to her companions, and they turned their attention once more to their beloved queen. Three of the women circled around to the far side of the bed, then they all hung their heads and intoned a ceremonial prayer to Usirian, god of the underworld. Ubaid listened to the low, mournful chant, as the sun sank low on the horizon and the light fled from the room. The prayer came to an end, and the chamber was plunged into a funereal gloom. As one, the handmaidens began their keening wail again, and bent over the queen's recumbent form.

Suddenly, there came a dreadful sound from the bed. It was a faint, wet, rippling crackle, like the popping of joints grown stiff from disuse. Then the keening of the handmaidens spiralled into a threnody of horrified screams.

Bone crunched and flesh parted with a sound like a knife through wet cloth. The two handmaidens closest to the head of the bed were hurled backwards in a welter of blood, their throats reduced to ragged pulp. Ubaid's stunned mind barely had time to register the horrifying sight before there was a blur of motion above the bed and the sickening sound of crunching bone. Two more handmaidens collapsed, their skulls crushed by swift and terrible blows.

There was scarcely time to breathe, much less react. The last of the queen's devoted servants seemed to reel away from the bed in slow motion, their hands rising to their faces as a lithe, bloodstained figure reached for them with gaunt, grasping hands.

The grand vizier stared in shock as Neferata lashed out at one of the handmaidens with an open hand. The blow crushed the woman's skull like a melon and flung her corpse against the far wall. The last of the handmaidens, younger and swifter than the rest, turned and fled towards Ubaid, her hands outstretched and her face twisted into a mask of absolute terror.

She managed less than a half-dozen steps before Neferata leapt upon her back like a desert lioness. Fingers tipped with long, curving claws sank into the handmaiden's throat. The impact jarred the golden death mask from the queen's face, its cold, smooth perfection falling away to reveal the snarling face of a monster.

The queen's face was horribly gaunt, her cheeks sunken and the flesh stretched like parchment across the planes of her face. Her eyes were twin points of cold, pitiless light, shining with animal hunger as she fell upon her prey. Neferata's shrivelled lips were drawn back in a feral snarl, her delicate jaw agape to reveal prominent, leonine fangs. The handmaiden scarcely had time to scream before the queen's head plunged downward and those terrible fangs sank into the young woman's throat. Flesh tore and vertebrae popped, and the girl's screams dwindled into a choking rattle.

Ubaid pressed a trembling fist to his mouth, biting back a scream of his own. His legs trembled, threatening to betray him completely as he backed towards the bedchamber door. No matter how hard he tried, he could not take his eyes from the handmaiden's body. He dared not turn and run.

Each step lasted an eternity. The handmaiden's body twitched as the queen worried at her throat, gorging on the young woman's blood. He had to be close to the doorway now, Ubaid thought. Another few feet at most, and then–

Suddenly the grand vizier realised that the sounds of feasting had stopped. Neferata's head was raised, her mouth and chin soaked in bright, red blood. His own veins turned to ice as she turned her unearthly gaze upon him.

'Ubaid,' she said, her voice liquid and menacing. The power of her stare left him transfixed. His heart laboured painfully in his chest. '*Loyal servant*. Fall to your knees before your queen.'

The grand vizier's body obeyed. His knees cracked painfully on the stone as he all but prostrated himself before Neferata's terrifying visage.

The queen smiled, her teeth slick with gore. Her eyes glinted cruelly.

'Now tell me all that has transpired.'

The gathering in the Hall of Regretful Sorrows was silent and subdued. The only sounds in the vault-like space were the soft sounds of the mortuary priests' robes as they went about their preparations to receive the body of the queen. Votive incense had been lit, and the proper sigils of preservation had been laid across the marble bier. Lord Abhorash stood at the foot of the cold slab of stone, his head bowed and his hands resting upon the hilt of an ancient ceremonial sword. Lord Ushoran and Lord Ankhat stood apart from one another, each lost in their own thoughts as they contemplated the difficult days ahead.

When news of the king's death became widely known it would send ripples throughout the entire land. It would require adroit manoeuvring to keep the other priest kings in check. Behind the powerful nobles, W'soran stood with his hands folded at his waist and his head bowed, as though in prayer. The old sholar had an impatient expression on his face. He now had unfettered access to Nagash's works, and he was eager to begin his studies. Behind W'soran stood young Lord Zuhras, who lingered close to the door as though he might bolt from the hall at any second. The king's cousin looked pale and stricken, though from grief or guilt, none could truly say.

They had been waiting for more than an hour already, having gathered long before sunset to view the body of the queen. It had already been decided that once Neferata's body had been laid in state, the word of her and Lamashizzar's death would be announced to the city. When the doors at the far end of the chamber swung silently opened, a stir went through the small assembly as they braced for the beginning of a new era.

None expected to see the queen emerge from the shadows of the Women's Palace, pale and terrible in her glory. Her beauty, once the gift of the goddess, now took on a divine power all its own. They did not see the dark blood that stained her white robes and painted her hands and face. Her eyes, dark and depthless as the sea, banished thought and replaced it with a yearning that was deeper and more all consuming than any they had known before.

Beside the queen came Ubaid, the grand vizier. He stepped past Neferata, head bowed and shoulders hunched. He descended the shallow steps that led to the waiting bier, and regarded the assembly with haunted, hollow eyes.

'Rejoice,' he said in a bleak voice. 'Rejoice at the coming of the queen.'

FOURTEEN

THE DARK FEAST

The Plain of Skulls, in the 76th year of Phakth the Just (-1597 Imperial Reckoning)

The warriors of the Forsaken had pitched their tents upon the Plain of Skulls, a broad, roughly triangular plain some three leagues north-east of the Sour Sea. As the only navigable terrain between the coastline and the village-forts of the northlanders, the plain was where the barbarians – or the Yaghur, as Hathurk knew them – and the Forsaken had met to do battle for centuries. By ancient custom, the warbands of both sides normally encamped along the northern and southern edges of the plain, but after a series of recent victories of the Yaghur, the northlanders were no longer abiding by the old rules. They had taken note of the absence of the Keepers, and believed that the strength of the tribes had been broken. The destruction of the Yaghur was finally at hand.

For the last month, Forsaken raiding parties had struck southward from the plain at will, destroying a number of lowland settlements and storming a pair of hilltop villages. They left behind heaps of charred skulls as offerings to their four-faced god, Malakh, and sent scouts further westward to test the defences of the remaining Yaghur villages. Unless they were driven off the plain, the Forsaken would decimate the Yaghur to the point that the survivors would have little chance of surviving the winter.

According to Hathurk, the war between the Forsaken and the Yaghur had nothing to do with resources or territory; there was nothing the Yaghur possessed that the Forsaken could possibly desire. Indeed, according to Hathurk, the Forsaken once ruled the entire coast, down past the great mountain where a narrow strait led to the great Crystal Sea. It was they who had witnessed the fall of the star-stone that had pierced the side of the mountain, and who had built a great temple-city to venerate their newfound god. They had used the power of the burning stone to dominate the surrounding tribes and carve out a kingdom of their own. In those days, *they* were known as the Yaghur, which in Hathurk's tongue translated as 'the faithful.'

But the kingdom's glory days were short-lived. The noble houses, which ruled from the temple-city on the southern flank of the mountain, turned paranoid and cruel. Madness infected the ruling clans, and soon the kingdom was torn by civil war. Clans fought over the god-stone buried beneath the mountain, and thousands died. Finally, the noble houses of the Yaghur were overthrown when an exiled prince returned from the northlands with the teachings of a new god: Malakh, the Dark One, Master of the Fourfold Path. Malakh's power gained the prince many followers, and in time they conquered the temple city and slaughtered the maddened Yaghur nobles in a grand sacrifice to their god.

Afterwards, the prince sealed up the tunnels beneath the temple city and led his people northwards, where they settled far from the mountain and its corrupting god. But the insatiable desires of Malakh turned out to be just as bad – if not worse – than the lunatic rule of the old Yaghur kings, and once again the people were torn by civil war. Eventually, a schism occurred. Those who rejected Malakh broke away and returned to the shores of the Sour Sea in a vain bid to reclaim the glories of the kingdom they had lost.

The war had raged ever since. The Forsaken would not rest until the last Yaghur had been offered up to their four-faced god. Malakh would be satisfied with nothing less.

Watch-fires flickered across the Plain of Bones, picking out the curved flanks of hide tents and tall, wooden trophy poles festooned with rotting human skulls. Here and there, warriors dozed drunkenly around the fires. As far as they knew, there were no Yaghur warbands for miles; had there been any, their scouts would have warned them long before.

Those selfsame scouts now crept silently towards the Forsaken camp, their eyes burning with necromantic fire. Nagash's warriors had hunted down every one, tracking them by their life energies across the dark, lifeless plain. Now the small, skeletal army was less than fifty yards from the Forsaken camp, crawling inexorably across the rocky ground with the tireless patience of the dead.

A hundred yards further south, Nagash and Hathurk waited with the Yaghur hetmen. The barbarians had taken too long to unite against the northlanders. After months of fighting, the hetmen could barely muster two hundred warriors against an enemy force almost ten times that size. Most were armed with nothing more than crude spears and clubs, and none wore anything resembling proper armour. Nagash wasn't surprised that the Yaghur had hardly ever won a pitched battle against the Forsaken; indeed, it surprised him that they'd survived as long as they had. The Keepers must have been hard-pressed indeed just to maintain an uneasy stalemate against their foes.

The hetmen themselves were armed and armoured with bronze wargear that had been brought from the northlands during the time of the schism. They nervously fingered tarnished bronze swords or clutched at the hafts of bronze-tipped spears and cast fearful glances at Nagash and his undead bodyguard. Hathurk had suggested to the necromancer that bribery would be the best way to win over the hetmen, but Nagash had opted for a more direct approach. When the village leaders had gathered to formally seal their alliance, he had arrived unannounced during the evening feast, riding upon a palanquin borne by the corpses of the High Keeper and his senior subordinates. That served to get the village leaders' attention with a minimum of expense and effort. The rest would hinge on the outcome of the battle that was about to unfold.

As before, Nagash sat upon the palanquin that had once belonged to the High Keeper, which in turn rested upon the motionless shoulders of his servants. It gave him a slightly better view of the battlefield. He could see his warriors crawling forward steadily under the fading light of the moon; another few minutes and they would be at the edge of the watch fires. The necromancer stirred, turning his burning gaze upon the hetmen.

'*The time has come,*' he said. '*The hour of your victory is at hand. We will slaughter the northmen and drive them from the plain, as I have promised.*'

The hetmen shared sidelong glances. Finally, one of them stepped forward. He was a large man for the Yaghur, with dark hair and a shelf-like brow. A third eye, covered with a cataract-like green film, tracked lazily from his forehead. His name was Aighul, and among the barbarians he was reckoned a mighty warrior. The hetman threw out his chest and clutched at the haft of his bronze axe, but he could not quite bring himself to meet Nagash's burning eyes.

'What about the rest of your promise?' Aighul replied. 'You said–'

'*I said I would give you the secret of the northmen's prowess,*' Nagash almost sneered, '*and so I shall. After the battle is won.*'

'And after you bow before great Nagash and accept him as the new god of the mountain!' Hathurk added, in the steely tones of a true believer.

Nagash fought the urge to slay each and every one of them. Men such as they weren't even fit for the slave dock at Zandri. They were little better than animals, unworthy of the attentions of a king. Even Hathurk's credulous worship disgusted him. And yet, for the moment, they were all he had.

'*Go now,*' he told the Yaghur. '*My warriors are nearly ready.*'

Aighul looked as though he was about to say something more, but at the end his nerve deserted him. He and the other hetmen nodded curtly and fanned out into the darkness to meet their warbands. Before long the Yaghur were on the move, loping across the stony plain with admirable stealth. Nagash watched their progress carefully. The barbarians moved much faster than his undead warriors, hence the need to hold them back until his own forces were almost on top of the camp.

Hathurk and his disciples crowded around the palanquin, their expressions earnest. 'How may we be of help, master?' the young supplicant asked.

'*By doing nothing and saying less,*' the necromancer hissed. '*I must concentrate.*'

The Yaghur had almost overtaken his warriors. Nagash willed forth his commands. As one, a mix of two hundred and fifty skeletons and rotting, shambling zombies reared up against the moonlit sky and closed in on the northmen sleeping around the watch fires.

Quick. Quiet. Nagash impressed his will upon his warriors. He'd learned long ago that the undead did not need to be guided through each and every movement of a given order; there were memories and reflexes that lingered in their rotting bodies, though he could not say precisely how. All he needed to do was provide the impetus, and the corpses would do the rest. Those that performed poorly made good sword-fodder so that the rest could fulfil his wishes.

Long, angular shadows crept towards the northmen. Nagash watched swords rise and fall; powerful hands clamped over mouths and tightened about throats. A few northmen thrashed in the grip of the zombies, but never for more than a few moments. Nagash smiled to himself, whispering an incantation into the night air. Most of the slain northmen rose slowly to their feet.

Now the fire, Nagash ordered.

Several of the skeletons turned towards the watch fires. They reached their hands into the dying flames and drew out pieces of burning wood. One by one, they raised their torches skyward, signalling the Yaghur.

Out on the plain, the barbarians saw the signal fires and broke into a ground-eating charge. Then one of the Yaghur, overcome with bloodlust, threw back his head a howled a savage war cry.

'*Idiots!*' Nagash snarled. More and more howls rent the night as the other Yaghur gave into their rage and bayed for the blood of their foes. Already, shouts of alarm were answering the cries from deeper within the camp. *Attack!* The necromancer commanded. *Kill! Burn!* His lips moved, hissing out another incantation.

The undead warriors surged forwards, moving with a sudden burst of speed and agility. Northmen staggered from their tents, sluggish from sleep and the lingering grip of wine. Most barely had time to gape in shock at their attackers before they were slain. Torches were pressed against the oily hides, and within seconds half a dozen tents were ablaze.

Howling like fiends, the Yaghur came charging into the camp. They swung their clubs at anything that moved, adding to the pandemonium. At Nagash's command, the undead pressed further into the camp. Speed was critical, the necromancer knew. The attackers had to stay ahead of the enemy's ability to organise a proper defence, or the defenders' greater numbers would quickly tip the scales against them.

And yet, many of the Yaghur were milling about the edge of the camp, tearing down tents and looting bodies! Nagash's fingers clawed furrows down the arms of his chair. *Forward,* he commanded the corpses carrying his palanquin. If the barbarians were still there when he reached the edge of the camp he would slay them where they stood!

More fires were spreading through the camp, but now came the sound of fighting as well.

Nagash gazed through the eyes of his warriors, and saw that the Forsaken were reacting quickly to the surprise attack. The northmen were huge, powerfully-built warriors, far larger than their deformed southern kin and almost as large as the giant, bronze-skinned fighting men of faraway Ka-Sabar. They wore leather kilts like the Yaghur, studded with wide disks of bronze, and broad belts hung with polished skulls and long chains of finger bones. Some of the warriors were bare-chested, their skin marked with elaborate scar patterns that wound from their thick necks all the way to their waists, while others wore heavy leather vests covered in layers of small, bronze squares.

They showed no fear at the sight of Nagash's warriors. Instead, they charged headlong into their midst, swinging huge axes or long-bladed swords and screaming the name of their strange god. Bones shattered; rotting bodies burst apart. The Forsaken waded through their foes, heedless of peril. They fought on despite terrible wounds, intent only on slaying as many enemies as they could before they were brought down.

In the darkness and the confusion the northmen even attacked one another, further adding to the chaos. Nagash knew that if the enemy's confusion could be fanned like the flames already consuming the camp, the Forsaken would ultimately defeat themselves.

Then the air over the centre of the enemy camp flickered with orange and red light, and series of small thunderclaps shook the air. Nagash felt the aether tremble with invisible energies, and knew that dozens of his warriors had been obliterated. Hathurk had warned him that the Forsaken warlords were often accompanied by a trio of witches, a custom that dated back to the earliest days of the Yaghur kingdom. Their power, he saw, was considerable.

On the heels of the detonations came the baying of horns. Nagash spat out a curse. The warlords were trying to rally their warriors and organise a counterattack. The necromancer knew that he had to deal with the enemy leaders, and quickly, or his meagre forces would be quickly overwhelmed.

The palanquin had nearly reached the perimeter of the camp. Snarling impatiently, Nagash rose from his seat and leap to the ground. Around him, Forsaken warriors were charging out of the darkness, their blades glinting hungrily in the firelight. The Yaghur attacked them with guttural shouts, but the northmen hacked the unarmoured warriors to pieces.

Snarling, Nagash swept his hand in a wide arc, and unleashed a fan of sizzling green bolts that cut down three northmen who sought to bar his path. He charged towards the centre of the camp, forcing his limbs to move at preternatural speed. The tents weren't laid out in neat lines, like a proper Nehekharan army camp, which forced him to weave his way left and right past one shelter after another. Bodies were strewn across the open ground between the tents, half-glimpsed in the firelight.

Another series of flashes lit the air above the camp, followed by a rumble of thunder. His warriors were being decimated. Nagash called back the survivors, drawing them in towards him in hopes that it would force the warlord and his witches to follow. He found a tent blocking his path and raced around it, coming upon a small, cleared area where eight or ten Yaghur were trading blows with six northmen. Nagash let fly with a volley of glowing missiles, spearing friend and foe alike. The survivors scattered in every direction, clearing the necromancer's path.

Moments later, Nagash found himself at the edge of a much larger, open square. Tall trophy poles marked the corners of the square, festooned with dozens of fresh skulls. Within the square stood perhaps a score of Nagash's warriors, engaged in a fighting withdrawal with a large force of northmen. At the forefront of the enemy warriors was a tall, powerfully muscled warrior, clad in bronze scale armour and swinging a huge, bronze sword. Runes had been engraved along the length of the heavy blade, and the air around the sword seemed to shimmer, like the haze over a desert dune.

At Nagash's arrival, the undead warriors halted their retreat and the Forsaken crashed against them in a howling wave. Over the heads of the warriors, Nagash and the enemy warlord locked eyes, and both recognised the other for who and what they were. But the necromancer spared the warlord only a moment's thought. He wasn't the greatest danger inside the enemy camp. Nagash reached out with his arcane senses, seeking the source of the magical energies that had destroyed so many of his warriors.

There! He sensed swirling vortices of power on the far side of the square, well behind the line of savage northmen. Here was the heart of the Forsaken host. He had to seize it quickly and tear it apart.

Nagash reached out across the camp, summoning every one of his surviving warriors. Then he uttered a powerful incantation, increasing the vigour of the warriors in front of him threefold. They surged forwards, into the Forsaken line, their weapons moving almost in a blur. The sudden push caught the northmen by surprise. Several of them fell, slain outright or bleeding to death from mortal wounds. The rest, including their warlord, found themselves on the defensive. It wouldn't last for long, Nagash knew, but it would give him the time he needed to deal with the witches.

Or so he thought. Almost at once he sensed tendrils of magical energy pulling at the forces contained within his invocation, seeking to dispel it. Angered, Nagash threw out his hands and hissed out another spell. A trio of burning green globes flashed from the space between his hands, arcing like arrows over the enemy line and hurtling towards the witches. But before they could plunge onto their targets, the spheres burst apart in thunderous detonations that buffeted the warriors struggling in the square. The witches' counter-magic was potent indeed.

Within moments, Nagash discovered that their offensive sorceries were deadly as well. Tendrils of dark mist coalesced out of the night air around his warriors and wrapped like ropes around their arms and legs. In seconds, they were thoroughly enmeshed, limiting their movements and the strength of their blows. The Forsaken warriors struck back with bloodthirsty shouts, breaking apart many skeletons in the front rank.

Nagash ignored his warriors' plight. He could not afford to become distracted in a contest of spell and counter-spell with the Forsaken witches. So long as the mists clung to his warriors, it meant one or more witches were occupied with maintaining the spell. That was one or more witches who weren't able to act directly against him. He hurled another volley of magical bolts over the warriors' heads. Again, the bolts were dissipated before they could reach their mark, but only barely so.

By this time, more undead warriors were converging on both sides of the square. Nagash launched another storm of sorcerous missiles, then unleashed his reinforcements on the northmen's flanks. The Forsaken found themselves beset on three sides. More of the northmen fell, and despite the exhortations of their warlord, the courage of the Forsaken began to waver.

Sensing his opportunity, Nagash hurled another volley of bolts - this time aimed right at the faces of the Forsaken warriors. Several of his own warriors were caught in the volley, but that mattered little to him. Men fell to either side of the warlord, their bodies consumed in burst of green fire; the warlord himself was driven back, but some kind of magical protection deflected the force of Nagash's bolts away from his body.

Through the gap created by the dead men, Nagash caught sight of the witches at last. They stood in a loose semicircle, clutching tall, wooden staffs topped with skulls and strings of ritual ornamentation. Nagash sent another stream of bolts hissing their way, and the witches quickly brandished their staffs and chanted counter-spells. The fierce energies burst about them, but once again failed to inflict any damage.

But magic was not the only danger threatening the witches. No sooner had they turned aside Nagash's latest attack than a flight of spears plunged into their midst from the northmen's right flank. One of the weapons struck the right-most witch in the chest. She collapsed, blood pouring from her mouth, and her sisters recoiled in surprise and fear.

The cries of horror from the Forsaken witches was the last straw for the northmen. The Forsaken warriors fell back in confusion, believing that they were on the verge of being surrounded and destroyed. The warlord retreated with them, roaring curses at his men, but no amount of shouting or threats was enough to get them to stand their ground.

With a snarl, Nagash drove his warriors forward, pushing them in a rough semicircle towards the warlord and the surviving witches. He let fly another volley of bolts, and watched as one of the witches was wreathed in green flame. The energies set her robes on fire and wracked her with terrible burns, but somehow she survived the necromancer's spell.

The Forsaken were in full retreat now, fleeing north through the square and into the maze of burning tents beyond. The witches held their ground, and the warlord retreated to stand among them. He turned, his eyes blazing with hatred, and Nagash prepared to crush them beneath an avalanche of sorcerous might. Yet no sooner had be begun the incantation than the last of the witches spat a savage string of syllables and smote the ground with her staff. The shadows around the two witches seemed to enfold them and their master like a cloak. It swallowed them up, and then simply vanished, right before Nagash's eyes.

What manner of sorcery was this? Nagash had never seen the like. Not even his druchii tutors in Khemri had ever hinted at such a thing. What else did these barbarians know that he didn't?

Nagash ordered his warriors to pursue the retreating northmen. Without their leaders, the rest would flee the destruction of their camp, possibly even going so far as to return to their homelands beyond the north edge of the plain. It had been a close-run thing, Nagash realised, much closer than he'd expected. His small force of warriors had been almost destroyed, and there was no telling how many of the Yaghur still survived. Had the battle in the square lasted another few minutes, the outcome might have been very different.

The necromancer made his way across the square, stepping over crushed skeletons and bleeding bodies. He made his way to the witch and stood over her, studying the woman's corpse carefully. She was dressed in fine, dark robes, and wore a curved dagger at her hip. A necklace of bronze plates, engraved with strange runes, rested against her collarbones.

Nagash knelt beside her and picked up her staff. The skull that capped the length of wood wasn't human. He studied it for a few moments in the flickering light before he realised that it was the skull of a huge rat.

Shouts split the air behind him. Nagash turned to see Aighul and the rest of the Yaghur hetmen come charging into the square. Most of them bore battle-wounds, and their weapons dripped with blood. Hathurk accompanied them, his eyes blazing with triumph.

'They're fleeing!' the supplicant cried. 'The northmen are running for home! It all happened as you said it would, master!'

Hardly, Nagash thought. He had underestimated the Forsaken. They were far more powerful than he'd expected. They'd won because the enemy had been overconfident and unprepared. Next time, things would be different.

And there would have to be a next time. The fighting would continue until the Forsaken had been conquered. There was no choice now. The campaign could take years, or even decades, but it would only end when one side or the other was broken. And Nagash intended to make them subjects of his growing empire. They would prove far more useful than the Yaghur.

Aighul approached the necromancer slowly, his expression a mix of fear and wonder. He stopped a few yards from Nagash and sank to his knees.

'All hail the god of the mountain,' he said in a hollow voice. The hetman bent at the waist, pressing his forehead to the blood-soaked ground. One by one, the other hetmen followed suit.

Nagash rose to his feet. Their obeisance meant nothing to him. He recalled how the barbarians had very nearly ruined the attack at the outset, and felt nothing but contempt for them.

Hathurk approached the necromancer, an ecstatic look on his crude features. He came right up to Nagash and bowed deeply. 'The hetmen are ready to receive their reward, master,' he said proudly.

Nagash suppressed an angry sneer. When he'd promised to give them the secret of the northmen's strength, he'd meant skills like metalworking and simple tactics. But such things were lost on these animals. No doubt they expected some kind of magical gift – or worse, a damned miracle!

A cruel idea came to him then. He looked at Hathurk and smiled, as a man might smile at an obedient dog.

'They want to make the strength of the Forsaken their own? Very well. Tell them this: the power of a man lies in his flesh and his bones. His heart is the fount of his strength. The liver is the seat of his courage. If you would become like them, you must consume them, down to the very bones.'

Hathurk's eyes widened in shock. 'You... you mean–'

'Tell them!' Nagash commanded. *'I command it! Tell them that they must feast upon the dead. It is the only way.'*

The supplicant stared at Nagash. A look of dread crept across his face. After a moment, the necromancer thought that Hathurk would refuse, but then the fool bowed to him once again and turned to give the hetmen the first commandment of their new god.

FIFTEEN

THE SHADOW OF THE HAWK

Lahmia,
the City of the Dawn,
in the 76th year of Phakth the Just
(-1597 Imperial Reckoning)

The news of King Lamashizzar's death took flight within hours of the announcement by the palace. Swift messengers raced across the Golden Plain, carrying word to Lybaras and Rasetra, and then past ruined Mahrak to the Valley of the Kings and the cities of the west. Within months, royal processions from each of the seven cities were underway, heading east to pay their respects to the dead king and to gauge the new state of affairs in the City of the Dawn. It was rare for a queen to assume the throne in the great cities of Nehekhara, and unheard of in Lahmia itself. Speculation was rampant on how this would affect the complex web-work of trade deals that the city had woven during Lamashizzar's reign. The priest kings hastened to Lahmia as quickly as they could manage, suspecting that those who reached the queen first would stand the best chance of profiting under the new regime.

Queen Amunet of distant Numas was first to arrive, having journeyed by barge up the River Vitae and deep into the mountains, where the great trade stations had been built around the shores of the wide Vitae Tarn. From there the Numasi had off-loaded two score of their fine steeds and rode swiftly through the twisting mountain passages until they reached the northern edge of the Golden Plain.

King Teremun of Zandri followed the same path and arrived less than a month later, leading a procession of northern slaves laden with gifts for the new queen. The delegation from Zandri had been bedevilled by bandit raiders as they crossed the plain, losing several of their number along the way before finding refuge within the city.

Next to arrive was dour, white-haired King Naeem of Quatar, accompanied by a solemn retinue of ash-daubed priests. Beset on all sides by the dispossessed hierophants of Mahrak, the Quatari ruler had spent his entire life trying to restore both his city and theirs, with minimal success. Had it not been for a quick-witted captain at the city gates, the delegation might have been taken for beggars and turned away.

Two weeks after the Quatari delegation came a much larger procession, led by King Ahmun-hotep of Ka-Sabar and a score of nobles clad in the old armour of the once-mighty Legion of Bronze. Though the city still lay mostly in ruin following the dreadful siege a half-century before, Ahmun-hotep intended to show his peers that he and his city remained a force to be reckoned with. His servants bore rich gifts for the queen that likely had been stripped from the royal palace itself, and the blood staining the tips of his warriors' spears told of the bandits who'd come to grief trying to wrest those treasures from Ahmun-hotep's grasp.

Curiously, the cities closest to Lahmia were the last to send delegations to honour the queen. First came King Shepret of Rasetra, hard-faced and armed for war, at the head of a procession of royal guardsmen armoured in glossy lizard-scale. Unlike the other delegations, who bore treasures of gold and precious stones, the Rasetrans brought with them the riches of the deep jungle: raw amber, polished thunder lizard horn and jars of exotic herbs found nowhere else in all of the land.

As lavish as the gifts were, they were also a message for the queen: Rasetra had regained much of its strength since the dark days after the war, driving back the lizard tribes and reclaiming much of their lost territory. In short, the Rasetrans meant to show the queen that Lahmia would be far better off treating them as friends and allies rather than rivals.

Last of all, more than three months after the arrival of the Numasi delegation, came the Priest King of Lybaras and his fierce warrior-queen. They arrived with even less pomp than the dour Rasetrans, attended by a retinue of nobles and spearmen clad in glossy plates of dark iron.

The sight was a shock to the Lahmian nobility. For years there had been rumours that the Lybarans had been hard at work searching for local sources of iron in the Brittle Peaks. Not only had they evidently succeeded, they had also divined the art of working the dense metal, something that even the Lahmian royal artisans hadn't been able to achieve. It was also clear that the rumours of cooperation with Rasetra was borne out in the martial skill of the warriors under the Lybaran king's command. Unlike Lahmia, the City of Scholars had dealt aggressively with the roving bands of raiders that had plagued the trade road within their sphere of control, and it was said that on more than one occasion the Lybaran queen herself had led expeditions to run down the largest and most stubborn raiders. She rode in full armour alongside the marching warriors, her hair bound back in tight braids and her expression as unsparing and fierce as her namesake.

Rather than keep the royal delegations at a lavish remove by housing them in tent cities, as Lamashizzar had once done, Neferata instead welcomed each procession into the royal palace. They were assigned luxurious quarters, as befitted their stations, and treated with generous, if sombre, hospitality. The opportunity provided by the queen wasn't lost on her guests, each of whom made use of the proximity to the throne to press for their individual agendas. For weeks, Neferata met each ruler in private, discussing matters of state deep into the night – all but the kings of Rasetra and Lybaras, who treated the queen's representatives with careful courtesy but chose to keep their own counsels nonetheless.

By the time all the kings and queens were assembled, Lamashizzar had been more than six months in the tomb. Rather than take part in a funeral procession the visiting rulers took part in a solemn ritual of remembrance in the great necropolis to the north of the city, then spent another six days attending lengthy afternoon councils and sumptuous feasts held in the great palace garden.

The guests used the council meetings to test the success of their private dealings with the queen and determine where they stood in relation to their peers. Each and every one soon discovered that, no matter how ruthlessly they'd pursued their agendas, not one of them had emerged in a better position than their peers. If anything, their strengths and weaknesses had been carefully exploited to neutralise their counterparts, creating a status quo that left each city prosperous and stable only so long as they fulfilled their obligations to Lahmia.

The net of trade and debt, first envisioned by Lamasheptra, then laid down by Lamashizzar his son, had finally been drawn tight by Neferata, trapping the great cities at last. And not one of Nehekhara's rulers could say just exactly how it had happened. They had understood the danger when they'd begun the journey to Lahmia, had plotted and schemed diverse ways to counter it, and yet their cunning had all come to naught when matched against the wiles of Lahmia's canny and seductive queen.

By the end of the sixth day it was clear to the visiting rulers that they had journeyed to Lahmia not just to bear witness to the passing of a king, but to also formalise the city's ascension as the centre of wealth and power in all Nehekhara.

In private councils, sometimes well into their cups, the royal guests confessed their dismay to one another in rueful whispers. They wondered how all their plans could have gone so wrong, pitted against a cloistered and untried queen. The rulers of Rasetra and Lybaras listened closely, but kept their suspicions to themselves.

The Hall of Kings glittered like a treasure vault in the slanting rays of the afternoon sun. The gifts of five great kings and queens had been heaped upon the gleaming marble floor, at the feet of towering basalt statues that flanked the long processional leading to the Lahmian throne. No less than eight of Nehekhara's lost gods looked down upon the supplicants of the court. The first two, closest to the chamber's great double doors, were grim, jackal-headed Djaf, the death-bringer, and faceless, hooded Usirian, who judges the worth of the souls of the dead. Sixty paces onward stood lion-headed Geheb, god of the earth and giver of strength, standing opposite Phakth, the hawk-faced bringer of justice. Yet another sixty paces further, at the feet of the wide steps leading to the great throne, rose sensuous, cat-faced Basth, giver of love and beauty; her feline eyes seemed to stare mischievously across the great hall at slender Tahoth, giver of knowledge and keeper of lore. Finally, towering to either side of the throne, stood Lahmia's patron goddess Asaph, giver of magic and architect of the sacred covenant, and mighty Ptra, god of the sun and father of all Creation.

The guardians of the throne faced westward, towards the sea. Sunlight streamed through high, rectangular openings set above the chamber's entrance, bathing the statues in golden light. Only the great throne room in Khemri had rivalled the chamber in splendour and regal glory; now it was without equal in all the land.

So, too, the great throne of Lahmia had been wrought from the same fine-grained, dark wood as the one that had once sat in the palace of Khemri. There was nothing like it in all of Nehekhara, and legends said it had been brought out of the deep parts of the southern jungles during the Great Migration of mankind. The throne was high-backed and deep, shaped in sinuous curves that suggested it had been grown rather than carved by the hand of man; its thick, rolled arms were glossy and smooth, polished by generations of royal hands. They felt warm beneath Neferata's touch as she leaned back in the ancient chair and studied the approaching figures of the Imperial delegation. Even at a hundred paces she could read their discomfort in the curt *swish-swish* of their slippered feet and the thin whistle of breath through their tightly-pressed lips.

The queen was clad in her richest robes of state: layers of rich saffron embroidered with gold and thousands of tiny pearls. A girdle of gold thread and lapis circled her narrow waist, and a thick necklace of gold plate circled her alabaster throat. Her lustrous hair had been bound up with golden pins and more strands of pearl, and thick bracelets of gold circled her slender wrists. Nestled in the crook of her left arm was the sceptre of Asaph, a heavy rod of solid gold wrought in the shape of a pair of twining asps and inset with tiny scales of onyx. Upon her face rested the cold, lifeless contours of her golden mask. It was the first time she had worn it since rising from her deathbed. She had resolved that the scheming barbarians of the far east deserved nothing more.

Sunlight shone from the mask's polished surface, almost too bright to look upon. Neferata felt its rays upon her bare hands and felt little more than a faint discomfort, like the fading ache of a *hixa* sting. Even Nagash and his immortals had grown to shun Ptra's searing rays, but the queen found that she could move about in the morning and afternoon with little trouble. She was nothing like the necromancer or his minions; somehow she had been reborn in a crucible of poison, sorcery and death. The interactions of the sphinx's venom with the powers of the elixir and the workings of Arkhan's rituals had transformed her into a being of flesh that existed beyond the reach of death.

She was no mere immortal. Neferata had become like unto Asaph herself, and the secrets of the world were laid bare at her feet. She could sense the passage of the sun through the sky and feel the rhythm of the tides through the stones beneath her feet. She sensed the presence of each and every living thing in the echoing audience chamber, from the members of her privy council who stood at the feet of her throne to the Celestial Prince and his retainers and even the stolid-faced royal guards who stood just outside the chamber door. She could hear their every movement, smell the scents upon their skin and taste the rich, sweet blood hissing through their veins.

It was blood, always blood, that was uppermost in her mind. If there was one weakness to her new existence, it was the endless thirst for human blood. It was the wellspring of her power, a thousand times purer and more potent than Nagash's petty brew, but almost as soon as she had drunk her fill of it, she found herself craving more. Neferata found that she had to drink each and every night to sustain her strength. Fortunately, with a city of souls at her beck and call she knew that she would never go without.

The queen smiled languidly behind the implacable curves of her mask and studied Prince Xian's young, handsome face with the cold intensity of a hungry lioness. His expression was set in a mask of calculated disdain as he and his retinue approached to within a dozen paces of the queen's privy council and came to an abrupt halt, as though noticing the Lahmian nobles for the first time. As before, the Scion of Heaven was accompanied by a fawning translator, a handful of imperious-looking bureaucrats and a silent, demure young woman whose face and hands were painted as white as Neferata's own. The queen could not be certain if she was the prince's wife or merely a favoured concubine. Her hands were clasped at her waist, and her eyes were focused on a point just behind Xian's heels.

Xian gestured almost imperceptibly with one long, golden fingernail, and his translator immediately took one small step towards the throne. 'The Scion of Heaven offers his condolences on the death of your husband, the king,' he said stiffly. 'He cannot help but observe your sorrow, so deep that even the simplest ceremonies are too terrible a burden to bear.'

Neferata's smile sharpened. 'The Scion of Heaven is mistaken,' she said simply, careful to keep her tone neutral and unaffected. 'I am conscious of my obligations as ruler and host. Has he not been treated with all due courtesy and respect?'

The translator paused, pressing his lips together tightly as he struggled for a proper response. 'It is to my eternal shame that I must inform you that your guards have refused to admit the Scion of Heaven's servants to prepare the hall for his arrival.' He spread his hands. 'Where is my lord and master to take his ease, while he indulges you with fine tea and civilised conversation?'

'There is but one chair in the Hall of Kings,' Neferata replied coldly, and watched with satisfaction as the translator shivered in response. 'And it is a place for conducting affairs of state, not indulging in idle chatter.' The queen waved her hand dismissively. 'Though the Scion of Heaven can be forgiven his misapprehension, since this is the first time he has been invited to attend upon the throne.'

One of the prince's bureaucrats let out a strangled gasp; the rest kept their composure, but Neferata could hear their hearts beating angrily in their chests. She couldn't have insulted the prince any worse if she'd walked up to him and slapped him across the face.

The translator was completely taken aback. Uncertain how to proceed, he turned and stared at Xian, whose own expression might have been carved from stone. Once more, the Son of Heaven gestured to the functionary with a tiny flick of one curved nail. The man bowed deeply to the prince, then drew a deep breath and turned back to the queen.

'The Scion of Heaven has the honour of bearing tidings from his divine father, the Emperor of Heaven and Earth,' the translator said with as much affronted dignity as he could muster. 'He wishes you to know of the great fortune bestowed upon the Empire in the form of the gold mines of Guanjian province. So great is their bounty that the value of gold is not as it was when your father incurred his debt to the Empire.' A tiny glint of satisfaction shone in the functionary's eyes as he bowed before the throne. 'A single payment remains to settle the matter between Lahmia and the Celestial Household, but it must be no less than triple the agreed upon amount in order to satisfy the terms of the debt.'

Silence fell across the great hall. The prince and his retainers watched and waited, expecting cries of outrage and growing ever so slightly concerned when none was forthcoming. Finally, after a long moment, the queen shook her head.

'No.'

Now the cries of outrage began in earnest, but it was the prince's retainers who shouted their anger at the insult to the Scion of Heaven's honour. One of the functionaries even went so far as to take a step forward and raise his fist to the queen. Before he could take a second step Abhorash was blocking the man's path. The tip of the champion's iron sword rested in the hollow of the bureaucrat's throat.

'Enough,' Neferata said, her voice carrying clearly over the tumult. 'Prince Xian, the insolence of your retainers offends me. They will remove themselves at once.'

The translator puffed up his narrow chest. 'It is not for you to dictate–'

'*Go,*' Neferata commanded, exerting her will. The Imperial functionaries fled, all but stumbling over the hems of their robes in their haste to obey the queen's command. Within moments, the prince and his woman were alone.

Neferata rose slowly from the throne. Her movements were fluid and graceful, as mesmerising as the movements of a cobra. She descended the stairs and approached the Scion of Heaven, who held his ground out of sheer, stubborn pride. The queen drew close enough to touch him, staring deeply into his dark eyes.

'What your father asks is impossible,' Neferata said softly. She exerted her will and listened with satisfaction as the prince's heart quickened in response. 'You know that as well as I.' The golden mask cocked slightly to one side as she studied him. 'You're a clever man, Prince Xian. Pragmatic too, else you'd have never agreed to come here in the first place. So perhaps there is a way to settle Lahmia's debt with a currency other than gold.'

Prince Xian frowned slightly. He hesitated but an instant before answering the queen. 'What have you to offer?' he said in fluent Nehekharan.

The queen took a step closer and laid a hand on his chest, right at the juncture of neck and collarbone. She could feel the pulse of blood vessels throbbing sweetly beneath the prince's skin. Her lips parted, brushing against the tips of razor-sharp fangs.

'For you, oh prince,' she whispered. 'I offer the gift of life eternal.'

Xian's eyes widened. She could sense the struggle within him, as reason warred with the seductive force of her will. He wanted to disbelieve her, to heed his father's wishes and close the trap around Lahmia, but his heart refused to obey.

A tiny frown creased the prince's smooth forehead. 'How?' he asked faintly.

Neferata held up a tiny, ceramic vial. Within lay a single dram of her blood. 'Take this,' she said. 'Return to your home in the city, and when the sun has set, drink it down. Then you will understand.'

Moving as though in a dream, the prince reached out and took the vial from her hand. The vigour stored within faded much quicker than Nagash's elixir, but its potency was a hundred times greater. She had tried it already on the members of the cabal, and was well pleased with the results. 'Return to me tomorrow,' she continued, 'and we will discuss our arrangement in more detail.'

Xian gripped the vial tightly. His heart bade him obey, but still his mind tried to resist. 'I... I cannot defy the will of the Emperor,' he protested.

'Might the Emperor's will not change when he hears of this?' Neferata said, tapping the vial lightly with a lacquered nail. 'Or with this power at his command, might a son not rise up to supplant the father, and become Emperor himself?'

'I...' the prince began. His expression grew troubled, but then slowly he nodded. 'I will think on this.'

Neferata smiled. 'Then go,' she said, 'but tell no one of what we have discussed.' Her gaze drifted to the woman standing in the prince's shadow.

On a whim, the queen said, 'She will remain here in the meantime, to vouchsafe your discretion.'

Xian turned and looked at the woman, as though suddenly remembering that she was there. 'Her?' he asked, clearly surprised by the queen's request. 'She is nothing to me.'

Neferata saw the woman stiffen slightly. 'Then she will remain here at my pleasure,' the queen said coldly. 'I thank you for the gift. Now go. Your servants await you.'

Xian turned back to her, as though to protest further, but with one last look in Neferata's eyes, the last of the prince's resolve was swept away. He sketched an awkward, uncertain bow, and then retreated dazedly from the hall.

The queen contemplated the woman. Her thin shoulders trembled faintly, but she continued to stare resolutely at the floor. Neferata frowned slightly. She reached out and touched a finger to the woman's chin and gently raised her head. For a moment they regarded one another, their expressions concealed by carefully constructed masks.

'What is your name?' Neferata asked.

The woman frowned slightly. The queen sighed. Naturally the woman wouldn't speak Nehekharan. 'Ubaid,' Neferata snapped. 'Show her to the Women's Palace and see that she's made comfortable.'

Ubaid hurried to the woman's side. The queen's displeasure had crumpled the once-proud grand vizier; he had bent beneath her will to the point that he was hunched over like a whipped dog. His eyes were wide and furtive, and his hands trembled as though with palsy. Silently he took the young woman's arm and led her into the shadows at the rear of the hall.

As they left the queen returned to the great throne and stared down at her privy council. Not for the first time, she found herself wondering who had sided with Lamashizzar. Lord Zurhas, the king's young cousin, had most likely been one of the king's supporters. Abhorash, perhaps? Certainly not W'soran; the king would never have given him the freedom to explore Nagash's works as she had. Or would he? Such an offer would have made for a powerful bargaining tool.

None of them knew how to react to her now. She could sense their unease, now matter how hard they worked to conceal it. On one level they were repelled by her transformation, while on another level they craved the power she possessed. Only Abhorash, the stoic master warrior, seemed unaffected by the allure of her newfound power. In the end, all of them would have to accept the poisoned cup, Neferata reckoned, whether they wanted it or not. She needed their support in order to rule the city; the only way she could guarantee that was if they shared the same degree of risk that she did. She now had Arkhan's notes in her possession, and Ubaid had led her to the vial of sphinx venom hidden in Lamashizzar's quarters. In time, Neferata was certain that she could reproduce the process.

Lord Ankhat waited until Prince Xian had left the hall before he spoke.

'It might work,' he mused. 'Much depends on the amount of influence he wields at home. The Emperor might simply send another, more powerful envoy to demand payment.'

Whatever his loyalties might have been, Ankhat had proven invaluable to her since Lamashizzar's death. It was he who concocted the story that a priest of Sokth, patron god of assassins, had crept into the palace to murder the king in reprisal for his treatment of refugees from Mahrak. As the story went, the assassin-priest had attacked the queen first, slaughtering her handmaidens and striking her with a poisoned needle, then fighting his way to the king's chambers and slaying him before being slain in turn by Abhorash and the royal guard. It was a cunning move, one that focused the need for revenge on a group of outsiders that were already held in contempt by much of the populace. More importantly, Neferata's recovery had been touted as nothing less than a miracle, reminding Lahmia and the rest of the land of her divine lineage. Support for her rule had been absolute.

It was also Ankhat who arranged for the disappearance of Arkhan's decapitated corpse. W'soran and even Abhorash had been adamant that the immortal's body should be incinerated, but at the last moment, Neferata found that she could not bring herself to permit it. Instead, Ankhat discreetly purchased a pauper's tomb in the great city necropolis and had the immortal interred there at the same time King Lamashizzar was being placed inside his own, far greater tomb farther north. Neferata felt she owed the ghastly creature at least that much.

The queen considered Ankhat's counsel and nodded thoughtfully. 'Perhaps, but it would take many months, possibly even years, for another delegation to arrive. That gives us time to build up the treasury and consolidate our power.' She shrugged. 'If the Emperor is a pragmatic ruler, he'll take our final payment and accept the fact that his gambit failed. If not... well, we will be in a far better position to defend our interests.'

Abhorash turned and looked up at her. He did that very rarely now, which hinted at his surprise. 'You mean war with the Silk Lands? That would be ruinous!'

'That is certainly not my intent,' Neferata said smoothly. 'But I will defend this city with every power at my command. You may be assured of that.'

'Then you should worry more about enemies closer to home,' Ushoran said quietly.

Neferata straightened. The Lord of Masks was infamous for his intrigues within the city, and she knew that he spent lavishly to maintain a vast network of spies within Lahmia and elsewhere. 'Enemies within the city?'

'At present, yes,' Ushoran replied. 'My sources tell me that the King of Lybaras is... uneasy about your ascension to the throne. And he's been sharing his concerns with others.'

The queen frowned. Ushoran liked to savour his revelations, but she wasn't in a patient mood. 'Such as?'

'The King of Rasetra, for a start. Since he's been here, he's also held late-night meetings with the King of Quatar and the Queen of Numas.'

'And what exactly are his concerns?'

Ushoran shook his head. 'That I do not know, great one. But it is safe to assume that Rasetra will be sympathetic, if for no other reason than the age-old friendship between the two cities. Quatar and Numas might not be receptive yet, but...'

Neferata sighed irritably. 'What lies at the heart of this? What are the Lybarans' concerns, exactly?'

The Lord of Masks shrugged. 'That I cannot say, great one. King Anhur has been very careful to avoid details.'

Lord Zurhas shifted uncomfortably, clearly torn between the desire to appear useful and the fear of gaining the queen's attention. 'Perhaps you could ask Queen Khalida? Surely she would tell you.'

Neferata sighed under her breath. How long had it been since she'd spoken to Khalida? Years, certainly. After a moment, she shook her head.

'There is no need,' she said, rising from the throne. 'As it happens, I had already planned on a pair of announcements at tonight's feast that will put an end to these intrigues. No doubt the Lybarans covet Lahmia's newfound power, but we've laid our plans with care. The treaties have been signed and sealed. Nothing short of war can break them, and no city in Nehekhara would contemplate such a thing.'

Neferata reached up and pulled away her mask. As one, the assembled nobles lowered their heads – in respect, to be sure, but not without a certain amount of fear as well. That was well, as far as she was concerned.

The queen smiled down at the men. 'Lahmia's time of glory is at hand. Savour this, and thank the forgotten gods that you were alive to see it.'

Neferata's guests were feted in the great palace garden that night, seated at the same wide, circular table that had served them during the long council sessions with Lamashizzar more than a half-century before. The feasting had begun an hour after sunset and had lasted well into the evening. Rich courses of fish and fowl, prepared with fiery spices imported from the Silk Lands, were served with jars of fine wine and bowls of thick, yeasty beer. Musicians and silk-clad dancers beguiled and entertained the royal guests between courses, allowing time for the food to settle and the potent drink to mellow their moods. Small braziers had been discretely situated around the wide clearing, filling the air with sweet-smelling, slightly narcotic vapours.

The queen sat in the tall chair that had once belonged to her husband and studied her guests from beneath heavy-lidded eyes. She pretended to eat a little when each course was served, and the servants were instructed to clear her dishes away first. Since her transformation, food and wine had lost their savour; in fact, even the smallest taste caused her throat to tighten and her stomach to knot in pain. No amount of lotus root or drugged incense could dull her senses, either. Fortunately, the small goblets of hot, red liquid Ubaid served her between courses more than made up for the absence of solid sustenance.

She watched the gathered rulers closely for signs of suspicion or discontent. King Fadil of Zandri was raucously drunk, laughing loudly and hissing salacious whispers into the ear of a pale-skinned barbarian concubine. To his left, Queen Amunet of Numas made no effort to conceal her disdain as she picked at a bowl of spiced eels with a long-tyned copper fork. King Naeem, grey-haired and gloomy beyond his years, sat amid a flock of querulous old priests who stolidly refused to share in the queen's entertainments.

That left the kings of Rasetra and Lybaras. King Shepret sat to Neferata's left, sipping from a jar of beer like a common soldier. The elderly Rasetran king, still hale despite the passage of years, had eaten well from all the fine offerings at the feast table, and had taken great pleasure in the procession of silk-clad dancers that had whirled past him during the course of the evening. Yet Neferata could not mistake the tension in the warrior king's shoulders, and the wary glances he cast about the table when he thought no one was watching. She also couldn't help but notice that the dagger hanging from the king's belt was anything but ceremonial.

The King of Lybaras sat to Shepret's left, almost close enough to touch, and yet they had spoken scarcely two words to one another since the feast began. Instead, Anhur had spent nearly the entire time in quiet, sometimes heated, conversation with his queen. Neferata hardly recognised her beloved cousin; her years in Lybaras had transformed her, not into a quiet, submissive queen, but into the fierce, radiant warrior she'd always longed to be. She had shed the soft flesh of a cloistered princess and become lean, tanned and muscular, with sword-scars on her hands and a Rasetran warrior's tattoo marked in red ink along the right side of her slender neck. Her black hair was done up in a score of tight braids and bound with a gold pin at the base of her neck, accentuating the sharp lines of her face. She was a scandal in royal society; not even the queens of warlike Rasetra were permitted to learn the ways of sword and spear, much less march with the common soldiery. But Khalida did as she pleased, riding, fighting and hunting like any man, and public opinion be damned. Supposedly the Lybaran people loved her for it, which filled Neferata with equal measures of pride and bitter envy. They hadn't spoken at all since Khalida had returned to the city. Even at the feast table she avoided Neferata's gaze. When she wasn't speaking to the king she was trading whispers with a young, nervous-looking woman that the queen was certain she'd seen somewhere before.

Had she offended Khalida somehow? Neferata couldn't imagine how such a thing was possible, unless her cousin somehow resented her arranged marriage to Anhur. She found herself studying the young Lybaran king and wondering if perhaps her relationship with her cousin might improve if Anhur were to have an unfortunate accident. The idea had its merits, she thought.

It was late in the evening now. Servants were emerging from hidden paths to carry away the last courses of the feast. Ubaid appeared at Neferata's side with another brimming goblet to slake her thirst. She sipped at the hot liquid as the servants finished their work, savouring the rush of strength and vitality that flooded her limbs and took the chill of the evening away.

When the servants had finished their work and withdrawn, Neferata returned the goblet to Ubaid's trembling hands and rose smoothly from her chair. The nobles of her privy council, who were seated either side of the queen, immediately set aside their drinks and gazed at her expectantly. Within moments her royal guests took note and paid heed as well. King Shepret studied her over the rim of his beer, his expression neutral. Anhur folded his arms tightly across his chest, his gaze darting uneasily between Khalida and Neferata. Only Khalida failed to meet her gaze; her cousin stared stubbornly at the tabletop, tracing patterns across the polished surface with a close-bitten thumbnail.

For a fleeting instant, she was tempted to use her power to bend these kings and queens to her will. It was so tempting, so easy... and yet, Ushoran's warnings about Rasetra and Lybaras gave her pause. If she tried, and somehow failed, the backlash might be catastrophic. And there was no sense taking such a risk when she had other sources of power to draw upon.

'Beloved friends,' she said, lifting her arms and smiling warmly, as though she meant to take them all into a wide embrace. 'Words cannot express how truly honoured I am that you made such a long and arduous journey to pay your respects to my husband, whom we pray has reached the company of his ancestors in the Lands of the Dead. His loss is a terrible blow to all of Nehekhara, but after speaking to most of you over the course of the last few months, I'm hopeful that his legacy of prosperity and renewal will continue to live on.'

Neferata allowed her smile to fade, transforming her luminous expression into one of wistful regret. 'If there is one thing I have learned from this awful experience, it's that there are still a great many Nehekharans who are still suffering from the horrors wrought by the Usurper. The breaking of the sacred covenant and the passing of the old gods have left a terrible wound on our collective soul. We no longer think of this as a blessed land, nor we a blessed people.'

That got the attention of King Amunet and his gaggle of priests. Their sullen expressions vanished, replaced with looks of genuine surprise and faint, dawning hope. That sent a ripple of interest through the other rulers as well. Anhur's bemused expression turned increasingly wary.

'Beloved friends, honoured kings and queens, I say that the gods are with us yet. The bloodline of Lahmia remains strong. The blessings of Asaph have not deserted us, even in these dark times! It was she, great goddess of beauty and magic, who persuaded great Ptra to take pity on our people and make this land a paradise.'

Neferata's gaze went around the table, meeting the eyes of each ruler in turn. 'Hear me, friends. The goddess lives on through me, as she has lived in each of my ancestors since the dawn of civilisation. We are not forsaken. If we come together and restore what Nagash cast down, perhaps we can forge a *new* covenant – one that will lead us into a golden age of rebirth.'

'Praise the gods!' cried an elderly hierophant. The old man rose to his feet, his age-spotted hands rising skyward. 'Praise be! We are delivered at last!'

The queen smiled fondly at the old man. Go on believing that, she thought. It will help convince the others.

'In the past, my husband believed it was wiser and more compassionate to focus on the needs of the living rather than the memories of the dead,' the queen continued. 'And it is not for me to question the wisdom of his policies at this late date. But now that our cities are well on their way to recovery, and we have a plan to ensure our continued trade and prosperity, I believe that now is the time we moved to erase the last traces of Nagash's infamy. Mahrak, the City of Hope, must be rebuilt. Khemri, the Living City, must be restored to her former glory once more.'

Everyone, even drunken King Teremun, stared in shock. Several of the priests began to whisper prayers of thanks to their gods, silent tears trickling down their lined cheeks. Neferata paused, letting the moment build, until finally King Shepret took the bait.

The old warrior-king of Rasetra put aside his beer and leaned forward, resting his elbows on the table. 'And how do you plan to oversee such a restoration?' he asked.

Neferata acknowledged the question with a respectful nod. 'In truth, I wouldn't presume to do such a thing at all,' she said, 'not when there are better people, like yourself, who have already demonstrated a desire to undertake the effort. Rasetra was born from distant Khemri; the bloodline of her royal house runs in your veins. By rights, it should be for you and your children to determine the city's future. I merely wish to share some of Lahmia's riches to make the task possible.'

Shepret didn't know how to respond at first. That wasn't nearly the response he'd expected. 'How... how much do you propose?' he asked.

'Ten thousand talents of gold each year, until such time as we agree that the city's reconstruction is complete,' the queen replied.

King Telemun gasped in shock. Queen Amunet's eyes went as wide as dinner-plates.

King Naeem drew in a long breath and pressed his palms against the tabletop. The look on his face hinted that he was afraid he might be dreaming. 'What of Mahrak, great queen?' he said. 'Surely you can do no less for the City of Hope.'

Again, Neferata nodded. 'Nor shall I. You shall have ten thousand talents of gold each year for you and Mahrak's surviving hierophants to use for the city's reconstruction.'

Pandemonium ensued. Mahrak's priests erupted in loud cries of joy, praising King Naeem and Queen Neferata with equal fervour. Queen Amunet rose from her seat and went around to speak intently to King Shepret, whose eyes were half-glazed with shock. King Telemun threw back his head and roared for more wine.

They were fabulous sums of money, far richer than either ruler could have reasonably hoped for, but in truth they were little more than half of what Lahmia had been paying annually to the Empire. Lahmia would still profit, and while Rasetra and Quatar would spend decades, even centuries, focusing their efforts on rebuilding two cities that would never again enjoy the wealth and power that they'd once possessed. By the time they realised they'd been duped, Lahmia's pre-eminence would be unassailable. It was the crowning triumph to decades of carefully laid schemes.

'*LIES!*'

The shout cut through the din like the peal of a war horn. Khalida was on her feet, hands clenched into fists and trembling with rage. Her face was pale and her expression anguished.

'Queen Neferata lies,' Khalida declared. 'It's not the blessings of Asaph that lend her beauty and unnatural youth, but vile necromancy! She consorts with monsters, and practises the damned sorcery of Nagash himself!'

Neferata stared at her cousin in stunned silence. 'Khalida?' she finally managed to say. 'How... how can you say such things?'

'I have a witness!' Khalida snarled. She pointed to the woman seated beside her. 'Aiyah was there when the pale-skinned creature appeared at the Women's Palace with your body in his arms! She witnessed the rituals, and the obscene bloodletting! It was a miracle she managed to escape the palace and reach Lybaras with the truth!'

Now Neferata knew where she'd seen the girl before. Aiyah the handmaiden would not meet the queen's eyes, as though she feared that her very soul would be forfeit if she did so. Betrayed, by a mere handmaiden? The very idea galled her.

'I don't know what the little fool is talking about,' Neferata shot back. 'You'd take the word of a handmaiden over that of the rightful Queen of Lahmia?'

Khalida continued, as though she hadn't heard. 'How long?' she demanded. 'How long had you been worshipping at the feet of the Usurper? I always wondered why you never aged, cousin. Did Lamashizzar know? Is that why he poisoned you?'

Neferata's hand came down on the table like a thunderclap. '*You go too far!*' she snapped, transmuting shock and sudden fear into burning anger. 'How *dare* you sit at my table, share my bread and salt, and then accuse me of such terrible things, when I alone in all of Nehekhara still bear the mark of the gods' favour!'

'Beware, cousin! If the gods still hear us, they will not suffer such blasphemy lightly!' Khalida shot back.

'It is you who blaspheme, Khalida!' Neferata cried. 'The innocent have nothing to fear from the gods!'

'Then challenge me,' Khalida said. 'Prove your innocence beyond a shadow of a doubt.' A glint of triumph shone in the warrior queen's eye. 'Let us cross blades, and see who the gods truly favour.'

Too late, Neferata realised she'd gone too far. Khalida had laid the trap, and she'd charged headlong into it. She did not dare refuse, especially not in front of a gaggle of priests and hierophants. It would undermine everything she had worked so hard to achieve.

'So be it,' she said numbly. 'Abhorash, bring me a blade.'

The preparations were made largely in silence. Lord Ankhat led Neferata away from the table to the far side of the garden clearing. For a wonder, there were no clouds overhead, and the queen marvelled at the vault of stars glittering coldly over the palace. Khalida followed several minutes later; King Anhur dogged her heels, whispering urgently, but she paid him no mind. She had bound back her voluminous sleeves with a pair of leather cords, and the hem of her feast robe had been pinned back so that it wouldn't tangle her feet. Neferata saw that Khalida was wearing sturdy leather sandals instead of slippers, the kind that soldiers wore on the battlefield. On any other day it might have amused her, but now the sight left her cold. *She was planning this all along,* the queen realised. *One way or another, this evening was going to end in blood.*

Abhorash appeared before her, gripping a bronze blade in his hands. The champion's expression was stricken. He held out the hilt to her; it took Neferata a moment to realise he meant her to take it. The leather wrapping felt cold against her palm. The weapon was short and straight, like an oversized dagger about two feet long, but it seemed to fit her hand well. She stared morbidly at the tip of the blade. 'Not iron?' she asked.

The champion shook his head. 'You'll notice that Khalida isn't using iron either,' he said, nodding slightly in her direction. 'Bronze is lighter and quicker. She was hoping you'd take iron and give her one more advantage.' He paused, pressing his lips together as if uncertain what to say next. 'Have you any training, great one? Any at all?'

'Don't be stupid,' Neferata snapped.

Abhorash grimaced. 'Then you're going to have to make this quick,' he said to her. 'You're faster and stronger than she is. She doesn't know it yet. Use that to your advantage.' He reached forward and gripped her wrists tightly, his gaze burning into hers. 'And when you strike, don't hold back. She's not your cousin any longer. Khalida will kill you if she can.'

Neferata pulled her hands away. 'Let's be done with this,' she said, and stepped into the circle formed by the assembled crowd.

Khalida gently pushed her husband aside and went to stand before Neferata. She carried a bronze sword nearly identical to the queen's, though Khalida held hers easily, as though it were an extension of her hand. Her face was emotionless now, her eyes cold and remote, like an executioner.

Neferata surveyed the crowd, seeking out the priests. There were formalities that had to be observed. 'Is there a priest or priestess of Asaph in attendance?'

The priests and hierophants shifted uncomfortably. The eldest shrugged his narrow shoulders. 'That honour falls to you, great one,' he said.

Neferata growled under her breath. She closed her eyes and raised her hands to the heavens, struggling to remember the proper words.

'Great Asaph, goddess of beauty and the mysteries of the world, we beseech you to preside over this contest of arms and judge it fairly, lending your strength to the righteous and casting down the false claims of the wicked. Let justice prevail in your name.'

'Let justice prevail,' Khalida echoed faintly, and rushed forward, her sandals gliding on the grass, as though hurrying to her cousin's embrace. Neferata saw the glinting tip of her blade at nearly the last moment and tried to leap aside. She swung her own weapon in a wide, clumsy block, and connected with a discordant clang of metal.

Khalida's blade flickered again, and the point tugged at the billowing sleeve of Neferata's left arm. The queen circled right, trying to get away from the slashing sword, her own weapon hanging forgotten in her hand. She felt a burning pain in her left hand and jerked it back with a cry. Khalida's blade had slashed cleanly across her palm. Neferata stared at the wound in horror, watching beads of dark blood well up from the cut.

But Khalida never paused. She leapt forward, grabbing Neferata's sword wrist and stabbing at the queen's chest. Neferata felt the point of Khalida's sword pierce her robe and sink into the skin beneath her left breast. Without thinking, she seized her cousin's sword wrist with her wounded left hand before Khalida could drive her weapon home.

They grappled for an agonising moment, nose-to-nose, feeling each other's gasping breaths against their skin. Khalida dug in her heels and pushed for all she was worth. Neferata could feel the muscles working in her cousin's arms as she tried to drive the sword deeper. Khalida's lips were drawn back in a rictus of fury, her dark eyes burning with battle-lust.

Cold terror clenched Neferata's throat. Without thinking, she drew upon her power and shoved Khalida backwards. Her cousin was hurled off her feet, flying back for nearly five feet before landing hard on her back. Khalida turned the impact into a backward shoulder roll and sprang swiftly back onto her feet. Blood glistened on the tip of her sword.

Now she knows how strong I am, Neferata thought. She won't make that mistake again.

They circled one another for a moment, contemplating their next moves.

Neferata's left hand ached dully, and the wound in her chest felt like it was on fire. Abhorash's words echoed dully in her mind. *You're going to have to make this quick.*

She stared at Khalida, her eyes pleading. 'Don't do this,' she whispered.

But Khalida was beyond hearing. With a snarl she rushed forward again, sword held low. She was on the queen in moments. Neferata tried to twist aside again, but felt the point of Khalida's blade dig into her hip. She cried out, groping instinctively for Khalida's wrist again, but the attack was only a feint. Swift as a snake, Khalida jerked the blade away and brought it around in a swift, looping motion, straight for the side of Neferata's throat.

She saw the blade arcing towards her out of the corner of her eye. With a scream, Neferata called upon her power once more and surged forwards, deeper into Khalida's embrace. Her cousin's sword missed its mark by inches, carving a furrow across the back of Neferata's neck.

The queen held her cousin for just a moment, and she could feel Khalida's heart hammering wildly through the thin fabric of her robe. Then they parted. Khalida took one step back, her expression slack. Her gaze fell to the hilt of Neferata's blade, jutting at a downward angle from her side. Slowly, wonderingly, she grasped the hilt with her left hand and with a strangled gasp, pulled the weapon free. Dark blood poured down Khalida's side.

Neferata watched in horror as her cousin sank to the ground. An agonised cry split the stunned silence. It was Anhur, his face a mask of anguish.

The queen fell to her knees beside Khalida. Her terror was gone, replaced with a bottomless well of sorrow. Without thinking, she pressed her hand to the wound in her cousin's side, but the bleeding would not stop. The warm fluid ran over her fingers and stained the sleeve of her robe. Khalida made a choked sound and tried to move, but she was already growing weak. Her eyes were open, searching wildly about for something or someone.

'Oh, gods,' Neferata whispered. 'Oh, great gods.' Her eyes burned, but no tears would come. She laid a trembling hand against Khalida's cheek, staining it with blood. 'Forgive me, little hawk. Please, please forgive me...'

She could still be saved, Neferata realised. She took her lower lip in her teeth and bit down hard, tasting blood. She bit until her lip was bitter with the taste.

Neferata took Khalida's head in her hands and turned it until their eyes met. She lowered her face, until all they could see was one another's eyes.

'Kiss me,' she said to Khalida. 'Kiss me, little hawk, and you'll live forever.'

Khalida stiffened. Tears welled in her eyes. Her head trembled, and her hands pressed weakly at Neferata's shoulders. When she spoke, her voice was almost too faint to hear.

'No,' she said.

'*Please,*' Neferata said. She pressed closer, and felt Khalida push back with the last of her strength. 'I never wanted this. I never wanted *any* of it, but Lahmia needs me. Please, let's kiss and be friends again, like before.'

Khalida resisted a moment more, and then Neferata felt her body relax. With a gasp of relief, the queen pressed her bloody lips to Khalida's.

Her cousin did not return the kiss. Khalida's body was utterly still.

After a long, painful moment, Neferata raised her head again and stared into Khalida's vacant eyes. Slowly, she became aware of people shouting, and a man's voice wailing in misery. Hands grasped Neferata's shoulders and pulled her away from Khalida's body. Her robe was heavy with blood.

Ankhat stepped close, whispering in her ear. 'Say something,' he urged. 'Everyone is waiting to hear the goddess's verdict.'

Neferata's gaze fell to her cousin's body, and felt her heart break.

'Justice is served,' she said in a hollow voice.

SIXTEEN

THE GLORY OF NAGASH

North of the Plain of Bones,
in the 96th year of Ptra the Glorious
(-1350 Imperial Reckoning)

Cold, dead hands seized the priests and dragged them towards the towering wooden statue of Malakh that stood in the hill fort's ceremonial square. Pieces of splintered wood, scavenged from the fort's shattered gates, had already been piled around the statue's base and soaked with pitch from the temple's own storehouses.

The Forsaken priests screamed and kicked, crying out to their god to bring down bloody vengeance on the invaders, but the skeletal executioners paid them no heed. The four old men were all that remained of the god's temple at Maghur'kan, the chief hill fort of the northmen's petty empire. Those members of the cult that hadn't died in the bitter defence of the main gate were dragged from the temple cellars and their bodies left to bleed out in the muddy street.

Every man, woman and child still living after the month-long siege of Maghur'kan had been herded to the edges of the square to bear witness to the death of their god. The night air trembled with their muffled wails. Most were so weak from hunger that they could manage little else.

Nagash sat upon a palanquin of polished oak at the southern end of the square, surrounded by the skeletal warriors of his bodyguard and a score of northmen vassals drawn from hill forts conquered during the long war. The struggle against the Forsaken hadn't lasted years, or decades, but *centuries* – nearly two hundred and fifty years since that first, confused night battle upon the Plain of Bones.

The northmen had proven to be mighty warriors, and their witches possessed of great skill and cunning. Nagash had lost count of the number of battles that had been fought down the years, but in most cases the Forsaken had given as good as they'd got. Ultimately, the path to victory had rested on the simple fact that the Forsaken had to eat, and his army did not. By keeping up constant pressure on one hill fort at a time, he prevented the northmen from adequately tending their fields and setting back enough food for the winters to come, until finally they had been so weakened by hunger and sickness that they couldn't resist Nagash's constant attacks. And so the northmen had been enslaved, one hill fort at a time, until only Maghur'kan remained.

The necromancer watched as the priests were lashed to the great totem of their god. Off to the east, near the circular wall of the hill fort, one of the Yaghur let out a bone-chilling howl. Children squealed in terror, burying themselves in their mothers' skirts. No doubt the barbarians were feasting well tonight.

When the ropes had been drawn tight, Nagash rose from his seat and stepped onto the stinking mud of the square. Heavy, leather robes, faced with polished bronze medallions inscribed with runes of protection, flapped about his lean limbs. A deep hood, its hem ornamented with tiny disks of gold, concealed all but the flickering flames of his eyes. There was a dry clatter of bone as his bodyguard made to follow him, but he held them back with a wave of his hand and a curt mental command.

His legion of undead servants had grown so vast that he could no longer keep them all under control at the same time. Most functioned more or less autonomously, operating on a strict set of commands according to their function. It was an arrangement he'd perfected out of necessity during the long campaigns in the northland. Unfortunately he'd yet to find a way to impose the same degree of control on his human minions without ultimately killing them. He was instead forced to rely upon intangibles such as loyalty and devotion, which, as far as he was concerned, was a kind of sorcery all its own.

Thus, the death of the priests was a ritual in more ways than one, Nagash mused, as he approached the condemned men.

Malakh's high priest had been lashed to the statue facing Nagash. He and the two senior priests to his left and right glared at the necromancer with pure, fanatical hatred.

'You have not won!' the high priest spat. The Forsaken spoke a purer, somewhat more cultured form of the tongue once spoken by the Yaghur. 'You will not defeat great Malakh by ending our lives! He is eternal! He will triumph after–' the holy man's curse faltered.

'*After my works are dust, and I am nothing but bones?*' Nagash chuckled cruelly. '*Your curses mean nothing to me, old man.* I *am eternal. What can your petty god do to one who has passed beyond life and death?*'

The high priest thrashed against his bonds. 'May pestilence find your house! May it burrow in the walls and consume your treasures!'

Nagash shook his head in disgust. The Forsaken had been worthy foes. He'd hoped for better from their high priest. He raised his right hand. The energies of the burning stone had permeated the flesh that remained, until it was swollen and foul with cancerous tumours. Black veins, thick and pulsing with unnatural life, penetrated muscle and tendon and sank their roots into bone, where they drew sustenance from the deposits of burning stone. He reached out and seized the priest's jaw, cutting off his tirade. Nagash's fingers left streaks of slime on the northman's cheeks.

'*There is nothing your god can do to me that I have not willingly inflicted upon myself,*' Nagash said. '*Malakh's days are done. Go and tell him, when your soul is wandering the wastelands beyond death's door.*'

Nagash released the high priest and withdrew a few steps. On cue, Thestus, the leader of his Forsaken vassals, came forward with a blazing torch in his hand. The northman, once the chieftain of a hill fort nearly as large as Maghur'kan, wore leather and bronze armour in the Nehekharan style, and his scalp had been shaved bare. His hard, craggy features showed no emotion at all as he approached the bound priests and held his brand aloft. It was important that the people of Maghur'kan saw one of their own feeding their god to the flames.

'Witness!' Thestus cried. 'Malakh rules here no longer! From this moment forward, Maghur'kan serves only Nagash, the Undying King!'

The high priest spat upon Thestus. The Forsaken warrior's only reaction was to bend low and thrust the torch into the wood directly beneath the holy man's feet.

Flames *whooshed* through the pitch-soaked wood, until the totem and the men tied to it were wreathed in hungry blue flames. The priests began screaming at once, their cries of agony piercing the night. From the narrow mud lanes of the hill fort, the Yaghur began to howl in reply. Nagash listened to the gruesome chorus for a moment, savouring the sound, then left Thestus and his warriors and headed to the opposite side of the square, where the warlord's great hall could be found.

The Forsaken built their halls the same way they built their barrows. It was large and dome-shaped, with a roof of wood and thatch, and the only building in the entire fort with a thick, stone foundation. As he approached the hall, dark, humanoid shapes glided from the shadows and paced along behind the necromancer. They wove back and forth in Nagash's wake like a pack of two-legged hounds, panting and sniffing at the sweet smell of roasting flesh.

There were no guards stationed outside the hall's large, round door; only a pair of lit braziers, vainly trying to hold back the shadows of the night. The Yaghur raised clawed hands to shield their faces from the hateful light; their eyes shone a pale yellow in the firelight, like a jackal's.

Nagash passed through the open door, noting the sorcerous wards that had been incised into its wooden foundation. Protection against misfortune, against pestilence and evil spirits... he felt not the slightest murmur of power from the old symbols. Perhaps they had died along with the men burning in the square outside.

Beyond the door was a wide passageway leading to the centre of the hall, flanked by branching corridors that ran left and right around the building's circumference. Tapestries hung along the walls, depicting glorious victories against the northmen's many enemies. Nagash saw human tribes defeated and enslaved, and fierce battles against hulking, green-skinned monsters that walked upright like men. He also saw one old, threadbare tapestry that depicted the Forsaken triumphing over a horde of rat-things like the ones he'd encountered in the wasteland.

Interestingly, there were no tapestries showing mighty victories over their old foes, the Yaghur. Nagash wondered what his long-time vassals thought of such an omission – if they thought of it at all.

At the far end of the passageway, Nagash entered a large, circular great room, dominated by a crackling fire pit in the centre of the space. A crowd of silent, grim-faced warriors stood around the dying flames, their scarred faces fixed in masks of anger and despair. They turned as the necromancer appeared, and retreated slowly to the perimeter of the room.

These were the Forsaken warlord's few remaining allies, as well as the survivors of his own personal warband, gathered together at Nagash's command to bear witness to Braghad Maghur'kan's submission.

Over the tips of the crackling flames, he could see Bragadh, the last of the Forsaken warlords. Even in defeat, the young leader of the northmen was proud and defiant, flanked on his right hand by Diarid, his scarred, grey-haired champion, and on his left hand by Akatha, the last of his witches. Akatha's two sisters had died horrible deaths during the battle at the fort's main gate. She had survived Nagash's sorcerous bolts only because of the heroism of another of Bragadh's champions, who had stepped in front of the blast and had died in her place. Like Bragadh, she was very young, perhaps twenty-five or twenty-six. In Nagash's day, as a priest in Khemri, they would have been considered little more than children. It was a sign of how badly the northmen had suffered during the last, bitter years of the war.

Nagash paused just inside the great chamber, pointedly ignoring the hateful stares of the Forsaken as he studied the many war trophies hung along the walls. Eventually his gaze came around to where Bragadh stood. The necromancer smiled coldly.

'*I had expected a throne, at the very least,*' he said.

The warlord nodded at the timber crackling in the fire. 'You're looking at it,' he growled. He was a huge, broad-shouldered giant, with a forked, red beard and a heavy, brooding brow.

Nagash inclined his head to the warlord. That kind of bitter spite was something he could understand. '*It is time,*' he said.

Bragadh raised his chin stubbornly. 'Let's hear your terms.'

'*Have I not already given them?*' Nagash countered.

'I want my people to hear you say them as well.'

Nagash considered the request. Bragadh had been a fearsome war leader in his time: bold, cunning and ruthless to a fault. The necromancer did not take him for a petty man; that suggested his allies did not necessarily support his decision to surrender.

'*Very well,*' Nagash said. '*You will receive the same terms as every other fort which has surrendered to me. To begin with you will reject the worship of Malakh from this night forward. In addition, two-thirds of your fighting men will return with me to my fortress, where they will serve in my army until death and beyond. The rest will remain here, along with the women and children, to tend the fields and grow the population. Two-thirds of each male generation will be called to serve, while the village will supply them with shipments of meat and grain twice each year. These are the only tithes that you will owe to me as your master.*'

The Forsaken glanced sidelong at one another. The terms were very generous, as far as Nagash was concerned.

Diarid folded his muscular arms. Like Bragadh, his long face was framed by a dark, forked beard, and polished finger bones were plaited into his hair. 'How will our people defend themselves against our other enemies?' he asked. 'You would leave us with too few warriors to survive.'

Nagash chuckled. '*I have walked your lands from one end to the other,*' he said. '*There are a great many graves here. Enough for a very large army indeed. They can be called to war at any time.*'

Diarid's dark eyes narrowed thoughtfully. The implication hadn't escaped the young champion. If any village were foolish enough to rebel, their own ancestors would rise up to punish them.

Bragadh nodded. 'All this you will swear to, if our villages submit?'

'*I would not have said so otherwise,*' the necromancer replied.

'No!' cried one of the Forsaken to Nagash's right. He was an older man, with streaks of grey in his beard, and a barrel-like body clad in bronze and leather armour. He stepped forward, shaking his fist at Bragadh first, then at Nagash. 'We are true men, not slaves!' he said. He turned to face Nagash, his expression savage. 'I would sooner choose death than to betray my god and serve the likes of you!'

Nagash regarded the old village leader for a moment. '*As you wish,*' he said.

At once, the Yaghur were upon him. Sleek, misshapen figures burst from the passageway, racing past their master and leaping on the man. Their bodies were hunched, naked and hairless, covered in layers of dried blood and filth, and they propelled themselves across the packed earth floor using all four limbs, like mad, bloodthirsty apes.

A baying chorus of terrible, ululating howls filled the great hall as they seized the old man in their clawed hands and dragged him off his feet. Jagged, rotting teeth sank into the barbarian's face and neck. He tried to struggle, screaming in terror and pain, but the creatures held him fast. Flesh tore like rotting cloth; hot blood sprayed through the air, and the man's screams became a choking death-rattle. The Yaghur tore at the man's body with their claws, ripping apart his armour to get to the warm meat beneath. Their howls transformed into slobbering, chewing sounds as the monsters began to feast.

'*Before the sun rises, every man, woman and child in his hill fort will be dead,*' Nagash said into the stunned silence that followed. '*The fields and buildings will remain, and will be given to someone with better sense than he.*' His gaze swept across the crowd. '*Your choice here is simple. Serve me, and your people will survive. They will even prosper, as well-tended vassals should. Otherwise, they will die, and their bones will serve me in the mines for centuries to come. Do you understand?*'

No one spoke. Finally, the witch – a tall, dark-haired woman with large eyes and a narrow, pointed face – folded her arms and glared at the men. 'Don't be fools,' Akatha snarled. 'The time for defiance has passed. We must be pragmatic. The True People must survive.'

One of the Yaghur raised his head as the witch spoke, blood drooling from his jaws. His flat nostrils flared, and he growled hungrily. After a quarter millennia of feasting on human flesh, the Yaghur had developed an especial love for the soft meat of women and children.

Bragadh glared hatefully at the ghoul, and the Yaghur quickly turned back to its meal. The warlord sighed. 'The witch speaks true,' he said wearily. 'We must all take the long view now, and look to our people's survival.'

Groans went up from a dozen throats as Bragadh walked around the fire pit towards Nagash. When he stood before the necromancer he drew the great, bronze rune sword from its sheath and sank to his knees.

'I am Bragadh Maghur'kan,' he intoned. 'Warlord of the True People.' He carefully set his blade at Nagash's feet. 'And I submit.'

For a moment, no one moved. Then, one by one, the village leaders came forward to lay their weapons at the necromancer's feet.

Nagash accepted the submissions in silence, his expression of triumph lost within the depths of his hood. Across the chamber, Diarid and Bragadh's chosen men watched with stricken expressions as they watched their honour and traditions laid at the feet of their long-time foe.

Only Akatha met the necromancer's eyes. Her expression was hard as stone. Pragmatic, but no less hateful for that, Nagash noted. *Well enough,* he thought. *So long as she serves.*

The Yaghur watched the ceremony with feral disinterest, chewing noisily.

The long procession marched from Maghur'kan just after sunset on the following day. First came Nagash, borne upon his oaken palanquin and attended by his skeletal bodyguard. Behind them came his vassal lieutenants, Bragadh, Thestus and Diarid, and the witch Akatha. They marched from their ancestral home with their heads high, but their expressions were bleak.

In their wake marched the columns of Nagash's infantry – human and undead, more than four thousand strong, their ranks replenished by the corpses of those they'd slain. Then, shoulders hunched and heads hung low, came the remnants of the once-mighty Forsaken host: four hundred barbarian warriors, stumbling from exhaustion and the pain of their wounds. Not all of them would survive the three-week march to the mountain. The Yaghur loped along the army's flanks, sniffing the air and waiting for the first of the barbarians to stumble.

South the column wound, through conquered territories that had lain under Nagash's hand for many decades. The hill forts were well maintained, the fields tended and the muddy lanes kept clean of filth. Silence and despair, heavy as a funeral shroud, hung over the entire region. Food and water were brought out for the human soldiers by hollow-eyed men and women, none of whom seemed to understand the simplest of questions posed by Bragadh or his kinsmen.

After the second week the army was close to the northern end of the Plain of Bones, and on bright, moonlit nights they could see a pall of dark grey clouds hanging low on the southern horizon. At first, the enslaved barbarians thought they were seeing storm clouds hanging over the Sour Sea, but night after night, the sight was still the same.

Three nights later the army had reached the Plain of Bones. The old battlefield had changed a great deal in the last two and a half centuries, as Nagash had pursued his campaign against the northmen. A wall of stone had been built across the narrow, northern approach to the plain, anchored on each end by a citadel garrisoned by human and undead soldiers. A wide gate in the centre of the wall creaked open as the army approached, and the warriors marched through a tunnel of stone some ten yards long before emerging onto a wide expanse of tortured earth. Every square foot of the plain had been churned by pick and shovel over the centuries, digging up the bones of those who had fallen there over the millennia and adding them to Nagash's undead army.

A pall of stinking, ashen cloud hung low over the plain, plunging it into perpetual darkness, and a heavy, almost tangible silence clung to the broken land. Even the baying of the Yaghur was muted beneath the churning shadow cast from the south.

From that point on, the army marched day and night through the perpetual gloom. Hard-bitten warriors who had endured the bitter siege and the torturous march south became unmanned as they stumbled through the nightmarish landscape. Some broke ranks and tried to flee, raving and screaming in terror before the Yaghur pulled them down. Others simply fell by the wayside, their hearts gone dead between one step and the next as the burden of fear and despair simply grew too heavy to bear.

Two days later, as they crossed the southern edge of the plain and began the long descent to the coast, the vassals got their first sight of the great mountain. *Nagashizzar*, it was now called, which in Nehekharan meant 'the glory of Nagash,' and a quarter millennium of constant labour had transformed it into a vast and impenetrable fortress. High walls girdled the wide slopes in seven concentric rings, each one higher and more forbidding than the next. Hundreds of towers clawed at the ashen sky, interspersed between barracks buildings, storehouses, foundries and mine works.

Wavering tongues of ghostly green fire flickered from scores of bronze forges, and twisting plumes of noxious vapours poured from countless mineshafts carved deep into the mountainside. The great barrow plain that once stretched westward towards the coast was now covered in vast piles of crushed stone and poisonous tailings from the mines, spilling down into the dark waters of the sea. To the north, where the Yaghur still dwelled, the marshland had turned into a poisonous waste, devoid of all life save for the flesh-eaters and their squalid lairs.

As the army descended onto the coastal plain the barbarians' fears mounted. Howls rose from the wasteland as the Yaghur sensed the return of their master, and shrill, wailing horns echoed them from the phantasmal towers. Down they went, across the lifeless slope and through the ruins of the old temple fortress, and then along a wide road of crushed stone that led to the first of the fortress gates.

Men began to wail in horror as they approached that dark portal. It yawned wide like the mouth of a hungry beast, eager for their souls. And, in a sense, they were correct.

Slowly, inexorably, the fortress gate swallowed them whole. The screams of the Forsaken echoed for a long time afterwards, until the huge gates crashed shut behind them.

As vast and ominous as Nagashizzar was upon the surface, the fearsome array of walls, towers and industry only represented a fraction of the fortress's true size. Much of the enormous stronghold had been burrowed into the mountain itself, with miles upon miles of tunnels, mineshafts, laboratories, vaults and storehouses. Night and day, Nagash's undead servants toiled in the darkness, extending tunnels and hollowing out still more chambers to support Nagashizzar's ever-growing population. No one knew for certain how deep the tunnels went any more, or even where many of them led. There were exploratory tunnels and deep shafts that had not been trod in a hundred years or more.

Deep, deep within the earth, in the very lowest levels of the mighty fortress, bare hands clawed relentlessly at dirt and stone. When at last they broke through into a vast, half-finished gallery, the exhausted tunnellers all but fell onto their snouts in the open, echoing space. They lay there on the smooth stone for several seconds, wringing their taloned hands and panting shallowly. Their smooth, pink noses tasted the dank air. Oil and metal, old bone and the teasing scent of man-flesh. Could this be the place the Grey Seer had sent them to find?

Yes! The Seekers caught the scent at almost the same moment. Quivering, they scrambled to their feet, wringing paw-like hands in excitement. They licked their noses, tasting the bitter dust. Sky-stone! Gifts from the Great Horned One, in numbers uncounted!

The Seekers froze, still as statues but for the wrinkling of their noses and the twitching of their ears as they searched for signs they'd been discovered. Always, always there was the risk that something vigilant waited in the darkness; some horror with teeth or blades to rend rat-flesh. Such was the way of life in the tunnels. Every one of the Seekers had secretly picked out which of their companions they could safely throw in the path of danger so they could make good their escape.

Nothing stirred in the abandoned gallery save for the Seekers themselves. Such luck! Such glory to the first one who carried the news back to the Council! Minds buzzing with dreams of power and schemes of treachery, the Seekers turned about and fled back the way they'd come, their long, pink tails twitching behind them.

SEVENTEEN

THE DEATHLESS COURT

Lahmia,
the City of the Dawn,
in the 96th year of Ptra the Glorious
(-1350 Imperial Reckoning)

By day, Neferata slept, yet she did not dream. Instead, the sounds of the great city washed over her, filling her mind with fragments of mortal life that existed beyond the cold palace walls.

Sailors shouted bawdy boasts to whores walking the city docks, or sang songs of foreign shores while they made their ships ready for another long journey at sea. Servants gossiped in the market squares, or haggled over the price of melons or grain. Beggars called out to passers-by, pleading for a copper or a crust of bread. A tavern-keeper opened his doors with a muttered prayer for a good day's custom. Lovers argued over an imagined slight. A thief jeered at the city guard as he made good his escape. A young mother sang a lullaby for her baby. An old man wept softly, mourning the wife he'd lost the year before.

She awoke at sunset, in the utter darkness of her bedchamber, her legs tangled in silken sheets. Her limbs were stiff and cold. Thirst tightened her throat. No matter how much she drank the night before, the thirst was always with her when she woke.

The faintest sounds of movement came from beyond her bedchamber door. Neferata swiftly wiped the tears from her cheeks as her attendants swept into the room to prepare her for the long night ahead.

Lamplight filled the room as the women went about their tasks with swift and silent precision. They were all priestesses of the highest order in the secretive Lahmian Cult: orphans raised within the precincts of the former Women's Palace and trained to serve the sacred bloodline of Asaph, as manifested in the person of the queen. Only the cult's inner circle knew the true nature of the living goddess whom they served, but by that point their hearts and minds belonged to Neferata alone. The initiates of the cult wore robes of purest samite and masks of fine, beaten gold, wrought in the image of Asaph herself.

She waited as the priestesses laid out her robes and drew open the heavy, bronze shutters that covered the windows and shielded her from the sun. A sea breeze stirred the curtains, caressing her icy skin, and she heard the distant murmur of waves. The riot of voices in the city below faded to a dull roar, not unlike the sound of the restless surf.

A priestess knelt by the side of her bed, her masked face carefully downcast. The mask she wore had been modelled on Neferata's own face, and wrought with exacting detail. With both hands she offered a golden goblet brimming with blood.

'For you, holy one,' she intoned in a hollow voice. 'An offer of love, and life eternal.'

Neferata took the goblet from the priestess and held it to her breast, savouring its warmth. The thirst grew suddenly, painfully sharp; her hand tightened on the metal rim, and she became horribly aware of the curved fangs pressing against her lower gums. As she did each night, she forced herself to remain still and calm until the feral impulse subsided. Slowly, deliberately, she raised the goblet to her lips and drained it in a single draught. Not one precious drop escaped her lips.

When she was done, she handed the vessel back to the priestess. The ritual would be repeated again at midnight, and once more just before dawn. Bloodletting in small amounts was a central tenet of the Lahmian Cult; from the lowliest acolyte to the most senior priestesses, each initiate surrendered a small portion each night as part of rituals intended to bring them closer to the goddess.

The cult had been a clever scheme on the part of W'soran, who envisioned it as both a cover for their predations and a safe haven from which to continue their rule over the city. Under Neferata's leadership it had also become a useful political tool as well, lending the Lahmian throne a degree of divine authority that the other Nehekharan cities lacked. The cult boasted a single, grand temple, converted from the Women's Palace during the latter days of Neferata's official reign. The temple's inner sanctum, a small complex of buildings in its own right, encompassed her private apartments and the palace's old central garden and still retained the opulence of its former existence. Nagash's tomes were kept in an arcane laboratory inside the sanctum, its doors sealed by physical and magical locks that only Neferata and W'soran together could open.

Fresh strength flowed through Neferata's limbs and lent her a small measure of warmth. She rose from the bed and spread her arms, allowing the priestesses to dress her. They garbed her in the raiment of an empress: robes of the finest Eastern silk, in layers of saffron, crimson and sapphire, embroidered with gold and silver thread and hundreds of tiny pearls. A girdle of fine, hammered gold was draped about her hips, its plates inset with dark, polished rubies. Deft hands slid precious bracelets onto her wrists, and a necklace made of heavy, gold links was fastened about her neck.

When the priestesses had completed the elaborate costume, they led her to the dressing table and bade her sit. Jewelled slippers were placed on her feet, and her eyes were darkened with kohl. All the while, Neferata stared out the open windows, listening to the sea. The steady whisper of the deeps soothed her mind as almost nothing else could.

As the priestesses worked, another pale figure slipped silently into the room and sat gracefully upon the edge of Neferata's bed. She was slim and delicate of feature, like the porcelain dolls from the land of her birth, and favoured elegant silk robes cut in the Eastern style. Her raven-black hair was swept up behind her head, held there with golden pins and a comb of polished jade. It drew attention to her slender neck, and emphasised her artful, elegant sense of poise.

Everything about her was carefully crafted, from the precise angles her hands made as they rested in her lap, to the patient, composed tilt of her pointed chin. She had been a courtesan once, expensively educated and trained from early childhood to be a companion to princes and emperors. Her purpose had been to moderate the baser appetites of noble men and elevate their public appearance with her refined manner. She had been an ornament, like a jewelled songbird that hovered about the shoulders of the wealthy and powerful. In those days, she hadn't even had a proper name. To her master, Prince Xian, she had simply been known as White Orchid. Neferata called her Naaima, and in her court she wanted for nothing.

The priestesses finished their work and withdrew as silently as they'd come. As they left, Naaima rose from the bed and went to her mistress. She ran slender fingers through Neferata's long hair, deftly teasing out the tangles, and then chose a silver-backed brush from the table.

'You called out in your sleep,' Naaima said softly, in the oddly lilting tongue of the Silk Lands. She drew the brush through Neferata's hair in long, smooth strokes.

Naaima slept in a luxurious bedchamber just across the corridor from Neferata's own. Centuries ago, when Neferata had persuaded her to take the poisoned cup, she had kept Naaima as close to her as she could, often taking comfort in the former courtesan's embrace while she slept. It did not last, however. As time wore on, Neferata felt only the coldness of Naaima's embrace, the deathly stillness of her body as she slept. There was no comfort to the found in the embrace of the dead.

The question irritated her. 'Perhaps I was dreaming,' Neferata said coldly. Even after two hundred years, the language of the easterners felt strange on her tongue. 'Do you always listen to me while I sleep?'

'Sometimes,' Naaima replied, ignoring the brittle edge in Neferata's voice. She was silent for a time as she finished her brushing, then gathered up a handful of golden pins. As she drew back Neferata's long hair she said, 'It sounded as though you were calling to a hawk.'

Neferata's body betrayed nothing. The pain was still sharp, even now, like a needle in her heart. The passage of years wore away the softer emotions first, she'd learned, while the harder, crueller ones endured.

'You must be mistaken,' she managed to say. 'I know nothing of hawks. Falconry never held any interest for me.'

'Of course,' Naaima replied smoothly. She did not pursue the matter any further. When she was finished with Neferata's hair, she went to the wooden box that sat on a pedestal in one corner of the room. Opening it, she drew out Neferata's golden mask. The delicate metal of the mask bore the weight of centuries upon its cold face. She studied it for a moment, frowning slightly. 'You should have a crown,' she said. 'You deserve better than this.'

'The crown is for the Queen of Lahmia,' Neferata replied. 'I am merely its ruler.' She beckoned to Naaima. 'Bring it here. I have work to do.'

She forced herself to hold still as Naaima slipped the mask onto her face. Every time she felt the touch of metal against her cheeks she was reminded of her own funeral. It reminded her now of nothing but death and loss. When it was in place she rose without a word and made her way from the chamber. Naaima fell into step a precise six paces behind her; the habits of a lifetime and were nearly impossible to overcome, and only became more so in the unlife that followed.

The corridors of the inner sanctum were funereal in their stillness. There were never more than three hundred acolytes and initiates of the cult at any one time, and they were swallowed up whole by the vast size of the temple complex. Neferata walked in silence down the dimly lit passageways, then across the broad expanse of the former palace garden. The trees and tall ferns grew wild and untended now, and many of the rare flowers had died without the care of the gardeners. Bats circled overhead, darting and dancing in the moonlight. She listened to their strange, almost plaintive cries, as she did every night, and wondered who or what it was they were calling for.

They crossed the wild garden, and then entered another set of silent, echoing chambers on the far side. Moments later they arrived at a pair of bronze doors, attended by silent, masked priestesses. Ubaid waited beside them. Though he still looked as young as the day he'd tasted Lamashizzar's elixir, his back was hunched and his hands trembled like that of an old man. His eyes were round and bright like polished glass. As Neferata approached, he managed a clumsy bow.

'The court awaits, holy one,' he said in a ragged voice. The former grand vizier sounded as though his inner workings had been crushed to pieces, then carelessly reassembled.

Neferata ignored him. With a curt nod, the priestesses pulled open the doors. Warm, yellow light poured over her as she crossed the threshold into the audience chamber. The blocks of polished sandstone and the lacquered wooden screens of the Hall of Reverent Contemplation had been dismantled and rebuilt within the inner sanctum when the Women's Palace had been renovated. She knew she would no longer have any need for the vast, echoing court chamber that she'd presided from in the palace proper, and she'd thought the familiar surroundings would be a comfort in the ages to come. How little she had known.

She climbed the back of the dais and stepped around the tall, wooden throne. It was the one concession to her ego that she'd allowed when she surrendered her crown. A vast fortune had been spent to hire a small expedition to scour the southern jungles for a match to the wood that had been used for the original throne, and a still greater sum paid to find and commission an artisan skilled enough to shape it into an exact copy of the original. The whole process had taken almost as long as the construction of the temple itself. Neferata had never gotten around to asking Lord Ushoran what had become of the artisan afterward. Certainly no one ever found the body.

Neferata settled gracefully into the ancient chair and surveyed the audience chamber. Lord Ankhat stood closest to the dais, attended by a pair of enthralled retainers burdened with stacks of ledgers and bundles of scrolls. Lord Ushoran waited at a careful remove from Ankhat, his expression distant as he meditated on his intrigues. This evening W'soran was present as well, accompanied by an enthralled young scribe who was busily copying down his master's muttered dictation. As always, Lord Zurhas lingered furthest from the throne, his arms folded tightly across his chest and a look on his face that said he would rather be gambling away his fortune in some squalid dice house.

Each one bore the marks of unlife in their own, unique way. Lord Ankhat, was, if anything, more lordly in mien than before, possessing a dominating presence that nearly rivalled her own. Ushoran, on the other hand, was just the opposite. He seemed more changeable, more chimerical than before. There were times that Neferata was certain his features looked subtly different from one moment to the next. Unfortunately for Lord Zurhas, his features were entirely fixed. Neferata couldn't help but think he turned more craven and rodent-like with each passing year.

Then there was W'soran. The old scholar had been the first to ask Neferata to drink from the poisoned cup, and since rising from his deathbed he had grown even more gaunt and skeletal than before. Now, centuries later, he was a hideous creature, more resembling a walking corpse than a man. The very sight of him filled her with dread. For the longest time, she was afraid that some error in the ritual had caused his transformation, and that he secretly hated her for it. But Lord Ushoran insisted that W'soran was actually *pleased* with what he'd become.

When she was seated, Naaima glided soundlessly around the dais and took her place at Neferata's right, head bowed and hands clasped at her waist. Moments later, Ubaid shuffled around to Neferata's left and cleared his gravelly throat.

'Pay heed to the throne of Lahmia,' the grand vizier intoned, his voice echoing in the nearly empty chamber. 'The court of Neferata the Eternal is convened. Let all bear witness to her glory.'

'The last of the annual tribute has arrived,' Ankhat said, scanning the contents of the ledger in his hands. 'Zandri has come up short again.'

Neferata sighed. 'What is the excuse this time?'

Ankhat shrugged. 'Pirates, of course. Cut down profits on the slave trade by nearly a third, according to them.'

Her eyes narrowed. 'Are they telling the truth, Ushoran?'

The Lord of Masks shook his head. His network of spies now reached from one end of Nehekhara to the other. Lahmia was the centre of the civilised world, richer by far than any of the other great cities combined. The yearly tribute to pay off the interest on their debts saw to that. There were a great many powerful people who resented that fact. 'Zandri's navy is as strong as ever,' he said. 'There hasn't been a pirate spotted in her waters for more than a century.'

'And does Numas support Zandri's reckless behaviour?' Neferata asked.

Ankhat snorted. 'Given how much we're paying them for grain? I should hope not.' The city of Numas, situated on the wide Plains of Plenty, had long been the chief food producer in Nehekhara. Now, with reports that the fertile banks of the River Vitae were shrinking, and the desert encroaching on the other cities more and more each year, their power and influence had grown tenfold. Even Lahmia found itself increasingly beholden to the distant city, as increasing numbers of bandit gangs drove farmers off the Golden Plain.

'Numas has given no sign of support for Zandri,' Ushoran agreed. 'The west has changed a great deal in the last two hundred years, and the only real common ground the two cities ever had was their brief allegiance to Nagash. If anything, I suspect that Zandri is growing bold in response to Numas's growing stature.'

'And does Numas pose a threat to us?' Neferata asked. Naaima chided her often that she saw potential threats everywhere these days. When one ruled a de facto empire, it was the only way to survive.

Ushoran gave another of his shrugs. 'Now? No. A hundred years from now? Perhaps.'

Neferata sighed. 'How quickly they seem to forget,' she growled. 'Three hundred years of peace and prosperity has evidently spoiled them. Perhaps a punitive expedition to Zandri is in order.'

Ushoran glanced at Ankhat, who shifted uncomfortably.

'For that, we'll need an army, I suspect,' Ankhat said.

Neferata straightened. 'What happened to the army we *had*?' she demanded.

'Three hundred years of peace and prosperity,' Ankhat replied. 'Lamashizzar began reducing the army right after the war, and it was allowed to wither ever since. There didn't seem to be a point to maintaining an expensive army when the trade policies were working so well, and besides, it's highly unlikely the dragon power has retained its potency after so long in storage.'

Neferata glowered behind her mask. There likely wouldn't be any more opportunities to buy the exotic powder, either. The Eastern Empire was still as secretive and isolationist as it ever had been, but Ushoran's spies in the trade cities hinted that there had been great upheavals inside its borders. Prince Xian Ha Feng, scion of the Celestial Household, had defied the edicts of the Emperor for two years after his first taste of Neferata's blood, effectively resolving the matter of Lahmia's debt to the Empire.

When he was finally recalled by his august father, the prince left for the Silk Lands with two more vials of the queen's blood, and promises of much more in the future. But shortly after Xian's return, all contact with the Empire abruptly ceased, and all foreigners were barred from its trade cities on pain of death. It would be more than a century before contact was restored, whereupon it was learned that the old emperor had met with sudden misfortune, and issues of succession had turned violent. Prince Xian disappeared into the chaos of the civil wars that followed, and none knew his fate. The current emperor's view on Nehekhara was one of benign disinterest.

'What have we been doing with all the money that was supposed to be going to the army?' she inquired.

'Some of it went to the navy,' Ankhat said. 'Most of it went to expanding the City Guard and adding patrols to the trade routes across the Golden Plain.'

'And much good that did us,' Neferata replied sourly. 'No wonder Zandri feels free to withhold tribute.' She pointed at Ankhat. 'That policy changes now. How long will it take to raise a new army and train it?'

Ankhat blinked. 'I don't know for certain,' he replied. 'I seem to recall that it took your father decades–'

'That was because he was negotiating with the damned Easterners,' Neferata said, and then cast a guilty look at Naaima.

'Abhorash could tell us,' Ankhat replied. 'If he was here, of course.'

Neferata glanced at Ushoran. 'What of Abhorash?' she asked. 'Any word?'

The Lord of Masks shrugged once again. 'There are rumours he was sighted in Rasetra last year,' he said, 'The last I knew for certain, he was heading into the jungles, but it's been twenty years now. He could very well be dead.'

Abhorash had been the last member of the cabal to accept the poisoned cup; later even than Naaima by more than a decade. Having witnessed the voluntary transformation of the rest of Neferata's cabal, he wanted no part of an existence that would prevent him from fighting on the battlefield. He believed that more than a hundred and fifty years of loyal service to the throne was enough to ensure that he would never betray the cabal, but Neferata was not convinced. Finally, she lost patience. When he came to the palace to receive his elixir from the queen, she gave him the poisoned cup instead.

He had been furious upon awakening as an immortal, and refused to accept what he had become. Incredibly, he'd denied his thirst for many nights, as though it were a sickness that could be overcome, until Neferata had begun to think the mighty warrior might actually waste away. But then, one moonless night, Abhorash succumbed. By the time the sun had risen once more, twelve people – men, women, even a small child – had been slain across the length of the city. Ankhat and Ushoran had scoured the city in search of Abhorash on the following night, but the champion was nowhere to be found. He'd fled the city, and no one in Lahmia had seen him since.

'Abhorash isn't dead,' Neferata declared. 'There's nothing in the southern jungles – or anywhere else – capable of killing him. When he discovers that for himself, I expect we will see him again.' She glanced at Ankhat. 'In the meantime, my lord, we need an army.'

Ankhat bowed. 'I will inform the queen of the new policy at once.'

A group of priestesses slipped into the chamber, bearing goblets to quench the court's thirst. Midnight already. They'd been discussing matters of state for six hours. The notion surprised and dismayed her.

Neferata accepted the first goblet and drank it down, then watched the others drink. The transformation affected each of them differently, she knew. They all dealt with the thirst in their own ways, and it was reflected in the way that they fed. Ankhat took the proffered cup, studied its depths, and then drank it slowly, like wine. Lord Ushoran took his cup in an almost absent fashion, his brooding mind distracted by one intrigue or another. He drank the blood in swift gulps; for him it was fuel, and nothing more. Zurhas eyed his goblet with dread, yet he accepted the cup with a grimace and drank it down in a single swallow. Naaima accepted hers with studied calm, as with everything else she did, and drank it without evident interest or emotion.

W'soran shook his head curtly, refusing the cup as he always did. Neferata wondered at his appetites, and how he managed to indulge them.

Once the priestesses had withdrawn, Neferata sighed. 'Is there anything else to discuss?'

Ankhat and Ushoran consulted their notes. 'More reports in Numas of strange clouds seen over the mountains to the east,' Ushoran said. 'King Ahmose is thinking about sending an expedition to find its source.'

'Much good may it do him,' Neferata said. 'Anything else?'

To her surprise, W'soran spoke up. 'I have a request,' he said.

'Go on.'

The old scholar raised his chin, almost in challenge. 'I would like access to Nagash's books for a time,' he said. 'I want to begin a new field of research.'

'And what would that be?' Neferata asked, though she had suspicions of what it might be.

'An aspect of necromancy,' W'soran began.

'We've discussed this before,' Neferata growled. 'Many, many times–'

'Not raising the dead,' W'soran interjected. 'Not that. My interest lies in raising spirits and communicating with them. If I recall, Nagash made some notes regarding summoning circles in one of his books.'

Neferata thought it over. 'And what do you hope to gain from this?' she asked.

W'soran shrugged. 'Knowledge, of course. What else?'

Her first instinct was to refuse, but she knew that W'soran would ask for her reasons, and she had none. 'Very well,' she said. 'But I expect to be kept apprised of your efforts.'

'Of course,' W'soran said, and gave a small bow of gratitude.

'There is also the matter of Khemri,' added Lord Ankhat. 'The rebuilding of the city is nearly complete, and the inhabitants are clamouring for a king. Will you approve of such a thing?'

The news surprised Neferata, though she chided herself that it had been centuries since she'd made her pledge to help the late King Shepret restore the ruined city.

'I see no reason why not,' she said at length. 'It's been almost four hundred years. Nagash is nothing more than an evil memory now. And the sooner that Khemri has a king, the sooner we can stop subsidising the city's construction.'

'Perhaps it's best to wait and see if the would-be king lives to claim the throne,' Ushoran said wryly.

Neferata turned to the spymaster. 'What does that mean?' she asked.

'The Queen of Rasetra is with child, but she has never been a woman of robust health,' Ushoran said. 'The pregnancy has been very difficult. From what I gather, there is little chance that the baby will survive.'

Ankhat nodded. 'She is here right now, in fact, praying at the temple.'

'What?' Neferata said, sitting straight upon the throne.

'She's holding vigil in the presence of the goddess, praying for her child's life,' Ushoran explained. 'A pity it will do her little good.'

Neferata did not reply at first. The silence stretched, until Ushoran began to look uncomfortable.

'Is there something wrong, great one?' he asked.

Again, Neferata did not immediately reply. When she did finally speak, it caught them all by surprise.

'Nagash is just an evil memory now,' she repeated. 'A legend. One that grows more nebulous each year.'

Ankhat frowned. 'So we hope,' he said warily.

Neferata nodded – thoughtfully at first, then more decisively. 'The baby will live,' she declared.

Ushoran gave her a bemused look. 'How can you be so certain?'

'Because I am going to save him,' Neferata replied. As she spoke, the idea took shape in her mind. 'The queen will remain here in Lahmia as our guest, for the duration of the pregnancy, and I will give her an elixir mixed with my blood.'

The news stunned the cabal. Ankhat and W'soran looked visibly shaken. 'What makes you think she would agree to such a thing?' Ankhat said.

'She travelled, heavily pregnant, for weeks, just for the chance to pray for her son's life,' Neferata snapped. 'That woman is prepared to do anything to save her child.'

Ushoran frowned. 'But to what end?'

'When the child is born, he will remain here until his majority,' Neferata declared. 'It's past time that the heirs apparent to the great cities came to Lahmia for their education.'

The spymaster gaped at her. 'Hostages. You're talking about hostages.'

'Not at all,' Neferata replied. 'I am talking about shaping the future of all Nehekhara. Think of it: what if, in a hundred years, we ruled an empire from here to Zandri, and we did so *openly*?'

'The other cities would never stand for it!' Ankhat exclaimed.

'They would if the kings supported us, and soon they will,' she countered. 'We've existed under the shadow of Nagash for too long. I'm *tired* of hiding. After everything I've done, everything I've *sacrificed*, all I've done is trade one prison for another.' Her fists clenched. 'No more. Do you hear? No more.'

She rose from the throne. 'Instruct the queen to draft the summons to the other cities,' she said. 'I will speak to the Queen of Rasetra personally. I want the first children here within the next year. Offer to lower their yearly tribute if you must.'

'And if they refuse?' Ushoran countered.

'They won't, once we hear how the temple saved the future King of Khemri,' Neferata said. 'We will show them that we are not the children of Nagash. We are something altogether different. In time, they may even worship us as gods.'

She left them in shocked silence, her mind whirling with possibilities. Naaima followed behind her, for once surrendering her composure and dashing after her mistress.

'You've frightened them,' she whispered in Neferata's ear as they rushed through the dark halls of the inner sanctum.

'We've all been afraid for too long,' Neferata replied. 'I meant what I said. I'm tired of skulking here, while the world turns without me. Perhaps Abhorash had the right of it all along, fleeing Lahmia and seeking his destiny elsewhere.'

'This has nothing to do with destiny, or with compassion,' Naaima replied, her voice taut. 'This is about Khalida–'

Neferata's hand blurred through the air, seizing Naaima by the throat. One moment they were racing through the inner sanctum, then the next Naaima was dangling from Neferata's iron grip in the middle of the passageway.

'Never speak that name again,' Neferata hissed. Her fangs glinted in the faint light. '*Never*. Do you understand me?'

It took all her strength to gasp out her reply. 'I... I understand,' Naaima said.

Neferata held her there for several agonising seconds, her face a mask of madness and rage. Slowly, one heartbeat at a time, the anger ebbed from her face, until she realised what she was doing. With a start, she released the former concubine. Naaima hit the floor hard and collapsed, clutching her throat.

'Forgive me,' Neferata said softly. 'I didn't mean to hurt you.'

Naaima shook her head. The pain she felt in her heart left her breathless.

'You can't bring her back,' Naaima gasped. 'Nothing you do will bring Khalida back. Why can't you see that?'

But there was no answer. Neferata was gone.

EPILOGUE

PORTENTS OF DESTRUCTION

Lahmia,
the City of the Dawn,
in the 98th year of Asaph the Beautiful
(-1325 Imperial Reckoning)

'Here they come!' the tutor roared in his leathery, field-of-battle voice. 'Get on your feet, boy! Get up!'

Four men in bronze scale armour hefted their weapons and charged across the training ground, their sandaled feet kicking up plumes of sand as they converged on their prey. The early morning sun slanted across the square, leaving much of the ground still in deep shadow except for where young Alcadizzar lay. Haptshur's pupil lay in his back in the rocky sand, half-covered by an overturned chariot. His bare legs were wrapped in the chariot's traces, and a heavy sack of grain – representing the body of his dead driver – lay across his chest. The young man's shield was strapped to his left arm, but his sword was ten paces away, back along the chariot's imagined trail. As a final touch. Haptshur had smeared pig's blood over his pupil's face, taking care to dab it liberally in the young man's eyes. The older warrior believed in making his lessons as realistic and messy as he possibly could – much like the brutal reality of the battlefield.

Haptshur's assistants likewise dispensed with any fanciful notions of honour or fair play – they had no intention of giving Alcadizzar the slightest chance of extricating himself and getting to his sword. They came at him all in a rush, intent on chopping him to pieces as quickly and savagely as they could.

Swathed in deep shadow behind a lacquered wooden screen, Neferata watched the oncoming collision with mounting concern. Accidents happened in training. Even wooden weapons were more than capable of breaking bones or fracturing skulls, and if an infection set it, the results were often fatal. It had never happened to any of Haptshur's royal pupils, but... She pressed the fingertips of her right hand against the screen's fragile wooden vine work, as though willing speed and strength into the young man's body.

Not that Alcadizzar needed it; despite his age, the Rasetran prince was already more than six feet tall, and more powerfully built than the burly Haptshur and his men. His mother had done everything Neferata had asked of her, remaining at the temple and drinking a vial of elixir each and every week until the baby was born, and its effects on the unborn child had been profound.

The young man's attackers covered the sandy ground in seconds, but Alcadizzar was already on the move. Cool and calm despite the angry shouts and the blood stinging his eyes, the young man paused for scarcely a moment to formulate his plan, and then sprang swiftly into action. Neferata watched as he got his hands underneath the heavy bag laid across his chest, then with a heave of his shoulders and arms he flung it backwards, over his head and into the path of the oncoming men. The projectile caught the attackers momentarily by surprise, but they recovered almost at once, dodging left and right out of its path, but the diversion bought Alcadizzar a few more precious seconds.

To Neferata's surprise, the prince didn't bother untangling his legs from the leather traces; instead, he drew back his muscular legs, propped his feet against the chariot's wicker rim, and heaved with all his strength. With a creak of wood and leather, the chariot rolled over onto its side, and Alcadizzar scrambled after it, disappearing into the open bed.

Now the prince's attackers pulled up short, suddenly without an easy target to reach. Alcadizzar had backed into the chariot like a cornered viper, and his foes could only come at him from one direction. Further-more, the upper side of the chariot provided a roof of sorts over Alcadizzar's head, preventing the men from raining blows down on him from overhead. They would have to come right at him, thrusting with their curved khopeshes, which made their task that much more difficult.

The three men spread out, communicating with one another using glances and hand gestures. One of the attackers nodded, rushing towards the prince, while the other two circled around the opposite side of the chariot. Neferata frowned. What were they up to? Then she understood. While one man kept Alcadizzar occupied, the others were going to grab the chariot and pull it back upright, disorientating the prince and leaving him open for a blow from his attacker.

But Alcadizzar had plans of his own. As the first man rushed in, stabbing awkwardly with his curved blade, his feet came down amid tangled loops of leather traces that the prince had trailed behind him. At once, Alcadizzar jerked back on the traces, and the man flew backwards with a yell. The prince leapt onto him like a desert lion, landing on his chest and pummelling him with one powerful blow after another. Snarling, the swordsman tried to counter-attack, but Alcadizzar caught his sword-hand by the wrist and cracked his fist across the other man's chin, knocking him senseless.

Just then, the chariot lurched, rolling back onto its wheels with a loud crash. The traces jerked tight, yanking Alcadizzar away from his foe, but not before he plucked the khopesh from the unconscious man's hand. He twisted onto his back as the traces dragged him across the sand, and began trying to kick his way free of the tangled leather straps.

It took the remaining attackers scarcely a moment to realise what had happened. They came racing around the back of the chariot, eager to avenge their fallen friend. Alcadizzar, his legs still trapped, did the only thing he could: he rolled across the sand towards the charging men, closing the distance more quickly than they'd expected. The men recovered swiftly, trying to circle around the oncoming prince, but the young man moved with preternatural speed. His wooden khopesh slashed through the air, feinting low at one man's calf, then cutting suddenly upwards and striking the man in the groin. The attacker fell to the sand with a muffled groan.

There was a *whack* of wood on flesh. Neferata missed the blow, but saw the angry red weal rising on Alcadizzar's right thigh. The prince didn't utter a sound at the painful hit; his sword blurred, reaching for the last attacker's left arm. The man pulled his arm out of the way just in time – and was caught by surprise when the prince's left leg swept into his right foot and knocked him from his feet. The man hit the sand with a whoosh of tortured breath as the wind was knocked from his lungs, and before he could recover, Alcadizzar had scrambled atop him and laid the khopesh's blade against his throat.

'Enough!' Haptshur cried. At once, Alcadizzar sat back with a grin and tossed the practice weapon aside. Within moments, the three men who'd been so intent on giving the prince a thrashing were slapping him on the back and laughing ruefully as they helped to unwind him from the dust-stained traces. Haptshur walked over, his leathery face beaming with pride, and tossed the prince a cloth to wipe the blood from his face.

'He has grown into quite the young man,' Lord Ankhat observed quietly. 'I'm certain his father would be proud if he could see him now.'

Neferata nearly jumped at the sound of the lord's voice. Ankhat was standing at the far end of the observation gallery, near the door that led to the secret corridor back to the temple's inner sanctum. He was careful to remain completely in shadow. Even so, the mere proximity of sunlight clearly made him uncomfortable.

'My lord Ankhat,' Neferata said smoothly. 'I didn't hear your approach.' Once upon a time, Naaima would have warned her, but she saw little of the former concubine these days. She kept to herself, spending her evenings in the wild garden or poring through the tomes in the temple libraries. Neferata had been offended at first, but then she had become preoccupied with Alcadizzar's birth, and after a while she hadn't missed Naaima's presence at all.

'Forgive me if I startled you,' Ankhat said with a mirthless smile. 'No doubt your attention was devoted entirely to the young prince.'

Despite herself, Neferata glanced proudly at the prince. He now stood next to Haptshur, towering head and shoulders over his tutor, his expression intent as he listened to the burly warrior's assessment of the fight. Even coated with dust and smeared with traces of blood, his face was handsome and refined, with a square chin, strong cheekbones and a sharp nose. Alcadizzar had black hair and dark, intense eyes that he offset with a brilliant, disarming smile.

'He is a wonder,' Neferata admitted. 'A true prince. One day, he will have the world at his fingertips.' Certainly he had been given the finest education in the land. Alcadizzar and the other royal children who now lived at the Lahmian court were lavished with the best of everything. The kings of the other great cities might resent sending their children to be raised in a foreign court, but they couldn't say that their sons and daughters weren't being treated as well – or in most cases, better – than they would have at home.

Ankhat studied Neferata intently. 'That day is close at hand,' he said. 'There have been letters from Rasetra. The king says that it's time for Alcadizzar to assume his duties as King of Khemri.'

'Now? Nonsense!' Neferata exclaimed. 'He's only twenty-five years old!'

'His father became King of Rasetra at his age,' Ankhat pointed out. 'People do not have the span of years that our fathers once did.'

'*He* will,' Neferata said. 'Look at him. See what the elixir has wrought! He'll live to be a hundred and twenty, perhaps more!'

Ankhat shrugged. 'Perhaps so, great one. Nevertheless, he has reached the age when he should be king in his own right.'

Neferata turned back to the practice field. Alcadizzar was walking away, still talking with his tutors and rubbing the thick dust from his bare shoulders. His smile was dazzling against his dark skin. Ubaid waited at the edge of the field with fresh clothes for the prince; at Neferata's command, the former grand vizier had been Alcadizzar's personal servant since childhood, allowing her to keep a constant watch over the boy. Even Ubaid seemed to have been charmed by the young prince's magnetism; in Alcadizzar's presence he seemed to recover a bit of his former poise and presence of mind.

'No,' she said, shaking her head. 'He's not ready yet. Tell the Rasetrans they cannot have him.'

Ankhat blinked. 'He belongs to them–'

'He belongs to *me*,' Neferata hissed. 'Were it not for me, he would have died in the womb! *I* made him what he is today, and I say I'm not finished with him yet!'

The full force of her will hit Ankhat like a gale. He visibly wavered underneath her stare.

'This is dangerous, great one,' Ankhat managed to say. 'The other kings already resent sending their children to live here as hostages. Refusing to return Alcadizzar will lead to repercussions.'

Neferata's eyes narrowed at Ankhat. Her lips drew back slightly, revealing her fangs. 'Are you threatening me?'

Ankhat bristled. 'I'm merely pointing out the risks of your... attachment to the young prince,' he replied. 'It is a danger to us all.'

'No,' Neferata said. 'That's where you're wrong. Alcadizzar is the future. Through him, we'll remake all of Nehekhara in our image, and rule over it until the end of time.'

The practice field was empty now. Neferata hurried down the length of the gallery, brushing past the stunned Ankhat.

'Tell the Rasetrans whatever you must,' she said to him as she went by. 'Khemri will have a king when I say it is time, and not before.'

Acrid smoke hung in a dense, blue cloud over the ritual circle in the temple's arcane sanctum. The incense braziers still burned after the long night's work, mingling with the candle smoke and the arcane vapours that W'soran had learned were efficacious in the summoning of spirits. Over the last twenty-five years he had summoned countless spirits from the bleak wasteland beyond death's door, until now he reckoned himself a master of the art. And yet his ultimate goal remained stubbornly out of reach.

The very thought of it galled him. W'soran had never been a strong man, but he reckoned that only one man in all of Nehekhara had ever rivalled him in matters of intellect. He was not accustomed to the notion of failure where his studies were concerned.

A glassy-eyed scribe shuffled up to him, holding out the transcript of the evening's ritual. W'soran snatched the papyrus from the thrall's hand and compared it to the invocations that Nagash had written in the yellowing tome open on the table before him. His lips pulled back in a snarl at the scribe's atrocious handiwork. The thralls made terrible assistants unless the lightest amount of pressure was brought to bear on their minds, but W'soran had little patience for such foolishness. He would have preferred the steady, tireless hand of a skeletal servant, and once again cursed Neferata's edict forbidding such creations. She was little better than her dead husband: ambitious, but too timid to make use of the tremendous power that lay in their hands. The specific tomes that governed the creation of the undead were locked away in another vault, along with Arkhan's notes on the transformation ritual he had used on Neferata. There they would remain until the end of time, if she were allowed to have her way.

'Stupid, moon-eyed bitch!' he muttered, smoothing out the papyrus next to the ancient page and reaching for an ink brush.

'The evening's work didn't go well, I take it?'

W'soran whirled, hands clenching into claws. Fleshless lips drew back, revealing long, needle-like fangs. He didn't recognise the bland features of the man standing just inside the doorway of the sanctum, but he knew the voice all too well. 'Ushoran!' he exclaimed. 'How did you get in here?'

Lord Ushoran gave the skeletal W'soran a ghostly smile. 'The door was unlocked long ago,' he said. 'You requested it, in fact.'

'Don't be impertinent!' W'soran snapped. 'You're not allowed here! If Neferata knew–'

Ushoran's smile turned cold. 'If she knew I was here, she'd no doubt be angry. I'll give you that. But that would be nothing compared to how furious she'd be if she knew what you were really up to.'

W'soran's anger vanished in an instant. 'What are you talking about?' he said, suddenly wary.

Ushoran sighed. 'You've been summoning and binding spirits for a quarter of a century. Do you mean to tell me that you haven't figured out how to do it yet?'

'Certainly not!' W'soran snapped. 'I mastered the art of summoning years ago!'

'Then I have to assume you're in here, night after night, not because you're still learning how to call up spirits – but because you're trying to call up a very specific spirit instead.'

W'soran cursed himself for a fool. Ushoran had led him right into the trap, and he'd never seen it coming. He affected a sneer, hoping it would hide his unease.

'What of it? Do you think Neferata would care if I was summoning one particular spirit over another?'

'Oh, yes,' Ushoran said. 'She most definitely would – if the spirit in question was Nagash.'

W'soran froze. How had he been found out? For a wild instant, he wondered if he were capable of killing Ushoran and disposing of the body. The Lord of Masks would often disappear for weeks, even months at a time. No one would notice his absence for a long while.

He slowly turned back to the table and began casually searching through the pile for another one of Nagash's books. There were offensive spells inside that would turn Ushoran to a blackened husk in seconds.

'How did you find out?' W'soran said, hoping to keep Ushoran distracted.

The nobleman gave a snort. 'It's my business to know things,' he replied casually. 'What I don't understand is why.'

'Why else?' W'soran exclaimed. 'Because we should have crushed the other cities long ago and built a new empire on their bones! The whole world is ours for the taking, and yet Neferata is content to hide behind her descendants and rule over a city of merchants! She might have had potential once, but killing that fool Khalida broke her nerve.' He waved his hand dismissively. 'Look at this foolishness with the Rasetran boy. Pure idiocy.'

'And how will summoning Nagash's spirit help us?'

The spell-book forgotten, W'soran whirled on Ushoran. 'Think of the knowledge he possessed! He was the only man in the world I would have called my equal. To this day I curse the fates that I was born too late to have journeyed to Khemri and served him!' He spread his hands, taking in the entirety of the room and its shelves of arcane tomes. 'With the knowledge at my command I could bind even a spirit as powerful as his to serve me.' He smiled a death's head smile. 'And then the world would truly change, Lord Ushoran. You may be assured of that!'

Ushoran was silent for a moment, his bland eyes regarding W'soran inscrutably. 'You've been at this a quarter of a century,' he said at last. 'Why haven't you been able to summon him yet?'

The answer stuck in W'soran's throat. It took an effort of will to get it out. 'I don't know,' he said.

'How is that possible?' Ushoran asked.

W'soran turned back to the tome. 'It's not difficult to summon a spirit in general,' he said, searching through the pages once more. 'The breaking of the covenant with the gods resulted in countless numbers of dead souls trapped between the world of the living and the lands of the dead; they wander in a kind of wasteland between the two, desperate for rest.' Suddenly he found the page he'd been seeking. He narrowed his eyes and quickly read over the incantation.

'Summoning a specific spirit is more challenging,' he continued, absently. His fingers traced the necromantic writing on the fragile page. 'One must possess a means of focusing the spell on that one spirit in particular.'

'Can't you just call the spirit by name?' Ushoran asked.

W'soran paused. He'd always taken the Lord of Masks for a dilettante. Perhaps there was more to him than met the eye. 'I suspected the same thing at first,' he continued. 'But either the name doesn't provide a strong enough connection, or the rituals I have to work with aren't as effective as they need to be.'

'All right,' Ushoran said. 'For the sake of argument, what would provide a stronger connection to the spirit?'

W'soran gave a bitter bark of laughter. 'A piece of his body would suffice. Failing that, perhaps a piece of a close family member, like his father.'

'Or his brother?'

W'soran paused. Slowly he turned to regard the Lord of Masks.

'Nagash's brother is entombed in a crypt outside Khemri,' W'soran said.

The Lord of Masks smiled and gave an offhanded shrug. 'That's not so great an obstacle as you might think.'

Now he had W'soran's undivided attention. 'You could do this?'

'If I put the right amount of gold into the right hands... yes, it's possible.'

Was this a trap? W'soran could not be sure. Temptation warred with his sense of preservation. Finally, he concluded that Ushoran already had more than enough to involve Neferata already. He didn't especially need anything more.

'Why would you do this?' W'soran asked.

The Lord of Masks gave another shrug. His expression was unreadable. 'As it stands right now, we're all hostages to fate,' he said. 'Neferata has seen to it that our fortunes are inextricably tied to her own. That can't be allowed to continue. We need to find a way to level the field against her before this affair with young Alcadizzar drags us all to our doom.' He regarded W'soran intently. 'Just be certain you have the means to control what you call up, sorcerer, or Neferata may well turn out to be the least of our problems.'

Nagashizzar, in the 98th year of Ptra the Glorious (-1325 Imperial Reckoning)

At first, the Children of the Horned God responded swiftly to the reports of god-stone buried beneath the great mountain. Within a year, packs of black-garbed scouts were pouring from the first, exploratory tunnel and scuttling silently through the lower tunnels of the fortress. Slowly, warily, they followed the bitter scent of the Horned God's spoor until finally they came upon the first of the active mine shafts. What they discovered in those dimly-lit tunnels sent the first scouts scampering back into the deeps in terror.

Glowing skeletons, they swore to their pack leaders. Skeletons that swung picks and hauled away stone, their bones glowing with god-stone dust. The first scouts who reported this were slain out of hand, for the pack leaders were foul-tempered, suspicious creatures that reacted poorly when they thought they were being mocked. The rest were sent back, and warned to return with proof if they valued their mangy hides.

And so the black-cloaks crept about the mine tunnels, whispering and watching and waiting for their opportunity. In short order, a trio of tunnel-creepers caught sight of a skeleton with a smashed foot that could not keep pace with its companions. As soon as the rest of the work party had disappeared around a bend in the tunnel the ratmen swarmed over the crippled thing. Knives flashed and teeth snapped; within seconds the skeleton had been expertly dismantled. The scouts smashed the thing's skull with a rock for good measure, then stuffed the glowing long bones into their packs and scuttled back into the darkness.

By the end of the day the bones had been snatched from the paws of the lowly scouts and were personally rushed back to the Great City by the pack leaders themselves. The sight of the bones stunned the Grey Seers, who by virtue of their own self-interest were knowledgeable themselves in the mining of god-stone. The bones were ground to powder and mixed with various potions to determine their potency. The results surpassed their wildest expectations. Even assuming that the scouts were wildly exaggerating their reports, the amount of dust found upon the bones hinted at deposits of god-stone beyond anything the Children of the Horned God had ever seen before. At once, the seers knew that the news had to be kept secret from the Council of Thirteen at all costs until they could determine the best way to exploit it. The pack leaders who had brought the bones to the Great

City were rewarded with goblets of poisoned wine, and all records of their testimony were destroyed, but by that point it was already too late. A dozen spies had already drafted coded messages detailing the discovery to their masters on the council.

The Council of Thirteen was the ruling body of the skaven, as the ratmen called themselves, and was comprised of the twelve mightiest lords of their subterranean empire. The thirteenth seat was a symbolic one, reserved for the Horned God himself. The coded messages sped by magical means to the far corners of the empire, and within days there were tangled intrigues afoot as the council members schemed to seize the mountain's riches for their own. Alliances were forged and subsequently betrayed; bribes and counter-bribes changed hands, and acts of assassination and sabotage abounded.

The great lords assembled expeditionary forces and hastily rushed them to the mountain, only to have them collide en route and decimate one another in an escalating series of ambushes and ruthless hit-and-run raids before ever reaching their destination. This went on for twenty-five years before the members of the council surrendered to reason and called for a gathering in the Great City to determine who had the best claim to the mountain's riches.

Of course, *every* lord had the best, most compelling claim. Many even had elaborately forged documents to prove it. Finally, the Seerlord, who was chief among the skaven's grey seers and a member of the council himself, came forward and explained in no uncertain terms how they had received signs from the Horned God that had led them to the mountain, and that the riches buried there belonged to the skaven as a whole rather than any one clan. He concluded his tirade with the very persuasive notion that every day they argued gave the skeletons more time to seize the stone for themselves.

That served to focus the council's attention. Within three more months, after another furious round of politicking, intriguing, bribing and assassinating, the skaven lords had agreed to an elaborate and complicated alliance of clans. Another expeditionary force was assembled, this time comprising warriors from all the great clans and their vassals, and a warlord appointed who would ultimately answer to the council as a whole. According to the terms of the alliance, every last piece of god-stone recovered from the mountain would become the property of the council, and would be shared evenly among the clans.

It was all a bunch of high-handed nonsense of course. Not one of the council members had the slightest intention of sharing such a huge treasure trove, but they were pragmatic enough to wait until they had the plunder in hand before the backstabbing began.

The mighty expeditionary force left the Great City with much fanfare, and Lord Eekrit, the warlord in command of the force, was urged by the council to return with his treasures as quickly as possible. The size of the skaven force was huge: equal contingents from each of the major clans made it the largest army of its kind in their race's history. With so powerful a force under Lord Eekrit's command, the council members felt certain that the looting of the great mountain would scarcely take more than a month to complete.

When Lord Eekrit finally arrived in the deeps of Nagash's mighty fortress, he was greeted by a small colony of scouts who had mapped out much of the mountain's lower tunnels and the routes to each and every mineshaft.

The number of shafts and the estimates of god-stone being pulled from them each day staggered Lord Eekrit. The wealth buried within the mountain was beyond his most avaricious dreams. It would take months to haul it all back to the Great City – perhaps even *years*. The treasure trove tempted him with feverish ambitions. He had visions of conquering the great mountain and claiming it for himself, ruling from the deeps like one of the great lords who sat upon the council; there was ample precedent for such things in his race's past. But the composition of the army made such an ambition nearly impossible. He could count on the rats of his own clan (and only then so far as he could make it worth their while), but the others would turn on him in an instant. The council had put a great deal of cunning into the creation of the expeditionary force, ensuring that they wouldn't be cheated of the treasure. Eekrit roundly cursed their conniving, black hearts!

At least victory would be swift and certain. His scouts assured him that there were only a few thousand skeletons working in the mines, and there wasn't a single one of them that stood a chance against a pack of stalwart clanrats. Lord Eekrit's force was almost fifty thousand strong, not counting the hordes of expendable slaves he could use to soften up any serious resistance. They would overrun the skeletons, clear out the lower tunnels, then push into the lower levels and see where all that precious stone was being taken. Nothing would stand in their way.

The gifts of the Horned God belonged to the skaven, and to them alone.

NAGASH IMMORTAL

DRAMATIS PERSONAE

NAGASHIZZAR

Nagash, the Undying King
Bragadh Maghur'kan, Nagash's captain
Diarid and **Thestus**, lieutenants to Bragadh
Akatha, last of the northern witches

BENEATH THE GREAT MOUNTAIN

Eekrit Backbiter, warlord of Clan Rikek
Hiirc, lord of Clan Morbus, Eekrit's lieutenant
Eshreegar, Master of Treacheries
Lord Qweeqwol, grey seer
Vittrik One-Eye, engine-master of Clan Skryre
Velsquee, grey lord of Clan Abbis
Shireep, scout-assassin
Kritchit, slaver

LAHMIA

Neferata, immortal queen of Lahmia, the first vampire
Ankhat, formerly a wealthy and powerful noble, now a vampire
Ushoran, the Lord of Masks, now a vampire
W'soran, a scholar and necromancer, now a vampire
Zurhas, a dissolute former noble, now a vampire
Abhorash, former captain of the Royal Guard, now a vampire
Naaima, a former courtesan from the Silken Lands, now a vampire
Ubaid, Neferata's chief thrall, Alcadizzar's personal servant
Alcadizzar, prince of Rasetra, hostage to the Lahmian court

THE OTHER CITIES

Ahmenefret, king of Lybaras
Asar, king of Rasetra
Heru, prince of Rasetra and heir to the throne
Khenti, a powerful Rasetran lord and Alcadizzar's uncle
Nebunefre, king of Quatar, Lord of the Tombs
Aten-sefu, king of Ka-Sabar
Inofre, grand vizier and regent of Khemri
Omorose, Queen of Numas
Rakh-an-atum, King of Zandri

UPON THE GOLDEN PLAIN

Faisr al-Hashim, chieftain of the bani-al-Hashim
Muktadir al-Hashim, Faisr's son
Bashir al-Rukhba, a wealthy and powerful chieftain
Suleima, bride of Khsar, the Hungry God, and Daughter of the Sands
Ophiria, Suleima's successor
Nawat ben Hazar, bandit leader

PROLOGUE

MOUNTAIN OF SORROWS

Nagashizzar,
in the 96th year of Geheb the Mighty
(-1325 Imperial Reckoning)

The mountain had many names, stretching back to the dawn of mankind.

The nomadic herders of the far northern steppes knew it as *Ur-Haamash*, the Hearth-stone; in the autumn they would drive their herds south and spend the winter sheltered at the foot of its broad, eastern slope. As the centuries passed and the tribes prospered, their relationship to the mountain changed; it became *Agha-Dhakum,* the Place of Justice, where grievances were settled in trials of blood. Nearly a thousand years later, after a long summer of murder, raids and betrayals, the first high chieftain was proclaimed from the mountain slope, and ever after the tribes knew it as *Agha-Rhul,* the Place of Oaths.

In time, the tribes grew tired of the constant cycle of migration from the northern steppes to the foot of the mountain and the shores of the Crystal Sea. One winter they built their camps just south-west of the *Agha-Rhul* and decided to stay. The camp grew, transforming over generations from a crude settlement into a sprawling, foetid, noisy city. The high chieftain's territory grew to encompass the entire coast of the inland sea and even reached north onto the great plateau, within sight of the bleak steppes from whence the tribes had come.

And then came the terrible night that the sky-stone fell from the heavens, and the mountain's name changed once more.

It came on a night when the awful bale-moon hung low and full in the sky; it arced earthwards on a hissing spear of greenish flame. When it struck the mountain the blow could be heard for miles; the force of the impact reverberated from its slopes and flattened villages on the far side of the Crystal Sea. The great city of the tribes was devastated. Buildings were shattered or consumed in eerie, green flames. Hundreds died, hundreds more suffered hideous diseases and malformations in the months that followed. The survivors looked northwards in terrified wonder at the glowing pillar of dust and ash that rose from the great wound carved in the mountainside.

The destruction was so sudden, so terrible, it could only be the work of a wrathful god. The following day the high chieftain and his family climbed the slope and bowed before the crater, offering up sacrifices to the sky-stone so that their people might survive. *Agha-Rhul* became *Khad-tur-Maghran*: the Throne of the Heavens.

The high chieftain and his people worshipped the sky-stone. They called themselves *Yaghur* – the Faithful – and over time their priests learned how to call upon the power of the sky-stone to perform terrible works of sorcery. The Yaghur became great once more and the high chieftain began to refer to himself as the chosen of the sky-god. His priests anointed him as a king and told the people that he spoke with the voice of the god itself. The priesthood of the sky-stone knew that, as the Yaghur kings prospered, their wealth and power would grow as well.

And so it went, for many generations, until the Yaghur kings grew decadent and mad, and the people suffered daily under their rule. Finally, they could take no more; they forswore their oaths in favour of a new god and cast down the king and his corrupt priesthood. The temple on the mountain was sealed up and the Yaghur went north once more, following the ancient pathways their ancestors had trod thousands of years before in search of a better life. When they spoke of the mountain at all in the years that followed, they called it *Agha-Nahmad*: the Place of Sorrows.

So it remained for centuries. The mountain became a desolate, haunted place, wreathed in poisonous vapours from the immense sky-stone buried within its heart. The Yaghur settled on a great plateau north of the mountain, devolving into a collection of tribes once more. For a time they prospered, but their new god proved to be just as hungry and cruel as the one they had left behind. The Yaghur were wracked by schism and civil war. In the end, those who sought to return to the old ways and worship the god of the mountain were cast out. They found their way back to the shores of the Crystal Sea and tried to eke out a living in the bleak wetlands, offering sacrifices to the mountain and burying their dead at its feet in hopes of winning back the sky-god's favour.

Their deliverance came, not from the great mountain, but out of the desolate lands to the west: a wretched, shambling corpse of a man, clad in dusty rags that had once been the raiment of a king. Feverish, tormented, he was drawn to the power of the sky-stone like a moth to the flame.

He was Nagash the Usurper, lord of the living dead. When the energies of the sky-stone were bent to his will he raised a legion of corpses from the Yaghur burial grounds and slew their priests in a single night of slaughter. He demanded the fealty of the coastal tribes and they bowed before him, worshipping him as the god of the mountain made flesh.

But Nagash was no god. He was something altogether more terrible.

* * *

More than two hundred years after the coming of Nagash, the great mountain had been transformed. Night and day the necromancer's minions had carved a vast network of chambers and passageways deep into the living rock, and mine shafts were sunk deeper still in search of deposits of glowing sky-stone. Seven high walls and hundreds of fearsome towers rose from the mountain slopes, enclosing foundries, storehouses, barracks and marshalling yards. Black chimneys belched columns of smoke and ash into the sky, mixing with the mountain's own vapours to spread a pall of perpetual shadow over the mountain and the sullen waters of the Crystal Sea. Polluted run-off from the mine works and the fortress construction spread across the empty burial fields at the base of the mountain and spilled into the waters of the sea, contaminating everything it touched.

This was *Nagashizzar*. In the tongue of the great cities of distant Nehekhara, it meant 'the glory of Nagash.'

The great hall of the Usurper lay deep within the fortress mountain, carved by skeletal hands from a natural cavern that had never known the light of the accursed sun. They had laboured under the mental guidance of their master, smoothing the walls, laying flagstones of black marble and carving tall, elaborate columns to support the hall's arched ceiling. And yet, for all its artistry, the great, echoing chamber was cold and austere, devoid of statuary or braziers of fragrant incense.

Thin veins of sky-stone glowed from the chamber walls, limning the towering columns and deepening the shadows in between. The only other light came from the far end of the hall, where a rough sphere of sky-stone the size of a melon sat upon a crude bronze tripod at the foot of a shallow dais. A sickly, green glow pulsed from the stone in slow waves, bathing Nagash's throne in shifting tides of light and shadow.

In the tenuous light the necromancer's robed form seemed to be carved from the same dark, unyielding wood as the chair itself. He sat as still as death, his cowled head turned towards the pulsing stone as though meditating upon its glowing depths. The hem of the cowl was stitched with complex chains of arcane symbols and the thick layers of his outer robe were faced with bronze medallions that had been enchanted with potent sigils of protection. The skin of his bare hands was dark and leathery, like that of a long-buried corpse, and the flesh beneath the robes was twisted and misshapen. In place of living eyes, twin green fires flickered coldly from the depths of his cowl, hinting at the cruel, unyielding will that animated the necromancer's grotesque frame.

Once, Nagash had been a mighty prince, scion of a great dynasty in a rich and civilised land. By tradition he had been forced to become a priest, where otherwise he might have risen to become king, and that he could not tolerate. He scorned the gods of his people, calling them parasites and worse, and sought a new path to power. And so he learned the secrets of dark magic, as practised by the cruel *druchii* of the distant north, and combined it with his knowledge of life and death to create something entirely new and terrible. The secrets of necromancy granted him the secret of eternal life, and dominion over the spirits of the dead.

In time, he seized his brother's throne and enslaved his wife, who was nothing less than the blessings of the gods made flesh. He subjugated the entire land, forging a kingdom the likes of which had not been seen in centuries, and *still* it was not enough. He sought to become something still greater… something very like a god.

Finally, the people of Nehekhara could bear the horrors of his rule no longer, and rose up in revolt. The war was more terrible than anything they had experienced before: entire cities were devastated and uncounted thousands were slain. The greatest wonders of the age were cast down and, in the end, even the sacred covenant between the people and the gods was sundered forever, but the power of the Usurper was broken.

With the kingdom in ruins, Nagash fled into the wastelands to the north, where he wandered, wounded and raving, for a hundred years. And there he might have perished at last – bereft of power, and without the life-giving elixir to restore his vitality, the sun and the scavengers eventually would have succeeded where all the kings of Nehekhara could not – but for his encounter with a pack of twisted monstrosities that were neither man nor rat, but some horrible combination of the two. The creatures were foragers of a sort, searching the land for fragments of sky-stone that they took to be gifts from their strange, horned god. Nagash slew the creatures in a wild frenzy; he sensed the raw power of the stone fragments they possessed, and so great was his need that he *ate* them, choking them down his shrivelled throat. And in that terrible moment, the necromancer was reborn.

His search for more of the burning stone, as Nagash called it, had brought him to the shores of the Crystal Sea and the slopes of the ancient mountain. And here, his schemes of vengeance against the world of the living had taken root.

From Nagashizzar he would reach forth to choke the life from the world and rule the darkness that would follow. And the first to die would be Nehekhara, the Once-Blessed Land.

There were tens of thousands of corpses labouring in the halls of the Undying King, each one driven to some degree by a fragment of Nagash's will. The demands upon his awareness created periods of cold reverie, scattering his thoughts like sparks from a flame. Time ceased to have any real meaning; his world turned upon the progress of construction and excavation, of coal fed to the great forges and metal hammered into the shapes of axes, spears and swords. From the moment of its construction, Nagashizzar had been arming for war.

Now the creaking of braided sinew and the groan of ponderous hinges intruded upon his meditations. His attention shifted, coalescing from thousands of scattered motes to focus on the towering doors at the far end of the chamber.

The doors – twin slabs of thick, unfinished bronze more than twenty feet high – parted just wide enough to admit four silent figures. They strode swiftly into the darkness of the hall, moving with purpose and a small measure of deference. Monsters prowled and snuffled in their wake: naked, filthy things whose bodies resembled those of men, but who loped across the stone floor like apes. The creatures kept to the deeper shadows of the chamber, circling the four interlopers like a pack of hungry jackals.

The leader of the four was a tall, broad-shouldered man, clad in bronze and leather armour in the Nehekharan style whose refinements clashed with the warrior's scarred, heavy-browed face. His wild mane of red hair and long, forked beard were streaked with grey; the skin around his deep-set eyes was etched by the weight of many years, but the warrior's thick arms were still corded with muscle. Once he had been Bragadh Maghur'kan, a mighty warlord and leader of the northern tribes that in ancient times had been called the Yaghur. Nagash had conquered the tribes after two and a half centuries of bitter warfare and made them vassals of his growing empire. Now the hill forts of the northern plateau tithed two-thirds of their men to guard the walls of the great fortress until they died and their bones were put to work in the mines.

Beside the former chieftain came Diarid, his chief lieutenant, and a shaven-headed barbarian named Thestus. Unlike Bragadh and Diarid, Thestus had descended from one of the first conquered tribes and had known nothing but servitude to the Undying King, and during the war had risen to command the necromancer's living army. He had been seconded to Bragadh, his former enemy, as soon as the former warlord had bent the knee. It was clear to Nagash that the two men hated and distrusted one another, which was exactly as he wished it.

The fourth member of the group was a woman, and she walked a measured two paces left and one pace behind Bragadh. Unlike the men, she disdained civilised attire, clinging stubbornly to the wool-and-leather robes of her former station. By tradition, the leaders of the northern tribes were counselled by a trio of fierce and cunning witches, who stood at their chieftain's side in times of peace and fought beside them in times of war. Akatha's two sisters had both died in the last battle of the war, when Nagash's warriors broke through the gates of Maghur and defeated Bragadh's exhausted warband. Despite her years, she was still lean and fit. Her narrow face might have been attractive once, but the years at Nagashizzar had hardened it into something like a blade: cold and sharp and eager to harm. Ever since Bragadh had bent his knee in submission she'd worn ashes in her tightly braided hair as a sign of mourning.

Nagash tolerated her continued existence because she tempered her hatred with flinty pragmatism that served to hold the barbarians' headstrong natures in check.

The northmen approached the dais and knelt. Akatha bent her knee slowly, making it yet another gesture of defiance that the necromancer simply ignored.

Joints crackled and muscles creaked as Nagash turned his head to regard Bragadh. With a conscious effort, he willed his lungs to draw breath. It rasped down his throat like wind skirling over stone.

'*What is the meaning of this?*' Nagash said in a sepulchral voice.

Bragadh raised his head slowly and met his master's gaze. Whatever else the barbarian was, he was not without courage. 'I come to speak of your army, great one,' he replied, speaking in badly accented Nehekharan.

Nagash's irritation grew. When Bragadh spoke of the army, he meant his kinsmen. His *living* kinsmen. It galled him to think that he still needed the assistance of flesh-and-blood servants; they reminded him that, despite everything, there were still practical limits to his power.

'*Is there an issue with their training?*' he asked, his broken voice somehow mocking.

Bragadh visibly steeled himself. 'The training *is* the issue, great one,' he replied calmly. 'There is no end to it. There are men within the spear companies that have known nothing else their entire lives.'

The northmen were mighty warriors, but they fought like animals, hurling themselves wildly at their foes without a thought to the larger battle at hand. Nagash wanted soldiers who could fight in disciplined companies and not break the first time they faced a cavalry charge. The northmen were commanded to learn the proper arts of spear and shield, how to march as a unit and respond to trumpet calls just as Nehekharan infantry did. The forges of Nagashizzar worked day and night to arm them with the weapons that were the equal of anything that the great cities could provide, for in time they would march in the vanguard of the vast host that would reduce his former homeland to ruins. Even now, hundreds of years after the war against the rebel kings, the taste of his defeat at Mahrak burned like a hot coal in his guts. It was not enough to defeat the Nehekharans; Nagash wished to destroy them utterly, to crush their armies and grind their cities to dust, so that no one would ever doubt that he was the greatest conqueror to walk the earth since Settra the Magnificent.

'*Are they not learning as they should?*' Nagash rasped. The question was as pointed and as menacing as a poisoned blade.

'They are not learning the ways of *war*, great one,' Bragadh declared. 'They march to the trumpets in their sleep, but most of them have yet to spill a foeman's blood. The purpose of an army is to *fight*.'

The necromancer's burning eyes narrowed to pinpoints. '*The army will fight when I command it,*' he replied. He recalled the Bronze Legion of Ka-Sabar and the companies of Rasetra, his greatest adversary during the war. He had no doubt they could grind the barbarians under their heel. '*Your companies are brittle. They are not ready to stand against veteran troops.*'

'That can only come with experience,' Bragadh countered. 'There are tribes of *rakhads* in the mountains, north of the great plateau. They are fearsome in battle, but as wild and undisciplined as we were, years ago. We could blood the warriors against them, great one. A short campaign, not far from the hill forts. The army would be easy to supply, and we could reap a fine harvest of slaves into the bargain.'

Nagash stared thoughtfully at the barbarian leader. There was some merit to the idea; in his day, the great cities would often stage small-scale raids against one another to give their young nobles the chance to spill some blood and see what battle was like first-hand.

But was that the only reason for Bragadh's request? After twenty-five years, the northmen had recovered the strength they'd lost in the long war against Nagashizzar; now they were better trained and better equipped than they had ever been before. Once they had left the shadow of the great fortress, would they not be tempted to rebel? It was possible, the necromancer thought.

His gaze shifted from Bragadh to his champion, Diarid, then to Akatha. Their faces betrayed no hint of treachery, but that meant little. The northmen were slaves, and what slave didn't dream of taking a knife to his master's throat?

Nagash was silent for a moment, considering. '*How large a force do you propose?*'

Bragadh's shoulders straightened. 'No more than five or six thousand,' he replied quickly, his voice growing eager. 'A warband that size would be small enough to manage in the mountains, yet easily strong enough to deal with a single tribe of greenskins.'

The necromancer nodded slowly. '*Very well,*' he replied. '*How quickly can such a force be assembled?*'

Bragadh smiled wolfishly. 'The warband could be on the march by the end of the day, great one.'

'*Good,*' Nagash replied. '*Then Thestus and the raiding force should be back at Nagashizzar by the end of the summer.*'

Nagash watched Thestus look up in surprise. The lieutenant's gaze shifted from Nagash to Bragadh. A faint grin pulled at the corner of his mouth.

Bragadh frowned, as though uncertain of what he'd just heard. 'Thestus? I don't understand.'

'*Your place is here, training the rest of the army,*' Nagash explained. '*Surely you didn't intend to lead the raid yourself?*'

Bragadh glanced over at his rival. When he caught the grin on Thestus's face, he ground his jaw angrily. After a moment, he said, 'Thestus is... a capable warrior. But he knows nothing of the *rakhads*. The only foes he has ever known have been his own people.'

Thestus bridled at the contempt in the warlord's voice. Nagash chuckled, a sound like grinding stones. '*One foe is the same as another,*' he observed. '*All men die in the same way.*'

'The greenskins are more beasts than men,' Bragadh declared. 'Sending Thestus against them would be a disaster!'

'*Then we will send no one,*' Nagash answered coldly. '*Your warriors will have to wait for battle until we begin the march on Nehekhara.*'

'And when will that be?' Bragadh demanded, forgetting himself.

'*Soon enough,*' Nagash replied. '*Do your work well, and you will hasten the day.*'

The tone of Nagash's reply made it clear that there was nothing more to be said, but Bragadh was not quite done. As the barbarians rose to their feet, he folded his muscular arms across his chest and scowled up at the necromancer.

'Forget the greenskins then, we will continue to train instead,' he said, 'but mark me, a knife can only be sharpened so much before it's worn down to a splinter. Men live to spill the blood of their enemies! If they aren't given a foe to test their strength against, they'll make one for themselves.'

Nagash stared down at the warlord. He leaned forwards slowly, his mummified hands clenching the arms of his throne. '*If there is blood to be spilled at Nagashizzar,* I *will spill it!*' he hissed. '*Caution your warriors not to crave death too much, Bragadh, or I will give it to them!*'

Thestus blanched at the tone in Nagash's ghastly voice. Figures stirred in the shadows: the misshapen forms of the necromancer's flesh-eaters edged towards the barbarians, their talons scraping across the stone floor. Long, black tongues lolled from their fanged mouths, and their pointed, jackal-like ears were pressed flat against their bald, bulbous heads. Wet, rasping growls rose from their throats as they readied themselves to pounce upon the northmen.

The barbarians glared hatefully at the flesh-eaters. Diarid's hand strayed to the hilt of his sword, but Bragadh forestalled him with a curt shake of his head. The warlord tore his gaze away from the monsters and looked up at Nagash.

'I hear, great one,' he said through clenched teeth. 'I hear and obey.'

Satisfied, Nagash leaned back against his throne. '*Then go,*' he said, dismissing the northmen with a wave of one leathery hand. '*And remind your warriors who is master here.*'

Bragadh bowed his head slowly, then turned his back on the flesh-eaters and stomped angrily from the hall. Still growling, the creatures made to follow, but Akatha paused and fixed the pack with a cold-eyed glare that stopped them in their tracks.

Nagash's eyes narrowed upon the witch. Akatha met his stare fearlessly, turning away only a heartbeat before the gesture could be construed as a challenge. She fell into step behind the warlord, never once looking back at the necromancer or his beasts.

The flesh-eaters watched them go, growling deep in their throats.

* * *

With miles of walls and hundreds of feet of crenellated towers, Nagashizzar was the largest and most terrible fortress ever built – but already there was an enemy gnawing at its roots.

Thousands of feet below the necromancer's great hall, in vast, dripping caverns and half-finished galleries, a mighty host had been gathered. The army was so huge it could not be contained in one place. It spread like a sea of dark-furred bodies through the deeps, waiting only for word from its master to flood the upper levels of the fortress and claim its treasures for the glory of the Horned God.

In one such teeming cavern, the master of the army stood atop a roughly hewn dais carved from the living rock and surveyed the stinking multitudes arrayed before him. Shifting, greenish light cast by god-stone lanterns played across a sea of armoured bodies. Naked, pink tails twitched restlessly; long snouts wrinkled, tasting the foetid air. Thin lips drew back from long, chisel-shaped teeth. Hungry, chittering whispers filled the echoing space with a malevolent, surf-like roar.

Eekrit Backbiter, Lord of Clan Rikek and master of the largest army of skaven assembled in the history of the Under-Empire, rubbed his clawed paws together expectantly and thought of the wealth and power that would soon be his. There was more god-stone buried within the mountain than his people had ever seen before. Its discovery had driven the scheming Grey Lords to paroxysms of treachery and murder that had consumed the Great Clans for decades before the Seerlord had finally intervened. The resulting alliance had led to the creation of the expeditionary force, comprised of massive contingents of warriors from each of the twelve Great Clans and their vassals. Arrayed against them – as far as the army's black-robed scouts were aware – were but a few thousand walking corpses toiling in the mines. No one had ever explained to Eekrit's satisfaction just where those corpses had come from, and what exactly they were doing with the god-stone they carved out of the mountain's heart. Old Vittrik One-eye, master of the host's war engines, once surmised that the skeletons might be the remains of slave workers from a long-dead kingdom, animated by energies from the very stones they mined and driven to toil in the mines for all eternity. Eekrit suspected the warlock was talking from the depths of one of his many wineskins, but wasn't so foolish as to point this out to the engine-master.

Truly, Eekrit didn't care who the mountain's skeletal inhabitants were. His warriors alone outnumbered them more than ten to one. The mountain would be his within a matter of hours; *keeping* it was likely to be a far more dangerous task altogether.

The dais was crowded with those who would be all too happy to poison his wine or slip a dagger between his ribs the instant it became profitable to do so. Just to Eekrit's right was his lieutenant, Lord Hiirc, a young and callow little fool from Clan Morbus, currently the most powerful of the Great Clans.

Outwardly, Hiirc didn't seem threatening in the least; he had no experience as a war leader, no especial prowess as a warrior, nor any notable murders attached to his reputation. He was sleek and well fed, his face marked with fine scar-tattoos and his chisel-teeth capped with gold, in the style of the obnoxiously rich. But Eekrit didn't mistake the veritable treasure-trove of god-stone amulets wound about Hiirc's scrawny neck; the idiot glowed from so much refined stone that he hardly needed lantern-bearers to find his way about in the darkness. Of course, Eekrit hadn't gotten a good look at the amulets themselves – that would have been considered rude – but he'd heard enough from his spies to know that the vast majority of them were wards of protection against everything from assassins' knives to ague. There were *clan lords* who weren't so thoroughly encased in protective spells, which spoke volumes to the crafty Eekrit. Clan Morbus wasn't protecting Hiirc; they were guarding his *position* within the army. Eekrit had no doubt that Hiirc's retinue was stuffed to the snout with 'advisors' far more experienced and capable than the young rat lord, who would then direct the course of the campaign from the shadows in the event that Hiirc found himself in control of the army.

Then there was the army's black-robed Master of Treacheries, Lord Eshreegar, who commanded the companies of scout-assassins. The scout-assassins were the army's eyes and ears – and its left-hand dagger, when the situation demanded it. Eshreegar's rats had spent years exploring the tunnels and chambers of the great mountain, until they knew it better than their own spawning-nests; for that reason alone Eekrit had made every effort to favour, flatter and outright bribe his way into Eshreegar's good graces. Eshreegar had accepted the warlord's many gifts with great pleasure and had deigned to provide a few choice secrets about the workings of his rivals, but Eekrit couldn't be certain exactly whose side the Master of Treacheries was on. The warlord had tried to hedge his bets on the march from the Great City by attempting to suborn several of Eshreegar's lieutenants, but the three rats who'd accepted his bribes had managed to suffer gruesome and wildly implausible accidents before the army reached its destination.

Lord Eshreegar crouched to Lord Eekrit's left, in whispered consultation with several of his black-robed dagger-rats. He was tall and lean for one of the rat-people, a veritable giant among the scout-assassins, who as a rule tended to be small, swift creatures. Though his reputation as a stalker and a slayer was legendary among the clans, the expedition to the great mountain was his first in command of a scout cadre. It spoke highly of his connections and reputation among the secretive assassin clans, if not necessarily his ability as a scout leader.

And then there was Lord Qweeqwol, the expedition's representative from the grey seers. Ancient, addled and canker-ridden, mad old Qweeqwol was believed by many to be well past his prime; most of the rat-lords in the Great City assumed that he had been chosen to accompany the expedition as a concession to the Council of Thirteen. Since the Seerlord was the driving force behind the great alliance that had made the expedition possible, the Grey Lords would be exceptionally sensitive to the slightest hint that the grey seers were arranging things to their own personal benefit. Few skaven imagined old Qweeqwol to be much of a threat in that regard.

Eekrit was one of the paranoid few. He couldn't help but take note that Qweeqwol had not only been Seerlord himself for more than *forty* years, he had voluntarily *retired* from that position in favour of Greemon, the current Seerlord. Most skaven thought that only confirmed just how far gone Qweeqwol really was. Eekrit wasn't so certain.

The warlord cast a wary glance over his shoulder at the aged seer. Qweeqwol was at the very rear of the crude dais, his wrinkled paws clutching a thick, gnarled staff of black cypress. The entire length of the staff had been carved with arcane sigils and inlaid with crushed god-stone, so that the air around the wooden shaft shimmered with a haze of magical energy. The white-furred skaven had his back to the proceedings, his pointed snout wrinkling as he studied the striations in the back wall of the cavern. Qweeqwol was muttering to himself, the sibilant words pitched just slightly too low for Eekrit to make out. When the warlord's gaze fell upon him, the seer straightened slightly. His mangy head turned to regard Eekrit; green light played across patches of bald, greying skin grown misshapen with pulsing tumours. Qweeqwol's ears were ragged and frail, as thin and fragile as wet parchment, and where his eyes had once been there were only blasted hollows, ringed by ancient, scarred flesh. Twin orbs of pure, polished god-stone, carved in the likeness of eyes, glowed from those ruined sockets. They fixed Eekrit with an eerie, unblinking stare.

It was all the warlord could do to keep his tail from lashing with unease. A cave-in, he thought. That was what he needed. A shower of sharp rocks on the heads of those who vexed him. Sharp, *poisoned* rocks. Yes, that would do. He should speak to Vittrik. Perhaps something could be arranged.

Lord Vittrik, the engine-master, was nowhere to be seen. Typically the warlock-engineer never strayed far from the glowing, spitting contraptions he and his clan-mates had brought from the Great City. The god-stone machines of Clan Skryre were legendary among the skaven; they were also notably capricious and often as deadly to their operators as to anyone else. All too frequently, the bronze casings of their fearsome weapons simply blew apart in the heat of battle, sending jagged splinters of glowing metal tearing through friend and foe. There were many clan lords who scorned the upstart warlocks and their unstable inventions; others feared them, believing that they could one day become among the most powerful of the clans, if only they could obtain enough quantities of god-stone to produce their machines en masse. Of all the clans, they had the most to gain from the success of the expedition. Eekrit thought that made Vittrik a natural ally, but the warlock-engineer was irritatingly oblivious to his overtures.

Fiery contraptions or no, if the Skryre clanrats couldn't master the simplest intrigues they would very soon find themselves extinct, Eekrit mused.

There was a stir from the scout-assassins. Lord Eshreegar was trying to get his attention, snout raised, paws resting atop one another, tight against his narrow chest. The towering skaven had to hunch his shoulders somewhat to lower his eyes to a level just beneath the warlord's.

'All is in readiness,' Eshreegar murmured. His voice was not unlike the sound of bronze being drawn across a whetstone. 'The scouts await your signal.' Which was a circumspect way of saying, *get on with it.*

Lord Eekrit flicked his ears in agreement, his tail lashing against his heels. He was garbed for war, cased in a heavy hauberk of bronze scales over a thick jerkin of tanned human hide. A heavy cloak, stitched with runes of protection against ambushes and betrayals, lay across his shoulders. An amulet inset with a palm-sized piece of god-stone hung from a golden chain around his neck. It was both a badge of rank and a token of the Horned God's favour. He reached up to stroke its polished surface with the tip of one claw.

Growling thoughtfully, Eekrit regarded the messengers that knelt at the foot of the dais. This would be no field battle, where he could stand atop a piece of high ground and take in the movements of his entire force. This assault would follow dozens of twisting paths through the labyrinthine fortress, directed by a steady flow of messages between Eekrit and his chieftains. He would be no closer to the battle than the dais upon which he now stood.

The warlord rested his paw upon the hilt of his sword. His ears flattened against the side of his skull. With a twitch of his tail, the air about Eekrit grew heady with musk. A stir went through the skaven assembled upon the dais; at the foot of the stone platform the messengers gripped their paws against their chests and raised their snouts. Pink noses twitched; lips quivered, revealing blunt, yellowed teeth.

Lord Eekrit stretched out his free paw. 'Go!' he commanded in a shrill voice. 'Carry my command to the chieftains! Swarm through the tunnels! Tear apart our foes! Seize the treasures of the Horned God! Strike-strike!'

Chittering and squealing, the messengers scattered in a blur of dark cloaks and whipping tails. They raced down narrow lanes between the great war-packs, sending a ripple of excitement through the restless horde. Within seconds, the runners were lost from sight. Then, from the far end of the cavern, came a blood-chilling chorus of bone whistles, rising and falling in an eerie cadence that never failed to set the warlord's fur on end. In response to the call, pack leaders snarled and spat at their warriors. The giant mass of furred bodies began to heave like an angry sea as the army began to move. Thousands of clawed feet scraped on stone; the air shivered with a cacophony of brass bells and clashing cymbals. Lord Eshreegar screeched a command to his scout-assassins and sent them racing after the mass of warriors, their black cloaks flapping about their flanks. The army's many scouts would be responsible for leading the scattered contingents of clanrats through the maze of tunnels towards their objectives. Lord Eekrit turned his attention to one side of the dais and beckoned for a goblet of wine.

The skaven were marching to war.

ONE

WAR IN THE DEEPS

Nagashizzar,
in the 96th year of Geheb the Mighty
(-1325 Imperial Reckoning)

The skaven horde came swarming up out of the bowels of the great mountain, pouring in a flood of snarling, snapping, sword-wielding bodies into the shadowy corridors and noisy mine works of Nagash's fortress. Guided by Lord Eshreegar's scout-assassins, they overran level after level in a headlong dash for the treasures that Nagashizzar contained.

Surprise was absolute. The lowest levels of the fortress were all but deserted, so the skaven were more than halfway to their objectives before they encountered the first of Nagashizzar's skeletal inhabitants. The handful of undead labour parties caught in the horde's path were literally crushed underfoot, trampled by the weight of thousands of charging, brown-furred warriors. The momentum of the charge was so great that the old bones were crushed to powder within moments. By the time the rear ranks passed over the same spot, naught but tendrils of dust remained.

The attackers reached the deepest of the mine shafts within minutes. The dank air trembled with the piping wails of bone whistles and the screech of skaven war cries as the clanrats erupted into the flickering light of the tunnels and fell upon the slow-moving skeletons. The disparity in numbers told against the undead labourers at once: the skaven came at their foes in packs, dismembering the skeletons with contemptuous ease. The initial encounters were over so quickly that actual skaven casualties occurred only in the aftermath, as the clanrats took to squabbling with one another over upturned carts of god-stone nuggets, or found a convenient, out-of-the-way spot to slip a knife into a troublesome rival.

As the invaders rose through the many levels of the fortress, resistance began to slowly increase. More and more, the skaven would burst into a strategic passageway and find a phalanx of skeletons waiting for them. Swords, spears, claws and teeth clashed with picks and shovels, or sometimes nothing more than bony, grasping hands. In each case, the defenders were quickly overrun, scarcely slowing the clanrats' headlong advance.

The first real fighting of the skaven assault occurred in the last, highest mine shafts. Almost two full hours had passed since the attack had begun, and the warriors of Clan Morbus, who had been given the honour of running the farthest to seize the most played-out of the mine shafts, found themselves up against packed ranks of skeletons armed with spears and wearing tattered but functional armour. Here the onslaught faltered, as the clanrats were forced to chew their way doggedly through the press of slow-moving foes. Before long the passageways became choked with heaps of bones and bleeding bodies, but the snarls of the chieftains – and the sharp jab of their blades – kept the clanrats fighting towards their goal.

The skeletons fought to the very last, giving ground only after they had been hacked to bits. The clanrats overwhelmed the remaining defenders at the very entrances to the topmost mine shafts, only to find the sloping tunnels dark and nearly devoid of treasure. The warriors who had been fighting in the front ranks slumped wearily against the tunnel walls and commenced to lick their wounds, leaving the rest to scuttle about in search of some kind of plunder. They cursed and spat, finding only a handful of nuggets in the deepest part of the shaft – which found their way unerringly into the paws of the much larger and cleverer clan chieftains.

It wasn't long at all before small parties of enterprising skaven began exploring the branch-tunnels that led to the upper levels of the fortress. All of the god-stone carved out of the upper shafts had to have been taken *somewhere*, after all. When the first few parties didn't return immediately, the rest of the clanrats took it as a sign that there were valuables up above, and the wretches were helping themselves to as much of it as they could. More small groups skulked off and when *they* didn't return, still more and still larger parties set off after them, until finally the chieftains took notice and took out their ire on the lackwits who remained behind.

That was when they heard the first, faint, blood-curdling howls – shrieks of madness and savagery the likes of which no skaven throat could make – echoing from the upper passageways. Moments later came a bare handful of hysterical clanrats, covered in gruesome wounds that turned foul with poison before the chieftains' very eyes.

A cold wind gusted down the branch-tunnels, filling the mine shaft with the dusty stench of old death. Over the frenzied howls of the approaching monsters came the eerie wail of horns and the *tramp tramp tramp* of thousands upon thousands of skeletal feet.

At first, the destruction of his servants in the lowest levels of the fortress escaped Nagash's attention; accidents occurred from time to time, and what was the loss of ten or twenty skeletons out of the teeming multitudes under his control?

It was only when the labour parties in the lowest and deepest mine shafts vanished that the necromancer realised something was amiss. *Treachery*, Nagash thought at once, immediately suspecting Bragadh and the northmen of some kind of coup. Furious, he drew upon the power of the burning stone, focusing his awareness on the skeletons toiling in the lower levels so he could come to grips with the scope of the attack. Even as he did so, three more of the mine shafts were overrun; dozens more skeletons were destroyed, but in the split-second before they ceased to exist, Nagash caught a glimpse of his foes. They weren't wild-eyed, bearded northmen, however; instead, he saw a seething mass of armoured, dark-furred bodies, wielding short, pointed bronze swords or cruel-looking spears. There was a flash of beady eyes, red with reflected light, and the snapping of curved, chisel-like teeth – and then darkness.

An angry hiss grated from Nagash's leathery throat. The ratmen! An army of them, loose in the deepest parts of his fortress! It had been centuries since he'd set eyes upon the filthy creatures, and then only in small, cowardly little packs. They slunk like jackals through the wastelands to the west of the great mountain, searching for pieces of burning stone. In those days he'd slain each and every one he'd found, whether they carried any stone on them or not. Their very existence offended him.

Somehow they had discovered the great lode of sky-stone buried within the mountain – his mountain – and they had come to lay their disgusting hands on it. Nagash vowed that when he'd slaughtered these interlopers, he would find the stinking holes from whence they'd come and wipe them from the face of the earth. Bragadh and his young warriors would have the blood they were thirsting for after all.

The lash of the necromancer's will resounded across the length and breadth of the fortress, and tens of thousands of skeletons swayed like wheat against its invisible weight. They answered the call to arms in silence, save for the creak of dried skin or the clatter of bone.

Not long afterwards came the ominous tolling of alarm gongs from the tallest towers of the fortress. The deep, shivering notes reverberated through the air and sent a chill down the spines of the living. Across dozens of marshalling grounds, companies of northern warriors paused in their training and looked skywards, wondering at the sound. How could there be an alarm when there was no enemy to be seen for leagues in any direction?

In the shadowy recesses of the great fortress, packs of Yaghur raised their heads and added their howls to the spine-tingling chorus. The noise rolled like an avalanche down the mountain slopes and across the grey sea, where it reached the ears of hundreds more of the flesh-eaters. Entire tribes emptied from their foetid lairs, loping like apes across the reeking, marshy ground in response to their master's call.

Within the fortress, living messengers ran back and forth from the great hall, carrying Nagash's commands to his barbarian troops. Meanwhile, the necromancer threw every available skeleton he could into the ratmen's path to slow them down while he assembled his spearmen into companies near the surface.

His rage grew as one mine shaft after another fell to the swarming creatures; their numbers were vast, easily as large as any Nehekharan army, and he had to concede that the assault was being carried out with speed and skill. Comparing the rate of their advance to the marshalling of his forces on the upper levels, Nagash could see that the ratmen would overrun all of his mine shafts – and possibly even reach the upper levels themselves – before his army was ready to act. Working quickly, he despatched several large companies into the upper mine shafts to slow down the enemy advance and keep the monsters bottled up below ground. Nagash meant to keep the ratmen penned up in the tunnels, where he could grind the horde to pieces under the relentless advance of his spearmen. He had no need of cunning manoeuvres or elaborate stratagems; Nagash planned to come at the trespassers head-on, crushing the ratmen under the weight of his troops.

The necromancer filled the upper tunnels with spearmen and hundreds of slavering flesh-eaters, then despatched Bragadh and his warriors to seal off the surface exits of each of the mountain's mine shafts. Any attempt by the ratmen to escape his advance – or outflank him along the surface – would be met with a thicket of barbarian spears. All too slowly, the units of his army moved into position, like pieces on a gaming board, while his rearguard troops in the upper mine shafts were slowly but surely cut down by the advancing ratmen. When the invaders finally broke through and swarmed into the mine shafts, Nagash turned his attention upon the Yaghur. Whispering words of power, he exerted his mastery over the foul creatures and stirred them to action.

Gripped by the necromancer's unyielding will, the flesh-eaters crept silently down the dimly lit tunnels towards the invaders. Though they could not be controlled as completely or as easily as the true undead, they were swifter, stronger and far tougher than his regular troops and their constant hunger made them keen predators. At his command, the flesh-eaters found places along the tunnels to lie in ambush for any advance parties of ratmen that ventured their way.

The Yaghur didn't have long to wait. The first, small scouting parties were swiftly overwhelmed, succumbing to the flesh-eaters' filthy talons and powerful jaws. Behind them came still more of the invaders, in ever-larger and less-cautious bands, until finally there were so many of the rat-creatures to contend with that the Yaghur couldn't possibly take them all at once. A handful of survivors managed to escape the flesh-eaters' clutches, fleeing back the way they'd come. With a mental command, Nagash ordered the first of his companies to advance, intending to strike before the clanrats could organise a proper defence.

Once again, the Yaghur struck first. The blood-spattered beasts erupted from the branch-tunnels hard on the heels of the dying ratmen, sowing terror and confusion through the enemy's ranks. The air shook with the baying of bone horns and the tread of marching feet. When the first companies of spear-wielding skeletons emerged into the upper mine shafts the stunned invaders lost their nerve and fled, trampling one another in their haste to escape. From his throne in the great hall many levels above, Nagash smiled cruelly and poured the energy of the burning stone into his lead companies, speeding their limbs and pressing hard upon the ratmen's heels.

The tide of battle, at first so overwhelmingly in favour of the ratmen, turned just as swiftly against them. The invaders fled back into the lower levels, spreading panic amongst their fellows. The necromancer's forces reclaimed one mine shaft after another; they slew so many ratmen in the process that they couldn't keep up with the survivors in the corpse-choked tunnels. The Yaghur, provided with a feast the likes of which their kind hadn't seen in centuries, required constant pressure to keep them focused on the battle at hand, slowing the pursuit still further.

Lord Eekrit was eating fermented musk-berries and preparing a letter to inform the Grey Lords of his great victory when the first of Lord Eshreegar's scout-assassins returned to the great cavern. At first, he paid no mind to their near-frantic whispers as they reported to the Master of Treacheries. The scouts had been ordered to continue their explorations of the levels beyond the mine shafts, in hopes of finding where the skeletons were storing the god-stone. From the sound of their voices, he surmised that what they'd found was far greater than anyone had expected.

The first intimation that something was wrong came not from Eshreegar, but mad Lord Qweeqwol. The old seer limped up next to Eekrit and leaned in close. 'It's begun,' he hissed, his scarred nose twitching. 'Time for battle. Fight-fight!'

Eekrit curled his lip in a bemused scowl. What in the Horned One's name was he babbling about? He glanced up, and caught sight of Lord Eshreegar. The Master of Treacheries looked like he'd swallowed a live spider.

The warlord glanced down at the bowl of half-eaten berries in his left paw. On impulse, he stuffed the remainder in his mouth and gulped them down. Thus fortified, he went over to the scouts. The black-robed underlings shrank back at his approach, their tails lashing apprehensively. At once, the fermented berry juice curdled in Eekrit's guts.

'What is going on?' the warlord asked, his voice deceptively mild.

The Master of Treacheries turned slowly to regard his commander. The skaven's whiskers twitched.

'There... ah,' Eshreegar began. 'There is a small problem.'

Eekrit's tail twitched. 'What kind of problem?'

'Ah...' the Master of Treacheries considered his reply carefully. 'It's possible there are more skeletons here than we thought.'

The warlord's beady black eyes narrowed on Eshreegar. 'How many more?'

Eshreegar stole a glance at his minions. The scouts focused their gaze on the cavern floor, as though contemplating an escape tunnel.

'Well. Perhaps... five or six,' Eshreegar said weakly.

The warlord's ears flattened against his skull. 'You and your rats have had years to scout this place,' Eekrit hissed. 'There were two thousand of the skeletons, you said. And now you tell me you missed five or six hundred more?'

Eshreegar seemed to shrink in on himself. His head drooped below the level of the warlord's snout. His whiskers twitched and he mumbled something under his breath.

'What was that?' Eekrit demanded. 'Explain yourself!'

'Not five or six hundred,' the Master of Treacheries said in a defeated voice. 'Five or six *thousand*.'

The warlord's eyes widened. 'What?'

'I said–'

Eekrit cut him off with an upraised paw. 'I *heard* what you said,' the warlord snarled. 'How... where...' He paused, breathing deeply. His paw clenched, as though ready to claw out Eshreegar's eyes. 'Where are they now?'

Speaking quickly, his voice pitched barely above a squeak, Eshreegar related what he'd heard from his scouts. 'Clan Morbus is in-in full retreat,' he finished. 'The upper shafts have been retaken.'

'And what of Rikek and Halghast?' the warlord demanded. They would be the next clans in line if the skeletons continued their descent.

Eshreegar spread his paws helplessly. 'There is no-no word yet.'

'Find. Out.' Eekrit growled.

The scouts leapt to obey without waiting for a word from their master. As soon as they were gone, the warlord stepped close to Eshreegar, until the two skaven were snout-to-snout. He sensed an opportunity here.

'The Council will want an explanation,' Eekrit hissed.

Eshreegar made a half-hearted shrug. 'One skeleton looks much like another,' he said.

'It is your business to tell the difference!' the warlord snapped. 'Do you imagine the Grey Lords will be sympathetic, Eshreegar?'

'No.'

Eekrit nodded. 'Just so. You will need allies if you hope to keep-keep your hide.'

The Master of Treacheries nodded. 'Of course,' he replied. 'I understand.'

The warlord nodded. 'Good. Then fetch a map. *Now*.'

Eshreegar gave a quick nod of obeisance and turned to bark orders at a nearby underling. The warlord folded his paws against his chest and began to pace, his mind working quickly.

The situation could still be salvaged, Eekrit thought. Five or six thousand more skeletons were an unwelcome surprise, but his force still outnumbered the enemy more than ten to one. That didn't even count the thousands of slaves attached to the army – fodder that he could use to bury the attackers by sheer weight of numbers if he wished.

So far, the enemy had provided him with a solid alliance with Eshreegar, and bloody humiliation for Clan Morbus. That would keep Hiirc and his minders in check for the foreseeable future.

A pair of slaves scuttled up onto the dais, carrying a large, rolled parchment between them. Eekrit smiled to himself as they unrolled the map at his feet.

Yes, the warlord thought. This might actually turn out better than he'd hoped.

Resistance increased steadily the deeper Nagash's forces went. The ratmen holding the lower mine shafts were fresher and forewarned of the counter-attack by streams of fleeing survivors from the upper levels. Nagash's warriors began to encounter more prepared defences and formed companies of warriors holding key tunnel junctions leading to the lower shafts.

Nagash drove his troops remorselessly forwards, determined to cleanse Nagashizzar of the invaders. When his companies encountered heavy resistance, he simply ground the ratmen down; gladly trading one of his warriors for one of theirs, until finally the creatures broke and ran. He had fewer of the Yaghur to call upon now; most of the surviving flesh-eaters were either too gorged or too exhausted to be much use. So far, the northmen had successfully held the ends of the mine shafts so that the retreating ratmen couldn't escape the necromancer's trap. With almost half of the mountain's mine shafts back in his hands, he had a sizeable reserve force of living infantry to call upon, but he was loath to trust them unless he absolutely had to.

What troubled Nagash was that he hadn't yet plumbed the depths of the enemy force. Every army had its breaking point, he knew; an invisible line where its leaders knew that they'd given all they had and it was time to pull back or risk destruction. Gauging an enemy's breaking point was a fine art, one that separated competent generals from great ones. Nagash knew without doubt that he was a great leader, but this subterranean battlefield offered him no clues as to the dispositions of his foe.

Though he had a god's-eye view of the battlefield from his own troops' perspective, he had no idea what the ratmen had waiting for him around the next bend in the tunnel. He'd expected fierce resistance in the upper levels of the mountain, then less organised resistance as he broke through the enemy's front line and encountered his reserves. But there didn't seem to be a front line that he could discern, not in the manner of a traditional field battle. This was an entirely different style of warfare – one that he began to suspect the ratmen were better capable of fighting than he was. They certainly seemed to know the layout of the lower tunnels as well as he did, which led him to wonder just how long they'd been hiding down there, biding their time until they chose to strike.

Hours passed and the fighting wore on. Nagash breached one defensive line after another. Now more than three-quarters of the way through the lower levels of the fortress, his troops had reclaimed all but a handful of the newest, deepest - and therefore richest - mine shafts. The enemy resistance grew clever and more determined. His lead packs of flesh-eaters were lured into five separate ambushes and badly mauled by dark-robed rat-creatures wielding knives and razor-edged obsidian darts, then a company of ratmen attempted to launch an attack at his flank through a network of half-finished tunnels. Or they *had* been half-finished, the last time he'd turned his attention to that part of the under-mountain. It appeared that the invaders had actually spent some time and effort in expanding the tunnels, displaying a kind of instinctive engineering skill that such monsters had no right to possess.

The advance began to lose momentum against a seemingly endless tide of screeching, furry bodies. His skeletons were within a few hundred yards of the next mine shaft, but no matter how many of the creatures his warriors killed, it seemed like three more sprang up to take their places. The necromancer's anger grew. For the first time, he regretted not entering the battle himself - but in the close confines of the tunnels, his sorcery would only be effective on localised portions of the battle. And as it stood now, he was literally miles from the front lines, with no swift way to reach the centre of the action.

Nagash leaned back against his throne and once again considered summoning the northmen. A flanking attack down the mouth of the lower mine shafts could well tip the balance... but then he remembered the steady look of defiance on Akatha's face, and his paranoia asserted itself once more.

He redoubled his attack on the rat-creatures, fuelling the lead companies with still more sorcerous power. The invaders had to be near the limits of their strength, he told himself. They *had* to be.

The counter-attack couldn't keep going much longer, Eekrit told himself. There *had* to be an end to the damned skeletons, sooner or later.

Hopefully sooner, the warlord thought nervously as he studied Eshreegar's map. The fighting was now less than five levels away. He fancied that if he opened his ears fully he could hear the faint sounds of battle, though he knew that it was just his imagination.

At least with the battle close at hand he had a better idea of how things were progressing. A steady stream of messengers were running to the front lines and making it back to report within minutes. He doubted the master of the damned skeletons had half so good a picture of the battlefield as he did.

The enemy had pushed his clanrats nearly all the way back to the caverns where they'd started from. At last count, he had only five mine shafts still in his possession, and one of those was about to fall. If he didn't manage to turn things around very quickly, he might as well ask Eshreegar to put a poisoned knife between his eyes. Better that than report his defeat to the Council.

The warlord turned to the Master of Treacheries. The counter-move had been Eshreegar's idea; no doubt if it succeeded, he would try to use it to balance his utter failure to determine the actual size of the enemy force. Unfortunately for him, Eekrit was increasingly certain that the revised estimate of five or six thousand skeletons was still woefully inadequate – not to mention the reports of howling, ogre-like creatures that seemed to accompany the skeletal spear companies like packs of jackals. When all this was over, Eshreegar would have a great deal of explaining to do, Eekrit thought.

'What are the reports from the slaves?' he asked.

Eshreegar paused for a whispered query to one of his scouts. With a curt nod, he turned back to Eekrit. 'All is in readiness,' he replied.

Eekrit gave the map one last look and then reached his decision. It was now or never.

'Send word to Clan Snagrit,' he ordered. 'Begin the retreat.'

The change in the tempo of the fighting was palpable. For more than an hour, the ratmen had been fighting tooth and nail – sometimes literally – to keep the skeletons from forcing their way into the next mine shaft. The branch-tunnels were choked with pieces of bone and heaps of furry bodies, and no matter how hard Nagash pushed his troops, the advance ground inexorably to a halt.

Both sides hammered at one another without pause, until the course of the battle was measured in mere feet gained or lost. And then, slowly but surely, the pressure against the skeletons began to ebb. First the ratmen were pushing hard against the skeletons, trying to drive them back; then their momentum dwindled until they were at a virtual standstill. It was only minutes later, when the invaders actually began to retreat back the way they'd come, that Nagash began to suspect that the ratmen had finally reached their breaking point.

The invaders withdrew quickly, but in fairly good order, careful not to create any gaps that Nagash could turn to his advantage. That convinced him the retreat wasn't a feint; had they been trying to lure him into an ambush, he would have expected to see a tantalising gap open in their lines to lure him into a killing zone. Sensing that the endgame was near, Nagash drove his companies forwards all the harder, pressing the enemy across the entire front in hopes of creating so much strain that it finally shattered. Then the slaughter would well and truly begin.

Nagash's companies reclaimed yet another mine shaft. There were only four left in enemy hands, the excavations begun so recently that they had yet to commence full operation – in fact, the mine shafts themselves had yet to be extended all the way to the surface of the mountainside. This served to limit the avenues of approach and channel the retreating invaders into fewer and fewer tunnels, which in turn permitted Nagash to focus his battered forces into larger, more powerful columns. The exhausted ratmen would have no reprieve as the undead warriors chased them inexorably into the deeps.

Level by level, the skeletal companies drove the ratmen back. From time to time, the enemy lines would halt and resistance would stiffen, but never for more than a few minutes at a time. Nagash's certainty grew: clearly the enemy's troops were exhausted and they had no reserves to call upon. Sooner or later, the leader of the ratmen would be forced to either sacrifice a rearguard so the rest of his army could escape, or else find a place to make a doomed, final stand.

Within an hour, Nagash's troops were closing in on the next mine shaft. Here the chambers and passageways were rudimentary in the extreme. Nagash's past philosophy of expansion was predicated on one thing only; access to the mountain's deposits of burning stone. His labourers first created exploratory tunnels to locate sources of *abn-i-khat*, then created galleries and chambers around the tunnels in anticipation of mine work to come. The necromancer knew that there were numerous natural tunnels and caverns throughout the lowest levels, as well as half-finished spaces that the enemy had been using for some time. If the ratmen hoped to outflank him through one of these natural approaches, he would be ready for them.

The spear companies reached the branch-tunnels leading into the fourth mine shaft and pressed onwards, forcing the ratmen back into the wide, echoing tunnel. The invaders continued to fall back across the dimly lit mine shaft – and then halted with their backs to the branch-tunnels at the far side. The loathsome creatures stood shoulder to shoulder, brandishing their weapons and snarling defiantly at the advancing skeletons.

Nagash smiled, already anticipating the final battle. He poured troops into the mine shaft, taking full advantage of the space to bring his greater numbers to bear against the enemy. No matter how fierce the ratmen thought they were, the fight would be a short one.

The two sides came together, not with a flurry of war-horns and the thunder of charging feet, but with a dreadful, appalling slowness. The ratmen watched the thicket of spears press in about them, one slow, implacable step at a time. Many became unnerved by the warriors' soulless advance, but there was nowhere left to run. Their angry snarls turned to panicked whimpers, then to shouts and screeches of terror as the bronze spear-points closed in.

In seconds, the screams and shouts of the living were drowned by the rising clatter of metal and wood, as swords and axes beat against spear-shafts and the rims of bronze-edged shields. Ratmen fell, pierced through the neck and chest, their blood slicking the stones. Bones cracked like brittle branches. The invaders had already learned to focus their attacks against the legs of the undead warriors; they toppled to the tunnel floor, rendering their spears all but useless and hindering the advance of the troops behind them.

More of the ratmen threw themselves desperately at Nagash's host. They came rushing through narrow passageways and rough-hewn tunnels, probing for a way to reach the army's flanks, but in each case their path was blocked by a phalanx of skeletal troops. Soon, Nagash knew, the ratmen would realise that there was nowhere left to turn and that defeat was imminent.

The enemy fought hard, matching Nagash's troops blow for blow. The battle raged across a two-hundred-yard length of mine shaft and at a score of smaller side-tunnels to either flank. The ebb and flow of the fighting absorbed the necromancer's full attention – so much so that by the time he saw the ratmen's trap, it was already too late.

To either flank of the undead advance, and a full two levels *behind* the front rank of the army, rough stone walls burst apart under the frantic claws of digging ratmen. Years before, the invaders had begun expanding side-tunnels in anticipation of their own mining operations in the depths of the mountain. Now their tunnelling masters skilfully turned those unfinished passageways to deadly knives aimed at the centre of the skeletal horde.

The ratmen broke through into the flanks of Nagash's forces at almost a dozen points. Whips cracked and a storm of snarling, snapping rat slaves tore into the packed ranks of skeletal warriors. Armed with picks, shovels, heavy rocks and bare paws, the slaves rushed in low, tearing at the skeletons' legs and lower spines. The skeletons, packed tightly into the narrow tunnels, couldn't bring their weapons to bear against the sudden onslaught and losses began to mount.

The first indication Nagash had of trouble was a sudden surge in ferocity from the ratmen inside the mine shaft. Where moments before the invaders seemed to be locked in a last, desperate stand, now they pushed forwards against the undead ranks with steadily mounting fervour. With sheer, bloody-minded ferocity the ratmen began to drive wedges into the skeletal companies. They scrambled over heaps of their fallen kin, their feet and legs coated in crushed bone and gore, and began hacking at every bony limb they could reach. Skeletons collapsed by the score and were crushed underfoot as the ratmen carved deeper and deeper into the enemy ranks.

What shocked Nagash more than the wild counter-assault wasn't the attack itself, as much as the waves of attackers that came pouring out of the tunnels and into the mine shaft. These warriors weren't the exhausted, desperate creatures he'd expected; they were fresh troops, well armed and eager for a fight.

For just a moment, the necromancer was incredulous. Somehow, somewhere, he had made a miscalculation. Thinking swiftly, he ordered his troops to redouble their efforts, determined to swallow up the enemy's counter-attack and smother it by sheer weight of numbers.

Nagash's awareness swept backwards, along the arteries that supplied his advance. It was then he saw the enemy's flanking attack and realised how he had been duped. The sheer scale and complexity of the ambush had been greater than anything he'd imagined his foes to be capable of. Worse, their numbers seemed endless.

The enemy had chosen to face his troops inside the mine shaft for the very reason that it would draw in as many of Nagash's warriors as possible. The branch-tunnels created choke points both into *and* out of the long tunnel, and now the pincers of the enemy's flanking movement had effectively cut them off from reinforcement. That left fully a third of his army isolated, and the rest strung out along miles of connecting tunnels where they couldn't bring their full strength to bear.

As Nagash watched, the enemy's flank attacks poured warriors into the tunnels in staggering numbers. They fought down the connecting tunnels in both directions, tightening the noose around the skeletons trapped inside the mine shaft. Immediately, Nagash ordered skeletons from the upper levels to push forwards, trying to batter their way through the enemy positions and link back up with the front lines, but he could already sense the tide of battle starting to flow away from him once more. After another moment's hesitation, he came to a galling decision.

The necromancer broadcast his orders to the horde. Within the mine shaft, half of the warriors formed a rearguard to hold the attacking ratmen at bay, while the rest began to withdraw back down the branch-tunnels towards the enemy's flanking units. He had to salvage what forces he could and form a defensive line until he knew the full extent of his enemy's dispositions.

It took almost three hours for his warriors to fight their way out of the trap. The enemy's flanking attacks were finally driven back, but not before the skeletal rearguard had been overwhelmed. The ratmen surged forwards, scrambling over heaps of shattered bones, and harried the withdrawing skeletons until they fetched up against fortified defensive positions three levels above. The invaders hurled themselves at the fortifications three times, only to be repulsed with heavy losses. After the third attack, the survivors paused, muttering and snarling to one another as they considered their next move. Nagash used the time to further reinforce his lines and prepare for more flanking attacks, but after half an hour the invaders slowly withdrew to their own hastily-formed lines.

The first battle of Nagashizzar had reached its bloody, inconclusive end.

TWO

MANIFEST DESTINIES

Lahmia, the City of the Dawn,
in the 97th year of Djaf the Terrible
(-1320 Imperial Reckoning)

Old Jabari grinned and picked up the wooden cup with one gnarled hand. He gave it a good shake, rattling the ivory dice inside. Alcadizzar had learned to hate that sound.

The scarred Rasetran bent forwards and squinted into the depths of the cup. 'Hmm,' he said cheerfully. 'Interesting.'

Alcadizzar folded his arms, glaring at the dispositions of his army. Four spear companies were arrayed in a slightly curving line before the oasis, their left flank anchored by the ruins of the old caravan post, their right covered by his chariots, situated on a low dune to the south-east. His archers still held the caravan post, despite repeated attacks by enemy skirmishers. The survivors of the last attack had retreated to the edge of a dune to the north-west, where it looked like they might be re-forming for another attack. In the centre, his companies were hard-pressed by enemy infantry, and his fourth company was on the verge of breaking. His reserves - a single company of spearmen - waited in the shade of the palm trees surrounding the oasis. He hesitated on committing them just yet, for the enemy cavalry had yet to make an appearance.

Jabari set the cup aside and plucked a wooden figure from the tray at his side. 'There's a thundering of hooves off to your left!' the tutor declared. 'Bronze glints in the noonday sun! There are shouts and confused cries from the ruins!' The Rasetran leaned across the wide sand table and placed the elegantly carved figure of a mounted horseman on Alcadizzar's flank - *behind* the ruins of the caravan post.

The prince's eyes widened. 'Where in the name of all the gods did *they* come from?'

Jabari shrugged his wide shoulders in feigned bewilderment, but his deep-set eyes glinted with mischief. In his prime, he had been Rasetra's

Master of Horse, and had ridden in more than a dozen campaigns against the city's foes. He pointed a scarred finger at the ragged, knife-like cleft carved through the sand off to the left of the ruins. 'Given the shouts of surprise coming from the ruins, I'd hazard a guess that they came galloping out of that wadi.'

'What? No, that's not possible!' Alcadizzar sputtered. 'Look – the far end of the wadi's in full view of my archers! We'd have seen them coming!'

Jabari nodded sagely. 'So it would seem, so it would seem,' he replied agreeably. 'Of course, there could also be a narrow branch connecting it to that larger wadi further north,' he pointed out, indicating a much wider cleft that curved behind the dunes further north. 'No way to tell from here, of course. Perhaps if your scouts had explored the area more thoroughly the day before you might have learned for certain.'

Alcadizzar sighed. 'Very well,' he grumbled. 'How many?'

Jabari smiled and picked up the cup again. The dice rattled. 'Thousands, your aides say. Many thousands!'

The prince's eyes narrowed suspiciously. Jabari always portrayed his aides as credulous nitwits. It hardly seemed realistic. He studied the sand table for a moment. The carved mahogany figure representing him and his retinue was positioned on a low dune just behind the oasis, dangerously close to the swift-moving enemy horsemen. 'All right. How many can *I* see?'

Jabari shook the dice cup. 'You can't tell. Too much dust.'

Of course, Alcadizzar thought sourly. He studied the battlefield a moment longer, then nodded. 'Shift the reserve company to the left, double-quick, and order them to attack the enemy horsemen.'

'Very well–'

'And I send *two* runners instead of one, to make certain that the order gets through,' Alcadizzar interjected. He wasn't going to make *that* mistake again.

Jabari's smile widened. 'I hear and obey, great one,' he replied. The tutor rattled the dice in the cup a few more times, considered the results, and then began shifting the positions of the troops on the table.

The prince reached for the goblet of watered wine resting on the edge of the table and sipped thoughtfully, his gaze wandering to the tall windows that lined the western wall of the chamber. There were few clouds in the sky, despite the summer season; the late afternoon sun outlined the dark hills beyond Lahmia's walls and sent shafts of mellow, golden light through the tall windowpanes. A good day to be riding, he thought wistfully, watching a caravan heading out through the city's western gate. The traders were leaving very late in the day; possibly there had been delays loading their goods, or perhaps they'd encountered difficulties obtaining the proper permits from the city magistrates. As it was, they would be lucky to make it up the winding hill roads and onto the edge of the Golden Plain by nightfall. From there, it would be a week to cross the plain – providing they had no trouble from the bandit gangs that roamed the area – and then on to Lybaras, or Rasetra, or even further west, past forlorn Mahrak and through the Valley of Kings to the great cities of the west. They could even be heading for Khemri, he realised, and felt a sharp pang of envy.

Some day, Alcadizzar told himself. Some day he would be ready. But *when*?

All roads in Nehekhara led to Lahmia, the opulent City of the Dawn. The wealth of the great city and the wise leadership of its rulers had led the Nehekharans out of the dark age wrought by Nagash the Usurper; indeed, the bloodline of its ruling dynasty was worshipped as the last vestige of divinity in a land that had been rendered bereft of its gods.

Lahmia's power and influence was so preeminent that it had become custom for the ruling families of the other great cities to send their young heirs to be educated at the City of the Dawn. They were borne to the great city, amid much pomp and ceremony, as soon as they were old enough to travel – all except for Alcadizzar, that was. His mother Hathor, Queen of Rasetra, had journeyed to Lahmia while he was still in the womb; her pregnancy had been fraught with trouble and the royal midwives were doubtful that she would deliver her child. Desperate, the queen turned to the only source of aid left to her, the Temple of Blood. There, she held a vigil in the presence of the goddess, praying for the prince's life.

Before the dawn – or so the story went – the high priestess of the temple came to Hathor, saying that her pleas had been answered. The goddess had spoken, and her child would survive. Every week afterwards, she was brought to the temple, where she was given an elixir to drink that had been blessed by the goddess herself. Two months later, almost to the very hour that the high priestess first spoke to her, Hathor gave birth to Alcadizzar. The queen had remained with him at the temple for a full year afterwards; then she placed him in the care of the Lahmian royal household and returned to Rasetra. Alcadizzar had never met his father, King Aten-heru, nor did he have any memories of his mother, who died in childbirth two years after returning home.

The insistent rattling of dice disturbed the prince's reverie. Alcadizzar turned back to the table and frowned. Jabari smiled, shaking the cup. 'What are your orders, great one?' he asked.

On the battlefield, Alcadizzar's reserve company had obeyed its orders with surprising speed, altering their formation to the left and charging over the open space behind the oasis to make contact with the oncoming enemy horsemen. Now both units were locked in melee. The spearmen had suffered the worst of it so far, having borne the brunt of the cavalry's charge, but now the horsemen's momentum was exhausted. Given time, the infantry would gain the upper hand.

Unfortunately, time was not a luxury that Alcadizzar's fictional army possessed. As the cavalry attack began, the rest of the enemy force renewed its attacks all along the length of the battle-line. The skirmishers had rallied and once more charged the caravan post, locking his archers in brutal hand-to-hand combat. In the centre, the enemy spear companies were driving forwards, despite terrible casualties, and his fourth company had broken at last. The survivors were retreating into the oasis and the triumphant enemy company was swinging to the right, preparing to attack his third company in the flank.

The prince took in the situation at a glance. His army was balanced on a knife edge. If he didn't shore up the centre, he was finished. 'Order the chariots off the hill,' he said to Jabari. 'Have them screen their movements behind the oasis, then swing around and charge the enemy spear company on our flank. I also send one of my senior nobles to rally the broken spear company and hold them in reserve inside the oasis.'

Jabari nodded sagely and rattled his dice. He peered into the cup. 'There is a problem,' he replied.

Alcadizzar gritted his teeth. There were *always* problems. 'What now?'

Jabari pointed to his reserve company. 'The commander of the unit has been killed, as well as his champion. The company is wavering.'

The prince leaned against the edge of the table, looming over the two innocuous-looking wooden figures. If the reserve company broke, the cavalry would be free to charge his chariots, preventing them from saving his centre. He had to either rally the reserve company somehow, or stop the horsemen. Preferably both. Unfortunately, he didn't have anyone left to commit to the fight.

Alcadizzar paused. That wasn't entirely true. He reached over the map and picked up a small, unassuming piece of wood carved in the shape of a sphinx, its fearsome head crowned with a king's headdress.

'I and my retinue will attack the enemy horsemen in the flank,' the prince said. He repositioned the sphinx next to his embattled reserve unit.

Jabari rubbed his weathered chin. 'Risky,' he said. 'Very risky. You could get a sword in your guts. And there's no one giving orders to the rest of the army while you're off playing soldier.'

'The rest of the army's committed.' He shrugged. 'Time for me to do my part.'

The old Master of Horse shook his head. 'A fine thing to say when you're talking about pieces of wood,' he grumbled, but for a moment there was a glint of admiration in Jabari's eye. 'Very well, great one. On your head be it.'

The dice rattled. Alcadizzar's tutor contemplated the results, like a long-lost oracle. First he moved the prince's chariots off the hill and placed them against the rear ranks of the flanking enemy spear company. Then he bent over the map and plucked Alcadizzar's archers from the caravan post.

'The enemy's skirmishers have taken the caravan post,' he told the prince. 'There's no way to tell how many of them are left, because none of yours lived to tell the tale.' Before Alcadizzar could protest, Jabari turned his attention to the chariots. 'Your charioteers have taken the enemy spear company by surprise; their initial charge has wrought terrible carnage on their rear ranks. So far, however, the enemy continues to hold their ground.'

Then the old tutor turned to the battle against the enemy horsemen. 'Your charge here likewise surprised the enemy,' he said. 'You and your bodyguard have penetrated the formation, but your foes are putting up a stiff fight. You are swiftly surrounded.'

Alcadizzar's eyes narrowed on Jabari. 'What about the spearmen?'

Jabari nodded. 'Your appearance has rallied them. They are pushing back hard against the enemy horsemen. Will you withdraw at this point?'

The prince frowned. 'Of course not!'

Jabari shrugged. He raised the cup. Dice rattled. He thought for a moment, then sighed.

'Most of your bodyguards have fallen, struck down by enemy swords and axes,' he said. 'You've been wounded, but remain in the saddle. Your spearmen are fighting to reach you, but they seem a long way off.'

'What about the chariots?'

'You have no idea,' the instructor said. 'They're the least of your worries right now.'

'But – surely I can see them?' Alcadizzar stammered.

'All you can see right now is dust and rearing horses,' Jabari said. 'Men are screaming. Blows are hammering at your shield and sword. It's all you can do to stay in the saddle.'

'My bodyguards–'

'They're gone,' Jabari said. 'All of them.'

Before Alcadizzar could reply, Jabari rattled the dice again. 'There is a terrible blow to your side. You tumble from the saddle. Hooves churn the ground all around you, missing you by inches.'

Alcadizzar's eyes went wide. 'Wait. That's not what I–'

'Men loom over you, shouting and swearing from their saddles. One of them raises his sword. And then...'

The prince's heart sank.

'There is a mighty shout from your right. Your spearmen hurl themselves at the enemy, frantic to save you from their clutches. The enemy horsemen are stunned by the ferocity of the attack and as dozens are killed, their courage breaks. They break off, fleeing back in the direction of the wadi.'

Jabari bent over the map, shifting the figure of the enemy cavalry back towards the winding gully. Alcadizzar's mouth was dry. Belatedly, he remembered the goblet of wine in his hand and took a quick drink.

The old cavalryman continued to work. 'Your men find you a horse that belonged to one of your bodyguards and put you on it.' Jabari turned his attention to the centre. 'When your messengers are able to reach you again, you learn that your chariots have broken the enemy spear company.' He picked up the unit's wooden figure and placed it at the foot of a dune well behind the rest of the enemy army. 'Your chariots are now poised to strike the next enemy company in the flank.'

The prince felt a flush of triumph. 'Give the order to charge!' he said. 'Meanwhile, I will lead the reserve company back to the oasis and attempt to rally the broken spear company there as well.'

At that point, the battle had turned. Alcadizzar could see that his troops were stronger and had momentum on their side. The chariots drove off a second enemy company before having to withdraw themselves, but by that point he had rallied the survivors of the fourth spear company and sent both them and the reserve spear company back into the fray. Their arrival tipped the balance, forcing the rest of the enemy army to withdraw. Jabari, ever stubborn, fought a bitter rearguard action against Alcadizzar's warriors. The sun had nearly set by the time the old tutor declared that the battle was finally over.

'A narrow victory,' Jabari declared, surveying the battlefield afterwards. 'You were very lucky. Do you know what you did wrong?'

'I didn't scout that damned wadi before the battle,' the prince said ruefully.

Jabari nodded. 'That's right. You should have never left those horsemen to get behind you like that. Always know the site of battle better than your enemy.'

Alcadizzar watched Jabari gather up the wooden figures from the table and set them on a shelf along the wall at the far side of the room. 'Was it a mistake to charge the enemy horsemen?' he asked.

The old tutor paused. 'What do you think?'

'It seemed like the best chance of winning the battle.'

'You could have been killed.'

The young prince shrugged. 'Isn't it a king's duty to protect his people to the death?'

To Alcadizzar's surprise, Jabari threw back his head and laughed. 'Most kings prefer it the other way round.'

'Well, *I'm* not afraid to die,' Alcadizzar said haughtily.

'That's because right now you've got nothing to lose,' Jabari said. 'Wait until you have a wife and a family. Wait until you have real people depending on you, not blocks of wood.'

Alcadizzar folded his arms stubbornly, stung by the dismissive tone in Jabari's voice. 'It wouldn't make a difference. When I rule Khemri, I'll defend the city with my life.'

'Then no doubt history will remember you as a great king,' Jabari replied. 'But your reign will be a short one, I fear.' He bowed to the prince. 'Congratulations on another victory, Alcadizzar. By tomorrow, I expect you to be ready to continue your pursuit of the retreating army... and take steps to deal with the peasant revolt that has broken out in your capital.'

Alcadizzar returned the bow, permitting himself a fleeting smile at Jabari's rare praise. 'Thank you, Jabari. I–' Suddenly the prince stood bolt upright, his brows knitting together in a frown. 'Peasant revolt? *What* peasant revolt?' He glanced about, searching for Jabari, but the old cavalry master had already slipped silently from the room.

With a sigh, Alcadizzar set his empty wine cup on the edge of the table. 'It never ends,' he muttered, shaking his head. 'Never.'

'All things end, master,' said a quiet voice from behind Alcadizzar. 'Or so the priests say.'

The prince turned at the sound of the voice. A gaunt, shaven-headed man stood just to the right of the doorway at the eastern end of the room, head bowed and hands clasped at his waist. His skin was a peculiar shade of pale mahogany, with the shadowy lines of old tattoos twining sinuously along his throat and the sides of his skull.

'Ubaid,' Alcadizzar said, addressing the man. 'Forgive me. I didn't realise you were there.'

'I didn't wish to disturb your study,' Ubaid answered. He was a man of subdued manner and indeterminate age, who had been the prince's personal servant since he was a babe. In all that time, Alcadizzar had never known him to smile, or frown, or sneer; his expression was leaden, his movements slow and hesitant. Ubaid had the aura of a man burdened by the weight of the world. If the man had a family – or a life at all beyond the palace walls – he had never spoken of it to Alcadizzar.

'You fought well,' the servant observed. 'Are you not pleased with your victory?'

Alcadizzar ran a fingertip along the metal rim of the cup, his handsome face pensive. 'Every victory just leads to another set of problems,' he grumbled. 'I fail to see the point any more.'

'The point is to learn,' Ubaid answered patiently. 'You are privileged to have the very best tutors in the land, master. Their wisdom is worth its weight in gold.'

'Really? It doesn't feel like wisdom any more, Ubaid. More like mockery.' Alcadizzar glowered at the miniature battlefield. 'Jabari never lets up. *None* of them do. What am I doing wrong?'

'Wrong?' For the first time in Alcadizzar's memory, Ubaid sounded faintly shocked. 'How can you say such a thing, master? The blood of the divine runs through your veins. You are stronger, swifter and sharper of mind than any of your peers, and you well know it.'

'Then why am I still here?' Alcadizzar rounded on Ubaid, his dark eyes flashing. 'I'm thirty years old! None of the other heirs remained past their eighteenth birthday. If I'm so much better than everyone else, why do I remain behind?'

Ubaid sighed. 'Is it not obvious? Because you are meant for greater things, Alcadizzar. You alone will one day rise to the throne of Khemri, greatest of the cities of the west. For all the work your father has done to resettle and rebuild Khemri, it will fall to *you* to restore it to its former glory.' The servant slowly straightened, folding his thin arms across his chest. 'The great queen has her eye upon you, master. She... expects great things of you.'

Alcadizzar had a hard time believing that the stiff, somnolent Queen of Lahmia paid him any mind at all. For the most part, the royal heirs lived in their own world, separate from the affairs of the court, attended by a select cadre of servants and tutors. In all his years at the palace, he'd been in her presence only a handful of times and she had scarcely spoken to him at all.

'I know very well what's expected of me,' the prince answered. 'Believe me, I do. It's all I've ever known.' He swept his hand over the mock battlefield. 'Tactics. Strategy. Statesmanship. History, law and commerce. Philosophy, theology and alchemy. Within these walls I've fought campaigns, forged alliances, crafted trade agreements and designed great buildings. I've learned to fight with sword and spear, learned how to ride, how to speak and sing and a hundred other things I can't ever imagine having a use for.' He leaned against the table and sighed. 'I'm ready, Ubaid. I *know* I am. Khemri is waiting for me. When will the queen let me go?'

The servant joined Alcadizzar at the table. He leaned forwards slightly, studying the prince's troubled face. 'A delegation from Rasetra arrived today, led by your uncle Khenti. He was in audience with the queen all afternoon.'

Alcadizzar scowled. He'd never met Khenti, but he knew from Jabari that his uncle was one of Rasetra's most powerful nobles, and a force to be reckoned with. 'What does he want?'

'Why, you, of course,' Ubaid replied. A strange expression passed like a shadow across the servant's face. 'He must be a very persuasive man. I've been told to prepare you for a second audience later tonight.'

Alcadizzar straightened, pulse quickening. 'An audience? In the royal court?' Such a thing was rare and portentous indeed.

Ubaid shook his head. 'No, master. At the Temple of Blood.' The ghost of a smile tugged at the corners of his mouth. 'You and your uncle have been summoned by the high priestess herself.'

'For you, holy one,' the priestess said, her voice muffled by the exquisite golden mask she wore. She bowed her head, lifting the golden goblet to Neferata with both hands. 'An offer of love and life eternal.'

Neferata favoured the priestess with a faint smile. She reached out with long, cold fingers and plucked the goblet from the supplicant's hands. The thin metal was deliciously warm to the touch. As always, the thirst cut through her like a knife. No matter how many nights went by, it never lost its razor edge.

Carefully, with perfect, unnatural grace, she raised the cup to her lips. Hot and coppery, yet ineffably sweet, it suffused her entire body in moments, filling it with heat and strength. She drank slowly but steadily, savouring the sensations of mortal life. When she was done, she licked a stray speck of red from the goblet's rim with the tip of her tongue, then handed back the empty vessel. She could already feel the blush of vigour fading, like heat seeping from the sides of a cooling kettle. In just a few hours the thirst would return, as sharp and cruel as ever.

'This isn't wise,' said Lord Ankhat, scowling into the depths of his own cup. In life, he had been a handsome, charismatic nobleman, with a charming smile and dark, piercing eyes. Slightly shorter than most Nehekharans, but trim and physically fit even into middle age, he acted with the casual authority of a man born to wealth and power. 'The Rasetrans are out of patience. Just give them the damned boy and be done with it.'

The nobleman's rich, commanding voice echoed in the dimly lit vault of the temple's inner sanctum. Above them, lit by shafts of moonlight that filtered through narrow gaps in the chamber's ceiling, rose the alabaster statue of Asaph, goddess of love and magic and ancient patron of the city itself. The blessings of the gods had allowed the Nehekharans to prosper amongst the desert sands for thousands of years, and in all that time, the sacred covenant between man and the divine had been made flesh in the eldest daughters of the Lahmian royal bloodline. Though the covenant had been broken centuries ago during the war against the Usurper, the power of the blood remained, and it was this that the temple purported to venerate.

In truth, the temple served as the secret heart of Lahmia's de facto empire, and provided both fortress and refuge for its immortal masters. When Nagash was defeated at the fall of Mahrak, more than four hundred years ago, the rebel kings of the east had pursued the Usurper's defeated army back to Khemri. The rulers of Rasetra and Lybaras meant to end Nagash's reign of terror for all time, but their erstwhile ally, young King Lamashizzar of Lahmia, had different plans. With the aid of the traitor Arkhan the Black, Lamashizzar found the blasphemous Tomes of Nagash and smuggled them out of the ruined city. The King of Lahmia sought the secrets of eternal life, but in the end his schemes were undone by his young queen, who had mastered Nagash's arts more swiftly than he. Though Lamashizzar had struck first, poisoning Neferata with the venom of the long-lost sphinx, she had been reborn through a combination of dark sorcery and blood.

With a gesture from Neferata, the priestess bearing the cup withdrew. She turned to a second priestess, who waited with downcast eyes and held a curved mask of beaten gold in her hands. The features of the mask were a cold reflection of Neferata's own, crafted by master artisans in her youth to conceal her divine beauty from unworthy eyes. She had been forced to wear it every day of her life when in public and, like her forebears, she was meant to wear it to her tomb. Neferata closed her eyes as the cool metal was pressed to her face, reminded, as she always was, of her own death, centuries before.

'Alcadizzar is not ready. Not yet,' she replied. Her tone was smooth and melodic, as soothing as cool water in the desert. It was not the sort of tone a sane man could resist, no matter what he felt in his heart, but Ankhat was unmoved.

'Then you're flirting with war,' the nobleman said darkly. 'Khenti all but spat at the queen's feet. He *demanded* we hand over Alcadizzar immediately. Do you understand what I'm saying?'

Neferata straightened swiftly and glared at Ankhat. Her full lips parted behind the concealing mask, revealing a pair of curved, leonine fangs. Though he couldn't see her expression, the force of her stare caused the immortal to stiffen.

'You forget who rules here, Ankhat.' Her voice lowered to a soft growl. 'Khenti can say all he likes to the queen. If he wants Alcadizzar, he will have to deal with *me*.'

A figure stirred from the shadows near the entrance to the sanctum. Lord Ushoran came forwards, holding his own empty cup loosely in his hand. Though distantly related to the royal family and in life a powerful nobleman himself, Ushoran was nothing like the dynamic, charming Ankhat. He was of average height, with bland, average features that failed to leave a lasting impression in the mind. The Lord of Masks was a man who loved his intrigues, and over the centuries his network of spies had spread all over Nehekhara.

'It is not merely Khenti that you contend with,' Ushoran said. 'My agents in Rasetra tell me that Aten-heru has warned his nobles that they could be called to arms at any moment. What is more, the king has sent a number of letters to the rulers of Lybaras, Ka-Sabar – even far-off Zandri.' He shrugged. 'It's possible that Aten-heru *expects* you to refuse him once again. It would give him something to rally the other cities around and force a confrontation between us and a coalition of most of the other great cities.'

'If that happens, we would be undone,' Ankhat declared. 'We have no means of enforcing our trade agreements and loan obligations at this point, also the other cities have grown increasingly resentful of the gold they pay us every year. Zandri has been testing our resolve for years now; if Aten-heru declares he'll no longer honour his obligations to us, the other cities will surely follow.'

'And what of the army?' Neferata demanded. 'It's been five years. Are they ready to fight, or not?'

Ankhat sighed. 'The process of rebuilding is a slow one. We've restored the army to its former size, but the troops are inexperienced. They're a credible threat to a weak city like Lybaras or Mahrak, but the Rasetrans are another matter entirely.'

Neferata beckoned, and another group of priestesses hurried from the shadows to set a carved mahogany chair at the feet of the great statue. There were never more than three hundred priestesses and acolytes in the temple at any time, and the highest of the orders served as her personal handmaidens. They were entirely her creatures, bound by Neferata's seductive allure and her implacable will. She settled lightly into the chair and allowed the priestesses to hover about her, arranging her golden vestments and tugging at the sleeves of her white silk robe.

'Alcadizzar must remain, whether Khenti wishes it or not,' she told the two lords. 'And the Rasetrans will have no choice but to accept it. You will see.' She waved the priestesses away. 'Now go. Khenti and his retainers are drawing near.'

Ushoran withdrew into the shadows without a word. Ankhat remained a moment longer, his eyes glinting angrily.

'Your obsession with this man is going to destroy us all,' he said to her. 'You mark my words, Neferata. One day, Lahmia will burn, and Alcadizzar will be the cause.'

Neferata straightened, swift as an adder, but before she could snarl a reply Ankhat was gone. Moments later, the great doors of the outer sanctum swung silently open to admit Lord Khenti and his retinue.

Khenti was a man of middle years, but like nearly all of Rasetra's noblemen, he was still in fighting trim. He was tall and broad-shouldered, with a swordsman's thick wrists and sinewy forearms, and a blunt, pugnacious face that harked back to Rakh-amn-hotep, the city's legendary warrior-king.

Neferata noted with some amusement that Khenti had chosen to attend the audience in full battledress; a heavy iron scale vest, no doubt obtained at great expense from the new foundries at Ka-Sabar, worn over a thick vest and calf-length kilt of thunder-lizard hide. His left hand rested on the worn hilt of a heavy khopesh sheathed at his hip and his dark eyes swept the shadows of the sanctum, as though expecting some kind of ambush. She studied the nobleman's belligerent expression and smiled mirthlessly, running her tongue along the needle-like tips of her fangs.

'Enter and be welcome,' she said to the Rasetrans. Her rich voice resonated through the sanctum, augmented only slightly by the power in her veins. Khenti's bodyguards slowed their swift pace almost at once, their shoulders relaxing and their hands sliding from the hilts of their weapons. Their master, however, was apparently made of sterner stuff; if anything, Khenti's suspicious scowl only deepened, though he no longer had eyes for anything but Neferata.

'Be at peace, and know that the power of the divine abides in the blood of the chosen,' she continued, focusing a bit more of her attention on Khenti. This close, she could hear the whisper of blood in his veins and measure the drumbeat of his heart. 'You honour us with your presence, Lord Khenti. Have you an offering to propitiate the memory of the gods?'

The nobleman grunted. 'I made my offerings to Ptra at noontime,' he said disdainfully, 'and at a proper temple, down in the city.'

Neferata gave a faint nod. Though the sacred covenant had been broken and the holy city of Mahrak ravaged during the war with the Usurper, the temples to the gods still lingered in most of the great cities. Attempts to spread Lahmia's cult across Nehekhara had so far met with little success. 'It is virtuous to respect the old ways,' she replied neutrally.

Khenti drew himself straighter, chin raised defiantly. 'Would that your queen did as well!' he declared. 'Bad enough that Lahmia holds the royal heirs of the other cities as hostage to its greed; now it denies Khemri its rightful king!'

Neferata folded her hands in her lap. 'Greed, my lord?' she said. Her smile widened. 'Am I mistaken, or was Khemri not rebuilt with Lahmian gold?'

Khenti folded his muscular arms. 'Don't play games of rhetoric with me, priestess,' he growled. 'Either the Queen of Lahmia gives up Alcadizzar, or else she admits that she's holding him as a prisoner and accepts the consequences of her mistake.'

Neferata chuckled. Aten-heru had been a fool to send Khenti, she thought. This was going to be simpler than she'd imagined. 'Blunt, but well said,' she told the Rasetran. 'I would expect no less from a man such as yourself.' She laced the words with another slight caress of power and watched Khenti relax slightly. He believed that he had the upper hand now. With the right words, she could make him believe anything she wished.

'The hour grows late, priestess,' Khenti said. 'Why is it you wished to see me?'

Neferata studied the Rasetran thoughtfully. 'You came here seeking the release of Prince Alcadizzar,' she said carefully. 'But there has been a misunderstanding, my lord. The queen did not speak of it, because it was not her place to do so.'

Khenti frowned. 'Not her *place*?'

She met his scowl coolly. 'Prince Alcadizzar is not a guest of the royal house. For the last twelve years, he has remained in Lahmia at the behest of the temple.'

For a moment, the Rasetran was too stunned to speak. 'The temple? How in the name of all the gods–'

'All will be explained in due course,' Neferata said, forestalling Khenti's outrage with an upraised hand. 'We await only the arrival of the prince. And see – he comes, even now.'

She could hear Alcadizzar's approach through the temple's ante-chamber; swift, sure steps, light and precise as a dancer's. Neferata could read much into those movements; after thirty years, she knew the prince more intimately than any lover. The prince was in high spirits, hastening to the audience with eagerness and keen interest. She straightened slightly, listening to the long, powerful drumbeats of Alcadizzar's heart, and felt her own pulse quicken in response.

He swept into the outer sanctum like a summer storm. The still air was suddenly tense with pent-up energy; heads turned at once, seeking the source. A stir went through the Rasetrans. Khenti's bodyguards sank to their knees at once, several of the warriors crying out in wonder at the sight of the prince. Khenti gaped at Alcadizzar for a moment, his eyes widening in disbelief. Then, with a shout of joy he strode forwards and gripped the prince's forearms in greeting.

Alcadizzar favoured Khenti and the bodyguards with one of his dazzling smiles. Taller even than Khenti and powerfully built, his presence filled the shadowy chamber with warmth, vitality and strength. Such was his charm that within moments the Rasetrans were smiling and laughing as though in the presence of a long-lost friend.

'Look at you!' Khenti marvelled, staring up at his nephew's face. He gripped Alcadizzar's muscular forearms tighter, as though fearful that the prince might be a mirage. 'Big as a damned thunder-lizard!' He rotated the prince's arms and studied his hands. 'You've been training hard, I see. Good.' The nobleman frowned questioningly. 'What about your studies? Has that old horse Jabari been keeping you busy?'

Alcadizzar chuckled. 'He vexes me every single day, uncle.'

'Good, good!' Khenti said with a laugh. 'There's no better campaigner in all of Nehekhara. If you can hold your own against the likes of him, there's no army in the land you can't defeat.'

'I can well believe it,' the prince replied. Absently, he waved for the bodyguards to rise from the floor. The warriors responded at once, admiration evident in their eyes. Neferata watched the exchange with bemusement, as she always did when Alcadizzar was in the company of lesser mortals. Though he'd been exhaustively educated in the social arts, the prince still had a disturbing tendency to ignore propriety and treat everyone, even *servants*, as his equals. It was degrading to watch, but Alcadizzar didn't care in the least, and the common folk worshipped him for it. Neferata couldn't fathom it; it was the one aspect of his personality that remained a complete mystery to her.

'How is my father?' the prince asked. Alcadizzar gave Khenti a wink. 'He hasn't forgotten about me, has he?'

'Certainly not!' Khenti said. 'He thinks of you always and awaits the day of your homecoming.' The nobleman seemed to remember Neferata, and turned back to the dais. His good humour evaporated like rain on the desert sands. 'A homecoming that's twelve years overdue.'

'Indeed,' Neferata said. She laced the word with power and savoured its effect on the assembled men. They responded to her at once, forgetting their high spirits and focusing on her once more. All except Alcadizzar. The prince favoured her with a bemused expression and one of his intense, curious stares, as though she were a puzzle that demanded a solution.

The intensity of his stare transfixed her. The power of his intellect was almost tangible, gripping her like a pair of invisible hands. Her dead heart raced. Was this how mortals felt when she addressed them? Did they feel this mixture of anxiety and exaltation?

Here was a man to give even the immortals pause, like one of the great heroes from Nehekharan legend. But it wasn't the power of the gods that coursed like lightning through Alcadizzar's veins, but Neferata's own dark magic. While he was still in the womb, his mother had been persuaded to drink an elixir of youth and vigour formulated by Neferata herself. It had made Alcadizzar a virtual god among men, like the mythical Ushabti of ancient times. Now, at last, his abilities were nearly at their peak. The time had come to reveal the destiny that awaited him – one she had built painstakingly for the last thirty years.

'Welcome to the Temple of Blood, great prince,' she said, nodding her head in greeting. 'It gives me great joy to see you here.' She extended her hand and pointed to a spot on the stone floor, not far from where Alcadizzar stood. 'It was not so long ago that your blessed mother knelt here and prayed to the goddess to bless you with health and good fortune.'

Alcadizzar nodded sombrely. 'Yes. I've heard the tale.'

'She was very brave,' Neferata said, affecting as much warmth in her voice as she could. She had to be careful with the prince; she knew from experience that his perceptions were much keener than normal men. 'Your mother was in ill health, but she braved the long journey from Rasetra to pray here, at the temple, in hopes of saving your life.' Neferata inclined her head to Khenti. 'You remember, don't you, my lord?'

Khenti's pugnacious face turned pinched, as though he'd bit into a lemon. 'Aye, I recall,' he said, disapproving of the deed but unwilling to speak ill of the dead.

Neferata smiled behind her mask. 'The goddess heard your mother's plea and was moved.' She gestured towards Alcadizzar with a sweep of her hand. 'And look at the man you have become! There is not another like you in all of Nehekhara, Prince Alcadizzar. *She* has seen to that. Now it is incumbent upon you to honour the great gifts that you have been given.'

Khenti frowned. He opened his mouth to protest, but Alcadizzar unintentionally cut him off.

'I'm deeply aware of my obligations to the people of Khemri,' the prince said, in that same, sombre tone. 'I've spent my entire life preparing for the day I become king.'

'So you have,' Neferata said, and there was no need to manufacture the pride in her voice. 'You will be a great king, Alcadizzar. But we at the temple believe that you are destined for much more.'

'Destined for what?' Khenti asked, having recovered his composure.

Neferata leaned back in her chair and fixed Alcadizzar with a steady gaze. 'What do you know of the Temple of Blood, my prince?'

Alcadizzar answered at once. 'The temple is based on the premise that the gods and their gifts have been taken from us, but the bloodlines they have blessed throughout Nehekhara's history remain. They are our sole remaining connection to the divine.'

'Preposterous,' Khenti sneered.

'And yet the proof stands before you,' Neferata said. 'Alcadizzar's mother came here after she'd spent months praying in vain at the old temples of Rasetra. It was here that her prayers were answered, were they not?'

Khenti's eyes narrowed, but he made no attempt to gainsay her. Alcadizzar, on the other hand, rubbed his chin thoughtfully and said, 'If the gods no longer take an active hand in our affairs, how is it that the goddess answered my mother's prayers?'

Neferata nodded approvingly. 'Remember, oh prince, the gods are gone, but the sacred bloodlines remain. Earlier, I spoke in figurative terms. The truth is that your mother spoke not to the goddess, but to the nascent power of the blood running through your veins.'

'I'm descended from a sacred bloodline?' Alcadizzar replied, both intrigued and dubious at the same time.

'One of the greatest and most venerated of all,' Neferata replied. 'We suspected as much when you were born, but it has taken many years to produce the evidence.'

She clapped her hands gently and a priestess appeared from the shadows, bearing a newly bound book in her hands. The priestess set the expensive tome in the prince's hands, bowed deeply, and then withdrew.

'Naturally, both of you are well familiar with the sacred ties between Lahmia and Khemri,' Neferata began. 'Since the time of Settra the Magnificent, the kings of the Living City have wed the eldest daughters of the Lahmian royal house, who were the living embodiment of the covenant with the gods.'

Alcadizzar opened the tome reverently and began to peruse its pages. 'So the blood of the royal heirs of Khemri was made sacred as well.'

'Just so,' Neferata replied. 'And the Lahmian royal house has gone to great pains to record each and every family line that has been produced as a result. The documents have been maintained here at the palace for many hundreds of years.'

Neferata considered the book in Alcadizzar's hands. The information within couldn't be proven beyond a shadow of a doubt, but Lord Ushoran was certain that it would survive all but the most learned scrutiny. All that mattered to her was that Alcadizzar himself believed it.

'Now, Rasetra's origins are well known; the city was originally a colony of distant Khemri, founded during the reign of King Khetep, some four and a half centuries ago.' During the time of my father, she thought. Neferata still remembered how King Lamasheptra had scoffed at the thought of the small settlement at the edge of the deadly southern jungle. It was their constant, ruthless struggle for survival that had transformed them into a warrior culture both respected and feared throughout Nehekhara.

'When King Khetep made ready to return home, he chose one of his ablest lieutenants, a nobleman named Ur-Amnet, to govern the new settlement. His son, Mukhtail, became the first king of Rasetra, and every king that followed is descended from his line.'

Now Khenti's interest was piqued as well. 'But Ur-Amnet was not part of Khemri's royal house,' he said. 'His family was a noble one, but its lineage uncertain.'

'Until now,' Neferata replied. 'We searched the records here at Lahmia and despatched agents to search for confirmation among the old temples at Khemri. Ur-Amnet is descended from Hapt-amn-koreb, who was a great warrior and Master of Horse to the mighty King Nemuret. Hapt-amn-koreb's lineage is murkier still, but after many years of searching, it was determined why – he was descended from Amenophis, fifth son of Settra the Magnificent.'

Alcadizzar closed his eyes for a moment. 'Amenophis was disowned by Settra during the tenth year of his reign,' he said, calling upon his years of study.

'Correct. He was suspected of assassinating his older brother Djoser. Though it was never proved, Settra cast him out nonetheless. But that is irrelevant. The bloodline remains true. You, Alcadizzar, bear the ancient birthright of the gods.'

'What does this mean?' Khenti asked, taking the bait.

'That depends on Prince Alcadizzar,' Neferata replied. 'There is a unique opportunity here to restore Khemri – and by extension, all of Nehekhara – to a measure of the glory it once possessed. If the prince proved himself worthy, we could witness the dawn of a new golden age of peace and prosperity, and put the dark memory of Nagash behind us forever.'

Alcadizzar raised his head from the book. 'What do you propose?'

Neferata leaned forwards. 'A new union,' she said. 'One not of flesh, but of spirit. Lahmia and Khemri can be united once more by the veneration of our shared bloodline.'

Khenti's frown deepened. 'No, I don't think–' but Alcadizzar placed a hand on his shoulder and the older Rasetran fell silent.

'What would Khemri stand to gain from such a union?'

'Why, all of the west,' Neferata said. 'Right now, Lahmia rules Nehekhara in all but name. What I propose is to divide the land between us. The trade and loan obligations of Zandri, Numas and Ka-Sabar would be placed in your hands. It would ensure Khemri's growth and prosperity for centuries, and restore a substantial measure of its political power in a single stroke.'

That got even Khenti's attention. He looked to Alcadizzar, who'd turned pensive once more.

'What would you require of me in return?'

'For the union to be consummated, you must pledge yourself to the temple,' Neferata said. 'Lahmia will have its high priestess, and Khemri its priest king.'

The prince sighed inwardly. 'How long would such an initiation take?'

Neferata felt a rush of triumph. She knew him better than he knew himself. 'That is up to you, of course,' she said. 'For most initiates, the path to the temple's highest rank is a long and difficult one. What might take them a lifetime, you could accomplish in a decade or less.'

'A *decade*!' Khenti turned to the prince. 'Khemri needs you *now*, great one. This... this is too much!'

'Khenti is perhaps right,' Neferata said slowly. Her eyes never left Alcadizzar's. 'It is a great deal to ask of any man. But the potential is equally great, is it not?'

The prince glanced at Khenti's worried face. 'What if I refuse?'

'Then your time here in Lahmia will be at an end,' she replied.

'I'm... free to go?'

'Of course,' Neferata said. 'The choice is yours, o prince. Do as you think best for your city and your people.'

Khenti gripped Alcadizzar's shoulders and turned the younger man to face him. 'You can't seriously be considering this,' he said. 'It's over! You're free! Come with me now, and we can be on the road to Rasetra by dawn!'

Alcadizzar stared down at his uncle, and Neferata could see the longing in his eyes. For a moment, her heart went out to him; she knew all too well what it was like to live as a prisoner, trapped in a gilded cage. One day he will thank me, though, she told herself. This is not just for me, or even for him, but for all of Nehekhara.

'What sort of king would I be if I put my own selfishness ahead of my city's future?' Alcadizzar said. His voice was heavy with regret, but he gripped his uncle's arms tightly. 'Khemri has survived for decades without me. It will last for a few years more.'

The prince turned to Neferata and bowed his head. 'I accept your offer,' he told her. 'Let Khemri and Lahmia be united once more.'

Neferata rose from her chair and joined Alcadizzar. Beneath the mask, her cheeks were wet with crimson tears as she placed a hand on his cheek. His skin felt hot beneath her fingers. She could feel the blood coursing through the flesh beneath. The thirst cut through her, slicing deep into her heart.

'As you wish, oh prince,' she said softly.

THREE

DEADLOCK

Nagashizzar,
in the 98th year of Tahoth the Wise
(-1300 Imperial Reckoning)

Moving as though in a dream, the barbarian witch crept towards the cavern wall. The rough stone had been scribed with angular northern runes in complex spiral patterns that radiated from the centre of the wall and covered an area broad enough for two men to stand abreast. Akatha paused before the strange sigil, her grey-tinged lips working as she murmured sibilant words of power. Arcane symbols had been painted on her cheeks and down the length of her arms in sinuous patterns; they shone a pale and ghostly blue through the fine layer of ash that had been smeared over her skin. Tiny charms of yellowed bone had been woven into her tangled, soot-stained braids, clattering softly with each measured tread. A faint, greenish glow emanated from the whites of her eyes.

Akatha raised her right hand and reached out palm-first towards the wall. Slowly, warily, as though testing the heat of a roaring furnace, she brought her hand close to the stone. Her eyes flickered shut.

She stood that way for several long moments, muttering the words of power. Suddenly, her body stiffened. Her eyes flew open, and she retreated swiftly and silently from the wall, back to where Nagash and her kinsmen waited.

The cavern was small and low-ceilinged, its floor sloping slightly downwards towards the rune-marked wall and the mountain's distant core. Nagash hadn't known it existed until just the week before; it had been separated from the fortress's passageways by little more than a few feet of solid rock at one part of the chamber's western wall. Akatha had discovered it during a casting of runes, as she'd sought to divine the invaders' next move.

Nagash stood just inside the narrow opening his labourers had dug into the chamber. At his back stood Bragadh, Diarid and Thestus, as well as a score of Bragadh's chosen warriors. Like Akatha, the warlord and his men were pallid and moved with an eerie, almost dreamlike grace. Their eyes shone faintly in the dimness, just as hers did, evidence of the potent elixir that Nagash had created to extend their life spans. Based on the same formula he'd used to create his immortals centuries ago, this elixir drew its power from a combination of stolen life force and the dust of the burning stone. It lent the northmen fearsome strength and vitality, though Nagash suspected that, once enough of the dust had collected in their bones, it would begin to change them in unpredictable ways. So long as they could take orders and lead their men in battle, he would continue to make use of them.

Hundreds of Bragadh's best fighting men waited along the passageways just outside the cavern, listening intently for the call to action. They all knew that, three levels below, the ratmen were launching yet another howling assault on the bastions protecting mine shaft number six.

Akatha approached the necromancer. Daring greatly, the witch met Nagash's coldly glowing eyes. 'They are nearly through,' she whispered, her voice flat and cold. 'A few minutes, perhaps. No more.'

Nagash raised a leathery hand and waved her aside. As much as her insolence irritated him, her sorcerous abilities had proven unexpectedly useful in the war against the ratmen. The barbarians, he'd discovered, had a long history of dealing with the creatures, and the arcane traditions of Akatha's extinct sisterhood contained several rituals that were designed to combat them. The necromancer's pride prevented him from stooping so low as to learn the barbarian rites for himself, and so the damned witch continued to survive.

The war beneath the mountain had raged for twenty-five galling years and showed no signs of ending. The ratmen were drawn like moths to the burning stone, and no matter how many thousands of the creatures he slew, there were always more to take their place. Losses on both sides had been staggering. The sheer amount of resources Nagash had expended thus far filled him with cold rage. The massive invasion force he'd carefully built for centuries was being squandered against a never-ending tide of vermin. When the war finally ended, it would take years, perhaps decades, to marshal another force capable of destroying Nehekhara. If he did not know for a fact that he'd broken the gods of his old homeland, he might have suspected some divine power bent on thwarting his dreams of revenge.

A faint sound echoed across the cavern – a scratching, scrabbling sound that Nagash and the barbarians had come to know all too well. With neither side willing to concede defeat, the course of the war had been measured in tunnels seized and levels taken. Passageways and branch-tunnels leading to the all-important mine shafts had been fortified by both sides, with cunning barricades and redoubts designed to hinder an enemy advance. Smaller tunnels were filled with rubble or sown with vicious traps to slaughter the unwary, forcing teams of sappers to reopen them in preparation for a major attack. Control of the deeps ebbed and flowed from one week to the next. Conquests were made and then lost again, as one side or the other exhausted itself in a punishing attack and then lacked the strength to hold on to what it had taken. In-between major assaults the two armies would pause for weeks or even months at a time, staging punishing raids against their enemy's forwards positions while they rebuilt their shattered forces.

From time to time, the two armies would try to break the deadlock with cunning stratagems. Most often they involved the digging of new tunnels to strike at the enemy from an unexpected direction – just as the ratmen were attempting now. The assault on mine shaft six was a diversion, meant to pin down the necromancer's troops so that another contingent of warriors could emerge behind them and cut them off.

It was a strategy that had served the ratmen well since the first day of the war, and one they returned to time and again when their frontal assaults had been stymied for more than a few months at a time. The tactic was effective because the creatures could dig tunnels with a speed and skill that beggared the imagination; by the same token, it was also largely predictable.

Nagash had known this was coming for several months now; he'd planned for it, in fact, reinforcing the defences around mine shaft six with every warrior he could spare and grinding down one frenzied assault after another. When the tempo of the attacks tapered off, he set Akatha to watching for the signs that the enemy was attempting another tunnel. This time he meant to turn their favourite tactic against them.

A part of the cavern wall across the chamber seemed to shimmer in the torchlight as the furious tunnelling stirred up a fine haze of rock dust. There was a faint crackling sound. Tiny fragments of stone began to cascade from the wall. Nagash smiled mirthlessly and clenched his fists. Power coursed through his limbs as he began a soundless chant, summoning up the energies of the burning stone.

The breach opened in a single instant, with a crash and a rumble of broken rock. A cloud of pale dust billowed out into the cavern, followed by the swift-moving silhouettes of ratmen. Hissing and chittering turned to squeaks of surprise as the attackers realised that they were not alone.

Words of power boiled up from Nagash's throat, reverberating painfully in the dank air. A surge of savage anticipation gripped him; since the war began, he had remained far from the front lines, directing the movements of his forces from on high rather than embroiling himself personally in one small part of the conflict. As a result, the ratmen had yet to suffer the full might of his power.

With a furious cry of exultation, the Undying King flung out his hands and unleashed a storm of death upon his foes.

Streams of hissing green darts leapt from the necromancer's fingertips, scything through the ranks of the stunned ratmen. The filthy creatures screamed as they were struck; their blood boiled, erupting from their bodies in glowing, greenish-black mist. Scores fell in the first moments, slain before their bodies hit the cavern floor.

Shrieks of terror rebounded across the chamber as the ratmen who escaped the first onslaught fled in panic back through the tunnel and fetched up against their comrades advancing in the other direction. Nagash followed after them, hurling another volley of magical bolts into the press. In the packed confines of the tunnel, the darts savaged the ranks of the ratmen. They collapsed where they stood like reaped grain, their corpses blackened by heat and hissing with escaping fluids.

The sight of so much terror and death filled Nagash with ferocious joy. The necromancer waded into the windrows of heaped bodies like a starving man welcomed to a feast. He seized corpses and flung them out of his way like straw dolls, his desiccated flesh buzzing with the unleashed energies of the *abn-i-khat.* Screams of pure, animal terror echoed from the roughly hewn walls. Nagash threw back his misshapen skull and howled with dreadful laughter as he hounded the ratmen into the depths.

Roaring wild oaths and battle cries, the northmen followed after their master. There was no way to know how far the tunnel went, but it was certain that it led back behind the invaders' front lines. The avenue of attack ran both ways, as the ratmen were about to learn.

Thoughts of strategy were lost on Nagash at the moment; he was caught up completely in the slaughter, hurling one burning volley after another at the retreating ratmen. His body was wreathed in a fierce nimbus of crackling green fire that grew fiercer with every spell he cast, until the corpses of the ratmen smouldered beneath his touch.

The pursuit stretched into an eternity of thunder, screams and bloodshed. Nagash waded through a sea of corpses, his body burning with unleashed power. The number of ratmen he slew passed all reckoning. He had grown so lost in the grim rhythms of the slaughter that when he finally emerged from the far end of the tunnel the transition took him momentarily aback.

Nagash found himself in a broad, low-ceilinged cavern packed with squalling, screeching ratmen. The terrified survivors had fled into the mass of warriors waiting their turn to advance up the tunnel, and their panic had spread like wildfire through the ranks. Pandemonium reigned as pack leaders fought to rally their warriors with snarled threats and the flats of their blades. Bone whistles shrieked and the urgent clash of brass gongs added to the cacophony.

The necromancer paused, taking his bearings. The closest of his undead warriors was *six* levels above him, below even mine shaft number seven. He was deep in enemy territory – possibly even behind the bulk of the ratmen army. In one swift move he'd turned his enemy's knife back upon their own throat. For the first time in decades, he dared to think that perhaps victory finally lay within his grasp.

With a triumphant shout, Nagash drew upon the burning stone and brought down a rain of fire on the milling ratmen. Burning bodies collapsed in heaps, adding fuel to the howling panic. He advanced on the stricken horde, his warriors filling the space behind him and forming up into companies of sword and axe-men. Dimly, Nagash could hear Bragadh and Thestus shouting orders over the din; their people's hatred of the ratmen ran so deep that their rivalry had all but disappeared in the face of the invasion.

A dull clatter arose at Nagash's back – the flat bark of sword and axe against the surface of bronze-edged wooden shields, rising in volume and intensity as one northman after another added their weapon to the din. Blue-tattooed barbarians threw back their heads and bellowed their bloodlust in a swelling roar that could be felt in the bones of man and rat-creature alike. In the confines of the cavern it was an awesome, world-shaking sound.

The noise rose to a fever pitch – and then, cutting through the tumult like a knife, came an unearthly, piping wail. Akatha's voice, charged with primitive magics and shaped by the ancient secrets of her sisterhood, calling for the spilling of blood and the harvesting of souls. As they had for thousands of years, the northmen charged at their foes not to the baying of horns, but to the cry of the witch's war-song.

A wave of shouting barbarians swept past Nagash in a thundering wave and smashed into the corpse-strewn ranks of the ratmen. The broad-shouldered warriors towered over their foes; their blows splintered shields and shattered swords. They carved their way through the enemy with as much joyous savagery as Nagash himself. Bragadh and his chosen warriors were in the thick of the fighting, spilling the blood of their foes with every stroke of their blades. The necromancer followed close behind them, hurling bolts of fire over their heads to fall upon the densely packed mob.

The ratmen, already well past the limits of their resolve, collapsed completely under the weight of the barbarian onslaught. A rout began: terrified warriors threw down their weapons and climbed over their fellows in an attempt to escape the oncoming northmen. The horde began to dissolve before Nagash's eyes as the ratmen died or fled into the dubious safety of the passageways on the far end of the cavern. The murderous northmen hounded them mercilessly and the melee seemed to swiftly recede away from the necromancer. Behind him, still more of the barbarians were charging into the cavern; Nagash paused, his own thirst for slaughter ebbing away as he tried to focus on the unfolding battle. From where he stood, he had two options: order his warriors to turn aside and cut off the ratmen on the levels above, or to press still deeper into the mountain in hopes of sowing further chaos and perhaps coming to grips with the leader of the enemy army.

He hesitated for scarcely a moment before reaching a decision, but the pause was enough to save him.

Across the cavern came a chorus of metallic-sounding shrieks, like steam bursting from a dozen copper pots. A furious, greenish glow filled the air at the far end of the chamber, and the battle cries of the northmen were transformed into screams of horror and pain.

In an instant, the barbarian charge came to a crashing halt. Warriors piled into one another around Nagash, shouting and cursing. The strange, hissing shrieks sounded again, followed by more screams and a gust of hot wind that carried the sickly-sweet reek of charred flesh. The flickering glow was getting closer, spreading over and through the ranks of Nagash's men.

The crowd of northmen surrounding Nagash began to surge backwards, towards the captured tunnel. Men were shouting in terror up ahead, exhorting their fellows in their own crude northern tongue. Furious, the necromancer forced himself through the press, searching for the source of the panic.

A figure loomed ahead of him. It was Bragadh, his face streaked with gore. The warlord's eyes were wide with shock. He shouted something in his native tongue, then remembered himself and switched to Nehekharan. 'Back, master!' he cried. 'You must go back–'

Before Nagash could snarl a reply, the shrieks rose again, louder and closer than before, and the necromancer saw a dozen northmen in front of Bragadh disappear in a roaring blast of green flame. The sorcerous power in the fire was as palpable as the heat he felt against his leathery skin. It ate through armour, clothing and flesh with appalling swiftness, gnawing the warriors down to blackened bones right before his eyes.

Like the lash of a whip or the flickering tongue of a dragon the flame receded with a thin hiss, vanishing even as the charred corpses of the northmen collapsed to the ground. With a shock, the necromancer realised that the hungry flames had carved a broad swathe through his troops, who were now in full retreat from the four contraptions of wood and bronze that squatted at the far side of the cavern.

The devices were each the size of a large war-chariot, and mounted on a wooden bed supported by a pair of bronze-rimmed wheels. A sturdy wooden yoke extended from the front of the bed, but where a set of horses would have been lashed to the post, there were four broad-shouldered ratmen with push-handles gripped in their clawed paws. Upon the wooden bed sat a sealed cauldron of cast bronze, whose curved sides shimmered with radiant heat.

Situated on the rear of the wooden bed, just behind the cauldron, was a large box of bronze and wood. Four long, almost oar-like levers extended from the box, alternating to the left and right. Two ratmen gripped each lever. In that strange, slow-motion clarity brought on by combat, Nagash saw the rats lift the great levers so high that they rose onto the tips of their toe-claws. There was a muffled *whoooosh* of indrawn air, like the sound of a great furnace bellows.

Four thick, bronze pipes ran from the box into the sides of the great cauldron and a long, oddly flexible pipe of some kind ran from the front of the cauldron and was threaded through arched bronze staples hammered into the wood. It extended for another six feet from the end of the yoke, terminating in a heavy-looking bronze nozzle held by a pair of curiously garbed ratmen. The creatures were swathed in heavy robes of leather and sturdy cloth, and wore leather gauntlets that reached all the way back to their knobby elbows. The skin of their snouts was bald and blistered from heat. Strange discs of some dark, glossy material were held over their beady eyes by a dark leather band, lending them an unblinking, soulless stare.

Nagash watched the mouth of one nozzle turn his way. Green fire flickered hungrily in its depths, mirroring the hungry leer of the ratmen who wielded it.

There was nowhere to run. Instinctively, Nagash shoved Diarid aside and called upon the power of the *abn-i-khat*. The wild energies burned at his fingertips, but at the last moment he hesitated to unleash his sorceries on the fire-throwers. If the cauldrons burst, even in such a relatively large space as the cavern, the escaping heat might consume everything in the chamber. Instead, he turned his attentions on the carpet of mangled bodies that lay between him and the ratmen.

The necromancer clenched one fist. '*Rise,*' he commanded, just as the bellows-rats hauled down their levers and another chorus of draconic shrieks filled the cavern.

Necromantic energies flowed from Nagash in a torrent, enveloping the corpses in an instant. The bodies of human and ratman alike reared up from the cavern floor, like mummer's dolls pulled by invisible strings. They caught the blast of sorcerous flames full-on; Nagash heard the buzzing sizzle of flesh and the sharp crackle of splintering bone as the heat consumed them. The ranks of the undead were cut down by the flames, but in so doing they absorbed or deflected enough of the blast to spare their master.

Once more the flames receded with a menacing hiss. Barely a handful of Nagash's newly-animated corpses remained.

Diarid clambered to his feet and stared at the enemy war engines in evident horror. 'We must retreat,' he said to Nagash. 'Quickly, before those things can draw another breath.'

Nagash clenched his corroded teeth. The barbarian was right. He hadn't imagined the damned ratmen could be so clever. Wordlessly, he ordered the remaining corpses forwards in a token charge against the war engines, then hastened swiftly back to the far tunnels.

His token force managed scarcely a dozen steps before they were incinerated. Nagash felt the heat of the flames wash over his shoulders, then abruptly recede. He glanced over his shoulder to see a semicircle of green flame playing across ruined corpses three-quarters of the way across the cavern. Realising that their quarry had retreated beyond their reach, the nozzle-rats were screeching at the wretches manning the yokes of their war engines, urging them forwards.

Diarid vanished into the tunnel. Moments later, Nagash reached the mouth of the sloping passage. Behind him, axles groaned as the war engines began to move.

The necromancer turned back to the ratmen, his rage building. Would the damned stalemate never end?

Nagash raised his arm and pointed at the oncoming ratmen. The fires of the burning stone had ebbed to little more than sullen embers. He'd expended too much, too quickly. Next time, he would be certain to have greater reserves to call upon.

His ragged lips curling with contempt, he spat a stream of arcane syllables. A handful of darts, larger and brighter than those he'd cast before, streaked across the cavern. They flashed past the nozzle-rats of one of the middle fire-throwers, missing them by a hair's breadth – and struck the bronze cauldron in a shower of hot green sparks. The cauldron resounded like a struck bell and then blew apart in a thunderous detonation. The crew of the war engine vanished in a ball of sorcerous fire. Jagged metal fragments slashed through the air, striking the engines to either side; less than a second later, they detonated too, showering the cavern with curtains of sizzling flame.

Hot air buffeted Nagash, tugging at his hood and the sleeves of his robe. For a long moment he stared into the depths of the holocaust he'd unleashed, then, muttering venomous curses, he withdrew into the darkness of the tunnel.

The long knife flashed in the firelight, silencing the pack leader's protestations. The warrior stiffened, beady eyes widening as he clawed at the gaping wound that stretched across his throat. He collapsed in a welter of bitter blood, legs and tail twitching horribly.

Lord Eekrit stood over the dying clanrat, his tail lashing in fury. The hem of his rich robe was soaked in gore.

'Anyone else?' he hissed, turning to glare at the trio of quivering pack leaders left on the dais. Four of their number already sprawled lifelessly on the steps behind them. The warlord gave the fifth pack leader a savage kick, rolling him off the dais to join the rest. 'Does *anyone else* expect me to believe that a *burning man* with eyes of *god-stone* killed four hundred of our best warriors *by himself*?'

The surviving pack leaders – all that remained of those who'd presided over the debacle earlier that night – stretched their rangy bodies across the stones and bared their necks to Eekrit. Ears flat, tails twitching feverishly, they filled the air with fear-musk and made no reply.

Eekrit had enough. No one was telling him anything useful, and his shoulder was getting sore from all the throat-cutting. 'Out of my sight!' he shrieked. 'Out-out! Tomorrow you fight in the front ranks, with the rest of the slaves!'

The three pack leaders scrambled off the dais, all but tripping over themselves in their haste to escape their master's rage. Once they were gone, packs of slaves hastened from the shadows to drag away the objects of Lord Eekrit's ire. The warlord watched them for a moment then turned away in disgust, flinging the bloodstained knife across the dais. It skittered over the stones, missing Lord Eshreegar's foot by a hair's-breadth. The Master of Treacheries never so much as twitched.

Like everything else in the great cavern, the dais had changed greatly in the past quarter-century. Slaves had built three-quarter-height walls from rubble and mortar, creating a proper audience chamber without completely isolating it from the cacophonous noise of the rest of the space. Rich rugs had been laid across the top, flanked by two gilded braziers that filled the partially enclosed space with a pleasing mosaic of light and shadow. Heavy tapestries hung from the walls, each one commissioned at great expense by artisans in the Great City. Tall, broad-shouldered warriors from Eekrit's own clan stood guard at every corner and to either side of the chamber's door, clad in armour of thick leather faced with bronze discs and clutching fearsome-looking polearms.

At the rear of the dais another, smaller platform had been built, upon which sat a fine and imposing throne made of teak and inlaid with traceries of gold. Growling under his breath, Eekrit stalked back to the throne and collapsed angrily onto its cushioned seat. 'Idiots,' he muttered darkly. 'I'm-I'm surrounded by *idiots*.'

The tunnel had been a masterstroke. It had taken weeks to gnaw through the hard granite closer to the mountain's heart, but it had positioned his army for a devastating thrust into the enemy's side. While a massive frontal assault pinned down the bulk of the mountain's defenders around mine shaft six, Vittrik's precious war engines would have been positioned to pour fire into the rear ranks of the enemy. Meanwhile, the rest of Eekrit's troops would have raced into the upper levels of the fortress, seizing key tunnel junctions and disrupting the flow of reinforcements from the surface. He'd fully expected to seize at least three of the enemy's upper shafts by the end of the day, possibly even more. With a little luck and the Horned God's favour, it could even have been the death-stroke that put an end to the whole war.

But of course it hadn't worked out that way. All he had to show for his efforts were another three thousand dead skaven and a raging fire in his painstakingly crafted tunnel that was *still* burning, hours after Vittrik's engines had been blown to scrap. If he cocked his ears just right, Eekrit could hear the sounds of crashing metal and panicked squeals in the distance as the drunken warlock-engineer took out his rage on his hapless slaves.

Lord Eekrit drummed his claws on the hard wood of the throne's armrest. What could he have possibly done to earn the Horned God's ire? Had he not made all the proper obeisances, given all the proper bribes? What had he done to deserve such a perplexing, miserable, *expensive* war?

True, he had personally profited greatly from the War beneath the Mountain, as it was being called back at the Great City. God-stone was being carved from the mine shafts under his control and shipped home in staggering amounts. His personal fortunes and those of his clan swelled with each passing season; they had grown so great that Rikek was now considered among the most powerful of the warlord clans. He could afford the best of everything, even sorcerous potions and charms of god-stone to preserve his handsome looks and youthful vigour. Eekrit had even begun to seriously consider buying his way onto the Great Council once the war ended. *If* it ever ended.

There was just no end to the damned skeletons. For every one his warriors killed, there seemed to be a dozen more ready to take its place. The northmen who'd apparently allied themselves with the walking corpses were at least something his people knew how to deal with. Long ago they'd had a running war with the humans over their meagre store of god-stone, and while the barbarians were fearsome warriors in their own right, the fact was that they had lost their war with the skaven all those centuries ago. They could be beaten. The corpse army, though, that was something else again.

The long war of attrition was consuming skaven lives at a horrifying rate. New companies of reinforcements were arriving from the Great City every month. When the first loads of god-stone had begun to arrive at home, there had been a massive swell of volunteers from the clans, each seeking to make their own fortunes in the war. Now most of those treasure-seekers were dead, spitted on enemy spears or eaten by the enemy's pallid corpse-takers, and their gnawed skeletons stood in ranks behind their foe's tunnel redoubts. All that Eekrit got from the clans now were mobs of terrified slaves and sullen criminals; he suspected that the Great City hadn't been so free of bandits in centuries.

So far, the Council of Thirteen had tolerated the bloody stalemate thanks to the wealth of god-stone Eekrit provided, but he knew that such tolerance had its limits. The Children of the Horned God had never fought so long and so bitter a war in the entire history of their people and their resources, however vast, were not without their limits. He had to find a way to break the deadlock, and soon, before the Grey Lords decided to take matters into their own paws.

Eekrit glanced sullenly at Eshreegar. 'What do you make of it?' he asked.

The Master of Treacheries shrugged. For once, Eshreegar couldn't be blamed for having no news to give the warlord; his scout-assassins had been covering the diversionary assault, many levels away from the disaster. 'We know that the northmen are accompanied by a witch,' he observed. 'It's said they have powers of divination. She might have predicted the attack.'

'Not that,' Eekrit growled. 'The burning man.'

Eshreegar's ears rose in surprise. 'You believe the pack leaders' tales?'

'The fools didn't have the wit to change their story, no matter how many throats I-I cut,' Eekrit grumbled. 'So I must assume they were telling the truth, strange as-as it seems.'

The black-robed skaven considered the warlord's question. 'A sorcerer-corpse, perhaps?'

Eekrit's whiskers twitched. 'Is such a thing possible?'

The Master of Treacheries shrugged again. 'Perhaps Qweeqwol knows.'

The warlord bared his teeth in disgust. 'Most days I'm not certain which side that-that lunatic is on.'

When the war had first begun, Eekrit had made a point of soliciting the old seer's advice, showing him the respect that Qweeqwol's station deserved; to do any less would have tempted the wrath of the Seer Council. All he'd gotten for his trouble were riddles, or rambling discourses on treachery and death – as though he needed an education on *those* subjects. Qweeqwol came and went as he pleased, roaming the caverns and the lower tunnels at will, even occasionally making token appearances along the battle-lines. It was as though the seer was searching for something, though what was anyone's guess. And yet, he wasn't *entirely* useless. Eekrit could think of at least three separate occasions over the years where Qweeqwol had taken an interest in the course of the campaign and supported Eekrit's strategies in the army's war councils. On two of those occasions, Lord Hiirc had very nearly turned the army's chieftains against him, but the seer had stomped into the middle of the proceedings and had the would-be rebels baring their throats with little more than a hard stare and a few well-chosen words. Come to that, Qweeqwol had also been instrumental in persuading Lord Vittrik to part with those precious war engines of his. It was as though the seer was pursuing an agenda all his own, but Eekrit hadn't the first clue what it might be.

A thought occurred to the warlord. He tapped a claw meditatively against the armrest. 'If this magical terror is half as deadly as those fools claimed it to be, perhaps I could appeal to the Seer Council for someone...'

'Younger?'

'Less insane.'

Eshreegar let out a high-pitched snort. 'Best of luck with that,' the Master of Treacheries said, his pink tail twitching.

The warlord's ears flattened in irritation. He raised a paw to summon a scribe, and was surprised to see one of his slaves already racing to the foot of the dais. Eekrit straightened.

'What is it?' he demanded.

The slave stretched himself out at the base of the steps – no mean feat, with the puddles of cooling blood scattered across the stones. 'New-new arrivals, master,' the slave gasped. 'From the Great City.'

Eekrit's whiskers twitched. Travellers to the mountain were rare, especially these days, and the next contingent of reinforcements weren't due for another few weeks. 'What manner of arrivals?' he asked.

'Warriors,' the slave squeaked. 'Many-many of them.'

Eekrit gave the Master of Treacheries a penetrating stare. Eshreegar tucked tail and head both.

'I-I don't know,' he said weakly. 'I've heard nothing.'

Eekrit growled deep in his throat. 'One day you'll have to tell me the story of how you came to be a master of scouts,' he said darkly. 'I imagine it's a *very* amusing tale.'

Without waiting for a reply, the warlord stalked down off the dais and across the audience chamber. His bodyguards fell into step behind him in ordered ranks, polearms held across their chests and tails lashing aggressively. The slave let out a startled squeak and dashed ahead of Eekrit to pull open the chamber's double doors.

Beyond lay a complex of walled spaces and narrow passageways, framed by three-quarter-height walls of mortar and stone, which included lavish living quarters for Eekrit and loyal members of his clan who served in his retinue. More bodyguards stood watch at strategic locations throughout the complex, ever vigilant for signs of treachery. They pounded the ends of their polearms on the stone floor as Eekrit approached, sending passing slaves scrambling out of the warlord's way.

The warlord's mind raced as he hurried through the maze of dimly lit corridors. He wasn't fool enough to assume that the sudden arrival of troops was a good sign, nor was he going to sit idle and wait for their leader to come and pay his respects. It was entirely possible that one clan or another – possibly Morbus, or even Skryre – had decided to alter the balance of power in their favour and claim the mountain's riches entirely for their own. The longer he waited to assert himself, the more time the new arrivals had to begin pursuing their own agendas.

The clangour and stench of the cavern steadily grew as the warlord left his clan's lair behind. The great space, once so vast it easily held as much as a quarter of the entire skaven expeditionary force, was now sub-divided into dense warrens of living quarters, foundries, storage sites and slave pens. The labyrinth of chambers and passageways spread outwards from the cavern for as much as a mile in every direction – an under-fortress to match the sprawl of towers and structures crowding the mountain slopes high above. There were even marketplaces stretching back along the wide tunnels that led to the Great City, where traders from the lesser clans gathered to provide goods and luxuries for the wealthier members of the expeditionary force. Eekrit couldn't even guess how large the population under the mountain had grown over the last two decades; in another ten years the under-fortress might become a subterranean city every bit as tangled, scheming and treacherous as anywhere else in the growing skaven empire.

Hot, dank air swirled around the warlord, reeking of scorched metal, offal and old, pungent musk. Skaven screeched imprecations at their slaves; somewhere a whip cracked and a young voice cried out in pain. Copper furnaces huffed and roared, sending up thin ribbons of acrid smoke and casting waves of pulsing green light across the soot-stained roof of the cavern. It was the sound and smell of civilisation, Eekrit mused. Whether the skeletons wanted it or not, the skaven were here to stay.

The warlord and his bodyguards cut like a knife through the crowds of labourers, slaves and clan warriors milling along the main arteries that led across the floor of the cavern. He headed for the broad square that lay just inside the cavern opposite the Skaven Gate, which opened onto the wide tunnel that led from the mountain back to the Great City. As they approached the square he could hear the deep buzz of voices up ahead.

Eekrit emerged at the side of the square opposite the Skaven Gate and, even knowing what to expect, the sight of the warriors assembled there stunned him. The entire assembly area was packed from one end to the other, and judging by the commotion over by the gate, there were still more arriving. Facing him were packs of towering, broad-shouldered skaven warriors, armoured in layered plates of bronze and wielding polearms with broad, curved blades. They were the *heechigar*, the elite storm-walkers of the warlord clans, rarely seen in the field unless–

The warlord felt his hackles rise at the sight of the two skaven standing in the shadow of the storm-walkers. One was mad old Qweeqwol. The aged seer was standing with his back to Eekrit, his knobby paws gripping the ancient wood of his glowing staff as he spoke in low tones to a tall, lean skaven lord.

Eekrit's tail twitched. The warlord clamped down hard on his musk glands. The skaven lord was older than he, and wore a fine harness of bronze plates chased with gold. Glowing tokens of god-stone hung about his neck, and another god-stone the size of a swamp-lizard egg shone balefully from the pommel of a curved sword resting at his hip. His lean, dark-furred head bore the marks of the battlefield: a triangular notch had been neatly sliced from the skaven's right ear, and a fearsome old scar spread down his cheek and across his throat like a jagged fork of pale lightning. But it wasn't the terrible scars, or the vicious sword and armour that struck terror into Eekrit's ruthless heart, it was the unassuming grey wool robe that hung about the lord's broad shoulders.

Eekrit's bodyguards snapped to attention at once, the butts of their polearms striking the stone in a single, well-practised motion. The sound caught the attention of the skaven lord, whose dark eyes narrowed coldly as they regarded the warlord. Noticing the sudden change, Qweeqwol turned about slowly and focused on Eekrit as well, his glowing green eyes unblinking and inscrutable.

Lord Eekrit clasped his paws over his stomach and approached the newcomer. Despite his best efforts, his whiskers gave a single, nervous twitch.

'An honour,' Eekrit managed to say. The back of his neck itched as he sank to his knees before the Grey Lord. His eyes were on a level with the baleful light at the pommel of the skaven's sword. 'A great-great honour, yes.' The warlord's fawning expression faltered. 'Ah, my lord–'

'Velsquee,' Lord Qweeqwol announced. 'Grey Lord Velsquee, of Clan Abbis.'

Eekrit stole a glance at the seer. Was the old fool smirking at him?

'My lord Velsquee,' he continued, pronouncing the name with care. 'Welcome you to the under-fortress.' The warlord bowed his head. 'How may I serve the Council?'

The Grey Lord stared coldly down at Eekrit. 'Under-fortress, eh?' he said. 'I suppose you've scratched out a lair for yourself somewhere in this nest.'

Eekrit gritted his teeth. The stonecutters had only just finished the last touches on his chambers. 'I would be pleased to make them available to you, my lord,' he managed to say. 'Will you be visiting for long?'

Velsquee rested a clawed paw on the hilt of his sword. 'As long as it takes to win this war,' he said with a wicked smile. 'This stalemate's gone on long enough. It's time for a change of strategy.'

FOUR

NECESSARY EVILS

Lahmia,
the City of the Dawn,
in the 98th year of Tahoth the Wise
(-1300 Imperial Reckoning)

The night air was sultry in the Travellers' Quarter, redolent with sweat, cooking spices and sour wine. Crowds of immigrants - mostly from the struggling cities of Mahrak or Lybaras, but also a few from as far away as drought-stricken Numas - mingled with dusty caravan drivers and scowling sell-swords as they plied the tightly-packed merchant stalls in search of everything from fine saddles to silver jewellery. The singsong chants of the merchants seemed to drift like smoke through the humid air, rising and falling over the muted buzz of the crowd.

The night bazaar stretched for six winding blocks through the quarter, and was anchored at the eastern end by a wide, paved square lined with ale-houses, wine-sellers and incense shops. Lord Ushoran sat at a table beneath a faded linen awning of a wine-seller's shop, idly fingering the cracked rim of a clay cup filled with date wine as he studied the faces of the passers-by.

Tonight he chose to wear the face of a well-to-do scholar: a dispossessed Lybaran noble, perhaps, driven from his home by the steady decline of the collegia there and forced to continue his studies in self-imposed exile. The serving girls and the other patrons of the wine shop saw a man of middle years, stooped with age, his pate gone bald save for a thin fringe of white. His nose was crooked, his eyes watery and deeply set. His cheeks were pocked from a bout of river fever, and starting to show the rude blush of a man who indulged in too much wine. A dark brown robe hung from his hunched shoulders, the fabric rich but faded from years of hard use. Around his thick neck hung a chain made of elongated links of gold, decorated with more than a dozen brass-rimmed lenses of glass and faceted crystal - one of the many tools of the scholar-engineer's trade.

In the past, he'd had to be far less ostentatious with his disguises, for there was only so much one could do with a change of clothing and a bit of face paint. He'd tried to blend with the teeming crowds, quickly dismissed and easily forgotten. Now, he was limited only by his imagination and he could switch guises with but a moment's concentration. Ushoran could cloud a mortal's mind simply by willing it, placing any image in his or her mind that suited him. It was a gift that none of his fellow immortals possessed and, more importantly, one that not even their supernatural senses could penetrate. Which was for the best, as far as he was concerned. He doubted that Neferata or Ankhat would approve of what he had become.

Ushoran was nothing like the acerbic, cerebral W'soran, but he still considered himself a scholar of sorts. Mysteries and secrets intrigued him, and the process of death and rebirth was one of the greatest mysteries of all. Though Neferata had forbidden the cabal to create immortal progeny of their own, he had made a few discreet experiments over the centuries and suspected that the others – especially W'soran – had as well. He'd made good use of the dozen or so safe houses he'd established throughout the city, with their deep cellars and sets of stout chains fixed to the walls.

Along the way, he'd learned a great deal. Their kind could only draw sustenance from living blood; animals could serve, but the vigour they possessed was far less potent than a human's. Starvation steadily weakened them, but did not bring extinction – merely a kind of nightmarish torpor, which could only be broken by the taste of blood. The vigour gleaned from living blood gave them strength and speed far surpassing any mortal, and allowed them to swiftly heal any wound save outright decapitation. If their heart was pierced, or rendered unable to beat, they became torpid until the offending object was removed. As a result, they were nearly impossible to kill. Fire inflicted lasting injury; direct sunlight sapped their vigour with terrible speed, and especially intense sunlight burned like a brand. Ushoran suspected that sorcery could harm them as well, but had to wait to test the theory himself.

Such qualities were common to all immortals. In addition were the unique gifts that manifested in Neferata and the rest of the cabal – those who were transfigured by the complex and gruelling mixture of poison and magical ritual that Arkhan the Black had used to resurrect the queen herself. Neferata's goddess-given beauty and allure had increased tenfold, lending her powers of seduction and mental domination far beyond mortal ken. Arkhan, the aristocrat and political creature that he was, demonstrated his own sense of eerie charisma and razor-keen perception. In life, Arkhan had been a well-known hunter and breeder of horse and hound, and Ushoran wondered if perhaps his gifts had developed along those lines as well. W'soran, the secretive former priest, was entirely the opposite. He had been transformed into a repellent, skeletal creature, more corpse than man, but his grasp of the arcane – and necromancy in particular – possibly rivalled that of the infamous Nagash himself. That left Abhorash, the former king's champion, and Zurhas, the feckless cousin to the late Lamashizzar. Abhorash had fled the city almost immediately after his transformation and Ushoran could only speculate on the particulars of his transformation, but given his dedication to the arts of warfare, Ushoran suspected that Abhorash had gained a degree of physical prowess equal to – or possibly greater than – the fabled Ushabti themselves. If true, there was no deadlier warrior anywhere in the world.

As for Zurhas, Ushoran hadn't a clue. The former nobleman seemed more furtive and rodent-like with every passing year. Perhaps his gifts extended to gambling and whoring, two of his favourite pastimes. It stood to reason. Every one of them had changed in ways that reflected their true natures, for good or ill.

Lost in thought, Ushoran didn't notice the lean, travel-stained man at first. He'd slipped from the crowd milling in the square with the practiced ease of a cutpurse and unobtrusively ducked beneath the wine shop's low awning. The man's flinty, appraising stare swept over Ushoran, stirring him from his reverie.

This was the one he'd been waiting for, Ushoran realised at once. The man had the look of a desert bandit, clad in dusty, tattered robes and ragged leather sandals held together with cheap twine. A battered khopesh and a pair of curved daggers hung from a wide leather belt about his waist, partly concealed by a thin, sand-coloured cloak that hung nearly to the man's feet. His face was narrow and gaunt, the leathery skin tanned a deep brown by years of exposure to the harsh desert sun. With his narrow chin, hooded eyes and brooding brow, he reminded Ushoran somewhat of a jackal – which, considering his profession, wasn't all that much of a surprise. The Lord of Masks met the tomb robber's gaze and placed a bulging leather bag on the table next to the wine. The coins inside clinked softly as he set the bag down.

Even then, with his reward in sight, the thief didn't immediately react. His gaze swept past Ushoran and studied the rest of the shop for a full minute, searching for signs of a trap. When he found none, the man wove among the tables and took the chair opposite Ushoran. He studied the Lord of Masks silently for a moment. Ushoran returned the stare with a placid smile.

The thief grunted to himself. 'You're not what I expected,' he said.

Ushoran chuckled. The thief and his companions had been hired through a sprawling network of intermediaries stretching all the way to Khemri, one entirely separated from his conventional network of informants and spies. He'd been careful and patient, building the links over a period of decades, until he was certain that their actions could not be traced back to him. The consequences of discovery – for Ushoran, and for Lahmia in general – would have been too terrible to contemplate.

'I hear that quite a lot,' the Lord of Masks said with a smile. 'Wine?'

The thief shrugged. Ushoran beckoned, and a girl quickly appeared at his shoulder with another cup of wine. About fourteen, the nobleman reckoned, admiring the girl as she bent over the table. Fine skin, firm of flesh and lean of limb. A bit old for his tastes; in the old days he might not have cared – the older ones lasted longer, after all – but now he could afford to be choosy. The girl met his gaze, smiled innocently, and hastily withdrew.

'To your health,' Ushoran said, raising his cup in a toast. He feigned taking a sip. The thief raised his cup and likely did the same. 'It's been months. I was beginning to grow concerned.'

The thief's upper lip curled in a sneer. 'There's a damned good reason why nearly all of the great pyramids are still intact, and Khemri's are the worst of the lot. Go barging inside and you'll be dead before you're ten steps past the door.' He shook his head. 'None of the other fools you hired made it past the first antechamber.'

Ushoran nodded. There had been four other gangs who'd accepted the job over the years. Khetep's pyramid had simply swallowed them up, one after the next. 'Truth be told, you were my first choice all along, but since you proved extraordinarily difficult to contact, I had to make do with lesser talents.'

The thief grunted noncommittally, but Ushoran caught a glint of pride in the tomb robber's eye.

The Lord of Masks spread his hands. 'So. What do you have for me?'

Once again, the thief glanced warily at the other tables. When he was satisfied that no one was watching them, he reached within his cloak and produced an old, wooden box the size of a small wine jar, which he set on the table between them.

Ushoran glanced sceptically at the box. 'That's all?'

The thief barked a laugh. 'If you'd wanted the whole thing, you should have said so,' he snarled. 'You're lucky we managed that much.'

The Lord of Masks sighed. 'I suppose it will do,' he said, though in truth W'soran would have to be the judge of that. 'You're certain it's him?'

The tomb robber shrugged. 'As certain as I can be,' he replied. 'It was the right tomb, sure enough, but... well, let's just say it wasn't your typical internment.'

Ushoran cocked his head quizzically. 'He wasn't interred with the typical grave goods?'

'Hardly.' To his surprise, the thief shifted uncomfortably. 'He wasn't even dead when they sealed him up.'

'Ah. I see.' Ushoran had heard tales of Nagash's brutal usurpation, but there had been no way to tell fact from rumour at the time. He picked up the heavy bag of coin and set it down beside the thief's cup. 'I'd say you and your people earned every bit of this.'

The man picked up the bag and hefted it. 'Only four of us made it out of that damned place,' he said grimly. 'There were traps everywhere. Poor Jebil died on the way out, just three steps from the entrance. Toppled over dead with a dart in his neck. Never did find out where it came from.'

Ushoran nodded sagely. 'Sad, indeed,' he agreed. 'And your three companions?'

A slow, wolfish smile spread across the thief's face. 'Well. The Golden Plain's a dangerous place,' he said slowly. 'Bandits everywhere, you know.'

'How tragic,' the Lord of Masks replied. 'I suppose you'll just have to keep their shares as well.'

'I suppose so,' the thief said, slipping the bag beneath his cloak. He rose quickly from the table.

Ushoran laid a hand on the wooden box. 'You aren't the least bit curious about this?' he asked.

'I couldn't care less,' the thief said, his attention already focused on the square.

'Well, I suppose that's it, then.' Ushoran leaned forwards, extending his hand. 'Safe travels, my friend. You have my thanks.'

The thief turned back to Ushoran, looking down at the immortal's outstretched hand as though it were an especially venomous snake. He started to sneer – but something in the immortal's eye gave him pause. After a moment's hesitation he reached out and gripped Ushoran's hand.

'I have your gold, and that's enough,' the thief growled. 'Goodbye, scholar. I don't expect we'll see each other again.'

With that he turned and slipped into the square without a single backwards glance. The thief blended into the milling crowd and within moments was lost to sight.

Ushoran watched him go with a smile. His hand was still faintly damp from the thief's sweaty grip. He raised it, palm inwards, to his face and breathed deeply, drinking in the man's scent.

'I hear that quite a lot, too,' the immortal said. He chuckled softly to himself and licked his palm lightly with the tip of his long, grey tongue.

The Temple of Blood was a fortress within a fortress. Situated within the walls of the Lahmian royal palace, the huge, roughly pyramidal structure fully enclosed what had once been the Women's Palace, where the daughters of the royal line were kept in virtual seclusion from the rest of the mortal world. The stepped sides of the temple were comprised of solid blocks of sandstone, each one twelve feet high and weighing many tons. The only entrance was sealed by a pair of immense bronze doors and was guarded day and night by a company of dour-looking warriors from the queen's lifeguard. To all outside appearances, the monumental structure seemed more impregnable than the royal palace itself, but, like much else about the temple, such impressions were deceiving.

The hour of the dead was fast approaching as Ushoran stole across the silent palace grounds towards the temple. There were few mortals about at such a late hour, allowing him to pass unobserved along the north wall of the mammoth structure until he reached the hidden entrance set cunningly into the stone. The door was very heavy, and set so snugly into its frame that its seams were nearly invisible to the naked eye. Pressing with both hands and exerting his unnatural strength, he swung the portal silently inwards, revealing a dark, narrow passage carved into the foundation stone.

There were at least a half-dozen secret ways into and out of the temple that Ushoran knew of; only Neferata herself could say if there were more. He followed the passageway through the temple's foundation, emerging a short while later into the ground level passageways that wound secretly among the storerooms, dormitories and halls of meditation used by the initiates of the cult. The immortal moved down the dark corridors swiftly and surely, aided by supernatural senses and more than two centuries of practice. Finally, many minutes later, he passed through another hidden door and into the temple's vast inner sanctum.

In truth, the inner sanctum was actually a sprawling complex of chambers that had once comprised the most opulent rooms of the old Women's Palace. It was here that Neferata ruled, issuing edicts from the Deathless Court through successive generations of Lahmian queens who were enslaved to her from birth. But that wasn't the only secret concealed within the inner sanctum's walls – and, in Ushoran's opinion, far from the worst.

There were many libraries in the former palace: small, quiet rooms piled with sumptuous rugs and surrounded by shelves atop shelves of histories, fables, romances and more. They were nothing like the one Ushoran now sought. It was located in a largely isolated part of the old palace, far from the corridors frequented by the temple priestesses and initiates. Its walls had been reinforced with slabs of dark, heavy granite, which in turn had been engraved with layer upon layer of arcane wards designed to keep out even the most determined intruder. The door, likewise, was stone, and far too heavy for mortal hands to open. It was also covered with potent runes of binding, strong enough to seal the library shut for all time, but for the last fifty years the sigils had been cold and inert. The Lord of Masks took a moment to compose himself, putting on the bland, neutral face that his fellow cabal members were accustomed to, then laid a hand upon the door and pushed it silently open.

As always, the chamber was dimly lit and wreathed with acrid incense smoke, shrouding the walls and ceiling in darkness and rendering the dimensions of the room uncertain. A dense arrangement of worktables and reading stands filled the chamber, piled with precise stacks of parchment and priceless, leather-bound tomes of varying size. Some of the books were fairly new, having been written within the past half-century, while others were larger and far, far older.

Ushoran eyed a stack of such volumes on a nearby table as he slipped inside the room. They had been bound in pale leather once, but the centuries had caused the covers to wrinkle and darken to a deep reddish-black. Their edges were ragged from age and rough treatment; in their time they had travelled with armies, and been fought over like ghastly treasures. Their thick pages were likewise roughened and rendered grey with age, but Ushoran had no doubt that if he were bold enough to turn back one of the covers, he would find the notes and diagrams within still perfectly legible, despite the passage of years. These tomes had once belonged to Nagash himself, plundered from his Black Pyramid outside the ruins of Khemri after the war. Some of the volumes were at least five hundred years old, Ushoran reckoned, and yet they lingered when other books would have long since turned to dust.

W'soran stood at the far side of the chamber, his macabre form lit by wan candlelight as he paced about the perimeter of a complicated magical circle that had been laid down with silver dust on the bare stone floor. He was a hideous figure, bearing more resemblance to a poorly mummified corpse than a living, breathing man. What little flesh he'd possessed had melted away, leaving his grey, parchment-like skin stretched tight against ropy sinew and sharp-edged bone. The immortal moved with a strange, angular gait, almost like a spider, and his bald head swung from side to side in furtive arcs as he surveyed the handiwork of his thralls. The circle was, in truth, more like a nested set of complex bands of magical runes, each one laid down with exacting precision and carefully arranged in relation to one another. It was the culmination of a half-century of effort, shaped by the most astute arcane mind in Nehekhara. Ushoran hoped that it would be enough.

W'soran's head rose as the Lord of Masks stole into the chamber. His fleshless lips were plastered against his teeth, exaggerating his needle-like fangs and lending the immortal a permanent snarl. He drew a rasping breath. 'Will you never learn to knock, my lord?'

Ushoran smiled coldly. 'I don't see why I should,' he replied. 'Neferata certainly won't.'

'Neferata,' W'soran sneered. 'She thinks of nothing but her young prince these days. I doubt she even recalls opening the library at this point.'

'Let us hope so. Because we both know what she would do if she realised what you've been up to these last fifty years.'

W'soran hissed derisively, but Ushoran caught a flash of unease in the immortal's deep-set eyes. Necromancy had been forbidden even when Lamashizzar was master of the cabal, but Neferata had even gone so far as to take the worst of Nagash's tomes and lock them away in a separate vault elsewhere in the inner sanctum. W'soran had been trying to circumvent her restrictions ever since. He had persuaded her to open the library solely to learn the rituals of summoning and communicating with spirits, and so far as it went, he had spoken the truth. If she knew precisely *who* W'soran intended to call up from the lands of the restless dead, her wrath would be terrible to behold.

Ushoran had known what he was up to from the beginning. W'soran had never been secretive about his ambitions. But instead of betraying the would-be necromancer, Ushoran had become an uneasy ally. As terrible as the risks were, he was certain that Neferata's obsession with Alcadizzar would ultimately lead to disaster. They needed leverage to persuade her to abandon her ridiculous scheme – or, failing that, the power to supplant her and seize control of Lahmia themselves.

W'soran's gaze fell to the wooden box tucked under Ushoran's arm. His pale eyes narrowed. 'Is that it?'

The Lord of Masks stepped forwards, setting the box on one of the tables. 'You tell me.'

W'soran made his way across the cluttered chamber, weaving among the tables and reading stands with his strange, spider-like gait. His ghastly face was lit with a dreadful sense of anticipation as he unfastened the catch and opened the lid of the box.

Ushoran folded his arms. 'I'd thought he would have brought more,' the Lord of Masks said with a scowl. 'Will it be enough?'

A faint, hitching rattle rose from W'soran's throat. It took a moment before Ushoran realised the immortal was chuckling to himself.

'Oh, yes,' W'soran hissed, reaching into the box with knobby, clawed hands. 'Yes. This will do.'

He lifted from the box a human skull, still covered in scraps of yellow flesh and matted black hair. The eyes were empty sockets, the nose, lips and ears gnawed down to little more than tattered nubs by the work of hungry tomb beetles. The jaw hung open, as though frozen in the midst of an agonised scream; the taut, leathery tendons of the jaw muscles stood out in sharp relief beneath the papery skin.

Buried alive, Ushoran thought, recalling what the thief had told him. The thought sent a chill down his spine.

'Is it him?' he asked.

W'soran nodded. 'Thutep, last true king of Khemri,' he said with certainty. 'And brother to Nagash the Usurper.'

'How can you be so certain?'

'Because his death is etched here.' W'soran traced a clawed fingertip along Thutep's skull, from forehead to chin. 'The agonies he suffered in the tomb left their mark in flesh and bone before Thutep's spirit passed into the dead lands.' He turned away from the table, still holding the king's skull, and beckoned with his free hand. At once a gaunt, robed figure shuffled out of the shadows near the circle, bearing a short stand made of bronze. As Ushoran watched, W'soran plucked the stand out of the thrall's hand and stepped carefully into the summoning circle. The would-be necromancer set the stand at its centre and placed the skull atop it.

Ushoran's eyes widened. 'You're going to attempt the summoning *now*?'

'Why not?' W'soran beckoned again, and another pair of thralls placed a heavy wooden lectern a few feet from the edge of the summoning circle. 'The hour is right, and the position of the moons propitious.'

'Well.' The Lord of Masks eyed the ritual symbols dubiously. 'Are you certain the wards will hold?'

'As certain as I can be,' W'soran replied. He opened the heavy tome resting upon the stand and began searching through its pages.

Ushoran fought the urge to start edging towards the door. This was what they'd been working towards for decades, after all. If the summoning worked, they would finally be in a position to challenge Neferata. 'But, what if... I mean, suppose there is an accident–'

The would-be necromancer glanced back at Ushoran. 'You wish to leave?'

Ushoran paused. The smug note in W'soran's voice was enough to steel his resolve. 'Certainly not,' he answered coldly. He folded his arms and drew a deep breath. 'Go on. Call to him. Let's see what he's got to say.'

W'soran's leathery cheeks wrinkled, creaking like old saddle leather as he attempted a smile. 'As you wish,' he said. Chuckling to himself, he turned back to the open tome and spread his skeletal hands wide. He drew a long, whistling breath and then began the invocation.

The arcane words rolled easily from W'soran's withered tongue and his voice grew stronger as he spoke, until the invocation rang from the chamber walls. Ushoran tried to follow the awful litany at first, but the words scarcely left an impression upon his mind. The passage of time seemed to slow, then failed to register altogether.

The temperature began to fall within the room. The chill came on quickly, like the cold of a desert night. Sheets of parchment fluttered atop the table next to Ushoran, stirred by a sudden breeze, and suddenly he realised that W'soran's voice no longer echoed through the shadow-haunted room.

At some point, the candles had gone out. What little illumination there was came from a pillar of pale, shifting blue light that hung in the air above Thutep's screaming skull. As Ushoran focused on the light, he became aware of a faint sibilance emanating from the circle, like the stirring of a nest of snakes. The more he listened, however, he realised that it wasn't hissing, but *whispering*. A multitude of voices, young and old; some of them were insistent, others fearful. Some were angry. *Very* angry.

W'soran's shout rode above the sea of voices. 'Come forth!' he cried. 'Nagash, son of Khetep, I call you! Nagash, priest of Settra's cult, I call you! Nagash, usurper of Khemri, I call you! Heed my voice and *come forth!*'

The chorus of spirits broke into wails at the sound of Nagash's name. Sheets of parchment flew into the air; a cold wind rose up, buffeting Ushoran's face. A heavy stack of books tottered, and then fell to the floor with a crash.

'Heed me!' W'soran shouted into the building gale. 'By the blood of your brother Thutep, I command it! Come forth!'

The pillar of light began to waver. Thin screams issued from it. Voices howled in despair, or spat curses, or begged for release. One of W'soran's thralls was hurled away from the circle like a straw doll; he flew more than ten feet through the air and hit one of the wooden tables with a bone-jarring thud.

W'soran flung a hand out towards the shifting column of light, as though he could steady it in his grip. 'You must obey!' he shouted. 'Show yourself!'

The wind continued to rise, until it roared in Ushoran's ears like a hungry lion. The voices of the dead swelled in volume as well, until he could make out individual voices, each one clamouring to be heard above the din.

Within the circle, Ushoran could see tendrils of smoke curling around Thutep's skull. The hair and skin were blackening, as though from the heat of a fire, even though the room was as cold as the abyss itself. The pillar of light was growing brighter, even as its outlines grew less stable. Ushoran felt a pressure against his chest – light at first, but growing stronger and more tangible with every second, until it felt as though dozens of hands were clutching at him. The more distinct they became, the more frantically they reached for him, as though he were becoming more substantial – more *solid* – to the ghosts themselves.

There was an anguished cry – for a moment, Ushoran thought he'd uttered it himself, but then realised the sound had come from W'soran instead. The would-be necromancer clenched his fists and spat a string of angry words and the pillar of light grew tall and thin, as though squeezed in a giant's fist. Ushoran felt the unseen hands clench desperately at his robes, and then they were torn away as the pillar vanished in a brittle crack of thunder.

Darkness fell. Ushoran heard W'soran mutter a sulphurous curse, and then the sharp sound of splintering wood.

By the time the thralls were able to relight the candles, W'soran was bending down and picking up Nagash's tome from the floor. The heavy reading stand had been smashed to splinters; jagged bits of wood jutted from W'soran's palm, but the immortal didn't seem to notice.

Ushoran smoothed his rumpled robes. Belatedly, he saw that they were torn in places. A chill went down his spine.

'What happened?' he asked.

W'soran inspected the ancient book carefully for signs of damage and then set it aside. The immortal stepped carefully into the circle and picked up Thutep's skull. 'I held open the doorway as long as I could,' he said absently, studying the grisly artefact. 'Much longer, and we might have lost the skull. The amount of energy focused on it was... considerable.'

'That's not what I mean,' Ushoran said. 'What went wrong? Why couldn't you summon him?'

The immortal did not reply at first. His shoulders tensed. 'I don't know,' he said at last.

'I thought you said–'

'I know what I said!' W'soran snapped. He turned to Ushoran, his withered face a mask of rage. 'The skull was the perfect link to Nagash. It should have worked! The rite has never failed me before. *Never!*'

Silent, shuffling thralls emerged from the shadows and went to work restoring some order to the wind-wracked library. Ushoran absently watched them as they worked, trying to force his stunned mind to function. 'If not the rite, then what else could it have been?'

W'soran shook his head slowly. 'An unforeseen complication. A... temporary setback. Nothing more,' he said. He stared at the skull for a moment more, then turned and placed it carefully into the hands of a waiting thrall.

'I must think on this,' he said at last. 'Perhaps it has to do with the vibrations of the third enumeration...'

The immortal's voice drifted away as he turned back to the summoning circle. He stroked his pointed chin with a clawed hand as he studied the dense bands of ritual symbols. It was not a dismissal as such, but Ushoran could see that he had been clearly forgotten.

That suited the Lord of Masks. He slipped silently from the library and swung the heavy stone door shut behind him. It was nearing dawn, and he had one last bit of business to attend to.

The tomb thief was clever and cautious, but nevertheless predictable. His scent led from the Travellers' Quarter to the Red Silk Quarter, down by the city docks. With little more than an hour to go until dawn, many of the district's dice houses and brothels had shut their doors. Dozens of revellers lay in the filthy streets, overcome by too much wine, or lotus root, or both. Bored-looking men from the City Guard checked each insensate form in turn; those who were clearly members of Lahmia's noble class were lifted from the gutter and urged on their way, while the others were efficiently searched for valuables and left where they lay. A few small knots of leathery-skinned sailors followed along behind the guardsmen, looking for stout bodies to fill the rowing benches of their merchant ships.

Ushoran took two long steps and leapt from the edge of the dice house's roof, clearing the narrow alley with ease and landing in a crouch on the pleasure house next door. He paused there for a moment, his hulking form hidden in deep shadow, nostrils flaring as he tasted the hot night air.

He followed the thief's scent to the far side of the roof, keeping low and creeping along on hands and feet like a jungle ape. It felt good to hunt again, he thought, feeling the salt breeze against his bare skin. He found it ironic that, despite what he had become, he had less opportunity to indulge his appetites now than he'd had as a mortal.

Ushoran intended to savour the next few minutes as much as possible. The failed attempt to summon the Usurper's spirit had left him deeply unsettled. He and W'soran were playing a dangerous game, one that could threaten Lahmia just as much as Neferata's obsession with Alcadizzar, but what other choice did they have?

Swift and silent, he paused at the low parapet and peered over the edge. The rooms on this side of the building looked out over the wide harbour and the slate-grey sea. Ushoran paused, his large, lantern-jawed head swinging from left to right until he caught the scent of his prey. In one fluid motion, he planted a wide, clawed hand on the parapet and swung out over the edge. For a delicious instant he hung in empty space, thirty feet above the ground, then he dropped like a cat onto the wide ledge of a window directly below.

The window to the bedchamber had been left open to let in the cool sea breeze. Ushoran's gaze swept across the dimly lit room. The air was still tinged with blue streamers of incense and lotus smoke. A trio of figures lay tangled in the silk sheets upon the low, wide bed.

Ushoran ran his tongue along jagged teeth as he climbed silently into the chamber. It was the work of a few moments to find the bag of coins he'd given the thief just a few hours before. He hefted the bag in his hand and smiled, then set it carefully beside the bedchamber door.

There was more than enough coin left to pay for the mess he was about to make.

FIVE

REVERSAL OF FORTUNES

Nagashizzar,
in the 99th year of Asaph the Beautiful
(-1295 Imperial Reckoning)

The fires could be seen from the tallest tower of the fortress, glittering like a necklace of rubies across the hilltops along the northern shore of the Crystal Sea. From the dark lanes that ran along the terraced mountain slope, hundreds of the Yaghur filled the night air with eerie, ululating howls as they caught wind of the devastation that had been wrought on their squalid homes.

Thestus folded his arms and studied the distant lights. 'I count six fires,' he said grimly. His skin was pale as chalk beneath the moonlight and his once-dark eyes were now the colour of eastern jade. But for a few tendrils of black hair that fluttered in the breeze rolling in from the sea, the barbarian stood with the statue-like stillness common to the undead. 'Judging by their positions, I would say that the largest of the Yaghur nests have been put to the flame.'

Nagash stood beside Thestus atop the narrow tower, his body shielded from the sea breeze by a heavy, hooded cloak. Ancient flesh crackled as he clenched his fists in rage. Dimly, the necromancer felt the leathery tendons of his right hand start to give way under the pressure; with an act of will he exerted his power and re-knit the corded flesh back together. The practice had grown so common over the last few years that he performed it almost without conscious thought. There was a sound like the tightening of dry leather cord, and his fingers curled inwards like a grasping claw. Too much of the ancient tissue had disintegrated, leaving the remaining tendons foreshortened. The realisation further deepened Nagash's fury.

'*Despatch ten companies of infantry,*' he snarled. '*Run the damned ratmen to earth and destroy them!*'

Behind Nagash, in the shadow of the tower's arched doorway, Bragadh answered coldly. 'Send the Yaghur if you want to chase the ratmen,' he said. 'It's their filthy holes that are burning, after all.'

Nagash rounded on the warlord, his eyes blazing angrily. Words of power rose to his fleshless lips, ready to form an incantation that would shrivel the barbarian like a moth in a candle flame. The necromancer's anger was palpable, radiating from his body in icy waves, but the warlord was unmoved. He stood with his fists clenched at his side, his expression icy and resentful. Diarid stood close by, his expression neutral but his body tense, as though ready to throw himself between Bragadh and the necromancer's wrath.

'*You forget yourself, Bragadh*,' Nagash hissed. '*More important, you forget your oaths to me.*' The menace in his voice was like a knife, poised and ready to strike.

Yet the warlord seemed heedless of the danger. His voice took on a hard edge all of its own. 'Not so,' he replied. 'Be assured, master, I have forgotten nothing. I remember all too well how I swore to obey you – while you, in turn, swore to protect the hill forts of our people. And look what came of *that*.'

Doom had befallen the hill forts of the northmen five years ago, not long after Nagash's failed counter-stroke against the ratmen. In one night, four of the largest of the barbarian settlements had been set upon by the enemy, who burrowed up into their midst and slaughtered every man, woman and child they could find. The hill forts' small garrisons were totally unprepared to deal with the savage raids, and without any sorcery of their own there was no way to predict when or where the next attack would occur. More settlements were attacked on the following night, and on the night after that. By the time that a messenger reached Nagashizzar with the news, nearly a dozen of the hill forts had been destroyed. Bragadh and his kinsmen had been beside themselves with rage. They begged Nagash for permission to march north and protect the hill forts; even though many of the barbarians hadn't seen their homes in decades, their rough sense of honour demanded that they take action. Nagash had refused outright. The barbarian companies were needed in Nagashizzar, helping to secure the mine shafts still under his control.

Instead, the necromancer had withdrawn to his throne chamber and begun working on a great and terrible ritual. The drafting of the sigil alone had taken days, marking out a great circle and hundreds of complex runes with *abn-i-khat* dust. Nagash had ingested still more of the dust, until his withered flesh was saturated with it. Then, upon the hour of the dead, he entered the great circle and began a fearsome incantation.

Once, long ago, he'd kept Bragadh and his barbarians in line with the subtle threat that their homeland was rich with the bones of their ancestors. Any rebellion by the hill forts could be crushed by the simple expedient of raising a punitive army drawn from the barrows of their own ancestors. Nagash now called forth the bones of the ancients not to punish the hill forts, but to protect them from further harm. Across the length and breadth of the barbarian lands, hundreds upon hundreds of skeletal warriors rose at Nagash's command and returned to the hills that had once been their homes.

When next the enemy raiders came pouring up from their tunnels, they ran headlong onto the swords and axes of the ancient dead. The few survivors were sent screeching back the way they'd come – only to return in greater numbers on the following night. Defeat followed defeat, but the enemy was undeterred. The raids grew more sporadic and more widely scattered; sometimes they inflicted more damage, sometimes less. Always they were chased off with substantial loss of life, but the tempo of the attacks never abated. They continued for months, then years, and slowly Nagash grasped the purpose of the enemy's strategy. Though they lost nearly every battle against his forces, they were succeeding in forcing him to maintain scores of large garrisons across the northlands. Relatively small raiding forces were requiring him to maintain thousands of undead troops, draining his energies at a constant and prodigious rate. Meanwhile, the incessant tunnel warfare beneath Nagashizzar ground on and on, further taxing his strength and dividing his attentions.

After five years, the strain had become severe. Worse, it had sowed seeds of discord among his barbarian troops. Nagash had watched Bragadh grow more sullen with each passing year; the damage inflicted on the hill forts had reduced the stream of new recruits to a mere trickle. Now the ratmen felt bold enough to strike at the heart of the Yaghur as well. The enemy was drawing a noose around the mighty fortress, one agonising inch at a time.

Before Nagash realised it, his deformed right hand was raised to strike at Bragadh. Lambent bale-fire crackled hungrily along the curved fingers, increasing in power with each passing moment. Bragadh never flinched; his resentful glare practically invited the necromancer's wrath.

Perhaps Bragadh wanted to be struck down, Nagash thought. Certainly, the enemy would wish it. There was no telling what repercussions such a blow would have on the rest of the barbarian army. The northmen worshipped Bragadh almost like a god at this point; to destroy him might incite the barbarians to open revolt. Though Nagash was certain that he could ultimately crush such an uprising, doing so would require troops that were desperately needed in the tunnels, and he had no doubt that the ratmen would take advantage of the crisis.

The noose around Nagashizzar drew inexorably tighter.

For a long moment, Nagash struggled to choke back his rage. Slowly, he closed his fist and willed the pent-up energies to dissipate.

'*The day will come,*' the necromancer grated, '*when you will regret having spoken thus. For now, you will simply* obey.'

Nagash reached out with his will and seized both of the barbarian warriors. Bragadh and Diarid went rigid, their eyes widening in horror as the necromancer used the power of his life-giving elixir to reach into their very souls.

'You are mine to command,' Nagash hissed. *'Now and forever more. And I say take your warriors and go forth.'*

Bragadh's body trembled as the warlord struggled against Nagash's grip. A low, agonised groan seeped past his tightly clenched lips. But no matter how hard he fought, the effort was futile. The warlord's trembling increased and his body began to bend, like a river palm in the face of a howling desert storm.

Just before Bragadh could succumb, a slender figure emerged from the shadows beyond the tower doorway. Bone charms clinked softly as Akatha interposed herself between the warlord and Nagash.

'This accomplishes nothing,' she said to the necromancer. Her voice was hollow and cold, but her steady gaze and straight-backed pose still held some of the witch's old defiance. 'Unless it is your intention to play into the enemy's hands.'

Fresh rage boiled up from Nagash's withered heart. His left hand shot out, seizing the witch by the throat. Visions of hurling the barbarian woman over the tower battlements danced before his mind's eye.

'You dare to speak thus to me?' he hissed. Ancient flesh along the back of the necromancer's hand crackled and flaked away as his bony fingers tightened around Akatha's neck. He felt her body stiffen, but her cool, penetrating stare never faltered.

'I do what I must,' the witch replied, her voice barely louder than a whisper. 'Despatching the great *kan's* warriors is pointless. If the raiders still remain, it is only because they have set an ambush for you.'

Akatha paused, drawing a tortured breath. 'The rat-things... have grown clever,' she managed to say. 'They are... forcing you... to waste your power on... futile gestures. You... cannot... *react*. You... lack... the strength.'

Her words only inflamed Nagash further. With an angry snarl he summoned still more power, dragging Akatha to the edge of the battlements as though she weighed nothing at all. Behind the necromancer, Bragadh let out a startled shout of protest.

More blackened pieces of skin crumbled away from Nagash's wrist in puffs of faintly glowing dust. The muscles and tendons lying along his arm looked like fraying cords of cured leather. All at once, he felt the bones of his wrist and hand shift ominously, as though threatening to burst apart beneath the strain. Without thinking, he summoned yet more power to force the bones into their proper place – and in that fleeting moment of concentration he understood that the witch spoke true. Whether the ratmen understood it or not, they were pushing him to the point of dissolution.

Nagash released Akatha. The witch half collapsed, slumping against the battlements. She looked up at the necromancer through a fall of tangled hair.

'The ratmen hope you will send warriors out into the hills,' she told him. 'Is it not obvious?'

Nagash had no answer. With an effort, the witch forced herself onto her feet. 'If you would strike at them, do so at a time and place of your own choosing and marshal your strength where it will do the most harm.'

The necromancer glared hatefully at the witch. The fact that Akatha was right only made him want to destroy her all the more. He relished the thought of forcing his will upon her and commanding the witch to cast herself from the top of the tower. She would struggle, no doubt, but that would make it all the sweeter. Yet was her destruction worth the power it would cost?

Nagash whirled on Bragadh and his champion. *'Send word to your companies,'* he told the warlord. *'Any warriors within the tunnels are to head for the surface and await my command.'*

Bragadh eyed the necromancer warily. 'What are you planning to do, master?' he asked.

'Something the damned ratmen will not expect,' Nagash replied.

The pale, crescent moon hung low in the sky to the west, casting its glow slantwise across the killing ground. Eekrit could hear the snarling howls and guttural barks of the flesh-eaters coming from a long way away, the maddened sounds carrying easily across the rolling, marshy ground. Like all skaven, the warlord could see perfectly in the darkness, and he searched the line of sickly yellow trees across from his hiding place for the first signs of the monsters' approach.

The raid on the flesh-eaters' foetid nests had unfolded with the mechanical precision of one of Lord Vittrik's tooth-and-gear contraptions. Unlike the campaign against the barbarian forts further north, Eekrit had no intention of digging his way directly into the monsters' foul burrows. Instead, his force, composed of the entirety of the army's scout-assassins and half a dozen chosen packs of clanrats, had emerged from tunnels at the base of each of their hilltop objectives and quickly surrounded them.

Once upon a time the hilltops had been ringed with protective wooden palisades, but centuries of neglect had reduced them to barely-recognisable ruins. At the appointed time, bone whistles had skirled faintly along the night air and the scattered companies had swept up and over the broad, flat-topped hills. The handful of flesh-eaters caught on the surface were swiftly and silently despatched, then the skaven spread out and located the many entrances to the monsters' reeking burrows. Heavy bladders of oil were brought up and emptied into all but a few of the tunnel mouths. By the time the first howls of alarm began to echo up from the darkness, the skaven had torches ready to toss in as well.

After decades of bitter fighting, the skaven had learned how much the flesh-eaters hated and feared the touch of fire. The oil went up with a hollow, hungry roar; from there it was merely a matter of lurking outside the unlit tunnel mouths and slaying the survivors as they emerged.

The fighting was as savage as it was merciless. No quarter was expected or given; the flesh-eaters were maddened by bloodlust and pain, and the skaven had come to fear and hate the unnatural creatures as they did little else. The monsters burst from the tunnels singly or in shrieking packs, many of them burning with sickly yellow flames, and Eekrit's warriors rushed in and cut them down with spear and blade. After five years of brutal raids against the barbarian tribes, the warlord's troops had become fearless, hard-bitten fighters – and Eekrit along with them, much to his surprise. Thanks to the thrice-damned Lord Velsquee, there had been little alternative.

Officially, Velsquee had no direct authority over the expeditionary force – or so he insisted to Lord Hiirc and the army's many clan chiefs. Eekrit retained his rank and title; Velsquee and his huge contingent of elite troops were merely there to observe the course of the campaign and to provide advice and assistance where needed. Of course, no one believed a word of it, but no one was willing to gainsay the Grey Lord, either. Meanwhile, Eekrit had been *advised* to go and harass the barbarians and the flesh-eaters, while Velsquee and that lunatic Qweeqwol discussed strategy and issued *recommendations* to the army from the comfort of Eekrit's own audience chamber.

Even now, five years on, there was much about Velsquee's arrival that Eekrit didn't understand. Clearly he and Lord Qweeqwol had been working together all along, at least insofar as the grey seers worked with anyone outside their own, secretive fraternity. But to what end? The warlord had no idea. At least, not *yet*.

Marsh grasses thrashed along the far end of the killing ground. Eekrit tensed, his paw drifting to the hilt of the sword resting on the damp ground at his side. The flesh-eaters burst from cover at a loping, four-limbed run, their eyes alight and their hideous faces contorted with bloodlust. Eight of the monsters emerged from the tree line and down into the marshy hollow where the raiders waited.

The skaven waited until their prey reached the very centre of the hollow. Black-robed shapes rose from cover, swinging braided leather cords above their heads. The slings made a thin, deadly whirring in the night air; the flesh-eaters halted at the sound, their gruesome heads swinging about in search of the sound, and that sealed their fates. Polished sling stones the size of snake eggs hissed through the air and found their mark; bones crunched wetly and the monsters collapsed, their limbs twitching.

More black-robed figures appeared from cover and raced silently across the marshy ground. They converged on the flesh-eaters; daggers flashed briefly beneath the moonlight as the scout-assassins finished off their victims, then the bodies were dragged swiftly out of sight. Whatever their shortcomings as scouts and spies, Eshreegar's rats were nonetheless *very* enthusiastic and capable killers.

Silence descended again. The ambushers resumed their murderous vigil, ears open wide as they strained to hear the faintest sounds of approaching troops. After several minutes, Eekrit let go his sword and relaxed once more.

'Another pack of stragglers,' Eshreegar whispered, close to the warlord's left side. 'Probably out prowling the wasteland at the foot of the mountain when we began the attack.'

Eekrit's tail gave a startled twitch. The Master of Treacheries had appeared at his side like a ghost. Calming his suddenly racing heart, the warlord gave Eshreegar a sidelong glance. The black-robed assassin was using a handful of marsh-grass to wipe the dark ichor of a flesh-eater from the edge of one of his knives.

'There's no sign of a response from the fortress?' Eekrit asked.

Eshreegar shook his head. 'Not since the alarm horns sounded, more than two hours ago. The main gate's still shut.'

The warlord raised his snout and gauged the height of the moon. 'If they don't march soon, it will be dawn before they arrive,' he reckoned.

'If they come at all,' the Master of Treacheries agreed.

Eekrit muttered irritably and considered his options. After destroying the flesh-eater nests, he'd brought together his forces and arranged them in an arc along the most likely avenues of approach from the distant fortress. Velsquee and Qweeqwol had been certain that the enemy would respond, probably with companies of swift-moving barbarian troops. In the dark and upon the unsteady, marshy terrain, Eekrit had expected to give the enemy a good mauling, then retreat to the safety of his tunnels, but that was growing less likely with each passing hour. To make matters worse, hungry packs of flesh-eaters were being drawn to the fires from lesser nests throughout the area; the longer his raiders remained in place, the greater the odds that they would be hit by the creatures from an unexpected direction, or find their escape routes cut off.

Beside him, Eshreegar raised his head, his ears unfolding completely as he listened to the seemingly random animal sounds echoing across the marshland. 'We've a runner from inside the mountain,' he said after a moment, then put a clawed paw to his mouth and made a sound very like the hiss of a large swamp lizard. The Master of Treacheries listened to the plaintive cry of a marsh owl and nodded to himself. 'He's heading this way.'

'Damn it all, what now?' Eekrit muttered. As hard as the campaign against the barbarians had been, at least he and his warriors had been far enough from the mountain that Velsquee couldn't stick his snout into things whenever he pleased.

Within moments came the sounds of loud rustling through the marshy growth behind the raiders. Gritting his teeth, Eekrit rose carefully to his feet and sheathed his blade as a breathless skaven came dashing through a stand of dead cypress trees. The messenger came up short as he recognised Eekrit and crouched in a posture of subservience, his head cocked to the side and his throat bared to the warlord.

Eekrit scowled at the hapless rat. 'Eshreegar, hand this idiot a brass gong,' he growled. 'Perhaps he could bang it for a while and sing us some songs.

I think there might still be a few half-deaf flesh-eaters who don't yet know where we're at.'

The messenger glanced nervously from Eekrit to the Master of Treacheries. 'I... I don't know any songs,' the clanrat protested weakly.

'I suppose we should thank the Horned One for small mercies,' Eekrit snapped. 'Did Velsquee send you here for a reason other than to vex me?'

The messenger wrung his paws. 'Oh, yes-yes, great lord,' he replied. 'I-I bear a message from him.'

'Well?' the warlord demanded. 'Must we torture it out of you?'

'No!' the clanrat squeaked. 'No-no, great lord! Grey Lord Velsquee, ah, *suggests* that you and your warriors return to the mountain at once! The enemy is about to attack!'

Eekrit frowned. '*About* to attack? And how does he know this?'

The clanrat's whiskers twitched. 'That-that he did not say.'

Eekrit cursed under his breath. 'No. Of course not,' he muttered. He waved a clawed paw at the messenger. 'Tell the great Velsquee that we appreciate his *advice* and we'll come straight away. Go.'

The messenger bowed his head and departed in a cloud of terrified musk. The noise he made thrashing through the undergrowth made Eekrit wince.

Eshreegar rose to his feet. 'Shall I tell the rest of the warband?'

'We certainly can't stay here any more,' Eekrit snarled. They probably heard that fool all the way back at the fortress.'

The Master of Treacheries produced a bone whistle and blew three eerie, piercing notes – the signal for the raiders to abandon their positions and return to the tunnels. As the skaven made ready to depart, Eekrit glanced towards the dark bulk of the mountain and wondered what else Velsquee knew but wasn't saying.

All labour in mine shaft six had come to an abrupt end. The labourers had set aside their dusty picks and shovels and taken their place in the ranks of the spear companies massing along the length of the cavernous tunnel. A handful of barbarian warriors, hastily returning from a long patrol through the treacherous passages of the lower levels, eyed the silent assembly with a veteran's sense of foreboding as they picked their way through the tightly packed columns and continued their long journey to the surface.

Moments later, a stir went through the spear companies at the centre of the mine shaft, and with a clatter of bone they shifted left and right as Nagash and the glowing figures of his wight bodyguard emerged from a nearby branch-tunnel. Behind the necromancer shuffled a score of broad-shouldered ratmen, their muscular bodies stained with gore and their filmy eyes glowing faintly green. They laboured under the weight of a massive bronze cauldron, appropriated from one of the necromancer's fearful laboratories. The cauldron's curved flanks were freshly incised with hundreds of angular runes and it was sealed with a heavy, ornate lid crowned with a cunning representation of four gaping human skulls. Faint wisps of vapour curled from the skulls' open mouths and deep eye sockets.

At Nagash's unspoken command, the rat-corpses bore the cauldron into the cleared space between the companies and set it upon the stone with a dolorous clang, then withdrew to the mouth of the branch-tunnel. As they did, the necromancer produced a bag of crushed *abn-i-khat* from his belt and began to pour out a glowing circle of power around the great vessel. The sigil was a simple but potent one, designed to shape the workings of a spell and increase its potency a hundredfold.

When all was in readiness, the necromancer stepped up to the great cauldron and pressed his ravaged palms against its surface. Then, in a low, hateful voice, he began his spell. For many long minutes, arcane words spilled from Nagash's fraying lips, filling the mine shaft with ominous power. A deep, low hissing rose from the depths of the great cauldron and its sides began to shimmer with steadily mounting heat. Thin wisps of smoke rose from the necromancer's desiccated hands, but Nagash did not relent. His chanting grew in speed and intensity, his glowing eyes focused intently on the boiling cauldron and its invisible contents.

Slowly but steadily, the vapours emanating from the leering bronze skulls began to take on a luminous, sickly, greenish-yellow hue. The tendrils of mist thickened swiftly, flowing heavily across the cauldron's lid and writhing like serpents across the tunnel floor.

With eerie swiftness, the flow of vapour swelled to a torrent, pouring from the skulls in a rushing flood and boiling about the ankles of the waiting skeletons. Its touch pitted bone, tarnished bronze and bleached wooden spear-hafts and shields, but the undead took no notice.

Nagash's incantation swelled in volume, and the mist seemed to react to the vehemence in his sepulchral voice. Within moments the mists stretched the entire length of the mine shaft, rising as high as the knees of the skeletons and roiling against the tunnel walls.

All at once, Nagash threw back his head and roared a stream of arcane syllables, and a charnel gust of wind swept down the branch-tunnels from the surface. It howled like a tormented spirit in the confines of the mine shaft and drove the heavy vapours ahead of it, down the branch-tunnels and into the lower levels, where the masses of the ratmen waited.

By the time Eekrit and his small force had collapsed the raiding tunnels behind them and reached the under-fortress, the entire camp was in a state of pandemonium. Alarm gongs clashed and bone whistles screeched, calling the army's reserves into action. Slave masters and their gangs were driving masses of panicked slaves into the upper access tunnels, lashing the backs of their wretched charges with whips or prodding them with wickedly pointed spears. The warlord even heard a cacophony of hisses and howling shrieks from Clan Skryre's quarter, hinting that their infernal machines were being hastily readied for action. Knowing how jealous Vittrik was of his unpredictable creations, the sound raised the hackles on the back of the warlord's neck.

Eshreegar paused beside the warlord, his ears open and his nose twitching. 'What's this?' he mused aloud.

'Nothing good,' Eekrit answered darkly. He considered the sounds of movement on the far side of the cavern; the main tunnels were likely crammed with skaven warriors rushing to battle. He had no intention of getting caught up in that chaos – especially with Vittrik's war machines coming up behind him. 'Get the warriors over to the eastern murder holes and wait for me there.'

'What about you?' Eshreegar said.

'I'm going to find out what in the Horned God's name is going on.'

The warlord broke away from the raiding party and dashed down the maze-like tunnels that subdivided the cavern. Minutes later he was standing outside his clan's former quarters. He'd expected to find Velsquee's personal guard standing watch outside the entrance, but the fearsome-looking storm-walkers were nowhere to be seen.

Tail lashing apprehensively, Eekrit pressed on, heading for the audience chamber. The cramped passageways were deserted, as was the hall itself. Eekrit stood at the threshold to the chamber and stared possessively at the throne at the far end for a moment.

Eekrit caught a hint of movement at the corner of his eye. He turned swiftly, reaching for his sword out of reflex, and saw one of Velsquee's slaves scuttling from a side-passage. The slave caught the sudden motion and let out a terrified squeak. Pungent musk filled the air.

'I'm-I'm on an errand for Lord Velsquee!' the slave bleated, his beady eyes wide. 'An important errand, yes-yes! Certainly not hiding. No, I'd never–'

'I don't care,' Eekrit snarled. He took a step towards the terrified slave. 'Where is Velsquee now?'

'Up-up, in the tunnels, with Lord Qweeqwol,' the wretch stammered. 'The seer said that the skeletons were going to attack, and Velsquee went with the *heechigar* to catch the *kreekar-gan.*' The fiery-eyed *burning man* had become a baleful legend among the ranks of the army's veterans.

Eekrit lips drew back from his chisel-like teeth. Qweeqwol had never been half so useful before Velsquee arrived. 'Go on,' he growled.

The slave shuddered and his ears folded back against his head. 'Velsquee laid-laid a trap for the *kreekar-gan*, but this time the skeletons have filled the tunnels with a killing smoke that slays-slays everyone it touches! Many-many are dead, and the rest are in flight! Already, the skeletons have taken mine shaft seven, and are drawing close to number eight!'

The news stunned Eekrit. If Velsquee had laid a trap for the *kreekar-gan*, he would have had his best troops gathered for the ambush. In those tunnels, there would have been no escape from any kind of killing gas.

The *heechigar* and the clan warriors of Velsquee's supporters – including the insufferable Lord Hiirc – had likely been decimated.

Like any sensible skaven, Eekrit's first instinct was to grab everything valuable he could find and not stop running until he reached the Great City. Yet the warlord also sensed a tantalising opportunity to regain some of his lost stature, if he could but find a way to check the enemy's advance. Eekrit's mind raced. He could use the murder holes to get in behind the skeletons, but what then? A few hundred warriors with hand weapons and a few torches wouldn't do more than slow them down. He would have to do something drastic.

An idea occurred to the warlord. His tail lashed as he formulated the outlines of a plan. It could work, he thought, his confidence growing. Of course, it could also get him killed. Even if he succeeded, Velsquee might have him poisoned just out of spite, but he would worry about that later.

Eekrit shook himself from his scheming reverie. 'You said the skeletons were moving on mine shaft eight,' he said, turning his attention back to the slave. 'Is there any chance of holding the enemy there?'

The warlord blinked in surprise. He was alone in the antechamber. The slave had fled while he had been lost in his own thoughts. Under the circumstances, that seemed to be answer enough for Eekrit's purposes.

Eshreegar gripped the sputtering torch uneasily. 'Are you certain this is wise?'

'Wise? No,' Eekrit muttered. 'But necessary. Of that, I'm certain.'

The warlord and his raiders were packed into a steep, roughly circular passage that had been gnawed through the hard rock that lay deep within the great mountain. The tunnel was one of several that had been dug over the last decade and set aside in case an enemy attack succeeded in overrunning the defensive positions around the lower mine shafts. The passages were small enough to avoid detection by the enemy, or so Eekrit devoutly hoped, but were positioned to allow for lightning raids behind the enemy's line of advance. The small skaven force had reached the uppermost limit of the tunnel they were in, right at the level of mine shaft seven. Only a foot of relatively soft rock separated them from the shaft itself. A small knot of skaven warriors stood ready, awaiting the order to create the breach.

Orange light flickered hungrily in the cramped confines of the tunnel. One skaven in twenty carried a lit torch – not nearly enough to suit Eekrit, but all that they had left after the raid against the flesh-eaters. The rest of the raiders were charged with ensuring that the torchbearers reached their targets. The rest was up to luck and the Horned God's favour.

From the look on Eshreegar's face, the Master of Treacheries was far from convinced. 'What about this killing smoke that the slave mentioned?'

Eekrit tried to give Eshreegar a nonchalant flick of his whiskers. 'If the skeletons have such a weapon, it would be down in the lower tunnels by now,' he said. 'The enemy will be pressing its advantage to gain as much ground as it can.'

The assassin shifted uncomfortably. 'But smoke gets *everywhere*–' he protested.

'Then hold your breath if you like,' Eekrit growled. With a curt nod, he ordered the digging party to go to work.

Eekrit focused on readying his weapon and clamping down hard on his own musk glands. The more he thought about the ways his plan could go awry, the more nervous he became. He was gambling heavily that the majority of the skeletons would have passed through mine shaft seven by now. If he was wrong, there would be no way for the small force to extricate itself – and he would have opened up a direct route for the enemy all the way to the under-fortress, many levels below. Not that he would live long enough to witness such a disaster.

Within minutes, the sound of splintering stone rose above the scrabbling claws of the warriors. Eekrit tried to forget about everything that could go wrong and just focus on living through the next few minutes.

The breach opened with a crash of falling rubble. Eekrit raised his sword. '*Forwards!*' he cried.

The skaven warriors who made the breach grabbed up their weapons and charged forwards, into the mine shaft. Eekrit and Eshreegar were hard upon their heels – and then, without warning, the three skaven at the front of the raiding party collapsed to the floor of the mine shaft.

Eekrit's blood turned to ice. He caught sight of a very faint, yellow-green tinge to the air. The killing smoke!

The three skaven writhed on the stone floor, clawing at their throats. Hideous choking sounds rattled from their gaping mouths for a few heartbeats and then their eyes rolled back and they went still. The skaven directly behind them turned and tried to flee back the way they'd come, crashing into Eekrit and Eshreegar. The scent of fear-musk was thick in the dank air – along with a very faint metallic tang, like burnt copper.

Eekrit snarled at the warriors, giving the skaven in front of him a rough shove that sent him sprawling onto his backside. 'Keep going!' he snapped. 'If the smoke is going to kill us, it's already too late! Go!'

Without waiting for the warriors to respond, Eekrit rushed past them, charging up the gentle slope of the mine shaft. The faint taste of burnt metal seared his throat and made his eyes sting, but no more. What little smoke remained in the mine shaft was too dispersed to be much threat – although he reckoned the dead warriors behind him would disagree.

After the glare of the torchlight, it took the warlord's eyes a few seconds to adjust to the gloom. He heard the skeletons long before he could see them – a rolling, clattering tide of wood and bone filling the mine shaft before him. It sounded like thousands of the damned things and they were all coming his way.

The warlord shook his head savagely, trying to blink away the last vestiges of the torch glare. The first thing he could make out were green pinpoints of light – a veritable sea of them – floating through the air in the tunnel ahead. As his eyes adjusted he made out the rounded tops of human skulls and the hard outlines of wooden shields. The undead warriors were bearing down on the skaven raiders in a relentless tide, but without any sense of formation. Their response was daunting in size, but largely uncoordinated. It wasn't much, he reckoned, but it just might be enough.

'Eshreegar!' the warlord cried. 'The supports! Fire the supports!'

'Now?' The Master of Treacheries gave Eekrit a wide-eyed look. 'But–'

'Do it!' Eekrit ordered.

Eshreegar looked as though he might argue further, but one look at the oncoming horde seemed to persuade him. Barking orders at the raiders, he dashed over to the thick wooden support closest to him and placed his torch against it. The heavy column, soaked in pitch to prevent rot, erupted in hungry blue flames within seconds.

Other skaven torchbearers dashed across the mine shaft, lighting every support within reach. Eekrit felt waves of heat play across his shoulder-blades. It was a start, but they had to reach a great many more of the wooden beams if they hoped to succeed. He raised his sword. 'Fire as many supports as you can!' he called out. 'Don't waste time on the skeletons! Go!'

With that, the warlord beckoned to Eshreegar and dashed forwards, hugging the right-hand wall of the shaft. Skeletons moved to intercept him; he screeched a fierce battle cry and lashed out at their legs with vicious sweeps of his sword. Bronze smashed against bone, and undead warriors toppled, their spears still jabbing for his chest and throat. Corroded bronze points stabbed into his armour, or were turned aside; he stumbled as another point gouged a furrow across his left thigh. Snarling, he threw his shoulder against the shield of the skeleton in front of him and knocked the undead warrior backwards against its companions. With a sweep of his sword he hacked off the warrior's lower legs, then ducked his head and plunged still deeper into the shifting mass.

More screeches and savage cries echoed across the mine shaft as the rest of the skaven raiders charged into the press of skeletons. They bent low and raced through the crowd at little better than knee-height, breaking leg bones and shattering joints with claw and blade. Others plied their torches as weapons, setting rotting cloth and shrivelled flesh alight. The skeletons hefted their spears and stabbed at the racing skaven, but the press of bodies left them with little room to bring their weapons to bear. Still, as swift as they were, the thicket of bronze points still drew blood among the raiders. Eekrit heard cries of agony as warriors were stabbed again and again by the enemy, yet still they pressed on.

The warlord forced his way further up the mine shaft, past one wooden support after another. There wasn't time to glance back and see if Eshreegar was still behind him; it was all he could do to keep pushing forwards, staying literally one step ahead of the skeletons and their spears. He tore wildly at the undead warriors, savouring the brittle crunch of bone. A spear dug into his hip, biting deep into the armour and driving him against the wall; he snarled at the sudden bloom of pain, seizing the spear haft with his free paw and smashing the skull of the skeleton that wielded it. Eekrit pulled the weapon loose and drove himself forwards with another angry shout.

More skeletons pressed against Eekrit; time blurred, the seconds stretching with the dreadful elasticity of combat. He blocked and parried, cut and thrust. He lost count of the number of skeletons that fell beneath his blade. All that mattered was staying alive from one moment to the next and putting one foot resolutely in front of the other.

Dimly, Eekrit became aware of a constant, breathy roar that rose above the clatter and crash of battle. Fierce heat prickled at the back of his neck and head, but he paid it little heed. Then, suddenly, a hand tightened on the back of his cloak and tried to pull him backwards. With a snarl, the warlord spun, brandishing his sword, and saw that it was Eshreegar. The Master of Treacheries was bloody and soot-stained and his head was silhouetted by a halo of raging flames.

'Enough!' Eshreegar shouted. 'It's enough! We've got to get out of here!'

For a moment, Eekrit didn't understand – then he saw the inferno stretching behind them. The pitch-soaked columns were fully ablaze and the fire had spread to the overhead beams as well. Sheets of hungry flame were shooting along the ceiling of the mine shaft, drawn towards the surface by thin draughts of air; as Eekrit watched, the fire raced overhead, reaching for the next set of supports in line. The intensity of the heat swelled in an instant, bearing down on him like a red-hot brand.

The skeletons were withdrawing as well, retreating farther up the mine shaft away from the skaven. From where he stood, Eekrit could see a few score of his raiders staggering like drunkards among the heaped bodies. Many of them had drawn their cloaks over their snouts to protect them from the heat. The warlord nodded, gasping for breath, and fished out a bone whistle. He blew three shrill notes and his warriors raced boldly back into the flames.

As he watched, several of the warriors' cloaks left trails of smoke and flame in their wake.

'It's possible that I didn't think this through very well,' the warlord said, shouting over the roar of the flames.

Eshreegar gave the warlord a look of pure irritation – and then his eyes widened in terror. 'Down-down!' he cried, jerking hard on Eekrit's cloak. Eekrit was pulled completely off his feet, just as the world exploded in a sizzling crack of thunder and a flash of blinding, green light.

When his vision returned, Eekrit was on his back, staring up at the inferno roaring overhead. Spots of awful heat burned across his chest, like hot coals laid atop the surface of his armour. His nerves jangled painfully, like glass shattered under a hammer blow. With a groan, Eekrit levered himself onto his elbows, and saw that a half-dozen of his god-stone charms had been melted into smoking, black lumps. They had saved him – just barely – from the blast of sorcery that had struck him from farther up the mine shaft.

Perhaps twenty yards up the smoke-filled tunnel, surrounded by skeletal spearmen and fearsome-looking wights, stood the infamous *kreekar-gan*. The figure was swathed in tattered grey robes and his face concealed within the depths of a voluminous hood. Twin points of green flame burned hatefully from its depths, their baleful glow fixed on Eekrit's stunned form. The burning man's mummified hands were stretched towards him, wreathed in a terrible aura of sorcerous power.

Beside Eekrit, Eshreegar moaned, and tried to push himself upright. The warlord had caught the brunt of the blast, but the Master of Treacheries had suffered a glancing blow that had battered him senseless. Eekrit scrambled to his feet, his body given new life by the terrifying figure of the burning man.

'The fire!' Eekrit yelled. 'Back into the fire!' He grabbed hold of Eshreegar's smouldering robes and began to drag him bodily down the mine shaft.

A howl of pure rage chased after Eekrit as he fled into the dubious safety of the inferno. The heat was nigh unbearable; after only a few seconds it felt as though his limbs were aflame. Every breath was an agony of heat and choking smoke. All around him, wood burst with loud, blistering cracks, showering the tunnel with burning splinters. Fragments of dirt and broken stone were falling from the ceiling in a growing tide as the overhead supports began to give way.

Eekrit's head began to swim. Where was the breach? He couldn't be certain how far he'd gone. Everywhere he turned, there was only fire. A curse came to the warlord's lips, but he hadn't the breath to voice it. There was a groan above him, a sound so deep he felt it in his bones, and it grew with every passing second. The sound was important, the warlord thought dimly, but he couldn't quite understand why.

It was impossible to breathe. Eekrit heard a pounding in his ears, growing louder by the moment. Who in the Horned God's name would be pounding drums in the middle of a roaring fire?

Eekrit turned about, trying to focus on the sound. Invisible hands plucked at him, pulling him this way and that. And then came a thunderous, splintering *craaaack* overhead and the warlord felt himself falling backwards into roaring darkness.

SIX

INITIATION RITES

Lahmia,
the City of the Dawn,
in the 99th year of Asaph the Beautiful
(-1295 Imperial Reckoning)

A dozen pale, blood-streaked hands held the golden goblet aloft. The high priestesses lay in a tight circle at the foot of the alabaster goddess, their golden faces upturned. Drops of red speckled their smooth cheeks and dappled the corners of their eyes like tears. Their chanting swelled, stoked to a near-ecstatic pitch by the curling clouds of lotus smoke that permeated the inner sanctum. As the rite neared its climax, Neferata, standing upon the dais, spread her arms wide and added her voice to the chorus. But it wasn't the goddess she sang to; the sole object of her attention was the handsome young man who stood before the offered cup, head bowed and hands clasped across his chest.

Her pulse raced as she watched Alcadizzar gather his focus and begin to chant. His rich, deep voice blended harmoniously with the rising and falling notes of the priestesses' chorus, increasing its power and urgency. At the proper moment, the prince raised his head and spread his arms in a pose identical to Neferata's. Alcadizzar's dark eyes met hers, and the intensity of his stare sent a frisson of desire through her.

The wide sleeves of the prince's white robe had slid back to his elbows, revealing tanned, muscular forearms and the thick wrists of a practiced swordsman. Reflected moonlight glinted icily off the curved dagger in his right hand. Still staring deeply into Neferata's eyes, he placed the point of the dagger against his left wrist and slowly drew it downwards. The razor-edged blade cut cleanly through the flesh, drawing a thin line halfway to the prince's elbow. The blood came a heartbeat later, welling up from the cut and spilling in thick streams down Alcadizzar's arm.

'*The glory of the goddess!*' cried the priestesses, as the prince's blood fell heavily into the goblet. '*Behold the gift of Asaph!*'

A shiver went through Neferata as she watched the prince's lifeblood mingle with the offerings of the high priestesses. Her chest heaved, drawing in breath and expelling it in short, ragged gasps. Behind her ancient mask, her mouth opened slightly, revealing the tips of her leonine fangs.

Alcadizzar bled into the goblet, adding to the offerings there until the cup was nearly brimming full. Then he took the goblet from the priestesses and they fell away to either side, opening a path for him to ascend the dais and offer the cup to Neferata.

'For you, holy one,' he intoned. 'An offer of love and life eternal.'

Neferata bowed her head solemnly, though her heart was racing and her body ached with sudden thirst. With slow, ceremonial restraint, she reached out to the prince and took the warm cup from his hands. Sighing faintly, she brought the goblet close. With a practiced motion, she shifted her mask slightly and raised the cup to her lips. The taste of the blood sent waves of delicious heat pulsing through her body. Knowing that part of its power came from Alcadizzar himself only added to its savour.

When she was finished, she raised the empty cup and gazed lovingly on Alcadizzar and the cultists. The prince closed his eyes and swayed slightly under the full weight of her stare. The priestesses cried out in exultation; several succumbed completely, collapsing onto the floor in a dead faint.

Neferata beckoned, and a high priestess emerged from the shadows to the right of the dais with another cup held carefully in her hands. At the same time, a second high priestess emerged from the left, bearing an ornately carved wooden box. The final act of the initiation was at hand.

The immortal took the cup from the high priestess, exchanging it for the empty goblet in her hand. It brimmed with a dark red elixir crafted from Neferata's own vital fluid. She turned back to Alcadizzar and offered him the cup.

'Drink, faithful servant,' she said, her words crackling with power. 'Drink, and know the power of the goddess herself.'

The prince opened his eyes. With solemn ceremony, he accepted the cup, and raised it reverently to the white face of Asaph. His gaze then fell to Neferata, and he brought the cup to his lips. In one long draught, he drained the goblet to the dregs.

As near to her as Alcadizzar was, Neferata could feel the transformative effects of the elixir on his body. The prince's heart raced and his muscles swelled with vigour. Heat radiated from him like metal drawn from the forge. Though he had partaken of the elixir almost a dozen times, first as an initiate and later as a priest of the temple, he had never had so much at once. The effect on him was profound. His mouth fell open and his eyes widened in shock. A low, almost bestial groan rose from his throat. He shuddered, his muscles tightening until every tendon stood out like taut cords beneath his skin.

Neferata could feel the torrent of emotions raging through the prince, tasting the fear, the wonder and the ecstasy as though they were her own. She felt it through the bond forged by the elixir, as though she and Alcadizzar now shared the same heart and mind. The intensity of the connection stunned her as well; for a moment she was as stricken as he was. It was an intimacy unlike anything she had known before.

They stared at one another for what felt like an eternity. At last, Neferata took a long breath and said, 'The blessings of the goddess fill you, Alcadizzar. Can you not feel the power of Asaph's gift?'

Alcadizzar replied in a subdued voice. 'I do, holy one.'

'You are one with the divine, now,' she said. 'Do you accept what you have been given, with all your heart?'

'I do.'

'Then show us your devotion,' she said. 'Prepare yourself.'

The prince nodded solemnly. He handed the empty goblet back to the high priestess and then, moving as though in a dream, he unbelted his robe and let it fall to the floor. As he did, Neferata turned to the high priestess carrying the box and gestured for her to come forwards. She opened the cedar lid and reached inside.

Clad now only in britches, Alcadizzar waited with his hands at his sides, breathing deep, calming breaths. Already, the wound on his arm had closed, thanks to the power of the elixir. Now he closed his eyes and prepared himself for the trial to come.

Neferata gently lifted out the contents of the box. The asp was blacker than night and around three feet long. In ancient times, the queens of Lahmia held court with two live asps curled about their wrists as a sign of Asaph's favour. The serpent obediently wound about her forearm and coiled a third of its length upon her open palm. Its unblinking eyes glittered like chips of onyx and it tasted the air with a flickering, blue-black tongue as Neferata turned to face the prince once more.

She extended her hand to him. 'Prove to us your devotion,' she said. 'Trust in Asaph's blessing, and you will prevail.'

Alcadizzar opened his eyes. His breathing slowed and his body grew still. She could sense the tightly harnessed energies of the elixir humming like plucked chords along his lean, muscular limbs. Slowly, gracefully, he raised his right hand, palm out, and extended it towards the coiled serpent.

At once, Neferata felt the asp grow tense. The serpent's head drew back slightly as the prince's hand came closer. The asp was one of the swiftest and deadliest serpents in all Nehekhara; a single bite could kill a grown man in less than a minute. But Alcadizzar showed no fear. For the last twenty-five years he had devoted himself to the teachings of the temple, learning through meditation and intense physical training how to harness the full power of both body and mind. The training was not unlike that which the great Ushabti received in ancient times; only instead of calling upon the blessings of the gods, Alcadizzar drew upon the power of Neferata's elixir.

Inch by inch, the prince's hand drew closer to the serpent. The asp's coils slithered across Neferata's palm, gathering tightly together. Its tongue angrily lashed the air. And then, without warning, it struck.

The asp's head darted forwards, almost too fast for Neferata's eye to follow. It closed the distance between her and the prince faster than the blink of an eye, mouth open and fangs distended.

Alcadizzar's hand snapped shut – and suddenly the asp spasmed, writhing impotently in his iron grip. As Neferata watched, the prince bent his head and kissed the serpent gently atop its head, and then carefully unwound the rest of its length from her arm.

'Asaph be praised,' she said softly, feeling a flush of heat across her face and down her slender neck. Quickly she mastered herself as Alcadizzar placed the asp back in its box. 'Bear witness, sisters!' she called to the other priestesses. 'The goddess has shown her favour! Behold Alcadizzar, the temple's first high priest!'

With cries of joy, the high priestesses rose up and gathered around the prince. They touched him lightly and whispered their congratulations as a new robe of purest samite was draped about his broad shoulders. He nodded his head and smiled a little sheepishly at the masked women, clearly uncomfortable being at the centre of such intimate female attention.

Neferata dismissed the priestesses with an unspoken command; they scattered like a flock of birds, vanishing quietly into the shadows. She stepped forwards and held out her hand to Alcadizzar.

'You are one of us now,' she said. 'It is time you were welcomed into the inner sanctum.'

The prince, his face flushed with triumph, gave Neferata a dazzling smile and placed his hand in hers. His eyes widened faintly in surprise.

'Your skin,' he said. 'It's so cold. Are you well, holy one?'

'I have never been better. Come.'

Pulling gently on his hand, Neferata led him from the dais and into the shadows behind the statue of the goddess. Her hand found the small wooden door set into the wall and pushed it open. Orange lamplight spilled through the doorway from the corridor beyond.

They walked in silence for a time, down the narrow, dusty passageways and through the richly appointed chambers of the inner sanctum. Alcadizzar studied each room with interest, drinking in every detail of his surroundings.

'This part of the temple is much older than the rest,' he observed, brushing his fingertips along the curved flank of a marble pillar.

Neferata nodded approvingly. 'So it is. We are walking in what was once the Women's Palace. Now these chambers are set aside for the comfort and edification of the temple's higher orders.'

'Hmpf,' the prince replied with a frown. 'A far cry from the bare walls and the wooden cot of an initiate's cell.'

'An initiate's purpose is to learn, not luxuriate,' Neferata replied. 'Now that you're enlightened, you may reap the rewards of your hard work and dedication.'

They passed through a long, columned gallery and found themselves at the edge of the former palace's old garden. Once it had been a carefully manicured refuge, with profusions of gorgeous, exotic plants, rambling gravel pathways and serene reflecting pools. Now, after centuries of benign neglect, it was a dense wilderness of dark fronds, glossy native vines and stands of Eastern bamboo. Frogs chirped to one another in the darkness, while late-summer cicadas droned from the depths of the bamboo groves.

New pathways had been worn through the undergrowth over the decades, lit by the faint glow of the moon. Neferata led the prince down one such track, navigating more by memory than eyesight. After several minutes, they emerged at the centre of the garden. Here, the area had been kept mostly clear and remained much as it had been centuries before. A dense carpet of soft, springy grass surrounded a broad, deep pool, ringed by old, well-tended ornamental trees. Neru was bright and full overhead, transforming the surface of the pond to quicksilver.

Neferata let go of Alcadizzar's hand and walked towards the still water. The tips of the thick grasses brushed her feet through the gaps in her sandals. 'This has always been one of my favourite places,' she said softly. So many memories, she thought, their edges blurring now with the passage of time. Neferata could not say for sure whether that was a blessing or a curse. 'The temple at Khemri will need a place like this as well. Remember that, when you lay its foundations.'

'That's a long way away,' the prince said with a sigh. 'It's possible that the temple won't even be completed in my lifetime.'

Neferata laughed at the notion. 'Don't be foolish. Of course it will!' She turned back to him. 'Look at how far you've come since joining the temple. In just a few more years, you'll be ready for the final initiation, and then the west will be yours.'

Alcadizzar walked towards the moonlit pool, his face pensive. 'But for how long?' he asked. 'I'm fifty-five years old. There is so much to do. I hardly know where to begin.'

Neferata joined him at the edge of the pool. 'Look at you,' she said, pointing to his reflection. 'Still as young and handsome as ever. That's the power of the divine, Alcadizzar. In ancient times, our people lived a much longer span of years. A man wasn't considered to be in his prime until he was *eighty*. You'll enjoy a life at least as long,' she said to him, 'as a hierophant of the temple, perhaps even longer.'

The prince looked at her wonderingly. 'Is such a thing possible?'

Neferata smiled behind her mask. 'That depends upon you, my prince. Tell me, if you could rule Khemri for a hundred years, what would you do?'

Alcadizzar smiled. 'Rebuild the city, for a start. There are still entire districts inhabited by nothing more than rats.' He folded his arms. 'After that, focus on the docks, and get the river trade with Zandri going again. If Lahmia would permit it, I'd build a trading post along the river, where it touches the Golden Plain to the north-west of here. That would bring goods to the west far quicker than the overland route through the mountains.'

'And avoid all those troublesome tolls passing the goods through Quatar,' Neferata noted wryly.

'There is that,' the prince answered slyly. 'After that... I don't know. There are so many things I'd like to do. Build a collegium, like the one at Lybaras, and a great library that would serve scholars and citizens alike.' His smile widened and his voice grew more animated as he continued. 'I'd rebuild the army, of course, and fund expeditions to explore the lands beyond Nehekhara. And of course there's the matter of stemming the growth of the Great Desert...' He spread his hands and gave a shrug. 'You see? I don't even think a century would be enough.'

Neferata slipped her arm around the prince's broad shoulders. 'Two centuries, then,' she whispered. 'Or *five*. There are... higher mysteries... that you have not yet plumbed, Alcadizzar. There is so much more I can teach you, if you are willing. Perhaps... perhaps you need not ever die at all.' She leaned close to him, intoxicated by his warmth. 'Think of it. You would be greater than Settra himself!'

'Or as terrible as Nagash.'

The woman's voice was melodious and yet forbidding, as cold and pure as the silvery tones of a bell. Alcadizzar and Neferata jolted apart like a pair of guilty young lovers, searching amid the surrounding trees for the source of the sound.

A lithe figure glided from the shadows on the far side of the glimmering pond. She was dressed in fine silken robes from the lands of the Far East and moved with an artful, almost mesmerising grace as she stepped into the moonlight. Her porcelain features were delicate and exotic, with high, rounded cheekbones and large, oval-shaped eyes. Jade pins glowed from her raven-black hair, bound tightly atop her head to reveal the slender curve of her throat. After spending so many years among the masked priestesses of the temple, the woman's uncovered face both disturbed and fascinated Alcadizzar.

'Death is what separates mankind from the gods, young prince,' the woman said. 'And for good reason. Immortality brings us nothing but misery.'

Neferata growled deep in her throat, like an angry lioness. 'Naaima!' she spat. 'What is the meaning of this?'

Suddenly, the serene atmosphere of the clearing was charged with tension. Alcadizzar stiffened, surprised by the vehemence in Neferata's voice, but Naaima's expression was implacable.

'There is news from Rasetra,' she said, glaring an accusation at Neferata. 'The old king, Aten-heru, is dead. He has gone into the realms of the dead, never having seen the face of his eldest son.'

Alcadizzar said nothing. A frown creased his brow, as though the young man was uncertain what he should feel. After a moment, he sighed. 'Who will rule in Aten-heru's place?' he asked.

'Your younger brother, Asar,' Naaima told him. 'He sends you his greetings and his love, and begs you to quit Lahmia and come home for your father's interment.'

The prince's frown deepened into a scowl. 'Home?' he said. 'No. I cannot. I am pledged to the temple–'

'Cannot?' Naaima said. 'You are to be the king of Khemri! There is *nothing* you cannot do! Leave this place, Alcadizzar. Now. Before it's too late–'

'*Silence!*' Neferata snarled, and this time Naaima flinched at the power in her voice. Eyes glittering like a serpent's, Neferata turned to Alcadizzar. 'Leave us,' she said curtly. 'Return to the inner sanctum and offer up prayers to the goddess for your father's safe passage into the underworld. It is the proper thing for a son to do.'

Alcadizzar hesitated for a moment, his gaze shifting from Neferata to Naaima as he tried to read the invisible currents of anger between them. When no further explanation was forthcoming, he gave a reluctant nod. 'Yes, holy one,' he said at last.

The prince withdrew quietly from the clearing, casting long glances over his shoulder at the rigid, angry figures of the two women.

Silence descended on the clearing. Neferata said nothing for a long while, until Alcadizzar's stealthy footfalls had faded from the garden entirely. Naaima waited for what was to come, her expression calm but her dark eyes glinting defiantly.

'I'm trying to recall the last time I saw you,' Neferata said at last. 'How long has it been? Forty-five years? Fifty? You've avoided me for half a century, and now here you are.' She began walking slowly towards Naaima, as if the former courtesan were a wild animal that was easily spooked. 'After everything I've done for you, this is how you repay me?'

'Yes,' Naaima shot back. 'How else? Long ago, you saved my life. Can't you see that I'm trying to do the same?'

'You know how important he is!' Neferata snarled. 'Alcadizzar represents the future! Together we'll lead Nehekhara into a golden age – an *eternal* age of peace and prosperity!'

'No. You won't.' Naaima shook her head sadly. 'Alcadizzar will never be your consort, Neferata, no matter what you think. Once he realises what you truly are, he will become your sworn enemy.' Tears glimmered at the corners of her eyes. 'He will have no choice. Can't you see that? All he knows is duty and sacrifice. That's the way you made him.' Naaima wiped at her cheeks. 'Then you will have to kill Alcadizzar, or let him go. Either way, Lahmia will burn.'

Neferata reached up and tore off her golden mask. Her fangs glinted coldly in the moonlight. 'What do you know of Alcadizzar, you Eastern slut?'

she said. 'It was *my* blood that saved him as a babe, when his own mother could not, and it's my blood that courses through his body even now! His first duty is to *me*, and no other!'

More tears stained the former courtesan's face. This time she did not bother to wipe them away. 'I'm sorry,' Naaima said. 'I know it must be hard for you, after everything you've lost. But Alcadizzar will not make you a queen again. He cannot. Nor will he ever love you.'

'Get out of my sight,' Neferata said. Her voice had grown as hard and cold as stone. 'Now. Or so help me, I'll rip out your traitorous little heart.'

Naaima closed her eyes in resignation. 'As you wish,' she said, with as much dignity as she could muster. She withdrew slowly, stepping back into the all-concealing shadows. Her voice rose like a ghost from the darkness. 'Always, I have loved you,' she said. 'And I will do so until the end. Remember that, when all the others have betrayed you.'

'I said go!' Neferata cried. She rushed forwards, claws raised. Night birds leapt from the branches of the trees, their forlorn cries echoing from the distant garden walls.

SEVEN

UNWELCOME CONCLUSIONS

Nagashizzar,
in the 99th year of Ualatp the Patient
(-1290 Imperial Reckoning)

'Hsst!' The scout-assassin raised a clawed paw and lashed his tail sharply. One ear was pressed against the rough, weeping stone of the tunnel, and his eyes were shut in concentration as he listened to the faint sounds vibrating through the rock.

A chorus of shrill, serpentine hisses echoed up and down the narrow passage, and the dust-covered sappers at the far end froze in place. Bits of broken stone spilled from their clenched fingers, the noise magnified a thousandfold in the tense air. Down the length of the tunnel, the rest of the skaven silently readied their weapons. They were close now; the sappers had been digging underneath the foundations of the tower for more than an hour and the last of the supports were nearly exposed. This was the point where things most often went wrong.

The scout-assassin held himself absolutely still as he waited for the sound to repeat itself. It might have been nothing more than wagon wheels rumbling across a paved roadway, just a few dozen feet above them – or it might have been a sudden fall of stone from a counter-sapping tunnel heading their way. A breach could fill the tunnel with roiling clouds of poison gas and spear-wielding skeletons – or worse, packs of howling, frenzied flesh-eaters. The campaign against the creatures' foetid nests had driven the flesh-eaters to new depths of savagery against the invaders – especially the distinctive, black-robed scouts. Better a swift death than to be captured by the monsters and dragged back to their hilltop lairs.

Long moments passed. Pink noses twitched nervously in the gloom. Clouds of fine, grey dust drifted through the air, stirred by the faint exhalations of the sappers and their guardians. One of the skaven stirred, ever so slightly, drawing savage looks from his companions.

By degrees, the scout-assassin relaxed. His paw lowered and the skaven let out a collective hiss of relief. Moments later, the soft sound of claws on stone resumed at the far end of the passageway.

Eekrit straightened as the sappers continued their work. 'That's the fifth one in the last ten minutes,' he muttered. The warlord grimaced as he tried to work a cramp from between his scarred shoulderblades.

Lord Eshreegar coughed faintly – the closest sound to laughter he could manage. 'Better than the alternative,' the Master of Treacheries answered. Five years after the inferno in mine shaft seven, his voice was still little better than a whispering rasp. 'The last time we had a breach, the flesh-eaters nearly made off with you.'

The warlord snorted in derision. 'They never laid a hand on me. Not that you noticed, of course.' Eekrit's sword paw clenched at the memory of the vicious, close-quarters fight. It had been a nearer thing than he cared to admit. He attempted a dismissive shrug, wincing as the scar tissue across his shoulders drew tight. 'I'm more like to die of a heart rupture from all these false alarms.' He bared his long teeth at the sharp-eared sentry, several dozen paces down the tunnel. 'I'm starting to think Velsquee's put him up to it.'

Eshreegar gave the warlord a sidelong glance. He had to turn his head to do it; the left side of his face was a patchwork of bald, pinkish scar tissue, and a golden skull gleamed in the ravaged pit where his eye used to be. 'We've been pulling down the burning man's towers for the last eight months,' the Master of Treacheries replied. 'We're outnumbered a thousand to one, and his warriors are getting better at catching us with every passing night. You think the Grey Lord needs to go to all the trouble of *bribing* an assassin to kill you?'

Eekrit glowered at Eshreegar. 'He might,' the warlord muttered darkly. 'It's been five years since we brought down mine shaft seven, and we're still alive. He could be getting impatient.'

There was no doubt in anyone's mind that Lord Velsquee certainly wanted Eekrit dead. By all reports, the Grey Lord had been near apoplectic when he'd learned of the mine shaft's collapse and the attendant destruction that had followed. The levels around shaft number seven had grown so honeycombed with side-passages and murder holes that the collapse touched off a wave of secondary cave-ins for more than a week afterwards. The aftershocks reverberated as far down as the under-fortress itself, and only the desperate efforts of the army's engineers prevented the loss of mine shaft eight as well. How the raiding party managed to escape the destruction and reach the safety of the lower levels, only the Horned God himself knew.

Had Eshreegar and a couple of his scouts not pulled Eekrit from the collapsing mine shaft, he would not have survived at all. As it was, both he and the Master of Treacheries nearly succumbed to their burns during the long weeks that followed. Eekrit's clan spent large sums on his behalf, summoning chirurgeons from as far away as the Great City to tend his injuries. Eshreegar's wounds were even more severe; the scout-assassins closed ranks around their leader and kept him in seclusion for more than a month until they were certain that he would survive. All the while, Velsquee seethed, wanting nothing more than to drag them before a summary trial and lay the entire blame for the disaster at their feet.

The Grey Lord was eager to divert attention onto Eekrit and the destruction of mine shaft seven and away from the disaster of his would-be ambush of the *kreekar-gan*. The enemy's poison cloud had decimated the army's best troops, including Velsquee's own storm-walkers, and sent the rest in a panicked retreat that the Grey Lord himself had been hard-pressed to stop. Mine shaft eight had fallen to the burning man's warriors and hasty defences around mine shaft nine, comprised of shattered warrior packs and terrified slave mobs, likely wouldn't have held for long, even with Velsquee and Qweeqwol personally in command. Though stories of Velsquee's heroic stand were now an established part of the lore surrounding the desperate fight, the truth was that the army had been pushed to the brink of defeat, and the lines had stabilised only after the collapse of the mine shaft had thrown the enemy advance into disarray.

Velsquee had gambled mightily and lost. The near-destruction of the *heechigar* and the severe losses suffered by many of the army's more powerful clans placed the Grey Lord in a precarious position, and it wasn't long before he was forced to abandon the notion of a show trial and focus on the intrigues of the army's many factions. The balance of power among the skaven lords shifted many times during the weeks that followed. It was only after concluding a hasty alliance with Clan Morbus – and a particularly brutal campaign of assassinations – that the Grey Lord was able to secure his position and restore order.

What mystified Eekrit for a long time afterwards was why Velsquee never made the obvious move of stripping him of command. The Grey Lord scarcely needed any real justification to do it, and no doubt Lord Hiirc thought that the alliance with his clan entitled him to the position. Eekrit could only surmise that he was being kept around to hold Clan Morbus in check. So long as he remained warlord, Morbus would have to contend with Clan Rikek first and foremost if they meant to claim the mountain for their own – but even now, five years after the army's near-defeat, neither clan had the strength to hold a clear advantage over the other.

As soon as Eekrit was fit enough to fight, Velsquee 'advised' that he resume his dangerous raids against the enemy – only this time, instead of striking relatively defenceless villages or flesh-eater nests, the warlord and his raiders were aimed straight at the enemy's heart. They struck at the towers and storehouses of the fortress itself, undermining their foundations or kindling fires in their bowels. From a purely military standpoint, the raids were a bold, aggressive strategy, meant to keep the foe on the back foot while the skaven army rebuilt its strength. They were also extremely dangerous. One in three of the sappers' tunnels were discovered by enemy search parties and losses among the skaven were heavy, but Eekrit couldn't deny that the tactic had proven successful. It also served to keep him far away from the corridors of power in the under-fortress, where his presence would lead to a number of awkward questions that Velsquee and Qweeqwol could ill afford.

At the far end of the tunnel, the master sapper paused and made a series of paw- and tail-signals. The message was relayed down the line, and within moments a handful of scout-assassins were creeping forwards with oil bladders to douse the sappers' temporary supports. Eekrit watched them pass and fought down a shudder at the sharp smell of the lamp oil.

'Any word from the under-fortress?' Eekrit asked in a low voice.

The Master of Treacheries folded his arms. His head shifted this way and that, making sure none of the sappers were within earshot. 'More reinforcements have arrived,' he answered in a low voice. 'Velsquee sent them straight to the upper levels. Mercenaries from the lesser clans plus another pack of monstrosities from Clan Moulder, and several large packs of slaves.'

'All bought and paid for by Lord Hiirc, no doubt,' Eekrit muttered. The alliance between Velsquee and Hiirc had opened Morbus's coffers and the clan had spent huge sums to replenish the army's decimated ranks. Most of the replacement troops were sell-swords from the lesser clans, lured to the killing grounds by the promise of coin and a share of the plunder from the mountain's vast store of god-stone. Others, like the bizarre beast-masters of Clan Moulder, or the fanatics of Clan Pestilens, joined the expeditionary force in hopes of enhancing their status amid the ever-shifting currents of skaven politics. They were a far cry from the fierce, well-armed packs of clanrats that had marched with the army at the beginning of the war. Most were dead within a few months, hurled against the enemy's defensive lines in one bloody assault after another, while Eekrit's raiders continued to gnaw away at the foe's sources of supply.

So far, Velsquee's two-pronged strategy seemed to be working. The enemy remained on the defensive, unable to replenish its losses, while the skaven managed to scrape together enough warm bodies to sustain a slow but relentless offensive. Much of mine shaft seven had been cleared over the past few years, and the skaven had pushed beyond it into levels that they hadn't reached since the beginning of the war. No one had seen the *kreekar-gan* at all since Velsquee's abortive ambush, and there hadn't been a major enemy attack for years. Victory now seemed inevitable, and the skaven lords were already manoeuvring to take full advantage of the aftermath. Between the mercenary companies and the slave troops, nearly half of the army had been bought with Morbus gold, and Velsquee couldn't kill them fast enough to blunt Lord Hiirc's growing influence. Eshreegar thought it was only a matter of time before the raiders were pulled from the front lines and his assassins put to work by the scheming clan lords.

'What of Velsquee's troops?' the warlord inquired.

The Master of Treacheries gave Eekrit a meaningful look. 'Another pack of *heechigar* arrived late last week,' he replied. 'They're still laired up with Lord Vittrik's engineers on the far side of the main cavern.'

Eekrit's eyes narrowed as he tallied the numbers. Velsquee had been quietly rebuilding his cadre of elite troops since the disaster, bringing them in a pack at a time and quartering them in the one place where they would be certain to avoid prying eyes – among the unpredictable and deadly engines of Clan Skryre.

'That brings Velsquee nearly back to full strength,' the warlord mused. 'And they're still working closely with the warlocks?'

'Nearly every day,' Eshreegar confirmed. 'There's no telling what tricks they've got up their sleeves now. You can bet that the *kreekar-gan* won't be able to slaughter them like he did last time.'

'Do you think the other clan lords suspect how many warriors Velsquee's got?'

Eshreegar shook his head. 'Unlikely. The Grey Lord's been careful, and the others are too focused on positioning themselves for the end game.' His tail flicked thoughtfully. 'I still don't understand why Velsquee's hiding his true strength. A show of force by the storm-walkers would secure his position and make the other lords think twice about siding with Hiirc.'

'That's true enough in the short term,' Eekrit agreed, 'but then it would only be a matter of time before Hiirc and the other clan lords began pressuring Velsquee to send them into action, and that's the last thing the Grey Lord wants. The *heechigar* are being saved for one task and one task only.'

'The destruction of the *kreekar-gan*.'

Eekrit nodded. 'Velsquee overplayed his hand last time. He had good reason to believe that the burning man was about to fall into his paws, and nearly lost everything as a result. This time, he's being much more careful.' The warlord's lip curled in irritation. 'I just wish I knew where he was getting his information from. Or *who*.'

The Master of Treacheries sighed irritably. 'He *does* have a grey seer at his beck and call, does he not?'

Eekrit's tail lashed angrily across the tunnel floor, loudly enough to draw apprehensive glances from the scouts. 'It's not Qweeqwol,' he replied. 'Velsquee would have killed him for failing to predict the poison cloud. No, the Grey Lord is getting his information from someone else.'

'Well, it's none of my rats,' Eshreegar declared.

'Of that I have little doubt,' Eekrit replied, his whiskers twitching sarcastically.

'Then who...' Eshreegar began. His good eye narrowed thoughtfully. 'It would have to be a traitor. Someone within the enemy's own ranks.'

The warlord nodded. 'And privy to the enemy's senior councils. Someone who has likely been close to the *kreekar-gan* all along.'

'But how?'

'I don't know for sure,' Eekrit admitted, 'but I'd bet Qweeqwol knows. He's been feeding Velsquee information since the beginning. How else does one explain the timing of the Grey Lord's arrival?'

The idea made Eshreegar's ears lie flat. 'But, that means–'

'That means Velsquee and Qweeqwol knew about the burning man from the very beginning,' Eekrit said.

'Then why not tell us?' said the Master of Treacheries. 'They want the god-stone just as much as the rest of us.'

The warlord sighed impatiently. 'Of course they do,' he snapped. 'They want *all* of it. You think it was an accident that Velsquee was the primary architect of the expeditionary force?'

Eshreegar frowned. 'I thought the grey seers were behind the alliance?'

The warlord raised a clawed finger. 'Yes, but Velsquee was their chief advocate among the Grey Lords. They came to him first, because he had the most influence on the Council. No doubt they agreed to split the riches of the mountain between them, once the rest of the clans had been bled white against the *kreekar-gan*'s horde.' The warlord shook his head ruefully. 'In fact, it wouldn't surprise me if the grey seers were behind the scouts who "discovered" the mountain in the first place, acting on information supplied by the traitor.'

Eshreegar folded his arms and considered what he'd been told. 'A brilliant scheme,' he admitted. 'Cunning and ruthless beyond belief.'

'Indeed,' Eekrit snarled irritably. 'I couldn't have done better myself.'

There was the sound of movement from the far end of the tunnel. The scouts were withdrawing back the way they'd come, followed closely by the sappers. They filed past Eekrit and Eshreegar quickly and quietly, eager to return to the relative safety of the lower levels.

The master sapper and his chief assistant were the last in line. 'It's-it's ready,' the grizzled veteran hissed. At a nod from Eekrit, the sappers knelt and began fishing a pair of torches from their shoulder bags. Within seconds they were striking fat, orange sparks from their flints. Eshreegar and Eekrit watched the hungry flickers of light with expressions of sick unease.

'So now you know Velsquee's plan,' Eshreegar said faintly. 'What do you propose to do about it?'

One of the torches sputtered to life in a flare of crackling flame. Eekrit all but flinched at the sight. His teeth clenched in disgust at the smell of fear-musk in the close confines of the tunnel. The scars along his paws and shoulders itched and ached. He could still remember the searing pain gnawing at his limbs; still feel the smoke clawing at his eyes and throat. The memories were as vivid now as they'd been five years ago.

Abruptly, the master sapper straightened, raising his blazing torch over his head. The flame made a fearful whoosh and flared angrily as it passed through the air only a few feet from Eekrit's face. Eshreegar made a choking sound and flinched a bit himself, haunted by his own memories of the inferno.

Angrily, the warlord reached out and snatched the torch from the master sapper's grip. The scar tissue on the back of his paw tightened painfully, but Eekrit forced himself to hold the brand steady.

'There is-is nothing to be done,' he said in a grim voice. The warlord stared hatefully into the hissing flame. 'Velsquee believes us powerless. With the support of Lord Hiirc, the Grey Lord no doubt thinks he has-has the upper hand.'

The master sapper and his assistant looked on worriedly as Eekrit left them, heading up the tunnel towards the oil-soaked supports. At a dozen paces from the tower's foundations he stopped, holding the fire before him like a naked blade.

'For now, we-we wait,' he said, staring into the fire. 'Sooner or later, Velsquee will have his reckoning with the *kreekar-gan*.' He drew back his arm, and with a snarl he hurled the torch through the air. The brand spun end-over-end and struck the closest support. With a baleful *whoosh* the wooden support was engulfed in a pillar of seething flame. Eekrit forced himself to stand still as the bloom of heat washed over him. He closed his eyes and counted slowly to five, then let out a slow breath and turned to face Eshreegar and his warriors.

'Let the burning man come. We shall see who survives the flames.'

The war-witch's song was all but lost amid the deafening cacophony of the fight. Across the mine shaft, four companies of northmen stood shoulder-to-shoulder, roaring oaths and hacking away with their blades in the face of a howling tide of wide-eyed rat-creatures. The enemy were unarmoured and carried little more than crude daggers or heavy rocks, but they attacked the towering barbarians with fearless abandon. Their eyes shone a pale green and phosphorescent foam flecked their gaping mouths. Whatever they'd been fed, it had driven them into a berserker fury that disdained all but the most terrible injuries. Even in death, the monsters seized the arms and legs of the northmen and tried to pull them to the tunnel floor. The barbarians had learned that to fall was to die; if they lost their feet they would be seized by a dozen pairs of hands and dragged into the mob. Those that did so were never seen again.

Standing at the opposite side of the mine shaft, Nagash could see that the barbarian formations were already dangerously close to breaking. For more than six hours the enemy had launched one wave after another against his defensive lines. Once they'd found the points guarded by his living troops, they had focused their efforts on them and increased the pressure. Skeletons had no need for food or rest, but flesh and blood did, and now the lack was beginning to tell.

It galled Nagash that he had to depend upon the barbarians at all. When the war began, the northmen comprised little more than a third of his vast forces. Now, decades later, nearly half of the army was flesh and blood. He was forced to position his companies with great care these days, and to stand ready to lend his own power when the situation became desperate.

A figure in battered scale armour staggered away from the raging fight and hurried across the tunnel towards Nagash. It was Thestus, his heavy sword notched and red-stained and every inch of his exposed skin covered in cuts and scratches. His pale face was worn and deeply lined; it had been more than a month since he'd last been given a draught of the necromancer's elixir and the hunger was taking its toll.

Thestus pushed his way through ranks of yellowed skeletons massed in reserve behind the main battle-line and came to a lurching halt before the baleful stares of the necromancer's wight guard. 'The line won't hold!' he said, shouting tonelessly over the din. 'Bragadh has fallen and the warriors are at their breaking point! If you would strike, master, strike now!'

For a long moment, Nagash did not stir. Tattered grey robes hung across the bony planes of his shoulderblades. The deep hood, stained by old soot and frayed along the hem, hung listlessly around his skull. His arms hung loosely across his waist, hands hidden within the depths of his long sleeves. An aura of power still crackled invisibly about his withered frame, but to Thestus the necromancer somehow seemed less substantial than the wights surrounding him.

There was a strange ripple of motion beneath the layers of rotting cloth; first the right shoulder, then the upper arm, then down through the elbow and the bones of the hand. Nagash's arm rose, sweeping in an arc to encompass the low-slung figures that crouched beside him. The air grew dense with sorcerous energies, plucking at the decaying raiment of the necromancer's bodyguards.

There was a dry, rustling sound in the shadows by Nagash's side, like the sound of old bones being stirred in a fortune-teller's bowl. Sharp points scraped against stone and a rising chorus of ominous, clicking sounds swelled at the necromancer's command. Clusters of small, oval green orbs glimmered balefully out of the darkness.

A single word slithered like a serpent across Thestus's mind, resonant with the tones of Nagash's sepulchral voice.

Go.

With a manic scuttling of bony limbs, a dozen fearsome-looking shapes burst into murderous life, like a pack of hounds unleashed by their master. They raced from the shadows with unsettling speed; gleaming figures of polished bone and thin plates of bronze, each as big around as a northman's shield. They raced across the tunnel floor on six segmented legs, their small, armoured heads swivelling left and right in search of prey. Their mandibles, each as long as a desert warrior's khopesh, trembled at the prospect of rending living flesh.

Had he been a denizen of distant Nehekhara, Thestus would have recognised them at once: they were monstrous replicas of tomb beetles, cunningly shaped from bits of broken bone and curved metal and animated with hideous unlife by the power of the burning stone. But while real tomb beetles were scavengers, feasting on the rotting flesh of the dead, these constructs had been built for war.

Directed by the necromancer's hateful will, the constructs' carapaces opened on cunning hinges, revealing thin, wing-like armatures made of metal and tanned human hide. They cracked like sailcloth as rope-like musculature shook them out and caused them to beat in a growing, bone-chilling hum. The constructs raced forwards, gathering speed, then, with a kick of their powerful hind legs, they leapt into the air and plunged like catapult stones into the midst of the enemy warriors. They landed in a welter of blood and broken bones, knocking the frenzied rat-creatures to the ground and slicing them apart with swift, scissor-like blows from their mandibles. Within moments, all was confusion behind the enemy lines, as the berserk rat-creatures turned on the scarab constructs instead of the thinly-stretched line of northmen.

The carnage was incredible. The scarabs severed legs and arms with terrible ease, and their razor-edged carapaces sliced through flesh and muscle as though it were old parchment. The constructs had no brain to speak of – only a series of commands carved into the inside of their skulls and animated by the necromancer's will. A small piece of *abn-i-khat* was lodged deep inside the thorax of each of the beetles, providing them with enough murderous energy to function for the length of a short fight. Nagash had envisioned them as shock troops, meant to carve their way through the enemy's defensive lines and open the way for his advancing companies. With enough time and resources, he could have built hundreds of the war machines; as it was now, he could manage barely a score, and those were being hurled into battle in a last-ditch attempt to stem the enemy advance.

He had come close to victory, five years past – bitterly, tantalisingly close. The poison vapour had slaughtered the enemy in the tens of thousands and sowed terror and confusion in their ranks. His undead warriors had pursued the fleeing ratmen into the very roots of the mountain, seizing rich mine shafts that he had not possessed in decades. Sensing that the enemy lay upon the brink of defeat, he pressed them closely with his skeletons, and it had proved to be his undoing. When the rat-creatures launched a desperate counter-thrust into mine shaft seven, Nagash had precious few reserves on hand to stop them. The collapse of the mine shaft had taken him entirely by surprise; it was by luck alone that he had escaped being ground to powder beneath tons of collapsing stone.

Cut off from reinforcements, his advancing troops were eventually stopped at mine shaft eight and destroyed over the course of several days by repeated enemy counter-attacks. The loss in resources had been staggering, so much so that when the enemy struck back the following week, the ratmen quickly regained mine shafts five and six, leaving Nagash in even worse shape than before.

Furious, he had lashed out at the enemy with a campaign of sorcerous attacks over the next few years, searching for the perfect weapon that would finally drive them from the mountain, but the damned rat-creatures adapted swiftly to every new tactic he employed, from poison vapours to blood-boiling plagues. The ratmen suffered terribly, and occasionally one of the upper mine shafts would temporarily fall to his warriors, but every time his forces lacked the strength to consolidate his gains, and in short order they were lost once again. And all the while, his supply of the precious *abn-i-khat* was dwindling away. Where once he'd thought himself secure for millennia thanks to the riches of the great mountain, now he was forced to hoard each and every particle of the glowing rock, spending it only when he must.

Nagash had grown so attuned to the ebb and flow of the sorcerous power in his bones that he could feel it trickling away while he directed the actions of the tomb beetles. Such exacting focus was necessary, because more than ever his existence depended on ingesting the stone. After so many centuries, his leathery flesh was all but gone, consumed by the rigours of time and the strain of countless sorcerous rituals. His bones, permeated by layers of stone dust, were held together now by pure sorcery and the necromancer's implacable will. At first, the amount of power required was negligible, but it had grown fractionally with each passing year.

Nagash directed the movement of his right arm once more, reaching into the depths of his left-hand sleeve. He found what he sought by virtue of the power it exuded against the bones of his fingers. Grasping the pieces of *abn-i-khat,* he drew them free and raised them to his hooded face. The faded sleeve fell away to reveal the bones of hand and forearm, blackened with age and centuries of arcane ritual. A faint green aura flickered about the outlines of his bones and glowed sullenly in the narrow joints.

There were two pieces of stone resting in his skeletal palm, shaped into thin discs like Nehekharan coins so that they lay flat against the bones. Angrily, Nagash closed his fingers about the stones and mentally intoned a swift incantation. There was a hissing sound as the *abn-i-khat* dissolved, its power leaching into his bones. Faint impurities curled from the gaps between his finger bones in thin wisps of smoke. Sorcerous energy flowed through him like molten metal, but its potency dissipated all too quickly. It flowed through him and was drawn away almost at once by the demands of his army, like water poured onto the desert sands.

Across the tunnel, Nagash saw Diarid force his way out of the press of barbarians. Though sorely wounded himself, the champion dragged the limp form of his master, Bragadh, behind him. From the necromancer's left, Akatha's war-song faltered as the witch caught sight of the wounded chieftain. Without asking for Nagash's leave, she pushed through the circle of the necromancer's bodyguard and rushed to Bragadh's side. For a moment,

Nagash thought to force her to return to her place, but his resources were stretched too thin as it was to risk a battle of wills with the barbarian witch.

Nagash's hooded head shifted fractionally, focusing on Thestus. Without lungs to draw air, or flesh to shape words, he used still more of his precious energy to impose his will on the barbarian. *Rally the northmen,* he commanded. *Restore the line.*

Thestus recoiled at the lash of the necromancer's will. 'But... what of the reserves?' he stammered. 'We must commit the spear companies, master! The men are exhausted; they cannot continue much longer–'

Obey, Thestus!

The barbarian cried out at the fury in Nagash's unspoken command. Black ichor welled up at the corners of his eyes and mouth. He staggered backwards, pressing a hand to his face, then turned away and stumbled towards the still-struggling barbarians.

Beyond the battle-line, the enemy's foothold in mine shaft four was shrinking fast. The maddened ratmen proved their own worst enemy against the armoured scarabs, hurling themselves into the path of their snapping mandibles or slicing themselves to pieces against the scarabs' carapaces. The gore-streaked constructs scuttled nimbly over heaps of ravaged corpses, driving ever deeper into the enemy ranks.

Nagash poured his rage into his sorcerous engines, doubling, then tripling their speed and strength. Still more wild-eyed ratmen poured from the branch-tunnels and hurled themselves fearlessly into the path of the scarabs, only to be cut down in turn by the buzzing, snapping war engines. The enemy assault had been stopped in its tracks, and for the first time in years, was being driven back upon itself.

The necromancer relished the sight of the slaughter. He drove the scarabs onwards, pushing for the branch-tunnels, eager to drive the knife deeper into the enemy's line. There was no way to tell what lay behind the hordes of drugged ratmen; could there be a flaw in the enemy line that he could exploit? If he could push even as far as mine shaft five and hold it for a day or so, he might be able to seize enough raw stone to turn the counter-attack into a general offensive. After five years of punishing retreats, the urge to strike back was almost unbearable.

Thestus's dreadful voice rose above the tumult, shouting orders to the exhausted northmen. The companies ordered their ranks and slowly pushed forwards over the heaped bodies of the ratmen. The constructs had nearly reached the mouths of the branch-tunnels; they had been designed with the cramped confines of the passageways in mind and would be at an even greater advantage over the enemy.

Nagash considered the waiting ranks of skeletons before him. He had five hundred spearmen immediately at hand, plus his fearsome wights. They could pass through the barbarian lines and push into the tunnels behind the scarabs. If they cut deeply enough, quickly enough, they might be able to cut off a large part of the enemy's troops...

Just then, the necromancer caught sight of movement out of the corner of his eye. A bloodied barbarian warrior had come running out of one of the branch-tunnels and was gasping out a report to Akatha and Diarid. The witch rose from beside Bragadh's unconscious form and reluctantly returned to Nagash's side. Her expression was grim.

'There is news from the interior,' she said, referring to the end of the defensive line anchored at the deepest part of the mine shaft. 'The ratmen have tunnelled around our warriors and emerged behind them. Our forces there have been thrown into confusion.'

Nagash rounded on the witch, his skeleton warping unnaturally with the sudden movement before reasserting itself. *Rally them,* he seethed. *The line must hold!*

Akatha groaned at the savage pressure inside her skull, but the witch did not falter. 'Bragadh himself might have been able to turn the tide, but now...' she shrugged. 'His wounds are deep. He requires a fresh infusion of your elixir before he can fight again.'

There is none to give! Nagash raged. *Thestus will go in Bragadh's place. The companies will follow him, or I will slay them myself!*

Akatha did not reply. Her cold stare was answer enough. Of all his servants, she understood best how precarious their situation had become.

Nagash turned back to the fight at the far side of the tunnel. The advantage he'd seen there had been an illusion; the bloody assault had been but a diversion to distract him from the enemy's flanking attack. He had been outmanoeuvred again.

A stream of deadly curses stained the aether. Once again, his position had become untenable. He could continue to fight, and possibly even repulse the new attack, but the cost in troops would be great. Caught between two axes of attack, it was even possible that the barbarians would collapse under the strain, and he might find himself cut off from the surface.

The enemy war leader was cautious and cunning, Nagash had to admit. His slow and steady advance was crushing the necromancer's troops, like the suffocating coils of a river python. The more he fought, the weaker he inevitably became. The only viable tactic left to him was to avoid battle as much as possible, but even that played into the enemy's hands.

Somehow, the enemy understood that the burning stone was the key to victory. Every day brought his forces closer to defeat, as the store of *abn-i-khat* dwindled. Before much longer, he would need to hoard the last remaining bits of stone not to fight, but to stave off his own extinction.

Trembling with fury, Nagash brought the bone scarabs to a halt at the edge of the branch-tunnels. He had to conserve his strength, to wait for his enemy to make a mistake. Then he would strike and he would not stop until he held the enemy war leader's beating heart in his hands.

Until then, he had no choice but to retreat.

EIGHT

MEDITATIONS ON LIFE AND DEATH

Lahmia,
the City of the Dawn,
in the 99th year of Ualatp the Patient
(-1290 Imperial Reckoning)

Lightning split the sky over Lahmia, burning white-hot against a backdrop of roiling black cloud. For a fraction of an instant the garden clearing was thrown into stark relief; each stunted, thrashing branch, each bent blade of grass, each frantic ripple across the wide, dark pond – then darkness rushed in and thunder beat at the back of Alcadizzar's head and shoulders. Rain lashed at his naked body, coursing down his forehead and into his eyes. After the heat of the day, the cold water wracked him with painful spasms in his arms and legs. It was all he could do to remain upright, focusing on the fading heat in his veins and drawing what little strength he could from it.

This is the day I die.

The thought echoed over and over in his mind. For seven days and seven nights he had been left alone in the garden to purify his mind and body and prepare for the ordeal to come. The high priestesses had stripped him of his robes and left him with neither food nor water; if he were worthy, the gifts of the goddess would be enough to sustain him.

This is the day I die.

Surprisingly, he'd felt no hunger. No thirst. After the first few nights, he'd felt no fatigue, either. The sun burned his skin by day, until he welcomed the thunderstorms that blew in from the sea at evening; then darkness would fall and the night air would chill him to the bone. The passage of time had become disjointed as he'd withdrawn deeper and deeper into his own mind. Meditate, the high priestesses had told him. When one had been cleansed of all worldly cares, only the goddess remained. That was the path to salvation.

And so he'd looked inwards, seeking the goddess. For the first time, he tried to put aside his dreams and ambitions, to stifle his hunger for a life outside the walls of palace or temple, but he found that he could not. The fact was that he didn't want to. He didn't want the gifts of the goddess. He wanted *Khemri*. He wanted to stride the world as a king and a conqueror, not spend his days pondering the mysteries of some esoteric cult. During the long years of study he'd tried to convince himself otherwise, that he could balance the duties of a hierophant with the drives of a monarch, but after the fourth day in the garden he could no longer deny the truth. Alcadizzar was no priest, and never would be.

The realisation had been a painful one. He could not turn aside now, not after pledging himself to the temple. He refused to forswear himself, even to save his own life. All that remained now was to endure as long as he could, and then go to the lands of the dead with his honour still intact.

This is the day I die, he thought calmly. Lightning flashed and the rain poured down, and he waited for the moment to come.

After a time, the storm's fury abated. Night drew on, with a bright, full moon rising above the sea to the east. The frogs began to sing from the depths of the garden and the cicadas murmured in the trees. Bats whirled high overhead, their darting shapes silhouetted against the starlight.

He was not aware of the high priestesses until they had emerged from the trees surrounding the clearing. Their golden masks shone like lamps beneath the moon, and their samite robes seemed to float about their bodies as they walked bare-footed across the damp grass. Alcadizzar smiled at the sight of them after so many days with nothing but his thoughts for company. Silently they glided up to the prince, forming a wide circle around him. Their eyes were flat and pitiless.

The prince straightened his back and turned his head up to the sky. He breathed deeply, tasting the night air. Salt and stone, green grass and murky water; these were the smells he would take with him into the afterlife.

Between one breath and the next, he felt her enter the clearing. He could feel her presence like a weight upon his soul. The pressure increased with every step she took, causing his pulse to quicken and a chill to race down his spine. He couldn't say how long she had affected him so; the connection he felt had grown slowly over the years, bound ever more tightly together with each ritual sharing of the goddess's cup. Until recently, he'd thought the bond was a measure of his devotion to the cult; now he wasn't sure what to believe.

The high priestesses seemed to share Alcadizzar's connection; they bowed their heads in unison as she approached the circle and two of the masked women stood aside to allow her to pass inside.

She glided silently across the grass to stand before Alcadizzar. From his perspective, she seemed to tower above him, like one of the lost gods. She wore a fitted golden breastplate engraved with twining asps, over a robe of white samite bordered at the hem and sleeves with bands of gold thread. A necklace of fiery rubies encircled her pale throat, glinting like fresh drops of blood. Her gold mask seemed to glow against the backdrop of her lustrous black hair. A broad-rimmed goblet was clasped reverently against her chest. Two high priestesses followed in her wake; one bore a second goblet in her hands, while the other held a heavy leather scourge.

For a moment she said nothing. He could feel her gaze against his skin like a caress. Gooseflesh ran along his arms and down the back of his neck. Alcadizzar gritted his teeth and tried to suppress a shudder.

Finally, she spoke. 'Prince Alcadizzar of Rasetra, you have spent seven days and seven nights in solitary vigil, purifying your mind and body of worldly desires. We have gathered here to elevate you to the temple's highest rank, but first you must demonstrate your devotion and piety in a trial of suffering. Do you understand?'

Alcadizzar nodded gravely. 'I do, holy one,' he replied, his voice roughened by disuse.

'You will be tested unto destruction, oh prince,' she said. Her voice was cold, but her dark eyes smouldered with suppressed emotion. 'It is the only way. If your heart and mind are pure, the blood of the goddess will sustain you.'

'I know,' he said. Alcadizzar summoned his resolve, determined to accept his fate with dignity. 'Let it be done.'

'Then rise, oh prince, and drink from the cup of the goddess.'

Alcadizzar took a deep breath and forced his cramped limbs to work. Slowly, carefully, he rose to his feet. Fiery pain blossomed from his shoulders all the way to his toes, but he forced the sensations into the back of his mind. Solemnly, he took the proffered cup and raised it to his lips. The metal rim was warm and the dark liquid soft. *Asaph's Kiss,* he'd heard it called by some of the priestesses. He drank, and this time the ritual offering was far more potent than he'd tasted before. Its heat spread through his body in an instant, taking away his pain and filling him with strength. His mind reeled, borne on a sudden wave of euphoria that seemed to emanate, not from the cup, but from *her.* She took the cup from his hands and he knew that she was smiling behind the curve of her mask.

'Do not be afraid,' she said softly – or perhaps she had merely *thought* it. He could not say for certain any more.

She withdrew from him then, and he felt it like an ache in his heart. It took all of Alcadizzar's concentration not to try and follow her. Instead, he focused on the high priestess who stepped up to take her place. Without a word, she offered him the second cup.

'Drink,' the priestess said in a husky voice.

He took the cup without fear and drained it in a single draught. The wine was sweet and spiced with a multitude of herbs, but not enough to hide the bitter taste of the poison within.

When he handed back the goblet, he met the masked priestess's eyes and was surprised to find that they were brimming with tears. Without thinking, he tried to give her a reassuring smile. She bowed her head and returned to her mistress's side. As she did so, the rest of the circle began a low, almost mournful chant.

The die was cast. Alcadizzar was surprised at how calm he felt. It might have been the effects of the elixir, but the prince wanted to think otherwise. Once more, he turned his face to the sky.

Forgive me father, he thought, and offered himself up for judgement.

The pain came on quickly. It began as a terrible burning in his guts that grew more intense with every passing moment, as though he were swallowing one hot coal after another. He clenched his jaw and kept silent for what felt like an eternity, thinking that eventually the agony would subside, but no such relief came. His body began to tremble uncontrollably and a strangled scream forced its way past his lips.

Moments later he was lying on the wet grass, his naked form curled into a foetal ball as the poison worked its way through his body. The muscles of his torso first began to ache, then, like the tightening of ropes, they began to contract and stiffen. The suffering spread through his limbs, then up his neck and along the muscles of his face. His screams became agonised gasps, whistling through clenched teeth as an invisible fist closed about his chest. Every beat of his heart was like a red-hot dagger driving into his ribs. Darkness began to crowd the edges of his vision, until he was certain that he was going to pass out, but somehow the promise of oblivion never came.

Hours passed. Slowly, gradually, the agony began to ebb away. It receded like the tide, shrinking from his head and limbs and drawing back into his chest. Little by little his aching muscles sagged; when his head bent far enough for his temple to touch the cool grass, the sensation was so shocking it caused him to cry anew.

Slowly, painfully, he began to draw ever-deeper breaths, despite the red-hot bands that still wrapped around his chest. Each gulp of air tasted sweet and cool, and though it made his throat ache, he found himself gasping for more. He scarcely noticed when two of the priestesses came forwards and knelt beside him. Still chanting, they each gripped one of his wrists and with surprising strength they lifted him until he was able to get his knees underneath him and sit back shakily upon his heels. Then the women drew apart, stretching his arms to their full length between them. Alcadizzar felt their small hands tighten upon his wrists and wondered hazily why – then came the first, fiery lash of the scourge.

The scourge's seven leather tails – each one a six-foot length of braided leather that was studded with dozens of tooth-like shards of glass – raked across his shoulders like the claws of a lion. The pain was so sudden and so intense that it left him speechless; his whole body spasmed under the blow and the priestesses who held him were nearly hauled off their feet. Alcadizzar scarcely had time to draw a single breath before the next blow struck. Hot blood spattered the backs of his outstretched arms and began to flow in rivulets down the small of his back.

The priestess who wielded the scourge was an expert. By the seventh stroke, the skin of his back was in tatters from the nape of his neck to the top of his waist. And still the blows kept coming, tearing implacably into flesh and muscle. The agony was beyond anything Alcadizzar had ever known. After the tenth stroke he thought he could stand no more and that surely he would pass out from the pain, but his mind and body stubbornly refused to succumb. He felt each and every blow as vividly as the first.

In the public squares and aboard the slave galleys of Lahmia, twenty lashes with a scourge was regarded as severe punishment. Forty lashes was a death sentence. After a hundred lashes, the priestesses finally lowered Alcadizzar's twitching body to the grass.

He could not say how long he lay there, his blood soaking into the sward. Alcadizzar's entire body felt as though it were on fire. His face was pressed to the grass; eyes open and mouth slack, breathing in shallow, ragged gasps. He could see the silhouette of a number of the priestesses, but could not hear their chanting for the roaring in his ears. Not long now, he thought. Soon the stars would go out and blackness fall like a shroud, and then he would cross over into the realm of the dead.

But then Alcadizzar heard her voice. 'Rise up, oh prince,' she said. It was as though she were whispering softly into his ear. He could almost feel her breath on his skin.

'There is but one final test, Alcadizzar. Rise up.'

Alcadizzar coughed weakly. It was the nearest to a laugh he could manage. And yet, there was something in her voice that compelled him to try. He tried to focus on his limbs, using the tricks of concentration he'd learned in his years at the temple. After a moment, the searing pain began to ebb. His hands and feet twitched, and then, unbelievably, they obeyed his commands. Slowly, weakly, he pulled his arms in close, and then, with a shuddering breath, he pushed himself up onto his knees. The ground beneath him was dark with blood.

'That's it!' he heard her say. 'Rise up, beloved! Rise, and come to me!'

Another breath and he was rearing shakily to his feet. Alcadizzar's head swam and he staggered backwards a step before catching himself. The pain flared again, clawing across his shoulders and down his back in lines of fire. His head swam, and for a dizzying second he thought he might fall to the ground, never to rise again.

'Here,' she said. Her words were like honey. 'Here I am. Come to me.'

Alcadizzar blinked dazedly, struggling to focus on her voice. She was just in front of him, radiant in gold and white, her left hand outstretched to welcome him. Her dark eyes gleamed with passion from the depths of her polished mask.

He drew a deep breath and pushed back against the tide of pain. His right foot twitched and then shuffled forwards a half-step. Another breath, and his left foot moved as well. A collective, indrawn breath went up from the assembled priestesses.

His strength began to ebb almost at once. Alcadizzar felt his knees start to tremble. Staying upright demanded more and more of his concentration, allowing jagged spikes of pain to shoot up his spine with every step. Yet he kept moving forwards, his eyes fixed on her pale, slender hand.

Alcadizzar's hand trembled as he reached for her. Her palm was cool and hard, like marble. The prince's eyes widened in awe as she gently pulled him close, as though to embrace him.

The sudden pain in his chest was sharp and cold, and for a moment it left him baffled. The chanting stopped. Then he looked down and saw the silver hilt of the dagger jutting from his breast. The blade had slipped effortlessly between his ribs, transfixing his heart.

Alcadizzar frowned in bemusement. She let go of his hand, reaching up instead to grip his ragged shoulder. He looked up at her, trying to speak, but his lungs would not draw breath. A terrible ache spread through his chest, dulling his nerves and stealing away his strength. His legs buckled. She lowered him back to the grass, one hand still gripping the hilt of the dagger.

Her perfect, golden face floated above him, serene and inscrutable. Sensation faded swiftly. The last thing Alcadizzar clearly felt was a sharp pang of regret. His gaze drifted to the firmament of stars glittering overhead as he waited for the end to come.

Yet darkness did not come rushing in. One moment stretched into another, without discernible end. His thoughts drifted, as though in a dream, his sense of regret transforming into a leaden feeling of pure, mindless horror. He had died, but was not dead. *He was not dead!*

And then, faintly, he heard her sigh, and watched as she slowly withdrew the dagger from his heart. Inch by inch, the bloodstained bronze emerged from his chest, until the point came free in a single, sharp tug.

All at once, Alcadizzar felt his heart clench. A spasm of agony wracked his chest. His back arched and his lungs filled with air. The prince returned to life with a wordless cry of pain.

Alcadizzar collapsed back against the grass, chest heaving as he gasped for air like a drowning man. The pain in his chest spread like a fire through the rest of his body and he was powerless to stop it.

Robed figures crowded in around him, their ecstatic cries drowning out his own gasps of pain. Alcadizzar glanced from one identical mask to another, trying to make some sense of what was happening. The pain made it nearly impossible to think.

Finally, his eyes met hers. She stared down at him, her entire body radiating a terrible, almost primal joy.

'You see?' she said to the priestesses. Her voice was husky, like the growl of a hungry beast. 'He was pierced by the knife, and yet he did not die! He is worthy, sisters! Alcadizzar has been chosen!'

And then, at last, the darkness rose up to claim him.

He awoke to gentle, perfumed breezes and the cool weight of silken sheets against his skin. After so many years sleeping on a simple priest's cot, the sensation was both familiar, and yet eerily strange at the same time.

Alcadizzar slowly opened his eyes. He lay upon a vast feather bed, larger and more sumptuous than anything he'd known in the royal palace. The hour was very late; he could tell by the hushed sounds of the city that it was close to dawn.

The prince drew a long, deep breath. His chest ached from front to back, all the way down to his bones. It reminded him of the time, many years back, when he'd been kicked in the ribs by a horse during one of his first riding lessons. Moving as though he was in a dream, he rose weakly on his right elbow and peered down at his chest. The room was plunged in shadow, but he could see enough to tell that he'd been bathed and wrapped in a robe of yellow silk.

Hesitantly, Alcadizzar pulled back the left side of his robe. The knife wound was visible as a neat, dark line of scar tissue incised into the flat plane of pectoral muscle just above his heart.

'It is sweet, is it not?'

Her voice rose from the shadows at the far end of the room, where gauzy curtains stirred languidly in the faint sea breeze. Alcadizzar blinked in surprise. As his eyes adjusted to the dimness, he could just make out the graceful curve of shoulder and hip as she leaned against the frame of one of the tall, open windows.

'Death is more than just an endless night,' she went on. 'It's cold and empty, in a way no living man can understand.' Silk rustled as she turned slightly, the perfect shape of her profile silhouetted against the pale, night sky. 'The air tastes like wine now, doesn't it? The feel of silk is like a lover's caress.'

She continued to turn, stepping away from the window's edge and regarding Alcadizzar's recumbent form. The faint glow of false dawn limned her in silver. Her dark hair was still bound up in tight curls, but she had divested herself of her jewels and ritual finery in favour of a simple, diaphanous cotton robe. Her eyes were pools of darkness, her cheek smooth and cold. The face of the goddess was inscrutable and alluring, pale as the death mask of a queen.

He watched as she took another step towards him. The breeze shifted the curtains behind her, letting in more of the outside light, and Alcadizzar's breath caught in his throat. Gooseflesh prickled his skin. The goddess's face was pale as alabaster and her perfect lips were quirked in a faint, enigmatic smile. The prince's mind reeled. Her unearthly features were not wrought from polished gold, but soft flesh and delicate bone.

'Blessed Asaph,' he whispered. 'The – the mask...'

Her smile widened. 'You have endured the Trial of Rebirth, oh prince,' she said, misreading the look of shock in Alcadizzar's eyes. 'We are one and the same now, so there is no further need for artifice.'

Before the prince could reply, she raised her arm and beckoned to the shadows at Alcadizzar's left. A robed figure shuffled painfully out of the darkness, clutching a golden goblet to his chest.

'Your body has already healed the worst of your injuries,' she said, 'but the ordeal consumed much of your strength. Drink this, and then we will discuss your future.'

The servant approached the bedside. His shoulders were hunched awkwardly, as though beneath an invisible weight. Though the man's head was downcast, Alcadizzar recognised the faded tattoos that wound sinuously about his shaven skull. 'Ubaid?' he said wonderingly.

Ubaid's head rose at the sound of his name. The old servant's expression was haggard, his lips slack and faintly trembling, but for all that, he hadn't aged a bit since he'd left the prince outside the temple some thirty years before. A tiny flicker of awareness shone in the depths of Ubaid's watery eyes as he offered his cup to the prince. It was all that Alcadizzar could do not to recoil from the pathetic figure.

'I – I don't understand,' he stammered.

'He is my gift to you,' she replied. 'Ubaid will accompany you to Khemri and help you in the construction of the temple.' Her perfect face clouded with a momentary frown, causing Ubaid's bony shoulders to tremble. 'Be assured, despite his wretched appearance, he is a man of many talents, and will serve you in a multitude of ways.'

It was all too much. The sense of unreality threatened to overwhelm Alcadizzar. He raised a trembling hand to his forehead. 'How... how can this be?'

'The power of the blood,' she explained, her tone growing slightly more insistent. Suddenly, she was standing at Ubaid's side, crossing the bedchamber in the space of a heartbeat. Her pale fingers gripped the rim of the heavy cup and plucked it from the servant's palsied hands.

'Drink,' she commanded. 'And all will be made clear.'

His hand moved without conscious thought, driven by years of obedience to the rites of the temple. But his eyes fell to the dark liquid shifting turgidly in the depths of the cup, and for the first time, the sight of it repelled him. Alcadizzar lurched from the bed, bare feet scuffing across the rug-covered floor as he staggered towards the open windows and the fresh sea air.

'You don't understand,' Alcadizzar told her. He paused just before the window and drew in a deep breath. 'I should have failed the trial. I meditated in the garden, and realised that I could not dedicate myself to the temple. By rights, I should have perished – and yet, here I stand!'

She did not answer at first. When she finally answered, her voice had turned hard and cold.

'You have a great destiny before you, Prince Alcadizzar,' she told him. 'Your sacred bloodline and the teachings of the temple spared you–'

Alcadizzar whirled. 'Then what of *him*?' He levelled a finger at Ubaid's pitiful form. 'Does he share in the sacred blood of kings?'

She recoiled slightly at the accusing tone of Alcadizzar's voice. 'Don't blaspheme!' she snapped, her eyes glinting angrily.

'How then does this poor man still live?' the prince demanded. 'Look how he suffers! He was an old man when I was but a boy; by rights he should have gone on to join his ancestors years ago. Yet he has aged barely a day since I first saw him. What manner of sorcery is this?'

'*Enough!*'

The bedchamber suddenly grew cold. Alcadizzar felt his body go rigid, as though an invisible hand had reached into his body and taken hold of his spine. The shadows deepened and within the darkness her pale skin shone like a brand. He felt his eyes drawn irresistibly to hers. Alcadizzar felt as though he were being dragged to the edge of a precipice; he gritted his teeth and fought with every ounce of his will, but slowly, inexorably, the prince was overcome.

Her voice caressed his aching skin. '*Drink*,' she said. The word sank into his flesh and made his bones ache with need.

One foot lurched forwards, then the other. It felt as though he were falling, drawn unerringly to the waiting cup. And yet, a small part of his mind rebelled against its pull. Terror lent his thoughts an icy clarity Alcadizzar had never known before.

'What are you?' he groaned.

Her smile was terrible. It sank into his heart like a knife.

'I am Neferata,' she said. 'And I have always ruled here.'

Alcadizzar tasted metal against his lips. He could smell the bitter tang of the liquid inside the golden cup.

'*You are mine, Alcadizzar*,' Neferata said. '*Together we shall rule Nehekhara until the end of time.*'

The prince gasped. Warm fluid poured into his mouth. He choked, spilling some of the elixir down his chin, but the rest found its way down his throat. His body responded at once, veins singing and muscles swelling with vigour. Once, the sensation had exhilarated him; now he felt nothing but terror.

Worse, Alcadizzar could feel her grip on him growing stronger by the moment. Her implacable will closed about his brain like a fist, slowly crushing all thoughts of resistance.

And then, abruptly, the crushing pressure was gone. There was a muffled ringing sound as the goblet bounced across the layered rugs and a howl of bestial rage rent the darkness. Alcadizzar staggered backwards, torn from Neferata's hypnotic grip. The shadows receded once more and he saw what had saved him at once.

It was Ubaid. The old servant had thrown himself at Neferata, catching her unawares and knocking her to the floor. He clawed at her face like an animal, his nails raking deep into her eyes. Dark ichor flowed down her pale cheeks and stained the old servant's fingers.

Alcadizzar cried out in horror and rushed forwards, intending to save Ubaid from the creature. But the servant rooted him to the spot with a stern glare. In that instant, a small measure of the old man's spirit seemed to return.

'Go!' Ubaid pleaded. 'In the name of all the gods! *Run!*'

Before the prince could reply, a slender hand shot upwards and seized the old man's throat. Ubaid's eyes bulged; cartilage popped wetly and blood burst from his lips. Then, with a monstrous howl, Neferata reared up, jaws agape, and sank her fangs into the back of his neck. With a single, convulsive wrench, she tore the old man's head from his shoulders in a fountain of crimson gore.

Ichor streaming from her wounded eyes, Neferata turned to Alcadizzar. A bubbling growl rose from her throat. In another moment, he would be lost.

Without thinking, the prince whirled and leapt for the open window. Neferata charged blindly after him, her nails rending the expensive rugs.

He tore through the thin curtains and lighted on the stone windowsill. A long way down spread the sloping flank of the great temple, then the walled expanse of the palace grounds. Beyond that lay the great hill, crowded with the villas of noblemen and wealthy merchants; then the sprawling coastal districts of the city itself. The great sea shone like a polished silver coin in the first, feeble rays of dawn.

Already, a plan was forming in the prince's mind. Once he escaped the city, he would have to make his way to Rasetra. He had to spread the truth about the temple and the evil that lurked in its heart. He had to warn the great cities about Neferata.

Cold fingers clutched at his robe. With a prayer to the gods upon his lips, Alcadizzar leapt into the morning air.

NINE

ACTS OF LAST RESORT

Nagashizzar,
in the 99th year of Usirian the Dreadful
(-1285 Imperial Reckoning)

Sound carried a very long way in the bare, stone halls of the *kreekar-gan*. The scout-assassins darted into the deep shadows at the first, faint sounds of movement in the corridor ahead. Ears wide, nostrils twitching, the veteran raiders gauged the nature of the threat. Paw-signs were passed along the line: *skeletons, small group, coming this way.*

Eekrit shrank back against the cover of a rough-hewn stone column. Eshreegar was close by, flattened against the far wall of the wide hallway. Next to Eekrit, one of the scout-assassins shifted silently into a fighting stance. A pair of needle-pointed daggers slid from the black sheaths at the skaven's belt. The warlord caught the movement out of the corner of his eye and gave the raider a baleful glare.

'Put those damned things away,' Eekrit hissed. 'You want to get us all killed?'

The scout-assassin was a young skaven named Shireep, one of a handful of new replacements from the Great City. His tail lashed in irritation at the tone of Eekrit's voice.

'We're here to kill the enemy,' Shireep replied, his eyes narrowing disdainfully. 'Lord Hiirc's orders were clear on that, were they not?'

Eekrit fought the urge to reach for his own blade. The newcomers were properly respectful to their master, Eshreegar, but they regarded the warlord with thinly veiled contempt.

Another of Hiirc's pawns, Eekrit reckoned. They were turning up with irritating regularity now that the end of the war was finally in sight. This one clearly had more ambition than guile, which either meant that Lord Hiirc was having a hard time finding useful allies, or else his position was strong enough now that he didn't care what Eekrit thought. The warlord feared that it was probably the latter.

'Up here, you take orders from *me*,' Eekrit snarled. He rose to his full height, moving close enough that the two skaven stood almost nose-to-nose. 'The *kreekar-gan* knows everything his skeletons know. Kill one of them – just *one* – and you'll bring the rest of the fortress down on our heads.' The warlord leaned still closer. 'Is that what you're after, ratling? Is it?'

Shireep's hackles started to rise. Eekrit tensed slightly, suddenly very much aware that the skaven's twin knives were just inches from his throat. But it was the assassin that blinked first. He shrank back slightly beneath the warlord's fierce gaze, ears folding tightly against his head. Without a word, he slipped the daggers back into their sheaths.

Eekrit gave the fool a disdainful flick of the ear and settled back against the column, quickly tugging his hood down over his snout and then tucking his paws deep within his wide sleeves. No sooner had he done so than the corridor was filled with a cacophony of scraping bone, clattering armour and the rattle of sword and shield.

Peering out from beneath the rim of his hood, Eekrit watched a pair of skeletons shuffle slowly into view. They were tall and broad of shoulder, still covered in places with scraps of rotting flesh, and their heavy, bronze blades were notched from hard use. The stench of decomposition hung about them in a suffocating fog. Eekrit reckoned that the warriors had been dead less than a week; it was likely that one or more of them had died by his own paw during the raids of the last fortnight.

The first pair of corpses shuffled past Eekrit's hiding place, nearly close enough to touch. Another pair followed, then another, and then yet another. The rattle of marching feet echoed from the walls and the warlord realised with mounting dread that this was no mere patrol. An entire company of undead warriors was marching past, no doubt heading for the barricades in the lowest vaults of the fortress.

Eekrit scarcely dared to breathe. His small force was heavily outnumbered, and there was nowhere to run. If even one of the scout-assassins were noticed, it would be the end of them all. He turned his head fractionally to see what the young fool next to him was doing, but of course he couldn't see a thing through the heavy folds of the dark hood. If he gives us away, I swear to the Horned One that I'll kill him myself, Eekrit thought balefully.

The ghastly procession seemed to continue for hours. Eekrit held absolutely still, fighting to keep his whiskers from twitching at the miasmic stench of decay. At one point, he thought he distinctly heard a sneeze somewhere close by; fortunately the sound was all but lost amid the noise of the march.

Finally, the last of the company shambled past and vanished into the gloom farther down the passageway. Still Eekrit waited, senses strained to the utmost, until well after the sounds of movement had faded away. This deep in the heart of the enemy's defences, there was no such thing as too much caution.

At last, Eekrit allowed himself to relax. His joints ached as his shoulders slumped and his paws slipped from the sleeves of his robe. Eshreegar and the other scout-assassins were moving as well, edging carefully back out into the corridor. The warlord drew back his hood and went to join the Master of Treacheries.

He found Eshreegar and a number of veterans crouched together, muttering softly to one another as they studied dozens of small objects scattered along the length of the passageway. The Master of Treacheries glanced up at Eekrit's approach, his good eye narrowed thoughtfully.

'What do you make of this?' he rasped.

There was a trail of debris littering the corridor. Eekrit saw pieces of rotting leather, bits of tarnished bronze scale – and bones. There were scores of bones, large and small, left behind by the shambling company of northmen. The warlord spied finger bones, ribs, even a few jawbones, their surfaces still glistening with vestiges of decay.

'Not holding together too well, are they?' Eekrit mused, prodding a curved rib bone with a clawed toe. That was troubling news, as far as he was concerned.

Shireep crouched next to Eekrit, his paws resting on his knees. His ears were folded against his skull and his tail was curled tightly around his feet. Clearly the brush with the northmen had unsettled him. 'What-what does it mean?' he asked in a subdued voice.

Eekrit gave the rib bone a kick, sending it skittering across the corridor. 'It means we're wasting time,' he growled. The warlord reached down and hauled Shireep to his feet by the scruff of his neck. 'Show us this secret chamber you've found.'

Shireep led the raiding party across the lower levels of the fortress, pausing only occasionally to check his bearings against the tiny runes scratched into the walls by previous scout parties. For the last year, as skaven forces closed in on the last of the *kreekar-gan*'s mine shafts, Eekrit and his raiders had been ordered to penetrate the lower vaults and storehouses of the fortress in preparation for the final assault. In addition to building a detailed map of the lower levels, the scout-assassins ambushed isolated parties of northmen or flesh-eaters, set fires in unguarded warehouses or laboratories, and otherwise sowed confusion among the enemy's ranks.

It was dangerous, nerve-wracking work; there was no way to create new tunnels inside the fortress itself, and for the first time, the enemy knew the territory far better than they did. Undead patrols were everywhere and the burning man could reinforce them with unsettling speed and efficiency. Eekrit had been forced to divide his forces into smaller and smaller packs in hopes of avoiding detection, sometimes despatching scout parties of three skaven or less into the most heavily patrolled areas. Many of them ventured into the dark vaults and were never seen again.

As bad as things were, Eekrit went to great lengths to make it appear even worse to Velsquee and the other skaven lords. After fighting for so long to defeat the *kreekar-gan* and his undead horde, now the warlord found himself struggling desperately to delay the inevitable. Over the last few years the skaven army had been entirely on the offensive, seizing one mine shaft after another in a series of brutal but ultimately victorious battles. The speed of the skaven advance had been so swift and decisive that Velsquee and the other warlords had been forced to relocate from the under-fortress to a temporary camp at mine shaft four, the better to coordinate the movements of their far-flung companies. Now they were massing a huge force opposite the enemy's final set of barricades and Velsquee was waiting for the opportune moment to strike.

Eekrit did everything in his power to keep the Grey Lord guessing. He left large gaps in his reports to Velsquee, and what information he did share hinted at the possibility of unseen enemy reserves and hints of deadly traps being readied in the fortress depths. It was a delicate balancing act, playing on Velsquee's calculating nature without exhausting his patience entirely. In the meantime, Eekrit was searching the fortress for anything that would give him leverage over Velsquee, Hiirc and the rest of the skaven lords. He knew perfectly well that the moment the war was over, his life wouldn't be worth a plugged copper coin. If Velsquee didn't strip him of his rank and title and have him executed outright, he'd be dangled like a prize before Hiirc and the other lords, like a piece of meat before a starving pack of ratlings. Either way, his future was certain to be as short and brutal as the Grey Lord could possibly manage.

The raiding party crept through the dark and twisting tunnels for more than an hour, heading into a series of large, low-ceilinged storehouses that the scouts had thoroughly explored many months before. Eekrit reckoned that the cavernous rooms had once held tools and supplies meant for the mine excavations going on in the lower levels. Here and there one could still find coils of rope and stacks of wooden pick handles, rotting wicker baskets and the sagging ruins of empty carts. As far as the warlord could tell, the chambers hadn't been used in decades; in fact, that had been the point of sending the young fool into this part of the fortress in the first place, so he couldn't report anything useful back to Lord Hiirc.

They were three levels above the enemy's barricades, and heading further into the heart of the mountain with each passing moment. Eekrit's impatience grew; he was just about to give the order to turn back when Shireep gave the paw-sign to halt. Eekrit and the rest of the raiding party settled onto their haunches, ears open and noses twitching for signs of danger. They were in the centre of one of the storage chambers, surrounded by musty darkness on all sides. Eekrit peered warily into the shadows around him; though he couldn't see any obvious signs of danger, there was something in the air that raised the hackles on the back of his neck. The warlord's paw crept to the hilt of his sword.

Faint sounds of movement drifted back from the head of the column. Shireep crept back to where Eekrit and Eshreegar waited.

'Up-up ahead,' the young skaven whispered. 'In the chamber next to this one. That's where I saw them.'

'Skeletons. You're certain?' Eekrit asked.

'Of course!' the scout replied, a trifle impatiently. 'A score of them, at-at least.'

Eshreegar leaned forwards. 'How do you know they're guarding something?' he asked.

Shireep sighed. 'Why else would they be all-all the way down here?' he replied.

Eekrit gave Eshreegar a sidelong glance. 'We'll see for ourselves,' the warlord said. 'Show us.'

Eshreegar passed orders to the rest of the raiding party to find hiding places in the deeper shadows surrounding the cavern, then Shireep led Eekrit and the Master of Treacheries to the threshold of the chamber just beyond. Through the wide entryway the air was as thick and dank as a tomb.

Shireep lowered himself to all fours, just to one side of the opening. He glanced back at Eekrit and Eshreegar, his ears folded tight. 'There are three skeletons watching the entrance,' he whispered. 'Once inside, move to the right along the outer wall.' Without waiting for a reply, the scout lowered himself even further, until his belly nearly scraped the floor – and then he was gone, flitting like a swift, silent shadow into the chamber. A moment later, Eshreegar darted after him.

The warlord shook his head, suddenly feeling very thick-limbed and clumsy. He waited for a space of ten heartbeats and then scampered after the two scouts as swiftly and as silently as he could.

Eekrit very nearly ran full-tilt into the side of a stack of rotting wooden boxes set just inside and to the right of the entryway. This particular storage space was still piled with decaying mounds of mining gear and other supplies. The sagging boxes and bulging wicker sacks provided the skaven with ample sources of cover, but the same could be said for the undead sentries scattered about the cavern. Opening his ears wide and scanning the darkness for the glowing pinpoints of unliving eyes, Eekrit scuttled into the narrow alley between the stacked supplies and the rough stone of the cavern wall where the others waited.

Eshreegar and Shireep traded a rapid series of paw-gestures, then they headed deeper into the cavern. For a time they followed the cavern wall, then abruptly cut left down a tunnel-like alley formed by tall stacks of sagging boxes. At times they even crawled through empty containers, or wormed their way through narrow gaps between tumbled stacks of spare roof-beams. From time to time, Eekrit caught passing glimpses of distant pinpoints of green light; the watchful, unblinking eyes of undead guards, standing watch over the conventional routes into and out of the cavern. The warlord tried to remember the last time that one of his scouts had searched the great storehouses. Had it been three months ago, or as much as six? Regardless, there hadn't been reports of activity then.

After nearly an hour of cautious travel, Shireep emerged warily into another narrow aisle, somewhere near the centre of the cavern. Across the aisle was a tall stack of rectangular support beams that rose twenty feet into the air. He pointed at the pitch-covered beams with a clawed finger. 'The wood is-is still strong,' he whispered. 'It will support our weight, but we should go up one at a time.'

At this point, Eshreegar stepped forwards. 'I go first,' he hissed, 'then Lord Eekrit, and then you.' The scout ducked his head in a nervous bow, and the Master of Treacheries crept silently up to the stacked beams. He studied them for a moment, tested their surfaces with his claws, then in moments he was climbing up the side of the pile. Seconds later he vanished over the top.

Eekrit drew a deep breath and flexed his scarred paws. The amulets he wore beneath his robes and the potions he drank nearly every day were supposed to maintain his youthful vigour in every respect, but the fact was that he'd never been particularly vigorous to begin with. Whiskers twitching grimly, he stepped up to the stacked beams and searched for a good set of pawholds.

Centuries later, chest heaving and muscles aching, Eekrit dragged himself onto the top of the pile. Shireep appeared at his side seconds later. He leaned over Eekrit, his beady eyes intent. 'Are you well, my lord?' he asked.

Eekrit pushed the skaven away. The question didn't merit a reply, and he didn't have the wind for it, anyway.

After a few moments, the warlord composed himself. When he rolled onto his belly, he found Eshreegar beckoning to him from the opposite side of the wide stack. His paws made a flurry of signals. *You need to see this.*

His discomfort forgotten, Eekrit squirmed forwards on his belly and settled down beside Eshreegar. The stack of roof beams rose nearly to the cavern ceiling, giving them a panoramic view of the dimly lit space.

Eshreegar pointed. Less than ten yards away, a space some twenty paces across had been cleared. A large, flat piece of stone, almost like a paving stone but the size and shape of a wagon wheel, had been lifted from the floor and set to one side, revealing a deep, dark hole. Small units of skeletons ringed the hole with shields and spears held ready, watching over the opening with deathless vigilance.

Shireep settled down beside Eekrit. 'You see?' he hissed. 'It-it must be important. A treasure vault, perhaps, or a cache of god-stone?'

The warlord flicked both ears in irritation. Ever since they had been ordered to scout the fortress, the raiders had been searching for the *kreekargan*'s god-stone vaults. Short of getting close enough to assassinate the burning man himself, seizing his dwindling hoard of the sacred rock was the surest way of ending the war that Eekrit could think of.

'No, I don't think so,' the warlord said thoughtfully. 'Look at the guards. They aren't there to keep people away from the hole; they're meant to keep something *inside* from getting *out*.'

'We're at the far eastern end of this level,' Eshreegar mused. 'What's beneath us at this point?'

Eekrit tried to visualise their position on the map of the fortress he'd memorised. After a moment, he shook his head. 'Nothing but rock,' he answered.

'Perhaps a mine shaft?' the young scout suggested.

'Don't be stupid...' Eekrit began – and then fell silent as a strange sound began to echo up from the darkness of the hole. It was a hollow, rhythmic clatter, thin and hollow and yet heavy at the same time. The warlord felt his hackles rise once more. He studied the waiting phalanxes of undead guardsmen, but they didn't react to the noise.

The rattling beat swelled in volume. After a minute, Eekrit thought he could see a faint, greenish glow radiating from the depths of the hole. Then a long, curved appendage, black as coal and engraved with glowing runes, extended over the rim and rested its tip on the cavern floor. Seven more appendages, equally long and curved like sword blades, extended around the circumference of the hole. They flexed upwards, dragging the rest of the thing's body into view.

It was a spider, long-legged and bulbous like the giant hunters of the swamps around the Great City – only this one had been fashioned entirely from the slender bones and teeth of some huge sea creature. The sight of the construct sent a thrill of pure terror through Eekrit's body. Shireep let out a muffled yelp and the pungent smell of fear-musk filled the air.

The construct was nearly the size of one of Lord Vittrik's war engines; easily the largest that Eekrit had ever seen. The *kreekar-gan* had seeded scores of similar constructs through the lower levels in the wake of his retreating forces, where they would lie in wait and ambush unsuspecting skaven. Of all the murderous weapons that the burning man had unleashed on the skaven, it was the constructs that filled the clan warriors with fear. A company of undead spearmen came at you face-to-face, in ordered, predictable ranks; even a wall of poison gas could be survived with enough caution and a little advance warning. But the constructs could be *anywhere*, sitting in the darkness with absolute, eternal patience, waiting for the perfect moment to strike. Some of them had even penetrated as far as the under-fortress itself.

Blade-like legs rattling against the stone, the construct lifted its bulbous abdomen from the hole. Like the rest of the body, it was formed from large, curving bones instead of flesh. The cold glow of sorcerous runes revealed a dark, huddled shape trapped inside.

Eshreegar stiffened. 'That's a skaven,' he hissed.

'Are you sure?' Eekrit squinted. He couldn't tell much at this distance.

'He's right,' Shireep confirmed. 'I can see a tail.'

'Slave or clan warrior?' Eekrit asked.

Eshreegar shook his head. 'Neither. He's wearing armour and decent robes. Probably a pack leader of some kind.'

Down by the hole, the units of undead guards moved aside to let the construct pass. It scuttled forwards with surprising speed, bearing its prize down a wide lane across the chamber and into the heart of the fortress. Within moments, it was lost from view.

'I thought the *kreekar-gan* didn't take prisoners,' Shireep said, his voice heavy with dread.

'He does now,' Eshreegar said grimly. 'The question is why.'

Eekrit studied the scene, putting the pieces together. 'Information,' he said at length. 'What else?' He pointed to the hole. 'That's a murder hole, just like the ones we used to dig in the lower levels. It probably comes out somewhere between mine shafts one and four, otherwise we would have discovered it by now.'

The Master of Treacheries shook his head. 'They couldn't have dug that deeply that fast,' he said. 'We searched this cavern just a few months ago and none of this was here.'

'Yes, it was,' Eekrit replied. 'It must have been. They just covered the hole with that slab and buried it under debris so we wouldn't find it.'

Shireep's eyes widened. 'That means they dug the tunnel long before we'd taken the upper mine shafts.'

Eshreegar gave Eekrit a troubled look. 'So the burning man expected us to capture the upper levels.'

'Or he *allowed* us to,' the warlord replied. Suddenly, the enemy's swift retreat made sense. 'Too easy. I *knew* it was too easy.' He turned to the Master of Treacheries. 'How fast can we get back to mine shaft four?'

'From here? Four or five hours, if we're lucky,' Eshreegar replied. 'A single messenger could make the trip faster–'

'There's no guarantee a message will reach the Grey Lord,' Eekrit replied. 'He'll take an audience from me, though. At least, I hope so.'

Shireep looked from Eekrit to Eshreegar and back again. 'I don't understand. What's happening?' the young scout asked.

Eekrit paused, staring at Shireep. He reflected that this was probably as good a time as any to cut the skaven's throat. One quick signal to Eshreegar, and Shireep would be dead before he knew what hit him.

The warlord started to raise his paw, but abruptly reconsidered. He could sort out Shireep later. If his suspicions were right, they were all going to be fighting for their lives in the next few hours, and he was going to need every able paw he could get.

He beckoned to the two scout-assassins to follow him. 'We've got to get back to Velsquee,' he told Shireep. 'The *kreekar-gan*'s laid a trap for the entire army and the Grey Lord's marched right into the middle of it.'

* * *

The rat-thing shrieked and squirmed in the grip of the spell. Runes carved into its scalp flared with crackling, greenish flames and the stench of burnt, greasy fur hung thick in the cold air of the necromancer's great hall. Nagash continued to chant, focusing his will to a razor-keen edge as he tried to carve out the knowledge he sought from the wretched creature's brain.

A roiling froth of memories and emotions flowed across the surface of his mind, rushing past almost too swiftly to grasp. The taste was bitter and strangely potent, utterly unlike the human essences he had consumed over the centuries. The thought processes were difficult to grasp, much less understand. The necromancer redoubled his efforts. This was the highest-ranking prisoner his constructs had ever caught. Such an opportunity might not come again for months, by which point it would be far too late. The war would not – *could not* – last for more than another thirteen days. His power – and by extension, his very existence – would not last beyond that point.

Glimpses of battles fought in the last few years flitted across Nagash's mind, yet when he tried to grasp them, they broke apart like quicksilver. *More power*, he thought, his anger mounting. *I must use more power.*

There had been no new supplies of *abn-i-khat* since the fall of mine shaft three, close to two and a half years ago, and the demands of the war had consumed his remaining stores at a prodigious rate. Like a miserly river merchant, he knew down to the ounce how much of the stone he had left. Every iota he consumed hastened the moment of his extinction.

Reluctantly, Nagash reached with bony fingers for the small leather bag hanging at his waist. With deft, spider-like strokes, he undid the thick cords securing the mouth of the bag and reached carefully inside. A moment later he drew out a fragment of stone the size of a sesame seed, pinned between the pointed tip of thumb and forefinger. A moment later, the piece of *abn-i-khat* flared like a hot coal. He absorbed the spark of energy hungrily and fed it into the ritual circle surrounding the tormented rat-thing.

At once, the creature's thoughts took on more weight and clarity, but Nagash knew the effects were temporary at best. He reached deeper into the prisoner's mind, mercilessly looting its memories. The creature's screams turned to a choking rattle. Bloody froth tinged the corners of its mouth and its tail lashed spasmodically against the stone floor.

Nagash saw the tunnels leading up to the stone barricades guarding the lowest levels of his fortress, only this time it was through the eyes of an invader. He saw companies of ratmen crouching in the bastions once held by his own warriors, and thousands more teeming in the echoing tunnels of mine shafts one, two and three. Excavation work at mine shaft four had been suspended, he saw, and the tunnel converted into the invaders' new base camp. Cook-fires burned by the score along the length of the passage-way, amid the small forges of field armourers and sprawling caches of weapons, ammunition and other supplies.

The necromancer seized on these memories in particular, sifting through them carefully for what he sought. And then he saw it – a huge pavilion of wood and tanned hides, situated roughly in the centre of the disorderly camp. Hulking, broad-shouldered ratmen stood guard at each corner and at the entrances to the enclosure. A steady stream of slaves came and went from within, bearing trays of food and jars of wine.

Nagash stopped chanting. Cold, mirthless laughter echoed through the minds of the barbarian immortals gathered in the hall. Released from the necromancer's sorcerous grip, the rat-thing's corpse slumped to the floor.

A dozen pairs of cold, unblinking eyes watched Nagash as he turned and slowly climbed the steps to his shadow-haunted throne. Bragadh, Diarid, Thestus and Akatha waited in a loose semicircle on the far side of the ritual circle, their pale flesh glimmering faintly in the dim light. Their robes were ragged and faded with time; the battered scale armour of the warriors was tarnished nearly black. Their faces were etched by the constant thirst for the necromancer's elixir. Grim and tormented as restless ghosts, they waited in uneasy silence for their master's command.

Eight of Bragadh's distant ancestors stood guard around Nagash's throne, gripping bared blades that flickered with baleful corpse-light. The wights were the first undead warriors that Nagash had raised from the barrows that had once littered the plain at the foot of the great mountain. These days they accompanied him wherever he went, for the enemy now infested the halls of his own fortress, skulking about and slitting throats with near impunity.

There were other things abroad in the halls of Nagashizzar as well. Nagash settled carefully onto his throne, his burning eyes sweeping the great hall for signs of intrusion. For some time now he had been catching glimpses from the corners of his vision: fleeting images of distant, glowing forms that vanished whenever he tried to focus on them. The figures seemed to follow him, dogging his heels like a pack of hungry jackals.

Of late, the sightings had grown more numerous. They seemed to be edging closer, as though sensing that he was reaching the limits of his power. Once, on a moonless night close to the hour of the dead, he had roused from his meditations and seen a figure staring at him from the shadows at the foot of the throne. A woman, clad in the finery of lost Khemri, pale-skinned and as beautiful as Asaph herself. Her eyes were pools of darkness, depthless and cold as death. By the time he'd roused himself from his throne the apparition was gone, but the memory of it troubled him still.

The last time he'd seen Neferem was in the barren wastes far to the west of Nagashizzar and the Sour Sea, when he'd wandered, raving and alone, after his defeat in Nehekhara. In life she had been Queen of Khemri and the embodiment of the sacred covenant between the Nehekharans and their gods; for that he had taken her from her husband and enslaved her, bending her divine power to his will. Later, when it suited his purposes, he destroyed her, breaking the power of the old gods forever. Now, her soul lingered in the dark limbo that lay beyond the realm of the living, unable to find her way to the afterlife now that the covenant with the gods had been broken.

Neferem had haunted his steps through the wasteland, watching him weaken with every passing night and savouring his torment. She spoke of the thousands of lost souls who waited for him across the threshold and the terrible reckoning he would face. But then the ratmen had found him, and from their corpses he learned the power of the *abn-i-khat.* She did not appear to him after that. As Nagash regained his strength, he had dismissed the apparition as a fever dream – the by-product of deprivation and a festering head wound and nothing more. What her return meant now, at the darkest hour of the war, he did not care to speculate.

The necromancer's burning gaze raked the shadows of the great hall. Finding them empty, he turned his attention to his lieutenants. The time had come at last. After five bitter years, he would finally put Bragadh and the others to the test.

The ratmen are at the barricades, Nagash declared, the words grinding together like stones in the minds of his immortals. *They have massed by the tens of thousands in the upper mine shafts. The final assault could come within days. The last battle of the war is upon us.* Nagash leaned forwards, his bony fingertips scraping across the arms of the black throne. *Now we shall strike.*

A ripple of unease passed through the assembled immortals. Bragadh looked to his companions and then gazed bleakly up at the throne.

'Death in battle is preferable to surrender,' he said, the words bubbling thickly from his throat. Both lungs had been ravaged by deep wounds during the defence of mine shaft four; the ratmen's poisoned blades had etched scars that never healed, despite the power of Nagash's elixir. 'The ratmen will pay a bitter price before we are destroyed.'

Nagash's burning eyes narrowed on Bragadh. *I do not speak of surrender, northman. When we attack, it will be to drive the vermin from the mountain once and for all.* The necromancer clenched a fist. *We will tear the heart out of the enemy in a single stroke and send the rest fleeing whence they came.*

Once again, Bragadh exchanged uneasy glances with Diarid and Thestus before facing his master. 'The enemy outnumbers our warriors almost a hundred to one,' he said, 'and there is little of the magic stone left. How can we possibly defeat them?'

'Bragadh speaks truly,' Thestus said, stepping forwards and resting his hand on the hilt of his sword. 'We cannot prevail here, master. If each of us killed a score of the creatures before we were slain, it would still not be enough.' He hesitated, uncertain how to proceed. 'Would... would it not be wiser to quit the mountain altogether? What if we took the army north, back to the hill forts? We could make war on the greenskins and replenish our depleted warbands. Then, when we had regained our strength, we could–'

There will be no retreat.

The words sliced like a knife into their minds. Thestus made a choking sound and staggered backwards. Dark ichor oozed from the corners of his eyes.

All is going according to plan, Nagash told them. *We are not so weak as the enemy has been led to believe, nor quite so desperate. Every defeat, every withdrawal for the last five years, was made with one purpose in mind, to lure the invaders into a trap from which they will never escape.*

Bragadh frowned. 'What trap, master?' he replied. 'We were told nothing of this.'

All the better to convince the enemy that they held the upper hand, Nagash replied. *The ratmen had to believe that our strength was nearly spent. The desperation of you and your men no doubt helped to convince them.*

Thestus spread his arms. 'But *why*, master? To what end?'

To tempt the enemy into carelessness, Nagash said. *The speed of our retreat has forced the enemy to pursue us, stretching their lines of communication and complicating their leaders' ability to control their troops. The leaders of the ratmen have been forced to leave the safety of their subterranean fortress and relocate to mine shaft four so they can direct the army and further their own petty schemes.*

The necromancer leaned back against his throne. *What they do not know is that there are hidden tunnels that open into all four of the upper mine shafts. The enemy has been too preoccupied to find them, and that will be their undoing.* Nagash pointed at Bragadh with a skeletal finger. *Tonight, you will quietly withdraw your warriors from the barricades, and we will lead them through the tunnels to mine shaft four. We will overrun the enemy's base camp, kill their leaders, and then fall upon the enemy army from the rear. By the end of the day tomorrow, the invaders will be in full retreat.*

Bragadh folded his powerful arms. 'A cunning plan, but a risky one,' he said. 'It will leave the barricades very thinly held. If we were to be cut off, even for a short while, the enemy could break through our defences and seize the fortress with ease.' He eyed the necromancer warily. 'Unless there are other reserve forces you've kept hidden from us as well.'

'It does not matter. Nagash is right. The time to strike is now.'

Bragadh turned, his dark eyes widening in surprise as Akatha stepped forwards. 'It's not your place to speak of such things, witch,' he said darkly.

'*I* decide my place in things, Bragadh, and you well know it,' Akatha replied. 'And I say we must attack. Our people were not born to cower behind stone walls, nor slink back to our hill forts and yield our possessions to the enemy.' She glared hard at Thestus, who visibly shrank beneath the witch's gaze. 'Let the Faithful hear the war-song and spill the blood of their foes, as is proper.'

'We will be beset from all sides!' Bragadh protested.

Akatha raised her chin defiantly. 'It has ever been thus,' she replied. 'Perhaps you have forgotten, Bragadh Maghur'kan, but I have not.'

'This could mean the end of us,' Bragadh told her. 'Can you not see that?'

The witch uttered a cold, mirthless laugh. 'I see more than you know, Bragadh,' she said. 'Never doubt that for a moment.'

Bragadh took a step towards Akatha, his hand falling to the hilt of his sword. An angry protest rose to his lips, but suddenly, all of the northmen froze, their bodies going rigid as though gripped in the fist of a giant.

Nagash studied his lieutenants in silence for a moment, watching them suffer under the weight of his terrible will.

Heed the witch, the necromancer told them. *For once, she and I are in accord. Prepare yourselves, for tomorrow the war ends, in victory or in death eternal.*

TEN

THE DISPOSSESSED

Lahmia,
the City of the Dawn,
in the 99th year of Usirian the Dreadful
(-1285 Imperial Reckoning)

Lord Ushoran walked slowly around the blood-spattered wooden frame, studying the gasping, wide-eyed wreck of a man hanging from its leather straps. The immortal pursed his fleshless lips and reached for the round knob of a long, gold needle that jutted from the angle where the man's neck and shoulder met. He twisted it ever so slightly and the victim's body tensed in agony. A thin hiss escaped the man's ragged lips; leather creaked as his back arched in a bow, bringing him up from the frame's central support. Flayed muscles knotted across the man's chest and shoulders, sending fresh rivulets of blood coursing down his bare torso.

The Lord of Masks smiled. Behind the bland illusion of his handsome nobleman's face, he ran his long tongue over the tips of his fangs. How he wished he'd taken more than a cursory interest in Nagash's books when they'd first come into King Lamashizzar's possession all those centuries ago. The necromancer's druchii tutors had been truly gifted in the arts of inflicting pain.

Ushoran continued to circle around the suffering man, his sandals tracking noisily through the puddles of dark blood congealing on the marble floor. The stench of death hung heavy in the chamber, its suffocating weight all but impervious to the braziers of incense that burned next to the dais at the far end of the room. Once upon a time, the Hall of Reverent Contemplation had been a grand and refined space, where the cloistered Queen of Lahmia would appear on high, holy days and give her blessings to the royal family and the city's most prominent nobles. After the creation of the temple and Neferata's elaborate, illusory funeral, the hall became her throne room, where she continued to rule Lahmia through the auspices of her Deathless Court.

All that had been forgotten since the treachery of Ubaid and the disappearance of Alcadizzar. Now the chamber was little better than a charnel house, devoted to the queen's insatiable thirst for vengeance. The floor beneath the dais was crowded with implements of torture: wooden racks and bronze cages, vats of oil, and tables lined with a grisly array of needles, hooks, saws and knives. Day and night, the chamber reeked like an abattoir. An ocean of blood had been poured onto its marble floor over the last few years, and the tide showed no signs of abating.

The Lord of Masks counted slowly to five and then twisted the needle once more. The man sagged back against the wooden frame with a ragged groan, his arms and legs trembling. He was a leather worker, according to his agents; by his lean, vulpine features and the dark, weathered cast to his skin, Ushoran reckoned he was from the desert tribes of the far west. A great many of them had turned up in the city over the last few years, seeking whatever work they could find in the Traders' Quarter. Most turned to thievery – something the desert nomads knew well – but this one had been carrying a leather satchel and proper tools when he'd been snatched from the street by Ushoran's men. Perhaps he'd lingered too long in his shop, finishing a belt or a set of fine boots for a caravan master or a ship's captain, or had decided to stop by one of the local wine shops and lost track of the time. Or perhaps he was new to the city, and ignorant of the risk of being caught out on the streets after dark. These days, most people knew that you didn't tarry in the Traders' Quarter or down by the docks after nightfall – not if you valued your life.

Ushoran paused for a few moments, listening carefully to the man's laboured breathing. There was an art to gauging how much real pain another person was suffering and how lucid they were from one moment to the next. When he judged that the time was right, he circled around to the front of the wooden frame and took the man's narrow chin in his hand. Ushoran was pleased to see the man flinch at his touch. He raised the leather worker's chin until he could gaze into the man's eyes.

'How long this lasts is entirely up to you,' Ushoran said. 'You understand? Answer my questions and the pain will end.'

The man on the frame drew a hitching breath. A thin whine escaped his lips. 'Don't – please... I don't know,' he whispered, the words almost too faint to hear.

Ushoran's fingers tightened on the man's jaw. 'No, no,' he said slowly, as though he were a tutor with an exceptionally slow pupil. 'You're a clever fellow. *Think.* This man has been seen in the Traders' Quarter before; he is tall and broad of shoulder, and has a grip like a blacksmith. Likely he was dressed like a commoner – even, perhaps, like a beggar – but he would have been handsome and well spoken, like a noble. Such a one would stand out from the crowd, yes? You may have only glimpsed him in passing. Just tell us where and when. That is all.'

The leather worker blinked at Ushoran, his dark eyes wide and unfocused. He groaned, a sound torn from the depths of his soul. Tears of frustration trickled from the corners of his eyes. 'Please,' he begged. 'I don't know. I... I swear it! Why... why won't you believe m-me?'

Ushoran sighed in mock disappointment. The fool was too proud to lie, even to spare himself further suffering. He would provide hours more entertainment before his young heart gave out. Careful to conceal any trace of pleasure, the Lord of Masks turned to glance at the dais.

'He is stubborn, great one,' Ushoran said to the apparition seated upon the ancient wooden throne. The Lord of Masks shrugged. 'On the other hand, it's possible that he is telling the truth. Shall we release him?'

Neferata studied the weeping man with the eerie, serpent-like stillness of an immortal. She had not worn her golden mask since the night of Alcadizzar's betrayal and her pale, otherworldly face was as cold and pitiless as the desert night. Likewise, the eternal queen disdained the gleaming finery of the temple; her white silken robe was dingy and tattered, stained at sleeve and hem with layers of grime and spots of old blood. In truth, she looked like a corpse freshly dug from its tomb, her unblinking eyes brimming with hate for the cursed world of men.

Ushoran watched her fingers slowly tense upon the arms of the throne. Long, curved claws scraped faintly over the priceless wood. A slender figure in a ragged priestess's robe stirred at the queen's feet. Like Neferata, the woman was as pale as alabaster, her cheeks smeared with dirt and dried blood. Sensing the change in her mistress's mood, the young immortal fixed Ushoran with a feral, catlike gaze and bared her fangs in a silent hiss. The Lord of Masks stiffened at the challenge, only just managing to refrain from baring his own teeth at the whelp in response. As Neferata's hatred of the mortal world had grown since the betrayal, so too had her distrust of her fellow immortals. Now she surrounded herself only with creatures of her own creation - women who had come as orphans to the temple and had risen through the ranks to become its first high priestesses. Their will and self-determination crushed long ago by Neferata's ruthless mental control, they were little better than animals, but their loyalty to the queen was absolute.

Lost in her dreams of vengeance, Neferata had withdrawn almost entirely from the affairs of the kingdom. In the wake of Alcadizzar's escape she had gone out into the streets herself in search of him; screams would echo from the Travellers' Quarter or the refugee slums in the dead of night and in the morning there would be another gruesome spectacle for the City Guard to find.

Wild tales of a savage, flesh-eating spirit gripped the populace. For the first time in centuries, terrified citizens flocked to the decrepit temples of Neru and Ptra, begging the startled priests for deliverance. When they proved powerless to halt the slaughter, the city nobles decided to take matters into their own hands. They pointed to the squalid population of immigrants in the western part of the city, accusing the former desert dwellers of unleashing a curse upon them all. Lost in the hysteria was the simple fact that the victims of Neferata's reign of terror had almost exclusively been immigrants themselves; the citizens had rioted, and the slums had burned for three straight days. It was only thanks to the sea breeze and the spine of hills that cut across Lahmia from north to south that the fire was kept from consuming the entire city. The air in the palace had reeked of smoke and burning flesh for a week. Afterwards, Lord Ankhat managed to persuade Neferata to restrain herself, but only after assuring her that the search for the prince would continue without pause. As a result, Ushoran had been allowed – nay *encouraged* – to indulge his secret appetites to a degree he had never before imagined possible. For every victim snatched from the street to answer the queen's relentless questions, three more found their way into his private houses of amusement.

At the foot of the gore-spattered dais, Lord Ankhat watched the spectacle with sour disapproval. He was the only principal of the Deathless Court who still paid any attention to affairs of state, managing the city and its affairs through a complex web of ministers and noblemen. Neferata's obsession with the young prince had badly strained her relationship with Ankhat, once her staunchest ally in the court. He kept his own counsel for the most part these days, making state decisions by fiat and abandoning all pretence of consulting with the queen. The once affable aristocrat had grown cold and aloof, eyeing everyone around him with a mix of suspicion and arrogant disdain.

Perhaps it was just the passage of time, Ushoran mused. With every year our powers increase, he thought, as do our appetites. We grow ever more territorial, ever more jealous of our prerogatives. Before long we will have grown too hungry and too paranoid to share the city between ourselves, and what then?

Ankhat folded his arms and glared at the luckless fool on the rack. 'This is ridiculous,' he spat. 'Doesn't anyone mark the passage of time any more? It's not been five weeks since he's been gone, or even five months. It's been five *years*. No one's seen or heard from him since. For all we know, his bones are lying in a shallow grave somewhere on the Golden Plain.'

Neferata fixed Ankhat with a smouldering glare. Ushoran cleared his throat. 'The facts do not support this,' he interjected. 'Rasetra has made no inquiries about the prince's wellbeing since his disappearance. Clearly, he has been in contact with them somehow–'

'Then where is he, spymaster?' Ankhat shot back. 'Khemri *still* lacks a king. You think he's taken up work serving tables in the Travellers' Quarter?' He turned and glared back at Neferata. 'What in all the world could be more important to him than the crown of the Living City?'

Ushoran turned his attention to his victim in an attempt to conceal his unease. Ankhat was right – Alcadizzar ought to be in Khemri now, well on his way to restoring the city's wealth and power. The fact that he hadn't claimed the throne filled the immortal with a growing sense of dread.

'Alcadizzar is here,' Neferata declared, in a voice as cold and hard as stone. 'I *know* it.' She leaned forwards, hands gripping the arms of the throne. 'Ask him again,' she hissed at Ushoran. 'Strip away his flesh until he speaks the truth. He will give up his secrets soon enough. They always do.'

Ushoran bowed to the queen and turned his attention to a table lined with gleaming tools. Behind him, he heard Ankhat snarl in disgust; there was a gust of icy wind as the immortal took his leave.

The Lord of Masks selected a long, serrated blade from the table and inspected its edge. The man on the rack started to thrash weakly against his restraints.

Neferata was right. Eventually the miserable wretch would talk. He would say whatever it took to make the agony stop, and leave the queen with yet another wild rumour to pursue. The orgy of blood and pain would continue.

As Ushoran returned to his labours, he silently prayed that the lost prince would never be heard from again.

The slow-moving caravan raised a pall of churning dust that stretched for half a mile down the arrow-straight course of the great trade road that travelled westwards along the Golden Plain. It glowed reddish-ochre in the sullen light of the setting sun, visible for leagues to the north and south.

Any bandit worth his salt quickly learned how to gauge the size and speed of a caravan based upon the trail of dust it left behind. This one was plodding along at barely more than a mile per hour; that meant laden wagons and slow, stolid oxen. Half a mile of dust wasn't much – the huge spice caravans that left the city every three months raised a trail that could stretch for up to a league or more, depending on the strength of the wind. Alcadizzar reckoned there were perhaps a dozen wagons, all told, plus outriders ahead and to the flanks. They'd left the city late in the day – far later than was wise – so by the time night fell they would be well beyond the reach of the Lahmian forts on the eastern edge of the plain. Easy pickings for a bandit gang that knew its trade; either the caravan master had taken leave of his senses, or there was more going on here than met the eye.

Nawat ben Hazar did not share in Alcadizzar's concern. The bandit leader fairly rocked in the saddle with anticipation, a gap-toothed grin stretching from ear to ear. 'Not long now,' he said, breaking into a wheezing chuckle. 'They'll hit the caravan just before sunset, when the fools are thinking of nothing but making camp and drinking a little wine.' He shifted his lanky body and glanced at Alcadizzar, who walked his horse just a pace or two behind Nawat and to his right. The bandit leader's dark eyes glittered beneath shaggy grey eyebrows. He tapped the side of his narrow nose with a grimy fingertip. 'Mark my words, *khutuf*. We'll have a bit of gold and meat for our bellies tonight.'

The prince nodded absently, his eyes still fixed on the drifting ribbon of dust along the northern horizon. The bandits knew him as Ubaid, a former soldier and exile from Rasetra, but Nawat called him – and any other man not descended from the tribes of the Great Desert – simply *khutuf*. In the dialect of the tribes, the name meant 'house dog,' and referred to the pampered pets of merchants and other fat, indolent city dwellers. Nawat never let his men forget that he was of a different breed than the rest of them. He was a *nazir*, a desert lion, who could trace his lineage back to the great chieftains of the *bani-al-Akhtar*, the fiercest of the desert clans. He was as lean and as tough as a strip of rawhide, his dark skin weathered and wrinkled by years of exposure to the unforgiving sun. Though he wore simple cotton robes of Lahmian cut – plundered from a spice trader's chest and now stained a uniform brown by the dust of the road – the wide leather belt of a desert horseman circled his waist. Its cracked surface was tooled with precise notches that signified the battles he'd fought as a tribal warrior, and the scores of men he'd killed.

Alcadizzar had no reason to doubt Nawat's claims. The bandit leader wore a fine pair of ivory-hilted daggers tucked into his belt and carried a sleek, curved sword of the type favoured by the tribes. The old bandit sat his stolen horse with the ease of a man born to the saddle, which was more than Alcadizzar could say for himself. But he doubted that Nawat had been exiled from his tribe for loving the chieftain's daughter, as the man so often boasted. He suspected it had more to do with the telltale black stain of lotus root on the bandit's few remaining teeth.

For certain, Nawat's days of glory were far behind him. His gang, such as it was, consisted of barely a score of hungry-looking men and women, clad in a motley assortment of grimy rags and bits of finer, recently stolen garb. Most of the band struggled along on foot, while Nawat and the best-armed men of the gang sat upon lean, dispirited horses stolen from the scenes of previous raids. Most of the bandits carried little more than short clubs of knotty wood or dull-edged bronze knives; none wore anything resembling useful armour. The gang had no bows or spears – not even so much as a shepherd's simple leather sling. They were far and away the most pathetic bunch of would-be raiders that Alcadizzar had ever seen, surviving off the leavings that larger, stronger gangs left behind, but they were also the only outlaws on the Golden Plain desperate enough to take him in.

Five years ago, Alcadizzar's only thought had been to escape from the City of the Dawn and warn Nehekhara of the evil that lurked in the depths of the Temple of Blood. Ironically, it was only by virtue of Neferata's terrible elixir that he had managed to survive the long drop to the palace courtyard; from there, his knowledge of the royal compound had allowed him to evade the guards and slip quietly into the city proper. By then, alarm gongs were clashing stridently within the palace, and startled City Guardsmen were prowling the early morning streets with cudgels in hand. The prince had spent his first day of freedom huddled inside an enormous ceremonial urn at the back of a potter's storage shed, his body trembling and his mind numb with shock as he struggled to make sense of everything he'd learned.

Neferata had responded swiftly and decisively to Alcadizzar's escape. Over the course of the day the search for him had intensified, and on several occasions he could hear the potter and his son arguing bitterly with City Guardsmen who came prowling through his shop. The prince tried to treat it as just another of the countless exercises that Haptshur, his battlefield tutor, had subjected him to. *You've been trapped deep in enemy territory with nothing but the robes on your back and your foes are hunting you. You must find a way to escape and return to your people.*

That was far easier said than done, of course. Alcadizzar had no weapons, no gold – not even sandals for his feet. Though his robes were now as filthy and torn as a beggar's, the rich, white silk would attract the attention of every watchman in the city. And it was safe to assume that his description was being circulated around the docks and at the city gates; there might even be a reward offered for his capture. To make matters worse, his nearest allies were in Rasetra, hundreds of leagues away. Even if he made it out of the city, he would still have a long and gruelling journey to reach the city of his people.

By the end of the first day, Alcadizzar had come to the conclusion that he would not be getting out of Lahmia any time soon. He would have to bide his time and gather resources while he waited for the search to eventually subside. That night, he slipped from the potter's shed and climbed silently onto the artisan's roof where freshly cleaned robes had been laid out to dry. Alcadizzar took a set of the son's robes, silently vowing to repay the family later, and then slipped into the crowded streets. The stained white robes were left in an alley deep inside the Travellers' Quarter, where he hoped they would convince the City Guard that he was trying to slip out of Lahmia with one of the many outbound merchant caravans. Instead, the prince made his way down to the teeming districts around the docks and looked for ways to earn some coin.

For nearly eight months, Alcadizzar, prince of Rasetra and would-be King of Khemri, lived like a harbour rat among Lahmia's busy docks. He looted and he stole; he gambled on games of dice and drank sour beer in reeking alehouses no City Guardsman dared enter. He killed his first man in a vicious, back-alley brawl, when a gang of sailors tried to pressgang him onto their ship. For a time he worked as hired muscle for one of the most notorious brothels in the Red Silk District, and there fell into the company of a gang of jewel thieves who preyed upon the old noble families who lived in the shadow of the royal palace. That association had ended in blood and betrayal on a moonless night in early spring; Alcadizzar had escaped with nothing more than a handful of copper coins and a dying woman's kiss. She'd been his first love, and she'd nearly been the death of him.

Finally, the prince judged that his time had come. He was certain that Neferata was still looking for him, but her attention was still fixed on the caravans and the Travellers' Quarter. The guards at the city gates had slipped back into their daily routine, and his description was changed from the night of his escape. He was much thinner now and his features were hidden beneath a full, black beard. Dressed in faded desert robes and laden with a leather pack filled with food, spare clothing and other supplies, he passed through the eastern gate in the middle of a torrential afternoon rainstorm. The guardsmen, scowling from the doorway of the gatehouse, waved him through without so much as a second glance.

But the prince soon learned that escaping the city was only the first of many challenges that lay between him and distant Rasetra. Beyond the watch-forts at the eastern end of the plain the land was wild and lawless, infested with roving gangs of outlaws that preyed on unwary travellers. His hopes of falling in with an eastbound caravan were quickly dashed, as the paranoid merchants and their hired guards feared that he might be a spy for the caravan raiders. Alone and on foot, Alcadizzar's skills were tested to the utmost over the next few months as he struggled his way across the plain. He was forced to fight for his life on more than one occasion, but his training and the lasting potency of Neferata's elixir saw him through.

The road became less dangerous but no less easy once he had left the Golden Plain behind. Alcadizzar made his way to Lybaras, thinking that Rasetra's ancient allies would lend him aid, but the prince found the City of Scholars in a sad and decrepit state. The famous collegiums were all but deserted and the Palace of the Scholar-Kings was closed even to its citizens. Alcadizzar lingered there for almost a month, waiting in vain for an audience with King Pashet, but the royal viziers refused to even listen to him. In the end, he left Lybaras as road-weary and penniless as he'd been when he'd arrived.

Finally, almost a full year and a half after his escape from the Temple of Blood, Alcadizzar passed through the formidable gates of Rasetra, the warlike city of his people. The prince was pleased to see that the city prospered under the rule of his younger brother, Asar. This time, he knew better than to approach the palace directly. He was sure that Lahmia had agents in the city and they were certain to be on the lookout for him. Instead, he made inquiries in the market, and that evening he found his way to the home of his uncle Khenti.

Though Khenti was an old man now, his strength gone and his vision fading, he recognised Alcadizzar at once. The prince was welcomed with tears of joy. Later, when he had told Khenti of what he'd seen inside the temple, his uncle wasted no time in arranging a secret meeting with Asar inside the palace.

Accompanied by Khenti, Alcadizzar was ushered into the king's privy council chamber, where he met his younger brother for the very first time.

Though Asar did not possess his brother's extraordinary physique and magnetic charisma, the kinship between the two could not be denied. Asar welcomed his brother warmly, and over goblets of strong southern wine Alcadizzar told Asar his horrifying tale.

This had been the moment that the prince had been waiting months for. Sitting in the filth of Lahmia's back-alleys, he'd envisioned his brother's face lighting up with righteous rage as he learned of Neferata's crimes. Swift messengers would be sent across the length and breadth of the land, spreading the news and summoning their armies to war. Alcadizzar would return to the City of of Dawn as a conqueror, at the head of a vast army made up of warriors from every city in Nehekhara.

But Alcadizzar was to be disappointed. The King of Rasetra listened to the prince's tale, his expression thoughtful. When Alcadizzar was finished, Asar took a long sip of wine, and then gave his brother a frank stare.

'Where is your proof?' the king asked him.

Nawat altered their course as the sun sank behind the hills to the west, aiming the bandit gang towards the distant trade road. If the old raider's instincts were correct - and Alcadizzar had to admit, Nawat was rarely wrong - then the caravan would be attacked just at sunset, while they were busy making camp. Timing was critical; if they arrived too early, they risked walking into the middle of a battle. Too late, and they would need torches to pick their way through the caravan's remains, which meant they would likely miss what few valuables remained.

Alcadizzar shifted impatiently in the saddle, his hand falling to the hilt of the sword at his hip. It had been the sword of his uncle Khenti, a heavy, bronze khopesh that had spilled the blood of countless lizardmen in its time. Asar had tried to provide him with a fine gelding from the royal stables and a suit of bronze scale to aid him on his mission, but Alcadizzar knew such things would attract unwelcome attention on the Golden Plain. Instead, he'd gone to Rasetra's horse market and purchased a sturdy Numasi mare, and then plied a desert trader with gold to part with one of his personal possessions.

The *rakh-hajib*, or raider's robe, was a heavy cotton outer garment re-inforced with bronze discs sewn into the inner lining to cover the wearer's vitals. It wasn't as good as proper armour, but it was proof against arrows, spears and knives. Best of all, it was discreet; he could not risk appearing too well equipped, or the bandits on the plain would think he was a spy for Lahmia's City Guard. Mistrust and paranoia were the only constants on the trade road leading to the City of the Dawn.

The same could be said for Nehekhara in general, Alcadizzar had learned. That night at the palace, Asar had laid out the political situation among the great cities. Though there was a great deal of resentment and discontent towards Lahmia, the centuries-old policies of King Lamashizzar and later,

Queen Neferata had been so effective at playing the other cities against one another that none of them were strong enough to challenge the Lahmians directly. Even Rasetra, which had clawed its way back from the brink of ruin after the war against Nagash and had rebuilt its powerful army, still lacked the resources for a protracted war against the Lahmians. And though many of the great cities now possessed iron weapons and armour that were the equal of Lahmia's, none of them had a counter for the fearsome dragon powder that Lamashizzar's army had used to destroy the Usurper's army almost five hundred years ago. Not even the Lybaran scholar-priests had succeeded in unravelling the secrets of the mysterious eastern powder, and no one knew how much of it the City of the Dawn possessed. As Alcadizzar knew first-hand, the Lahmians guarded their secrets jealously.

Of course, a coalition of armies would almost certainly triumph against the Lahmians, but there was too much ambition and too little trust among the other cities to make such an alliance possible. Of the great cities, only three were strong enough to present themselves as possible rivals to Lahmia's power – Rasetra in the east, plus Zandri and Ka-Sabar in the west – but none were willing to take the first step and risk standing alone in the face of Lahmian reprisal. It would take something truly portentous and terrible to persuade the rival kings to put aside their ambitions and come together in a common cause against Lahmia. Alcadizzar's discovery was just such a revelation – but only if it could be proven beyond a doubt. Without proof, the other kings were just as likely to suspect that it was nothing more than a Rasetran ploy to trick them into a ruinous war.

Asar had made it clear that he believed every word of the prince's story and vowed to send agents to uncover proof of Neferata's crimes – but Alcadizzar knew that such efforts were doomed from the start. No stranger to the city would stand a chance of penetrating the palace compound and slipping undetected into the temple – and none of the temple's high priestesses could be persuaded to betray their mistress's secrets. That left only one possible alternative. If the great cities needed proof of Lahmia's hidden evil, then Alcadizzar would have to obtain it himself.

He had remained as his uncle's guest for many months, formulating his plans, then slipped quietly from the city amid the guards of a merchant caravan bound for Lybaras. Six months later he found himself, once again, friendless and alone, upon the lawless expanse of the Golden Plain.

Alcadizzar had thought that slipping back into Lahmia would have been a simple matter. It had been years since his escape; for all that the rest of the world knew, he might as well have been dead. But Neferata still hadn't given up looking for him; if anything, her search had turned far darker and more terrible than before. The city docks and the poorer districts lay under a constant pall of dread. The streets were all but deserted after dark, because people were disappearing almost every night and were never seen again. Informers were everywhere, searching for men who matched his description. The City Guard had tried to detain him at the west gate; when no amount of gold would dissuade them, he'd been forced to draw his sword and fight his way out. Mounted riders had scoured the trade road for weeks afterwards, searching for him. He'd only managed to escape by fleeing deep into the abandoned farmland, where the bandits held sway.

He'd known from his early days inside the city that there were two kinds of bandits on the Golden Plain. There were desperate, pitiful folk like Nawat's band of cutthroats, and then there were the descendants of the desert tribes who had migrated there in the years after the war against the Usurper. Nagash's armies had shattered the once-proud tribes, and the loss of their patron god Khsar had forced them to abandon the burning sands that had sheltered them for centuries. In those days, Lahmia had been the richest of all the great cities, and caravans journeyed there from as far away as Zandri to partake in the exotic goods of the distant east. Where there was wealth, there was banditry, and the desert tribes were superlative caravan raiders. They struck like lightning out of the scrub forests that now grew wild across the plain, taking what they pleased and vanishing before the City Guard could respond. There were also many former desert dwellers living inside Lahmia as well, eking out a miserable existence in the city slums. The Lahmians regarded them with suspicion and thinly veiled hostility, suspecting them of spying for the raiders out on the plain.

Alcadizzar saw at once that the desert tribesmen had the potential of becoming powerful allies against the Lahmians, but they were a clannish and secretive bunch at the best of times. He had spent a year on the plain trying to earn their trust, but to no avail. When Nawat had agreed to accept him into his gang, Alcadizzar had joined up in the hopes that the old raider might still have some friends within the tribes, but if he did, Nawat refused to speak of them.

The prince suppressed an irritated sigh. Another dead end, he thought, watching the gang slink across a wide, stony field that had once grown corn and wheat for nearby Lahmia. He was better off on his own, he reckoned. Perhaps it would be easier to move about inside the city now. It had been another full year – surely Neferata was growing tired of the search.

Just then came the distant, skirling cry of a horn, off to the north. Nawat sat straight in his saddle, listening, then nodded in satisfaction. 'It's begun,' he said to the gang. 'They're a little early. We should pick up the pace a bit.'

The old raider nudged his horse into a faster walk and the bandits limped along in his wake as best they could. Alcadizzar touched his heels to his mount and she responded at once, breaking into an easy, ground-eating trot. He searched the darkening sky above the road where he knew the caravan to be. After a few moments, he frowned. 'No signal arrow,' he said, half to himself.

Nawat turned to the prince. 'What's that?'

Alcadizzar gestured in the direction of the road. They were less than a mile away now, their movements concealed by a line of low, wooded hills. 'The caravan hasn't called for help.'

The old raider straightened in the saddle. Every caravan within easy riding distance of the Lahmian watch-forts kept a bow and a pitch-soaked arrow close to hand, in case of attack. A fire arrow shot skywards would have a troop of Lahmian cavalry riding to their aid within minutes. Nawat rubbed his chin. 'Maybe the arrow failed to light,' he mused. 'It's been known to happen.'

'You think so?' the prince asked, sounding dubious.

Nawat shrugged. 'What else?'

They rode onwards in tense silence for a bit longer, drawing closer to the base of the hills. A horn sounded again – two short notes, then a long one, repeated in quick succession. Alcadizzar stiffened. He knew that sequence all too well. Moments later, another horn answered, perhaps a league to the west.

'Those are cavalry signals,' Alcadizzar told Nawat. 'The caravan had a troop of horsemen trailing them.'

'Where the dust trail from the wagons would hide their presence.' Nawat muttered a curse and spat into the dust. 'When did the *khutuf* get so clever?'

Alcadizzar could hear other sounds coming from the far side of the hill now: the faint clatter of blades and the shrill, woman-like shriek of a dying horse. The caravan had been nothing but bait, drawing the raiders into a deadly ambush. The prince thought quickly, considering his options. He reached down and loosened his sword in its sheath.

Nawat cursed again and turned his horse about. 'We've got to get out of here,' he snarled to his gang. 'Back to camp, and quickly. If the Lahmians catch us–' Suddenly, the old raider's mount shied sideways as Alcadizzar spurred his horse to a gallop and charged up the wooded hillside.

'Ubaid!' Nawat called after him. 'What in the seven hells are you doing?'

The long-legged Numasi mare lunged up the slope in graceful bounds. Alcadizzar gave the horse its head, letting it find its own way amid the gnarled, spiky trees. The sounds of battle grew louder as he reached the hill's summit and plunged down the other side. He drew the heavy, bronze sword with a graceful sweep of his arm and tried to catch glimpses of the battle unfolding along the road below.

Alcadizzar could see seven or eight wagons – wide-bodied, wooden affairs with four wheels and high, wicker sides. Half a dozen archers stood in each one, drawing back yard-long reed arrows and loosing them at the swift-moving horsemen circling in the open ground north of the road. The desert raiders were armed with quivers of bronze-tipped javelins and short, recurved bows made of polished horn; they drew and fired on the move, sending broad-headed arrows thudding into the wagons' flanks. But instead of plunging through the painted wicker they stuck fast, or the shafts broke from the impact. No doubt the wicker was a screen, concealing a wall of wooden shields that protected the archers to just above the waist.

The bodies of riders and horses alike littered the ground before the wagons and the gaps between them. A favoured tactic of the desert raiders was to race in among the wagons and strike down their drivers with a few well-placed javelins. The Lahmians had waited until the raiders were virtually in their midst before springing their trap, cutting down the first wave of raiders at point-blank range. The rest had drawn up short in the killing ground north of the road, where they offered more targets for the swift-firing bowmen.

The caravan guards – Lahmian soldiers clad in the motley gear of hired blades – had withdrawn behind the wagons as soon as the attack had begun, and now they were making short work of the wounded raiders who'd had their mounts shot out from under them during the first charge. Alcadizzar caught sight of a dozen of these soldiers surrounding a large knot of dead horses and their riders. As he watched, a lean, robed figure darted up from behind one of the fallen mounts and flung a javelin at one of the Lahmians. The soldier screamed and fell, clutching at the shaft protruding from his chest. Arrows hissed through the air, but the raider had already ducked back down out of sight and the shafts passed harmlessly overhead.

A shout went up from the raiders north of the road. Alcadizzar watched in surprise as a dozen of them broke from the group and charged the line of wagons. Horse-bows twanged; one of the Lahmian archers pitched over backwards with an arrow in his eye. The raiders closed the distance swiftly, their mounts fairly gliding over the stony field. They plunged fearlessly into a storm of arrow fire. Horses screamed and plunged to the ground; their riders leapt free, only to be shot in turn. Only two of the brave riders made it past the wagons, hurling javelins at their tormentors as they raced by. Alcadizzar watched them rein in for a moment on the other side of the line, their heads turning this way and that as though searching for something. One of the riders fell a second later with an arrow in his throat; the second man caught sight of the mound of dead horses that the Lahmians had surrounded, and spurred his horse towards them with a cry of challenge. Three arrows struck the man in quick succession, piercing him in the leg and chest. Still, he struggled onwards, driving his mount forwards, until another pair of arrows struck him in the side and sent him plunging to the ground. The raider's horse came to a stop, its flanks heaving – but then a whistle caused its ears to perk up. At once, it started to trot towards where the stranded raider was hiding, but was brought down by a well-placed Lahmian arrow.

Now Alcadizzar understood why the desert raiders hadn't simply withdrawn as soon as the ambush had been sprung. Their chieftain had been brought down in the first charge and was now trapped by the Lahmians among the bodies of his retainers. Honour demanded that they rescue him, or die in the attempt.

The Lahmian soldiers pushed forwards, tightening the noose around the desert chieftain. To the west, Alcadizzar could hear the faint thunder of hooves. The cavalry would arrive in moments and then the raiders would have no choice but to withdraw; the chieftain's fate would be sealed.

There was no time to think. Alcadizzar raced down the slope, angling his course towards the downed chieftain. With the latest rescue attempt having failed, the Lahmian archers had turned their attention northwards once again. He might succeed where the gallant raiders had failed.

The prince broke from the concealing woods at a full gallop, his horse kicking up a cloud of dust as she raced across the level ground towards the encircling soldiers. The Lahmians didn't see him at first. Alcadizzar crossed the intervening distance in the space of a few heartbeats. By the time one of the soldiers on the far side of the circle caught sight of him and shouted a warning, it was already too late.

Alcadizzar plunged into the circle of warriors, his bronze sword flashing. Blood spattered in a wide arc as he split one soldier's helmet and carved into the skull beneath. The prince jerked his blade free with a bloodthirsty shout and struck another man in the shoulder, the sword cutting through the warrior's leather armour and shattering his collarbone. Screams rent the air; Alcadizzar spurred his mount forwards, leaping over the bodies of horses and men. He caught sight of the chieftain, hunched down next to his dead stallion, a sword and dagger clenched in his bloody hands.

The prince leaned down, extending his left arm. The desert chieftain's face was hidden behind a chequered headscarf, but his dark eyes glinted fiercely as he gripped Alcadizzar's forearm and swung easily onto the back of his horse. There were shouts all around them as the Lahmians surged forwards; with a cry, Alcadizzar spurred his mount once again – not northwards, into the teeth of the enemy bowmen, or southwards, towards the wooded hill but west, down the length of the caravan and in the direction of the oncoming Lahmian cavalry.

Arrows hissed through the air as the wagons flashed by. An arrow struck Alcadizzar in the left side, but the point failed to penetrate the rings of mail sewn into his raider's coat. Only a few of the archers could fire on him at any one time, and the speed of his horse made him a difficult target.

In less than a minute he reached the last wagon in line and was galloping out into the open. Shouts rose behind him and he expected a fusillade of arrows to rain down on him, but just then the Lahmian cavalry arrived on the scene, their yellow silk standards flapping in the wind. He charged full into their midst, dashing straight down the column of charging riders. The Lahmian archers had no choice but to hold their fire, and within moments Alcadizzar had vanished in the churning dust cloud kicked up by the cavalry troop.

A fist pounded at the prince's shoulder and laughter boomed in his ear. 'That was boldly done!' the chieftain said. Alcadizzar glanced over his shoulder and saw that the raider had pulled aside his headscarf. He was a young man, no more than twenty-five or so, with a handsome, tanned face and a brilliant smile that was more than a little mad.

'I am Faisr al-Hashim, of the *bani-al-Hashim*,' the young man said. 'And I am in your debt, stranger. Ask of me anything, and it is yours.'

A half-mile down the trade road, the prince reined in his mount. In the distance, the Lahmian cavalry were chasing the rest of the bandits northwards. Alcadizzar glanced back at the chieftain. Nawat and his rabble were forgotten; this was the opportunity he'd been looking for.

'Anything?'

The chieftain laughed again, drunk from his close brush with death. 'Anything, upon my honour! What is your heart's desire?'

The prince smiled. 'I wish to ride with the *bani-al-Hashim*.'

ELEVEN

INTO THE TRAP

Nagashizzar,
in the 99th year of Usirian the Dreadful
(-1285 Imperial Reckoning)

'Out of the way, damn you! *Move-move!'* Eekrit laid about with the flat of his blade, striking shoulders and backsides. The clanrats yelped and snarled, glaring back at the warlord with pure murder in their eyes – then lowering their heads and squeezing against the walls of the narrow tunnel once they realised who he was.

Eekrit drove onwards, shouldering his way through the press of armoured bodies. The journey from the lower levels of the fortress had taken nearly twice as long as expected. After successfully dodging enemy patrols and slipping past the *kreekar-gan*'s barricades, they'd emerged into a scene of utter pandemonium at mine shaft one. Some kind of massive troop movement was under way, with the army's assault troops being pulled from the battle-line and replaced with yowling mobs of slaves. Every passageway to the lower levels was packed tight with snarling, cursing skaven going in one direction or the other, slowing movement to little better than a crawl. Eekrit was exhausted already from fighting his way through one crowded passageway after another. His arms ached and his patience had long since worn thin. The only thing preventing him from using the sharp end of his blade was the fact that the maddened clanrats would likely turn on him in an instant. The army had enough problems already without touching off a bloody melee within its own ranks.

The warlord shoved his way to the front of the pack, with Eshreegar and the rest of his raiders close at his heels. The leader of the clanrats started to hiss a curse as Eekrit stalked past, but a glare from the Master of Treacheries left the warrior cowering in a cloud of fear-musk.

Just past the clanrats was yet another shuffling mass of stinking fur and rustling armour, but this time Eekrit pulled up short. It was a pack of the Grey Lord's *heechigar*, standing shoulder-to-shoulder and probably thirty rats deep. The warlord paused, his narrow chest heaving. His whiskers twitched, sensing the movement of air currents up ahead. They had to be close to their goal now, he reckoned, and the storm-walkers were moving along at something approaching a slow march. At the moment, that was good enough for him. Eekrit fumbled for his scabbard twice before he finally managed to put away his sword.

'How long?' he asked, as Eshreegar came up beside him.

The Master of Treacheries took a deep breath, focusing his tired mind. 'Seven hours,' he replied. 'Maybe a bit more.'

Eekrit spat a sulphurous curse. 'The *kreekar-gan*'s probably on the move right now. The attack could begin at any minute.'

Eshreegar cocked his head at the warlord. 'How can you be so sure?'

'Because it's the worst possible thing that could happen,' Eekrit growled. 'That's been the one constant in this whole, miserable war.'

They followed the *heechigar* for several minutes before a bone whistle blew up ahead, and the storm-walkers surged ahead at a loping, rattling trot. Moments later, Eekrit found himself standing at the mouth of the branch-tunnel leading into mine shaft four.

The army's base camp had expanded dramatically in the weeks since the raiders had last been there. Huge piles of food and supplies, separated by clan and guarded by anxious packs of warriors, stretched from one end of the long tunnel to the other. Smoke from cook-fires and hissing furnaces created a bluish-black haze along the roof of the mine shaft; the air was hot and reeking from the copper stink of the swordsmiths' forges. The slave pens that he could see had been emptied and units of heavily armed warriors were hastening down the narrow lanes to the call of screeching bone whistles or the bark of clan chiefs.

Eshreegar surveyed the chaos and scowled. 'What in the Horned God's name is going on?' he said.

Eekrit wasn't quite sure what to make of it himself. 'We'll know soon enough,' he replied, and set off at a trot for the Grey Lord's pavilion.

They made better time cutting across the mine shaft and reached the sprawling collection of wood-and-hide enclosures within a matter of minutes. A pair of *heechigar* stood watch at the pavilion's main entrance, nervously clutching the hafts of their fearsome-looking polearms. Their hackles bristled as Eekrit and the raiders approached.

Eekrit was in no mood for displays of dominance. 'I must speak with Lord Velsquee at once,' he said without preamble.

'Lord Velsquee is meeting with the war council,' rasped one of the storm-walkers.

The warlord glared up at the broad-shouldered warrior. 'How convenient,' he replied. 'I'm on the war council.'

The two *heechigar* exchanged sly looks. 'That's not what we were told, black-robe,' the burly guard said, baring his teeth in a lopsided sneer. 'Aren't you supposed to be past the barricades, sniffing up the *kreekar-gan*'s bony arse?'

'You shut your teeth,' Eshreegar warned, his voice low and full of menace.

The storm-walker's smile broadened. 'Do your worst, one-eye.'

Eshreegar stepped forwards, a pair of cruel-looking knives appearing in his paws as if by magic. His answering smile was wicked and cold. 'You asked for this,' he told the storm-walker. 'I want you to remember that once I'm finished with you.'

'*Enough,*' Eekrit snapped, and the tone of his voice was enough to get even the *heechigars'* attention. 'We don't have time for this.' The warlord stepped up to the towering guard. 'You listen to me,' he told the storm-walker. 'The leader of the army's scouts has an urgent message for the Grey Lord and the council. If he doesn't get that message *immediately*, then Velsquee will hold the both of you responsible. Do you care to take the blame for the army's defeat?'

The guard's eyes narrowed, searching Eekrit's face for signs he was bluffing. Finally, the storm-walker shrugged. 'No need for that,' he muttered, and then sent his companion into the pavilion with a jerk of his head.

Eekrit and Eshreegar fumed in silence, tails twitching, for what felt like an eternity. Finally, the second guard returned. 'All right,' he said, with no sign of deference. 'You two come with me.'

The Master of Treacheries tensed again at the guard's insolent tone, but Eekrit forestalled him with an upraised paw. 'Lead on.'

They followed the storm-walker past the hanging hide flap and into the noisome darkness of the pavilion. Foul-smelling incense – some acrid swamp fungus that was currently fashionable in the Great City – curled listlessly about the ceiling of the narrow antechamber beyond. Slaves from a number of the army's prominent clans abased themselves as Eekrit passed by.

The *heechigar* led them down a maze of twisting, close-set passageways, fashioned to suit skaven sensibilities and confound would-be assassins. After several minutes, they emerged into a slightly larger antechamber, this one laid with expensive rugs and stinking of slightly less acrid smoke. More slaves, these belonging exclusively to Velsquee, crouched silently in the far corners of the chamber as they awaited their master's summons. Another passageway opposite led deeper into the pavilion. From somewhere beyond came the faint murmur of voices.

As they entered the chamber, the hide flap across the room was pulled aside. Eekrit came to a sudden halt as he caught sight of the skaven lord who'd come to meet them.

Lord Hiirc was clad in rich robes embroidered with gold and silver thread. Tokens of burning stone gleamed balefully from fine chains around his neck. Like Eekrit, the lord of Clan Morbus could afford the best charms and potions that money could buy back at the Great City. He looked like a skaven barely half his true age, Eekrit noted irritably. Hiirc's gold-capped teeth glinted coldly as he spoke.

'What in the-the Horned God's name are the two of you doing here?' he said. His voice was thin and shrill, like a poorly tuned whistle. The lord's fur was tangled and unkempt, and his ears twitched apprehensively. Eekrit wondered at his appearance, but then realised that it was very early in the morning for the clan lords, who were accustomed to the luxuries of camp life.

'There's going to be an attack, Hiirc,' Eekrit snapped. 'The *kreekar-gan* has led us into an ambush.'

Hiirc's ears folded back against his skull. 'Is that so?' he hissed. 'And how exactly do you know this?'

Eekrit growled under his breath and took a step towards Hiirc. His paw drifted to his sword hilt. He wanted nothing more than to bury his blade between the fool's beady eyes. The *heechigar* sensed this at once and let out a warning snarl, moving to place himself partially between the two lords. Eshreegar shifted slightly, paws at his sides.

The warlord caught himself at the last moment. However much he wanted it, painting the hide walls with Hiirc's blood would only complicate things with Velsquee. Eekrit paused, took a deep breath, and told his erstwhile second-in-command what he'd learned.

Hiirc listened carefully to the story, even nodding thoughtfully at the description of the tunnel mouth and the captured clan chief. When Eekrit had finished his report, the Morbus clan lord snapped his fingers. Instantly a slave appeared, bearing a bowl of wine on a silver tray. Hiirc took the bowl and sipped its contents.

'Is that all?' he asked.

Eekrit stared at Hiirc. Even the *heechigar* seemed shocked.

'Isn't that enough?' the warlord snarled. 'What is-is so hard to understand, Hiirc? The burning man and his warriors are likely moving through the tunnels even as we speak. They could attack at-at any moment–'

'We know,' Hiirc replied, his tail lashing smugly. 'We've known for hours, in fact.'

'You *know*?' Then, suddenly, Eekrit understood. 'The spy. Of course.'

Hiirc shifted uncomfortably. 'I-I don't know what you're talking about.'

Eekrit cut him off with an upraised claw. 'Don't be more of an idiot than you have to be, Hiirc,' he snapped. 'There's been a traitor in the enemy's ranks all along. How in the Horned God's name did you get the warning so quickly?'

Hiirc finished the wine and tossed the bowl back onto the slave's tray. 'That's none of your concern,' he shot back. 'Velsquee's summoned our best troops. When the burning man attacks, he'll walk right into a trap. In an hour, two at most, the war will be over,' he said. Hiirc bared his golden teeth in a malicious smile. 'Which means your services to the army are no longer required.'

Before Eekrit could reply, Hiirc snapped his fingers once again. This time the hide flap behind him was drawn aside and twelve more storm-walkers filed ponderously into the room.

Eekrit glared at the broad-shouldered warriors. 'What is the meaning of this?'

Hiirc turned to the leader of the *heechigar*. 'Escort Lords Eekrit and Eshreegar to the under-fortress,' he commanded. 'Confine them to the warlord's lair and guard them closely.'

The storm-walkers surrounded the two skaven. Eekrit bared his teeth, furious that he'd allowed Hiirc to trap him so easily. With the rest of the scout-assassins behind him he might have made a fight of it. But now...

Eekrit folded his arms in resignation. 'Lord Velsquee will hear of this.'

Hiirc's ears fluttered with amusement. 'It was the Grey Lord himself who ordered this.' He waved a paw in dismissal to the guards. 'Remove them by one of the side entrances,' he ordered. 'If you even *think* they might give you trouble, hack them to bits.'

The *heechigar* leader grunted in assent and nodded to his warriors. Lowering their polearms, they herded their two prisoners past Hiirc and back the way they'd come, past the hide flap and into another adjoining room connected by three branching corridors. Down a side-corridor they went, passing into another labyrinthine set of passageways that finally led them to an exit on the far side of the pavilion.

Outside the enclosure the air still rang with shouted orders and the shrill cry of whistles as the storm-walkers and the army's veteran clanrats prepared their hasty ambush. Eekrit paused, surveying the scene. The rest of the scout-assassins were nowhere in sight, and with so much noise there was no way to call for aid.

A sharp bronze point jabbed the warlord in the shoulderblade. 'Move,' said the storm-walker behind him.

The phalanx of guards started off towards the opposite side of the mine shaft. Eshreegar fell into step beside Eekrit. He gave the warlord a sidelong look.

'Any brilliant ideas?' he asked.

'I'm *thinking*,' Eekrit muttered.

The Master of Treacheries leaned closer. 'There's a slave trader in the under-fortress who owes me some favours,' he whispered. 'If we can get to him, he'll smuggle us back to the Great City for a price.'

Eekrit walked along in silence, considering his options. After a moment, he looked up and considered the hulking forms of the storm-walkers.

The warlord took a deep breath. 'Eshreegar, how much gold have you got?'

The preparations for the attack took hours to complete. Swift messengers carried orders to the barbarian companies, withdrawing them from the barricades and assembling them in four large contingents along the deserted storage chambers close to the approach tunnels. Large packs of flesh-eaters – nearly all that remained of the debased Yaghur tribes – prowled the tunnels around the assembled warriors, hunting for enemy scouts who might spoil their master's plans. The northmen, some four thousand strong, left behind a mere thousand skeletal warriors to man the barricades and hold the enemy at bay.

As the warriors gathered, Nagash went to the secret vault that contained the last of the *abn-i-khat*. The windowless stone chamber, carved from the very bedrock of the mountain, was large enough to rival the vast treasure houses of the kings of old Khemri; now its shelves and marble plinths sat empty but for a single, small table at the far end of the vault. There, flickering like a pair of baleful eyes, sat two fist-sized lumps of burning stone.

Nagash paused but a moment at the threshold, surveying the dark, empty place. Once a measure of Nagashizzar's wealth and power, now it spoke only of defeat and a long, bitter decline.

At length he entered the echoing vault, his bony footsteps making faint, scraping sounds upon the stone. His body moved with an unnatural gait more akin to a beast or a reptile than to a man. His arms and legs, unmoored by muscle or sinew, moved like serpents beneath the parchment-like folds of his ancient robe. His wight bodyguard followed at his heels, ghostly green fire flickering across their tarnished armour and down the length of their deadly blades.

The macabre procession halted before the table and Nagash spread his skeletal hands possessively above it. The magical stone seemed to respond to the necromancer's desires, flaring like coals in a furnace. The light of the burning stone played across the surface of the bronze and leather breastplate that they rested upon and the long, straight, double-edged blade that lay before it. The armour had been wrought by the smiths of the northmen and enchanted by Nagash's own hand; each scale had been inscribed with a rune of protection to turn aside the spells and blades of his foes. The blade had been taken from an ancient northern barrow during the long war of subjugation, and had been wrought from obsidian in the days before men knew how to shape metal. The art of its making was a mystery even to Nagash; there was terrible power coiled within, a hunger for life that was depthless and cold as the abyss itself.

Nagash plucked the stone orbs from their resting place and weighed them in his hands. At once, the left-hand orb was wreathed with a shimmering green mist that soaked into the necromancer's blackened bones. At once, he stood straighter, his skeletal frame drawing together tightly as the arcane energies leapt from joint to joint. He craved more, but with an effort of supreme will he put his hunger aside. He had measured out each and every ounce according to his battle plan. Nothing would be held back. Either he would defeat the ratmen once and for all, or be destroyed in the process.

At his command, the wights gathered around him. For the first time in more than a century, they set aside their bared blades and reached for the wargear resting upon the table.

Slowly, with unspoken ceremony, the risen dead garbed Nagash for war. The weight of the armour upon his chest reminded him of ancient times, of past glories won beneath Nehekhara's burning sun, but the memories filled him with a strange sense of foreboding. As the champions went about their work, cinching cords and fastening ties, the necromancer found himself studying the vault's shadows for pale figures and ghostly, accusing faces.

'I should not be here,' Akatha said, her voice echoing hollowly in the confined space of the tunnel. 'I belong with Bragadh. It is an ill-omened thing to send a chieftain to battle without a witch to sing for him.'

Nagash said nothing. Rock bubbled and hissed beneath his fingertip as he traced a magical circle on the floor. The tunnel had no exit – it merely ended at a rough-hewn wall of granite, some three feet thick. Magical runes had been etched into the surface of the rock and inlaid with *abn-i-khat* years ago; they formed a tall, wide arch, broad enough for two men standing abreast. His wight bodyguard formed a protective barrier between him and the archway, their dark blades held ready.

Behind the necromancer came the muted rattle of weapons and armour as his warriors awaited the call to battle. The tunnel was, in truth, a long, spiralling ramp that bored down through the bedrock and terminated at the far end of the mine shaft. Three others like it had been sunk through the stone on the opposite side of the shaft, each packed with a thousand northmen and led by Bragadh, Diarid and Thestus. A fifth tunnel, which had been opened months ago to allow his constructs to enter the mine shaft in search of useful prisoners, had been quietly sealed up just a few hours before to maintain the element of surprise.

Akatha stood with folded arms to Nagash's right, her expression hidden behind a fall of ash-stained hair. Her pale skin shone with unnatural vigour, throwing her ghostly blue tattoos into sharp relief. She had drunk deep from the necromancer's cup, along with Bragadh and the other immortals, just before joining their mortal kinsmen in the fortress depths. The necromancer had been generous with his elixir, restoring his lieutenants to their former might. The witch radiated arcane power, like the churning clouds of a fierce desert storm.

'What is it you wish me to do?' she asked. 'If I am not to sing the war-song, then what?'

Nagash finished inscribing the last of the ritual symbols. Kneeling amid them, he reached past the runes and etched a glowing green circle in the rock. He had consumed the most burning stone of all, and the sensation of raw, unbridled power filled him with a terrible, mirthless joy. The cold hilt of the obsidian blade fairly trembled in his hand, its ancient spirit stirring at the prospect of battle.

The necromancer straightened, calling to mind the words of the ritual he'd created years ago and held in reserve in anticipation of this very moment.

Bear witness, he said to her. *Behold the vengeance of Nagash.*

The incantation reverberated through the necromancer's brain, fuelled by the power of the burning stone, and the runes carved into the rock blazed with light. Within moments, thin wisps of smoke rose from the sigils carved into the rock wall, and the temperature in the crowded tunnel began to rise. The northmen closest to Nagash began to shift uneasily and mutter blasphemous prayers as the wall began to blacken and a malevolent hissing sound filled the air.

Focusing his will, Nagash raised his left hand and slowly made a fist. The air shimmered with heat. When he reached the end of the incantation he punched his fist at the wall and unleashed a fraction of his pent-up energy; the iron-hard granite contained within the arch exploded outwards in a furious crack of thunder.

Hundreds of razor-edged fragments scythed through the mine shaft around the breach, followed by a roiling wall of blinding dust, heat and rushing air. The few ratmen unlucky enough to be caught within the blast were killed instantly; their pulverised bodies were caught by the shockwave and hurled dozens of feet through the air. Stacked crates and wicker baskets were torn apart, their contents scattered across the mine shaft and in some cases ignited by the searing air.

A string of three more blasts ripped through the lower end of the mine shaft as the runic arches inset into the remaining assault tunnels detonated as well. A cyclone of dust and howling, furnace-like air roared up the shaft towards the ratmen's pavilion, punctuated by the roaring war cries of the northmen.

Attack!

Nagash's command echoed in the minds of his bodyguards and lieutenants. The wights swept forwards in a silent, deadly wave, their movements lent unearthly speed by another of the necromancer's incantations. Nagash followed them, his burning gaze searching the battlefield for foes, and the barbarians came charging in his wake.

The necromancer glided like a ghost through the heat and the swirling smoke. Ahead of him ranged the wights, moving so swiftly their feet scarcely seemed to touch the ground. Shouts and screams filled the air. Nagash could hear the charge of Diarid's barbarian warriors off to his right and the shouts of Bragadh's barbarians to his left. Thestus and his men were somewhat ahead and to Bragadh's left; his lieutenants were entrusted with blocking any would-be rescuers advancing from the enemy forces in the upper and lower mine shafts. They would protect his flanks while he and his warriors raced to the pavilion and killed every rat-creature he found there.

For the first few minutes, the only ratmen Nagash found were the twisted and torn bodies of those caught by the initial blast. Shrill cries and panicked screeches sounded ahead and to either side of him, lost behind mounds of supplies and churning wisps of dust. His wight bodyguards had caught up to the rear edge of the smoke cloud he'd created; they were nothing more than wavering silhouettes, tinged by faint haloes of green grave-light. The undead warriors raced on without pause through the scalding cloud, driven by the hateful will of their master.

Nagash charged into the whirlwind after them. The hot dust filled his hood and blew it back from his blackened skull. It sang against his stone blade, causing it to utter a low, crystalline moan. His robes and the thick leather underlayment of his armour began to smoulder in the superheated air, but the necromancer scarcely felt its touch. He could dimly sense Akatha and the barbarians some distance behind him, loping like wolves in the dust cloud's wake.

They were some three hundred yards from the assault tunnels when Nagash heard screams and shouts in the dust clouds up ahead. Corpse-light flickered in sweeping, deadly arcs, and the cries of the ratmen were cut short. A heartbeat later he came upon the first of the corpses. The ratmen had been cut down in mid-stride as they stumbled blindly through the dust. Their fur had been burnt away, along with their ears and their deep-set eyes. Many were still toppling to the ground as the necromancer rushed past.

And then, without warning, there were ratmen everywhere. They came screaming out of the veil of dust from all sides, their snouts blistered and bleeding and their chisel teeth bared. Wight blades flickered through the air, slicing through armour and sinking into flesh. The blades froze the blood and silenced the hearts of those they touched; Nagash watched ratmen stagger beneath the blows, their last breaths billowing in jets of glittering vapour as they fell.

Still more of the creatures charged Nagash from left and right. Those that had managed to avoid being blinded by the storm rushed directly at him, their swords raised to strike.

He met them with a cruel laugh and a blasphemous incantation. Streaks of green fire burst from the skeletal fingers of his free hand, scything through the ratmen on his left. The creatures collapsed, shrieking in agony as their bodies boiled from the inside out.

No sooner had the sorcerous bolts sped from his hand than Nagash was turning to face the ratmen charging from his right. Roaring, exultant, he raised his obsidian blade and fell upon them. His sword flashed in blurring arcs, biting into armour, flesh and bone and snuffing out the life within. Their blows turned aside from his enchanted armour, or shattered against its scales. He beckoned to the wretched rat-things, daring them to do their worst, his burning eyes mocking them as they died beneath his blade. When there were no foes left to kill, he spun about and stalked back through the dust clouds, hunting down stumbling, blinded ratmen and slaying every one he could find.

The fight lasted barely a minute. One moment Nagash was lost in an ecstasy of slaughter and the next he was standing amid piles of lifeless bodies, watching the surviving ratmen fleeing deeper into the dust cloud, towards the distant pavilion. The necromancer's bloodthirsty howl shook the aether as he and his wights set off after the retreating ratmen.

Nothing could stop him now.

Velsquee nervously fingered one of the god-stone tokens hanging from his neck as he watched the oncoming dust cloud. It filled the wide mine shaft from one side to the other, roiling up from the depths and swallowing everything it touched. A hot wind, dry as bone and reeking of charred flesh, blew full into the Grey Lord's face. Around him, the *heechigar* hunched their shoulders and eyed one another apprehensively. They'd all known to expect an attack, but nothing quite like this.

At the far end of the killing ground they'd established around the former pavilion, a black-robed scout-assassin emerged from one of the camp's narrow lanes. Wisps of smoke rose from his scorched clothing and blood dripped from his blistered tail. The young skaven paused, chest heaving, and searched for the Grey Lord among the tightly packed ranks of storm-walkers. Velsquee let go of the token, took a deep breath, and beckoned to him.

The scout dashed over, making only the most cursory obeisance before the Grey Lord. Up close, Velsquee could smell the skaven's burned flesh and the bitter reek of fear-musk.

'He is-is coming!' the scout gasped in a ragged voice. 'The *kreekar-gan* comes!'

'I can see that, Shireep!' Velsquee snapped. 'Tell me something useful! How many does he have with him?'

'A-a few thousand,' the scout replied. 'No more. Two-two columns on the left, one column on the right. Humans. No bone-men.'

The Grey Lord nodded. It was more or less what he expected. 'How far away?'

The scout pointed back the way he'd come with a trembling paw. 'Just-just the other side of the cloud. Two hundred yards, maybe less.' Eyes wide with terror, Shireep reached out and grabbed Velsquee's sleeve. 'We can't-can't stay here! The cloud, it-it burns! By the Horned One, it *burns*! We have to get out of here!'

With a snarl, Velsquee tore his paw from Shireep's grip. In one swift move, he drew his sword from its sheath and slashed at the terrified scout. The enchanted blade sank into Shireep's chest, and the skaven collapsed with a groan.

'There will be no retreat!' Velsquee screeched, brandishing his gore-stained blade for all the storm-walkers to see. 'The *kreekar-gan*'s magic cannot harm us. The trap has been set, and he is marching to his doom! This is our moment of victory!'

As one, the *heechigar* cheered the Grey Lord, their lusty shouts echoing from the walls. Velsquee passed between the ranks of storm-walkers and beckoned for a messenger. The young clanrat scampered over and cowered at the Grey Lord's feet.

'Tell Lord Vittrik and Lord Qweeqwol that it's time,' Velsquee said. 'And pass the word to the left and right flanks to close in.'

The messenger repeated what he'd been told in a high-pitched voice, and then raced back in the direction of the former pavilion.

Velsquee returned to the font ranks of the *heechigar*, his rune-etched sword held at his side. The dust cloud was much closer now, the screams within louder and more distinct. In a few more minutes it would be upon them.

The Grey Lord reached again for the god-stone token around his neck.

Nagash's sword chopped into the edge of the ratman's shield, carving through the bronze rim and splitting the wood beneath, before lodging in the bones of the warrior's forearm. The creature stiffened and let out an agonised shriek as the ancient weapon consumed his life essence.

A spear dug into the necromancer's side but could find no purchase among the enchanted scales. A sword struck his right shoulderblade and snapped in two with a discordant clang. The ratmen attacked from every direction, clambering over the bodies of the slain to try and reach him. Many were half-blinded by the searing dust cloud, but still they came on, their raw faces twisted into masks of hatred and rage.

Nagash's bodyguards fought in a loose semicircle around their master, each one beset by a half-dozen foes. They had pursued the retreating ratmen through the veil of dust, overtaking and killing nearly a score of the wretches before stumbling into another, much larger mob of the creatures just a hundred yards or so from the pavilion. These ratmen were just as ravaged by the dust cloud as the others, but they were far from panicked. Indeed, they almost seemed to be laying in wait for Nagash's arrival. They swarmed the wights and quickly isolated them; then the rest of the mob turned their attention on the necromancer himself.

Cursing the ratmen in ancient Nehekharan, Nagash swept his left hand in a wide arc, unleashing a storm of sizzling green bolts into the multitude. A dozen of the creatures fell screaming, but still more closed in to take their place. Snarling, he put a skeletal foot on the fallen skaven's shield and tore his weapon free. An enemy dagger slipped beneath the heavy sleeve of his armour and scored his upper arm. An axe crashed into his chest and was turned aside in a fan of sorcerous sparks. Nagash caught the axe-arm a glancing blow with his sword, slicing off the ratman's thumb and snuffing out his life like a candle.

A two-handed spear thrust struck Nagash in the back, and this time the blade found a chink in his armour. The triangular point punched between the bonze scales and through the leather underlayment, lodging fast between his ribs. Snarling, the necromancer tried to turn and reach his attacker, but the canny ratman dug in his heels and held on fast, effectively trapping Nagash like an insect impaled on a pin.

Sensing their opportunity, the ratmen closed in. A sword chopped into his upper thigh, carving a notch into the ancient, blackened bone. Nagash stabbed the sword-wielder through the throat, but another of the enemy leapt upon his outstretched sword arm and clung there, effectively trapping it. More blows rained upon his torso and back. Then the tip of another axe blade clipped his spine, just beneath his skull, and he realised how dangerous his situation had become. He threw off the creature that had grabbed him and swung his sword in a wide arc, catching one ratman as he leapt forwards and slicing open his throat, while mentally forming the words of another incantation.

Suddenly, the dust clouds immediately surrounding Nagash changed their course, rushing towards him and spiralling around his body in ever-swifter circles, until he was entirely hidden within a howling, opaque column of pulverised stone. With a crack of thunder, the column collapsed – only to reappear again a dozen yards back. The ratman who'd impaled the necromancer found himself staring at his bare spear-point, while Nagash emerged from the smaller column of dust directly behind him.

Laughing, the necromancer unleashed another storm of sorcerous bolts that wrought havoc among the mob of rat-creatures. A score of his attackers died where they stood, and the rest turned and fled. The retreating ratmen sowed panic among their fellows and within moments the entire mob was in full flight, disappearing into the swirling dust cloud.

Nagash paused a moment to assess his strength. He still possessed sizable reserves of power, though he'd spent far more than expected since the attack began. His wights awaited him, tireless and deadly as ever, though their armour was badly battered and their bones had been chipped and scored in dozens of places by enemy blades. What was more, he could hear more sounds of fighting off to his left and right. His flanking columns had come under concerted attack. What should have been a swift, devastating raid on the enemy camp was rapidly turning into a pitched battle. The question was whether or not the ratmen were present in sufficient numbers to save their leaders from destruction.

Onwards. Quickly! The swifter they reached the pavilion, the greater the chance that the plan would succeed.

The wights turned without hesitation and fell in alongside Nagash as he rushed through the swirling dust. He could still hear the panicked cries of the ratmen somewhere ahead. Just a few dozen yards more...

Nagash didn't notice the sudden thickening of the dust clouds until he was well within it. An instant later he felt the unmistakeable sensation of passing through a membrane of magical energy – and then he and his wights burst through the gritty cloud and into open air.

They were standing at the edge of a wide, cleared space possibly two hundred paces square, its edges clearly defined by the churning walls of dust held at bay by a powerful magic ward. A hundred paces away, safe from the dust's touch, stood hundreds of hulking, heavily armoured ratmen, arrayed in ranks eight warriors deep and holding heavy bronze polearms at the ready. Standing at the centre of this powerful formation stood a tall ratman in gold-chased armour. Tokens of burning stone glittered like a constellation of stars around his dark-furred neck and a larger, oval stone blazed from the hilt of his curved sword.

Yet it wasn't the fearsome sight of the waiting enemy warriors, or the baleful figure of the enemy warlord that gave Nagash pause. It was the forest of bare, wooden stakes that spread across the cleared ground a few dozen paces beyond the ratmen. The hide walls of the vast pavilion, Nagash saw, had been taken down, and the furniture within had been cleared away. All that remained was a high, broad dais, at what would have been the centre of the enclosure. More ratmen moved atop the platform; Nagash could not make out what they were doing, but there was no mistaking the seething aura of magical energy gathered there. This was the source of the magical ward protecting the enemy leader and his warriors.

Raising his sword in challenge, Nagash drew upon the power of the *abn-i-khat.* Sorcerous thunder rolled in counterpoint to the incantation that reverberated in the necromancer's mind. The air about him crackled with energy, gaining intensity until arcs of green lightning lashed angrily all around him. Nagash stoked the power of the magical storm until its fury threatened to consume him, then flung out his hand and unleashed it on the enemy warriors.

Faster than thought, the curtain of lightning raced across the open ground, its arcs of fire carving channels in the bare rock – and then Nagash felt the power atop the dais flare into life. Invisible energies attacked his spell, unravelling its weave with a deftness that the necromancer never thought possible. The arcs of lightning paled, diminishing swiftly from one moment to the next, until finally fading from existence just a few feet from their intended target.

Incredulous, Nagash roared a second incantation. Arcs of sorcerous power burst from his extended hand and sped at the dais, but the bolts detonated harmlessly against a second, smaller ward that surrounded part of the platform.

Reflexively, the necromancer summoned up a portion of his power to guard himself from a counter-blow from the dais. When no such attack came, he hurled another volley of bolts, this time aimed at the enemy warlord. Once again, the wizard atop the dais deflected the attack. Whoever the ratman was, his mastery of the burning stone's power was impressive; not as great as Nagash's own, to be sure, but countering a spell required far less power and control than it did to cast one.

The ratmen had once again surprised him. Here was a skilfully prepared defence that would cost him dearly to overcome, and he was left with no other choice but to assault it. The leaders of the enemy army were finally within his grasp. Here was the victory he'd sought for nearly a hundred years.

Nagash gathered his wights to him and then turned his attention to the dust storm raging about the square. He dispelled the magic holding the burning cloud together and scattered it with a wave of his hand. The veil parted, revealing Akatha and the thousand northmen who had been following along behind him. They were less than twenty yards away, and when they saw the waiting ratmen they charged forwards, filling the air with their war cries.

The necromancer turned his gaze back to the enemy warlord. He let the power of the burning stone flow along his limbs and levelled his sword in challenge at the distant figure.

Attack!

'Here they come!' Velsquee snarled. 'Get back in line, damn you! Stand fast!'

Pack leaders repeated the Grey Lord's orders along the length of the formation, shoving and cursing recalcitrant warriors back into their proper place. Discipline reasserted itself swiftly: backs straightened, tails uncurled and ears unfolded as the northmen came charging across the killing ground. The sight of the *kreekar-gan* and his champions had been bad enough, but the sorcerous duel that had raged over the storm-walkers' heads had left them badly shaken. The sight of a flesh-and-blood enemy did much to restore the veteran warriors' resolve.

Velsquee took a deep breath and tried to calm his racing heart. The thunderous magical barrage had shaken him as well, even though he'd known that Qweeqwol was ready to counter whatever the burning man threw at them. He'd heard all the stories about the ferocity of the *kreekar-gan*'s magic, but actually experiencing it was something else entirely. The grey seer had assured Velsquee that he was up to the task of countering the burning man's sorcery. At the time, the Grey Lord had no reason to doubt the master wizard. Now, however, he wasn't so sure. He suspected it would come down to whoever ran out of power first. In that, at least, he was certain that they held the upper hand.

The humans were a mere thirty paces away now. The air shook with their howling battle cries. Nagash's terrifying lieutenants led them; green fire blazed malevolently from their eye sockets and leaked from rents in their ancient, tattered armour. Their bony jaws gaped in a macabre echo of the howling northmen that flanked them.

He couldn't see the burning man any longer, but a rattle of detonations over the heads of the *heechigar* told Velsquee that he was still close by. Qweeqwol was going to have his paws full holding the *kreekar-gan* at bay, but that would be enough. In a battle of flesh and blood, sword and polearm, the skaven were certain to win, because he had an advantage that the burning man didn't.

The northmen were nearly upon them. The rock floor trembled beneath their tread, and the air shook with their savage cries. Velsquee planted his heels and brought up his enchanted blade. One of Nagash's wights was running directly at him, its movements swift and fluid as a serpent's. The black blade in the skeletal lord's hand shone like polished midnight.

Vittrik's aim had better be good, the Grey Lord hoped.

The two sides came together in a rolling crash of metal, flesh and bone. The northmen in the front rank struck the wall of polearms and were killed almost immediately, cut down by the storm-walkers' heavy blades. The second rank of barbarians suffered a similar fate, but now Nagash's lieutenants were past the enemy's long-hafted weapons and striking at the ratmen with their fearsome blades. The northmen quickly followed suit, hacking with sword and axe at the wooden hafts of the enemy's weapons and forcing their way deeper into the opposing formation. The clangour of battle became punctuated by the thudding of metal against flesh and the screams of the maimed and the dying. Northmen and rat-creatures fell by the score. The enemy line bowed backwards at the fury of the barbarians' charge, but refused to give way.

Nagash unleashed another storm of magical bolts, this time aimed at raking the top of the dais. The streaks of fire arced over the melee, falling like thunderbolts, but once again they were dispelled before they could find their mark. Again and again he struck at the foe, but each time the enemy sorcerer was able to counter the spell. The battle raged back and forth across the killing ground, with neither side able to claim the upper hand. Frustrated, the necromancer switched tacks and turned his magic on his bodyguards. He added to their vigour, increasing the wights' speed and strength, and this time the enemy made no move to counter him. His lieutenants tore into the ranks of the ratmen, toppling enemy warriors left and right, but he knew that they were too few in number to carry the fight alone. Beside the necromancer, Akatha sang the war-song of the northmen, stoking the bloodlust of the barbarian warriors.

As the battle raged, a lone figure appeared to the left of the killing ground. It was one of Bragadh's northmen, his armour battered and bloody and his right arm useless at his side. He caught sight of Nagash and Akatha and ran to them, his expression grim.

'Master!' the warrior shouted. 'Master! Lord Bragadh says that the ratmen are attacking from the tunnels in great numbers! Thestus has been driven back, and Bragadh is hard-pressed! He asks for Diarid to lend his strength to them, or else they cannot hold!'

Nagash turned and glared at the messenger. *There will be no retreat!* The power of his thoughts was such that even the barbarian's living mind could not help but feel its weight. *Bragadh must hold to the last! To the last!*

The wounded northman staggered beneath the lash of the necromancer's black thoughts. 'But... Diarid...' he stammered.

Diarid had problems of his own. Nagash could hear the sounds of battle off to his right clearly enough. Both flanks were being hard pressed. Before he could reply, however, a chorus of dry, crackling hisses echoed across the killing field, followed by a drumbeat of hollow detonations and a chorus of agonised screams.

The necromancer whirled, just in time to see a trio of small green globes loft into the air from the dais. They flew high overhead, trailing thin plumes of smoke and a crackling hiss, before plunging into the ranks of the northmen. They struck with a flash of greenish light and a *whump* of hot air, bathing the warriors around the impact point with a gout of sorcerous fire. The ravening flame scoured its victims down to bone in seconds and sowed panic among the barbarians close by. The northmen wavered under the onslaught, and with a hoarse shout the ratmen began to push back, forcing the barbarians and wights onto the defensive.

At once, Nagash saw the full scope of the trap the ratmen had laid for him. The tide of battle was shifting quickly; in another few moments the ratmen would have a decisive advantage.

The moment of truth had come.

Nagash turned to Akatha. *This ends now,* he told her. *I will kill the warlord of the ratmen myself.*

The necromancer raised his obsidian blade and strode forwards. Barely a dozen yards separated him from the rear ranks of the northmen. Another three yards past that, and he would be in the thick of battle. He oriented himself on the last place he saw the enemy leader, and headed that way. From the dais, another volley of fire-globes lofted into the air on hissing streaks of fire. Nagash prepared a counter-spell, thinking that he might be able to at least dissipate the sorcerous power of the flames.

He did not sense the death-bolt until it was already upon him.

The spear of magical energy struck Nagash squarely between the shoulder-blades. The protective wards woven into his armour flared to life, attempting to turn aside the blow, but the power behind the spell was too great. Bronze scales glowed red-hot as the bolt transfixed the necromancer, tearing through his body and erupting from the front of his scale breastplate.

Nagash howled in anger and pain. The impact of the bolt spun the necromancer halfway about and threw him to the ground. Such a blow would have turned a living man to ash; as it was, Nagash's spine and ribcage had been shattered, and his access to the power he'd consumed was suddenly disrupted. For the first time in centuries, the necromancer felt a moment of horror as his vision blurred and the blackness of oblivion yawned before him. It was only by a supreme effort of will that he was able to claw his way back from the brink.

The vision of darkness faded just as Akatha launched a second attack.

The bolt of power sped from her fingers like an arrow; Nagash uttered a counter-spell, but there was little power behind it. He deflected enough of the witch's attack that his armour absorbed the rest, leaving behind a palm-sized patch of melted bronze scales across his chest.

Instinctively, Nagash flung out his hand and unleashed a stream of glowing darts at Akatha, but again, there was little power behind the spell; once again, the unseen rat-wizard atop the dais wove a counter-spell to nullify it. The darts flashed and popped harmlessly about the witch's body. Akatha threw back her head and laughed.

Nagash struggled to regain his feet. His limbs wavered, threatening to collapse beneath him, but with an angry cry he forced himself upright. His voice echoed hollowly in Akatha's mind.

The traitor reveals herself at last.

That gave Akatha pause. She studied him intently from behind her fall of hair. 'You knew?'

There were too many coincidences. No enemy is so lucky in war. He took a step towards her. *You were careful, and clever. I suspected, but I could never be certain. Until now.*

Nagash reached out his hand. His skeletal fingers made a fist, as though closing around the witch's heart. *Body and soul, you are mine to command, witch. You have broken your oath to me, and thus your life is forfeit.*

He reached into her, seizing upon the potency of the elixir that gave Akatha her power – but when he tried to wrest it from her, nothing happened. A magical ward, subtle but potent, prevented him from draining her vitality. The witch laughed again, a sound both joyous and full of contempt.

'Did you imagine I'd forgotten?' Akatha replied. 'You damned fiend. The witches of the north forget *nothing*.' Her fingers brushed a small token of burning stone hanging about her neck. 'I've had centuries to plan your demise, Nagash of the Wastes. Nothing has been left to chance.'

She swept her hand in a vicious arc, hurling another bolt of power his way. His weak counterspell did little to deflect it. The spell bored into his midsection, disrupting his spiritual corpus even further. Darkness, cold and empty, began to seep into the corners of his vision. Nagash staggered, but did not fall.

It was you who brought the ratmen here.

Akatha's pale lips curved in a mirthless smile. 'Their love of the burning stone was well known to us,' she hissed. 'I began sending visions to their seers from the first night I set foot in these accursed halls. It took years, but eventually they came.' The witch chuckled cruelly. 'How sweet it was, watching the vermin undo everything you'd built.'

Nagash struggled to regain his strength. The darkness ebbed from his sight, but did not vanish completely. Akatha stood alone; Bragadh's messenger had fled when the witch unleashed her first spell. Behind him, the sounds of fighting had grown desperate. The northmen were on the verge of breaking. The necromancer began a new incantation, feeding it power a bit at a time.

When you heard my plan to attack the pavilion, you believed that your time had come.

The witch raised her hand, preparing to cast another spell. 'At first, I thought that I had been found out,' she said. 'Why else go to all the trouble to dig the tunnels in secret? Then, when you ordered me to accompany you, I wondered if perhaps you were leading *me* into a trap.'

Nagash's burning eyes narrowed on Akatha. *I was.*

They lurched and staggered from the darkness and the smoke behind the barbarian witch, eyes flickering with green fire. The corpses of dozens of ratmen, their bodies covered in black blood from the bite of the wights' killing blades. Akatha didn't hear their halting steps over the tumult of battle until their hands were reaching for her throat.

They seized the witch, dragging her nearly off her feet. Akatha screamed in fury, struggling in their grip. The bolt she'd meant for Nagash ripped through their ranks instead, turning many of them to ash. Claws and fangs tore at her pale skin. She struck back with an immortal's super-natural strength, breaking bones and crushing skulls with her fists. The witch fought like a desert lion, but the undead were implacable. They kept coming for her, reaching for her, until finally a hand closed about the magical token around her neck and ripped it free. Akatha's body went rigid in an instant, gripped by Nagash's hateful will.

I knew that the enemy would be forewarned, he said to her. His voice was cold and cruel. *I counted upon it. Now the enemy's best troops are here, facing me, instead of at the barricades.*

Laughter filled Akatha's mind. *Darkness waits for you, witch. Darkness eternal. Go there, knowing that your life – and your treachery – have given me the final victory.*

Nagash reached inside the witch's undead body and took that which belonged to him. Akatha, last witch of the northlands, uttered one final scream, then was gone. The ratmen pulled down her shrivelled husk and began to tear it limb from limb.

High above, in the dark vaults of the fortress, a stir went through the ranks of the undead manning the barricades. Obeying their master's command, the spear companies began to pull aside the barriers that separated them from the tunnels below.

The going was slow at first, but before long the sounds of movement began to echo down the passageways from the levels above. One company of spearmen after another began to file into the vaults, their bones wreathed in cobwebs and the dust of decades. Long had they waited in secret, marshalled in great halls far from the eyes of the northmen or the spies of the invaders. They were Nagash's reserves, clad in the best weapons and armour the foundries of Nagashizzar could make and held ready for the last battle, whether it was fought within the mine shafts, or the great hall of the necromancer himself.

Behind the spear companies came a score of fearsome, armoured war engines, shaped in the guise of scarabs, or scorpions, or swift desert spiders. Some were the size of round shields, while others were larger than chariots. As the barriers were pulled aside they clattered without pause into the dark tunnels and began to hunt.

The slave-rats opposite the barricades were caught entirely unprepared. They had been rushed into position to take the place of their betters, and the slave masters had been told that they would not be sent into battle. A counter-attack from the enemy was the very last thing they expected.

The constructs attacked without warning, leaping from the shadows or falling from the ceiling into the midst of the slaves. Scores were dead before the slave masters understood what was happening. Most reacted as best they could, trying to rally the terrified slaves with curses, threats and the touch of the lash. Others panicked and ran, and their slaves fled moments after.

By the time the spear companies struck, there were already gaps in the enemy battle-line. Runners were sent to the lower levels, begging for re-inforcements, but by then it was already too late. The relentless slaughter broke the slaves, who turned on their masters and ran, desperate to escape the oncoming skeletons. Nagash's warriors followed, tireless and implacable, heeding their master's call.

The energy of the reclaimed elixir replaced a portion of the power that Nagash had lost. It was not enough to restore his shattered bones, but it lent strength to his limbs and allowed him to focus once more.

The necromancer turned back to the battle. Between the ratmen and the globes of fire, his warriors had been reduced to little more than two hundred men. The wights alone were keeping the ratmen from driving the barbarians back, but now there were less than a handful left. Two of them were trading blows with the enemy warlord, whose armour appeared to be proof against the effects of the wights' deadly blades.

Nagash ordered the undead ratmen into the battle, directing them to work their way around the flanks of the enemy formation. Then he spread his arms and spent another portion of his waning power to raise the bodies of the northmen who'd been slain. The necromancer sensed a flare of power upon the dais as the rat-sorcerer grasped what Nagash was doing, but his attempts to counter the spell were feeble at best. Hundreds of bodies stirred fitfully, then began to climb back to their feet. At the same time, more globes of fire arced over the struggling warriors and plunged into the ranks of the newly raised undead. Scores of the slow-moving corpses were caught in the detonations; seconds later their charred bones collapsed to the ground and did not rise again.

Nagash glared at the far-off dais. Between the rat-sorcerer and their damned fire globes, the enemy could withstand anything he threw at them. They had to be destroyed, and quickly. The enemy would move to counter any further attempt to raise more undead warriors, and the northmen would not last much longer.

The necromancer called upon his fading reserves of power once more. The incantation reverberated through his mind. From the dais, he sensed a surge of power as the enemy began his counter-spell, but the move was a fraction of a second too late.

Streamers of dust raced across the killing ground and entwined themselves about Nagash. They swallowed him up like a desert whirlwind; then he vanished from sight.

The rat-sorcerer was still casting his counter-spell when the necromancer emerged from the veil of dust onto the centre of the dais. Nagash found himself standing in the midst of a score of slave rats, who screeched in panic and scattered in all directions when they saw the terrifying figure in their midst. He saw the enemy sorcerer at once, standing close to the edge of the dais and raising a gnarled wooden staff over his head as he cast his spell. To the necromancer's left, a large group of ratmen was lifting fire-globes from straw-filled wooden boxes and loading them into the baskets of a trio of small metal catapults. Standing to one side of the catapult crews was an old, bent-backed ratman whose shrivelled frame seemed two sizes too small for the ornate bronze armour that he wore. A multitude of strange metal devices and glowing tokens of burning stone festooned the ratman's war harness, reminding Nagash somewhat of the engineer-scholars of far-off Lybaras. The ratman turned at the panicked cries of the slaves and his one eye widened in shock.

Nagash wasted no time with elaborate spells. As the one-eyed rat-creature let out a warning screech, the necromancer seized a slow-moving slave rat by the scruff of his neck and hurled him at the nearest crate of fire-globes. The impact upended the crate, sending three glowing, glass orbs bouncing across the stone. The catapult crew screeched in terror; the quicker ones leapt for the bouncing globes, while the rest fled for their lives. None of them were quite fast enough.

One of the globes bounced high and came down with a thin, brittle crack. There was a malevolent hiss as the mixture inside mixed with the open air and then the globe detonated. Half a dozen ratmen disappeared in an expanding ball of fire that touched off the remaining globes in a cacophonic drumbeat of explosions.

Velsquee had just about convinced himself that they had the upper hand when the air around him was suffused with bright green light and the noise of the battle was drowned out by a flurry of angry blasts emanating from the dais. The Grey Lord felt a wave of heat prickle the back of his head and neck; on reflex he cast a quick glance over his shoulder at the source. What he saw stunned him. One entire corner of the dais, including Vittrik's catapults and their crews, had vanished in an expanding ball of flame. Molten shrapnel from the war engines buzzed through the air, trailing glowing arcs of green fire.

The momentary lapse in concentration nearly cost him his life. The *kreekar-gan*'s skeletal champions were uninterested in explosions or balls of fire. They took advantage of the distraction, though, and pressed their attack against Velsquee. One blade slipped easily past the Grey Lord's guard and was only just turned aside by the plates of his enchanted armour. The second wight's sword sliced at his neck and it was only the Horned God's luck that it failed to kill him. Instead of slicing through his neck, the blade glanced off the rim of his thick gorget and tore a long, cold gash from his right jawbone to just behind his ear.

Velsquee staggered from the blow, screeching in pain at the sword's icy touch. The last of his god-stone tokens went dark, its power vanishing in a puff of smoke as it deflected the blade's deadly magic. The battle against the two enemy champions had been the hardest fight of his life; the wights were fast as serpents and ferociously skilled. He'd managed to land a number of blows against them that would have killed a living man, but the wights took little notice. In return, he'd been wounded several times, and only the quality of his wargear had saved him from certain death. As it was, an ominous sensation of cold was spreading through his body and sapping his strength. Sooner or later, his guard was going to slip, and the fight would be over.

There was nowhere to run, even if Velsquee wished it. The enemy had driven a wedge partway into the storm-walkers formation, its point aimed squarely at him. To his left and right, the *heechigar* were locked in combat with the northmen, and more storm-walkers formed a jostling wall of flesh behind him. The hafts of their polearms battered his shoulders as the *heechigar* struggled to bring them to bear.

The wights surged forwards, preparing to strike again. Suddenly, Velsquee had an idea. As the enemy champions lunged at him, the Grey Lord dropped into a crouch. The movement didn't faze the wights in the least; they simply shifted their aim and lowered the points of their blades. But now the storm-walkers behind the Grey Lord had room to bring their heavy weapons to bear, and they began hacking desperately at the skeletal warriors. The wights shifted targets effortlessly, bringing their swords up to deflect the fearsome polearms – and giving Velsquee the opportunity to attack their spindly legs.

The burning stone set in the pommel of Velsquee's blade flashed angrily as he chopped through the knees of the champion to his left. The wight toppled, still slashing and stabbing at his foes. Its black blade struck the Grey Lord's right shoulder at the same time Velsquee's sword swept down and crushed its skull. The wight's spirit uttered a despairing wail and its body collapsed into a heap of mouldering bones.

Now the tables were turned. The remaining wight was beset by three attackers, and no amount of speed and skill was enough to hold them all at bay. The skeletal warrior's blade stabbed one *heechigar* through the throat, but the second warrior's polearm crashed through the wight's left shoulder, severing the arm and shattering ribs like kindling. Velsquee surged upwards, slicing off the wight's sword arm and then chopping off the champion's head. In a fit of pure spite, he grabbed the bouncing skull with his free paw and flung it at the barbarians with a curse. The northmen immediately opposite him recoiled at the sight of their fallen champions, giving the Grey Lord a moment's respite.

The battle still raged unabated. Velsquee reckoned that the northmen had suffered the worst, but they were still stubbornly hanging on. The Grey Lord glanced about, searching for the *kreekar-gan*, but the enemy sorcerer was nowhere to be seen.

Behind him, the explosions had ceased, but part of the wooden dais was still ablaze. Velsquee spat a bitter curse at Vittrik and his damned inventions. The Skryre lord had assured him there would be no accidents. There was no sign of Vittrik or Qweeqwol from where Velsquee stood. If the human witch had failed and the old seer had fallen, the army was in dire peril indeed.

The Grey Lord turned back to the second rank of storm-walkers and grabbed the arm of one of his lieutenants. 'Push forwards!' he told the warrior. 'The northmen must be close to breaking!' He pointed to the dais. 'I'm going up there to find Lord Qweeqwol!'

The *heechigar* nodded curtly and reached for the bone whistle hanging about his neck. Velsquee pushed past the burly warrior and began working his way back through the formation. A grim sense of foreboding quickened his steps. Despite all their careful planning, something had gone terribly wrong.

Nagash focused his will and reached for the power of the *abn-i-khat*. Slowly, cautiously, he took stock of his battered body. The chain of explosions had struck him like an invisible wall of stone, smashing bones and flinging him like a child's doll to the far side of the dais. Once again, his armour had spared him from the full force of the blasts, or else his body would have most likely been torn apart.

As it was, the damage was still great. His bronze armour was scorched nearly black, and was pierced in more than a dozen places with jagged pieces of metal from the enemy's wrecked catapults. The red-hot shrapnel had wounded his corpus in ways a mere blade could not, costing him much of his magical reserves.

Slowly, unsteadily, Nagash rose to his feet. Thin tendrils of smoke curled about his ravaged frame. Flames licked at the corner of the dais where the catapults once stood. The war engines were gone; their frames had melted in the heat and the tension of their own tightly-wound springs had ripped them apart. Nothing remained of the old rat-engineer and his crews except smears of ash and a few blackened chunks of bone.

The rest of the dais was covered in smouldering bodies and melted pieces of bronze. Nagash searched among them for the rat-sorcerer. After several long minutes, the necromancer found him.

The wizard's body lay sprawled on the steps of the dais, opposite where the catapults had been sited. He was by far the oldest ratman Nagash had ever seen, with patchy white fur and a face covered in a patchwork of deep wrinkles. Like Nagash, the rat-sorcerer had been caught in a storm of red-hot shrapnel from the exploding catapults. Despite the many protective talismans wrapped about his robed body, a single piece of metal about a foot long had penetrated the sorcerer's wards and lodged in his neck. His blood spread like a crimson carpet down the dais's wooden steps. The sorcerer's eyes, made from polished orbs of burning stone, fixed Nagash with twin pinpoints of cold green light. Hungrily, the necromancer reached for one.

A scuff of claws on wood brought Nagash's head around just in time to see the enemy warlord rushing at him, his curved sword held high. The necromancer surged to his feet, bringing up his obsidian sword just in time to block the ratman's downwards blow. The force of the impact drove Nagash back a step, nearly sending him tumbling down the steps of the dais.

The enemy warlord was a fearsome figure at close quarters, his fine bronze armour streaked with blood and hung with a half-dozen charred magic tokens. His scarred face was contorted in a mask of pure, bestial rage as he unleashed a storm of terrible blows against Nagash's head and upper chest. The warlord's skill with the blade was great, and the necromancer, in his weakened state, was hard-pressed to match him.

Nagash tried to drive the ratman back, feinting at his face and then slashing quickly at his legs. The obsidian blade rang against the warlord's armour but its magic turned the sword aside. The ratman refused to give ground, however. With a vicious curse he took the blow on his leg and chopped down with his sword. The magic blade sheared through the necromancer's weakened armour and buried itself in his left shoulder.

The necromancer reeled from the blow. Darkness seeped back into the corners of his eyes. Without thinking, he reached up with his left hand and seized the warlord's sword wrist. Snarling, he turned in place, pulling the warlord off his feet and throwing him down the steps of the dais. The ratman lost his grip on his sword and landed hard, sprawling onto his back.

Nagash reached up and pulled the warlord's blade free from his shoulder. Casting it contemptuously aside, the necromancer glared coldly at his foe. The ratman was struggling to stand, though it was clear that he was in terrible pain.

It was a pity there wasn't time to savour the moment. Nagash raised his hand, calling upon one last mote of power. At the bottom of the dais, the warlord looked up at the necromancer. An expression of shock registered on the ratman's face, and then he ducked, covering his head with his arms.

Nagash laughed at the warlord's futile attempt to save himself. He was still laughing when the glowing green orb struck the dais just behind him.

Green flames were spreading swiftly along the wooden steps by the time Eekrit and Eshreegar reached the edge of the dais. Shielding his face against the heat, Eekrit squinted into the blaze in search of the *kreekar-gan*'s body. Other than some scraps of charred leather and some blobs of molten bronze, there was no sign of him. The burning man had vanished.

'You missed!' the warlord snarled.

The Master of Treacheries scowled at Eekrit. 'I tried to tell you those orbs are heavier than they look, but you wouldn't listen.'

Around them, the *heechigar* were skirting the flames and rushing to Velsquee's side. Off in the distance, towards the upper branch-tunnels, the sounds of battle were growing more intense.

'See if you can find the rest of our raiders and get them heading into the lower levels,' Eekrit said. 'Be quick. We don't have much time.'

Eshreegar nodded and vanished silently into the shadows. Moments later the storm-walkers returned, carrying Velsquee on a makeshift stretcher made from the Grey Lord's cloak and two polearm hafts. Despite his pain, when he caught sight of Eekrit he tried vainly to pull himself upright.

'What in the Horned God's name are you doing here?' Velsquee rasped. 'You're under-under arrest!'

'It's well for you that I'm not, my lord,' Eekrit answered coolly. 'Another moment and you would have been dead.'

The Grey Lord glared at him. 'You were guarded by a dozen *heechigar*. How did you possibly escape?'

Eekrit flicked his tail smugly. 'How else? I bribed them with more gold than they'd earn in a lifetime,' he answered. 'Storm-walkers or no, they were still skaven and every child of the Horned God has his price.' He folded his arms. 'We had to fight our way through a barbarian warband that was blocking the lower branch-tunnels. We finally drove them back, but by then it was too late. We saw the explosions and ran to the dais as fast as we could.'

'What happened to the *kreekar-gan*? Did-did you destroy him?'

Reluctantly, Eekrit shook his head. 'When Eshreegar found an unbroken fire-globe at the bottom of the far side of the dais, we thought we had our chance. I've no doubt we hurt him, but somehow he escaped.'

'How-how can you be so sure?' Velsquee demanded.

'Because the damned corpses are still fighting,' Eekrit snapped. They're all over the mine shaft. Our warriors are in full retreat. If we don't get out of here right now, we're going to be cut off from the under-fortress.'

'No!' Velsquee protested. 'We-we can hold them here!'

'That's exactly what the burning man wants you to think,' Eekrit shot back. 'We have to withdraw, while we can still salvage this situation. Otherwise, the *kreekar-gan* could drive us from the mountain entirely.'

For a moment, Velsquee looked as though he was going to argue further, but then his body was wracked with a spasm of pain that left him gasping and semi-conscious. The Grey Lord lay back against the stretcher. It was a few moments before he could master himself enough to speak.

'The army is yours, Warlord Eekrit,' Velsquee told him. 'Do as you see fit.'

Eekrit drew a deep breath. From this moment forwards, the decision to retreat would be laid squarely on his shoulders. Even half-delirious from pain, Velsquee was careful to cover his own tail. Gritting his teeth, he bowed to the Grey Lord, then turned to the storm-walkers.

'You,' he said to one of them. 'Find a pack leader with a whistle and tell him to sound the retreat. The rest of you carry Lord Velsquee to the under-fortress and find him a healer. Go!'

The *heechigar* obeyed with gratifying speed. In moments, Eekrit was alone on the burning dais, tasting ashes on his tongue. The battle was lost and possibly the war as well. Much depended on how steep a price the burning man had paid for his victory.

Thinking bitter thoughts, the warlord turned to leave. Just as he did so, something stirred beneath a pile of dead slave rats just a few feet to his right.

Eekrit's paw flew to the hilt of his sword. There was a high-pitched moan from the pile of corpses, then a pair of bodies rolled away to reveal the burnt and bloody face of Lord Hiirc.

'Is-is he gone?' Hiirc asked. The skaven lord clawed his way out from under the pile of bodies, his eyes darting frantically around the dais. 'The-the burning man. Is he gone?'

The warlord stared at Hiirc in surprise. Slowly, his eyes narrowed. 'Oh, yes,' he said. 'The *kreekar-gan* has fled. There's no one here now but you and I.'

'Thank the Horned One,' Hiirc exclaimed, too rattled to recognise Eekrit's voice. He let out a fearful groan as he turned away from the warlord and took in the devastation around him.

'Listen carefully,' he said to Eekrit. 'When we get back to the under-fortress, you must tell everyone that I fought the burning man.' Hiirc nodded to himself. 'Yes. I *fought* him, and-and I was *winning*. But then that fool Vittrik dropped one of the fire-globes, and the blast knocked me out.' He turned back to Eekrit. 'You can remember that, can't you?'

The skaven lord froze. His eyes widened as he recognised at last whom he was speaking to.

Eekrit smiled cruelly. 'Oh, yes. I'll remember every word.' He took a step towards Hiirc, his blade rising slowly. 'By the time I'm done, they'll be talking about your heroic death from here all the way back to the Great City.'

TWELVE

CHILDREN OF A HUNGRY GOD

The Golden Plain,
in the 101st year of Sokth the Merciless
(-1265 Imperial Reckoning)

The bani-al-Hashim rode northwards for nearly a week, beyond the abandoned farmlands and into wild country where few Lahmians had ever dared tread. They moved only at night and burned no fires, eating unleavened bread and sleeping on the cold ground, because that was the tradition the *bani* had brought with them out of the desert. In ancient times, the children of the desert had to be wary of gathering in great numbers, lest they draw the attention of their many foes.

By the time Faisr al-Hashim and his people reached the rolling foothills along the northern edge of the great plain, there was already a vast city of brightly coloured tents pitched along the grassy slopes, their roofs rippling like banners in the chilly autumn wind. Dawn was breaking and herds of lean-limbed horses were stirring in the lower meadows; their guardians, keen-eyed youngsters armed with javelin and bow, straightened in their saddles and nudged their charges out of the path of the new arrivals. Faisr and his warriors, nearly a hundred in all, nodded to the young men and women as they passed, and favoured their herds with a polite degree of predatory interest. The sentries puffed out their chests and accepted the compliments with raised lances and their best, most intimidating stares.

Alcadizzar rode alongside Faisr al-Hashim and nodded solemnly at the sentries as the *bani-al-Hashim* went by. He was dressed in layered desert robes and a chequered headscarf like the rest of the tribe's warriors and after twenty years among the desert raiders he sat in the saddle nearly as well as they. If the youngsters realised he wasn't a true son of the desert, they gave no sign of it.

As they left the last of the herds behind, the prince turned his full attention to the vast tent city spread out before him. Older women and mothers in dark robes were already stirring, coaxing the cook-fires back to life and making preparations for the morning meal. Young children were dashing among the narrow lanes, fetching wood or water. Dogs raised their heads and barked wildly, warning their masters of the *bani-al-Hashim's* arrival.

'Ah, curse the luck,' Faisr muttered as he surveyed the vast assembly of tents. Like Alcadizzar and the rest of the warriors, the lean desert raider was swathed in heavy robes of black and dark blue to keep out the morning chill. His headscarf hung loosely about his shoulders, leaving his bearded face bare. Cold or no, one did not approach a gathering of tents with one's face covered, unless one meant to spill blood.

Faisr winced. 'We're the last to arrive. That's a dozen pieces of gold I owe Muktil, the old thief.'

Alcadizzar chuckled. 'Give him two dozen, then, for pity's sake. When was the last time he rode against the caravans? We're late because we were busy filling our bags with Lahmian gold.'

Faisr threw back his head and laughed, his dark eyes sparkling. 'True enough! And maybe I'll have you give him the coin, just to watch him squirm.'

Every one of Faisr's warriors sported clinking bags of coin and rich ornaments, from jewelled daggers to gold earrings, worn to catch the eye of prospective mates and to show the gathered tribes how the *bani-al-Hashim* had prospered since they'd last met. Over the last twenty-five years, the tribe had gone from near-extinction to one of the wealthiest and most famous of the desert clans. Though the *al-Hashim* bloodline was an ancient and venerated one, it had fallen on ill luck over the last few generations. Faisr al-Hashim, the only son of the last chieftain, had a reputation of recklessness and impetuosity – both counted as virtues among the desert clans, but not exactly the best qualities one wanted in a leader of men. His time as chieftain might have been brilliant and altogether brief had it not been for his chance meeting with Alcadizzar. The prince could counsel the hot-headed bandit leader in ways that a tribesman would have never dared to do, and his knowledge of Lahmian military tactics was worth its weight in gold. With a relatively small number of fighting men, the *bani-al-Hashim* had gone on to perform a string of brilliant raids that were the envy of the rest of the tribes.

'Where do we fit into all this?' Alcadizzar asked, waving his hand at the tents.

Faisr nodded proudly towards the centre of the sprawling settlement. 'A space will have been left for us, close to the chieftain's tent. We'll rest and take our breakfast while the women and children make camp, then there will be horse races and games of dice until the gathering this evening.' He winked at the prince. 'And drinking. *Lots* of drinking.'

Alcadizzar's nose wrinkled. 'Not *chanouri,* I hope. I'd rather drink salt water.' The desert raiders' favourite libation was a mix of fermented mare's milk and sour date wine. He had tried it once, on a dare, and was sick for hours afterwards.

'Effete city dweller,' Faisr waved a hand disdainfully. 'I suppose we can persuade a child to part with his wineskin so you don't go thirsty.' The chieftain turned and regarded Alcadizzar thoughtfully. 'Are you certain you want to go through with this?'

The question surprised Alcadizzar. '*Me*? All I'm risking is my life. You've got much more to lose than I.'

'Hmph,' Faisr replied, but didn't deny the prince's assertion. If Alcadizzar failed the trials to come, Faisr would lose face among his fellow chieftains. That was a fate much worse than death.

The long procession of riders edged their way slowly into the sprawling settlement. Mothers watched the mounted warriors with wary interest, while the children gawped and pointed at the glittering trophies the riders wore. Faisr nodded respectfully to the elders he met along the way, guiding the procession unerringly down the close-set lanes. Each tribe's place in the settlement was determined by its status and relative strength, with the most prominent tribes closest to the gathering tent at the centre of the camp.

There had been many gatherings since Alcadizzar had joined Faisr's band, but this was the first that he had ever been permitted to attend. The prince studied every detail of the great camp, trying to gauge the power and prosperity of the tribes. He knew from Faisr that there were nearly two-score tribes of varying size living on the great plain, moving constantly to confuse would-be enemies of their size and strength. Here, Alcadizzar counted tents, jugs of water and loaves of bread being laid out for the morning meal. He then weighed that against the number of horses grazing the fields below to separate the women and children from the fighting men. Even by a conservative estimate, the numbers surprised him. There weren't hundreds, but *thousands* of them – a force to be reckoned with, in the right hands.

There was still much about the tribes that he did not know. Though he was Faisr's most valued lieutenant, the chieftain was careful to keep tribal business and tradition to himself. For all of his contributions to the welfare of the tribe, Alcadizzar had remained an outsider.

Not that the past decades had been a total loss. The tribesmen were wary about their own politics, but made free with news about the Lahmians. The atmosphere within the city grew more nightmarish and oppressive with each passing year. More and more citizens were disappearing in the night and all manner of outlandish stories were being told in the wine houses. It wasn't enough to stay off the streets after sunset; now people were being taken right from their very homes, never to be seen again. Only the aristocracy seemed to be safe, which naturally fomented all sorts of suspicious rumours in the poorer quarters of the city.

The plague of disappearances had grown so severe that it was even having repercussions on Lahmia's economy. Fewer and fewer caravans made the journey to the city each year, and those that did rarely stayed for long. The slums were emptying out as well, depriving the docks of their labour force.

The exodus had grown so severe that the government was now imposing a substantial 'departure tax' on citizens attempting to leave the city for any reason. Once the greatest city in Nehekhara, now Lahmia's citizens lived as virtual prisoners within its walls.

The reign of terror that gripped Lahmia hadn't gone unnoticed by the other great cities, of course, but a few chilling stories and the misery of the common folk weren't enough to provoke the other kings to war. Neferata's puppet rulers managed the dance of trade and diplomacy as well as ever, playing the other cities against one another and keeping them too off-balance to risk an open confrontation with Lahmia. Alcadizzar kept in regular contact with his brother, apprising King Asar of everything he learned about the goings-on inside the city, but the word from Rasetra was always the same: *give me evidence.*

Slipping inside the city now would be dangerous in the extreme; escaping Lahmia with damning evidence of Neferata's crimes would be nearly impossible. Alcadizzar knew that the desert tribes had ways of getting word to and from their kinfolk within the city walls, but such secrets were not shared with outsiders.

That would change tonight, Alcadizzar vowed to himself.

True to Faisr's word, the tribe had a spot reserved for them: a great square of sunlit hill-slope just north and east of a vast meeting tent of dark blue linen. In keeping with tradition, Faisr and his warriors ringed the open space and remained in their saddles while the tribe's women and children dismounted and unpacked the tents. In less than an hour, the first tent poles were going up, and the thudding of wooden mallets filled the air. Faisr's tent went up first, followed by those of his lieutenants, and then the rest of the tribe. Finally, the *ani mukta,* the oldest mother of the tribe, called out that the camp was ready and the desert warriors eagerly dismounted.

By that point, a crowd of men from the other tribes had gathered around the *bani-al-Hashim,* standing a polite distance outside the perimeter of horsemen and shouting greetings and friendly jibes to Faisr's men. When the old mother dismissed the menfolk a cheer went up from the crowd; the tribesmen came forwards to embrace Faisr and his kinfolk, and the celebrations began in earnest.

The tribesmen spent the rest of the day outside the sprawling camp, lounging on ancient rugs down by the grazing herds. Faisr and the other tribal chiefs shared bulging skins of date wine and *chanouri,* and boasted of the daring raids they'd made against the city dwellers over the last few months. Boys and girls were sent down to the herds to fetch horses for the men to admire and haggle over, while young maidens came and went bearing platters of flatbread, cheese and olives. Laughter and rude jokes filled the air. Men had their best horses brought up from the herds and soon the ground shook with the pounding of hooves as they raced back and forth across the slope. Cups of dice were produced and bags of finger bones, and fortunes were gained and lost. Alcadizzar kept to a corner of the vast rug laid out for Faisr and his personal guests and sipped sparingly from a small skin of wine. He pretended to admire the new horses born to the tribal chiefs and offered a cheer or two when one of the *bani-al-Hashim* took part in a race, but mostly he sat back and observed the people around him.

Alcadizzar noted that most of the chiefs drank little and gambled not at all. Though they talked and joked as raucously as their warriors, their dark eyes were keen and wary. They studied the herds of their peers, gauging their strengths and weaknesses. Alliances were made over the purchase of colts, or the arrangement of breeding rights. Lesser chiefs came and went, kneeling and kissing the rough hem of the ancient rugs before they sat beside their betters. Perhaps half a dozen younger chieftains sat around the edge of Faisr's rug, enjoying his hospitality and offering him gifts of friendship. By comparison, the rug next to Faisr's belonged to Bashir al-Rukhba, currently the richest and most powerful of the desert chiefs. There were more than a dozen men crowding one another upon the great rug, each one vying for the great chieftain's attention. Bashir sat in the centre of it all with a look of mild agitation on his bearded face. When he tired of someone's presence he waved a hand at one of his three lieutenants, who shooed the lesser chieftain away like a mother would chase off an especially stubborn crow.

By the end of the day, Alcadizzar knew several important things. Firstly, that Faisr al-Hashim, while admired by the younger chiefs, had little in the way of political influence among the tribes. Bashir, whom Alcadizzar knew by reputation to have once been a formidable raider, held sway over the others by virtue of the size of his retinue and the wealth he'd pain-stakingly acquired. Also, judging by the way Bashir studiously ignored Faisr during the afternoon, it was apparent that there was little love lost between the two men. If the state of affairs troubled Faisr at all, he was careful not to show it.

Finally, as the sun began to settle to the west, a stir went through the assembled warriors. Alcadizzar straightened, just as the lesser chiefs all rose in a great flock and took their leave of Bashir, Faisr and the rest of the great chieftains. The prince looked about, frowning in bemusement – and then saw the dark-robed figure approaching the rug of Bashir al-Rukhba.

The man was tall, and moved with strength and purpose. He was clad in black desert robes, shot through with golden thread that shimmered in the mellowing sunlight. He carried no weapons, which surprised Alcadizzar, for that was a badge of manhood among the tribes. What was more, his face was covered, but not in a conventional fashion. His headscarf had been wrapped loosely about his head to form a kind of hood, and a thin veil of black silk covered his entire face. In his hands, he carried a large, ornate goblet made of gold. The sight of it stirred memories that made the prince's hair stand on end. He caught himself just before his hand closed on the hilt of his sword and forced himself to relax.

Alcadizzar glanced over at Faisr. When he'd caught the young chieftain's eye, he whispered, 'Who is that?'

The lesser chieftains stared at Alcadizzar as though he were a fool. Faisr scowled. 'The chosen of Khsar, the Hungry God. He serves the Daughter of the Sands.'

'Who?'

Faisr waved his hand in agitation. 'Hush!' he warned, and said no more.

The chosen man made no obeisance to Bashir; rather, he stood at the edge of the chieftain's rug and the great chief came to him, edging his way across the ancient mat. He bowed deeply, touching his forehead to the hem of the rug and the hooded man bent, offering his cup. Bashir straightened, accepting the goblet and taking a small sip of its contents. As he did, the chosen one murmured something and the great chief nodded in return.

Then it was Faisr's turn. The hooded man approached and Alcadizzar's chieftain edged forwards. He bowed and accepted the goblet, and the priest spoke softly to him. The words were in the tongue of the desert people, too soft for the prince to make out. Faisr nodded, and murmured a short reply. For a moment, Alcadizzar felt the weight of the chosen one's stare, and then he moved on to the next chieftain in line.

Faisr rose without a word and his lieutenants followed suit. Alcadizzar's head swam with questions, but he knew that this was neither the time nor the place to ask them. Bashir and his retinue were already heading back up the slope towards the settlement; the day's festivities were clearly at an end.

Alcadizzar fell in beside Faisr. After they'd walked for a bit, the prince turned to the chieftain. 'What happens now?' he asked quietly.

Faisr grinned. Despite having drunk his weight in spirits, his steps were swift and sure. 'We prepare for the gathering. Then the fun really begins.'

Alcadizzar nodded. He jerked his chin at Bashir, who was striding among his retinue some way ahead. 'He doesn't like you very much.'

'You noticed?'

'He wasn't exactly subtle,' Alcadizzar replied. 'Will he be a problem?'

Faisr chuckled grimly. 'Oh, yes,' he said. 'You may count upon it. Don't take it too personally, though; he just wants to try and keep me in my place.'

'He's going to try to have me killed. How do I not take that personally?'

Faisr laughed and clapped the prince on the shoulder. 'This is a world of suffering and strife, my friend. Death surrounds us every day. Would you rather be known as a man who died choking on a olive pit, or one who perished at the hand of an assassin, struck down by the order of Bashir al-Rukhba?'

Alcadizzar frowned. 'I would rather be known as a man who lived a long and happy life, surrounded by his wife and children in a richly-furnished mansion.'

The desert chieftain sighed. 'You city dwellers,' he said, shaking his head bemusedly, 'have some strange notions about life.'

They dressed in their finest robes for the gathering of chiefs. Faisr gifted Alcadizzar with new garments of fine, white linen, and an over-robe of midnight-blue silk plundered during a raid a few months earlier. Outside, darkness settled over the tents, and in the distance, groups of young girls paced the perimeter of the camp on horseback, shaking silver bells and singing to the face of the rising moon to keep the evils of the night at bay.

Faisr raised a warning hand as Alcadizzar reached for his sword. 'We carry no weapons,' he said solemnly. 'You may wear a dagger, to cut meat or settle the odd quarrel, but nothing more. If you need a blade later, we'll send for it.'

Alcadizzar swallowed his misgivings and nodded, tucking his jewelled knife into his belt. He straightened, and Faisr studied him intently for a moment, making certain that nothing was amiss. The chieftain nodded. 'It will serve,' he declared, then his expression turned grave. 'I must ask, are you certain you wish to proceed? There is no shame in withdrawing at this point. You can stay here in the tent until the end of the gathering, and tomorrow things will be no different between us.'

The prince sighed. He wanted to tell Faisr that there was nothing the chiefs could do to him that was any worse than what he'd endured in the gardens of the Temple of Blood. Instead, he waved impatiently at the tent flap. 'Lead on.'

Faisr bowed, favouring Alcadizzar with a dazzling smile. 'As you wish, my friend.'

The chieftain led Alcadizzar out into the cold night. The sky was clear and bright with starlight. Neru's face was full and bright, shining her blessings down upon the camp. Sounds of revelry drifted through the air from the surrounding tents; muted laughter and women's voices mingled with the chanting songs of the desert. The prince drank in the sounds and the smells of smoke, leather and canvas, and smiled contentedly. It felt more like home to him than any palace or mansion ever had.

The gathering tent loomed large in the darkness. Two smaller tents had been pitched to either side of its single entrance, flaps drawn back on all four sides and lashed down in 'caravan fashion', so those within had a clear field of view in every direction. Rugs had been laid down in each, and small braziers had been lit to keep the night's chill at bay. Nearly a score of tribesmen took their ease beneath the tents, sampling platters of food and drinking wine offered to them by demure maidens. More desert warriors milled about in small groups outside, speaking to one another in low tones. They all turned and bowed their heads in respect as Faisr went by.

'Wait here for a time,' the desert chieftain said, indicating the caravan tent to his right. 'Eat and drink, or don't, as it suits you. Once the business of the night is done, I'll send for you.' Without waiting for a reply, Faisr ducked his head and stepped inside the gathering tent.

Alcadizzar watched Faisr disappear from sight and suppressed a sigh of irritation. The desert gatherings apparently shared one thing in common with the courts of Nehekhara; both involved a lot of sitting around and waiting. Scowling, he found a clear patch of rug inside the tent and settled upon it. A young girl edged towards him at once, holding out a bowl of sour-smelling *chanouri*. The prince held up a hand so the girl wouldn't see him wince. 'Perhaps a bit of watered wine?' he asked.

And so the prince waited, watching Neru chart her course across the sky as the hours passed. His neighbours mostly kept to themselves, their minds intent on whatever grievance or request they intended to present to the gathered chiefs. Within the tent came a steady drone of muted conversation, punctuated by the occasional shout or peal of laughter. Once, Alcadizzar heard angry shouts break out and for a moment he thought a riot had erupted amid the gathering, but the other tribesmen paid the noise little mind, and within a few minutes the disturbance had subsided as quickly as it had begun.

One by one, the men seated around him were summoned into the presence of the chiefs. Some audiences lasted longer than others and nearly always the men emerged with stoic faces, giving no sign as to whether their wishes had been honoured or not. Once, a pair of black-robed men emerged from the tent, half-carrying one of the petitioners. The tribesman was doubled over in pain, one hand pressed against his belly. Blood ran freely between his clenched fingers. Alcadizzar listened to the man's muffled curses as he disappeared into the night.

By midnight, he was alone in the tent. The maidens had withdrawn and the coals in the braziers were nearly spent. The sounds of conversation within the tent showed no signs of abating. The prince sighed and sipped at his wine, wondering if Faisr had gotten so deep into his cups that he'd forgotten Alcadizzar was waiting outside.

Beyond the gathering tent, the rest of the camp had fallen silent. The night air was still and cold, luminous with the light of the full moon. Alcadizzar breathed in the chill air, grateful for the way it cleared his head and focused his senses.

Little by little, a sense of unease crept up the back of the prince's neck. He was being watched.

Alcadizzar continued to breathe deeply, careful to show no outwards sense of alarm. As his eyes searched the deep shadows beyond the empty caravan tent opposite his, he drained his watered wine and set the cup aside. He casually rested his empty hand on top of his thigh, just inches from the hilt of his dagger, and waited for his unseen observer to reveal himself.

Minutes passed, and the sensation did not abate. If anything, it seemed more focused, more intent. Alcadizzar thought he saw a flicker of movement in the shadows near the wall of the gathering tent. He shifted slightly, presenting his right shoulder to the oncoming figure. His fingertips slid to the jewelled pommel of his dagger.

There! He could see a slender figure outlined against the flank of the great tent, creeping slowly and somewhat tentatively his way. Alcadizzar could see no weapons in the figure's hands, but the sheer weight of his stare was astonishing. Was this a sorcerer, or some restless spirit that haunted the dark hills north of the great plain?

After a moment, the figure paused, still well hidden in the shadow cast by the tent. Alcadizzar felt gooseflesh race along his forearms. Finally, he could stand no more.

'I see you there,' he said, rising slowly to his feet. 'What sort of man are you, to skulk in the shadows like a jackal? Are you thief, or assassin? Show yourself!'

The figure recoiled at the sound of his voice. Alcadizzar thought he might turn and flee into the darkness – but then, the person straightened his shoulders and took a bold step forwards, into the moonlight.

Alcadizzar's eyes widened. The figure before him was short and lithe, clad in fine, black robes shot through with silver thread that shimmered faintly in the light. This was no assassin, nor a restless, hungry spirit, but a young girl of about fourteen years, her face wreathed by the folds of a silken headscarf. She had a long, coltish face and a sharp nose, and large, leonine yellow eyes. A sinuous line of henna tattoos climbed up the right side of her slender neck, and traced its way along her jawline.

The prince stared at the girl in surprise. She studied him as a scholar would an ancient scroll, as though he wore his deepest secrets upon his sleeve. Not even Neferata had reached so deeply into his soul. He tried to speak, to ask who this girl was and what she wanted with him – but just then the entry flap of the gathering tent was drawn aside, and a black-robed servant stepped out into the night. The spell broken, the girl retreated at once, slipping back silently into the shadows.

The servant, unaware of the girl's presence, beckoned to Alcadizzar. 'Faisr al-Hashim bids you to join him,' he said.

Alcadizzar searched the darkness beyond the tent, but the girl had vanished. The servant paused, his brows knitting in a frown. He started to beckon again, but Alcadizzar shook his head, as though to clear it. 'Lead on,' he replied.

The prince followed the servant into the hot, noisy gloom of the great tent. He had expected it to be sub-divided by cloth partitions into discrete chambers, as he'd seen Faisr do with his own tent; beyond the entrance was a small antechamber, where a pair of maids came forwards with golden bowls and cloths to ritually wash his feet and hands. When the ritual was done, the servant led him onwards, past another tent flap and into the presence of the chiefs.

Alcadizzar had expected a large, open space, layered in fine rugs and thick with a haze of incense, where the chiefs lounged in small cliques as they'd done earlier in the afternoon. To his surprise, he found himself standing at the edge of a circular space containing an immense wooden table, large enough to accommodate almost two-score chiefs with room to spare. The surface of the table was covered in a thin sheet of gold, hammered by the hands of an artist into curious, uneven contours. The prince stared at its surface for several moments before he realised that the play of shadow and light created by the contours suggested the rolling dunes of a desert. Long, curving lines had been etched into the gold; he knew from his studies that some of them matched the ancient caravan routes that had crossed the Great Desert in ancient times. Other lines were less obvious in their meaning. Perhaps they represented the nomadic paths of the desert tribes themselves.

The perimeter of the chamber was crowded with high-ranking tribesmen from each of the clans, who sat upon rugs and observed the proceedings with interest. The air was hot and thick, almost stifling, and spiced with the aromas of food and *chanouri*. Alcadizzar felt the eyes of the entire assembly fix on him as he followed the servant to the great table.

Faisr rose from an ornately carved chair as Alcadizzar approached and went to stand beside him. The servant indicated for the prince to stand a few feet from the edge of the table, where the gathered chiefs could take their measure of him. Alcadizzar met the gaze of each and every man seated at the table, and found not a single mote of warmth or welcome in their eyes. A few, like Bashir al-Rukhba, glared at him with obvious contempt.

Then the prince felt a familiar prickling along the back of his neck. He stiffened, his eyes drawn to the shadows on the opposite side of the great table. There, he saw the silhouette of a robed woman seated upon a wooden chair similar to those used by the chieftains. Her face was hidden in the gloom, but Alcadizzar knew she was staring at him with the same intensity as that of the girl he'd seen only minutes before. At her side stood Khsar's chosen one, the hooded man that he had seen out on the hillside that afternoon. Instead of a golden goblet, the chosen one now held a tall, black staff in his right hand. Though apart from the rest, Alcadizzar noted that there was an empty space at the table so that the woman had a clear view of the proceedings.

Faisr laid a hand on Alcadizzar's shoulder. 'Here is the man I spoke of,' he said to the assembled chiefs. 'Ubaid has ridden as a friend to the *bani-al-Hashim* for twenty years, as our customs require, and in that time he has acquitted himself as a warrior and a cunning raider. Look you the marks upon his belt,' Faisr said, pointing to the dense rows of kill-marks inscribed in the leather. 'Fifty men, dead by his hand! He has earned the esteem of my people and has shed his own blood on our behalf many times. Indeed, he has saved my life not once, but *three* times.' The young chieftain spread his hands and winked at the other chiefs. 'Of course, he still rides like a soft-arsed city dweller, but no man is perfect, eh?'

Many of the chieftains laughed and Alcadizzar accepted the jibe with a self-deprecating grin. Bashir and a handful of other chiefs just stared at Faisr, their faces set in stony masks.

'Ubaid's loyalty and honour are beyond question,' Faisr said. 'He has put aside his past and has embraced the ways of the desert. I tell you, he is like a brother to me and deserves to be a part of my tribe.'

'He is an outsider!' Bashir cried. The chieftain leaned forwards and pounded on the golden table for emphasis. 'A city dweller! For all we know, he could be a spy for the Lahmians!'

At once, Faisr's chosen men were on their feet, shaking their fists and shouting angrily at Bashir. Bashir's men quickly followed suit, yelling at Faisr's men. Daggers were drawn, their blades glinting in the lamplight. The chiefs caught in between took turns yelling at Bashir, at Faisr, and at one another.

Faisr let out a lusty shout and leapt upon the golden table. With a flourish, he drew his dagger and levelled it at Bashir. 'If any man doubts Ubaid's worth, then put him to the test! Challenge him, by wit, by blade or by horse!'

Alcadizzar saw Bashir smile hungrily at Faisr's outburst and understood that this was the opening the older chief had been waiting for. He rose from his chair, his hand reaching for his own knife – when suddenly, Khsar's chosen man stepped from the shadows and brought his staff down upon the table with a thunderous blow.

The entire crowd was struck silent in an instant. The chiefs all but leapt from their seats, their eyes wide with shock. Even Bashir looked stunned.

When the hooded man was certain that he had everyone's undivided attention, he straightened slowly and drew back his staff. Alcadizzar saw that it was thick and obviously heavy, shaped from a kind of black wood unlike anything he had seen before. The faces of monstrous spirits had been carved into the wood, their fierce, inhuman expressions contorted into masks of rage and mindless hunger.

'Hearken unto the Daughter of the Sands,' the chosen one intoned. His voice was rough and deep, rumbling like the warning growl of a lion. At once, the spectators all sank to their knees. Bashir's face paled with rage, but even he sank back into his chair. Alcadizzar hesitated, unsure how to proceed. Faisr quickly sheathed his dagger and the prince followed suit.

Slowly and painfully, the robed woman climbed from her chair. She was very old, Alcadizzar saw at once, her leathery face creased in a complex tapestry of wrinkles. As she stepped into the lamplight, the prince was startled to see that her eyes were a leonine yellow, just like those of the girl he'd seen outside.

The old woman approached the chiefs, and her eyes rose slowly to Faisr's. 'Were you raised in a wine shop, Faisr al-Hashim?' she growled. 'Get off my table, boy.'

To Alcadizzar's surprise, Faisr hung his head like a child. 'My apologies,' he said, and hopped back down onto the rugs next to Alcadizzar.

The woman's gaze turned to Alcadizzar; once again, he felt his skin prickle with the intensity of her stare. 'You say that this one has observed all the customs of adoption?'

'He has,' Faisr replied.

'He has lived among your tribe for a span of twenty years?' she asked.

'As I said before, yes,' the chieftain replied.

'He has fought at your side and shed blood for the sake of the tribe?'

'Many times.'

The old woman's eyes narrowed on the prince. 'And in all that time, he has never given you cause to doubt his loyalty, or his devotion?'

'Never once,' Faisr answered proudly.

Alcadizzar found himself struggling to meet the woman's stare. There was much that Faisr did not know about him. The chieftain was unknowingly risking his own honour on his friend's behalf.

'Has he put aside his past life,' the woman asked, in a voice as pitiless as the desert sands, 'and devoted himself entirely to the ways of our people?'

Before Faisr could answer, Alcadizzar cut in. 'As much as any man can forget his people and the place of his birth,' he said. Faisr shot him a sidelong look, but the prince ignored him.

The Daughter of the Sands stared at Alcadizzar for a long moment. 'Then let it be so,' she declared. 'From this day forwards, you are one of the *bani-al-Hashim*.'

The assembled chiefs glanced at one another in amazement. Only Bashir al-Rukhba felt bold enough – or angry enough – to speak. 'But the customs of adoption are meant only for desert dwellers!' he protested. 'They are for adopting a man of one tribe into another, not... not this!'

The old woman turned and glared at Bashir. 'An exception was made once before, Bashir al-Rukhba,' she said coldly. 'Or have you forgotten?'

Bashir stiffened. 'I have not,' he replied.

'Then you must presume to know the will of Khsar better than I,' the old woman snapped. 'Is that so? Do you mean to gainsay me?'

All at once, the air in the tent was fraught with tension. Alcadizzar saw Bashir's warriors shrink back from their chief, their expressions stiff with fright.

Bashir's gaze fell to the tabletop. 'No,' he answered in a subdued voice. 'I would never do such a thing, holy one.'

'Then our business here is concluded,' said the Daughter of the Sands. 'The hour is late and my bones ache. Let an old woman have her rest.'

As one, the chieftains rose from the table. Nervous murmurs rose from their warriors. The atmosphere was still tense and unsettled. Something momentous had happened, Alcadizzar knew, but he had no idea what. His thoughts were interrupted by a tug on his sleeve.

'It's done,' Faisr said. For the first time since Alcadizzar had met him, the chieftain sounded shaken. 'Let's go.'

Alcadizzar turned to follow Faisr from the tent. As he went, he once again felt the stares of the entire assembly upon him, but they were as light as a feather compared to the weight of the old woman's gaze upon his back. It took an effort of will not to hasten his steps and run headlong into the night.

Faisr and Alcadizzar were quickly surrounded by members of the tribe as they departed the great tent. A few offered quiet congratulations, but most were silent as Faisr led them all back to the tribe's tents. Once there, some of the older tribesmen began stoking a fire and rousing their youngest sons to fetch wine and *chanouri*. Across the camp, the rest of the tribes seemed to be following suit, hewing to tradition and indulging in one last celebration before they scattered to the winds on the morrow.

But Faisr was in no mood to celebrate. The chieftain stood for a moment, staring into the depths of the fire his warriors were coaxing to life, then plucked a wineskin from a passing boy and stalked off into the darkness. Without thinking, Alcadizzar followed.

Faisr said nothing as he made his way through the camp. He avoided the tents of the great clans and their fire-lit gatherings, and before long he emerged from the camp onto the hillside's lower slopes. He led Alcadizzar down the hill towards the silent horse herds, finally settling down on the cold, damp ground not far from where they had lounged just twelve hours before.

The chieftain acknowledged the herd's sentry riders with a wave of his hand, then pulled the stopper from the wineskin and passed it to Alcadizzar. The prince took it and squirted a swallow's worth into his mouth, then handed it back.

'I take it that didn't go as planned,' he said.

Faisr chuckled ruefully. 'Observant as ever,' the chieftain replied, and filled his mouth with wine. He gulped it down and drank again.

'Who was that woman?' Alcadizzar asked. 'A priestess of some kind?'

The chieftain let out a snort. 'The tribes have never had much use for priests,' he said. 'Instead, we have the Daughter of the Sands. She is given to Khsar, the god of the wastelands, as his bride. She is the arbiter of his laws, and when she speaks, it is with his voice. Do you understand?'

Alcadizzar frowned. 'Yes, but...' He chose his words with care, uncertain how devout Faisr was, not wishing to cause offence. 'The covenant with the gods was broken centuries ago.'

Faisr shook his head. 'Forget about the covenant. That was made between the gods and *your* people, the Nehekharans.'

The prince nodded thoughtfully. Many Nehekharans thought of the desert folk as barbaric cousins, but the truth was that they were an entirely different race of men, whose history and culture stretched back thousands of years before the birth of the great cities.

'So... the tribes still enjoy the blessings of Khsar?'

Faisr threw back his head and laughed. 'Blessings? If Khsar doesn't burn your eyes from your head or suck the marrow from your bones, that's a blessing,' he said. 'He is the god of the desert. His breath gives life to sandstorms. The Hungry God gives no blessings, Ubaid. Only tests. By those tests we are made strong, or else we perish. There is nothing else.'

Alcadizzar spread his hands. 'Then... what? Am I being tested?'

Faisr didn't reply at first. He frowned up at the sky and then took another drink. 'It's possible,' he said. 'Or perhaps there is a test yet to come.'

'I don't understand.'

The chieftain sighed. 'Once in every generation, a daughter is born to the tribes with the eyes of a desert lion. It has always been thus. Such women have the ability to look into a man's soul and see what the fates have written there. For that reason alone, they have great influence among our people.'

The thought sent a chill down Alcadizzar's spine. 'When I was waiting in the caravan tent outside, I saw a girl with those same eyes,' he said softly.

Faisr gave him a startled look. 'You didn't touch her, did you?'

'What kind of question is that?'

The chieftain relaxed slightly. 'Forgive me. It's just that it's considered terrible luck to lay hands on one of Khsar's chosen.' He sighed. 'That would have been Ophiria. She will become the Daughter of the Sands when Suleima dies. Did she say anything to you?'

Alcadizzar shook his head. 'No, but I will remember those eyes for the rest of my life.'

Faisr shook his head. 'In all my time as chieftain, I've never known Suleima to take a hand in tribal matters. Now, in a single stroke, she affirms your adoption into the tribes and upsets the old order of the chiefs. Rebuking Bashir like that will cost the old jackal dearly.'

'The Daughter of the Sands has that much power over the chiefs?'

Faisr shrugged. 'These days, yes. It wasn't always so. The Daughter of the Sands used to serve as an advisor to the *alcazzar*, the chief of chiefs, but there hasn't been one of those since Shahid the Red Fox died during the war against the Usurper.' The chieftain shook his head. 'The seers were the reason that the tribes came here from the desert, centuries ago.'

Alcadizzar stared at Faisr, his curiosity piqued. 'Why is that?'

Faisr glanced over at the prince and started to reply, but then appeared to think better of it. 'That's a tale for another time,' he said with a tired grin. 'Too many revelations might spoil the wine, eh, Ubaid?'

Faisr raised the wineskin to his lips and took a deep draught, but Alcadizzar caught the haunted look in the chieftain's eye nonetheless.

Alcadizzar looked away, out over the sleeping herds. What had Ophiria and the old woman seen when they looked at him? How much did they know? The words of Faisr came back to him once more.

The Hungry God gives no blessings, only tests. By those tests we are made strong, or we perish. There is nothing else.

THIRTEEN

THE PRICE OF VICTORY

Nagashizzar,
in the 102nd year of Tahoth the Wise
(-1250 Imperial Reckoning)

'When is Lord Velsquee coming back?'

Eekrit sighed, rubbing a paw wearily over his eyes. He didn't like where this conversation was heading. 'Four months, if he encounters no trouble. Why?'

'Because the *kreekar-gan* is getting ready to attack.'

The warlord beckoned with a claw and a trio of slave rats scuttled from the shadows of the throne room. Two of the slaves carried a carved wooden chair between them, which they set on the rug-covered floor behind Eshreegar. The Master of Treacheries nodded his head to Eekrit in thanks and took a seat. Of all the skaven left in the under-fortress, he alone was permitted to sit while Eekrit presided from the throne. The third slave climbed the dais with a golden tray bearing two bowls of wine. The warlord chose one bowl for himself and then the slave served Eshreegar the other.

Eekrit's whiskers twitched as he breathed in the wine's heady vapours. 'You've been wrong in the past,' he pointed out. 'Sometimes *spectacularly* so.'

'As you never cease to remind me,' Eshreegar replied. He swirled the dark liquid in his bowl for a moment, then drained half the contents in one long draught and wiped his whiskers clean on his sleeve. 'The signs are there, nonetheless.'

'Such as?'

Eshreegar frowned at the warlord. 'Spear companies, for a start. Some of my scouts went over the barricades a few nights ago and got as far as mine shaft two. The ones that made it back said there were four or five companies of bone-men there. Looked like they'd just arrived recently.'

Eekrit shifted uncomfortably on the throne. 'How recently?'

The Master of Treacheries finished off his drink and beckoned for another. 'There was no mould on the bones or wrappings, so they couldn't have been in the lower tunnels for more than a day or two.' The air in the active mine shafts was so hot and humid that mould was a constant problem.

'Not a good sign, I grant you.'

'There's more.' Eshreegar turned to an approaching servant and traded his empty bowl for a full one. 'One of the survivors said he saw at least two war engines at the far end of the mine shaft. Big ones.'

Eekrit winced. 'Any chance he could have been mistaken?'

'Not likely. It was Joreel who spotted them. You remember him, don't you? He was one of the old hands.'

The warlord's tail lashed irritably. 'Yes, I remember Joreel, damn it. It hasn't been *that* long.'

Eshreegar snorted. 'Thirty-five years, almost to the day,' he said. He carefully avoided making eye contact with the warlord, but the tone in his voice said it all. *Much has changed since then.*

Indeed it had, Eekrit thought bitterly. With Velsquee incapacitated by his injuries and Hiirc dead, the task of saving the army had rested entirely in Eekrit's paws. The days following the failed ambush at mine shaft four had been a nightmarish ordeal of chaos, confusion and death. By the time he had managed to convince the surviving clan lords of his authority and organise a credible defence against the burning man's attacks, the skaven had been driven all the way back to mine shaft eight, and almost half of the army had been destroyed. Even worse was the loss of materiel; for all intents and purposes, the army's entire baggage train had been captured or destroyed when mine shaft four had been overrun. Even with access to merchants at the under-fortress, the army would have a hard enough time feeding itself in the near term, much less fighting the enemy.

Weeks passed before Eekrit was able to return to the under-fortress, only to find Velsquee gone. The official explanation was that his injuries required the attentions of the best chirurgeons in the Great City, but it was obvious to Eekrit that the Grey Lord was trying to get as much distance from the debacle as he could. Velsquee would make certain that the blame for the defeat rested squarely on Eekrit's shoulders. It was the skaven way.

Eekrit fought back the only way he could – by making certain that regular shipments of god-stone found their way to the Great City. He still clung stubbornly to the notion that the *kreekar-gan* could be defeated and then the mountain would be his. So he endured Velsquee's expert slanders and the inevitable disgrace that the Council heaped upon him. He knew that he could never go back home, at least not until he was wealthy enough to reform his image.

The warlord also went out of his way to publicly thank Velsquee for his many years of helpful 'advice' during the long war, plus his continued support for the expeditionary force – whether such support still existed or not. Eekrit even went so far as to hire an orator to deliver a grandiloquent speech to the Council of Thirteen to commemorate the day that the army first departed from the Great City, and went to great length to extol Velsquee's virtues as a warrior and a leader. Finally, he made sure that the Grey Lord received a regular allotment of god-stone from the mines and made very sure that the other lords on the Council knew about it.

Velsquee got the message. His fortunes were tied to the great mountain, whether he wanted it or not, so it was in his best interests to support the expeditionary force as much as possible.

The fact was, Eekrit needed all the support he could get. The great clans had grown weary of the long war beneath the mountain; many had lost so much blood and treasure over the last forty years that their positions on the Council had become vulnerable. In the months and years following the defeat at mine shaft four, the alliance of clans that made up the expeditionary force began to unravel. Clan Morbus was the first to withdraw its warriors, followed by the survivors of Clan Skryre soon after. Eekrit hadn't the power or influence to stop them. All he could do was try to lure as many of the lesser clans as he could to take their place, plus whatever mercenaries his depleted fortunes permitted.

All the while, the *kreekar-gan* continued to batter away at the skaven. With new stores of god-stone in his possession, he hurled wave after wave of skeletons and flesh-hungry corpses against Eekrit's defences. The days of digging murder holes and launching bold flanking moves were long gone. The most Eekrit could do was hold what he had and inflict as many losses on the enemy as possible.

His warriors destroyed the enemy by the hundreds, but it was never enough. The burning man never relented. As his losses mounted, Eekrit was forced to surrender one mine shaft after another. Slowly but surely, the skaven were being driven from the mountain.

All they had left now was mine shaft twelve. If that fell, the enemy would be at the tunnels to the under-fortress itself.

Eekrit drank deep from his bowl. 'It's just four months,' he said, swirling the bitter dregs. 'We can hold.'

'With what?' Eshreegar said. 'I wouldn't give a ratling's fart for half the hired swords you've got manning the barricades. The instant one of those bone-engines comes charging down on them, they'll turn tail and won't stop running until they reach the Great City. Then all you'll have left are a few thousand poorly-armed clanrats and whatever slave packs you can scrounge.'

The warlord's paw tightened on the wine bowl. 'We'll collapse the upper branch-tunnels if we have to. That should slow them down a bit.'

Eshreegar shook his head irritably. 'You'll just be delaying the inevitable.'

Eekrit scowled at the Master of Treacheries. 'I don't think so,' he snapped. 'The *kreekar-gan* has all but one of the mountain's mine shafts under his control. With that much power he should have crushed us years ago. Why hasn't he?' The warlord shook his head. 'I don't think he's as strong as he wants us to believe.'

'And yet here we are, hanging on to the under-fortress by our toe claws.'

Eekrit jabbed a finger at Eshreegar. 'No one's seen the *kreekar-gan* since the fight at mine shaft four. Why is that? All we ever see these days are skeletons and shambling corpses.' He leaned forwards. 'Our problem isn't that the burning man's so much stronger; it's that we've been getting weaker by the year. When Velsquee shows up with the reinforcements he promised, all that will change.'

The Master of Treacheries let out a snort. 'I'll believe that when I see it, and not before.'

Just then, the double doors at the far end of the chamber creaked open and a slave came scampering through. He dashed to the foot of the dais and stretched himself upon the stones. 'Master-master!' he said breathlessly. 'The Grey Lord has come! Velsquee is-is here!'

Eekrit straightened, ears fluttering in surprise. 'In the great square? Now?'

'No-no master. He-he waits without!' the slave replied.

Eshreegar rose from his chair and carefully set his wine bowl aside. 'I don't like the sound of that,' he said quietly.

The warlord shot Eshreegar a hard look. 'Let him in,' he snapped at the slave. As the skaven dashed back to the double doors, Eekrit felt the hackles rise on the back of his neck.

Moments later, the doors opened wide, and Grey Lord Velsquee made his painful way into the great hall. Despite the best elixirs and sorcerous charms gold could buy, Velsquee's fur had gone almost uniformly white and his face was deeply lined by years of strain. The Grey Lord still stubbornly wore his fine suit of armour and curved sword, though his fighting days were now far behind him. The chirurgeons had worked wonders, but Velsquee's shattered hip had never set properly. He leaned heavily on a gnarled cypress cane as he limped towards the dais. Behind him came a dozen heavily armed *heechigar*, marching with exaggerated slowness so as not to overtake their master.

Eekrit fought down a sense of foreboding at the sight of the storm-walkers. The places along the great hall where his bodyguards customarily stood were conspicuously empty, because every able-bodied skaven was needed to man the barricades. He glanced at Eshreegar and noted that the Master of Treacheries had retreated a few steps away from the throne and turned slightly to face the *heechigar*. His arms were folded, paws tucked into his sleeves.

Remembering himself, Eekrit quickly rose from the throne, but Velsquee waved for him to stop. 'Sit down, whelp,' he snapped, his voice rough with age. He nodded at Eshreegar's seat. 'This one will do.'

The warlord waited until Velsquee had settled himself in the chair before he sat back upon the throne. His throat suddenly felt very dry.

'Welcome back to the under-fortress, my lord,' Eekrit grumbled. 'Forgive me for not greeting you in the great square with the fanfare you deserve, but you've arrived much, *much* earlier than expected.'

Velsquee winced as he tried to get comfortable on the hard wooden seat. 'I moved much faster without an army to slow me down,' he said in a cold voice.

There it was, stated in bald terms. Eekrit shook his head slowly, not quite willing to believe what he'd heard. 'You... you travelled on ahead of the army, you mean.'

The Grey Lord growled. 'It's over, Eekrit. The Council of Thirteen doesn't want any more to do with this place. They call it the *Cursed Pit* these days. I couldn't get one other Grey Lord to support the call for more warriors.'

'What about all the god-stone buried here?' Eekrit asked. 'We've been at it nearly eighty years, and we've barely scratched the-the surface!'

'And look what it's cost us,' Velsquee shot back. 'It's even got the grey seers at each others' throats.' He shook his grizzled head. 'No, Eekrit. It's done. The Council sent me here with an official declaration dissolving the alliance of clans and disbanding the expeditionary force.'

Eekrit stared at the Grey Lord. 'This is lunacy,' he snarled. 'We can still triumph here, Velsquee. You haven't been here in almost forty years! I *know* we can defeat the *kreekar-gan*–'

'You know nothing of the kind, ratling!' Velsquee shouted, half-rising from his chair. 'Qweeqwol tried to warn me, but I wouldn't listen–' the rest of the outburst was lost in a fit of terrible, racking coughs that left the Grey Lord wheezing and doubled over with pain. Eekrit gestured frantically for a slave, who rushed a bowl of wine to the struggling skaven.

Velsquee took the bowl with a trembling paw and drank deeply. Eekrit waited until the old skaven had composed himself before he continued.

'Qweeqwol warned you of what?'

The Grey Lord didn't reply at first. His gaze wandered the room, lost in memories of the past. Finally, he sighed and rubbed a paw across his whiskers.

'Qweeqwol saw a great deal more than just visions of god-stone buried beneath this damned mountain,' he said. 'The god-stone was immaterial to him. He lent his influence to the alliance of the clans and marched with the army because he'd seen what the burning man planned for the world. If the *kreekar-gan* wasn't stopped, it wouldn't mean the death of the skaven. It would mean the death of *everything*.'

The haunted look in Velsquee's eyes made Eekrit's blood run cold. 'How could such a thing be possible?'

The Grey Lord shook his head. 'I don't know,' he replied. 'I didn't believe a word of it at the time.'

'Have you told the Council of this?' Eekrit asked.

Velsquee's eyes widened. 'Are you mad? Those fools would think I'd finally gone soft. There would be a dozen daggers in my back by the end of the day.'

'But if Qweeqwol was right...'

'Qweeqwol also said this, the burning man could not be defeated by the hand of the living,' Velsquee replied. 'The *kreekar-gan* is not bound by the laws of life and death. He can only be defeated by someone like himself, who is dead, yet lives on.'

The Grey Lord sighed. 'Qweeqwol thought he had the answer. He was sick, you see. A corruption of the blood. The Horned One alone knows how he managed to live so long.' Velsquee shook his head bitterly. 'Qweeqwol thought it was a sign. We know better now, of course.'

Eekrit fought the urge to beckon for more wine. He glanced at Eshreegar. 'My scouts tell me that the *kreekar-gan* is getting ready to launch another attack.'

'Can you hold him off?'

The warlord gritted his teeth. 'Perhaps.'

'Then if you'll listen to one last piece of *advice* from me, you'll clean out every scrap of god-stone you can from the mine shaft and clear out before the burning man strikes. Leave the mercenaries behind as a rearguard. If you move quickly enough, they won't realise they've been abandoned until it's too late.'

Velsquee's bald words stunned Eekrit. Before he could reply, the doors at the end of the hall swung open yet again and the same slave came dashing towards the dais. He wove his way nimbly around the *heechigar* and prostrated himself before the skaven lords. 'Master! Master!'

'In the Horned One's name, *what now*?' Eekrit snarled.

'A-a message from the barricades!' the slave cried. 'A corpse-man has come!'

The corpse-men were the *kreekar-gan*'s barbarian lieutenants. There were only three left, as far as Eekrit knew, and none of them had been seen in more than a decade. The news sent a chill down the warlord's spine.

'How many?'

The slave hesitated, glancing uncertainly from Eekrit to Velsquee and back again. 'How-how many what?'

'Warriors, you wretch!' Eekrit snapped. 'The corpse-man isn't standing in front of the barricades *by himself*, now is he?'

The slave's ears began to flutter nervously. Fear-musk spread through the air. 'But-but he *is*, master. The corpse-man came alone. He says he bears a message for-for you.'

'Terms? Your master wishes to offer us *terms?*'

The *kreekar-gan*'s lieutenant looked as though he had just climbed from a dusty crypt. Though tall and broad-shouldered, the northman's face was gaunt and etched by dozens of battle scars. His black hair was tangled, and layered with dust and grime. The corpse-man's armour of leather and bronze was notched and torn by countless blows, and still bore the stains of past battles.

The northman stood just ten feet from the foot of the dais, where Eekrit and

Velsquee sat. The burning man's emissary bore no weapons, but Eekrit knew all too well how swift and strong the corpse-men were. Velsquee's *heechigar* virtually surrounded the creature, their polearms ready to strike. Eshreegar was nowhere to be seen, but Eekrit knew that the Master of Treacheries was lurking somewhere in the shadows, just a quick knife-throw away.

Words rasped from the emissary's mouth. 'Remove your warriors from the mountain and abandon your mine,' the corpse-man hissed, 'and henceforth my master will provide you with *abn-i-khat* in exchange for slaves and other tribute.'

Eekrit's eyes narrowed. He assumed that *abn-i-khat* was what these monsters called the god-stone. 'Tribute?' he snarled. 'You insult us, corpse-man! The Under-Empire pays tribute to no one–'

The Grey Lord cut off Eekrit's protest with an upraised paw. 'You are saying that your master is willing to trade with us. Is that it?' Velsquee asked.

The emissary turned his head fractionally to regard the Grey Lord. If the corpse-man recognised the sudden tension between the two skaven on the dais, he gave no sign. 'He will trade with you, yes. But your warriors must leave here, and you must abandon your mine. Those are his terms.'

'This is a joke!' Eekrit spat. 'Surely you don't–'

Once again, Velsquee interrupted. This time his voice was hard as stone. 'What Lord Eekrit wishes to say is that the Under-Empire will accept your master's terms. We will remove our warriors immediately, and cease work on our mine. When will you provide the first shipment of god-stone?'

'You will receive one half-pound of *abn-i-khat* for every hundred pounds of metal or slaves that you provide. The sooner you deliver them, the sooner you will receive your stone.'

Velsquee did not hesitate. 'Done. When will we meet your master to seal the bargain?'

'There is no need,' the corpse-man hissed. 'Remove your warriors and empty the mine before dawn tomorrow; that will be enough.'

'And if we don't?' Eekrit snarled.

'Then by sundown your corpses will be mining stone for my master.'

Eekrit started to rise from the throne, his paw reaching for his sword, but the Grey Lord forestalled him. 'Take the emissary back to the barricades!' he commanded, and his storm-walkers quickly obeyed. They closed ranks around the corpse-man, effectively isolating him from Eekrit or anyone else, and marched him out of the room.

Eekrit rounded on the Grey Lord the instant the double doors closed. 'Have you lost-lost your mind?' he shouted. 'After all-all we've done here, you're just going to-to *surrender*?'

Velsquee's cane crashed to the floor of the dais as the Grey Lord shot to his feet. Crippled or not, his paw closed around the hilt of his sword. 'Mind your tongue, ratling!' he snarled back. 'I've given them nothing that they didn't already possess! This is a victory for us, not a defeat.'

'But the *kreekar-gan* is bluffing!' Eekrit shot back. 'Can't you see that? Do you imagine he sent that mouldering corpse to talk to us because he's suddenly grown tired of fighting? If he could have driven us out as easily as he claims he can, we'd be fighting for our lives right now. The only reason he's negotiating is because he's *weak*.'

'Then answer this, can you beat the burning man with the warriors you have on hand?'

Eekrit paused. 'I... don't know.'

'Then it doesn't matter how damned weak he is,' Velsquee said. 'Because there'll be no more help coming from the Great City. I can guarantee you that.'

The two lords stared at one another for a moment. Finally, Eekrit relented and sat heavily back down upon his throne. 'I need a drink,' he growled.

'That's the first intelligent thing you've said in the last ten minutes,' the Grey Lord replied. He bent painfully to retrieve his cane, then settled heavily back into his own seat with a sigh. '*Think*, ratling. Before that corpse-man turned up, we were getting ready to abandon the mountain altogether. This way, we still get access to the god-stone, and at a cost that no one on the Council can object to. And since the expeditionary force has been officially disbanded, who does that place in charge of all output coming from the mountain?'

Eekrit eyed the Grey Lord. 'You and I.'

Velsquee smiled. 'That's right. We're both about to become obscenely rich.'

The warlord thought things over while a slave poured him some wine. 'That's all well and good,' he said at last, 'but it still leaves us with a problem.'

'Which is?'

'The fact that the burning man is going to end life as we know it.'

'Yes. Well. Assuming Qweeqwol was right, of course.'

'Did you ever know him to be wrong about such things?'

'Honestly? No.'

'Then what do you propose we do?'

'At the moment, there's not much we can do,' Velsquee replied. 'But we can turn this situation to our advantage. Someone will have to stay here at the under-fortress to supervise the exchange of goods between us and the *kreekar-gan*.'

'By which you mean *me*,' Eekrit said.

'You may as well,' Velsquee replied. 'You're not rich enough yet to buy your way back into the Council's good graces. In the meantime, you and your black-cloaked friends can see what you can learn about the *kreekar-gan* and his plans. Find out his weaknesses, then, when the time is right–'

'We stick a dagger between his ribs,' Eekrit said.

Velsquee smiled mirthlessly. 'Just so, ratling. Just so.'

FOURTEEN

BLOOD AND SAND

The Golden Plain,
in the 103rd year of Basth the Graceful
(-1240 Imperial Reckoning)

The Lahmian watch-forts along the eastern edge of the Golden Plain were stout, sturdy affairs, having changed little since their creation almost a hundred years before. The first two had been built athwart the trade road, where it descended from the plain and wound through the wooded hills on the way down to the city. Four more had been built in quick succession, two to the north and two to the south, stretching in an arc that would allow Lahmian cavalry patrols to venture deep into the wilderness to either side of the road and interdict the bandit gangs that preyed on the western caravans.

Each stronghold was built according to the same specifications: a high, outer wall made of stone, wide enough at the top for four men to walk abreast, with a massive wooden gate made from cedar logs and secured with iron pins as long as a man's forearm. Within the compound were stables, barracks, a forge and storehouses piled with enough stores to sustain a garrison of a thousand men for at least a month. In the centre of the compound sat a squat, thick-walled citadel, containing the fort's armoury, its apothecary, quarters for its officers, a small cistern and a small shrine to the Temple of Blood. In the event the walls were taken, the entire garrison could retreat into the citadel and hold out for weeks, if need be; more than enough time for a rescue force to arrive from the fort's neighbours and drive the attackers away.

It was a sound design – and a formidable stronghold for an attacking force to overcome – but much depended on the discipline and determination of the men tasked with the fort's defence.

For the first few decades, the forts were a great success. Captains were paid lavish rewards for bandit heads, so they were aggressive and cunning in their patrols. Hundreds of outlaws were slain and hundreds more fled the plain for easier pickings elsewhere, until only the swiftest and cleverest of the caravan raiders remained. The desert tribes never came within a day's ride of the forts and were far too wily and swift to be caught out by a patrol of city-bred horsemen. As the pickings grew slim, the rewards dwindled as well and the patrols rode out less and less. And since no outlaw band had ever been so foolish as to mount a direct attack on the strongholds, a sense of complacency became inevitable. Late-night sentries found better ways to pass their time than walking the ramparts, like playing dice in the marshalling ground, or sneaking a cup or two of beer from the fort's ample stores.

Once upon a time, it had been a scourging offence to allow the ground to become overgrown within a thousand paces of the forts. At the northernmost of the strongholds, dense underbrush and young trees had been allowed to creep to less than a dozen yards from the outer walls. With so much cover, the warriors of the *bani-al-Hashim* could have approached the fort on a full moon night and none would have been the wiser.

As it was, Alcadizzar waited for a cold, moonless winter night before attempting the raid. First, a pair of archers was sent forwards to watch the ramparts and ensure that there were no sentries about. They watched for nearly an hour; when no guards were spotted, one of them let out the low cry of a hunting owl. Immediately, a quartet of tribesmen was sent forwards, carrying a light, slender ladder between them. Within minutes, the ladder was resting against the outer wall and Alcadizzar had waved the assault party forwards.

A dozen of the tribe's quietest, most efficient killers crept up the ladder and over the wall. Armed with powerful, compact horse-bows and long knives, they hunted down the sentries one by one, then went to open the outer gate. It was foul luck alone that they were discovered moments later, when a soldier came stumbling sleepily from the barracks to empty his bladder and caught sight of them. The Lahmian let out a yell a half-second before an arrow found his throat; instead of taking the entire fort by storm the desert raiders found themselves with a pitched battle on their hands.

'They fought well,' Sayyid al-Hashim said, and then shrugged. 'For the first few minutes, at least.' The stocky desert warrior paused to wipe blood from his eyes with the back of his hand. A deep cut across one temple had soaked his headscarf and turned his shoulder crimson.

Bodies littered the open ground between the barracks and the outer gate, feathered by thick, red-fletched arrows. Most were clad only in their linen under-tunics; others had died in little more than their britches. They'd grabbed whatever weapon was close to hand and rushed out to fight the dozen men of the assault party. Still more bodies were heaped around the open gate, where the tribesmen had held the Lahmians at bay long enough for the rest of the raiding party to arrive. Six of the assault party had been slain, and a seventh writhed on the ground with the broken haft of a spear buried in his guts. Alcadizzar knew each and every one by name and made a silent promise to the gods that their widows would be well taken care of.

He and Faisr stood beneath the archway of the outer gate, surveying the bloody scene. They were both clad in breastplates of thick leather armour and skirts of flexible bronze mail, and wore round bronze skullcaps beneath their silk headscarves. Faisr glowered at the bodies of the dead soldiers, his hand clenched about the hilt of his sheathed sword. It had gone against his impetuous nature to hang back with Alcadizzar and let his tribesmen do all the fighting. By the time they had rushed into the fort with the raiding party's small group of reserves, there was no one left to fight.

'What happened then?' Alcadizzar asked.

Sayyid nodded in the direction of the citadel. 'As soon as the first of our brothers came running through the gate, the city dwellers turned tail and shut themselves up inside there.'

The raiders had pulled a pair of wagons into the marshalling field and turned them onto their sides, providing them with some cover from the desultory arrow fire coming from the citadel. The rest were hard at work looting the fort's outbuildings. Tribesmen were shouldering past Alcadizzar with bundles of armour, stacks of swords and shields, jars of beer, and pretty well anything else that wasn't nailed down. Nervous whinnies from the fort's stable told the prince that several of the tribesmen were relieving the cavalry squadron of their mounts as well.

Alcadizzar rubbed his chin. By any reasonable measure, the raid could already be counted as a huge success and a humiliating blow for the Lahmians. He'd wanted to test the defences of the watch-forts and see how the desert raiders took to proper military tactics; he'd been satisfied on both counts. But the idea of leaving the fort intact stuck in his craw; he'd hoped to disarm the defenders and turn them out into the countryside, then put the stronghold to the torch.

'Have they sent any signals?' the prince asked.

Sayyid shook his head, scattering ruby droplets around his feet. 'None.'

Faisr sighed. 'It will be dawn in just a few hours,' he said. 'Signal or no, we have to be miles from here by first light.'

Alcadizzar nodded at the chieftain. When he'd first met Faisr, the young bandit would have probably opted to remain, more than willing to gamble his life and the lives of his men in an all-or-nothing assault on the citadel. But now, at seventy, the chieftain was wealthy and powerful and the *bani-al-Hashim* was considered the greatest of the tribes. Though his courage and his ambition remained undimmed, he also now had far more to lose.

Faisr al-Hashim had aged well, despite the hard life of a nomadic raider. The desert tribes still largely enjoyed the longevity of years that the ancient Nehekharans once had. Now comfortably middle-aged, the handsome chieftain had a touch of grey in his beard and streaks in his raven-black hair; years of squinting against the sun and wind had etched deep wrinkles around his eyes, but his body was still strong and his steps swift and light.

By contrast, Alcadizzar seemed to have aged hardly at all. By his reckoning, he was a hundred and ten years old, but he possessed the physical qualities of a man still in his prime. Though Neferata's elixir had long since faded in strength, it had not disappeared entirely. He was still stronger and swifter than any normal man and his wounds healed with extraordinary speed. Perhaps it was because he'd been fed the blasphemous liquid while still forming in the womb – Alcadizzar had numerous theories, but no real answers. Though Faisr and his fellow tribesmen could not have failed to notice, they never questioned it, either. Such was the loyalty – and the secretive nature – of the tribes.

Certainly, he and Faisr had become a fearsomely effective pair since Alcadizzar's adoption into the tribe. As the chieftain's prominence had grown in the wake of Bashir al-Rukhba's decline, he had entrusted much of the tribe's raiding strategies to the prince, which allowed Alcadizzar to refine his tactical skills and test the capabilities of the desert raiders to their fullest. The *bani-al-Hashim* had quickly become the scourge of the Golden Plain and, more importantly, had earned the respect and support of many of the other tribes.

All of which made the problem before Alcadizzar that much more irksome. Their choices for dealing with the stronghold were limited. They couldn't very well starve the garrison out and the only way inside was through the single reinforced gate. No doubt there was timber in the fort that could be put to use as a battering ram, but breaking through the gate would be costly and then the soldiers inside would fight like trapped rats. The prince shook his head, thinking of great commanders like Rakh-amn-hotep, who sent thousands of men to their deaths during the war against the Usurper. He'd lost six brothers tonight and had no interest in losing any more just to make a point.

He was just about to tell Sayyid to complete the plunder of the fort and then instruct the raiders to withdraw, when the stocky warrior straightened and pointed a finger at the citadel. 'What's that?'

The prince glanced past the upturned wagons, and saw that the citadel's heavy gate had been partially raised. A hand was extended from beneath the gate, holding out an empty sword scabbard for all to see. Alcadizzar blinked in surprise.

'They want to parley,' he told Faisr.

The chieftain was just as surprised as he. 'Why?'

Alcadizzar shrugged. 'We'd have to ask them.'

'It's got to be a trick,' Sayyid growled. It was well known among the tribes that the city folk had no conception of honour.

Alcadizzar could hardly argue with the veteran warrior, but his curiosity was nevertheless piqued. On impulse, he said, 'Let me talk to them.'

'Are you mad?' Sayyid exclaimed. 'They'll shoot you full of arrows!'

The prince managed a grin. 'I'm not worried. The Lahmians are terrible shots. Faisr remembers. Don't you, chief?'

Faisr grunted, and then slowly, his face split in one of his dazzling smiles. 'I remember,' he said. 'All right, Ubaid. See what they have to say. We can't leave until we empty the stables, anyway.'

Alcadizzar nodded in gratitude to the chieftain, then strode towards the overturned wagons. 'Parley!' he cried to the tribesmen, pulling his headscarf away from his face. 'Let the city dwellers send out their emissary.'

No one stirred within the stronghold until Alcadizzar had emerged into view from around the wagons. He crossed the open ground between the barricade and the stronghold and stopped at the halfway point, arms folded. A moment later, a stunned-looking Lahmian in a lieutenant's iron scale armour ducked underneath the gate and stepped warily into the marshalling ground. From the look on his face, the soldier expected to be filled full of arrows at any moment.

'What do you want, city dweller?' Alcadizzar shouted.

The Lahmian officer drew a long breath. 'My captain, the honourable Neresh Anku-aten, wishes to discuss terms.'

Alcadizzar fought to keep his expression neutral. Who did this aristocrat think he was? 'Tell your captain that he is not in a position to dictate terms. He has nowhere to go.'

The lieutenant paled. With an effort, he managed a nod. 'Captain Neresh is well aware of this,' the Lahmian replied. 'But he wishes to avoid further bloodshed.'

'Then tell the honourable captain to surrender!' Alcadizzar shot back.

'He will, so long as you guarantee safe passage for his men,' the lieutenant replied.

For a moment, Alcadizzar wasn't certain he'd heard the man correctly. 'Your captain wishes to surrender?'

'Only if his terms are met. He is adamant on that.'

Alcadizzar didn't reply at first. It didn't make any sense. His mind raced, trying to divine what the captain was thinking. Why abandon a perfectly secure stronghold when all he had to do was wait for a few more hours? If it was a trick, he was hard-pressed to discern it. Finally, the prince spread his hands.

'Very well,' Alcadizzar told the man. 'Tell your captain that he and the garrison are free to go. If they leave their weapons and armour inside the stronghold, they may leave freely. Upon my honour, no harm will come to them.'

The lieutenant eyed Alcadizzar dubiously for a moment more, then ducked his head in a quick bow and hurried back inside the stronghold.

Alcadizzar waited, still not quite daring to believe what he'd been told. But a few minutes later, the stronghold's gate began to creak upwards. When it was fully open, the first survivors of the garrison emerged into the night air, clad only in their under-tunics and britches. They filed past the prince with downcast eyes, heading for the gate.

Over the next few minutes, nearly a hundred and fifty Lahmian soldiers marched by – more than double the small force that Faisr had brought with him. Last of all came the fort's captain, a tall, black-haired noble whose handsome face was twisted in a bitter scowl. He stopped in front of Alcadizzar and inclined his head curtly to the prince.

'You are the leader of the raiders?' he asked.

Alcadizzar shook his head. 'I serve Faisr al-Hashim the Great, chieftain of the *bani-al-Hashim*.'

'My men will come to no harm?'

'Have I not already given you my word, Captain Neresh?'

The Lahmian grunted in reply, as though not quite daring to believe what he'd been told. 'I suppose you have my thanks then,' he grudgingly said.

Neresh made to leave, but Alcadizzar's curiosity got the better of him. He stopped the captain with a touch on his arm. 'A question, captain?'

The Lahmian turned. 'What is it?'

'Why surrender?' the prince asked. 'You must have known we couldn't have taken the stronghold without a fight.'

Neresh's expression turned bitter. 'Of course,' he replied. 'That wasn't the point.'

The Lahmian sighed. 'Eventually you'd have broken down the gate. Once inside, the fight would have been bloody, I promise you that.'

'I have no doubt as to your courage, captain,' Alcadizzar said. 'Which is why this confounds me so.'

Neresh sighed. 'Perhaps we could have held the stronghold. Perhaps not. What is certain is that many of my men would have died, and that would have been a terrible crime.'

Alcadizzar frowned. 'When is it a crime to defend the honour of one's city?' he asked.

The captain stared at Alcadizzar for a moment, his expression haunted. 'That's something I've been asking myself for a very long time,' he said, and turned away.

Alcadizzar watched the captain go. Forty years ago, such a reply from one of the city's nobles would have been inconceivable. Had the spirit of Lahmia's citizens truly sunk that far?

The prince followed after the captain, considering the possibilities. He found Faisr still standing at the outer gate, speaking tersely with a dust-stained rider. Belatedly, Alcadizzar realised the man was clad all in black.

'Things have changed,' Alcadizzar said to Faisr as the chieftain turned his way.

'Yes they have,' Faisr agreed. His expression was sombre. 'We have to go. The Daughter of the Sands is dead.'

* * *

According to custom, the tribes never gathered together at the same location from one gathering to the next. This time, it was decided by Suleima's last wish that the tribes would gather far to the north and west, at the very edge of the Golden Plain. This was wild country that had never been tamed by any man, Lahmian or otherwise, with unspoiled woods and a bubbling spring in the centre of a thicket-bound forest. It was hard going, even for the desert horsemen, but the tribes pressed doggedly on, determined to honour Suleima's passing.

The *bani-al-Hashim* now numbered almost four hundred warriors, born from many advantageous marriages to the other tribes or adopted into the ranks over the years. This far from Lahmia, they rode in their full panoply. Silk standards crackled in the cold wind blowing off the mountains and their fine robes fairly glowed in the sunlight. Gold and silver twinkled at ear, neck and wrist, from the buckles of their wide leather belts and the scabbards of their swords.

The raising of the tents was a sombre affair. The men touched neither wine nor *chanouri*, out of respect for the dead, nor did they tempt the fates by gambling. In the afternoon, the chiefs all came together and offered gifts to their ever-hungry god: stallions' blood, gold and silver coin, fine iron swords taken from the Lahmians, and more. Then they went into the forest to gather wood for a funeral pyre.

In the camp, the women were baking bread mingled with ash for the ceremonial meal at sunset. The children had been left to watch the herds at the edge of the forest, several leagues distant, so the tent city was eerily silent. The men kept to their tents, resting after the long night's ride and waiting for the funeral rites to begin.

Alcadizzar spent the long afternoon alone in his tent, musing over the raid at the fort. All the tribes were abuzz with the news, and jealous at the wealth of plunder that the *bani-al-Hashim* had taken – not just weapons and armour, but fine horses and a chest full of coin that had been kept inside the fort's stronghold. He had little doubt that several of the other tribes would be tempted to raid the other forts now, eager for loot and bragging rights. He had little doubt that the first few attacks would be successful, even forewarned as the Lahmians were sure to be. What interested him was how the city dwellers would respond at that point. With perhaps as many as half of their watch-forts put to the torch, they would have to respond in some fashion – either a massive military campaign to punish the tribes and drive them from the plain, or else a retreat back to the safety of the city walls. When he'd begun planning the raid, Alcadizzar had thought the former response was likely. But after speaking with Captain Neresh, he suspected the latter.

Year by year, little by little, Lahmia had been growing increasingly isolated. The caravans had dwindled to a fraction of their former numbers and the waves of immigration from poorer cities like Mahrak and Lybaras had ceased entirely. Though Lahmia still maintained its preeminence in Nehekhara by virtue of its economic and financial influence – and, he suspected, because Neferata was twisting the minds of the other cities' emissaries – its position was becoming increasingly tenuous. News from the few desert immigrants left inside the city spoke of a pervasive atmosphere of terror. Deaths and disappearances were a way of life; anger and frustration at the impotence of the City Guard had given way to the cynical belief that the royal court was actually in league with the monsters. Even the Temple of Blood was coming under suspicion, something that would have been unthinkable twenty years before. But the more restless the populace became, the more the Lahmian king tightened his grip on the city. The gates were guarded zealously, day and night, and none could pass through without papers signed by one of the royal viziers. Even an approach from the sea was fraught with risk, as the Lahmians patrolled the beaches and the dockside day and night.

The prince reclined against the cushions and rubbed at his eyes. How much longer, he thought? How many years had he already sacrificed for the sake of his duty? How many more must he give up before he could finally begin the life he'd craved since childhood?

Soon, he told himself. It has to be soon. The city is falling apart from within. Cracks will start to appear. Have faith, and wait a little longer.

'Faith,' the prince muttered. 'Faith in what?'

'The gods of Nehekhara are gone,' spoke a woman's voice. 'Believe in yourself, if nothing else.'

Alcadizzar whirled, scattering cushions and nearly tangling himself in his own robes. Across the tent from him sat a young woman, clad in black silk robes. A black neckscarf framed her sharp-featured face and contrasted against the burnished gold of her eyes. The line of henna tattoos along her jawline and down her slender neck reminded him at once of that night outside the gathering tent, twenty-five years before.

The prince stared at her in shock. 'How did you get in here?'

Ophiria sniffed derisively. 'Had you a wife and a few daughters, I would never have gotten within a mile of your tent,' she said. The seer spread her hands, taking in the well-appointed but otherwise empty tent. 'You have no one to watch out for you. You don't even keep a *dog*. Do you enjoy being so lonely?'

Alcadizzar scowled at her. 'What do you want?'

Ophiria leaned back slightly, tucking her feet beneath her knees. 'You could be a proper host and offer me some tea, to begin with,' she said, with a haughty tilt to her chin.

The prince stared at her blankly for a moment. 'I don't think you should be here,' he said.

Ophiria merely blinked at him with her sphinx-like eyes. 'Remember to put a bit of honey at the bottom of the cup before you pour the water,' she said.

Alcadizzar sighed and went to the silver tray that one of Faisr's daughters had brought him a short while ago. The water in the brass kettle was still quite warm. He poured her a cup of tea while he tried to collect his thoughts.

A few moments later, Alcadizzar set the small, ceramic cup before the seer. Ophiria took it in both hands and raised it to her chin. She breathed deeply, and a faint smile crossed her face. 'Treasures from the far east,' she murmured, and took a tiny sip. She raised her eyes to Alcadizzar. 'Thank you.'

'Why are you here, Ophiria?' Alcadizzar asked.

The seer arched a slender eyebrow. 'You know my name? Then you must know that in a few hours, Suleima will be gone, and I will be given to Khsar as his new bride. After that, you and I will never have the opportunity to speak like this.' She took another tiny sip of tea. 'Before that happens, there are some things you and I must discuss.'

Bemused, Alcadizzar settled onto the rugs across from Ophiria. 'What is there to talk about?'

Ophiria peered at him over the rim of the cup. 'For starters, why have you lied to Faisr all this time? What is your real name?'

The prince was taken aback. 'My name? Why, it's–'

'Carefully now,' Ophiria said. Her voice was soft, but her eyes glinted coldly. 'Do not presume to lie to me, city dweller. Especially when so much is at stake.'

Alcadizzar paused. Suddenly, his mouth had gone completely dry.

'Very well,' he said. 'My name is Alcadizzar. I am a prince of Rasetra.'

'You lie.'

Alcadizzar's eyes widened. 'No! It's the truth–'

'You are no prince,' Ophiria said, cutting him off with a raised finger. 'I see you resting upon a throne, with a crook and sceptre in your hands. You are a king.'

Alcadizzar clenched his jaw. 'In time perhaps, but not yet. There is something that must be done first.'

'And what does this task of yours have to do with my people?'

Ophiria's gaze was sharp and direct, like a poised blade. It unnerved him, to a degree, but at the same time he found himself eager to finally be able to speak of the secrets he'd kept for so many years. After a moment, he reached his decision. Without a word, he went back to the tray and poured a second cup of tea, then sat before Ophiria and told her everything.

She listened to it all in perfect silence, nodding at times and sipping her tea. When his story was done, she stared at him thoughtfully.

'And what happens once you've obtained this evidence of Neferata's crimes?'

Alcadizzar sighed. 'Then the other great cities will have no choice but to take action. We'll march on Lahmia, and–'

'I mean, what happens to my people once you've used us to get what you're after?' Ophiria said.

The prince shifted uncomfortably. 'Well, I would go to the chiefs and ask for their help,' he said. 'I suppose Faisr will be angry with me, but I will beg his forgiveness. The evil at Lahmia's heart threatens all of Nehekhara. Everything I've done has been for the good of the entire land. I hope he'll understand that.'

'And if the chiefs help you, what then?'

'I don't understand.'

Ophiria put down her cup and leaned forwards. 'Once you've driven out these creatures and claimed your throne, what becomes of the people who adopted you as one of their own, twenty-five years ago?' She swept her hand through the air, gesturing at the walls of the tent. 'Will you bring us to your city and keep us at court like trained hounds?'

A pained expression came over Alcadizzar's face.

'I see,' he said in a hollow voice. 'You think I see the tribes as just a means to an end. That as I soon as I've gotten what I want from them, I'll forget my oaths and cast them aside.'

'It's happened before. Many times.'

'That's true,' Alcadizzar said. 'But not by me. I'm no city dweller, Ophiria. This is my home, as it has been for many years. These are *my* people. Let me ask you a question now, what is it that the tribes truly want? Tell me, and if it's in my power, I will give it to them.'

Ophiria studied him carefully, searching for any sign of deception. Her expression softened, and she leaned back. Her gaze fell to the teacup.

'We want forgiveness,' she replied.

'What?' the prince gave her a baffled look. 'Who am I to forgive you anything?'

'On the contrary,' Ophiria replied. 'I think you're the man we've waited hundreds of years to meet.'

Alcadizzar shook his head. 'I don't understand.'

'No, of course not.' Another ghostly smile crossed Ophiria's face. 'You've only been with us for a quarter-century. We haven't given up *all* of our secrets.' She sighed. 'Have you ever wondered why the tribes came here, so long ago, and why we still remain?'

'Of course. I've asked Faisr about it several times, but he never would tell me.'

The seer nodded. 'That is because he was ashamed. It is a hard thing for any man, least of all a chieftain, to admit that his people are oathbreakers.'

Alcadizzar straightened. 'Oathbreakers? What do you mean?'

Ophiria sighed. 'The people of the desert live and die by their oaths, Alcadizzar. It has always been thus. Khsar is a terrible and pitiless god, but our oaths to him allowed us to prosper in a land that confounds and kills other men. We lived in the Great Desert for centuries and we were content. Then came Settra, the Empire-Maker, and we were sorely tested.'

The prince nodded. 'I've studied his campaigns. The desert tribes came the closest to defeating him of any army he ever faced.'

'Yes,' Ophiria agreed. 'Long and bitter were the battles and many brave men were lost. But Settra's armies were endless. We won every fight except the last, but that one defeat changed everything.' Her face twisted into a grimace. 'The Empire-Maker brought together the surviving chiefs and made them swear powerful oaths to him. Oaths to serve his kingdom and to protect it unto death. We swore it before Khsar, mingling our blood with his sacred sand. And we honoured that oath for many hundreds of years,' she said, then her face grew troubled. 'Until the Usurper came.'

'I don't understand,' Alcadizzar said. 'Your people fought the Usurper during the war. In fact, desert riders under Shahid ben Alcazzar saved the host of Ka-Sabar at the battle of Zedri.'

'That is true,' Ophiria said. 'And we harried his retreating army for many days afterwards. But then the Usurper sent his lieutenant, Arkhan, to claim vengeance. He struck at our very heart, falling upon Bhagar with his army. Shahid fought like a lion, but when his own brother was slain by Arkhan, his heart was broken. To our everlasting shame, the Red Fox surrendered to the enemy and cast aside the honour of his people.'

Ophiria brought up her knees and hugged them against her chest. 'And so Arkhan took from us our beloved horses – the one and only gift Khsar ever truly gave us – and he slew them all. After that, we became his slaves, toiling in the desert to build his black tower and to die upon his sacrificial altar.'

'And when the war ended?'

'The Usurper was overthrown, but what did that matter? We had broken our oath to Settra, and Khsar took no pity on us. The desert, which had once been our refuge, now turned against us. Our wells dried up and storms erased all our safe routes through the desert. Soon it was clear that we could not remain in the desert and survive.

'And so the tribes left the desert in shame. They travelled first to Khemri, intending to offer themselves as slaves in hopes of redeeming their honour. But the city was in ruins, its people fled.'

Ophiria picked up the teacup and drained it to the dregs. Staring into its murky depths, she said, 'Just then, when all hope was lost, the Daughter of the Sands went into the ruined palace, where Settra himself once ruled. She knelt before the dais where the great throne had stood and sought guidance. That was when she received the prophecy. She said that Settra had come to her in a vision, and told her to seek the City of the Dawn. There we would find the next king of Khemri and the old oath would be made new again.'

Alcadizzar listened, and a chill went down his spine. 'That seems very difficult to believe,' he said.

'And yet, here you are,' Ophiria said. 'Suleima saw it, too. That was why she intervened at the gathering all those years ago. She saw our salvation in you.'

The prince was silent for a long while. Outside, the sun was setting and the camp was beginning to stir. Ophiria set aside the teacup. 'The hour grows late, Alcadizzar,' she said. 'And you haven't answered my question.'

Alcadizzar sighed. His hand fell to the knife at his waist. 'Give me your hand,' he said.

'Why?'

The prince drew his knife. After a moment's pause, he drew its edge against the palm of his left hand. He gritted his teeth at the sting and watched beads of blood swell up from the cut. 'I have no sand of the desert,' he said. 'So I must ask for your hand instead.'

Ophiria studied him for a moment, her face inscrutable. Slowly, she held out her hand.

Alcadizzar clasped it at once. Her skin was smooth and very warm.

'By my blood and by my honour, when I am king in Khemri, the sacred oath will be made new again,' he said.

Ophiria smiled and withdrew her hand. 'So be it, son of Khemri.'

'But first, Lahmia must fall,' Alcadizzar said. 'My own honour requires it.'

The seer stared down at the bloody imprint on her palm. She closed her hand.

'Watch the skies, oh king,' she said. Her voice had a strange, distant quality that made the hairs prickle on the back of his neck. 'Look for the sign. A pennon of fire across the night sky, forked like the tongue of the asp.'

Alcadizzar frowned. 'When?'

'In the fullness of time. When the pennon fills the night sky, wait in the woods to the north of the city and Lahmia will deliver itself into your hands.'

'I–' A thousand questions raced through Alcadizzar's mind. But before he could ask them, Ophiria was gone, ducking out of the tent as silently as she'd appeared.

It was growing dark inside the tent. Alone in the growing gloom, Alcadizzar clenched his cut hand. 'I will. By all the gods, I will.'

FIFTEEN

THE CROWN OF NAGASH

Nagashizzar,
in the 105th year of Djaf the Terrible
(-1222 Imperial Reckoning)

The great chamber had been carved from the heart of the mountain with a single purpose in mind. Shaped purely by sorcery, it was precisely octagonal in shape, and measured a hundred and twenty-eight feet across from side to side. The soaring, arched ceiling reached its apex a hundred and twenty-eight feet from the flat, stone floor, above an octagonal pit sixteen feet across. Every inch of the chamber's surface - walls, floor and ceiling - had been inscribed with thousands of lines of precise runes. Each had been inlaid with the dust of the burning stone, causing them to pulse in precise, arcane patterns. Many of the runes were part of a complex formula designed to focus the magical energies of any ritual performed inside the space. Other runes, laid in concentric patterns along the floor and around the border of the chamber's sole doorway, were part of a series of complex wards designed to keep the spirits of the restless dead at bay. Of all the brooding towers and shadow-haunted vaults of Nagashizzar, this place had taken the longest to create; more than twenty years of tireless research and complex incantations had been employed and now, at last, its arcane purpose was about to be fulfilled.

At the far end of the great chamber, opposite the arched doorway, stood a towering throne carved from the living rock. It rose like a jagged stalagmite from the chamber floor, and was flanked on all four corners by squat, stone pillars topped by rune-etched braziers of thick bronze. Fist-sized chunks of burning stone sent up a pulsing, greenish mist from each of the braziers, wreathing the awful skeleton seated upon the throne.

Nagash had been carried into the sanctum upon a golden palanquin as soon as the chamber had first taken shape and had rested upon the throne ever since. His crushed bones had been fitted back together by a combination of sorcery and silver wire, but despite this, his grip on the physical world had continued to deteriorate. The damage wrought by Akatha during the battle at mine shaft four had proved impossible to repair; the broken bones would not fuse together again, no matter how much power Nagash employed. Far worse, though, had been the scorching heat of the ratmen's damned green fire. Had the fire-globe struck him directly, Nagash was certain that he wouldn't have survived; as it was, the sheer heat of the blast had somehow damaged his skeleton's ability to store the energies of the burning stone. The power leached from his bones constantly now. At first, Nagash had been forced to consume more *abn-i-khat* on a daily basis in order to survive; now he required new infusions every minute, or his skeleton would disintegrate.

The victory at mine shaft four had been a narrow one. Despite losing many of their leaders, the enemy had managed to finally restore their lines at mine shaft eight; Nagash had not the forces necessary to overcome them. He had fallen well short of his goals and for the first few years after the battle, the necromancer had grimly prepared for the inevitable counter-assault. But, inexplicably, the enemy never managed to regain their strength. They remained on the defensive, allowing him to fight a war of attrition and slowly wear away at their defences. Within thirty-five years, his warriors had reached the last of the enemy's mine shafts, but Nagash could press no further. His forces had been reduced to just a thousand skeletons and a pair of war engines and he lacked the power to create any more. Despite the enemy's battered state, he was not confident he could overcome them, and any day could see the arrival of reinforcements that could well seal his doom.

As much as it galled him to do so, the only option was to negotiate. He mustered every warrior he could outside the enemy barricades as a show of force, let the enemy's scouts get a good look, and then sent Bragadh to offer terms. The very idea of treating with the ratmen as equals felt like a defeat of sorts, but Nagash was determined to at least profit from the exchange.

The vermin capitulated at once, never realising how precarious the situation truly was. Nagash reckoned that a few decades of trade with the ratmen was a small price to pay for a steady stream of slaves and raw materials that would allow him to rebuild Nagashizzar and restore his decimated army. A final reckoning with the ratmen could wait. At long last, Nagash could turn his attention back to Nehekhara and the vengeance he was due.

The necromancer's burning gaze swept across the great chamber. Around the edge of the great pit in the centre of the room, Bragadh, Diarid and Thestus were arrayed at cardinal points around a ritual circle of pulsing runes. Their droning chant reverberated through the air, intoning the first of the five great incantations Nagash had taught them. The ritual chant stoked the energies of hundreds of pounds of *abn-i-khat* that had been painstakingly gathered and arranged in layers inside the pit. A twining column of sorcerous fire rose from its depths, whirling and pulsing in the air above the pit like the heat of a vast forge.

Beyond the hissing column of flame, Nagash could see pale, nebulous shapes hovering beyond the chamber door. The ghosts of the past had lingered there for years, watching and waiting for his demise. Was Neferem there, he wondered, or Thutep, or that damned priest Nebunefer? He hoped so. He wanted them to look upon his labours and despair.

Nagash studied the roaring furnace. He felt its heat and the currents of power that flowed within it. Far above, beyond the surface of the great mountain, the dreadful green moon burned full and bright. Satisfied, he turned his attention to his immortals.

All is in readiness, he told them. *Attend to the crucible.*

Resting on the floor at the foot of the dais was a great crucible of stone. Shaped by sorcery and weighing many tons, its mouth had been etched with a thick band of magical runes that corresponded to the second great incantation. Silently, the immortals withdrew from the furnace and proceeded to a pair of low, broad tables set to either side of Nagash's throne. From there, they gathered flat, hexagonal plaques of pure *abn-i-khat* and placed them carefully inside the crucible. The plaques were arranged in a specific order, so that the runes etched into their surface came together to form a complex sigil, one that Nagash had spent many years creating.

Once the burning stone was in place, the immortals filled the crucible with alternating ingots of lead and a silvery-grey metal unlike anything known to humankind. It was far stronger than bronze, and the secrets of working the metal with hammer and anvil were unknown even to Nagash. The skaven said it was called *gromril,* and claimed to have plundered it at great cost from an underground realm far to the north. He had recognised its value at once.

When the last of the gromril had been laid in the crucible, the immortals took up position around the stone vessel and, at Nagash's command, began the second great incantation. Power crackled in the air between them, until finally, with a ponderous sound of grating stone, the crucible began to move. It dragged slightly across the floor, then rose slowly into the air. Bragadh, Diarid and Thestus raised their arms, hands outstretched, and began to guide the floating vessel towards the waiting furnace.

It was slow, difficult work. The massive crucible, suspended solely by the power and will of the novice sorcerers alone, inched along at a wearying pace. Finally, hours later, the vessel slipped over the edge of the pit and into the roaring column of unnatural flame. The crucible bobbed like a cork over the magical updrafts, rising easily towards the ceiling, until it floated nearly ten feet above the surface of the floor. Ribbons of flame boiled along the crucible's rough surface and poured over the vessel's rim. Slowly but steadily, the runes etched into its surface began to glow with mounting intensity.

The second great ritual ended; now the third began. This time, Nagash began the rite, quickly subordinating the immortals as they worked to keep the crucible poised in the heart of the flame. Soon, a turbulent, multi-hued glow began to emanate from inside the vessel as the elements within were forced to combine. Impurities boiled away in hissing bursts of poisonous steam as Nagash patiently worked his will upon the molten materials. The mists surrounding the throne dissipated swiftly as the powerful ritual consumed them.

For hours Nagash shaped the metal. When at last he judged that the molten ore was ready, he commanded his immortals to bring forth the moulds.

Bragadh, Diarid and Thestus returned to the long tables beside Nagash's throne. Each one lifted a heavy block of obsidian and struggled to carry them back to the roaring flames. Each of the immortals made four trips in all, until twelve blocks of glossy stone stood at the edge of the glowing pit.

The three immortals were moving with great difficulty now. Their ancient armour and tattered robes were starting to disintegrate from the proximity to the furnace. Bragadh's dark hair was gone, singed away, and his skin had taken on the colour of brittle parchment. Still, the northmen returned to their places around the pit and the fourth great incantation began.

Once again, the immortals reached out with their magic and gripped the floating crucible. Guided by Nagash, the vessel was pulled from the furnace. Bragadh, Diarid and Thestus limped around the perimeter of the pit as the crucible shifted, closing in around the vessel from three sides. Balancing the huge container precariously, Nagash and his immortals tipped it towards the first of the moulds. The fiercely glowing ore rose thickly to the brim and then a thin, precise stream of metal fell from the vessel and splashed onto the mould's fill hole. Air howled like a tormented spirit as it was forced from the mould by the seething metal and currents of uncontrolled magic whiplashed through the air. Thestus and Diarid staggered as they were struck; their armour flaked away like ash, the flesh beneath blackened in an instant. The two immortals recoiled in agony, but Nagash froze them in place. Once begun, the rite had to be seen through to the end.

When the first mould was filled, Nagash moved on to the next. One by one, the blocks were filled, and the three northmen bore the brunt of the merciless heat and the wild magic. It flayed their flesh and burrowed into their bones, but the necromancer would not relent. He forced them to return the crucible to the fire and then ordered them to begin the fifth invocation.

Diarid and Thestus limped painfully to the first mould, while Bragadh staggered like a broken puppet towards the table on Nagash's right. With charred hands he gripped the haft of a stone hammer and then made his way painfully back to his kinsmen.

Now came the most difficult part of the rite. Still concentrating on the rite and holding the immortals in place, Nagash turned his attention to his own shattered body. After a moment, his finger bones twitched, then, with a hollow, scraping sound, his elbows and knees. The dust of years seeped from his joints as the necromancer rose slowly to his feet.

One step at a time, Nagash descended from his throne. Tendrils of wild magic wrapped about his skeletal frame, creating livid, thread-like arcs of power along his bones. As he approached the first pair of moulds, Bragadh lifted his ravaged arms and struck the first stone block. Pent-up energies blazed from the stone, leaving glowing scars along Bragadh's forearms, but the northman lifted the hammer to strike again.

On the third blow, the mould split apart. The two stone halves fell to the floor with a crash; within one lay the curved, red-hot surface of a dark metal breastplate. Nagash turned his gaze to Diarid and the northman reached for the armour with bare, trembling hands. Dead flesh sizzled as he gripped the metal and pulled it free. Then Diarid turned and laid the breastplate against Nagash's chest. Moments later, the second mould was broken open, and Thestus lifted the armour's backplate free. When the two pieces were joined together, their seams fused in a flash of blazing, green light. The heat was agonising, far worse than anything Nagash had known as a mortal, but still he commanded the immortals to continue.

For hours, the process continued. One piece of metal after another was laid atop Nagash's skeleton and fused into place, creating a suit of all-enclosing armour more complex than anything human hands could produce. When the metal cooled, its surface was rough and black as night. Though designed with surpassing cunning, the armour itself was plain, even ugly. Like everything else in Nagashizzar, it was not made to please the eye, but to serve its master's purpose.

As the pieces of armour were sealed about him, Nagash felt the change at once. The constant draining of power from his bones ebbed... then stopped entirely. The uncontrolled energies contained within the chamber's layered wards began to flow towards him, sinking through the armour and becoming trapped there. His strength increased with every passing moment, far surpassing that of mortal men.

Finally, the last pieces of armour were fitted over Nagash's feet. The heavy, stone hammer fell to the floor of the chamber with a dull thud. Bragadh's ruined body swayed unsteadily on bony feet. The strain of the great rite had all but destroyed him and his kinsmen, reducing them to pathetic collections of pitted hide and brittle bones. Their faces – what was left of them – were frozen in masks of unspeakable torment. Compelled by Nagash's will they gathered before him.

The necromancer raised his armoured hands and studied them, savouring the power that pulsed like living blood beneath the dark metal. Only his skull had been left exposed; it seemed to float above the throat of the breastplate, wreathed in ribbons of cold, sorcerous flame.

You have done well, Nagash told the suffering immortals. *Better than I expected. But now your usefulness is at an end.*

The necromancer held out his hands and, with a thought, stripped the immortals of their power. In an instant, their remaining flesh shrivelled and their bones collapsed as their souls were cast into the realms of the dead. They departed from the mortal plane with awful, soul-wrenching moans, drawing a cruel laugh from Nagash.

Go and tell Neferem that she will never know vengeance, he said to the wretched ghosts. *I am Nagash, the Undying King! Death has no dominion over me!*

When they were gone, the necromancer turned his gaze to the chamber doorway. The lingering spirits were nowhere to be seen.

One day, they would be made to suffer, he vowed. One day, when the world was his, he would call them back from the bleak lands and enslave them for all time. He savoured the thought for a moment, but then set it aside.

Nagash strode through the tangled piles of bone that had once been his champions and headed towards the crucible. He plucked the stone hammer from the floor.

There was one thing left to be done.

At the edge of the furnace, Nagash extended his open hand. The massive crucible wavered amid the flames and then obediently drifted towards him. The enormous pile of burning stone that had fuelled the rite had been nearly consumed; the crucible was floating much lower in the air than before. Only a small amount of the magical ore remained, bubbling away in its depths.

Nagash drew the crucible from the fire and set it upon the floor with a bone-jarring thud. Baleful green vapour rose from the molten ore within. As it cooled, the necromancer stared into its seething depths and began a sixth incantation, one far greater and more complex than the rest. The liquid metal stirred in response to the incantation, its components ordering itself in response to Nagash's commands.

After half an hour, the metal had cooled enough to hold a rudimentary shape, a rough disc, the size of a small shield. Nagash continued to pour magical energy into the metal, until he was aware of every mote and its position in relation to the rest. He was creating a structure within, similar to the one he'd built into the Black Pyramid centuries ago, although far more sophisticated and refined.

When the structure was locked in place by the solidifying ore, Nagash reached into the crucible with his left hand. The red-hot metal came away easily from the polished surface of the vessel. The necromancer turned the disc-shaped ingot this way and that, inspecting it for any flaws. Satisfied, he uttered a swift incantation. Dust and ash rose from the floor, surrounding him–

–and were swiftly torn away by the teeth of a howling wind, high atop Nagashizzar's tallest spire. Thick, heavy clouds roiled overhead, almost close enough to touch. The great fortress spread beneath him in a dense profusion of towers, manufactories, curtain walls and hulking redoubts. To the west, the poisoned sea heaved restlessly, churned by the dreadful occultation occurring high above.

Nagash cast his gaze skywards, to the ghostly smear of green light seeping like a bloodstain through the heavy overcast. He raised the disc of steaming metal overhead like an offering and spoke words of power that punched a whirling tunnel through the clouds. The bale-moon was revealed in all its terrible glory, eclipsing the face of Neru and blazing like the glaring eye of a malevolent god.

A few paces away, illuminated by the ghastly glow, sat a hulking bronze anvil. Beneath the awful moonlight, Nagash laid the disc on the anvil and lifted the stone hammer. As the words of the seventh and greatest of the night's incantations rang through his mind, he began shaping the red-hot ore.

Each ringing blow reverberated through the stones of Nagashizzar, down into the mountain and through the dark depths of the mines. It rippled through the earth like the beating of a terrible heart, reaching into stone crypts and worm-ridden graves the length and breadth of the young world. Mouldering bones twitched, stirring up the dust of ages. Bruised eyelids fluttered and blind eyes slithered in their sockets, searching for the source of the portentous sound. In the desert, packs of jackals forgot their carrion and filled the air with their chilling cries.

Slowly but surely, the glowing metal bent to the necromancer's will. The work was difficult, for Nagash was no metalsmith, but for the object to serve its purpose, it had to be shaped by his own hand and mind. The smithing was every bit as much a part of the rite as the incantation itself.

As the wide, heavy circlet took shape, Nagash poured not just magical power into the metal, but memories as well. From his bitter days as hierophant in Khemri, to the violent overthrow of Thutep, to his years of iron-fisted rule over all Nehekhara. He infused it with his lust for Neferem and his hatred for the gods of the once-Blessed Land; with his slaughter of the people of Mahrak and his fury at the betrayal of the army of Lahmia. More than anything else, he filled the metal with his lust for vengeance and his desire to rule over all mankind.

The hammer fell tirelessly, fuelled by hatred and ruthless ambition. There was no beauty or grace in the crown Nagash forged, only a dark and eternal purpose: to draw a veil of night over the world, and rule as king over a realm of the dead.

Forged by dark magic and infused with Nagash's necromantic essence, the crown would magnify his powers a thousandfold. It was both a symbol and a potent tool, one that would seal the doom of the great cities of Nehekhara.

The green moon passed across the sky as Nagash worked, heedless of the ambitions of necromancers and men. By the time that the last hammer blow fell, the clouds had passed westwards and dawn was paling the sky to the east.

The stone hammer was charred black, riven with hundreds of cracks. When Nagash tossed it aside it struck the flagstones and shattered with a splintering *crack*.

Nagash the Undying, lord of Nagashizzar and Master of the Wastes, gripped the jagged, smouldering crown and raised it like a challenge to the eastern sky.

The necromancer placed the dark crown upon his brow. Darkness fell over the great mountain like a funeral shroud.

SIXTEEN

A HOWL FROM THE WASTELAND

Lahmia,
the City of the Dawn,
in the 105th year of Djaf the Terrible
(-1222 Imperial Reckoning)

The tale of Ptra's virtuous wife Neru and his jealous concubine Sakhmet were well known to the people of Nehekhara, even in an age bereft of gods and their blessings. While Ptra the Father ruled in the heavens, so the stories went, Neru the Mother tended the gardens of the afterlife, and welcomed the souls of the dead who had earned their place in paradise. In the garden she was attended by her many daughters and guarded by a pack of ever-vigilant sphinxes, but when her husband's daily labours had ceased and he passed beyond the rim of the world to the west, she would rise from the garden and watch over her beloved children by night, keeping them safe from the beasts of the wild and the spirits of the waste. And each night, the vindictive Sakhmet would follow in her wake, glaring balefully at the children of the gods and scheming to usurp Ptra's beloved wife. Most nights, Neru would triumph, her swift feet guiding her across the heavens - but once in a great while, Sakhmet's wiles would bedevil her, and the Green Witch would usurp Neru's place in the sky. When that happened, all the land trembled in fear, as the creatures of the darkness and the deep earth would rise up and work their evils on mankind.

Never before in human history had Sakhmet usurped Neru during the year of Djaf, god of the dead. The implications, thought W'soran, were momentous indeed.

In keeping with her spiteful nature, Sakhmet did not follow a predictable course through the sky. A great many priests had attempted to divine it, particularly those of Settra's Mortuary Cult, who had devoted themselves to the resurrection of the souls of the dead. Of them all, Nagash had come the closest to predicting her movements, drawing on the accumulated observations of the cult and applying formulae more complex and visionary than any other liche priest had attempted before. An entire volume of Nagash's tomes was dedicated to his observations and they predicted an occultation during the one hundred and fifth year of Djaf's ascendancy.

True to the Undying King's predictions, that fateful night had arrived.

W'soran had begun his preparations for the night's ritual many months in advance. The proper sigils were studied, refined, and laid out on the floor of the sanctum with a mixture of quicksilver and ground human bone. The ancient skull of the cursed king, Thutep, was brought forth, and still more rituals were performed upon the relic, to better attune it to W'soran's spells. His thralls combed the dockyards and the slums in search of young children, who died each night beneath the necromancer's sacrificial knife. Their life energies boiled within W'soran's shrivelled veins, held in readiness for the coming eclipse.

Over the last few days, he'd sensed it: a growing disturbance in the aether, like the rising wind before a fierce summer storm. Each evening, Sakhmet's course came closer and closer to matching Neru's. W'soran noted each observation with care, his shrivelled lips drawn back in a death's-head grin as the celestial pieces slid neatly into place.

Tonight, the conditions would be ideal. W'soran could not possibly fail. When Sakhmet's power parted the veil between the realm of the living and the realm of the dead, he would call forth the spirit of Nagash.

The ritual's first steps were begun at sunset, just as the Green Witch appeared on the horizon. A dozen thralls attended upon the necromancer, clad in robes of red and black, their breasts marked in chalk with arcane sigils of power. Incense was lit in braziers of polished bone. As the first, telltale ripples spread through the aether, W'soran began the first of seven rituals of warding, preparing the chamber for the whirlwind to come.

The preparatory rites took many hours, while Sakhmet stalked Ptra's wife across the heavens. Beyond the temple walls, the people of the city shuttered themselves inside their homes and prayed to the forsaken gods for protection, sensing that something terrible was approaching. Trading ships at anchor in the harbour threw offerings of gold and silver into the dark waters; even the City Guard abandoned their nightly patrols and retreated to the safety of their barracks. As far as they were concerned, anyone foolish enough to ignore the signs and go about on the streets tonight deserved whatever fate befell them.

By midnight, Neru had reached her zenith and Sakhmet had crept up behind her like an assassin, nearly close enough to touch. Jackals gibbered and howled in the rocky lands south of the city, while off to the north-west a strange, otherworldly display of lights roiled and flickered on the horizon. And then, in what seemed like the space of just a few moments, the Green Witch overtook her prey, smothering Neru's light with her own and bathing the earth in a bilious green glow.

Deep inside the temple, a gust of wind rose inside the windowless sanctum, stirring the clouds of incense into ghostly shapes and plucking at the pages of Nagash's tomes. The aether began to roil.

And then, a faint, tolling sound, like the portentous note of a temple bell. It reverberated in the necromancer's bones. W'soran sighed in satisfaction, the breath rattling in the back of his throat. Dusty robes flapping, he rushed to the lectern that had been placed before the summoning circle. His thralls shuffled forwards, obeying W'soran's will, and formed a semicircle to either side of him. The necromancer's hands rested lightly upon the ancient pages of the tome.

Another bell-like note rippled through the aether, rhythmic as a hammer upon an anvil, or a fist against a door. W'soran raised his arms. 'I hear you,' he rasped. 'Lord of the Dead, I hear you. Come forth!'

W'soran began to chant the first of the invocations he had prepared, focusing his energies on the yellowed skull of Thutep in the centre of the summoning circle. Timing was critical, for the occultation would only last until dawn, and the great rite would take hours to complete.

Words of power rolled easily from W'soran's lips as the invocation took shape. Stolen energies flowed from his body into the cursed king's skull and the necromancer felt his perceptions beginning to expand, reaching beyond the walls of the sanctum and into the dark lands of the dead. As he worked, the aether continued to tremble with hammer-like blows, each one louder and more penetrating than the one before.

The physical world grew dim to W'soran's eyes. A bleak, twilit plain stretched before him, lit by a vague, greyish luminescence. The air within the sanctum turned cold and dank in the space of a single instant. The breath of the chanting thralls made ghostly plumes of vapour in the air. Glittering frost radiated outwards from the summoning circle across the stone floor.

Time ceased to have meaning. Gradually, as the invocation reached its conclusion and W'soran's mind adjusted to his new-found perceptions, he realised that there was movement upon the plain. A vast multitude of shadowy figures surrounded him, stumbling wearily through the dimness. In the echoing silence between the hammer blows, W'soran thought he heard faint sounds – the desperate cries of the lost, begging for release.

All at once, W'soran felt himself teetering upon a precipice. The twilit plain pulled at him, threatening to tear his soul from his shrivelled body. But the necromancer was prepared for this. Quickly he began a second incantation, one that created an arbitrary threshold between the realms within the confines of the ritual circle.

The hammer blows were coming faster now. The vibrations from one blow had barely ended before the next one began and they exerted a strange kind of weight on W'soran's soul. The necromancer could not account for it, but neither could he let it stop him. He forged ahead with the second incantation, drawing deeply from his reserves of stolen vigour.

There was a crash. Several moments passed before W'soran could discern whether it was a physical or a spiritual sound. Still chanting, he turned his head, and with an effort, the boundaries of the sanctum swam into focus. Ushoran leaned drunkenly against one of the heavy wooden tables, knocking a stack of scrolls and leather-bound books onto the floor. Just then, another ringing blow thundered through the aether, and W'soran saw the immortal's face twist into a grimace of almost childlike terror.

Ushoran's lips moved. W'soran could not hear his voice over the keening of the dead, but he could read what they said. *That sound! What is it? What's happening?*

W'soran felt a flicker of surprise. How could Ushoran sense what was happening? For a moment he nearly lost control of the second incantation. Swiftly the necromancer tore his attention away from Ushoran and focused once more on the summoning circle.

Doom. Doom. Doom. W'soran was buffeted by the ringing blows. His bones felt as heavy as lead. The necromancer redoubled his efforts, shouting the words of the invocation into the aether. Slowly but surely, the threshold took shape.

The unearthly pressure was mounting. W'soran could almost feel his bones beginning to warp beneath the strain. Snarling, he launched into the third invocation as soon as the second one was complete. His spirit responded to the arcane commands, extending from his body according to his will and approaching the threshold he'd created. The wails of the lost grew louder, tearing at his senses.

DOOM.

W'soran pushed his spirit onwards, drawing ever closer to the precipice. He could feel the emptiness of the space beyond and, for the first time in ages, the immortal felt afraid. This was what awaited him, should his mortal body be destroyed. The thought chilled him to the core. And yet he did not turn back.

DOOM.

At the threshold, the power of the bleak land increased tenfold. W'soran struggled against its terrible pull. His reserves of power were reaching their limits; before long the ritual's demands would begin to consume his physical body, until there was nothing left to anchor his soul. Then he would become one with the lost, trapped for eternity on a plain without end.

DOOM.

W'soran could not last much longer. He summoned up the last of his strength and crossed partly over the threshold, into the realm of the dead.

At once, the spirits of the lost sensed his presence. They turned on him in an instant, grasping at his soul like drowning men. Hundreds upon hundreds, dragging him under...

W'soran fought back. He lashed at them with his sorcerous might. *Nagash! Undying King! Master of life and death! Hear me! I, W'soran, summon you forth!*

His command echoed through the emptiness. The spirits that surrounded him recoiled for an instant at the utterance of the Usurper's name, but then they fell upon him with a vengeance. Their keening wails were now tinged with anger.

Come forth! I command you!

DOOM!

The last blow was discordant and terrible, a splintering crash of shattered stone. And then something vast moved upon the face of the aether and the realm of the dead trembled. The spirits receded from him, wailing in misery and fear.

His power all but spent, W'soran tried to draw back from the threshold – but he was held there, transfixed by a force of will a thousand times greater than his own. The twilit plain vanished, replaced by the vision of an ancient, smoke-wreathed mountain, its splintered flanks bathed in unholy, greenish light. A vast fortress crouched atop the mountain, and upon the tallest tower of that fortress stood a giant, clad in armour that glowed with icy, sorcerous flames. The giant gripped a jagged metal crown in his armoured fist and when his face turned skywards, W'soran saw only a leering skull, wreathed in necromantic flames. Bale-fires burned from the depths of the skull's eye-sockets, scorching W'soran with their glare. The immortal gazed into their depths and saw the end of the world of men.

W'soran writhed like an insect in Nagash's grasp, howling in terror. Then came a crushing impact that blotted out the immortal's senses, plunging him into oblivion.

W'soran lay upon his back, shoulders pressed hard against the floor of the sanctum. His ears roared with the fading echoes of the aetheric storm and the incense-laden air crackled with the dissipating energies of the massive ritual. Gasping in shock, the necromancer's parchment-thin eyelids fluttered as he tried to push himself upright – but a cold hand tightened about his throat like a vice and slammed him roughly back against the stone.

The rough impact jolted W'soran's senses. His vision snapped back into focus and he found himself staring into Neferata's snarling, blood-stained face. Spatters of gore dotted her slender arms and the front of her dust-stained robes. The heavy wooden lectern lay in pieces around them, shattered by the queen's fearsome blow.

'W'soran,' she said. Her voice was little more than a low, liquid growl. 'You withered fool. What have you done?'

The necromancer writhed like a serpent in Neferata's grip. A blistering incantation came to mind, powerful enough to crush the queen's bones to powder and hurl her carcass the length of the chamber – had he but the strength to cast it. The rite had consumed every mote of his carefully hoarded power, leaving him helpless before Neferata's wrath. But instead of fear, the realisation only filled him with rage.

W'soran's ragged lips drew back, baring his fangs in a death's-head grin. 'You felt it, too, didn't you?' he wheezed. His narrow chest heaved with ghastly, wheezing laughter. 'You felt it in your bones, just as I did. The master's fist upon the door!'

Neferata understood at once. W'soran could see the flicker of realisation in her dark eyes – and perhaps, the briefest glimmer of fear.

The queen glanced back over her shoulder. Belatedly, W'soran realised that they were not alone. Ushoran still leaned against the wooden reading table, glaring angrily at Lord Ankhat, who stood just inside the sanctum's entrance with a heavy iron sword in his hand. Neferata's white-robed progeny circled the room, their jaws and clawed hands dripping with fresh gore. W'soran's thralls had been ripped apart and left to bleed out their precious fluids upon the stone.

Ankhat looked to the queen and frowned. 'I told you he was behind this. He's been trying to call back Lamashizzar, somehow. He's all but admitted it!'

'Lamashizzar? Do you think I would call that capering fool my master?' W'soran's voice rose to a shriek. 'No, I speak of Nagash, the Undying King! I have seen him!' His laughter echoed from the walls. 'All this time, I have searched for him, but I was looking in the wrong place! He could not be found among the souls of the dead because *he still reigns upon this earth!'*

Neferata's fist tightened about W'soran's throat. 'You *lie*,' she hissed. 'Nagash was destroyed–'

'Not so,' the necromancer croaked. 'He escaped the battle at Mahrak; his body was never found.' He pointed a clawed finger at Ankhat. 'Ask him. He marched with the army to Khemri. He knows!'

'This is some kind of trick,' Ankhat snarled, but the look in his dark eyes belied the nobleman's bravado. 'He is nowhere in Nehekhara. We searched from one end to the other!'

'Imbecile!' W'soran sneered. 'All this time, the Undying King has been rebuilding his strength in secret, far from the eyes of men. He has taken a great mountain and made it his fortress. I have seen its towers wreathed in the smoke of countless forges, where his servants make ready for the day of Nehekhara's demise! And that day swiftly approaches! Already, Nagash is clad in the panoply of war, and he holds a dark and terrible crown in his hand! The days of mankind are numbered–'

Neferata snarled. Her hand closed tighter, until the necromancer's leathery tendons creaked, and his spine began to bend.

'Let him come,' she said, pitching her voice so Ankhat and Ushoran could hear. 'When he arrives outside my gates, your head will be there to welcome him.'

But if Neferata thought to see W'soran quail in fear, she was disappointed. The necromancer merely grinned, his eyes glittering defiantly. 'Do it!' he spat. 'Tear my head from my shoulders, just as you did to Ubaid. With my last breath I will utter a curse so terrible that Lahmia will be blighted until the stars have burned down to embers.'

The queen snarled in fury, and for a fleeting instant, W'soran thought that she had seen through his bluff. But then he felt her grip loosen ever so slightly and he knew that he had won. More laughter bubbled from W'soran's throat.

'He is coming,' the necromancer hissed. 'And when he does, you will grovel like a worm at his feet.'

Neferata bent over the necromancer, until their faces nearly touched. Her charnel breath gusted cold against his face.

'A pity you shall never see it.'

The queen's empty hand snatched up a splintered length of the wooden lectern. W'soran's eyes went wide. His cry of protest transformed into a wordless scream of rage as she drove the dagger-like fragment into his heart.

Ushoran's nails etched deep scars into the wood of the table at his back as he fought to maintain an outwards appearance of calm. His head still ached from the dreadful, bell-like tolling that had brought him to the sanctum. The blood in his veins, so freshly stolen from a young beggar mere hours before, had now lost its heat. His limbs felt as heavy as lead. From the tense cast of Ankhat's face, it was clear that the nobleman had been profoundly affected as well. Ushoran's gaze fell to the iron sword in Ankhat's hand and he debated whether he could slip through the door of the sanctum and escape before the nobleman could strike. If he tried, though, and failed, it would only confirm his complicity in W'soran's crimes. It was all Ushoran could do to maintain his bland facade and conceal his mounting desperation.

Neferata rose slowly from W'soran's limp body. 'Find a barrel and stuff him inside,' she said to Ankhat. 'Then bury him beneath the temple.'

Ankhat scowled at the necromancer's skeletal form. 'That should be easy enough. Is there any place in particular you want me to put him?'

'Somewhere that no one will ever find him,' the queen replied. Then Neferata turned to Ushoran.

'And what role did you play in all of this?' she demanded.

The Lord of Masks raised his hands in protest. 'None whatsoever, great one,' he said quickly. 'I'm no necromancer, as you well know.'

Neferata took a step towards him. Her priestesses stopped pacing about the sanctum and turned to face Ushoran, their expressions disconcertingly intent.

'And yet, here you are,' she replied.

'Clearly we shared the same idea,' Ushoran said, thinking furiously. The best lies, he knew, always began with a splinter of truth. 'When that awful pounding began, I naturally assumed that W'soran would have some idea of what it was. As did you, apparently.'

The queen's eyes narrowed. 'And you happened to know exactly how to find him.'

The Lord of Masks affected a shrug. 'It is my business to know such things, great one.'

'And yet you have no word of Prince Alcadizzar,' the queen snapped. 'How is that, my lord, after all these years?'

Ushoran paused, considering his reply with care. He'd escaped one snake pit and stumbled into another. 'We will find him, great one,' he answered. 'I'm sure of it.' He licked his lips. 'With every passing day, I become more convinced that you are right, and he is somewhere close by. Just a... a few more interrogations and I am sure we will learn something of value.'

Suddenly, Neferata was at his side, her dark eyes peering hungrily into his own. Ushoran's fists clenched reflexively; he smothered the instinct to bare his fangs at the queen's wordless challenge.

'I am pleased to hear it,' Neferata growled. 'Because my patience is wearing thin. I confess that it's confounded me why your network of spies has been so successful in every other inquiry except the one that matters to me the most.'

Ushoran kept his voice under careful control. The slightest sense of nervousness was certain to be misinterpreted. 'No one is more confounded by Alcadizzar's disappearance than I, great one,' he said.

'I hope so. I hope the matter has your *undivided* attention,' the queen said. 'Because if he isn't found soon, you will come to *envy* W'soran's fate.'

Later that night, as the hour of the wolf approached, the wind came howling in from the sea, tossing about the ships at anchor and rattling doors along the city streets. Lahmians crouched around their fires, many whispering prayers to Neru and ringing silver bells in hopes of keeping the unquiet spirits at bay. Strange sounds echoed from the darkness outside: angry mutterings and groans, frantic screams and the mocking laughter of jackals. Fingers scratched at the doors of wine shops and pleasure houses and tentative steps paced across the rooftops of many homes, as though searching for a way inside.

In the city's vast necropolis, one spirit in particular woke in darkness, summoned across the wide gulf by a call he was powerless to deny. Bony hands twitched, scrabbling at the sides of a simple, stone casket. On the exterior of the casket's lid, complex sigils carved into the stone and inlaid with silver started to glow with heat. Tendrils of steam curled from the protective wards as the will of the spirit contained within fought against its bonds. Within seconds, the silver inlay began to bubble and then drip in molten streams down the sides of the casket. There was a creak of tearing metal as the lead seal covering the seams of the lid slowly gave way, followed by a crash as the stone lid was hurled aside and broke into pieces on the mausoleum floor.

The figure within did not move at first, as though listening to the call that had summoned him out of the darkness. It was his master's voice, commanding him to rise and serve, as he'd done in centuries past. Once upon a time, the thought would have filled him with dread; now, he felt only triumph and a sense of savage joy. If it meant a release from that endless plain and the wailing of the damned, he would serve Nagash gladly, and drown the world in nightmares.

Ligaments creaking, the mouldy skeleton sat up in the casket. His robes hung about his bones in tatters, held in place more by layers of grimy cobwebs than anything else. Beetles and swift, brown spiders scuttled from burrows dug into the desiccated flesh of his ribcage as he gripped the edge of the casket and climbed his way out.

Standing amid the broken shards of the casket's lid, the skeleton reached into the casket and drew out his skull. The few scraps of flesh that still clung to the bone were dark and curled like patches of old leather. Green fires guttered balefully in deep-set eye sockets and grave-mould clung to his blackened teeth. A stub of broken vertebrae hung stubbornly from the base of the skull, the lower knob sheared halfway through by a powerful sword-stroke.

Slowly, haltingly, the skeleton turned the skull about and lifted it onto its severed neck. The sheared ends gripped together at once, bound by sheer force of will. With a faint, grating sound, the head turned left and right, studying the cramped confines of the pauper's tomb that he'd been sealed into. Bitter, ethereal laughter echoed in the dank space.

The figure bent, hands searching the darkness inside the casket once more. Finally, the fingers closed about a familiar hilt. The skeleton drew out a long, double-edged iron sword, its surface spotted with rust and sheathed in layers of cobwebs, and growled in satisfaction. Then he turned his attention to the crypt's narrow door.

On the third blow, the thin stone slab broke apart and fell to the ground. Arkhan the Black strode into the night air and raised his sword to the bale-moon gleaming above the western horizon. Then he turned his face to the north-west, where his master waited, and went to serve him.

SEVENTEEN

PREPARATIONS OF WAR

Nagashizzar,
in the 106th year of Asaph the Beautiful
(-1211 Imperial Reckoning)

A black-robed scout-assassin emerged from the wide, shadow-filled lane across the great cavern and skittered silently up to Lord Eshreegar. The two conversed quietly for a moment and the Master of Treacheries nodded stiffly. As the scout disappeared back into the shadows, Eshreegar turned his hooded head and nodded to Eekrit. The skeletons were coming.

Eekrit could feel Nagash's minions approaching long before he saw the green glow of their eyes, or heard the dry rustling of their steps. He felt it in his old joints and in the back of his throat, as the thick, reeking air of the great cavern turned cold and dank as a grave. Gritting his teeth and leaning heavily on the gnarled cypress cane in his paw, he rose painfully from the wooden chair his slaves had brought down from the great hall. Behind him, the shackled herds of greenskins noticed the change as well and filled the echoing space with a rising chorus of growls, barks and shrieking cries. Slavers snarled at the drug-addled beasts, lashing at their scarred backs with metal-studded whips to keep them in line.

Within moments, a pair of eerie grave-lights emerged from the gloom. Bone rasped along rough, slimy stone. A figure emerged, clad in mouldy rags and carrying a rust-spotted iron sword. Eekrit had seen this particular corpse several times before, but couldn't say for certain what it was. It radiated power, like one of the *kreekar-gan*'s wights, but held far more intelligence than the rest. Its teeth were black and jagged as splintered ebony, giving its skull a permanent, broken snarl.

Behind the figure marched a long line of hunched, yellowed skeletons, swathed in rotting fragments of clothing and scraps of mouldy flesh. They moved in pairs, each carrying a heavy wooden chest between them. Their knobby skulls turned this way and that, snouts raised as though sniffing the air for their lost clan mates. Though Nagash no doubt held thousands of human skeletons in thrall, it apparently amused the liche-king to send skaven corpses to trade with the Under-Empire.

'By the scales, damn you,' Eekrit snarled, pointing with his cane to the towering wood-and-bronze apparatus at his right. Every three months, it was always the same. As the black-toothed creature glared hatefully at the skaven, the skeletons slowly turned, staring at the scales as though they'd just sprung up from the cavern floor. Then, one pair at a time, they shuffled over and set down their burdens for appraisal. Eekrit waved a paw impatiently and a small gang of skaven hurried forwards to weigh the chests of god-stone and tally the results. The former warlord surveyed the process with a sour look on his face and wondered once again if he hadn't made a terrible mistake.

'A poisoned cup or an assassin's knife has to be a better fate than this,' he muttered to himself.

'Not from my experience,' Eshreegar replied, as he joined Eekrit near the creaking scales. Though nearly blind now from age and his injuries during the war, his hearing was as keen as ever. 'But, each to their own.'

Eekrit glared at the Master of Treacheries. 'Shall we trade places, then?' he sneered. 'I could give orders to your scouts and send reports back to Velsquee, while you stare at mouldy ledgers and put up with... with *this*–' he waved an arm at the noisome herds of shifting greenskins, 'each and every day.'

Eshreegar folded his arms and sighed. 'Well, Velsquee isn't exactly happy with the reports, for what it's worth.'

'No, I expect he isn't,' Eekrit said, tail lashing irritably. The liche-king had begun rebuilding his strength the very day that the trade agreement had been set and he hadn't stopped since. The foundries ran day and night, spewing vast clouds of choking fumes into the air above the mountain, while gangs of undead labourers bored dozens of new mine shafts deep into the mountainside. Toppled towers and collapsed buildings had been rebuilt at an ever-increasing pace, as a growing number of northern barbarians were sent to serve in the liche-king's halls. Looking back now, it galled him to think how close they'd been to victory. He should have listened to his instincts from the outset and thrown everything he'd had into one, final attack. It would have been far better to have tried – and possibly failed – than to sit amidst this rubbish heap from one miserable year to the next.

The appraisers went to work opening each of the chests. Green light flared brightly from each one; within lay carefully stacked ingots of refined god-stone. At a half-pound of stone for every one hundred pounds of flesh or treasure, the skaven had learned to maximise their profits early on by trading in big, muscular greenskins and crates of heavy ores. The wealth they were reaping from the mountain was nowhere near the amount they had mined during the war, but was still a fabulous sum by any normal measure. The sight of so much of the precious stone in one place never failed to set Eekrit's nose twitching.

One by one, the chests were weighed; two scribes – one from Velsquee's clan, and one employed by Eekrit himself – noted down the value in their ledgers. When the process was complete, they would be placed under heavy guard until the morrow, when a contingent of Velsquee's *heechigar* would come to collect them and carry them back to the Great City. There, Velsquee would sell the stone to the other clans and share the profits with Eekrit and Eshreegar. Eekrit had no doubt that Velsquee was robbing them blind in the process, like any self-respecting skaven would. Despite this, the former warlord had already amassed a sizeable fortune over the last few years. Another decade or so and he might be able to buy his way out of exile.

There certainly didn't seem to be any point in staying. Nagash had grown far too powerful. If mad old Qweeqwol had been right about the necromancer's designs, Eekrit didn't want to be anywhere near the mountain when the liche-king put his plans into motion.

'So many chests! Such *magnificent* wealth! It-it is pleasing to the eye, yes?'

Eekrit blinked, roused from his reverie by the nasal voice to his right. He glanced over at the wiry, younger skaven who had sidled up beside him. His ears flattened slightly in irritation. 'Don't start, Kritchit. I'm not in the mood.'

Kritchit wrung his knobby paws and gave the former warlord his most unctuous smile. Eekrit thought the slaver looked like a half-chewed lump of gristle. His shoulders were hunched, the left slightly higher than the right, and there was a noticeable hunk of flesh missing from his left thigh, which caused him to drag the leg when he walked. Kritchit's head and arms were patterned with dozens of old scars and his ears had been chewed down to mere nubs. He was a genuine horror to look upon and reeked of spoiled meat besides. For years he and his band of savages had taken Velsquee's gold and scoured the mountains for human and greenskin slaves. He was cunning, ruthless, and as greedy a wretch as Eekrit had ever met.

'Mood? How can your mood be anything but grand, my lord?' Kritchit spread his paws, taking in the long line of chests. 'Are you not *blessed*? Is this not a great bounty of wealth laid before you, greater than any conqueror's due?'

Eekrit's eyes narrowed angrily. 'We carved this much out of the mountain every *day* during the war.'

Kritchit chuckled. 'Oh, no doubt, no doubt,' he said patronisingly. 'But this here... this is a gift, yes? Dropped like ripe fruit into your outstretched paw. Did you sweat, and suffer, and bleed for this treasure? No, certainly not. You had but to recline here, in luxury, while my bold raiders and I hunted day and night on your behalf.'

The former warlord folded his arms. 'You're doing this for Velsquee, not me,' he growled. 'I'm nothing more than a *clerk*.'

Kritchit sighed with theatrical weariness, ignoring Eekrit's reply. 'The life of a raider is a hard thing, my lord. Much deprivation. Much danger. Days and nights in the cold, open spaces, without so much as a burrow to shelter in.'

'Really? I had no idea.'

'And the greenskins... there are only a few herds left and those are the meanest, cleverest of them all.' The slaver shook his scarred head sadly. 'There was much fighting. I lost many good warriors. Some were like littermates to me.'

Eshreegar made a disgusted sound. 'That's it,' the Master of Treacheries said. 'I'm killing him.'

The former warlord forestalled Eshreegar with an upraised paw. 'One share, Kritchit. Same as ever.'

Kritchit drew himself up to his full height, which had the unfortunate effect of making him seem a bit lopsided. His right paw fell to the butt of the coiled whip that hung from his belt. 'Where is-is the justice in that?' he said. 'I do all the work, take all the risks! I have warriors to pay, kinfolk to bribe. I-I have *expenses*.'

'One share, Kritchit.'

'It's been one share for the last ten years! You know how much things cost these days?' Kritchit pointed to the milling herd of slaves. 'These beasts killed a dozen of my warriors when we took their camp and then mauled two more-more on the way here! How do you expect me to-to replace them?' Kritchit licked at his long, front teeth. 'Three shares, this-this time.'

'Am I speaking too quickly for you, Kritchit? Should I use smaller words? One. Share.'

'Two shares!' The slaver swept his paw at the line of chests. 'Look-look at all that! Velsquee will never miss it!'

Eekrit sighed. 'I've changed my mind,' he said. 'Eshreegar, kill him.'

'Now, look here–'

Eshreegar had a knife drawn and was bearing down on Kritchit when a commotion suddenly erupted at the far end of the cavern. Greenskins bellowed and snarled, shaking their heavy chains and stirring up the entire herd. The slavers shouted back, their whips hissing malevolently through the dank air. Eekrit turned and saw a column of burly, armoured skaven shoving the slavers aside as they forced their way into the cavern from one of the wide tunnels that led from the mountain towards the Great City.

'What's this?'

Eshreegar paused, knife poised to strike Kritchit. He squinted his one eye at the distant skaven. 'Velsquee's *heechigar*,' he grunted. 'They're early.'

The storm-walkers poured into the cavern in a great column, polearms at the ready. Behind them, Eekrit caught sight of a gang of bent-backed slaves carrying a swaying wooden palanquin. His eyes widened.

'By the Horned One. What's he doing here?'

'Velsquee?' Eshreegar asked. 'After all this time?'

'So it would seem.' The former warlord's tail lashed agitatedly. For the life of him, he couldn't fathom why the old Grey Lord would risk the long and arduous journey from the Great City and that made him very uneasy.

Eshreegar gave a discreet cough. He nodded his head at the slaver. 'Do you still want me to...?'

The former warlord glanced back at Kritchit. 'No,' he told Eshreegar. Then, to Kritchit, he said, 'What luck! Here is Grey Lord Velsquee, no doubt come to partake of all those *luxuries* we're so famous for here.' He gestured to the palanquin. 'You should go at once and demand your extra shares from him. My lord is famous for his compassion and generosity.'

Kritchit shuddered from his whiskers to the tip of his tail. 'Oh, no!' he squeaked. 'No, I-I would not dream of-of imposing on Lord Velsquee.' The slaver gulped. 'No. One share will-will do.'

'Truly, Kritchit, you're an example to us all,' Eekrit sneered. 'Now get your gang moving and hand over the slaves double-quick.' The former warlord sighed irritably. 'I have guests to entertain.'

Eekrit and Eshreegar reached the great hall just ahead of Velsquee. The former warlord brandished his cane and snarled orders at the few slaves he had left, sending them scurrying to clear the worst of the rubbish out of the passageways before the Grey Lord arrived. While they worked, Eekrit had Eshreegar force open the one door to the hall that still hung on its hinges; the old skaven managed to shove it most of the way before the rotted wood tore free from its mountings and crashed to the floor in a cloud of dust and mould. After that, there was nothing left to do but stand by the dais and wait.

Minutes later, a company of storm-walkers came tramping up the passageway and filed into the hall. Velsquee was borne along in their wake, riding in a litter carried by eight exhausted-looking slaves. They passed between the ordered ranks of the *heechigar* and carefully lowered the chair to the floor, just a few feet from where Eekrit waited.

Velsquee rose from the padded seat with great care, his trembling paw leaning heavily on a rune-carved cypress cane. Eekrit reckoned that the Grey Lord was nearly two hundred years old now, his span of years extended by sorcerous means to well past that of a typical skaven. He could no longer bear the weight of weapons and armour, instead wrapping himself in layers of heavy, grey robes. His white fur had thinned around his paws and face, revealing the wrinkled skin beneath, and his ears hung listlessly against his skull. Grunting in discomfort, the Grey Lord found his feet and took a slow step forwards. Glowing charms of god-stone strung around his neck clinked softly together as Velsquee surveyed the mouldy, rotting tapestries and the pile of worm-eaten wood that had once been Eekrit's expensive throne. When he spoke, his voice was a bubbling rasp. 'How the mighty have fallen, eh, Eekrit?'

Eekrit's tail lashed, stirring up more dust. 'We wouldn't want Nagash to think we still had a claim to the mountain, would we?'

The Grey Lord chuckled, breath wheezing past his lips. 'Just so. Just so.' He raised a palsied paw to wipe at his mouth. 'Have you any wine?'

Eekrit sighed. 'Wine we have, my lord. Bowls, however, are in short supply. I have my slaves looking for some now. Forgive me, but we had no idea you were coming.'

Velsquee grunted. 'No. Of course not. That was the entire point. No one knows I'm here.'

'Not even the Council?'

'*Especially* not them.' Velsquee took a few halting steps towards the two younger skaven. 'As far as those idiots know, I've taken ill and retired to my sickbed.'

The news surprised Eekrit. The journey to the mountain from the Great City and back again took many months. Velsquee was risking a great deal; by feigning illness for so long, his rivals on the Council would think him easy pickings and begin manoeuvring against him. By the time he returned home, Velsquee might find his power base swept away and assassins lurking in every shadow.

'What in the Horned One's name is going on?' Eekrit blurted.

Velsquee leaned with both paws upon his cane. 'Your reports over the last few years have been very troubling,' he began.

'So you've read them, have you?' Eekrit snapped. 'At what point did you first become concerned? Was it the mention of the *legions* of undead warriors Nagash has raised? Or perhaps it was the *vast necromantic ritual* the liche-king performed on the Night of the Horned God, some *eleven years ago*?'

Velsquee's eyes narrowed. The *heechigar* filled the audience chamber with threatening growls, their paws tightening on the hafts of their polearms.

'Now is not the time for sarcasm,' the Grey Lord said.

Eekrit paused, drawing himself back from the brink. 'I'll keep that in mind,' he said grudgingly.

'Good,' Velsquee said. He sighed. 'You've stated in your reports that you no longer think we can defeat Nagash.'

Eekrit met the Grey Lord's stare. 'That's right. He's far stronger now than he was before the war and not just in the number of warriors at his command. His necromantic powers have increased as well.' He pointed a claw in the direction of the great cavern. 'Did you see those skeletons? Did you *feel* the cold clinging to their bones? They're much more potent than the ones we've faced before.' The former warlord shrugged. 'He's got too much god-stone in his vaults and he's had time to improve his defences throughout the tunnels. Even with the full weight of the Under-Empire arrayed against him, I doubt we could prevail.'

The Grey Lord nodded. At length, he said, 'I think you are right. In fact, I've suspected it for some time.'

Eekrit clenched his fist. Anger and frustration threatened to overwhelm him. He forced himself to speak as calmly as he could. 'Then why are we still here? Why continue feeding him slaves and increasing his strength?'

'Because it allows us to maintain a presence near the centre of the liche-king's power,' Velsquee said.

'To what end?'

The Grey Lord glanced at the nearest storm-walker and nodded, sending the *heechigar* striding swiftly from the chamber. 'Ever since the end of the war, there have been troubling reports from the Seer Council,' Velsquee said. 'Visions of darkness and death, spreading like a stain across the face of the world. They were vague things at first, but ever since the Horned God's Night, the clarity and intensity of the visions have increased.'

Eekrit felt his hackles rise. 'So Qweeqwol was right all along.'

The Grey Lord's expression turned bleak. 'Given the things I've heard recently, it's possible that the mad old rat may have understated things quite a bit.'

Eekrit laughed helplessly. 'Then what in the Horned One's name do you think *I* can do about it?'

Velsquee did not answer at first. A few moments later, the storm-walker returned, labouring under the weight of a long, narrow case cradled in his powerful arms. He walked carefully across the chamber to stand beside the Grey Lord and set the case on the floor between him and Eekrit. Its surface was covered with intricate runes of protection; its lid bore thirteen elaborate magical seals.

The former warlord squinted at the case's grey sides. 'Is that made of *lead*?' he asked.

'It is,' Velsquee said grimly. 'And sealed with potent sorceries to boot. Otherwise we would all be dead right now.'

Eekrit shrank back slightly from the container. 'What's inside?'

'A weapon,' the Grey Lord said simply, but there was a trace of awe in the old skaven's voice. 'A weapon more terrible than anything our people have made before. The finest warlock-engineers in the Under-Empire gave their lives to make it. I commissioned its forging in secret, just after the end of the war. It took nearly all my wealth and influence to see it finished.'

Eekrit stared at the case, feeling the first stirrings of greed at the power contained within. 'Such expense,' he murmured, feeling the temptation to reach out and touch the enchanted lead.

Velsquee shrugged. 'All the gold in the world doesn't make much difference if you're dead,' he said. He nodded at the case. 'If any weapon in the world can destroy the liche-king, it's this one. And I'm leaving it here with you.'

'*Me*?' Eekrit said. '*Here*? Right under the-the liche-king's nose?'

'Better here than the Great City, hundreds of leagues away,' Velsquee snapped. 'Do you imagine that you could get close enough to Nagash to kill him at this point?'

The former warlord glanced sidelong at Eshreegar, who snorted in disdain.

'Of course not,' Eekrit said. 'We'd get turned to ash – or worse – before we got within a mile of him.'

'I suspected as much,' Velsquee replied. 'But the liche-king is marshalling all this power for a reason. Sooner or later, he'll put it to use. His armies will march and great spells will be cast.'

Eshreegar folded his arms. 'Providing us an opening,' the Master of Treacheries said.

Velsquee nodded. 'And when the moment is right, you must strike.' He pointed to the case. 'Among the many enchantments worked into the seals is a spell that will alert me and the Seer Council when the case is opened. When that happens, we will gather in the Great City and lend you all the aid we can. In the meantime, we will see to it that you receive the very best potions and amulets to maintain your health and vigour. We wouldn't want you dying of heart failure before the task is complete.'

Suddenly the case didn't seem nearly so attractive any more. In fact, Eekrit felt a bit sick just looking at it. 'How am I to know when the moment has arrived?' he protested.

The Grey Lord shook his head. 'I have no idea. Not even the seers can say for certain.' He sighed and made his way slowly back to his litter. 'Watch and wait, Eekrit, watch and wait. And one more thing.'

'What is that?'

Velsquee settled back onto his chair. 'Remember Qweeqwol's warning. Only someone who is dead himself has any hope of defeating the liche-king.'

At a gesture from the Grey Lord, the slaves lifted the litter onto their shoulders. Without a word of farewell, Velsquee turned about and departed the great hall, probably for the very last time. Stunned, Eekrit turned to Eshreegar.

'Oh, no. Don't give me that look,' the Master of Treacheries protested.

'Why not? You're the master assassin.'

'He didn't say the job called for an assassin,' Eshreegar snarled. 'Just some stupid bastard who's already dead – and doesn't know it.' He folded his arms irritably. 'That could be either one of us.'

Try as he might, Eekrit couldn't very well deny it.

EIGHTEEN

PORTENTS OF DOOM

Lahmia,
the City of the Dawn,
in the 107th year of Ptra the Glorious
(-1200 Imperial Reckoning)

Down in the temple quarter, the great prayer lamps had been lit for the first time in hundreds of years. From his perch atop the square roof of a nobleman's residence close to the royal palace, Ushoran could hear the faint chanting of the priests and the frightened, almost pleading cries of the throng that filled the great square outside the decaying temples. Elsewhere, the great city was dark and still, even though the hour was early by Lahmian standards. He could remember a time when the market squares and the pleasure districts were noisy and bustling well past midnight, and richly-appointed palanquins would come and go at all hours between the houses on the city's great hill and the gambling dens down near the docks. Now the houses were shuttered; the houses of pleasure had shut their doors. Even down in the harbour, the crews of the trading ships went below and barred the hatchways leading to the upper decks. Those citizens who weren't begging for deliverance down in the temple quarter were huddled in the darkness, fearful of the terrible omen that stained the eastern sky.

No one could say for certain what it was. Certainly no one alive in Nehekhara had ever seen such a sight. It stretched like a streamer of glowing smoke across the heavens, a twin-tailed pennon of shifting, opalescent colour arcing high above the course of Neru and vengeful Sakhmet. The head of the pennon was rounder and brighter than the rest, shining with nearly the same intensity as Neru herself. It reminded Ushoran of a glowing catapult stone, like the orbs of bone that fell from the sky at Mahrak, so many centuries ago. He remembered the dread he felt, watching them hang suspended in the air over the battlefield, wondering when they would fall.

A palpable sense of doom hung over the city. Lahmia's citizens were growing desperate; they'd been afraid for much too long, trapped within the walls of the city and watching friends and neighbours go missing, night after night. Ushoran's agents warned him of angry murmurs in the market squares and the wine shops. People had lost faith in the king and the divinity of the royal bloodline. Offerings at the Temple of Blood had been dwindling for years, then dropped off altogether when the celestial portent appeared. The people of Lahmia were no longer looking to their rulers for succour, which was a very bad sign indeed.

It would only be a matter of time before Neferata noticed the lack of offerings at the temple. Edicts would be issued through the palace, demanding the worship of the people. Blood would flow, but it would be in the gutters of the city rather than the offering bowls of the temple.

At the moment, however, that was the very least of Ushoran's problems.

The Lord of Masks crouched on the edge of the building's high roof and launched himself into the air. The steep hill dropped away beneath him and for a dizzying instant he seemed to hang suspended in the warm night air. Ushoran's lips drew back in a ghastly grin as he plunged earthwards, tasting the salt breeze as he fell towards the close-set roofs of the houses sixty feet below. He landed easily, broad feet splayed across the baked mud bricks, propelling himself forwards on all fours like a loping jungle ape and leaping skywards once more.

Rooftop to rooftop he went, from one quarter to the next, down the long slope and eastwards, towards the docks. The further he went, the more the city's decline became apparent. The nobles' quarter was still relatively clean and small groups of paid watchmen stood at the street corners to preserve the illusion of order. The neighbouring district, where the city's wealthier tradesmen and ship owners lived, was filled with walled homes that had been turned into small fortresses over the years and were now showing signs of increasing decrepitude. More than once, Ushoran's preternatural senses detected groups of night watchmen prowling the courtyards of the wealthier homes, or peering into the darkness from shadowed rooftops. None marked his swift and silent passage - or if they did, they huddled in fear and dared give no alarm, for fear of drawing attention to themselves.

Where the money ended, the city's decline became sharply apparent. Past the tradesmen's district were the modest, single-storey homes of Lahmia's ship fitters and dockhands, which Ushoran had come to know well. Once, in the heyday of trade with the Silk Lands, the district had been bustling and well kept, if rough about the edges. Now it was dark and squalid. Piles of refuse rotted in the alleyways and behind the shuttered shops and the mud-brick walls of the homes were pitted and crumbling from neglect. Many of the families kept dogs in their courtyards and homes, to keep thieves - and packs of hungry rats - at bay. One began barking hysterically as Ushoran landed upon its master's roof, prompting others to take up the cry as well. By the time he reached the far end of the district, the air was full of their harsh, yapping cries.

Further east, conditions grew steadily worse. Poor neighbourhoods where unskilled day labourers had once been able to live and eke out a meagre existence had become despair-ridden slums. Empty, crumbling homes presided over streets filled with puddles of liquid excrement that had seeped to the surface from blocked or broken sewer pipes. It was not uncommon to find corpses rolled into the filthy gutters, where they would fall prey to rats or packs of hungry dogs. The people living in the decrepit buildings were little better than animals themselves. For a while they had offered Ushoran some interesting sport, but he'd quickly tired of their dead eyes and scrawny, battered bodies.

Beyond the slums lay the sprawling merchant districts, markets and pleasure dens that were fed by the sea trade and catered to rich and poor alike. This was the true heart of the ancient city, where the people of Lahmia made and lost their fortunes, celebrated victories or drowned their sorrows with wine, lotus or the pleasures of the flesh. During the glory days of Lamashizzar's reign, when the city was the richest in the civilised world, the shops never closed and throngs of people from all over Nehekhara would ebb and flow through the streets in a human tide. No more; now most of the merchants and wine-sellers barred their doors at sunset and the dens of vice were frequented only by the wretched and the desperate.

Ushoran alighted upon the roof of a shuttered wine-seller and crouched there, listening intently. The murmur of the multitudes in the temple district and the chorus of barking dogs at his back blended together into a surf-like rumble of distant noise. The immortal closed his eyes, breathing deeply and tasting the air for a very particular scent. His head turned slowly left and right, searching for telltale sounds among the streets and alleyways between him and the docks.

He crouched that way for hours, arms wrapped around his knees, listening and tasting the scents of the furtive world around him. He heard the shuffling footsteps of beggars, the phlegmatic murmurs of drunkards and the tremulous invitations of street-corner whores. Once, he cocked his head at the sounds of a scuffle in a nearby alley. Fists pounded into flesh and a man grunted in pain. When Ushoran heard a pair of voices arguing over the man's meagre possessions he settled back down with a scowl and continued his vigil.

Finally, well past midnight, came the sounds that he had been waiting for. Off to the south-east, perhaps four or five streets away, the strangled shout of a man, followed by the frantic, hysterical shrieks of a young woman. Then, moments later, Ushoran caught the coppery, acrid scent of fresh blood.

The immortal sprang into motion, leaping across alleys and rooftops in the direction of the screams. By the time the woman's shrieks came to an abrupt end, Ushoran was only two streets away. The smell of spilled blood burned in his nostrils and set his cold flesh tingling. It drew him unerringly, like iron to a lodestone.

At the last moment, as he crossed the rooftop of a dice house that rose above the source of the tantalising scent, the immortal considered his appearance. Hastily he shrouded his true features with the bland, noble facade he presented to Neferata and the rest of the Blood Court and then leapt lightly down into the alley yawning before him.

He landed amid piles of refuse, startling a pack of enormous rats that had been gathering near the lifeless body of an emaciated woman near the mouth of the alley. Her body lay sprawled in the stinking slime, her shabby robe undone and the side of her head crushed in like a broken wine jar. The whore's face was frozen in a wide-eyed rictus of terror, her cheeks spotted with droplets of fresh gore.

'She wouldn't stop screaming.'

Ushoran turned at the sound of the high-pitched, nasal voice. To his right, less than a dozen feet away, a heavyset man lay sprawled in a pile of rubbish, limbs contorted in death. The corpse's head had been pulled back and the thick neck torn open, exposing glistening bits of broken cartilage. Blood soaked the front of the corpse's brown robes and spattered the rubbish pile in a wide arc to either side of the body.

A slender figure in dark, filthy robes crouched over the man's ravaged corpse, dark blood drooling from his chin. Zurhas had changed a great deal since Ushoran had seen him last. His flesh was white as a corpse and glowed with a translucent sheen under the faint moonlight. Dark veins crawled up his narrow throat and across his bald, bulbous skull, pulsing with stolen life. The skin had drawn tight around Zurhas's face, emphasising his pointed cheekbones, receding chin and prominent, angular nose. His eyes were dark and beady, with tiny pupils that reflected the light like polished coins. More than anything else, he reminded Ushoran of a pale, hairless rat. He even clasped his strange, unusually long-fingered hands to his chest in a curiously rodent-like manner.

'I didn't want her,' the immortal told him. 'I told her to be quiet, to go away, but she wouldn't listen. She screamed and screamed, so I had to quiet her.' Zurhas unfolded his hands and gestured towards the dead woman. Drops of cooling blood dripped from dark, curved claws. 'You may have her, if you wish.'

Ushoran stared at Zurhas. There was no mistaking the gleam of madness in the immortal's rodent-like eyes. Not for the first time, he debated the wisdom of his plan. But time was running out. Neferata's patience was very nearly at an end. Something had to be done, and quickly, before it was too late.

'I have already fed,' the Lord of Masks replied. He managed a bland smile. 'But the offer is appreciated.'

Zurhas shrugged and turned his attention back to the dead man at his feet. 'This is the one I wanted,' he explained. 'He cheated at dice. Not once, but many times.' He touched a claw to one long, slightly pointed ear. 'Shaved dice make a very distinctive sound, I have learned. A shame I could not hear it when I was younger. How different my life might have been.' He leaned over the dead man and dipped two fingers into the gaping wound. Zurhas drew them out again and began licking the tips clean with delicate flicks of his bluish tongue. 'Are you any good at dice, Lord Ushoran?'

Ushoran's smooth brow showed the slightest hint of consternation. 'I don't much care for gambling.'

Zurhas rested his hands on his knees and stared up at the Lord of Masks. 'And yet here you are,' he said. 'Why else go to all the trouble to find me?'

Ushoran felt his hackles rise, purely as a matter of pride. 'Trouble? Nothing could have been simpler–'

To his surprise, Zurhas let out a wheezing snort. 'You have been searching for weeks,' the immortal said. 'I have watched you creeping across the rooftops, wearing one guise or another.'

For a moment, Ushoran was too stunned to speak. His mind reeled. If Zurhas had seen through his guises, what about Ankhat, or Neferata? 'I... I had no idea you were so perceptive,' he managed to say.

'I don't see why you should,' Zurhas replied. 'None of you ever paid the least attention to me.' He showed his teeth in a ghastly, jagged smile. 'I bet you couldn't even tell me the last time I attended the queen's court.'

Once again, the Lord of Masks bristled. 'As I said, I don't much care for gambling,' he answered stiffly.

Zurhas shrugged his narrow shoulders. 'Honestly, neither did I,' he said. 'But I wasn't smart enough for the priesthood, nor brave enough to be a soldier, so what else was there to do?' The immortal chuckled grimly. 'At least when I had coins to wager and a pair of dice in my hand, people paid attention to me.'

'You rode with the king's bodyguard at the Battle of Mahrak,' Ushoran pointed out. 'I remember that clearly.'

'Oh, yes. Yes, indeed,' the immortal said. A small, bitter smile tugged at his bloody lips. 'My father paid Lamashizzar a handsome bribe so I could join the king's retinue. He reckoned it cheaper than paying for another year of gambling debts – and if I were to die on the battlefield and spare them future embarrassment, so much the better.'

Zurhas sighed. 'There was no chance of that happening, of course. The dragon-staves saw to that. I watched the battle from behind a wall of iron-shod infantry, and watched the Usurper's champions shot to bits from fifty yards away. The most I suffered were saddle sores and red eyes from the clouds of dragon powder.' He shook his head. 'Afterwards, when the battle was done and everyone was looting the enemy's siege camp, I had my one moment of glory. I found a chest full of gold coin hidden in one of the tents belonging to Nagash's immortals. Everyone else had missed it, but I turned it up straightaway. You can't hide gold from a gambler. My father knew that lesson well.'

The immortal spread his stained hands. 'I saw a great deal of the king after that. Spent most evenings in his tent, drinking wine and pissing away my new-found wealth.' Zurhas let out a low hiss. 'He was the worst cheat I'd ever seen, but then, he could afford to be. He was the king.'

Zurhas's gaze fell to the gambler's contorted body. He studied it in silence, as though seeing it for the first time.

'By the time we reached the Living City I hadn't a coin to my name, but I was still one of Lamashizzar's personal guests.' He sighed again. 'I flattered myself that he and I had become friends. One night, he asked me for my help. *Asked* me, as though he and I were equals. Naturally, I agreed. And then the next thing I knew, we were following Arkhan the Black into the heart of Nagash's pyramid. By then, of course, there was no turning back.' Zurhas glanced up at Ushoran, his deep-set eyes strangely haunted. 'We carried Arkhan's body and Nagash's tomes back to camp in the dead of night. The whole way, I wondered when Lamashizzar would turn his dragon-stave on me. But he never did.'

Ushoran tried to sound sympathetic. 'Whatever else, he was still your cousin.' And some menial tasks were too delicate to trust to slaves, the Lord of Masks thought.

'I should have refused him,' Zurhas said. 'When we returned to Lahmia, I should have told the king I wanted no part of his schemes.' He scowled. 'But what would that have got me? A knife in the back, or poison in my cup, most likely. As long as I kept playing the game, there was the chance my luck would turn. The king would need me for some important task, and I would become someone of value – someone like you, or Lord Ankhat.'

'Is that what you want, Zurhas?' Ushoran asked. 'To be someone of import? A person of power and influence?'

'No chance of that now,' Zurhas replied. 'Neferata saw to that.'

The Lord of Masks smiled grimly. 'What if I were to tell you that the queen's luck had finally turned?'

Zurhas gave Ushoran a sidelong look. 'What do you mean?'

'Is it not obvious?' Ushoran spread his hands. 'The signs are all around us. Look how the city has suffered, ever since she became obsessed with that fool Alcadizzar. She thinks of no one but herself now and Lahmia has been pushed to the edge of revolt. The time is ripe for change.'

The immortal stared up at Ushoran, his beady eyes bright with fear. 'You cannot challenge her,' he said. 'None of us can. She is too powerful.'

Ushoran smiled. 'Perhaps. But what if we had help?'

Zurhas frowned. 'I don't understand. What kind of help?'

'An alliance,' Ushoran said. 'With the one being on earth powerful enough to tip the scales against Neferata – the Undying King.'

'Nagash?' Zurhas recoiled from Ushoran, eyes widening in fear. 'You don't know what you're saying!'

'He lives, Zurhas! How I do not know, but ever since the Battle of Mahrak he has been biding his time in the wastelands, gathering his strength!' Ushoran pointed to the north. 'You felt his presence during the night of the Green Witch, the same as the rest of us. Do you deny it?'

Zurhas reluctantly shook his head. 'No,' he replied.

'For ten years, I have had agents searching the wastes for Nagash's fortress,' Ushoran said. 'The cost was enormous, but in the end, I found it.' He took a step towards Zurhas, his voice lowering almost to a whisper. 'He is very near, Zurhas. Just a few weeks' ride north along the coast. And he is preparing for his return to Nehekhara. My agents have seen the smoke from his forges. Soon, very soon, his armies will march once more.'

'What does that have to do with us?' Zurhas protested. 'Lahmia was neutral during the war.'

'Up until the moment we betrayed Nagash, you mean,' Ushoran shot back. 'Do you imagine he has forgotten? No, Lahmia will be the first city to feel Nagash's wrath – unless we reach an accommodation with him first.'

'What kind of accommodation?'

Ushoran smiled. 'Simply this. If he helps us depose Neferata and seize control of the city, then Lahmia will ally with him in his campaign against the rest of Nehekhara.'

Zurhas frowned, clasping his hands together against his chest. His eyes narrowed thoughtfully. 'What about Ankhat? He is loyal to the queen.'

'Ankhat is loyal to whoever holds the crown,' Ushoran replied. 'If Neferata falls, then he will change sides quickly – or else he will suffer the same fate. With Nagash behind us, he won't stand a chance. Think on that! There would be no more need for secrets, no more skulking about in the shadows. We would rule the city openly, and the people would worship us as gods!'

Zurhas stared at Ushoran for a moment, his expression growing ever more suspicious. 'Why tell me any of this?' he asked.

'Because I can't do this alone,' Ushoran said. 'Someone must go to the Undying King and negotiate the alliance. I cannot go, because Neferata requires my presence at the temple every night. You, on the other hand, could leave the city for weeks at a time, and not raise anyone's suspicions.'

On impulse, he reached out and gripped the immortal's arm. The flesh beneath the grimy robe was hard and cold as marble. 'Don't you see? This is the moment you have been waiting for, Zurhas. Your luck has finally turned. Now the future of the entire city rests in your hands.'

Zurhas's gaze fell to his bloodstained palms. After a moment he gave a faint smile. 'We would share the throne?' he asked.

The Lord of Masks smiled. 'We would discuss matters of state and make important decisions jointly, but the crown would be yours alone. I don't care for that kind of attention.'

Zurhas nodded. Then his smile turned wicked. 'You're taking a great risk,' he said. 'What is to stop me from making my own deal with Nagash and taking everything for myself?'

Because you haven't the wit or the nerve, Ushoran thought. Why do you think I picked you in the first place? He affected a nervous grin, and tried to cover it up with a shrug.

'The advantage is yours. But I make a far better friend than an enemy,' Ushoran replied.

Zurhas laughed – a ghastly, barking sound, like the cry of a jackal – and slapped Ushoran on the shoulder. 'You're right, of course,' he said, but the wicked gleam never left his beady eyes. 'I just wanted to make certain we understood one another.'

'Of course,' Ushoran said. He had already begun laying plans for Zurhas's demise, just as soon as the deal with Nagash had been finalised.

'When do I leave?' Zurhas asked.

'As soon as we can manage,' Ushoran replied. Time was growing short. He could sense that Neferata's patience was nearly exhausted. If something didn't happen soon, he would be the one hanging from the torture rack in the queen's audience chamber. 'I must draft documents for you to present to Nagash, detailing the terms of the alliance. I will provide you with a number of trusted agents to serve as your retainers, along with falsified letters of transit that will allow you to leave the city.'

'If Nagash's fortress lies to the north, why not travel by boat up through the straits?'

Ushoran shook his head. 'Too conspicuous. Lord Ankhat has agents of his own, and they watch the docks closely. Better to travel overland, with as small a group as possible. Your retainers have been well trained; they will find you suitable shelter by dawn and guard you during the heat of the day.' He gestured at Zurhas's tattered clothing. 'We will also need to find you garments suitable for a royal envoy.'

'Of course,' Zurhas said. His smile widened, revealing a mouthful of jagged, discoloured teeth. 'We wouldn't want to give a bad impression.'

The immortal threw back his head and cackled at the sky. Ushoran smiled, masking his contempt. He had to work with the tools at hand, he reminded himself. Once the alliance was sealed and Neferata dealt with, there would be ample time to dispose of Zurhas.

The dice had been loaded from the start, and the fool hadn't suspected a thing.

The hooting of an owl echoed from the woodland to the south-west of the bandit camp. Alcadizzar was awake at once, casting aside his heavy cloak and rising silently to his feet. Around him, the dozen tribesmen who'd stood the daytime watch slept on, heads resting upon their saddles and hands gripping the hilts of their swords.

Their camp was ten yards inside the tangled forest that stretched along the foot of the mountains north of Lahmia's cramped necropolis. Faisr and the rest of the night watch crouched under the shadows just inside the tree line, peering warily across the rough ground that stretched in a crescent almost half a mile south and west in the direction of the city's western trade road. The Crystal Sea was a cobalt-blue line stretching along the horizon to the east. Lahmia's central hill, ringed with white manors and the towers of the royal palace, rose just above the line of broken ridges to the south. A mounted party heading north from the city would be hidden from view as they passed through these foothills. Faisr and the rest of the *bani-al-Hashim* agreed that it made an ideal spot for an ambush.

The twin-tailed comet blazed in the sky above the distant city, bathing the ridgeline and the rocky ground with pale blue light. His Lybaran tutors had spoken of such sights and had voiced many theories as to their purpose in the cosmos. Some believed that they were fragments of broken stars, careening across the heavens. Others insisted that they were portents of occult knowledge; arcane riddles posed by Tahoth, the god of knowledge. Whatever the truth about their origins, the celestial philosophers all agreed that they were harbingers of conflict. Fire and tumult followed in their wake.

This was the pennon Ophiria had warned him about, all those years ago. He'd known it from the first night that Faisr had pointed it out to him, weeks before. Alcadizzar had asked the chieftain for a dozen tribesmen and had ridden off before first light, racing eastwards as fast as his horse could carry him. Two weeks later, Faisr had joined him with another dozen warriors, and they had been waiting ever since – for what, Alcadizzar could not say.

Not a single human soul had passed through the foothills since Alcadizzar's arrival. The area was desolate and foreboding, home to packs of jackals that stole into the city's necropolis each night to forage for scraps. The tribesmen had found evidence of hunting trails through the woods when they'd first arrived, but the paths were overgrown and hadn't been used in many years.

The cry of the night owl echoed from the woods again, low and insistent. Faisr listened closely as Alcadizzar settled down on his haunches close by. 'Riders approaching, moving fast,' the white-haired chieftain said. He gave Alcadizzar an appraising look. 'Is this what you've been waiting for?'

'It is,' Alcadizzar replied. 'It must be.' He leaned over and tapped one of the tribesmen on the shoulder. 'Yusuf, go and wake the others.'

The warrior nodded silently and vanished back into the trees. The rest of the night watch went to work stringing their powerful horn bows. Faisr loosened his sword in its scabbard and made quick adjustments to his raider's robe, but his eyes never left Alcadizzar. 'Ubaid, you know I trust you above all others,' he said. 'When you asked for a dozen of my best men, I gave them to you without question. When you said you were bringing them *here*, of all places, I did not so much as bat an eyelash. But perhaps now you could explain to me just what in the frozen hells is going on?'

Alcadizzar's stomach fell. He'd known this was coming, sooner or later. How could he possibly explain more than eighty years of deception? What would Faisr do when he realised he'd been lied to all along?

He sighed. 'All will be made clear, chief. Once the arrows have flown and the riders are dealt with, I'll explain everything. You have my word on it.'

Faisr narrowed his eyes, but gave a reluctant nod. 'After, then.'

The rest of the raiding party came up from camp and settled quickly into position. Black-fletched arrows were driven into the sandy soil next to each crouching archer. A horse whickered softly a few yards behind them; Alcadizzar turned to see half a dozen men mounted and ready, just in case any of the riders escaped the initial ambush. The desert warriors were all chosen men, each one a veteran of countless raids. They knew their trade as well or better than Alcadizzar himself. All he could do was ready his blade and wait as the sound of hoof-beats echoed across the broken ground from the south.

Sound travelled strangely along the foothills. The thunder of hooves reverberated through the night air for many minutes before the first riders came suddenly into view, rising out of a patch of dead ground a hundred yards to the south-east. Alcadizzar counted six men, all clad in dark robes and dun-coloured headscarves, riding hard towards the north-west. They were travelling in a tight group, paying no mind to the dark woods or the concealing terrain surrounding them. They were trading caution for speed, clearly thinking that there was nothing to fear this far from the city. Alcadizzar glanced at Faisr and bowed his head respectfully. The honour of springing the ambush belonged to the chieftain.

Faisr accepted the honour with a nod and a predatory grin. He gauged the riders' approach and raised his hand. Bowstrings creaked as the archers chose their marks. The riders made easy targets, silhouetted by the light of moon and comet as they drew closer to the tree line.

Forty yards. Thirty. Twenty. At just under twenty yards the riders started to draw away again as they altered course to skirt the dense forest. Alcadizzar clenched his fist.

'Loose!' Faisr hissed.

Sixteen bowstrings snapped and sang. Heavy, broad-headed arrows flickered through the air, almost too fast for the eye to follow. At such close range, every shaft found its mark. Horses screamed and thrashed, hurling men from the saddle as they crashed to the ground. One rider struggled to his feet, cursing furiously, his left arm hanging limp; a pair of arrows struck him in the chest, pitching him onto his face. A second man dragged himself free from his dead horse and tried to flee, heading south towards the distant necropolis. A single tribesman rose to his feet, arrow drawn back to his chin. He tracked the fleeing man for a moment, the razor-edged arrowhead drifting fractionally skywards. The bowstring thrummed, and a second later the running man seemed to twist in mid-air, clawing at the shaft which had sprouted between his shoulderblades. He staggered, gave a strangled cry, and then collapsed.

Faisr waited for a dozen heartbeats, scanning the ambush site for movement.

Satisfied, he waved his tribesmen forwards. A dozen men put aside their bows and rushed forwards, steel in hand. They began to move among the fallen bodies, despatching wounded men and horses with swift, efficient blows.

Alcadizzar let out a long, silent breath. The ambush had gone much better than expected. Hopefully, his instincts were correct and he hadn't just cut down half a dozen innocent men. 'We will have to search them all,' he said to Faisr. 'Any detail, however small, could be significant.'

Faisr folded his arms and scowled. 'Significant to whom? Who are these people?'

The moment had come. Alcadizzar could delay no longer. But before he could speak, the stillness of the night was shattered with a savage, inhuman howl.

Out on the killing ground, the desert warriors had made their way into the midst of the stricken riders. Alcadizzar turned just in time to see a gaunt figure rear up from beneath a fallen horse, flinging the dead animal into the air as though it were a child's toy and scattering the three tribesmen who had closed in around it. The bluish glow of the comet shone from the figure's chalky skin, lending its long, clawed hands and hairless skull a strange, ghostly radiance. It snarled like a maddened beast, jaw gaping hungrily, and Alcadizzar felt a chill race down his spine.

The tribesmen reeled in shock at the sight of the creature – all that is, except for Faisr ali-Hashim. The sound of his sword rasping from its scabbard shook the tribesmen from their stupor. 'Slay it!' the chieftain cried. 'In the name of the Hungry God, strike the creature down!'

The *bani-al-Hashim* surged forwards at Faisr's command, shouting war cries and brandishing their swords. They rushed at the monster from all sides. Blades flashed, slashing at its neck and chest, but the creature wove like a viper between the blows, dodging them with hideous ease. Pale hands lashed out with unnatural speed; where they struck, armour ruptured, bone shattered and organs burst. Men crumpled, coughing blood, or their broken bodies were flung backwards like chaff in a rising wind.

Six men died in the blink of an eye. The surviving tribesmen faltered, stunned by the ferocity of the creature. A bowstring sang, then another. The blood-spattered figure spun out of the path of the first arrow, but the second took it high in the right hip. It staggered for a moment, spitting curses, and then two more arrows punched into its shoulder and chest. A fourth shaft transfixed the creature's throat, the broad arrowhead bursting from the back of its pale neck in a spray of thick ichor. The tribesmen let out a yell of triumph – but their hope was short-lived. With a gurgling growl, the monster seized the arrow with one clawed hand and ripped it free.

More arrows hissed through the air. Spitting ichor, the creature dodged first one, then another, but the next one punched through its left thigh. It snapped the shaft in two with a sweep of one hand and then suddenly turned and ran, heading south towards the city necropolis.

'A horse!' Alcadizzar cried. The monster was already well out of bowshot, racing over the broken ground faster than the swiftest mortal could manage. A tribesman dashed from the woods, leading Alcadizzar's horse by the reins; with a loud cry, he leapt into the saddle and dashed off after the monster at a furious gallop.

He couldn't let the thing reach the necropolis. Once it got in among the close-set mausoleums, there would be no way to find it. Alcadizzar spurred his mount onwards, riding hard over the broken ground.

At first, the distance shrank quickly, until the pale-skinned creature was little more than a dozen yards away. But the ridgeline was coming up fast and the horse was struggling to clear the rough terrain. No matter how he tried, Alcadizzar could not close the gap any further.

And then, with a wild laugh, Faisr came racing past him, his lean desert horse gliding like a ghost over the rocks. The chieftain held a short, barbed javelin in his upraised hand; as the creature started to ascend the ridge just ahead, Faisr charged to within a dozen paces of the thing and let fly. The missile sped like a thunderbolt and struck the monster in the back, just below the left shoulderblade. It let out a despairing wail and fell forwards, sliding face-first back down the steep slope.

Faisr was already standing over the creature's body when Alcadizzar reined in at the base of the ridge. He leapt from the saddle, sword ready, but it was clear that the monster was finished; the chieftain's javelin had taken it through the heart. Faisr glanced up and smiled ruefully as Alcadizzar approached.

'I despair of ever making a proper horseman out of you, Ubaid,' he said. Gripping the shaft of the javelin, he used it as a lever to roll the creature onto its side. 'What in the name of the Hungry God is this thing?'

Alcadizzar approached the monster warily, his mind drifting back to that blood-soaked night in Neferata's bedchamber. 'A servant of Neferata,' he said. 'A man, transformed by black arts into a blood-drinking beast.'

The prince raised his sword. The heavy blade flashed down, severing the fiend's head with a single stroke. Surprisingly, the creature's body spasmed beneath the blow, as though some shred of vitality still lurked in its limbs. It trembled spastically for a moment and then finally went still.

Summoning up his courage, Alcadizzar bent and retrieved the monster's severed head. Here was the proof he'd been seeking for almost a century. At long last, the fate of Lahmia's secret rulers was sealed.

Faisr studied Alcadizzar's grisly trophy. 'It's done,' he said. 'The arrows have flown; six of our brothers lie dead upon the sand. Now you owe me an explanation.'

The prince stared up at the starry sky. The twin-tailed comet seemed to ripple just overhead, like a battle-pennon. Alcadizzar offered up a silent thanks to Ophiria, then drew a deep breath and met the chieftain's eye.

'The first thing you must know,' he said, 'is that my name is not Ubaid.'

NINETEEN

CROOK AND SCEPTRE

Lahmia,
the City of the Dawn,
in the 107th year of Ptra the Glorious
(-1200 Imperial Reckoning)

Within a week of Alcadizzar's ambush, a band of Faisr's best riders spurred their mounts and headed southwards, bearing grim tidings for the King of Rasetra. The tribesmen bore not just the head of the foul thing they'd slain outside Lahmia, but also several scroll cases that had been found amid the creature's possessions. The letters within revealed a danger altogether more terrible and far-reaching than the cabal of blood-drinkers inside Lahmia. Nagash the Usurper, Tyrant of Khemri, still walked the earth, some five hundred years after his defeat at the Battle of Mahrak. It appeared that Neferata's hidden court had somehow learned of the necromancer's existence and sought an alliance with him against the other great cities. Along with the horrifying evidence, Alcadizzar included a letter of his own, meant to be copied and circulated throughout the land, exhorting the royal houses to marshal their armies and cleanse the land of Lahmia's evil once and for all.

Alcadizzar's younger brother, Asar, now an old and powerful king in his own right, sent emissaries with copies of the letters to every corner of the land. Rasetra called upon a vast and complex framework of secret treaties, some many decades in the making, compelling the Nehekharan kings to march eastwards and assemble upon the Golden Plain without delay. When the news from Lahmia was made known, not a single ruler dared to renege on his or her obligations. To do so would have cast their lot with the Lahmians, which would have invited certain destruction from the other great cities.

Six months after the stolen letters left Alcadizzar's hands, the armies began to move. The terms of Rasetra's treaties indicated not only when each host was to start their march, but also which roads and how many supplies they would be required to carry with them. Each movement was part of a vast and complicated schedule devised by Alcadizzar, Asar, and the veteran warlords of Rasetra, designed so that each element of the coalition would arrive upon the plain at more or less the same time. Facing the possibility of trade penalties if they failed to meet their time of march, the great cities wasted little time in preparing their hosts for war. The Rasetrans, it appeared, had learned a great deal from the financial warfare of the Lahmians, some four centuries earlier.

By the end of the year the armies began to gather upon the great plain. The first was the host of Rasetra, led by Asar's heir, Prince Heru. Ten thousand of the city's vaunted heavy infantry, plus two thousand swift war-chariots drawn by lean jungle lizards. Next came the scholar-warriors of Lybaras, whose fearsome siege engines would be pitted against Lahmia's walls; their train included a dozen huge catapults, eight ballistae and four armoured fire-throwers, all drawn by teams of surly, groaning oxen. They were met at the centre of the plain by a surprising sight – the assembled warriors of all the desert tribes, some eight thousand of the finest light cavalry in the land, clad in burnished armour and billowing silk robes. The sons of the distant sands welcomed Prince Heru and the Lybaran king, Ahmenefret, with gifts of gold, perfumed oils and wine, and directed the tired warriors to campsites that had been prepared for them along the dusty trade road.

Two days later, just as the sun was setting and the chill of the winter evening was settling on the sprawling camp, came the clarion call of trumpets and the ringing of silver bells. Chanting and singing to Neru, goddess of the moon, there appeared from the gloom some five thousand priestly warriors from the once-great city of Mahrak. The *Hurusanni*, or Devoted, as they were called, patterned their weapons and training on the legendary Ushabti of ancient times. This was the first time the order had marched to war since its founding, some two hundred years past, and they greeted the camp with joyous shouts, eager to come to grips with the evil things that lurked in nearby Lahmia. The shaven-headed youths took their place alongside the road and spent the rest of the evening in meditation and prayer.

Hours later, as Neru shone high above the camp, the warriors of the three armies awoke to the rumble of marching feet bearing down upon them out of the darkness to the west. Men shrugged on their armour and reached for their weapons; desert tribesmen went galloping from the camp into the night, their expressions tense. Veterans and novices alike shared uneasy glances as the tramp of armoured feet grew louder. The warrior-priests of Mahrak began intoning prayers of abjuration, meant to hold the hungry spirits of the wasteland at bay. Then they saw them; white figures, marching in silence down the road, their lacquered armour glimmering in the moonlight. Their helms were fashioned in the shape of jackals' heads, the sacred visage of Djaf, god of the dead. They were the fabled Tomb Guard of Quatar: five thousand heavy infantry, led by their king, Nebunefre, Lord of the Tombs.

After the arrival of the warriors of Quatar, the armies settled in to watch the trade road and wait for the rest of the western armies to arrive. Over the next few days a pair of small caravans were spotted, laden with goods for markets in Lybaras and Mahrak. The Lahmian merchants and their wares were seized at once and all the useful items were distributed amongst the three armies.

At the end of the week, long ribbons of dust were spotted off to the west. Two days later, columns of proud Numasi cavalry, ten thousand strong, came trotting into the camp, led by their queen Omorose. The desert warriors paced alongside the cavalry on both sides of the road, prancing and pirouetting their smaller, nimbler mounts, and shouting good-natured challenges to the dour horse soldiers. Behind them, marching to the thunder of heavy kettledrums, came the warriors of Ka-Sabar's Iron Legion; fifteen thousand heavily-armoured spearmen and four thousand archers, their sweaty faces caked with ochre dust stirred by the columns of Numasi cavalry. Their king, Aten-sefu, marched in the front rank with the rest of his travel-stained warriors, his armour virtually indistinguishable from that of his men.

The next day – a full week ahead of schedule – came the host of Zandri. Two thousand archers, four thousand spearmen and another five thousand pale-skinned northern mercenaries, all brought by barge up the River Vitae as far as the north-west edge of the Golden Plain, then marched overland through rough country to the armies' marshalling point. Their king, Rakh-an-atum, brought with him rich gifts of gold and silver for the gathered kings and a necklace of fine pearls for Queen Omorose – a not-so-subtle display of the city's burgeoning wealth and potential influence.

Within the space of seven days, a force of more than sixty thousand warriors had been assembled from six widely separated cities – a feat of planning and coordination unparalleled in Nehekharan history. Only Khemri was yet to be accounted for, and several of the kings – Rakh-an-atum in particular – doubted that their contribution would amount to much, if anything. The once-great city was still not much more than a Rasetran colony, administered by generations of viziers over the last four hundred years. The process of reconstruction had been long and difficult and was still far from complete, thanks in no small part to meddling on the part of Zandri and Numas themselves.

Yet at dawn on the day of Khemri's expected arrival, a fanfare of brass horns roused the warriors from their slumber, followed by the surf-like sound of cheers echoing down the western trade road. Dazed soldiers stumbled out into the cold morning air to behold a joyous and colourful procession of two hundred chariots rolling into camp, each one manned by the lord of one of Khemri's noble houses. The noble lords and their retainers were not armed and armoured for war, but instead were clad in their finest feast garments. As they rolled by, they tossed handfuls of coins to the dumbfounded soldiers, laughing and chanting 'Alcadizzar! Alcadizzar!' at the top of their lungs.

Behind the chariots came columns of javelin-wielding light infantry, clad in pristine white tunics and polished leather armour, followed by rank upon rank of spearmen. Six thousand infantry all told, plus another two thousand slave auxiliaries armed with slings and short swords. A meagre showing by military standards, but the warriors of Khemri marched with their heads held high, cheering Alcadizzar's name. They were followed by a parade of wagons larger than any trader's caravan, each one painted in bright, celebratory colours and laden with wine and gifts. On this day of days, the people of the Living City were determined not to make a poor showing before the other cities. They had spared no expense, held nothing back, for this was the moment they had been waiting for since the birth of King Aten-heru's eldest son, a hundred and fifty years ago.

Khemri would have a king once more.

Ever since he was a child, Alcadizzar had dreamed of the day he would become king. He had pictured sun-drenched streets lined with cheering throngs, scattered with glittering coins and offerings of fragrant oils and a solemn ceremony in the ancient palace built by Settra himself, surrounded by friends and noble allies. There would be feasting and celebrating for a week afterwards; the people of the city would come and pay their respects each day, laying gifts at his feet and praising his name. Princesses of distant cities would make his acquaintance each evening, plying him with their charms and vying to become his queen.

'Hold still, great one,' the priest said, gripping his chin firmly and shaking Alcadizzar from his reverie. A fingertip, covered in thick, black kohl, was inching towards his left eye. 'You may wish to cast your gaze upwards for just a moment.'

Alcadizzar swallowed quickly and looked up just in time. The kohl was warm and gritty and smelled of charcoal. It felt as though the priest was slowly and mercilessly grinding it into his lower eyelid. He clenched his teeth and forced himself to remain still, holding his arms stiffly out to his sides while another pair of priests fussed with the starched, knee-length kilt that had been wrapped tightly about his hips. He hadn't taken a single step since putting it on and it was already starting to chafe.

The air within the tent was near to stifling and redolent with the scent of horse manure, cooking grease and thousands of unwashed bodies. A small group of slaves bustled about, eyes downcast and scalps glistening with sweat, packing chests, rolling up rugs and taking away empty chairs to be loaded with the rest of the army's baggage. Faisr and Prince Heru were forced to stand in one corner of the tent, poring over a map rolled out on the last remaining table. Outside, the air shook with shouted orders, the creak of axles and the complaining bellows of oxen as the vast army continued the process of breaking camp. The timetable for the march to Lahmia would not be denied, regardless of the petty needs of aspiring kings.

'So long as the weather holds – and there's no reason to suspect it won't – the vanguard of the army should reach the Lahmian watch-forts at the eastern edge of the plain in just over three weeks,' Prince Heru said. 'How close can we get before we risk running into mounted patrols covering the trade road?'

Faisr chuckled. 'We've spent the last year discouraging the Lahmians from leaving the forts at all,' he said. 'If you march the last thirty miles by night, they'll never see you coming.'

Heru glanced up at Faisr. 'You're certain? Because the whole campaign hinges on seizing the eastern pass,' the Rasetran said. 'If the Lahmians get warning that we're on the way, they could rush a few thousand men into the gap and hold it against ten times their number.'

'Trust Faisr,' Alcadizzar interjected. He tried to nod reassuringly at the desert chieftain, but the priest still had his chin in a vice grip. 'The tribes know the Golden Plain better than anyone and they've made certain that Lahmia has no idea we're coming. They've intercepted every message sent by Neferata's agents since the armies began to march, and ambushed every patrol the Lahmians have tried to send down the trade road. We owe them a great debt for all they've done so far.'

Faisr accepted the praise with a grave nod of the head. The last ten months had been a tumultuous period for the chieftain and for the desert tribes in general. Alcadizzar's revelations in the wake of the ambush outside Lahmia had thrown the tribes into chaos. Faisr himself had been furious over Alcadizzar's long years of deception and when the truth became more widely known, several ambitious chieftains tried to paint Faisr as complicit in the prince's deception. But Ophiria intervened, revealing her oath to Alcadizzar and declaring the prince to be the fulfilment of Settra's prophecy.

After that, the political manoeuvring began in deadly earnest. The chieftains had heard the news about Neferata and the discovery about Nagash, and knew that the winds of war would soon begin to blow. The tribes had to unite under a single leader, as they hadn't done since the death of Shahid ben Alcazzar, the last Prince of Bhagar. A gathering was called, up in the mountains along the northern edge of the plain, and the chieftains met in Ophiria's tent to press their claim. The competition was fierce, but the outcome was never really in doubt. Seven days later, the Daughter of the Sands appeared and declared to the tribes that Faisr al-Hashim had been acclaimed Prince Faisal, first among the chieftains of the *bani-al-Khsar.* Faisr had accepted the title with uncharacteristic humility and grace, quickly winning over all but the bitterest of his rivals, and had worked tirelessly ever since to prepare his people for what was to come.

Over time, Faisr had forgiven Alcadizzar for his deceptions, but it had created a rift between them that had never truly healed. At Alcadizzar's insistence, the chieftain was among his closest advisors, but otherwise they saw little of one another. Of all the sacrifices he'd been called upon to make in his life, losing Faisr's friendship and respect had pained the prince most of all.

'On the night before the vanguard arrives, my warriors will seize the forts,' Faisr continued. 'The two forts covering the pass we will hold onto; the rest we'll burn. Then your troops can carry on through the pass and secure the far side.'

Heru gave the chieftain an appraising look, then shrugged. 'Then, all else being equal, we'll be outside the walls of Lahmia in twenty-three days. What do we know about the state of the Lahmian army at this stage?'

Gold bracelets were being slipped onto Alcadizzar's wrists and a belt of heavy gold links was drawn around his hips. The priest had gotten some of the kohl in his eye, and it was starting to burn.

'We outnumber them, that's for certain,' he said through gritted teeth. 'And the quality of their troops is poor, to say the least. They might be counted on to hold the city walls for a time, but once the Lybarans have made a breach, they won't be able to hold us.' Finally, the priest finished with the kohl, and Alcadizzar turned his head away with a sigh.

'What about the dragon powder?' Heru asked.

'The Lahmians haven't raised any companies of Dragon Men since the last war,' Alcadizzar said. 'That tells me they don't have any dragon powder left.' He gave Faisr a knowing look. 'It's Neferata and her ilk we need to be concerned about.'

Heru grimaced. He'd seen the severed head of the monster first-hand. 'And how many of those creatures are there?'

Alcadizzar belatedly realised that the priests had stepped back and were surveying their handiwork. With a scowl, he lowered his arms.

'Honestly, I don't know,' he told Heru. 'Not many, else they couldn't have remained secret for so long. If we're lucky, there are no more than a handful of them. Even so, there's no telling how much harm they could do us if we're not careful.'

The tent flap drew aside once more. A nervous-looking priest entered. 'It is nearly time,' he announced.

'Prince Alcadizzar is ready,' the senior priest replied.

Alcadizzar glanced down at his bare chest and arms. 'I feel naked,' he muttered.

Heru laughed. 'It's traditional,' he replied. 'And likely more comfortable in Khemri, which sits at the edge of the Great Desert.'

Faisr let out a snort. 'No desert dweller with an ounce of sense would be caught in public dressed like that. He looks like an overgrown babe.'

They all shared a chuckle at that. The priests shifted about nervously. Heru noted their discomfort and waved Alcadizzar towards the tent flap. 'Lead on, uncle,' he said. 'The sooner the ceremony is done, the sooner you can put your robes back on.'

A priest rushed forwards to draw the tent flap aside, admitting a brief gust of dusty air. Alcadizzar stepped out into the confusing swirl of an army preparing to march. Men dashed about purposefully in every direction. Some carried chests, or clay jars, their brows sheened with sweat; others marched in tight groups, turned out smartly in full armour and clutching their weapons tightly. Still others stumbled bewilderedly down the trade road, half-wearing their wargear and clutching the rest against their chests, searching vainly for their parent units. Voices laughed and cursed, bawled orders or cried out in confusion. A pall of dust hung over everything, churned up by thousands of shuffling feet. No one paid the least attention to Alcadizzar and his retinue. He glanced around bemusedly, fighting the sudden urge to sneeze.

'This way, great one.' The senior priest hurried up beside Alcadizzar and indicated a narrow lane running south between rows of campaign tents. Feeling a bit like a farmer's prized ox, he allowed himself to be herded along by the holy men. Heru and Faisr fell into step to either side of him.

The young prince cast a sidelong glance at his uncle and smiled ruefully. 'Not quite what you expected,' he said.

Alcadizzar grimaced. 'There are a few things missing, I admit. A city, for example. Cheering throngs. A procession of chariots.' He frowned at the priests. 'You'd think we could have managed the chariots, at least.'

'We needed them more in the vanguard.' Heru chuckled. 'I suppose we could round up some spear companies and order them to cheer for you, if that would make you feel better.'

'How about a company of dancing girls? Do we have any of those in the army?'

Heru arched his eyebrows in mock disdain. 'Who do you think we are, a bunch of decadent Lahmians?' The Rasetran shrugged. 'Look, it could be worse. I managed to talk the priests into dispensing with the formal ceremony, at least. Otherwise we'd still be at this by sunset.'

To Alcadizzar's surprise, Faisr glowered at the priests and grunted in agreement. 'Not the best way to begin one's rule, perhaps, but a necessary one,' he said. 'The army must have a clear leader, and the other kings won't accept the authority of a mere prince, no matter who he may be.'

'Look at all the trouble I've had from Zandri and Numas already,' Heru added. 'They've complained about everything from their place in the order of march, to the number of wagons allocated for their baggage. Imagine what they'll be like when we're camped outside Lahmia.'

Alcadizzar raised his hands in surrender. 'I know, I know,' he replied. He'd expected Rakh-an-atum and Omorose to try and assert their authority at every step. The last thing they wanted was to see Khemri regain its former power, so they would try to undercut him in any way they could. It wasn't enough to focus on the immediate problems of the campaign; if he wanted to succeed, he had to begin anticipating the challenges that would arise in the months and years to come. Not for the first time, Alcadizzar offered a silent prayer of thanks to the spirit of his long-dead tutor Jabari.

The priests led him to the far end of the lane. Beyond the last cluster of tents stretched a wide field of trampled earth, dimpled by horse hooves and rutted by wagon tracks. The sun was almost directly overhead, causing the shifting curtains of dust to shimmer as they drifted across the open ground. Beyond, wavering like some desert mirage, was the sight of a gleaming white pavilion, surrounded by a silent, watchful crowd of perhaps a hundred people.

The senior priest waved the procession to a halt and gauged the position of the sun with a practiced eye. 'A bit slower now, great one,' he said, smiling in satisfaction. He clapped his hands, and the rest of the priestly retinue swiftly formed ranks to left and right of Faisr and Heru. When they were in position, the holy man raised his hands to the sun and across the field came a ragged cheer, punctuated by the clash of cymbals and silver bells. The senior priests nodded gravely and set off towards the waiting pavilion at a steady, measured pace.

Alcadizzar's mind was a riot of conflicting thoughts and emotions. He ought to be happy, he thought. The moment he'd been preparing for his entire life was unfolding before his eyes. But all he could think about were the thousand and one tasks that needed tending to between here and Lahmia. As hard as he tried to savour the moment, he found it almost impossible to focus.

They'd crossed nearly half the field in tense silence, squinting through the shifting dust, when Heru abruptly spoke. 'So, have you given any thought to a wife?'

Alcadizzar blinked, shaken from his reverie. 'First this, and now you're trying to get me married, as well?'

Heru chuckled. 'Just trying to make conversation,' he said. 'Traditionally, you'd be marrying a daughter of Lahmia, you know.'

'Really?' Alcadizzar replied archly. 'My Lahmian tutors *never once* mentioned that.'

Heru let out a snort. 'Point being, that's one tradition likely to go by the wayside. Unless you still intend to respect Khemri's ancient ties to Lahmia after you've torn it stone from stone.'

'Doesn't seem much point, when you put it that way,' Alcadizzar said dryly.

'Exactly,' Heru replied. 'Father wants you to choose someone from Rasetra, of course. Strengthen the ties between east and west, that sort of thing. Or you could choose someone from Zandri or Numas. *That* would certainly roil the pot.'

'I'd rather marry for love than political gain.'

'Very funny, uncle.'

Alcadizzar sighed. 'If you must know,' he said, glancing sidelong at Faisr, 'I'd planned on marrying a woman of the desert tribes.'

Heru's eyes widened. 'Ah,' he said diplomatically. Instead, it was Faisr who blurted the obvious question.

'Why would you do such a thing?'

There was an edge to Faisr's voice, as though the chieftain half-believed he was being mocked.

Alcadizzar looked his old friend in the eye. 'Because they are my people,' he said. 'Bound by ties of blood and honour. Those are the bonds that matter most to me.'

The answer surprised Faisr. 'Well,' he began, momentarily at a loss for words. 'I... suppose such a thing is possible. But she would have to be very desperate indeed to settle for such an abysmal horseman.'

'Surely not desperate,' Heru protested, but his eyes glittered wickedly. 'Maybe just... slow of mind.'

Faisr scratched at his bearded chin thoughtfully. 'There is a woman of the *bani-al-Shawat* who was kicked in the head by a horse...'

Ahead of the nobles, the senior priest came to a sudden halt. They were only twenty yards or so from the pavilion now, close enough for Alcadizzar to see the expressions of the Khemrians who had gathered to witness his ascension. They ranged from richly clad nobles to common soldiers, standing shoulder-to-shoulder to welcome their new king. Many wept openly, beaming with pride as they chanted ancient songs of blessing to Ptra, father of the gods and patron of their city.

From the midst of the chanting crowd emerged a tall figure clad in robes of white and gleaming cloth of gold. Sunlight blazed from the golden mantle set about his shoulders and the head of the tall staff clutched in his right hand. Atop the staff was a great golden orb, borne on the shoulders of four rearing sphinxes – the seal of Ptra, the Great Father himself. It caught the light of the noonday sun and shone so brightly that it was almost painful to look upon. Shepsu-amun, the Grand Hierophant of Ptra, left the crowd and went to join the waiting procession. He bowed to the senior priest, who returned the gesture and swiftly stepped aside. The hierophant took the priest's place at the head of the procession, smiling briefly at Alcadizzar before turning back to the pavilion.

The cheering crowd suddenly fell silent. Behind Alcadizzar, the noise of the army camp had faded to a dull roar. He was suddenly aware of the heat of the sun on his scalp and the caress of the dusty breeze across his shoulders and face.

At some unseen signal, the crowd around the pavilion parted to the left and right, revealing a stocky, middle-aged man, clad in robes of samite and bearing the gold circlet of the Living City's Grand Vizier. His name was Inofre, the latest in a long line of regents who had rebuilt Khemri from nothing while Alcadizzar had lived as a hostage in Lahmia. Hands clasped at his waist, he cried out in a clear, powerful voice. 'Hearken! The people of the city cry out for succour from the blazing sands and the evils of the night! They gather before the throne to receive the wisdom of the gods, but it lies empty! Where is the great king?'

The crowd raised their hands to the sky, taking up their part in the ancient rite. 'Great god of the sun, where is our king?'

Shepsu-amun raised the blazing staff of Ptra and answered. 'The young king, Thutep, has gone into the dusk and resides with the spirit of his ancestors, until the day when the sons of Man cast off the bonds of death.'

'Who, then, will lead us?' Inofre replied. 'The enemies of the city gather about us even now. Has the Great Father forsaken us?'

At this, the hierophant threw back his shoulders and laughed. It was a rich, joyous sound, a bright counterpoint to the solemn rite. 'Fear not, people of the city, for Ptra hears you! He has sent a man of honour and courage to lead you through the dark times to come.'

'Who is this man?' Inofre asked.

'Alcadizzar!' Shepsu-amun declared proudly. 'A prince of royal blood, son of Aten-heru, King of Rasetra.'

'*Alcadizzar!*' shouted the crowd. '*Alcadizzar!*'

Inofre beckoned. 'Then let him come forth, to receive the instruments of rulership and accept the accolades of his people!'

The hierophant nodded and approached the white pavilion at a slow, stately pace. Alcadizzar followed behind, his heart fluttering in his chest. It was as though a great weight was settling about his shoulders – the mantle of history, stretching back to the time of Settra himself. He could feel the stares of the assembled crowd as he passed by. Inofre had cautioned him to keep his gaze fixed straight ahead, but he couldn't help but look from side to side, meeting the eyes of the people around him. *My* people, he thought. The thought was surreal, after so many years living alone among the tribes.

Suddenly, Shepsu-amun stepped to Alcadizzar's left and the prince found himself standing before an ancient throne of dark, polished wood. The throne of Khemri, a relic of ancient times recovered from the Usurper's camp at the Battle of Mahrak by the Rasetrans and returned to the Living City centuries later. Upon its surface rested the ceremonial instruments of rulership – a miniature shepherd's crook, wrought in pure gold, and a gleaming sceptre surmounted by a golden sun-disc.

Alcadizzar took a deep breath and reached for the sceptre. The shaft was warm to the touch and fitted easily into his palm. Next he took up the crook, crossing the two objects over his heart. Then, moving as though in a dream, he took his seat upon Settra's great throne. As he did, the hierophant turned to the crowd.

'The king has come! People of Khemri, look upon Ptra's chosen one and rejoice!'

Raucous cheers rose into the air. Seated upon the throne, Alcadizzar could see past the small crowd and back across the field where the great army was breaking camp. The sight called to him in a way that no throne ever could.

Alcadizzar rose to his feet. The Grand Vizier bowed once again. 'What is your will, great one?' he asked.

The king unceremoniously pressed crook and sceptre into Inofre's hands. There were many hours of hard riding ahead before the army would camp for the night, and then many hours more going over details of the attack on the city with Heru and his fellow rulers. If he was lucky, his coronation feast would consist of a bit of unleavened bread and a cup of watered wine. The thought made him smile.

'Bring me my horse... and a proper set of clothes,' the king said. 'There's work to be done.'

TWENTY

A STORM FROM THE WEST

Lahmia,
the City of the Dawn,
in the 107th year of Ptra the Glorious
(-1200 Imperial Reckoning)

The fires could be seen from the western quarters of the city; a shifting curtain of dull, orange light dancing along the tops of the hills that bordered the eastern edge of the Golden Plain. Families ventured furtively out onto their rooftops, or, daring greatly, gathered in the rubbish-strewn market squares to wonder at the sight. Most believed that the scrubland on the far side of the hills had caught fire; the previous summer had been an unseasonably dry one and the woodland was little more than tinder. Others, however – mostly wide-eyed vagrants, but not a few priests as well – saw an otherworldly significance in the baleful light. They warned the crowds that the wickedness at the heart of the city had grown so great that the gods had chosen to return and mete judgement upon Lahmia. The fire would build like a great wave behind the hills, until it finally overtopped them and came crashing down on the city, scorching it from the face of the earth. Grim-faced men of the City Guard did their best to silence the fearmongers, but the best they could do was slow the spread of hysteria. By midnight there were mobs converging on the temple district and riots were sweeping through the Travellers' Quarter.

This time, the hysteria was justified. The madmen were closer to the truth than anyone – except Ushoran, and a handful of others, mortal and immortal – suspected.

The Lord of Masks wiped the last of his tools clean and slid them clumsily into their loops on the wide leather wallet. Behind him, his evening's entertainment gave one final spasm against his restraints and then expired, his death-rattle echoing in the chilly confines of the cellar. Ushoran bared his teeth at the sound, his anger at the waste of such exceptional flesh momentarily eclipsing the panic that churned in his guts.

Now he knew why he hadn't heard anything from his agents in the west for nearly a year. It was possible that the great cities had finally grown tired of paying their yearly tribute to Lahmia; Ushoran had known all along that, sooner or later, revolt was inevitable. It was the timing that disturbed him. What could have possibly forced the great cities to put aside their differences now, after hundreds of years of rivalry? He could think of only one thing.

Ushoran hadn't heard from Zurhas since the immortal had left the city a year ago. Something had gone very, very wrong.

Footfalls thumped hurriedly across the floors of the house as his thralls gathered his personal effects together. He'd had a plan for escaping the city for the last several years, against the day that Neferata's patience would finally run out. There were forged letters of transit in a bag upstairs that would get him onto a boat in the harbour or pass him through the city gates; he hadn't yet made up his mind which course he would choose. Escaping to the east would put him well beyond Neferata's grasp, but his future in one of the Silk Land's coastal trade cities was uncertain at best. Conversely, he would prosper more easily in one of the other Nehekharan cities, but only if he could slip past the armies that were even now only a few hours from the city walls. He could do it alone, of that he was certain, but that would mean leaving his thralls and nearly all of his other possessions behind.

Ushoran carefully rolled the wallet into a tight cylinder and bound it closed with a braided cord of human hair. The Lord of Masks stroked the stained leather protectively. He could start anew in some other place. He could be anyone he wanted to be. All he needed were his tools. The rest he could do without.

West it was, then. If he moved quickly, he and his thralls could slip through the city's west gate, then turn northwards just as Zurhas had done. From there, they could take refuge in the city's necropolis, scouting a safe path through the enemy patrols that would take them into the wooded hills to the north-west. He knew of narrow game paths that would take him onto the Golden Plain, far north of the trade road. If he encountered any trouble along the way, he could abandon the thralls to their fate and make his escape.

Upstairs, the footfalls had gone silent. All was in readiness. Clutching his tools against his chest, the Lord of Masks raced up the mud-brick stairs to the house's ground floor. The quicker he was beyond the city walls, the better.

When he'd purchased the house, decades ago, the cellar stairs had been accessible through an archway at the rear of the building. Since then, he'd had the entrance hidden behind a cunningly wrought disguised door. Ushoran pressed the door's latch with the tip of a claw and pushed it wide. Beyond was a large storeroom, piled with an assortment of wooden boxes and empty clay jars – placed there to contribute to the illusion that real people actually lived in the building. An archway opposite opened onto a short corridor that led to the house's gathering room. His mind buzzing with the myriad details of his escape plan, Ushoran hurried to join his thralls.

He did not note the stink of spilled blood at first. His nose was deadened to the scent after the evening's entertainments. It was only when he emerged into the gathering room and stepped into a wide, tacky pool of gore that Ushoran realised the house had, in the space of a few heartbeats, been transformed into an abattoir.

The bodies of his thralls were scattered about the room. It looked like a battlefield: heads split, limbs severed, torsos slashed and entrails spilled across the floor. Blood painted the white walls in looping streaks and explosive spatters. Gore was splashed across the ordered rows of leather packs and saddlebags that had been set beside the door.

Ushoran froze, momentarily stunned by the suddenness and ferocity of the assault. A slight movement to his left caught the immortal's eye.

Ankhat sat at the gathering room's crude wooden table, idly tracing shapes with a fingertip through the spots of blood pooled across its rough surface. A red-stained iron sword lay on the table next to him, within easy reach.

The immortal fixed Ushoran with a steady, implacable stare. 'You have some explaining to do, my lord.'

Ushoran bared his teeth in a silent snarl, like an animal at bay. Mind reeling, he tried to compose himself, only to realise with an icy shock that he wasn't cloaked in his customary disguise. Ankhat could see him for what he really was, and showed not the slightest surprise.

'What is the meaning of this?' hissed the Lord of Masks.

Ankhat leaned forwards in his chair. 'Now that,' he said, 'is a *very* interesting question, considering the circumstances.'

Ushoran grew very still. His hands slowly closed into fists. How much did Ankhat know? The noble was swift and deadly with a blade, but Ushoran knew he was far stronger. Could he kill Ankhat? Possibly.

'How did you find me?' Ushoran said. He edged towards the table a fraction of a step.

Ankhat did not answer. Instead, Neferata's icy voice spoke from the darkness beyond the door.

'We have known about your secrets for quite some time,' she said, gliding like a pallid wraith into the blood-streaked room. Her retinue of maidens followed in her wake, fanged mouths gaping hungrily at the scent of so much carnage.

Neferata stalked towards Ushoran, her tattered robes swaying hypnotically with every languid step. Her eyes were pools of darkness, empty of human feeling.

'While your agents watched the kings of the great cities, Ankhat's agents were watching you,' Neferata continued. 'In truth, your appetites meant nothing to me, so long as you were useful.'

He never saw the blow. One moment, Neferata was several feet away – the next, he was being hurled against the far wall with a thunderous crash. Fragments of whitewashed mud flew across the room.

Neferata's fist tightened like a vice around Ushoran's throat. Her face was expressionless as she pushed him harder against the wall. Fragments of brick ground against his back.

'But now the forts along the plain are burning and an army has seized the eastern pass. A soldier from one of the forts escaped and lived long enough to bring us the news.' Her fist tightened further. 'I think you have disappointed me for the last time, my lord.'

Ushoran gripped Neferata's slender wrist and fought with all his strength for enough air to speak. 'I... did... not... know!' he gasped. 'My... agents... slain...'

Neferata's eyes narrowed angrily. 'Do you expect me to believe that this vast network of agents you've boasted about for so many years was undone so quickly and thoroughly that you received *no* warning whatsoever?' Quick as a viper, she drew back her arm and slammed Ushoran back against the wall, sending more clay fragments spraying around the room. 'Now you're insulting my intelligence.'

The Lord of Masks pawed desperately at Neferata's wrist. 'You're... right,' he hissed, his mind racing. 'Not... the... agents. The... messages... intercepted.' His eyes widened. 'Bandits... on the... plain. The... desert... tribes...'

'And why would a gang of flea-bitten thieves suddenly take an interest in your couriers?' Neferata snarled.

There was only one answer Ushoran could think of. '*Alcadizzar*,' he croaked.

For a moment, it looked as though Neferata's icy mask would crumble. Her eyes flashed angrily, but she abruptly released the Lord of Masks, allowing his misshapen body to slide heavily to the floor. 'Explain,' she demanded.

Ushoran drew a deep breath. The more he considered the notion, the more things started to make sense. 'The tribes... wouldn't care,' he began. 'Unless someone gave them a reason to.'

Neferata scowled at him. 'Alcadizzar? A prince among thieves? Is that your explanation?'

Wood creaked as Ankhat leaned back against the rough-hewn chair. 'As much as I hate to admit it, the idea is not as far-fetched as it sounds,' he said. 'The desert tribes have ancient ties to Khemri, going back as far as Settra himself.'

'They must have been sheltering him all along,' Ushoran said. 'He was under our noses, hiding right outside the city. The tribes have always been secretive and hostile to outsiders. Every attempt to infiltrate them came to nothing. If Alcadizzar could have convinced them of his lineage, though, he might well have won them over.'

'And now the little prince has managed to turn the other great cities against us,' Ankhat said, casting an accusing look at Neferata.

'How?' Neferata demanded. 'We've kept them at one another's throats for centuries.'

'Does it matter?' Ushoran interjected. 'The enemy is nearly at our gates. The question is, can we defeat them?'

For several, agonising seconds, neither Ankhat nor Neferata spoke and Ushoran began to fear he'd overreached. But then Ankhat sighed heavily, breaking the tension.

'The army is not trustworthy,' he said reluctantly. 'We can count on the royal guard, of course, and most of the noble companies, but that's all.'

'The people of Lahmia will defend their city,' Neferata snarled. 'Call up the citizen levies. Anyone who does not answer the summons will be slain out of hand.'

'The moment we start executing people, we may as well open the gates and invite Alcadizzar in,' Ankhat said flatly. 'The city will tear itself apart.'

Neferata glared angrily at Ankhat, but the immortal didn't waver. Finally she growled. 'How many, then?'

'Twenty thousand,' Ankhat replied. 'Two thousand cavalry, a thousand archers, and the rest infantry.' He shrugged. 'They're inexperienced, but it doesn't take much skill to stand on a wall and stick men with a spear.'

'Will that be enough?'

Ankhat shrugged. 'I have no idea. We don't really know what we're dealing with yet.'

'We can guess,' Ushoran said. 'There have been no reports from the west for many months. If Alcadizzar has roused Zandri, Numas, Quatar and Ka-Sabar, we could be facing as many as fifty thousand men. If he's won over Rasetra and Lybaras as well – and there's no reason to think he hasn't – then the number could be much higher. All they would need to do is create a breach in the walls and it would be all over.'

Neferata shot a look at Ankhat, expecting the immortal to challenge Ushoran's dire assessment. When he did not, her expression turned grim.

'There must be a way to stop them,' she said. 'There *must* be. I'll die the true death before I give up this city – and I'll see the rest of you die with me!'

Ankhat stiffened, his eyes narrowing angrily. He started to rise from the chair, his hand drifting to the hilt of his sword.

Ushoran's eyes widened. If Ankhat turned his blade on Neferata, then all would be lost. With her maidens at her back, she would destroy them both.

'There might be a way!' he shouted. 'But there will be a price, great one.'

Ankhat paused. Neferata turned to Ushoran, her eyes glinting like polished onyx.

'Tell me,' she said.

The vanguard of the army moved in good order down through the wooded hills and reached Lahmia's walls by midnight; the leading companies of the army's main body, Alcadizzar and Heru among them, joined up with them just before dawn. By the time they arrived, Faisr's tribesmen had preparations for the army's sprawling camp well under way, marking positions for tents, enclosures and corrals by torchlight.

Alcadizzar leaned back in the saddle with a grimace, trying to stretch his lower back. They had been riding since just after dawn the day before and he ached from his shoulders to his toes. The chariots and spearmen of Khemri filed past in weary ranks, heading for their assigned spot at the centre of the camp.

Heru drew up alongside the king, looking as relaxed and alert as though he were on an afternoon ride. Leather creaked as he leaned forwards in the saddle and surveyed the distant city. 'A strange sort of homecoming,' he said to Alcadizzar. 'How long has it been?'

Alcadizzar sighed and tried to count the years. Eighty, perhaps? Ninety? He was too tired to be sure. After a moment, he shrugged. 'Longer than you would believe.'

'Has it changed much?'

The king straightened, waving his arm at the cramped farmland nestled between Lahmia and the hills at their back. 'The last time I was here, this was a shanty town,' he said. 'Or what was left of one. Refugees settled here from Mahrak and Lybaras after the war against the Usurper, but they'd been mostly chased off or had found lives inside the city by the time I was born. When the bandits chased all the farmers off the Golden Plain, the lucky ones managed to resettle here.' The farms were dark now, their inhabitants having fled yet again for the dubious safety of Lahmia's walls.

Heru nodded towards the city. Columns of smoke, dull black against the grey predawn sky, rose from various quarters and wreathed the broad flanks of Lahmia's central hill. 'It looks like someone's started ahead of us.'

Alcadizzar nodded. 'Faisr's people in the city tell me that Lahmia's on the verge of revolt. After everything her citizens have suffered, Neferata will have a difficult time finding troops to man the walls.'

'All the better,' Heru said. 'The Lybarans should be here by midday. If they work through the night tonight, they can have their catapults ready to fire by tomorrow. All we need do is wait for them to make a breach.'

Alcadizzar said nothing for a moment, his gaze fixed on the smoke-wreathed hill. He couldn't yet see the walls of the palace that ringed its summit. Was Neferata there, standing atop the Temple of Blood and planning the destruction of his army?

'Faisr should already have pickets out,' he said. 'Pass the word to him that I want the posts to the north-east doubled. Then tell the captains I want half the companies to get some rest, while the others make camp. We'll switch them at noon and then start digging defensive positions.'

Heru frowned. 'You think the Lahmians will try an attack?'

The king looked north-east, to the rolling ground beyond the city where Lahmia's vast necropolis lay. 'Neferata has little choice,' he replied. 'If she hasn't realised it yet, she will before long.'

The Rasetran let out a snort. 'We've got the better part of thirty thousand men here, and more arriving every hour. If Neferata tries a sortie today, we'll cut her to pieces.'

Alcadizzar glanced at his nephew, his expression sombre. 'It's not a daytime attack that I'm worried about.'

It took hours for a group of temple acolytes to prise away the mortar sealing the flagstones in the temple cellar and reveal the cavity beneath. The space was just large enough to hold a large, earthen grain jar, its wide mouth capped and sealed with lead.

Ankhat had followed Neferata's commands to the letter, Ushoran thought, watching the acolytes grip the jar's four thick handles and haul it out of the hole. The cellar was one of the smallest and deepest of the chamber's storehouses and had been filled with everything from barrels of dried fish to bales of mouldy cotton. No one but rats had ventured there for years; even if the cellar had eventually been cleared out and put to another use, no one would have had any reason to suspect that anything had been buried beneath it. The Lord of Masks stole a glance at Ankhat, who stood above the hole and supervised the excavation with a tight, angry scowl on his face. He had been loudly, almost violently opposed to Ushoran's plan, but Neferata had overridden him. The city had to be saved, regardless of the risks.

The acolytes set the jar on the cellar floor with a heavy *thump* and stood back, shoulders heaving. Ankhat dismissed them with a wave of his hand. The mortals bowed swiftly and withdrew, eager to return to the light and warmth of the upper levels.

Ushoran listened to the acolytes' footsteps fade away down the corridor. Within moments, the immortals were alone. The Lord of Masks folded his arms, expecting Ankhat to vent his displeasure further, but the nobleman said not a word. Instead, he walked up to the jar and struck it with his fist.

The jar's thick, curved side shattered beneath the blow, sending palm-sized fragments skipping across the flagstones. Wreathed in a thin veil of clay dust, Ankhat reached into the jar and dragged W'soran's body free.

The necromancer's skeletal body was filthy with dust and mould and had been folded into a foetal position in order to fit into the tight confines of the jar. The jagged end of the wooden shard that Neferata had used to stab him protruded from the back of his grimy robes.

Ankhat's lip curled in disgust. He glared at Ushoran. 'There he is,' the immortal snapped. 'You're the one who wanted to free him, so you can do the rest.'

Ushoran gave Ankhat a disdainful stare, but went and knelt by W'soran's body. Carefully, he gripped the necromancer's fragile-looking arms and straightened them. Fabric crackled; dust puffed from wrists, shoulders and elbows. W'soran's skin was as thin as parchment and his bones little more than twigs. He worked gingerly, fearing that they might snap off if he used too much force.

Once the arms were free, Ushoran straightened out the necromancer's torso, until his body more or less lay flat. W'soran's face was little more than a snarling death's-head, his fangs bared in a tight-clenched grimace. The Lord of Masks stared into the necromancer's desiccated face and paused. He vividly remembered another night, in another cellar, hundreds of years ago, when Lamashizzar had plucked the stone from Arkhan's heart. He remembered the howl of madness as the immortal had clawed his way back to wakefulness, after having been paralysed for only a few months. W'soran had been trapped, fully aware, in the prison of his own mind for some twenty-two *years*. Would he have any sanity left?

The Lord of Masks reached out his hand and grasped the length of wood that jutted from W'soran's ribs. He plucked it free with a quick jerk of the wrist and tossed it across the cellar.

A faint tremor went through W'soran's bony frame. Ushoran settled back on his heels and waited for the howling to begin.

Moments later, the necromancer's eyelids snapped open, and Ushoran found himself staring into W'soran's dark, pitiless eyes. There was no madness there that Ushoran could see; just the cold, calculating intelligence of a serpent. Not a single sound escaped his ragged lips: no cry of terror, or anger, or relief. The lack of reaction chilled him far worse than Arkhan's tortured howls ever did.

For the first time, Ushoran feared he'd made a terrible mistake. Did they dare place Nagash's forbidden tomes into W'soran's hands?

Did they have any other choice, Ushoran thought? They would need an army to defend the city from the invaders. If the living would not answer the call, then the dead would have to march in their place.

TWENTY-ONE

FIRE IN THE NIGHT

Lahmia,
the City of the Dawn,
in the 107th year of Ptra the Glorious
(-1200 Imperial Reckoning)

Screams and the tramping of running feet rose from the narrow streets that surrounded the royal palace. Lahmia had lapsed into a shocked silence when the rising sun revealed the vast army camped outside its walls; now, with the coming of night, the city was trying to tear itself apart once more. The City Watch was patrolling the streets in gangs, armed not with clubs but with bared blades, under orders to kill any citizen roaming the streets after dark.

Neferata's high priestesses filed silently into her bedchamber as the last rays of the sun sank below the hills to the west. She did little more than sip from the proffered cup; just enough to quicken her limbs and whet her hunger to a razor's edge. Silent and sombre, the masked thralls drew her gently from the bed. This was a duty they had not performed for many years, not since the escape of the Rasetran prince, and they went about their work with slow, almost ritualistic care.

Deft fingers plucked at Neferata's stained clothes, peeling them away. Golden basins were brought in; they bathed her pale skin and then rubbed it with fragrant oils that had once been held sacred by the priestesses of Asaph. Neferata said nothing, her expression distant as she gazed out through the bedchamber's tall windows at the restless sea. The striped sails of trading ships spread in a wide arc from the mouth of the harbour, fleeing eastwards on the receding tide.

The thralls wrapped her in robes of dark blue silk and bound them with a girdle of plain, woven leather. A spearman's supple leather sandals were placed on her feet, secured in place by laced straps that reached as high as her knees.

When she was dressed, the priestesses guided her to a chair and began to work on her hair. Fingers teased and tugged at the mass of knots and tangles. Outside, darkness spread across the surface of the sea. By now, she knew, her warriors would be gathering at the city's southern gate, and W'soran would have begun his preparations for the great ritual. The sands were slipping through the hourglass.

Neferata waved her hand at the thralls. 'Time is wasting. If it won't come loose, cut it off. I care not.'

The thralls paused. There was a faint murmur of voices and the hands drew away. Neferata steeled herself for the cold touch of the knife – but instead felt another pair of hands take up where the thralls had left off. Deft fingertips unwound one tangle after another, drawing it down around her shoulders and her back. The sensation brought back memories Neferata had buried long ago.

She turned her head slightly to the side. 'Listening to me as I slept, again?'

The fingers paused for a moment. 'No,' Naaima said quietly. 'Not for a very long time.'

'What then?' Neferata demanded. 'If you've come to gloat, then say your piece and be gone.'

'No,' Naaima said again. She resumed her work, pulling at a stubborn knot at the base of Neferata's neck. 'What's done is done. I take no joy in seeing Lahmia brought to this.'

'Why shouldn't you?' Neferata said bitterly. 'It's not your home.'

To the queen's surprise, Naaima answered with a low chuckle. 'Of course it is,' she said. 'Lahmia has been my home since the day you set me free, all those years ago.'

Neferata looked away again, out into the darkness. 'If only he had listened,' she said hollowly. 'How different Nehekhara would be now.'

'It was not his fate,' Naaima replied. 'Such things cannot be changed, no matter how we might wish it.'

Neferata fell silent. Frightened screams drifted on the sea breeze.

'Are you still angry with me?'

'No,' Naaima said. 'Not any more. Does that comfort you?'

'I no longer know the meaning of the word.' The queen sighed. 'Why did you never ask to leave? Did you think I would have refused you?'

Naaima teased out the last of the knots and picked up a silver brush from the dressing table nearby. 'Is it so hard to understand?' she said sadly. 'Because I love you.'

'Then you have made a grave mistake.'

'As I said, we cannot change our fates,' Naaima replied. 'Once upon a time, you gave me the world. Ever since, I have waited to give it back.' She put down the brush and came around to kneel at the queen's side.

'Come with me to the east,' she said, taking Neferata's cold hands in hers. 'There is a ship waiting for us in the harbour. We can settle for a time in one of the trade cities, or leave them behind and travel the empire itself. Think of it–'

Neferata frowned. 'You think I'd abandon Lahmia?' she said. The queen pulled her hands away. 'My family has ruled this city for millennia.'

'All things end,' Naaima replied. 'Come away with me. Please. When the sun rises tomorrow, Lahmia will be no more.'

The queen stared down at Naaima, peering into the depths of the immortal's pleading eyes. Slowly, her expression hardened into a cold, defiant mask.

'Not while I still walk the earth,' Neferata said.

The queen rose from her chair and turned away from Naaima. The priestesses waited in silence, hands clasped at their waists, their expressions hidden behind their masks of gold.

She went to them, raising her arms as if in welcome. Next to them, laid out upon the silken bed, waited her armour of polished iron.

The view from the western gatehouse showed the invading army arrayed in a wide arc from north to south, their camps set in the fallow grain fields just a few dozen yards out of bowshot from the city walls. The darkness made it difficult to gauge the size of the host, but judging by the number of tents and cook-fires alone, W'soran reckoned that their numbers were vast - probably fifty thousand or more. For once, Neferata had shown a modicum of sense, the necromancer thought. Her pathetic excuse for an army wouldn't have stood a chance against such a force.

W'soran ran his fingertips along the yellowed pages of the great tome cradled in his left hand and smiled possessively. The taste of vindication was sweet. Even trapped in the stifling darkness of his prison, he had known that this day would come. Now the forbidden tomes were his. The final secrets of the necromantic art lay within his grasp.

He turned away from the gatehouse's narrow windows, satisfied that they would provide him with the vantage point he required. The large chamber dominated the upper storey of the gatehouse and normally served as a barracks and common room for the guardsmen who stood watch along the western wall. At Neferata's command the wide, rectangular room had been emptied of cots, tables and chairs, and the guardsmen forbidden to enter on pain of death. A trio of thralls - Neferata's possessions, which galled W'soran no end, but there was no time to create more of his own - waited at the far end of the room, ready to serve his every command. The bloodless corpses of two young men were piled in a heap near one of the chamber's two doors, their faces contorted in masks of terror and pain.

The ritual circle had been inscribed on the floor in blood, copied exactly according to the notes and diagrams in Nagash's tome. W'soran studied the complex incantation with an expectant smile. He had been waiting for this moment for centuries.

'Is all in readiness?'

The necromancer's head jerked up in surprise. He hadn't heard Neferata's approach. The queen had entered through the door to his left, attended by her maidens. The former priestesses were a fearsome sight, clad in dark robes and leather armour reinforced with thin strips of iron. Fresh blood darkened their lips and dripped from their chins. The queen herself was more forbidding still: her torso was cased in a flexible breastplate of polished iron scales, a heavy skirt of leather banded with iron covered her from hips to knees. Hinged iron bracers encased her forearms, heavy enough to block swords and shatter bones. Her face and hands had been cleansed of filth and gleamed like marble in the torchlight. She was radiant, beautiful beyond compare, but her eyes held nothing but death. It was the first time he had seen her since that night in the sanctum, more than twenty years ago. He had looked forwards to the meeting, eager to heap upon her all the bitterness and hate that had sustained him in his prison, but the sight of her now gave the necromancer pause.

'The circle is prepared,' he said curtly. 'But the effects will be limited. The tombs of the nobility are warded with powerful spells of protection, which require more time to circumvent.'

A flicker of irritation crossed the queen's face, but she nodded. 'Very well,' Neferata said. 'The enemy's pickets have been slain. Ushoran waits in the necropolis, and Ankhat is leading the army through the south gate even now.'

Neferata strode to the gatehouse windows, surveying the battlefield. 'And you will guide them from here?'

'It will serve,' W'soran replied.

'Then begin.'

The necromancer gave the queen a sepulchral smile. 'As you command,' he said, and sketched a quick, faintly mocking bow. Neferata took no notice, her gaze fixed on the distant enemy.

No doubt searching for her lost prince, W'soran thought, his lip curling into a sneer as he turned his attention to the necromantic circle. With luck, he would find Alcadizzar first. How sweet it would be to present the queen with his still-beating heart.

W'soran took his place before the circle. His gaze fell to the incantation writ upon the page before him. Teeth bared in a death's-head grin, he began the ritual of summoning.

The cook-fires of the enemy camp twinkled in the darkness, little more than a mile away. From where he stood on the rocky plain just outside Lahmia's southern gate, Ankhat could only see perhaps a third of the enemy force, but even that seemed far larger than the small force under his command.

The last of the spear companies were marching down the coastal road, moving to take their place at the far end of the battle-line. The warriors were well armed, each man carrying an eight-foot spear and short sword, and wearing a shirt of iron scales over a thick leather tunic. In addition, each spearman bore a rectangular wooden shield with a round iron boss in the centre; in battle, each man would stand shoulder-to-shoulder with his companions and form a solid wall of wood and metal to protect the formation from enemy attacks. Helmeted heads glanced his way as the company went by; the faces Ankhat saw were young and frightened. None of them had ever seen battle before. Would they remember their training when they came to grips with the enemy and the blood began to flow? Ankhat had his doubts. Most had answered the call because they had families in the city and knew that their loved ones would be punished if they didn't obey.

The exception was the soldiers of the royal guard. A thousand men strong, they were clad in heavier armour and wielded fearsome, sickle-bladed polearms instead of spears. Most of them were from families whose sons had guarded the royal palace for generations and were given payment and privileges far above what a typical spearman received. Their courage and skill were unquestioned, as well as their devotion to the royal family. Ankhat had placed them in the centre of the battle-line, in hopes that their example would inspire the rest.

He had twenty-five thousand men in all, including the chariots of the city's nobility. Had he a few hundred veterans among them, they would have constituted a formidable force; as it was, he feared that they would break if pressed too hard. Ankhat knew he had to take full advantage of the element of surprise and to keep the battle-line moving forwards, deeper into the enemy camp. If the spear companies were halted, and their casualties began to mount, the attack would quickly fall apart.

To his left, the last spear company turned off the road and settled into place. Moments later, the chariots emerged from the southern gate, bouncing and clattering down the road in a line of two abreast. They galloped down the length of the battle-line, moonlight flashing from the fearsome sickle blades fixed to the hub of the iron-rimmed wheels. Each war machine carried a driver, two archers, and the chariot's master, who bore a shield and either an axe or sword. Many raised their weapons in salute as they passed; here and there, a spearman forgot himself and cheered in reply, only to be silenced by a cuff to the head and a curse from his sergeant.

The chariots turned off the road past the battle-line and rumbled off to a position a few dozen yards behind and to the left of the farthest company. When the spear companies finally engaged the enemy, the chariots would attempt to sweep around and take their foes in the flank, forcing them to retreat or else be struck from two sides. It wasn't much, as battle tactics went, but it would serve. So long as the companies closed with the enemy and did their level best to kill them, that was all that really mattered.

Ankhat drew his iron sword and waited for the call of the trumpets. He had drunk little since waking, anticipating the bloodletting that lay ahead.

Tonight, the fate of Lahmia would be decided, not by the living, but by the dead.

Ushoran crouched in the shadow of an ancient stone crypt, his senses straining to detect the first telltale signs of magic. The northern edge of the enemy camp was some three miles distant, hidden from view by the rolling terrain that surrounded the necropolis. If Neferata's pets had succeeded in killing the invaders' sentries, then they would have little warning of the coming attack.

Not for the first time, the Lord of Masks wondered if W'soran could be trusted. He had only agreed to aid Neferata if he were given the forbidden tomes of Nagash and the queen had no choice but to agree. Now that he had what he'd been after all along, what was to stop him from fleeing the city the moment the opportunity arose?

Of course, he could ask himself the same question. He'd been attempting that very thing when Ankhat and Neferata had caught him. And now here he was, alone and outside the city at last. He could slip into the hills and be halfway across the Golden Plain by dawn if he chose.

As he sat among the crypts, the wind shifted, carrying to him the scents and sounds of the unsuspecting camp. Thousands upon thousands of men; he could almost hear the blood singing in their veins. The thought of tearing into their midst, claws slashing, teeth snapping, of rending flesh and snapping bone, sent shudders of anticipation through his misshapen frame. He suspected that W'soran – indeed, all of the immortals – felt it as well. They had existed in secret for too long, furtively stealing scraps from the city streets, or sipping discreetly from golden cups. Here at last, they could cast aside their masks and walk the earth as gods.

Ushoran tensed, feeling a faint tremor in the air. The vibrations grew stronger, seeming to come from everywhere at once. He felt it against his cheeks and the pads of his clawed feet. The immortal crouched lower, placing his palm against the ground, and felt the tremors quicken into a grinding, surf-like rumble.

He recognised it at once. It was the sound of stone scraping against stone, of hands pushing aside hundreds of mortuary slabs or forcing open long-sealed doors. An instant later the noise was echoing among the tombs as the risen dead burst from their resting places and lurched forth into the night.

Skeletal feet scraped and clicked over the rocky ground. Ushoran began to see figures moving stiffly among the tombs; bony shapes clad in rags and patches of grave mould, with pinpoints of greenish light gleaming in the depths of their eye sockets. They were the corpses of the city's poor, laid to rest in crude stone mausoleums and bereft of the grave goods that Lahmia's wealthy citizens were buried with. Though they bore no weapons and carried no armour, there were thousands of them, sweeping past

Ushoran in a lurching, staggering tide, heading towards the unsuspecting enemy camp.

The Lord of Masks let out a low, hungry growl and let the tide carry him along. Behind him, the chilling cries of jackals filled the air, drawn by the smell of rotten flesh. They loped along in the wake of the skeletal army, jaws agape, as if sensing the carrion feast to come.

Horns sounded, echoing wildly from the north. Alcadizzar straightened, his dinner forgotten, wine cup halfway to his mouth.

Prince Heru sat bolt upright from the narrow cot where he'd been napping. Oil lamps filled the king's campaign tent with warm, steady light; a trio of braziers had been lit to stave off the night's chill. The Rasetran glanced sharply about, taking his bearings. 'Those are our horns,' he said with growing alarm.

Alcadizzar nodded. He sat at one of the two large tables set to one side of the tent, where a large map depicting Lahmia and the surrounding area had been laid out and marked with the dispositions of the army. He'd been certain that a night attack was coming. Neferata had nothing to gain by holding the walls and letting her smaller force be decimated by weeks of fighting. A night attack, on the other hand, offered advantages. Aside from the potential of surprise, her troops would not have to worry as much about Alcadizzar's archers and she and her monstrous allies could intervene directly in the fight.

There was also the danger of a simultaneous attack from the city's necropolis. He had to assume that if Neferata could defy death, much like Nagash had done, then she could command the dead as well. Against that possibility, he had given the battle-hardened Rasetrans the job of securing the army's left flank. In the centre, facing the city's western gate – and the likeliest route of attack by the Lahmians – he had placed Ka-Sabar's Iron Legion. On the right, close enough to offer support but otherwise out of the way, Alcadizzar had placed the troublesome Zandri infantry and mercenaries. The Numasi cavalry and the desert horsemen were held in reserve, as well as the Tomb Guard and the much smaller contingents of troops from Khemri and Mahrak.

Heru leapt to his feet, swiftly buckling on his sword. Outside, shouted orders and cries of alarm filled the air. 'What in the name of the gods happened to our pickets?'

'Dead, most like,' Alcadizzar replied. 'The night belongs to Neferata and her ilk. Or so they think.' He studied the map one last time, committing the placement of units to memory, then rose and pulled his own sword from its hook on the nearest tent-pole.

'Let's not waste time on what's gone wrong,' the king continued. 'We suspected something like this was going to happen. Remember the battle plan.' Buckling on his sword, he rushed to the tent flap. 'Runner!' he called.

In moments, a young boy from Khemri appeared, his eyes wide with excitement. 'Yes, great one?'

'Get to the Lybarans and tell them to get their catapults to work on the left flank. Go!'

The boy bowed quickly and dashed from the tent, narrowly avoiding Faisr, who was rushing to find the king. The great chieftain's face was grim.

'The left flank is under attack,' he said. 'Lahmia's necropolis has given up its dead, and they are marching on us in vast numbers!'

Alcadizzar had never heard Faisr sound worried in his entire life. The realisation sent a chill down the king's spine, but he tried to remember old Jabari's teachings and push the fear aside. 'Take your riders and flank the corpses,' he said, in as steady a tone as he could muster. 'Find the sorcerer that's controlling them. Go!'

The great chieftain nodded curtly and hurried back out into the night. Alcadizzar turned to Heru. 'Let's go!'

'Us? Oh, no,' Heru protested, placing a hand on his uncle's arm. 'I'm going to go lead my people. Your place is here.' Without giving Alcadizzar a chance to reply, he brushed past and shoved the tent flap aside. 'I'll send a report on the situation as soon as I'm able. Just get those Lybarans moving, eh?'

'I will,' the king said, but before he could say any more, Heru was gone.

Alcadizzar clenched his fists. Off to the north, he could hear the faint roar of battle. The sound called to him, setting his blood afire. With a frustrated sigh, he went back to the map table and studied the positions of his troops.

Just then came another wave of trumpet calls – this time, however, from the south. Alcadizzar's eyes widened.

'Runner!' he called again. His carefully prepared plan was threatening to come apart at the seams.

Just ahead of Ushoran, a man was brought down by a trio of skeletons. The warrior fell with a shout, slashing wildly with his sword and shearing off several ribs from the nearest corpse. The skeleton took no notice, its finger-bones clawing deep into the warrior's throat. Arterial blood jetted into the air. The second corpse pulled the sword from the dying man's hand and the trio continued on, seeking another victim.

The undead horde flooded into the enemy camp in a silent, shambling tide of bone, tearing apart anyone and anything that got in their way. The enemy fled before them, bellowing and cursing in fear. Those that stood their ground and tried to fight were quickly overwhelmed. Here and there, tents were afire, bathing the battleground in garish crimson light. Off to Ushoran's right there was a blaze of sparks as a skeleton kicked its way through an abandoned cook-fire and kept going, its rotting clothes burning greasily about its legs and waist.

Ushoran threw back his head and howled like one of the hungry spirits of the waste. He thirsted for the taste of hot, bitter blood.

There was another line of tents up ahead. Several skeletons had already reached them and were clawing at their sides. Beyond them, Ushoran heard a throaty roar of challenge; the Rasetrans had finally chosen to turn and make a stand. Grinning evilly, the immortal picked up speed, loping past the slower skeletons, between the tents, and into the open ground on the other side.

The Lord of Masks let out a grunt of surprise. Some twenty yards past the nearest tents was a long, somewhat irregular line of barricades, formed of tall wicker baskets filled with packed earth and rock. The Rasetrans had formed up behind the barricades, thousands strong; firelight flickered balefully off a thicket of spear-points that stretched as far as Ushoran's eye could see.

It was a sight that would have given the stoutest heart pause. But not the dead; the skeletons looked upon the enemy line and were unmoved. The horde came on, filling the open ground before the barricades and throwing itself against the enemy line. Spears jabbed and thrust, but could find no purchase. Fearless, mindless, the undead clawed at the earth-filled baskets, climbing onto them and reaching for the warriors on the other side. Men shouted oaths and struck at the corpses with spear butts, or the metal-rimmed edges of their shields. Smashed limbs and broken skulls were hurled back upon the oncoming tide, but the advance never faltered.

For the moment, the enemy line was holding, smashing apart the corpses as they clambered onto the barricade. Snarling hungrily, Ushoran broke into a run. Calling upon the power in his veins, he gathered himself and leapt like a cat, clearing the struggling mass of skeletons and coming down on the far side of the barricade. Two men fell screaming underneath the immortal; a spear punched through his hip and the wooden haft snapped in two. Ushoran felt nothing but a savage, bloodthirsty joy. With a sweep of his hand he tore a man's guts out and hurled his screaming body high into the air. Another blow crumpled a warrior's helmet and pulped the skull beneath.

Shouts, screams and curses thundered in Ushoran's ears. The enemy charged in from all sides, jabbing at him with their spears. Laughing wickedly, the immortal swept the weapons aside like twigs, clawing for the soft flesh behind them. Leather and armour tore like cloth beneath his talons. The scent of blood filled his nostrils.

Roaring like a hungry lion, the immortal plunged deeper into the mass of screaming warriors, sowing terror and death as he went.

The barbarian came at Ankhat with a furious bellow, eyes wild and bearded mouth agape. He was a giant, like all the men of the far north, broad of shoulder and thick of limb, clad in a heavy leather tunic and protected by a wooden shield the size of a chariot wheel. The northman brandished a fearsome, single-bladed battle axe in his knobby fist, drawn back to strike at the immortal's head.

He might have been trudging through wet sand, as far as Ankhat was concerned. The immortal darted forwards just as the axe fell, its blade tracing a broad, languid arc. His sword flashed upwards, chopping through the barbarian's thick wrist, then down again in a backhand stroke that smashed the northman's hip. The warrior crumpled, his bold yell transformed into a scream of mortal agony.

The barbarians threw themselves at the advancing battle-line without thought to order or discipline. They came charging out of the darkness of the camp in ragged mobs, smashing bodily into the shield wall and hewing at the heads and shoulders of their foes. Many times they were struck through by spears at the moment of impact, but the pain of their injuries only made them fight the harder. Men fell screaming, clutching at split skulls or ruined faces, or struggling to stanch the blood pouring from gaping throats. Others pressed forwards, filling the gaps in the line, and the companies continued to advance.

Another brute rushed at Ankhat, bloodshot eyes glaring hatefully over the rim of his shield. The immortal fixed the barbarian with a haughty stare and bared his fangs; the northman pulled up short, shouting in terror. Ankhat took off the top of his head with a single, swift stroke. More of the mercenaries crashed into the line of guardsmen to the immortal's right; men grunted and cursed, hacking at the giants with their polearms.

'Forwards!' Ankhat cried, adding his own voice to the din. Trumpets were pealing up and down the battle-line, urging the men onwards. The immortal cut the legs out from under a charging barbarian, then stabbed the throat of another who was locked in battle with the guardsman to his left. He had lost track of the number of foes he'd slain since the advance began. Twenty? Thirty? They all blurred together in a magnificent haze of screams and spilled blood. Part of him longed to leave the slow-moving companies behind and truly indulge his hunger. What a slaughter he might have wrought then!

Now, abruptly, the tide had shifted. The barbarians were withdrawing, racing back towards the camp at the bellowing sound of deep-throated horns. The Lahmians, flush with success, flung insults and jeers at the retreating mercenaries. Ankhat, whose eyes were far keener in the dark, saw why; the enemy had finally managed to restore some order in the camp and the rest of the northmen had been formed together in something approaching a proper battle-line, some twenty yards away. As the Lahmians approached, they roared in challenge, striking their weapons against their shields and sending up a thunderous clatter of metal and wood.

Ankhat grinned hungrily, levelling his sword at the enemy. 'At them!' he commanded, and the guardsmen shouted in answer. He turned to the trumpeter beside him. 'Signal the chariots to advance and wheel right!'

Here was the moment that they would break the northmen. Ankhat sensed it in his bones, like a lion studying his prey. They must have squandered almost half their number already; what remained couldn't hold once the chariots took them in the flank. The barbarians would break and run, leaving the centre of the enemy army dangerously exposed.

Ankhat growled in anticipation of the bloodshed that would follow.

The young messenger was pale and trembling. Ochre dust and streaks of someone else's blood caked his bare forearms and calves. He'd been out on the battlefield less than thirty minutes.

'Rasetra is-is giving ground,' the boy said, his voice hitching as he gasped for breath. 'The-the barricades on the r-right have been overrun. The-the dead are walking, and-and worse–'

Alcadizzar bit back his impatience. The boy was only twelve or so, he reminded himself. There were horrors walking the field that few grown men could face, let alone a mere boy. He gripped the child's arm reassuringly.

'Put that aside, lad,' he said, in as persuasive a tone as he could muster. 'You're a soldier in the army now. I need you to do your duty. Do you understand?'

The messenger drew in a deep breath and visibly calmed himself. 'Y-yes, great one. I understand.'

'Good. Then show me on the map here where Prince Heru's troops are.'

The boy nodded. 'They're here, more or less,' he said, tracing an arc that roughly paralleled the line of barricades, but was anywhere from seventy-five to a hundred yards behind them.

Alcadizzar gritted his teeth. Another hundred yards and the attackers would be at the edge of the inner camp. 'Can Prince Heru hold them?'

The messenger paused, consulting his memory. 'He said that they are outnumbered and making a fighting withdrawal, and need reinforcements urgently. He also told me to ask you where the damned catapults were. He said to tell you in those words.'

'I can well believe that,' Alcadizzar said. He'd already sent two more messengers to get the Lybarans' weapons in action. What was the point of dragging them halfway across eastern Nehekhara if they weren't put to use? 'Well done,' he said absently, his gaze poring over the battle map. 'Have the servants give you a cup of wine and catch your breath.'

As the messenger withdrew, the king took stock of the situation. Zandri had sent urgent messages saying they were under heavy attack from the south-east, but Alcadizzar didn't know how much stock to put in the reports. Meanwhile, on the left flank, Rasetra was in grave peril. Ka-Sabar, however, reported that the centre, facing the city's closest gate, was silent.

What was Neferata up to? Where was the main threat? Was it the attack on the left, or on the right, or was there something else entirely that he'd overlooked? He longed to grab a horse and go review the battlefield for himself, but he knew that would only complicate things further. It was just like one of Jabari's maddening exercises – only this time, his orders were getting real men killed.

Alcadizzar sighed. He needed to re-orient his troops to deal with the threats to his flanks. Ka-Sabar's heavy infantry could be wheeled around to support Rasetra, but that would leave the centre wide open. Did he dare take the risk?

He didn't see much choice. The threat to the centre was pure speculation, while the ones on the flanks were all too real.

Alcadizzar motioned to three of the messengers who were waiting quietly just inside the tent. He pointed to the first one. 'Carry this message to Queen Omorose. Tell her that the Numasi must counter-attack on the right. Swing wide and take the enemy in the flank. Go!'

As the boy rushed out into the night, Alcadizzar turned to the second messenger. 'Go to the reserves. The forces of Khemri and Mahrak are to move up and hold the centre. Ride with them; when they are in position, inform King Aten-sefu that the Iron Legion is to pull back and support Prince Heru on the left.'

The second boy nodded hastily and raced outside. The king studied the map and nodded to himself. It was a risk, but a calculated one. He still had the Tomb Guard in reserve, just in case.

Alcadizzar reached out and gripped the third messenger's arm. 'Go to the Lybarans. Tell them to get their cursed machines working, or I'll head back there myself and start firing *them* at the Lahmians.'

Farther west, at the rear of the enemy camp, there was a sudden flare of bluish light. Moments later, a half-dozen globes of fire were hurled skywards, arcing over the invaders' tents before plunging to the ground off to the north-east. The balls of pitch exploded on impact, showering the area with hungry blue flames. Scores of slow-moving, lurching corpses were caught in the blasts, their rotting flesh sizzling and their bones cracking in the intense heat.

W'soran watched the battle unfolding from the safety of the gatehouse and hissed in satisfaction. The ritual had worked to perfection; he could *feel* the vast horde moving along the plain below, as though his mind were bound to each and every one by an invisible gossamer cord. There were thousands of them, far more than the pitiful display the mortal defenders of the city could manage, and they were eating their way deep into the enemy's flank. The bursts of fire only served to better illuminate how desperate the enemy's position was; now he could see that his undead slaves had overrun a long line of barricades and driven the mortals back almost as far as the inner core of the camp. No doubt that little fool, Alcadizzar, was somewhere in there, frantically trying to find a way out of the noose that was tightening around his neck.

Still more globes of pitch fell among the undead host. More skeletons fell, consumed by the flames, but they felt no pain at their demise and neither did W'soran. He could lose many hundreds more and scarcely feel the loss. There would be more than enough to complete the destruction of the invaders.

As the globes of burning pitch passed over the camp, W'soran noted a commotion in the centre of the enemy's positions. Armoured troops were pulling back and heading to the north, undoubtedly in a vain attempt to save the doomed flank. All that remained in the centre were a few companies of lightly armoured troops.

The necromancer smiled mirthlessly, revelling in his new-found power. He turned to Neferata, who stood with her retinue of maidens at a window to his right. 'They are growing desperate,' he croaked. 'Soon their troops will grow tired, while mine will not. They will give in to their fear, while mine feel none. They cannot hope to win.'

Neferata studied the panoramic spectacle of the battlefield. If she'd heard W'soran, she gave no sign. Her eyes were distant, her expression grave. 'The time has come,' she said coldly. The queen glanced over at the necromancer. 'You have done well. Press the attack upon the right. I will deal with Alcadizzar.'

W'soran gave a deep, slightly mocking bow. 'Of course,' he said. 'I should have expected no less. And what will you do when you find him?'

There was no reply. When he straightened, the queen and her maidens were gone.

The man's head came away with a crunch of cartilage and a torrent of blood. Ushoran flung the grisly trophy at the enemy battle-line, then bent to drink deeply from the liquid still jetting from the corpse's neck.

Balls of fire hissed overhead, plunging well behind Ushoran and among the rear ranks of the undead. The noise of battle rang in his ears and beat at the bones in his chest; a grinding, surf-like roar of shouts, screams and hoarse battle cries. The enemy line was giving ground slowly but steadily, being forced ever backwards in the direction of the centre of camp. Somehow, their discipline held together despite the relentless pressure of the skeletal horde. Twice now they had launched counter-attacks with chariots in hopes of breaking up the undead advance, but the walking dead simply shrugged off the losses and pressed onwards with single-minded intent.

Ushoran's muscular arms and torso were matted with gore. Blood and bits of flesh drooled from his gaping jaws. Never, in all his long existence, had he imagined anything so glorious as this. He'd killed hundreds of men in the space of the last hour, smashing, clawing, biting and tearing in an orgy of bloodletting and slaughter. All the many nights he'd spent in cellars across Lahmia, drawing out the pleasure of a screaming victim's death agonies... it paled in comparison to this.

The Lord of Masks tossed the headless body aside. His body was near to bursting with vigour. Laughing cruelly, he advanced on the enemy line once again. The enemy warriors in front of him shouted and screamed, recoiling at his approach; many of them had been given ample opportunity to witness what he was capable of. Several flung spears at him, which he batted carelessly aside.

Snarling, Ushoran broke into a run. He wasn't interested in foot soldiers any longer; this time, he meant to find the man commanding this rabble and tear him to pieces.

Just short of the enemy's front rank he gathered his energies and bounded into the air. The battle-line was much thinner than when the battle began; he cleared the remaining ranks with ease and landed on the other side.

There were wounded men everywhere; soldiers who had staggered out of the battle-line and were trying to tend their injuries. Ushoran tore into them with savage glee, savouring their screams as he ripped into them with claw and tooth. As he did so, he searched for men on horseback, who would be riding behind the battle-line and shouting orders or encouragement.

There! Off to his right, some fifty yards away, a large group of horsemen was moving in his direction. Some carried torches, perhaps to draw the eye of the soldiers more easily. Among them he could see a fluttering standard; no doubt the enemy leader on this part of the battlefield. Like a hungry lion he charged at the oncoming riders, letting out a guttural roar as he approached.

The sound had the desired effect. The horsemen scattered before him, spreading out left and right with surprising speed. Directly ahead, Ushoran could see the enemy standard and a group of armoured riders surrounding it. The riders stood their ground, drawing their swords and grimly preparing to receive his charge.

A powerful impact struck him in the side, hard enough to stagger him. Ushoran reached down and felt the thick stub of an arrow jutting from his ribs. Two more missiles struck him in the left leg, knocking it out from underneath him. He fell, tumbling, and still more arrows hissed past his head.

Ushoran was on his feet in an instant. Horses were dashing past him to the left and right, their riders aiming powerful horn bows at him. He realised with a shock that they weren't proper cavalry, but robed desert riders. They fired at him as they went by and nearly every missile found its mark. In seconds, he was struck no less than eight times, in his chest, abdomen and arms.

The immortal scarcely felt the pain. Snarling, he snatched at the shafts, trying to yank them free, but the heads were barbed and refused to pull away. Worse, each arrow seemed to have a bulb of clay just behind the barbed head; when it struck the target, the bulb shattered, covering the area with a patch of sticky fluid the size of his palm. The sharp reek of the substance filled his nostrils at once. *Pitch.*

Ushoran's joy was transformed to terror in the space of an instant. Two more arrows hit him – one dangerously close to his heart. He whirled about, seeking an avenue of escape.

Two more riders thundered past. Too late, Ushoran saw the torches guttering in their hands. The Lord of Masks had just enough time to scream before his body was enveloped in a sizzling column of flame.

'Forwards! Forwards, damn you!'

A Nehekharan spearman reached over the top of the wicker barricade and stabbed at Ankhat. The immortal knocked the point aside with his sword and crushed the man's skull with a quick, backhand stroke. Around him, the warriors of the royal guard were hacking at the barricade's defenders with their polearms, but making little headway.

Ankhat was furious. Just half an hour before he'd thought victory lay in his grasp. They'd met the barbarian battle-line and held the fools in place while the chariots swung around and struck them in the flank. Panic had taken hold and the mercenaries had turned and run. Exultant, Ankhat had let the Lahmians pursue their broken foes and they had slaughtered the lumbering northmen as they fled.

And then, without warning, the charging Lahmians had come upon the barricade. A fresh line of troops – Nehekharans this time, not wild-eyed barbarians, waited with spears and bows, and unleashed a fierce volley of shafts point-blank into the faces of the oncoming Lahmians. Fortunately for Ankhat's men, the sheer inertia of their charge carried them into the enemy fortifications before they had time to register their shock. Had they time to think, the tired troops might have broken under the storm of arrow fire.

But now the attack had bogged down. Ankhat's men were tired and the enemy fresh, and they defended the barricade with dogged determination. He had tried to signal the chariots to find the end of the fortifications and swing around it, but could not be sure if the message had been received or not.

Furious, the immortal prepared to make another leap onto the barricade. He'd tried three times before but had been thrown back. Enemy spears had struck him twice, but hadn't managed to pierce his vitals.

The royal guardsmen were attacking the enemy with great courage, but even they were beginning to falter. Something had to be done, and quickly, or all would be lost.

Thinking quickly, Ankhat sheathed his sword and took hold of the wicker basket in front of him. It was almost as tall as a man and packed with hundreds of pounds of dirt and stone; he dug his fingers deep into its woven surface and summoned up all of his strength. With a savage cry he heaved the basket into the air and onto the defenders, who fell back with shouts of dismay.

The barricade was two baskets wide. At once, Ankhat pushed forwards and seized the next as well. A spear jabbed at him from the left, scoring his cheek, but the immortal paid it no heed. He grabbed the basket and flung it skywards just like the first, creating a narrow gap in the enemy's defences.

Suddenly, far off to the left, came the sound of trumpets. Ankhat felt a surge of savage joy. The chariots had come through at last! But then he realised that the sounds were coming from the Lahmian side of the barricade, rather than the opposite, and the signals were not ones that he was familiar with.

His bloodlust called to him to press forwards, but his instincts said that something had gone very wrong. The enemy pushed forwards, trying to seal off the breach. Gritting his teeth, Ankhat fell back, drawing his sword once more.

Now more horns were sounding to his left. These signals he knew and the sound caused his heart to sink. The spear companies on his flank were sounding the retreat!

Ankhat turned and shoved his way through the ranks of his own guardsmen. He had to see what was happening. Dragging his trumpeter with him, he made his way to the rear of the formation and peered into the darkness.

What he saw filled him with anger and dismay. The plain to the south was full of warriors, racing back in the direction of the city. Horsemen were charging through their midst, cutting down the fleeing men with spear or sword.

Ankhat understood what had happened in an instant. Enemy cavalry had counter-attacked in great numbers, scattering his chariots and striking his spearmen in the flank, just as they had done to the barbarians. The inexperienced soldiers had panicked and the result was a rout.

The attack had failed. There was no way his surviving companies could press forwards with enemy cavalry sweeping around behind him. Now he had to focus on getting back inside the city before he was completely surrounded.

Ankhat quickly took stock of the situation. There was no chance of reaching the south gate – the terrain favoured the cavalry, allowing them to outmanoeuvre the retreating infantry and cut them off. Their only hope was to pull back and withdraw to the north-east, hoping to reach the city's western gate.

They'd done all they could, Ankhat thought bitterly. It was up to W'soran and his undead warriors now.

Alcadizzar glanced up as the tent flap was pulled aside. Faisr rushed into the tent, beckoning to the servants for a cup of wine. 'You sent the Iron Legion just in time,' he said, taking the offered cup and draining it to the dregs. 'Another few minutes and we would have been lost.'

'Prince Heru?' the king inquired.

'Still fighting with his kinsmen. The Rasetrans are a courageous bunch,

I'll say that for them. They've paid a steep price in blood tonight, and the fighting's not done.'

Alcadizzar pointed at the map. 'I just got a message from Omorose. The Numasi have broken the attack on the right. How bad are things on the left?'

'Bad.' Faisr shook his head. 'The dead just keep coming. You kill one and three more take their place.'

'What about the necromancer? Can't you find him?'

The chieftain shook his head. 'He's not out there. Some brave souls even circled around the horde and searched the necropolis. We found one of the monsters leading the horde and hurt him badly, maybe even destroyed him. It didn't make any difference.'

The king turned his attention back to the map, frowning thoughtfully. 'He has to be out there somewhere,' he mused. 'Everything Rakh-amn-hotep wrote about the undead is that the risen corpses can't think for themselves. They have to be guided by the necromancer who raised them. So he has to be in a place where he can see enough of the battlefield to give them proper commands.'

At that moment, a wide-eyed messenger stumbled into the tent. Gasping for breath, he bowed to Alcadizzar. It took a moment for the king to understand that the boy was from Khemri and thus one of his subjects.

'Great one! The centre is under attack!'

Alcadizzar straightened. 'Attacked? How? By what?'

'Creatures!' the boy said. 'Pale creatures in armour, with the faces of women.'

The king gave Faisr a knowing glance. 'How many?'

'I-I don't know! Four or five, perhaps. But they're killing everyone! Killing them, or driving them mad. The Devoted have lost many men already.'

'Where did they come from?'

'The-the western gatehouse, we think. Some say they jumped right off the city wall, as though it was nothing more than a stepping-stool!'

Alcadizzar began to see what was happening. Neferata had been watching the battle unfold from the gatehouse, gauging his response. The attacks on the left and right had both been feints, meant to weaken the centre. Now she had entered the fray – and he knew where she was heading.

The king rose to his feet. 'Gather your people,' he said to Faisr. 'We're going to finish this.' Then he beckoned to two of his messengers. 'You, fetch my horse,' he said to one young boy. 'And you, I want you to carry a message to the Lybarans as fast as you can.'

Neferata and her maidens walked beneath the moonlight and chaos and death rode in their wake.

They came upon the enemy battle-lines like wives welcoming their husbands home from battle; arms outstretched, faces lit with desire. Men looked upon their faces and lost all control. Some fled screaming, while still others turned their blades on their fellows in a mad fit of jealousy and passion. The few men of iron will who could not be swayed, who remembered their oaths and tried to put an end to Neferata and her maidens, were torn apart by the immortals' talons.

A company of javelin throwers charged at Neferata and let fly; white-robed priests from Mahrak leapt between her and the oncoming missiles, screaming in horror even as they shielded her with their bodies. A moment later the javelin throwers had drawn their short swords and were locked in combat with a company of spearmen, warriors whom they had perhaps shared a meal with just a few hours before. Their faces were contorted into masks of agony and disbelief. They *knew* that what they were doing was wrong, but were powerless to stop it.

Within minutes, the queen and her maidens became separated by the wild melee. Neferata would catch glimpses of them from time to time, walking calmly among the slaughter like the eye of a raging summer storm. They moved steadily westwards, towards the centre of the camp. The place where, she was sure, Alcadizzar waited. At long last, she would see him again.

A quartet of chariots came rumbling out of the darkness, heading straight for her. The queen met the gaze of the driver in the lead chariot. The man's eyes widened, his expression suddenly transformed from anger to utter, mindless desire. He cast a jealous glance over his shoulder at the other charioteers, and with a snarl, he hauled upon the reins. The chariot veered sharply right, into the path of those behind it, causing a horrendous collision. Horses fell, shrieking in fear and pain, and the air was filled with pieces of broken wood and broken men.

Miraculously, the driver of the lead chariot survived. He staggered to his feet, blood pouring from his face and from a deep cut on his arm. The man rushed to Neferata, hands reaching for her face. Without breaking stride she caught the man's wrists and pulled him close, tearing out his throat with a single, vicious bite.

Slingstones buzzed through the air like angry bees. Several struck sparks off Neferata's iron scales; another buried itself in her forehead with a dull, smacking sound. Grimacing irritably, she plucked the round stone free with thumb and fingertip and tossed it aside.

Off to her left, a woman screamed. Neferata turned to see one of her maidens stagger, clutching at a javelin that had struck her in the heart. Men rushed to her as she fell; several began hacking at her body with their swords, while the others fought to possess her. Even in death – the true death – she continued to spread havoc among the enemy.

Minutes later, another maiden fell, this time crushed to pulp beneath the weight of a tumbling chariot. By now, panic and confusion had taken hold and most of the enemy were fleeing in terror, racing back towards the centre of camp. Five women had broken the hearts and minds of thousands of warriors in a matter of minutes.

Neferata watched the enemy roll away from her in a swift tide, leaving behind a field littered with fallen weapons, helmets and shields. The queen laughed mockingly, delighted at the ruination of her foes. Alcadizzar had underestimated her power and now all of Nehekhara would pay the price.

TWENTY-TWO

LAST STAND

Lahmia,
the City of the Dawn,
in the 107th year of Ptra the Glorious
(-1200 Imperial Reckoning)

The battle had shifted. From his vantage point at the gatehouse, W'soran could see that Ankhat's attack on the left had been broken by the sudden appearance of enemy cavalry. Most of the Lahmian troops had turned and fled, only to be mercilessly ridden down long before they reached the safety of the city gates. The rest, now anchored at the far end of the line by the city's royal guard, had pivoted towards the south-east and were now slowly withdrawing northwards, under pressure both from enemy spear companies and increasingly large numbers of cavalry. Fortunately for Ankhat and his men, their path to the western gate was largely clear, thanks to the chaos wrought by Neferata and her maidens. In the centre, the queen and her companions had put the weakened enemy to flight and were driving inexorably into the heart of the invaders' camp.

On the right, the necromancer's forces had been brought to a grinding stalemate by the timely arrival of fresh troops from the enemy's centre. That was still good news for Neferata, for as long as the undead kept the bulk of the enemy's infantry pinned down, then Lahmia still had a chance at victory, but W'soran felt cheated nonetheless. It was his sorceries that had made the attack possible in the first place! The victory should be his as well.

W'soran leafed through the pages of Nagash's tomes, looking for a spell or ritual that might tip the balance of the fight in his favour. If there was some way to increase the speed or strength of his troops, perhaps...

A strange sound from the west caused the necromancer to pause. It was a thin, high-pitched whistling, faint but growing louder moment by moment. He frowned, trying to place the noise, when it passed just above the gatehouse and seemed to plunge into the city beyond. A second later came a huge, muffled *thump* and a crash of falling brick that reverberated through the stones beneath his feet.

The necromancer's eyes widened. With a cry, he shut the book and scrambled for the rest of Nagash's tomes, resting on the floor by the ritual circle just a few feet away, just as a chorus of similar whistles rose into the sky from the west.

The next catapult stone fell short, hitting the ground with a dull thud and then crashing into the western gate. W'soran heard the sound of splintering wood below as he gathered the ancient books into his arms. He turned and raced for the nearest door just as four more catapult stones, each the size of a small chariot, came smashing through the gatehouse wall.

Ankhat turned at the sound of grinding stone and watched in horror as the top of the western gatehouse collapsed in a torrent of dust and broken rock. Another catapult stone whistled through the air, and by sheer bad luck, came in at a shallow angle and struck the face of the western gate. The immortal could hear the sound of splintering wood from where he stood, some two hundred yards away.

The royal guards and the surviving spear companies were paying for every step they took in blood. Arrows fell among their ranks in a steady rain and enemy cavalry kept nipping at their flanks. He had lost track of the number of charges they'd suffered since the withdrawal began, but the field before them was littered with the bodies of horses and men.

There were only two companies of spearmen left on their right. The royal guard had suffered terribly, having lost more than two-thirds of their number, but their resolve never wavered.

The one thing that had held them together thus far was the realisation that Neferata herself had taken the field, and had put the entire enemy centre to flight. From his place at the rear of the retreating guardsmen, Ankhat searched the darkness off to the north-west for any sign of the queen, but it was hard to make out anyone amid the swirling mass of panicked troops. The amount of death and destruction she had left in her wake was both awesome and terrifying at the same time.

Just then, as the last echoes of the gatehouse's collapse faded away, Ankhat saw the swirling mob off to the far right simply melt away, like morning mist. Men scattered in every direction, revealing the pale forms of Neferata and two of her maidens, stalking inexorably westwards through the carnage they'd wrought.

For a moment, Ankhat's spirits lifted – and then he saw the solid wall of enemy horsemen approaching Neferata from the centre of the camp.

The desert horsemen rode knee to knee, an uncharacteristically tight formation for the swift-moving raiders, but it ensured that nothing would get past them and into the midst of the undefended inner camp. Alcadizzar and Faisr rode side-by-side at the centre of the formation, searching the swirling mass of panicked troops in front of them for any sign of the undead. Warriors from Mahrak and Khemri scattered to the left and right at the riders' approach. The look of confusion and fear on their faces was an unsettling sight, but the horsemen clutched their powerful bows tightly and forged ahead through the press.

Catapult stones whistled overhead, falling on the distant gatehouse. A cheer went up from the riders as the gatehouse was demolished; moments later, another chorus of shouts and cheers off to their left told Alcadizzar that his intuition had been correct. The necromancer's ritual had been disrupted and Lahmia's dead were returning to their original state.

There was little time for relief, however. Ahead of the horsemen, the mob of panicked troops suddenly cleared away, revealing the wide trade road and the rocky fields that led up to the city gate. Hundreds of bodies lay everywhere, many locked together in mortal combat. The warriors of Mahrak and Khemri had all but destroyed one another, their minds twisted by Neferata's seductive glamour.

Alcadizzar saw her at once. She and two other pale-skinned monsters were walking towards them across the corpse-strewn fields, less than a hundred yards away. Even from so great a distance, he could feel the weight of their predatory stares against his skin. Even the horses felt it. They rolled their eyes and tossed their heads with fright, causing their riders to exchange worried glances and murmurs of concern, for the horses of the desert tribes were famed for their courage and high spirits.

The king raised his hand, and Faisr called for the riders to halt. 'Don't let them get close enough to look in their eyes!' he warned.

As he said this, Neferata's maidens let out a piercing wail and broke into a run, racing across the broken ground like desert cats. Their grace and speed was mesmerising. In the blink of an eye, they had covered half the distance between them and the horsemen.

Faisr shook himself from his momentary reverie with a fearsome curse. 'Loose!' he roared at his men.

The order galvanised the tribesmen. Four hundred bows drew back as one, and a moment later the air was full of hissing, black-fletched arrows. The riders were all expert shots, hand-picked from among the tribes. The shrieking maidens were hit dozens of times; both fell, struck through the heart, their bodies tumbling limply to the ground.

An uneasy silence fell. Neferata came to a stop well beyond bowshot, hands at her sides. Alcadizzar straightened in the saddle. 'Wait here,' he said gravely.

Faisr gave the king a shocked stare. 'Are you mad?' he exclaimed. 'She deserves no better than the other two got.'

But the king shook his head. 'No. This one thing I have to do myself.'

Alcadizzar spurred his horse forwards. Off in the distance, he could see more troops converging on the scene: warriors of Ka-Sabar and Rasetra on the left, and a ragged force of Lahmian infantry on the right. Neither side was close enough to interfere.

The king reined in, some thirty yards from the waiting queen, and slid from the saddle. Drawing his sword, Alcadizzar went to face her.

She stood, silent and still, and watched him approach. The closer Alcadizzar came, the more he began to doubt the wisdom of his decision. Could he withstand her power? The gifts of the elixir were long gone, now. He had only his strength of will and his courage to sustain him – just like every one of the hundreds of dead men who littered the field around him.

He came to within ten yards of her and stopped, not daring to get any closer. A faint smile tugged at the corners of her mouth. Alcadizzar felt his mouth go dry. She was even more beautiful than he remembered. How was that possible? Even the drops of blood that glistened on her cheek seemed to accentuate her features, like a spray of brilliant rubies.

Neferata's smile widened and set its hooks in his heart. Her voice was dark and rich, like spring honey.

'You never should have left,' she said. 'All those wasted years, and see how it all ends?' She spread her arms. 'Here we are, back to where we began.'

Alcadizzar felt a brief spark of anger at Neferata's tone. He clung to it desperately, like a man lost in a cold and empty wasteland. 'You think to tempt me now? Here? Amidst all this death and horror? You have much to answer for, Neferata.'

'I answer to no one,' Neferata replied haughtily. 'That is the privilege of a queen.' She gestured at the carnage around her. 'And this? This means as much or as little as we wish it to.'

Alcadizzar shook his head. 'Every ruler in Nehekhara is watching us,' he said, his voice full of scorn. 'If I accepted what you offer, they would kill us both.'

'They wouldn't,' Neferata said. 'Kneel to me. Accept my gift and they will clamour for it as well. Become my consort, and see how quickly they sheathe their blades and beg for my forgiveness.' She held out her hand to him. 'It's not too late, Alcadizzar. Take my hand and the world will be ours.'

For a fleeting moment, it all made perfect sense. Alcadizzar looked into Neferata's dark eyes and saw the desire burning there. She reached out to him. His gaze fell to her bloodstained hand – and the sight of it reminded him of all the men who had cheered his name only a week before, but now lay dead in the field around him. His anger returned, scouring the queen's glamour from his mind.

Alcadizzar raised his sword. 'Take your gifts with you to the grave,' he said. 'I want no part of them.'

Neferata grew suddenly, unnaturally still. The smile faded from her face. As Alcadizzar watched, the desire in her eyes transformed into something sharp and cruel.

Suddenly, she was right in front of him, screeching in fury, her talons raking at his face. Fiery pain exploded across his left cheek. The king was hurled backwards, hitting the rocky ground hard enough to knock all the wind out of him.

Alcadizzar's mind reeled. It had been too long since he'd tasted Neferata's elixir. He was nowhere near as fast as he'd once been. Neferata, on the other hand, was both swifter and stronger than he'd imagined possible. A moment after he'd hit the ground she was looming over him again. An iron-hard blow from her open hand swatted the sword from his numbed fingers; a second one struck him across the face and stunned him nearly senseless.

On your feet, boy! Get up! The voice of Haptshur, his old battlefield tutor, echoed in his head. Unable to breathe, scarcely able to see, he rolled in the direction of the blows and lashed out with his right leg as hard as he could. The kick connected with Neferata's leg and knocked the queen off her feet. Still moving, Alcadizzar scrambled onto his hands and knees and crawled after his lost sword.

He nearly made it. The blade was only a few feet away, lying atop a knot of bloodstained corpses. Alcadizzar lunged for it – just as a hand closed painfully about his ankle. Neferata jerked him backwards like a hound on a leash, dragging his chest, arms and face over the rough ground.

Snarling, the king lashed out with his free leg, but missed. His flailing hands closed on the wooden haft of a dropped javelin. Gripping it with bloodied hands, Alcadizzar twisted onto his back and flung it at Neferata with all his strength. She saw it coming at the last moment and tried to knock it aside with her left hand; instead of striking her in the chest, the bronze point hit her in the shoulder, forcing its way between the iron scales and sinking deep into the flesh beneath.

Neferata hissed in rage, groping for the haft of the javelin with her off-hand to pull it free. Alcadizzar twisted in her grip, wrenching his ankle painfully as he fumbled among the corpses for another weapon. He saw another wooden haft jutting out from beneath a nearby body and seized it. Alcadizzar wrenched it free, and found himself gripping a gore-spattered hand axe. With a yell, he swiped at Neferata's hand, chopping deep into her wrist and nearly cutting off his own foot in the process. The queen let out a shriek of rage, her nerveless fingers losing their grip around Alcadizzar's ankle.

Bounding to his feet with a roar, the king hurled himself at Neferata, hacking savagely at her with the axe. The bronze blade rasped and rang against the queen's iron armour, ripping scales free and scoring the thick leather beneath. More blows fell upon her arms, shoulders and neck, but her armour turned aside the worst of the impacts. Still, Alcadizzar did not relent, driving the queen inexorably backwards as he searched for an opening to deliver a fatal blow. He struck her twice more, tearing into her armour, and Neferata staggered, her foot catching on a body sprawled in her path. Before she could recover, the king lunged forwards and struck her across the side of the head. The axe blade bit deep, cracking bone from temple to jaw and snapping her head around from the force of the blow.

The wound would have been enough to kill a normal man outright. Neferata staggered, her ruined armour flapping loosely about her torso. Alcadizzar rushed forwards, aiming a swift, backhand blow at her neck to end the fight.

But the blow never landed. A hand closed about his wrist – Neferata's *right* hand, the one he'd nearly severed a moment before. The broken bones and severed muscles had already knit together again.

Neferata's head came back around. Dark, thick blood flowed from the ghastly wound Alcadizzar had inflicted. Yet even as he watched, the split bone began to close back together. She gave the king a mocking, lopsided smile, then gripped the haft of the axe with her left hand and plucked the weapon from his grip as though he were a child.

Her fist drove into his side, cracking ribs despite his armour and lifting him from his feet. Another blow crashed into the side of Alcadizzar's head, blinding him with pain. Again and again she struck him, pummelling his shoulders and torso while she held his arm fast with her right hand. All the strength went out of his legs and he collapsed like a rag doll, landing roughly on the ground.

He did not feel Neferata sink down onto him, straddling his waist. Her hands gripped the collar of his bronze scale armour and tore through the thick leather backing as though it were parchment, exposing the king's throat. She bent down, her own iron scale vest hanging loosely from her shoulders, until her charnel breath blew coldly against his face.

'I take it back,' she whispered. 'All of it. Every gift I ever gave you.'

She seized his chin and forced his head to one side, exposing the pulsing artery in his neck. Alcadizzar tried to speak, but only managed a strangled grunt. His hands fumbled weakly at his waist.

'What do you know of the grave?' Neferata murmured. 'I have stood upon the threshold of death and glimpsed what lies on the other side. Do you know what waits there? Darkness. Nothing more.' She bent down further, until her lips brushed lightly against his throat. 'Think on that, as the light fades from your eyes.'

Alcadizzar scarcely felt the tips of her fangs sink into his skin. His concentration was focused on one thing only: gripping the hilt of the jewelled dagger thrust into his belt. With the last of his strength he pulled the blade free and drove it into Neferata's side, piercing her heart.

'No!' Ankhat shouted, watching from a distance as Neferata's body went rigid, then toppled over onto her side. Moonlight winked balefully from the ruby-studded hilt of the knife that jutted from her ribs.

At the same moment, the enemy let out a roar – part cheer, part horrified shout – and the horsemen spurred their mounts, racing towards the fallen combatants. When they moved, the enemy infantry on their left moved as well, scrambling and stumbling over the bodies of the slain in an effort to reach the spot where Alcadizzar and Neferata lay tangled together.

'The queen!' Ankhat roared. 'To the queen!'

The last survivors of the royal guard – fewer than sixty men, every one of them wounded to one degree or another and exhausted to the bone – let out a defiant shout and charged, true to their oaths to the last. The survivors of the remaining spear companies took up the shout as well and within moments they were running across the battlefield as well.

The enemy cavalry reached the pair moments before everyone else. Robed riders leapt from their saddles and went at once to Alcadizzar, seizing him by the arms and dragging him towards safety. A half-dozen more drew sabres and made for Neferata, clearly intending to make sure she never rose again.

Ankhat leapt among the swordsmen, his iron blade flickering. Two men fell at once, their throats slashed open, while the others tried to encircle him and strike from different angles. An arrow thudded into his shoulder; he snarled like a cornered animal and took a swordsman's arm off at the elbow.

The royal guard caught up to him seconds later, charging at the mounted warriors with polearms levelled. Horses reared and screamed; arrows flew, and men fell dying on both sides. Ankhat despatched another swordsman with a cut to the head and drove the rest back, away from the fallen queen. The Lahmian spearmen rushed in, brandishing their spears and trying to reach Alcadizzar, only to be met by the oncoming enemy infantry. Men stabbed and swore, tearing at one another like starving animals fighting over a bone. All sense of order dissolved into a vicious, four-sided brawl.

Ankhat cut a man's legs out from under him and pushed his way to Neferata's side. Two enemy soldiers grabbed her body by the ankles, dragging her roughly towards them; with a shout, the immortal lunged forwards, slicing the hands off one man and driving the other back. More arrows hissed past. Each one found a mark in the swirling mob, but Ankhat couldn't say whether they hit friend or foe.

The enemy infantry drove back the Lahmians, creating a wall of flesh and metal between them and Alcadizzar. Ankhat didn't care about the fallen king. All he could think about was keeping Neferata out of enemy hands. He stood over her, slashing and stabbing at every man who came too close.

More enemy troops were arriving every moment, closing in from both left and right. Before much longer, they would be surrounded and then none of them would escape.

The enemy pressed in around him. His blade never stopped moving, trying to hold back the tide. Horns sounded off behind Ankhat and to his left. More enemy cavalry were closing in. The end was nearly at hand.

Ankhat took his eyes off the enemy for just a moment, glancing down at Neferata's body. They would want her head for a trophy, he knew. Perhaps at least he could deny them that.

He raised his sword to strike – and then, without warning, came an eruption of screams and shouts from behind the enemy infantry to his immediate left.

It was as though a storm was tearing through the tightly packed enemy soldiers. Ankhat saw pieces of men flung through the air: severed limbs, helmeted heads, hands still clutching the hilts of weapons, all trailing streamers of blood. The killing was swift and relentless, carving its way step by step towards where Neferata lay.

Suddenly, the enemy horsemen that accompanied the king hauled on their reins and spurred away, shouting in confusion at the unexpected attack. The enemy infantry saw that and panicked, scattering in every direction to escape the fate of their comrades. The surviving Lahmians – barely a handful of guardsmen and a few score others – drew back in a tight circle around Ankhat, staring fearfully in the direction of the slaughter and wondering if they were next.

The last of the enemy soldiers drew back like a curtain, revealing a tall, broad-shouldered man with pale skin and close-cropped black hair. He was armoured in nothing more than a dirty, knee-length leather kilt and a sleeveless jerkin, of the type favoured by those who lived and hunted in the southern jungle. The man wielded a pair of huge, dripping khopeshes in his scarred hands; every inch of him was streaked and stippled in gore. His face was handsome but severe, with a square chin and a thin-lipped mouth set in a permanent scowl. He strode fearlessly towards the Lahmians, heedless of the thousands of enemy warriors surrounding him.

Ankhat stared at the man in wonder. 'Abhorash?'

Lamashizzar's former champion and captain of the royal guard strode up to Ankhat and took in the situation at a glance. 'Get the queen out of here,' he said simply, as though he'd never been gone from the city a day, let alone the last hundred and seventy years. 'I will cover your retreat.'

Abhorash spoke in a voice that brooked no dissent. The four surviving royal guards leapt to obey, lifting Neferata's body and shielding it with their own. If any of them realised that she was not the queen that they knew and served, they gave no sign whatsoever. The spearmen were already falling back towards the ruined western gate in a ragged mob. Back across the field, the horse archers saw their prey escaping and shouted angrily. Bowstrings hummed and arrows plunged towards the guardsmen holding the queen.

Abhorash's twin swords flashed, weaving a web of flickering bronze, and knocked every one of the arrows aside.

The horsemen gaped in shock. No one attempted to stop the Lahmians after that.

Every movement was agony. Groaning between clenched teeth, Ushoran dragged himself another torturous foot, reaching the summit of the wooded hill just to the east of the city necropolis.

The sounds of battle had faded some time ago. It could have been minutes, or it could have been hours; Ushoran could no longer say for sure. The pain pushed such trivial details aside. But there was no question of who had won. Of that much he was certain. Which was why he was trying to get as far away from the city as he could.

The fire had eaten into him from his head to his calves, burning away his hair and much of his skin, and cooking the flesh beneath. When the torches had hit him, he could think of nothing but running, as though the fire was something he could actually escape. That had only fanned the flames more. He had pounded at them until his hands were scorched and raw, but nothing would put them out. Finally, after running for what seemed like ages, his legs gave out beneath him. He collapsed on the ground, howling in agony, and waited for the flames to finish him.

Yet he did not die. Eventually, the fire burned itself out, but the final death did not come. Eventually, through the blinding haze of pain, he realised that he could move his legs a bit. His body, despite the damage, was slowly healing itself. Ushoran didn't know whether to laugh or cry.

When he came to his senses, he realised he was no longer alone. A pack of jackals surrounded the dip in the rocky ground, studying him with flat, yellow eyes. Apparently they couldn't decide if he was carrion or not. He wasn't all that certain either. But he knew that, sooner or later, it would be dawn. If the noonday sun didn't finish what the fire began, it would only be a matter of time before some enemy patrol stumbled onto him and chopped off his head. And so he'd crawled, foot by foot, out of the depression and towards the hills to the west, in search of a place to hide.

Now, having reached the top of the hill, the immortal rolled weakly onto his side and looked back the way he'd come. Ushoran could see a vast field of bones stretching from the edge of the necropolis to nearly the centre of the enemy camp. At some point, W'soran's ritual had failed and his army had literally fallen apart where it stood. From the angle where he lay, he could just see the western gate; when he glimpsed the destruction there, he suspected what had occurred. He wondered if the necromancer had managed to escape the massacre.

There was no sign of Neferata or Ankhat, but the ground between the camp and the western gate was piled with corpses. It was clear that both sides had suffered terrible losses, but in the end the invaders had prevailed. Even now, columns of troops were marching down the trade road and through the rubble of the western gate; columns of smoke were rising from Lahmia's western districts as the sack of the city began.

Abruptly, the smothering darkness receded. Neferata opened her eyes with a gasp that very nearly rose to a scream. She fell back against a cold marble floor, her entire body trembling with the shock of what she'd endured.

Ankhat knelt beside her, his face grave. A ruby-hilted dagger hung from one hand. With a scowl, he tossed it aside. 'You're safe,' he said to her. 'For now, at least. We thought it best to wait until we got here before doing something about the knife.'

Neferata glanced wildly about. She was in a shadowy, vaulted chamber, far from the battlefield. 'Where are we?' she managed to say.

'The palace. Abhorash insisted we bring you here.'

Neferata frowned, uncertain if she'd heard Ankhat correctly. 'Abhorash?'

'Yes. He's returned,' Ankhat replied. 'Without him, all of us would have been lost.'

Grimacing, the queen forced her body to sit upright. She was resting in the centre of the great hall, with the royal dais at her back. At the far end of the chamber, the great double doors lay open, revealing the dimly lit vestibule beyond. Past the vestibule, the entrance to the palace lay open. The sky outside was tinged red with flames.

Abhorash stood a short distance away, surrounded by four men in the armour of the royal guard. The guardsmen were stripping away Abhorash's bloodstained tunic and fitting him with the iron breastplate and pauldrons of a captain of the guard. She knew the dour champion at once, despite the passage of years. The queen inclined her head to him. 'We owe you a great debt, captain,' she said, with as much dignity as she had left.

Abhorash glared at her. 'I didn't come here for you,' he snapped. 'The city was under attack and I swore an oath to defend it. At least here I can meet death with something of my honour intact.'

Neferata scowled at him. 'Still as arrogant and sanctimonious as ever,' she growled. The queen turned to Ankhat. 'What of Alcadizzar?'

The immortal shrugged. 'His people dragged him away. I have no idea if he was alive or not.' He gripped her arm. 'Forget about him. The city is lost. The enemy could be here at any moment.'

The queen snatched her arm away. 'Then here is where they'll find me. If Lahmia is to die, then I die with her.'

'Good,' Abhorash declared. 'It's long past time this nightmare came to an end.'

Ankhat took a step back, glaring at the both of them. 'Die, then,' he snapped. 'Let the damned mortals cut off your heads and parade them through the streets! I don't intend to give them the satisfaction.'

Ankhat's vehemence surprised Neferata. 'Where is there to go?'

'Anywhere but here!' the immortal cried. 'There is more to the world than just Lahmia – or even Nehekhara, come to that. Who knows? I might go north. The barbarians there would worship me like a god.' He sighed, shaking his head. 'We should have scattered to the winds long ago. Lahmia might have survived if we had. Now...'

'Now, what?' Neferata demanded. 'We've lost everything, Ankhat. What's left?'

'Eternity,' the immortal answered. 'We have nothing but time, Neferata. Time enough to do whatever you wish.'

Neferata turned and studied the red-lit sky beyond the vestibule. Her expression hardened. 'Time enough for vengeance,' she said.

'If you wish,' Ankhat said. 'Do as you will. But I am leaving this cursed place and hope never to return.'

The queen glanced back at the immortal. She was transformed. Her face was a cold, pitiless mask.

'There is a ship waiting in the harbour,' she said. 'I will take it and abide for a time in the east. I have a great deal of thinking to do.'

Ankhat nodded. 'A new beginning, then.'

'No,' the queen said. 'An ending. From this moment forwards, there will be nothing but endings between me and this world.'

Outside, a horn sounded. Abhorash nodded sombrely to the guardsmen, who bowed and offered him his blades. The grim-faced immortal turned to Neferata.

'The enemy is here,' he said. 'These good men have sworn to fight by my side until the last. Together, we'll make our stand here, as befits the royal guard. If the gods are kind, perhaps I will be rid of your damned curse at last.'

Neferata glared at the champion as he turned and made his way from the great hall and out into the vestibule, where his four companions waited. After a moment, she turned to say her farewells to Ankhat, but the immortal was already gone.

The last queen of Lahmia stood alone in the great hall where her dynasty had ruled for millennia. She turned, glancing back at the royal dais, and looked one final time at the empty throne.

'Endings,' she vowed, her voice hollow. 'Nothing but endings.' And then the shadows swallowed her and she was gone.

'This is madness,' Prince Heru said. 'You should be resting, uncle. The chirurgeons say you are lucky to be alive.'

'I'll be fine,' Alcadizzar said tightly, mindful of the pain in his side and the stitches in his cheek. He sat stiffly in the saddle of his horse as he climbed the winding road up to the royal palace. A hundred warriors of the *bani-al-Hashim* rode in his wake, arrows nocked, searching the shadows for danger. 'This is something I need to do.'

'Like you needed to fight Neferata single-handed?' Heru said. 'We saw how well that went.'

The king grunted. 'I won, didn't I?'

Heru frowned. 'I don't know. It's looking more and more like a draw.'

The riders rounded the final turn and approached the entrance to the palace compound. It was early morning and the fires had burned their way down the hill and across the city, where smoke now rose from the dockyards. Soldiers roamed the streets, looting what they could and wrecking what they couldn't. Screams and shouts echoed from nearly every street. When the victorious armies were done, the richest city in Nehekhara would be picked down to its bones and its people, who had suffered so much under Neferata's reign of terror, would be carted away in chains, to serve their conquerors as slaves. Such was the brutal reality of war.

Alcadizzar guided his horse through the palace gates and reined in. The scene before him was breathtaking in its devastation.

Smoke still rose from the narrow windows of the Temple of Blood. As many as two hundred acolytes and priestesses lay on the ground around the temple's entrance, their bodies riddled with wounds. They had been dragged from the temple during the night and executed, one after another. There was no way to know if the army had done it, or if it had been the work of the Lahmians themselves.

The same could not be said of the royal palace. It was obvious to anyone what had happened there. The steps leading to the great hall were covered in bodies, in some cases piled four or five deep. 'The Lahmians didn't surrender the palace easily,' he observed.

Heru grunted. 'That bastard with the swords,' he said. 'He and some of the royal guard held the door until dawn. Took enough wounds to kill a hundred men, but never gave an inch.'

'What happened to him?'

Heru looked uncomfortable. 'We don't know. At dawn, the guardsmen dragged him back inside the vestibule while we regrouped for another charge. By the time we got inside they were gone. We're searching the palace for them now.'

'What about Neferata?'

The Rasetran sighed. 'We don't know about her, either. The last anyone saw of her, she was being carried into the city by the royal guard. We expected to find her here, but...'

Alcadizzar shook his head. 'Is there anything we *do* know?'

'Well, we managed to secure the city treasury,' the prince said. 'Zandri and Numas are already petitioning for their share, of course.'

The king stared at his nephew. 'I don't care about the gold,' he said. 'Did you find any books?'

Heru's expression darkened. 'Not yet. If they're anywhere, they're probably inside the temple and the upper levels are still burning. The men found some large chambers on the lower levels that looked like they might have been vaults, but there was nothing left inside.'

Alcadizzar nodded thoughtfully. 'We'll keep looking, just to be certain. Neferata couldn't have learned necromancy from nothing. Lamashizzar must have somehow brought some of Nagash's tomes back from Khemri after the war. If they're here, I mean to see them destroyed.'

'And then?'

The king sighed, thinking of distant Khemri and the work that lay ahead. A tired smile spread across his face. 'Then we go home.'

The two men fell silent, contemplating the wreckage of the palace. The wind shifted, blowing from the sea and carrying the scent of salt and ashes.

TWENTY-THREE

THE USURPER

Lahmia,
the City of the Dawn,
in the 107th year of Ptra the Glorious
(-1200 Imperial Reckoning)

For seven days and seven nights, Alcadizzar's men searched the city for Neferata and her followers, and for the hiding place of the infamous tomes of Nagash. They combed the palace and the smouldering ruins of the temple from top to bottom, and though a great many hidden passageways and chambers were discovered, no sign of the city's secret rulers was found. Even Neferata's puppets, King Sothis and Queen Ammanura, had vanished, though several witnesses claimed that they had fled to the temple garden after the city gates had fallen and taken poison to avoid capture by the invaders.

After a week, Alcadizzar privately conceded defeat. Jars of oil and barrels of pitch were brought up from the docks and the great palace was set alight. The roaring flames burned long into the night, rising like a pyre atop the high hill as the invaders marched out through the broken western gate. They left behind a wasteland of empty streets, pillaged shops and burned-out homes, roamed by vultures and packs of fat-bellied jackals.

Laden with plunder and files of weary, hollow-eyed slaves, the allied armies made slow progress across the Golden Plain. Faisr's people rode ahead, each one bearing a message that the tribes had been waiting to hear for centuries. By the time the soldiers reached the centre of the plain a vast tent city awaited them; wives raced out from the camp on swift horses to welcome back their husbands, filling the air with songs of joy. The long exile in the east was finally at an end.

Upon reaching the tent city, Alcadizzar offered his fellow rulers the hospitality of his tent and bade them stay as his guests for a while, to celebrate their victory and talk of Nehekhara's future. As the matter of Lahmia's vast treasury had yet to be settled, Alcadizzar's allies could not very well refuse.

For a full week, as the last of the desert tribes filtered down from the far reaches of the plain, Alcadizzar entertained his guests with horse races and martial contests by day and lavish feasts by night. During the feasts, young women of marriageable age from the tribes would join the royal guests and provide entertainment, as was their custom, in the form of conversation, dance and song. It was during these feasts that Alcadizzar came to notice one young woman in particular: Khalida, a maiden of thirty years, who was named after the legendary warrior-queen of Lybaras. She was tall, dark-haired and slender, like most women of the tribes, but her eyes were a rare, vivid green, like polished emeralds. Her voice was deep and earthy, and she laughed often, but what captured Alcadizzar's interest most of all was her keen wit. She was astonishingly well read, conversing with kings and champions on matters ranging from horsemanship to history. One night he had found himself in a lively debate with her about Settra's early campaigns against the tribes that had lasted until nearly midnight, until her brothers had been forced to politely separate them for propriety's sake. He'd looked forwards to seeing her ever since.

Over the course of the week, the political manoeuvring intensified. Numas and Zandri pressed shamelessly for a lion's share of Lahmia's gold and promised close ties of trade and friendship in return. Mahrak and Lybaras appealed to Alcadizzar's scholarly nature, pleading for gold to restore their libraries and temples. Ka-Sabar promised a steady supply of good iron, drawn from the deeps of the Brittle Peaks, in return for trade agreements that would keep their forges working for generations to come.

Prince Heru told Alcadizzar he could keep Rasetra's share of the gold, just so long as he could take Khalida home with him. The king of Khemri refused, much to Heru's amusement.

Alcadizzar played the game of diplomacy with great skill, forging profitable alliances with Ka-Sabar, Quatar and Lybaras, while keeping Mahrak at arm's length and establishing an understanding with Zandri and Numas, his closest and most ambitious neighbours. In the end, Lahmia's plundered gold was split seven ways, with equal shares going to each of the cities. Faisr's tribes received a slightly larger portion of gold than the rest, but forfeited their share of slaves, since their laws forbade it. The following day, Alcadizzar's guests took their leave, marching for home laden with riches and bound by new political ties to Khemri. Whether Alcadizzar's peers had realised it or not, a new era had begun.

The armies began to move at dawn, starting with Zandri and Numas; by sunset, the last of the Lybaran companies had departed, driving their slow-moving wagons westwards. Only the people of Khemri remained, waiting to escort their king to his new home. After days of celebration, a sense of relative calm settled over the tent city, as the tribes prepared their meals and contemplated breaking camp the following day.

Alcadizzar sat inside his tent, wrapped in heavy robes and sipping tea from a fine porcelain cup as he reviewed the particulars of trade agreements he'd signed with Ka-Sabar and Numas the night before. His broken ribs ached and the rest of his body was stiff and sore, from his eyebrows to the tips of his toes. His duties as a host had left him more drained than the battle outside Lahmia, or so it seemed

There came a scratching at his tent flap. Out of habit, Alcadizzar started to rise from his chair and see to it, but Huni, one of his new royal servants, rose smoothly from his place near the entrance and went to see who was outside. There was a brief murmur of conversation, then the servant returned with a look of consternation on his face.

Huni prostrated himself before the king. 'There is someone who wishes to speak with you, great one,' he said. 'I told her that you have retired for the evening, but she is most insistent.'

Alcadizzar glanced up from his documents. 'Who is it?' He thought of Khalida, his pulse quickening.

The servant frowned. 'I do not know,' he replied. 'All she will say is that she is the Daughter of the Sands–'

'Gods above,' Alcadizzar swore, straightening in his chair. 'Send her in at once!'

Huni leapt to his feet and dashed for the tent flap. He pulled it aside with a bow, and Ophiria entered, followed by her hooded servant, the chosen of Khsar. She arched an eyebrow at the king.

'My apologies,' Alcadizzar said, sheepishly. 'This is... unexpected. Ah... may I offer you tea?'

The seer's lips quirked in a faint grin. 'You may.'

Huni hurried to the brass kettle, only to be waved away by the king. Alcadizzar poured the cup himself and brought it to her, his mind racing. 'I wasn't aware you'd arrived in camp,' he said, trying to work out what was going on.

'I've been here since before *you* arrived,' Ophiria said, her golden eyes studying him over the rim of the teacup. 'You were too busy entertaining to notice.' She glanced around the tent. 'Shall we sit, or is it your habit now to drink tea standing up?'

'Yes – I mean, no.' Alcadizzar sighed irritably. Ophiria flustered him more than all the kings of Nehekhara combined. 'Please. Sit.'

The seer lowered herself gracefully to the piled rugs, cradling the teacup in her hands. Alcadizzar had seen her many times over the years, at tribal gatherings, but hadn't actually spoken to her since the night of Suleima's funeral rites, some forty years ago. Other than a few streaks of grey in her hair and some wrinkles at the corners of her eyes, she hadn't changed a great deal since then.

Alcadizzar sat across from her. His gaze went from Ophiria to her servant and back again. He wasn't certain how to proceed. The bride of Khsar, as a rule, did not visit other men's tents.

'To what do I owe the honour of this visit?' he asked.

Ophiria gave him a sphinx-like stare. 'We have matters to discuss,' she said.

'I… see,' Alcadizzar replied. The seer sipped her tea and said nothing. Finally, the king turned to his servants. 'Leave us,' he said.

Huni and the rest bowed and slipped silently from the tent. Ophiria waited until the last one was gone before she spoke.

'Congratulations on your victory over the Lahmians,' she said.

Alcadizzar shrugged stiffly. 'It was a hollow triumph at best,' the king said. 'Neferata escaped.'

'Her fate lies elsewhere,' the seer said cryptically. 'Her power has been broken for now and my people are free to return home. That is victory enough for me.' She sipped her tea, glancing over at the papers piled on the table. 'The past few days have been profitable, I trust?'

'It's a good beginning,' the king allowed. 'There'll be more to do once I get to Khemri, of course.'

'And what are your plans, now that Lahmia is no more?'

Alcadizzar took a deep breath. 'Well. Finish rebuilding the city, to begin with. Hopefully find a wife, and have children. Try to live like a normal person, for the first time in my life.'

Ophiria let out a snort. 'There's nothing normal about you, Alcadizzar,' she said. The seer finished her tea. 'What do you think of Khalida? Does she interest you?'

The king's eyes widened. 'You know about her?'

She rolled her eyes. 'I was the one who suggested she attend the feasts in the first place,' Ophiria said. 'As it happens, she's my niece. And she could use a husband who's read as many books as she has.' The seer gave him an arch look. 'Assuming you were serious when you told Faisr you wanted to marry a woman of the tribes.'

Alcadizzar bristled a bit. 'After all this time and everything I've done, you *still* doubt my sincerity?'

Ophiria set down her cup and sighed. 'No. I don't.' Her expression turned sombre. 'You've been a man of your word in every respect, Alcadizzar. I wouldn't be offering you my niece if you weren't.'

'Well, what's all this about, then?' the king asked.

The seer's golden eyes met his. 'It's about Nagash,' she said simply.

Alcadizzar stared at her. 'What have you seen?'

Ophiria was silent for a moment, her expression thoughtful, as though uncertain how much she ought to say.

'The Usurper is coming,' she said at last. 'Even now, he prepares his armies for war.'

The king's heart sank. 'How soon?'

'Years; possibly even decades,' Ophiria said. 'Nagash does not measure time as we mortals do. He has not forgotten his defeat in the last war and will not act this time until he is certain of victory.'

'Then he cannot be defeated?'

Another faint smile crossed the seer's face. 'That depends on what you do with the time you're given. From this moment forwards, every day is a gift. Use them wisely.'

Alcadizzar sighed wearily. 'All right. What am I supposed to do?'

Ophiria shrugged. 'I'm no strategist,' she said. 'How was he beaten the last time?'

'The other priest-kings combined their forces against him.'

'Well, then, perhaps you should start there.'

The king scowled. 'You're a seer. Is that the best you can do?'

'Don't be impertinent. It doesn't work that way,' Ophiria snapped. She rose to her feet. 'I've told you all I can, Alcadizzar. Rule well with the time you are given. Prepare Nehekhara for Nagash's coming. All the world depends on it.'

As she turned to leave, the king called out to her. 'Wait!'

The seer stopped at the tent flap and scowled at him. 'There is no more to tell, Alcadizzar. I can't share what I haven't seen.'

The king shook his head. 'Never mind that. What about Khalida?'

'What about her?'

Alcadizzar frowned. 'Now who is being impertinent?'

Ophiria grinned. 'She resides in the tent of her father, Tariq al-Nasrim. Call upon her if you like. She loves to read. Promise her all the books her heart desires and you should do well.'

By night he crept across the wasteland like a spider, clutching his precious cargo to his chest and stealing the life of any living thing that came too near. North and west he went; at the end of each night, just before the paling of dawn, he would scuttle into a shallow cave or a hillside crevice and open his senses to the aether, like a ship's captain taking a bearing from the stars overhead. The crackle of necromantic energies pulsed invisibly in the distance, always seemingly just beyond the next set of hills.

Three weeks after his narrow escape from the city's gatehouse, W'soran crested a splintered ridgeline and caught his first glimpse of the great fortress. The ancient mountain was as large as Lahmia itself, ringed about with seven high walls of black basalt and hundreds of slender, blade-like towers. It dominated the horizon to the east, crouching like a dragon beneath a vast pall of ashen cloud, along the edge of a dark, fog-shrouded sea. Though he was still a great many leagues away, the sight of his destination filled the necromancer with a terrible, hateful joy.

The path around the shores of the great sea was a long one, fraught with dangers. Twisted, scaly creatures lurked in the marshes that bordered the sea's western shore, but worse were the packs of howling, pale-skinned monsters that infested the hills to the north. Once they'd caught his scent they hounded him without pause, tracking him through the hillside thickets like hungry jackals, until finally he was forced to turn and fight. He slew scores of them with blasts of necromantic energy and still dozens more with his claws and needle-like fangs, until finally the survivors fled in terror. After that, the creatures continued to test him, pacing at his heels and trying to herd him into places of ambush, but they never risked an open battle with him again.

Finally, after many weeks, W'soran crossed through the territory of the flesh-eaters and reached the far shores of the wide sea. He came upon the ancient ruins of a large temple that had once barred the path along the sea's eastern shore. Beyond the ruins, the shoreline along the base of the mountain was covered in treacherous mounds of crushed stone and wreathed in tendrils of poisonous yellow vapours; a lifeless waste made by human hands, living or dead.

A wide road of black stone carved through the wasteland like the path of a knife, leading to the first of the mountain's forbidding walls. This close to the mountain, there was no day or night; just an endless, iron-grey gloom that neither sun nor moon could shine through, allowing the necromancer to travel on without pause. The air throbbed with the sounds of industry: hammers and bellows, the groan of wheels and the rumble of spilled rock. Beyond that, however, there were no shouted commands, no weary curses or barked laughter, as working men might make in the lands to the south. The fortress hissed and rumbled and banged, but for all that, there were no sounds of life within.

As he approached the gate, a horn wailed from a nearby tower and the great black portal grated open. In the darkness beneath the gate's arch waited a dozen skeletal figures, wreathed in icy mist and flickering green grave-light. The wights leered at him balefully, gripping blades marked with runes of death and damnation. Leading them was a rotting skeleton in ragged robes; the liche's eyes flared hatefully at the sight of W'soran, as though it somehow knew him. A malevolent hiss slipped past its splintered teeth.

Undaunted, the necromancer smiled coldly. 'I am W'soran, from the city of Lahmia to the south, and I am known to your master.' He lifted the heavy leather bag clutched to his bony chest. 'I bear him gifts and news that will be of great interest to him.'

The wights said nothing. After a moment, they withdrew. The liche reluctantly lifted a bony hand and beckoned for W'soran to follow.

Traversing the vast fortress took hours, first across narrow lanes under the ashen sky, then down dank, twisting corridors carved into the mountain's flanks. Higher and higher they climbed, and the closer W'soran came to the object of his quest, the more he felt the weight of the Undying King's power pressing against his skin. It permeated the rock and hissed invisibly through the air, filling up his skull until it was almost impossible to think. It gripped him and pulled him onwards, like an irresistible tide.

At last, W'soran found himself in a vaulted antechamber, high upon the slopes of the great mountain. Before him, towering doors of unfinished bronze groaned on their hinges, opening just wide enough to admit him. Green light flickered hungrily within. The wights flanked him to either side, heads bowed towards the open doors. They offered no instruction, for none was required.

Gripping the leather bag tightly, W'soran strode into the presence of the Undying King, followed closely by the silent, black-toothed liche.

The great, columned hall beyond was vast, larger by far than the pitiful chambers of Nehekharan kings. Shadows writhed along the walls, stirred by pulsing veins of glowing green stone that wound across the surface of the rock. More green light pulsed from a sphere of the same glowing rock, resting atop a corroded bronze tripod at the foot of a stone dais. Sorcerous power radiated from the rock like heat from a furnace, but its intensity paled before the conflagration of power that was Nagash himself.

The Undying King sat upon a great throne of carved wood, cased in the intricate black armour that W'soran had glimpsed on Sakhmet's night, so many years ago. Pale green flames wreathed the king's leering skull and arced along the rough surface of his crown.

W'soran made his way towards the king's dais. Hunched, growling figures paced him from the shadows along either side of the hall – flesh-tearing beasts, like the ones who had hounded him along the hills north of the great sea. Of course they served the Undying King, the necromancer reckoned. Every creature within sight of the great mountain, living or dead, likely bent its knee before Nagash's might.

W'soran did so as well, falling onto his knees before the dais. The burning skull did not move an inch in response to the immortal's presence. There was no need; Nagash's awareness filled the echoing space, invisible and all-consuming. A portion of it fell upon him, much as a man might note the passage of an ant beneath his feet.

The immortal raised his hands to the figure upon the throne. 'Great Nagash,' he cried. 'Undying King! I am W'soran, who witnessed your triumph on Sakhmet's night, twenty-two years ago.' W'soran fumbled open the leather bag before him. Reaching in, he drew out the first of the leather-bound volumes inside. 'I have come bearing tokens of my devotion – your own necromantic tomes, looted from the Black Pyramid centuries ago and held by lesser hands in Lahmia ever since.'

This time, the burning skull did move fractionally, glancing downwards at the offered tome. The Undying King's awareness focused upon W'soran, scorching his mind like a heated iron.

'I bring news also,' W'soran croaked. 'The City of the Dawn has fallen; the bloodline of the treacherous Lamashizzar is no more.'

The skull inclined further, until W'soran found himself staring up at the orbs of fire that seethed from its eye sockets. Nagash's awareness burned like acid along the immortal's bones, threatening to consume them.

'There is more!' W'soran exclaimed. 'A... a usurper has claimed your throne, great one! A man of Rasetran blood sits upon the throne of Khemri! Alcadizzar is his name and he claims descent from Settra himself!'

There was a creaking of metal. Nagash leaned forwards upon the throne, looming over W'soran. The ancient tome flew out of the immortal's hand as an invisible fist gripped him, smashing him back onto the stone floor. The necromancer's veins burned and claws of fire sank into his brain. A voice, cold and soulless as stone, reverberated through the hall. W'soran screamed in ecstasy and terror.

'*Tell me of this usurper,*' the Undying King said.

TWENTY-FOUR

THE LAST LIGHT OF DAY

Khemri,
the Living City,
in the 110th year of Djaf the Terrible
(-1163 Imperial Reckoning)

Heads turned as Inofre, King Alcadizzar's Grand Vizier, led the small procession of nobles down the length of Settra's Court. Though it was late afternoon, the resplendent throne room was still crowded with petitioners and embassies from the far corners of Alcadizzar's empire, from the horse lords of Numas to the merchant princes of distant Bel Aliad. They had been waiting for hours to speak with the great king; with the evening drawing on, most would be turned away until the morrow. For the moment, however, all eyes were upon the tall, handsome lord who followed after Inofre and the three strange, iron-bound chests carried by the noblemen who trailed in the lord's wake.

Alcadizzar straightened slightly on Settra's ancient throne as the procession approached the dais, dragging his mind away from worries about the trade negotiations that were planned for later that night. He'd only returned from Numas that morning, reviewing the new irrigation plan that they hoped would restore the city's parched grain fields. He was tired beyond words and his body was a mass of aches – particularly the ribs that Neferata had broken, some thirty-seven years ago. They never had healed quite right, despite the best efforts of the chirurgeons.

Thirty-seven years, he thought, suppressing a grimace. *Where had the time gone?*

The king stole a guilty glance to his right. Khalida sat upon her throne, serene as always, her left hand resting upon Alcadizzar's right. They had instituted the tradition upon their marriage, moving her throne from its customary place – set further to the right and two steps lower than the king's – and placed them side by side. Her hand upon his was meant to signify that they ruled Khemri jointly, that her opinion counted for as much as his.

The touch of her fingers was light and cool, as though Khalida was loath to rest the full weight of her hand upon his. Things had been strained between them for a long time now, ever since the last war with Zandri, some five years ago. The expansion northwards into the barbarian lands over the past two decades had provided more lucrative routes for the slave trade that had once made the coastal city so wealthy. When Alcadizzar had finally conquered the bellicose city after a lengthy and difficult campaign, he discovered that their coffers were completely empty and the citizens on the verge of starvation. King Rakh-an-atum had taken ship with many of Zandri's nobles and fled to parts unknown, leaving Alcadizzar in possession of a city on the verge of anarchy. Since then, he had spent much of his time there, helping to restore order and improve the lives of its citizens, leaving Khalida to return to Khemri and manage the city's affairs alone.

Holding the empire together demanded more from him with every passing year. In the beginning, the horrors of what his fellow rulers had seen at Lahmia and the threat posed by Nagash had been a potent force for unity, allowing him to forge powerful alliances based on mutual defence and free trade. Free at last from Lahmia's crippling economic policies, the great cities flourished. Alcadizzar invested his city's wealth as wisely as he could, returning Khemri to its former glory. Vast amounts of coin were spent on improving roads across the entire country, and connecting east and west via trade along the River Vitae. The great collegia at Lybaras were restored and then similar centres of learning were founded in Khemri as well. Scholar-engineers were put to work creating methods of irrigation that drew water from the Vitae and restored arable land that had been reclaimed by the desert centuries earlier.

As Khemri's fortunes rose, Alcadizzar made certain that the rest of Nehekhara's fortunes rose as well. Peace and prosperity brought stability, and increased his influence over the entire land. What started as an alliance grew into a confederation of cities, then a short-lived commonwealth, and then, after a combination of statecraft and military manoeuvring, into an empire. Through it all, though, Ophiria's warning remained uppermost in his mind. Everything he did, ultimately, was geared towards preparing the land for Nagash's eventual return.

Those preparations grew a little more difficult with every passing year. The memories of Lahmia had faded with time. Now there were powerful men around the empire who had begun to chafe under the elaborate – and expensive – military obligations they were compelled to maintain. There were even whispers that perhaps Nagash's interests had turned elsewhere and no longer posed a threat to Nehekhara. Some even went so far as to allude that Nagash had never been a threat at all, but merely a potent fiction that Alcadizzar had used to gain control of the great cities. He found himself travelling more, visiting cities and speaking directly to the nobles who lived there, reminding them of their shared duty to defend the land. So far, the tactic was working, but at what cost?

Alcadizzar reached over and touched Khalida's hand, brushing the smooth skin with his fingertips. He smiled. His wife glanced over, stirred from some reverie of her own and managed a strained smile before looking away again.

The king frowned, trying to think of something to say, but was interrupted by Inofre's voice.

'Great one,' the Grand Vizier intoned, 'your loyal subject Rahotep, Lord of the Delta and Seeker of Mysteries, has returned in accordance with your commands and wishes to give an account of his efforts in the lands of the barbarians.'

Alcadizzar pushed his fears aside and summoned up a warm smile for the nobleman standing at the foot of the dais. 'Of course,' he said. 'Welcome home, Lord Rahotep. This is a pleasant surprise; unless I am mistaken, your expedition was not expected back for another two weeks.'

Rahotep bowed to the king and smiled in return. The two men shared the same interests in learning and exploration, and had been friends for many years. The young lord was a famous adventurer, renowned throughout Nehekhara for his travels to the far corners of the world. Thanks to his efforts, Nehekhara's northern border now extended for hundreds of leagues past Numas and had opened valuable trade routes with the barbarian tribes beyond the World's Edge Mountains.

'The past winter was a mild one,' Rahotep answered, 'and the mountain passes opened sooner than expected.' He turned and beckoned his retainers forwards. 'It also helped that I was halfway through the mountains when the snows began to thaw.'

Alcadizzar leaned forwards, his eyes widening. Rahotep had his undivided interest now. 'You met with the *annu-horesh*?'

The fabled explorer swept out his hands and made a dramatic bow. 'I enjoyed their hospitality for the entire winter,' he said proudly. 'They have showed me wonders beyond compare, and offered us assurances of friendship and trade.'

Excited murmurs swept through the court. The *annu-horesh* – literally, the mountain-lords – had been discovered by Rahotep more than a decade ago, but the stout, bearded folk had been slow to warm to the Nehekharans. The barbarians who lived at the foot of the mountains regarded them with awe and spoke of their surpassing skill as warriors and craftsmen.

'Their king, Morgrim Blackbeard, sent you these gifts, as a gesture of his respect,' Rahotep said. With a flourish, he opened the first chest and drew out the most magnificent sword that Alcadizzar had ever seen. It was a huge, two-handed khopesh, but Rahotep held the blade as though it weighed no more than a river-reed. Its edge looked keen enough to cut stone; the metal had a sheen to it like molten gold. The weapon caught the light of the braziers and shone like the morning sun. Gasps of wonder echoed throughout the hall.

Alcadizzar stared at the sword in wonder. 'What is it made of?'

'Iron,' Rahotep said, 'but made into something far lighter and stronger than anything our smiths can forge.' He laid a hand gently against the flat of the blade. 'The true magic lies in the way the blade was washed in gold. The bond radiates heat and light, and is anathema to the evils that dwell in the darkness.' The explorer indicated the remaining chests. 'There is armour as well, shaped by the same processes. Truly a gift for the greatest of Nehekharan kings.'

'Beautiful,' the king agreed. 'It's a great shame that my sons could not be here to see it. Prince Asar is hunting with his uncle in the desert and Prince Ubaid–'

'Asar and my father are in Ka-Sabar now, as guests of King Aten-sefu,' Khalida interjected coolly. 'And Ubaid's interests run to horses and hawks these days.'

The queen's tone stung Alcadizzar. 'Of course. Hawks and horses. How forgetful of me.' The king sighed inwardly and beckoned to a group of robed men standing off to the right of the dais. They wore metal skullcaps, like priests, and gripped staffs of cedar or sandalwood.

'Suleiman,' the king called. 'What do you make of this?'

A tall, dignified, older man stepped forwards, joining Rahotep and peering closely at the blade for several moments. He reached out and lightly touched the sword, just as the explorer had done, and his eyebrows rose. 'Truly a marvel,' he said to the king. 'A form of elemental sorcery unlike anything we have seen before. There are no runes in its shaping; it is as though the very essence of the sun has been worked into the metal.'

Alcadizzar nodded sagely, even though his knowledge of magic was still very limited. The knowledge had been brought to Nehekhara from the far north, by intrepid sailors and explorers like Lord Rahotep, and given to learned men to emulate and master. In the first decade of his reign, Alcadizzar had founded a collegium of magic in Khemri, knowing full well that the other cities would waste no time creating their own. Without the gifts that had once been granted them by the gods, it was imperative that the Nehekharans find new sources of power to counter Nagash's foul magic. The forges at Ka-Sabar were making small amounts of enchanted arms and armour each year now, which were purchased and stored in armouries across the land.

Rahotep smiled at the king. 'The mountain-lords save their runes for truly powerful weapons,' he said. 'Morgrim swore to me that a blade like this requires no great skill to make.'

'Indeed?' the king said. 'Then would the mountain-lords be willing to teach us how to make them?'

The explorer spread his hands. 'It's possible. King Morgrim has invited you to be his guest at his hold, to share the tales of our two peoples and discuss how we may work together in the future.'

Alcadizzar brightened. The prospect of meeting the mountain-lords and seeing their creations excited him. 'How far a journey is it to the World's Edge Mountains?'

'Six weeks, if the weather is cooperative,' Rahotep answered. 'We could travel there in the early autumn, and winter there until the passes open again.'

Six weeks, Alcadizzar thought. It could be done. If the trade negotiations were concluded quickly enough, it was just possible. He turned to Khalida, smiling hopefully – only to find her already watching him, her expression bleak.

Slowly, deliberately, she withdrew her hand.

'The king may do as he pleases, of course,' she said without being asked and looked away.

Alcadizzar's heart sank. 'We will consider the invitation,' he said, turning back to Rahotep with a half-hearted smile. 'You have my thanks for your efforts on behalf of the empire, my lord. I look forwards to hearing a fuller report on the morrow.'

Rahotep bowed gracefully and withdrew. Servants came forwards from the shadows to take charge of the king's magnificent gifts. Alcadizzar watched the explorer depart through the crowd of restless petitioners and felt the bitter sting of envy.

No sooner had Rahotep gone than Inofre reappeared, hurrying down the processional towards the throne. The Grand Vizier gripped his hands together nervously, and his sweaty face was pale. Alcadizzar frowned, seeing that Inofre was alone.

'Well?' the king asked. 'What now?'

Inofre looked from Alcadizzar to the remote face of the queen. 'A great host of desert riders have arrived and are making camp south of the city,' he said. 'Ophiria is with them. She says you must come to her at once.'

A hot wind, reeking of burnt metal and ash, howled like a tormented spirit around the top of the high tower. The Lahmian stood as still as a statue, his eyes glittering with fear as Nagash stood before him. The Undying King reached out and gripped the side of the necromancer's face, the tip of his armoured thumb hovering just beneath W'soran's eye. Slowly, deliberately, Nagash pressed the tip of his thumb against W'soran's withered flesh and drew it downwards, etching a glowing green line into skin and bone.

'*Go forth,*' intoned the Undying King, '*into the lands of men, where the name of Nagash has been forgotten.*' He etched the first part of the sigil all the way to the bottom of W'soran's jaw, then lifted his thumb and began the second mark, clawing a curve along the line of the necromancer's cheekbone.

A faint tremor shook W'soran's skeletal frame as Nagash etched the sigil of binding into his face. The Undying King could taste the necromancer's agony, and noted with approval how W'soran fed upon the suffering, as he had been taught. When the Lahmian had first arrived at Nagashizzar, his skill at necromancy had been rudimentary at best. It had taken many years of instruction to mould him into a potent and useful servant. Arkhan, by comparison, had improved much more swiftly, perhaps because his sojourn in the lands of the dead had given him a greater facility with spirits. Because of this, and because Nagash knew of his skills as a warlord, Arkhan would have overall command of the Undying King's host. W'soran – and the dozen barbarians he had bequeathed his peculiar brand of immortality to – would serve as Arkhan's lieutenants and champions and take charge of individual legions as the liche saw fit. He would need every necromancer at his disposal to control the vast army that Nagash had created. The effort would tax their abilities to the utmost.

'*Go you to the great cities and cast them down,*' Nagash continued, weaving the incantation that would bind W'soran to his legions. '*Cast down the palaces of the proud kings. Cast down the temples of the fallen gods. Fill every well with dust and every road with ash. Let the winds carry the lamentations of the people to the far corners of the world.*'

Nagash drew his hand away. The sigil of binding pulsed fitfully against W'soran's grey skin.

'*In the name of Nagash the Undying, go forth, faithful servant, and conquer.*'

The necromancer wove unsteadily on his feet for a moment, but then bowed his head. 'It shall be done, great one,' he said in a hollow voice. 'I swear it.'

Nagash turned away. The wind hissed across the jagged surface of his armour as he strode to the edge of the tower and looked down upon his assembled host.

They had been marching out from the depths of the fortress for days, and would continue to do so for several days more, taking their places along the shores of the dark sea. The long shoreline had been cleared of debris for leagues to the north and south, where huge ships of bone waited to carry the army to Nehekhara.

The shoreline glittered coldly in the wan moonlight, reflecting off countless spear-points and tarnished helms. Hundreds of companies of spearmen and archers, hordes of skeletal cavalry and sickle-bladed chariots, and huge, thundering engines of war; it was his hatred for the living given form, as vast and pitiless as the desert sands.

The Undying King raised a smoking fist to the heavens. '*Now let the end of the living world begin.*'

TWENTY-FIVE

HOLDING BACK THE DARKNESS

Khemri,
the Living City,
in the 110th year of Djaf the Terrible
(-1163 Imperial Reckoning)

Nagash is coming.

The warning sped to every corner of Nehekhara, sent from the collegium of sorcery in Khemri to each of the great cities, and thence to the ears of the empire's vassals. Within hours, horns were sounding from the palaces, summoning their fighting men to war.

A strategy had been devised decades before in anticipation of the Usurper's return, its particulars refined every year by a war council convened by Alcadizzar in Khemri. Each city's army had a specific role to play in the grand strategy, plus a strict timetable in which to complete their assigned tasks. It was similar in some ways to the complex movement of armies that occurred during the Lahmian campaign almost forty years prior, but altogether more complex and difficult to achieve.

During the first few months after Ophiria's arrival at Khemri, a steady stream of messages flowed from the palace to the collegium and back again. Alcadizzar worked day and night from the relative seclusion of his personal library, communicating with his vassal kings and directing the mobilisation of the empire. Roughly four weeks after receiving Ophiria's warning, the armies of Rasetra and Ka-Sabar had assembled and were on the march, both rushing northwards to reach their assigned places ahead of the Usurper's forces. Meanwhile, on the river docks outside Khemri, every barge the city's merchants owned had been pressed into service, while the city's army mustered in the fields to the south.

There were hundreds of decisions, small and large, to be made each and every day. Alcadizzar quickly learned that being able to communicate with his allies across such vast distances was a double-edged sword. He was deluged with questions, requests, clarifications and reports at every turn, until it became a challenge just to sift through the flood and determine which messages needed attention and which did not.

Ironically, the more Alcadizzar knew, the more he worried about the things he didn't know. Where were Nagash's forces? How large were they? How fast were they moving? He reviewed his battle plans over and over, looking for hidden flaws that the enemy could exploit.

The king was standing before a large wooden table in the centre of the library, studying a detailed map of the empire, when he heard the door to the library quietly open. He sighed inwardly, rubbing at his eyes. 'Yes?' he asked, expecting yet another handful of messages from the collegium.

'Inofre says you haven't left this room in days. Is something wrong?'

Alcadizzar turned in surprise at the sound of Khalida's voice. His wife stood close to the library's door, surveying the cluttered desks and reading tables with a mix of scholarly interest and mild apprehension. She was dressed simply, as was her habit when not attending court, clad in dark cotton robes and silk slippers. A desert headscarf was wrapped loosely about her braided hair. It accentuated the worry lines that creased her forehead and etched the corners of her eyes.

Too exhausted and too surprised to think properly, Alcadizzar shook his head and said, 'No more or less wrong than the day before.'

'Then why are you still awake? It's well past midnight.'

Alcadizzar frowned. He had no idea it was so late. The library had no windows, being in the centre of the royal apartments, so there was no easy way to mark the passage of time. He ran a hand over his face, trying to rub the tiredness away. 'Going over reports,' he replied dully. 'Making sure there's nothing I've missed.'

Khalida joined him beside the map table and peered closely at his face. 'You look ten years older,' she murmured. Her fingertips lightly brushed his temples. 'There's grey in your hair that wasn't there a month ago.'

The king managed a half-hearted smile. 'That's what you get for marrying such an old man,' he joked.

Khalida scowled. 'Be serious,' she said. 'You're exhausted. I can see it in your eyes.'

The smile faded from Alcadizzar's face. He looked down at the map, eyes sweeping over symbols and notations that he'd burned into his memory over the past weeks. He shook his head. 'It weighs on me,' the king said. 'Every moment of every day. When I try to sleep, all I can think of is this damned map.'

'I know,' Khalida replied. 'You always fret like this before a campaign.'

'Not like this,' he said, shaking his head. 'This isn't about taxes, or trade, or expanding the borders of the empire. This is about life and death – or something altogether worse than death.' Alcadizzar sighed. 'The empire is depending on me. If I fail, then every living thing from Lybaras to Zandri will suffer.'

Alcadizzar was surprised to feel Khalida's arms slide about his waist and draw him close. It made him think of the first time she'd embraced him, on the road to Khemri with the tribes. He'd thought desert women were quiet and pliable back then, Ophiria notwithstanding. Khalida had shown him how utterly wrong his impressions were.

'You will not fail,' she told him, in a voice that brooked no dissent. 'This is the moment you've been preparing for. It's the whole reason the empire exists.' She rested her head on his shoulder, and her voice softened. 'In all my life, I've never known a man more devoted to anything.'

The words stung, whether she'd meant them to or not. He put his arms around her. 'I'm sorry.'

'For what?'

'For letting all this come between us,' Alcadizzar replied. 'I've been a poor husband these past few years.'

'But a great king,' Khalida said. She reached up and wiped at her cheek. She gestured at the map. 'Look at all you've done.'

'I'd give it all up in an instant if you asked me to.'

'You wouldn't,' Khalida said, laughing weakly. 'Don't be stupid.'

The king laughed along with her. 'I'm not,' he protested. 'Once this is over, things will be different. No more travelling. No more campaigns. No more pacing the floor at all hours of the night. We'll finally do all those things we dreamed about.'

'You'll take me to the Silk Lands in a barge made of gold?'

Alcadizzar smiled. 'If you wish.'

'And you'll make the Celestial Emperor bow before me?'

'He won't need much encouragement, once he sets eyes on you.'

Khalida chuckled and hugged him tight. 'Promise?'

The king smiled. 'With all my heart.'

'I'll hold you to that,' she said. 'So. When do we march?'

'*We?*'

Khalida disentangled herself and gave Alcadizzar a stern look. 'You expect me to stay here? I've ridden with you on every campaign since we were married and I do not plan on stopping now.'

The very idea filled Alcadizzar with dread, but he knew that there was no point in arguing. Even the authority of kings had its limits.

'Zandri's forces have already left and are travelling upriver now,' he said, tracing his finger along the length of the River Vitae. 'The Numasi are on the move as well, they should be here in two weeks. Another two or three days to load their army and ours onto the barges, then we'll be ready to go.'

Khalida nodded. 'And the rest?'

'The Iron Legion left Ka-Sabar two weeks ago and are headed north to Quatar. Rasetra's forces left at roughly the same time and Heru reports that they'll be at Lybaras in another week or so.' He folded his arms. 'There's been no word from Mahrak in weeks. I fear the Hieratic Council is reconsidering its role in the plan.'

The queen nodded. Though she hadn't been directly involved in drafting the battle plan, she'd pieced it together over the years, and knew it as well as any of the other rulers. 'It's not hard to understand. You've placed them in a difficult position.'

'It wasn't by choice, but they don't seem to believe that,' Alcadizzar said. 'They've been suspicious of my motives ever since I started the sorcerer's collegium. But abandoning the city is the only realistic option. If they won't join Rasetra and Lybaras, at least they could withdraw to the Gates of the Dusk, where they could hold the eastern end of the Valley of Kings for many weeks – certainly long enough for their people to reach the far end of the valley and take refuge in Quatar.'

'It's not that easy a decision for them. They're trying to preserve their faith,' Khalida pointed out.

'Not if they manage to get themselves killed in the process,' Alcadizzar retorted. 'It will be a bitter irony if the Hieratic Council's own mistrust and paranoia proves to be their downfall.'

'If that is their fate, then there's nothing we can do,' Khalida said. 'But they may surprise us yet. There is still some time left before Nagash's army crosses the Golden Plain.'

Alcadizzar nodded, but his expression was doubtful. 'We can hope,' he said. 'At this point, it's all we can do.'

Propelled along the dark waters by sweeping oars of bone, the undead fleet took two long weeks to cross the narrow straits and reach the ruined harbour at Lahmia. They arrived in the dead of night, concealed by a spreading stain of ashen cloud that swallowed the light of the moon. In the years since the fall of the city it had become home to squatters and bandit gangs from all over eastern Nehekhara – desperate men and women who laughed at the legends of the Cursed City's past. W'soran stood upon the deck of his transport ship and listened to their screams as the undead host spread silently through Lahmia's narrow streets.

Hour upon hour, the heavily laden ships came and went from the great stone quays, pouring a steady flood of spectral troops into the city. It was well past daybreak when W'soran's turn came to disembark, riding upon a palanquin of bone that moved like a spider on eight long, segmented legs. He rode the undead engine through the preternatural gloom, making his way up the hill to the remains of the royal palace. There he remained over the next several days, while the army slowly gathered on the plains south of the city.

The necromancer amused himself by picking through the ashes of the old temple, both from curiosity and for the simple reason that he knew Arkhan would not come within a mile of his former prison unless he had to. Sharing control of the army – and the glory of victory – with the damned liche galled W'soran no end. For years he had tried to think of a way to engineer Arkhan's demise – certain that the liche planned the same fate for him. At Nagashizzar, under Nagash's unblinking gaze, he could not think of a way to destroy the liche without considerable risk to himself, so W'soran had bided his time, waiting for the invasion to begin. Though Arkhan's necromantic skills might be marginally better than his at present, W'soran now had the advantage of numbers on his side. His seven progeny together accounted for control of nearly half the army. All he had to do was watch and wait for the right opportunity to push the damned liche into the enemy's hands.

As W'soran expected, Arkhan kept to his own devices, haunting some other part of the city until the army was ready to move. One by one his immortal retainers gathered at the palace as their contingents debarked in the harbour. The old throne of the city was long gone, likely consumed in the temple fire years ago, and the copy that Neferata had made was nowhere to be found, so W'soran had his warriors search the palace for a suitable chair to place upon the royal dais and waited there for Arkhan to attend him and discuss strategy.

A day and a night passed. Then another. W'soran's ire grew. Finally, on the third day, he despatched one of his immortals to find Arkhan – only to discover that the liche had taken the warriors directly under his control and headed west two days before.

Furious, W'soran roused the rest of the host and chased off after him, determined not to let Arkhan reach Khemri first and deprive the necromancer of the honour of capturing Alcadizzar. The vast army lumbered and lurched up the narrow pass and onto the Golden Plain, spilling like a dark stain across the barren fields. The necromancer drove his troops forwards ruthlessly, marching both day and night; the dust and ash stirred by their marching feet was drawn upwards by W'soran's magic to perpetuate the vast sea of cloud that shielded them from the burning sun.

It took more than three weeks to finally catch up with Arkhan, clear on the other side of the desolate plain. W'soran's cavalry caught sight of the liche's forces drawn up in fighting order some ten leagues west along the trade road, not far from where it branched south-west towards Lybaras. A league away, with their backs to the Lybaras road, waited a Nehekharan army.

The necromancer's infantry caught up with Arkhan's troops some four hours later. W'soran commanded them to halt a short way behind the liche's forces and then led his palanquin forwards in search of the broken-toothed bastard.

Arkhan sat astride a huge, skeletal horse, surrounded by a group of mounted wights near the centre of his battle-line. Unlike W'soran, who had retained his sigil-marked robes, the liche had traded his filthy rags for bronze and leather armour. A tarnished bronze helmet covered his skull, its skirt of leather and bronze rings surrounding his face and neck like the lower part of a cowl. The liche's snarling face turned to the necromancer, green eyes burning from their bony sockets. With a creak of leather he raised his hand and pointed a bony finger at the distant army.

'*Explain this,*' Arkhan grated.

W'soran brought the palanquin to an abrupt halt. 'Isn't it obvious?' he snapped. 'Some of that misbegotten rabble in Lahmia must have escaped and carried a warning to Lybaras. You didn't think they would just sit and wait for us to show up outside their walls, did you?'

A guttural hiss slipped past the liche's rotten teeth. '*Lybaras and Rasetra both,*' Arkhan declared. '*It would have taken weeks to muster them, much less march all this way to meet us. How is that possible?*'

'How should I know?' W'soran shot back. 'The Lybarans have all manner of strange devices, do they not? Perhaps they spied us coming from a long distance away.'

'*You're an even bigger fool than I remembered,*' Arkhan sneered. '*You swore to Nagash that the great cities were divided. That they couldn't muster a proper defence against us.*'

The necromancer felt a moment of unease as the implications of what the liche was saying finally sank in. From this moment forwards, if anything went wrong on the campaign, Arkhan would try to blame W'soran for it.

'You call that a proper defence?' the necromancer shot back. 'I always suspected you were a coward, Arkhan. That's a *fraction* of the army I nearly defeated at Lahmia, years ago!'

Arkhan leaned back in his saddle and considered W'soran for a long moment, until the necromancer began to wonder if the liche would be foolish enough to reach for his sword.

'*Indeed?*' he said at length. '*Then your legions should have little trouble defeating this one.*' He raised his hand; all at once, his entire force turned to the right and began to march northwards, out of the path between W'soran's forces and the enemy.

W'soran glared at Arkhan, furious that he had let the liche outmanoeuvre him so easily. 'Very well,' the necromancer hissed. 'Pull your warriors back to the north-east and keep them out of my way. You can manage that much, can't you?'

Arkhan did not deign to give him an answer, merely turning his horse about and heading off to the north. W'soran clenched his fists, sorely tempted to blast the liche from his saddle and settle things once and for all. Reluctantly, he stayed his hand. Now was not the time, not with an enemy army just a few miles distant.

Seething, he turned his palanquin about and returned to his waiting legions. With a few curt orders and a string of mental commands, the army began forming into battle-line. Archer companies clattered forth to take up position in front of the spear companies, while cavalry and chariots took their places at the flanks.

As they were assuming their places, W'soran studied the enemy force.

Truthfully, the force seemed at least as large as the one Alcadizzar had led against Lahmia – perhaps eighty to a hundred thousand warriors. He spied heavy infantry in the centre and on the flanks, screened by large units of archers to the front and chariots to the south. Just behind the battle-line were perhaps two-score small, wheeled catapults, arranged in alternating ranks to fire over the heads of the infantry. A formidable force, the necromancer allowed, but woefully outnumbered against the assembled legions of undead. With a mirthless smile, W'soran ordered his archers and spearmen forwards.

The tightly packed spear formations descended the sloping ground towards the enemy troops. Minutes passed as the two forces drew together. W'soran could dimly hear trumpets calling back and forth along the enemy battle-line. When the advancing skeletons were perhaps a thousand yards away, the necromancer saw men begin working the winding arms on the Lybaran catapults. The necromancer issued another command and his archers picked up their pace, trotting ahead of the spear companies to provide covering fire for the last few hundred yards before contact. At two hundred yards, they came to a halt and drew back their bowstrings in a single motion, then unleashed a hissing storm of arrows into the ranks of the enemy infantry. Many fell upon upraised shields or glanced off rounded helms, but others slid through narrow gaps and buried themselves in flesh and bone. Holes opened in the ranks as men fell, wounded or dying.

The skeletal archers prepared for a second volley, but now the enemy bowmen responded, sending up a shower of their own missiles. They plunged down among the lightly armoured archers, punching through dusty ribcages and bleached skulls. Where the arrows struck, there was a tiny white flash and the skeletons collapsed to the ground.

The flashes caught W'soran's attention at once. Whatever it was, it snuffed out the magic animating the corpses like pinching a candle flame. It had to be magic of some kind, the necromancer realised with alarm.

Down on the field, the skeletal archers unleashed another, more ragged volley of arrows. Almost immediately, the Nehekharans fired back, and hundreds more of W'soran's archers were destroyed. With a snarl, he ordered the survivors to retreat. As the archers turned about and trotted through narrow gaps between the spear companies, W'soran issued curt orders to his retainers. The immortals raised their arms and began to chant, casting the first incantations of the battle.

The spear companies pressed forwards, undaunted by the punishment suffered by the archers. At five hundred yards, a trumpet blew from the enemy battle-line, and all twenty catapults went into action. Clutches of smooth, rounded stones the size of melons fell among the spear companies, crushing shields and shattering bones. Knots of spearmen simply ceased to exist, as though flattened by the stomping feet of an invisible giant.

A hundred yards later, the catapults fired again, then a hundred yards after that. The lead companies of spearmen were all but destroyed, but there were still thousands more ready to take their place. At two hundred yards, another shower of stones fell, plus a flight of enemy arrows that sowed yet more carnage through the ranks. Snarling, W'soran raised his hand to the sky and all eight immortals unleashed their incantations simultaneously. Necromantic power surged through the undead spearmen, filling their spindly limbs with a momentary burst of additional vigour. They surged ahead in a silent mass, weapons levelled, charging across the last two hundred yards faster than either the enemy bowmen or the catapults could react.

The enemy archers saw the danger approaching and retreated at once, snatching unfired arrows out of the ground by their feet and racing back to safety behind the heavy infantry. Moments later the Nehekharan battle-line roared in challenge as the undead spearmen crashed against their upraised shields and the battle was truly joined.

The Rasetran army was clad in heavy armour of leather and bronze plates and they wielded iron-bladed hand axes or heavy maces with deadly skill. Their shields were marked with runes of protection; their weapons with symbols that crumpled skeletons with every blow. W'soran and his retainers responded with another series of incantations that speeded the attacks of their spearmen, until the bronze spearheads jabbed into the enemy like the heads of vipers. The slaughter on both sides was terrible to behold, but the Nehekharans stood their ground against the onslaught.

W'soran lashed at the undead legions with the force of his will, hurling the entire host at the stubborn foe. To the south, skeletal cavalry and chariots charged into the mass of Nehekharan horse, touching off a wild, swirling melee. Companies of archers and spearmen advanced behind the undead cavalry, striking the Rasetrans from the flank and unleashing volleys of arrows at the struggling Nehekharan horsemen. To the north, another force of undead cavalry and infantry were swinging around the enemy's left flank. Trumpets sounded a desperate call for reinforcements, as the enemy left began to bend backwards under the pressure. Before long the undead charioteers would be able to swing past the struggling infantry and strike at the Lybaran catapults at the rear of the army.

Still the Rasetrans fought on, stubbornly refusing to give ground against the onslaught. The Lybaran catapults continued firing over their heads into the rear ranks of the undead, along with the archer companies, but ultimately the effort was a futile one. The skeletons felt no fear or pain. They did not know the meaning of retreat. They fought until they were destroyed, whereupon the next warrior in line took their place and the battle went on. Slowly, inexorably, the undead host began to spill around the flanks of the struggling army, like a pair of jaws that would soon close and swallow the living warriors whole.

After nearly an hour of fighting, the Nehekharans reached the breaking point. Their flanks had nearly collapsed and their infantry companies had taken a terrible mauling. Suddenly, trumpet calls sounded up and down the battle-line, and the withdrawal began. With a steady, disciplined tread, the companies fell back a step at a time, angling slightly back towards the south-west.

Sensing victory, W'soran urged his troops to redouble their efforts. More incantations were cast – but this time, to the necromancer's surprise, their effects were dispelled by cunningly directed counter-magics. Furious, W'soran searched the aether for signs of the enemy spellcasters – but before he could locate them, there was a sudden surge of magical energy and the ground before the struggling warriors seemed to erupt into a howling wall of blinding dust and sand.

W'soran drove his warriors forwards, into the howling sandstorm, but perversely, the sounds of fighting dwindled rather than intensified. The enemy was in full retreat, shielded by the concealing storm. The necromancer switched tactics, marshalling his retainers to dispel the storm. Within minutes, the spell was unravelled, but swirling clouds of dust still obscured the field of slaughter, making it difficult to gauge the enemy's position.

By the time the dust had cleared enough to see, the necromancer was left cursing in disgust. The Rasetrans had pulled back with surprising speed – even the catapults had managed a rapid withdrawal, towed down the trade road by teams of horses. The enemy cavalry had wheeled about and followed in their wake, screening the weary infantry from pursuit.

W'soran glared sourly at the retreating Nehekharans. He'd won, at best, a minor victory. As long as the enemy army remained intact, it still posed a threat. Now he would be forced to chase them, all the way to Lybaras and beyond if he must. That would cost precious time, while the cities of the west marshalled their forces on the other side of the Bitter Peaks.

The necromancer spat a curse at the mortals. At the bottom of the slope, Arkhan was walking his skeletal horse amongst the piles of enemy dead, no doubt searching for some piece of evidence that could be used to damn him before the Undying King.

Already, the campaign was proving to be a long and a bitter one.

TWENTY-SIX

TIDES OF BONE

West of the Golden Plain,
in the 110th year of Khsar the Faceless
(-1162 Imperial Reckoning)

The spirit wailed like a damned soul, wracked by the binding sigil and the force of Arkhan's will. It wavered like a luminous thread of smoke above the body it had inhabited in life, that of a young, handsome Rasetran clad in finely wrought iron armour. Dried blood coated the prince's square chin and spread down the front of his breastplate like a coating of rust. An arrow jutted from the side of his throat.

With an angry sweep of his hand, the liche dispelled the summoning ritual, returning the prince's spirit to the realms of the dead. He spat another string of arcane syllables and the bloodstained body jerked, as though startled. A groan escaped from the prince's lungs, forcing a stream of thick congealing blood from the corpse's slack mouth. Grave-light flickered from the depths of the man's filmy eyes. The dead man climbed stiffly to his feet; with a growled command the liche sent the corpse to join the ranks of the Undying King's army.

Hours had passed since the battle with the Nehekharans and the bulk of the undead army remained close to the corpse-strewn battlefield. Arkhan had been forced to wait until nightfall to interrogate the spirits of the enemy dead; after his abrupt departure from Lahmia several weeks ago, W'soran refused to let him out of the necromancer's sight. Even now, he sat upon his ridiculous palanquin just a few yards away, sneering under his breath while Arkhan worked.

Arkhan would have liked nothing better than to twist the necromancer's head off his bony neck and feed his old bones to the jackals, if they would have them. The battle with the Nehekharans had confirmed his suspicions that W'soran didn't know the first thing about war. The necromancer had simply thrown troops at the mortals until the much smaller army had no choice but to retreat - and had taken substantial losses in the process.

Unfortunately, if he killed W'soran now, he couldn't be certain how the immortal's progeny would react, and Arkhan could not effectively command the vast army without them. If the battle with Rasetra and Lybaras was any indication, he would need all the warriors at his disposal to conquer the great cities.

The enemy was far better prepared than they had any right to be and now he knew the reason why.

W'soran stirred from his reverie as the dead Rasetran prince shuffled past. 'That's the eighth one,' he snapped. 'How many more do you intend to question? We're wasting valuable time.' He waved his skeletal hand to the south. 'Every hour we spend here allows the Lybarans to get another mile closer to their city.'

'*That is the least of our concerns,*' Arkhan snarled. '*All of Nehekhara is up in arms. They somehow knew we were coming while our ships were still sailing down the strait!*' He pointed to the prince's walking corpse. '*They've been preparing for our coming since Lahmia fell, nearly forty years ago. How is that possible?*'

'It's not,' W'soran said flatly. 'The very idea is absurd. Alcadizzar is many things, but he's not an oracle.' He snorted in derision. 'The spirit must have lied to you.'

Arkhan's fists clenched angrily. '*The ritual compelled him to speak the truth.*'

'Then he was mistaken,' W'soran snapped. 'What does it matter? Nehekhara must be conquered and Alcadizzar brought back to Nagashizzar in chains. The Undying King has commanded it and we must obey.'

It matters a great deal if we're marching into a trap, you fool, Arkhan thought. '*The Nehekharans know we're coming,*' Arkhan insisted. '*What is more, they're armed with weapons and magic that we had no idea they possessed.*' He folded his arms. '*We've lost the element of surprise and today's battle shows that we can't depend on numbers alone to defeat the enemy.*'

W'soran studied him warily. 'What do you suggest?'

'*We still have one advantage the mortals cannot match: our troops are tireless and can march longer and faster than anyone else. The Rasetrans and the Lybarans were put in our path to slow us down, while the cities of the west marshalled their troops. If we move quickly, we can still catch them unawares and defeat them one city at a time.*'

'How?'

'*We divide the army. You take a third of the host and keep Lybaras and Rasetra at bay, while I head west at once and strike for Khemri. If I can take Quatar and the Gates of the Dawn by storm, I can be at the Living City within three weeks. Once Alcadizzar is defeated, the rest of the cities should fall easily.*'

The necromancer shook his head. 'Oh, no. You think I'm going to waste my time on this side of the Brittle Peaks while you march into Khemri and claim all the glory?'

Arkhan glared at the immortal. '*We cannot leave Rasetra and Lybaras free to act while we march into the Valley of Kings,*' he grated. '*If they marched into the valley behind us, we would be caught between two forces, with little room to manoeuvre.*'

Even W'soran could see the danger in such a situation. 'I'll send four of my retainers to keep Rasetra and Lybaras occupied,' he said. 'That's almost a third of the army. More than enough to hold the Nehekharans at bay.'

'*Very well,*' Arkhan said grudgingly. He didn't want W'soran anywhere within a hundred leagues of him, but for the moment, he needed the fool's cooperation or else the entire invasion was in peril. '*We leave at once.*'

The liche turned on his heel and headed for his horse, thoughts of murder dancing in his head. If W'soran wanted to be in the thick of the fighting, he would be happy to oblige him. The battlefield could be a dangerous place for the unwary.

The people of Khemri turned out in a vast, cheering throng to see their king and queen off to war. Down at the docks, the last few companies of Khemri's army had been loaded onto the barges, along with the horsemen from Numas and the desert tribes. The barges from Zandri had arrived the day before; now the river was crowded with a fleet of brightly painted craft that stretched westwards as far as the eye could see.

Outside the palace, the royal guard was drawn up in their chariots, awaiting the command to depart. The slaves of the royal household waited on the steps of the palace; each one had been given a gold coin to cast upon the ground at the feet of the king, as an offering to Ptra the Great Father, god of the sun.

At the appointed hour, brass horns shook the air and outside the palace compound the people of Khemri roared in response. Moments later, the royal procession emerged into the bright sunlight. First came Inofre, the Grand Vizier, dressed in all his finery, leading the rest of the king's viziers, followed by the king and queen.

Alcadizzar wore the golden armour gifted to him by the mountain-lords, and shone with all the fury of the sun. The crook and the sceptre had been left upon Settra's throne; in their place the king held his golden sword of war. Beside him, Khalida was the dark to the king's light, clad in a gold-chased iron breastplate and a heavy skirt of iron scales over her flowing cotton robes. A desert headscarf hung loosely about her face; a horseman's bow and quiver were slung over her shoulder.

Behind the king and queen walked Prince Ubaid, their youngest son. The prince's head was downcast as he followed them out onto the steps of the palace, his handsome face screwed up into a fierce scowl as his parents turned to face him.

'Why must I stay behind?' he complained, as though the matter hadn't already been explained to him a dozen times.

'Because you're too young,' Alcadizzar reminded him. 'Your older brother Asar is sixteen and he's not fighting, either.' The crown prince had left Ka-Sabar not long after the call to arms had been sounded and returned with his uncle to Bel Aliad, where he would remain until the war was over.

'But Ophiria is going along,' Ubaid protested. 'And she's *old*.'

Alcadizzar sighed. 'If I could command Ophiria to stay, I would. But the Daughter of the Sands goes where she wishes.'

The prince folded his arms. 'I wish I was the *Son* of the Sands, then.'

Khalida placed a hand on her son's shoulder. 'Someone must stay behind to reassure the people while the army is away,' she said solemnly. 'You and Inofre will rule the empire until our return. Are you up to such a great task?'

Ubaid's head lifted proudly. 'Of course,' he said, with all the solemnity a nine year-old could muster. 'Does that mean I can stay up all night like father does – and eat my meals in the library?'

Khalida gave Alcadizzar a sidelong look. 'That's the privilege of being a ruler, I suppose,' she said. The queen bent and kissed him gently on the forehead, causing the young prince to squirm. 'We'll be back as soon as we can, dearest,' she said.

'I know.'

Alcadizzar knelt beside his son and embraced him. 'Be brave, and rule wisely,' he said. 'And don't empty the treasury while I'm gone.'

'All right.'

The king smiled and kissed his son farewell, and then took Khalida's hand. Together they descended the stone steps. Gold flashed and chimed at their feet. The king and queen smiled broadly at the royal household and the waiting guards.

'I heard a messenger came last night,' Khalida said under her breath.

Alcadizzar nodded. 'News from Heru. They encountered Nagash's vanguard four days ago. The first battle happened yesterday.'

'And?'

The king drew a deep breath. 'They lasted an hour,' he said through clenched teeth. 'Between them and the Lybarans, they had close to a hundred thousand men, and Heru said they were outnumbered at least five to one.'

'Great gods,' Khalida cursed. Her smile never faltered. 'Where are they now?'

'Retreating south, towards Lybaras.'

'They were supposed to delay Nagash for *weeks*,' the queen hissed. 'What now?'

The couple reached the bottom of the steps and turned to wave one last farewell to Prince Ubaid. The boy broke into a wide grin and waved back.

'We hold to the plan,' Alcadizzar replied. 'And pray that Quatar can hold the Gates of the Dawn. Otherwise, there will be nothing to stop Nagash from seizing the west.'

* * *

True to Arkhan's word, the undead host moved like locusts down the western trade road, darkening the skies with their passage. While four of W'soran's immortals pursued the eastern armies southwards, the liche raced for the Valley of Kings with all the speed his slow-moving force could manage.

First, however, came Mahrak, seat of the Hieratic Council and once known as the City of the Gods, where Nagash had been defeated during the first war.

What little that Arkhan knew of the city's fate dated from Lamashizzar's reign, centuries ago. In those days the city had largely fallen into ruin, following the end of the sacred covenant and the decimation of the ruling council. W'soran claimed that Neferata had supported the restoration of the city during her reign, but that Mahrak was still but a shadow of its former glory. At this point, however, Arkhan didn't trust anything the necromancer told him, so he approached Mahrak expecting to find bristling fortifications and a determined army ready for battle.

The truth, he discovered, was somewhere in-between. Two weeks after the battle with Rasetra and Lybaras, the undead host arrived at Mahrak just after sunset, and found a city much diminished in glory, but with its walls and gates fully intact. Thousands of white-robed warriors stood atop the battlements, ready to defend the city to the death.

Arkhan made every effort to oblige them.

Through the night, his warriors surrounded the city, cutting off every avenue of escape and forcing Mahrak's defenders to spread themselves all along its perimeter. Catapults were dragged into place and smaller war engines assembled at strategic points around the city. Within hours, the first probing attacks were launched against the city walls, testing the strength of the defenders' organisation and resolve. Arkhan kept them up all through the following day, keeping the mortals on edge and giving them no chance for rest.

That evening, just after sunset, the attack began in earnest.

Catapults hurled shrieking missiles high overhead, targeting the tops of the walls and the city's gatehouses. Multi-legged war engines raced for the walls, followed by scores of skeletal companies equipped with crude ladders. Showers of arrows fell amid the ranks of the dead, striking down warriors by the dozens, and sporadic catapult fire from inside the city carved swathes of destruction through the oncoming companies. But the survivors pressed on, heedless of casualties and undaunted by the towering walls rising before them. War engines scuttled up the stone face like spiders, stabbing men with their forelegs and flinging their screaming bodies off the battlements. Bone ladders rattled against the walls under the covering fire of arrows; skeletons climbed for the battlements with daggers or hatchets clutched between their rotting teeth. The city defenders flung rocks down at the attackers, or waited along the walls with clubs or axes to fend them off. The undead snatched at them with their bony hands, seizing men by the arms and necks and pulling the defenders with them as they toppled off the wall.

Once the assault began, it never let up. Arkhan gave the defenders not one moment of respite. Necromantic energies crackled in the night air, lashing the battlements with searing bolts of power, or animating the bodies of the fallen and turning them on their fellows.

Arkhan expected to carry the walls in just a few hours and one of the gates shortly after that, but the defenders of the once-holy city were made of sterner stuff than he imagined. They defended every foot of the walls with their blood; if the undead did not falter, then neither did they. Two hours passed, then four, and then six, and still the gates remained in the defenders' hands.

Slowly but surely, however, the sheer weight of numbers began to tell. By dawn of the following day, most of the city walls had been cleared and fighting was concentrated around both city gates. By noon, the east gate fell, only to be retaken minutes later by a furious counter-attack. Back and forth the fighting went, with both gatehouses changing hands as much as a dozen times throughout the bloody afternoon. By nightfall, however, the eastern gate fell again, and this time there was no mortal left alive to reclaim it.

Arkhan's troops poured into the city and for the next three days and nights they slaughtered every living thing within Mahrak's walls. The temples were put to the torch, and the corpses of the slain were raised up and pressed into the ranks of the conquering army, restoring a portion of the warriors Arkhan had lost.

Five days after the undead host reached Mahrak, the City of the Gods was no more. Nothing was left but heaps of broken bones and scorched rubble; a vast, bleak testament to the vengeance of Nagash.

TWENTY-SEVEN

AT THE GATES OF THE DAWN

The Valley of Kings,
in the 110th year of Khsar the Faceless
(-1162 Imperial Reckoning)

A week after the fall of Mahrak, the undead army reached the eastern edge of the Valley of Kings. At the mouth of the valley stood the Gates of the Dusk: eight towering stone pillars, each a hundred feet tall and older than Nehekhara itself, arrayed to either side of the wide road that wound through the base of the broad valley floor. In Arkhan's time, an unfinished wall had stretched across the valley up to the first pillars of the ancient gate. Since then, it had been replaced with something altogether more formidable – a towering bulwark of closely-fitted stone that rose more than thirty feet high, with hulking bastions rising every quarter mile to the north and south. A brooding gatehouse had been built across the road, just a hundred yards east of the obelisks, and the entrance sealed by twin slabs of solid basalt more than ten feet wide and fifteen feet high.

Prepared for another bitter assault, Arkhan hurled a dozen companies of skeletons and ten war engines at the city walls. Shielded by layers of necromantic incantations, the companies crossed the open ground before the walls without challenge and climbed swiftly onto the battlements. The liche waited upon his horse just out of bowshot, listening for the sound of fighting that never came. There were no guards upon the battlements, or within the fearsome gatehouse. The huge and costly fortifications, no doubt built over many years to secure the eastern end of the valley, were completely deserted. The garrison – if in fact there had ever been one – had likely been withdrawn to Mahrak and died there in the city's defence.

There was no fathoming the ways of priests, Arkhan thought, as he led his wights past the Gates of the Dusk.

At that same moment, more than a hundred leagues to the north, Alcadizzar and the armies of the west were emerging onto dry land once more.

The trip upriver had gone without incident – other than a lengthy and brutal battle with seasickness among the desert tribesmen – and within a few weeks the first of the river barges reached their destination. After the first week of the journey the fleet had headed up the Golden River, a tributary of the Vitae, and into the depths of the Bitter Peaks. There, at the river's end, they came to a small outpost that stood sentinel over a series of stone docks that would have been the envy of any major city. They had been built during Alcadizzar's reign for a single purpose – to move an army as quickly and efficiently as possible to the eastern side of the mountains.

Few men outside of Khemri knew of the existence of the docks; fewer still knew of the narrow road that had been carved a hundred and twenty leagues through the mountains to the south-east. Caches of food and water had already been put in place along the route, allowing Alcadizzar's forces to travel light and move faster still. So long as the weather held, they would reach the Gates of the Dusk in just under two weeks.

They had learned of the fall of Mahrak while en route up the river; Ophiria had seen it in a vision and spoke of the slaughter that Nagash's troops had wrought. From Mahrak, Alcadizzar was certain that the army would continue into the Valley of Kings in an attempt to break out into western Nehekhara. With the armies of the east now trapped in Lybaras by a sizeable force of Nagash's troops, the way seemed clear to proceed to Quatar, and then beyond to Khemri itself.

What the enemy did not know was that the Gates of the Dawn had changed a great deal since the Usurper's reign, and that the armies of Quatar and Ka-Sabar stood ready to repel them. When Alcadizzar and his armies reached the Gates of the Dusk, the trap would snap shut.

They just had to reach the western end of the valley in time.

The Valley of Kings had once been a vast burial ground, where the early Nehekharans had laid their people to rest prior to the creation of the great cities. Grand tombs had been dug into the valley's steep slopes and the valley floor had been crowded with sandstone shrines and clustered mausoleums.

Now there were only piles of broken stone and blackened rubble stretching for hundreds of miles – the remnants of a months-long running battle fought between the armies of the Usurper and the rebel kings of the east, some six hundred years before. Arkhan remembered the gruelling pursuit across the valley. The retreating easterners had toppled statues and broken apart the mausoleums to create improvised redoubts for their archers and spearmen, while Mahrak's priests bedevilled his cavalry with cunning illusions and deadly magical traps. The rebels had made Nagash's forces pay dearly for every foot of ground, forcing the immortals to break open the tombs along the valley slopes in search of more bodies to fill their thinning ranks. The pursuit had lasted for two gruelling weeks and was some of the hardest fighting of the war.

This time, Nagash's warriors were moving in the opposite direction, towards the Gates of the Dawn and the city of Quatar. During the days of Nagash's reign, the western end of the valley had been sealed off by fortifications even greater than the ones that had been built at the Gates of the Dusk, but the Lybarans had found a way to demolish them in an attempt to slow Nagash's advancing army. Given what he'd seen at the Gates of the Dusk, Arkhan had to assume that something similar had been built at the western end of the valley, and that it would be well defended. Quatar's famous Tomb Guard had been charged with protecting the Gates of the Dawn for millennia; since the Valley of Kings was the only way to move an army across the Brittle Peaks, it was certain that they would be manning the battlements and watching for his approach.

The Gates of the Dawn had to be taken by storm. Now that all Nehekhara was up in arms, Arkhan knew that he had to move quickly before the western kings could unite into a single, massive army. Every day he lost fighting in the valley allowed his enemies to grow stronger, which was something he could not permit.

Arkhan bent all his power to speeding the march of his army. W'soran, not to be outdone, commanded his progeny to do the same. Shrouded in swirling darkness, the undead host raced westwards, past the shattered tombs of the ancients.

Moving day and night, Nagash's army crossed the Valley of Kings in a mere seven days, but the demands of the march and the broken terrain had spread the host over more than ten miles of ground. The cavalry was in the lead, the skeletal horses picking their way easily over the broken ground, followed by scores of clattering war engines and loose companies of loping, axe-wielding skeletons. Farther back were the tighter formations of the spear companies and then finally the catapults and the rest of the large siege engines. Arkhan rode with the rest of the horsemen, his glowing eyes burning in the dark as he tried to catch a glimpse of the distant gates. When he reached them, there would be no pause for preparation – he would simply unleash his warriors on the wall in a rising tide of metal and bone, until the Tomb Guard were swept aside. Whatever defences the enemy had in place, Arkhan was certain they could be swiftly overrun.

He was wrong.

The first thing Arkhan saw was sparks of fire blazing against the darkness, scores of watch fires, burning in the night. They were arranged in three lines, and at different heights, with the first row of fires some twenty feet above the valley floor, the next at forty feet, and the smallest at around sixty feet above the ground.

Moments later, the liche vaulted his horse over a heap of broken sandstone and found himself galloping across a wide expanse of cleared ground, more than a hundred yards long. After days and nights of negotiating the rubble-strewn terrain of the rest of the valley, the transition was jarring.

Then, he understood, just as the first blazing missiles flew from the enemy's defences; they'd reached the killing ground at the edge of the fortifications.

Crackling balls of pitch shot skywards on trails of fire, seeming to hang in the air for long moments before plunging like thunderbolts amidst the skeletal horsemen. The missiles exploded on impact, catching desiccated skin and dried bone alight and transforming riders and mounts into firebrands. Snarling, Arkhan redoubled the speed of the cavalry, racing his horse archers as close to the wall as he could manage.

As the fires multiplied along the killing ground, Arkhan saw the wall – the *first* wall, made of slabs of granite that rose twenty feet above the valley floor. Archers along the wall and its squat, brooding gatehouse unleashed a torrent of arrows at the oncoming horsemen, their enchanted arrowheads wreaking havoc among the undead squadrons. A hundred yards behind the first wall, a second wall rose to a height of forty feet, reinforced with stone bastions every two hundred and fifty yards along its length. Then, another hundred yards further on, Arkhan could just make out the black bulk of the third and final wall; sixty feet of sheer basalt, sealing off the Gates of the Dawn.

Another ball of fire crackled just overhead, spilling motes of burning pitch onto Arkhan's shoulders. With a curse, he ordered his horse archers to fire one volley at the men on the first wall and then withdraw out of range. The enemy's defences were far stronger than he'd imagined possible. He would have to waste precious time until the rest of the army arrived before he could contemplate an assault.

His plan in tatters, Arkhan wheeled his horse around and retreated from the killing ground, his mind seething as he contemplated his next move.

The western army stopped only when absolutely necessary to spare the horses and feed the men. Everyone, from the king to the lowliest spearman, was dull-eyed with fatigue, but they had made good time along the mountain road and had crossed the Gates of the Dusk in only ten days. As the warriors sat alongside the trade road that wound along the rubble-strewn valley, they could still see the lingering pall of smoke that hung over the dead city of Mahrak to the north-east. It was a grim sight, reminding them of the threat that loomed over all Nehekhara.

Alcadizzar was resting his head against the side of his chariot when Suleiman, his chief wizard, came riding up the column on a borrowed horse. His arcane robes were stained brown with road-dust; lines of grit stood out sharply along the creases of his neck and the deep wrinkles around his eyes. His polished metal skullcap flashed brightly in the morning sun.

'A message from Quatar,' the wizard said without preamble, leaning heavily on his staff. 'Nagash's army is at the Gates of the Dawn.'

Alcadizzar sat forwards, instantly alert. 'How many?'

'A hundred thousand at least,' Suleiman replied. 'But more are arriving each hour. It could be many times that number.'

The king nodded gravely. 'Can they hold the gates?'

Suleiman nodded. 'For now.'

'Any word from Lybaras?'

'Heru says that the city is still besieged. Reinforcements are on the way from Rasetra, but are not expected to arrive for almost a month.'

Alcadizzar rubbed his aching eyes. So long as Heru and the Lybarans could hold the city, then they were drawing away thousands of warriors that his own army would not have to face in the valley. That would have to be enough.

The king looked to the west, contemplating how hard he could push his exhausted men. 'Tell Quatar to give me ten days. Tell them to do whatever they must, but I need ten days.'

The first wall fell after two days of near-constant attacks. Arkhan ordered the skeletal companies forwards under a hail of arrow fire and a relentless barrage from the catapults that had been rushed to the battlefield. The defenders fought back tenaciously, using their own arrows and catapult fire to wreak havoc among the undead horde. Arkhan saw quickly that it wasn't just white-armoured Tomb Guard who were manning the walls, but iron-clad heavy infantry from Ka-Sabar as well. They hurled sandstone blocks down on the skeletons, or doused them with pots of burning pitch; they smashed skulls and hacked off arms, or split ladders in half with polearms and axes.

One assault after another was repulsed, but Arkhan was relentless. Finally, the catapults succeeded in making a breach around noon of the second day, and the liche ordered his cavalry through the gap. At that point, the defenders knew they had to retreat, or risk being cut off. They pulled back in good order, leaving some four thousand of their dead and wounded behind. Arkhan made certain that they were the front ranks of the next assault.

The second wall held out much longer than the first. It was too high for ladders, and so thick that it shrugged off all but concentrated catapult fire. Arkhan raked the battlements with blasts of sorcery and repeated attacks by swift war engines, but each one was repulsed. Four attempts to batter down the gate were likewise defeated, crushed by heavy stones dropped from the gatehouse, or burned to ash by streams of burning pitch. Finally, after five days of effort, Arkhan persuaded W'soran to send in his immortals. The risk was great, since they were integral to the spells that animated and controlled the army. The death of even one would cost the undead host tens of thousands of troops. But the gamble paid off; the immortals scuttled up the wall like spiders, concealed from view by a wall of sorcerous fog conjured by W'soran. Within an hour, shouts of alarm sounded from along the wall as the second gate groaned open. The wall's defenders launched one ferocious attack after another in a desperate attempt to retake the gatehouse and seal the gates, but to no avail. The survivors fled to the third and final wall with Arkhan's cavalry right on their heels.

After a week of constant attacks, Arkhan pulled back his forces and contemplated the final obstacle in his path. The third wall was too tall to climb and too thick for catapults. That left only the gate, which was made from two slabs of polished basalt some two feet thick.

For two days, the grim defenders atop the third wall peered into the gloom, nervously clutching their weapons as they waited for the final assault to begin. By the third day, some atop the wall began to hope that the enemy had finally given up. King Alcadizzar and his forces had to be very close by now.

And then, just past noon, they felt it, a faint, rhythmic tremor, vibrating through the stone beneath their feet. One slow beat after another, like the tread of giant feet.

The bone giants weren't built for height. They were relatively short – only about twelve feet tall at the shoulder – but very wide, with massive arms and four thick, stubby legs. There were six of them, each one composed of thousands of man-sized bones and plated with every piece of scavenged metal that Arkhan's skeletons could find. Between them they carried a battering ram made from a sandstone column that was fifteen feet long and weighed tens of tons. The ground shook beneath their feet as they made their way through the second gate and towards the remaining wall. Several dozen smaller war engines scuttled along in the giants' wake, their spindly legs crusted with old gore.

Assembling the giants had required the efforts of not just Arkhan, but W'soran and all three of his immortals as well. The cost in time and energy had been great, but Arkhan reckoned it a small price to pay if it got them past the Gates of the Dawn.

The liche sat upon his warhorse and watched the giants lumber off into the distance. Trumpets were already sounding the alarm atop the wall as the juggernauts became visible through the gloom. Most of the army's cavalry and a few large skeletal companies stood ready on the far side of the second wall. The rest – belonging to W'soran and his immortals – waited in the space between the first and second walls, safe from enemy catapult fire. Arkhan turned to W'soran, who sat upon his palanquin at the edge of a ritual circle inscribed upon the ground. Six large clay jars rested in the centre of the circle; the necromancer's three progeny stood at different points around the perimeter, waiting to begin the ritual.

W'soran clutched a large, leather-bound tome in his bony hands. It was one of the ancient books of Nagash, returned to him by the Undying King just before leaving Nagashizzar. The necromancer searched through the pages for the proper ritual, then turned to Arkhan. 'When shall we begin?'

The liche gauged the distance between the giants and the wall. They would be in catapult range any moment. '*Now*,' he grated. '*I will go forwards and lead the cavalry through the breach.*'

'Of course,' W'soran said, with only a hint of a sneer in his voice.

Arkhan spurred his horse forwards, heading for his wight bodyguard and the waiting cavalry. The necromancer muttered a curse at his retreating back and then turned to his progeny. With nothing more than a curt nod, he raised his arms and began to chant.

The three immortals joined in at once, adding their power to the rite. The energy built from one minute to the next, until the air above the circle crackled with unseen power. The heavy jars, each one as big as a grown man, began to tremble. Their lids rattled – slightly at first, but then louder and more energetically with each passing moment. W'soran's voice increased in pitch, the words spilling from his lips in a buzzing crescendo. And then, with a crack of shattering clay, the lids of the jars burst apart at once, and thousands upon thousands of black tomb beetles erupted from their depths. They rose into the air, joining together in a swirling, oily-black cyclone that wavered for a moment above the ritual circle, then sped westwards, climbing swiftly until it broke like a hungry wave over the battlements.

Shouts and agonised screams echoed from the top of the wall as the giants bore down upon the last gate.

The desert tribesman crouched and marked lines in the sand with the point of his knife. 'The enemy is through the first and second walls,' he said. 'The first wall has a breach, here, and the gates are open. Most of the enemy army is between the first and second walls.'

Alcadizzar studied the markings in the gloom. He was crouching beside his chariot, surrounded by his closest advisors: Khalida, Ophiria, Suleiman and Faisr's eldest son, Muktadir. They were a quarter mile from the Gates of the Dawn, close enough to hear the sounds of battle in the distance. 'What are they doing now?'

'Hammering at the third gate with something very large. I could not see what. They are also using some kind of magic to blind the men atop the wall. It looks like a shimmering black cloud.'

Alcadizzar looked to Suleiman. The wizard shook his head. 'It could be anything,' he said. 'But it means that at least some of their necromancers are busy performing the spell.'

'It appears we have arrived just in time,' Muktadir observed. He was tall and rakishly handsome, as his father had been. Upon Faisr's death, just five short years after the fall of Lahmia, Muktadir had risen to take his place as the great chieftain of the tribe. 'We should strike quickly, while they are focused on taking the third gate.'

'Agreed,' Alcadizzar said. He turned back to the tribesman. 'Does the enemy have any sentries on the first wall?'

The warrior smiled wolfishly. 'None.'

Alcadizzar returned the smile. 'Good. Suleiman, can you and your wizards conceal our approach as far as the first wall?'

The wizard scratched his chin. 'If they are distracted with their own rituals, then yes.'

'All right,' the king said. 'We'll put archers along the first wall. They'll fire as soon as the attack begins. I'll lead the chariots through the first gate. Muktadir, take your tribesmen and heavy cavalry through the breach. The infantry will follow behind us as quick as they are able. Look for their necromancers. If we can destroy them, we'll end this battle quickly.' He rose. Behind him, the army spread out across the valley in a vast battle-line, its ends hidden in the gloom. Part of him would have liked to have said something inspiring, right at the brink of battle, but circumstances prevented it. If they survived the next few hours there would be plenty of time for speeches later, he thought. 'Suleiman, you ride with me.'

Muktadir and his kinsmen mounted their horses and departed quickly, while Suleiman summoned a messenger and composed instructions for his fellow wizards. Alcadizzar took Khalida's hand and turned to Ophiria. 'Any last words of advice?' he asked the seer.

The Daughter of the Sands was an old woman now, having served the tribes for more than a hundred years. Her face and hands were deeply wrinkled, but Alcadizzar could still see the coltish lines of the girl she once had been.

She looked up at the king and shrugged. 'Don't get killed.'

Despite the tension in the air, Khalida snorted in laughter. Alcadizzar gave Ophiria a mock frown. 'What would we have ever done without you?'

The seer leaned forwards and rested a hand on the side of each of their faces. Tears shone in her eyes. 'Khsar turn his face from you in the battle to come,' she said in a wavering voice. 'Let him unleash his hunger upon the foe, and gnaw their bones in his teeth.'

Alcadizzar smiled. 'Keep safe, Daughter of the Sands. Until we meet again.'

With that, the king and queen climbed into their chariot. Suleiman climbed clumsily after them, then came the chariot's two young bowmen. When all were aboard, Khalida tugged at the reins and the war machine clattered off into the darkness.

Ophiria watched them go, knowing how the battle would end.

The giants drew back the ram once more and smashed it against the gate. Arkhan could feel the concussion almost seventy-five yards away. The thunderous blow shook the stone slabs on their hinges and brought down another shower of powdered mortar from the arch above the gate. The huge constructs worked entirely unimpeded; every man atop the wall was beset by the buzzing storm of scarabs, or the swiftly-moving war engines. Another few blows, he thought, and the gates would start to crack.

Arkhan turned to his cavalry and, with a thought, ordered a slow advance. Thousands of skeletal horsemen started forwards, walking slowly over the hard ground.

Another blow echoed across the field, followed by a brittle shower of broken rock. Not long now, he thought.

* * *

The archers went in first, racing up to the wall and disappearing through the gate. Within minutes they were spreading out across the top of the wall. After the last bowman had vanished, Alcadizzar ordered the cavalry forwards. Beside him, Suleiman clutched his staff and chanted in a low voice, muffling the sound of the wheels and the thudding of the horses' hooves. Other wizards were doing the same with the infantry companies approaching behind them. With luck, the enemy would not know they were in danger until the charge began.

Khalida crouched low behind the armoured rim of the chariot, reins gripped loosely in her hands. She'd strung her bow and had it ready upon her back. Alcadizzar leaned forwards and gripped her shoulder. 'We'll charge as soon as we emerge from the gate. No time and no point waiting for us to get into formation.'

She nodded, intent on guiding the chariot through the approaching gate. Everything was strangely calm. The king gripped the hilt of his golden blade.

Khalida snapped the reins as they entered the tunnel, bringing the horses to a canter. The sound of the wheels was deafening inside the tunnel; it seemed impossible that no one else could hear it. Within seconds, they had crossed through the first wall and emerged on the other side. At that moment, the queen drew her headscarf across her face and let out a wild, ululating battle cry. The horses broke into a charge.

Alcadizzar drew his sword. The blade of the mountain-lords blazed in the darkness, like a splinter of the sun.

'For Khemri!' he shouted. 'For Nehekhara! *Forwards!*'

The ritual occupied W'soran's total focus, guiding the scarabs and stoking their hunger with the slightest touch of his power. It required a delicate touch: too much, and the scarabs burned out, too little and they became tired and docile.

He did not realise that the army was under attack until arrows started hissing all around them.

Flashes of white peppered the ranks of the undead, toppling a skeletal warrior with each hit. Two shafts thunked into the back of his seat, while another struck one of his progeny in the shoulder. The immortal howled in pain, snapping the shaft of the arrow in his frantic efforts to remove it. He tore the arrow free with a convulsive wrench, leaving a smoking hole in his breast.

The other immortals ducked for cover and the ritual came undone. Cursing, W'soran whirled about, searching the darkness for the source of the arrow fire.

Trumpets wailed to the east, followed by the swelling thunder of horses' hooves. The killing ground behind the undead host was packed with horsemen and chariots – tens of thousands of them – and they all seemed to be charging his way. At their centre was a man in golden armour, brandishing a fiery sword. W'soran's heart went cold.

'Alcadizzar!' he cried.

The ram struck home again. This time Arkhan could see the cracks radiating through both doors, stretching all the way from the inner edge to the hinges. A shower of rock fragments fell to the ground, leaving a shallow crater in the surface of the right-hand gate. Arkhan hissed in anticipation and drew his sword.

And then, without warning, the angry buzzing that had filled the air for nearly half an hour fell ominously silent. Arkhan looked up to see a shower of tiny, black insects pattering along the battlements and coursing like rain down the sheer wall. The screams from above fell silent.

Arkhan whirled his horse about, as though he could peer down the tunnel of the second gate and see what had interrupted the ritual. And then he heard the wailing of war-horns – not from the wall, but from the *east*, back the way he'd come.

It wasn't possible, the liche thought. The closest mortal armies were trapped at Lybaras, hundreds of miles away.

And then he heard the rending crash of a cavalry charge striking home and knew for certain that, somehow, his forces were under attack.

Alcadizzar's sword sketched an arc of fire through the air and carved through two skeletal warriors as the chariot thundered past. Behind him, his two bowmen were firing as fast as they could draw arrows; the enemy was so tightly packed together that every shot almost guaranteed a hit. Suleiman was roaring incantations over the din of the battlefield, hurling bolts of power into the undead ranks.

Around the king, the chariots of the royal guard had formed a wedge and driven deep into the enemy's reserve formations. Heavy cavalry off to the left and right had smashed into the rear of the spear companies, smashing warriors to the ground with swords, axes and horse hooves. More arrows hissed overhead as the archers on the first wall adjusted their aim to fire over the heads of the Nehekharans.

The initial attack had gone well. Against a mortal army, the result would have been chaos, but the undead simply turned about to face their new foe without a moment's shock or hesitation. It would not be long at all before the cavalry was forced back by the sheer numbers of the enemy.

Alcadizzar turned to Suleiman. 'The necromancers!' he cried. 'Where are they?'

The wizard scowled at him for a moment, trying to understand the king over the din of battle. Suddenly, his face brightened, and he closed his eyes for a moment in concentration. 'There!' he cried, pointing off to the north-west.

A thrown spear clattered loudly off the side of the chariot. Khalida yelled out a curse at someone or something, but Alcadizzar couldn't see what. He searched the battlefield to the north-west – and then he saw it. A strange palanquin made of bone, with legs like a spider, crouching behind a pair of spear companies just thirty yards away. There was a throne atop the palanquin and the king caught sight of a skeletal figure lurking behind it.

Alcadizzar slapped Khalida's shoulder. 'That way!' he yelled, pointing with his sword. 'That way!'

The chariot lurched to the right, its axle-blades scything through the legs of several slow-moving skeletons. The rest of the king's royal guard responded at once, changing course to follow him. Up ahead, the two spear companies saw what was happening and formed into line, linking their shields together and levelling their spears.

Immediately, they became a target for the archers on the wall. Arrows hissed over the chariots and struck the formation; where the enchanted bronze struck bone, a skeleton collapsed in a flash of white. Then Suleiman raised his staff and bellowed in a furious voice. The end of his staff flared like a torch, and a volley of tiny, glowing darts tore into the undead. Dozens fell, their bones incinerated by blasts of intense heat.

Then the chariots crashed into the battered line, smashing skeletons from their feet or grinding them beneath metal-shod wheels. Alcadizzar chopped at skulls and smashed collarbones; every bite of his enchanted blade toppled another skeleton to the ground. The royal guard added their weight to the charge as well, striking at the enemy with bow and blade. In less than a minute, one of the two spear companies was all but destroyed.

Alcadizzar smashed another skeleton to the ground and saw there was nothing standing between them and the palanquin of bone. 'Forwards!' he shouted in Khalida's ear. 'Forwards!'

The queen shouted something in reply and lashed at the reins – and then the world dissolved in a blast of heat and greenish light.

Arkhan saw the explosion and let out a sulphurous curse. If W'soran was using sorcery like that, then it meant he was under attack.

The liche led his troops through the second gate and emerged into a scene of pandemonium. Enemy cavalry and chariots had struck his companies from the rear and were being caught by arrow fire from along the first wall as well. The spear companies had no archers to support them, as they were all still on the wrong side of the second wall, and so they were suffering heavily. To make matters worse, large companies of enemy infantry were pouring through the first gate and trying to form a battle-line on the other side.

He caught sight of the pennons flapping above the chariots. *Khemri*? Here? But how? The realisation filled him with a momentary surge of panic. Alcadizzar had turned the entire valley into a trap and he'd walked right into it. Now he was caught between two powerful forces, with few options left.

Cheers rose from the third wall behind Alcadizzar, followed by the first volleys of arrow and catapult fire as the defenders sprang into action. The attack on the Gates of the Dawn had failed, and possibly the entire invasion along with it. Unless he counter-attacked at once, it was likely that he would never break out of the noose that was tightening around his neck.

Arkhan tried to catch sight of W'soran among the chaos. He caught a glimpse of two of the necromancer's immortals, charging at the wreckage of a destroyed enemy chariot. His first instinct was to try and reach them. If they were lost, then most of the army went with them. But on the other hand, this could be the opportunity he was looking for to be rid of that idiot W'soran and his pets once and for all.

The battle was already lost. The question was whether he would try to save W'soran, or let the bastard hang. When put that way, the answer was an easy one.

With a shout, Arkhan urged his mount forwards. He would lead his troops as far north along the wall as he could, then swing around and try to force his way around the edge of the enemy flank. If he was lucky, he could drive through the gap in the first wall and make good his escape.

Someone was dragging him backward. A voice shouted wildly in his ear. Alcadizzar shook his head and tried to open his eyes.

The chariot lay on its side amid a tangle of dead horses, just a few feet away. Blood was everywhere, but the king couldn't tell whose it was. His sword lay on the ground beside the overturned vehicle, gleaming in the darkness.

And then he saw the slender, bloodied arm poking out from beneath the chariot's battered hull.

'Khalida!' the king screamed. He twisted in the grip of whoever held him, pulling himself away. A boy cried out – one of his archers? – and someone grabbed for him again. He tore himself away and scrambled forwards on all fours, trying to reach his wife's hand.

He had almost reached her when he heard a hiss above him. Behind him, the boy screamed. Battlefield instinct caused him to roll to the side, out of the path of the axe that buried itself in the ground beside his head.

Alcadizzar rolled onto his back. A shrivelled, almost skeletal man stood above him, clad in rough, barbaric robes and bits of bronze armour. Swift as a viper, the creature ripped the axe from the ground and rounded on him. That was when he saw the creature's fangs, and understood what he was facing.

There was a shout and a flare of white light and the creature screamed, clutching at the side of its face. Alcadizzar saw his chance and lunged for his sword. The monster caught the movement and snarled, chasing after him. An arrow punched into its back, the enchanted metal hissing in the dead flesh, but the creature barely broke its stride.

Alcadizzar's hand closed on the hilt of the sword and he continued to roll as the monster charged at him. The king rose in a kneeling position and swung the enchanted sword at the creature's midsection. It ran right into the blow and the magical blade parted armour and cloth as though it were paper. The blade sheared the thing in two; the power of its magic shrivelled the creature in an instant, like a leaf caught in a flame.

A dark shape leapt like a cat onto the upturned side of the chariot. It was another of the creatures; its attention was directed upon the wizard, Suleiman, and one of the king's two young archers. It spat a string of arcane syllables and flung out its hand, and a bolt of greenish lightning leapt for the wizard. But Suleiman was prepared, and raised his staff, blocking the energy with a counter-spell. The bolt detonated with a thunderclap, leaving Alcadizzar's ears ringing.

Alcadizzar's second archer – the same boy who'd tried to drag him to safety – saw the monster and drew the short sword at his hip. With a cry he charged at the thing, swinging wildly. The creature snarled at the boy and pointed a clawed finger; there was another flash of light and the archer's body burst into flames. As the boy collapsed, thrashing and screaming, Suleiman unleashed a sorcerous bolt of his own. The monster deflected the blast with his own counter-spell, hissing in disdain – then his body went rigid as an arrow from the first archer thudded into his forehead. White steam erupted from the creature's gaping mouth and it fell over onto the ground. Alcadizzar lurched forwards and finished it off with a blow to its neck.

Around them, the tempo of the battle was changing. Cheers were rising from the Nehekharan warriors as the skeletons seemed to be withdrawing – no, not withdrawing, but *collapsing* where they stood. As the blood-drinkers died, Nagash's army died with them.

And then an invisible fist seized the overturned chariot and flung it into the air as though it were a child's toy. It struck Alcadizzar a glancing blow and sent him sprawling.

The king rolled quickly onto his back, and saw two more of the emaciated blood drinkers. They stood at the far end of a magical circle, beside a trio of small, sealed earthenware jars. One of the creatures was clearly a barbarian, but the other wore remnants of Nehekharan robes and clutched a battered leather tome to his chest. The creature seemed to smile at Alcadizzar and lifted his bony hand.

'Beware, great one!' Suleiman cried, rushing forwards to stand between the monster and his king. 'See to Khalida! I'll protect you!'

The Nehekharan laughed, and a bolt of energy leapt from his hand. Suleiman brandished his staff – but the fire ate through it like dry wood and clawed deep into the wizard's chest. Suleiman let out an agonised groan and fell to the ground.

'Pathetic,' the Nehekharan blood-drinker hissed. He turned to Alcadizzar, and managed a predatory smile. 'I have been looking for you, boy,' he snarled. 'I just might be able to salvage this disaster if I drag you back to Nagashizzar.' He gestured to the other blood-drinker and spoke in a strange, guttural tongue.

The monster was on Alcadizzar in an instant, seizing his wrists with uncanny strength. Hissing, the creature clenched his hands, until the king felt the bones in his wrists grate together. He groaned in pain but refused to let go his sword.

There was a loud cry, and the surviving archer came to the king's rescue. He appeared at the monster's side, chopping his short sword into the blood-drinker's left wrist. Bones snapped; the creature snarled in irritation and struck the boy a backhanded blow, crushing his skull. But Alcadizzar was able to free his sword-hand and bury the burning blade in the monster's face.

The next thing he knew, he was lying on his back, with smoke curling from his breastplate. His ears were ringing and every nerve in his body hummed with pain. The Nehekharan blood-drinker lowered its hand, a look of mild surprise on his face. Evidently the magic forged into his armour by the mountain-lords had saved him from the necromancer's blast.

Alcadizzar tried to rise, but his legs refused to work. The blood-drinker smiled and said something, but the king couldn't make out the words. Then, languid as a snake, the monster started to walk towards him. Desperate, Alcadizzar raised his sword and hurled it at the monster with all his strength, but the blood drinker dodged it with contemptuous ease.

The creature took another step – and then, as clear as day, the king heard the *twang* of a bowstring. Then came a choked scream as the blood-drinker reeled backwards with one of Khalida's arrows in his eye.

The monster screamed in agony. White steam curled from the ruined eye socket. He fell backwards, fetching up against the clay jars as he fumbled for the arrow shaft. He seized it in his right hand and with a shriek of pain he wrenched the arrow free. Thick ichor bubbled down the side of his face.

Shadows danced at the corners of Alcadizzar's vision, Dimly, he sensed men crowding around him and the queen. His gaze was fixed on the monster, who shouted and cursed at him from just a dozen yards away. With a final, angry howl, the creature turned his back on the king and smashed one of the jars at his back. To Alcadizzar's horror, a tide of glossy black beetles poured from the vessel and engulfed the necromancer's body. Moments later, the insects burst into the air in a buzzing cloud and flew off to the north. Of the necromancer, there was no sign.

Alcadizzar fell back onto the ground. Someone was shouting his name. He turned and saw a pair of royal guardsmen helping Khalida to her feet. She was reaching for him, her eyes wide with fear.

The king's gaze drifted past her, to the clouds roiling in the sky. As he watched, they began to fade, dispersing like smoke on the wind.

His vision faded. The last thing Alcadizzar felt was the warm touch of sunlight on his cheek.

TWENTY-EIGHT

THE EDGE OF VICTORY

Lahmia, the Cursed City,
in the 110th year of Phatkh the Just
(-1161 Imperial Reckoning)

Though Nagash's army had been defeated at the Gates of the Dawn, Alcadizzar's injuries threw the western army into disarray. The king's chirurgeons debated whether to try to treat his injuries on the battlefield, or send him to Quatar, many miles away. The rulers of Numas and Zandri both attempted to take charge of the army in the king's absence, issuing conflicting orders from different parts of the battlefield that took hours for the paralysed forces to sort out. By the time Queen Khalida had recovered enough from her own injuries to take charge, the last remnant of Nagash's army had broken out of the trap and fled eastwards down the Valley of Kings.

By dawn of the next day, it appeared that the king would survive his injuries. Alcadizzar awoke with his wife beside him and dispelled any notion that he would be sent off to the gloomy city of Quatar for his recovery. Instead, he ordered the army to strike camp and pursue their retreating foes.

Nagash's army withdrew from the Valley of Kings and continued eastwards, where two weeks later it was joined by the remnants of the undead forces that had laid siege to Lybaras. Though the undead had succeeded in breaching the city's walls, the timely arrival of reinforcements from Rasetra had broken the siege and slain two of W'soran's four surviving progeny.

Pursued now by the combined armies of east and west, Nagash's warriors fought a bitter, running battle all the way back to the ruined city of Lahmia. Companies of spearmen and cavalry were sacrificed to stage vicious ambushes and night attacks on the Nehekharans, while the rest marched tirelessly onwards towards their goal. Again and again, Alcadizzar tried to pin down the enemy with attacks from his cavalry, but the undead army simply shed another sacrificial rearguard, like a lizard giving up its own tail, while the rest escaped. Fields of shattered bone stretched along the great trade road for miles.

The last battle was fought at the edge of the Golden Plain, just miles from the Cursed City. W'soran's surviving immortals and their skeletal warriors had occupied the decrepit forts guarding the narrow pass that led to the city, and held off the Nehekharan armies for weeks before they were overcome. By the time Alcadizzar reached Lahmia, the city was deserted. Arkhan and the last remnants of Nagash's vast host had boarded their ships and escaped.

Lahmia's docks had not been so alive in decades. Men from Zandri and Khemri – seamen and rivermen, who knew the ways of boats and the sea – were walking the city's old quays and inspecting the scores of silent, fat-bellied troop ships that the enemy had left behind. As Alcadizzar watched, a number of intrepid souls had found a pair of large skiffs that were still mostly seaworthy and were in the process of towing one of the huge troop ships up to the docks.

It was a sunny day in early spring, warm and damp with the promise of rain. The city still smelled of cinders, almost forty years after its fall. The king sat astride a lean desert horse and watched the activity on the docks from an empty square a short way uphill. A small group of royal guardsmen sat their horses a discreet distance away, allowing him to be alone with his thoughts. The chirurgeons encouraged him to ride when he could, saying that exercise would help speed his recovery.

Alcadizzar had his doubts. He leaned back in the saddle, wincing at the pains in his knees, hips and back. The chirurgeons had all done their best, he knew. He suspected that the aches he felt had less to do with the blood-drinker's magic and more to do with the fact that he was a hundred and eighty-nine years old. The power of Neferata's elixir was just a memory now, but he still seemed to age far slower than his peers. He looked like a man no more than a hundred – past the prime of his life, but with a good many years left in him, if he was careful. A time when most men put aside their work and tried to enjoy all the good things they'd earned.

Hoofbeats drummed along the cracked cobblestones across the square, shaking the king from his reverie. He glanced over to see Ophiria walking her horse towards him. Her hooded servant, the chosen of Khsar, reined in at the edge of the square, a discreet distance from both the Daughter of the Sands and the royal guardsmen.

The king managed a tired smile as the seer came up alongside him. 'This is a surprise,' he said. 'I hadn't expected to see you inside the city.'

Ophiria scowled suspiciously at the empty buildings along the square. Rather than find lodgings inside Lahmia, like the rest of the army, the tribesmen had pitched their tents up on the Golden Plain, near the ruins of the border forts. They shunned the city, convinced it was truly cursed ground.

'You didn't look as though you were coming out any time soon, so I decided to come in after you,' she replied.

Alcadizzar chuckled and spread his hands. 'If you're expecting tea, I'm afraid you'll be disappointed.'

The Daughter of the Sands smiled sadly. 'No,' she said. 'No time for that now, I'm afraid. I've come to say goodbye.'

The king sighed. 'I'd hoped that Muktadir and his riders would stay with us a while longer.'

Ophiria shook her head. 'Muktadir is a good son. He promised his father on his deathbed that when Nagash returned, the tribes would help drive the Usurper from the land. That promise has been kept and now he longs to return home, where his new wife waits for him.'

Alcadizzar nodded. 'I understand,' he said, a little wistfully. 'Truly, I do.' He glanced over at the seer and gave her a mischievous grin. 'The barges are waiting to carry you back to Khemri.'

Ophiria grimaced. 'Never again, by the gods!' She put her hand to her belly. 'I'd rather be dragged to Bhagar from the back of a horse.' The seer shook her head. 'The next time I want to see a man tortured I'll have him carried to the river and tied to a barge for a week.'

The two shared a rueful laugh. Alcadizzar reached over and took her hand. 'Safe journeys, Ophiria. You will always be welcome at the court in Khemri.'

Ophiria studied the king for a long moment. 'You are a good man, Alcadizzar, and my people owe you a great deal. For that you have my thanks.' She glanced away from him then, looking down the hill at the docks. 'You are contemplating another voyage,' she observed.

The smile faded from Alcadizzar's face. 'The war's not over yet,' he said gravely. 'As soon as we can put together a fleet, we're going after Nagash.' He pointed down at the abandoned ships. 'My men are examining those bone ships to see if we can rig them with oars or sails. We'll head up the strait, find the Usurper's lair, and deal with him once and for all.' He sighed again. 'Then, perhaps, I can finally rest.'

'I hope so,' Ophiria replied, her voice sad. For a moment, it looked as though she were about to leave, but then she paused, as though there was something more she wanted to say.

Alcadizzar frowned. 'What is it? What's the matter?'

Ophiria did not reply at first. She stared out at the sea for a time, as though wrestling with what she ought to say. Finally, she turned to the king. 'Will you do one thing for me, before you go?' she asked.

'Of course. Anything,' Alcadizzar said.

'Send Khalida home,' she said. 'That's all.'

'That's all?' Alcadizzar said, his eyes widening. 'Can't I do something simple instead, like emptying out the sea, or counting the stars in the sky?' He chuckled. 'She'll never go, especially not after what happened at the Gates of the Dawn.' The brush with death had wiped away all the years of tension and resentments that had grown up between them. Now they rarely spent more than a few hours apart each day. 'If you think she should go back to Khemri, then you should tell her.'

'She won't listen to me. I'm just her aunt.' Ophiria protested.

'You think she'll listen to me? I'm just her husband,' Alcadizzar said. He frowned. 'What's all this about?'

'Nothing.' Ophiria shifted uncomfortably. 'Her children need her, that's all.'

The king gave the seer a long look.

'You've seen something, haven't you?'

Ophiria grimaced. 'I shouldn't have said anything.' She jerked on the reins, trying to turn her horse about.

The king bent down and took hold of the horse's bridle. 'Too late for that now,' he said gravely. 'What is it?'

Ophiria stared at the king. 'If you go north to face Nagash, you will triumph,' she said slowly. 'But you will not return.'

Alcadizzar let go the bridle and sat back, stunned. 'I don't believe it.'

The seer nodded in understanding. 'I'm sorry. But that's the way of it.'

'No,' the king said. 'You're mistaken. I can't die now.' He took in the ruined buildings of the square with an angry sweep of his hand. 'First Lahmia, then Nagash, and now this? I've given *everything* for this land, Ophiria. Everything I've done was for Nehekhara's sake. A hundred and eighty-nine years, and hardly a day of it was ever truly mine.'

'You're a great king,' she said sadly. 'Perhaps the greatest Nehekhara has ever known.'

'But what about *me*?' Alcadizzar said. 'Where is the justice in this? There's so much I've waited to do. I've hardly even begun.'

'I know,' Ophiria said sombrely. 'Believe me, Alcadizzar. I know what it's like to sacrifice everything for a higher calling.' She shook her head. 'But we cannot choose our fate.'

'Then what's the point?' Alcadizzar cried. 'What's the point of all this horror and suffering, if not to earn the right to live as we wish, for however many years we're given?'

A tear trickled down the seer's wrinkled cheek. 'I cannot say,' she replied. Ophiria reached forwards and laid a hand on his cheek.

'Goodbye, Alcadizzar, King of Kings. I wish you well, in this life and the next.'

The Daughter of the Sands tugged on the reins, turning her horse about and heading back across the square. The king watched her and her hooded servant head west, deeper into the city, until the two riders were lost from sight.

Evening was drawing on when Alcadizzar arrived at the palace. Thunder rumbled faintly to the east, heralding the coming storm.

The king found Khalida deep amid the ruins of the Temple of Blood, surrounded by her maids and a cadre of keen-eyed guardsmen. The ancient garden at its heart had survived the worst of the fire, and was now a tangled, green wilderness.

Most of the paths through the garden had vanished, swallowed up by ferns and creeping vines. Only the widest, stone-flagged paths survived. One led straight to the centre of the garden, where Khalida rested by the bole of a gnarled old tree and tossed breadcrumbs into the brackish pond nearby.

Alcadizzar strode softly over the thick grass and settled down beside her. The queen turned, smiling, and kissed his cheek. 'There you are,' she said. 'Have you been down at the docks all this time?'

'Mostly,' the king said, his gaze wandering about the clearing. 'What are you doing here?'

'I heard a rumour that there were still fish in the pond,' Khalida said. 'Giant carp, the colour of gold coins. I've been trying to coax them out with some crumbs.'

Alcadizzar turned back to Khalida. He reached up and gently swept a strand of dark hair away from her face. 'How do you feel?'

The queen smiled. 'A little better every day.' She had broken two ribs and an ankle when the chariot flipped during the battle and they had been slow to heal.

'Are you up for a long journey?' the king asked.

Khalida's smile faded. 'Why?'

Alcadizzar leaned forwards and kissed her gently on the lips. 'Because I think it's time we returned to Khemri.'

Khalida's expression turned sombre. 'What about Nagash?'

The king was silent for a long moment. 'We've beaten him. His army has been destroyed. That's victory enough for me.' He put his arm around Khalida and pulled her close, careful of her ribs. 'I've fought enough for two lifetimes. Now I just want my wife and children beside me.'

The queen looked up at him. 'Do you mean it?'

'With all my heart.'

Khalida smiled. 'Then let's go home.'

Three weeks after escaping the Cursed City, Arkhan the Black beached his ship of bone on the shores of the Sour Sea, beneath Nagashizzar's shadow. He marched into the fortress with fifty thousand warriors – a formidable army by mortal standards, but little more than a tenth of the vast host he had been given.

When Nagash learned of his army's defeat, his wrath was terrible to behold. The sound of his fury thundered through the halls of the fortress and sent tremors through the tunnels below. For seven days and seven nights the air above the mountain roiled like an angry sea and spat forks of green lightning that lit the blighted land for miles.

And then, after the seventh night, the thunder subsided, and the mountain grew still. An ominous silence descended over Nagashizzar, more fearsome and portentous than all the days of fury combined.

* * *

'I don't like the looks of this,' Eshreegar muttered as the black-toothed liche emerged from the tunnel.

It had been a month since Nagash's army had returned to the fortress in defeat. Many times, while the fortress halls had been all but empty of the undead, Eekrit and Eshreegar had debated on whether the time had come to unseal Grey Lord Velsquee's chest and make use of the weapon inside. Each time, Eekrit's instinct was to wait, fearing that, even without an army, Nagash was still far too powerful to face. The storm of fury that had wracked the fortress - nay, the entire *mountain* - upon the army's return convinced Eekrit that he'd been absolutely right.

Beneath the mountain, it was still business as usual. Nagash's hunger for slaves had shown no signs of abating, and the work in the mines continued without pause. Across the cavern, the latest shipment of greenskins snorted and bellowed in their guttural tongue as the undead arrived to make their trade.

Eekrit's ears twitched. Something was different. There were many more skeletons this time. A *great* many more, in fact, all carrying chests or stacks of flat, square boxes, sealed with lead. As the liche looked on, the skeletons carried half of the chests over to the scales, as usual, then deposited the rest at Eekrit's feet.

'What's all this?' he asked.

The liche turned to Eekrit. His skull was blackened in places, his armour scorched and battered. He looked as though a giant had grabbed him by the ankles and used him to beat out a rather stubborn fire.

'*My master wishes to make a new arrangement,*' the liche grated. One leg dragged slightly as he stepped forwards and indicated the chests and boxes arranged before Eekrit. '*In addition to the usual amount for slaves, he will pay double for you to carry these chests to the source of the River Vitae and empty their contents into the water.*'

Eekrit eyed the boxes warily. Each one was marked with a complex pattern of runes and arcane symbols. 'What's inside them?'

'*Death,*' the liche said.

'Ah.' Eekrit replied. He spread his paws. 'We, ah, have never heard of this river.'

'*It feeds all of Nehekhara,*' the liche said. '*Its source is a tarn, high in the mountains to the south-west.*'

'Where-'

'*Find it,*' the undead creature rasped. '*Unless you do not wish to have the stone?*'

'No!' Eekrit said. 'I mean - yes, we want the stone.' He glanced at Eshreegar. 'No doubt something can be arranged.'

'*There will be more,*' the liche said. '*Deliver them all to the tarn, and you will be well paid.*'

'I am glad to hear it,' Eekrit replied, though he felt anything but. 'What is all this for, if you don't mind me asking?'

The liche glared at him.

'The Nehekharans will die before they serve my master,' he said. *'And so they shall have their wish.'*

TWENTY-NINE

RED AS BLOOD

The Tarn of Life,
in the 110th year of Tahoth the Wise
(-1155 Imperial Reckoning)

It took nearly a year to find the place that the liche had spoken of. First they found the wide, swift-flowing river, many hundreds of miles away to the south-west; then they followed its course up into the treacherous, unforgiving mountains. Many were the scouts who were lost along the way, taken by avalanches, or swift, silent wyverns, or stabbed by their fellows when their rations ran low. They negotiated thundering cataracts, scaled sheer cliffs and swung over bottomless crevasses, until finally, after much suffering and hardship, they reached a vast lake, its surface as smooth as glass and coloured a dark, depthless blue. They found the ruins of twelve great temples along its shores, so ancient and so long abandoned that they were little more than crumbling shells of pitted sandstone, the idols within reduced to shapeless knobs of white marble.

This was the tarn they had been paid to find; the birthplace of the great river that fed the lands to the west, all the way to the distant sea. With nervous paws they broke open the seals on the twelve boxes they had carried with them on the journey, and they emptied the burning man's poison into the dark depths. Then they scuttled away into the darkness, heading back to the great mountain where their reward awaited them.

Halfway back to the mountain, the first of the scouts began to sicken. By the time the expedition reached the tunnels that would lead them around the shores of the Sour Sea, only the strongest of the scouts were still alive. Two managed to reach the great cavern beneath the mountain and gasp out their report to Eshreegar before their insides turned to mush.

Eekrit and Eshreegar split the fortune in god-stone between themselves and sent out the second expedition six months later.

* * *

Over time, the wily scouts learned to adapt to the dangers of the long trip up to the tarn. Rikkit Sharpclaw had survived the past three expeditions to the lake, which made him the natural leader of the pack. The last thing he did before leaving the mountain was to spend some of his accumulated wealth to hire a score of shifty-eyed clanrats from one of the visiting slaver gangs. He told them he needed the extra muscle to protect the valuable cargo he was carrying up into the mountains. The clanrats took his coin and snickered to one another at the deal they were getting. Five gold coin apiece to help carry some boxes? Compared to hunting greenskins up north, that sounded like a holiday to them.

After nine expeditions to the tarn over the last five years, the scouts knew the route very well. They knew how to avoid the sudden avalanches, where to be watchful for the fearsome wyverns and how best to negotiate the waterfalls and the yawning chasms. Rikkit was cautious as ever – more so this time, perhaps, because rumour had it that this was to be the last expedition to the lake. He had no intention of getting himself killed with so much unspent wealth hidden back at the mountain.

The expedition reached the tarn right on schedule. The early spring night was cold and clear, and a full moon smiled at its reflection in the still water below. The clanrats gaped at the size of the lake and the ominous, silent ruins, but followed the scouts without question as they worked their way around the shore and up a narrow path that led to a high cliff overlooking the tarn.

Rikkit breathed in the cold, clear air and smiled at the clanrats. 'Here is-is where you earn your keep,' he said. The scout pointed a claw at the edge of the cliff. 'Set the boxes over there.'

Wary, the clanrats crept to the edge of the cliff and set the boxes at their feet.

Rikkit smiled. He motioned to the one of the other scouts, who produced three pairs of hammer and chisel and tossed them to the hirelings.

'Open them,' Rikkit said.

The clanrats eyed one another uneasily, but were not in any position to argue. Taking the tools, they cut away the lead seals securing each lid and levered the boxes open. Caustic green light spilled from each container, washing over the hirelings.

Rikkit's smile widened. This was the part he really enjoyed. The scout reached into his robes and pulled out a fat bag of gold coin. At once, he had the clanrats' undivided attention.

'Now, here's where you lot can earn yourself some extra coin,' he said, tossing the bag onto the ground. 'The clanrat that tosses the most of those things into the lake gets the gold.'

Rikkit didn't need to tell the clanrats to begin – all at once there was a snarling, scratching, kicking scramble to grab hold of the contents of each box and hurl them into the water below.

Each box contained a flat disc of pure god-stone, each about the size of a small shield. The surface of each disc was carved with hundreds of strange, arcane symbols and the discs themselves seethed with pent-up magical power. The scouts hissed with laughter as the hirelings seized the heavy discs – each one worth a Grey Lord's ransom – and fought for the privilege to toss them into the depthless tarn below.

Amid savage grunts and yowls of pain, the first discs were hurled into the air. They glowed balefully as they fell, spinning like tossed coins. They hit the water of the tarn with a bubbling hiss, like hot metal plunged into a quenching vat, and sent up a plume of acrid, faintly glowing steam as they sank out of sight.

Once it was down to the last few discs, the knives came out. Clanrats screeched and toppled over the cliff, clutching at the blood pouring from their chests. Two of the hirelings fell together, grappling over a disc up to the moment they hit the surface of the water, forty feet below.

When the last disc was gone, the three survivors turned on one another. After a few minutes, only one clanrat was left. Rikkit laughed loudly, scooping up the bag and tossing it to the victor. The scouts were already taking bets as to how long the fool would last before the sickness took him. Whispering and chuckling amongst themselves, the skaven scuttled back down the narrow path, their thoughts already turning to the long journey home.

By dawn, the surface of the great tarn was as red as fresh-spilled blood.

The great river was the source of life for all Nehekhara, in ways both great and small. Its waters nourished a verdant belt of arable land that stretched through the high desert for more than a thousand miles, providing so much food that cities like Numas, Khemri and Zandri grew rich trading wheat, rice and beans with their neighbours to the east. The river supplied fish for the river cities as well, and water for making wine and beer. Its countless tributaries, many deep underground, spread across the land like threads in a tapestry, feeding distant oases and tiny, hidden springs that sustained merchant caravans and desert nomads alike.

For years, Nagash's poison had spread to every corner of Nehekhara, spreading through the soil into the crops, and from the crops into animals and people alike. Men filled their bellies with the liche-king's curse every time they drank a cup of wine, or sipped greedily from a spring in the great desert. By the time the final set of discs sank into the waters of the tarn, the poison was curled like a sleeping viper in the flesh of every living thing.

The final set of discs completed Nagash's elaborate curse and set the wheels of death in motion. The waters of the tarn turned crimson; the stain flowed down the roaring cataracts and into the River Vitae, where in time it was witnessed by horrified fishermen and river traders all the way to distant Zandri. It was the Undying King's sign that the doom of Nehekhara was at hand.

Within days, the crops in the fields began to wither and die. Not all at once, but by degrees, driving the farmers into fits of desperation as they struggled to save their livelihoods. Livestock who ate the tainted crops soon sickened and died. The disease was horrible to behold; it was a slow, agonising death, as the bodies of the victims rotted from the inside out. Agony led to madness, and madness to death, but the process was neither merciful nor swift.

Not long afterwards, the first Nehekharans began to suffer as well. Hardest hit were the river cities, particularly Khemri. Alcadizzar the Great, ruler of the empire, summoned his chirurgeons and his wizards, and bent every effort to locating the source of the disease and uncovering a cure. The sick were taken from their homes and placed in the temples, in hopes that they would not spread the disease to others. And yet, despite their best efforts, the plague continued to spread.

As the crops failed, food prices soared. Even those who were healthy now faced the prospect of starvation. Cities began hoarding food, leading to riots and more bloodshed. Alcadizzar used all his power to try and maintain order amongst his vassal kings. For a while, he succeeded. Food was rationed, but everyone, from highest to lowest, was fed. As the plague spread to distant cities like Quatar and Ka-Sabar, the infected were removed as humanely as possible and isolated in tent cities outside the walls.

And then Ubaid, the king's youngest son, fell ill.

Alcadizzar summoned a legion of chirurgeons to attend upon his son. Every wizard and oracle in the land was consulted in search of a cure. The king himself spent night and day at his son's bedside, while he thrashed and bled, and screamed in pain. Once the disease was far advanced, not even the milk of the poppy could dull the young prince's suffering. He begged his father to make the pain go away; later, in the grip of madness, he begged his father to end his life. When he died at last, almost a month later, he did so with a curse upon his lips.

By then, the plague was everywhere. The great cities shut their gates to outsiders, and shut the infected up in their homes to try and hold the sickness at bay. Gripped with fear and half-maddened by grief, Alcadizzar sent Asar, his only surviving son, away from the city and into the Great Desert to live with the tribes, where it was hoped the plague couldn't reach. The king's heir travelled through a land fraught with violence and unrest, as gangs of bandits waylaid travellers in search of food. After many brushes with death, Asar and his retainers reached the safety of the Great Desert and camped for the night at an oasis known only to the tribes.

The very next day, the prince fell ill. His retainers, many sick themselves, struggled to care for him, but his conditioned worsened. One night, in the grip of madness, the prince slipped from his tent and wandered out into the sands, never to be seen again.

When the news reached Alcadizzar, he was devastated. Over the course of a year, he had watched the plague spread through his empire, and now it was dying before his eyes. Nothing he did slowed the spread of the disease in the slightest. Fresh, untainted water, locked away in cisterns, jars and wells, was now worth its weight in gold. Riots tore through Khemri every day, as the panicked citizens searched for some way to escape the sickness. They clamoured outside the gates of the palace, begging their great king to save them.

As the second year of the plague wore on, the begging of the people turned to angry shouts, and then from shouts to bitter curses as the disease claimed more and more lives. The fact that the king himself seemed impervious to the disease only fuelled the bitterness of his citizens even further.

The months passed and the supplies of food dwindled. Men turned into savages, murdering their neighbours for a crust of bread or a cup of stale wine. Alcadizzar opened the palace's meagre food stores to his people, but his gesture of goodwill spawned a bloody riot that left hundreds of his citizens dead. They rampaged through the palace, stealing whatever they could, while the king and queen and a handful of royal guards barricaded themselves in the kings' apartments and waited for the chaos to subside.

One week later, Khalida contracted the plague.

The sickness came upon her much more slowly than the rest. For a time, she tried to hide her suffering from her husband, but within a month her condition had grown too visible to ignore. Alcadizzar summoned his chirurgeons once more. He sat at her bedside and wiped the blood from her eyes, and listened as she groaned in her sleep. As her condition worsened, he went to the ancient temples and prayed in vain for the gods to save her life.

Khalida lingered in pain for many months, wasting away upon her sickbed. When her suffering had grown so great that she no longer recognised her own husband, the chirurgeons offered to give her a cup of undiluted poppy to ease her into the next life. Alcadizzar took the cup himself. He lifted it to his wife's lips and sat with her into the night, as her moans faded and her breathing grew ever more shallow. She passed into the realms of the dead shortly thereafter, heedless of the grief-stricken man at her side.

Alcadizzar sent for the mortuary priests and helped them prepare his beloved for the tomb. The last of the horses had died months before, so the king and a pair of acolytes pulled the wagon carrying her body out into the city's necropolis, where a modest crypt awaited. There was no grand pyramid for Nehekhara's greatest king. Alcadizzar had resisted the idea of commissioning one, and Khalida, being born amid the desert tribes, scoffed at the notion of entombment. But in the end, Alcadizzar could not bring himself to lay her upon a wooden bier and set her alight, as was the practice among her people. The tomb at least held out hope that perhaps one day she might rise again.

For a time, Alcadizzar contemplated taking the poisoned cup and joining his family in the afterlife. But then, a few days after Khalida had been laid to rest, an exhausted messenger rode into the city from distant Rasetra. How he had managed the long journey alone was a feat of courage and endurance unto itself, and he was already half-dead from the plague by the time he arrived. The message he bore was from King Heru. An army of the undead had emerged from the Cursed City to the east and was slaying everything in its path. Lybaras had already fallen, its few remaining citizens ruthlessly put to the sword. Rasetra would be next.

The message was more than two months old. Alcadizzar knew that Heru had been dead long before his warning reached Khemri.

From that moment on, the king put thoughts of the poisoned cup aside. Instead he brought forth his armour and his golden sword, and turned his eyes eastwards, searching for the approaching darkness.

THIRTY

ALL IS DUST

Khemri,
the Living City,
in the 110th year of Asaph the Beautiful
(-115 Imperial Reckoning)

When the time had come, the last of the king's household went into the great necropolis and sought out Alcadizzar in the tomb of his beloved wife.

'The darkness is coming,' the faithful servant said. His name was Sefru, and in better days, he had been an attendant in the royal stables. His linen robes had been carefully cleaned and his skin anointed with fragrant oil, so that his spirit would present a pleasing appearance when he went to join his ancestors in the lands of the dead. A vizier's circlet of gold sat uneasily upon his narrow brow, and he carried a shield and spear in his trembling hands.

The king was clad in his armour of gold; his gleaming sword rested upon the stones at his feet. He knelt by the marble bier where Khalida's body lay and held her cerement-wrapped hand in his. Hunger and grief had ravaged the king's once powerful frame. Alcadizzar's face was gaunt, eyes sunken and cheeks hollowed as though by a long and merciless fever. He had the look of a man who longed for the peace of the grave.

While the servant waited, the king rose slowly to his feet. Gently, he laid his wife's hand upon the bier, and then bent to press his lips against the wrappings that covered her cheek. Dry lips rasped faintly against the cerements.

'Not much longer now,' he whispered to her. 'Watch for me in the dusk.'

Then the king took up his sword and headed out into the dying light of day.

It was high summer and a chill wind was blowing from the east, carrying the dank scent of the grave. The sky from horizon to horizon roiled with thick, purple-black clouds, spreading implacably westwards towards Khemri. At that moment, the radiance of his golden armour made him seem somehow small in comparison to the vast darkness that was arrayed against him, but he stared up at the gathering clouds with a grim sense of anticipation. He had been waiting for this day ever since his beloved wife had gone.

As the wind began to howl amid the crowded tombs, Alcadizzar made his way south, through the necropolis and across the low hills that separated the city of the dead from the great trade road. It was there that the sons of Khemri had chosen to make their stand against the coming night.

There were perhaps a thousand men, all told, armed with everything from spears to farmers' scythes. A few carried shields, but no more; it was unlikely that their gaunt frames could have borne the weight of armour in any case. Most were sick to one degree or another and the rest were beyond caring. Not a one of them expected to live out the day.

On the far side of the city, men and women with the strength to travel were still leaving the city, hoping to make it on foot all the way to Zandri, some two hundred leagues to the west. There had been rumours for weeks that ships were leaving with refugees, hoping to find safety in the far north. No one knew if the rumours were true, but a faint chance was better than no chance at all.

It was for the same reason that men clutched spear and axe and stood facing the darkness to the east. Every minute they stood and fought was a gift to those who sought succour in the west. It was little enough, they knew, but better that than nothing at all.

There were no cheers as the king and his servant arrived; no shaking of spears or clashing of shields. None of that mattered to Alcadizzar. It was enough that they had come to stand beside him, when all the others had fled. He stood before them, with the roiling darkness at his back, and lifted his sword to the sky.

'Woe to us that we have lived to see this day,' he said. 'Our strength is spent, and our hearts are broken. Nehekhara is no more.'

The king's voice carried clearly over the keening wind, and the men stirred from their reverie and listened. Some wept, knowing that the end had come.

'We go now into the dusk, where our ancestors await,' Alcadizzar said. 'Let it be written in the Book of Ages that when the world ended and darkness swallowed the land, the men of Khemri did not falter. No, they went into the night with spears in their hands, fighting to the last.'

The wind rose, as though in reply, howling like the spirits of the damned. Alcadizzar felt the cold breath of the grave upon his neck. He turned, and saw a wall of shadow rushing towards him like a desert storm.

'To the last!' he cried once more and then the light failed, and darkness swallowed the world.

Within the veil of shadow, the howling of the wind was dulled to a muted roar. Alcadizzar could dimly hear the shouts of the men behind him. 'Stand fast!' he cried, but he could not be sure if he was heard.

One moment stretched into another, as the wind roared, and the cold sank like knives into his skin. Faint points of light emerged out of the gloom; unblinking eyes of grave-light, glowing from sockets of bone. Ragged figures took shape, clad in scraps of armour and rotting cloth. They marched forwards in their thousands, clutching spears and cruel, tarnished blades.

The air above the undead seemed to shimmer. Moments later he heard the hiss of arrows flickering invisibly overhead. Men screamed in agony as they were struck; others cried out in terror and despair. Alcadizzar gripped his sword in both hands and shouted.

'For Khemri!' he cried, his voice muted by the shadows. 'For Nehekhara!' And then he charged, hurling himself into the arms of death.

Alcadizzar's sword made burning arcs in the darkness as he leapt at the army of the undead. He swept aside spear-points and hacked through armour and bone, severing arms and shattering ribcages. The skeletons he struck flared like banked coals for an instant and then collapsed lifelessly to the ground.

Onwards he went, driving deeper into the horde, not knowing or caring if his men followed him or not. He swung his blade wildly, connecting with two or three skeletons with every swing, waiting for the inevitable spear that would find a seam in his armour or pierce his exposed throat. But no such blow ever came. Indeed, not a single blow struck him at all. The skeletons recoiled from him as if afraid to strike him.

The king chased after them, slashing wildly. 'Fight me, damn you!' he shouted at them. He hacked through a skeleton's spear haft and severed its hand. 'This is what you came for, isn't it?'

He was growing weary now. His strength had fled him long ago, when his first son had died. Still he drove himself forwards, practically throwing himself upon the enemy's spears. 'What's the matter?' he cried, his voice breaking. 'Here I am! *Kill me!*'

But the enemy drew back from him, retreating away into the darkness as if in a dream. Alcadizzar screamed in despair, running after them, begging the spirits of the damned for release.

Suddenly, a tall, skeletal figure in bronze armour loomed out of the darkness, a black, double-edged sword in his hand. Cold radiated from the liche's body in waves, leeching all the heat from the king's wasted body.

Undaunted, Alcadizzar leapt at the liche, slashing at its torso. The undead monster blocked the stroke with ease, striking sparks from the flat of his iron blade. Shouting defiantly, Alcadizzar pressed his attack, chopping at the liche's head and neck, but each blow was turned aside. With the last of his fading strength, the king lunged, thrusting the chisel point of his sword at the monster's heart, but the liche was too fast for him. The iron blade swept down in a ringing parry that wrenched the glowing weapon from Alcadizzar's hands.

Stunned, the king fell forwards, right into the liche's grasp. A cold, armoured hand closed about his throat. Distantly, he could hear the screams of his men as they were overwhelmed by the undead.

The liche lifted Alcadizzar by the neck, until he could stare into the king's face. A ghastly laugh hissed between the monster's blackened teeth.

Alcadizzar struggled in the liche's grip. 'What are you waiting for?' he snarled. 'Go on! Kill me, and be damned!'

'*In time*,' Arkhan agreed. '*But not today, Alcadizzar of Khemri. My master wishes you to suffer a short while longer.*'

They stripped the king of his gleaming armour and cast his treasured sword into the sands. His hands were bound in chains of bronze and he was given into the keeping of a dozen wights, who locked him inside an enclosed palanquin made of polished bone. The last he saw of Khemri, its streets were teeming with corpses, and the living were being dragged from their homes and slain.

The palanquin was borne on the shoulders of a dozen skeletons, which carried him east through a silent, empty land. Time lost all meaning within the sorcerous gloom; Alcadizzar drifted in and out of consciousness, unable to say for certain whether it had been weeks or months since he'd first been taken. From time to time the palanquin would stop; bony fingers would seize his jaw and pour a trickle of fiery liquid down his throat. He coughed and sputtered, but the skeletons did not relent until they'd gotten some of the potion down his throat. Whatever it was, it nourished him enough to keep his emaciated body alive.

On and on they carried him, past the charnel house that had once been Quatar, and on into the Valley of Kings. Past silent Mahrak they went, and along the trade road to fallen Lahmia. They carried him through the Cursed City's broken gate and down to the docks, where once upon a time an old woman had told him of his fate and he'd chosen to hide from it instead.

The skeletons placed him on a ship of bone and took him north, up the narrow straits and into a dark and restless sea. In time, they beached upon a shore of broken stone and bore him across poisoned fields that reeked of burnt metal and bitter ash.

The further they went, the more that Alcadizzar felt the weight of an invisible presence studying him from the darkness. He could feel a malevolent intelligence scrutinising him, an implacable, hateful will that was both utterly alien and disturbingly human at the same time.

They passed through the gates of a vast fortress and into narrow lanes that led up the slopes of an ancient, desecrated mountain. Alcadizzar soon lost track of all the twists and turns that the skeletons took as they rose ever higher through the levels of the fortress. At one point they entered into an echoing, humid tunnel that led them deep into the heart of the mountain. Nagash's awareness – for the malevolent presence could be nothing else – grew steadily more intense, until Alcadizzar's nerves were raw with apprehension.

At last, when he thought he could stand it no more, he heard the groan of hinges and the grating of a pair of massive doors, and soon the hollow sound of skeletal feet marching down a long and echoing hall. Finally, the rocking movements ceased and he was lowered with a jarring thump that reverberated through the vaulted space beyond.

A key rattled in the palanquin's lock. The sliding panel was drawn aside and bony hands dragged him from his months-long prison. Agony flared from his cramped joints, wrenching a bitter cry from his parched throat. Green light seared his eyes. He blinked, but no tears would come.

Alcadizzar struggled in his captors' grip nonetheless. Without warning, they released him; his legs, weakened by captivity, betrayed him. He fell to the smooth, cold flagstones with a groan, shaking uncontrollably as his cramped muscles twisted into knots.

He lay there for an eternity, lost in suffering and shivering like a babe. And then a voice, jagged and rough like broken stone, sawed through his haze of pain.

'*Behold the usurper,*' said Nagash, the Undying King.

Nagash's prisoner was a pathetic wreck of a man: a pallid, trembling skeleton clad in filthy linen wrappings. Metal grated on metal as the Undying King rose to his feet and descended the steps of the dais. Nagash reached out with a gauntleted hand and seized the mortal by the throat, lifting him from the floor as though he weighed no more than a bundle of twigs.

'*You are the man who seized my throne and united the great cities against me?*' Nagash twisted the human this way and that, studying him like a piece of meat. '*I had expected better.*'

With a disdainful hiss, he tossed the mortal aside. Alcadizzar collapsed to the floor with a strangled groan, his body curling back again into a foetal ball. The liche-king chuckled, savouring his foe's pain.

'*Alcadizzar of Khemri, lord of a dead land,*' he declared. '*Does the title please you? It was yours, in truth, from the moment you chose to defy me.*'

Metal clattered softly as the Undying King clasped his gauntleted hands behind his back. He paced slow circles about Alcadizzar's trembling body, eyes burning with malice.

'*Nehekhara's fate was sealed the moment I was betrayed at Mahrak, centuries before you were born,*' Nagash told him. '*Though they drove me into the wasteland, I prevailed. Alone, I built a new empire, with a single purpose in mind: to take my revenge upon the great cities, and to enslave their people until the end of time.*'

With a disgusted hiss, Nagash dug the toe of his metal boot into Alcadizzar's shoulder and forced him onto his back. He leaned forwards, slowly increasing the pressure on the mortal's chest until his breath wheezed past his lips. Alcadizzar's eyes opened as he struggled for breath. Nagash fixed him with a mocking stare.

'Your victory at the Gates of the Dawn meant nothing,' he sneered. *'I sent my army to destroy Nehekhara only because I wanted the great cities to know that it was* I *who had brought them to ruin.'*

'That... explains... why we destroyed them... so easily,' Alcadizzar gasped. 'The... trade road was... littered with bones.'

Nagash glared down at the fallen king. *'Five hundred warriors, or five hundred thousand; it makes no difference to me.'* He leaned down, putting his full weight on the mortal's chest. *'I can make ten times that now. All of Nehekhara is mine to command.'*

Alcadizzar let out a strangled groan. After a moment, Nagash rose, and pulled back his foot.

'Tell me,' he said. *'Did you wonder, when your people sickened and died, why you alone managed to survive? When your wife and children writhed on their sickbeds, and begged you for release, did you pray to the forsaken gods that you would be next, if only to assuage the guilt that gnawed at your soul?'*

Nagash knelt and gripped Alcadizzar's jaw, squeezing his pallid flesh until the mortal's eyes snapped open again.

'You survived for no other reason than because I wished it,' the Undying King said. *'The doom I unleashed upon Nehekhara was aimed with care. Of all the living things that walked the land, I saw to it that you alone would be spared. I wanted you to watch everything you ever loved turn to dust. I wanted you to understand, most of all, how futile your struggles have been. You cannot defeat me, mortal. I am Nagash. I am eternal. And before you die, you will deliver your people into my hands.'*

Alcadizzar let out a choked growl, writhing in Nagash's grip. 'I'll die before I betray my people again.'

Nagash rested the tip of his clawed thumb against Alcadizzar's cheek, just beneath his eye. *'The choice is not yours to make,'* he said.

The last king of Khemri began to scream as Nagash carved the first ritual symbol into his skin.

A tower had been built at the summit of the mountain, taller and wider than any of the hundreds of spires that towered over Nagashizzar. Potent necromantic runes had been carved into its walls, both inside and out, spiralling upwards to join with the complex summoning circle that had been laid out in molten silver across the tower's flat top.

On the night of the new moon, Nagash ascended to the top of the tower with Alcadizzar and three wights in tow. In his hands he clutched the glowing sphere of *abn-i-khat* that had rested at the foot of his throne for hundreds of years. At long last, its purpose would be fulfilled.

A restless wind moaned above the high tower and the clouds above were depthless and dark. The pulsing radiance of the burning stone spilled across the curving lines of silver and lent them an ominous, squirming life.

Nagash stepped to the centre of the circle and knelt, placing the sphere within a bowl-shaped depression in the stone. Two of the wights crossed to the far side of the circle, dragging Alcadizzar's semi-conscious form between them. The mortal's body was a raw wound, carved with hundreds of arcane symbols from his forehead to the tops of his feet.

The wights lowered Alcadizzar to his knees at the edge of the circle, at a spot where the major lines of the sigil met. Nagash rose and crossed the circle to join them.

'*Now comes your true moment of glory,*' Nagash said, glaring mockingly at the king. '*For you will be the key to awaken not just those who died of the plague, or at the hand of my warriors, but Nehekharans who have slept in their tombs for millennia, even unto great Settra himself.*' The Undying King held out his hand, and one of the wights handed him a long silver needle. Nagash studied it for a moment and then drove it deep into the juncture of the mortal's neck and torso. Alcadizzar stiffened in pain, the muscles of his body going rigid as stone.

'*The art of magic – even necromancy – is about symbols,*' Nagash said, as the wight handed him another needle. '*Symbols form connections, tying one concept to another. And the more powerful the symbol, the greater its potential effects.*'

Alcadizzar hissed sharply as the second needle slid into the other side of his neck.

'*I do not want to merely animate the bones of our people, you see. I intend to summon back their spirits and bind them to their remains, as I have done to my servant Arkhan, and bind them to me forever. But such a monumental effort requires a uniquely resonant symbol to focus the ritual's power. A symbol such as the ruler of the Nehekharan empire, to whom all the land – living and dead – must offer their fealty.*'

All was in readiness. Nagash took his place at the opposite side of the circle. The wights withdrew, disappearing into the tower.

The Undying King raised his arms in triumph to the suffocating sky. '*Perhaps you will live long enough to see your wife and children again,*' he said. '*If I find her pleasing enough, perhaps I shall take your woman as my consort.*'

Alcadizzar howled in helpless fury as the great ritual began.

'It's been going on like this for days!' Eshreegar shouted over the raging wind. Lightning rent the sky above the mountain, briefly illuminating the master assassin's anxious face. He pointed up to the top of the great tower, just across the narrow courtyard where he and Eekrit crouched. 'Nagash went up there with his prisoner on the night of the new-new moon, and he's been there ever since!'

Eekrit gripped his cloak tightly about his chest and scowled up at the top of the tower. It was bathed in a nimbus of green light so intense that it lit the underside of the boiling clouds overhead. Thunder crashed, rolling like an avalanche down the narrow lanes of the fortress. The former warlord cursed, ears folded back against his skull.

Eshreegar seemed unmoved by the tumult. 'You see that door at the base of-of the tower?' he shouted. 'It leads to a chamber with a black altar. Greenskins are being dragged up from the mines and sacrificed *every hour.* This is worse than anything we've seen before!'

Eekrit turned his scowl onto Eshreegar. 'That much is clear,' he snarled. 'But what in the Horned God's name do you expect me to do about it?'

'Velsquee's chest! We should open the chest!'

The former warlord growled under his breath and glanced once more up at the tower. His tail lashed apprehensively. 'No! Not yet!'

'Can you think of a better time than now?' the Master of Treacheries exclaimed.

Eekrit jabbed a claw at the maelstrom up above. 'Preferably when he's not capable of doing things like *that*,' he snapped.

Eshreegar frowned worriedly, but he didn't try to argue. 'You think we should let him finish whatever he's doing?'

'You honestly think we can stop him?' Eekrit shot back. He shook his head. 'No. We wait until he's done. Until he's got nothing left.'

'And then?'

Eekrit cast one more glance up at the churning, green-lit clouds, before heading for the mouth of the tunnel that would carry them back to the under-fortress.

'Then we open the damned box,' he growled.

It was like forging a chain. Day by day, night by night, shaping one unbreakable link at a time.

The incantation was the longest, most complex ritual Nagash had ever performed. Centuries had gone into perfecting the invocations and bindings contained within. The last, most crucial piece of the puzzle had eluded him for ages, until Alcadizzar had provided him with the answer. It was an irony he would savour long after the fallen king was gone.

The ashen wind howled above the tower, forming a whirling, lightning-ravaged funnel over the ritual circle. The storm had grown steadily since the ritual began, fuelled by the power of the incantation until it spread westwards across the length and breadth of Nehekhara. It was the harbinger of the great ritual, the vehicle by which Nagash's summons would reach across the dead land.

At the centre of the circle, the great sphere of burning stone was all but gone, its composition altered by Nagash's will into a glittering black dust that rose in a long, whirling tendril up into the maw of the storm. Barely a pebble-sized fragment of the *abn-i-khat* remained and it was vanishing steadily before his eyes. For weeks, the storm had carried the black dust across the dead land, where it had sought out the corpses in the streets and in the tombs of the silent necropolis.

Across the circle, Alcadizzar rested on his knees, locked in place by Nagash's paralysing needles and the power of the great ritual. His eyes were open, staring up into the whirling wind tunnel. Green light seethed within their depths. The Undying King wondered what vast and awful vistas the mortal looked upon. Did he stare across the gulf, searching for his wife and children in the twilit realm of the dead?

Nagash could sense the spirits gathering on the other side of the veil. They were drawn by the bond of fealty they owed to Alcadizzar, the first link of the necromantic chain Nagash had forged. When Sakhmet rose in a few hours and usurped Neru's place in the heavens, he would draw that chain taut, and draw the spirits of uncounted ages back into the living world.

Raw power flowed into the Undying King from the sacrificial altar at the base of the ritual tower. The life energy of the greenskins had sustained him during the month-long incantation, adding to the enormous quantities of burning stone he had consumed before the ritual began. The incantation consumed energy at a fearsome rate, far more than his calculations had suggested. At this stage, with the most demanding part of the rite about to begin, his reserves of energy were almost completely gone. Every mote of power he gained from the black altar was consumed almost from the moment he received it.

With a crackling hiss, the last of the burning stone blackened and flew up into the air. Within hours, it would be settling in some distant corner of Nehekhara, just as the sun dipped below the horizon. It was all coming together precisely as he'd ordained.

Soon, Nehekhara would rise again. The kings of ages past would gather at Nagashizzar and bend their knee before the throne of Nagash, and darkness would descend upon the world forevermore.

Night fell across Nehekhara. Neru rose in the east, ever following in the footsteps of her husband, Ptra. Sakhmet, the jealous concubine, followed at her shoulder, burning green with envy.

Upon the ritual tower, the final phase of the incantation began. Buoyed by the stolen life energies of his greenskin slaves, Nagash clenched his fists and spat words of power at the sky. The storm raged above his head, howling like the souls of the damned.

Layer by layer, he could feel the veil between the realms grow thin. The chain was complete, starting with Alcadizzar and linking to the motes of dust spread across Nehekhara, then leading back to the circle of silver and Nagash's crown. As Sakhmet rose in the night sky, the Undying King began to draw that chain tight, pulling at the spirits of the dead.

Hour after hour, as the Green Witch crept closer to Ptra's loyal wife, the tension on the sorcerous chain grew tighter. The power of the ritual spread throughout the dead land, from the narrow streets of cursed Lahmia, to the cold forges of Ka-Sabar and the empty docks of Zandri. It reached into the dark crypts, settling upon the cerement-wrapped corpses of beggars and kings alike. Ancient limbs trembled, stirring the dust of ages.

Nagash's voice rose as the ritual neared its climax, the Undying King staring upward through the whirling funnel of cloud to the clear sky beyond. Neru was directly overhead, and Sakhmet was just behind her, moments from seizing the goddess by the throat. Exultant, he shouted the closing phrases of the incantation to the Green Witch, high above.

'*Let the veil of ages fall away!*' the Undying King commanded. '*Let the dark lands give up the lost! Let the dust fall from the eyes of the kings and of the heroes, and of the queens sealed within their tombs! Let the people cross the threshold of night and return to the lands of the living! Let them rise from their beds of stone! Rise! I command it! Rise, and serve your master! Nagash, the Undying King, commands it! RISE!*'

Lightning cracked like a slave master's whip, lashing at the silver lines of the magic circle. Thunder pealed, shaking the tower to its foundations. Nagash poured the last of his power into the storm; the wind rose in pitch and the trapped cyclone broke free at last, recoiling violently into the sky. Nagash stood unshaken amid the maelstrom, roaring his triumph at the sky.

Already, he could sense the first, tentative tugs at his awareness as the dead of Nehekhara began to open their eyes.

The first to stir were those whom Arkhan's warriors had slain. From the blood-spattered collegia at Lybaras, to the fields outside Khemri and beyond, the bodies of the last Nehekharans began to move. Heads turned, glowing green eyes looking eastwards as though in response to some distant summons. Groans leaked from rotting throats as the dead lurched clumsily onto their feet in answer to Nagash's call.

These corpses were quickly joined by others, clawing their way out of barricaded homes or from the loose, sandy soil of mass graves that surrounded nearly every one of the great cities. Men, women and children, struck down in their tens of thousands by Nagash's plague, broke free of their makeshift tombs and emerged into the night.

In the great necropoli, dead hands beat at stone lids and mausoleum doors. Dust billowed from the entrances of the mighty pyramids as the great kings and their retinues woke from centuries of slumber. They rode from their crypts on chariots of gold, drawn by teams of skeletal horses, surrounded by entire armies of faithful warriors who had gone into the tomb to serve their masters in the afterlife. Retinues of shrivelled liche priests followed in the wake of each royal chariot, bearing the canopic jars of their monarch and chanting invocations of power to speed his journey to the east.

Beneath Sakhmet's baleful glare, the great cities of Nehekhara gave up their dead. Tormented howls and groans of rage rose into the still air as beggars and kings alike struggled in vain against the sorcerous chains that bound them. Nagash commanded them, and they had no choice but to obey.

Tireless and implacable, the dead of Nehekhara made their way eastwards through the night. The greatest army the world had ever seen began to converge on distant Nagashizzar.

Above the great fortress, the whirling tunnel of cloud collapsed in upon itself, swallowing Sakhmet's light and plunging Nagashizzar into darkness. Off to the north-west, packs of flesh-eaters howled exultantly in the night.

Nagash had fallen silent at last. Faintly glowing smoke leaked from every seam of his enchanted armour. At the very last, the ritual had nearly undone him; it had taken almost every last mote of power he possessed, but in the end, he had triumphed. He could feel the risen spirits of Nehekhara surging like a dark tide across the land, moving in answer to his summons. At long last, his vengeance was complete.

The Undying King lowered his eyes to regard Alcadizzar. The green light had faded from the mortal's eyes, leaving only emptiness in its wake. Nagash approached the fallen king and gripped the first of the silver needles. A faint tremor through the metal spoke of a pulse and told him that, somehow, the last king of Khemri yet lived.

Nagash withdrew first one needle, then the other. Alcadizzar's body collapsed bonelessly onto the stones. The Undying King studied the wretch for a moment, tempted to consume the last of Alcadizzar's life force and leave his body to rot atop the tower. He raised his smoking hand, clawed fingers clenching into a fist, but at the last moment he decided to spare the last living Nehekharan instead. So long as Alcadizzar lived, he might still provide some sport, once Nagash had regained a modicum of his power.

The Undying King turned as the trio of wights emerged from the depths of the tower. With a thought, he ordered Alcadizzar thrown into a dungeon cell, and then departed, making his way back to his throne room. There he would wait, slowly regaining his strength, until the first of his undead subjects arrived.

Eekrit sat at the edge of his throne with a wine bowl in his paw. After so many weeks of raging wind and groaning earth, the silence in the great hall was eerie and oppressive. Before him, upon the dais, sat Velsquee's lead box.

'Well?' Eshreegar said, breaking the silence. 'What are you waiting for?'

The former warlord scratched at his chin. The very sight of the box filled him with a sense of foreboding. 'We've got no idea what's inside this thing,' he said.

'Velsquee said it was a weapon, didn't he?' the Master of Treacheries said. 'A weapon made especially to kill Nagash.'

Eekrit sipped his wine thoughtfully. 'That's what worries me,' he replied. 'If what's in that box can kill Nagash, what in the Horned God's name will it do to *us*?'

Eshreegar's one eye widened. 'I... hadn't considered that.' He covered his snout with one paw. 'What are we going to do?' he groaned.

Eekrit glared at the chest. After a moment, he raised the wine bowl and drained it to the dregs, then tossed it over his shoulder.

'We're going to do what any skaven would,' he said. 'We're going to find someone else to do the dirty work for us.'

Alcadizzar lay in darkness, waiting to die.

He did not know where he was, or how he'd come to be there. His awareness had taken shape very slowly, seeping in from the edges of his fractured mind. With it came memories of grief and a sense of loss too great to endure. The pain of it all cut into him like a dull knife, digging into his vitals inch by relentless inch, until he thought his heart would burst.

Slowly, he became aware of a soft, white light filling the narrow cell. A figure knelt beside him, just beyond the edge of his vision. And then from the depths of his pain, Alcadizzar felt a gentle hand touch his cheek.

Tears welled up in his eyes. 'Khalida?' he whispered. He struggled to move, his hands slipping on the cell's slimy floor. With an effort, he moved his head and tried to peer up into the face of the person beside him. The nimbus of white light made it difficult to see details, but he could make out the fall of dark hair and the slope of a woman's shoulder.

Alcadizzar lifted a trembling hand, trying to touch her. At once, the apparition withdrew. With a despairing cry, he tried to follow, drawing his knees up beneath him and weakly pushing himself upright.

The apparition had retreated across the cell, until she stood next to the heavy wooden door. Alcadizzar tried to crawl over to her, but before he had the chance, there was the grating of metal as an ancient lock was turned and the cell door groaned open.

Two short, furtive creatures shuffled into the room, dragging a heavy, rectangular chest between them. They took no notice of the apparition whatsoever, focusing their beady eyes solely upon him. Alcadizzar blinked in the uncertain light, trying to make sense of the strange figures. They looked like two enormous rats, clad in filthy robes and walking upright like men. He looked to the apparition for guidance, but the indistinct figure only watched in silence.

The ratmen laid the chest on the floor of the cell and, with great trepidation, they set about breaking the seals that held it shut. They looked at one another uneasily, then without a word they drew back the lid of the box and took several quick steps backwards.

As the lid flew open, a terrible light filled the room – it was a kind of poisonous greenish-black, and gave off heat like the touch of sunlight. The terrible glow radiated from a weapon of sorts: a crude-looking, single-edged sword with a curved blade and long hilt that would just barely take a pair of human hands. Strange runes had been etched along its length and it had been crafted out of a mottled, greenish-grey metal unlike anything Alcadizzar had seen before. It was also deadlier than anything he'd ever known. The sword *radiated* death. It was the kind of weapon that could kill a god.

Or an Undying King.

Alcadizzar's eyes rose from the sword and regarded the apparition. He could not say why, but it seemed as though she was waiting for him.

And then he understood. She wanted him to take up the sword. Khalida was giving him a chance to make things right before it was too late.

With a deep breath, Alcadizzar reached into the chest. The hilt of the sword was hot to the touch and caused his hand to tingle painfully as he took hold of it and lifted the blade free. Heat, prickly and unpleasant, flooded his limbs, filling his muscles with strength.

Alcadizzar turned to the apparition. 'I'm ready,' he said, accepting his fate at last.

The apparition slipped silently through the doorway. He followed after, determined to redeem himself in the eyes of his beloved.

Eekrit and Eshreegar watched the human race from the cell, sword in hand. They turned to one another with identical looks of surprise.

'Who was he talking to?' Eshreegar asked.

'Who knows?' Eekrit replied. 'You saw his face. He's mad as a white rat.'

'Do you think he knows where he's going?' the Master of Treacheries said. 'We'd best follow along and make sure.'

Nagash lay shrouded in deep shadow, resting like a corpse upon his dark throne. The flames that normally wreathed his skull had been extinguished; his burning eyes had shrunken to cold sparks glowing from the depths of his eye sockets. His mind had slipped into a near trancelike state, pulled into millions of tiny fragments by the souls he'd bound to his will.

Already he was looking ahead to what he would do with the undead legions at his command. They would scour the land from north to south, killing every human, greenskin and rat-creature no matter where they tried to hide. Then he would turn his attentions to the east, and amuse himself with the destruction of the Silk Lands. When they were dead, he would continue eastwards, searching out the living and destroying them, until at last he came round again to Nagashizzar, and the entire world had been rendered as lifeless as a tomb. It might take a thousand years, or ten thousand. It mattered not to him.

As he brooded, a dim, white radiance took shape at the far end of the hall. At first, Nagash thought it was one of his wights, but as it came closer, he saw with surprise that it had the figure of a woman. The sight bemused him and he tried to focus his dulled senses upon it.

Slowly but surely, the image grew clearer. Details emerged. Dark hair, and pale skin. Eyes like polished emeralds, and the golden headdress of a queen.

Nagash tried to stir, but his limbs felt like lead. '*Neferem,*' he hissed.

The ancient Queen of Khemri drew nearer. She was not the withered husk that she had been when he'd sacrificed her at Mahrak, but the radiant beauty that he'd first seen on the day of his brother's ascension. The sight of her sent a chill along his bones.

'*You are bound to me once more,*' the Undying King said. '*Even now, your bones shamble across the desert to bow at my feet.*'

Neferem reached the bottom of the dais and raised her chin defiantly. *I have no bones for you to command, usurper,* she said. *They were burned to ash when you broke the sacred covenant at Mahrak. You have no power over me.*

'*Then I will bind your spirit instead,*' he snarled. '*I am like unto a god now. All of Nehekhara bows its head to me.*'

To his surprise, Neferem smiled coldly and shook her head.

All but one.

And then the apparition vanished, scattering like smoke before the onrushing figure of Alcadizzar, last king of Khemri. Bellowing with rage, the mortal charged up the stone steps with a glowing sword in hand and brought it down upon Nagash's skull.

Fear and rage galvanised the Undying King. At the last moment he brought up his arm to ward off the deadly blow, catching the sword against his armoured wrist. Instead of turning the blade aside however, there was a flash of searing green light, and the sword's edge bit clean though metal and bone, severing the hand with one blow. It fell to the dais, its clawed fingers twitching spasmodically.

Nagash shrieked in agony. The fell blade's power clawed at his bones. For the first time in ages, the spectre of death sent a chill down his spine.

Yet even in his weakened state, Nagash was not completely without power. As Alcadizzar drew back his sword for another blow, the Undying King raised his other hand and spat sulphurous words of power. Fearsome energies leapt from his fingertips, bathing the mortal's body in jagged arcs of fire that would strip the flesh from his bones in an instant.

But the sorcerous bolts washed harmlessly over Alcadizzar, deflected by runes of protection forged into the glowing sword. Undaunted, he lunged forwards, shearing the blade through Nagash's ribs and severing his spine.

Nagash screamed in pain and terror. The sword's unnatural energies leached the very power from his bones. Already, he could feel his strength ebbing away. Cursing, he lunged forwards with his one remaining hand and seized Alcadizzar by the throat.

The mortal king struggled in Nagash's grip. Blood flowed freely down his neck where Nagash's claws bit deep into his skin. The Undying King put all of his remaining strength into his fingers, trying to crush Alcadizzar's spine.

Alcadizzar's knees began to buckle. His eyelids fluttered. But just when it seemed that he was about to fall, he raised his sword with the last of his failing strength and brought it down on Nagash's arm. The fell blade sliced through the armour, severing the arm at the elbow – then a backhand stroke slashed across Nagash's neck, severing his head.

A hideous, rending scream echoed through the hall. The last thing Nagash saw, as the fires faded from his eyes, was the ghostly apparition of Neferem standing at the foot of the dais. Her smile was terrible to behold.

Darkness waits, she said.

Nagash's death reverberated through the aether like the tolling of a broken bell. The power of his ritual shattered, sending shockwaves through the legions of the dead. Thousands of corpses collapsed to the earth, their spirits drawn back once more across the veil of death. These were the souls of those who had died during the days of the plague and the bloodshed afterwards, who had been buried without the customary rituals of the mortuary cult.

The rest ground slowly to a halt, no longer at the mercy of Nagash's implacable summons. They had been restored to the living world, and now were free to act as they pleased.

The great tomb kings reined in their golden chariots and surveyed the empty land around them. Their burning gaze fell upon the legions of the dead. Without hesitation, the corpses bowed before their masters, responding to ancient loyalties that had guided them in life.

Some kings commanded more loyalty than others. The strong eyed the weak and ancient ambitions once more occupied their thoughts.

Skeletal hands gripped tarnished khopeshes and raised them to the baleful moon. Bone horns wailed as the tomb kings went to war.

Metal rang on metal, striking fat, green sparks as Alcadizzar hacked at Nagash's still form. The burning fell blade hacked through the Undying King's armour, tearing the ancient skeleton to pieces and hacking up the wooden throne beneath.

Finally, his body spent, Alcadizzar stumbled back a step and looked upon the carnage he'd wrought. His hands were numb and tingling from the awful energy of the sword, as though its power had seeped into his body like poison. Repelled by its corrupting touch, Alcadizzar let the blade tumble from his hand.

'It's done,' he gasped. 'Thank the gods, it's done.' He looked about, searching for the apparition. 'Khalida?' he called. 'Beloved? Where are you?'

He had to find her. He had to show her what he'd done. More than anything, he needed her to forgive him. Alcadizzar cast about looking for something he could show her, to convince her that he'd made things right. His gaze fell upon Nagash's grinning skull.

Alcadizzar bent and tore the jagged metal crown from Nagash's skull. Gripping it to his chest, he turned and staggered from the dais. The blade's poison was working its way through his body, killing him from within.

'Khalida!' he called mournfully. 'Forgive me. Please.' Clutching the crown of the Undying King, Alcadizzar staggered from the great hall.

EPILOGUE

LAND OF THE DEAD

Nagashizzar,
in the 110th year of Djaf the Terrible
(-1151 Imperial Reckoning)

Alcadizzar haunted the halls of Nagashizzar for days, calling plaintively for a woman that only he could see. His mind shattered by guilt and the torments he'd suffered at the hands of Nagash, he eventually found his way through the fortress gates and onto the shores of the Sour Sea. Still clutching Nagash's crown, the last king of Khemri disappeared into the wastelands in search of redemption.

There are those who believe he wanders there still.

They searched the fortress for the largest furnace they could find and filled it with charcoal from the enormous bins that stood outside the forges. Eshreegar and Eekrit took turns working the bellows, until the fire breathed like a living thing and the heat scorched their whiskers. Then they went and raided the nearest mine shaft for all the sky-stone they could carry.

'Are you sure this is necessary?' the Master of Treacheries said.

'Without doubt,' Eekrit said, tossing a hunk of sky-stone into the furnace.

Eshreegar winced. 'Think of the wealth you're throwing away! Enough to buy your way back into good graces with the Under-Empire three times over! Enough to make yourself a Grey Lord if you wish!'

Another chunk of stone flew into the furnace's roaring maw. 'The mountain is mine now, Eshreegar,' the former warlord growled. '*All mine.* At this point, I'm richer than the Horned God himself.'

The Master of Treacheries eyed the flames dubiously. 'What if Velsquee goes back on his word and forgets he ever agreed to give you the mountain?'

Eekrit sniffed. 'He can either have the mountain or the fell blade. Not both.' They had recovered the sword and tossed it back into its lead container with as little physical contact as possible. Now it was hidden deep within the bowels of the mountain, where only the two of them would ever find it. 'If he's smart, he'll take the blade back and call it even, and Velsquee is nothing if not very, very smart.' He threw another two pieces of stone into the furnace, then gestured at the bellows. 'Stoke the furnace while I get the cart.'

Eshreegar sighed and went to the long, wooden lever. With a grunt, he leapt up and grabbed it, then pulled down with all his weight. Air flowed into the furnace, causing it to roar. Within minutes, the sky-stone turned molten and the heat within changed from orange-white to a bright, baleful green.

Eekrit returned a moment later, dragging a small wooden cart. Piled within was every piece of Nagash's armour and bone they could find. The former warlord stared down at the remains and shook his head. 'I still don't see how we missed his right hand. It couldn't have just crawled off on its own.'

Eshreegar shook his head. 'We searched every inch of that dais. If it were there, we would have found it. Nagash's prisoner must have taken it with him, along with the crown. Nothing else makes sense.'

Eekrit sighed irritably. 'Perhaps.' He reached in and rummaged through the pile.

'Do you really think this will destroy him for good?' Eshreegar asked, eyeing the roaring furnace.

'I have no idea,' Eekrit replied. 'This is for my own personal pleasure.'

He grunted in satisfaction, and pulled Nagash's grinning skull from the pile. Eekrit stared at it for a long moment, peering into the depths of its empty eye sockets.

'I've been wanting to do this for a very long time,' he said, and tossed the skull into the flames.

High above the ancient mountain, a plume of faintly glowing smoke rose from one of the fortress's many chimneys. Ashes from the seething fire below rose into the air and were scattered on the high winds, spreading across the bleak and blasted land.

Riding high on the swift-moving wind, the ashes travelled for miles before falling back to earth. One mote in particular rode the currents westwards, tumbling through the updraughts over the Brittle Peaks and then gliding lazily downwards again in a long, surprisingly straight path along the bloody line of the dead River Vitae.

Over the silent land of Nehekhara, the tiny mote of ash drifted, until it came to the vast city of the dead that lay beside the river just east of Khemri. There it began to settle, waving this way and that like a leaf on the breeze, until at last it alighted upon the tip of a towering black pyramid, whose matt black sides seemed to swallow the light of the sun.

By some curious trick of the air currents, the mote of ash was drawn inside the pyramid, slipping through narrow airshafts until it reached the very heart of the giant crypt. There, in an octagonal chamber whose walls were carved with hundreds of complex runes, sat an open sarcophagus of black stone.

Silent, unobserved, the mote of ash settled within the sarcophagus of Nagash, the Undying King.

And there it waited.

PICKING THE BONES

For days, Nehekara had been shrouded in gloom. Clouds of ash and the dust of broken tombs had been drawn up into the air by the power of Nagash's ritual, blotting out the light of sun and moons alike. Summoned by the will of the Undying King, the risen dead had marched towards Nagashizzar beneath a veil of never-ending darkness.

At the time, riding out from Khemri with countless thousands of revenants at his back, Arkhan had turned his burning gaze to the clouds and imagined them continuing to spread, seeping like a great stain across the face of the entire world. Nagash's final victory was at hand, and the days of the living were numbered.

So it had seemed. But then the unthinkable occurred.

Now the mantle of cloud was roiling like an angry sea, churned by a bitter wind blowing from the desert to the south. The great pall of darkness was ebbing slowly, creeping eastward like an outgoing tide. The great ritual had been undone. Arkhan had felt his master's demise, as had every one of the risen corpses across the land. The fact of it had been seared into his bones.

Arkhan did not care how it had happened, or why. All that mattered now was reaching Nagashizzar, and claiming all that remained.

The liche rode north and east through the barren foothills of the Brittle Peaks, making for the river of blood as fast as his skeletal horse could carry him. Nine black-armoured wights galloped in his wake. They were all that remained of the hundred that had ridden into Khemri with him, just a few months before. The others – along with the rest of his army – had been sacrificed on the Great Trade Road to buy his escape. From the flashes of green light that lit the undersides of the clouds, and the brittle thunder of detonations to the south, the fighting had yet to abate.

The dark riders galloped across a stretch of treacherous, rocky flatland, then reached the base of another low, rounded hill. Arkhan hissed, gripping the reins and putting his heels to the horse's flanks, as if the mount still had flesh and nerves to respond to his urgings. The undead horse lunged up the slope, sinew creaking and heavy bones knocking hollowly together. Though slower than living horses, the undead creatures were tireless and strong. Arkhan had ridden day and night, racing the receding gloom, and meant to keep on going until their hooves splintered and their leg bones split. Quatar and the Gates of the Dead were closed to him, so he would have to take the longer, more circuitous route through the wasteland north and east of the great river. That would give the forces east of the Brittle Peaks a sizeable lead in the race to the fortress.

The army that Arkhan had led from Nagashizzar many months before had been far smaller than the mighty invasion force he had commanded against Alcadizaar: barely sixty thousand strong, and composed of spearmen, archers and swift-moving cavalry. He had been compelled to divide the force even further once it had reached Lahmia. Nagash's orders had been explicit: slaughter the last survivors of the Nehekaran people and capture Alcadizaar within six months, and return the defeated king to Nagashizzar before the new moon of the seventh. And so, from Lahmia, he'd despatched two of his lieutenants and twenty thousand warriors to head southwest, to wipe out the last dregs of humanity in the plague-ravaged cities of Lybaras and Rasetra. Then, at Quatar, after passing the ruins of Mahrak and scouring the Valley of Kings, Arkhan had sent another lieutenant and ten thousand warriors south to wipe out the desert dwellers at Bhagar and the city of Ka-Sabar. At Khemri, once Alcadizaar's pitiful army had been destroyed, a fourth lieutenant had taken ten thousand warriors north to destroy Numas, and then two smaller detachments were sent south and west to deal with Bel Aliad and Zandri by the sea. He'd heard nothing from his subordinates since then, but had no reason to believe that they had failed in their tasks. Now he imagined every one of them doing just the same as he: racing across the empty land, avoiding the wrath of the risen priest kings where they could, and thinking of the power now left unguarded at the Undying King's mountain fortress.

Hooves drumming the dead earth, the dark riders crested the hill. On the far side was a long, gentle slope, and beyond, perhaps a mile or so away, was the dark ribbon of the great river.

Arkhan and his bodyguard pressed on, their mounts gathering speed as they swept down the rocky slope. As he went, he studied the horizon to the north and west, looking for telltales of battle, or the dust trail of an army on the march. If the force sent to Numas had survived, it stood to reason that it would be following much the same course as he. But try as he might, Arkhan's burning gaze could not penetrate the gloom that lingered past the river's opposite bank.

The wide river shone a glossy black in the darkness. Once the source of all life in Nehekara, now the River Vitae ran red and thick as clotting blood. Arkhan urged his mount to greater speed, spurring it not with his heels now, but the lash of his will. The wights flogged their horses as well, filling the air with their wailing cries.

The dark riders thundered down the slope. As they approached the turgid waters, Arkhan raised a bony fist and began to chant. The invocation hissed past his jagged teeth, calling to the magic coursing through the aether. The skeletal horses leapt ahead, their hooves flashing over the dusty ground. Faster and faster they went, and the spaces between hoofbeats lengthened, until they scarcely touched the earth at all.

In moments, the dark riders reached the foot of the slope and onto the reeking bank of the river. Still gathering speed, the horses plunged into the river – but instead of sinking, they seemed to glide across the surface of the poisoned water. Their hoofbeats left curls of glistening vapour in their wake. Swift as a loosed arrow, light as the desert wind, the dark riders crossed the wide river in a matter of moments.

Arkhan reined in his mount on the far bank. The liche slumped in the saddle, his senses reeling. The invocation had been something of an improvisation on his part, and the strain had been profound. His wight bodyguards formed a protective ring about him, their glowing eyes searching the shadows along the hillsides to the north.

The liche allowed himself a few moments to regain his wits before pressing on. Silence stretched upon the riverbank. Far in the distance, a jackal howled in the wastes.

There was a faint creak of sinew. One of the wights stirred slightly, its skull turning to the northwest. Arkhan was alert in an instant. With a thought, he focused on the wight and saw through its eyes.

For several moments, there was nothing to see. Arkhan grew puzzled, unsure what the wight thought it had seen. But just as he was about to draw back, the shadows along the hilltop seemed to ripple.

Arkhan hissed a furious curse, his bony hand reaching for the iron sword at his hip as the first arrows went flitting past.

The enemy broke from the hillside shadows with the first volley: a score of skeletal horse archers, garbed in the black leather armour of Nagashizzar. The revenants fired as they rode, sending a steady rain of black shafts sleeting through the circle of dark riders.

Snarling, Arkhan wheeled his horse about. An arrow thudded into the saddle, just behind his hip, while another blurred past less than a finger length from his eyes. He felt one of his wights take an arrow through the arm; another was struck in the side. The liche flung out his hand and sent a volley of his own howling through the oncoming horsemen. Three of the horse archers were torn apart by a stream of fiery darts, sending glowing fragments of bone tumbling over the ground.

More arrows snapped through the air in reply, but by then the dark riders were on the move, galloping upslope into the hills to the northeast. Arkhan fought to contain his fury. The horse archers were skirmishers, likely covering the flank of a larger force – the detachment from Numas, or possibly Zandri – just beyond the hills to the north. And now their master knew exactly where he was.

Arkhan crested the hill just ahead of his bodyguards. On the far side, the hill descended into a winding gully, thick with shadow. Already, the liche could hear faint sounds of pursuit echoing from beyond the hills to the northwest, as more skeletal horsemen joined in the hunt. With the river to his right, the only direction he could go was north and east, which made the enemy's task that much easier. But the skeletons were not infallible; if he moved fast and used the gullies to his advantage, there was still a chance of escape.

Once again, the liche began to chant. The aether was still suffused with necromantic power in the wake of Nagash's ritual, but the torrent of energy was difficult to control. The invocation was not as well contained as before, sending waves of agony coursing through his skeletal frame, but it was enough. The dark riders' undead steeds raced ahead, coursing like quicksilver down the narrow path. The pursuing riders vanished from sight.

Arkhan sustained the incantation as long as he dared, until it felt as though his bones would splinter from the strain. The riders wound about the feet of the low hills, working their way alternately north and east in hopes of throwing the enemy off their trail and forcing them to abandon their pursuit.

But the dark riders' respite was short-lived. Soon the hills echoed with the clatter of hooves as more and more enemy cavalry units joined in the hunt. Arkhan listened to the sounds of pursuit and tried to puzzle out their relative positions. As far as he could tell, the hunters were spread out in a rough semicircle some two miles across and perhaps a mile or so behind him. All it would take would be for one enemy rider to spot them, and the semicircle would start to close around them like a pair of jaws. They had to stay ahead of the cordon and keep to cover, or all was lost.

For two more miles, their luck held. Arkhan followed one narrow hill-path after another – until, without warning, the riders emerged from a steep-sided gully into a wide, sloping plain several miles across. The north edge of the plain was bounded by a tall, rocky hill, while to the south the liche saw only broken, treacherous ground that sloped steeply back towards the river. Off to the east, perhaps two miles distant, the hills crowded in again, forming a valley that rose up and out of sight.

Arkhan snarled a curse. Two miles, and no cover – a bad proposition, to be sure, but there wasn't a better one to be had. Hissing between his teeth, he led his wights onto the plain and then began to chant.

Almost at once he found himself struggling with the incantation. The energies of the spell twisted in his grasp like an adder, threatening to destroy him, but he would not relent. Heat began to build along his bones like irons held in a fire, but, step by step, the horses began to pick up speed. Within moments, the riders were flying across the plain.

The valley drew nearer. Arkhan's bones sizzled. Wisps of foul-smelling smoke seeped from the seams in his armour. The agony was terrible, but he would not relent. Each second carried them further to their goal.

They were only a few hundred yards from the mouth of the valley when the enemy found them. There were no shouts of triumph, or braying of horns; simply a swelling rumble of hooves behind the dark riders as more and more of the pursuing cavalry poured eagerly onto the plain.

Arkhan could feel his concentration slipping. More and more power was leaking past the edges of the spell and scorching his body and soul. It felt as though his bones might fly apart at any moment. He held the incantation together for two seconds more, then relinquished his grip. The change in speed was sudden and dramatic, but just a moment later the dark riders entered the mouth of the valley and once more vanished from sight.

Once inside, Arkhan saw that the valley curved slightly northward and appeared to narrow at its far end. Past that, they would have more options, more opportunities to throw the enemy off their trail. Or so the liche chose to believe.

The undead horses lunged up the slope, their hooves kicking up thick plumes of sand and dust. Arkhan knew that the enemy would be pushing their own mounts for all they were worth, trying to catch sight of him again. It would all come down to a matter of seconds, he thought. Part of him was tempted to try the incantation again, but he knew that he'd already pushed his luck too far. Another attempt could well destroy him. Yet would that be any worse than what would happen if the enemy caught him?

Arkhan weighed the risks. It proved to be his undoing.

He did not see the enemy soldiers until it was far too late. Ranks of spearmen waited at the valley's narrow end, closing it off completely. Their shields and their tattered rags were covered in layers of thick dust, and their statue-like stillness rendered them nearly invisible in the gloom. Stunned, Arkhan reined in just a hundred yards short of the enemy battle-line.

More dust and sand exploded around the dark riders. Undead skirmishers clattered to their feet all around Arkhan, brandishing barbed javelins and tarnished khopeshes.

Arkhan's wights circled protectively around their master. Dark swords, glimmering with fell magics, hissed from their sheaths. The liche glanced back the way he'd come, only to see the first of the pursuing cavalry galloping into view.

There was nowhere to run. Though Arkhan still clutched his battered, iron blade, he had little desire to use it. The thought of a glorious, last stand quickly lost its savour when one knew exactly what awaited them in the realms of the dead.

A change of tactics was in order. With an angry hiss, the liche put away his sword. He nudged his horse forward, out of the protective ring of his bodyguards, and took a few steps towards the nearest skirmisher. Arkhan leaned down, peering into the pinpoints of light that served as the skeleton's eyes.

'Send me someone with a working set of lungs,' he said, speaking to the

liche that lay behind the skirmisher's glowing stare. *'I have a proposition to discuss.'*

Arkhan saw almost at once that the situation was not quite as grim as it appeared. The pursuing horsemen had filled the western end of the valley, but had come to an abrupt stop well outside bowshot from the battle-line of camouflaged spearmen. At once, the liche realized that he hadn't stumbled into the middle of one army, but *two*. The spearmen to the east were likely part of the force he'd sent to Numas, while the horsemen to the west had originally been sent to Zandri.

It also suggested that the ambush he'd stumbled into might not have been meant for him at all. That was good, Arkhan thought. It gave him more leverage. He sent one of his wights back down the valley to call for a representative from the milling horsemen.

The two mouthpieces arrived within minutes of one another. From the east came a heavy cavalryman on a snarling, black cadaver of a horse, while from the west rode a horse archer with skin like saddle leather and a few wisps of black hair floating about his rotted pate. Arkhan left his wights behind and walked his horse down the valley to a point about mid-way between the two forces.

'Lord Khamenes,' Arkhan said, greeting the heavy cavalryman – or rather, the liche who controlled him. *'And Lord Shiwat,'* he said to the horse archer. *'We find ourselves in interesting times.'*

The heavy cavalryman tilted his helmeted head quizzically. Leathery flesh creaked as the man's mouth struggled to form words. *'You... have... no... army,'* Lord Khamenes said. Whether it was an observation or an opening gambit to the negotiations, Arkhan could not tell.

'We were beset on all sides when the ritual failed,' Arkhan replied. *'The risen dead turned on us, and upon one another. No doubt the same happened at Numas.'*

The cavalryman made a growling sound that might have been a sneer. *'Yes. But we... fought... them off. You... did not.'*

Now it was Arkhan's turn to sneer. *'You were born in Khemri. You recall all the great kings of legend, going back to Settra himself?'* The liche pointed to the south. *'They're still fighting each other, out on the trade road. All of them, plus scores of petty rulers you've never heard of. And I was in the middle of it.'*

'I scarcely fought at all,' said Lord Shiwat. The withered horse archer glanced from Arkhan to the heavy cavalryman and back again. *'Zandri was empty when I arrived. The survivors of the plague had taken to the sea. So I left.'*

Arkhan eyed the horse archer. Was Lord Shiwat subtly suggesting that he now possessed the larger army? It was possible, Arkhan thought, but unlikely. Shiwat had never been known for subtlety – or for much of anything else, for that matter. When Nagash had needed new generals in the wake of his failed invasion, he had tried to summon his immortals – men like Arkhan, from the old days at Khemri – back from the realms of the dead. But most of those dread warriors no longer had a body to return to. Their flesh and bones had been burned to ash by the vengeful priest kings at the end of the war. Only a handful of immortals had escaped total destruction and were able to rise again: most were lesser souls like Shiwat and Khamenes, who were too obscure and unimportant in those days to catch the priest kings' attention.

And then there was Raamket, the Red Lord, and his companion Aten-heru. They had been among the wickedest and most powerful of Nagash's lieutenants, and when they had fallen, some ninety years after Nagash's defeat at Mahrak, their bodies had been preserved as trophies rather than burned. Arkhan had sent Raamket with the detachment to Ka-Sabar, and Aten-heru with the force headed to Rasetra. He would have given much to know where they were now.

'*Why are you here?*' Khamenes asked Arkhan. '*The wasteland is no place for a small group of riders.*'

'*No worse than Quatar and the Gates of the Dawn,*' Arkhan replied. '*The dead there remember me well. It's possible I could have slipped past them in time, but ironically, that is the one thing I can ill afford right now. Nagash is no more, and all his secrets are free for the taking.*'

'*The Undying King has fallen?*' Khamenes said.

'*Do not dissemble,*' Arkhan snarled. '*You know it, as well as I. Even Shiwat felt it, clear on the far side of Nehekara. Something happened. I don't know what. But Nagash is gone.*'

'*Then how is it we are still here?*' Shiwat asked.

Arkhan turned to the horse archer. '*A good question,*' he said, trying to conceal the surprise from his voice. '*I do not know for sure. Perhaps the power of the great ritual was enough to give our forms permanence. Nagash may have planned it that way all along.*' Privately though, Arkhan doubted it. He couldn't imagine Nagash giving up that kind of power over one of his subordinates. More than likely, the effect had been unintentional.

'*And the others?*' Khamenes said.

Arkhan shrugged. '*Those that died during the plague did not last once the ritual ended. The magic binding their souls was all that kept them in the land of the living. But the older ones – those interred with all the preparations and rituals of the Mortuary Cult – they were more resilient. They provided a strong vessel to house a resurrected soul. It's possible that they might endure forever.*'

'*With no one to control them,*' Shiwat observed.

Khamenes glared at Arkhan. '*Which is why you are so desperate to reach Nagashizzar.*'

'*Of course,*' Arkhan replied. '*Nagash's secrets are there for the taking. I expect that Raamket and the other eastern lieutenants are hastening there even now.*'

'But you want the throne for yourself,' Khamenes hissed.

Arkhan glared back at the cavalryman. *'I have no intention of serving Raamket or anyone else, in this life or the next.'*

The heavy horseman nodded slowly. *'Nor I,'* Khamenes agreed. *'Which presents us with a problem.'*

Shiwat's man edged his horse closer, until he sat almost between Arkhan and Khamenes. *'You said something about a proposition.'*

Arkhan bowed his head in acknowledgement. *'As I said before, Raamket and the warriors I left in the east are rushing to claim Nagashizzar even now. I would bet my soul on it. And even if I get to Nagashizzar ahead of him, I can't hold him off with just a handful of wights.'*

'So you need me to deal with Raamket,' Khamenes interjected.

'You? You think you can defeat the Red Lord alone?' Arkhan's laugh echoed up and down the valley. *'No. It would take both your armies, plus the walls of Nagashizzar, to hold Raamket at bay.'*

The heavy cavalryman's lips curled back in contempt, but Khamenes did not try to argue the point. *'And what would we gain from such an alliance?'*

Arkhan spread his arms. *'Power. What else? I know where Nagash kept his secret tomes in Nagashizzar. I know how to get past all the traps he laid to destroy would-be thieves. Most of all, I know how to interpret his notes and perform the great rituals.'*

The horse archer leaned towards Arkhan. Shiwat's greed gleamed in the corpse's beady eyes. *'You will share them with us?'*

'Better that than bend the knee to Raamket. Do you not agree?'

Neither of the corpses spoke for a moment. Arkhan could only wait and see if they would take the bait. Khamenes was the dangerous one. His intelligence did not match his ambition. If he decided that he could deal with Raamket himself…

Shiwat spoke first. *'How would the power be shared between us?'*

Arkhan spread his hands. *'Perhaps we can discuss it on the march. Every moment we wait, Raamket draws closer to the prize.'* He looked to Khamenes for agreement.

The heavy cavalryman sat stiffly in his weathered saddle, shrivelled lips drawn tight. His green eyes blazed with irritation, but there was a degree of calculation there as well. *'Agreed,'* Khamenes barked. The corpse turned his horse about. *'Bring up your warriors, Shiwat. You will cover my right flank as we advance. Any warrior that cannot keep up will be left behind.'*

Arkhan hissed in satisfaction. His chances of reaching the great mountain had risen considerably. *'Shall I ride with you, Khamenes?'* he asked.

'Go wherever you like,' Khamenes snarled. *'So long as you stay out of my way.'*

Khamenes set a brutal pace through the wastelands north of the dead river, driving his warriors through the treacherous ground with ruthlessness and an impressive degree of sorcery. Shiwat struggled to keep up. From time to time, Arkhan wondered if Khamenes was doing it to try and provoke Shiwat into overextending his necromantic powers, as he had very nearly done in the chase up the valley. If Shiwat managed to immolate himself, Khamenes could then try to seize Shiwat's forces for himself, and have one less rival to share the throne with.

Arkhan took Khamenes at his word and kept out of the liche's way. The air was thick with treachery. He had no doubt at all that his erstwhile allies would turn on him the instant they had access to Nagash's tomes. Even Shiwat, dull as he was, was no doubt hatching schemes of his own. During the journey, he did what he could to play the two liches against one another. With careful planning and a little luck, they would turn on each other first, giving him enough advance warning to deal with whoever survived. Khamenes was more clever and a more potent necromancer, but Shiwat's army was larger. No doubt Khamenes hoped the brutal march to Nagashizzar would at least even the scales somewhat.

The armies never stopped marching. Day and night, they worked their way through the wasteland, following routes scouted out by Shiwat's horse archers. Warriors and horsemen were lost along the way, their bodies wrecked by falls, or pulled down in the dark by packs of hungry jackals, or blown away by sudden, savage windstorms that swept the wastes from the west. The losses were small but steady, slowly bleeding away the strength of both armies, until Arkhan worried that they might not be able to face a real threat once they reached the great mountain.

Khamenes accepted the cost without hesitation, and left Shiwat with no choice but to do so as well. The march was brutal, but effective. Two months after forming their unsteady alliance, Shiwat's scouts reached the marshlands west of the Sour Sea. Once again, Khamenes drove his army into the marshes without a second thought, but the murky terrain and the twisted denizens of the swamp threatened to swallow his troops whole. After two days, the liche was forced to pull his army out of the marshland and follow Shiwat and Arkhan around its perimeter.

After a week, the armies left the marshlands behind and entered the hilly country of the flesh-eaters. The ghouls, driven almost to extinction during the war against the rat-men, howled hungrily from their nests as the armies went by.

With every passing day, Nagashizzar grew larger and more ominous on the eastern horizon. Arkhan studied the grave-lights glimmering from dozens of fortress towers and wondered what he would find inside.

The armies crossed the northern edge of the Sour Sea, and were only a few miles from the great road that led to Nagashizzar's main gate, when Shiwat's forces lurched to a sudden halt. Arkhan gathered his wights about him and pushed through the packed ranks of skeletons, seeking the liche and his retinue.

Shiwat was far forward along the line of march, along with the rest of his cavalry. The liche was clad in heavy scaled armour much like the harness that Arkhan wore, and carried a wicked-looking bronze khopesh at his hip. Half a dozen heavy horsemen formed a protective cordon around their master, where he sat upon the summit of a low hill.

Arkhan edged up the hill to join him. From their vantage point, he could see the northern road that climbed the hills in the direction of the Plain of Grass, and trace its route southwards up to the towering arch of Nagashizzar's main gate. Astonishingly, the huge portal lay open, as though inviting the armies inside.

The bulk of Khamenes's forces were more than a mile to the west, jammed up along the narrow paths that wound through the hill country. Shiwat was blind to the opportunity before him. He could have easily used his spearmen to block Khamenes in the hills and raced into Nagashizzar alone. Instead, his gaze was turned southward, studying the misty surface of the Sour Sea.

'What is going on?' Arkhan asked, drawing up beside Shiwat. In reply, the liche pointed a bony finger to the south.

Arkhan bit back his irritation and studied the sea's surface. For a few moments, all he could make out was shifting currents of mist. Finally, off to the southeast, he caught sight of something low and broad amid the layers of vapour. Then he saw the brief flash of oars, and understood what he was looking at: a troop ship, one of the wide-bellied troop barges Arkhan had used to sail his army to Lahmia months ago. And it wasn't alone.

There was a disturbance at the foot of the hill. Khamenes had arrived, with a squadron of heavy cavalry at his heels. The liche forced his way past Shiwat's bodyguards and lurched up the slope, his eyes blazing. *'What is the meaning of this?'* he snarled.

'It's Raamket,' Arkhan declared. *'He's landing his troops on the eastern shore.'*

'What should we do?' Shiwat asked.

Arkhan studied the shoreline where Raamket had already beached a handful of troopships. The Red Lord was hurriedly forming up a large force of fast-moving cavalry, which could make good time crossing the slopes beneath the fortress walls. Fortunately, it appeared that only Nagashizzar's main gate was open, so the race was still anyone's to win. The liche gauged distances and weighed the odds. He likely wouldn't get a better opportunity than this.

'We must hurry,' he said. *'Gather your horsemen. While Shiwat's infantry moves to block Raamket's advance, we seize the gate. Quickly!'*

Without waiting for a reply, Arkhan spurred his horse and charged down the far slope of the hill. His wights swept Shiwat's warriors aside as they raced for the northern road. Seconds later, Shiwat and Khamenes were in hot pursuit, just as Arkhan hoped.

It was the work of only a few minutes to break free from the packed ranks of Shiwat's army. Arkhan drove his horse onward, gaining speed as he raced for the dark ribbon of the roadway. Cavalrymen closed in on him from all sides – Shiwat's horse archers, plus a leavening of heavy cavalry that had formed part of the army's vanguard. They closed in around him like a fist, gradually slowing him down until Shiwat could catch up. The liche was not quite as dense as he appeared.

They reached the north road and turned southeast, hooves clattering on the crushed stone surface. Horns wailed in the distance. Raamket had caught sight of his rivals. Shiwat's infantry was already quick-marching down from the hills and spreading out to form a battle-line facing the Red Lord's approaching cavalry. The enemy horsemen might break through the hasty defensive line, but by then it would be too late.

Arkhan and his erstwhile allies charged down the north road, passing the ancient, slumped ruins of the old Yaghur temple fortress. The towering gate of the fortress loomed above them. Grave-lights shone balefully from the ominous bulk of the outer barbican, like the hungry eyes of a leviathan. The open gateway beckoned, only a couple of miles ahead. It was an impossible stroke of luck. Arkhan had never known the gates of Nagashizzar to be left open. He had originally planned to distract Shiwat and Khamenes with efforts to scale the fortress walls, while he slipped away and entered Nagashizzar using more secret means.

Now he would wait until they were inside the fortress walls. Once past the barbican, he would utter the incantation to seal the main gate, separating his rivals from the bulk of their warriors. He would slay Khamenes first, then turn his attentions to Shiwat. And then, if he had enough strength left, he would seize control of their armies and turn them on Raamket.

The first of Shiwat's cavalry reached the gate and disappeared into the darkness beyond. The outer wall – the first of seven curtain walls that climbed the slopes of the fortress – was more than sixty feet thick at the base, and was traversed by a high, arched tunnel that led to an inner gate. In the past, the tunnel had been lit by grave-lamps, which burned coldly from metal sconces set high in the tunnel walls. Those had gone dark, somehow, and the tunnel was as lightless as a tomb.

Arkhan and his wights raced past the gate moments later. The air within was cold and dank, and reeked with fumes from the mountain's many idle forges. The darkness within was oppressive. There wasn't even a faint glow of grave-light at the far end of the tunnel from the inner courtyard.

The liche felt a chill settle into his bones. He couldn't see the lights of the inner courtyard. That was impossible. Unless...

Arkhan reined in his horse with such violence that the undead mount skidded ten feet along the paving stones. By the time his wights had clattered to a stop, he had already turned about and was racing back the other way as fast as the undead beast could carry him. Khamenes and Shiwat flashed by, shouting in alarm.

He couldn't see the inner courtyard because the inner gate was shut. They'd ridden headlong into a trap.

Sorcery stirred the aether. There was an earth-shaking groan and the gates of Nagashizzar began to close. Arrows hissed through the darkness. One thudded into his horse's backside, sinking deeply enough for the arrowhead to grate against bone. Arkhan shouted an incantation of his own, trying to speed his mount further, only to find the spell expertly countered by some unseen foe.

The fortress gates were closing, but their great bulk did not move easily. Had he been another ten yards further down the tunnel, he would not have made it in time. As it was, the sides of the gates were almost close enough to touch as Arkhan raced by. Khamenes and Shiwat appeared moments later, driving their mounts with all the will they possessed.

Many of Shiwat's horsemen were not so lucky. Two were caught between the swinging gates and crushed to powder. The rest were trapped in the tunnel, at the mercy of the hidden archers.

Outside, the walls of Nagashizzar had come alive, raining destruction on the armies at their feet. Arrows, javelins and sling stones rained down on Shiwat's infantry and Raamket's horsemen alike. As Arkhan emerged onto the battlefield, there was a rumble from the barbican as a handful of catapults went into action. Smooth stones the size of chariots arced overhead, plunging down onto Shiwat's battle-line and wreaking havoc on the tightly packed companies. The liche responded with a blast of sorcery, raking the battlements with a storm of greenish lightning, to no apparent effect.

Arkhan kept going, ignoring the chaos of battle to his left. He raced for the ruins of the temple fortress, gauging them to be outside the range of Nagashizzar's defences. Within moments, the retreating horsemen drew the attention of the defenders on the walls. The rain of arrows picked off a dozen of Khamenes's trailing horsemen before the rest were out of reach.

Khamenes and Shiwat reined in around Arkhan, who had taken shelter beneath the temple fortress's gate arch.

'You lied!' Khamenes roared. *'You said Nagash was gone! Now he thinks we have rebelled against him!'*

Arkhan's mind raced. The brush with destruction had left him rattled. Out on the slopes, Raamket's horsemen were in swift retreat, racing for cover from the endless volleys of arrows. Shiwat's infantry were pulling back as well, though more than a third of them had already been destroyed.

'Nagash is gone, you idiot,' Arkhan snapped. *'We would never have made it this far otherwise.'*

'Then how else do you explain this?'

'Isn't it obvious?' Arkhan said. *'Someone has reached the fortress ahead of us.'* He glared up at the mountain. Who could it have been? Aten-heru? Bhashan? It didn't seem likely. Bhashan wasn't much brighter than Shiwat, and Aten-heru didn't make a move without Raamket's blessing. Who did that leave?

Whoever it was, he had control of Nagashizzar, and worse, Nagash's hoarded knowledge. The fact that he was using arrows instead of enslaving them outright suggested that he didn't have access to the higher rituals yet – but that was only a matter of time.

Shiwat completed the withdrawal of his surviving troops. The slope near the gatehouse was covered in smashed skeletons and scattered bones. The liche turned to Arkhan. *'What now?'*

Arkhan bit back a curse. Things had just gotten a great deal more complicated. *'Now we talk to Raamket.'*

The Red Lord came to the parley in person, just as Arkhan expected he would. Aten-heru stood at his side, along with a modest bodyguard of a dozen heavily armed wights – and a pair of spokesmen. The pitch that had been used to preserve the bodies of both liches, hundreds of years ago, had ruined their lungs and vocal chords.

They stood a few hundred yards from the ruins of the temple fortress, just within the shadow of the main gate, yet beyond the reach of the wall's catapults. Raamket and Aten-heru had run a gauntlet of missile fire to reach the parley site, and had lost a number of warriors along the way.

One of the spokesmen dismounted clumsily from his horse and sank to his knees in front of Raamket. At the time of his death he had been a boy of twelve or thirteen, slightly built, with high cheekbones and curly black hair. Much of his skin from the neck down was missing. It had likely gone to help make Raamket's new cloak, Arkhan mused.

Arkhan stood a few feet away, flanked by spokesmen for Shiwat and Khamenes, who hid themselves in the ruins at his back.

The boy's face twisted in a long, grotesque grin. *'I'm not here to negotiate,'* Raamket said. *'You can either surrender your forces to me, or I'll kill you and take them anyway.'*

Arkhan gave the Red Lord a death's-head grin. *'You can't win, Raamket. Fight us, and even if you win, I guarantee there won't be enough left of your army to conquer Nagashizzar. Unless you'd rather settle this with a duel? If so, I would be happy to oblige you.'*

Raamket bristled. His lips drew back in a snarl, revealing teeth that had been filed to points and were now stained a dull grey. The pitch had dyed his skin black, but otherwise had left his features reasonably well preserved. His large hands clenched in anger, but he refused to rise to the bait.

'What do you want?' the boy's corpse said.

Arkhan glanced from one liche to the other. *'First, where is Bhashan and his army? Did you leave him in Nehekara?'*

The boy gave a ghastly chuckle. *'Bhashan is still in Nehekara, yes. Or what's left of him, at least. His army now belongs to me.'*

Arkhan's gaze turned to the distant fortress. Bhashant had been sent to wipe out Lybaras, which would have left him closer to Nagashizzar than even Raamket or Aten-heru. If not him, then who was lurking behind those walls?

'Be that as it may, you still do not have enough forces to breach those walls, Raamket. You need all the help you can get.'

The Red Lord was unimpressed. *'If I need more troops, I will make them.'*

Arkhan shook his head. *'Time is not on our side, Raamket. Whoever is in control of the fortress is plumbing Nagash's secrets even now. Before long, he will have the power to enslave us. No, the sooner we capture those tomes, the better off we will be.'*

Aten-heru leaned forward. In life he had been a lean man with the face of a jackal; the dried pitch had drawn back his lips into a permanent, predatory sneer. His spokesman, a short, broad-shouldered Rasetran, croaked, *'And once we have the tomes, what then? We each take a share?'*

'Exactly,' Arkhan replied. *'Nagash is gone. We are the Lords of the Dead now. Let us divide the world between us, just as the priest-kings did for centuries in Nehekara.'*

It did not take long for Raamket to reach a decision. His faults were many, but indecisiveness was not one of them. *'Very well. How do you propose we take the fortress?'*

'First, we probe the enemy along a wide front. We gauge his numbers and strength. We will focus our attacks at the main gate and along several hundred yards of wall to either side. You take your forces and attack along the wall closer to your landing site. There are three lesser gates along that length where you can put pressure on the enemy's defences. We identify weak spots along the line, and then we attack.'

Raamket turned in the saddle and surveyed the imposing fortress. After a moment, the Red Lord glanced at Aten-heru, who gave a reluctant nod.

'Very well,' the boy said. *'It will take six hours to disembark the rest of my troops. After that, the attack begins.'*

Arkhan watched as the spokesmen mounted up, and the Red Lord braved the gauntlet of arrows once more. As the riders dwindled in the distance, Shiwat's mouthpiece turned to him.

'Raamket will betray us the first chance he gets,' he said.

Arkhan chuckled. *'I never expected otherwise. But he doesn't know the fortress like I do. Those gates nearest his landing site aren't real. They're decoys, meant to tempt an invader to try and outflank the main gate. He will lose thousands of troops trying to take them, while we cross the wall farther north, on the other side of the main gate, and fight our way into the fortress.'*

Shiwat seemed convinced, but not Khamenes. The heavy cavalryman eyed Arkhan warily. *'And then we divide Nagash's tomes amongst ourselves.'*

Arkhan gave the corpse a black-toothed smile. *'You have my word upon it.'*

The assault on the fortress ebbed and flowed like the tides. One wave after another crashed against the walls, raising ladders made of scavenged bones and surging upwards to try and seize sections of the outer wall. The undead fell in droves, struck down by the steady rain of spears and arrows, or smashed to bits by bouncing catapult stones. Ladders were pushed away from the walls by metal-tipped poles, hurling scores of attackers to the rocky ground, only to see them raised by the same bony hands a few moments later. The assault would continue until most of its strength had been spent, and then the survivors would withdraw to make way for a fresh wave to resume the attack. It was a tactic that Nagash and his lieutenants had perfected over the centuries, whereby even a superior enemy force could be ground to dust by sheer, unrelenting pressure.

The battle for Nagashizzar had been raging for hours, and the defenders showed no signs of breaking. The fortress walls and an inexhaustible supply of missiles had managed to keep the attackers at bay and inflict a tremendous amount of casualties. Losses had grown so great that Shiwat and Aten-heru were now fully occupied with raising up new skeletons to keep the battle going. The carnage had in fact grown so great that hungry packs of flesh-eaters had begun slinking about the edges of the battlefield, sniffing for marrow and tendon to fill their aching bellies.

There were signs that the pressure was starting to take its toll. Raamket's forces had spread further along the wall than Arkhan had hoped, striking not just at the false gates but at empty stretches of wall as well. They had reached the top of the wall almost a dozen times in the past few hours, and the defenders were finding it harder and harder to drive them back again. At the same time, fighting around the main gate had been exceptionally fierce, but the strength of the enemy's counterattacks had begun to wane. An hour before, a suicide raid by a company of Kahmenes's spearmen had managed to force their way atop the barbican and set fire to several of the catapults. The wind off the Sour Sea continued to fan the flames, wreathing the gatehouse in thick clouds of grey smoke.

Arkhan stood atop a ruined length of wall at the temple fortress, far to the rear of the assault. Without troops to command, he had relegated himself to countering the enemy's spells, a role that Khamenes and the others were all too pleased to relegate to him. They were as close to the front lines as they dared, waiting for the moment their warriors would carry the walls and the race for the prize began.

What the fools didn't realize was that the role Arkhan had chosen placed him in a perfect position to read the tides of battle and pinpoint the location of his foe. The enemy necromancer had cast a flurry of deadly spells during the early hours of the assault, striking from the top of a high tower that Nagash himself had once used in the war against the rat-men. Arkhan had countered most of those spells with ease; in general it was far easier to negate an incantation than to perform one. Over the course of the next six hours the necromantic duel continued, and Arkhan had learned quite a bit about his foe: a powerful and skilled necromancer, but lacking Arkhan's degree of experience. His incantations were complex designs, rather than the simple, brutally effective ones that worked best on the battlefield, which made them all the easier to negate.

Over time, the barrage of deadly spells began to abate. The enemy devoted more and more energy into incantations that were meant to replenish his mounting losses. Arkhan interfered with most of those as well, letting only as many succeed as he thought would keep the battle going. Even those had dwindled to a trickle now, and the source had shifted, relocating from the tower to a chamber deep within the mountain.

The battle was entering its final phase. Now was the time to put his plan into motion.

Out on the slopes, Khamenes was ordering another wave of spearmen to attack the walls close to the barbican. To the south, Raamket had dismantled several of his transport ships and used the parts to construct a trio of ponderous siege towers, which were slowly approaching the outer wall. The liches sensed that the tide had turned in their favour. They would be waiting to pounce at the first sign of a breach.

Arkhan made his way down from the ruined wall. His horse waited at the bottom, surrounded by his ever-vigilant wights. The liche climbed into the saddle and led his riders away from the battle, back into the hills to the northwest. Not even the flesh-eaters took notice of their passing.

Arkhan had not fought in the war against the rat-men, but he knew its history well. For years he had collected tribute from the repulsive creatures in the sullen peace that had followed, and supplied them with the discs of *abn-i-khat* that had turned the River Vitae to poison.

During that time, he had learned a great deal about their underground network. Including the ones they'd used to stage raids on the flesh-eaters at the height of the fighting.

Shiwat and Khamenes had marched past a half-dozen entrances to the great mountain and never known it. There was an old, abandoned flesh-eater nest not more than a mile from the ruins of the temple fortress. Around its base, Arkhan quickly found a trio of muddy holes that might have looked like sinkholes to an untrained eye. Two of the tunnels had collapsed over the years, but the third one descended to a rocky side-tunnel fifteen feet below the marshy ground.

The liche got his bearings quickly and set off with his bodyguards through the darkness, moving as swiftly as he dared. Even with his knowledge of the labyrinthine tunnels, it would take hours to reach his goal. After all his efforts to undermine the fortress's defence, he now found himself hoping that the defenders managed to hold out just a little while longer.

From the mouth of the tunnel, it was three miles to the lower levels of the mountain's mine works. Veins of *abn-i-khat* glowed poisonously from the walls of the mineshafts, illuminating the toppled forms of hundreds of skeletal miners. The workers had collapsed all at once when their master had been destroyed.

Once inside the mine works, Arkhan made his way back towards the surface. He passed through dark, deserted halls and echoing vaults; past storehouses stocked with armour, weapons and ammunition enough for a hundred wars and shuttered laboratories that had once witnessed all manner of blasphemous experiments. He moved like a ghost through the vast mountain crypt, drawing ever nearer to his prey.

The antechamber to the great throne room was empty. Arkhan suspected that every available warrior had been sent to the outer wall. The liche drew his sword. At his unspoken command, his wights formed a wedge behind him. Fell blades shone balefully in the darkness.

Arkhan raised his left hand and uttered a simple incantation, and the doors to the throne room groaned inward. Grave light gleamed coldly in the chamber beyond. The air stank of old blood and putrefying flesh.

The corpses of a dozen barbarians lay sprawled on the marble floor, their throats expertly slit open and their faces frozen in masks of terror and pain. They surrounded a large, complicated ritual circle, its precise lines drawn with a mix of chalk and *abn-i-khat* dust. Five gaunt, pale figures in filthy brown robes stood at cardinal points around the circle. Once they had been men of the northern barbarian tribes, but now they were monsters. Rotting blood painted their cheeks and blackened their bony chins. At the sight of Arkhan they raised clawed hands and hissed like vipers, exposing vicious, needle-like fangs.

At the far end of the chamber, seated upon the throne of the Undying King, was the blood-drinker W'soran. The necromancer looked even more corpse-like since he'd fled the battle at the Gates of the Dawn, some fifteen years ago. His skin, once grey and thin as parchment, had now turned nearly black, like a mummy that had lain for centuries in a desert tomb. Thin, cracked lips were drawn back in a permanent snarl, and his teeth were nearly as black and jagged as Arkhan's. His right eye, which had been put out by an arrow during the battle, had grown back as a milky-white orb without iris or pupil. His left eye was black as a chip of polished obsidian, and burned with a cold, all-consuming hate.

To the left of the throne sat a trio of tall, rounded jars, of a type that Arkhan knew all too well. Spread about W'soran's feet and spilling down the steps of the dais were ancient, leather-bound tomes, many open to diagrams of ritual circles, or detailed notes written in a careful, precise hand: the tomes of Nagash, the Undying King.

Arkhan stalked into the vast room like a desert cat, his sword held low at his side. His wights spread out around him, pacing their master step for step.

'How stupid I was,' the liche said. *'Of course it would be you. How long did you cower in the north, waiting for your chance to slink back into Nagashizzar? You pathetic bag of bones! You're worse than the rat-men!'*

W'soran rose from Nagash's scarred throne. 'Bold talk from a traitor,' the blood-drinker sneered. 'I mean to continue the Undying King's plan, while you and your ilk circle the mountain like jackals, come to pick at his bones!'

He extended a skeletal finger at the liche. 'I am your lord and master now!' he shrieked. 'Bow to me, or suffer my wrath!'

Arkhan threw back his head and laughed. The dreadful, joyous sound echoed in the vast hall.

'This is a gift from the forsaken gods,' he exulted. *'How I have longed to send your soul screaming into the Abyss! Come to me, you misbegotten worm. Come and face your doom.'*

W'soran shrieked an incantation in reply, and green lightning leapt across the room. Arkhan dispelled it with a few snarled words and rushed towards the throne.

As one, the blood-drinker's servants leapt to defend their master. Arkhan tore one part with a bolt of sorcerous fire, and then the rest were upon him. The creatures looked frail, but they shared W'soran's blood, and were swift as snakes. Claws raked at his arms and chest, ripping through scale mail and leather with ease. The liche struck back with his sword, but his target dodged nimbly aside. A moment later the wights joined the fight, lashing at the blood-drinkers with their rune-etched blades.

Arkhan stabbed at another of W'soran's blood-drinkers, ripping a deep wound in its side. The creature howled in pain, recoiling from the blow, and the liche lunged past, searching for W'soran.

There was a flash of sickly green light and a clap of thunder. Arkhan was blown from his feet. Heat scorched his bones and consumed him with pain. W'soran's bolt hurled him backwards into a blood-drinker and a pair of his wights, sending them all crashing to the floor.

A mortal might have died at once from the sheer agony of the blow, but Arkhan had suffered worse in his time. Snarling, he struggled upright. The blood-drinker he'd knocked down reached for his throat. With a curse, he buried his blade in the side of its skull and levered himself to his feet.

Another bolt of power sizzled through the air. This time, however, Arkhan was ready. He turned the deadly spell aside and responded with his own, raking W'soran and the throne with a torrent of burning darts. W'soran tried to deflect the attack, but hours of constant spellcasting had left him weak. Several of the darts punched through his chest and buried themselves in the back of Nagash's throne. W'soran screamed, clutching at the smoking wounds, but did not fall.

Bones clattered across the marble floor as one of Arkhan's wights was torn apart. Another fell victim to a bolt of magical fire. Three of W'soran's servants still survived, but they all bore ghastly wounds from the wights' fell blades. Arkhan ignored the blood-drinker's servants. Instead, he snarled an invocation and leapt through the air like a loosed arrow, plunging down upon the dais with his sword held high.

Arkhan crossed the intervening space in the blink of an eye, but W'soran was still faster. With an angry cry, he dodged to one side and Arkhan's blade buried itself deep in the back of Nagash's battered throne. W'soran responded with outstretched hands and a ball of magical fire that the liche only barely dispelled, leaving his scale armour shimmering with spent heat. The concussive force of the blast sent Nagash's heavy tomes flying off the dais and skidding across the polished floor.

With a roar of fury, Arkhan gripped his sword with both hands and heaved with all of his supernatural might. The sword was buried deep and refused to come free, so he picked the chair up by the blade and smashed it down onto W'soran. The blood-drinker barely had enough time to get his arms up in front of his face before the chair struck. The throne flew apart with a rending crash and flung W'soran from the dais.

Grinning like a daemon, Arkhan leapt after W'soran, but the blood-drinker scuttled away from him like a grotesque spider. The liche sent a storm of magical bolts chasing after him, leaving a trail of tiny craters along the polished marble floor.

Arkhan uttered a malicious laugh. '*Your power is ebbing, W'soran,*' he hissed. *'I've spent hours wearing you down. You cannot fight me and maintain Nagashizzar's defences at the same time.'*

W'soran barked a command. One of his servants snatched up a fell blade from a fallen wight and charged at Arkhan. The blood-drinker's sword blurred through the air, but the liche weaved away from the blow and chopped off the servant's sword-hand. His return stroke bisected the creature's skull. And at that moment, W'soran struck.

The bolt of necromantic force struck the corpse of W'soran's servant first. Rather than shield Arkhan from the blast, however, it prevented him from seeing the attack coming until it was too late. Its power consumed the corpse in an instant, converting it to energy and adding fuel to the attack.

Arkhan tried to dispel the bolt's energy even as it enveloped him. His armour began to melt at once. The leather beneath it blackened and caught fire. The impact was so intense, he felt no pain – just a gale of power that began to rip his soul free from its moorings and hurl it into the outer darkness.

W'soran cackled in triumph, despite the strain etched on his skeletal features. He held nothing back; all of his remaining power coursed through the bolt that was slowly ripping Arkhan apart.

'You've underestimated me for the last time, Arkhan the Black,' W'soran sneered. 'I am the greatest necromancer in the world. Beg my forgiveness. Plead with me for mercy, and perhaps I will destroy your soul instead of consigning it to the Abyss.'

Arkhan fell to his knees. It took every last iota of his will just to stay upright. The power of the spell was too strong; there was no chance of turning it aside. His burning armour fell away and the skeleton beneath began to blacken. He could not speak, could not move. Darkness, absolute and eternal, began to close in around him.

It was all he could do to focus upon a single thought, and distract W'soran long enough for his last surviving wight to chop its blade into the blood-drinker's neck.

W'soran spasmed. Ichor gushed from his gaping mouth. His spell failed as he staggered, reeling away from the wight's blow. Arkhan's bodyguard pulled its fell blade free and made to strike again, but W'soran lashed out with his fist and struck the wight in the side of its helmet. Bronze crumpled under the blow, and the bodyguard's skull shattered into pieces.

Dimly, Arkhan watched W'soran turn about. The blood-drinker's eyes were wide with fear. Ichor poured from the deep wound in his neck. His stained lips moved, but no words came out. For a moment, he glared hatefully at Arkhan, then lurched towards the dais.

Arkhan summoned the last reserves of his strength. He tried to rise, to grip his sword, to curse at the stricken W'soran. The blood-drinker reached the steps of the dais and fell to his knees. One dripping hand reached for the jars at the foot of the throne.

No! Not again! Fuelled by rage, Arkhan managed to raise his hand. His jaws worked, spitting out a few arcane syllables, and three magical darts leapt from his charred fingers.

Two of the darts struck home, blasting a pair of the jars to ash. The third struck W'soran's outstretched arm, ripping flesh from bone but not preventing him from pulling the lid from the last jar.

Arkhan watched in helpless fury as the blood-drinker was engulfed in a boiling cloud of swarming beetles. They hung there for a moment, filling the chamber with their buzzing song, and then darted in a glistening stream past the open doors of the throne room and out of sight, taking W'soran with them.

Arkhan stumbled through the darkness of the deep tunnels, clutching his prizes tightly to his chest. His armour was gone, and his robes hung about him in tatters. His sword belt barely hung about his hips, causing the blade to clatter against his legs with every halting step.

He had lost count of how long he had been walking through the depths of the great mountain. By now, Raamket and the others would have reached the throne room and found the remains of his wights. No doubt they were searching for him, expecting him to be plundering Nagash's sanctums, or poring through his vaults. They could look for days before they realized he was nowhere about, though he expected their own greed would cause them to forget about him soon enough.

They were welcome to the fortress and everything in it. They could have the mountain and the *abn-i-khat*, if they were bold enough to try and use it. By now, the rat-men had to know of Nagash's demise. Soon enough they would return in their thousands to claim the burning stone. After Raamket and the others were finished betraying one another for Nagashizzar's treasure, they would be easy prey for the creatures.

Arkhan had what he'd come for: three of Nagash's tomes, chosen randomly from the pile. It didn't matter that he might not be able to use the knowledge contained within, so long as no one else could as well. He'd taken crucial bits from the puzzle of Nagash's masterwork, ensuring that no one would be able to master his most potent rituals. He would take them to his tower in the depths of the great desert and seal them away in the deepest vault he had.

There would be no other master of the undead. For the first time in centuries, he was free.

Moonlight shone faintly down the rocky tunnel ahead. Up above, the world waited. Soon enough, it would tremble at the sound of Arkhan's name.

THE NEHEKHARAN PANTHEON

The people of the Blessed Land worship a number of gods and goddesses, both major and minor, as part of an ancient pact known as the Great Covenant. According to legend, the Nehekharans first encountered the gods at the site of what is now Mahrak, the City of Hope; the timeless spirits were moved by the suffering of the tribes, and gave them succour amid the wasteland of the desert. In return for the Nehekharans' eternal worship and devotion, the gods pledged to make them a great people, and would bless their lands until the end of time.

Each of the great cities of Nehekhara worships one of the great deities as its patron, though devotion to Ptra, the Great Father, is pre-eminent. The high priest of a Nehekharan temple is referred to as the *Hierophant*. In every city but Khemri, the high priest of Ptra is referred to as the *Grand Hierophant*.

In addition to the priesthood, each Nehekharan temple trains an order of holy warriors known as the *Ushabti*. Each Ushabti devotes his life to the service of his patron deity, and is granted superhuman abilities in return. These gifts make the Ushabti among the mightiest warriors in all the Blessed Land. Since the time of Settra, the first and only Nehekharan emperor, the Ushabti of each city have served as bodyguards to the priest king and his household.

The fourteen most prominent gods and goddesses of Nehekhara are:

Ptra: Also called the Great Father, Ptra is the first among the gods and the creator of mankind. Though worshipped all across Nehekhara, the cities of Khemri and Rasetra claim him as their patron.

Neru: Minor goddess of the moon and wife of Ptra. She protects all Nehekharans from the evils of the night.

Sakhmet: Minor goddess of the green moon, also called the Green Witch. Ptra's scheming and vindictive concubine, who is jealous of the Great Father's love of mankind.

Asaph: Goddess of beauty, magic and vengeance. Asaph is the patron goddess of Lahmia.

Djaf: The jackal-headed god of death. Djaf is the patron god of Quatar.

Khsar: The fierce and malign god of the desert. A cruel and hungry god worshipped by the tribes of the great desert.

Phakth: The hawk-faced god of the sky and the bringer of swift justice.

Qu'aph: The god of serpents and subtlety. Qu'aph is the patron god of Zandri.

Ualatp: The vulture-headed god of scavengers.

Sokth: The treacherous god of assassins and thieves.

Basth: The goddess of grace and love.

Geheb: The god of the earth and the giver of strength. Geheb is the patron god of Ka-Sabar.

Tahoth: The god of knowledge and the keeper of sacred lore. Tahoth is the patron god of Lybaras.

Usirian: The faceless god of the underworld. Usirian judges the souls of the dead and determines if they are fit to enter into the afterlife.

THE NEHEKHARAN CALENDAR

The Nehekharan calendar operates on a twelve-year cycle, with each year in the cycle devoted to one of the major gods in the Nehekharan pantheon. For example, the 62nd year of Qu'aph (-1750 Imperial Reckoning) represents the year of Qu'aph in the 62nd calendar cycle.

ABOUT THE AUTHOR

Mike Lee's credits for Black Library include the Horus Heresy novel *Fallen Angels,* the Time of Legends trilogy *The Rise of Nagash,* the Warhammer 40,000 novel *Legacy of Dorn* and the Space Marine Battles novella *Traitor's Gorge.* Together with Dan Abnett, he wrote the five-volume Malus Darkblade series. An avid wargamer and devoted fan of pulp adventure, Mike lives in the United States.

YOUR NEXT READ

SKAVENTIDE
by Gary Kloster

Beyond the mountain range of the Adamantine Chain, Aqshy lies destroyed. Noxious fires light up the horizon, death skitters in the smoke, and a wasteland of horror threatens the entire realm. Humanity has but a single hope: the Reclusians of the Ruination Chamber. These Stormcast Eternals, though few in number, are the only force capable of enduring the perils of this dark era, for their souls are already broken.
